P9-DNS-513

THE SNOW MOUNTAIN

ALSO BY CATHERINE GAVIN

The Devil in Harbour
The House of War
Give Me the Daggers
Madeleine

THE SNOW MOUNTAIN

CATHERINE GAVIN

PANTHEON BOOKS
A Division of Random House
NEW YORK

FIRST AMERICAN EDITION

 Published in the United States by Pantheon Books, a division of Random House, Inc., New York. Originally published in Great Britain by Hodder and Stoughton, Ltd., London.

Library of Congress Cataloging in Publication Data

Gavin, Catherine Irvine.
The Snow Mountain.
I. Title.
PZ3.G24Sn3 [PR6013.A83] 823'.9'12 73-19752
ISBN: 0-394-49179-3

Manufactured in the United States of America

TO HELEN PEERS

PETROGRAD 1914-1918

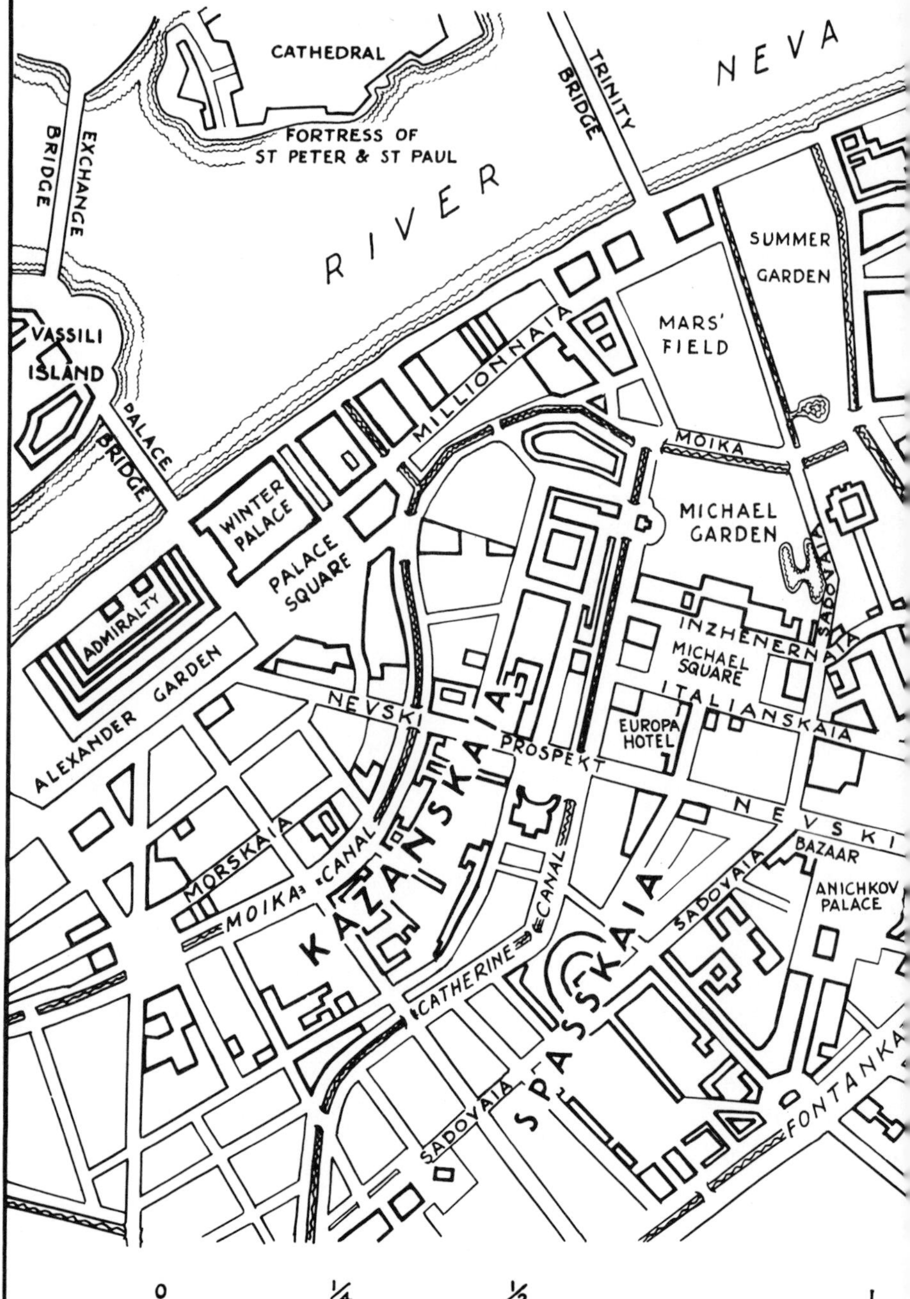

CATHEDRAL
FORTRESS OF
ST PETER & ST PAUL
NEVA
RIVER
TRINITY
BRIDGE
EXCHANGE
BRIDGE
VASSILI
ISLAND
PALACE
BRIDGE
SUMMER
GARDEN
MARS'
FIELD
MILLIONNAIA
MOIKA
MICHAEL
GARDEN
WINTER
PALACE
PALACE
SQUARE
ADMIRALTY
ALEXANDER GARDEN
INZHENERNAIA
MICHAEL
SQUARE
SADOVAIA
ITALIANSKAIA
NEVSKI
PROSPEKT
EUROPA
HOTEL
NEVSKI
BAZAAR
ANICHKOV
PALACE
MORSKAIA
MOIKA
CANAL
KAZANSKAIA
CANAL
CATHERINE
SPASSKAIA
SADOVAIA
SADOVAIA
FONTANKA

0 1/4 1/2 1
Mile

RIVER NEVA
To THE FINLAND STATION
To THE SMOLNY
SHPALERNAIA
SHPALERNAIA
DUMA
TAURIDE GARDEN
SERGIEVSKAIA
FURSHTATSKAIA
KIROEHNAIA
TAVRICHESKAIA
PANTELEIMONSKAIA
LITEINI PROSPEKT
LITEINAIA
TRANSFIGURATION SQUARE
BASSEINAIA
LITEINI PROSPEKT
PROSPEKT
ROZHDESTVENSKAIA
SUVOROVSKI PROSPEKT
LIGOVSKAIA
CANAL
PROSPEKT
ZNAMENIA SQUARE
NEVSKI PROSPEKT
NICHOLAS STATION
MOSKOVSKAIA
VLADIMIRSKI CHURCH
YAMSKAIA

I

THERE WAS ONE DAY, and perhaps only for an hour of that one day, when they were all within sight of each other on the broad expanse of water where the Neva flows into the Gulf of Finland. Some of them had not yet met. They were strangers among the thousands of Sunday holiday-makers who had come out from St. Petersburg in the ferry steamers which normally plied between the islands, and in light craft of all sorts, to see as much as they could of what the Russian newspapers had been calling for nearly a week an historic occasion. But the Grand Duchess Olga was there, happy and excited, aboard the little *Alexandria,* and so was Simon Hendrikov, in the bodyguard of her father, the Russian Czar. Simon's parents and the two schoolgirls in their charge were on the deck of a steamer close behind the barrier of river police boats guarding the waterway along which the imperial yacht would pass. And Richard Allen was there, waiting inconspicuously aboard the British flagship, HMS *Lion,* long before Joe Calvert, who knew none of them as yet, moved away from the parapet of the Nicholas Bridge.

The Czar of All the Russias and his family were going to lunch aboard the *Lion* with the British Admiral and his officers. This was the historic occasion, the apex of a week of tremendous celebrations in St. Petersburg marking the visit of the First Battle Cruiser Squadron to Kronstadt, after a long goodwill voyage begun nearly five months earlier at the French port of Brest. The Royal Navy was showing the flag in the North Sea and the Baltic, and on this same Sunday when Sir David Beatty was to play host to Czar Nicholas II, Admiral Sir George Warrender was receiving the German Kaiser aboard his own flagship at Kiel. In Russia the Duma, which had suffered many things at the hands of the Czar since its mild attempts at parliamentary government began, had stolen a march on him by sending a delegation to greet Admiral Beatty at the Gulf port of Reval; but this was only a prelude to the festivities at St. Petersburg. All the British ratings had been entertained by the Russian Admiralty in the People's Palace. The Municipality gave the officers a banquet at the Tauride Palace, in a setting even more splendid than that of the luncheon party previously given by the Czar in his own home at Czarskoe Selo. Now, after a week of rising excitement, of feasting carried out in perfect June weather, came the imperial visit to the squadron at Kronstadt, to be followed later in the day by a Royal Navy ball.

Of all the group of young people whom fate and history were to link together, Joe Calvert was the one who saw and heard the least that day. This was because he started for Kronstadt late and unprepared, without binoculars, a young man who had spent exactly five days in the Russian capital as a vice-consul of the United States of America. He had gone with one of his new colleagues to the Nicholas Bridge, joining the crowds looking on and even cheering as the two British light cruisers berthed in that stretch of the Neva got under way, dressed overall, and departed to join the rest of the squadron at Kronstadt.

"Just listen to the girls!" he said, as squeals and shrill goodbyes broke out. "They won't forget the Limey sailors in a hurry."

"Jack ashore!" said Edward Murchison. "Jack's going to remember Petersburg as a wide open town, a damn sight better fun than Devonport on a wet Saturday night. Or even Newport News, for that matter."

"Petersburg put on a great show for them, you've got to allow."

"Sure did," said Murchison amiably. He was pleased with himself and with the world. He had served two years in the American consulate at St. Petersburg, and had earned so many reprimands from the consul that he had more than once feared his next posting would be to Siberia, and behold! his orders had come through for Berlin and a return to the western world. He had never even attempted to understand the Slav mentality, and yet, with this kid already on the spot to take his place and his bags packed to go, he was inclined to envy Joe Calvert, who had the whole Russian experience before him. He wondered what Calvert would make of the alternate brilliance and fecklessness of a society in which he might or might not find a place, the snowy winter streets and the white nights of midsummer, the ballet and the gipsy singers, all backed by the daily drudgery of the consulate.

"What do you say we follow them downstream for a bit?" Joe Calvert said. He was fascinated by the sight of the two cruisers, running west between the rose-purple of the granite embankments on the city side and the rose and white façades of the university on Vassili Island. "Come on, Murchison! The fun's all over here, and there's still time to catch that steamer by the steps."

"What, that leaky old ferry?" But Ned Murchison, after consulting his watch and reckoning that they could 'just make it' before the Czar's arrival, allowed himself to be persuaded. He was sentimental, although he would never have admitted it, about going on one last trip down river, looking back beyond the Nicholas to the Trinity Bridge, to the Alexander, to all the bridges of the Neva which opened to let the freighters go upstream; looking back at the statue of the Bronze Horseman and the slim golden spires against the blue. Unsentimentally, he warned Joe Calvert to look out for his watch and wallet and keep his jacket buttoned up, as they ran down the granite steps and aboard the crowded ferry, where a shaggy man in an embroidered peasant blouse was playing the fiddle on the after deck, and some girls were already dancing. In fact the jackets of both young men were buttoned almost to their choker collars. They were tall and lanky, American dandies of 1914, immaculately turned out in light grey suits and straw boaters.

Joe Calvert's name, which was to become familiar and sometimes execrated in St. Petersburg, was only known to two persons in the crowd that day. Madame Hendrikova, the language teacher, had heard it from the American consul, who wanted her to give the new arrival Russian lessons, and she had mentioned it to her husband, the professor. As it happened, the Hendrikov party was not far away from Joe when the ferryboat shut off her engines at the order of a police patrol. Professor Hendrikov had reserved places for his wife and the girls in one of the pleasure-boats chartered by the university for the occasion, and from the deck of this craft, lying low in the water, the two schoolgirls looked up curiously at the noisy crowd aboard the ferry, and the bottles of vodka being handed round. Madame Hendrikova signed to them to move away from the rail and under the shelter of an awning.

"But mother, we can't see anything, back there!" protested her daughter.

"I promised your headmistress you wouldn't make yourselves conspicuous, when I asked her for a holiday."

"It's not as if we were wearing our Xenia fancy dress," said the other girl defiantly. They had been close friends for several years, Darya Hendrikova and Marya Trenova, Dolly and Molly to their classmates at the Xenia School, and although the friendship had begun to wane they were united that day in the silent determination to see Lieutenant Simon Hendrikov in the uniform of the Garde Equipage.

On the other side of the police barrier, on the deck of HMS *Lion*, Richard Allen was waiting for the show to begin in far greater comfort than Joe Calvert or the Hendrikov party. It was like him to be at the centre of events, ostensibly in attendance on the British Ambassador, while back in the embassy on Suvarov Square some junior members of the staff who had not been invited to the revels wondered resentfully how Captain Allen had got away with it again. With the modest posting of temporary military attaché, Captain Allen kept his distance from the Ambassador, while giving his full professional admiration to Sir George Buchanan's fine appearance in his gold-laced diplomatic uniform, and the poise of Lady Georgina, his stately wife.

"Who did we pull out of the imperial lucky dip today?" he inquired *sotto voce* of a young man in naval uniform, who answered with a smothered laugh:

"His sister and the Kirills: it might have been worse."

"Not much worse." Captain Allen surveyed those members of the imperial family who had been invited to meet their august relatives under the protection of the British flag. The Czar's younger sister, Olga Alexandrovna, was likely to be a popular guest, especially as she had turned up alone, without either her husband, the much disliked Prince Peter of Oldenburg, or the handsome colonel who was the third member of their unconventional ménage. A rawboned, rangy woman in her middle thirties, with a plain face and an underslung jaw, she was talking pleasantly to one of Beatty's flag officers: her laugh rang out from time to time. No problems there, thought Richard Allen, and looked thoughtfully at the Grand Duke and Grand Duchess Kirill. They were talking to nobody, but standing a little apart, she with the look of offended dignity only too familiar on the faces of the imperial ladies. Their marriage had been a resounding scandal of some years back, when she, as a divorced woman, had married the Czar's cousin Kirill, the scandal being compounded by the fact that her divorced husband was none other than the Czarina's brother. They had been banished from the Empire by the Czar, and although he relented after a time and permitted them to return, the wrong still rankled in his wife's unforgiving heart. All the British diplomats aboard the *Lion* knew the problem, the more acute to them because the Grand Duchess Kirill had been born a British princess: either the Czarina would ignore her former sister-in-law or she would favour her with the frigid smile that blighted conversation. The very best that could be hoped for, thought Richard Allen, was that the former sisters-in-law would kiss the air four inches from each other's cheeks and call each other by their nursery names. He was never sure of his ability to keep his own face straight when he heard the Czarina addressed as 'Sunny'—she who looked so miserable, or the Grand Duchess called 'Ducky' when her long neck and dramatically poised small head occasionally made her look like an indignant swan.

"Did we have to have the Kirills?" he said, still in a lowered voice, and the naval attaché reminded him:

"Of course we did. He's the commander of the Garde Equipage, and he'll probably be the next chief of the naval staff. And anyway, who else is there?"

Richard Allen shrugged. He knew as well as the other man that the Czarina, Alexandra Feodorovna, had quarrelled with nearly every member of her husband's family since she entered it twenty years ago. With some, the quarrels had been on religious grounds, with others because of what she called loose living—and no doubt about it, outside the charmed circle of the ruler and his family, the Romanovs had a talent for living loosely. His uncles, his cousins, even his only surviving brother, had bedevilled the Czar's peace of mind with their morganatic marriages, their bastard children who had to be legitimised and ennobled, their years of foreign exile until the inevitable pardon was forthcoming. Who, in such a crew, could be invited to meet, or particularly wanted to meet, the religious and strait-laced Czarina?

"It's all gone well so far," said Allen. "I'd like to see this particular show go with a swing."

"I think we can safely leave that up to Beatty."

"To Beatty and the girls."

"The little Grand Duchesses? The older two?"

"All four of 'em, from what I hear. People say they were wonderful hostesses at the Czarskoe Selo lunch last Wednesday."

"I expect it was a change for them. Poor little devils, they don't have much of a life!"

By way of reply, Richard Allen silently indicated a small yacht which had appeared on the bright waters of Peterhof bay. It was nearly eleven o'clock, and all through the British squadron crisp orders rang out. Aboard the flagship the marine band lifted their bugles to their lips. The guests drew back in a semi-circle behind Admiral Beatty and his flag officers. It was a great moment for Sir David Beatty, who had scored a huge personal success in Russia, where since the disasters of the war with Japan the image of an admiral was that of an obese elderly man with a white beard and a marked incompetence in seafaring and the art of war. Admiral Beatty was only forty-three, and looked much younger, clean-shaven and debonair, with his headgear set at the famous 'Beatty tilt'. There were cheers from the Russian pleasure-boats as he stepped forward, and the twenty-one gun salute began.

"Here they come, bang on time," said Ned Murchison.

"Say, I read where the Czar had a terrific yacht," said Joe Calvert. "I never knew he travelled in a paddle-wheeler!"

"That's the *Alexandria,* she's only a tender. The *Standart* can't put in to Peterhof, and neither can the *Polar Star.*"

"Peterhof's the summer palace?"

"One of them. Watch him now!"

Nicholas II swung himself nimbly up to the frenetically holy-stoned deck of HMS *Lion* as the bosuns' pipes shrilled and the imperial standard was broken out. He was wearing the British uniform of an admiral of the fleet and all his British decorations. As always when the Czar appeared before a British regiment or ship's company, however disciplined, there was a perceptible wave of recognition that the Russian ruler was so like George V as to pass for his twin brother. They had the same neat features, inherited from the Danish sister princesses who had given them birth, the same short, slight bodies and the same trim brown beards. Only the Czar's dark eyes, unfathomable and sad, were in striking contrast to King George's straight blue gaze.

The Emperor and the Admiral saluted and clasped hands. It was the high point of the occasion, urgent in its symbolism, and yet the eyes of all the spectators were already turned on Alexandra Feodorovna, waiting to follow her husband. Then there were murmurs from the critics on ship and shore, and no applause: the Czarina, with her talent for doing the wrong thing, had hidden her face from her husband's subjects behind a white lace parasol.

There were other critics, like Professor Hendrikov, who were talking instructively about bread and circuses. St. Petersburg had been convulsed for a month past by strikes and lockouts, when the shrieking streets had been cleared again and again by Cossack charges, and only the arrival of the British sailors had changed the ugly mood to one of holiday. "Beatty's visit is worth its weight in gold to Nicholas," said Professor Hendrikov, but neither his daughter nor her friend was listening. The girls had taken off their hats, much to Madame Hendrikova's displeasure, and Dolly's fair curls were pressed close to Mara's sleek dark head as they craned their necks to look at the *Alexandria.*

"Oh mother, I can see Simon, close beside Her Majesty!" gasped Dolly, who had the binoculars. "Don't you want to look?"

"Let Mara have the glasses first, dear."

"I don't need them, thank you, Vera Andreievna, I can see quite well."

"Then you must have exceptionally long sight," said Dolly's mother with a smile, and Mara blushed. It was true that she could see Lieutenant Simon Hendrikov, although the other officers standing to attention on the *Alexandria*'s deck were almost a blur: the long vision which made his blunt features clear to Mara Trenova was the vision of first love.

The transfer of a tall woman of forty-two, for long a martyr to sciatica, from a paddle-wheeler in mid-channel to the deck of a battle cruiser was not easy to accomplish gracefully, and the Czarina appeared to hesitate, but a gloved hand appeared from nowhere—as a white-gloved hand always did—to take the furled parasol, and Alexandra's huge picture hat was not even disarranged when she appeared on the deck of the *Lion* and graciously extended her own hand for Admiral Beatty's kiss. The spectators watched eagerly to see who would follow her up the awning-protected companionway. There had been very little cheering for the imperial couple: now there was a groan of disappointment, like a long sigh or growl coming over the water, when no small boy in a sailor suit appeared behind his mother.

"The Heir? Where's the Heir?"

"Where's Alexis Nicolaievich?"

"What are they saying?" Joe Calvert asked.

"They want to see the boy—the Czarevich," said Murchison. "I guess he's sick again. He doesn't often get to appear in public."

"Is that right?" said Joe. "I knew he had one bad illness, was it a year ago, and that monk fellow, Rasputin, cured him; I thought it was for keeps. Will Rasputin be along with them today?"

"Keep your voice down, for God's sake," said Murchison between his teeth. "Don't ever mention that name in a crowd like this!" And lowering his own voice, he said in a whisper, "He's in Siberia."

"Where's the Heir, the pretty dear?" said a fat woman wedged close to Joe, whose shawl smelt abominably of fish. "Where's little Alexis?"

Obviously not to be seen that day. Not even carried in the arms of his *diadka*, the sailor nurse who had carried him, before the eyes of a horrified people, through all the previous year's celebrations of the Romanov tercentenary. The thousands who stared at the nine-year-old Alexis had seen only a pale face beneath bright hair, a thin hand clutching the *diadka*'s shoulder, and then the pathetically dangling legs. Last year's rumours sprang to life again in the boats behind the police barrier, well out of bomb and hand grenade range: helpless cripple, semi-paralysed, idiot child, unfit to reign.

But there came the four Grand Duchesses to take their places behind their father and mother. Across the heat haze rising from the water, they could be seen only as a dazzle of white dresses and white picture hats as big as the Czarina's. Olga and Tatiana wore hats adorned with white ospreys, while the two younger girls, Marie and Anastasia, had wreaths of white and pink roses instead of feathers. The four sisters, so near in age (the eldest eighteen, the youngest just thirteen), were not quenched by the over-elaborate fashions of the times. They were overflowing with health and good spirits and the absolute assurance of enjoyment ahead. The Family enemies relaxed into smiles, the British naval officers and diplomats were beaming, and it was with difficulty that the ship's company looked solemn for the playing of the two national anthems. The Czar, like the Admiral, stood stiffly at the salute. But his sombre eyes looked away from the flags and the bunting, past the Russian double eagle and the white ensign, down the hidden years into the future.

* * *

Far away from St. Petersburg, another luncheon party had been arranged for a royal personage. He and his wife, who did not share his titles or his honours, were to be the principal guests at a banquet in the Governor's Residence of a small provincial capital which had been for four hundred years under Turkish rule.

Forty years of western influence had enlarged the population and added some new buildings to the dusty little town, but had hardly altered its appearance. Mosques and minarets still lifted their heads beneath the mountain peaks, and the Turkish bazaar was still a centre of the local life. But there were new influences at work in the town, influences which had seeped across the border from free Serbia, and these went by the name, at least, of liberty and independence. The prince in whose honour the banquet was to be given appeared to some to be an obstacle to these influences and a monster of reaction.

He had known, for he was not a fool, what he might be risking by going to the mountain town, and one threat to his life was made when his procession started on that Sunday morning. But he survived to take the route to the Residence, a route about which there had been some difference of opinion, and it took him past a modest provision store, outside of which stood a nineteen-year-old boy armed with a pistol. There the prince and his wife were shot dead, and by the time the first toast was drunk aboard HMS *Lion* their bodies were lying on two iron bedsteads in the Residence, strewn with flowers hastily taken from the vases arranged along the luncheon tables in the hall below.

The news travelled slowly beyond the mountain range. In the town of fifty thousand persons the mayor, the chief of police and the military governor were all disputing responsibility for the security arrangements which had so sensationally broken down, and there was an outbreak of street rioting and looting which did nothing to help the authorities in their attempt to round up the criminals. The youth who fired the two fatal shots had been seized and beaten up by the police, but refused to implicate others in the plot, although at least one had been caught when he jumped into the dry bed of the Miljacka river, after swallowing a cyanide capsule which failed to work. It was some time before the news of the double murder was telegraphed to Austria, whence the dead man had come. It had not even reached Vienna when Lieutenant Hendrikov and his brother officers of the Garde Equipage ate lunch ashore, listening to the sound of music floating across the water from the British ships.

The *Alexandria* had been ordered to return to HMS *Lion* at half past three, but it was almost half past four when the imperial family was ready to embark. The Czarina came aboard exhausted, and was helped by a maid of honour to a comfortable wicker chair, but the Czar appeared to be in excellent humour, and his four daughters were in wild spirits. They all crowded to the rail, laughing and waving their bouquets as their new English friends cheered them on their way. Then there was a concerted rush to put the flowers in water, for the pretty girls, always kept in the background, were touchingly grateful for any little presents they received. The bouquets, very wilted as to petals, were reverently arranged in vases on the Czarina's table. She complained of the strong perfume.

"You're so tired, mother," said the Grand Duchess Tatiana, carefully arranging cushions at the Czarina's back. "Wouldn't you like to have some tea?"

"I'd rather wait till we get home." Alexandra paused, frowning, to listen to her husband teasing his daughters.

"Oil on Mashka's dress," he said with mock severity. "The Imp has a run in her stocking, and even Tania has coal dust on her shoes. You three look as if you'd been in the stokehold."

"So we were, all except Olga," said Marie.

"Olga stayed on deck, flirting with Georgie Battenberg," said Anastasia, and Mademoiselle Schneider, in attendance on the Czarina, said "Girls, girls! Young ladies, if you please!" But this was automatic, and made no impression; teasing about flirtations, like the flirtations themselves, was encouraged by the parents of the four Grand Duchesses, as a normal and innocent outlet for the romantic ideas of growing girls.

"I don't care," said Olga, "Georgie was so nice today, they all were." She took off her matronly hat with a sigh of relief, and stabbed the two pearl-headed hatpins through the crown. "Thank goodness we don't have to be dressed up any longer! But I hate to have the party over, it was such fun."

"Why should it be over?" cried Anastasia. 'The Imp' was the most daring of the sisters, and often showed the most initiative; now she began to clamour for just one hour's extension of their outing, just a short sail across the Gulf and back before they need go home!

"What does mamma say?" asked the Czar, and his wife, supine in the wicker chair, turned her careworn face to his.

"Baby will be missing us," she said.

"He's got half a dozen people to amuse him," said the Czar. His manner was unusually breezy, as if the British admiral's uniform he wore, and the company of King George's officers, had been a stimulus to his reserved personality. He bent over Alexandra's chair, and with his fingers made a bracelet round her wrist. "I do think we might run over to Terijoki and back again, just to get the fresh air. And the girlies would enjoy it."

In the scales Alexandra perpetually balanced in her mind, the claims of the girlies were as nothing compared to the claims of Baby, as she still called her growing son. But the touch of her husband's fingers, the rarity of his caress in public, at once stirred the deep sexual response Nicholas could always arouse in her. With a blush, and a submissive smile, the Czarina said, "Well, just for an hour then. Tatiana, tell them to bring us tea."

There was no room for tea-tables and the elaborate service of the *Standart* aboard the little *Alexandria,* but tea was served in glasses, quickly and informally, and within twenty minutes after the imperial guests had left HMS *Lion* the paddle-wheeler was passing Tolbukin Light, where the British squadron was half hidden by the fortifications of Kronstadt. It had been a very hot day, and the Czarina owned the sea breeze was refreshing, the breeze which lifted the flattened gold hair of the Grand Duchess Olga and stirred the white laces at her throat as she stood by the rail with Lieutenant Simon Hendrikov.

It was an article of faith among all the young officers of the

Guard that the Czar's second daughter, Tatiana, was the most beautiful of the four sisters. Marie, called Mashka, or sometimes Bow-Wow, was at fifteen much afflicted by puppy fat, and Anastasia, the Imp, offered no certain promise of beauty. But Tatiana Nicolaievna, at seventeen, was said by the older courtiers to be even more beautiful than her mother, in the legendary days when the Czarina, as Princess Alix of Hesse-Darmstadt, was the admired 'Sunny' of a little German court. Tatiana's red-gold hair was richer in colour than her mother's, her eyes a warm amber instead of Alexandra's cold grey-blue, and her smile was warm and loving. Simon Hendrikov, like his brother officers, admired her from afar. But the one he adored was her older sister, less classically beautiful with her tip-tilted nose and Slavic cheekbones, but also less acquiescent and far more exciting in the vivid shift and domination of her moods.

"Why didn't you come aboard the *Lion,* Simon Karlovich?" she was saying, in the impulsive way some of the courtiers called abrupt. "You met the English officers last Wednesday, didn't you?"

"My orders were to return to shore, Your—Olga Nicolaievna." Lieutenant Hendrikov had served in the *Standart* for only three months, not long enough to be accustomed to the order never to say 'Your Imperial Highness' when talking to the girls.

"But you're going to the ball tonight, I hope?"

"I was lucky enough to get one of the invitations, yes." Simon took his courage in both hands. "Madame—Olga Nicolaievna—may I have the very great honour and pleasure of a dance with you?"

The girl stared at him in honest surprise. "Why so formal? Of course I'd love to dance with you again, Simon Karlovich, but you see . . . my sister and I aren't going to the ball aboard the *Lion* after all."

"But I understood you—"

A smiling mask seemed to have dropped over the pretty face of the Czar's eldest daughter. "There will be two thousand guests in the British ships tonight," she said. "It was thought—not really advisable for us to go."

The young man understood at once. Although the 'white nights' were not yet over, there would be two hours of darkness in the Gulf of Finland. There would be shadows, patches of light and shade beneath the fairy lamps, along the decks of the two battle cruisers which were to be lashed together for the final entertainment Admiral Beatty intended to offer to all those who had shown such lavish hospitality to the men under his command. There were, aboard the cruisers, too many places where an assassin, come aboard in the great crowd of guests, could lurk until he found the right opportunity to fire at, to draw his knife on, just one girl, or one of two girls, whose only crime was to bear the name of Romanov.

He felt rage rising in his heart. But Simon Hendrikov had been well schooled since he joined the *Standart*; he too could smile, and affect nonchalance in the presence of the constant menace which hung over the heads of those he had sworn to serve. He said, "The Admiral and his officers will be very disappointed."

"Oh, so are we all! My little sisters pestered the life out of our cousin, Prince George of Battenberg, wanting to know how *Lion* was to be 'tied up' to *New Zealand,* as they called it, and how the guests were going to get from one ship to the other, and what they were going to have for supper—that was Mashka, of course!"

Olga looked smilingly over her shoulder at the plump girl, who was sitting between her father and mother at the flower-laden table, and enjoying a plate of cream cakes.

"I don't know about the supper," Simon said, "but I did hear the Englishmen were having trouble in getting enough champagne for the ball tonight. After all the Petersburg hospitality, supplies are beginning to run short in the city."

"Perhaps it's a good thing they're leaving soon. Are you going in the *Polar Star* to Björkö, to see their tactical manœuvres?" She stumbled over the technical words, and laughed at herself.

"On Wednesday, yes." The young man spoke so glumly that Olga laughed again, at him.

"Cheer up, Simon Karlovich, don't look so sad! I'll keep that dance for you, next time we're at a ball together. Maybe next winter, when the court balls begin again, or maybe sooner, who can tell?"

"Are there going to be court balls next winter? Really?"

"Yes, really, didn't you know? The Czar and the Czarina" (the girls always spoke of their parents by their titles) "decided long ago that as soon as my sister Tatiana was seventeen, we could start going to balls together. We did go to two last winter, but they weren't our *own* balls of course. Next year they will be."

"And given in the Winter Palace?"

"Just as they were in the Czar Alexander's time."

"May I take your tea glass, Olga Nicolaievna?" Simon asked.

"Thank you."

The glass, in its wrought silver holder, was put on a tray carried by one of the sailor servants, and Simon again looked into Olga's eyes. She was a tall girl, and he was not much over medium height, strongly built rather than slender: on a ballroom floor, he remembered all too well, her face was very close to his.

"Thank you for your promise, Olga Nicolaievna," he said. "But at the Winter Palace, I'm afraid, you'll be too far away from me. You'll be near the thrones, with princes begging you to dance with them—it won't be like our last waltz at Livadia, fifteen days ago."

"Exactly fifteen days ago? Are you sure?"

"It was the night before the *Standart* sailed for Constanza, I know that."

"Oh, Constanza!" Olga, to her annoyance, felt her cheeks grow warm. "Is it really only two weeks since we all went to Rumania? It seems much longer, doesn't it? Such a lot of things have happened since."

"Things have happened to *you*, Olga Nicolaievna?"

She heard the new, rough note in his voice, and thrilled at the thought of telling Tatiana all about it, in the bedroom which they shared at Peterhof. The sisters loved to gossip about their carefully permitted flirtations, and this was flirtation with a vengeance, something more in earnest than Olga had ever known before. She said,

"I mean, there's been so much to do, since we came back! First there was the King of Saxony's visit, well, I know that wasn't very exciting; and then this wonderful time with the English squadron, and next month the French President is coming on a state visit, and Tatiana and I are going to ride with the Czar at the grand review!" She clapped her hands. "It's almost too much for just one summer!"

"So you're happy, Olga Nicolaievna?"

"Why shouldn't I be?" she said, with a quick return of her imperious manner. "I have everything in the world to make me happy; everybody tells me so! Look, Simon Karlovich, we're nearly at Terijoki, see the club-house and the church! Come and look, you two; you wanted to see Terijoki, didn't you?"

Not only the two younger girls, but the Czar himself, who had been walking up and down the deck with one of his officers, came up to stand beside Olga at the rail, and Simon respectfully drew back. The Grand Duchess Tatiana remained beside the Czarina's chair, and fanned her mother with a small silk fan.

"Nice place, Terijoki," said the Czar. "I had some first-rate tennis there last year."

From the water the little Finnish town looked charming, with the tall steeple of the Orthodox church rising three hundred feet above the harbour. Terijoki was in the Czar's Grand Duchy of Finland, only three miles by land from the Russian frontier posts, and a favoured spot for the rich inhabitants of Petersburg to build their summer dachas. The members of the Terijoki Yacht Club had set their club-house behind green lawns running down to the water's edge, covered, on this hot June Sunday, with tea-tables shaded by gay parasols. The little *Alexandria* could go so close inshore that the imperial ensign was clearly seen from the club-house, and the members left their tables and hurried down to the edge of the lawn to cheer their monarch and his family. The Czar saluted automatically. The three Grand Duchesses waved their handkerchiefs; they loved to be recognised and feel part of the people, but the Czarina called her younger daughters to her side. She detested any appearance of what she called 'currying favour', or even worse, 'publicity'.

The *Alexandria* turned away to port, and Anastasia, on her way to rejoin her mother, said sorrowfully, "Must we really go back to Peterhof now, papa?"

"What an Imp you are! Of course we must. Here ends your cruise in Finnish waters, girls, but don't be down-hearted! We'll be off to sea in the *Standart* in another couple of weeks."

The Czar, with a smile for Simon Hendrikov, resumed his walk. He was fanatical about his need for exercise, and five hours of near-immobility aboard HMS *Lion* had tried him severely. Olga laughed at the expression on Lieutenant Hendrikov's face.

"Are you glad to hear about the *Standart,* Simon Karlovich?"

He made her a little bow. "Very glad."

"But you knew it was on the programme, didn't you—the summer cruise?"

"On the programme, yes, but you missed it out of your wonderful summer, Olga Nicolaievna. You jumped straight from Admiral Beatty to President Poincaré, and for all I knew the cruise had been cancelled—"

"Why should it be?"

"In case somebody might be coming from Rumania."

Simon Hendrikov knew that he had been presumptuous when he saw the Grand Duchess Olga's dark brows, so much darker than her fair hair, meet in a straight line across her eyes. But she ignored his stammered words of apology, and smiled again, saying, "I can't imagine anything at all that would make the Czar cancel the summer cruise. It's the best thing that happens in the year, for him and the rest of us. We're going to Björkö first, where you'll see the British squadron at their manœuvres on Wednesday, and then right down the Gulf to Hangö Head. Have you ever been there, on your own, I mean? It's your first tour of duty on a *Standart* cruise, I know."

"I've never been to Hangö, Olga Nicolaievna. But I do know Björkö, as it happens. My father and mother have a little dacha in that direction, not far from Koivisto village."

"They have? Could we go and see it? Would your parents mind? We've none of us ever been inside a real country dacha, just those awful villas that pretend to be dachas, between Czarskoe Selo and Pavlovsk. Where is yours? Is it far from the harbour? Could we get there on foot?"

The torrent of eager questions fascinated Simon. He had been for too short a time in the imperial entourage to know what boundless curiosity the four Grand Duchesses, and even their little brother, felt in the homes of everybody who lived outside the court circle. During the two months spent at Livadia, their palace in the Crimea, while the *Standart* was in harbour at Yalta, there had been little opportunity for the girls to go about among the people: they went, guarded always by the security police and in automobiles, from one princely Crimean estate to the other. But a dacha, his father's little dacha by the river-side—that his princess should want even to look at it was outside his scope of belief. He managed to say that his parents would be honoured beyond words—

"But they're not there now, are they? I thought your father was a professor in St. Petersburg."

"So he is. They went there with my sister Dolly at Easter, when I was at sea . . . and to tell you the honest truth, Olga Nicolaievna, I don't know what sort of state the place is in, shut up since the spring . . . I'd have to arrange to get it cleaned, and everything."

"Oh no, that would spoil it all! People are always cleaning up for us, and putting out flags, and offering us the holy ikons, and turning out the guard. Couldn't we just walk to your dacha at Koivisto, and take a picnic basket from the *Standart,* and have tea there? My sisters would be absolutely *thrilled,* and so would Alexis be, I know."

After all, he thought, she was still a schoolgirl, with a schoolgirl's sudden enthusiasms, in spite of the voyage to Constanza and the rumours of her engagement to the Rumanian prince which had aroused his jealousy. He said,

"As far as walking goes, that's easy; you wouldn't even have to go through Koivisto village. There's a path from the shore along the riverside, and it isn't far. But remember, won't you, that it's just a little place, a little old wooden cottage, not a grand dacha like the ones round Terijoki—"

"That doesn't matter! It'll be such fun to look forward to! I'll tell the others as soon as we get home. We'll keep it a secret, won't we, Simon Karlovich—my sisters and I, and you and Alexis, nobody else?"

"As Your Imperial Highness wishes." He couldn't help but call her that, she was his princess, who talked to him, and would let him walk with her by the river of his boyhood holidays, and he stood at the salute as she smiled and turned away. The *Alexandria* was coming up to Peterhof quay, and the Czarina was being helped out of her wicker chair. The last thing he heard Olga Nicolaievna say as she joined her sisters was, "What have you all done with my horrible hat?"

* * *

The sightseers who went out from St. Petersburg to look at the British officers and their imperial guests made their way back to the city long before the first course was over at the luncheon tables aboard the *Lion.* Slowly, on that hot afternoon, the capital filled up again: family parties strolled in the Summer Gardens or in Mar's Field, and young people studied the shop windows in the

Nevski Prospekt. The factory workers and mechanics went back to their crowded homes on Viborg Side or the Lines near the Maly Neva. By contrast the Austrian capital was empty when the news of the double murder in the mountain province reached the city. The news of the tragedy had to be broken first to the Emperor, Franz Josef, for the dead man had been his heir-apparent, and the eighty-four years old Emperor was on holiday at his favourite place, Bad Ischl. His subjects had a carefree afternoon in the Weinerwald or the Semmering, drinking wine in the flowery gardens of rustic inns and listening to music. They trailed back to the city in the early evening, young girls arm in arm with their sweethearts, and young fathers carrying sleeping children on their shoulders. By that time the telegraph had begun to send its message of murder across the world. It reached the Czar and his ministers, the British Admiral and his officers, when the great ball aboard the two cruisers had just begun. It reached the young Grand Duchesses in their protected home at Peterhof, and it reached some to whom the name of murder was not horrible, in the slums of Petersburg. Soon the whole world knew that a student terrorist, of the same breed if not of the same nation as those who had hunted the Romanov Czars for so long, had shot and killed the Archduke Franz Ferdinand, and his wife the Duchess of Hohenberg, in a place few people had ever heard of called Sarajevo.

2

THE HOTEL EUROPA, seventy-five years old in 1914, continued to be the most fashionable hotel in St. Petersburg. Connoisseurs in living might extol the cuisine and the general unpredictability of the Hotel de France on the Morskaia, and the new rich of the rising business community might prefer to spend their money and show off their women in the Astoria, but neither could seriously challenge the Europa. It had been built as part of Rossi's great complex in the heart of the capital, with the park, the squares, the theatres all harmonising in their architecture and their façades of yellow ochre, and on the hot July night when Joe Calvert came in from the Nevski Prospekt some of the dust from the street seemed to be dyed the same gold in the westering sunlight. He stood blinking on the threshold of the bar. It was entered from the lobby of the Europa, through the main door on a street leading to the former Michael Palace, but the tall windows opened on the Nevski Prospekt, and they were open now, in spite of the noise of trams and droshkies, to let the warm summer air come in.

Joe surveyed the place with well-concealed amusement. The words 'American Bar' had recently been added, in gilt letters, to the glass doors, but the interior was like no saloon he had ever seen in America. The long mahogany bar, the brass rail, the white-coated barmen and the array of bottles behind them were not to be found in the Europa, where the atmosphere was more like that of an English club. Waiters in tail coats moved quietly between the tables and the heavy saddlebag chairs, set not too close together in a room heavy with the scent of Russian cigarettes and bright with the uniforms of a colourful army. There were no women to be seen. Ladies, sometimes perfectly respectable ladies, took tea in the Palm Court of the new Astoria; the Europa's bar, whether American or not, remained a strictly masculine preserve.

"Are you making up your mind to have a drink, Mr. Calvert?"

said a voice from behind the pages of *Vechernaya Vremia,* and Joe turned round with a smile.

"Oh, good evening, Captain Allen. Sorry I didn't see you at first. How are you?"

"Very well, thanks. Won't you join me, unless you're meeting somebody?"

"Nobody at all." Joe Calvert settled his long body behind the corner table where the man from the British Embassy was watching him with quizzical eyes. Captain Allen was as unobtrusive as ever in a dark civilian suit, with his blond hair carefully brushed and his blond moustache close-clipped. His nondescript face reminded Joe of the rubber toys of his childhood, which could be squeezed into any shape by skilful fingers.

"How about some vodka?" Richard Allen said, beckoning to a waiter. There was a small carafe of vodka in a bowl of ice, with one glass, on the table, flanked by another ice bowl containing a little pot of caviar, and a plate of sliced black bread.

"Vodka seems to be an acquired taste, and I haven't acquired it yet," said Joe. "I'd like a sherry cobbler."

"Do you think they'll know how to mix it, here?"

"Oh, they should," said Joe softly. "I gave them a lesson myself, a few days ago. No point in calling it an American Bar if they can't mix American drinks, is there?"

Captain Allen laughed. Young Calvert wasn't quite the 'new boy' he had thought him at the American Embassy reception last night, when the consular staff, pressed into service for the Fourth of July, had been over-eager in trying to make things go. Young Calvert looked fine-drawn and pale this evening, as if the rising tension in St. Petersburg had communicated itself at last to the one foreign colony which had remained in splendid isolation since the murder at Sarajevo.

"That was a very good party your chargé d'affaires gave us yesterday," he said. "I enjoyed myself."

"Why, thanks. We did our best, Independence Day and all that, but we couldn't measure up to the great shows you people put on when the Navy was here. Congratulations, by the way; I hear your Admiral was a roaring success in Moscow."

"Roaring being the appropriate word," said Allen. "He's got a fine, powerful voice, has Admiral Beatty, and the story goes that when he spoke out of doors in the Sokolniki Park he could be heard inside the Kremlin. Anyway he made a great impression, and we've all survived—even His Majesty. I suppose you heard about the Björkö foul-up, at the tac. exercises in close order?"

"I did hear there was some trouble aboard the *Polar Star,*" said Joe discreetly.

"That's putting it mildly. The damned yacht sailed too close to the cruisers, and was nearly swamped in the wash when they turned. The Czar and his entourage were clinging to the rail, knee deep in water, God knows how they weren't drowned."

"Sounds like a court of enquiry for somebody."

"Not necessarily. It's only a few years since Admiral Nilov ran the *Standart* aground, and all the imperial family had to be taken off in boats. Aground in the Gulf of Finland, on a summer cruise! The Czar himself stopped the Admiral from committing suicide over that one, and there was never any question of a reprimand."

"The Czar seems like a pretty cool customer."

"Cool, or apathetic." Captain Allen paused while the waiter put Joe's sherry cobbler on the table. "There's an element of farce in the Russian character, as you'll soon find out. They put on great shows and ceremonies, and then something goes wrong out of sheer inefficiency, as it did aboard the *Polar Star* last week, and everybody behaves like knockabout comedians in the music halls."

"It might be rather an endearing trait."

"I certainly hope they'll stick to the comedy line for the next few weeks."

"Even during the French state visit?"

"There'll be some unrehearsed funny turns during that visit too. By the way, what are they saying in France about President Poincaré's trip to Russia? Your last posting was to Lyon, didn't I hear you say last night?"

"My last posting and my first, I only left Washington in January '13. Well, I can't say there was much interest expressed in Lyon, one way or another, but I had Paris leave before coming here, and the Parisians were full of it; some approved, but the Socialist newspapers were dead against it. Said the French President ought not to consort with—you know the sort of stuff they write," said Joe, looking cautiously around. The bar was full of Russian officers, none of whom showed any interest in the two foreigners in their quiet corner.

"I know the stuff all right. But talking about consorting, quite a lot of people here see it the other way round. The monarchists are saying the Romanov ancestors will turn in their graves when Nicholas welcomes the president of a republic to his palace. However, there's nothing they can do about it, France is the ally of Russia, bound by solemn treaties going back to the last reign. Then the Socialists—Social Democrats *and* Social Revolutionaries, argue like their comrades in France. They think the alliance with France is bound to lead to war."

"But isn't your own country part of that alliance?" asked Joe Calvert.

"Of the Triple Entente, yes," Richard Allen said.

"Meaning just good friends, eh?"

"Something like that."

"And what are we?"

"The Americans? Nothing, so far. But you just might be called upon to keep the ring in Europe, one of these days."

"That's not very likely."

"We shall see. I'm glad President Wilson has appointed an ambassador to Russia at last. Not that your chargé d'affaires hasn't done extremely well, but still—two years without any ambassador at all, and just because your Congress revoked some eighty-year-old trade agreement with the Russians, that everyone here had forgotten for generations!"

"It was a pretty convincing vote by Congress—three hundred to one, as I recall."

"When do you expect the new man in St. Petersburg?"

"Mr. Marye? Not for a while yet. The Senate has to advise and consent to his appointment first. He'll probably arrive at the end of September or the beginning of October."

Richard Allen considered that, with his pale eyes as round as glass marbles beneath lifted brows.

"So there'll be no American Ambassador in Russia for the next eight weeks. Too bad!"

"There won't be much doing in the holiday season."

"I'm not so sure. What are they saying at your shop about the murders at Sarajevo?"

"Oh that." At Joe's shop, if by 'shop' Allen meant the US consulate, the current problem had nothing to do with international politics, but with the labour troubles of an American

concern called the Stepeezi Shoe Company, recently established in St. Petersburg. Joe had spent the afternoon drafting a memorandum to the parent company in Philadelphia. It was written on approved consular lines and he was rather proud of it, but it was hardly on the level of a Note exchanged between the Great Powers. "Sarajevo?" he said, "you should have asked our chargé d'affaires about that, last night."

"I did," said Captain Allen, "but every day counts in a Balkan crisis, and it's a week since the Archduke and his wife were killed. I don't like the way the Austrians are hanging in the wind. If they want to pin the final responsibility for the murder plot on the Serbian government, I should have thought both the Ballhausplatz and the Hofburg would have shown their hands by now. After all, Franz Ferdinand was the heir-apparent to the throne of Austria-Hungary."

"You wouldn't think so by the way they buried him," said Joe. "A scrambled lying-in-state and a midnight drive through a thunderstorm to a private vault at Artstetten. I read in our press digest that the coffins were nearly toppled into the Danube before they got there."

"Yes, well, that's the Austrian idea of drama, they've never recovered from Mayerling. And the Archduke wasn't really popular in Vienna. That morganatic marriage stuck in more throats than the Emperor's."

"Well, if he wasn't all that important, why should they want to involve the Serbs in it? They've got three of the Bosnian gang in custody now, and this fellow Princip is known to have done the actual shooting—why not just string him up, and call it quits?"

"Because unfortunately," said the Englishman with a wry smile, "we're dealing with the Near East, not the Wild West. Will you excuse me, please?" He got up and shook hands with a tall Russian officer, who had greeted him on his way out of the bar. They chatted for a few minutes, which Joe employed to order the little carafe of vodka to be refilled.

"That's very kind of you," said Allen, sitting down again just as the waiter's careful pouring ended. "I hope you'll forgive me for not introducing you to Count Bronski. He doesn't speak a word of English, and unlike most of them he doesn't speak French either."

"I was admiring your Russian," said Joe. "I saw you were reading the evening paper when I came in, but the way you speak it—gosh! How long have you been attached to the British Embassy?"

"Oh, not so very long on this tour of duty," said the Englishman easily, "but as a matter of fact I was born here. My father came from Lancashire: he set up some of the first textile mills in Russia, in the Czar Alexander's time."

"That sure gave you a head start with the language. And maybe you could advise me—" Joe looked at his pocket watch. "Or am I detaining you? Maybe you're expecting friends, or going out?"

"I *am* expecting guests, and we're dining at Cubat's. But being Russian, they'll be at least an hour late, so there's no hurry. You're taking a long time to finish your sherry cobbler."

"Well, I—the thing is, I've been invited to my language teacher's house tonight."

"Ah, you've acquired a language teacher. Good."

"And as people here seem to eat at all hours, I don't know if I'll be crashing into the middle of *their* dinner, or have to hang around until they finish it, or just go hungry."

"That depends on the man who's going to teach you Russian," said Allen, looking amused.

"It's a lady. Madame Hendrikova, she lives on Vassili Island."

Allen whistled. "You must be quite a linguist, Mr. Calvert. Vera Andreievna can pick and choose her pupils, and one thing she insists on, they must all have what she calls a language brain."

"You make me feel as if I were going to sit an exam tonight. So you know Madame Hendrikova?"

"Only very slightly. I've been to their apartment twice, but that was as her husband's guest, not hers. And I haven't met any of the family. I believe they've got two very pretty daughters, and a son in the Marine Guards, but I imagine they fight shy of papa's political evenings."

"I thought the husband was a history professor."

"*And* by way of being a politician. Rather a swell in his day, an elected member of the First Duma, but after that little flutter in the parliamentary line was closed down by imperial ukase, Karl Hendrikov was warned that he would lose his professorship if he went on with it. I suppose he's what we'd call a Liberal, and you a Democrat; at any rate, he still writes for the Liberal paper,

Rech, and Vladimir Nabokov was one of the guests the first time I went there. Nowadays he seems to have taken up with Kerensky, the Labour leader—the barrister who made such an impression in the Lena Goldfields case. You won't meet Monsieur Kerensky tonight, though. He's politicking somewhere in Siberia. According to the papers, he was attending a schoolteachers' congress on the day Franz Ferdinand was shot. At a town in the Urals called Ekaterinburg."

"That's all right with me," said Joe. "I don't feel equal to meeting any Russian politicians yet, Liberal *or* Labour."

"You'll have a very pleasant evening. They'll probably ask a crowd of relatives and friends to meet you, and the samovar will be filled and refilled until midnight. You're wise not to have any dinner! But let me get you another of those cobbler concoctions. By the way, I thought you Americans went in for cocktails, made with gin?"

"Oh, we do," Joe Calvert assured him. "I was just keeping my head clear for Madame Hendrikova. No, not another, thanks. And thanks for the briefing, too. I think I'll go up to my room and have a wash."

"That's right, you're staying in the hotel, aren't you?"

"Only until I find a flat. And I suppose that means until I can speak enough Russian to hire a maid."

"It won't take you long. I've got a small flat of my own in the Italianskaia, about five minutes' walk from here. Number 365, an easy one to remember, just think of the days of the year. After President Poincaré gets safely back to Paris, maybe we could fix up a bridge four there some evening?"

"I'd like that," said Joe, shaking hands. "But poker's my own game."

"I rather thought it might be."

* * *

The Hendrikovs lived in the Fourth Line of Vassili Island, a wide street set at right angles to the University Quay, where two rows of tall apartment buildings faced each other across stone pavements with grass verges planted with linden trees. The limes were just coming into flower, and the sweet scent of the blossom was mixed with a faint but distinct smell of salt sea and tarry ropes. Joe sniffed it appreciatively as he paid off his driver. The

Hendrikov flat, he was told by an obsequious porter, bowing very low, was two stairs up, if the *barin* would give himself the trouble to ascend the staircase, since alas! there was no elevator. The stairs were well carpeted, and solid mahogany doors indicated that there were two apartments on each floor. He rang the Hendrikovs' bell. A tidy girl with a broad face and her hair in two plaits, wearing a white apron, curtseyed as she opened the door. He hung his straw boater on a stand in the hall and was shown into a pleasant family room where two girls rose to greet him with curtseys far more graceful than the maid's.

"Good-evening," Joe said as he made his bow. "My name's Calvert, from the US consulate. I've an appointment with Madame Hendrikova . . . "

"Good-evening, sir," said the fair girl politely. "Please sit down."

"Thank you." The two girls had been sitting at a round table, covered with a red plush cloth, with open books before them. Joe took a chair opposite, and said, rather at a loss:

"Uh—it's been a beautiful day, hasn't it?"

"Beautiful," the dark girl repeated. He could have sworn they were laughing at him. As a rule Joe was immediately at his ease with girls, but there was something disconcerting in the way those two were staring, as if some strange creature had been released in their familiar room. And yet they were very attractive, the fair one, with her curls tied back by a black ribbon bow, extremely pretty; the dark one, with her black braids wound round her head, also pretty in a more severe style. They had the same hazel eyes, neither brown nor green, and on the strength of that resemblance Joe decided to say:

"Are you Madame Hendrikova's daughters?"

"Oh no, sir," the fair girl managed to say, "my older sister Betsy is married, and lives in Denmark. I'm Darya Hendrikova, and this is my friend Marya."

"Mara Trenova," the dark girl said. "We are pupils of the Xenia School."

"Is that a boarding school?" said Joe.

"Yes, but now we have holidays."

"I see," Joe glanced round the room, seeking inspiration for what he could say next. It was well furnished in mahogany, with glass-fronted bookcases, a mirrored sideboard and a china cabinet, but there were also some execrable examples of still-life painting which included one enormous canvas, a 'problem picture' of the Nineties, representing a young woman with a baby at her breast and no wedding ring, staring morosely into a dying fire. No inspiration there! Joe was about to venture, "Are you going on to college?" when Darya helped by saying, "Please to excuse my mother. She had another pupil, but I think now she is coming." The sounds of farewell, and of doors shutting, could be heard from the hall. In another moment a little stout lady, with fair greying hair screwed up on the top of her head, and her face pink from exertion, burst into the living-room.

"My dear Mr. Calvert," she said effusively, "I'm so sorry to have kept you waiting. My last pupil was over half an hour late for his lesson. I hope Dolly and Molly have been entertaining you?"

"They've been very nice," said Joe, and Dolly said something in Russian which made her mother turn on her with a snap.

"Dolly, it's very rude to speak your own language in front of somebody who doesn't understand it!"

"What did she say, madame?"

"Please excuse a silly girl, Mr. Calvert. You are the first American my daughter ever saw, and what she said was that you don't look at all as she expected."

"I should have worn a war-bonnet and wampum, maybe," said Joe good-naturedly.

"Aha! You can be silly too! This is well," said Madame Hendrikova. "Come now, we must talk about your work. I have a little room far, far away," she waved her hand to indicate the other corner of a not very large flat, "where I receive my pupils, but tonight we shall sit in my husband's study. He too has been looking forward to meeting you."

With another snap of "Dolly! tell them to make the tea!" the little lady ushered Joe through a connecting door into a room lined with books on open shelves where Professor Hendrikov rose courteously from behind a laden desk. He was not a tall man, though decidedly taller than his wife, with a high scholar's forehead, growing bald, and clumps of hair arranged behind his ears. With his greying moustache and imperial, and something flowing about his collar and tie, he reminded Joe of a bust of Shakespeare which had stood in his school library at home.

It was about Joe's home that Professor Hendrikov began to talk gently, discovering that he was an only son, that his father had 'sort of retired', while his mother was active in women's club affairs, and getting some idea of the home in Baltimore, Maryland, where Joe had been born and his parents still lived. He nodded approvingly at Joe's description of the brick-paved streets, where the old trees thrust their roots up strongly and made the bricks uneven, and the suburban houses with wide stoops and porch swings where pretty girls and their beaux sat on summer evenings, playing mandolines and sometimes singing in harmony, while younger kids played in the middle of streets where only an occasional horse and buggy ever came.

"And you're a university graduate, I'm told?" he said.

"Yes sir, A.B. Princeton. Princeton 1911, I majored in French Civilisation."

"Dear me," said Professor Hendrikov. "Already we have something in common. My own subject is French history, from the Revolution to the present day."

"Donc, attention, monsieur!" interrupted Madame Hendrikova, *"parlons français!"*

"Bien, madame."

She led the American briskly through an account of his daily life in Lyon and his short holiday in Paris, and then exclaimed "*Assez!* The grammar is very good, the accent not; I think we shall work in Russian-English, not Russian-French."

"That's fine with me," said Joe. "I wasn't planning on working any other way."

"Then the sooner we start the better. Normally I see my students twice a week, Mr. Calvert, but you I should like to see three times a week for what remains of this month, until we go on holiday to Finland."

It was agreed that Joe should come to the flat on Mondays, Wednesdays and Fridays, beginning next day at six o'clock.

"It's really very unfortunate," fretted Madame Hendrikova, "that you're starting on the eve of the holiday season. We go to the dacha in one month from today, Sunday the second of August; would it be possible for you to come and spend a week with us at Koivisto, talking nothing but Russian, as far as you are able?"

"My dear Vera," said her husband, "you're forgetting that

Betsy and Hans are coming all the way from Copenhagen to spend August with us, and you've already invited so many relatives we'll have to board them in the village. I don't think that would appeal very much to Mr. Calvert."

"It's very kind of you, madame," said Joe, "but in any case it wouldn't be possible for me to get away from Petersburg. I'm the new man here, and the junior vice-consul; my Paris leave is all I rate this year."

"Then I shall set you a great many exercises to do in August," said his teacher. "And now come and have some tea."

When they returned to the living-room the table had been spread with a white cloth, and Dolly was presiding over a samovar set at one end. To Joe, the room seemed to have filled with people all talking at once, who presently resolved themselves into Cousin Timofey, a violinist under Glazunov at the Conservatoire; Cousin Arkadeiv, a laboratory assistant to the great Mendeliev; Cousin Boris, who was a junior curator at the Museum of Russian Art, and at least four plump female cousins dressed up for the occasion in evening blouses bedecked with lace inserts and tucks. They spoke in French to Joe, and were all very friendly and welcoming, a great deal more so than the stuffy businessmen of Lyon, not one of whom would have dreamed of inviting a young American into their bourgeois homes.

The maid and another girl of the same sturdy peasant type came and went with platters of food, until presently the whole table was covered. There was a dish of sliced white fish of some unfamiliar sort, and another of Baltic herring; various salads, including cucumber with an oil dressing, and cubed beetroot; black bread, and bread sprinkled with poppy seeds, and saucers of raspberry jam, which some of the company mixed with their tea instead of lemon. Dolly Hendrikova left her place behind the samovar to offer Joe a plate of ginger snaps, bought especially for him, she said with her little curtsey, at the English Shop on the Nevski Prospekt.

He looked up at her, smiling. She was really very pretty, with those clear eyes, and the soft features on which life had left as yet no mark, and the fair shining ringlets which had escaped from her severe black bow.

"You have such ginger cakes in Baltimore?" asked Cousin Timofey, and to please Dolly Joe said yes, monsieur, he was crazy about them, and took a second from the plate she had left near him.

"Russia must be very strange to you, monsieur."

"It is, a bit, but I hope to be here for a good long while, and see something of the country."

"What do you find most difficult to get accustomed to?" persisted Timofey. "The food? The wine? The hours we keep?"

"The calendar," said Joe unexpectedly.

"The *calendar*?"

"You know why. It's the fifth of July in America, yesterday was our Independence Day, but here it's only the twenty-third of June. I've been in trouble at the consulate already, for getting the dates mixed up."

There was a general laugh, under cover of which Joe thought he heard Professor Hendrikov mutter, "I wish we could put the calendar back to the first of June, for all of us." But he was not sure that he had heard aright, for Madame Hendrikova, reverting to English, broke in emphatically:

"There now, Mr. Calvert, we've found a good topic for your first Russian lesson: after the alphabet, the days of the week and the months of the year. But tonight already, you shall learn how to address Russians, and be addressed: you shall no longer say to me, Madame Hendrikova, but Vera Andreievna, using the patronymic; and to my daughter, Darya Karlovna, and so on. You shall use each time the person's Christian name and his father's name; it is more correct Russian usage than the other."

"But what if you don't know a person's father's Christian name?" parried Joe.

"Then you shall listen until he is called by it, and then you shall remember it. Now we take your own case. Your Christian name is Joseph, so?"

"Right."

"And your father's?"

"It's George, as a matter of fact. George Alexander Calvert."

"Thus we see," said his new teacher, "that your name in Russian is Yusuv Yurievich, and so, from now on, you shall be known here."

"To Yusuv Yurievich!" cried the musician, raising a glass of what looked more like yellow wine than tea. But the rechristened Yusuv said very decidedly:

"I'm sorry, madame, but I don't think I'd know myself as Yusuv What-d'you-call it. I'll go on being plain Joe Calvert, if you don't mind."

There was a shout of laughter, even louder than before, and though Madame Hendrikova shook her head, the American was pleased. He had asserted himself, and they liked him for it; Joe felt himself accepted into the friendliest group he had yet met in St. Petersburg. The talk broke out again like Niagara Falls: it was almost a shock when a new, deep voice cut through the gabble and a young man said from the door:

"What a row you're all making! I could hear you from the end of the Fourth Line!"

* * *

Simon Hendrikov told the droshki driver to wait for ten minutes, say a quarter of an hour, and when the man demurred he offered him double fare for the return trip to the Morskaia, which was accepted. A young officer going to one of the smart clubs or hotels on that fashionable street would be good for a big tip as well as double fare when the drive was over, and the *isvoschik* got contentedly down from his seat and gave his scraggy horse a nose-bag. On his way to the front door Simon looked up at the unlighted, open window on the second floor, and listened for a moment to the babble of talk. They were sitting in the dark as usual, smoking and talking about art and the artist's duty to his public, or so he was prepared to bet. Indoors, the staircase was well lighted, and as he reached his own landing a man in naval uniform came running downstairs from the floor above. He wore the badges of a commander's rank. Simon saluted, received a pleasant "Good-evening" and, while feeling for his latchkey, watched the stranger go on downstairs and out of the building. There had been something oddly familiar about his face.

He opened the living-room door without a sound. There they all were, his family and the cousins, the eternal hangers-on, their faces only visible by the tiny points of light from their cigarettes. He told them he could hear the row they were making from the end of the Fourth Line, and flicked the electric light switch by the door.

"I wish you wouldn't do that, boy!" The professor was blinking in the crude white light. Suddenly they were all shown at their worst, sitting round a littered table with dregs in their glasses, the women with tousled hair, the men irritable. Simon himself was immaculate in his summer uniform. He had square features, crisp hair more chestnut than brown, and clear hazel eyes like his sister's. His mother said, "You're late."

"I know, mother, but something came up at the last moment, I'm very sorry." Simon pulled his sister's hair, said something in Russian to Mara which made her smile, and then went round the table greeting all the company in French and kissing the hands of the ladies. He shook hands with Joe Calvert and bade him welcome to St. Petersburg. It was a finished performance of ease and good manners, but Simon Hendrikov's restless impatience was clearly held in check beneath the surface.

"Father, could I speak to you alone?" he said when the circle of the table was complete. "I've got a droshki waiting, I mustn't stay too long."

"But Simon—" Madame Hendrikova was silenced by her husband's gesture. "Come into my study, boy," he said very gravely indeed.

"I've told them to make fresh tea for Simon, mother," said Dolly, pulling a heavy brass ceiling lamp down to the table. Joe jumped up to help her, and some of the women began lifting the scattered plates from the centre of the cloth.

"Don't trouble, Mr. Calvert, I know the way of it," said Dolly. She held a match to the lamp wick and replaced the large white shade. A smell of paraffin, accompanied by a soft golden light, diffused itself through the friendly room. Dolly switched off the lights in the chandelier. "Papa is so old-fashioned," she confided to Joe, "he likes the oil lamp better than anything more modern."

"I don't blame him." But the spell was broken. One or two of the women murmured that they ought to be going home.

"Nonsense, it's not eleven o'clock yet," said the hostess automatically. "Simon and his father won't be long, I'm sure."

"Are you?" said Cousin Timofey. "Simon looks wrought up enough to be breaking the news of a general mobilisation."

"Good God!" said the museum curator. Two of the older women crossed themselves, and Simon's mother, very pale, told Timofey that was a horrible thing to say. It was over in a moment, for Simon and his father came back smiling, the young man putting something in his pocket as he closed the study door.

"You must sit down and drink a glass of tea with us, Simon," said Madame Hendrikova, imperative in her relief.

"All right then, but I really mustn't stay more than a few minutes. I'm invited to supper at the Yacht Club, and I don't want to be late."

"The club on Krestovski Island?" asked the professor.

"No, father, the Yacht Club on the Morskaia."

"And then on to the gipsies, no doubt," said Mara Trenova.

Simon gave her an indifferent look. "Possibly," he said.

Joe Calvert missed none of it: the delight of the liberal professor at his son's entrée to the most exclusive club in Petersburg, and the disappointment in the girl Mara's face. She came here to see him, and now he's walking out on her, Joe thought. Too bad!

Dolly intervened hastily. "Well, as long as you *are* here, give us some court gossip," she said. "When is the Grand Duchess Olga's engagement to be announed?"

Simon was fitting a black Russian cigarette into an amber mouthpiece.

"What engagement is that?" he said.

"Oh, come on, now!" "Simon, don't be silly!" The voices broke out in a gush of relief, as if a court romance put the hint of war a long way off. "We all know you went to Constanza for the great meeting with Prince Carol, and that she liked him very much—"

"She *met* Prince Carol at Constanza, that's all anybody knows." The young officer scowled. A handsome kid with one hell of a temper, thought Joe Calvert; with that build he should be useful in a scrap.

"I heard Olga Nicolaievna was going to marry the Prince of Wales," said one of the ladies.

"But Monsieur Sazonov prefers the Rumanian match," said Professor Hendrikov. "Our foreign minister thinks it would advance Russia's plans in the Black Sea. On to Constantinople! The old Byzantine dream will never die."

"Are princesses still made to marry for political reasons? Sounds like the Middle Ages," said Joe.

"The Romanovs are *living* in the Middle Ages," said Mara. "The Empress Dowager has a great deal more influence in the family than Sazonov," said Madame Hendrikova, "and *she* would like to see her eldest granddaughter married to the future King of England."

"I've been told," said Cousin Timofey, "that the young lady herself favours the Grand Duke Dmitri."

Simon pushed his chair back and got up. "What a pack of gossips you all are!" he said. "Next time I'm here, I'll expect to find you holding a spiritualist seance, or telling fortunes with the tarot cards."

"And you get plenty of occult influences at court, don't you?" Mara said.

"You know nothing whatever about the court, Mara Ivanovna," Simon retorted. "Mother, I must go. I'll leave the rest of you to your old wives' tales. Good-night!"

"Simon darling, when shall we see you again?"

He was too warm-hearted to resist the appeal in his mother's voice. He stooped and kissed her.

"I hope to get a few hours' city leave before the cruise to Finland starts, but I'm not sure. They're keeping us pretty close to barracks this week. Oh, that reminds me! I meant to ask you something, mother."

"Yes, what is it, dear?"

"Those new people who moved into the flat just overhead, have they a son in the Navy?"

Madame Hendrikova laughed. "What an idea! The Martovs have a son in the cradle, barely three months old. They're quite a young couple; but of course you haven't seen them yet. What made you think they had a son in the Navy?"

"Oh, nothing. Just a man I met on the stairs, he must have been a visitor. He reminded me of somebody, that's all." Simon twisted the door handle irresolutely. "Well, good-night again."

"Good-night, Simon Karlovich." It was almost a chorus, and after that nobody spoke until the door of the apartment closed. Then Cousin Timofey said with a sarcastic laugh:

"Who would have thought your son would turn out to be such a supporter of the court, Karl Leontovich? Simon has become a monarchist since he was promoted into the *Standart.*"

"Imperial favour means a lot to a young man with his own way to make in the service," said the professor.

"How does Simon stand in Rasputin's favour?"

What might have been an argument was stopped by the girl Mara. She got up, and looking only at Madame Hendrikova, said, "Many thanks for your hospitality, Vera Andreievna. I really must go home now, I live so far away, and my mother will be anxious about me."

"May I have the pleasure of seeing you to your home, Mara Ivanovna?" said Joe. He didn't know what prompted his offer, the girl might live ten miles out in the country for all he knew, but he didn't like to see a woman humiliated, even if it was her own fault for showing her feelings all too plainly, and then needling the guy until he turned on her in front of everybody. Anyway it was a good move, because Mara smiled, and the other Russians burst into a shout of laughter. "Aha! he has begun to use the patronymic!" "Your pupil will do you credit, Vera Andreievna!" It was a small joke, but they made the most of it to relieve the tension which Simon had brought into the room.

"Please don't worry about me, monsieur, I'll get a tramcar at the bridge," said Mara.

"Let us all three walk along to the new bridge together," said the professor. "We can hardly expect our foreign guest to know one bridge from another yet."

His getting up was the signal for a general departure. Mara went away with Dolly, and came back wearing a tightly fitting blue serge jacket over her dress of the same material, and a cream straw hat not unlike Joe's own. The professor took up a shapeless homburg, and while the other guests lingered chattering on the landing, they went out together to the Fourth Line. Here, after the dimness in the linden-shadowed living-room until Simon's entry, it was surprisingly light.

"Not as light as it was two weeks ago," said Professor Hendrikov in answer to Joe's comment. "If you had been here at the time of the summer solstice, you could have stood where we are now and seen the sun sinking into the Gulf of Finland while the light of a new day was dawning in the east. But I think that at the beginning and the ending of what we call 'the white nights' the colours are even more subtle than at the melodramatic moment of the solstice."

He was right about the subtle colour of the white night. From Strelka Point the river and the city seemed to have taken on the colours of a clouded pearl, shading through rose to lilac above the deep violet of the granite embankments. The sky above was palest grey, pierced on each side of the Neva by the golden spires of the Admiralty and the Cathedral of St. Peter and St. Paul.

"Listen!" said Mara Trenova.

A carillon, delicate but insistent, rang across the river from the cathedral belfry.

"It's a tune, isn't it?" said Joe.

"It's the chime of *Gospodi pomiloui*, 'Lord have mercy upon us,'" said the professor. "It rings every quarter hour. If we waited here for another quarter, we should hear the hymn the bells play at midnight. *Kol slaven nach Gospod v Sion*, 'How glorious is our Lord in Sion'. My wife shall teach you the Russian words."

Joe glanced down at Mara. She was looking up the broad reaches of the Neva, and he could see tears on her black lashes. Instinctively he slipped his hand through her arm. She looked up at him, surprised, and her face softened in a smile.

"Shall we walk on a little ways?" said Joe. "There's another tram stop at the far side of the bridge."

"I'd like to." Mara said nothing more about her mother's anxiety. Walking slowly, the girl between the two men, watching the deepening of the grey light on the stone harmonies which the Romanov empresses and their architects had built to realise the great Peter's dream in granite, stucco and water, they passed through the squares beyond the bridge into the Nevski Prospekt.

"Now I know where I am," said Joe. "Here's the Morskaia, with the Astoria Hotel at the end of it, and once we're across the Moika canal, the Europa's just a few blocks further on. Say, the Petersburgers certainly enjoy taking a walk at night!" The Nevski was almost as crowded at midnight as in the early evening. The shop windows were lighted and electric lamps shone down on the steady movement of trams and traffic.

"Walking by night is one of our pastimes, winter or summer," said the professor. "You'll soon know your way around St. Petersburg, Mr. Calvert!"

"Do you know the names of all the canals?" asked Mara. She had slipped her hand from Joe's arm when they entered the Nevski Prospekt.

"I know three. We've crossed the Moika, we're coming up to the Catherine, and the Fontanka's quite a distance down the avenue. Professor, I wish you'd tell me the name of that church on the canal bank. It's different from all the other buildings in the city, and yet it looks familiar, somehow."

The professor smiled. "That's because you've seen pictures of the church of St. Basil in the Kremlin. They're very much alike—this one is called the Church of the Resurrection—and I agree with you, it is not in keeping with all our eighteenth-century and neo-classical façades."

"The Byzantine dream again, eh?" said Joe, studying the domes and Greek crosses, the polychrome rhomboids of blue, green, yellow and amber, all shifting in their colour values as the electric lighting from the Prospekt challenged the darkening night. "Is it a very old church?"

"One of the newest in the city," said Mara. "The Romanovs put it up in memory of Alexander II, on the spot where he was killed. Its other name is the Church of the Spilled Blood."

"Killed?" said Joe. "You mean murdered."

The professor interposed. "It's an old story, Mr. Calvert, and not one we should be proud to tell our foreign friends. A story of student terrorists, led by a fanatic from Odessa—"

"And by a girl from the aristocracy, Sophia Perovskaia," said Mara. "After they killed the Czar, she was hanged for her share in the plot. Imagine the cruelty of hanging a woman!"

"If you plan to blow up an emperor, you'd better be prepared to pay the price," said Joe. "Murder solves nothing, Miss Trenova! Do you think the shots Princip fired at Sarajevo last week will give the Bosnians their independence?"

"I admire Sophia Perovskaia," said Mara violently, "and I honour Gavrilo Princip for what he did. The Bosnians have lived under an imperial tyranny for too long—just as we live in Russia. Oh, what's the use of talking, I'll only make the professor angry! Thank you both for escorting me—and good night."

Before either man could stop her Mara ran across the street, dodging the traffic, and they saw her boarding a tram on the far side of the Nevski Prospekt.

"That was an abrupt departure," said Joe dryly. "Has she really got a long way to go? Will she be all right?"

"Of course she will. She doesn't like any of us to escort her to her own front door. Poor Mara! She lives in a miserable neighbourhood, and she's alternately proud and ashamed of it."

"She wasn't ashamed to say she honoured the Sarajevo murderer."

"Poor girl," the professor said again, "I don't think she quite knew what she was saying. She's very unhappy about her own future, now that she's come to the end of her schooldays and has no prospect of going on to the university—but Mara Ivanovna's personal problems can't possibly interest you!"

"I want to understand, if I can, sir. But you mustn't stand here by the canal, being jostled by all these night walkers! Come back with me to my hotel and let me offer you a drink before you start back home."

He wanted the drink, he didn't want to go on talking; even for a young man of twenty-five it had been a long day, with the routine office work overlaid by a host of new impressions, but the Russian jumped at the chance of continuing the conversation. When they were settled in the Europa bar, as crowded still as when Joe sat there with Richard Allen, and now enlivened by the sound of orchestral music coming from the supper room, he observed with a sinking heart that Professor Hendrikov looked fit for another hour of talk.

"You are right," the older man was saying earnestly, as he sipped appreciatively at the brandy Joe had ordered. "You want to understand, you ought to understand this country where you have been appointed to serve your own. And I believe Mara Trenova's story may contribute just a little to your better knowledge of our difficulties. To begin with, her father, Ivan Trenov, was a schoolmaster here in Petersburg. I knew him very slightly: he was a clever man. Very active in the Teachers' Union, but apart from that not politically inclined. Now, after the troubles in 1905, when between the Duma and the *zemstva*—rural councils you might call them—it seemed as if Russia was set on a more liberal course, an imperial edict invited the Teachers' Union to propose any reforms they wished to see in our school system. Trenov was one of the authors of the proposals finally submitted. They were studied by the Czar's ministers, if not by the Czar himself, and they were used, Mr. Calvert, each separate reform in the petition—remember one may only address the Czar as a petitioner—was used as a weapon to attack the very men who had drawn it up. Many teachers were arrested, many more lost their jobs. As my talented young friend Alexander Kerensky says, it was a trap for those who had taken the word of the Czar at its face value."

"Was Mr. Trenov among those arrested?"

"He was. His case was heard, with others, by the Court of Appeals, and he was among the majority who were acquitted. But not one was reinstated in his old position; there was no job anywhere for those men in our Russian schools. Trenov kept his head fairly well until he realised the truth. Then he went back to the law courts, demanding justice; was arrested again, resisted arrest, and wounded a police officer—the wretched man was armed—and after another trial he was exiled to Siberia."

"Is he still in Siberia?"

"His conduct on the march was such that he was sent to the prison reserved for our most dangerous convicts, on Sakhalin Island, and he died there three years later."

Joe drew a long breath. "When did all this happen, sir? How old was Miss Trenova at the time?"

"Let me see. The Court of Appeals heard the teachers' case in 1907, as far as I remember. Mara Ivanovna is nineteen now, so she would have been twelve then. Left virtually fatherless at twelve years old! I don't know how she and her mother would have survived if it hadn't been for some old cousin, a wealthy woman, who paid for Mara's education at the Xenia School. I believe the mother has a tiny annuity; enough to live on by herself in their pathetic flat near the Vladimir church. Indeed I think the mother spends most of her time at church, or attending funeral services, to hear the priest singing the *panikhidia,* and reciting the *kontakion* with the rest of the faithful."

"Poor woman. It's a tough story, professor, and I can see how it would make Trenov's daughter very bitter, but even so, it's not an excuse for condoning murder."

"That affected you unpleasantly, I see. Wild talk, Mr. Calvert! I'm accustomed to it from my students. Nine times out of ten it means nothing."

"But what if the tenth man is Gavrilo Princip?"

"Ah." Professor Hendrikov looked cautiously round the American Bar. There were fewer officers than there had been earlier, and three tables had been pushed together to accommodate a large party of men in white tie and tails, some wearing decorations and all absorbed in their own conversation. "Princip, yes. He set a match to a bonfire last week in Sarajevo: let us pray that the fire brigade comes along and puts it out before the flames are out of control."

"You don't really think the assassination will lead to war, do you?"

"We shall know better in a day or two."

It was exactly what Captain Allen had implied, when he wished that "the Ballhausplatz and the Hofburg would show their hand". Joe shook his head doubtfully. "Even so," he said, "it would only be another little Balkan war like last year and the year before. I have an uncle in the State Department. He's got one of the desks in the East European section, and his view is that the Balkan wars can always be localised: the real danger in that area is Turkey."

"I must respect the views of the State Department," said Hendrikov politely, "but speaking as a mere citizen of Petersburg, I saw and heard some alarming things in this city during the last 'little Balkan war' as you call it. The Bulgarians were the heroes of the hour then; now, of course, if the Austrian government can pin responsibility for Gavrilo Princip's act on Serbia, it'll be the Serbs. But last year we had a hothead from Bulgaria as the guest of the city, a general no less, called Radko Dmitriev, and he made speeches about the great Slav brotherhood, and how Russia alone had the right to interfere in the domestic quarrels of the Slavs. Of course he was only drumming up help from Russia for the Bulgarians, but he did go so far as to promise to lay Constantinople at the feet of the Czar . . . and His Majesty has always been a dreamer of the Byzantine dream."

"That's very interesting, and I wish we had more complete reports of all that in Washington, but in any event the Russians didn't march, and the war was localised and ended quite soon. Why shouldn't it happen that way again?"

"It should," said the professor heavily. "If only we had stronger men at the head of affairs. Sazonov is very clever, but the cabinet is responsible to the Czar and not the Duma: they will be overruled if the generals can overpersuade the Czar. I wish Stolypin were alive today. He was a man of great authority."

"Stolypin was the prime minister. But my God! he was assassinated too!"

Joe Calvert's head was aching, and in spite of the long brandy and soda his throat was parched. He thought sheer fatigue must be responsible for his sudden qualm of fear.

"Stolypin died in hospital, after a murderous attack upon him in Kiev," said Professor Hendrikov. "In Russia, all too often, the good men die young."

3

THE FINE SUMMER DAYS went quietly by, and the diplomats breathed more easily. It began to be hoped that the Sarajevo murders would be indemnified by the payment of some sort of reparations by Serbia, and of course by the execution of the young men now held in custody. What was not immediately known was that there had been a quiet exchange of letters between the aged Austrian emperor, Franz Josef, and his good friend and ally, Wilhelm II, the German Kaiser. The old man wrote to his ally a few days after the double murder, personally and almost ruminatively, to say that his primary policy objective in the affair must now be the isolation of Serbia. To which the Kaiser, with the full approval of his Chancellor, Bethmann-Hollweg, replied that Austria could count on Germany's full support if punitive action against Serbia should bring her into conflict with Russia. He added a few days later that this support would be forthcoming even in the event of 'a European complication', for the price of German support of Austria-Hungary in the Balkans was to be Austrian support of Germany against France.

Thus the famous 'blank cheque' was issued, a document which was literally a matter of life or death to millions of men and women who were young in 1914, and who were then, in their various ways, enjoying the pleasures of a remarkably warm summer. In Britain the perennial trouble in the Balkans seemed remote. Britain's troubles lay nearer home: there was a threat of civil war in Ireland, where Ulster was preparing to resist Home Rule. Sir Edward Carson's speeches encouraged the formation of an Ulster Provisional Government, and sums of money collected in America encouraged the arming of the Irish National Volunteers. This did not spoil the average Englishman's enjoyment of a sporting summer, in which the fight between two famous boxers, Georges Carpentier and 'Gunboat' Smith, aroused at least as much interest as the strife beyond the Irish Sea. A torrid Henley was followed by the tennis championships at

Wimbledon and the Eton and Harrow match at Lords. Society went to the Rose Show in Regent's Park and looked forward to the state ball at Buckingham Palace and the naval review at Spithead towards the end of July; meanwhile, the fruit ripened in the Kentish orchards, and trainloads of happy Cockneys went off on their annual cherry-picking holiday. Across the Channel a sex drama, revealed when Madame Caillaux, the wife of the Finance Minister, shot and killed the editor of the *Figaro,* was absorbing the attention of the Paris press.

Even in Russia, where the Czar and his ministers conferred daily on the Balkan situation, a new sensation had eclipsed the assassination of Franz Ferdinand. This was an attempt on the life of Rasputin, the *staretz*, or 'man of God', whose influence at court was believed by most literate Russians to be the influence of the devil. Joe Calvert had been warned, aboard the ferry bound for Kronstadt, not to say his name aloud in a Russian crowd, and this no doubt was wise advice to a foreigner, but the name, in all its variants, rang in the streets of every city in Russia when it was known that he, Grigori Efimovich Novik, Grisha, called Rasputin, had been stabbed in his home village of Povrovskoe by a young woman who drove a knife into his stomach, with a cry of "I have killed the anti-Christ!" Rasputin was in hospital in Tiumen, and lay there at the point of death; about his assailant the reports were far less clear. Her name was given as Khinia Gusseva, her age as twenty-six. She had been taken to prison, she had been taken to a lunatic asylum, she had been torn in pieces by the devoted villagers of Povrovskoe. She had been paid to kill Rasputin by his enemies, said one report. Another said she was a Petersburg prostitute who had been rejected by Rasputin after sharing in many of the orgies which went on at his apartment, or in the bath houses of the capital. All of these reports were censored by the Czar's police, and the news telegraphed round the world was that the stabbing of Rasputin was the act of a madwoman.

The ship's officers and members of the Garde Equipage assembled on board the imperial yacht *Standart* on the day the news was released were a silent company. Sidelong glances and one or two bawdy references to Gusseva were as far as anyone cared to go in comment. Simon Hendrikov, after only three months' service aboard, had not yet decided which of the naval officers owed their appointments to the Czarina's interest—this meant they venerated, or said they venerated, Rasputin as a holy man—and which of them, being there by merit or seniority, were prepared to jeer at the priest's convenient doctrine of committing the sins of the flesh deliberately, in order to obtain salvation. It was part of the wretched web of intrigue which the Czarina's faith in Rasputin had woven about the court that even in her floating home, the *Standart*, which her children preferred to all their father's palaces, there could be no honesty between one man and another.

It was the day appointed for the start of the cruise down the Gulf of Finland, and as the morning passed without orders from Peterhof it began to be rumoured that the cruise would probably be cancelled. Rasputin must have died in Tiumen, the grief-stricken Alexandra Feodorovna must have refused to consider a holiday: the only matter for conjecture now was, one humorist dared to say, how long would the court mourning last? Simon could tell, by the look on several faces, that there were still officers in the *Standart*'s company who would exult in the death of the Czarina's evil angel.

Shortly after midday it was announed that the summer cruise would start as planned, but with a few hours' delay to enable the Czar to visit the new dry dock at Kronstadt. Simon's spirits rose immediately. Since going to his home in the Fourth Line to ask his father for the key of the dacha at Koivisto, he had thought of nothing but the picnic so impulsively proposed by his princess, and how it could possibly be brought about. He was no more interested in the knifing of an unsavoury religious maniac in Siberia than in the assassination of the Austrian Archduke; at twenty-three, his heart was set on just one thing: the chance to spend an afternoon in the company of Olga Nicolaievna.

It seemed hours before the *Alexandria* came alongside, and he saw her on deck, standing rather in the rear, with her head bent over the stiff bouquet of carnations which told him that the eldest Grand Duchess, instead of her mother, had accompanied the Czar on his tour of the dry dock built to accomodate two newly purchased Dreadnoughts. The Czarina was sitting in a deck-chair, listening to a fat, pasty-faced young person called Anna Virubova, her closest woman friend. The Heir to the Throne was standing at the rail between his father and one of his two sailor nurses, waving and laughing to his friends, the whole ship's company of the *Standart*, and at the sight of his happy face the long tension of the day was suddenly relaxed.

Alexis Nicolaievich was nearly ten years old, and tall for his age. He had inherited his mother's grey-blue eyes and red-gold hair, which in the boy might darken to copper as he grew to manhood. Whatever ailment had kept him from the luncheon in H.M.S. *Lion*, he now appeared to be the picture of health, and although he was rather pale, his clear complexion gave the lie to the persistent rumour that he had been born with one skin too few.

From the deck of the little *Alexandria* he looked up delightedly at the splendid Danish-built *Standart*, sleek in her black paint with the gilded bowsprit and stern, and started up the ship's ladder behind his father, at the very moment the Czar was piped aboard. Nobody really saw how the accident happened. The sailor attendant, Derevenko, was close behind the child, and a petty officer called Gordienko had stretched out both hands to help Alexis aboard, when suddenly he seemed to slip between the two men, and stumbled heavily on one rung of the ladder. He was saved from sprawling by the petty officer, but his involuntary "Oh!" reached the ears of his father, who was shaking hands with Commander Sablin.

"What happened, Alexis?"

"Nothing, papa. I hit my foot against the ladder, that was all."

"What a silly thing to do."

"I'm *all right*, papa."

"Of course you are." But the Czar took the child's hand and held it tightly until the ladies of his personal staff had come aboard. Then, when the formal greetings were over, he marshalled them all below, and to the disappointment of the officers the imperial family was seen no more that evening.

It was perhaps understandable, for a stiff breeze was blowing up the Gulf of Finland, and even the splendid steam yacht was rolling a little as she headed west by south. The escort of torpedo boats, the only security measure the Czar permitted on those cruises, was bucketing up and down along the line of the horizon. So the white awnings above the decks were furled, the folding chairs and tables put away, and no pretty girls appeared to ask eager questions about navigation or renew acquaintance with old friends. The balalaika orchestra was summoned to one of the ornately furnished saloons, but only played for half an hour, the Czarina complaining of headache, and the stewards, sent to offer evening tea, reported that everyone had turned in early. Simon Hendrikov did the same. He slept soundly, happy in the knowledge that his princess was not far away, and awoke once only during the night, when he thought he heard a child screaming in pain. But all was silent, except for the normal sounds of a ship at sea, and Simon dismissed the dream, to sleep again.

The wind fell during the early hours of the morning, and when the Czar came on deck for his usual brisk constitutional the *Standart* was lying in a beautiful little Finnish bay, where the birch woods came down close to the water's edge. He chatted amiably with the officers of the Garde Equipage, and groaned audibly when the courier boat from St. Petersburg came alongside with the morning's load of letters, reports, and documents requiring the signature of the man who, in spite of the Duma and the Council of the Empire, was still the final arbiter of all affairs in Russia. When the Czar went to his private quarters, Marie and Anastasia came on deck. They had friends among the sub-lieutenants, and presently a noisy game developed, involving the squealing and shouting and racing round the housing which their parents not only tolerated but encouraged aboard the yacht. It was in the middle of the fun, when Simon for some reason was required to time their activities with a stop-watch, that he received an unexpected summons from the Grand Duchess Tatiana.

He turned over the stop-watch to another man, and went below with his uniform cap under his arm, following the steward who had been sent to fetch him through the magnificent suite of saloons until they came to a cabin fitted up as a writing room, where Tatiana Nicolaievna was sitting behind an ormolu desk. One of the young officers from the wireless cabin was standing at attention by her side.

"Good morning, Simon Karlovich," she said with the smile and the studied charm so oddly mature in a girl of seventeen, so often contrasting with her sister Olga's more slapdash ways. "Will you excuse me one moment? I've been writing telegrams for the Czarina, and they must go at once." She counted the sheets of paper, while Simon thought what a picture she made, with that glorious hair against the emerald green silk hung instead of paper on the walls of the writing room. He had time to wonder how many of the telegrams were directed to the hospital at Tiumen, where Rasputin (so the men in the courier boat had said) was beginning to rally from his stomach wound.

"Ten, that's right. These may go off now, and thank you, Ivan Ivanovich."

When the wireless officer had left, the girl relaxed in her velvet armchair, and smiled again at Lieutenant Hendrikov. "I want to give you a message from my sister Olga," she said. "She's sitting with our little brother. I don't know if you heard that Alexis wrenched his foot rather badly as he came aboard yesterday, and Dr. Botkin wants him to stay in bed all day."

"Wrenched his foot? Just coming up the ladder?" He couldn't help saying it, or seeing how the smiling mask came down over Tatiana's lovely face, just as it dropped over Olga's when she talked by implication of security at the British squadron's ball.

"Yes, it was most unfortunate," the young Grand Duchess said. "Especially since we're now so near your home, I mean your father's dacha in Finland, which my sister says you kindly invited us all to visit!"

"Your visit would be a great honour for my family and me, Tatiana Nicolaievna."

"Then shall we arrange for this little excursion to take place today, Simon Karlovich? The Czar has given his permission, and perhaps you could arrange with Commander Sablin about the launch, and where you would like to be put ashore?"

Simon bowed. He had an intuition that the prompt arrangements for what was to be a surprise picnic had been devised as a means of getting the noisy youngsters ashore and procuring silence for the boy who didn't seem able to stay well for a couple of weeks on end. He said, "I will make all the arrangements, Your Imperial Highness. At what time would it be convenient for us to start?"

He had to use her title, all orders to the contrary: there was something regal about this girl with the red-gold hair, who was planning his day for him, and for her sisters, with such aplomb. He remembered having heard that Tatiana was sometimes called 'The Governess' by her sisters, because of her ability to plan for them, her fondness for timetables and exactitude—the exactitude which made her say immediately:

"That depends on the distance between your dacha and the anchorage, Simon Karlovich. As far as my sisters' leisure is concerned, I should say about half past two."

* * *

It was barely half past two when three glowing girls came on deck to join him, the 'Little Pair', as Marie and Anastasia were called in the Family, childishly dressed in pinafore frocks with wide sailor hats, and carrying osier baskets. Olga Nicolaievna wore a white middy blouse with a navy blue tie and a white duck skirt. All three were wearing white buckskin shoes with heavy leather soles.

"Simon Karlovich! Are those the right kind of shoes?"

"We could wear our tennis shoes, you know!"

"Is it far to the dacha? Are we going into the village? Are there other people living close to you?"

"Be quiet, you two," said Olga. "Simon Karlovich, my sister Tatiana is so sorry she can't join the party. She really feels she ought to stay aboard with the Czarina and my brother."

"How is Alexis Nicolaievich feeling now?"

"Very sorry for himself," said Olga frankly, "but Dr. Botkin thinks he'll be much better in the morning." She turned to the man who was waiting to help her down into the launch. "You're Petty Officer Gordienko, aren't you? I do hope you aren't blaming yourself for my brother's stupid accident?"

The man saluted and said nothing.

"Because it was all his own fault really," Olga went on. "He was so excited about the cruise he simply didn't look where he was going; I think he must have picked that up from me!"

Gordienko bowed. He said to Lieutenant Hendrikov: "At what time shall the launch return, sir?"

Simon looked enquiringly at the Grand Duchess. "Shall we say five o'clock? It's not quite half an hour's walk to the dacha, twenty minutes if we walk fast."

"But we don't want to walk fast, this is our holiday! Five o'clock will be quite soon enough."

"Five o'clock, Gordienko."

"Very good, sir. And which of the men shall go with you, to carry the basket?"

"I'll take that myself." Simon already carried beneath his arm a large box wrapped and tied by a famous Petersburg confectioner, at which the Grand Duchess Marie's huge blue eyes—'Marie's saucers' as they were called in the Family—grew wider than ever in anticipation.

They were set ashore in a sandy cove, one of the many which broke the rugged Finnish coastline, with no sign of life about it, not even the wooden sauna which would have revealed the presence of a summer dwelling hidden by the evergreens. A narrow path led from the cove up through the trees.

"Where exactly are we?" Olga said. "I know we haven't passed Björkö yet."

"No, we cruised across the Gulf to the southern shore last night, and then turned north. We're about one mile west of Koivisto village, call it thirty miles east of Terijoki."

"It feels like three hundred miles from Terijoki. Remember the Yacht Club, and all those smart little tables on the lawn? This is the real country, isn't it?"

"I'm glad it pleases you, Olga Nicolaievna."

"I love the Finnish countryside."

It was impossible to hurry along that path, which wound between thickets of pine and birch until it emerged upon the bank of a river, little more than a trout stream, which flowed to the sea through stony shallows and deep pools of clear amber water. There were wild flowers growing in profusion, which made Marie and Anastasia begin excitedly to plan how they would fill their baskets, and there was above all, hardly broken by their chattering, the deep and healing silence of the Finnish woods. Olga walked very quietly on the carpet of pine needles. Simon brought up the rear, carrying the picnic basket, which was heavy: he was glad when they reached the clearing where his parents' summer cottage stood.

He had been right in telling Olga that it was not in the least like the smart villas at Terijoki. The Hendrikov cottage was built of pine logs, hand hewn, with a stone chimney at one gable end and a pile of firewood at the other. A flight of four wooden steps led up to a verandah with a shingle roof, protecting the door, on each side of which a small window of four square panes gave the front of the cottage something of the simplicity of a child's drawing. There was no attempt at a garden, but the grassy ground which sloped very gently to the river had been roughly scythed, and smelt of new mown hay.

"Is this it?" "What a marvellous place!" "Oh, Simon Karlovich, aren't you lucky!" The enthusiastic exclamations broke out behind Simon as he laid down his burdens and produced the key he had requested from his father. "Just a moment," he said hurriedly, and this was the anxious moment, when he let himself into the cottage without knowing what state it might be in. Madame Hendrikova had long ago decided that as a member of the intelligentsia she had a soul above housekeeping, and the occasional country girl who was all the help available in Finland appeared to share her views. But Dolly's neat hands must have been at work before they left at Easter, for the living-room was very tidy, and across the tiny hall he could see through an open door that his parents' bedroom was in good order too. The place was hot and stuffy, but that was remedied at once by throwing up the sash windows, and then his eager guests were jumping up the steps to join him.

"It really is delightful, Simon Karlovich," was Olga's quieter comment while her sisters squealed their admiration, and Simon looked round the log-walled living-room, hung with *rya* rugs in vivid colours, trying to see it with the eyes of a girl accustomed to the formal grandeur of Peterhof and Czarskoe Selo. There was a long table in the middle of the room with a runner of Finnish linen down the middle and set about with stools, and a copper lamp swung on chains directly overhead. There was a magnificent stone fireplace, with iron firedogs set wide enough apart to hold six-foot logs, with a bearskin stretched in front, pale brown on the back and shading to cream on the extended paws. A small brick cooking stove, also wood-burning, was built on one side of the great stone hearth.

"And where does everybody sleep?" said inquisitive Marie.

"Mashka, I really am ashamed of you—"

"But Olga, it's the very first time we've ever been in a real house!"

"My parents sleep across the hall, Marie Nicolaievna. There's nothing much to see but beds and books."

"What a lot of books!"

"My father uses this for the overflow from our flat in Petersburg."

"He must be *very* clever to have read all those."

"And just look at the beds, so cosy, with those lovely puffy quilts," said Anastasia. "You should see the beds we have to sleep on, Simon Karlovich!"

"*Anastasia!*"

"Well, what's wrong with that, everyone must sleep somewhere," said the *enfant terrible*. "We sleep on beastly little camp beds at home. Because the daughters of Alexander the First did it, we have to do it too!"

"Well, never mind about all that, let's think about having tea," said Marie, to cover Olga's vexation.

"Tea already!" the latter said. "Why, it isn't half past three!"

"We ought to get started on it," said Marie. "You never know, somebody might be sent to fetch us back—"

"That's true. Let's see what's inside our basket, then."

The picnic basket, opened on the greensward, was found to contain two kinds of sandwiches and a large plum cake. There were also glasses, carefully packed, china plates and linen napkins, and to Anastasia's despair, a vacuum container full of milk.

"But we ought to have *tea* at a picnic!" she protested.

"We can make tea indoors," said Simon recklessly. "My mother has a spirit stove somewhere. I'm sure I can find it, the fire would take too long."

He found it easily inside the wooden dresser, and his delighted visitors, rummaging, discovered a teapot and teacaddy, which Olga appropriated, and Finnish pottery mugs, pronounced to be "much nicer than those rotten glasses from the yacht". The tea was infused, the long table set, and next to the cut cake in the centre of the linen runner Simon set the box of chocolates which he had brought from St. Petersburg.

"Two chocolates each after tea, girls, and we'll take the rest home to Tania and Baby," Olga said.

"Huh!" said Anastasia. "Baby won't be allowed to eat sweets today."

"Why not?" asked Simon. "I should have thought chocolate was just the right prescription for a wrenched ankle."

"He'll enjoy them tomorrow," said Olga, with an imperceptible glance of warning at her sister. "Have some more cake, Simon Karlovich."

"It *is* good," said Marie, helping herself. "We get much nicer teas on the *Standart* than we do ashore."

"That's because we always have some horrible cakes that Catherine the Great enjoyed," said Anastasia.

"This is my sister's day for giving us a lecture on Russian history," said Olga lightly. "Now who's going to do the washing up?"

"Washing up?"

"Yes, of course; we can't leave this lovely place untidy."

"But we've got to go now, and make the posies for mamma and Anna."

"Dishes first."

Eventually they all did the washing up, by the simple process of rinsing the mugs and plates in the river and drying them with one of the table napkins. Then the two younger girls caught up their osier baskets; they were impatient to be off.

"Where does that road lead to, Simon Karlovich?" asked Olga, pointing to a road of sorts, many times broader than the track from the shore, which began at the cottage clearing.

"First to a farm, and then across the river by a bridge, and then back on the other side of the water to Koivisto," Simon said. "That's the way my parents drive up, when they come here on holiday."

"I see. All right, you two, keep to the road or the river bank, and don't go out of sight, please."

"Oh, but Olga, we want to go into the woods to gather berries."

"The bilberries aren't ripe yet, I saw them all green beside the path." She turned to Simon as the girls ran off. "What a blessing it isn't the mushroom season. We wouldn't have been able to keep track of them then."

He was enchanted by the way she said 'we', for the first time linking them together, two adults, jointly responsible for two harum-scarum children.

"Where would you like to sit, Olga Nicolaievna? You haven't got a hat, and the sun's so strong."

"I love sitting in the sun." But she got up, and moved to the verandah, folding her white skirts carelessly to sit down on the top step, motioning to the young man to sit on one of the steps below.

"There's just one drawback to your paradise," she said. "The midges. Wouldn't you like to smoke?"

"If I may."

"Of course. And since there's nobody here to be shocked, I think I'll smoke myself."

Simon got up at once to offer her his cigarettes and strike a match. She looked up at him with a smile. He was very good-looking, with his chestnut hair growing so crisply above his broad forehead, and his clear hazel eyes, but the Grand Duchess Olga saw handsomer men every day of her life among the officers of her father's Guards. What appealed to her in this man was his solidity, not only the strength of his square shoulders and vigorous body, but in the feeling he gave her that here was a man to be relied on. She leaned backwards in a luxurious stretch, and said,

"How marvellous to get away from the botanists!"

"What botanists, Princess?"

"Don't you know that expression? That's what the Czar calls the plain clothes police, who're always slinking about when he goes on his long walks. He says he can spot them a mile away, peering at flowers and pretending to be interested in shrubs. You must have seen them in the Crimea, Livadia was swarming with them!"

"I suppose I did."

Simon sat down again and looked away from her, across the shining river. He was remembering, almost with guilt, the hour he had spent in the Commander's cabin after his talk with Tatiana, drawing a map of the route they would take from the launch to the dacha and back, showing the farm and Koivisto village, and answering detailed questions about the Finnish farmer and his family, their names and ages, but quite unable to give answers about their political opinions, about which he knew nothing. Olga might think, poor darling, that the summer woods were free of 'botanists', but the invisible guards were bound to be there, the bars were still up round the golden cage. He muttered something like, "It's better to be careful." He was remembering that this young girl, when she was younger still, not yet sixteen, had been a witness of Stolypin's murder in the theatre at Kiev. Everybody knew the story, how the murderer and his victim, dabbled with blood, had been removed, and the horrified audience, streaming back from the stairs and foyers (for it was an interval) had poured into the auditorium, believing that the Czar himself was shot. Then, while they sang the national anthem, spontaneously, full-throated, while the fourteen-year-old Tatiana cried hysterically in the anteroom, the Grand Duchess Olga stood steadfastly beside her father in the imperial box, as proud a Romanov as any woman who ever graced the throne. He said, trying to speak naturally, to pick up the cue she had given him about Livadia:

"Do you think you'll be going back to the Crimea, later in the year?"

"It isn't very likely."

"But—it was announced that Prince Carol of Rumania, and his mother, the Crown Princess, would be returning your visit to Constanza."

"How you harp on that visit to Constanza! It only lasted for one day."

"I was in hell that day . . . because everybody said your engagement would be announced at the end of it."

"That was the idea, I believe."

"So what happened? For God's sake tell me what happened, Princess!"

"Why do you call me Princess, Simon Karlovich? You know my name, why don't you use it?"

"Because you *are* a princess, just a girl: Grand Duchess seems so old and settled, it makes me think of a tall, stout lady, very proud and hung about with jewels, giving orders to everybody—not like you."

In spite of herself, Olga giggled. "You're drawing a wonderful picture of somebody I know."

"Please don't tease me, Olga Nicolaievna, it means so much to me."

She relented. "Very well, I will tell you, and why shouldn't I? Some of my real friends know, and you are my friend, aren't you? We sisters think of everybody in the *Standart* as our good, true friends—and you'll never know how glad I was to get back aboard the *Standart* after that horrible day at Constanza. Poor people—they put on such a show for us, building that wretched pavilion specially, down by the sea; and the old Queen, Carmen Sylva, had forgotten her Orders, and the King was furious with her . . . and then Prince Carol, and the awful proposal. I asked for time to think. So Monsieur Sazonov said his say, about how much I could do for Russia as Queen of Rumania—and of course

Carol's wife will be Queen some day—and the Czarina had a heart attack, at least she said it was a heart attack, and it was only papa, I mean the Czar, who stood by me. He said he would never force me into a marriage against my will, and he knows I never want to marry any foreign prince, and have to make my home away from Russia. Why should I, Simon Karlovich? After all, I *am* a Russian, and I mean to live and die in Russia!"

She was a Russian of the Russians then, in spite of all the German blood, going back through generations, which the spiteful said had drowned the tiny proportion of Slav blood left in the reigning house. She was a Russian, and also a thorough Romanov: through the girl's young face came the look, the features pictured on a hundred canvases in the galleries of the Winter Palace; and in a gust of admiration and relief Simon Hendrikov seized her hands and began to kiss them.

"So they sent my answer to Bucharest, and Prince Carol and his mother won't come to Livadia this year . . . Oh, Simon Karlovich, why does it mean so much to you?"

He lifted his head from her hands and said hoarsely:

"Because I want you to stay my princess—stay a happy girl—because I can't bear to think of you as the wife of any man."

It took a moment for the full sexual implication of his words to reach her. It was the physical relationship, from which she had shrunk with Prince Carol, which had roused this storm of feeling in the young man almost kneeling at her feet. Olga's first impulse was to pull her hands away, to run to the river, calling to her sisters that it must certainly be time to start back to the launch. But then it was too late, for Simon Hendrikov was kneeling no longer. He rose and pulled her up into his arms.

* * *

It was not until after she had gone to bed, and was listening to Tatiana's quiet breathing in the next berth—'the Big Pair' shared a stateroom afloat as they shared a bedroom ashore—that Olga was able to live in memory the thrilling moments of Simon Hendrikov's embrace. It had literally lasted for moments only, for he released her as soon as they heard the sound of the young voices coming round the bend of the river. Then Olga went to meet the girls with exaggerated praises of the wildflowers they had found, and Simon, at Anastasia's suggestion, went back into the dacha to see if he could find some sewing silk to tie up the posies. He found it in Dolly's neat workbox, in the back bedroom she had been accustomed to share with her sister; looked into his own small bedroom, and wondered what his father would say if he knew who his guests were on this summer afternoon. He had told the professor that he wanted to give Captain Prince Somebody a few hours' fishing—he knew that for a title his father would give up half a dozen keys.

They were all sitting on the grass when he went out with the green silk reel, and Marie had begun to arrange the harebells, the trefoil and campion into the little nests of coloured mosses which her strong hands wove with such delicacy. The four little Finns from the farm were sitting cross-legged, and devouring plum cake.

"They can't speak Russian," said Anastasia.

"Their parents can, I know." To Olga, lining the osier baskets with bright moss, Simon's voice sounded forced and far away.

"May we give them some of your lovely chocolates, Simon Karlovich?"

"They're your chocolates now, Marie Nicolaievna."

"Two each, then," said Olga. "Just what we had ourselves, share and share alike."

The silent little, tow-headed Finns looked blissful as the young ladies gave them the chocolates. They hung about, waiting for whatever might happen next while the Grand Duchesses had one more look inside the dacha ('just to remember everything') and then stood waving while Simon's party went off back down the path. The Finnish children were a help, thought Olga, as the *Standart,* that floating palace, steamed west and by south again towards the roadstead of Reval. They made everything seem so ordinary.

Everything was normal, too, though in a tragic way, when they were back aboard the yacht. It only required the deep, anxious silence which hung over the imperial suite, and the lady-in-waiting on duty rising with her finger to her lips as the girls entered, to tell them that their brother was no better, and Tatiana coming in pale and despairing, whispered that he was worse.

"Is it as bad as the Spala time?" asked Olga, when the older sisters were alone in their stateroom. They both dreaded a recurrence of the fearful attack of 'internal bleeding', as they had been taught to call it, which at Spala in Poland, in 1912, had left Alexis crippled for a year.

"Oh, we must pray it won't be nearly as bad as that!"

"But we do pray, Tania: if our prayers were heard, he'd be the healthiest boy in all the world."

She was unknotting the sailor tie, unfastening the middy blouse and the white skirt stained with grass. "The Little Pair want to give him their flowers and sweets, can they?"

"Mamma won't let anyone but herself see him tonight."

"Oh Lord," said Olga with resignation. "So we're in for it all over again. Why doesn't papa order them to put about and take us back to Peterhof?"

"The doctors are here on board with Baby. There's nothing they can do for him at Peterhof that they can't do here. And think of the publicity, just before the French state visit!"

"Of course, we can't risk the publicity, can we?"

The four sisters had been trained from their brother's babyhood to keep him from bumps and bruises. That bump against the ship's ladder, which would have meant nothing to any one of them, had resulted within two or three hours in a dark blue swelling over the place where his ankle struck the wood, then in further swelling and intense pain as the bruised blood seeped into his ankle joint and then through the tissues of his leg, which was already hideously cramped against his abdomen. The girls had petted him and prayed for him through all his attacks, had sung lullabies and told him fairy stories, even wept for his pain, but thanks to their mother's excessive prudery in physical matters, they had never been told, in so many words, the nature of his malady.

"How's mamma bearing up?" Olga picked up her white cambric dressing gown, and heard someone turn on the bath water in the next cabin. Her hands still smelled of moss and flowers.

"Mother? Wonderful with Baby, of course, she always is, but feeling so wretched and depressed. As she says, if only Father Grigori were well and close beside us, or even able to remember us in his prayers!"

"*Can't* he remember us in his prayers?"

"He's only been conscious for short intervals since they took him to hospital. But Ania had a much more hopeful telegram from the chief surgeon, just over an hour ago."

"So they think he's going to live?"

"Oh yes, he'll live, thank heaven."

"Well, good, in a day or two he'll be able to telegraph himself. After all, Grigori Efimovich was in Siberia when Alexis was so ill at Spala. He cured him by telegram that time; why shouldn't he do it this time too?"

"What an unfeeling thing to say!"

Olga considered that judgment, hours later, after the wretched evening had worn away. The Czarina remained by her sick child's bed, the Czar escaped to dine in the mess, while the girls sat on deck and chatted quietly as the *Standart* sailed into the twilight. No, she was not unfeeling—unsympathetic, perhaps, to her mother's cult of Rasputin, whose magnetic eyes and shaggy, greasy locks had become increasingly repulsive to the adolescent girl. But her deepest feelings had been aroused that day, and as never before, in the arms of Simon Hendrikov.

His kisses were not the first to kindle her Romanov blood. At her very first dance, on her sixteenth birthday, Olga had given her lips trustingly and happily to the young prince, little more than a boy himself, whom she believed her parents had chosen to be her husband. It had been the perfect setting for romance, like a scene in one of the English novels the Czar liked to read aloud to his family, among the roses and heliotropes of Livadia, high on a marble balcony above the sea. There had been other episodes since then, the natural outcome of the carefully encouraged flirtations, but none of them had so much moved her, had so kindled her sexuality, as that brief embrace in the wild Finnish countryside, under the pale skies of the north. Olga fell asleep wondering how Simon would look, what she would say, when they met on deck next day.

But the next morning was given up to pomp and ceremony, in which the Grand Duchess and the Marine Guards officer each had different parts to play, when the Czar received the mayor and military governor of Reval aboard the *Standart*. The Czarina came on deck and walked through her own part in the ceremonial, and when it was over Olga and Tatiana were allowed to sit with their little brother while the pale empress sat in the fresh air on deck. Alexis was out of pain, for the doctors had unwillingly given him morphine at midnight, but sleepy and very languid. Tatiana brought her balalaika and played to him softly. Both girls thought it a great advance, a hopeful sign, when the boy's heavy lids were raised and he said, in almost his normal voice, "I think I'd like to learn to play that thing!"

He was able to be dressed in his sailor suit, although the cap with its brave *Standart* riband lay pathetically askew on his bright hair when Derevenko carried him on deck as the yacht entered Peterhof bay. The unsuccessful cruise had lasted only six days instead of fourteen, because of the French state visit, although it was understood that this was only an interruption. The Czar said as much, talking cheerfully to Commander Sablin at the approach of the tender, and as the imperial ladies went down the line of officers, saying goodbye, Simon seized his chance to say to Olga when he bent over her hand:

"I look forward to the next part of the cruise, Princess."

"I hope we can begin again where we left off," she answered, and hid her smile at the quick look of delight in his eyes. The Czarina, immediately ahead, heard nothing: she was saying lugubriously to Anna Virubova that she didn't think they would ever be all together in the *Standart* again.

"Speak for yourself, my dear," said the Czar. "I'll be at sea tomorrow, for the welcome to President Poincaré." He was quite nonchalant about the French state visit, although the courier boats had brought him reports twice daily about the increasing tension in the capital. While the investigation of the Sarajevo murders was still being studied in Vienna, the President of the French Republic was not a welcome guest in Petersburg. Raymond Poincaré, a Lorrainer, had seen the province of his birth invaded by the Prussians in 1870 and torn from France by conquest: for him, even more than for most of his French contemporaries, 'the gap in the Vosges' was a phrase full of poignant meaning. To fill that gap, to bring Alsace and Lorraine back to France, was known to be the aspiration of Poincaré and other Frenchmen sworn to *la revanche*: might this honoured guest not use his visit to France's ally to persuade Russia into a war with Germany? The Cossacks were clearing the streets of the capital of anti-Poincaré demonstrators while the Czar and his family entered the immense grounds of Peterhof and were driven to their summer home at Alexandria Cottage.

It was a cottage only by courtesy, being more like a large country house, but compared with the other imperial residences it was a gay and frivolous little dwelling in a mixture of styles. There were mullioned windows wreathed in creepers, there were white-painted balconies with blue curtains and pink and white sun screens in a bright contrast to the yellow stucco of the house. It looked both welcoming and peaceful to the travellers from the *Standart*, for the gardeners usually working beneath the rose pergolas and linden alleys had been drafted to swell the army of men who were bringing the lawns, the avenues and the fountains of Peterhof to the last pitch of perfection in honour of President Poincaré.

The representative of the French Republic was to stay in Peterhof palace itself, the supreme achievement of the great Peter and his challenge to Versailles; and there on the next evening, following his safe arrival on board the battleship *France*, Monsieur Poincaré was entertained by the Czar at a banquet in the Empress Elizabeth salon. For the young Grand Duchesses the chief pleasure of this occasion was the sight of their mother restored for a few hours to her legendary beauty, with her splendid cold profile and glorious hair enhanced by the traditional dress of a Russian empress. Alexandra Feodorovna wore a diamond tiara over the long lace veil which fell over her bare shoulders, revealed by her low-cut brocade gown, and above a many-stranded diamond collar and necklace, ropes of pearls, her favourite jewels, reached almost to her waist. It was a hot evening, and when she held out her hands to her younger daughters, who had begged to clasp the pearl and gold bracelets on her wrists, they were shocked by the chill of their mother's touch.

The next day the French President visited St. Petersburg, and as a protest demonstration the tramcar and train drivers went on strike. This was no inconvenience to Monsieur Poincaré, driving up the Nevski Prospekt in a carriage and four: he smiled affably and raised his silk hat repeatedly to the cheering groups paid and stationed at every corner by the police. It was an inconvenience to Richard Allen, who, unable to find a droshki, had to walk some distance between his flat on the Italianskaia and the British Embassy, and also to Mara Trenova, who had to walk still further from her depressing home near the Vladimir church to the equally depressing classroom where she was taking lessons in shorthand and typewriting. Her fellow-students were as discontented as herself, young men and women who had been unable, for a variety of reasons, to enter the university, and were starting adult life with a grudge against society. In the shabby tea-room to which they repaired at the end of the day, they eagerly discussed the strikes which were said to be breaking out in the major factories of the capital and the rumours of a general mobilisation which had been rife for some days past. They carried their rumours and complaints home with them, to be repeated in the cheap food stores and round the supper tables of the poor and the dispossessed. But President Poincaré held a grand diplomatic levée at the Winter Palace, at which the only guest who appeared to be under some constraint was the envoy of Austria-Hungary, and drove back in state to Peterhof when the day was over.

Those responsible for his safety began to breathe more easily. The worst was over. There had been no 'incident' in Petersburg, not even the shadow of another Sarajevo, and nothing lay ahead until the hour of his departure but the long series of ceremonial occasions, toasts, and protestations of undying friendship between France and Russia. There was a luncheon given by the Czar at which no ladies were present, there was the singing of the Evening Hymn by the Guards in the summer camp at Krasnoe Selo, and finally, on the morning of the last day of the state visit, there was to be a great review of those same Guards, the flower of the Russian Army.

The Grand Duchesses Olga and Tatiana waited in one of the wooden dachas, which were part of the cantonments at Krasnoe Selo, to play their part in the review. From earliest childhood they had been present at the summer manœuvres which their father enjoyed so much, feeling himself to be a soldier among soldiers and at his ease, but this was the first time that, as the Colonels-in-Chief of two crack regiments, they would ride alongside the Czar as he reviewed his troops. The little room where they stood waiting, with its one window looking into a clump of birches, seemed to be remote from the great camp, but in fact the girls could hear all the noise of the preparations, from the moving into place of the cavalry regiments to the sound of carriage wheels as the privileged spectators were driven up to the grandstand.

"How much longer, Tania?" said Olga, going closer to the open window. "It's terribly hot in here."

Tatiana consulted her wrist watch. "Fifteen minutes, if they're punctual . . . Olga, *don't* lean on the window sill! You're sure to get a smear or dust on your sleeves, or something!"

She herself was immaculate, standing just as her mother's dresser, lent for the occasion, had made her stand while the heavy uniform was smoothed and folded to her slenderness. Olga scrubbed at her elbows with her handkerchief and pulled her tunic down. "No harm done," she said nonchalantly. "Do you think we dare undo our collars?"

"No, the hooks are far too stiff to fasten again. It *is* hot, though!" The tunics of their regiments, worn above dark riding skirts, were far heavier than their usual summer dresses, Olga's with frogs across the breast and embroidered cuffs, Tatiana's with heavy epaulettes. On a table in the centre of the room lay their white gloves and riding crops, beside Tatiana's Uhlan helmet with its drooping plume and Olga's Hussar hat with its thick chinstrap.

"I wish mamma was here," said Tatiana. "She told me this morning she hadn't been inside this place for years."

"She's got to drive with Monsieur Poincaré. But isn't it odd to think that she and father actually lived here, nineteen years ago, the whole summer before I was born? I bet they were happy then, don't you?"

"They're very happy in each other now."

"Yes, but—" There was no need to elaborate upon that 'but'. Olga looked round the little sitting-room, so unsuitably furnished for its country setting. The young Empress of Russia had exercised the fatal taste of all minor German royalty for the London furniture of the Nineties, and had shopped extensively on the Tottenham Court Road.

"The place looks all wrong somehow. Not a patch on the Hendrikovs' dacha at Koivisto."

"That really impressed you, didn't it? Listen—are they bringing up the horses?"

"No, but somebody's creaking about outside." Olga opened the door leading to the little anteroom, where an ADC remained on duty. He had his back to the Grand Duchesses, and seemed to be barring the way to a plump woman with an ingratiating smile.

"Anna Alexandrovna, what are you doing here?" demanded Olga.

"Oh, my darlings, I only came to wish you luck—"

"It's all right," said Tatiana quietly. "Madame Virubova may come in." And, as the ADC stood aside, she added, "I should have thought you'd be in the grandstand by now, Ania."

"But my place is reserved, Tania dearest; I can climb up there at the last moment. I can wait here for ever, if there's the least little thing I can do for you."

"What should there be?" said Olga indifferently. She turned back to the window and took a deep breath of the fresh air.

"But aren't you, confess now, just the least little, teensy weensy bit nervous?" said Madame Virubova.

She had a curious way of talking, as if her tongue were too thick for the small mouth in what was still a babyish face, overlaid by fat. There was the same disproportion in Madame Virubova's figure. At thirty-two she had sloping, girlish shoulders above a short torso and huge thighs, painfully outlined, on this blazing July day, by her clammy, clinging chiffon skirts. She had taken off her gloves, and Olga shied away from the moist pink fingers stretched out to her own breast.

"Don't touch me, Ania. You know I hate being pawed about."

"Angel, I think you must be just a wee bit uncomfy, because your ribbon is askew—"

"Leave it alone!" The mirror showed Olga that the scarlet ribbon of the Order of St. Catherine, which with its diamond star was the prerogative of the empress-consort and her daughters, lay in a perfect line across her tunic.

"You're terribly excited, pet, and I don't wonder. I told your dear mamma only this morning that you ought to have had a chance to practise for such a grand review."

"We don't have to practise," Olga said. "It comes to us quite naturally."

"Very well, girlies. I see you haven't any use for your poor old faithful Ania. But do do your best, won't you, out there in front of all those men? Don't do anything to spoil your father's memories of Krasnoe Selo!"

"What do you mean by that?" said Tatiana. "You mean when he lived here with the Czarina, long ago?"

"I mean his happy days with Mala Kchessinskaia." Anna

Virubova kissed her hand to the two girls, and manœuvred her spreading hips through the doorway. Olga shut the door behind her with a bang.

"You were awfully rude to her, Olga."

"I don't care, she makes me sick. How mother can bear to have her about, I simply do not know."

"Oh, come on now, you used to enjoy going to parties at her house when we were little."

"My sense of smell can't have been developed in those days. When do you suppose she washed her armpits last?"

A heavy knock on the door changed Tatiana's shocked *"Olga!"* into "Five minutes! Let's put on our helmets! We can't keep papa waiting!"

"We won't." The chinstraps were adjusted, the white kid gloves pulled on. A long look in the wall mirror was entirely reassuring. But before they left the close little room, which now indeed smelled far from fresh, Olga said uncertainly:

"What do you suppose she meant about Kchessinskaia?"

"The ballerina?"

"Who else?"

"Oh, don't fuss about it, Olga, you know how Ania likes to drop little hints which never mean anything! And everybody knows that Kchessinskaia—"

"Is Cousin Andrei's mistress," Olga finished for her. "And has been, almost since the time that I was born."

* * *

The vast parade ground at Krasnoe Selo was hardly an amphitheatre, but the ground sloped at either end into a rise where, at the end where the cantonments were established—the headquarters, barracks, dacha, church and theatre—a grandstand had been put up for the guests at the review. It was already filled with women in picture hats and their escorts, many in brilliant uniforms, when a barouche drawn by four grey horses and escorted by Cossacks came up the long avenue and halted beneath a silken canopy. In it were the Czarina and the President of the French Republic, and facing them, the young Grand Duchesses Marie and Anastasia.

In the silence of almost reverent attention sixty thousand troops, horse and foot, stood fast while the Czar and his elder daughters rode on to the parade ground. The regiments stretched out as far as the eye could reach, to the belt of trees which marked the summit of the rising ground at the far side, and only the faint but constant jingle of harness was heard as the Czar halted and raised his hand in salute. Two little white-gloved hands flashed up behind him as a massed military band broke into the 'Marseillaise', and the French President stood up in the barouche with his silk hat in his hand. While the Czar's mount fidgeted and tossed her head, the black and the bay which carried the Grand Duchesses stood motionless during the playing of the French and Russian national anthems. Then the imperial riders, saluted and escorted by the generals of the Guards, turned to pace along the front rank of the foremost regiment, while the band played the traditional *'Kol slaven'*, the hymn which the fortress bells of St. Peter and St. Paul played at midnight and noon.

The Czar, surrounded by his generals, wore the uniform and insignia of a colonel of the Regiment of the Transfiguration. It was the highest rank he had reached during his father's reign, when after training in the Hussars he had been gazetted colonel in the Preobrazhenski, and out of sentiment he had promoted himself no higher when he became Czar. The Transfiguration Regiment was in front, with the girls' regiments immediately behind: Olga's Hussars of Elizabethgrad, Tatiana's Uhlans of Vossnossensk. All the three regiments were inspected by the Czar. The spectators, through the binoculars which became necessary, saw Tatiana's face grow pale with nervousness and assume some of her mother's hauteur: Olga was flushed and smiling. Before the review began she had been innocently excited at the thought that Simon Hendrikov would see her mounted, dressed as a soldier, wearing the Order of St. Catherine, but as she rode down the lines behind her father she was too much carried away by the vastness of the assembly to think of any one man in it. Under the wide pale Russian sky, in the huge plain that smelt of dust and harness oil and horse manure, secure in her side saddle on the familiar black mare, Olga Nicolaievna knew a physical felicity only matched by the exaltation of her mood. As they turned and rode back to the saluting base, to the silk-canopied barouche where her mother's parasol dipped in approval, to the smiling faces, becoming more distinct, in the red and gold draped imperial stand, Olga's heart was beating faster in the first public triumph of her life.

The march-past began, and now, in honour of the French President, the Russian troops came up in quick time, to the tune of the 'Marche Lorraine' followed by 'Sambre et Meuse'. Some of the better-informed Russians in the grandstand shrugged their shoulders: they knew that these were melodies to which the soldiers of France had traditionally gone into battle, but not all the company grasped that significance—the tunes were catchy, that was enough. The infantry marched past in faultless alignment, by columns of four, of eight, sixteen, thirty-two; the regimental colours were dipped to the Czar and his daughters, a group as motionless as Peter the Great and his bronze horse miles away on the Neva embankment. And the French President, who had been visibly moved at the playing of the 'Marche Lorraine', said to the Czarina:

"Your daughters are magnificent, Madame—all your daughters!"

The younger girls giggled, and the Czarina, with the pinched and patronising smile of which Poincaré had had more than enough, replied, "My older girls are very fond of riding, and His Majesty is the best of teachers."

"And you, Altesse," persevered the President, smiling at Marie, "do you enjoy riding too?"

"Very much, Monsieur le Président."

"Oh, but my sister's a terrific gymnast!" burst out Anastasia. "She's very strong. She can lift a man right up off the ground—an ordinary-sized man, that is," she concluded, with a doubtful glance at the President's bulk.

Poincaré's lips twitched. "Your Imperial Highness has inherited the prodigious strength of the Czar Alexander III," he said to Marie. "I shall have to be very careful not to offend you!"

Alexandra Feodorovna closed her eyes. Tormented by headache to the point where the flags and the uniforms turned in her brain like a vast wheel of colour, she found it no longer endurable to look at the tableau of her husband and the girls on horseback. They were more relaxed now, and Nicholas had turned from one to the other with a smiling remark as the long lines of marching men advanced and wheeled. She saw Tatiana smile in return, and that was bearable, for Tatiana was her favourite daughter, and there was something deeply satisfying in seeing her own young beauty revived in the slender girl on the bay mare. But Olga's gay glance at her father gave his wife a pang of jealousy which, as she looked at them once more from beneath her tilted parasol, she told herself was jealousy for Alexis. Olga's strong, slim shoulders in the military tunic, Olga's long, strong legs just moulded by the riding skirt, were to the mother's obsessed mind an insult to Alexis. He had never sat a horse and never would. He walked in the gardens, when he was well enough, holding the bridle of Vanka, the donkey bought for him at Cinizelli's circus. Sometimes, with his sailor nurse in close attendance, he drove little Vanka in a donkey cart. But the doctors were absolute in forbidding him to ride. It was Olga, not Alexis, who rode beside their father to review the troops.

The Grand Duchess Marie unobtrusively passed a bottle of smelling salts to the Czarina.

"It's nearly over now, mamma," she said gently. "Do watch the cavalry!"

The bugles were shrilling for the sensational finale of the Guards' review, when the cavalry regiments charged en masse towards the saluting base. They came shouting, and with such élan that spectators who were at Krasnoe Selo for the first time shuddered at the thought that the Czar and his entourage would be swept aside or ridden down by an irresistible tide of horses and men. Then at the last moment the riders checked, the horses in the front rank curvetted in a salute, and silence fell over the sun-soaked plain. The voice of the Czar was clearly heard in the traditional shout of approval:

"Well done, children! Well done!"

And sixty thousand men gave the deep-throated reply:

"Happy to serve Your Imperial Majesty!"

4

JOE CALVERT WAS GLAD the tramcar strike had ended. On the morning after the battleship *France* sailed from Kronstadt, carrying President Raymond Poincaré on his next state visits to the northern capitals, Vice-Consul Calvert, that tiny cog in the diplomatic machine, caught a tram outside the Europa at eight in the morning and went off to his Russian lesson.

With the permission of his consul, he had arranged to visit Madame Hendrikova at half past eight on three mornings a week. It meant arriving late at the consulate, but Joe had already seen enough of Russian unpunctuality to realise that a lesson set for six in the afternoon might not begin until seven, as her tardy students prolonged Madame Hendrikova's working day. And both she and Joe were fresh, first thing in the morning, ready to do a good hour's work in her little room at the far end of a corridor, where the only sounds were the footsteps of the Lettish servants going between the kitchen and the living-room. There, Joe supposed, Dolly and her father were having breakfast, but he neither saw nor heard them; after having been catapulted into the family life of the Hendrikovs his own plan for work now kept them at a distance. By and by, but certainly before they left for Finland, he wanted to invite Dolly and her parents to dinner and the French play at the Alexandrovski theatre. He was hardly up to a Russian performance after barely three weeks' instruction in that language, but he knew he was making progress, although his teacher was sparing of her praise.

He had mastered the Cyrillic alphabet and its pronunciation, and was acquiring the rudiments of the complicated grammar, with a small vocabulary. Joe Calvert had no difficulty in reading one word on the billboards outside the newspaper kiosks as the tram went along the Nevski: *Voina! Voina!* That meant 'war', he knew; but the papers could hardly be announcing an outbreak of war, for there was no undue concern on the faces of his fellow passengers. They wore the blank look of indifference Joe had become used to in a certain element of Petersburg society, and he supposed, at that hour of the morning, they were minor members of the empire's vast bureaucracy going unconcerned to their routine work.

When he reached Vassili Island he was sufficiently disturbed to buy a copy of *Novoie Vremia,* and was feeling in his pocket for change when he heard his own name spoken breathlessly and found Dolly Hendrikova at his elbow.

"Oh, Mr. Calvert, are *you* buying the newspaper?"

"Yes, though I can't read much of it yet, Darya Karlovna—"

"Father sent me out to get the special edition—"

"This is an extra? Because of this word here, *voina,* war?"

"One of his friends at the paper telephoned—"

"You mean war's been declared?"

"No, thank God, no! This says 'Danger of war', not 'Declaration of war'—"

She was out of breath and flushed with hurry; pretty Dolly, in a blue cotton dress without hat or gloves, and little wisps of fair hair escaping from the tortoiseshell clasps meant to hold her curls in place. Joe saw with amusement that she was wearing a scuffed pair of dancing slippers, as if she had been sent off half-dressed along the quays.

"Come on," he said, "we'd better get along to the flat and out of this crowd; see, everybody's going to work as usual."

Dolly looked at the office workers making for the Exchange and the Academy of Science, and nodded in agreement.

"So they are," she said, "and you're coming to your lesson with my mother?"

"That was the idea. And maybe, as we go, you'd tell me what the trouble is? People have been talking about the danger of war for nearly a month now—"

"Yes, but *last* night," said Dolly earnestly, "in the *middle* of the night, they waited until the French President had sailed from Kronstadt, the Austrians sent an ultimatum to the Serbian government. My father says if the Serbs don't accept it, it means war."

"But what was the ultimatum?"

"It's in the newspaper. Oh, let's hurry, please!"

In her flat-heeled slippers Dolly was almost running over the uneven paving, and Joe remembered to ask:

"How is your friend, Darya Karlovna? I mean your school friend, Miss Trenova?"

"I haven't seen her for a week. She's doing a secretarial course, you know."

"So your mother told me."

"One of the visiting lecturers at school promised to find a position for her, as soon as she's qualified."

"That's good." They were in the Fourth Line by this time, and Professor Hendrikov's grey head was to be seen at his study window. Dolly waved the copy of *Novoie Vremia*, which Joe had passed on to her. The porter, with his most obsequious bow, opened the front door for them.

Madame Hendrikova, without waiting for the slow Lett maid, pulled open the door of the apartment. "You had Mr. Calvert to look after you," she said to Dolly. "That was good."

"I'm glad I was early this morning," said Joe.

It was still not half past eight, but Madame Hendrikova was ready for her day's teaching, every hair in place, a plain silver watch pinned to her white blouse, and her satin belt drawn taut above her sweeping skirt. "You must have a cup of tea with us, Mr. Calvert," she said calmly, "and my husband will tell us the news from Vienna."

She took a fresh teacup and filled it from the samovar, indicating to Joe and Dolly that they should sit down at the breakfast table. The chair the young man took was the one occupied by Simon Hendrikov during his brief visit to the supper party late in June. Joe remembered Madame Hendrikova's distress at the mere hint of a general mobilisation, and marvelled at her calm when the hint seemed so likely to become reality.

"May I have some more tea too, mother?" said Dolly. "I'm so thirsty."

"No wonder; you ran out before you'd finished your breakfast."

They smiled at each other, and Dolly, after a furtive glance at the sideboard mirror, pushed back her dishevelled hair with her fingers. Professor Hendrikov, almost as untidy as his daughter in a shabby alpaca jacket, had been scanning the newspaper closely since he took it from Dolly's hand. Now he looked over his spectacles at his wife and said:

"It's all pretty much as Kolia told me on the telephone.

Except that the ultimatum wasn't sent to Belgrade in the middle of the night, as I understood him to say, it was sent yesterday evening. But here comes the bombshell. Austria requires a judicial investigation in Serbia itself, conducted by Austrian officials as well as Serbs—" He threw up one hand in a gesture of despair.

"A new investigation into the plot?" said Joe.

"Yes."

"And you think the Serbians won't accept the Austrian officials?"

"I'm certain they will not. It would be too great a blow to their national pride and sovereignty."

"Maybe they'll swallow their pride rather than risk a war."

"They swallowed their pride in 1908, when the Austrians annexed Bosnia and Herzegovina. They won't do it a second time." Professor Hendrikov struck the table suddenly, so that the china rattled, and raised his voice. "What a farce! What an imposture! The Emperor Franz Josef has one foot in the grave, and the King of Serbia is deranged to the point where his son has just been named as Regent. Why should two old dotards gamble with the lives of a whole generation of young men?"

Joe Calvert looked at Dolly and her mother. Both were pale, and the girl's eyes were full of tears. It's the son, of course, he thought, that kid in the Marine Guards, they're thinking what he's in for, if the Serbs reject this damned silly ultimatum. He felt out of place, the neutral, the citizen of a great republic above and beyond a squabble in the Balkans. He said to Madame Hendrikova:

"It's very upsetting news, madame, and I'm sure you don't feel like giving me a Russian lesson this morning. Let's just cancel this one, and try again on Monday."

"Certainly not!" The little lady got up briskly, and Joe jumped to his feet. "There is nothing like hard work in a crisis, monsieur, and I hope you intend to work hard this morning. I set you a lesson on the use of adjectives—hard, soft and mixed."

"I've studied it, madame."

"Then come along; we're ten minutes late already."

But before Joe followed his teacher to her workroom he said to her husband:

"Look here, sir, I know I'm only a greenhorn, and maybe I'm too optimistic, but I don't see why this ultimatum *has* to lead to war. Maybe the Serbs will be sensible, and accept all the terms, or maybe the Great Powers will take the whole thing to the Court of Arbitration at the Hague and settle it round a conference table like the Agadir crisis. Say! Is there a time limit to that ultimatum?"

"Forty-eight hours."

"Well, the great thing is to keep them talking and not shooting off any guns."

"Yes, but the very timing of the ultimatum shows the Emperor and his friend the Kaiser want to prevent talks between the allied Powers. Sent at the very end of Poincaré's visit, making it impossible for him to consult the Czar! Sent when the French chief of state and the French prime minister are both out of the country together and on the high seas—"

"But good Lord, sir, don't they have wireless telegraphy aboard the *France*?"

"You mean nations should take great and vital decisions by wireless telegraphy?"

"Why not, if it's to stop a war?"

Dolly looked up, and she was actually smiling. "It's no use," she said. "Papa thinks of statecraft in terms of pens, ink and paper. And speeches in the Duma, very correct and proper."

"Oh! Well! I'm keeping Madame Hendrikova waiting. Maybe we could have another talk on Monday?"

Joe saw as he left the room that Dolly had gone to her father's side and put her fresh cheek against the lined cheek of the history professor whom History had overtaken.

* * *

Street fighting broke out again in Petersburg that day. The bridges of the Neva were raised to keep the workers on the Viborg Side from demonstrating in the main arteries of the city, and heavy police casualties were reported at the council of ministers presided over by the Czar. No time was wasted on such domestic details by Nicholas II and his councillors, who like every other cabinet in Europe were concerned only with the Austrian ultimatum to Serbia. It was impossible to hold their meetings at Alexandria Cottage, and the Czar walked to and from the great palace, reluctantly leaving the summer warmth of the long avenues for the council chamber.

His daughters, confined to the environs of the Cottage, lamented their father's absence as much as his decision to postpone the second part of the summer cruise. He was the best of playfellows in his leisure hours, and without him Marie and Anastasia took to the tennis court and played endless singles, complaining of the heat. Even when they stopped to mop their faces and drink lemonade they had nothing to say about the business which kept their father at Peterhof. The Czarina stayed with Alexis, who was still confined to bed, and Tatiana was in devoted attendance on her mother. No one seemed to realise the gravity of the situation but Olga. The young Grand Duchesses were not encouraged to read the newspapers, but the papers were there, on a table in the little library, and she read them in the peaceful, silent afternoons, to the thump of tennis balls and the pleasant sound of a pony, wearing leather boots, drawing a mower over the lawns round Alexandria Cottage.

Olga was thankful for two mercies, not small: that Father Grigori, called Rasputin, was far away in Siberia, and that Anna Virubova, although much closer at hand, had gone home to her own little house at Czarskoe Selo, for those were the two who most regularly encouraged the Czarina to meddle in politics. So far she was keeping quiet, even at the family tea which her husband never missed, although many more dispatches than usual were brought in while they sat over the teacups. It was a sight to which all the girls were accustomed: the ADC on duty bringing in the news agency digests for the next day's press in their long white envelopes, and their father pulling at the thread of orange-coloured silk passed under each seal for easy opening. He read each report as calmly as he had always done, and folded it with care, but without making any comment on the contents. Alexandra Feodorovna watched him intently, but she asked no questions: Nicholas II had been brought up to believe that it was discourteous to mention politics in the presence of ladies.

It was Olga, impulsive as ever, who made the first oblique comment on the painful situation. On Saturday, when the forty-eight hours of the Austrian ultimatum were beginning to run out, the Czarina lunched with her girls on one of the pleasant balconies of the cottage. A vegetarian herself, and proud of the fact that she took no interest in food, she ate only a few mouthfuls and drank a sip of mineral water, and even the healthy appetites of the girls were quickly satisfied. At last Alexandra Feodorovna, abandoning her pretence of tranquillity, said to Olga:

"I feel so much for poor dear Helen today! Write her a little note of sympathy, Olga, and a courier can take it over to Pavlovsk."

"Which Helen?" Olga said perversely. "Cousin John's wife?"

"Don't be silly, dear; yes, Helen of Serbia, of course. Poor thing, my heart bleeds for her, a stranger in a strange land—"

"She's been married to John Romanov for at least three years, mamma."

"But I'm sure her heart is in Belgrade today, where her poor father is so much afflicted, and her brother the Regent faced with such a terrible responsibility! Tell her we are all thinking of her and her gallant little country—"

"I don't think I can quite say that, mamma."

"What *do* you mean?"

"I think Serbia has been a very quarrelsome little country, since old King Peter came to the throne. And we all know *how* he came to the throne—after King Milan and his queen were stabbed and hacked to death in their own palace, only ten or eleven years ago."

"Olga! Where did you hear such a horrible thing?"

"It's a matter of history, mother."

"But I thought you were so fond of your cousin Helen!"

"I am, I like her very much. But I don't see why Serbia should be called a gallant little country just because one of the princesses married our cousin John!"

The Czarina closed her eyes. "Please don't argue, Olga," she said. "Write as I tell you, and sign all your initials, in that pretty way I like so much. Go indoors and do it now."

The Grand Duchess Olga obeyed. She wrote a few affectionate lines to the anxious young princess at Pavlovsk, in the firm, almost masculine hand with the wide spaces between the words which was her characteristic. But she omitted the girlish signature of OTMA, which the four sisters had adopted from the initials of their names, and almost for the first time in family correspondence signed herself "Olga" with the broad sweep of a ruler signing a document of state.

It was a firmer signature than the 'Nicholas' which her father appended, some hours later, to his order for the preliminaries to mobilisation in four military areas of Russia. For the Serbian government, after long deliberation, refused the one clause in the ultimatum which demanded an Austrian share in a new judicial investigation. When this refusal was sent to the Austrian envoy in Belgrade he immediately asked for his passports, and diplomatic relations with Serbia were broken off.

* * *

It had been the tradition through more than one reign that the Krasnoe summer ceremonies should end with a performance in the little theatre, presented by the new graduates of the Imperial Ballet School. This year, on the hot July evening when peace hung in the balance, there were to be two additions to the programme: the great aria from Glinka's 'A Life for the Czar', and the mazurka from Act II of the same opera, to be danced by Mathilde Kchessinskaia.

When the Grand Duchess Olga was told that, as had happened at several of the summer ceremonies, she must take her mother's place at the theatre, she felt a double surge of pleasure. Anna Virubova's poisoned words had left enough impression for the girl to wish to watch her father as he watched the dancer, but above all, the pent-up anxiety of the previous days made her long for a private word with the Czar. As it turned out, she was dressed and sitting in the motor for ten minutes before Nicholas came to join her, and then he was followed by the ADC on duty. With the brief remark, "More rotten telegrams!" the Czar switched on the roof light of the car, dispelling the gentle summer dusk, and all through the short drive to Krasnoe Selo he read the telegrams one by one, making very brief notes on each with his gold pencil, and handing it over to be filed in a leather wallet by the ADC. It was impossible to interrupt him, and Olga sat silent while they drove through Krasnoe Selo, the Red Village, until they reached the theatre. There the court official who was also the theatre director was waiting, with a bouquet of roses for the young Grand Duchess in his hand.

It was a quaint little place, like an overgrown dacha, with fretwork carving and a curtained piazza set about with pots of flowers. Protocol required that certain courtiers should greet the monarch in this piazza, and then the Czar and his daughter entered the theatre by a covered private way which led past the stars' dressing-rooms, where lights were shining behind drawn blinds. The ante-room to the imperial box was so bright that Olga's eyes were dazzled: she was aware of ladies curtseying, and then all other impressions were obliterated as Simon Hendrikov stepped forward to take her light cloak from her shoulders.

She gave him her hand to kiss, and said:

"I hardly expected to see *you* here."

"I moved heaven and earth to be posted to the theatre guard tonight."

"I mean, I didn't expect you to be still at Krasnoe Selo."

"We're moving off to Petersburg tomorrow."

"Oh, then you'll see your family. Unless they've gone to the dacha already?"

They smiled at one another, as much alone in that crowded ante-room as if they stood again among the wild grasses by the Finnish river.

"My family? I don't think they plan to go to Koivisto yet . . . I saw you at the review, Olga Nicolaievna. You looked marvellous." His eyes said, And you look marvellous tonight.

"I'm afraid the *Standart* cruise is off for the time being," said the girl.

"It was in the orders of the day. I suppose it can't be helped. But if all this blows over—"

"Oh, Simon Karlovich!" said Olga, very low, "pray, pray that it will!"

"Come along, my dear," said the Czar at her elbow. "Ten minutes late already, and I asked for a short programme tonight!"

In his terrible preoccupation, Nicholas had hardly noticed how the girl was dressed. Now, as he handed her to the front of the imperial box, he was at once aware of a hum of pleasure and approval, as the very critical audience assessed the charm of that young figure in a simple, pink chiffon dress, bowing and smiling to them all. Olga's only ornaments were a single strand of pearls, banding her upswept golden hair, and the bouquet of roses which she carried in her left hand. The unexpected meeting with Simon had left her flushed and pleased.

"How very nice you look," murmured the Czar. "Young Hendrikov seems to be badly smitten. Are you going to turn out to be a heartbreaker, my dear?"

It was the familiar tone of family banter, but Olga was glad that the house lights were dimmed at that moment, and the orchestra began an overture. The performance started, no better and no worse than others she had seen before, with the new graduates of the ballet school dancing in the perennial hope of imperial patronage as eagerly as if no Serbian batteries were being mounted along the high frontier on the way to Sarajevo. When the interval came she and her father remained in the imperial box; cousins came, and courtiers came, and made their bows, leaving the girl just time to say,

"I'm looking forward to Madame Kchessinskaia's dance."

"But you saw her dance the mazurka last year, at the Maryinski."

"I missed most of it. Don't you remember? Mamma felt faint, and Tania and I went back to the ante-room with her."

"So she did, poor mamma." The Czar spoke abstractedly, and Olga wondered if he realised, as she had come to realise, that her mother's faintness and palpitations always came on when she herself was not the centre of attention. But, on that night of the tercentenary celebrations at the Maryinski theatre, had Alexandra Feodorovna had a special reason for resenting the dancer's presence on the stage? She said breathlessly:

"Do *you* admire Kchessinskaia's dancing?"

"She's Russia's only *prima ballerina assoluta,* dear."

"Yes, but, some people say her style is terribly old-fashioned, and too formal and cold for modern audiences. Do you agree with that?"

"I must say I prefer the old choreography to the new." It was one of the Czar's characteristically noncommittal answers, and Olga was surprised when he went on to say, "It was in this very theatre that I saw her dance before the public for the first time."

"Madame Kchessinskaia? When was that—before you and mamma were married?"

"Oh, long before. About a thousand years ago."

"You're not very flattering to the lady. Why, how old is *she*?"

"She must be over forty now."

But the dancer, revealed in a shaft of golden light when the curtains swept aside, looked little older than a girl. She was small and slim, with a piquant face and brilliant eyes, and the mazurka which she had danced so often was out of all her repertoire the theme best suited to her genius. Mala Kchessinskaia was of Polish blood, and the celebration of a Polish triumph in the scene of the mazurka struck an emotional fervour from her performance which overshadowed its technical skill. She curtseyed her thanks for what was very nearly an ovation without glancing in the direction of the imperial box, where the Czar, after applauding politely, sat with his hand covering his bearded mouth.

The real ovation came ten minutes later, when the greatest baritone in Russia finished Glinka's magnificent aria in which Ivan Susanin, surrounded by the enemies of his young emperor, proclaims his duty to give his life for Russia. It was the final expression, the emotional catharsis, of what every man and woman in the theatre had felt under the mounting pressure of the passing days. They stood up to cheer the singer, they turned spontaneously to cheer the Czar. In a moment the evening became his triumph, as the theatre echoed to the national anthem.

And when his daughter followed him down the covered way which led past the stars' dressing-rooms, she saw him look across the courtyard at one window, and lift his hand to his cap in a salute to Mala Kchessinskaia, who stood there silhouetted against the lighted room with her own hand at her lips.

It was a fleeting impression, only visible to Olga's watchful eyes, and swiftly obliterated by the scene in the piazza. The ADC who had accompanied them to the theatre was there, with a new sheaf of telegrams in his hand, and the Grand Duke Kirill and his wife were there with one or two other members of the Family. It was Kirill who took the Czar aside and spoke to him urgently: Olga could hear nothing but names—"the Kaiser—the German Ambassador—Sazonov"—and then her father glanced in her direction.

"Kirill and Ducky will take you home, Olga. Tell mamma I'm going straight to the palace to hold an emergency council; I hope it won't last long."

With that he got into the car waiting with its motor running in front of the rose-hung door, and the Grand Duke Kirill, with cold ceremony, bowed Olga into his own limousine. His stately wife took her place beside the girl. She felt tongue-tied, a schoolgirl again on the short journey home, during which only the performance was discussed by them, in words suited to the understanding of a child of ten. Olga almost ran into the hall of Alexandria Cottage as their motor drove away.

The Czarina appeared at once from one of the reception rooms. She was wearing a robe of heliotrope silk, cut in the flowing style she preferred, neither a teagown nor a negligée, which gave her a look of perpetual invalidism.

"Where's your father?"

"He went straight to the palace to hold an emergency council."

"At this hour of the night?"

Olga glanced at the clock. It was after midnight.

"Has there been more news from Vienna?" demanded the Czarina.

"I don't know, mamma. I only heard them say something about a message from the Kaiser."

"That madman!" exclaimed the Czarina. "He's at the bottom of all this, of course! Nastia" (to the lady-in-waiting who had followed her into the hall) "I want to telephone to the palace at once!"

"Mamma, do you think that's wise, if they're in conference?"

The Czarina wrung her hands. "Heaven knows what may be decided, if I'm not consulted! Oh, if Father Grigori were only here!"

Olga looked round the hall. They were not alone—but then they never were alone; besides the alarmed lady-in-waiting there were two footmen on duty, immaculate in livery, their hands encased in white cotton gloves, and an ADC was standing at attention on the landing upstairs. "Where's Tatiana? Gone to bed?" she asked.

"Yes, she went to bed an hour ago, she wasn't feeling well. You run along now, lovey, and don't wake her up to start gossiping."

"I never felt less like gossiping in my life." But the Czarina had no more attention to give to the daughter she had dismissed like a tiresome child. As Olga went upstairs, trailing her cloak, with the roses of her bouquet dropping petals on every step, she heard her mother saying eagerly:

"Nastia! Get Anna Alexandrovna on the telephone! Arrange for a car to bring her here as soon as possible!"

But it was not until many hours and several telephone calls later that Anna Virubova arrived at Alexandria Cottage. The

Czar himself had come and gone by that time, arriving in the dawn and breakfasting alone with his wife before returning for a long morning's work at Peterhof. The cars came and went along the avenues, bringing new counsellors in and out of uniform to discuss the news already being flashed around the world: the declaration of war on Serbia by Austria-Hungary.

By the time that Madame Virubova came the Czarina was distraught, and her daughters shocked into silence. They submitted to be kissed and cried over by the plump, untidy woman, and then sat down near the drawing-room window, making a pretence at embroidery, while their mother whispered with her Ania at the far end of the room. They were sewing in silence when the car came up the drive and Nicholas II got out alone.

"There's papa!" called Anastasia, jumping up and scattering the basketful of sewing silks.

"Wait!" said Olga. "Wait until he comes to tea." It was nearly five o'clock, and two footmen had already come in to arrange the tea-table.

From the window, the girls saw their father stoop to pat two of his favourite collies, decoratively grouped beside the open door, and then they heard his footsteps, heavy and slow, crossing the hall and diminishing on the stairs.

"Let's put our work away," suggested Marie. "Papa won't be long."

The clock struck five, and Alexandra Feodorovna came forward, with Ania at her heels, to light the spirit-lamp beneath the silver kettle. The women waited in silence until the lid began to dance.

"Shall I make the tea, mamma?" asked Olga.

"We'll wait a few minutes longer for papa."

They waited. The gold clock, adorned with tiny statuettes of Cupid and Psyche, struck the quarter after five. The Czarina, with a sigh, turned down the flame beneath the kettle.

"Papa was alone, wasn't he?" she said.

"He came in alone, mamma."

"Tatiana, run, darling, and remind him that it's tea-time. Tell him Ania is here, and wants very much to see him."

"I'll go!" said Olga, before her sister could get up. It was the chance to speak to her father alone for which she had been waiting since they drove together to the theatre at Krasnoe Selo. She ran upstairs, along a corridor, and stopped at the study door before which, even in the informality of Alexandria Cottage, two gigantic Ethiopians in their picturesque dress stood guard. Olga looked round for an ADC on duty: there was none.

The Ethiopians bowed to the Czar's eldest daughter, but stood squarely in front of her father's door. Men of their race had guarded the privacy of the Russian monarch since the days of Catherine the Great, and they were jealous of their privilege. But when Olga said urgently: "I have a message from Her Imperial Majesty!" the men bowed low, and simultaneously opened the two leaves of the gilded door.

The Czar's study was a pleasant, airy room, with large windows giving a fine view of the Gulf of Finland. Besides the neatly arranged desk it contained one table covered with papers, and another nearly concealed by an ordnance map of Turkey and the Balkans. Engravings of military subjects hung on the walls, and the furniture was very simple. There were half a dozen leather chairs and a deep sofa, in one corner of which the Czar was half sitting and half lying. His uniform tunic was open at the throat, and his face was more haggard and worn than Olga had ever seen it. On a table near his hand was a tray with cognac and seltzer water, and a half-empty glass showed that the Czar, the most abstemious of men, had felt the need of a stimulant.

"Papa, I'm very sorry to disturb you, but mamma said—"

"You don't disturb me, dear; come in and sit down."

Looking at those burning eyes she felt helplessly certain that the worst had happened, and Russia was at war. But she plunged on with the message:

"Mamma said to tell you that Ania's here, and wants very much to see you. We hoped you'd come to tea—"

Nicholas managed to smile. "Ania can wait," he said. "How nice and cool you look! Sit down and tell me what my girlies have been doing all this long hot day."

"Papa, please don't make babies of us all. Please tell me what is happening. I must know, I have a *right* to know," said Olga, more vehemently than she meant. "Has Austria declared war on Russia? Have you ordered a general mobilisation?"

The Czar sat up and drained his glass. "We're not at war," he said, "don't worry your pretty little head about that."

"I asked you not to treat me like a child, papa. After all, I'll be nineteen in November."

"You still seem like a little girl to me."

"But only a few weeks ago you thought I was old enough to be married, didn't you?"

"I told you I would never force you into marriage, Olga, and I kept my word."

"I know you did, but at the beginning you thought it would be all right to give me in marriage to a boy I hardly knew, and send me off with him to a strange country, away from all of you! If I was old enough to be the Princess of Rumania, surely I'm old enough to know what's happening to my own country?" She used the word *rodina,* motherland, and saw the exhausted man before her bite his lip.

"Very well," he said, "you know, of course, that the Austrians have declared war on Serbia. They ordered a general mobilisation this morning. And very much against the will of my military staff, who wanted us to reply in kind, I ordered a partial mobilisation of our army."

"What does that mean, exactly?"

"It means that thirteen divisions will start moving west to the Galician frontier"

"Including the Guards we reviewed at Krasnoe Selo?"

"Including certain Guards divisions, naturally."

"But the Austrians aren't threatening *us!*"

"Not directly. Not today."

"And if they don't attack us, ever, could you order those thirteen divisions back to barracks—back to all the towns and provinces they came from?"

"In theory I could, but technically it would be very difficult. It's a problem of train transport, which I doubt if you would understand."

"Father, it would be better to send these men home if they had to walk every mile of the way, rather than send them to the front to die for Serbia."

"Now you're talking foolishly, my dear. Hadn't we better go to tea?"

"Please wait." Olga had not accepted the invitation to sit down. Now she moved across the room to where a huge globe, mounted in a brass stand, stood between the two long windows.

"You know," she said, and spun the globe as she spoke, "I'm old enough to remember 1905."

"Are you really?" said the Czar, with an attempt at a light tone.

"Yes, really. I was just the same age then as Alexis is now, and he's supposed to be very bright. I'm sure he'll be able to remember 1914 all his life."

"And what does my equally bright Olga remember about 1905?"

"I remember the troops leaving for the war against Japan, dead drunk. I remember the troops coming back—those who came back—maimed and blinded. I know Japan defeated us terribly at Mukden, and destroyed our navy at Tsushima Bay. What will happen if the Japanese declare war on us again, and attack us in the east while our army marches west?"

"God's will be done," said the Czar, and stood up stiffly. "I learned long ago to bow myself to His punishments."

"But that's just fatalism, father! Don't you believe God expects us to work to help ourselves?"

"Somebody has been teaching you Protestant doctrines," said Nicholas dryly. "Speaking of which, I'm a great deal more concerned about the British than I am about the Japanese. I'm waiting for my beloved cousin Georgie to announce his intention of standing by France and me—"

"But the King of England has to wait for his parliament to decide, doesn't he? We learned that in our history class—"

"That's their beastly idea of liberty," agreed the Czar. "—Sunny, my love, I'm so sorry to have kept you waiting!"

The Czarina, with a swirl of draperies, was in the room, red patches on her cheeks and neck marking the nervous rash which afflicted her in moments of extreme stress. Her confidential friend, perspiring and humble, curtseyed deeply to the Czar.

"We couldn't wait any longer, Nicky," said Alexandra Feodorovna. "Ania had a telegram from Our Friend, from Father Grigori, with a message for you which you ought to read at once . . . Olga, go downstairs, and supervise the children's tea."

"Olga has taken to grand strategy like a duck to water," said the Czar. "I don't think Father Grigori can have anything to say to me that she can't hear too. Where is this telegram?"

The Czarina had it ready in her hand. Nicholas took the message—it was very short—and the colour rose in his pale face.

"Is this impudent telegram in answer to one from you?" he asked his wife. She, in her turn, coloured at his tone.

"Ania telegraphed to Tiumen on my behalf," she said. "After the Austrian declaration, I thought Our Friend ought to know that we are truly horrified at the very thought of war. I begged him to help us with his counsel—and you have it there."

Nicholas turned to Madame Virubova, who had burst into tears.

"Anna Alexandrovna," he said icily, "will you in future remember that I am capable of ruling my country without your interference, or that of Father Grigori? I shall destroy this piece of impertinence, and as a kindness to you both I'll try to forget that it was ever sent."

"What does it say, father?" Olga asked, and ignoring his wife's gesture of protest the Czar read Rasputin's telegram aloud:

"Let Papa not plan war, for with the war will come the end of Russia and yourselves, and you will lose to the last man."

5

AUSTRIA-HUNGARY DECLARED WAR on Serbia on July 28 by the western calendar, exactly one month after Princip fired the fatal shots at Sarajevo. But whereas the opening crisis had been counted in days and weeks it was now counted by hours, and the Czar's insistence that the mobilisation of his army should be only partial proved as ineffectual as Olga's pathetic suggestion that if there was no attack from the west the Russian troops might walk home if train transport failed.

When the Austrians presented Europe with a *fait accompli* by bombarding Belgrade on the next day, Nicholas II could not stand out against his eager generals. At dawn on Friday, July 31, the general mobilisation began in Russia, along the East Prussian as well as the Galician border. The immediate result was general mobilisation in Germany, and an ultimatum from Germany to Russia to stop the preparations for war. When the ultimatum expired at seven o'clock on Saturday evening, Germany declared war on Russia.

At almost the same hour, hundreds of miles to the west, there was a sudden alarm in Luxemburg, the tiny Grand Duchy which lay between Belgium and Germany. There was a point in the Luxemburg territory—barely one thousand square miles in extent—where the railway lines from Germany and Belgium crossed, and this railway station with its adjacent telegraph office was invaded and occupied by a German lieutenant and one infantry company of the 69th Regiment. The station was called Les Trois Vierges, the virgins being Faith, Hope and Charity.

It was a miniature act of aggression, with very little damage done, for the Luxemburg army was barely three hundred strong and composed largely of postmen and railway workers. But it was none the less conclusive, because the neutrality of Luxemburg had been guaranteed by all the Powers, including Germany, and the young girl who was the ruler of the little country was justified in asking the German soldiers to withdraw. But the Germans stayed.

The Czar told his family the sad little story late in the evening, while he waited to give an audience to Sir George Buchanan, the British Ambassador. He still had no great hopes of help from Britain, where the cabinet was in almost continuous session, although the French were standing firm to the Russian alliance and had mobilised during the afternoon. "Probably only another beastly telegram," he said of the message which the ambassador was bringing from King George V. Tonight, at least, the Czar did not take refuge in his study. He had spent half an hour with his boy, and then seemed glad to sit in the last amber of the sunset with his wife and daughters, forbidding the lamps to be lit. In the dusky drawing-room, where her husband's cigarette made a little point of red, Alexandra Feodorovna was all loving attention and all patriotism. She had had a bad fright when Nicholas tore up Rasputin's telegram in a weak man's sudden gust of rage: tonight, with the die irrevocably cast, she stormed at her cousin the Kaiser, the arch-plotter behind the senile Austrian emperor, and lamented the bad luck which had sent the Czar's mother, the Empress Dowager Marie, travelling home across Germany at such a time.

"She's not alone, Sunny," the Czar reminded her. "Xenia is with her, and all their people; they'll be well taken care of, I'm sure. Their special train may even be at Wirballen by this time."

"But what if they stopped in Berlin to see Felix and Irina? Really I think *they* might have left for home as soon as the Austrians issued that wicked ultimatum! So inconsiderate of Felix not to be more careful of Irina, in her state of health!"

In the half dark, side by side on the sofa, Marie and Anastasia unobtrusively nudged each other. Their cousin Irina, daughter of their father's sister Xenia, had recently married Prince Felix Yusupov, and in their experience whenever a young married woman was 'in a state of health' it meant a baby was on the way. For both girls, but particularly for Marie, weddings and the subsequent arrival of babies were the two most important topics in the world.

"Don't worry too much about Motherdear," said the Czar. He knew only too well his wife's steady jealousy of Motherdear, as the Empress Dowager liked her children to call her: it had been one of the penalties of his early married life. To cover her insincerity he began to tell his daughters about that other family of royal girls in Luxemburg, and the ordeal which the eldest, still only twenty, was facing on that July night.

"Are they related to us, papa?" asked Marie.

"Are they, Sunny? Haven't they relatives in Baden?"

"I only know that this girl's mother was a Braganza."

"But why should the Germans invade Luxemburg?" asked Tatiana.

"They want to cross Luxemburg and Belgium to invade northern France," said her father.

"Why don't they just cross the Rhine?" asked Olga pertly.

"Because it would take them too long to reduce the forts the French built along their eastern frontier after they lost Alsace and Lorraine, Now, chicks, I've got to see that tiresome ambassador—"

"Come on, girls," said Tatiana, rising, "let's go to bed."

They wished their father good-night affectionately. There had been tears earlier in the evening, when the Czar told them war was declared, but now all four were too tired to show emotion. They kissed their mother's hand and left the room.

Olga halted in the hall.

"I wonder if there are any pictures of that Luxemburg girl in the library. Let's have a look and see."

"But all our photograph albums are at Czarskoe Selo," objected Marie, a devoted collector of the family snapshots.

"There wouldn't be any in *our* albums, silly, but I think I know where to find one in papa's collection," said methodical Tatiana.

"Oh, don't let's start hunting for photographs tonight," whined Anastasia. "I'm so sleepy. I want to go to bed.'

"You want to look your best at the Winter Palace, do you?" said Olga.

"That's not *fair!*" said the child, flinching at the tone. "I think it'll be *awful* at the Winter Palace tomorrow with all those people staring!"

"Staring at papa, perhaps, but not at you."

"Here you are," said Tatiana, lifting a green leather album from one of the bookshelves. "I knew I saw it here . . . Oh, thank you!" The inevitable pair of white-gloved hands took the heavy album from her own; a footman, accepted rather than recognised, had been switching on the lights in the library.

"Put it on the round table, please . . . What a neat index papa keeps! 'Marie Adelaide, Grand Duchess of Luxemburg, born 1894'—just a year older than you, Olga! 'Succeeded 1912', yes, he did say she was twenty now. Page sixty-three." She turned the pages of the Czar's neat collection of pictures presented to him by minor foreign royalties. The Grand Duchess Marie Adelaide had signed the stiff cabinet photograph taken on her accession day, showing a girl with a sweet, serious face, her hair puffed out over a wire frame under a top-heavy hat.

"That hat's even worse than ours."

"But she looks rather nice, doesn't she?"

"I wonder why she isn't married." That was Marie, of course; but Olga, pointing to the opposite page, said, "Here she is with her sisters."

The sepia print, obviously reproduced from a painting, was captioned 'Christmas at Castle Berg'. It showed six girls, scarcely a year apart in age, wearing tailormade costumes and flat, round caps, standing round a little donkey cart laden with Christmas trees and gifts for the poor.

"Six of them!"

"*Les six vierges,*" said Anastasia with a giggle.

"And they haven't got an Alexis, bringing up the rear."

"That's why Marie Adelaide's the ruler, isn't it?"

"So papa explained."

"I didn't know girls *could* be rulers."

"What about our great-grandmamma, Queen Victoria?" asked Tatiana.

"Oh well, that's history," said Anastasia, and yawned. The younger girls' interest in the Grand Duchess of Luxemburg was yielding to fatigue, and they were ready to follow Tatiana through the far door of the library and up to the private staircase to their rooms. But Olga sat on at the round table with the pictured face of that other girl before her, the girl who, with her little army of market-gardeners and postal clerks, had suddenly become the symbol of resistance to German aggression. And for the first time in her eighteen years Olga Nicolaievna wondered what it would be like to be a ruler—and a girl.

The thought of Marie Adelaide was still uppermost in her mind when they all met for a hasty breakfast before the age-old ceremonial of a Romanov Czar at war laid its iron hold upon them, and she gasped with pity when her father told her that the whole of Luxemburg, capital, villages and countryside, was now in the hands of the Germans.

"Oh, the poor girl! She couldn't hold out against them?"

"It would have meant a wholesale massacre." The Czar rose from the table with a word to his wife, and left the room abruptly. Alexandra complained,

"How can you talk about Luxemburg, Olga, without even asking about poor granny?"

"Is there news of granny? Has she reached the border safely?"

"Your grandmother is still in Germany," said the Czarina, with an awful calm. "We've just heard through the Danish Embassy that she was arrested in Berlin by order of the Kaiser."

"Granny's in prison? I don't believe it!"

"She's under arrest at the station," said Tatiana. "She's with Aunt Xenia, in their special train."

"I don't blame Olga for refusing to believe it," said her mother. "To me it's absolutely incredible. Imagine a monarch arresting an empress! Willy must have gone out of his mind."

"Granny under arrest!" repeated Olga. "But what does father mean to do? How can we get her home again?"

"Naturally the Danish relatives are doing all they can."

"I'm sure they are." It was no time to speak of the British relatives, although the Empress Dowager had been visiting her sister, the widowed Queen Alexandra, in Britain before she started back to Russia via Berlin. It was quite evident, from the silence of the Czar himself, that the British Ambassador had brought him no satisfactory message in the night hours. Olga took a sip of tea and pushed away her plate.

"Don't let it destroy your appetite," said Marie. "I'll back granny against the Kaiser any day."

"I'll back granny against the whole German army," said Anastasia, and even the Czarina smiled. She reminded the girls that they must leave for St. Petersburg in just over an hour, to attend the ceremony of the Czar's oath to the Guards, and must try to cheer up Alexis, once again to remain behind in bed, before they left.

The girls were already in their little brother's room when their father joined them. Nicholas had been working with his secretaries, going over what must be done that morning in the Winter Palace, and studying the first plans for the more complicated rituals and ceremonials which awaited him in Moscow. He had been persuaded, much against his wife's will, to receive the members of the Duma, that debating society—for it was very little else—with which he was so frequently in conflict; and this was an innovation which had to be planned with no guidance from protocol. From his study he had been called to his wife's dressing-room, to discuss what jewels Alexandra should wear for her first appearance before the mass public for over a year. Against the opinion of the Mistress of the Robes, who argued for a rope of pearls at least, he upheld the Czarina's wish to wear no ornaments of any kind on a progress which would take them by water to St. Petersburg, and then on foot through what might well be hostile crowds.

"Her Majesty will wear jewels in Moscow, but not today," he told her attendants, as he dismissed them from the room. Then he took the trembling woman in his arms and kissed her passionately, whispering that she must be calm, and help him through his ordeal at the palace, that he relied upon her absolutely, in all things . . . and knew, as he felt her immediate physical response, that he had one hold over her which never could be broken while they lived. He had withheld his caresses since the affair of the telegram from Rasputin, not by calculation but from sheer fatigue; Nicholas realised now, as he heard her broken murmurs for forgiveness, that she had gone in fear of his displeasure for days past. He forced her mouth open with his lips, and moulded his body close to hers, so that when he released her she looked at him with the adoration of a bride, and whispered, "Such kisses—and in the daylight too! Sweet Childie, how happy you make me!"

So she was happy, for an hour at least, and as the Czar paused outside his son's bedroom door he knew that Alexandra was not the only one; the sound of happy laughter was coming from inside. His sweet silly girls were certainly amusing their brother, for Alexis's laugh rang louder than the rest.

They must have been acting some sort of charade for him, as the Little Pair, especially, loved to do, for they were all standing against one wall, while Alexis, giggling, was propped up on his pillows. Monsieur Gilliard, his Swiss tutor, was smiling by the bedside, with what looked like a picture book in his hand. He rose and bowed when the Czar came in.

"Well, young man," said the Czar fondly, "what are you up to, this fine morning—teasing your sisters?"

"They look so funny, all dressed up with their hats and gloves on," said the little Czarevich. "But they do look very nice and tidy, and I'm proud of them!"

"Thank you, Sir," said Anastasia, dropping a curtsey.

"Only why can't I go to the Winter Palace too?"

"Because you want to go to Moscow, don't you? The doctors say if you have a few more days' rest in bed, you'll be quite able for the journey."

"It's always a few more days," said the child.

The Czar glanced at the young tutor. "How was the walking exercise this morning?"

"Very promising, Sir. Alexis was able to walk right round the room between Nagorny and myself."

"So you see, Alexis! You'll be running about and playing again in no time," said his father. "And while we all go off to work, you're having a marvellous holiday from lessons—"

"I was doing my lessons when all these girls came bursting in."

Monsieur Gilliard held up the book with the bright cover. "We were reading *Heidi,* in the French translation," he explained. "Alexis is making good progress in his French."

"*Heidi*'s a girl's book," said Marie.

"I don't care, I like to read about Peter scrambling on the mountain with the goats," said the boy who was never allowed to scramble unless someone held his hand. "Papa, can I have a pet goat when I'm quite well again?"

"It seems to me you've got a sizeable menagerie already." The Czar surveyed the big grey cat, sleeping through all interruptions at the foot of his boy's bed. There were three dogs in the room, one asleep—Ortipo, Tatiana's bulldog, which snored—Eira, the Czarina's snappish little Scotch terrier, and Joy, the King Charles spaniel which Alexis loved best of all. "What would you do with a goat, boy?"

"Milk it, like Heidi and Peter did," said Alexis, and the laughter began again, so that the Czar told his daughters rather sharply that enough was enough, and they were supposed to leave for Petersburg in five minutes.

"Why do they get to go in the motor today, and not in the yacht with mamma and you?" the boy said, as his sisters came up to kiss him goodbye.

"Because we want them to be at the palace when we arrive," said the Czar. But when the girls had gone, and Monsieur Gilliard had tactfully left the room, he took his son's hand, with the long fingers so like Alexandra's, tenderly in his own, and said,

"I wish you were a bigger boy, Alexis."

"And a stronger boy—don't you?"

"You're getting stronger every day. I mean, if you were older, if you were sixteen and had taken the oath of allegiance to me, you could have joined me in the oath I must take to the Guards today."

"Monsieur Gilliard told me what you were going to say."

"Will you think about it, Baby, while I'm gone? And pray for me?"

"I'll pray for you and Russia," said the child.

* * *

"Alexis has a lot more nerve than we have," said Marie, as the motor rolled down the avenues of Peterhof. "He asked point-blank what we've been wondering about—why we're going to town ahead of papa and mamma."

"You heard what father said," Olga reminded her. "It's because they want us at the palace before they get there."

"Yes, I know, but *why?* We always follow them, walking two by two, just like the pictures of those English girls in the school stories Aunt Victoria sends us."

"Pooh!" said Anastasia with her sharp look, "I've worked it out already. If *they* appear alone, without any of us tagging along behind, it won't be so noticeable that Alexis isn't there at all. You know that's what worries them really; we don't count."

"We're on our way to a religious service, Imp," said Tatiana. "It's hardly the time to be sarcastic, is it? Especially when we think about poor granny."

The Little Pair subsided, as they always did when 'The Governess' took that tone, and the two older girls exchanged glances. They knew, if the younger ones did not, that there was another possible reason for the change in their routine. Four girls in white dresses, walking for however short a distance through a city seething with discontent, were simply four more targets for a bomb or a bullet, and while Olga and Tatiana had learned to master fear for themselves since Stolypin was murdered before their eyes in the theatre at Kiev, they were both sick with anxiety for their father and mother. This visit to the Winter Palace for the ceremony announcing the beginning of a war would be almost the first the sovereigns had dared to pay to their former home for nearly ten years.

The little procession of three motor cars took longer than was necessary to reach its destination, for the drivers kept away from the main arteries of the capital and chose side streets along a route decided on at the last possible moment. The girls tried to recognise the few familiar landmarks through the smoked glass windows: there were none until they came to Suvarov Square, with the British Embassy on one corner and the Marble Palace on the other, and the spire of Peter and Paul rising into the summer blue on the far side of the Neva. From there it was a short drive along the quays, past the magnificent homes of their kindred, with nearly every one of whom the Czarina had systematically quarrelled, to the river entrance of that great palace, with its thousand rooms, its hundred staircases, which Rastrelli had built for a Russian empress and autocrat.

The aged Mistress of the Robes and the Governor of all the Imperial Palaces, General Voieikov, got out of the first car and stood ready to greet the Grand Duchesses: the armed police guard got out of the third car and closed in behind the girls, who were scarcely given time to notice, as they ascended the short flight of steps, that a dense crowd had already gathered on the Palace Quay.

"How many people have been invited to the ceremony?" Olga asked the Governor as he escorted her through the hall leading to the Ambassadors' Staircase. It was empty except for a guard of the Cossacks of the Escort, standing between the pillars and at regular intervals up the grand staircase itself, their red caftans vivid beneath the white stucco angels which started from the walls.

"Five thousand, Your Imperial Highness, and most of them—using another entrance of course—have already taken their places in St. George's Hall. Outside, I'm told there are a hundred times that number in the Palace Square."

"How strange that everything should be so silent here."

"The walls are very thick, *Altesse.*"

Down corridors between those thick walls, which for two hundred years had held so many secrets of blood and lust, the four sisters were conducted to a suite of rooms which had been the private apartments of their great-grandfather, the Czar-Liberator Alexander II. Their maids were waiting in the dismal Blue Bedroom where his neglected wife, the Empress Marie, had dragged out her last days, to offer basins of scented warm water, damask towels, eau de cologne, hairpins and curling tongs, as toilet necessaries after the short motor drive from Peterhof.

"She didn't have much of a view, did she, great-grandmamma Marie?" said Anastasia, going to the window. It overlooked a cheerless stone courtyard and another wing of the vast palace, in which the anonymous windows were shrouded with thick net. There was nothing to be seen but a patch of blue sky overhead, such as a prisoner might have pined to see.

"The Empress Marie Feodorovna was a sad invalid," said Madame Narishkina, the Mistress of the Robes. "But also a model of deportment. An example to *you,* Anastasia. Come into the Gold Parlour, young ladies, if you please."

In the immense parlour a table had been spread with more unnecessary luxuries in the shape of candied fruits and violets, and rich little cakes such as the girls were never allowed to have at home. Marie stripped off her gloves with enthusiasm.

"Mamma and papa were married here, weren't they?" she said when she had enjoyed two glacé apricots and a macaroon. "No, not here in the Gold Parlour, silly! In the chapel, of course."

"Yes, and they *saw* each other for the first time in the chapel, when Aunt Ella was married to poor Uncle Sergei."

"I remember Aunt Ella telling us that."

"Mamma was only twelve."

"But where *is* the chapel, Olga? Do you know?"

"I was taken there once or twice when I was a little girl, but I couldn't possibly find my way back there alone."

"Mamma was dressed for her wedding in the Malachite Hall," said Marie, reverting to her favourite subject. "Shall we see that today?"

"Yes, we shall," said Tatiana. "You'll see the Empress Anna's mirror where mamma watched her reflection when they put the bridal diadem on her head. As you will too, Bow-Wow, when your turn comes."

"Oh-h!" said Marie blissfully. "But don't you have to wear false hair?"

Olga bit back a laugh. Somehow it was impossible to picture Fat Little Bow-Wow decked out in the traditional cloth of silver and red velvet mantle of a Romanov bride, with the artificial ringlets framing her round, honest face.

"Well, I must say, our ancestors had more room in their palace than we have in ours," said Anastasia. "No wonder great-grandpapa Alexander was able to keep his mistress and three brats in a set of rooms right over his poor wife's head!"

"Anastasia!" "Anastasia Nicolaievna!" Both Tatiana and Madame Narishkina fell upon the culprit, and How dare you use such language, and Who told you such an abominable story, mingled with Marie's giggles and Anastasia's spirited defence.

"Well, he married her, didn't he, just as soon as his wife died? She was his morgantic, no morganatic, wife, just the same as the Archduke's, that we were all so sorry for when he was killed at Sarajevo, wasn't she? And she was lovely, Princess Catherine Dolgoruki—"

Olga moved away, out of earshot of the inevitable lecture on behaviour befitting an Imperial Highness which Madame Narishkina was preparing to deliver, and went into the next room, which, although small, was known as the White Ballroom. It was almost bare of furniture, except for the gilt chairs set round the walls, and the iridescent sparkle which the sunshine struck from the prisms of the chandeliers was reflected in the inlaid parquet of the floor. Olga would have said the room was empty, although in fact there were footmen as well as Cossacks on duty, motionless and unobtrusive. She was quite unaware that their eyes followed her as she walked gracefully down the room and looked across the Neva to the bridge.

Candied apricots and court gossip—they seemed to sum up the future that had been waiting for herself, when she emerged from the schoolroom less than six months before. And now Russia was at war, bound no man knew where, and least of all the man, who, his daughter's newly critical heart told her, had drifted or been urged downstream into the worst danger of all. The Grand Duchess Olga wished passionately that the Czar's first act, after

Germany declared war, had not been to seal himself to the fight in this ancient palace where he and his were surrounded by so many emblems of death. She was not a fanciful or a superstitious girl, having inherited the strong nerves and commonsense of the indomitable little lady who even at that moment was sitting in her train at a Berlin railway station, ignoring the insults and obscenities hurled by a mob of German louts from behind a police barrier only two yards away. But the Winter Palace had never been a fortunate home for the Romanovs. Here the terrorist Khalturin had tried to blow up the state dining-rooms, with Alexander II inside, and had succeeded only in killing innocent soldiers and servants instead. Here Alexander II, after escaping so many attempts on his life, had been brought back to die after the bombs were thrown on the spot where the Church of the Spilled Blood now stood, and had died in the arms of his morganatic wife, the Princess Catherine Dolgoruki. And there were other, and worse, associations than the tale of royal assassinations. When Olga told her father that she could 'remember 1905', she had spoken only of the war with Japan. But she could also remember, as a terrified child, hearing what happened outside the Winter Palace on the Bloody Sunday of that unhappy year, when a procession of workers, crossing the Palace Square to present a petition to the Czar, had been fired on by the troops and ridden down by the Cossacks, so that a peaceful demonstration had turned into a near-massacre. Olga could remember the courtiers saying that the Czar was not to blame, he was at his palace in the country: it was his uncle, the Grand Duke Vladimir, who had given the fatal order to fire on the crowd. But the Czar, as Autocrat, was ultimately responsible, and although Bloody Sunday had led to the October Manifesto which ended the autocracy and led to the establishment of the Duma, more than a year elapsed before Nicholas II dared to set foot in his loyal capital of Petersburg. Now here, nine years later, was another Sunday, bloodier in its implications than any which had gone before, and what sort of reception would the Czar and his consort have today?

Tatiana came up behind Olga and slipped her arm round her sister's waist.

"The general wants us to take our places in St. George's Hall," she said.

"I want to see papa and mamma disembark."

"I do too."

"They can't be much longer, can they? . . . What's that noise?"

It might well have been the roar of an angry crowd. Tatiana turned imperatively to one of the waiting footmen.

"Open the window, please!"

The man wrestled with the single pane set in the double window, which could admit fresh air to the White Ballroom on a winter day. Now the warm breeze of summer rose off the Neva, lined on its further shore by spectators, and there was no mistaking the sound which greeted the *Alexandria,* just visible below the Palace Quay.

"They're cheering! Oh, thank God!"

Olga clutched her sister's hand. In the eager clasp they both betrayed the depth and secrecy of their anxiety.

Between the escorting police boats, up the river teeming with craft, the *Alexandria* reached the landing stage, and the Czar and Czarina stepped ashore. Alexandra had made a supreme effort to be gracious and to conceal her own tortured anxiety. She was smiling as she laid her hand lightly on her husband's arm, as it had lain at their wedding and their coronation, and allowed him to lead her towards the palace he had once intended to be their married home. She was dressed in white, with a long white ostrich boa on her shoulders, and wore a tulle hat which showed her red-gold hair.

"Doesn't she look wonderful today?" said Tatiana.

"Yes, she does."

"Come on, you two!" called Marie from the ballroom door. "Or else the general will have a fit!"

General Voieikov, trying to conceal his impatience, led the girls quickly through the maze of corridors and reception rooms to St. George's Hall. From the great room of state, where five thousand men in uniform and women in gala dress had assembled, there came a murmur of anticipation which echoed the sound of cheering from the Palace Square. Although the ceremony was to be religious, with an altar set up in the hall to hold the ikon of the Virgin of Kazan, brought from the national sanctuary on the Nevski Prospekt, it was not possible for five thousand members of the Russian nobility to maintain a devotional silence for long. They moved and murmured, chattered, criticised, acknowledged the presence of their friends with waves or bows, while those nearest the closed french windows jockeyed for position to see the vast crowd in the enormous square.

The young Grand Duchesses (walking, to Olga's irritation, two by two like the English schoolgirls of Marie's joke) were led to their places at the left of the altar. There they were hemmed in by the Family, led by the stately Grand Duchess Marie Pavlovna, known to the girls as Aunt Miechen, who considered herself to be, after the two empresses, the third lady in the land. She gave them an all-embracing, condescending smile; and Olga, smiling back, remembered with secret amusement Simon Hendrikov's definition of a Grand Duchess as 'a tall stout lady, very proud, and hung about with jewels'. Aunt Miechen to the life! She remembered that Aunt Miechen's husband, now dead, was that Grand Duke Vladimir who had given orders to open fire on Bloody Sunday.

There was someone else in the serried ranks of the Family whose smile was instant and affectionate. The Grand Duke Dmitri, tall and fair and engaging, wearing the uniform of the Chevalier Guards, gave Olga the encouraging nod of an elder brother, which was how when they were children—he being only four years her senior—she had been taught to regard him. There had been a later time, at that first dance at Livadia and for a while thereafter, when Dmitri's kisses, his gaiety, and his attentive companionship had led the adolescent girl into a happy fantasy of becoming, some day, Dmitri's wife. The realisation that the dashing young cavalry officer, the toast of the Petersburg nightclubs and the theatre dressing-rooms, would never feel more than a cousinly affection for a girl whose upbringing was more like that of an English parsonage than a Russian court, had brought Olga some pain and even some secret tears. She had conquered her feeling for him in silence: it was still strong enough, as the Orthodox clergy's processional began, with chants and swinging censers, for Olga's first prayer to be for Dmitri's safety.

The Czar and his consort entered St. George's Hall, where now at last five thousand Russians bowed and crossed themselves in devout unity. Alexandra's public smile had disappeared, but she was more composed than many of the witnesses had expected, and during the long Te Deum she was ready with a grave but encouraging look whenever her husband seemed to ask for her support. The chants, the ritual took their prolonged way, and St. George's Hall grew thick with incense. Then the court chaplain read the manifesto by which the Russian Czar informed his people that the country was at war. Nicholas stepped towards the ikon of the Virgin of Kazan. A copy of the Gospel was held out to him, and he solemnly laid his right hand upon it.

"Officers of my Guard, here present, I greet in you my whole army and give it my blessing. I solemnly swear that I will never make peace so long as one of the enemy is on the soil of the motherland."

It was the oath which his ancestor, Alexander I, had sworn when the enemy was Napoleon Bonaparte—an oath redeemed by Russia's victory. To all his hearers, superstitious and dependent on signs and tokens and influences both mystical and occult, the words seemed like a happy omen. Nicholas himself seemed to have gained in stature by repeating them. With his curiously impassive dignity he walked down the hall, the french windows being opened at his approach, and passed alone out to the balcony.

He stood there, dwarfed by the gigantic pillar in the square topped by the statue of that same victorious ancestor, between the People outside and the Court within, while the Court applauded, and the People yelled themselves hoarse. They cheered their beloved Little Father as he had never been cheered in his life before. They roared their execration of Germany and their confidence in the might of the Russian army. And then, in the square where the workers had fallen under the bullets of 1905, and while the bells of Peter and Paul chimed, "Lord, have mercy on us", they sang the national anthem.

God save the Czar! For that day, at least, Bloody Sunday was forgotten.

6

AMONG THE ASSEMBLY OF Russians invited to listen to the oath taken by Nicholas II, there was only one foreigner. He was the French Ambassador, Monsieur Maurice Paléologue, representing Russia's great ally. Within two days Russia had other allies, one a little nation fighting for its life, which was Belgium; the other, the guarantor of that little nation's independence, which was Great Britain.

The game of ultimatums was nearly over. During all that Sunday when St. Petersburg clamoured its enthusiasm for the war, the King of the Belgians and his ministers discussed the reply they should send to the German government, which demanded free passage for its troops across the little country. Next day, the day that Germany declared war on France, King Albert, his cabinet and his parliament resolved to resist the German invasion. Belgium had six army divisions and Belgium would fight.

That Monday was a Bank Holiday in England, traditionally a day for going to the seaside. Some Englishmen went in other directions, as Reservists and Territorials were called up, and all the members, without exception, of the House of Commons assembled in the historic chamber to hear the Foreign Secretary declare that it would be a sacrifice of Britain's good name and reputation before the world to run away from the obligations of the Belgian Treaty. The tumultuous applause of the vast majority of the House indicated its complete approval.

At eight next morning, August 4, the Germans invaded Belgium, and later in the day the British ultimatum was received in Berlin. It charged Germany to uphold the treaty of Belgian neutrality, signed in the previous century by Prussia among other powers. The German Chancellor dismissed the treaty as 'a scrap of paper', and no answer was sent to the British ultimatum. With a much briefer time-limit than the ultimatum sent by Austria-Hungary to Serbia, the British challenge expired at midnight. Britain declared war on Germany, the last knot in the rope of alliances and ententes had been tied, and the midnight bells rang out across a continent under arms.

At the American Embassy and consulate in St. Petersburg, by comparison with these excitements, all was stagnation. President Wilson had given a press conference on the day Germany declared war on France, but on August 6 his wife died, and for the period of her funeral there was no further statement from the White House. Joe Calvert, professionally concerned only with the fortunes of an American sewing-machine company's Russian outlets, was delighted to hear Richard Allen's voice on the telephone one mid-August morning.

"Joe? You free for lunch today, by any chance?"

"You bet I am!"

"Care to come along to my place, about one o'clock?"

"It's a date."

Their few brief conversations had always been in this laconic style, due as much to the erratic Petersburg telephone system as to their respect for official business, as the friendship developed between the two young men. Thus they had arranged meetings at the Mourina golf course, laid out by the British colony about twenty miles from the capital, and evening poker sessions at Richard Allen's flat. This was the first time Joe had visited the flat by day, and as he walked along the Italianskaia he thought how splendid the street was, with its harmonising façades of yellow ochre, compared with the shabbiness of his new friend's home.

Captain Allen's flat was decidedly a bachelor establishment, kept barely tidy by an elderly daily maid. The living-room, which had two windows on the Italianskaia, gave absolutely no indication of its owner's tastes and personality, except for a few books by William Le Queux and E. Phillips Oppenheim, and a china tobacco jar with a regimental crest which stood next to a rack of well-seasoned pipes on the writing desk between the two windows. The table used for the card games was now covered with a coarse linen cloth and set for luncheon with a modest selection of *zakuski*, the Russian hors d'œuvres, the inevitable vodka decanter, and a large glass jug into which, when Joe arrived, his host was pouring bottles of chilled Danish beer.

"That looks good, on a hot day like this," said Joe as they shook hands.

"I remembered you weren't very keen on vodka. Pull up a chair, Joe, and fill your plate. There's nothing coming but boiled sturgeon and potatoes, the only dish Varvara knows how to cook."

"This is very good." Joe helped himself to caviar, and took a gulp of the cold beer. "Say, Dick, I wanted to call you days ago, but I figured you'd have too much to do to spare any time for poker. Fact is, I wanted to tell you how right you were, that night we met back at my hotel, when you talked about America having to keep the ring in Europe, one of these days—"

"Was that what I said?"

"You sure did. And right off, President Wilson told the press that the United States stands ready to help the rest of the world as a mediator in this great international crisis—wasn't that what you meant?"

"Something like that."

"Well, anyway, you were pretty smart. You saw the war coming, when I just couldn't believe it, and now you people are in it yourselves, right up to the neck."

"In your own words, Joe, we sure are."

"Anyway, you're the heroes of the hour in Petersburg."

"We've Admiral Beatty and his jolly tars to thank for that. More beer?"

"Please." The cool gold Tuborg foamed in the fluted glass. "Say, are you going to Moscow for the imperial visit?"

"Me? Good Lord, no! That particular junket's only for top-drawer diplomats, not for the likes of me. And what a waste of time the whole dead ceremonial is—the Czar going off to Moscow to ask God's blessing on the war, and drag his family round every shrine and chapel in the Kremlin, when he should be here in Petersburg, taking advantage of the goodwill of the Duma."

"The Duma certainly seems to be solid for him right now. But so does everybody."

"Yes, Nicholas is riding high, but how long will it last? I wouldn't bet on his popularity after the first defeat. Just one defeat like Liège—"

The slipshod maid brought in the fish platter and a pot of coffee, which she deposited with a grunt by her employer's hand, and the conversation turned to the German capture of the great fortress of Liège, which the Belgians had believed to be impregnable. And as they talked, Dick Allen studied his guest's face, so open, even ingenuous; the brown eyes so candid: was it really possible, when it got down to brass tacks, to convey to this boy a disingenuous suggestion, on which much might yet depend? He stirred his coffee thoughtfully.

"Joe, have you found a flat yet?"

"I only wish I had! I've looked at more dumps from the office list, and they're either miles out, or filthy dirty, or I'm expected to muck in with the family . . . I don't know what to do. I can't go on living at the Europa much longer, it's in a higher bracket than my allowance scale. The other guys are beginning to think I'm a millionaire—"

"How would you like to take over this dump of mine?"

"*This* flat? But what about you?"

"I'm going away from Petersburg for a bit."

"Back to England?"

"Why to England?"

"I thought you might be going back to rejoin your regiment."

"I haven't been any use to the regiment since I stopped a Boer bullet at Spion Kop. You haven't noticed? I still limp a bit when I'm tired."

"I did notice, on the golf course; I thought you'd a stone in your shoe. The Boer War, eh? You must have been just a kid."

"Twenty-one. But that's water under the bridge, old boy; I'm leaving Petersburg because I've been posted. I'm going to the Legation at Stockholm."

Joe nodded. It seemed to him like a demotion, this transfer from one of the nerve centres of the spreading war to a remote and neutral country like Sweden. He thought it tactful to say nothing.

"I don't want to give up the flat," Dick Allen was saying in his placid way. "It isn't up to much, I know, but I've got all my stuff here—I hope you don't mind that—and I'd like to be able to come back some day. And it *is* very central and convenient."

"What would you want for rent?"

"Well, first you ought to look at it, we'll do that in a minute. You've seen the bathroom, the kitchen's not much better, but Varvara knows her way about in it, and I think she'd like to keep the job. There's a fair-sized bedroom and a little one, both looking out on the courtyard, and that's all. I certainly wouldn't want a big rent from a careful tenant."

He named a weekly sum which made Joe raise his eyebrows. "That's less than I'm paying for my cubbyhole at the Europa."

"Wait until you see the bedrooms. The little one's just a cubbyhole too."

The old-fashioned flat was speedily inspected. There was a single wardrobe in each of the bedrooms and built-in cupboards for linen and china in the hall.

"And what's that door?"

"That? It's the door on to the service stairs. They're supposed to be used for deliveries, but the tenants are always complaining that the delivery men use the front entrance."

"And the stairs lead up from the courtyard?"

"That's right." They went back to the living-room, and Dick Allen started to fill a briar from the tobacco jar. Joe waited until the match was struck.

"Look here, Dick," he said, "I'd like to rent your flat, it's very much the sort of place I'd hoped to find. But the rental you're asking just isn't realistic. Where's the catch in the deal?"

"There isn't any catch," said Dick. "There is just one slight string attached."

"Let's hear about it."

"I might have to come back from Stockholm, from time to time. And then, if it wouldn't cramp your style in any way, I'd like to be able to use the smaller bedroom. I'd like to keep one key, and come and go without bothering you or Varvara—"

"Or any of the neighbours?"

"Well, yes."

"Because you'd be using the service stairway."

"Exactly."

Joe squared his shoulders. "Now get this," he said, "I wasn't born yesterday. I may be just a freshman around here, but I do know that a foreigner renting a Petersburg apartment has his name on the police files, and may be liable to police surveillance. What you're asking me to do is to front for you, whatever it is you're up to; and when all is said and done I'm an officer of the American Foreign Service, a low man on the totem pole of a neutral power. I can't, and I won't, cover for anything I don't understand. I think you'll have to tell me more about your job in Stockholm."

"Assistant military attaché, the same as here."

"I don't think," said Joe Calvert, and his Maryland drawl was suddenly very pronounced, "that you British really need such a heavy military representation in a neutral country like Sweden. One military attaché would seem to be enough."

Dick shrugged. "Then let me put it this way. Very few men among our allies—very few, that is, in Russia, and certainly none in gallant little Serbia and gallant little Belgium, have twigged that this is going to be a war of propaganda as well as a war of manpower, transport and weapons. But we know how good German Intelligence is, and how long their brightest boys have been working on the idea of starting revolution—yes, actual revolution, the overthrowing of the state—behind the frontiers of their enemies. We're vulnerable in Ireland, where the Germans counted on civil war, in British India and in Egypt. But Russia is the most vulnerable of the lot, especially in Poland, Finland, and perhaps the Caucasus and the Ukraine. Joe!" he said emphatically, "what I'm going to tell you now might be considered classified, but I have to take the risk: after all, it's something the American Foreign Service has probably worked out for itself: five of the German Embassies in Europe are key points in the propaganda network. Stockholm is one of them. As you know, Baron von Lucius is the ambassador to Sweden, and he has a staff of the Kaiser's best men around him. We've decided to increase our representation in Stockholm, just to keep pace with them, and that's the reason for my transfer. I may have to act as a courier between there and here from time to time, or the King's Messengers may act as liaison officers instead: it's as simple as all that."

"Very simple indeed," said Joe, "unless you use the word 'espionage' instead of 'propaganda'." He laughed. "All right, Dick, you don't need to tell me any more. When do you expect to leave St. Petersburg?"

"Next week—the twenty-second."

"Then it's a deal. I'll take over the flat on the twenty-third, for one quarter only, and we'll see how things work out."

"Good enough!"

"The way people are talking, the war mayn't even last three months. The Russians say they'll be in Berlin in six weeks' time."

"And the Germans are planning to celebrate Christmas in Paris. God! Lord Kitchener's the only realist among the lot. As soon as he took over at the War Office, he said he would begin his plans on the assumption that the war would last three years."

"Three *years!*"

"Or maybe four."

* * *

Simon Hendrikov was one of the few young Russian officers who was not convinced of a lightning victory. He was indeed profoundly depressed when he returned to his parents' home in the Fourth Line on the night before his entrainment for the front, although with true Russian fatalism he accepted the destiny which had placed him in the one battalion of the Marine Guards called up for active service. The *Standart* had been laid up for the duration of the war, and the Grand Duchess Olga was with her family in Moscow.

As he turned in at the gate he saw another officer emerging from the building, and recognised the man who had passed him on the stairs a few weeks earlier. As Simon saluted briskly the other man stopped, and after saying "Good evening!" in the same pleasant way he added, "Haven't we met before?"

"We've seen each other, sir, right outside my own front door."

"Oh, you live here, do you? Then you're Professor Hendrikov's son; my cousin Madame Martova told me about you. My name's Yakovlev, Commander in the *Askelod.*"

"A cruiser, isn't she? Wasn't *Askelod* one of the guard ships when His Majesty opened the new dry dock last month?"

"Yes, and I remember now, you were one of the Garde Equipage on duty."

Commander Yakovlev was very frank and agreeable, much more so than Dr. Martov or his wife, as far as Simon knew the Martov neighbours. It was unusual for a naval officer of higher rank to be so pleasant to an unknown junior, and Simon wished the commander, "Good luck, sir!" with sincerity. But as he went upstairs he was still haunted by the man's resemblance to somebody, and somebody in the Service at that. Out of uniform the resemblance would have been less striking. Then he dismissed the matter as he entered the flat, and Dolly came running to meet him, jumping up to kiss him and clasping her hands behind his neck.

"Here, you're choking me!" Simon protested. "Look at you, all dressed up! Are you going to a party?"

"Mother and I are going to dinner with Plain Joe Calvert!"

"With *who*?"

"You know, the nice American who's studying with mother. You met him the first night he came here, before the cruise."

"Tall, dark, speaks good French? I remember him."

"He's asked us to dinner at the Europa, along with a friend of his from the British Embassy, who's going off to Stockholm."

"Simon! my dear boy, what a nice surprise!" said his mother, who had hurried from her bedroom at the sound of his voice. 'What a shame we'd planned to go out! Of course we could cancel it, couldn't we, Dolly?"

"Cancel it?"

"We could telephone to Mr. Calvert and explain about Simon's visit—"

"But mother, he's got seats for the theatre! And we can't telephone to Mara, to tell her not to meet us outside the Gostinnoi Dvor!"

In the face of Dolly's open disappointment, Simon took a quick decision. There was no need to tell his family that he was on entrainment leave; that could wait until the early breakfast time, and then, as soon as the fuss started, he would be gone. "You mustn't give up a theatre evening on account of me," he said. "I've got an all-night pass. Go ahead and enjoy yourselves, and I'll have something to eat with father. Where is he, by the way?"

"At the Public Library. Oh, Simon, this does seem so unfair to you! Should we call Cousin Timofey or Cousin Boris, and ask them to come round and entertain you? Papa is so depressed these days. Mr. Calvert invited him too, of course, but he says it's the wrong time to be going to parties—what do you think?"

"I think Petersburg's gone party mad, and father doesn't know there's a war on," said Simon lightly. "It'll be nice to spend an evening with him, just the two of us, and we'll have the samovar boiling when you come back. And mother, shouldn't you finish dressing if you're going out to dinner? Dolly looks all ready for the road, so don't you want me to get you a droskhi?"

"Lena went out to fetch one." When the flurry of departure was over Simon went into his own narrow bedroom to change out of uniform. As he put on an old pair of trousers and a soft peasant blouse of the sort he wore at the dacha he wondered how many of his brother officers, on their last all-night leave in St. Petersburg, would be spending it exclusively with their families. He had been invited to join more than one group, bound either for the Islands and the gipsy singers, or for Cubat's restaurant and the ladies of the town, and when he thought of an evening alone with his father, who always talked above his head, Simon half regretted his refusal. But then no girl would do but the one girl, in rank so far above him, unattainable, who was now taking part in that foolish charade in Moscow; and he sat down on the edge of his bed with the embroidered shirt in his hands, to think of their last meeting. All the officers and ratings who had served in the *Standart,* from the Black Sea duty earlier in the summer until the cruise to Finland, had paraded at Peterhof quay to receive the farewells and good wishes of the imperial family before dispersing to their different barracks. Olga Nicolaievna had come down the lines of men in blue immediately behind her father and mother. He heard her greeting the senior officers much as her parents did: "We'll be thinking of you"—"Good luck!"—"May we meet again soon." But when she came to him, Simon saw the golden head droop and the blue eyes mist over, and when she held out her little hand for his kiss he heard Olga murmur, "God bless you, Simon Karlovich!" It was all he needed, of pleasure, feasting and love, before leaving for the front.

He had been so casual, and so prompt in sending his mother and Dolly off to Joe's dinner party that neither one suspected that this leave was the last, and Dolly chatted happily as they drove down the Nevski Prospekt to the big bazaar opposite the Europa Hotel. Mara Trenova was waiting there, for Madame Hendrikova had insisted that the two girls must enter the hotel together, and under her chaperonage. Joe and Dick Allen were waiting for them in the lobby. Joe was unusually nervous; he had invited Mara Trenova at Dick's own request, and was uncertain how that unpredictable young lady would choose to behave in company.

"Don't you know some nice English girl you'd like to have meet the Hendrikovs?" he pleaded when the farewell party was being planned.

"I'd like to meet Ivan Trenov's daughter, and see if she runs true to form. Her father was a bit of a firebrand, I've been told. Is she?"

"I think she's a bit of a pill," said Joe, and then, repenting, "No, she isn't really. She's an attractive girl, and clever too, I think. But if one of us says something that doesn't please her, she's quite capable of getting up and walking out of the restaurant and going home."

"That wouldn't worry the other diners, Russians love scenes. Go ahead and invite her, Joe!"

So now he was ushering Madame Hendrikova into the Europa's vast restaurant, one stair up and with its ceiling two storeys high, and the girls were walking behind their chaperone as demurely as if they were once again the Dolly and Molly of the Xenia School. All the ladies wore high-necked dresses, but no hats, and for the first time since he had met Dolly, Joe saw that her curls were brushed up and pinned on the top of her head. Mara's dress was plain, but her manner was relaxed, and she obviously intended to be a charming guest. As the food and wine were brought Joe realised that another person determined to be charming was that usually lackadaisical individual, Captain Richard Allen. It was strange how a well-cut dark suit, starched linen, and a touch of pomade on his hair and moustache seemed to have transformed him into a man about town. Dick's French was not as good as his Russian, but fluent enough to allow him to embark on a series of jokes and anecdotes which started off the evening well.

Mara and Madame Hendrikova listened with amusement, but Dolly looked round the room very often, and twice whispered to Joe that it was wonderful. The place indeed was crowded with handsome men and women who were apparently determined to forget the war, and the orchestra was playing selections from *The Merry Widow*. There was champagne on every table, and Joe had ordered it as a matter of course. Dolly's hazel eyes sparkled as she took her first sip, and wished Captain Allen a safe journey to Sweden.

The conversation turned to the stage, and the French play they were to see at the Alexandrovski theatre. On this Mara was opinionated, and spoke rather too long about Meyerhold's theory of audience participation, but the only slight ruffle on the surface harmony came later, and was innocently caused by Joe himself. In one of the pauses between the courses he asked Mara how her secretarial training was progressing.

"Pretty well, I think. The instructors say I have fair speeds already, in both shorthand and typewriting."

"Great, and you must be pleased to know you've got a job waiting for you." He meant to add, "When exactly do you graduate?" but she interrupted him with:

"Who told you I had a job waiting for me?"

"Darya Karlovna said something about it."

"What a chatterbox you are, Dolly!" It was said with a touch of the cold venom which had repelled Joe when Mara condoned the Sarajevo murders, and Dolly said defensively:

"I only told Mr. Calvert that one of our lecturers had promised to find a position for you. I didn't know it was a secret. I didn't even mention the person's name."

"Of course it's not a secret," said Mara, and was able to smile. "It was Professor Rostov who kindly offered me his help. He was a friend of my father's, in their student days."

"Which Rostov is that—the historian?" said Richard Allen.

"No; Lev Andreivich Rostov, the distinguished chemist."

"Is *he* teaching at Xenia now?"

"Oh, certainly not. He came just once, as a guest lecturer, when he was on a short visit to Petersburg. He works in Stockholm now. Perhaps you'll meet him there, Captain Allen."

"I wouldn't know how to talk to a distinguished chemist."

Then the cutlets were served, and Joe turned to Madame Hendrikova with a question about the dacha at Koivisto. "My daughter Betsy and her husband are staying there," she said. "We want to wait here until we know what Simon's orders are. Of course we hope he'll remain in Petersburg for as long as possible." It was the only reference to the war which had been made so far, except for Madame Hendrikova's warm greeting of Dick Allen, when Joe introduced him. "I'm proud to meet one of our allies, monsieur," she had said. "I've always admired Britain; now, more than ever." But Dick had only bowed and smiled; he had not made any comment on Britain's entry to the war, although every day now the trains which had carried the cherry-pickers to Kent in July were carrying the British Expeditionary Force to the ports of embarkation for the

Continent. In the company of three Russian women, two of them very young, the Englishman and the American had steered the conversation clear of politics, so that Joe was taken by surprise when Dick said, over the coffee:

"You must have brought your new student on very quickly, madame, since he's already taken to attending the sessions of the Duma."

"The Duma!" said Madame Hendrikova. "You never told me that!"

"Captain Allen exaggerates," said Joe. "I attended *one* session of the Duma last week, and as I understood about two words out of every hundred, I didn't tell you because I thought you'd laugh at me."

"Have all foreign consuls the entrée to the Duma?" asked Mara.

"I doubt it, Mara Ivanovna. I'm afraid I was a little above my station, but I did manage to get a pass for the diplomatic box at the Tauride Palace, when they were debating the war credits. I couldn't understand much of it, but I could watch their faces, and find out what the Deputies look like, what they sound like—the men I read about in our press translations every day."

"I think that was very clever of you," said Dolly. "But how did you find out what was happening?"

"From a Frenchman sitting right next to me. He explained that the Socialists were refusing to vote the military credits, and that worried me some, because in Germany the Socialists did vote the war budget, same as all the other parties. But it seems to be true enough, because it was repeated in our press digest next day."

"Did your press digest give our Social Revolutionary party's reasons?" Mara asked.

"Not in so many words, no. Those digests have got to be kept short."

"I can tell you in so many words," said the girl, and again the flash of her dark eyes was cold. "The SRs refrained from voting the war credits because they refuse to accept responsibility for any Czarist policies. And the spokesman said, "We invite democracy to defend its native soil against invasion. *Workers and peasants, defend your country! We will free it afterwards!*' "

* * *

While the Czar and his retinue paced through the Moscow ceremonies, which had more than a touch of the old Byzantine splendour about them, the Grand Duke Nicholas Nicolaievich, an experienced soldier, assumed the supreme command of the army and established his GHQ, called the Stavka, on the Moscow-Warsaw railway at Baronovichi. There was nothing to fear on the eastern front, for in spite of Olga's forebodings Japan had declared war on Germany. In the west Italy, allied by previous treaties with Germany and Austria-Hungary, decided on neutrality and the strategic advantage of sitting on the fence.

Along with this good news, the imperial family were thankful to know that the Empress Dowager, after her ordeal at the station in Berlin, had been allowed to journey on to St. Petersburg via the Scandinavian countries with her daughter Xenia, her granddaughter Irina, and Irina's husband Prince Felix Yusupov. They were all safe at the Anichkov Palace, tired and angry after their adventure, and the Empress Dowager, furious with the Kaiser, could hardly wait for the Russian victory parade through Berlin. It *must* happen before Christmas, everybody said so; the Allies in the West had great faith in 'the Russian steamroller', which was the new propaganda phrase. And with the slow, cumbrous advance of a real steamroller the Russian armies moved forward to East Prussia and Galicia, groping for the enemy.

As soon as the fighting began, the Czarina threw herself heart and soul into humanitarian plans. In her early married life she had tried to improve the hospital services of her new country, and her working guilds, summer crèches, and orthopædic institutes for children had been heartily ridiculed by Petersburg society. Now, while her daughters pestered her to let them learn to drive ambulances, to go to the front as nurses, or even to practise pistol shooting, she conferred alone with her sister Elizabeth, the head of a successful nursing sisterhood in Moscow.

Elizabeth, or Ella, of Hesse was the childless widow of the Grand Duke Sergei, the Governor of Moscow, who during the revolutionary troubles of 1905 had been blown to shreds by a terrorist's bomb. Ever since, the Grand Duchess Elizabeth had worn a most becoming habit and a sweet martyred smile, but she had her full share of Teutonic efficiency, and was of real help in organising her sister's always emotional plans. The Grand

Duchesses were only told that their share in the plans would be explained as soon as they got home.

They knew already that the Winter Palace, which was to have been the scene of Olga and Tatiana's brilliant début, was being transformed into a vast depot for medical supplies and surgical apparatus, and that the splendid Catherine Palace at Czarskoe Selo, the Czar's Village, fifteen miles from St. Petersburg, was to become a military hospital. But there were no changes as yet at the Alexander Palace, joined to the Catherine by vast and linking parks, and this was the home they were bound for, the palace they knew and preferred to any other. The first hour after they got back from Moscow was spent romping through the familiar rooms, greeting the entourage, the servants, the officers of the Guard, and petting the beloved cats and dogs which had been brought back from Peterhof. They were all children again for that one hour, perhaps for the last time in their lives.

One of the uncomfortable aspects of the imperial family's housekeeping was the parents' decided preference for eating in almost any room other than the formal dining-room in their private apartments. That night the Czar's choice fell on the library. Alexis, exhausted after the trip from Moscow, was having supper in bed and feeding titbits to his adored spaniel Joy, and without his chatter the library's sobriety had a calming effect upon the girls. They were ready to be attentive when, the folding table having been taken away by the footmen, the Czar said gravely:

"My dears, you realise that I'll have to be away from home a great deal in the future."

"Oh papa, must you?"

"Of course. I'll have to be at GHQ very often, and visiting our brave soldiers at the front. So I think there are some things we ought to settle as soon as possible." He cleared his throat. "Mamma and I have been so touched, so comforted, by your willingness to help us now in any way that young girls can. And this is one way we talked over with your aunt Elizabeth: the provision of hospital trains for the wounded."

"A hospital in a train!" marvelled Anastasia.

"You know there has been heavy fighting in East Prussia—"

"But we're winning, papa?" said Tatiana.

"It's certainly a very hard-fought fight," said the Czar in his oblique way. "And that means a heavy casualty list. The

Commander-in-Chief tells me trains converted to hospital use are needed urgently. Mamma and I are each donating one such train: may we give four more, at your expense and in your names?"

"Oh papa, *yes!*" "What a marvellous idea!" "And one for Baby, too!" The happy clamour brought a smile to the Czar's drawn face. But Olga said,

"How much would it cost?"

"You don't mean you would *grudge* the cost?" said the Czarina.

"Oh no! Please!" Olga flushed with dismay. "I only meant, can we really afford it?"

"Most certainly you can."

"Well but, papa, how are we to know? We only get twenty roubles a month each, for pocket money. I asked Mr. Gibbs, and he said that was two pounds in English money, or ten dollars in American, which really isn't very much."

"Is there a single want of yours which isn't satisfied?" flashed the Czarina. "You have dresses, furs, jewels—"

"Yes, I know, mother, but sometimes I think it would be fun to go into the Gostinnoi Dvor and buy a pair of gloves I chose myself."

The Czar held up his hand. "That's beside the point," he said. "Each one of you girls has an annual income from the Apanages established by the Empress Catherine II. It's administered for you by a special office of the Household, and the accounts will be rendered to you as you attain your majority. Does that satisfy you, Olga?"

"Well, I *must* say," the Czarina interrupted, "when I was a girl in Darmstadt, my sisters and I were never present at any discussion of money matters—"

"No, mamma," said Tatiana hastily, and gave a slight shake of her head at Olga. She knew, as if she had shaped the words herself, that her quick-tempered sister was about to say, "I don't suppose there was much money to discuss at the court of Hesse-Darmstadt!" The tactful girl went on:

"Thank you so much, papa, for explaining it all to us, and of course we'll be delighted to donate the trains. But we do want to work ourselves as well. I know you laughed at us for wanting to go to the front, but surely we can do war nursing here at home?"

"I think you can, lovey, and that's what mamma has in mind for you."

"The Big Pair and I are going to be nurses," said the Czarina impressively. "Tomorrow morning we'll go over to the other palace and meet the lady who's going to instruct us—not a nurse, but a qualified surgeon, one of the best in St. Petersburg. And when we've passed our examinations, then we'll be able to work as nurses in the wards."

"But mamma, you're a wonderful nurse already," said Anastasia.

"I've certainly had enough practice with you children," said her mother sadly. "But for military nursing we must study anatomy and physiology, and operating theatre techniques, and much else, before we can really help our brave wounded. And isn't that just what you wanted, girls?"

"Oh *yes*," said Olga from her heart, and Tatiana kissed her mother's hand. But the Little Pair set up a clamour: "What about us?"

"You can make bandages, and sew for the troops. But you're too young to be nurses; yes, Mashka, fifteen really is too young."

"Well, it's too bad," said the honest girl, "because I was planning to be a heroine."

"What sort of a heroine, Bow-Wow? A lady soldier?" teased the Czar.

"No, a historical heroine like in our English story-books. They're all about girls who refused to betray state secrets, even under the threat of torture—real heroines."

"You'd better stick to your sewing basket," Olga told her. "Because we don't know any state secrets, and no one in the world is going to torture *us*."

"It was only a joke," said Marie humbly. But the Little Pair felt no temptation to be funny next morning, when they were left behind in their schoolroom for a French class with Monsieur Gilliard, while their sisters started on a new career. Nor did the Big Pair feel anything but solemn when they were conducted through the magnificent rooms of the great palace which Rastrelli had built for Elizabeth I, and which had been added to and made even more magnificent by the imperial Catherine whose name it bore. The girls knew the state rooms well, although in recent years these had only been used for family baptisms or weddings, and it was strange to see the rooms, with their gilded walls and painted ceilings, set out with high, hard hospital beds. In the operating theatre, which made Tatiana shiver, they met the lady of title who was not only a surgeon but a surgery professor, and liked the way she spoke to them as students and not as Imperial Highnesses. They were given textbooks, and told to go home and study them in preparation for some practical instruction that afternoon.

After that it was only a matter of hours before even the hands of two inexperienced girls were useful when the first ambulances drew up before the Catherine Palace hospital. The fighting in East Prussia flared into a six-day battle in a wilderness which the Germans decided should be called Tannenberg. In Galicia the Russians won a victory at Lemberg for which bells were rung in a capital which had changed its name from St. Petersburg to Slavic Petrograd, and in the rejoicings it was easy to make light of the defeat at Tannenberg—a battle which had made the Germans order six corps eastward from the fighting on the Marne meant to end in the fall of Paris. Certainly the Allied High Command in France was not at once aware of the significance of Tannenberg, in which the proud façade of Russian patriotism was wrecked.

The occupants of the Alexander Palace were almost as well protected as the Allied High Command from a knowledge of the meaning of the Tannenberg disaster. There were only so many casualties which the Catherine hospital could hold at any one time, only so many hospitals in Petrograd which the Czarina and her daughters could visit. They had not yet seen the hideous confusion of the front, where men died for lack of medical care and horses in the antique ambulances fell dead between the shafts as they dragged their loads of wounded to the railhead. They saw enough, within the rococo rooms of their ancestral palace, to turn Olga and Tatiana Nicolaievna from girls into women.

In the days after Tannenberg they worked all round the clock at the task they had assumed. In their off-duty hours, they went to their sitting-room (or sometimes to their bedroom, for their mother often invaded their sitting-room, to scribble her endless letters on their own chaise-longue) and asked each other questions from their lecture notes and textbooks. It was Tatiana, with her practical mind, who assimilated scientific knowledge faster, but Olga was the steadier in the wards, the calmer and more warmly compassionate in the face of sights and sounds which could not be kept from the knowledge of Imperial Highnesses. And when the long day came to an end they were ready, although the Czarina often protested, to return after dinner to the Catherine Palace and take their turn at washing the instruments used in the operating theatre, which was always in service.

They were very simple girls, and hardly understood, as yet, that the war had brought them a new freedom, being discovered by thousands of other girls in the sheltered homes of Europe. The Czar's daughters had never been allowed to make any friends of their own age—"For surely," the Czarina often said, "four sisters are quite enough company for one another!"—and now they had other young nurses to talk to, and drink tea with when they had ten minutes of leisure; and young army doctors, to whom they gave the same eager friendliness as the officers of the *Standart*. They were free to come and go between the palaces, unescorted for the first time in their lives, with only the sentries presenting arms at the gates, and the Cossacks of the Escort, patrolling the avenues day and night at a distance of fifty yards apart, to remind them of their rank. And their mother, whose possessive jealousy had kept them tied so close to her, was now unable to account for every moment of their days.

The Czarina was in better health than for some time past. She still complained of sciatic pains, but said no more about her palpitations, nor of her heart, which apparently could not only enlarge or contract at will, but even move from one side of her body to the other. She had reacted emotionally to the defeat of Tannenberg, and while her husband reminded his family that he was born on the birthday of the long-suffering Job, and repeated with the prophet, "All the evils I foresee descend upon my head", the Czarina valiantly told her children:

"We did everything we could to avert this war, and so we may be certain God will give us victory!"

There came a night in September, with the first breath of autumn chilling the long hot summer of 1914, when the Grand Duchess Olga, returning alone from the hospital to the Alexander Palace, was ushered in by the side door and climbed the long flight of stairs leading to a gallery where sentries stood between the marble statues on the upper floor of the private apartments. There a footman, sweeping off the hat with coloured feathers worn by tradition since the Empress Elizabeth's reign, informed her that the Grand Duchess Marie wished to see her 'on an important matter' as soon as she returned.

"Ask Her Imperial Highness to come to me."

Olga went into her sitting-room, hiding a smile. Fat Little Bow-Wow's important matters—she probably had an essay to write for Professor Petrov and had stuck in the middle of it! She took off the cape she wore above a plain white overall, and flung herself down in one of the chintz-covered armchairs. She noticed that the cretonne screens round the tall porcelain stove had been removed and that there was a faint warmth in the room.

"Can I really come in, Olga?" Marie, at the door, was certainly wearing an important face.

"Of course you can! Is anything the matter?"

"Where's Tatiana?"

"She hasn't finished yet, the car went back to fetch her. I came right home to have a bath, as soon as I was through.'

"You're tired." Marie came to sit on the arm of her sister's chair. "Was it awful today?"

"Pretty awful. Be a pet, Mashka, and take my hairpins out."

"I will in a minute. But I've got a message to deliver, to you and Tatiana."

"Who from?"

"Father Grigori."

Olga sat upright. "Has *he* been here?"

"About an hour ago. About half past nine. He was very sorry to miss seeing you."

"Who *did* he see?"

"Why, papa and mamma, and Baby of course, and us. And Olga, he kissed Anastasia and me!"

"Kissed your lips?"

"No, he kissed us on the forehead, like he does Baby, and gave us his blessing."

"He should have been down on one knee, kissing your hands."

"He doesn't even do that to mother."

Olga sighed. "You'd better tell me all about it," she said. "How was he looking?"

"Just the same as ever, with his high boots and peasant blouse—you know. Mamma seemed so happy to see him again, and kept telling us it was a miracle. She sent for us, after he'd been with

Alexis—I mean we went down to the drawing-room, and they were all three there, papa, mamma and Father Grigori."

"And did papa seem happy too?"

"Oh yes, very. Why?"

"Because I know he wasn't pleased with a message Rasput—Father Grigori sent him, just before war was declared."

"Papa told us Alexis was asleep when they went into his room. So Father Grigori said not to wake him. He made the sign of the cross over his head, and whispered, "Now the Little One will soon be well." Then mamma kissed Father Grigori's hand, and cried."

"But Alexis *is* quite well again."

"I know. He was playing outdoors with Joy all afternoon."

The dark blue eyes met Olga's in a searching look. It struck the elder sister that Fat Little Bow-Wow was not quite the harum-scarum schoolgirl she had been. She's beginning to watch and wonder too, she thought, and saw that the round childish face was thinner, the Slavic cheekbones more clearly defined, since Marie had started out to be a heroine by curbing her appetite for chocolate and cakes.

"Father Grigori has a talent for turning up every time that Alexis is really on the mend," she said. "But what was his message to us?"

"He said he was very pleased you'd started to train as nurses."

"That was kind of him."

"But he wants you to visit the hospitals in other cities, not just in Saint—Petrograd; with mamma, of course, and he wants you always to wear your uniform as Sisters, with the red pectoral cross."

"What nonsense," said Olga. "Dressing up to visit other people's hospitals, indeed! Anyway we're only allowed white overalls until we've passed our certificate exams."

She stood up, shaking down the rumpled overall, as if she meant to argue this point with Rasputin then and there. "Is he still in the palace?" she asked.

"He went away with papa and mamma to pay a late call on Ania."

"Oh—" Olga nearly said, "Oh no! So that's going to start all over again!" It had been one of the blessings of the Czarina's preoccupation with war work that she had practically suspended those evening visits to Madame Virubova's discreet little house at the corner of Srednaia Avenue, just outside the palace grounds, which were the subject of gossip, as Olga well knew, to the imperial entourage. If she meant to drag the Czar to the Srednaia again, with Rasputin leading the way—! "Sorry, Mashka," she said, "I didn't quite hear what you were saying."

"You were whispering too." But Marie did not raise her voice: whispering seemed to have come into fashion in the Alexander Palace since Rasputin's return. "I only asked you why mother makes such a fuss of Ania, when she's usually so strict about divorce."

"Oh, but the Virubov marriage was dissolved, they weren't divorced. And anyway, the poor man's gone. He had a terrible experience at the battle of Tshusima Bay, and went off his head soon after they were married. I was about twelve then; I remember him being sent away to a sanatorium in Switzerland."

"Yes, but why should mamma call Ania 'our eldest daughter'? She has a very nice father and mother of her own."

"But *our* mother feels responsible for the whole thing. Ania had fallen in love with General Orlov, and mother thought he was too old for her. So she urged her to marry Lieutenant Virubov, and ever since, she's felt guilty about the consequences."

"Ania's always falling in love with somebody," said the Grand Duchess Marie. She looked at the double doors of the sitting-room, and lowered her voice further still. "Olga, don't be angry—but honestly I sometimes used to think she'd fallen in love with father."

* * *

The Czar went off to Baranovichi, and in his absence Rasputin did not appear at the Alexander Palace. Nor did the Czarina pay any evening visits to 'Our Lady of the Avenue', as some of the courtiers called Ania Virubova. She sat at home with her girls, sewing, and writing her name on the holy pictures they all signed in turn, which were intended for the troops. But Ania was with her for part of every day, and most often when the Czarina visited the restored crypt chapel beneath the palace hospital, where rapt with religious exaltation she would lie on the cold stones to pray.

Insidiously, through Ania's messages, Rasputin's influence was re-established. As he suggested, Olga and Tatiana went with their mother to visit hospitals behind the lines as soon as they passed their nursing examinations at the end of October, earning the right to wear white veils, and the nursing sisters' white aprons with scarlet pectoral crosses. They went to Vilna, where the Czarina's sciatica was so acute that she had to be carried up the hospital stairs, an unregal progress which mystified the soldier patients. They went to Pskov, where the Grand Duke Dmitri's sister Marie, known in the Family as Marisha, was on the staff of a huge hospital of twenty thousand beds. These were all filled. The sight of the wounded lying on pallets along the corridors, and the misery of the refugees wandering homeless, drove Olga frantic for fresh opportunities for service.

"Tania and I want to help the old people, mother. And the babies! Nobody's doing anything about them."

But this had not been foreseen by Rasputin, and Alexandra Feodorovna snubbed her impetuous daughter.

"You always want to run before you can walk, Olga. Try to become a really good nurse; that's quite enough for a girl barely nineteen."

"Marisha isn't only nursing, she's helping to *organise* that enormous hospital. You said yourself she was fighting a good fight against incompetence. And she's only five years older than I am."

"Five very important years in a young woman's life. You're an inexperienced girl compared with Marisha."

"Yes, well, Marisha's been married and divorced and had a baby. Is that the right experience for running a hospital? Do I have to be married and divorced before I can run a charity?"

"I shall talk to your father about the wilful, disagreeable spirit you're showing these days—"

"All right, I want to talk to him myself."

As usual, it was the diplomatic Tatiana who did the talking, at the first family dinner after Nicholas II returned from his latest trip to GHQ. Her gentle "We only want to do more to help you, papa," was far more persuasive than Olga's excitement, and the Czar looked hopefully at his wife.

"What do you say, Alix? Really I think we might let them be seen and heard a little more."

"But what in the world could they do? Olga is far too young to preside over a sewing circle, as Motherdear did in the war with

Japan." The girls burst out laughing, and even the harassed Czar smiled.

"Frankly I don't see Olga presiding over a sewing circle at any age," he said. "But I don't see why they shouldn't be the nominal heads of two of the relief committees."

"Your sisters are the proper persons to take charge of the relief committees," said the Czarina. "If Olga Alexandrovna had remained in her married home instead of going off to nurse at Kiev—"

"My sister Olga is doing very well in her hospital at Kiev, I saw that for myself three weeks ago. And Xenia is too busy to do war work, with that great household of boys—"

There was nothing, and her husband knew there was nothing, which silenced Alexandra Feodorovna more completely than an allusion to the Grand Duchess Xenia's large family of sons. Her first child had been a girl, Irina, born in the same year as Olga Nicolaievna. Then, while daughter after daughter was born to the Czarina, waiting in hope and despair for a son and heir, Xenia had given birth to no fewer than six sons, big, noisy, healthy boys whom the Czarina, in her terrible jealousy, had declared too rough to be fit playmates for her own ailing Alexis. She sat sulking now, while the girls overwhelmed their father with thanks, and finally said crushingly:

"Well, I hope you're satisfied, Olga. I think you must want to curry favour and court popularity, like your Aunt Miechen. Isn't it enough that your new photographs are on sale at every street corner in the Nevski Prospekt?"

"Like the Biograph Girl's!" said Anastasia, and the Czarina's sarcasm was drowned in happy giggles as the family got up from table. It was very soon settled that Olga should be the president—the 'nominal president', her mother insisted, of a relief committee for soldiers' families, while Tatiana took on a committee for refugees. It was a new escape for the girls to go at least once, and more often twice a week to the Winter Palace, where the committees met and donations were received. They drove to town accompanied only by one of their mother's younger ladies-in-waiting, and at the Winter Palace they quickly dispensed with protocol and fuss. The members of Petrograd society who had joined the relief committees because it was the fashion to be charitable without getting one's hands dirty, were soon amazed at the programme of work laid out for them by two very young and very determined girls who, so far from being 'nominal' presidents, sheltering under the wing of some white-haired general, stood up and addressed their committees with clarity and force. "True Romanovs both," was the general opinion. "How very different from their wretched mother!"

Eight hours a day in hospital, four hours a day on the committee work—it was enough to give Olga Nicolaievna dreamless sleep at night, unplagued by thoughts of the Galician front into which Simon Hendrikov and his brother officers of the Garde Equipage had disappeared weeks ago. Perhaps only the girls and Alexis slept soundly during those November nights at Czarskoe Selo, after the new offensive on the western front had fallen into bloody collapse, and the Russian High Command turned to face a new threat to the south and east. In the Ottoman Empire, Enver Pasha and his Young Turks had dragged the Sultan into the war on the side of Germany, and while the winter snows began to fall on the great plain of Petrograd, Russian troops were struggling through blizzards in the mountain passes of Eastern Armenia. By Christmas, the date each belligerent had sworn to celebrate in the enemy's capital, it was clear that Lord Kitchener had been right in predicting a long war. In western Europe the trenches, waterlogged and rat-ridden, stretched from the Channel to the Swiss frontier, and the terrible toll of First Ypres had been added to the casualty lists. The Russians had lost over a million men. And steadily new volunteers joined the ranks, above all from the British Empire, where young men were still loyal to the motherland. They called the war 'the Great War' now, for it had become a global struggle in which two men had already been forgotten: Franz Ferdinand in his tomb at Artstetten, and Gavrilo Princip, rotting in his Austrian prison.

7

IN PETROGRAD, IN EARLY January, the wan daylight did not filter through the falling snow until nine o'clock in the morning, and many shops and places of business did not open their doors until ten. There was plenty of time, said Madame Trenova, for Mara to accompany her to a brief memorial service in the Vladimirski church, a *panikhidia* for three young men of their neighbourhood who had fallen on the Turkish front.

"I wouldn't call any of your services exactly brief, mother. And I don't want to be late at the office," said Mara. She was standing in front of a little cracked wall mirror in the kitchen which was also their living-room and her own bedroom, pulling a woollen cap down over her ears and adjusting its strings inside the narrow fur collar of her black cloth coat.

"You needn't stay for the mass, dear. But it would please the boys' mothers so much to see some young people present. So dreadful not to have a proper funeral!" whimpered Madame Trenova. She was a tiny, mouse-like woman, darting round the small apartment with something of a mouse's agility, piling the teacups into a basin to wait for water from the tap on the landing, and slipping into her own slit of a bedroom for a thick scarf to twist round her head. Without a hat she looked like any of the shawled, shabby women who thronged the stone staircase of the apartment building on Yamskaia Street which had been her refuge since Ivan Trenov was marched off with the convict gangs to die at Sakhalin.

"Come along then, at least it isn't far," said Mara, for the Church of Our Lady of Vladimir occupied most of the huge square near their home. Crossing the street, she took her mother's arm, for the square as usual was crowded and the going difficult on the lumpy, frozen snow. There were crowds outside the small shops and round the fish and vegetable barrows by the church; crowds not yet formed into orderly patient queues, although food shortages were now beginning to be felt. There were hawkers' carts, and vendors of old clothes with ten capes on their backs, four fur hats on their heads; and in the grey-faced, dark-clothed crowd there were also women pickpockets and men who, in spite of the wartime ban on vodka, had somehow contrived to become uproariously drunk. The scene through which Mara piloted her mother might have been sketched by Dostoievski, it was the St. Petersburg of Raskolnikov and Prince Myishkin, and Dostoievski himself had died in the Yamskaia, in a flat very little more luxurious than Madame Trenova's mousehole. The two women loosened their coat collars thankfully in the warm air of the church.

"Are you coming home to lunch today, Mara?" her mother whispered, before they went inside the nave.

"I shouldn't think so. This is press day, don't you remember? We'll probably all go out and have a bite at 'The Red Sarafan'."

"Well, be sure to have a proper meal, you're getting much too thin. Don't let them work you too hard . . . "

Any bite at 'The Red Sarafan' would be more filling than a midday meal at the flat, which usually consisted of a bowl of soup or kasha and a small piece of smoked fish, a scanty diet for a girl who for years had been fed on the good plain fare of the Xenia School. Mara said nothing, but let the familiar whimper about overwork die away as she piloted her mother to the ikon of St. Dmitri. One of the dead soldiers had been called Dmitri, and there the mourners had gathered, most of them in tears. Madame Trenova's easy tears began to flow too, and Mara lit a candle and put it in her mother's hand.

There were sorrowing groups in other corners of the church, and a constantly shifting line of shawled women standing with clasped hands and moving lips before the great golden ikonostasis, representing the temple veil, which stood between the altar and the nave. All three gates were shut: the two through which the deacons might pass during the rites of worship, the third which opened only to the priest or to a Czar on the day of his coronation. Above the flickering candles Mara Trenova studied the glory of gold and imagery which was almost the only colour in the lives of the drab women standing or kneeling below it. She had seen the doors of the ikonostasis open many times, and had once truly believed that when the priest's gate was opened after the consecration, the sight of the altar beyond was the revelation of heaven to the faithful. She believed in nothing now, except that religion was the opium of the people, and the words of the priest, singing the *kontakion,* meant less than nothing to Ivan Trenov's daughter.

Give rest, O Christ, to Thy servant with the saints:
Where sorrow and pain are no more;
Neither sighing, but life everlasting.

It was the right time to go; the mourners were all absorbed in the chant and would never miss her. Mara touched her mother's arm, made a little movement of her head towards the door, and went away down the stone flags on tiptoe. The priest was still singing, inaudible by the time she reached the door, but whether she believed in them or not she knew the words by heart:

All we go down to the dust,
And weeping o'er the grave we make our song:
Alleluia! alleluia! alleluia!

As she hurried back across the square, a clock above the market stalls reminded Mara that the girls of the Xenia School must then be filing into their chapel, a copy of the Church of the Nativity at Bethlehem, to sing their morning hymns. She could picture Dolly Hendrikova, condemned to another year of school, trailing the absurd skirts of the school costume along the steps of the great grey marble staircase and shivering, as they all did in January, in the low-cut boned bodice and the white lawn sleeves and apron. She was delighted to be done with all that mummery, and she didn't care if she never saw the Hendrikovs again, or Plain Joe Calvert either, with his champagne and his Hotel Europa dinners. Now she was a worker, and though her hands were stained with nothing worse than carbon paper Mara felt, every time she went down on an errand to the printers in their cellar below her office, that she was one of a community of real workers, proletarians, just as every time she joined in the arguments over the tea glasses and *pirozhki* in 'The Red Sarafan' she felt herself accepted by creative artists. Alleluia! Alleluia! Mara Trenova was free at last.

The publishing house where Professor Rostov had found her a job was within walking distance of her home, occupying nearly the whole of one of the short, dingy alleys near the Nicholas station, off the Znamenia Square, one of the beating pulses of Petrograd. Known as The Children's Castle, it published school textbooks and juveniles, but was best known for its pocket editions of the Russian classics which, on thin grey paper and in type small enough to strain any child's eyesight, were sold tied up in orange ribbon with slabs of chocolate by the leading confectioners of the capital.

Almost as bland as the 'candy classics', as they were known to the trade, was the children's magazine put out monthly by the house, and a weekly review for adults which went out to a fairly large mailing list, and which was known as *Castle Comments.* When Mara was getting her bearings in her new job, she was surprised to find that so much business was done through the mails, for large consignments of the pocket classics, orange ribbons, chocolate slabs and all, were sent off regularly to addresses in the country, and the readers of *Castle Comments* were assiduous in writing to the editor, Jacob Levin. The review was the reverse of *avant-garde.* The criticisms of music and the ballet were fresh and interesting, but no historian more recent than Karamsin, no poet more revolutionary than Zhucovski, was ever made the subject of a leading article. It appeared that admirers of Karamsin and Zhucovski were numerous in the provinces, and the letters to the editor were full of page references and paragraph numbers which Mara was expected to check and compile for Jacob Levin. She had been his secretary for nearly three months.

He was not in the office when she arrived breathless from the Vladimir church, but this was normal on press day, when he and his elderly assistant came in at the same time as the printers. Their coats and fur hats were hanging on the wall of the big, dingy office on the second floor, and the clatter and stamp of the antiquated Wharfedale presses could be heard and felt all through the building. She stole a quick glance at the newspaper on Levin's desk. The headlines scarcely ever varied. Retreat—Strategic Withdrawal—Commission Demanded by the Duma—Lack of Air Support in the North—she could have written them blindfold. Mara tackled a basketful of morning mail.

It was not until Sergiev brought her a glass of tea from the samovar which bubbled continually at the end of the corridor that Mara Trenova realised she was famished, and that the morning hours had sped away.

"Thank you, Sergiev," she said gratefully. "Mr. Levin's staying down there a long time, isn't he?"

"He had a row with the foreman printer," said Sergiev. "One of the presses broke down in the middle of the run."

"It happens every week, doesn't it?"

Sergiev laughed hoarsely. He was an uncanny creature, barely four feet tall. Sergiev was a hunchback, with a lined and twisted face: he might have been any age from fifteen to forty, and was employed at The Children's Castle as a copyboy and general drudge.

"Every week, and Mr. Levin fixes it," he said. "Have you heard what the carters are saying in the alley?"

"No, what?"

"They say the German woman has been shot."

"What German woman? Sergiev! Not the Czarina?"

The hunchback nodded. "It happened out at Czarskoe Selo. Six thousand men she had to guard her, I've heard tell. Police and soldiers, Cossacks, Garde Equipage and all. But they got to her, oh yes, they got to her . . . just as they'll get to *him* some day."

"Is she—dead?"

"Dead or dying, does it matter?" Sergiev looked gloatingly at the pale face close to his own. "This is good news, not?"

"I suppose so. But who did it, Sergiev? Have they caught the assassin? Was it at the hospital, or in the grounds, or where?"

"Does it matter?" he said again. "Think of it, Mara Ivanovna! Rasputin's crowned mistress—gone!"

"I wish *you'd* go, and find out the details. It's probably only a silly rumour," she called after him, as Sergiev tossed his huge head and left the room. Why she added that, she didn't know; she was shocked, and there was no reason to be shocked, for death always stalked the Romanovs, and Alexandra Feodorovna deserved it more than most. Still, Mara's head was throbbing as she rolled fresh paper and carbons into her high typewriter, and when she had written the date under the letterhead she took her hands from the keyboard and pressed them to her brow, and thought of a beautiful and tragic woman, lying dead.

She heard Levin's heavy step in the corridor, and the creak of the opening door, but although she raised her head Mara neither rose nor turned round. In a moment she felt the touch that made her shiver, the caress of a maimed hand on the nape of her neck, and she said, "You startled me."

"Don't be silly, you were expecting me, weren't you?"

"Yes."

She felt Levin's indrawn breath above her hair. "You reek of incense, girl, where have you been?" he said easily, as he moved round the desk to his own big chair.

"Mother dragged me to a service at the Vladimir this morning."

"Aha! That accounts for it. Now let's get to work."

Mara passed a file of letters and notes on copy paper across the desk, and he read them quickly. Jacob Levin was a short, powerfully built man, with greying hair cut as short as possible, and a square, self-contained face. The top joints of the middle finger of his right hand were missing, the result of an accident when he was a journeyman printer in Odessa. Mara had at first found the stump repellent; she came to have a perverse pleasure in watching how dexterously he held his pen.

"Right; now take dictation, please." He began to talk, not too quickly, expanding the annotations he had made upon the file; and as he dictated he watched Mara Trenova, with her dark head and sharp profile bent over the shorthand notebook. He thought she was shaping up very well indeed.

Rostov had ended a short written report on her background with the words, "Clever, conceited, resentful and deprived—could become a useful recruit, with the proper training." Levin was an experienced trainer. Offhand and impersonal, he had let the girl settle to the office routine for a few weeks. Then he took her along to 'The Red Sarafan' and waited while Mara Trenova adapted to the group of failed authors, unpublished poets and hack reviewers who made the restaurant their rendezvous. One night, when after two glasses of yellow wine she had become voluble and excited about the latest rumours of corruption in high places, he had escorted her home with her cold hand comfortably tucked inside the pocket of his greatcoat, and asked her pointblank:

"Are you going to fritter away your time jabbering about politics, like that crowd in the 'Sarafan', or do you mean to do something about it?"

Mara told him proudly that she intended to apply for membership of the Social Revolutionary party. He barked with laughter.

"The SRs! Why the SRs?"

"It was my father's party, when he was alive. And I think the SRs mean to do most for the people."

"For the peasants, or so they say. They don't reach the proletariat of the factories."

"Well, at least their leaders are in Petrograd, and not in Zürich or Geneva, like the Bolsheviki."

He had stopped at a street corner then, and taken her by the shoulders. "I bet you heard that argument at one of Professor Hendrikov's social evenings," he said. "I can just see you, lapping up his milk-and-water liberalism."

"But Professor Hendrikov isn't an SR. He was elected to the First Duma as a Constitutional Democrat—a Kadet."

"He has plenty of SR friends, though: he practically thinks he invented Alexander Kerensky. Was *he* your inspiration, Mara? Kerensky? He's young, and not bad-looking in his way; a lot of girls have fallen for him."

She was quite oblivious to the cold and the snow, he saw with professional approval. Exalted by her own fervour, she told him that her inspiration for years had been the great women of the SRs, who had conspired, killed, borne torture and exile, even gone to execution, so that some day Russia should be a better place to live in. The names came tumbling out, Vera Figner, Vera Zazulich, Perovskaia who had died for her share in the assassination of Alexander II, Dora Brilliant who had helped Kaliaev, the killer of the Grand Duke Sergei, Maria Spiridonova, for the past eight years an exile in Siberia . . . Levin had kissed her then for the first time, roughly, their cold faces colliding rather than caressing, to put an end to the scene.

He remembered it, as he watched her across the desk, and when he finished dictating and took out his cigarettes he said casually:

"There's a rumour floating around the building, about an incident at Czarskoe Selo—"

"An *incident*! Sergiev told me the Czarina had been murdered."

"The Czarina, did he? We'll have to get Sergiev to churn out some fiction for our readers, one of these days. The way I heard the story, it was the Czarina's dear friend, Madame Virubova, who was the victim of—circumstances."

"I told Sergiev to go out and get the facts. He must have gone to buy an evening paper."

"He won't get any facts from the newspaper, if the censorship has been clamped down. Cigarette?"

"No thank you."

"Mara. Was that why you were looking like a sick cat when I came in—because you thought the German woman was dead?"

"Why should I care about her death?"

"What was the matter with you, then?"

"I was just trying to picture—trying to imagine what it would be like to be the—the person who put a weapon in her pocket and went out deliberately to take a life—"

" 'In *her* pocket.' Still thinking of the great SR heroines?"

"Perhaps I was."

"Have *you* ever handled firearms?"

"Never in my life."

Levin drew a Nagan revolver from his jacket pocket and laid it on the desk between them. Mara looked at it fearfully.

"Is it loaded?"

"Yes, of course it's loaded, not much use if it weren't. Pick it up. Like this, see? You've got five fingers, not like me."

The mutilated finger seemed to be no handicap as Levin's hand closed on the revolver. He pushed it closer to the girl. Mara Trenova took it up cautiously and without touching the trigger. It was warm with the heat of Levin's body.

"It's very heavy."

"Too heavy for you, maybe. All right, now you've got something like the feel of it, and if it stops snowing I'll take you out to the marshes on Sunday and teach you to fire it. Where the hell has Sergiev got to?" Levin put the weapon back in his pocket and opened the office door. "Hey! You out there! Anybody seen Sergiev? Eh? Oh, he's coming."

The hunchback came stumbling in, carrying a newspaper. "I went over to the station, and then I had to wait for the delivery truck," he grumbled. "And it's not the Czarina they got, it's the Virubova woman."

"As I could have told you, you damned fool, if you'd come to me with your silly story. Clear out now, and get your dinner, I'm too busy to be bothered with you."

Mara was rubbing her right hand, still tingling from its contact with the gun. "So it's actually in the paper?" she asked.

"Yes, here it is, page four, they've been told not to give it much of a play. Mara! They claim it was a rail accident, not far from the station at Czarskoe Selo."

"A *rail* accident! Not an attempted murder?"

"Listen to this. Yesterday afternoon, a number of passengers were injured, etc., including Anna Alexandrovna Virubova, daughter of, etc, a former maid of honour to Her Imperial Majesty (now a matron of dishonour, they might have said), trapped under wreckage, etc, received nearly fatal injuries but has survived the night. Well! That should put a stop to Her Imperial Majesty's cosy evenings with Rasputin, for some time to come!"

"What about the other people who were hurt?"

"Just a list of names, mis-spelled; what more did you expect for the common herd?"

"But what caused the accident?"

"Doesn't say. An accident, eh? on the best policed line in all Russia. Couldn't have been a bomb on the line, or a length of track torn up, or a grenade thrown from the embankment. Perhaps it *was* an accident—maybe the driver was drunk."

Mara shook her dark head. "It's never an accident," she said positively, "when it's anything to do with one of *them*."

* * *

But it can't have been an accident. The Grand Duchesses Olga and Tatiana, looking at each other aghast in one of the hospital offices in the Catherine Palace, shared the thought of Mara Trenova, although they were careful not to put it into words. If one of them had spoken out, it might have been to say, "Do you suppose it was something meant for *us?*"

They knew much of the long record of terrorist activities against the Romanovs when the imperial family travelled by train. Bombs on the permanent way, bridges blown and dynamite charges left in tunnels had been part of their forebears' occupational hazards, culminating in the tragedy near Borki in 1888. They knew every detail of that attempt, which caused nearly three hundred casualties, because their father had been in the train, a young man of twenty, and he had often told them how his own father, the Czar Alexander III, a man of colossal strength, had saved his wife and children from maiming and suffocation. They were in the dining car when the terrorists blew up the train.

The Czar had taken the whole weight of the iron roof on his powerful back and shoulders, allowing his family and their attendants to crawl to safety, but sustaining the damage to his kidneys which brought about his early death.

There had been no man of similar strength in the train wreck outside Czarskoe Selo, and now Anna Virubova lay unconscious, her left leg broken, her right thigh crushed, and with multiple injuries to her head and shoulders.

"The Czarina wishes absolutely to send for Father Grigori," said Tatiana, in the soft voice which could be as implacable as her mother's when she chose.

The army doctor who had brought them to the little office where one of the few telephones in the palace hospital had been installed, sighed and shook his head.

"Her Majesty was in a state of acute hysteria," he said. "She became much calmer as soon as His Majesty the Czar arrived. The interference of another person—*any* other person—might easily revive her distress."

"The Czar also wishes Father Grigori to be sent for. Not on my mother's behalf, but on the patient's."

"The patient should be left in peace for her last hours. You heard the opinion of three doctors, nurse: Madame Virubova is dying."

"My brother has been at death's door more than once, and Father Grigori's prayers have saved him."

"Then the telephone is at the disposal of Your Imperial Highness."

"Thank you." Tatiana ignored the sarcastic tone. She called the switchboard operator and gave the number of Rasputin's flat in Petrograd. The doctor listened. She knew the number by heart, of course, no hesitation there! He remembered the rumours circulating about those two pretty girls and Rasputin. The fellow had slept with them both, and their mother too: soon it would be the turn of the younger ones. Disgusting if true, revolting if lies! Tatiana was saying:

"When? About an hour ago? No thank you, I'll see to it myself." She turned to Olga. "His housekeeper says he's at a dinner party at the Hotel Europa. One of the cars must go in and bring him here at once."

"Doctor—" said Olga appealingly, and the doctor, with an

unwilling bow, said he would attend to the matter. "But may I remind you, nurses, that this is a military hospital, where discipline can not be disrupted for the sake of one civilian patient? Or two, however exalted the second one may be? You both left your duties to comfort Her Imperial Majesty. Now you will please return to your wards immediately."

"How rude he was to us!" said Tatiana, in the corridor, and Olga wondered if they could blame the man, when her sister lingered until she saw an orderly on his way to the stable garages, where the imperial cars were parked. She fully expected a few angry looks when she returned to her own ward, for the patients' supper had been served while the girls tried to calm their frantic mother, and one young nurse muttered "Don't *hurry,* will you?" when Olga arrived only in time to help with the removal of the dishes. But then quiet fell on the ward as the patients, all surgical cases, were settled for the night, and the lights were dimmed, and the nurses left on duty sat down by their tables to sew before each in turn went to her own supper.

Olga, because of her long absence in the late afternoon, was the last to go, and there was no one in the little refectory but two servants who brought her food and tea. No sign of Tatiana, no one to tell her if Ania Virubova was alive or dead; the Catherine Palace was as silent as it had been for many years before the war. She looked at the watch pinned to the bib of her apron. If Rasputin really was at the Hotel Europa, and not carousing in the city, there was almost time to have brought him to his devotees by now. Olga crossed the great landing and gently opened the small shutter which allowed her to look out of the heavily covered window. It was a clear, sparkling night with no snow falling, and she could see all down the gardens, where the trees were heavy with snow, and all the follies, statues and bathhouses of the Romanovs were encased in wood against the bitter frost. One of the imperial cars came up the driveway, where even the wheels of the ambulances had not broken the snow crust, and stopped, just below Olga's window, at the steps leading up to the main entrance to the palace. She watched, sick with foreboding, while Rasputin got out.

Dressed for his dinner party, he was not wearing the rough peasant clothes which appealed so much to his imperial patrons. His tall figure was clad in a long tunic of purple silk, with a jewelled belt, breeches of fine cloth, and high boots of the finest polished leather. In the starlight his long black hair shone with brilliantine. He stood on the bottom step, looking up at the splendid palace as if he owned it, and spread his arms out, Olga thought in rehearsal of a blessing, like the wings of some gigantic coloured bird. Or it might have been in an attempt to keep his balance, for as a footman left the seat behind the driver and came running round the limousine to put a fur *shuba* round Rasputin's shoulders, the monk staggered and caught at the fellow's arm to steady himself. To the watchful blue eyes at the window, it was clear that the holy man was drunk.

It was not until much later, when he called them into his own study, that Nicholas II described to his elder daughters the miracle that 'the man of God' had wrought in what was all but a chamber of death. The Czarina was already in a drugged sleep, and the girls more exhausted by her emotion than by their long day's work, but the usually impassive Czar was strangely excited as he told how Rasputin entered Anna Virubova's room, ignoring everyone but the woman in a coma on the hospital bed.

"Poor mamma knelt to him and tried to kiss his ring," said Nicholas II. "But he withheld his blessing. He didn't call her 'Matushka Czarina' Mother Empress, as he usually does, nor bow to me and call me 'Little Father', he simply fixed his glowing eyes on Ania, and held out those wonderful long hands towards her. Then he said her name, 'Annushka!' three times over, and her eyes opened and she recognised him. She whispered 'Father Grigori!' and he said 'Rise!'"

"He didn't say 'Arise, take up thy bed and walk,' by any chance?" said Olga, and Tatiana quickly covered the levity.

"But poor Ania couldn't rise, could she, papa?" she said.

"Those idiots of doctors told us she would never move again. But at the sound of *his* voice she lifted her head and shoulders from the pillow, she even smiled. One of the doctors came forward to take her pulse, and poor mamma got up and tried to speak. Then Father Grigori said, 'You will keep her. Russia needs her still!' and fell back against the wall with the sweat pouring down his face. I thought he would be the next to faint—"

"I hope they gave him something to drink," said Olga.

"—They brought him wine in the ante-room, and mamma and I said a prayer of thanksgiving with him. Oh, how grateful we should be, my darlings, for the divine intervention that saved his life last summer! I may have been born on the birthday of the long-suffering Job, but tonight I have been privileged to be the witness of a miracle."

The daughters kissed their father's hand and went to bed almost in silence. Tatiana went to sleep at once, but Olga lay awake for an hour, trying to think what this new victory for Rasputin might mean for all of them, and wondering if there would be an investigation of the railway accident and what it would reveal. She might have been comforted if she could have heard the doctor who had spoken so bluntly about hospital discipline telling a colleague about Rasputin's 'miracle', ending with the words:

"It was the clearest—the very damnedest—case of hypnotism I ever saw."

Hypnotised or not, Anna Virubova recovered. The news was broken to her than even when discharged from hospital she must spend weeks in a wheel-chair, or on a couch; when she began to walk it would be on crutches, and she might never walk without a support again. Ania accepted the verdict with pious resignation. She had regained the full attention, even the doting care, of Alexandra Feodorovna, and in spite of the pain of her terrible injuries her fat face lit up with pleasure when the Czarina sat down beside her with a bowl and spoon, and fed her as tenderly as she had fed her own babies.

Every bed in the palace hospital was needed for the wounded, and as soon as possible Ania was taken by ambulance to her own little house, where a nurse called Sister Akulina was detached from the hospital to care for her. Soon 'Our Lady of the Avenue' had a new entourage, all followers of Rasputin. Sister Akulina, a Siberian, had been cured of convulsions by Rasputin when he visited her convent near Ekaterinburg, and Peter Badmaiev, sometimes called a Siberian and sometimes 'a Mongolian herbalist', or even a Tibetan, came at Rasputin's instance to dose Ania with some of his brews made from wild plants and herbs. Anastasia, the first of the Grand Duchesses to meet Badmaiev, reported to Olga that he was 'a funny little man, with a tall peaked hat', who had made her taste a drop of some dark green stuff called Essence of Black Lotus, which made her feel quite funny.

"I don't think mamma and papa would like you to drink some

queer stuff out of bottles, unless Dr. Botkin knew and approved."

"Oh, but papa had some too! He drank a wine glassful of Tibetan Elixir and enjoyed it. Peter Alexandrovich says it'll make him sleep better when he's at the front."

Olga said no more. She thought there must be a queer new group at the little house on the avenue, where the Czar and Czarina visited every night—they who visited nobody—and where she never went herself if she could help it. Olga was too kind-hearted not to be sorry for Ania, a grotesque figure with her heavy and now twisted limbs sprawled on the sofa, but she always felt stifled if she spent longer than twenty minutes in the little sitting-room which was at once cold and heavy with the stale smoke of innumerable cigarettes, and where three of the four walls were covered with enlargements of Ania's own snapshots of the Czar. As for Alexis, he was not allowed to visit Ania at all, much as she begged to see him. He had been ill so often himself that he was very sensitive to the suffering of others, and would certainly have cried himself sick if he had seen her in the first weeks after the accident.

The boy was now quite well and strong, and growing fast. He had begun to learn English and the balalaika, and enjoyed playing in the snow, especially with a captured German machine-gun which the Commander-in-Chief had sent him in the early days of the war. The great improvement in Alexis was the chief gain of late January and February, while the military situation deteriorated on all fronts, and the Duma, outraged by the incompetence which was sending Russian troops unarmed to their deaths, was clamouring for the creation of a War Council on a broad basis, to include Deputies, bankers, industrialists and representatives of the war ministry.

The Duma and the Czar had long been irreconcilable, all the more so because in the Czar's own home his wife kept insisting that the manifesto which created the Duma had been 'wrested from him' in the aftermath of Bloody Sunday, and that in the eyes of God he was still the autocrat of his anointed coronation. She told him a good deal more than that in the weeks following Rasputin's 'miracle', and now her criticisms were not kept to their private hours, but voiced in front of the embarrassed girls.

She began, characteristically, by criticising various members of the Family. It was a sore point with the Czarina that Nicholas II had recalled his brother Michael to Russia at the beginning of the war. The Grand Duke Michael, know to his relatives as Floppy, was an exile for the usual Romanov reason of a morganatic marriage, in his case with the extra distinction that his wife, Countess Brassova, had been twice divorced before the birth of their illegitimate child. But the Czar was determined to forgive 'Misha' and have him back, and now Misha, or Floppy, was commanding a division in the Caucasus, a long way from the salons of Petrograd or the Puritan lady of Czarskoe Selo. There were other targets, nearer home, for her growing malice. The Grand Dukes came under steady fire: Dmitri, once a great favourite, "now so *fast*, and coming on leave so often, he ought not to have the honour of being your aide-de-camp, Nicky," Sergei, "mixed up in that dreadful artillery scandal," Kirill, "using his position at the Stavka to connive with Nikolasha." And Nikolasha himself, the C-in-C, "incapable of winning a victory," and "trying to undermine your popularity with the troops". The young Grand Duchesses saw a case of pathological jealousy developing at their family table, day after winter day.

The Czar bore it all calmly enough until the day came when the hysterical woman attached Mala Kchessinskaia, and then the worm turned. In the Duma and the popular press there was a mounting outcry against the War Minister, who was held responsible for the terrible shortages of munitions, artillery, and even food and clothing for the troops. But the War Minister was a strong adherent of Rasputin, and so in the Czarina's eyes could do no wrong. She asked point blank that the Minister of Justice should take proceedings against certain persons who had accepted bribes for placing orders for artillery with different firms in Russia and abroad. And among them she named Madame Mathilde Kchessinskaia.

The Czar laid down his table napkin (they were about to finish luncheon) and said, "I really don't believe that's true, Alix. Kchessinskaia has no need to take bribes from anybody, she must be one of the highest-paid dancers in the world."

"So brave to go *on* dancing, at her age," said the Czarina. "But perhaps she doesn't get all the money she needs from her protector, your cousin Andrei."

"She was dancing like an angel, only last July at Krasnoe Selo," said Olga, and her father gave her a grateful glance.

"I don't think these details can really interest the younger ones," he said, though 'Marie's saucers' were round with the determination not to miss a word. "Have you any documentary evidence of this bribe-taking—names, dates, places, that sort of thing?"

"One doesn't need documentary evidence when a matter like this becomes common knowledge!"

"I think you'll find the Minister of Justice will," said the Czar, "before you can persuade him to take legal action against your 'certain persons'. As for Mala Kchessinskaia, she isn't even a business woman, let alone a cheat. I remember the night I met her first—long before you and I were married, Alix—and my father said to her, a lovely girl of eighteen, 'Be the glory of our Russian ballet!' And that's exactly what she has been, and *all* she has been, from that day to this."

He left the table with a bow to his wife and went to his study; the girls scattered hastily to their different occupations. But before the Czar left for the front that night he kissed his eldest daughter with especial tenderness, so that she knew her few awkward words of championship had touched his heart. She must have been uppermost in his mind on his journey into Poland, for his first letter from the front, addressed to the Czarina, was so completely lacking in the usual endearments and implicit sexual allusions that she showed it at once to Olga and Tatiana.

My beloved Sunny [the Czar wrote from Warsaw]

I wish you would direct the Zemstvo Red Cross to look at once into the situation of our wounded in this area. I was horrified to find upon arrival at Warsaw that nearly twenty thousand wounded from the recent battles have been lying untended in and around the Vienna railway station for several days. I personally ordered up all the available ambulance trains, and into Olga's train, which happened to be the first to arrive, I put several wounded officers known to me, among them Olga's old flame from the *Standart,* Lieutenant Simon Hendrikov. He has a severe chest wound, and the doctors don't hold out much hope for him, but the train will go straight through to Czarskoe Selo, and you may be able to patch him up. The courier is leaving now. I will write tomorrow.

Your loving old hubby,
Nicky.

8

OLGA WAS THANKFUL THAT this letter arrived so late in the evening that she soon had a chance to be alone. When the Czar was at GHQ the two elder girls had to sleep with their mother in turn, in the big double bed in her bedroom on the ground floor. It was too cold for their Russian blood in the winter, for the Czarina shared the liking of her grandmother Queen Victoria for cold and draughty rooms, and they were often awakened during the night as the restless woman turned on her pillows, or tiptoed in and out of the private chapel by a door on the right side of the bed. On this particular night it was Tatiana's turn to sleep downstairs, so Olga had the comfort of solitude in a warm room, with the door of the porcelain stove open to show the burning birch logs, and the snoring of the bulldog, Ortipo, the only sound in the February night.

She sat, propped up on a hard pillow, in the narrow bed prescribed for her by tradition, with the bright hair Simon had loved spilling over her white nightgown, and thought about the hospital train which her money had bought and which bore her name, crawling across the frozen countryside from Poland into Russia. She thought of the young officer who had kissed her hand in farewell six months before, and of whom she had heard nothing, enquired nothing, until now when by the most fortunate of all chances he was coming back to her. *If* he came back to her—if the doctors were wrong, as they had been wrong in Ania's case, about his chances of survival. If he were to come back only to die.

Olga Nicolaievna had seen death in many forms since the summer evening when sixty thousand men, vigorous and well, had shouted, "Happy to serve Your Imperial Majesty!" The first time, death had come horribly to a soldier on the operating table, in the middle of surgery intended to save his life, and Olga, threading the needles in the operating theatre, had watched appalled as the red tide of a violent hæmorrhage flowed across the table and dyed the sterile sheets. Since that day, at the end of November, she had watched others die more slowly and more tranquilly, often feeling a sense of total unreality as death came into the clean, well-tended wards so far from the battlefield. And Simon had been one of those who had lain for days without attention, not even on a pallet in a hospital corridor, but among other wounded men laid out like half-slaughtered animals in a railway yard. "If only I were older," she thought desperately. "If only there was more that I could *make* them do!"

She knew already—she could not fail to know—the real power she exercised over the very limited public she was allowed to meet. At a big war charities concert given in Cinizelli's circus a little surprise had been sprung upon her—probably by Aunt Miechen, who enjoyed showing up the inefficiency of what she called 'the Grand Court'—in the presence, which she had not expected, of all the ambassadors and Ministers in Petrograd. Before the performance, the Grand Duchess Olga had 'made the circle' for the first time in her life. Young, blushing but very dignified, she had remembered all the names and faces, had said something appropriate to each one, and at the end even Aunt Miechen had swept her a little curtsey of approbation. The experience had lent her courage to ask the huge audience to give generously, and the giving had exceeded all expectations.

It was the same, on a smaller scale, at her weekly meetings in the Winter Palace. People gave large purses to the young Grand Duchess, and like Tatiana with her Refugee Committee, she checked the accounts most carefully, and kept lists of the various relief centres to which the money was destined. But how could she be sure that the money ever got there—that it didn't stick to a score of paws along the line, just as surely as the credits voted for armaments had gone in bribes and faked manifests? How could she, at nineteen and unmarried, embark on such a career of active good works as had already earned for her mother and Aunt Ella the ridicule of Russian society? How could she get away from society, and reach the people?

On her bedside table Olga had several volumes borrowed from her father's library, dealing with recent Russian history and Russian thought. She found them heavy going, for as the best of her tutors had noted, the Grand Duchess Olga's intellectual powers—much greater than those of her sisters—had never received the right nourishment and training. But the librarian was delighted to lend them. Every month he sent what he considered the twenty best books published in several languages to the Czar's study; every month the books came back with the pages uncut. The Czar said he had no time for reading now; and in any case his tastes ran to English lady novelists with such melodious names as Mrs. Henry Wood, Mrs. Humphrey Ward, and Florence L. Barclay. So the librarian, bored with inactivity, was delighted to advise the Grand Duchess Olga, and even to let her take away—surreptitiously—a copy of *Anna Karenina*, prohibited by her mother as likely to cause 'unhealthy curiosity'. *Anna* had gone back as furtively as she had come, Olga's healthy sexual curiosity not having been much enlightened thereby; but the romantic poets remained; respectable as Russian classics, they were always on Olga's bedside table.

It was to Lermontov that she turned when the logs burned low, and the sleeping dog stretched himself full length on the rug. There was something in her father's letter that had made her think of a Lermontov poem about a soldier, which she had learned for recitation to Professor Petrov when she was twelve. The soldier had been shot in the chest like Simon Hendrikov. Olga had forgotten the title, but the verses began:

> I want to be alone with you
> A moment quite alone

and she found them easily in the book on her table:

> And yet if someone questions you
> Whoever it may be—
> Tell them a bullet hit me through
> The chest—and did for me.
> And say I died, and for the Czar,
> And say what fools the doctors are,
> And that I shook you by the hand,
> And spoke about my native land.

" 'And say I died, *and for the Czar*,' " she repeated aloud, and oh God! what a long way they had all come from that night in the rose-decked theatre at Krasnoe Selo, when the audience rose cheering at "A Life for the Czar"! How many lives given already? How many more to lose?

*   *   *

Simon Hendrikov's battalion had been moved up to the line of the Vistula during the abortive advance of November, and there it survived until the engagement which reduced it to the strength of a single company. He vividly remembered being brought in to Warsaw, and laid on the floor of what had once been a station waiting-room, so it seemed logical to suppose he had been taken away from there by train. But of the train itself he could remember nothing, except a great deal of pain and jolting, and the occasional comfort of some cool liquid held to his mouth, until he became aware that he was in a clean, high hospital bed with white muslin screens around it, under a lofty ceiling where naked Loves and Graces played in a transparency of milky cloud. His right shoulder and arm were splinted, his wounded breast very tightly bandaged, but his head was almost clear. He said to the man in a white coat, with the stethoscope dangling round his neck, "Where am I?"

"In the Catherine Palace hospital at Czarskoe Selo."

"They brought me here from Warsaw? So near Petrograd? My family—?"

"Your family knows your whereabouts, lieutenant. They'll be allowed to see you in a day or two, if all goes well."

"Why not—today?"

"We've got to get you in better shape first. Don't worry, you'll be taken good care of. I've got you down on my list as a PP, so you get top treatment, Lieutenant Hendrikov."

"What's a PP?"

"Palace Pet. Sent on to us by order of the Czar, travelling in the Grand Duchess Olga's hospital train, enquired for every few hours by the most exalted ladies in the land—we know the form! Now just let me listen for a moment, and then you can go back to sleep."

He moved the stethoscope over Simon's bandaged chest, and nodded. "You've been very lucky. The bullet smashed your shoulder-blade but missed your lung. Expect you'll have some trouble with the arm for a bit, but it'll come all right in time. Now here's Nurse Vera with some liquid nourishment. Good-bye."

A little dark-haired nurse held a feeding cup to his lips with something bland and warm in it, and while he was trying to tell her that she had the same name as his mother Simon drifted off into a haze from which he was only roused by a cool wet cloth on his forehead and the sensation that his bandages were being undone. He opened his eyes to see a tall ward sister, with grizzled hair, lifting away the sterile dressings.

"I'm afraid this will be uncomfortable, lieutenant; I'm sorry," she said, not unkindly. " . . . Now hold the bottle steady, nurse, and pay the tape out evenly."

The treatment prescribed for a chest wound, still in danger of septicaemia, was to plug it with medicated tape taken from a bottle of disinfectant. Simon bit his lips on a groan. His eyes filled with water, and through the blur he saw a face he knew, intent on nothing but the task in hand. The sight connected with the doctor's words 'the Grand Duchess Olga's hospital train', and Simon said tentatively:

"Princess?"

"No talking, please," said the ward sister. "The dressings, nurse."

But when the bandaging was done to her satisfaction she went away at once, and the young nurse, clearing the dressings tray, had a moment to bend over Simon and whisper, "I'm Tatiana Nicolaievna. My sister and I are very glad you're safe!"

"Is she here? The Princess?"

"She'll come to see you in the morning. Now try to rest."

He rested, ate a little solid food, drowsed, asked to be shaved and was refused; slept. And in the morning there she was, and he wasn't dreaming. His Princess, dressed in white, just as he remembered her, was standing beside his bed.

"How are you, Simon Karlovich?" It was the most conventional of greetings, but her lips were trembling, and Simon could only gesture with his left hand. Olga guessed what he wanted, and put her own hand in his, so that he could carry it to his lips and kiss the palm and fingers, rougher than they had been. Then she put one hand on his hot brow, and stroked his unshaven cheek, and Simon whispered, "My darling—*dushenka moya*—" Then he saw her tears, and could say no more.

But that was the only moment of weakness. Next morning when she came Simon was better, all the better for being shaved, and very thankful to be shaved, since Olga was accompanied by the Czarina, herself looking worse than some of the patients, and leaning heavily on a stick.

"My poor boy," said the Czarina, in the motherly tones her children loved when they were ill, "we are all so sorry for you! So very glad you're off the danger list today!"

"Thanks to Your Imperial Majesties," said Simon, with the slight movement of his head which had to do duty for a bow.

"Do you feel much pain in your shoulder this morning?"

"I don't feel much of anything, Madame."

"And your arm?"

"I don't seem to be able to move it yet, but the doctor says that'll come."

"Of course it will. And now a happy surprise! Your own mamma will soon be here to see you. I sent a car into Petrograd to fetch her, half an hour ago."

"I don't know how to thank Your Majesty for so many kindnesses."

"We have to take specially good care of our old friends from the *Standart*."

He was a Palace Pet, no doubt about it. Simon could see in his mother's eyes that she thought so too, when she told him about the telephone call from the Czarina's lady-in-waiting, and the limousine with the footman which had so impressed the porter of their apartment building in the Fourth Line, and of the kind promise that his father and Dolly should be brought to see him next day. Not a word—and for this Simon adored her—did Madame Hendrikova say of the long winter of anxiety, and of the terror they had all felt for him after the last fighting on the Vistula; no, Simon was on the mend, thank God, and they could now look forward to the future.

But after this promising beginning Simon suffered a relapse, and some days of fever and great pain went by before his father was allowed to see him along with Dolly, on a special day's leave from school and revelling in the comforts of the palace hospital as she had once revelled in the luxury of the Europa restaurant. She was wild to leave school and start war nursing.

"It's a nasty messy job, Dolly, you wouldn't stand it very long."

"Other girls can stand it, so why not me?"

"I suppose that means Mara Trenova has started nursing, and so you do too."

"Mara? No, she really did get a job. I saw her at Christmas and she said how busy she was. And once I saw her on the Nevski with a rough-looking man, an older man—she was so busy talking to him that she didn't see me."

"I feel sorry for that poor little mother of hers," said the professor. He kept still while Dolly chattered, with eyes only for his boy. He hardly realised who the young nurse was who came in so quietly, until he saw his daughter rise and sweep the newcomer her graceful Xenia curtsey. Then he got up hastily and bowed, while Simon said:

"Your Imperial Highness, may I present my sister Darya, and my father, Professor Hendrikov?"

"I'm so glad to know them both," said Olga with a smile. "Do forgive me for interrupting you! Our chief surgeon sent me with a message to you, professor. She would like to see you before you leave the hospital."

"Your chief surgeon is a lady, Madame?"

"A very clever and capable lady, sir."

"I hope this doesn't mean she has bad news for us?"

"I'm sure it doesn't," Olga smiled. "The lieutenant is making very good progress now. But Darya Karlovna!" looking at the blushing girl, "you and I have met before. Didn't you present a purse of money to me, from the girls of the Xenia School, after the concert in the circus?"

"Yes if you please Your Imperial Highness," said Dolly in one breath, and her brother came to her rescue.

"Dolly is envious of the young nurses here, Madame. She seems to have ambitions in that line herself."

"Have you really?" said Olga. "But aren't you still at school?"

"I'll be eighteen in March, please Your Imperial Highness, and my father says I can leave school at Easter, if I pass all my exams."

"Then let's see what can be done at Easter," Olga said. "I'm sure you'd like Darya Karlovna to work near her home, professor? My cousin Dmitri Pavlovich has put his home on the Palace Quay at the disposal of the British Red Cross, and I know the charming English ladies taking charge of it are looking for Russian probationers. Will you allow her name to go forward—if she passes her exams?"

It was said with the smile Simon adored, so saucy and so lively, with the flash of perfect teeth in the pretty Russian face, and Olga quickly cut short their thanks. "The orderly in the corridor will take you to the chief surgeon when the visiting hour is up," she said. "Good-evening to you all!"

"Isn't she *wonderful*?" whispered Dolly, when the light footsteps died away across the ward.

"No Romanov ever came in a more charming guise," her father said.

"You should have *seen* her at the circus, Simon! She was wearing the most beautiful blue dress—"

"I've seen her a hundred times wearing beautiful dresses," Simon interrupted. "Last summer, before this rotten mess began."

"Does she nurse you herself?" said Dolly.

"God forbid!" Simon closed his eyes. It was bad enough to have Tatiana Nicolaievna at his bedside twice a day, assisting in the painful stuffing of his wound with tape. But to have Olga involved in the intimacies of the bedpan and blanket bath was worse than unthinkable.

Professor Hendrikov thought they were tiring the boy. He told Dolly to kiss her brother, and took her to wait in an anteroom while he went to see the surgeon-in-chief. Installed in one of the smaller reception rooms of Catherine the Great, where the modern desk and filing cabinets were in odd contrast to the baroque splendours of the walls and ceilings, the princess told him that his son's right arm was at present entirely paralysed, but that when the wound was sufficiently healed the paralysis might be overcome by 'electric therapy'.

"It is a new technique in Russia, at least in military hospitals," she said. "As a matter of form I should like your consent to its use on Lieutenant Hendrikov."

"I'll consent to anything that'll do him good. Electrical techniques, eh? Isn't the apparatus very difficult to install, in an eighteenth-century palace?"

"I believe there have been certain problems," admitted the princess, "but our engineering section solved most of them within the first three months."

"I'm inclined to wish I had been allowed to visit the Catherine Palace before the engineers took over." The professor hesitated. "Equipping it as a hospital must have cost a fortune."

"It most certainly did."

"At the public expense, princess?"

"Entirely at the expense of Their Imperial Majesties."

* * *

Next morning Simon's bed was rolled out of the screened alcove and into a long ward where it became one of twelve beds, arranged in two rows of six. Here he had the company of other men, just when he felt ready for it, but with no special privileges of receiving visitors, imperial or family. The only suggestion that he was still a Palace Pet came from the doctor who had given him the nickname, and who, on his first visit to Simon in the ward, remarked as he moved away:

"Remember, if you want some hypnotic treatment, lieutenant, we've a direct line to Rasputin."

The man in the left hand bed snickered, the one in the right said "Hush!" and the doctor was out of earshot before Simon found the right retort. He had heard the rumours about Rasputin and the Czarina—who had not? but he had never expected to hear, in an imperial palace, the kind of gibe that would have brought dirks out of their scabbards in the Marine Guards barracks. He himself was a model of frozen respect when the Czarina, tired and limping, made her next round of the wards. He saw that, however tender and maternal she could be when alone with a man on the danger list, her invincible stiffness and reserve prevented her full communication with badly wounded men. He remembered those, flung with himself into the charnel house of the railway station at Warsaw, who had raised themselves to kiss the Czar's shadow as he passed.

Alexandra Feodorovna, as a nursing sister, was still the empress he had known from afar at Livadia and aboard the *Standart*. She had the same pinched smile for every man she spoke to, and the same mechanical form of words. That morning it was, "Are you feeling a wee bit more comfy today?" and Simon could see some of the men winking behind her back as she walked down the line of beds. That day each man received a holy picture, signed on the back by the Czarina and her children, and obviously much care had been taken to fit the pictures to the names of the patients. Simon was touched to receive the image of the Apostle Simon

Zelotes, and propped it respectfully against a little flower vase on his bedside table.

The Grand Duchesses must have been kept busy in their own wards, for Olga no longer accompanied her mother, and the taping of Simon's wound was taken over by Nurse Vera. As he grew stronger every day, the fact of not seeing her became a mild obsession: he could hardly believe that she had stroked his gaunt cheek and let him call her 'darling'. All winter long, in the snow and slime of the front, Olga had been the vision of his romantic idealism. He had believed in her as a spirit, just as many young men in other lands believed in the Angels of Mons. But now he had seen her again, neither an angel nor a princess, but simply a tired young nurse with a bedraggled apron, and a veil not as crisp as it might have been, and desire moved again in Simon Hendrikov's body, and the days without her took a long time to pass.

Presently he was promoted to a wheel-chair, and passed the mornings in an oval room, ornately decorated, which looked out through tall windows down the avenue leading from the main entrance to the palace. Here as many as fifty men, walking wounded or in wheel-chairs, could gather round tables laid out with table games like chess and dominoes, magazines and playing cards. These were largely neglected for the favourite Russian pastime of talking, and talking, of course, about the war. There was resignation rather than defeatism in the talk, for although the thinking of all of them had been conditioned by the débâcle of Tannenberg, although the first great flame of patriotism had been extinguished in 1914, never to be revived, there was a degree of optimism in the air. Two million more Russian recruits had been called to the colours, and the Grand Duke Nicholas was preparing for a new advance. The British and French, with troops from the British Empire, were about to come to Russia's aid in the Turkish campaign by moving in to the Black Sea, so that the capture of Constantinople, the realisation of the Byzantine dream, seemed to be a matter of weeks. By the time Simon's electrotherapy treatments started the Russians had captured the great Austro-Hungarian fortress of Przemysl, and the victory bells were ringing in Petrograd for the first time in many months.

There was always the ominous undertone that even though

Galicia was entirely conquered, it had been by the bayonet and not by fire-power, while only force of numbers and great courage had taken the Russians across the Carpathians and into the vast plain of the Danube which lay below. But the overtone was all exultation, and Simon Hendrikov's exultation was that he now saw the Grand Duchess Olga every day.

The new electrotherapy wing had been installed in the Cameron gallery, which her Scottish architect had added to the great Catherine's palace, and the door of Olga's ward was set at right angles to the circular ante-room, hung with portraits of the nineteenth century, in which the patients waited to be summoned to their treatments. It was easy for Nurse Olga to slip out for a few minutes, once the timetable was established, and chat with Lieutenant Hendrikov, so far improved by now that he was wearing uniform, with his arm in a sling, and able to walk to the electrotherapy department on his own two feet.

In those brief meetings they took up their friendship again, as it had been in the previous summer at Livadia, but now as two human beings, not as the pretty princess and the dashing lieutenant of an operetta. The old etiquette was forgotten, for Olga insisted that Simon, as a patient, should remain seated, while she stood by the door left ajar "in case ward sister pounces!" she said. And every time he went back to his own ward Simon Hendrikov wished that she was just Olga Romanova, an ordinary girl, a young nurse of the kind Dolly was cut out to be, warm-hearted and true; and that theirs could be the very ordinary romance of a wounded soldier and the girl he met in hospital.

But she was Olga Nicolaievna, the eldest daughter of the Czar. The reminders of it were everywhere, in this resplendent palace of her ancestors.

Even the nineteenth-century portraits in the ante-room reminded him that the Romanov line went back for three hundred years, through Russia's greatest era of expansion and power. They were not good paintings, and some of them were highly imaginative, but the more recent ones had the merit of showing members of the Family in their younger days, before they assumed the sceptres and sashes of authority. One or two of them reminded Simon of Yakovlev, the naval commander he had met in the Fourth Line, and who now presumably was aboard the *Askelod* off the Island of Lemnos, the cruiser having been sent to represent Russia in the Allied attempt to force the Dardanelles. Yes—he had caught the resemblance at last: Commander Yakovlev had a certain look of Alexander II, the Czar-Liberator, and perhaps even more of Alexander III, who had been Olga's grandfather.

The Romanov look, written clearly on her own face.

Well, the Grand Dukes had scattered their seed lavishly across Russia; there was no reason why Yakovlev should not be a Romanov by-blow. But Olga's was the blood imperial: her place was in the circle round the throne.

She looked very little concerned with her imperial heritage on the bright day at the end of March when she met him, not—as so often—before his treatment, but afterwards, just as he left the electrotherapy department.

"How would you like to go for a drive with me, Simon Karlovich?"

"A drive? This morning?"

"Yes, quite a lot of the other men have been out since the weather turned so fine."

"I know—but you did say a drive *with you*, didn't you?"

"Sister has given me the rest of the morning off, and the doctor says you can go. I wish we could take a sleigh and a troika, but the cold and the jolting might be too much for you. We'll take a limousine, and go gently round the parks. If you would like, that is."

"If I *like*!"

"Then we'll meet on the ramp in twenty minutes, and Ivan will take care of you."

There was always an Ivan, not very far away, and although the hospital orderlies didn't wear white cotton gloves like the palace footmen, there was always a pair of hands ready to serve an Imperial Highness. The orderly made Simon sit down, brought him his own uniform cap and gloves, a heavy hospital cape, a scarf and a pair of felt *valenki* big enough to fit over his hospital shoes, and finally, against Simon's rising protests, a wheel-chair, in which Lieutenant Hendrikov was taken into the fresh air for the first time in many weeks.

The big car with the imperial arms on the door was waiting on the ramp built for the convenience of Catherine II in her unwieldy old age, and Olga got out to help Simon, hampered by his splinted arm, to climb inside.

"Roll up the window, Ivan," she said imperatively. "The lieutenant must *not* catch cold." She told the driver, "Go very gently round the parks, and then bring us back to the hospital."

The orderly, before closing the door, put two cushions deftly behind Simon's shoulder and splinted arm, and laid a fur-lined lap robe over his and Olga's knees. The big car glided down the ramp and started along the roads through the park, which were kept sanded for such outings. The snow sparkled in the sunshine with iridescent lights of pale gold and blue: the surface was still hard, but the sheathes of ice were dropping off the birch twigs, and the twitter of birds was beginning to be heard.

"This is wonderful," said Simon Hendrikov.

"I thought you'd like it. But are you quite comfortable?"

"Very, thank you, except that I'm wrapped up like an Eskimo."

Olga laughed. "We mustn't risk a chill for you. Have you ever been in the park before? It used to be open to the public at certain times before the war."

"I came here just once with my father, when I was a little kid. He used it for a history lesson, of course."

"I'm not too sure of all the history myself. But look, there's the Chinese Pavilion, doesn't all that red and gold look pretty in the snow? And the Turkish Bath with the pink minaret on the other side of the lake? They didn't care how they mixed up styles and places, did they?"

"I remember the 'Girl with a Pitcher' best, from the Pushkin poem."

"Do you love Pushkin too?"

"I do, in spite of having to learn reams of him by heart at school."

A plate glass partition divided them from the chauffeur in the imperial livery. Olga picked up a speaking tube and told the man to take the road leading past the 'Milkmaid' statue.

"There she is, your Pushkin heroine!"

But Simon had no eyes for the 'Girl with a Pitcher'. He had Olga beside him, living and warm, with a sable coat concealing her white uniform, and a peaked sable hat instead of her nurse's veil. He said impulsively: "How lovely you look in furs! I never saw you wearing furs before."

"It was summer when we met first, Simon Karlovich."

"At Livadia. But that hat—it does look a bit like uniform. It makes me think of the morning you rode on to the parade ground at Krasnoe Selo, and your regiment cheered you—"

Olga said quietly, "Do you know that the Hussars of Elizabethgrad were completely wiped out at Tannenberg?"

Simon held out his hand to her, on top of the lap robe, and she put her gloved hand into it. She sighed, and then he realised how tired she looked: pale, with shadowed eyes, and he blurted out:

"You look absolutely exhausted."

"What a nice compliment."

"It is; I know you're tired because you're doing far too much. How many hours did you spend in hospital yesterday?"

"I *am* a little tired, that's why Sister gave me half the morning off, but it's nothing to do with the hospital. I had to go into Petrograd last night to help my sister Tatiana, and we didn't get back until nearly two o'clock."

"Help her, what with?"

"She's chairman of the Refugee Committee, it's a terrific job. And so many refugee trains came in yesterday afternoon that the committee simply couldn't cope: the shelter at the Narva Gate was overflowing. We ordered the emergency barracks on Golodai Island to be opened, and somehow they got food and bedding for them all."

"Who's 'they'?"

"Some of Tatiana's committee, and some Americans who've started working for it too. The American Ambassadress brought a motor car full of tinned food, and a Mr. Calvert from the consulate helped to distribute it. He's a man about your own age, very tall."

"I think I know him. Joseph Calvert, dark-haired, with a sallow face? He's been taking Russian lessons from my mother."

"Really? He speaks Russian very well. And he was a great help at the barracks—I liked him."

"But it took you and Tatiana Nicolaievna to get the barracks opened. You were the only two who could really cope?"

"Oh no, but when we're there the others work harder, instead of just—philosophising. Sometimes I think we Russians are rather too fond of talking, instead of doing."

"You ought to be at one of my parents' evening parties. Talk about talk!"

"I'd love to come! I'd love to see your home in Petrograd. Is it as nice as the dacha?" Simon smiled and shook his head.

The car had left the Catherine park, and crossing the avenue went into the other vast park which surrounded Olga's home, Quarenghi's masterpiece in honey-coloured stone, with its two wings balancing the central building, reached through the state entrance by a flight of steps and colonnades.

"It really looks prettier in summer," said Olga apologetically, "when the deer are wandering about the park, and the swans are on the lake. Still, the children enjoy skating in the winter—"

"Don't you?"

"I've no time for skating any more."

They had been driven round the front of the palace to the garden side, where the flower-beds were covered with fir branches against the frost and the captured German machine-gun, prominently displayed, was protected by a tarpaulin. Beside the lake a miniature toboggan run, perhaps twenty feet high, had been constructed on a wooden framework, the top of which could be reached by a fireman's ladder.

"Why, there's Alexis Nicolaievich!" said Simon. "Playing on the snow mountain."

"He's crazy about snow mountains, we all are," said Olga. "But as he told me this morning, 'it's no fun without papa'."

"Let's stop and watch them, may we?"

"If you're sure you won't be chilly?"

"With all these wraps, *and* a footwarmer?"

The car came to a standstill. Across the snow they saw Alexis appear at the summit of the snow mountain, and set his toboggan at the top of the ice chute, which was about three feet wide. A tall man in sailor's uniform sat firmly down on the long toboggan and took Alexis in his lap. With a squeal of delight from the boy they shot down to the bottom, where another man in a fur cap and fur-collared overcoat helped Alexis to his feet. Clapping his hands, the boy ran off round the base of the mountain to start all over again. He was quickly pursued by the sailor.

"That's not Derevenko, is it?" asked Simon.

"No, that's Nagorny, it's his week on duty. He takes such good care of Alexis!"

Simon remembered the last cruise on the *Standart*, and the

little boy's accident on the ladder. "Is it quite safe for Alexis Nicolaievich?" he said uneasily.

"Oh quite; he's not allowed to go down alone. You should see him with Marie, she never brakes with her heels, and Nagorny does."

"He's looking splendid, and he's having great fun," said Simon. "I was crazy about snow mountains myself, when I was a kid."

"Really? Where was yours?"

"Well, we didn't have a private one, we went to the public parks. The best snow mountain in Peters—Petrograd, is always the one in the grounds of the Tauride Palace. It's about three times as high as yours."

"Yes, well, there aren't so many grooms this year, to keep the buckets of water going. This one looks a bit patchy to me already."

But now the attention of the Czarevich had been attracted to the stationary car, and he came running up, waving to his sister. Nagorny was running alongside, and the other man was not far behind Nagorny. It struck Simon Hendrikov that they were a lonely little group, hurrying across the expanse of snow with the great bulk of the palace behind them, and a spaniel, barking, bringing up the rear.

"Olga, come and play on the snow mountain!" The child stopped, embarrassed at the sight of his sister's companion, and Olga opened the door on her side of the car.

"Alexis, this is Lieutenant Hendrikov. You remember him last summer at Livadia?"

Alexis bowed.

"I remember you, lieutenant, and my sister Tania told me all about you. She said you'd been wounded, but you were very brave and didn't cry."

"Well, no," said Simon awkwardly.

"Where are you going to? Can I come for a drive with you?"

"We're on our way back to the hospital," said Olga.

"Well, just *to* the hospital, then, and home again," said the child, sure of his welcome, and climbing into the car.

"Be careful! Don't jostle Simon Karlovich's arm, whatever you do!"

"And Zilchik and Nagorny must come too."

"The more the merrier," said Olga resignedly. "Lieutenant

Hendrikov, this is my brother's tutor, Monsieur Gilliard. (Alexis, you are *not* to call him 'Zilchik'). Nagorny, get in front beside the driver. Oh, not the dog too!"—for Alexis, with a shout of "Joy! Joy!" was dragging his pet into the car. The dog, which had been rolling on the snow, immediately jumped on to the lap robe.

"We're imposing on you, Olga Nicolaievna," said the Swiss tutor, as the car started, "but you know how Alexis enjoys even a short spin—"

"Of course I do. But I thought you were going for a drive every afternoon in this fine weather?"

"We drive thirty versts some afternoons," said Alexis to Simon. "Where were you wounded, Simon Karlovich? Does your arm hurt you much?"

"On the Vistula, Alexis Nicolaievich, and it's getting better all the time. What do you do on such long drives?"

"I'm studying the railway system of the Petrograd suburbs," said the boy importantly. "Zilchik won't allow me to go into the city."

"There are plenty of railway lines to study outside Petrograd," suggested Simon.

"Oh yes, and I make notes of the bridges and tunnels, and the stations, and the repairs to the tracks, and everything."

"I'm afraid it's only lessons in a pleasant form," said Monsieur Gilliard, "but it's excellent practice in mapping and memorising details, and we enjoy talking to the people we meet, don't we, Alexis?"

"Have you a model railway, Alexis Nicolaievich?" said Simon.

"Yes, a huge one, all over the nursery floor. I move my troop trains on it, and my hospital train too."

"You'll be a great soldier, when you're a man."

The boy hung his head in the sudden shyness of ten years old. Then he recovered, and gave Simon his sister's saucy smile, which in his rosy face was a boy's grin, and said:

"Anyway we take a different route each day, and the policemen can't keep up with us, it's lovely!"

They had made a short circle of the park, and the car stopped again near the garden entrance of the palace. The Czarevich and his party got out with many good-byes and thanks, the boy turning to wave several times before he trudged off across the snow, with his hands deep in his overcoat pockets.

"He's grown a lot this winter," Simon said. Olga was picking wet brown and white hairs off the lap robe.

"That miserable dog!" she said. "I wonder Alexis doesn't take *him* down the snow mountain."

"I don't think anybody'll go down this snow mountain again, unless the frost comes back," said Simon. "Look, it's beginning to melt."

The sun of an early spring, even of the chilly Russian spring, was at high noon. The fir trees round the lake were shedding their loads of embossed snow, and where the ice chute had been patchy there was now a tiny rivulet of water.

"It doesn't matter," said Olga, and slipped her hand once again into Simon's. "It only means the winter's over now."

9

ON THE NIGHT RICHARD ALLEN returned to his flat in Petrograd the spring thaw was well established, and a steady rain was washing the last grimy slush from the pavements of the Italianskaia. There were few pedestrians about at ten o'clock, and Joe Calvert, waiting in the living-room with a good fire in the stove, imagined that every footstep, heard so faintly through the double windows, marked the arrival of his friend.

The flat was still very much a bachelor apartment, and Joe had added very little to it except a score of books and a few prints of old St. Petersburg. The belongings left behind by Captain Allen—referred to as his 'stuff'—had not amounted to much beyond his golf clubs and his fishing tackle, for Dick had been a dedicated fisherman in the rivers of Finland on his occasional summer leaves. Joe had bundled this sporting equipment, along with a butterfly collection which surely dated from Dick's schooldays, into the wardrobe in the smaller bedroom. Nobody had occupied it during his tenancy, which had been extended for a further six months after the original three. Nor had he heard anything of his landlord, barring an exchange of letters about the extension of the lease, until Dick's telephone call had reached him at the consulate in the afternoon.

The ring at the front door bell took him by surprise. The bulky figure on the landing surprised him too, and he said, "Good evening, sir," in Russian, uncertainly, and then the man took off his fur hat, laughing, and was Dick.

"You son of a gun," said Joe, punching the visitor on the arm as he took him into the lighted living-room, "what's happened to the cloak and dagger stuff? I was expecting you to tippy-toe up the back stairs and slide through a secret panel in the service door."

"I took a chance," said Dick. "D'you think any of the neighbours would have recognised me?"

"No," said Joe more seriously, "there's not much fear of that. Put on a bit of weight, haven't you? And how about that beard?"

In the light of the crude electric chandelier he saw a Russian *bourgeois,* a stout, prosperous merchant in a fur-collared coat, with a well-trimmed moustache and beard—surely darker than the moustache Joe remembered—and gold pince-nez. Dick laughed.

"The beard I can't remove without a razor. The overweight is easily disposed of." He took off the heavy overcoat, and the padded jacket and waistcoat underneath, and stretched luxuriously.

"That's quite a load to carry around," he said, flinging the garments on a chair. "Well, Joe, and how are you? Got a drink for me?"

"Sure, the vodka's all ready, and I've even got some ice." Joe indicated a drinks tray, waiting on the writing desk.

"Vodka, eh? Breaking the wartime prohibition order?"

"Doesn't affect me, this is one of your own bottles," Joe retorted. "Thanks for leaving me the bar."

"What's that you're having yourself?"

"Imported bourbon and branch water. Even the consular staff lives in luxury since the new ambassador took over."

"Mr. Marye. I hear he's doing very well, and I hear great things of *you,* Joe."

"You must be well informed in Stockholm. You came on from Stockholm, I suppose?"

"Actually I've been in Moscow. Came up on the night train, in time for breakfast at the Astoria."

"It was nice of you to call me, especially when you didn't have to. It was part of the deal, wasn't it, that you were to keep your key, and come and go whenever you wanted?"

"Yes, but I wanted to be sure of seeing you, and I didn't want to upset any of your private plans."

"Such as?"

"Such as having a pretty lady to dine and sleep."

"That wouldn't have happened. I might have had some guys in for a poker session, but that's about all."

"Leading a celibate life, are you?"

Joe shrugged. "I wouldn't say that, exactly. But there's been nothing—nobody—that mattered at all." He grinned. "Maybe I'm waiting for Dolly Hendrikova to grow up."

"Ah! How is that sweet child?"

"She's just started nursing at the Grand Duke Dmitri's hospital."

"*His* hospital?"

"Well—his palace. The British Red Cross project. Dolly's brother's in hospital right now, out at Czarskoe Selo. He was wounded on the Vistula, end of January or beginning of February, I forget."

"It seems a long time since your party at the Europa."

"Doesn't it, though?"

"Have you seen much of the other girl, Mara Trenova?"

"Just once since then, at the Hendrikovs' Christmas party. She's going great guns in some publishing house, The Children's Castle I think it's called."

"H'm, the 'candy classics'. That sounds rather a sugary diet for the fiery Trenova."

"Top up your glass, Dick?"

"Thanks."

Joe had been in the Foreign Service long enough to know that the preliminaries were now over. When he thought the friendly silence had lasted long enough, and Captain Allen, predictably, had filled and lit his pipe, he said easily:

"So what brings you to Petrograd, Dick? You're not going to throw me out of the flat, I hope?"

"Can't, until the end of May, and don't want to anyway. You like it here, eh? Old Varvara looking after you all right?"

"She gets by."

"Good. As to what brought me back to Petrograd, well, that's quite a long story. And I can't even begin to tell it you until I know if you still feel the way you did last August."

"In relation to the war?"

"In relation to American neutrality. You remember the day I offered you a sub-lease of the flat, you reminded me that as an officer of the American Foreign Service you couldn't 'front' for anybody—I think that was your word—unless you knew what you were getting into. Do you still feel that way?"

"Look," said Joe, "we had no ambassador in Petersburg at that time. Petrograd I mean, damn it! Things have been a lot different since Ambassador Marye came. He really got the American colony together and started to organise charities.

There's an American hospital for Russian wounded now, and an American crèche for babies, sort of tied in with the Grand Duchess Tatiana's Refugee Committee; it seems to me we've come out pretty strong on the Russian side."

"Yes, but only for Russian charities, Joe! What about Russia in the war against Germany?"

"Now see here," said Joe, "President Wilson spelled out where he expects us to stand on that, just about the time you left for Stockholm. I think it was the first public statement he made after his wife died. He said, 'Americans should be neutral in fact as well as name, impartial in thought as well as action.' I know those were the words, I memorised them."

"Yes, I remember," said Richard Allen. "Well?"

"But Mr. Page, our ambassador to the Court of St. James, he came right out and begged to disagree. He said, 'A government can be neutral, but *no man* can be.' And he'd been a very close friend of President Wilson."

"It sounds like the end of a beautiful friendship to me," said Dick flippantly. "Joe, I think I see what you're driving at. You've come down on the Page side, and not on the President's?"

"As a man, I have. Way I see it, the Germans have been the aggressors all along the line. They want to take over the world, and sooner or later we'll have to line up with the guys who're out to stop them. That's my own opinion, Dick, in confidence, strictly unofficial; but just remember, I want to help every which way there is."

"Thanks, Joe," said the Englishman. "That makes things easier."

He leaned forward in the creaking wicker chair.

"There's one thing I want to ask you first, and then I'll tell you my story. Did you ever hear of an organisation called the Green Men?"

"Here in Petrograd?"

"Or in Moscow, or anywhere in Russia."

"Would they be Moslems?"

"I hardly think it's likely. Why?"

"Green's the Prophet Mohammed's colour, and there's been a lot in the press about the new mosque near the Finland Station."

"Apart from that, you've never heard of the Green Men?"

"Sorry; never."

"Right. Well, I was sent to Stockholm because our Intelligence had become interested in the Green Men; it was believed to be a propaganda network—well, espionage, since you prefer that word—planning to start a revolution in Russia by spreading the rumour that the Czar would betray the nation by making a separate peace with Germany."

"Because of Tannenberg?"

"Partly, and partly because the Czarina was German born, and has a brother fighting on the German side."

"Do you really think it matters to the Russian peasants, the bulk of the population, that Ernest of Hesse is a German princeling in the Kaiser's army? They've probably never even heard the fellow's name," said Joe.

"It's up to the Green Men to make it matter. And it could be done by way of Rasputin."

"He's been lying low since he came back to Petrograd."

"He wasn't lying low in Moscow a few nights ago," said Dick. "Didn't you know he'd gone to Moscow?"

"You bet; it was well advertised in the newspapers. Seems he took a vow last summer after he recovered from the wound that woman gave him, to make a pilgrimage to one of the shrines in the Kremlin."

"His pilgrimage took him to a nightclub called 'Yar', a few evenings ago. And I was there."

"You went to Moscow to keep an eye on Rasputin?" said Joe.

"Yes, I was sent to Moscow to get a line on his contacts, if I could. The brute is so well guarded in his apartment here, with an army of plainclothesmen protecting the Little Father's beloved Grigori, that it isn't easy to get close to him. Especially after the stabbing in Siberia. So my assignment was to start fresh as a Moscow businessman—I know the milieu pretty well—and find out, if I could, how the money was flowing from Germany, through Stockholm, into the hands of Rasputin."

"I don't believe he's all that interested in money. But go on!"

"It wasn't too difficult to get to meet him in Moscow, and I saw some interesting faces in his entourage. But within forty-eight hours the whole thing blew up at the 'Yar' nightclub."

"You went there with him?"

"I was there, but not with him. He came in late, and very

drunk, with his hangers-on—men and women too—and after he'd drunk another bottle he began to sing and dance and howl like a Siberian wolf, breaking glasses and upsetting tables and crockery, until at last the manager and his staff intervened. Rasputin barricaded himself behind the furniture and made a wild speech at the pitch of his voice, saying they dare not touch him, he was protected by the Little Father and the Little Mother, 'Matushka' as he calls her, who ate out of his hand—but he didn't say 'hand'. 'I can make the old girl do anything I want', he yelled, 'I've got what she likes best!' And then, just in case any of us had missed the point—he exposed himself."

Dick Allen grinned savagely at Joe's face of disgust.

"The manager had sent for the police by this time," he went on, "and they arrested him. They had to."

"You mean Rasputin's in *prison* in Moscow?"

"No such luck. He was arrested in the name of General Djunovski, the chief of the gendarmerie, supported by General Adrianov, the Prefect of Police. But in spite of that he was released at once, pending an investigation into the affair at the —very—highest—level."

"Guess who," said Joe.

"Exactly, guess who. And if, after these public insults to herself, the Czarina goes on protecting Rasputin—if at least a hundred witnesses are overruled, or never get a hearing—if the press censorship is clamped down on the story—then it may mean the fall of the monarchy."

"And Russia will leave the war."

"Exactly."

Joe Calvert got up and poured himself more bourbon from the bottle imported by the American Embassy. He knew they had come to the crux of the matter—the desperate anxiety of the western Allies that Russia should continue the fight. The month of March had brought them two major reverses: the massacre of Neuve Chapelle and the failure of the Royal Navy to force the Straits of the Dardanelles, the gateway to Constantinople and the Black Sea: if Russia made a separate peace now the victory of the Central Powers was assured.

"You're kidding yourselves," he said.

"We're what?"

"Kidding yourselves, if you think the Russian monarchy

depends on Rasputin. Sure, the empress protects him—and I wouldn't bet on those two Moscow cops keeping their jobs—because she believes he's a holy man, and a holy man who has the power to cure her boy whenever he gets sick. But that's only part of it, Dick! You can't say the future of the Russian Empire depends upon a mad monk and a kid! For my money—and I've been following the whole thing pretty closely—the real danger to the monarchy, and the prosecution of the war, lies in the rotten, I mean rotten to the core, relationship between the Czar and the Duma."

He was still standing by the drinks tray, and Dick looked up at him consideringly. The greenhorn of last summer had acquired authority; he spoke as if he was sure of himself, and knew what he was talking about. Young America comes of age, thought Richard Allen, and answered seriously:

"I think you attach too much importance to the Duma."

"And why not? God damn it, why shouldn't the Duma be important? I know it's not the House of Commons. I know it isn't Congress. But it's all they've got as an elected assembly, a debating forum, and every time they pass a resolution he dislikes, the Czar simply winds up the session. He sulks out there at Czarskoe Selo and won't even receive the Ministers. That's where the inefficiency of this country begins, Dick—in the Alexander Palace at Czarskoe! That's why all the war supplies they bought from their Allies, and from us; coal, guns, munitions, are rusting and rotting on the docks at Archangel, because they can't even run a railroad efficiently! The Duma votes for a Munitions Council, the Czar says no dice. They try to sort out the arms shortage by indicting the War Minister—"

"And he's protected by the Czarina and Rasputin," Dick interrupted. "It's no good, Joe; everything comes back to those two—"

"—And the Green Men. I wouldn't care if your Green Men were as thick on the ground as the Green Mountain Boys in Vermont in 1775, I still say you can't pin every muddle in this country on Rasputin. You can't blame him for all the quarrelling between the Army Medical Service and the Zemstvo Red Cross, the like of which I've never witnessed in my life. Nor for the way the civil servants oppose everything that the county councils try to work out along with the town councils to get quarters and food for all those wretched refugees. Don't worry, Dick; I'll keep my ear to the ground for anything I can hear about your Green Men, but I think they're a damned sight less important than the Bolsheviki."

"Most of whom are now living in Switzerland."

"Don't you believe it! Those five members of the Duma who were tried and found guilty of conspiracy against the Empire—tried in a regular court of justice, and not by Rasputin—and packed off to Siberia only last month were Bolsheviki, meeting in 'illegal assembly', as the prosecution called it, to debate Lenin's 'Defeatist Thesis' that the victory of Germany will mean the downfall of the Czar. That's it, short and sweet! Lenin may be living in Zürich, but his instructions to Russian socialists to work for the defeat of Russia have been in circulation as an underground pamphlet for at least the last six weeks."

"Have you seen one?"

"No, but I—what in hell is that?"

A tremendous explosion, which made the wooden shutters rattle and the porcelain stove shake in its brick foundation, sent its sound waves echoing across the city.

Both Joe and Dick were on their feet, but neither spoke. Some flakes of whitewash fell from the ceiling, and they could hear a trickle of dust behind the walls. Then the babble of an excited house broke out, and the doors were slammed, and feet ran up and down the stairs.

"Terrorists!" said Joe. "The Winter Palace!"

"A hospital depôt now—"

"But the girls go there," said Joe. "The young Grand Duchesses. I met them both there, the night they opened a barracks for the refugees—you stay still," he went on urgently. "I'm going up to the attics to find out."

"You won't see much from a building this high." But Joe was out of the flat by the back door and running up the service stairs to the attics, which he knew were divided into boxrooms and a few bedrooms for menservants, whom few tenants in the Italianskaia had employed since the outbreak of war. There he found a dozen people who had had the same idea as himself, and some had already opened two or three skylights and climbed up on chairs or storage chests to scan the sky. It was brilliantly illuminated by tongues of flame, which flickered against the rainfilled clouds and the dust of the great explosion to cover Petrograd with a lurid purple pall.

Joe took his turn at peering out, listened to the opinions of his neighbours (one of whom was convinced that the Kaiser's Zeppelins had got through to Petrograd) and hurried back to Dick.

"Well?"

"It's not the Winter Palace, that's for sure. It's a whole lot further to the east."

"Oh my God!" said Richard Allen. "Can it be the Arsenal?"

Joe stood aghast. The Arsenal of Petrograd occupied two huge building complexes, one on each side of the Liteini Prospekt near the Alexander Bridge across the Neva.

"If it's the Arsenal half the Liteini Prospekt must have gone up too," he said. "And it's awful goddamned close to our embassy. I think I ought to go and see."

"I'm coming with you."

Richard Allen began to put on his padded garments and gold pince-nez, the accoutrements of the Moscow merchant. As the legal tenant of the flat, he checked the heat of the porcelain stove and made sure the kitchen light was out while Joe fetched his own overcoat and fur hat. Before Dick opened the front door he stopped in the dark little hall and said to the American:

"You've caught Russian fever now, like the rest of us. You hear a bang and you think of a bomb. You feel a blast and the first word you say is 'Terrorists!' "

"Oh, for God's sake, cut it out!" said Joe.

"Because if it *is* the Arsenal, then the only word is 'sabotage'."

They met nobody on the staircase, everybody was in the attics or the street. Wherever the fire was, it was blazing wildly enough to send umbered shadows dancing on the yellow and white façades of the Italianskaia as the two young men hurried towards Sadovaia Street. There was no question of getting through to the American Embassy, for heavy police patrols were already clearing the main arteries for the passage of the fire engines and ambulances, likely to be quite inadequate to a disaster assuming an epic scale. At least three policemen assured Joe that the embassy was not in danger, neither was the Tauride Palace nor the Smolny Convent, all of which were in the same locality: the explosion had taken place at the Okhta munition works on the east side of the Neva.

"I'm afraid there's no doubt about it," said Dick, who had been making his own enquiries among some of the more responsible elements into the crowd that was fast degenerating into a rabble. He spoke in French; English would hardly have been in keeping with the personage he was trying to create, and Joe answered in that language, "It really is the Okhta?"

"Yes. The most important explosives factory in Petrograd, perhaps in the whole of Russia. And this in the middle of the advance! The factory that made everything from rifle bullets to machine-gun parts, and where the workers hardly ever went on strike! The munitions crisis will be twenty times worse than it was before."

"They'll have to make an effort to bring on the Archangel stores."

"Which will be a mere drop in the bucket compared to the weekly production of the Okhta."

"You going to blame this on Rasputin too?"

Dick bared his teeth in a grin. They were slowly forging their way southwards through the crowd, in the direction of the Nevski Prospekt. Here and there old men and women were kneeling at the edge of the pavement, crossing themselves and praying aloud.

"They're praying to Saint Andrew and Saint Catherine to intercede for them," said Dick. "They say the explosion is a sign of God's wrath with Russia. This means another spiritual crisis, of course. Another excursion into the dark night of the Russian soul. All this, right on top of the Dardanelles—!"

"Where are we heading for?" said Joe.

"We might as well go back to the Astoria and have a drink—I've got a room there, by the way, in the name of Shulkov, and I'm expecting a call from Moscow within the next hour. If the Okhta disaster doesn't foul up the whole telephone system, that is."

"I might try calling our embassy, just to make sure—" Joe began, and then, pointing across the street, he interrupted himself to say, "Look, Dick! Isn't that Mara Trenova?"

"You've got better sight than I have, old chap. That girl in the red fox hat, holding on to a fellow's arm, beside the tram stop?"

"She's not holding on to him, stupid, she's *struggling* with him! My God, he's going to hit her! It *is* Mara Trenova, I tell you!"

"He hasn't hit her, and she's got away from him," said Dick, peering short-sightedly at the lighted corner of the Nevski, where the surging crowd made it difficult to judge the movements of any two figures as the tram cars set down and took up their passengers. "Look, Joe," he said, himself grasping the American's arm, "even if it is the Trenova girl, don't interfere. You haven't been seeing her, so keep it that way. There's enough trouble afoot tonight without getting involved with—"

He had meant to say 'with one of Russia's eternal victims', but the far-fetched phrase died on Dick Allen's lips as Joe gave him a light slap on the shoulder, said, "Call me at the consulate tomorrow!" and threaded his way through the crowd on their side of the pavement with a footballer's grace. He had never lost sight of the red fox hat, and soon caught up with Mara, walking stiffly and as if blindly, back up the Nevski in the direction of the Winter Palace.

"Good evening, Mara Ivanovna," he said as he came abreast of her. "Can I be of any help?"

She looked up at him, startled, and he saw tears and dirt on her pale face.

"Mr. Calvert!" He had spoken to her in Russian, and she hardly knew how to address him, having heard him object, in what seemed like another life, to "Yusuv Yurievich." She said uncertainly, "Thank you, I'm very glad to see you, but I don't need help."

"I was afraid you were in some kind of trouble—or distress."

"I'd just—just heard of a friend's death. Well, not a friend exactly, just someone I knew . . . It shocked me."

"*Not* Simon Hendrikov?"

Her sudden peal of laughter, cutting through the noise of the avenue, was as shocking to Joe as her stained face and bare hands, which he now saw were bruised and bleeding at the base of the palms.

"Oh no, not Simon Karlovich, Mr. Calvert. He's making splendid progress, with the whole imperial family to fawn over him and feed him with black grapes and champagne. No, just an acquaintance. Somebody you would never have dreamed of knowing—"

"Come on now," said Joe, "you don't know what you're saying. You got caught in that crowd, didn't you, and everybody was pushing and shoving like mad, and you stumbled and hurt yourself, wasn't that it?"

"My coat," said Mara, looking down at the wet stains above her knees, "yes, somewhere back there, I must have fallen—it was silly of me."

"Not silly at all, on a night like this." Joe looked about him. They were nearly at the Hotel Europa. He couldn't take her in there, bedraggled as she was, and the few teashops still open were crammed with soldiers and their girls. "We're just five minutes from my place," he said. "Come back and wash your hands and let me make you a cup of tea."

"Oh, but—"

"And don't tell me you were hurrying home to mother, because you were walking in the opposite direction."

"All right." Mara made no further protest, but let him take her arm, and walked round the corner to Joe's flat as if it were quite natural for her to go alone to a man's rooms. In the flat he helped her off with her coat, and gently drew the torn woollen gloves from her hands.

"Let me take your hat too," he said. "Red fox. The colour suits you."

"One of Dolly Hendrikova's cast-offs. Just right for me."

"You're not a cast-off person. Don't rate yourself so low, and now come and wash those hands."

He showed her to the bathroom, found her a clean towel and a bottle of iodine, and went to the primitive kitchen. The samovar from which Varvara drank tea all day long was not quite cold, and he had a hot glass of tea, well sugared, ready and waiting when Mara Trenova came out of the bathroom, looking much refreshed.

"Sit in the basket chair and drink your tea," he said. "And don't let any false modesty stop you from telling me this: were your knees cut too? Because if so, you're going to need more first aid."

"No, it's all right. My coat and skirt and things protected them."

"Somebody really barged into you, to make you fall like that."

"I suppose so." He was watching her, drinking the sweet tea greedily. She had accepted the version of someone knocking into her just as she accepted his first suggestion that she must have stumbled and fallen in the crowd. Joe wondered if either version was the truth. He remembered the short thick-set man struggling with her in the half-darkness at the corner of Sadovaia Street.

"This is Captain Allen's flat, isn't it? You told us about renting it, that night of the dinner at the Hotel Europa."

"That's right. I've been here ever since."

"It's very nice. And Captain Allen, is he still in Stockholm?"

"Still in Stockholm." Mara put down the empty glass and said, in her prickly, defensive way:

"I was very sorry not to be able to return your hospitality. But really I can't invite anybody to my humble home."

"I told you already, don't underestimate yourself."

Joe pulled his own chair up to Mara's and took one of the abraded hands, now brown-streaked with iodine. She let him stroke it gently, and seemed to relax, but he felt that she was still trembling.

"You had a bad fright," he said. "Were you anywhere near the munitions factory at the time of the explosion?"

Mara shuddered. "Near enough."

"Then no wonder you were scared, I didn't like it much myself."

"Do you think they've got the fire under control by now?"

"If they haven't, a whole lot of tenements must have been gutted. God! I hope they got the people out in time." He slipped his arm round her thin shoulders.

"This friend of yours, whose death upset you so, was he killed in action?"

"I suppose—you could say—he died for what he believed in."

"That's as much as any man can do. Mara! Please don't cry!"

But she wasn't really crying, she was looking at Joe Calvert with the unfocussed look which had alarmed him on the Nevski Prospekt. And while she murmured, "You're very sweet to me," it changed unmistakably into a look of invitation. He leaned forward and lifted her out of the basket chair and into his embrace.

He kissed her cheek and then her lips, cradling her in his lap and feeling her warm against his chest and thighs. She was very light, but there was a strength in her arms as she locked them round his neck which told Joe that Mara Trenova was his for the taking, God knew for what reason, but certainly not for love. And he loved her no more than his occasional café pick-up, but there was something about her, something corrupt and bitter, which had fascinated him since the night they met. Now she was in his arms, and to the bitterness was added the aphrodisiac of a strangely mixed perfume, compounded of his own soap and some cheap scent like appleblossom, and a chemical smell which reminded him of the lab. at school.

He raised his head and saw that she was watching him between her half-closed lids. As he met that calculating look, so far removed from tenderness or even lust, he identified the smell. It was picric acid.

Picric acid, extensively used in the manufacture of explosives, whether explosives were made in the Okhta Works or in some cellar in the back alleys of Petrograd.

He didn't know, didn't want to know, what she had been doing. It was none of his business, whatever Dick might think. But he also knew he couldn't take Mara Trenova to bed, as she obviously meant him to do, to consume him, to blur his perceptions of—what? Feeling like his Bible namesake escaping from Potiphar's wife, feeling like a chilled, emasculate, useless fool, he kissed Mara lightly and said:

"You're feeling better now, aren't you? Come on, cheer up, and I'll take you out to supper at 'The Bear.'"

10

THE PIOUS RUSSIANS WHO knelt to pray in the streets of Petrograd on the night of the munitions factory disaster, and crowded the churches of the capital next day, were soon justified in their belief that the tragedy was a bad omen for the war. Within a matter of days the western Allies and the troops of the British Empire were defeated in their first attempt to attack Turkey by land in Asia Minor and Gallipoli. Although Enver Pasha and the Young Turks might have dragged Sultan Mohammed V into a dangerous adventure, a far great man than Enver was prepared to confront Turkey's enemies, and on the heights called Ariburnu, above the landing beach which came to be known as Anzac Cove, Colonel Mustafa Kemal repelled the western invaders and took the first giant step into his own dramatic future.

On the heels of Kemal's victory, the German advance began. It came a few days too late for Italy, for the Italian government, convinced that the Russians had defeated Austria, slipped down off its congenial position on the fence of neutrality and stabbed Austria-Hungary in the back with a formal declaration of war. Then the German war machine went into action in the northern sector of the long front. The immense German superiority in weapons and fire-power was felt once more, and while in Flanders the battle of Second Ypres was raging, the Russians had to surrender the great fortress of Przemysl, the prize they had held for two months only.

At the time the Germans began their drive through Poland, the Russian casualties amounted to four million men, and it became necessary to consider calling up the Second Category, the *opolchenie,* of untrained men between the ages of eighteen and forty-three. It was an extreme measure, for the Second Category had only been called up twice in Russian history—in 1812 against Napoleon I, and in 1854, during the Crimean War. There was now not a town, not a village, not an *isba* in Russia which had not given its toll of young men to the war.

June came round again, the war was nearly a year old, and in spite of the lengthening shadows over the Empire there were girls in Russia who still nursed a secret happiness. One was the Grand Duchess Olga, who by good fortune had her sweetheart close to her. Simon Hendrikov, discharged from hospital and pronounced fit for light military duty, was in the Marine Guards barracks at Czarskoe Selo, one of the élite body—now largely composed of war veterans—whose special duty was to protect the imperial family. As the summer dawn broke earlier and earlier, the Czarina was edified by her eldest daughter's early morning visits to the little Znamenia church near the palace. Olga had always been less willing than her sisters to give herself up to the long services, the frequent hours of prayer which fed the Czarina's mystical fervour, and the mother encouraged the humble walks on foot to the Znamenia and the brief devotions which, Olga declared, sustained her all day long in hospital and city.

The real refreshment, of couse, was the half-hour she spent with Lieutenant Hendrikov before they went to their respective duties. Their meetings were not furtive, for they walked openly in the park, and fed the deer now turned out for the summer, and gathered branches of lilac, purple and white, for the wards of the palace hospital. The 'botanists' knew all about their idyll, for the secret police were botanising as usual among the shrubberies and the rose parterres, and the Cossacks cantering along their perpetual round of the avenues of Czarskoe Selo knew something about it, for they often saluted the young officer of the Garde Equipage who had just saluted his princess before she entered the gates of the Catherine Palace. The three girls who made up the rest of the group which had once signed itself OTMA may have suspected it, but they said nothing. The Czarina was in a state of exalted ignorance, for she had but two aims in life at that time, to get the Grand Duke Nicholas removed from the supreme command, and to contradict the foul lies, as she called them, which were circulating in Petrograd about the sainted Father Grigori's behaviour in a vile Moscow nightclub, where of course he had never set his holy foot.

The Czar was at GHQ at Baranovichi.

There came a fine June day when Olga was relaxing contentedly after a night on duty at the hospital. She had slept undisturbed for most of the morning, her mother being at a Red Cross meeting in the city. Then she had a wing of chicken, a peach and a glass of wine, played the nursery piano to Alexis's balalaika, and saw the boy off for a drive in his donkey cart, Alexis holding Vanka's reins and Marie sitting watchfully beside him. Anastasia had received an imposition from Monsieur Gilliard and was dolefully studying French verbs.

"Come on, you silly kid, and I'll hear your pluperfect subjunctives," Olga called at last. Tatiana was at the hospital, and Olga had taken a leisurely bath in the solid silver tub used by all the sisters, and washed her hair with a lotion scented with her favourite essence of tea rose. The four girls had no personal maids, but they had several attendants, young women of good family who, but for the war, might have become maids of honour to the Grand Duchesses. One of them was brushing Olga's bright hair as she sat near the window in her white cambric wrapper and listened to Anastasia stumbling through the subjunctive mood.

It was a drowsy, peaceful scene, broken suddenly by a knock at the door.

"Come in!" said Olga.

The door opened to admit a fair-haired young footman, who had only recently entered service in the private apartments of the palace. He bowed apologetically.

"Your Imperial Highness, Father Grigori requests the honour of an audience—"

"Stand back, little brother!"

Rasputin motioned the footman from his path. He strode into the pretty feminine room, almost stumbled over a footstool, and clutched at the back of a chair to steady himself. Wearing the coarse, knee-length tunic of a peasant with a worn leather belt and high boots, his hair matted and greasy, he automatically raised one dirty hand in blessing.

"Where's Matushka?" was all he said.

Olga had risen to her feet, tying the ribbons of her wrapper across her young breast, while the French grammar in her lap fell to the floor, and Anastasia, who had risen too, moved a step backwards in dismay. The girl with the brush stood petrified behind Olga's low chair.

"*What* did you say?" asked the Grand Duchess disbelievingly.

"I said, 'Where's Ma?' Where *is* the old girl?" said the monk.

Olga looked at the footman, standing at attention by the open door. "Go to the Commandant of the Palace," she said. "Tell him to call four Cossacks of the Escort and bring them to me at once. And hurry!" She turned furiously on Rasputin. "Her Imperial Majesty is at the Winter Palace," she said. "Your spies should keep you in better touch with her movements. And His Majesty, my father, forbade you years ago to enter these apartments."

Rasputin's eyes narrowed. He took two steps towards Olga, and she felt the smell of stale brandy and foul breath.

"So!" he said. "Little kittens are growing long claws, are they? Little Olga plays at being the great Catherine, eh? What would a sceptre feel like in that pretty hand? No, no!" He changed to a wheedling tone. "Your faithful Grigori was only joking. But Olga Nicolaievna, lovey, little sister, Grigori needs Matushka's help. Batiushka Czar is far away, out of reach, and I need help today—"

"What sort of help?"

"My boy," the monk said cunningly, "my only son. They say he must be called up with the Second Category. A soldier, Grigori's boy Mitia, the mainstay of the family, the poor little family at Povrovskoe! This must not be. Tell Matushka she must write a line, an order to set the poor boy free—"

"Other men's sons have gone to the war, and given their lives for their country," said the Grand Duchess Olga. "Why should yours be exempt?"

"Ah, now you argue, now you're willing to bargain, like a country girl!" said Rasputin. His magnetic eyes, half closed, travelled all over her body with the sensuous look which had overcome the resistance of a thousand silly women in the so-called society of Petrograd. "And what a lovely country girl you'd be. Gold hair, white breast, strong legs to clasp your lover with, when the handsome lieutenant takes you into the bushes after the village fair—"

"You're wasting your time, glaring and grimacing," Olga said. "I'm not a subject for hypnosis." The first shock of the monk's appearance was over, and she was completely in command of the situation. Rasputin seemed to feel it by instinct. He said, more calmly, "I'll ask Matushka to give me my son back as I have often given her back her own. And you, little sister, I'll give you something extra, to make up for having offended you: I'll tell you the secret of the Green Men."

"Who are they?"

"What, you've never heard of the Green Men? They're friends of mine, good friends. Most of them live in Sweden, with the trolls who dig the precious metal from the secret mines. But *their* friends, my friends too, they live in Russia. Some here, some there, some in Siberia. *I* call them the Greenishes. Wouldn't you like to know what Batiushka Czar should call them?"

"I neither want to know nor care," said Olga. She had heard the tramp of the Cossacks coming down the gallery, and sighed with relief. The fair-haired footman flung the door open, the Commandant and his escort came in.

"In what way may I serve Your Imperial Highness?" the soldier said.

"Order your men to take Grisha Rasputin and escort him from the palace and the grounds," said Olga. "He is to be put out at the gate leading to Srednaia Avenue, where he has friends. He is never again to be admitted to this part of the palace. Warn the sentries accordingly, and you—" she turned like a fury on the footman, "you there—what's your name—Ivan! You are dismissed for a grave breach of trust, and if I ever hear of you in the imperial service at any time or place, I'll have you flogged."

It was the Romanov temper, which had skipped a generation: the rage which the Commandant, at least, was old enough to remember in Alexander III. He saluted hastily. He said, "Happy to serve Your Imperial Highness!" and ordered his men to take Rasputin and the footman from the room. The young man walked out in silence. Rasputin could be heard swearing horribly all the way to the top of the stairs.

"I'll get dressed now, please," said Olga to the young attendant. The girl was thankful to hurry away to the big dressing-room next door, to lay out the first summer cotton that came to hand, and Anastasia moved closer to her sister.

"Olga—won't mamma be terribly angry?"

"Probably."

"Because you know she's going to say just what *he* said, that he's saved Baby, over and over again—"

"Alexis is very tired of being called Baby, or haven't you noticed? Why don't you run away, and see what he and Marie are up to? I think you know your verbs quite well enough by now."

"Oh, thank you, Olga!" The child was glad to escape. When Olga was dressed she went downstairs to the library, where nobody would think of looking for her, and persuaded the librarian to lend her one of the forbidden books, so as to compound her act of defiance. Protesting, he gave her Tolstoy's *Resurrection,* which she had dipped into furtively before, and then he sat down to work at the Czar's neglected stamp collection, while Olga took her place by the open window and began to turn the pages of the book.

She was quite incapable of reading the text, because her brain was occupied by the scene with Rasputin and its inevitable consequences. He went straight to Ania, and she telephoned to mother at the Winter Palace, she thought. Then mother went directly to the Srednaia, to get a full account of my misdeeds. Well! I'm glad I did it; it was high time.

Olga mechanically turned the pages of *Resurrection,* looking at the illustrations by Leonid Pasternak, showing the thief and prostitute Maslova in the courtroom and on her way to Siberia. Maslova stood alone in the emptying courtroom 'After the Sentence', behind her stood a guard with a drawn sabre, his heavy left hand on her arm. She wondered if the Cossacks had hustled Rasputin out like Maslova, delighted—she was sure of it—to have her authority to lay rough hands on the charlatan. I wish I could send him to prison, she thought, and looked vengefully at the pictures in *Resurrection* of the prisoner gangs stumbling through the Siberian snow to Tiumen, to Ekaterinburg. Poor Maslova, more sinned against than sinning! Her fate seemed remote from the life of an Imperial Highness, safe in her father's palace of Czarskoe Selo, who had nothing to fear but the sound of her mother's limousine purring round the long driveway by the lake.

It came, and there was a silence as if the palace held its breath, which lasted for perhaps a quarter of an hour. Then Tatiana, rather out of breath herself, appeared at the library door.

"Oh, there you are!" she said to Olga. "I've been looking for you everywhere."

"You're back early."

"Mamma telephoned to the hospital. She wants to see you in the drawing-room."

The private drawing-room of the Czarina had been decorated at the time of her marriage in pale green, with spindling Chippendale furniture. Through the years innumerable portraits of her family had been added to the walls, which were dominated by a huge painting of Marie Antoinette, for whom the Czarina had a special cult. There were flowers in profusion, and among the nick-nacks on the glass-topped tables a number of devotional books and slim volumes of poetry, all bound in limp mauve leather and embossed with the Czarina's favourite emblem, the swastika. The Czarina herself was standing by an étagère of mauve sweetpeas, forced in the palace hothouses. She was still wearing the dust cape she used for motoring, and twisting a long pair of beige suede gloves between her hands.

"Olga!" she said, and by the very tones of her voice her daughters knew that she was in a state of barely suppressed hysteria. "Olga, I sent for you—I want to hear the truth from your own lips—could you, dared you, insult Our Friend today, here in this very house?"

"I'm sure you've already heard the truth, with a few additions, from himself and Ania," said Olga.

"Never mind about Ania; leave Ania out of this. Father Grigori, the best friend we've ever had or ever will have, came here in great distress to ask a favour of myself. You repaid him for years of prayer on our behalf, for interceding at the throne of the Most High for Baby's very life, by sending for soldiers to remove him from our home like a common thief—"

"Or a common drunk," said Olga. "He may have sobered up before you ran to comfort him at Ania's, but he was tipsy when he lurched into my bedroom, where I was sitting only half-dressed—"

"Drunk!" cried the Czarina. "That's a lie! So you have joined the pack too, Olga: the enemies who are hunting Father Grigori down! 'Grisha Rasputin', he says you called him—the insolence, the disrespect—"

"That's what he calls himself," said Olga, "when he's drinking and singing in the bath houses, naked with the women of the town."

"Olga!"

"And if there's a pack," said Olga mercilessly, "it's a pretty big one. It's composed of all the Duma, half the High Command, most of the daily press, my grandmother—and my father."

The Czarina collapsed into an armchair, and waved back Tatiana, who had started to her side.

"Tania, go to your room and rest, darling—"

"Stay where you are, Tatiana," Olga said. "Let's have this out once and for all; it affects you as much as it does me. You can remember, and maybe the Little Pair can too, the night five years ago when Rasputin came into our rooms when we were all in our nightdresses, and he tried to tickle us and play kissing games with us, until the nursemaids ran to bring our governess to make him stop. Oh yes, we had a governess then! Madame Tutcheva, the only educated woman who ever took charge of us, and she complained to papa about Rasputin, and papa forbade him ever to come near our rooms again. Of course you had your revenge; you sent our governess away, and today Rasputin was too drunk to remember the rule, or thought he could take a chance while papa was at the Stavka. And then he must have bribed that new footman to admit him by the private stair—"

"So you took it upon yourself, you had the impertinence, to dismiss one of my servants—"

"I would dismiss the Commandant of the Palace himself if he betrayed us to Rasputin. Mother, when will you understand that by the favours you show to this *strannik*—for that's all he was, a wandering hedge-priest, living by charity and his wits until *you* raised him up—you're destroying the people's faith in you, and in all of us? Stolypin made my father send him home to Siberia once. After what he did today, mightn't it be possible to have him sent back again?"

"The people's faith!" cried the Czarina, catching at the words. "What people? The good Russian men, the peasants, worship Father Grigori as they worship their Little Father the Czar. The people who hate him are only certain people in Saint—Petrograd: that rotten town, not an atom Russian, and I know who they are! Aunt Miechen and her horrible sons, and Nikolai Mihailovich, who has detested me since I was a girl of seventeen, when your father fell in love with me; and Paul's wife, and even Dmitri now! All the people hate *me*, because they know I have a strong will,

I don't change my mind, and that they can't bear! But I am strong because I'm blessed by Grigori! I can even bear the wounds you've dealt me, Olga! Oh, my heart . . . my heart!"

Clutching the right side of her body, the Czarina fell heavily across the arm of her chair. Tatiana ran to kneel beside her mother.

"Palpitations," said Olga, tugging at the long embroidered bell pull. "I'll tell them to send the doctors. She'll be all right."

She said a word to the anxious ladies-in-waiting in the anteroom and went upstairs. It was a long time until anyone came near her. Then she rang for her girl attendants, enquired for the Czarina and was told Her Majesty was resting comfortably in bed. Olga said she would like to have a supper tray in her own room at eight o'clock. She had been on night duty for a week, and so was not due back at hospital until eight next morning.

A tray of eggs and fruit, with the pot of coffee she had especially asked for, made its appearance in due course, and Olga fetched her cigarettes from the pocket of her hospital cape. For the first time in her life she smoked in her own bedroom in the palace. And as she smoked she thought over the scenes of the day, not without a sense of triumph, and not without reflection on Rasputin's curious references to the Green Men and the Greenishes. Was he merely babbling because he had drunk too much brandy? Or were the Green Men real, who if they were Rasputin's friends could only be ranged on the side of evil? She was trying to think of German regiments which wore green jackets—huntsmen, Jägers—when, the tray having been removed and fresh coffee brought, Tatiana at last came in.

"Olga, this has been a dreadful day!"

"You missed the worst of it."

"Oh yes, sweetie, I know Father Grigori was very naughty, and deep down inside her mamma knows it too, but still—to have him thrown out!"

"I was only sorry I couldn't do it with my own hands.'

"Olga, why do you say such things, when you know how it upsets mamma? She's sent the most dreadful telegram to Baranovichi."

"Where I should think father has other things on his mind than Rasputin and me."

"Maybe, but why don't you come downstairs now, and say you're sorry, and then you can both kiss and make up?"

"Because I'm not sorry, and I'm not a baby now, Tania. I did my best to tell her the truth tonight, but if she won't listen—"

Tatiana, with a gesture of despair, went into the dressing-room. When she came out she had her nightdress and wrapper over her arm.

"Going to bed already? It's only nine o'clock"

"I know, but mamma's in such a nervous state, and they don't want to give her veronal. I think she might sleep if I went to bed . . . I'm sorry, Olga. I know it's your turn, but she wants me to sleep with her tonight."

"You're very welcome. And you might take your snoring bulldog with you, if you want to do me a real favour."

"You don't have to quarrel with me too," said Tatiana sorrowfully. "Come along, Ortipo."

The Grand Duchess Olga had one more visitor before the palace clock struck half past nine. This was the Heir to the Throne, who in white pyjamas and carrying his big grey cat in his arms, slipped into her room with a quick glance behind him.

"Alexis!" exclaimed his sister, "you ought to be in bed and sound asleep."

"I can't go to sleep in the daylight," said the boy, "so when Zilchik went down to dinner I thought I'd come along and see you."

"Cat and all?"

"Yes, I brought Pussy too, in case you were feeling a bit lonely. I'd like him to stay with you all night."

"That's very sweet of you, Alexis." The big spoiled cat, now sniffing suspiciously at the place where Ortipo had been lying on the rug, was as welcome to Olga as the snoring bulldog, but she knew the gift of his company was the most important Alexis had to offer, and she pulled the boy close to her and gave him a hug.

"Olga, is it true you've been very naughty?"

"I don't think so. I think I've been very sensible, but then grown-up people have different ways of looking at the same thing."

"I expect so." The beautiful blue-grey eyes, so like their mother's, were turned thoughtfully on Olga's face. "I wish papa were here."

"Oh, so do I."

"But anyway I brought you my sugar ration." From the pocket

of his pyjama jacket Alexis produced a small white linen package and handed it to Olga. "That's my handkerchief for tomorrow morning," he said anxiously. "It's perfectly clean."

It was, but the effect was somewhat spoiled by the collection of assorted nails which the Czarevich, an inveterate hoarder, had wrapped up with two cubes of beet sugar, and Olga stifled a giggle.

"Are the nails for me too?"

"No, just the sugar. Don't you want to eat it now?"

"You eat one bit and I'll save the other for my last cup of coffee. You're sweet, Alexis, but honestly Monsieur Gilliard will have a fit if he comes up and finds you're not in bed."

"All right." Alexis crunched contentedly. Then he flung one arm round Olga's neck and gave her a sugary goodnight kiss. His lips were close to her ear when she heard him whisper, "I don't like Father Grigori very much myself!"

When he had gone she settled down to *Resurrection,* which the librarian had thoughtfully sent up to her room.

"The cell in which Maslova was imprisoned," she read, "was a long room twenty-one feet long and sixteen feet wide, occupied by fifteen persons. Two-thirds of the room was taken up by shelves used as beds. By the door there was a dark spot on the floor on which stood a stinking tub—" She laid the book down in disgust. So those were the conditions of women prisoners, politicals or criminals, on the long road to Siberia! The dimensions of the room she shared with her sister were almost exactly the same as the den occupied by Maslova and her fourteen companions in misfortune. But this beautiful room, into which Rasputin with his foul breath had stumbled, affected Olga now as something like a prison cell. She threw her hospital cape round her shoulders and went into the broad gallery, warm with the sunset light.

Alexis was not the only wakeful one among the imperial children. The door of the Little Pair's bedroom was ajar, and through it Olga could hear Anastasia, in a very good imitation of her own voice, declaiming:

" 'You are dismissed for a grave breach of trust, and if I ever hear of you in the imperial service at any time or place, I'll have you flogged.' " The dramatic pause was filled by Marie's uncontrollable giggle.

It was a great temptation to go in and say "I don't think it's very kind of you to imitate your own sister!" but Olga conquered it. The complaint would be so exactly in their mother's tone of martyrdom, and after all, what did it matter? She went on, past the two men on duty at the entrance to the bedroom corridor, to the top of the main staircase of the Alexander Palace.

In Quarenghi's beautiful Palladian design the two wings of the palace, the one occupied by the Czar and his family, the other by the suite and by occasional guests, were joined on the outside by a colonnade and an enormous paved court and on the inside by the State apartments which were so seldom used. Only a few chandeliers were lighted above the well of the stairs, and the vast rooms of state were dark, but when the Grand Duchess appeared on the staircase lights sprang up above her head; and hands in white cotton gloves carried candelabra from room to room until at last each one was brilliantly lit, to honour the passage or anticipate the whim of a girl in a cotton dress, with a nurse's cape lying loose on her young shoulders.

Olga entered the great Crimson Hall. The Cossacks and the footmen were already there, immobile, brought at her approach from their supper or their wine, sixteen of them ordered by fours against the marble walls. She walked slowly beneath the portraits of the reigning empresses, Catherine I, Anna, Elizabeth, Catherine II, who had all done better for Russia than most of the men who followed them. And among the Russians there was a stranger face, not strange to Olga, although it was younger far in the picture than in the photograph which always stood on her mother's writing table. It was a state portrait of her English great-grandmother, Queen Victoria.

Queen at eighteen. A constitutional monarch, bred to that idea of democracy Olga often heard her own father deride. Who told her prime minister on the day of her accession—their English tutor had taught Olga the words—"It has long been my intention to retain the present ministry at the head of affairs." What calm, what self-possession! Supposing Victoria had had to say "It has long been my intention to retain Rasputin at the head of affairs"?

Never.

The great entrance doors, meant for ambassadors, were swung open as Olga approached. And now a major-domo, or a chamberlain, or some minor functionary with a gold chain of office round his neck was bowing, and asking if he should send for a limousine—

"No thank you. No."

She crossed the courtyard in the shadow of the great nude statues of games players, which they called Babochnik and Svayachnik, and walked slowly towards the palace gate. It was a beautiful white night, still rosy in the west, and the sky above as purple as the lilac blossom she had gathered the day before with Simon Hendrikov. The guards at the gate could see her coming; she heard the words of command rapped out by a sergeant, and saw a young officer emerging hurriedly from the guard house on the other side of the public avenue. For a moment she hoped that by one chance in a thousand Simon Hendrikov was the commander of the guard. Then, as the great gates with her father's monogram on the grilles swung slowly open, she recognised another man and stood still as he saluted her.

"Happy to serve Your Imperial Highness!" he said breathlessly. "May my men have the honour of providing an escort to the hospital?"

The word roused Olga from her reverie. "No thank you, Captain Vlashkov," she said with a smile. "I'm not going to the hospital, not just yet. In fact I'm not going anywhere. Good night!"

She turned away, hearing the clink of swords in scabbards and the clang as the gates were shut at her back. And Olga Nicolaievna walked towards the palace where lights sprang up at the passing of a girl who wasn't going anywhere, with the sick conviction that they were all bound hell-for-leather on the road to nowhere.

* * *

"At four o'clock, you say, my granddaughter comes off duty?" The agreeable, coaxing voice of the Empress Dowager came along the telephone wires from Petrograd to the palace hospital at Czarskoe Selo. "No . . . no, princess, certainly not. I wouldn't dream of asking any privileges for her. Don't say anything until she's free. Then you might ask one of your assistants to tell her she is to come straight to me instead of returning to the Alexander Palace . . . What's that? Yes, I myself will inform Her Majesty. Just tell the Grand Duchess one of my own cars will be waiting to bring her here. . . . Thank you very much, princess. . . . What a noble work you are doing for our brave men."

The Empress Dowager listened with a smile to the farewells, dictated by protocol, of the chief surgeon of the palace hospital, and laid down the telephone. She had got her own way again, as she had been getting it for nearly fifty years—ever since a pert little princess, born Dagmar of Denmark, had arrived in St. Petersburg as the bride of the future Czar Alexander III. A beautiful dancer, a superb skater, she had been dancing and skating over all the trials and difficulties of her great position from that day forward, and although she had always kept aloof from politics she had more political sense in her little finger than her daughter-in-law the Czarina had in her whole mystical and muddled brain.

It was only half past two, at least two hours before Olga could be with her, but the Empress Dowager, ramrod straight at sixty-eight, had never yielded to the temptation of an afternoon nap. Before she left the desk where her telephone stood she wrote several letters, and carefully re-read the evening paper which had prompted her telephone call to the palace hospital. Then with a lady-in-waiting she walked for some time in the gardens of the Anitchkov Palace, her city home for many years—the Anitchkov, that world within a world, with the vibrant life of Petrograd flowing past it on one side, along the Nevski Prospekt, and the Fontanka Canal flowing past Quarenghi's splendid portico on the other.

Marie Feodorovna had never been as beautiful as her sister Alexandra, now the Dowager Queen of England, but she had what the French called *du chien*: a lively little face with large dark eyes, a twenty-inch waist still, and a great deal of attraction. She had never relaxed into old ladyhood, nor into boudoirs and negligées, and she was trim and erect in a plain black dress with a pearl 'dog collar' when she sailed across the carpet of the Red Drawing-room to greet her granddaughter with a kiss.

"Now tell me what you've been doing, you naughty girl, to get your name in the papers!"

"*My* name in the newspapers?" Olga looked genuinely astounded. "Granny—is it something to do with my Soldiers' Committee?"

"Committee indeed! It's something to do with that awful man Rasputin! You didn't know? Read this."

Olga read, on the front page of *Vechernaia Vremia,* an editorial complimenting her on having 'the clarity of vision and the energy' to take the advice consistently given by the Suvorin group of newspapers and 'banish the charlatan Rasputin from the imperial palaces'.

"Banish!" said Olga. "Palaces! He'll be back."

"I'm afraid he will, he or another like him. Rasputin is not the first, you know. Are you old enough to remember Philippe Vachod?"

"Monsieur Philippe, the Frenchman? Who gave mamma a bell that rang when evil influences came anywhere near her? She has it still."

"No doubt," sniffed Marie Feodorovna. "But my concern is with you, Olga. It's most unpleasant to see my grandchild's name all over the front page of a rag like this—and heaven knows what *Grashdanin* and *Rech* will make of your exploit. You had better tell me yourself what happened."

As she described Rasputin's invasion of her bedroom, Olga had the pleasure of seeing anger take possession of her grandmother's little crumpled face, and ended triumphantly:

"Anyway I don't care, I've got father on my side!"

"You've heard from him? Your mother told me she had telegraphed."

Olga took a crumpled telegram from the pocket of her apron and held it out. The Empress Dowager read aloud:

" 'My girlie must remember all Our Friend has done for Sunbeam and forgive his mistake, which will not be repeated. Kiss mamma, sisters, Baby from loving old papa, and be agooweeone.' H'm! That's clear enough, at all events." She peered again at the telegram through her gold lorgnette. "Is that an English word, *agooweeone?*"

"Four English words, it means 'a good wee one'. Don't you remember, that's what mother used to say to Alexis when he really was a baby, 'Sleep well, and be agooweeone'?"

"Yes, but your father needn't telegraph to you as if *you* were a baby. It doesn't matter! He obviously means to send Rasputin away this time."

"Does he? I only hope you're right, grandmamma."

"Your mother knows about this telegram?"

"It arrived before breakfast, and she read it first."

"I talked to Tatiana too, this afternoon. She said your mother refused even to see you before you went to hospital."

"It was all my fault!" cried generous Olga. "I said far too much yesterday, I was so angry about Rasputin, and I made her ill. She has one of her terrible headaches today."

"Or a backache, or a stomach ache, or pains in all her limbs. There never was a greater sufferer than your poor mother. Oh, I knew how it would be, when she and Nicky were engaged! She had to go off at once to take a cure for rheumatism at Harrogate. And a few months later, when she came to us at Livadia, when your dear grandpapa was dying, she complained all the time of pains in her legs. Pains in her legs indeed! A young princess, twenty-two years old, does not permit herself to have pains *anywhere,* when the ruler of her future country is passing away!"

"But you're such a Spartan, grandmamma! Mother tells us her health was ruined by having five babies, so close together, and nursing us all."

"I had a large family too, and I was never a penny the worse for it . . . Of course I ate raw ham," said the Empress Dowager reflectively.

"Raw *ham*?"

"Every day, before I got out of bed. It's the best thing in the world for morning sickness. Remember that, my dear, when your time comes."

"I don't believe my time will ever come."

"No? Well, we'll see about that, and as quickly as we can, too. But now ring for tea, Olga, I know you always enjoy an Anitchkov tea; at least you did when you were in the schoolroom. And take off your veil so that I can see your hair. H'm! When did you last have it properly dressed?"

A retinue of servants brought in tea tables and trays, and while they were in the room the old empress contented herself with saying, in French:

"How do you suppose the story of what happened yesterday appeared in the papers today?"

"I've been wondering about that."

"Which young lady was in the room with you at the time?"

Olga told her. "But she would never have given the story to the press," she said. "She wouldn't know how to, any more than I do."

"No, I don't believe she would. The general—impossible. One of the Cossacks?"

"I think it probably was the fair-haired footman. I sent him away too, you see."

The Empress Dowager smiled. "I didn't know that. Dismissing the staff—no wonder your mamma was angry."

"He betrayed his trust," said Olga obstinately.

"Yes, well, that can't be helped now. What I'm concerned with is *your* future. First of all, I'm not going to have you exposed, day after day, to your mother's sighs and sulks."

"Mother can't help sighing and sulking, it's in her nature."

"I know it is." Marie Feodorovna closed her lips firmly on what she wanted to say, which was, 'And I've had to put up with her sulks for twenty-five years, ever since poor Nicky fell in love with her. Especially after she came among us as his wife, determined to set the Family at loggerheads, and snub the whole of Petersburg society!' Reminding herself that Olga was the woman's daughter, and that the woman, according to her lights, was a most devoted mother, she contented herself with saying, "She inherited her difficult nature from your other grandmamma, Princess Alice. All that religious fervour, all that wild enthusiasm for some 'man of God' or another, all that domineering tactlessness—" She pulled herself up short.

"Did you know my other grandmamma?"

"Yes, quite well, when my sister Alix was first married and living in England. Queen Victoria used to be very cross with Alice of Hesse, until of course her tragic death sanctified *her*. But all that doesn't concern *you*, my dear. I only want to see you happily married, and established in a home of your own."

"Easier said than done, granny dear."

"That sounds rather melancholy. You don't regret sending away the Rumanian prince?"

"Oh *no*!"

"I'm glad, I could never picture you in Bucharest. Olga Nicolaievna to be the future queen of that semi-Oriental, self-indulgent little country—!"

"Married to that semi-Oriental, self-indulgent boy."

"Your mother pressed it because of the Orthodox religion, didn't she?"

"I suppose so."

"Does the faith you were baptised in mean a great deal to you?"

"If you mean the Christian faith, it does. If you mean the

Orthodox form of worship, I don't think it means any more than the Lutheran service did to you, when you gave up your church to marry my grandfather."

"I wish to heaven," said the Empress Dowager piously, "that your mother's conscience, all those years ago, had been as accommodating as yours. After all, as I used to say to her, what do the rites matter? It's only another way of worshipping our Saviour. You agree? Then, my darling, let me tell you about a little plan I've made for us. You've been nursing for nearly a year without a break. It's June, the best time for a trip to Denmark. Suppose you and I take a little holiday, and visit Copenhagen? It's a long time since you've seen your Danish relatives."

"Granny, you're sweet, but I can't give up the hospital just because you think I need a holiday."

"And then we might spend a week or two in London. You could do even more good in London than you're doing here," said the old lady cunningly. "The English know so little about Russia. Or rather, what they do know is all bad propaganda, spread by that wretched Socialist, Ramsay MacDonald. You see I realise what is going on! If you were there, the eldest daughter of the Czar, going about with Queen Mary to all those wonderful public works of hers, meeting the people who count—the Ministers—the generals—you would show them another side of Russia, wouldn't you?"

"Possibly. And among the people who count, would you include the Prince of Wales?"

"He's at the front with his regiment, my sister writes."

"But if you and Queen Alexandra asked especially, he could be brought home at a day's notice, couldn't he?" Olga laughed. She got up and kissed her grandmother's delicately powdered cheek. "Oh darling, you never give up! I believe you're still trying to make a match between me and poor David of Wales."

Marie Feodorovna caught at Olga's hand, noted automatically that the nails were untended, and whispered,

"To see you Queen of England, Olga! My dream ever since you were born!"

Olga pulled her chair closer to her grandmother's. "Listen, dear," she said, "I told my father I would never marry away from Russia. And now I know I can never marry without love. David was fifteen and I was fourteen when we were last in England, that time at Cowes; what possible feelings, grown-up feelings, could there have been between us two? Now he's twenty-one, and I'm nearly twenty; and if our families make us marry, then we're forced into a loveless marriage—just as Aunt Ducky was forced in her first marriage, or poor Aunt Olga with the Prince of Oldenburg. Haven't you see enough of that, granny, close to home? Oh, I know you were one of the lucky ones. You accepted the man your parents chose, and you've often told me you and grandpapa were happy together. But it doesn't always work out that way, and this is 1915, after all, not 1866. The Prince of Wales only wants to get himself into the firing line, I'm sure he doesn't want to marry now, and I'm also sure the King and Queen won't force him into marriage."

"If they don't, they may live to regret it," said Marie Feodorovna. "Princes and princesses should marry young, it's their first duty, and if Georgie and May don't arrange the right match for that boy soon, he may lead them a pretty dance when he grows older."

"I'm sure I'm not the right match, granny dear."

The Empress Dowager sighed. "I only want you to take a little time and think it over. But in the meantime, here's what I want you to do—"

She asked Olga to spend a month with her at the Anitchkov Palace. It was too tiring for a girl, going from hospital to those endless committee meetings, those visits to refugee shelters, those charity performances; and then there were the battleship launchings, two within the next two weeks. Why stay at home to be scolded and treated like a child? It would be so convenient to be in Petrograd. "And it would be company for me," the old lady said wistfully. The girl realised that she was lonely with her elderly court in the enormous palace.

"Granny, you're very sweet to ask me, but I can't give up my job, even to please you. It would be deserting, just like a soldier at the front."

"You make too much of that most unsuitable 'job', as you call it."

"Perhaps I do. Tania's a better nurse than I am, and I think Marie'll be better than both of us, when she starts next September. But I've got to go on trying—"

"Don't be ridiculous, child. There are ten hospitals in

Petrograd where you can give your services for a few weeks, if it means so much to you, and I know a dozen young ladies who'd be delighted to take your place at the Catherine Palace. You might very well spend every morning at the British Red Cross hospital; that would please our Allies, and Dmitri would like it too, I'm sure."

A lovely smile brightened Olga's face. "Dmitri's hospital!" she said slowly. "I'd forgotten that. Yes, that might work out very well."

The Empress Dowager fiddled with the gold watchguard looped into her black silk belt. "Olga," she said, "is there a definite reason for your wishing not to leave Russia? You've been looking very happy lately. You ought to look exhausted, and I must say your grooming has been shamefully neglected, and yet you're prettier than ever. Almost as if you were in love. Do tell me, Olga—is it Dmitri?"

"Dmitri and I are the best of friends. But there's no more between us than that, nor ever will be."

"I know when you were children your parents thought it would be a happy match for you."

"It didn't work out that way," said Olga lightly. "Remember Dmitri's four years older than I am. As we grew up, his fancy fell on my cousin Irina, not on me."

"But she preferred Felix Yusupov, I don't know why."

"Felix and Irina seem to be very happy, and now they've got a dear little girl. Mashka's perfectly foolish about that baby! What does it feel like to be a great-grandmother?"

"It makes me feel like an ancestor, my dear. And don't try to change the subject, we were talking about you."

"We *are* having a heart to heart, aren't we? Please, granny, don't plan any more marriages for me. I don't want Dmitri, I don't want the Prince of Wales, I don't want awful Carol—"

"Then what *do* you want?"

"Only to be loved."

II

THE SUNLIGHT OF THE white nights still lingered over Petrograd, but inside 'The Red Sarafan' it might well have been midwinter. The little restaurant was always dark, lit only by oil lamps and occasionally by candles, and always crowded for half the day and half the night.

Above the door on a little alley, not much cleaner or more inviting than the alley which housed The Children's Castle, a street sign swung. It was the kind of sign which elsewhere in that district of illiterates showed the wares the wretched shops were selling, but instead of a leg of pork or a loaf of bread the restaurant sported a painting of a buxom peasant girl wearing a scarlet sarafan, a bright pinafore dress with shoulder straps over an embroidered blouse. The girl was laughing; a handkerchief was tied over her fair hair, and her strong arms were akimbo. It was an image which had no relation to the regular customers of 'The Red Sarafan', who were almost all undernourished, unhealthy and discontented.

They were also noisy. There was always somebody holding forth at 'The Red Sarafan', somebody reciting his own poetry (usually beginning with exclamations like 'Howl!' 'Kill!' 'Dogs!') or somebody singing to the balalaika; and the noise of the performers and the critics round the wine-stained tables made it possible for many private conversations to go on in the alcoves at the back of the room. There on a summer night sat a square-shouldered man who looked better fed than any other there, who indeed had put on weight since the winter: the editor of *Castle Comments*, Jacob Levin.

He had just refilled the glass of his secretary, Mara Trenova, who had joined him, hot and thirsty, a few minutes before.

"Feeling better?" he said indulgently.

"Much."

"You looked as if you needed that. Everything cleared away at the office?"

"Sergiev was just locking up when I left."

"Good." It was the evening of press day, they had earned their glass of wine.

"Jacob, I've got something to tell you."

He had something to tell her too, but you couldn't beat Trenova. She *had* to talk first, blurt out whatever was in her mind; it was one reason why Levin had given her so many black marks on her last report.

"What is it, Mara?"

"My mother's going to spend the rest of the summer in the country."

"Where in the country?"

"Oh, not too far from here. At Koivisto in Finland, the Hendrikovs have a dacha there. It seems they've taken pity on my mother, so lonely, daughter out at work all day—"

"And half the night, eh?"

"—And so they've asked her to keep the place open, keep it tidy, be a sort of housekeeper in fact, just for the professor and his wife. Dolly won't be going there this summer, she's too busy nursing."

"Meantime Dolly's brother is rising in the world."

"Rising, how?"

Levin flicked his thumb and finger at the evening paper, folded at the programme of tomorrow's ceremony, the launching of the battle cruiser *Poltava* at the Vassili Island yards. "In the suite of HIM the Czar," he read aloud, "HH the Grand Duke Dmitri Pavlovich, ADC; Admiral Nilov, Commander Sablin; in the suite of HIH the Grand Duchess Olga, Madame This, Countess That, Lieutenant Simon Hendrikov."

"That old snob of a professor will be overjoyed," said Mara.

"You're not very civil to your mother's benefactor. But what about you? Shall you stay on all by yourself in the Yamskaia?"

"Yes, of course, I've nowhere else to go."

"That might have certain definite advantages." Levin yawned, stretched his legs, and shouted to the panting waitress to bring more wine.

"Mara, let's get down to business. Here's *my* news. I'm off to Moscow at the end of next week—no, not on a business trip—for good."

"Jacob, why?" He saw her eyes dilate in the candlelight, and that was all.

"Two reasons. One, now that it's official about the Second Category, I mean the call-up in September, I stand a fair chance of being combed out and sent off to the marshes round Lake Naroch, mutilated hand and all. Two, that our publisher and boss has had a strong hint from a friend across the river, you know, in that establishment near Peter and Paul, that *Castle Comments* ought to suspend publication for a while."

"But why to Moscow?"

"Ah yes, that's reason three. The Party thinks I'll be more useful there than here."

"Will you take me with you, Jacob?"

"I think the Party may have other plans for you."

"I'm not a member of the Party. I'm perfectly free to look for a position with some other publication, or anywhere I can find a job."

"Oh no, you're not."

His maimed hand fastened on hers with the touch she found perversely exciting, and beyond the spear of candlelight Mara saw the crowded room swinging in a maze of heat.

"Listen," said Levin, "there's no need to drag this out. When Rostov recruited you at the Xenia he sent you to me because he thought Ivan Trenov's daughter, full of fire and guts, might have considerable revolutionary potential. My first job was to kick all that SR nonsense out of you—the heroines of *Narodna Volnia*, the Czaricides, and all the beloved comrades whose names have been consigned to oblivion by most of us. You learned fast enough, and it's only a matter of time till you can be accepted as a Party member. But in another way you've been a disappointment. You turned out to be useless as a comrade for direct action."

"Give me time," said Mara resentfully.

"You've had six months. And I knew you would be hopeless with a gun the first time I took you out to the marshes for target practice—remember?"

Mara looked away. She remembered the winter Sunday, and the long tramcar ride along the main road, lined with wooden houses which grew shabbier with every verst, on the way to the Finnish frontier. And then the waste land, half marsh and half scrub pine and birch, where they were out of earshot, out of sight of anything but the shore ice of the Gulf of Finland, and all her limbs seemed to freeze as she stood there firing at the target, with only the Nagan in her hand for warmth. She remembered the dingy *traktir*, half way to the city, where coarse food and contraband vodka had warmed her as if she were recovering from frostbite. There Levin had taken her to bed, and the surrender of her virginity, which she had anticipated as a moment of romance and beauty, had become a brutal, painful struggle in a room with dirty blankets and a red-hot stove. Yes, she remembered the marshes.

"You're no use at all with firearms," Levin repeated. "You couldn't hit a barn door at ten paces, and as for throwing a hand grenade, you can't even throw a tennis ball! Admit it now, if you were to stand outside the Vassili-Ostrov works tomorrow, when the Czar and his retinue go by, what chance would you have of eliminating any one of them? Even the little Grand Duchess—or her ADC?"

"I thought the Party line was against assassination, for the present."

"It is, because we want Nicholas the Bloody to work out his own damnation. But you couldn't pull the trigger, could you now?"

She shook her head.

"And then that night at the Okhta Works—you lost your head and made a scene in the street, just because you'd seen young Stepan blown to pieces when he placed the charges wrong! A kid you hardly knew, and yet you were sobbing and carrying on because Stepan had the guts to give his life so that children not born yet would have a better life than ours—"

Mara crushed down the thought of the children who had been killed in the Okhta disaster, when the fire licked through the workers' tenements across the Neva. She said painfully:

"You've said all that before, Jacob. You only want to go on punishing me because I went home that night with Joseph Calvert—"

"And how many nights since then?

"Not so very many. Joe Calvert is really what you try to be—a dedicated professional. His job comes first, and I come nowhere, so there's no cause at all to be jealous."

"Jealous!" said Levin, and his coarse face crinkled in a smile. "Trenova, you could go to bed with half the Baltic Fleet for all I care! If you like going to bed with me, fine, but it doesn't give us any claim on one another. We're comrades in the struggle, and that's all."

"In that case," said Mara, trying to keep her voice steady, "I think it's time I went home. I'll come in to the office tomorrow morning, and pick up my wages."

"Sit down," said Levin, dragging her roughly backwards as she rose, "I haven't finished talking to you. Drink your wine and listen to me."

Mara picked at the fastening of her shabby satchel, her head lowered.

"You can't be allowed to walk out with your nose in the air, like some little bourgeoise stenographer whose sister's husband has found her a job in one of the Ministries. You know too much. You're in it with us now."

"You can trust to my discretion, Jacob, absolutely."

"I trust nobody. I watched you making your discoveries—oh, you were sharp enough for that! You looked like a cat with a saucer of cream when you found out about the messages from Lenin going out to the cells in the provinces along with the candy classics, tucked in between the pages of *Pikovaya Dama* and *Voina i Mir*. And then the code in the *Comments*, in the Letters to the Editor—how did you find that out, by the way?"

"I worked out all those page and paragraph references for myself."

"You see? You're sharp enough, as long as we keep you away from firearms. Now here is what you do. You come in tomorrow and get your money, just as you said. In the evening we have a final celebration in my room at the Hotel du Nord, before the train leaves for Moscow. You have a couple of days to see your mother off to Finland, and on Monday you start your new job at *Pravda*."

"But I don't want to work for *Pravda*! *Pravda*'s liable to be raided any day!"

"No, they'll be in the clear for a bit, now that the editor's been sent to Siberia, along with the Bolshevik Five. There's practically a new staff at *Pravda*, and they need all the help they can get. I've recommended you as an editorial assistant, chiefly on the strength of those fillers you've been writing for *Comments*. You've got a flair for that sort of thing—that and caption writing. You'll get on all right." Levin slapped his pockets, feeling for his cigarettes.

"What if I absolutely refuse to work for *Pravda*? It's a Bolshevik paper. And I'm not a Party member."

"You will be," he said. "And you won't be going among strangers. I've fixed a job for Sergiev, quite a good one. He doesn't mean to be a copyboy for ever."

"I hoped I was going to see the last of Sergiev tomorrow. Frankly, Jacob, he makes my flesh creep—"

"That's too bad, because he'll be there to keep an eye on you. Sergiev reports on you, you report on Sergiev, and the Party member on the staff reports on both of you. That's how it's done, my dear, and very effective too: now let's have something to eat and another bottle."

Which was possibly why Mara Trenova was loitering, next morning, with two weeks' salary from The Children's Castle in her purse, at the Vassili Island end of the Nicholas Bridge. For during the leisurely drinking of the second bottle of Crimean wine, which along with the heat and noise of 'The Red Sarafan' had made her head spin more than ever, Jacob Levin had talked so much about firearms, her own inefficiency with firearms, and the uselessness of firearms in getting rid of all the evils which preyed on the workers of Russia, that Mara had come, almost in a state of trance, to the place where she could see the Czar's procession pass from the launching of the battle cruiser *Poltava* from the Vassili-Ostrov yards. As usual, neither the time of the launching nor the route to be taken had been announced in the press, but the island site narrowed the possibilities of arrival and departure, and Mara had guessed correctly that the carriages and the cavalry would not cross the new Palace Bridge. So she left the tram herself at the Admiralty stop, and walked down river and across to the island by the Nicholas Bridge, which Dolly Hendrikova and she had once known so well as the way back to the Xenia School after a holiday. She knew she had guessed right when she saw the crowd of spectators behind the police cordon. 'They' had gone by, an old apple-seller told her, but 'They' would be coming back this way again; and Mara stood on the kerb and reckoned how many paces it was from there to the carriageway, and at what moment some better marksman than herself would raise his gun and fire.

Her head was splitting, between the effects of last night's wine and her loathing of the night ahead (but it would be the last night) in Levin's shabby room in the old Hotel du Nord, opposite the Nicholas Station, where so many revolutionaries had lived under so many aliases, and her dread of the future. She had been expecting carriages and Cossacks, and the motors came up so quietly that she almost missed the Czar as he went past, saluting mechanically, with smudges so dark beneath his eyes that they looked like bruises.

"Retreat, retreat—how can the Little Father smile?" growled a man in the crowd, but the cheerful applewoman called out, "Look at the sweetings! Look at the lovely couple!" and Mara realised that the noise coming up with the hoofbeats was one name, shouted by five thousand shipbuilders, suddenly unanimous:

"Ol-ga! Ol-ga! Ol-ga!"

The Grand Duchess Olga, flushed with success, was driving in an open motor car with her cousin the Grand Duke Dmitri Pavlovich. She had a bouquet of flowers in her lap, and one white-gloved hand waved steadily at the crowd. At her grandmother's desire she wore a very small hat, so that her face could be seen, and she remembered to look up, from time to time, at the windows of the high buildings on the embankment, where students and office-workers, not all of them friendly, had waited to see the Czar go past. Olga's was a new face to them, a young and pretty face, a change from the sour, set faces they knew too well, and some of them applauded, even against their will.

"*She* launched the battleship," said a well-informed man in the surging crowd round Mara Trenova. "The workers asked for her, at the last minute. Said they thought she'd bring good luck—"

"Can't bring any worse luck than *he* does!" said a cynic.

"Look at her with her best boy, will you?" cried the applewoman. "When's the wedding, lovey dear?"

The Grand Duke Dmitri, overhearing, took Olga's free hand in his own and sketched a kiss. He was easily the handsomest young man in the Family, tall, with regular features and thick blond hair, and the one who most resembled the Czar Alexander II, the liberator of the serfs. He grinned companionably at his cousin as the car turned right on the Nicholas Bridge, and told her she looked wonderful, had risen to the unexpected occasion at the launching 'like a real trouper', and God! how he could use a drink.

The watching faces disappeared from the windows facing the Neva, the crowd scattered, the show was over. But Mara Trenova, when the carriageway was clear, walked out from the kerb into the middle of the street and calculated that for any marksman who, unlike herself, could hit a barn door at ten paces, the distance would have been ten paces—exactly.

* * *

The Czar, who knew the jealous scene his wife would make if he stayed in the city to lunch with his mother, drove straight back to eat consommé and mutton cutlets at Czarskoe Selo. In Olga's honour, her grandmother had arranged a luncheon for thirty guests in the Anitchkov Palace, with a *zakuski* table filled to overflowing for the gentlemen, and sprays of Crimean roses at each lady's place. The launching of the *Poltava* was not needed as the excuse for a party, because the pleasure-loving old lady had given several such luncheons since her granddaughter had come for a holiday to Petrograd. She obstinately called it a holiday, for although Olga spent four hours every day on duty in the wards of the hospital on the Palace Quay and three in the committee rooms of the Winter Palace, there was time for hairdressers and manicurists and above all dressmakers to be brought in bevies to the Anitchkov. Olga accepted all they did for her with pleasure: she knew, as one female to another, that it was her grandmother's way of spiting the Czarina, who—as the older empress said with a sniff—"always dressed those poor dear girls as if they were an English parson's daughters".

Olga enjoyed the party, as she enjoyed everything these days. Her grandmother invited girls of her own age, and their brothers or young husbands at home on leave, to all of whom she was her friendly, lively self. The younger generation went home and told their parents that Olga Nicolaievna was very different from what her mother had been, years ago; and it was high time that casual charmer, Dmitri Pavlovich, took himself in hand, just as his bosom friend Prince Felix Yusupov had done, and settled down to matrimony with that delightful girl. Before the launching lunch was over there were knowing smiles on many faces when

Dmitri took Olga into one of the window bays to admire the view over the Fontanka Canal, which both knew by heart. But there was nothing loverlike in what the Grand Duke said:

"What time d'you come off duty tomorrow, Olga?"

"Twelve o'clock as usual, why?"

"Could you come down and see me when you're free? I won't keep you long. Olga, I've *got* to talk to you alone. Not in a mob like this."

"But my father's going back to the Stavka at Baranovichi tomorrow morning early. Aren't you going too?"

"Well, that's just it. There may not *be* any Baranovichi by tomorrow."

"Oh, my God," she said. "The German advance! Is it so bad?"

"So bad the C-in-C is thinking of moving the Stavka to the Dnieper river."

"I'll join you as soon after twelve noon as I can."

"Thank you, dear."

Olga took her leave of the company and went to change her dress. It was one of her grandmother's orders that she was not to drive through the city in her nurse's uniform, which was to be kept at the hospital, just as her grandmother had ordained that on public occasions the Grand Duchess was to be accompanied by two ladies-in-waiting ("And *young* ladies," she insisted, "not some of those old frumps of your mother's, stumbling about and peering through their spectacles") and also by an ADC. It had been the simplest thing in the world to persuade the Czar that a devoted former member of his own bodyguard, Lieutenant Simon Hendrikov, was just the right person to be his daughter's ADC.

Once inside the Winter Palace, it was also a simple matter to shake off the ladies-in-waiting. They too were involved in committee work for the different war charities, and in that great warren of the Romanovs most of the committee members spent their time hunting about for meetings which might be held in any of the thousand rooms. The Malachite Hall was their final rendezvous, and provided Olga was there at the end of the afternoon, pensively inspecting the famous door knobs made of great red balls of garnet held by golden claws, or looking at her reflection in the Empress Anna's bridal mirror, no lady would have dared to question where she had been in the meantime.

Within an hour of her arrival from the Empress Dowager's luncheon, she was leaving the Winter Palace by an unpatrolled staircase which led to the doorway of the New Hermitage.

Simon Hendrikov watched her coming down the steps, in the shadow of the ten grey granite monolithic figures which guarded that doorway, and thought how slim and light she looked by contrast, and how clever she had been to wear an inconspicuous summer dress, grey-green like carnation leaves, and a hat with a veil of the same shade. He hoped he was equally inconspicuous in the undress uniform of the Garde Equipage, with a flat cap, and without the aiguillettes of an acting ADC. Olga was his only concern, that day and always, as he stepped forward to salute her, and to refrain, with difficulty, from kissing the laughing face so nearly on a level with his own.

"I did it! I did it! I don't have to be back until five o'clock! Now we can go for a real walk!"

"You're sure you'll be all right?"

"Of course. Who's going to recognise me, dressed like this?"

"Half Petrograd saw you this morning, it seems to me."

"Yes, but people were expecting to see me then, they aren't now," she answered sensibly. "Hurry, Simon! We ought to get away from here!"

"This way, then." He led her down from the river front of the palace, where the sentries were on duty, along the side of the Winter Canal, between the great buildings and out to the Millionnaia. He felt better when they were away from that princely street and crossing the vast Square where her ancestor, Alexander I, stood high on his column. There were a great many men about, coming and going to the General Staff Headquarters with portfolios under their arms, none of whom gave a second glance to the young officer and the girl by his side.

Olga looked over her shoulder at the Winter Palace. "It looks so different from here," she said. "I wish they hadn't painted it that hideous shade of ox-blood red."

"My father says Rastrelli meant it to be porcelain blue."

"Rastrelli was crazy about porcelain blue, look at the Catherine hospital. Aren't you glad to be away from there?"

"As long as I can be in Petrograd with you."

"Petrograd!" she said. "Imagine being free to *walk* along the Nevski Prospekt, and when the shops are open, too!"

They had emerged on the great avenue at the level of the Police Bridge over the Moika Canal, and Olga looked longingly at a cinema on the far side of the street.

"Is that the only cinema in Petrograd?" she asked.

"No, there's another one. The Parisiana and the Piccadilly, they're called. I don't know why they both have foreign names."

"Allied names, at least. And where's the Astoria Hotel?"

"It's at the far end of the Morskaia."

"I suppose we couldn't go there and have tea?"

"Good heavens, *no!*"

Olga laughed. "It's all right," she said, "I realise you think people would know me there. And I don't really want tea, I only wanted to look inside. I remember three years ago, when the Astoria was opened, I nearly broke my heart because they wouldn't let me go to the gala dinner with the British Ambassador and Lady Georgina Buchanan. Oh well! This is much more fun, isn't it?"

And Simon, touched and adoring, wondered if there was another girl in Petrograd who was getting as much fun out of walking down the Nevski Prospekt on a fine summer day, amused at everything, and finding such ordinary things so new and strange. He felt increasingly confident that no one would recognise her, even when she stopped beside one of the street kiosks and mischievously pointed out a selection of postcard photographs of herself in nurse's uniform, all veil and white apron, with nothing but a tip-tilted nose and a firm chin turned to the camera to indicate the girl inside the dress.

"It doesn't do the Grand Duchess justice," he said hastily, and almost pulled her away from the stand. Olga said with a giggle, "Justice! It's a libel! Jaguelski really is a rotten photographer—he makes all of us look awful except my sister Tatiana, and nobody can spoil *her*."

"Nobody can spoil you, Princess." He didn't mean photography, and she knew it; she gave Simon the smile he loved before she turned away to identify, with delight, the famous English Shop which purveyed so many things to the imperial children, from picture puzzles and tennis balls to golden syrup for schoolroom tea and the round brown cakes of Pear's soap which had once been a feature of their bath time. `He got her past the Hotel Europa without incident, and then, of course, she wanted to cross the street and buy something, anything, in the bazaar called the Gostinnoi Dvor.

Simon was afraid, for her sake, of the old, rambling, two-storey building, with its warren of tiny shops dating from the eighteenth century. Unable to rid himself of the idea that they had been followed, he suggested that there were better shops in the Passage, only a few minutes' walk from where they stood. And there he led her, past a basement tearoom with cheap saffron buns in the window, and a men's outfitter showing shoddy summer suits, for the shops on the Nevski grew dustier and less inviting the nearer they came to the Fontanka Canal. But inside the Passage there was a perfumer's, and a jeweller's, and a shop with suede handbags in pastel colours, and there was a theatre, presenting *The Three Sisters*, and far down the Passage there was one of Petrograd's two cinemas, announcing a matinée performance of William Farnum in *Young Lochinvar.*

"A movie! An American movie! Oh, Simon, do let's go!"

He hadn't the faintest idea what the title meant, but Olga was quick: she looked at the stills in their glass case outside the door, and of course the lurid coloured bills were showing cowboys, one with a girl perched behind him on the saddle and the dust rising beneath the horses' hoofs.

"You can't want to see a show like this," he said.

"Oh, but I do. We never get to see a decent movie! Don't you remember those awful evenings at Livadia, in the riding school?"

"With 'short selected subjects for instruction and amusement'?"

"Selected by my dear mamma," she said, and Simon choked on a laugh. The Czarina's selections, and more particularly the cuts Her Majesty made in any item remotely romantic or exciting, had caused some ribald comment in the Guards' mess at Livadia. He realised that Olga for the first time had said 'mamma' instead of 'the Czarina'.

"We did once get to see Max Linder," he reminded her.

"Simon, I want to see *this* show! And hurry, it's going to start in five minutes!"

"Well, come inside the lobby, then, don't stand about outside." The lobby was empty. The woman in the little kiosk said the house was nearly full. But Simon was able to get two seats in the back row, with a chance of being seated on the aisle himself, and at least the house lights had been dimmed before they went inside.

It was amazing how many young people had preferred watching William Farnum to walking in the Summer Garden on such a fine afternoon. They applauded the pianist, coming in and settling her beads and bangles before attacking a tinny piano; they applauded frantically the extinguishing of all the lights as the credits began to roll up on the screen: William Farnum in *Young Lochinvar*, based on the famous poem by Sir Walter Scott. The distributors had balked at the expense of translating the sub-titles into Cyrillic characters, and the audience sat in docile ignorance until the picture began. And then it turned out to be a very simple story, as easy to understand in Calcutta as in Petrograd or in New York.

They saw the little dusty cow town in the Wild West, where a rancher forbade his only daughter to have any dealings with one of his cow hands,

"He's a low-livin', no-account coyote"

said the sub-title, and Simon whispered to Olga:

"You speak English, don't you?"

"I thought I did."

"Is that Farnum, the peasant?"

"S-sh."

Simon smiled. While the screen father ranted at his daughter, and told her she must marry another rancher,

"A great guy, with ten thousand head of cattle"

his eyes were for his princess and not for the star. She had folded back her veil, and her charming profile, nose tilted, lips parted, was lifted in complete absorption to the screen. Olga paid no attention to her surroundings, although the cinema was small, with hard wooden seats, and the atmosphere, thick enough to cut with a knife, was made up of sweat, scent, hair-oil, cachous and stale fish. There was enough light from the flickering images on the screen to show that most of the audience were boys in uniform, young enough to be the first draft of the Second Category, with their arms around their girls. Greatly daring, Simon slid his own arm behind Olga, cushioning the hard back of the unpadded seat, and to his joy she moved slightly towards him, so that he felt her slimness and her warmth against his side, while she never took her eyes from the screen.

A grand wedding was planned at the ranch house, beginning with a barn dance. The unwilling bride and her groom stood up together. William Farnum appeared in the doorway and told the scowling rancher that he claimed a dance.

"Let's you and me really show 'em how, honey"

was what the sub-title made the dashing cow hand say. He danced the girl through the open door, threw her on his saddle, jumped up in front of her, and rode away triumphant with his friends cavorting all around them.

"Young Lochinvar wins his bride!"

The show was over. The audience clapped and cheered, and Simon Hendrikov got the Grand Duchess Olga Nicolaievna through the lobby and into the Passage ahead of the stampede of her father's troops.

"Oh Simon! Oh! wasn't it heavenly! How I wish I could tell my sisters all about it!"

"You enjoyed it better than the short selected subjects?"

"Don't be silly, there's no comparison. William Farnum, wasn't he marvellous? I only wish I'd understood the words."

"They must have been in American."

"Probably. And now, before we go back—can't we just *walk* through the Gostinnoi Dvor?"

She was terribly persistent, with the Romanov persistence, but Simon still refused to take her up those ramshackle wooden stairs and through those crowded corridors where the exits were so few. Luckily, Olga was attracted by the outdoor booths, set between the wall of the bazaar and the trees on the verge of the Nevski Prospekt, and he followed her from one to another, from the ice-cream stalls to the soft drink stands, and from there to the little cart where a fat woman in a white apron was selling the meat patties called *pirozhki*.

"Simon, do look at the chocolate books!"

They were neatly arranged on a candy stall, the familiar slabs of chocolate tied by orange ribbons to the little books bound in greyish paper, and Simon said, "That's funny! I never saw them on sale in the bazaars before. My sisters and I used to buy them out of our pocket money, at a rather fancy confectioner's on the Island."

"I know, Konradi's. Aunt Olga used to have parcels of them sent from there, and we were given them when we went to lunch with her on Saturdays."

"Would you like to choose one now?"

"Oh please! But you choose, that used to be half the fun of it, having someone else choose, and not knowing what you would find inside."

"That's why they're bound in a plain paper."

Simon bought the packet on the top of the pile, and gave it to the smiling girl.

"Want to open it now, or wait until you get back—?" He couldn't say aloud "get back to the Winter Palace", but that was what he meant. The holiday afternoon was very nearly over.

"Now, of course, I can't wait." She untied the orange ribbon carefully and lifted the little book from the wrapped chocolate. "Lermontov's *Poems*, how gorgeous, they're my favourites. . . . Oh Simon, look!"

She was holding something out to him in the shadow of the trees, and he saw dismay invade the face which had been, for so short a time, so happy. He took the thing in his hand, the cartoon which had been folded between the leaves of Lermontov. It was a viciously clever drawing of a gigantic Rasputin, holding two tiny figures on his knees. One, in military uniform, with his face vacant above his beard, was the Czar Nicholas II. The other, wearing a crown, and a dress cut so low that her almost naked breasts were rubbing against Rasputin's tunic, was the Czarina.

They were both clutched in Rasputin's giant hands, shaped like claws. Underneath, four words were written:

"The Ruler of Russia."

* * *

"How dashing it feels," said the Grand Duchess Olga, "to be drinking champagne in a bachelor's apartments, and before luncheon too!"

"It would be more dashing still," suggested the Grand Duke Dmitri, "if you didn't mean to rush away to have lunch with your grandmamma."

"You think I ought to go on drinking champagne, and then spend the afternoon with you?"

"Something like that." The young man looked at his guest with amusement. She had arrived rather late; the bells of Peter and Paul, just across the Neva, had chimed the '*Kol slaven*' at midday, and two quarters, before Nurse Olga had come off the ward, changed out of uniform, and run down the private staircase of the palace he had turned into a hospital to Dmitri's own apartments on the ground floor. Now she was affecting sophistication, and quite delightfully. She had even complimented him on the big living-room—he refused to call it by any more formal name—which he had designed in collaboration with the men who had made the stage sets of the Imperial Russian Ballet famous in every civilized capital in Europe.

Dmitri had come back to the palace which his widowed father had left empty, following on a second and typically Romanov morganatic marriage, after the Czarina had made it clear that he was no longer a welcome inhabitant of the Alexander Palace at Czarskoe Selo. The cause of the trouble had been his intimacy with Prince Felix Yusupov, then a bachelor himself; 'decadent, and degenerate' being two of the mildest adjectives 'that German *hausfrau*', as he thought of her, had applied in their wild-oat days to Yusupov. So Dmitri Pavlovich had left his 'Uncle Nicky' and 'Aunt Alix', as he called the rulers who were in fact his cousins, and behold! Yusupov was now a model husband and father, and he, Dmitri, was about to appeal for help to the eldest of the long-legged girls who only yesterday were making sand-castles on the beach at Livadia. He respectfully offered his cigarette case to Olga Nicolaievna.

She was sitting in an armchair entirely covered with zebra skin, which unlike her mother's furniture had not come from the Tottenham Court Road, and which made a striking background to Olga's golden head. Dmitri touched the pale silk of her summer dress.

"Pretty frock," he said, "you do look so pretty since you came to Petrograd. Olga, don't you think it's time you gave up the hospital?"

"Stop nursing? Why on earth should I?"

"The men don't like it, and it's not fit work for you."

"But it *is* fit work for your own sister, Marisha, and my Aunt Olga at Kiev?"

"They both took up nursing to get away from Petrograd, Marisha because of her divorce and Olga Alexandrovna because she wanted to escape from a miserable marriage. But you and Tatiana are young girls, the daughters of the Czar, and please forgive me, Olga, 'cheapen' is a horrible word to use, but some of the men think it cheapens you to go among them as a servant, washing their feet and bandaging their wounds—"

"They haven't read their Bibles, then."

"They don't read the Bible, they kneel to their ikons. And they think the Czarina should be like an image in an ikon, all pearls and gold. They simply don't understand it when they see her in an apron and a veil."

"That's true enough," said Olga thoughtfully. "I remember at one of the first hospitals we ever visited, at Vilna I think it was, one of the wounded men called me over just as we were leaving the ward. And he said, 'Little sister, who's the old lady the boys carried in on their clasped hands?' I told him it was the Czarina, Alexandra Feodorovna, who was too lame to walk upstairs. He got quite angry. He said, 'You lie, little sister, everybody knows Alexandra wears cloth of gold, and lives in a palace eating off gold plate and praying for our souls: she wouldn't come here in an apron, like my old woman back home, to see the likes of us.' "

"You see?" said Dmitri.

"Yes, I do see, and I think it's very hard. If we did stay in our palaces and brought out the gold plate instead of our nice English china, you know what the left-wing press would make of that. If Tatiana and I empty slops, and go down on our knees to scrub floors, then we're told we're making ourselves too cheap. It's so unfair, so miserable, that everything we say or do is wrong!"

"I've never found it easy to be a Romanov."

"Oh, *you*!" she said resentfully. "Is that what you asked me to come here for, to give me a sermon about nursing?"

"No. Your father meant to telephone to you this morning. What did he say?"

"He only said he wasn't going back to Baranovichi."

"Right, and now tell me, how long are you going to stay at the Anitchkov?"

"Indefinitely, I imagine—why?"

He answered her obliquely. "You had a row with your mother about Rasputin, didn't you?"

"The biggest row of my life. But father patched it up when he came home."

"Of course. And what you did was splendid, Olga; the night

the newspapers reached GHQ with the story, we asked His Majesty's permission to drink your health."

"And he granted it?"

"Yes, he did."

"Sometimes I think I'll never understand him," said his daughter.

"But as I remember," said Dmitri, cautiously refilling Olga's glass, "you were rather fond of Grigori Efimovich, when you were a little kid."

"Yes, then, maybe, but not after I was old enough to understand his very convenient message: that the more you sin and the worse you sin, the more certain you are of redemption."

Dmitri laughed. "Olga, would you say I was crazy if I asked you to go back—oh, not tomorrow, but next week—to Czarskoe Selo?"

"But why?"

"Because the children need you, and because some of us are very worried about your father's health."

"Father isn't ill, is he, Dmitri?"

"It's not so much that he's ill as that he's taking medicines that make him ill."

"Badmaiev!" She spoke the name so loudly that Dmitri came quickly to her side and took the half-empty champagne glass from her suddenly limp hand. "Olga!" he said, "are you all right? I didn't mean to frighten you. I didn't know you knew."

"Rasputin's friend," she said with trembling lips. "Anna Virubova's friend! Oh yes, I knew. Anastasia came home from the Srednaia with a story about meeting him along with father, and how father was going to take a bottle of Tibetan Elixir to the front with him—Dmitri, are they drugging him?"

"I'm afraid so. I hadn't heard about the elixir, but Badmaiev has been sending him some stuff to take for—for a stomach complaint we've all been suffering from, and it makes Uncle Nicky wildly excited and then terribly depressed, and—well, the doctors are worried, that's all; and I thought you could help."

"How, please? Even if I go with them to Ania's every time they visit her, and make sure father doesn't leave with a bottle of dope in his pocket, how can I stop *any* of that gang, say Sister Akulina, smuggling out the stuff to mother at the hospital? How can I check all the couriers that travel between home and GHQ? My mother would send on any medicine, any wine, as long as it was blessed by Father Grigori! Dmitri, I'm sorry, but it isn't my responsibility! If only we could get rid of Rasputin—"

The slim young man in the grey civilian suit, so quietly distinguished in the bizarre décor of savage colours which Bakst had created for him, sat very still on the arm of Olga's chair.

"How would you propose to get rid of him?" he said.

"By persuading father to send him back to Povrovskoe."

Dmitri relaxed. "That has been tried," he said.

"This might help in the persuasion." Olga opened her big silk bag and handed her cousin the package Simon had bought outside the Gostinnoi Dvor. The slab of chocolate was unopened, the orange ribbon tied again round the *Poems* of Lermontov, the cartoon called 'The Ruler of Russia' was ready to slip out and hand to him. The young man examined it in silence.

"Where did you get this, Olga?"

"A friend bought it for me."

"Nice friends you have, I must say."

"It wasn't done on purpose! My friend bought it from a stall on the Nevski Prospekt, out of a hundred other chocolate packs. Sold on the public street, Dmitri, and the police don't even interfere!"

"They will now, don't worry, I'll see to that." He dropped the little book and the cartoon in his pocket. "I'm sorry you had to see that rubbish, or even know it existed. Selling on the streets, that's new."

"New?" Olga caught at the word. "You mean you've actually seen that—that trash before? Are there other pictures like that going the rounds?"

Dmitri could have told her that he had seen far worse, that the police, civil and military, had their work cut out to suppress the pornographic drawings of the Czarina, Anna Virubova, and Rasputin, sandwiched together in a writhing climax of arms and legs. He had too much respect for Olga's integrity to put her off with a lie or a caress. He only answered her with one word, "Yes."

* * *

Two anxious days followed for Olga. Marie, whom she consulted by telephone, told her papa was taking a new kind of tea, imported from Outer Mongolia by Badmaiev, which would cause Divine Grace to descend upon him. Some of this was given to

Sunbeam, as Alexis was still called by his parents, but the boy spat it out of the schoolroom window and refused to take any more.

"And don't *you* take any, Bow-Wow—nor Tania, nor Imp—"

"It's far too precious for the likes of us. Olga, when are you coming home?"

"Soon, but I've several things to do in Petrograd, and you know how granny is. She keeps saying she'll miss me terribly—"

"We miss you here," said Marie, and Olga laid down the telephone feeling that Dmitri was right: her first duty lay at home with the other members of OTMA, and with Alexis. But there were engagements to fulfil, including a charity ballet performance at the Maryinsky Theatre, and she carried them out attended by her two ladies and by her acting ADC, Lieutenant Hendrikov.

During those two days the tremendous German advance started which was to result in the recapture of the whole of Galicia and Bukovina, and in the north a part of Courland as well. To train the Second Category and transport them to the front was obviously going to demand a major effort from a War Ministry which so far had made nothing but mistakes, and a big comb-out of all the garrison troops began. Even Simon Hendrikov, so recently discharged from hospital, was ordered to report to a medical board.

Whatever he felt about his interview, he was smiling when on the third afternoon, Olga having found another opportunity to escape from the Winter Palace, his princess joined him in the shadow of the New Hermitage.

"I've got a droshki waiting on the Millionnaia."

"Oh, wonderful, I've never ridden in a droshki. But I thought we were going to your home this afternoon?"

"If you still want to. But as it's quite a long walk to the Fourth Line, I thought you'd rather drive."

"Of course I want to! I've been looking forward to it!"

But on the pavement of the Millionnaia, while the *isvostchik* was whipping his weary old horse towards them through the dusty sunlight, Simon said urgently:

"You do understand, don't you, that my mother and father won't be there? They went to Finland yesterday. I—I didn't tell them there was a possibility you might honour our home with a visit—"

"Oh, don't, Simon, you sound like someone presenting a purse of gold to a war charity! Darya Karlovna will be there, she told me so this morning. Let's get in."

The droshki set them down under the linden trees of the Fourth Line, and the porter, bowing low, looked inquisitively at the veiled lady accompanying Professor Hendrikov's only son. Simon opened the door of the flat with his latchkey, and scowled at the sight of strapped trunks and tin boxes blocking the rather narrow hall.

"What a mess," he said, "I didn't want you to see the place like this. And Dolly ought to be here to welcome you."

"With the ikon and the bread and salt?" she laughed. "I think this is fun. Am I to come in here?"

Simon was holding open the door of the living-room. The bay windows were wide open, and the Island's summer smell of lime blossom, tar and salt water filled the room. For that reason it was at once more pleasing to Olga than the Grand Duke Dmitri's splendid living-room where scented pastilles burned, and heavy net curtains shut out the light and air.

"I told you it wasn't as nice as the dacha," said Simon, watching anxiously as she walked round the big table to inspect the bookcases and the 'problem picture' of the young mother and her child.

"The dacha's special. But this is such a friendly room, Simon. It feels as if a lot of people had enjoyed eating and talking and living here. . . . Do you suppose vodka was *her* downfall?" she said mischevously, tilting her head at the picture of the girl with the baby and the ringless hand.

"You're very quick, Olga Nicolaievna. Most people don't see the vodka bottle until they've looked two or three times. If they bother to look at all, that is."

"The artist was clever, he hid the bottle on the floor by her skirt. Poor thing! I suppose that's what they call narrative painting."

"Talking of narratives, I telephoned my father about that movie we saw. He promised to look out Scott's poem for me, but I don't see anything like English poetry here. It may be in the study."

Olga followed him into the professor's study, where all was unnaturally tidy, with nothing on the desk but a big calf-bound volume of Scott with a paper stuck between the pages.

" 'Lady Heron's Song' from *Marmion*," Simon read aloud. "How clever of your father to know where to look!"

"You read it, Olga, Read it and tell me what it says."

Olga read:

> "O, young Lochinvar is come out of the west,
> Through all the wide border his steed was the best,
> And save his good broadsword he weapons had none,
> He rode all unarm'd, and he rode all alone.
> So faithful in love and so dauntless in war,
> There never was knight like the young Lochinvar."

"It's very long," she said, reading on silently, "But—yes, I understand it now. They took a tale of chivalry and made a Wild West movie out of it, and why not?"

"That verse you read, what does it say, in Russian?"

She translated to the best of her ability. And Simon asked if Lochinvar had been a prince or a nobleman.

"No, just a soldier, I think. It says he had a sword."

"And he was faithful to the girl he loved."

" 'So faithful in love and so dauntless in war'," said Olga. "Like you, Simon."

"Oh, my darling!" The word had been spoken at last between them, spoken and avowed; and Olga was in Simon's arms, close held, with her lips parting beneath his eager lips, which he lifted from hers only to say again and again, "I love you!"

She took her hat off and laid her cheek against Simon's with a sigh of happiness. And now he was free to touch her hair, her bare throat, at last her breast, until desire was made manifest in both their bodies, and Olga broke away from him with a gasp—

"Dolly—"

"Dolly won't be home until four o'clock," Simon said roughly. "Don't be afraid, the maids are here. But I wanted to be alone with you, we're never alone, I had to tell you that I love you—"

"Tell me again."

At that whisper of acquiescence Simon almost lost his head. But he drew Olga gently to the battered old leather sofa, for once not covered with piles of students' essays, and there in his arms the princess whose one desire was to be loved heard that she was adored, idolised, worshipped, but above all had the heart's whole love of Simon Hendrikov. She held his head between her hands, feeling the blood beating in his temples and touching his crisp chestnut hair, watching his hazel eyes grow dark, tracing with one finger tip the square lines of the face that pleased her more than any other, until Simon interrupted his long-suppressed words of passion to say:

"I was such a fool a year ago, Olga! That day in the country, by the river, saying I was jealous of any marriage planned for you! Wanting you to stay for ever a young girl, so that I needn't picture you the wife of any other man! I wonder how I dared to say it—I, who have nothing to offer you, not even a Baltic title, let alone a name descended from Rurik—"

"The Romanovs aren't descended from Rurik. We're just a bunch of parvenus compared with him."

"Try telling any courtier that. I'm a man without a title, or estates, or money—"

"You have your good broadsword, like young Lochinvar."

Olga smiled, and Simon even laughed, until the meaning behind her words struck him, and he said almost in awe, "You mean you don't care that I'm not a baron or a prince? That if it were humanly possible—but I know it's not—that you would marry *me*?"

"Yes I would, my darling."

He kissed her until the breath almost left her body, and then he said, "But why me? Why me, *dushenka*? There must be a thousand men like me, ready to fall in love with you: why should I be the one?"

"Because we're right for each other."

Simon knew that, beyond all hoping, it was true. The Czar's daughter and the professor's son, in the simplicity of their view of life and the harmony of their physical natures, were the right match for each other. But even in his triumph Simon felt that he had said too much, had forced her to her own avowal, and between kisses he begged Olga to believe that he would have waited—would have been silent in the present as in the past—except that they would be parted very soon.

"*What* did you say?" Olga raised her head from Simon's breast. "Why should we be parted soon? You're coming back with me to Czarskoe Selo next week."

"Darling, no. I had a medical board this morning, while

you were at the hospital. I've been passed fit to rejoin my battalion, or what's left of it plus the new intake. They're stationed at Odessa now."

"But that's ridiculous! You're not nearly fit for active service yet!"

"No, but Odessa's only a replacement depot."

"It's also a staging point for the Turkish front. Next month you may be sent to Armenia or the Caucasus, or—anywhere!"

He thought it was entirely possible.

"I shall speak to the Czar at once," said Olga.

"Darling, don't. You have to understand, I must go where I'm sent, it's all in the line of duty. And I owe my life to His Majesty. Without him I would have died in that filthy station yard at Warsaw. And look what I've got, along with my life! Four wonderful months of seeing you nearly every day. Those early mornings in the park, and being in your escort here in Petrograd, and now this—this joy."

"Such a short joy!" said Olga, and there were tears on her dark lashes. "But Simon, it won't be for ever that we'll be apart. You'll get leave, you'll come home; *we* may go to Livadia in the spring, and travel by Odessa . . . and the war must end some day. Then I think there'll be big changes for us all. I don't know what they'll be exactly, but a lot of the old rules and traditions are being thrown overboard already, and who knows what the future may have in store for you and me?"

With his lips on hers Simon heard the door-bell ring. "There's Dolly, ten minutes early, confound her!" he said. "Darling, stay where you are." There were voices in the hall, a man's, a girl's, not Dolly's, and some guttural words from the Lettish maid. Simon hurried out.

"What's the matter?" he said. "Whose is the—good God, Mara, what are you doing here?"

The porter and the maid were pushing a heavy leather portmanteau into place alongside the pile of luggage already in the hall, and Mara Trenova, slightly out of breath, was flexing the fingers of her right hand.

"A bit too heavy for the young lady, *barin*," said the porter. "I carried it upstairs for her." His cap was in his hand, his eyes darting in all directions. Simon gave him a coin.

"All right, Stepan," he said. "Now, watch out for Darya

Karlovna, I'm expecting her any minute. She'll come in a droshki, tell the driver to wait . . . Well, Mara Ivanovna," he said as the man withdrew, "that wasn't much of a welcome, was it? I didn't know you were coming to stay with us."

"Don't be ridiculous, Simon, of course I'm not. I brought mother's portmanteau, it's to go to Finland by carrier with Madame Hendrikova's luggage. You did know mother had gone to Koivisto, didn't you?"

If he had heard it, Simon thought, it was in another life, the life before the one begun less than half an hour ago. He stammered that of course he knew, it was a fine idea, the weather in Finland was fine too, he thought, and at last, "Won't you come in?" The Lettish maid asked if she should bring the samovar.

"Yes—no—yes, it doesn't matter," Simon said. He ushered Mara into the living-room. The Grand Duchess Olga had not stayed in the study, and he was glad of that. She was looking at the books in the glass-fronted bookcase, wearing her hat again, like any friend of Madame Hendrikova's who was paying a social call. Mara looked at her with amazement. Then the Xenia training told; she swept her curtsey, while Simon said, "Your Imperial Highness, may I present my sister's friend, Miss Mara Trenova?"

"How do you do," said Olga cordially. "I know who you are, Dolly's clever schoolfellow, she's often told me about you."

"I'm flattered, Madame."

"You're not doing nursing work, are you?"

"I'm obliged to earn my living, Madame."

Simon opened his mouth to explain about The Children's Castle and shut it again. He knew quite well who published the candy classics, and by consequence the cartoon of Rasputin as the ruler of Russia. Suddenly aware that the high collar of his tunic was undone, he explained that Mara Ivanovna had an interesting job on a literary review.

"But I left it last week," said Mara. "I'm starting another job next Monday."

"I think that's wonderful," said Olga. "Imagine being so independent!"

"I wouldn't care to change jobs with Your Imperial Highness." It was Mara at her worst, defensive and gauche, and Simon was not surprised at the slight frost in Olga's "Really?" and the deliberate misunderstanding in her reference to war nursing. He thanked heaven that Dolly came in then, happy in her greeting to both guests, and was followed by the beaming maid, who brought the samovar nobody wanted and made an immense clatter with the tea-things.

"Stepan said you wanted the droshki to wait?" said Dolly.

"Yes, so that Her Imperial Highness may go straight back with me to the Winter Palace," Simon said. It was nearly an hour before they need meet the ladies-in-waiting, but this situation, with Mara Trenova's dark eyes travelling from one to the other, was too complicated for him. Olga was quite at her ease. She had sat down, at Dolly's shy request, to sip at a glass of tea, and looked up smiling at the mention of the palace.

"Lieutenant Hendrikov has been showing me parts of Petrograd I've never seen before," she said, "and the Fourth Line is one of the pleasantest of all."

"I can show you other streets not nearly so pleasant," said Mara Trenova. "Where I live myself, for instance. You wouldn't like that much."

The Grand Duchess raised her eyebrows at the tone, and Dolly said, "But, Mara Ivanovna, your apartment's very nice. So—compact."

"I imagine Her Imperial Highness has very little idea of how the poor live," said Mara.

"On the contrary," said Olga, 'I see the poor every day. Those who come to the hospitals to visit the wounded, and many of the soldiers' families my care commitee tries to relieve. My sister and I visit the refugees at the Narva Gate shelter, every week of our lives."

"We all know the Narva Gate—shelter, do you call it? The refugees *you* see have been bathed and clothed and fed and taught the words of thanks to say to the kind visitors. They're not representative."

"Perhaps not," said Olga. "But when we go as near the front as we're allowed, we take our turn to work in barns and stables without water, with only straw for beds, where the refugees come in—sometimes wounded, always covered with sores and lice, always half starving. Have you ever worked in any place like that?"

"No."

"You should try it some time."

"Madame, I don't have to go to the front to see people covered with sores and lice, and starving, I could show you sights like that not two miles from the Anitchkov Palace."

"Where?"

"If we take that droshki, waiting outside, and cross the Neva, past the Xenia School and the Maryinski Theatre—which of course you know very well indeed—we'd come to the Jews' Market, where the people your grandfather deprived of their rights live in a stinking ghetto. We'd go on down the Zabalkanski, and I'd show you what they call civilian barracks, with the tiny rooms, the *kamorki*, where three or four families live together, with one chair and one table for ten people, and only their rags of washing hung on lines from wall to wall to separate them for the sake of decency. That's where the workers live, Your Imperial Highness, that's the kind of den they go back to from the war factories—"

"And you were never in a place like that in your life," Simon interrupted. "You got all that out of some subversive book."

"But there *are* such places?" the Grand Duchess asked.

"Yes, there are, unfortunately," Simon said, "but the people in the *kamorki* are the real down-and-outs, the 'dark people', the kind of riff-raff you find in any great city, not only Petrograd."

"But I'm concerned with Petrograd," said Olga. "Mara Ivanovna, would you like to take me to the Zabalkanski now?"

"She's not going to take you anywhere!" said Simon angrily. He was suddenly furious with Mara for her ill-timed arrival and her strident introduction of a theme he knew only too well. And Olga had been provoked into accepting her challenge! He recognised her reckless tone, though he had seldom heard it before: it was the voice her sisters would have called "Olga never saying No to a dare."

"There's nothing to be afraid of in the Jews' Market, or the Zabalkanski either," said Mara, as if she read his thoughts.

"All right, Mara Ivanovna, we all know you're a rebel," he said. "But it's my duty to protect the Grand Duchess, and I won't allow her to be jostled in the Market, or exposed to the insults any lady would risk in the *kamorki*, where even the Petrograd police won't go. It's no use, Your Imperial Highness," he said, as Olga impatiently took up her bag. "If you insist, I shall telephone to the guardroom of the Winter Palace, and a detachment of the Convoy Cossacks will be here in just as short a time as it takes them to saddle up. You must decide if you want their escort, or if you'll come back in the droshki with me."

He turned to the window, to make sure the droshki was still there. The driver was sitting patiently on his box, chewing sunflower seeds.

When Simon looked round, all the girls were on their feet, and Olga was pulling on her gloves. She was still intent on Mara Ivanovna, and seemed to ignore her sarcastic smile.

"Simon Karlovich called you a rebel," she said to the other girl. "Are you more than that? Are you a revolutionary?"

"You would be a revolutionary, Madame, if you lived in the Zabalkanski."

"Perhaps I should," said Olga Nicolaievna. Then her irrepressible gaiety flashed out as she added, "But don't you think my name's against me?"

12

LIEUTENANT HENDRIKOV RECEIVED his movement orders for Odessa three days later, one day after he had been in attendance on the Grand Duchess Olga at another battleship launching, this time performed by the Czar himself. They had no opportunity for anything but a formal and public leave-taking, and the speed of Simon's removal from the scene sent Olga home to the Alexander Palace with anger in her heart.

She remembered Rasputin's gibe at her as "a country girl . . . when the handsome lieutenant takes you into the bushes—" and wondered if the spies of the *staretz*, or perhaps Anna Virubova herself, had told him about the morning meetings in the park with Simon, which they had never attempted to keep secret. Then, if Rasputin told her mother, how easy it would have been for Alexandra Feodorovna to drop a hint at the War Ministry, where the Minister owed her so much, and have the inconvenient lieutenant sent from Czarskoe Selo to Odessa. It was just the sort of feminine tit-for-tat her mother would enjoy, and Olga's head was high, her greeting cool, when she reappeared in the mauve boudoir. But her sisters squealed with joy at the sight of her, wearing one of the beautiful dresses their grandmother's couturier had made, and she, in turn, exclaimed at the sight of Marie in a probationer's overall.

"You've started in hospital already, Mashka?"

"Last week. I didn't tell you on the telephone, I wanted it to be a surprise."

"And how's it going? Aren't you exhausted? We were, at the start."

"Oh, I am too! Last night I went with papa and mamma to spend the evening with Ania, and I was so tired I fell asleep on the sofa and had no idea what was going on!" Marie gave Olga a significant look.

"You poor old thing," said Olga lightly. "I thought you weren't going to start nursing till September."

"I couldn't wait after I heard about Nurse Cavell."

"Who's she? Oh, that poor woman in Brussels, yes, I read about her."

"I've started a scrap-book about Nurse Cavell." And Marie showed her sister a blurred newspaper photograph of Edith Cavell, the matron of the Red Cross hospital in Brussels, who had just been tried and found guilty by the Germans of assisting English, French and Belgian soldiers to escape over the Dutch border.

"I thought heroines had to be beautiful—and young," she said. "*She's* fifty!"

Olga looked at the thin, self-contained face beneath the nurse's bonnet. "She looks very calm and brave, doesn't she? I think she's wonderful, Marie."

"Imagine saving the lives of two hundred men! Why can't *we* do things like that!"

"Two hundred would be something," said Olga grimly. For this was at the time when the Russians had surrendered Warsaw, and after Warsaw, Vilna, and the loss of millions of men had been in vain.

"Do you think the Germans will really dare to shoot her?" said Marie, still thinking of the heroine.

"Granny says the Germans are equal to any devilry."

"We must all pray for her," Tatiana said.

If her young deputy couldn't keep from falling asleep on Anna Virubova's sofa, Olga felt it was high time she was there to act as watchdog. She proposed herself as a companion to her father and mother every time they went to visit the lame woman, and sat up bored but alert while Sister Akulina handed round the insipid refreshments, to which the Czar sometimes added a bottle of cherry brandy, carried in the pocket of his tunic. There was never any sign of Rasputin, or Badmaiev; a young officer called Soloviev was present once or twice who spoke familiarly of them both, but no mysterious Tibetan cordials were offered, and Madame Virubova's conversation was as boring and banal as it had ever been. It was hardly possible to think of the crippled woman, now obese from lack of exercise, as dangerous, and yet Olga's intuition told her where the danger lay. It lay in the telephone which linked Anna Virubova with Rasputin's flat and with the palace. It lay, at the very end of the long coil of intrigue, in the double bed where a passion unquenched by years and suffering was consummated, and where on the dark verge of sleep the Czar heard his wife's whispers, prompting him to act like Peter the Great, like Ivan the Terrible—to be Russia's saviour.

From half-hints dropped by Ania, from conversations halted when she went in to her mother's boudoir, Olga realised that the new intrigue centred on one thing: her mother's jealous hatred of the Commander-in-Chief. All her persuasions were directed at getting the Czar to relieve him of his command and send him to the Caucasus with some meaningless title like Viceroy, while the Czar took over the supreme command himself. But the Czar appeared to be in no hurry to act, or to visit the little provincial capital of Mohilev, to which the Stavka had removed from Baranovichi. The governor's house, standing in the woods above the Dnieper river, was ostensibly being made ready for the Grand Duke Nicholas Nicolaievich and his staff. Meanwhile the Czar transacted business with his Ministers, played with his boy, went for long walks with his ADCs, and at night read aloud to his wife, whose failing health had caused her to give up nursing at the palace hospital.

On the day when Nicholas II told his family, in his quiet way, that he intended to assume the supreme command, Olga escaped from her mother's open jubilation in the course of the afternoon. It was very hot, and she went into the park with a novel and a parasol, hoping for an hour alone, in a rose arbour near the entrance to the palace and with the book closed on the rustic table, to collect her thoughts. She was surprised to hear male voices from the arbour, one of them the eager voice of her brother Alexis.

"Olga!" he called as soon as she came into view, "do come here! See who I'm entertaining! Monsieur Rodzianko!"

They were all on their feet as Olga came up; Alexis, and his Russian tutor, and the President of the Duma, Michael Rodzianko, who had once jovially described himself to Alexis as 'the biggest, fattest man in the whole of Russia'. He was not looking jovial now; the polite smile which accompanied his bow was forced, and as she gave him her hand to kiss Olga said, in an attempt at gaiety, "Are you playing truant from the Duma, *monsieur le président*?"

"He came to see papa, and papa's too busy to talk to him," Alexis interrupted. "So he came out with me instead."

"It's not quite as bad as Alexis Nicolaievich makes out," said Rodzianko, with a laugh as forced as his smile. "My audience with His Majesty had to be postponed for half an hour. And I've been in the hands of an accomplished host—"

Olga looked at the silver tray on the rustic table, which held chilled wine, fruit and cakes, and smiled. "The Czar had a number of audiences to give this afternoon, I know," she said. "May I join your party?"

"We shall be honoured, Madame."

"Alexis," said the Russian tutor pleadingly, "our lesson should have begun half an hour ago—"

"All right, I don't mind coming now, if Olga's going to sit with Michael Vladimirovich. Good-bye, sir," said Alexis, holding out his hand to Rodzianko, "I'm most awfully glad to have seen you again."

"What a charming child," said the President of the Duma, as the boy and his tutor hurried off towards the house. "I'm glad I arrived in time to spare him half an hour of Russian grammar. He tells me the subject doesn't appeal to him at all."

"We'll never make a scholar of him," said Olga, and the tall, stout man surveyed her with appreciation. He was uncomfortably warm in the black frock coat required for an audience with the Czar: she looked as cool as springtime in a thin dress of greenish grey. It was the dress she had worn to walk with Simon on the Nevski Prospekt.

"I last had the pleasure of meeting Your Imperial Highness at the launching of the *Poltava*," he said, and began to compliment her on her great personal success that day. But Olga cut him short in her characteristic way. "Monsieur Rodzianko," she said, "you know so much: can you tell me anything about the Green Men? Do you know who they are, and what they do?"

Rodzianko sat astounded, silent under her blue direct gaze until he dared be silent no longer, and then he chose his words with care.

"As it happens I do know a great deal about that—organisation. You will permit me to say that I am surprised Your Imperial Highness has ever heard of them."

"Rasputin mentioned them."

He remembered then—the story so well publicised in the Petrograd press, of this girl's confrontation with Rasputin. He made up his mind that she deserved the truth, whatever use she made of it, or however far, in that palace of intrigue, she was to be trusted. He spoke as precisely as he would have spoken in the Duma:

"The Green Men are a body controlled by German agents in Stockholm, but operating in this country. Their object is to obtain places of power for their associates through the manipulation of Rasputin, and also to enrich themselves by the financial transactions of which his staff obtain inside information. Am I making myself clear, Madame?"

Olga nodded.

"The leader of the group is the banker Manus, one of the few Jews who has a residence permit and the right to do business in the capital. He has a confederate called Manuilov, a journalist and suspected forger, already enriched by the sale of stolen state papers. There are other names, equally unsavoury, which I need not mention to Your Imperial Highness. They are a decided menace to the good government of Russia. They meet weekly for dinner at Rasputin's apartment on the Gorokhovaia, where he is lavishly entertained by Manus, at whose expense the dinners are supplied."

"Did the police find out all this?"

"The details were given me by an Englishman, who has been working on the Stockholm connection. We have checked with our sources here, and the facts are true."

"Do you intend to make any arrests?"

"Arrest the friends of Rasputin?"

Olga's eyes fell. She might as well have said, arrest Rasputin.

The statesman leant across the table, and spoke urgently. "Madame—Olga Nicolaievna—you've already proved your strength and courage. Do, I beg you, give me your support in the matter which brought me here today. I asked for an audience by telephone—I knew His Majesty was unwilling to grant it, just as now he is unwilling to see me—because he thinks of me as an upstart, a challenger to his authority, and too often as the voice of doom. I've warned him for years about Rasputin, and His Majesty has never paid the least attention to my warnings. If I told him what I've just told you about the Green Men he would only laugh at me. But I haven't come to complain of Rasputin today. I've come to warn him that if he persists in his intention of taking command of the armies he will put himself in a desperate situation. He will be blamed for every defeat and every failure. If he dissolves the Duma—as he is almost certain to do, as soon as we oppose his wishes—the workers of Petrograd will come out on strike. Not at our call, but because they have men behind them who know how to profit from every difficulty. Strikes in the war factories mean more defeats, more blame for the Commander-in-Chief. In the end, it will cost him his command—if not his throne."

He saw that he had touched her to the heart, for Olga's face was very pale, and her voice shook as she said, "Do you really think the dynasty may be endangered?"

"On my solemn oath, I do, Madame."

"Then *you* must tell him so, and not you alone! Get the generals—get all the leaders of the Duma to put their views before him. He's not unreasonable, but—" She stopped, but they both knew what her next words would have been, 'But he only listens to my mother.'

"Will *you* speak to him, urge him to see reason, as only a daughter can?"

"But he treats me like a child!" she said. "Whenever I talk politics he laughs at me. But I will tell him, you have my word for it, that he mustn't quarrel with the Duma, because the Duma represents the people, whom he loves."

Rodzianko looked at the pretty, flushed face admiringly. "Madame," he said, "I wish to God *you* were the Heir to the Throne!"

* * *

"The fat fool had a great deal to say for himself today," the Czar observed tranquilly to his wife, when the whole family met at the dinner table. "He threatened me with dire consequences if I dissolve the Duma."

"As you will, of course, darling."

"Certainly, if they continue to make seditious speeches about me."

Three of his listening daughters took his words as gospel, and even Olga knew better than to interpose at such a moment.

As far as the supreme command of the army went, she was not sure of her ground. It was surely significant that even the headquarters had been moved in the general retreat from the advancing Germans, but it had been a basic principle of the scanty instruction in history she had received that Russia *always* tempted her enemies to advance deep into the country and then destroyed them. Think of Poltava! Think of Napoleon, driven back to the Beresina! These were the classic examples which the Czarina, in her exaltation, was never tired of quoting. But Olga was unable to persuade herself that her father was the reincarnation of Peter the Great or General Kutusov.

Everything fell out as Rodzianko had predicted. The Duma President was snubbed, the Duma suspended, the strikes began. The members of the Family telegraphed, asked for audiences, wrote letters of protest at the whole business of the State's being left to—Who?—while the Czar took up the exacting duties of supreme commander. The Czar smoked and smiled: was silent, and prepared to leave for Mohilev.

Olga tried once, though she knew it was useless, to make him change his mind. All she got for answer was an allusion to the birthday of the long-suffering Job, and the solemn words: "Perhaps a scapegoat is needed to save Russia, and if so, I mean to be the victim. Come to the Znamenia church and pray with me, my dear."

The last person to try was the Grand Duke Dmitri, and he, reckless as ever, took a special train from Mohilev to beg 'Uncle Nicky' to leave 'Nikolasha' in command. It was two hours after his arrival before he was able to reach Olga by telephone.

"Dmitri! Where are you?"

"At Pavlovsk. Listen, Olga, I've *got* to have a talk with Uncle Nicky. I've called half a dozen times, and he won't even come to the telephone—"

"What do you expect me to do?"

"Fix it up for me. Beg Aunt Alix to let me come over in the car—"

"She won't listen to me, and neither will he, if it's about Mohilev."

"Of course it's about Mohilev! It's going to be an absolute disaster if he throws out Nikolasha. The troops adore Nikolasha, they'll follow him through thick and thin—"

"Several millions of them have followed him to their deaths in the past twelve months."

"Yes, we've had defeats, terrible defeats, but Nikolasha's not the *emperor*! If we have another summer like this one, the troops will throw your *father* out, and then where'll we all be? He's got to stay in the rear where he can't do any damage—"

Olga lost her temper. "Now that's quite enough of that! You make my father sound like a perfect fool! Who are you to judge, at your age, and only an ADC? My father had a thorough military training—"

"Yes, just enough to make him look good at the summer manœuvres at Krasnoe Selo. He had a few years in the army when he was a youngster, just like me, he doesn't know a damn thing more about how to handle troops in action than I do."

"But he'll have General Alexeiev as his Chief of Staff, won't he?"

"Oh, to hell with Alexeiev! Olga, if you love me, you'll get me an audience today, before nightfall—they're waiting at Mohilev to hear—"

"*I* can't do it, but maybe Tatiana can."

As usual, Tatiana could. Dmitri was invited to a family dinner that evening, and then to play billiards with the Czar. There were no equerries present. The click of balls became the murmur of voices, and eventually Dmitri emerged from the billiard room with a radiant face. The elder girls were hovering in the green drawing-room; he seized them round their waists and danced them troika-fashion to the private door.

"It's all right!" he exulted. "Thanks to you two. What a pair of bricks you are! Uncle Nicky's given me his absolute promise to call off the whole thing and let Nikolasha stay. Hurrah!"

Two days later the Czar blandly and characteristically broke his promise to Dmitri, and placed himself at the head of his armies.

For once it seemed as if the evils of the long-suffering Job were to be spared the Czar. He took the supreme command at the Stavka, with General Alexeiev as the effective commander in the field, exactly at the moment when the German advance lost its impetus after five devastating months. The winter was not far away, and behind the frozen lines the Russian generals had time to plan the campaign of 1916, with only one new anxiety in the south, where Bulgaria had entered the war on the side of the Central Powers.

All was so calm at Mohilev that the Czar took the great decision, only six weeks after his first arrival, to fetch Alexis from the schoolroom to share his life at the Stavka and his visits to the troops. The boy, of course, was wild to go. He had been in excellent health for months, and was feeling neglected by his busy sisters; soldiers, real fighting soldiers, seemed likely to be better playmates than the few little boys he was ever allowed to meet. His mother, equally of course, was in terror for Sunbeam's safety, but he set off with such a retinue of doctors, tutors, sailor attendants and orderlies that 'the womenfolk', as he loftily called them, could hardly feel anxiety when he left them in his father's care.

He had adopted a device for himself that autumn, something in the style of the Prince of Wales's *Ich Dien*, but not so terse. "Prayer to God and service to the Czar will never be in vain" was to be the boy's motto, and he scrawled it on the flyleaf of all his schoolbooks, often with the signature *Alexis* beneath it in a variety of fancy capital As and underlining, as if the writer were practising for the time when he would sign himself Alexis II. He was very much the Czarevich when he kissed his mother's hand on the station platform, and gravely saluted his admiring sisters. He was extremely proud of wearing the uniform of a private soldier, complete with military cap and top boots, "instead of those kiddy sailor suits I used to wear," he said.

The letters from both father and son made delightful reading to the ladies left behind at Czarskoe Selo. Alexis had a camp bed in his father's room at Mohilev, with a *lampadka* burning constantly in front of his favourite ikon. He had a typewriter, and a silver bowl for his bedtime fruit instead of a silly china saucer. The girls read with resignation that he also had a new kitten, called Zubrovka, for which he wanted a collar and a bell.

To these practical details the Czar added that the troops cheered Alexis wherever he appeared, and the publicity pictures ("this sort of thing seems to be needed now") were excellent. The Allied liaison officers enjoyed his chatter and fun, and he had had the time of his life at Reval with the British submariners who had penetrated the German sea defences in the Baltic. At

Odessa he had been almost mobbed by the townspeople. It was all a huge success, though Monsieur Gilliard might shake his head over neglected lessons, until the day when the letter said "Alexis has a little cold . . . we are giving up our visit to Galicia . . . we are going back to Mohilev" . . . and then the telegrams.

Then the telegrams. Very severe bleeding from the nose, summon the specialists, we are on our way home. Bleeding can not be stopped, he is growing very weak, pray for him. And then the last, pathetic message, from Vitebsk: please let there be nobody at the station when we arrive tomorrow.

There was 'nobody' in the official sense, no courtier, no station master, when the blue imperial train drew gently into the private station at Czarskoe Selo. Only the tragic mother, the anxious girls, were there to see the faithful sailor, Nagorny, step warily to the ground with the half-conscious boy, wrapped in blankets, in his arms. Nagorny had held the Czarevich against his shoulder all through the terrible night, when to let the boy lie back upon his pillows might have been fatal.

They took him, with the blood still oozing from the plugs inserted in his nose, back to the palace where his hospital bed was waiting for him. Professor Feodorov, who had cared for him in other attacks, was in attendance, and he told the parents not to give up hope. The head cold, with the sneezing and catarrh, had unfortunately caused a tiny blood vessel to break inside the Czarevich's nose, but the doctors would proceed to a cauterisation of the nostrils, which would give relief.

The haemorrhage was halted, the boy had spoken and even taken a little beef tea, when Rasputin in his peasant dress arrived at the Alexander Palace. He was escorted to the forbidden bedroom floor as an honoured guest. He smiled at Alexis from the doorway of his room and made the sign of the Cross in the air. "God bless you, little Aliesha," he said in his resonant voice, "you will soon be well and strong again." He added to the unshaven Czar, the weeping Czarina, "Don't be afraid, my dears. Nothing will happen to the Little One." And then stood, with an exaggerated air of humility while the imperial couple knelt to kiss his hands.

"So Rasputin wins again," said Olga, alone with Tatiana in the room from which she had had Rasputin ejected in the summer. "Along he comes when that poor kid is cured, and gets away with all the credit."

"How do we know when the cure took place? Father Grigori prays for Baby all the time, he told us so. Today he blessed him and promised he would be well. And he *is!*"

"Rot!" said the Grand Duchess Olga. "They've been feeding us up with tales like that for years. Today you and I *saw* it happen. The doctors cauterised the nose, the bleeding stopped. Not by faith healing. By medical science!"

"What does it matter, if Baby's going to be all right? Honestly, I can't think straight any more—"

"I can," said Olga. "I think this is the worst thing that's happened to Alexis yet."

"Oh, Olga, it's nothing like the Spala time! He seems quite comfortable already—sitting up in bed, and asking to see Joy, and his cat."

"Yes, but don't you see? All the other times the internal bleeding began because he fell, or knocked himself against something, like last summer on the *Standart*. He hurt himself outside and then he started to bleed inside, that's what we were always told. But this time it was only a cold, Tania! He didn't trip, or bruise himself. He only sneezed, or blew his nose, as anyone might do! And that made him bleed so much he nearly died last night! Just because of a cold in the head!"

"Oh, it was far worse than a cold. He burst a blood vessel in his nose, the doctors said."

"Yes, but *why* did it burst? I'm going to find out the truth this time, Tania; we've got to know."

"You know they don't like us to ask questions. Mamma used to tell us it was because Alexis is a boy, and we're girls, so he's made differently from us—"

"Yes, she made a big sex thing out of it, trust her. Do you remember all her blushing and stammering about what she called the curse of womanhood? And telling us, even this year, that the stork had brought Irina a dear little baby? I'm going to tackle Feodorov tomorrow morning."

But Professor Feodorov was far too skilled in turning aside questions on the Czarevich's health to reveal anything to Olga. It was Dr. Botkin, officially her mother's physician, but who often cared for the children too, who told her the truth at last. Perhaps he was exhausted by the strain of the child's dangerous haemorrhage, perhaps he was weary of the long dissembling, or perhaps he felt compassion for the girl of twenty who knew nothing of her own fatal inheritance, but he told her, in the privacy of his little study, that there was a scientific name for her brother's malady, which as far as medical science knew, was incurable.

Haemophilia. The female always the carrier, the male always the sufferer. A disease where a blow, a fall, a bruise could cause the internal bleeding which knotted the muscles, cramped the limbs, stopped—as she had seen so often with Alexis—the very power to walk.

"You say the *female* is the carrier, *she* transmits the disease? Then it was mother who gave this—awful thing to Alexis?"

"That's been her tragedy, Olga Nicolaievna."

"But how did *she* get it?"

"From her own mother, one of whose little boys died of it. And *she* carried it from Queen Victoria, who also lost a son through haemophilia."

"And Aunt Irene, is she a carrier too? Is that why *her* little boy died, and Waldemar is—delicate?"

"Alas, yes, that's the reason why."

"But Aunt Victoria, she must be all right? The Battenberg boys are both strong and well, I know!"

"Yes, because Princess Victoria is not a carrier. Not every woman, in every family, transmits the malady. Sometimes it skips a generation and then reappears in the next—"

"I see," said Olga, and Dr. Botkin wondered at her calm. "It's like that game called Russian roulette, they say our young officers used to play. Hold the pistol to your head, fire, and with any luck the chamber will be empty! Am I a carrier or am I not? Get married and find out!"

"Dear Olga Nicolaievna, I know this has distressed you very much . . . I do beg you won't tell Her Majesty what I've disclosed to you in confidence—"

"No, no, of course not," Olga said almost abstractedly. She was putting the thought of her mother aside for a time: the guilt, the self-tormenting she had undergone explained so much. "Alexis is the one who matters. Can he be cured?"

"I told you, my dear young lady, that no cure has yet been found for haemophilia."

"But doctor, those other boys you spoke of, they died when they were younger than Alexis—little children, and he's at an age when he can be sensible, and learn to take great care of himself, can't he?"

"That's what we'd all begun to hope. But this new attack, the haemorrhage starting from a winter cold, the most ordinary of ailments . . . this has shown us all, all the Czar's medical advisers, that the life of the Czarevich hangs by the merest thread."

He allowed her to weep then, with her head on her folded arms, crouched over his work table; while the only words he could hear under the tangle of Olga's golden hair were "My father! Oh, my poor father!" It was all new to her, the thought that her brother might die young, and never reign. Dr. Botkin, like the Czar and the Czarina, had lived with that thought for nearly twelve years.

When Olga raised her head at last, and felt for her handkerchief, and pushed her hair back from her wet eyes, he knew that she was fully aware of that other thought, which he had not dared to put into words. She voiced it at once, and with a smile which gave him pain to see.

"Thank you, Dr. Botkin," said the Grand Duchess Olga. "I'm grateful to you for telling me the truth. My sisters and I *have* wondered, and worried, and made wild guesses, for a long time now. Do many of the people who are closest to us, know?"

"Monsieur Gilliard does, but he's the soul of discretion, as you're aware. None of the Family, I think."

"And I'll say nothing to my sisters, at least, not just now. But they'll have to be told some day, and probably quite soon. Because I understand quite well what you've been trying to tell me—that not one of us is a fit wife for any man."

13

A FEW WEEKS AFTER THE bitter truth of her inheritance was told to Olga, she received a new and surprising proposal of marriage.

With great self-command, she told Tatiana nothing of Dr. Botkin's revelations. When asked, she answered "I couldn't get a thing out of him we didn't know already!" and Tatiana had not persisted; she was deep in the old farce of pretending that the sudden return of the Czarevich was due to "a really bad cold; poor darling, he wanted to be at home in his own bed!" Watching the faces of the courtiers as they listened to the story, Olga began to wonder how many of them believed it. She had a feeling that there were smiles and raised eyebrows behind their backs, just as in hospital there was often an ugly ripple of laughter in the wards when some man roughly declined the offering of a holy picture, and said "How about a good tumbler of vodka, little sister, that's more in my line than your saints!"

The sad and funny thing in the latest fiction about the boy's illness was that the last place where Alexis wanted to be was in his own bed. He wanted to be back at Mohilev, in a man's world, and much more than his sisters' he wanted the companionship of 'Zilchik', his tutor, who had been with him at Mohilev and could endlessly discuss with him the garrisons they had visited and the soldiers they had met. Failing Zilchik Alexis made do with Olga. In spite of his bouts of illness and the constant petting and pampering, there was a tough, unsentimental streak in the boy which found its counterpart in his eldest sister, and to her, when they were alone, he was able to communicate what it felt like to go aboard the British submarines, lying sheathed in ice in Reval harbour, or to see the Russian wounded in the field dressing station at Rovno humbly touching the Czar's greatcoat as he knelt on one knee beside their stretchers and wished them well.

At Odessa in November he had seen Lieutenant Hendrikov,

one of a detachment of the Garde Equipage which had resumed its old duties as a bodygyard. "And I'm jolly glad Simon Karlovich was there," he said importantly, "because the people really went wild at Odessa, and he helped to keep them back from the car. Honestly, Olga, it was *me* they wanted to touch that time! They kept shouting out 'The Heir! the angel! the pretty boy!' all the way to the parade ground. Papa was so pleased."

"I'll bet he was."

"I asked Simon Karlovich if he wanted to send his love to you, and he said you knew all about that already. What did he mean?"

"Now, Alexis, don't be sly, and let's have a game of dominoes!"

"I'm sick of dominoes. Papa plays every evening with the ADCs, and when I've finished my lessons he makes me play too."

"It's high time you had lessons to do again."

"That's what Zilchik says."

The boy was not supposed to laugh, or sneeze, or do anything which might start another nasal haemorrhage, but it was difficult to keep him quiet when his new cat, Zubrovka, arrived in a basket from Mohilev (the satin lining torn to shreds) and promptly began to fight with Pussy, the grey Persian. Anna Virubova had just given Anastasia a little Pekinese called Jimmy, and when Jimmy and Joy added their barking to the fray, the sickroom, so-called, became, said the Czar, more like a bear garden. Entirely reassured about his heir's recovery, he went back alone to the Stavka at Mohilev.

Once more established as the man of the family, Alexis decided to keep a diary. Kind-hearted Marie helped him to rule the lines in a new book stamped '1916', and he started out in the footsteps of all his royal and imperial ancestors, who had been trained to keep diaries in their own schoolroom days. But with so little to chronicle the entries soon tailed away into the classic Forget What Did, and Alexis, teased by his sisters, announced that he would make a proper start as a diarist when he went back to Mohilev. His father wrote that he was greatly missed at GHQ.

With the man of the house in bed by seven o'clock, the evening in the private apartments seemed long and intensely feminine. Madame Virubova, who called in her wheel-chair twice during the day, spent four hours with the Czarina every evening, talking about her imaginary love affairs and listening to the stories of Alexandra Feodorovna's happy childhood in Darmstadt, which had long ago reduced her daughters to strangled yawns. There was reading aloud, that favourite occupation, although the girls missed their father's attractive voice in the readings, and their mother's choice set Olga's teeth on edge. Alexandra Feodorovna had discovered an English book called *Through the Postern Gate,* over which she shed sentimental tears. The action took place mainly in a garden which, the Czarina said, reminded her so much of her sister's garden at Walton-on-Thames, where she and her future husband had once spent some happy and carefree days. Olga took the book upstairs after the first emotional reading aloud. It was not very long, and she finished it before she went to sleep.

"What did you think of it, childie?" her mother asked next day.

"I thought it was awful. It nearly made me sick."

"Sick? That beautiful, tender story?"

"Very tender, just like underdone beef. That awful heroine, with her 'stately presence', and poor 'Guy, slight and boyish', that she played with on the beach when he was six and she was sixteen, and called him 'Little Boy Blue'! How *could* he fall in love with a woman who kept on saying 'Why was I not your mother?' Enough to put any man off for life, I should have thought."

"Ten years is no great difference between a woman and a man."

"Oh yes, it is, mamma, but that's not the point; what's so false is the way Christobel keeps *on* about feeling like his mother, even after he's grown up. 'I knew my Little Boy Blue had no mother'—she can't stop talking about it, ever."

"You don't know what *you're* talking about," said the Czarina, whose presence at that moment was very stately indeed. "When you meet the right man, Olga, you'll find out that every woman has the feelings of a mother for the man she loves. He's her first child, it's such a beautiful relationship . . ."

Olga heard the fantasy out in a polite silence. When she turned away to return Mrs. Barclay's masterpiece, in its mauve binding, to its place next to *The Rosary,* she formed with her lips the one word 'Bosh!' which caused Anastasia to burst into a fit of laughter and be sent from the room in disgrace.

After this lesson in love it was refreshing to find the Czarina in an unsentimental mood when the offer for Olga's hand was received.

It came out of the blue, on a day of heavy snow, with a twenty-four hours' warning which caused some surprise at the Alexander Palace.

"Olga," said her mother, coming unannounced into the girls' sitting-room, "I've had an extraordinary letter from Aunt Miechen."

"Goodness, what does *she* want?"

"Wants to come to tea tomorrow, to have a confidential talk with me, and especially wants to have a word with you."

"Me? What have I been doing wrong?"

"You know that best yourself," said the Czarina darkly, and Olga began to think aloud about her recent committees and receptions—had she forgotten a name, a face, or an attentive word to one of Aunt Miechen's friends? "I can't think of anything," she said, "We'll have to wait and see."

"You'll be sure to be at home?"

"What's tomorrow? Thursday; yes, I'll be at home."

"And try to make yourself look nice, you're getting far too fond of slopping round the house in uniform."

Olga grimaced, but next afternoon she took care to brush her hair to its liveliest gold, and put on a dark red dress made for her most important public functions. It was only four months old, and seemed too loose already; Olga drew the waist-belt a notch tighter, and asked her attendant to bring a single strand of pearls.

Aunt Miechen, otherwise the Grand Duchess Marie Pavlovna, widow of the Czar's Uncle Vladimir, believed in keeping her relatives up to the mark: a dress had to be more elaborate, a tea more festive, when she graced the Alexander Palace with her presence. This seldom happened, except on state occasions, for Miechen and the Czarina had been at daggers drawn since the seventeen-year-old Alix of Hesse, painfully shy and stiff, had been unmercifully snubbed by the handsome young married woman on her first appearance in St. Petersburg society. The awkward princess had become the adored wife of the Czar, but Marie Pavlovna, self-confident, brilliant and worldly-wise, still treated her as a girl from the country, and her daughters as Cinderellas who were never even invited to the ball.

Aunt Miechen had a daughter of her own, married and

living in Greece, and three sons for whom she had once been very ambitious. They were not young men now, and Kirill, the eldest, was the man who had cut his own career short by marrying the divorced wife of Alexandra Feodorovna's brother. The second, Boris, who was nearly forty, had for long lived the totally uninhibited life of a Romanov bachelor, and the third, Andrei—not rash enough to risk a morganatic marriage—had spent many happy and domesticated years with the ballerina, Mala Kchessinskaia, and the son she had borne to him.

That any one of these grand-ducal cousins could be the subject of a confidential talk with the Czarina was beyond Olga's imagination. Probably another attempt to get mamma to give a ball, she thought; for Aunt Miechen was the most brilliant hostess in Petrograd, and while the sovereigns sat drinking their own cherry brandy with Anna Virubova her salons were always filled with outstanding people in diplomacy and in all the arts of which she was the patron. Olga knew the great lady was arriving by train from town, and that a half-company of cavalry had been sent to escort her to the palace. She waited until she heard the horses clattering across the great forecourt, and a few minutes more, and then went quietly down to the green drawing-room, waiting for her mother's summons.

It came in less than a quarter of an hour: a bell ringing, a maid of honour curtseying, and then the Grand Duchess Olga was admitted to her mother's mauve boudoir and kissing the air exactly one inch from Aunt Miechen's cheek.

"How are you, my dear? Not too busy, not too tired, I hope?"

"Thank you, aunt, I'm very well. And you?"

"Aunt Miechen is in splendid form," interrupted the Czarina. "She has come to us with the most remarkable proposal I have ever heard."

"Perhaps you would like to explain matters to the dear girl?" beamed Aunt Miechen, and the Czarina snapped, "Tell her yourself, Marie. I'll have nothing to do with it."

Olga looked interrogatively at her father's aunt. Marie Pavlovna wore a dark blue dress of fine cloth, with a sapphire brooch and earrings, just visible beneath her tiny sable bonnet. She was a robust, handsome woman in middle life, whose vigour made the Czarina's once dazzling beauty seem sickly and faded. She smiled.

"Come and sit beside me, Olga dear, and don't stand looming over me like a young giantess." The Grand Duchess reached forward and took Olga's hand. "The fact is, I'm here to speak for my son, your cousin Boris. He begged me to come here myself and open the—the matter nearest to his heart, on his behalf. He has just told me, and of course his brothers, what none of us suspected: that ever since you left the schoolroom, his heart has been given to you."

"I never suspected it either," said Olga. "I can't even remember when I saw my cousin Boris last."

"He respected your youth, my dear, and your great devotion to our wounded heroes. He wanted to wait until you were at least twenty, before he spoke."

"But he hasn't spoken yet," said Olga. "What am I supposed to do? Say 'Oh, Aunt Miechen, this is so sudden'? Isn't Boris brave enough to do his own courting?"

"So you will give him permission to address you, when his military duties permit?" said Aunt Miechen swiftly.

"Oh certainly, he may *address* me," Olga said, over her mother's furious gesture. "Then I can ask him one or two questions myself."

"Such as?"

"Well, Boris is twice my age; doesn't he really think that's rather too big a difference?"

"Not where there's a genuine attachment—"

"If Boris can convince me that there *is*! And then, Aunt Miechen, I should want to ask him if that Zina person, that lady who has shared his home here for so long, will pack her bags and leave before Boris is married, or if she'll stay on and make it a *ménage à trois*."

"Olga, let me tell you, no well-brought up girl ever referred to such subjects in *my* young day—"

"Probably not in your young day: at the court of Mecklenburg-Schwerin, wasn't it?" said Olga, who knew that Aunt Miechen hated to be reminded of her German provincial origins. "But there's a war on, aunt, or hadn't you realised it? I know all Boris's Zinas and Zizis are just meant to be fun, a young man sowing his wild oats—and poor old Boris has had time to sow a whole provinceful of wild oats—but that doesn't mean a modern girl can close her eyes to it."

"Boris will be grateful for your interest," said his mother, her nostrils quivering. "May I tell him that the Grand Duchess Olga does not entirely reject his addresses?"

"Tell him to ask my father, if he's such a stickler for etiquette. I think I know what father's going to say."

"*I* shall write to Nicky tonight," said the Czarina, getting a word in at last. "I shall tell him that a used-up, half worn out, blasé man has dared to propose—at second hand—to a pure girl half his age—"

"My dear Alix, how you love to dramatise yourself," said Marie Pavlovna, rising with amazing swiftness from her sofa. "I'm sure poor Nicky will understand, far better than you do, how important it is to get dear Olga settled in a home of her own, and with a member of the Family, who understands all her little fads and fancies—"

"You make me feel like an old maid, Aunt Miechen."

Miechen laughed, a hard little laugh. "Scarcely an old maid at twenty," she said, "but the years pass, faster than you realise. You're too thin now, and you ethereal blondes don't keep your looks for ever. Haven't you found it so, Alix? . . I shall tell poor Boris not to give up hope. If Nicky will kindly grant him leave from his duties, perhaps he will be able to storm Olga's hard heart himself—and to assure her that any little difficulty she may feel sensitive about will of course be cleared away before the wedding."

"Aunt Miechen managed a great deal better than we did," said Olga, when her mother returned from making the adieux which protocol required. "We were rude and excited, but she kept so cool. She made it sound as though she'd won."

"She's had a long training in duplicity."

"I wonder how Madame Zina Rashevskaia would like hearing herself called a little difficulty, something to be swept under the carpet to the tune of wedding bells?"

Olga laughed as she said it, but it was a bitter laugh, and the Czarina said remorsefully, "I shouldn't have let Miechen upset you. I oughtn't to have sent for you, only I wanted to let her hear you speak your mind yourself. Otherwise she would have said I wanted to keep the whole thing a secret, and have something else to blame me for."

"She didn't upset me, mother."

"You stood up to her so well, lovey, far better than I did at your age. Now I must get a letter off to your papa—there's a courier leaving for Mohilev at six, I know."

The Czarina sat down at her writing desk and opened her well-worn letter case. Olga said, "You're not going to write him all of that, are you?"

"Why not?"

"Oh, I don't know."

Alexandra paused with the pen in her hand. "Don't worry, dear," she said. "I won't tell papa what other thoughts have filled your little head and heart. Even the best of men can't understand that a young girl has holy secrets which others cannot share—"

It was the exact, the sickly note of 'Little Boy Blue', and Olga said rebelliously. "*What* holy secrets? What are you talking about, mother?"

"Don't you still think rather too often about Dmitri? I had so hoped you were beginning to get over that! He's not reliable, my dear. Felix got him into a wretched set, and they say he's undermined his health with drinking and late hours—"

"Dmitri's a darling, and I won't listen to a word against him. But Boris! Mother, you don't know how humiliated I feel, to have been proposed to by Miechen, on behalf of Boris Vladimirovich!"

"Of course the whole thing is Aunt Miechen's idea. She thinks that by marrying you Boris would be nearer to the throne."

"How could that be? I'm not in the succession to the throne! In Russia, no woman ever is."

There was silence in the mauve boudoir, where the Czarina sat in her flowing mauve teagown, so exactly matched by the scented Parma violets massed in the shallow bowls by Baccarat. Then she said carefully, "Boris wants to call himself the Czar's son-in-law, that's all."

* * *

Olga had hardly time to consider all the implications of the Grand Duke Boris's second-hand and second-rate proposal when the Grand Duke Dmitri, on the following day, came on the telephone.

"Dmitri! Where have you gone to ground this time?"

"I'm back at Pavlovsk. Special leave to see Marisha, she's got a week off from her hospital at Pskov."

"Oh good." In any other house than the Czarina's, it should have been possible to invite two favourite cousins to come to dinner, but Olga knew better; she asked discreetly, "When shall we see her—and you too, of course?"

"My last visit wasn't a great success, was it? . . Olga, are you there? What we were wondering was, could you come to tea with all of us at Pavlovsk this afternoon? . . Splendid! Try to come about four, and you and I can have a long talk first."

There was for once no need to give notice of her movements, for the Czarina had announced that she would be engaged all afternoon with Monsieur Goremykin, the venerable prime minister. More and more, since the Czar became Commander-in-Chief, she had tended to think of herself as the regent, summoning Ministers from Petrograd to secret conclaves, after which the couriers were sent flying with long unpunctuated letters to Mohilev. Olga ordered a troika and a sleigh for half past three. It was a beautiful winter afternoon of hard, glittering frost, the very day to drive behind horses along the short two miles to the palace of Pavlovsk.

Two pairs of white-gloved hands made the bearskin lap robe secure round Olga's waist and attached it by loops to the side knobs as soon as she was settled in the sleigh. She was wearing the sables which Simon had admired, with the addition of a sable muff which she held up to her face, in the classic gesture of a Russian lady, as a protection from the frost and from any lumps of frozen earth and snow which might be thrown across the screen of bright blue netting on each side of the sleigh. The driver, himself shapeless in furs, cracked his whip as they dashed out into the avenue. The sleigh bells began to ring.

The way to Pavlovsk lay between an avenue of Christmas trees, pines thickly embossed with the long winter's snow, on each side of which lay the handsome houses of those members of the Family whose ancestors had followed the Romanov empresses to Czarskoe Selo in the bygone days. The girl wondered if there was one of those houses left which her parents could enter as friends, one in which the Czarina's folly had not made half a dozen enemies. She was glad to be going to Pavlovsk, where a few congenial people lived remote from politics: Dmitri's grandmother, the widowed Queen of Greece, and the young Serbian princess who had married Prince John Romanov, and now Marisha, who like Olga asked only to be loved. There was no pomp at the beautiful yellow palace built by the son of Catherine the Great, no Cossacks, no secret police. Two sentries presented arms as Olga's sleigh swept through the iron gates, and two more came to attention at the entrance to the palace. But almost before the footmen had helped his cousin free of the bearskin lap robe, the Grand Duke Dmitri came running out to greet her, shrugging himself into his grey overcoat, and saluting, with his hand to his fur hat, before he kissed the hand in the little white glove.

"What an entrance!" he said admiringly. "My frost princess, you should live surrounded by furs and snow!"

"And tall guardsmen!" she mocked him. "Where's Marisha?"

"Sound asleep, but Helen meant to wake her as soon as we saw the sleigh. Come on, let's go for a walk. It's not too cold for you, is it?"

"*Walk?* Look at my shoes!"

"The paths are hard, you won't get your feet wet. And there's something I want to show you in the park."

She said "All right!" and tucked her hand companionably through the arm he offered. It was still daylight, although the ghost of a full moon had already appeared in the February blue, and a freshet of water could be seen among the ice of the little Slavianka river. A few wax candles, which the dowagers of Pavlovsk preferred to electricity, were lit in the windows of the palace.

"It hasn't changed much since his day, has it?" said Dmitri, looking up at the statue of their ancestor, the Czar Paul I, which stood alone in the forecourt.

"D'you know that if I'd been a boy they were going to call me Paul?"

"After *him* or after my father? I suppose my papa was still in favour, back in '95."

"Granny says it was after the emperor. She was against it, just to annoy mother, I imagine; but when you consider that Paul I was murdered by his own son, it didn't seem a very good omen for Paul II."

"Sometimes I'm sorry you weren't born a boy," said Dmitri.

Olga laughed. "What an ugly little wretch he was," she said, still looking at the statue. "Isn't that a grotesque nose! That's supposed to be what I inherited from him."

"You've a very pretty nose," said Dmitri, studying the charmingly tip-tilted profile under the becoming sables. "Do you remember when you used to call it 'my humble snub'?"

"Of course I was only fishing for a compliment. But oh, Dmitri, people *are* beginning to grow old when they start saying 'Do you remember'!"

"Wait till you see what I've got to show you, down here in the park."

"How *is* Marisha, Dmitri? Exhausted, I suppose?"

"She's been working awfully hard at her hospital, but she looks well in spite of it. She's bobbed her hair!"

"*Bobbed?*"

"Cut it short, round by the ears. It's the latest fashion abroad, and I must say it suits Marisha."

"We'd never be allowed to cut our hair."

"Dear Olga, not *your* lovely hair!"

Olga stopped short at the top of the path leading down to the Slavianka. "Is this what you wanted to show me?" she said incredulously, and Dmitri laughed. In the wide, safe space between the frozen river and the little Temple of Friendship which Cameron had built, the prettiest of all the follies of the Pavlovsk park, there stood a magnificent snow mountain, far higher than any ever seen at Czarskoe Selo, with its ascent ladder frozen into the rear, and toboggans protected by a tarpaulin at one side.

"Alone I did it!" said Dmitri. "Well—almost alone, with the assistance of Marisha and four creaking stablemen, veterans of the battle of Plevna, I'm inclined to believe—"

Olga giggled. "Oh, come on, they couldn't be as old as that. It really is a beauty, though!"

"The poor little kids were playing on such a miniature one, I couldn't bear to see it. So we started in with river water and buckets, and that's how we ended up. You should have heard the nurses shrieking when I took the kids down on the toboggan!"

"I'll bet! Alexis would be wild with envy."

"Want to have a run yourself?"

"All bundled up in furs? I haven't tobogganed since I was in the schoolroom."

"That's not so long ago. Come on, I'll help you up."

There was something in the frosty air, the solitude, the unusual sense of freedom, which made Olga willing, as ever, to accept the unspoken dare. She hardly needed Dmitri's hand to guide her up the ladder, he pulling up the toboggans with his other hand, until they stood together on the little platform at the top.

'It *is* high, Dmitri! You go first, like you used to do!"

"Right."

He crammed the fur hat down on his blond head and was off, the runners of the toboggan striking sparks from the snow chute that was as hard as iron, flying down and down to brake and stop by the barrier formed by a hedge of young fir trees.

"Come on!" he shouted up to the excited girl, and Olga answered with a mock-dramatic cry as she launched her toboggan:

"Farewell, my youth!"

Then she felt the joy of that almost flight, that headlong, downward dash through particles of ice that stung her cheeks to crimson, down through depths of green and blue where the snow took on the colours of the sea, until she too braked to safety, and held out her hands to Dmitri.

He lifted her off the toboggan and into his arms. He kissed her as he had never kissed her in his life before, and Olga, hungry for love and aching with the strain of the months since Simon went away, responded to Dmitri's kisses. She put her arms round his neck like the child she still was, thrilling as he stooped from his great height to hold her closer still, as if their two bodies, so embraced, could hold back the oncoming darkness of the Russian night.

It was possible that if Dmitri Pavlovich had spoken the right words then, had turned to lead her up the path back to the palace in the shelter of his arm, the course of two lives might have been altered, and one life saved. But all he said when he released her was, "Darling Olga, that was fun! No, don't let's go back just yet. There's something I want to say to you while we're alone. Something about your father."

"We can talk indoors, surely. It's too cold to hang about in the snow."

"Come inside the Temple, then, it's warm in there."

He pushed open the door of the hall used for concerts before the war; now dismally empty with its seats piled round a statue of

Catherine the Great as Ceres, goddess of plenty, but certainly not cold.

"You're right, the stoves are hot. I wonder why?"

"Helen had them lit this morning, in case the kids got their clothes wet tobogganing," said Dmitri.

"I hope she had candles brought in too, if you're going to keep me here long." Olga felt chilled and irritable, somehow and against her will defrauded.

"Cigarette?"

"Thanks." It was dark enough inside the hall for the match to light up Dmitri's smoothly handsome face. "Olga, this isn't going to be easy to say, and all I can do is blurt it out: I hear you've refused to marry Boris Vladimirovich."

Over a heart-beat of anger she retorted, "How quickly gossip travels in the Family!"

"Gossip! Isn't it true?"

"Of course it's true. Oh, I didn't say no to Aunt Miechen, not in so many words, because I thought it was impertinent of her even to make the offer, but she knew what I meant all right. I wouldn't touch her precious Boris with a ten-foot pole."

"Olga, d'you know *why* that proposal was made, just at this time?"

"Not for love of me, I'm sure."

He brushed that aside. "Because Boris, with all his faults, is not a fool. He gets around, he meets more people than I do. He's quite aware that things are going very badly for your father—both at the Stavka and in Petrograd."

Olga was silent. She had picked up a child's toy, a windmill abandoned on one of the piled chairs, and was whirling it with her forefinger.

"We who're close to him at GHQ—Olga, please believe me, I hate to tell you this—we know he's not equal to the responsibilities of a Commander-in-Chief. He doesn't even try to do a fair day's work! He sees Alexeiev in the morning, and some others of the Staff as well, and he always has luncheon with members of the different Allied missions. But in the afternoon he does gymnastics, or goes for a long walk if it isn't snowing. In the evening he pastes snapshots into his albums, or sits for a couple of hours over some kind of puzzle, or a game of patience. His last big activity, when Alexis was at GHQ, was listening to Alexis say his prayers."

"You don't have to be cruel and sarcastic about religion."

"I'm being cruel to be kind. Religion's at the root of all the trouble—not our own true Orthodox faith, but the vile perverted superstitions Uncle Nicky's picked up from Rasputin. Do you know he never goes for a walk without Rasputin's walking stick, or gives an audience without holding an image Rasputin sent him in his hand? Your mother told him to comb his hair with Rasputin's comb before he took any important decision, and he *does* it, Olga, he *uses* the filthy thing, I've seen him do it! Last month your mother sent him a little bottle of wine from Rasputin's saint's day feast—Saint Grigori, can't you picture it? and Uncle Nicky was so excited he drank the stuff straight out of the bottle—"

"Drank that wine!"

"Ah!" said Dmitri, "that hit you hard—I thought it would."

"Do you wonder?" said Olga. "I told you when we were at your apartment in Petrograd that I couldn't possibly keep mother, or Ania for that matter, from sending anything Rasputin wanted sent, to Mohilev. Oh, my poor father? How did it affect him, the feast day wine?"

"It didn't affect him right away. But when it was time for *zakuski*, about an hour later, he drank a glass of vodka, which as you know he very seldom does, and ate nothing. He maundered all through luncheon about a character in a book called Little Boy Blue, and a little red gate and a brick wall covered with fruit outside your aunt's house at Walton—it was embarrassing. The Allied generals couldn't help exchanging glances—they probably thought poor Uncle Nicky was drunk."

"I wish he had been," said Olga sadly. "But Dmitri, I don't think it's so terrible to go for long walks in the afternoon, even at the Stavka. It's no worse than spending a whole morning making a snow mountain, is it? And things will change as soon as the thaw begins. Father will get away from Mohilev and be with troops again, and everything will be quite different."

"But whether he's at Mohilev or at the front, he won't be at home or in Petrograd, and that's where the real danger lies."

"You're thinking of my mother, aren't you?"

"Of course I am. She's not even regent, but she's behaving as if she were the sovereign. Believe me, Olga, I've learned to quail—and so has Uncle Nicky—at the sight of the couriers arriving with her letters from Czarskoe Selo. Dismiss this

Minister, promote that one, stop the trial of the War Minister and his conniving wife—there's nothing too great or too small for her to interfere in. And only two days ago she asked him to accept Goremykin's resignation and make Boris Stürmer prime minister—"

"Goremykin was coming to see her this afternoon."

"Probably signing his resignation this very minute. To make room for Stürmer—with the German name and the German sympathies. Can't Aunt Alix realise that it's fatal for her to make that man her protegé?"

Olga threw the little windmill on the floor. The sunset light had almost died away, but the full moon was shining brighter, and the Russian colours of the windmill's sails, white, red and blue, were turned in its pallor to a uniform silver grey.

"What d'you expect me to do about it?" she cried in the high petulant voice of a schoolgirl.

The young man moistened his lips. "To see straight, Olga. Because if things go on the way they are, with Aunt Alix and Stürmer and Rasputin running the country, we're heading straight for revolution. A far worse revolution than the disturbances of 1905."

"Have you tried saying this to my father?"

"Have *I* tried! Everybody has tried—my own father, and the older cousins like Nikolai Mikhailovich, and poor old Nikolasha before he got shopped to the Caucasus, and Rodzianko speaking for the Duma, time and time again. None of us did any good. Nothing will do any good at all . . . unless the Czar can be persuaded to abdicate."

"Abdicate!"

"Yes, Olga. Give up the throne, and take Aunt Alix to live quietly at Livadia, away from war and politics . . . before anything worse can happen to them."

"Do you remember the grand-ducal oath you took when you were sixteen? The Romanov tradition, that the girls get a diamond necklace on their sixteenth birthday, and the boys pledge allegiance to the Czar as head of the Family, as well as sovereign? Does your allegiance include asking your sovereign to give up his crown?"

"I don't care a damn for any outworn tradition. What concerns me is the future of our House—and Russia."

"But the House of Romanov comes first with you? I see." Olga laughed scornfully, but her face was grave, and her cousin's silence forced her to say, "If father really were to abdicate, is Alexis old enough to be crowned Czar?"

"Alexis is the Heir, and some people think he could reign with a council of regency until he comes of age."

"But you don't?"

"I know what's the matter with Alexis. Do you?"

"Dr. Botkin told me, after they had to bring him home before Christmas. How did *you* find out?"

"Indirectly, from something one of the British officers said about the Spanish royal family. He'd been an attaché at Madrid before the war, and he learned that two of King Alfonso's sons suffer from haemophilia. Apparently they don't make any secret of it there."

"Unlike us. And did this man say the boys got it from Queen Ena?"

"Alas yes, she's what they call a carrier, through her grandmother Queen Victoria."

"Like my poor mother." Before the pity in Dmitri's face she said with a kind of bravado, "At least it's got nothing to do with *your* side of the Family!"

"No. But you understand why we daren't try to rally army support to poor little Alexis, because—"

Dmitri left the sentence unfinished. But Olga could fill it in with the words of Dr. Botkin: "because the life of the Czarevich hangs by the merest thread."

"After Alexis," the Grand Duke went on, "the next in the line of succession is your Uncle Michael. I remember the prayers for him in church as heir-apparent, years before Alexis was born."

"Poor old Uncle Misha, with his famous morganatic wife!" said Olga. "Do you think he'd be much of a success as Floppy the First?"

"No, I don't. And that's when we come to the ambitious Boris and his two brothers, the grandsons of the Czar-Liberator."

"You're a grandson of the Czar-Liberator too, Dmitri."

"But I'm not ambitious, dear."

"You can't mean that *Boris* wants to be the Czar?"

"No, but he rather fancies himself as the consort of the reigning Czarina."

It took a moment for his meaning to sink in. Then Olga, seizing the lapels of her cousin's greatcoat, and striving to see his face in the brightening moonlight, exclaimed "Me! You think I could succeed to the throne, and reign as the Czarina? You're out of your mind."

He took her in his arms again, in an attempt to regain the physical harmony they had both felt at the bottom of the snow mountain.

"No, I'm not crazy, dear. You are the logical choice. You're Uncle Nicky's eldest daughter, and you've made yourself immensely popular since the war started. Everybody admires the way you stood up to Rasputin. And remember how those sailors and those shipyard workers cheered you at the *Poltava* launching? Remember the Allied ambassadors applauding, that night at the concert in the circus? You made more friends in the one month you spent at the Anitchkov than your mother did in more than twenty years in Russia. Don't shake your head! I know all about the Law of Succession. Paul I declared by imperial ukase that no woman could reign in Russia after him, because he hated his mother, the great Catherine. Your father need only sign a rescript revoking that ukase, and a new law stands."

"Do you think he would ever sign a ukase making over the throne to me? My mother wouldn't let him, to begin with."

"She can be stopped from interfering, by force if need be," said Dmitri. "What we are planning could be the dawn of a new day for Russia."

"Planning!" she echoed. "Do you realise that what you're saying is high treason?"

"It won't be treason if the plan succeeds. If you stand fast on the letter of the law, we'll make your father sign the ukase when he signs the act of abdication. If he refuses, the army will carry you to Petrograd and the Winter Palace, as her soldiers did for Catherine the Great."

"She usurped her husband's throne, and later had her husband killed," said Olga. "Aren't we a charming family? Now you and your friends want me to usurp my brother's throne, in the expectation that he'll die an early death. Who *are* your friends, by the way? You didn't dream this up all by yourself."

"I'm not at liberty to reveal their names."

"Except for Boris Vladimirovich, who seems to have shown his hand too soon."

The Grand Duke plucked up courage. She had objected, of course, and made a girl's fuss; but the deed was done, and at least she had not refused point blank. He said urgently, "I know all this has been a shock. But think it over, Olga; try to see it from everybody's point of view. Uncle Nicky will be perfectly happy with Aunt Alix at Livadia, and poor little Alexis may well be thankful to be spared the burden of the crown. Whereas you, Olga—strong and generous-hearted—"

"I don't want to think about it any more just now. Let's go back and talk to the Queen and Helen and Marisha . . . B-rr! I'm cold, and I can hardly see the way to the door."

"It's over this way; take my hand."

"If you were an experienced conspirator you'd have a dark lantern to light us back."

"The moon is bright enough." Dmitri pulled open the door. Between the Temple of Friendship, garlanded in carved grapes, and the river, the snow mountain reared up its great height in the moonlight, and Olga shivered again.

"That thing looks like a scaffold now . . . Dmitri!"

"Yes?"

"I don't know much about how the army put Catherine on the throne, a hundred and fifty years ago. Mother always made cuts in Professor Petrov's lessons, because she said Catherine was a disreputable woman . . . Don't laugh! I do know it was Prince Orlov, Catherine's lover, who engineered the *coup d'état*."

"Well?"

"If I agree to your plan, depending absolutely on my father's abdication, do you intend to play Orlov to my Ekaterina?"

"If you want me to."

"And if I tell you I'll have nothing whatever to do with it?"

Dmitri sighed. "Then I suppose I'll have to think of something else."

14

"WE OUGHT TO SAY, 'Thank God for our good dinner!' as we used to do when we were little, eh, Dolly?" said Simon Hendrikov.

"It was a wonderful dinner, Joe!" said Dolly, and Joe Calvert beamed. They were all sitting round the table in Joe's rented flat in the Italianskaia, with the windows open to the summer night.

"Glad you enjoyed it," he said. "I can't flatter myself you were treated to home cooking, but I wouldn't wish Varvara's efforts on to any of my guests. Specially when it's a celebration for Simon Karlovich's return to Petrograd."

"I'm flattered," Simon said, "but isn't it something new for the Europa to send out meals to private houses?"

"I wouldn't know. I fixed it up with them about six months ago, and they've been sending food round ever since."

"I wrote to you about the lovely dinner Joe gave father and mother and me at our New Year," said Dolly, with a faint touch of complacency, and Simon agreed with a smile. During a pleasant evening he had been quietly amused by his sister's little proprietary airs towards Joe Calvert, and Joe's devoted attention to everything Dolly said. He had never imagined having an American brother-in-law, but from hints dropped by his parents, and Dolly's sparkling eyes, he thought this might come to be. After all, Dolly was nineteen now, and prettier than ever.

"You were saying you hadn't seen Mara Trenova since her mother's funeral," Joe began, when Varvara had lumbered out with a tray of dishes, and Dolly pouted.

"*Not* a very cheerful subject for a celebration, poor Madame Trenova's death," she said. "It was very sudden, just three weeks ago. The Finnish doctor said she must have had a heart condition for a long time."

"And never had a check-up, I suppose."

"Probably not. Mara travelled to the dacha with papa and me.

We buried her at Koivisto, you know: it seemed the best thing to do. And at least she wasn't alone, mamma was with her when she had the last attack."

Joe changed the subject. "Any chance of your getting to the dacha before your next posting, Simon Karlovich?"

"If I'm very lucky. You've been there, haven't you?"

"Your mother kindly asked me for the Easter weekend. My first break for over six months, and I surely did enjoy it."

"More than I enjoyed *my* Easter," Simon grumbled. "I expected to be back at Czarskoe Selo by the end of March."

"Simon was looking forward to the Easter reception, and exchanging the resurrection kiss with all the little Grand Duchesses," said Dolly slyly. ". . . Never mind, Simon, you'll be there tomorrow, and they'll soon be back from their visit to Mohilev."

It was too much to expect shiftless Varvara to draw the cloth, and Joe set a tray with bottles and glasses on the white damask. It was new, like the damask table napkins, for he had recently replenished Dick Allen's modest stock, and bought some delicate glasses to replace the tumblers Varvara regularly smashed. There was even a bowl of ragged flowers in the middle of the table and another on the writing desk, in Dolly's honour, for Joe was trying to make the bleak little flat seem more like a home.

The telephone rang sharply.

"Who can that be, at eleven o'clock at night? Will you excuse me, please?" said Joe.

He picked up the telephone. "Who? . . Good Lord, we were just talking about you. How are you?" he put his hand over the mouthpiece and said "It's Mara Trenova!" Simon, with interest, watched the back of Joe's neck slowly turning red.

"He's *what*? . . . I didn't even know he was in Petrograd. Where did you . . . well, have you called a doctor? . . . But surely if he's as bad off as you say . . . All right, I'll come as fast as I can. What's your number on the Yamskaia? . . Right, I'm just leaving."

He hung up without a word of goodbye, and turned to the Hendrikovs.

"That was Mara," he repeated unnecessarily. "She's got that friend of mine, you met him once, Dolly, Richard Allen, at her apartment. He's been in some sort of accident, cut his arm or something, and she wants me to come and take him away. Extraordinary girl!"

"He's the Englishman father knows, isn't he?" said Simon. "Where do you suppose she met up with him?"

"Or why she didn't call a doctor. Look, I'm really sorry about this, but I guess some funny business has been going on. She made it seem like Dick had been drinking hard, and I just don't believe it."

"I'll come with you," said Dolly, jumping up. "If there's been an accident, I can help."

"I'll come too," said Simon. "I'll get a droshki from the rank outside the Europa."

"Before we go anywhere," said Dolly, very much in charge, "I think we should put out some sheets to air. Perhaps Captain Allen ought to go to bed as soon as we bring him back."

"I hate to have our evening end like this." But Joe got fresh bed linen from the cupboard in the hall, and helped Dolly to spread it out in the warm living-room before they all went downstairs. Not much was said until they found a droshki. There was a traffic jam at the corner of the Nevski Prospekt, where three soldiers in well-worn uniforms were objecting to being refused entrance to a tramcar.

"That's one of the stupidest things they've done yet," said Joe. "Depriving the military of the right to ride the streetcars."

Simon made no reply. There was much else to get accustomed to in this city from which he had been absent for nearly a year, above all the endless queues for food and fuel. There was now very little meat on sale, although the Europa Hotel had sent a leg of roast lamb to Joe Calvert's dinner table as a matter of course. Lena, his mother's one remaining maid, had told him that the great subject of rumour in the food queues was the scandal of the municipal cold storage depot beyond the Baltiski railway station, where the refrigerators were overflowing with rotting animal carcases, once intended as beef for the army, and now, because of the lack of transport to the front, fit only to be taken to the glue factories by horse-drawn carts.

The square in front of the Vladimir church smelled as if some of the carcases had been piled there too, for the street cleaners had come out on strike, and beneath the empty market stalls and on the cobbles there was a thick layer of straw and vegetable refuse. Some beggars were pawing it over in the hope of finding food.

"It's a lousy section for a girl like Mara to be living in," said Joe. "I thought she'd got a worthwhile job with some newspaper."

"She's not with a newspaper at all now," Dolly said. "She's employed as a stenographer in a commercial office—hides and tallow, I think she said."

"Can't be much money in hides and tallow these days."

There was a knot of loungers in front of the tenement where Mara Trenova lived. They muttered and moved unwillingly aside at the arrival of a droshki with an officer in the uniform of the Garde Equipage, but a girl in nurse's dress was rightly a privileged person, and Dolly, followed by Joe, went unmolested up the steep stone stair. Simon remained standing by the droshki, to make sure, he said, that the *isvoschik* didn't pick up another fare. In fact he wanted to avoid the irritation of a meeting with Mara Trenova.

The bell pull outside the door of her flat was broken, and the tongue waggled uselessly in Joe Calvert's hand. He knocked on the thick panel. After a few minutes the door was slowly opened, in the semi-darkness it appeared by nobody. Then Joe looked down and saw, somewhere between his waist and his shoulders, the huge head of a hunchback with suspicious eyes peering through a tangle of dark hair.

"Mara Trenova sent for me," said Joe, and then she was there, saying "Thank you, Joe! What, Dolly, you too?" and drawing them into a room with an empty grate, a kitchen table covered by a checked cotton runner over oilcloth, and a long sofa or daybed on which Richard Allen lay breathing heavily. One arm, bandaged with strips of towelling, lay across his chest, and a tin pan full of blood-stained water stood on the kitchen table.

Dolly Hendrikova began to examine the bandages, and Joe asked Mara what in the world had happened.

"*I* don't know," she said with an affectation of bravado. "I was at 'The Red Sarafan' with my friend Mr. Sergiev" (she indicated the hunchback, standing like a sentry by the kitchen door) "when we saw Mr. Allen arguing with some men at the entrance. We thought he'd been drinking, which was none of our business, but when we left ourselves a few minutes later we saw him leaning against the wall with blood dripping from his sleeve.

I brought him here for first-aid treatment, but then he became unconscious, and the best thing I could think of was to send for you."

"Quite right," said Joe, and Dolly, looking up, said, "You were smart to put on a tourniquet, Mara. The bleeding seems to have stopped. Is there another piece of towelling, please?"

"Plenty. How lucky you could come along, Dolly! Were you spending the evening at Mr. Calvert's flat?" Dolly was tearing up a strip of towel, and Mara went on without waiting for an answer, "It was only a shallow cut inside his arm."

Joe looked at the hunchback and then at Mara. Another year of independence, of God knew what else, had changed her greatly. Her sharp features were sharper than ever beneath a thick black fringe, for Mara, though not for reasons of fashion, had cut her hair short, and the heavy leather belt she wore gave an almost masculine look to her dark jacket and skirt.

"I was sorry to hear of your bereavement," he said.

"Thank you. And thanks to Dolly's parents, my mother had one good year—perhaps the happiest she ever had, since my father died."

"Are you going to stay on alone in this apartment?"

"For the present, yes . . . See, now he's coming round."

Dolly had laid a cloth soaked in cold water on Dick's forehead, and as the drops ran down his cheeks he moaned and stirred on the couch.

"He looks younger than when I saw him last," said Dolly in a whisper.

"He's shaved off his moustache, that's why." Joe thought that a thin blue suit, which might have been worn by anybody, instead of the padded garments of the Moscow merchant, also made Captain Allen look slighter and younger; and at that moment the Englishman opened his eyes and said, "Good Lord! All of you! Awfully sorry to be such a nuisance! Where have you brought me to?"

"You mustn't talk, Mr. Allen," said Dolly Hendrikova.

Dick levered himself up on his sound elbow, gave a groan, and set his teeth.

"Dolly, don't you think he needs a doctor?" said Joe, and Mara hastily intervened.

"It would take too long. No doctor is ever in a hurry to come to the Yamskaia—"

"I've got nine American doctors cooling their heels not very far away," said Joe, "and a droshki waiting outside. Dick!" he said urgently, as Captain Allen succeeded in sitting up, "do you think you can make it as far as the street?"

"I can try."

"That's the best plan!" cried Mara. "What do you want now, Dolly? Material for a sling? Will this do?" She took a whole, clean roller towel from a cupboard, cut it open with the kitchen shears, and held safety-pins while Dolly arranged the makeshift sling.

"I hope to God his wound doesn't open again, jolting over the cobbles," muttered Joe. He braced himself beneath Dick's weight and remembered thankfully that Simon was waiting in the street below. Dolly put her arm around Dick's waist.

"Thank her—please," Dick gasped, and Mara Trenova said, "It's all right!" She spoke in English, and the silent hunchback scowled. "You were kind to me when I was in distress, Joe. I'm glad I could do something for your friend."

* * *

It was not till the following evening that Joe heard the complete story of the incident at 'The Red Sarafan'. By that time Dick was in good heart, having been doctored and nursed all round the clock by members of a newly arrived American Red Cross team who had volunteered to care for prisoners of war in Russia. Varvara, amazed and dismayed at finding her former master in the spare room bed, had slippered in and out all day with glasses of tea and bowls of buckwheat gruel, and although he had been ordered to remain in bed Dick had felt able to get up in the afternoon and make a laconic telephone call to the British Embassy.

"They're sending a car for me in the morning," he told Joe, swirling round in one of the new glasses the very small ration of bourbon and branch water which Joe allowed him. "They want me to rest up there for the next few days."

"I should hope so. You must get leave for a couple weeks, and go fishing. Well no, not fishing with that arm, but you could go to one of the embassy dachas, couldn't you?"

"I could not. In a couple of weeks' time I expect to be in Archangel, not exactly a holiday spot."

"What're you going to do in Archangel?"

"An interpreting job."

"Something to do with your pleasant evening at 'The Red Sarafan'?"

"No, that was a hangover from my last assignment. Just a hunch I had, which didn't quite pay off."

"I'll say it didn't. Now come clean, Dick, you always tell your story backward; begin at the beginning."

"All right, I'll come clean, but just let me ask you one question. In your Service, is everything so compartmentalised, as well as departmentalised, that you don't know what problem your colleague in another branch is working on?"

"I'm not quite sure I follow your thinking," said Joe cautiously.

"Well, here's an example. There was a very decent chap here before you, Murchison I think his name was?"

"Ned Murchison. He was posted to Berlin when I came to Petersburg in June '14."

"Right! I remember wishing him luck at the Fourth of July party, where I met you for the first time. Now, you're both in the consular service, you're both neutrals, you could communicate by diplomatic bag, but tell me, have you ever heard of Ned Murchison from that day to this?"

"He could be posted to Jericho for all I know."

"Precisely. Well, that's the way we operate too. Not on a personal but on a departmental scale. In other words, I may have wasted the two years I spent loosely attached to our Legation in Stockholm, trying to track down the flow of German gold from Germany to Petrograd."

"I'd hardly call them wasted years."

"They were, because I was concentrating on the flow of German money from Stockholm to the ring running Rasputin. Now I know the really big German bribes go through Stockholm and out again to Bern and Zürich."

"To the Social Democrats in exile? The hard-core Marxists?"

"Exactly, to the Bolsheviki. As a matter of fact, to two chaps living in Switzerland for years. Of course, Whitehall knew all about it. Even I was told that Baron von Romberg, in Bern, was one of the German ambassadors whose embassy covered an intricate spy ring. But Bern was in one Whitehall dossier, and Stockholm was in another, and it wasn't until I picked up a cross-reference in Reval that I started to follow up the trail myself."

"The cross-reference being Alexander Keskuela," said Joe tranquilly.

"*Eh?*"

"We've got considerable material on him in our embassy files. We're not as dumb as some of you think we are, you know."

"Then you know that Alexander Keskuela, born in Esthonia, arrived in Switzerland September 1914, is one of the key contacts with the man who calls himself Lenin. Vladimir Ilyich Ulianov, author of the 'Defeatist Thesis' that Russia should be defeated by Germany to prepare the way for the class war. Keskuela was on to that as soon as the stuff was printed. He got £20,000 out of the German government, cash down, to finance Lenin's and all the other Bolshevik publications, as long as they hewed to the same party line."

"That about the figure we've got."

"What have you got on Parvus?"

"Nothing."

"Oh well now, Parvus. He's a bird of a very different feather. Keskuela has this excuse, he's an Esthonian patriot, and thinks the downfall of Czarism will mean an Esthonian Socialist Republic. Parvus is an old pal of Trotsky's. They were in the first Petersburg Soviet together, back in '05, but after a turn as financial adviser to the Young Turks, he got to like his little comforts, and by the spring of last year he was nicely established in a suite at the Baur au Lac, one of the most expensive hotels in Zürich. His official reason for living in Switzerland is that he's running a translation bureau called the Scientific Institute. The profits wouldn't pay for even a chauffeur's room at the Baur au Lac if it weren't a front for the German-Bolshevik finance machine. Parvus is the man who distributes the money to finance strikes in the Russian war factories. The railway workers, the chaps at the Baltiski, the Putilov, the Obukhov works—Parvus, sitting pretty in the Baur au Lac, is the man who brought them all out. He'll foot the bill for Lenin to come back to Russia, when the right time comes."

"Which will be when?"

"Perhaps never, if this summer's offensive succeeds. But there's no reason to suppose it'll succeed any more than the great attacks of 1914 and 1915. Less."

"In other words, German money is behind the Social Dems. and their Bolshevik leadership, inside and outside of Russia. And the right time for Lenin to stage a *coup d'état* will be when the Czar's regime collapses from its own inertia."

"That's one way to put it," said Dick Allen, and lay back on his pillows.

"You getting tired?"

"No, carry on."

"If Parvus and Keskuela are both outside Russia, what took you to 'The Red Sarafan' last night?"

"Some news I had about one of Parvus's young men at the Institute. He and his mother left Russia for Switzerland a few years ago, ostensibly for the kid to study at Zürich University, and they bought a villa on the Dolderberg outside the town. I know young Boris came back to Russia for a few months last year, but since then he took out Swiss citizenship, which means he can come and go to Germany as he likes. We believe he's one of the couriers between Lenin and his paymasters in Berlin, so when we picked up his trail on the way back to Petrograd I thought I'd like to check on who he was seeing here."

"A youngster, is he?"

"Twenty-eight and looks younger, according to his description. Medium height, fair-haired, slim: everything we have on him stresses his marked resemblance to Alexander Kerensky, the Labour leader."

"That's an odd coincidence."

"My information was that this fellow Boris might try to make contact with one of Lenin's agents at the 'Sarafan' last night—it's a notorious meeting-place for the comrades, and I wonder it's never been raided by the Okhrana. So I went there for a look-see. I had some food and a half bottle of wine—which was sealed, and opened at the table—and listened to the music for a while. Then I had some brandy, brought in a glass, and after that I knew I had to get outside fast. There was a scuffle at the door, but I don't remember much until you were there in Mara's kitchen, and you know the rest."

"Somebody slipped you a Micky Finn, I guess."

"Somebody tried to knife me, and I don't mean just a slash up my inside arm. Joe, was I delirious, or was there really some sort of a dwarf hauling and shoving at me, when Mara got me up those stairs?"

"There was a poor misshapen creature along with her, called Sergiev, she said."

"Could it have been Sergiev who was carrying the knife?"

"In that case I don't see Mara acting as the good Samaritan."

"I'm not so sure. They say there are a lot of women like Mara in Switzerland—Russian exiles, fagging for the Bolsheviki, making the tea and copying the manifestoes. Women who would stick a knife in your back one minute and dry your feet with their hair the next. I don't think Mara Trenova's made up her mind if she wants to be a revolutionary or a saint."

* * *

The Russian summer offensive of 1916 *had* to succeed. Nobody connected with the plan of campaign, from the Czar and his effective commander in the field, General Alexeiev, and all the epauletted and bemedalled officers of the Stavka, to General Brusilov, chosen to spearhead the attack, dared to envisage anything less than total victory.

For some of them, and perhaps most of all for the Czar, it was a matter of personal prestige. It was galling to think that the only conspicuous Russian success since winter ended the German advance in 1915 had been achieved by the Grand Duke Nicholas, recently relieved by the Czar of the supreme command. Sent to a remote theatre of operations, 'Nikolasha' had distinguished himself by the capture of the key Turkish city of Erzurum, and followed it up by taking Trebizond on the Black Sea. It was proof of what nobody had really doubted, that the Grand Duke was a first-rate professional soldier, but scarcely a matter for great rejoicings. Meantime the French were engaged in the catastrophic defence of Verdun, and the British were about to open the equally catastrophic battle of the Somme. A Russian offensive on the grand scale would relieve the pressure on both the western Allies, and it was Simon Hendrikov's bad luck that he reported at Czarskoe Selo at this precise moment of history, when the advance was all that mattered, and nobody was interested in the return of an officer from the replacement depot at Odessa. The Guards were stationed, as a combat unit, in the Lithuanian sector of the front, where the enemy invariably attacked in great strength, and subject to the calculated losses, Lieutenant Hendrikov might expect to become a replacement there himself. Meanwhile, the papers confirming his captaincy were lost somewhere in the files of General Staff Headquarters.

The members of the imperial family seemed preoccupied too, in their different ways, when Simon saw them for the first time after they all came back from Mohilev at about ten o'clock one summer night. It was true that it was late, and only a few of the privileged courtiers had been invited to be at the station, but Simon could remember arrivals and departures when all the Grand Duchesses had made a point of greeting the members of the bodyguard by name. Now Tatiana seemed more intent than ever on her mother's comfort, while the younger girls and Alexis were equally concerned with sorting out the leashes and baskets of the various pets. The maids and valets were swarming round the luggage, and the Grand Duchess Olga, the last to leave the train, made her way round them without a look to right or left. Only a sidelong glance, and the corner of a smile, helped Simon to persuade himself that she had seen him in the uncertain light of the station lamps.

Next morning, long before the bugles sounded for parade, he went to their old rendezvous at the Znamenia church. He hardly dared hope that Olga would come to meet him. Their second parting had been much longer than the first, and this time he had not returned as a wounded hero, but simply as a run-of-the-mill subaltern who had spent a year shuffling papers in a transit camp outside Odessa. He had no right to hope that the Czar's daughter would be faithful to the memory of a few passionate words spoken in his father's study on another summer afternoon.

He knew that Olga's correspondence, as she neared her twenty-first birthday, was still as strictly supervised as when she was ten years old, and his only way to send her messages had been through Dolly. He wondered if she thought of their relationship as something in a story or a play, as illusory as *Young Lochinvar*, and in one sense Simon Hendrikov had not been as faithful in love as Farnum's cowboy, or the hero of Scott's poem. He had been physically unfaithful to his hopeless ideal not once but many times during the drudging months at Odessa, and he wondered if Olga, too, would some day break under the strain of a romantic love with no hope of sexual fulfilment. He had heard it said more and more often that she would end by marrying her cousin Dmitri.

There the wondering ended, for she was coming towards him between the birch trees, with the early morning sun sending her long shadow ahead of her on the wet grass. She was thinner, and looked taller, dressed as he had never seen her dressed before, in a short skirt with a plain white silk blouse, and one of the new belted jersey coats slung round her shoulders. She was smiling as she came, but he saw that Olga's face was graver; the old eager friendliness was gone.

"Simon!" she said, and gave him her hand to kiss. "I knew you would be here this morning! But what a long, long time you've been away!"

He was too diplomatic to say, "Every time I put in for leave it was refused!" He said, "It's been ten times as long for me," and saw Olga frown at the courtier-like speech.

"I was hoping you would come for Easter," she said.

"I had a railway pass for Easter, but then there were the troops from Erzurum to shift, and all Easter leave was cancelled."

"I had the most beautiful Easter egg for you, painted with the Marine Guards' emblem."

"May I have it now?"

"I gave it to Alexis, he's collecting regimental eggs."

"I had a beautiful egg for you too."

"Keep it until next year."

"But what about the Easter kiss?" and Simon took Olga in his arms.

She had kissed him in the shelter of the Znamenia church last summer, with kisses as fresh as the lilac which grew round the walls, but now Olga put her hand against Simon's chest and said mischievously:

"Too late, it'll soon be midsummer! Don't you remember your Pushkin—

'Gone is the resurrection kiss
But yet to come: you swore it me!' "

"*Do* you swear it me, Olga darling? Do you?"

"Yes."

* * *

Twenty minutes later the Grand Duchess Olga strolled home through the Alexander Palace park, swinging her jersey coat by its collar and humming a little tune. She felt exhilarated, lightened in the heart which had been heavy during the week at Mohilev. It was not her first visit to the Stavka, and while her sisters exulted in the freedom of the woods and river (always accompanied by the mob of ragamuffins whom Marie attracted from the peasants' and railway workers' huts) Olga had watched and worried over the future. She saw that what Dmitri said was true: the Czar was not soldier enough, not man enough, to cope with the duties of a Commander-in-Chief. He was as much interested in acquiring a sun-tan, or in rowing on the Dnieper, as he was in the strategy of the summer offensive, and when they all attended the showing of a French film made on the battlefield of Verdun, Nicholas II had no professional comments to make. He showed only the tepid interest which he might have shown in *Young Lochinvar*.

Olga herself was hardly aware of the damage done to her spirit by the veiled suggestions of her cousin on the day of their last ride down a snow mountain. She had brooded over a possible future which contained both her father's abdication and her brother's death until she was hardened to both these ideas, and to the thought that it might even be her duty to allow herself to be proclaimed empress to save the nation from a revolution. But if her ambition was kindled—and Olga Nicolaievna was a true Romanov in her ambition—it was quenched almost immediately by the knowledge of the taint in her own blood, the game of Russian roulette that she must play if she ever dared to marry. There was no one to whom she could open her heart, not even her understanding grandmother, for the Empress Dowager, sick of her children's involvement with Rasputin, had gone off to Kiev. She had a child there too, her own daughter Olga, to whom the war had brought freedom: over the Czarina's anger and Rasputin's open disapproval, Olga Alexandrovna had won the Czar's consent to ending her miserable marriage by divorce.

But now Simon Karlovich had come back, and perhaps some day she would tell him her troubles. Even in that brief encounter by the church, Olga had felt they were still as right for each other as she had felt in Petrograd: that he was the man she could rely on through whatever troubles lay ahead. Meantime, it was a beautiful summer morning, and as she came near the garden entrance of the palace she saw the family breakfast table being set on the wide balcony where the Czarina liked to sit in the early morning sun. Closer at hand, she saw Alexis standing near the lake. He had his spaniel Joy at heel and was holding a basket of bread, for Alexis loved to feed the deer which wandered freely in the park. The little fawns were nuzzling up to him to be stroked. The boy had grown very much since the New Year, and while waiting for new uniforms to be made he was dressed for the first time in well-cut dark blue suits, like an English schoolboy. He was wearing a dark suit now, with a white shirt and a blue tie, and looked more like a youth of sixteen than a boy barely twelve. He was tanned from the river excursions with his father, and his hair glinted like copper in the sun. It struck Olga that if the doctors were wrong, and his health continued to improve, Alexis Nicolaievich would soon be a man. He might even be the Czar of All the Russias in ten years' time. How had she dared to think of usurping his inheritance? But then Olga thought of what she might be in ten years, an unmarried woman of thirty, a mere appendage at a young imperial court! Who would Alexis bring home as his bride, and what consideration would he have for his old maid sister? I'm not my brother's keeper, she thought impatiently. If my father abdicates, I shall do whatever I think is best for Russia.

15

THE GRAND DUCHESS Anastasia's fifteenth birthday was due to fall in June, a year short of the time when she would receive the traditional diamond necklace and be presented to society at a court ball. Marie, a year earlier, had good-naturedly allowed her ball to be postponed indefinitely, but the *enfant terrible* of the family was clamouring for 'a real grown-up dance' that summer.

"And I want it before, not after, my birthday," she said, "because all the handsome young officers will be going off to the front. After all, Olga and Tania had plenty of fun before the war, now it's my turn!"

A ball was ruled out, but the Czarina consented to a small dance in the great unused state rooms of the Alexander Palace, and Olga invited Simon Hendrikov at their very first meeting by the Znamenia church. She was looking forward to the dance as eagerly as the birthday girl. A real dance, with a string orchestra, and new dresses for them all—the Grand Duchesses had been deprived of such gaieties for years. And then, even while the chefs were preparing the cake and the ball supper, and the hot-houses were being ransacked for roses and heliotrope, news was received at GHQ which caused the Czar to cancel his youngest daughter's party.

It was not the news of the Battle of Jutland. That had already been greeted with angry tears by the Grand Duchesses, who still remembered a happy day aboard HMS *Lion*, and the attractive young British sailors of whom so many had met their death in the cold waters of the North Sea. But Russia, with her own warships penned up at Kronstadt, where the German submarines kept their doomwatch outside the harbour, was remote from the inconclusive battle between the Royal Navy and the German High Seas Fleet. It was the news of Lord Kitchener's death which shocked the world.

Kitchener, Britain's Secretary of State for War, and a man of immense prestige, had been personally invited by the Czar to visit the Russian battlefronts and report to his own government on the essential needs in military co-operation and supply. He died on his secret voyage to Archangel, going down with HMS *Hampshire* when the cruiser struck a mine off the coast of Orkney; and with him perished, in the long Atlantic rollers under Marwick Head, the only initiative Nicholas II had ever taken as Commander-in-Chief. He made his usual, fatalistic references to the birthday of the long-suffering Job, and desired his wife to cancel the dance for Anastasia.

Who wept, and said it was a great shame, and they never had any fun; but who became more reasonable when Tatiana quietly reminded her of court festivities which had taken place at the time of other tragedies, and the very bad impression this had made on all classes of society.

"But it's not like court mourning, is it?" said the child.

"No, but the British Ambassador and his party couldn't possibly come, unless it were made a matter of absolute protocol, and you wouldn't want that, would you?"

"It's not as if Lord Kitchener were a *relation*."

"Cheer up, Imp," said Olga. "We'll plan something nice for your birthday itself, and then you can have a lovely dance in the winter, along with Marie."

The Czarina herself had other ideas. "It does seem too bad to put it off, after all the preparations. Such a disappointment for poor Anastasia, and Sunbeam, too, was looking forward to it! His first dance, and really it was time he had some ballroom practice!" Their mother thought she would telegraph to Mohilev.

"I'd leave it, mother," counselled Olga. "I think papa has really made up his mind this time. Lord Kitchener was someone very special."

"Perhaps," said the Czarina with a shrug. "But Father Grigori told Ania his death may be a blessing in disguise. You know Our beloved Friend dreads what England may do in the peace negotiations. Later on Lord Kitchener might have done Russia harm."

"The Germans would love to hear you say that, wouldn't they?"

Olga's barb, planted where the Czarina was most sensitive, provoked another clash between the mother and the daughter, already parted by Alexandra's jealousy of her husband's love for Olga, and the youth and beauty of her eldest child. For several days the Czarina sulked, and spoke to Olga only in the presence of others. This was noted by the whole court—that strange, disaffected court, cut off from the intimate life of the imperial family by the empty rooms of state, and yet aware of every least shift of allegiance, every facet of disagreement in the little group of people they were pledged to serve.

Olga told Simon Hendrikov the whole thing, at the meetings they contrived early and late in the two palace parks. In the woods by the Chinese Pavilion, among the sedges on the verge of the lake near the Turkish bath-house, she blurted out the story of the drowned Lord Kitchener, and the drowned British sailors, and her horror at the increasing death toll of the war. Simon soothed her and kissed her, falling in love with her all over again, but now in a different way—as if their love was not hopeless, but might some day be openly acknowledged in a world of change. He was not to know how much Olga Nicolaievna left unsaid, nor that the story of the quarrel with her mother was her justification for her vision of herself as the reigning empress.

But Simon was gone within a month, not to the northern sector of the front but to the Stohod river. There what was left of the Imperial Guard was to advance to Kovel, one of the objectives of Brusilov's offensive which now began.

It relieved the German pressure on Verdun, but in all other respects it followed the pattern laid down in 1914 and 1915: a brilliant start, the routing of the Austrians, the capture of half a million prisoners who clogged the trains and the highways. And then the whole thing slowing down: no guns, no shells, no transportation, and the Germans moving east with disciplined precision. In all, the Germans had to take fifteen divisions from Verdun and the Somme to crush Brusilov. It was popular to blame the Czarina for the defeat: she, the German traitor, and her creature Rasputin, had ordered the Czar to 'stop the massacre' just when 'victory was within the Russian grasp'. It was true that Rasputin intervened. It was not true that victory was possible. The Guards stood on the Stohod and died almost to the last man.

In the two previous winters of the war, the coming of the snow had seemed to blanket Russia from the outside world. The snow slowed up all the reactions to the war, giving the generals time to plan, the war profiteers time to send their money out of the country, and giving even the young survivors time to marry and engender children in a false dream of peace. But not in 1916. That winter everything moved faster, except where the dead lay on the battlefields and on the vast steppes remote from the fronts where the Little Father Czar was still only at one remove from God. In Petrograd, from the warm, well-provisioned clubs and restaurants to the slums of the Lavra and the Zabalkanski, everybody knew that something was moving under the surface and would presently burst in fire through the snow.

Joe Calvert knew it, just as he knew, as soon as he heard of Kitchener's death, what sort of 'interpreting job' it was that took Richard Allen to Archangel almost before he was fit to travel. Joe was in his seat in the public gallery of the Duma, where he was now as familiar a figure as the ushers, on the day at the beginning of November when Miliukov, the Kadet leader, openly denounced the Czarina for engineering Stürmer's appointment to the Ministry of Foreign Affairs as well as the premiership which he already held, and Joe heard the Duma's deep-throated roar of approval. Joe met all the speakers, Rodzianko, Purishkevich, Alexander Kerensky, and reported on them weekly in the painstaking, pedestrian letters to his uncle which without his knowledge were now being read by the Secretary of State.

A naval commander who, by courtesy, bore the name of Yakovlev knew it, even while his ship, the *Askelod*, was on her way from Devonport to the new Russian harbour of Murmansk, and Mara Trenova knew it, hurrying between the hides and tallow merchant's office where she earned a modest salary, to the cellar where *Pravda* was printed, where she earned nothing but the satisfaction of believing that as a copy editor and caption writer she was helping to bring about the Revolution. And a man in Switzerland, who went by the name of Lenin, and who had once despaired of ever seeing the Revolution, began to think his hour was not far off.

The Czarina was doing everything possible to hurry on that hour. Launched on a Valkyrie ride of power, supported by her dark angel Rasputin, she went from excess to excess. After making Stürmer Foreign Minister, she forced the Czar to accept a man named Protopopov as Minister of the Interior, with the control of the Okhrana and the civil police. Protopopov was suspected of being a syphilitic, as such treated by Badmaiev, the

'Tibetan wizard', who had brought him to the attention of Rasputin. He was known to have been in touch, immediately before his appointment, with leading German agents at Stockholm. The Duma clamoured for his dismissal as well as Stürmer's.

"The Czar rules and not the Duma." So the Czarina wrote again and again to her husband at Mohilev, her self-will strengthening with every warning from Rodzianko, every letter from her relatives, every appeal to send Rasputin away and interfere no more in politics. Olga, alone in the Family, believed that Rasputin was not the key to the situation. He had fed Alexandra Feodorovna's mystical religious fervour, it was true. But far more than mysticism, the dominant in her nature was the will to power. Much stronger than her weak-willed husband, she now demonstrated, as she made and unmade Ministers, that she shared the same personality, the same manic drive to power as the man she hated—her first cousin, Kaiser Wilhelm II.

One woman came from as far away as Moscow to make a personal appeal to the Czarina. This was her sister Ella, the widow of the Grand Duke Sergei and now the Mother Superior of the Martha and Mary convent, a nursing sisterhood which had done much good in the city where the Grand Duke was assassinated. She arrived by train, rather late in the evening, tired but still beautiful in the pearl-grey robe of fine wool with the white wimple and veil of the habit designed for her by a famous painter. Rooms had been prepared for her in the visitors' wing of the Alexander Palace, as if to keep Ella at a distance from her sister, and there her nieces kept their Aunt Ella company while she ate some supper and asked her usual impersonal questions about their hospital work. Then she went to the Czarina, who received her in cold state, with two ladies-in-waiting and a gentleman usher in the drawing-room, before Ella was taken to the mauve boudoir for their private talk.

It did not last long. All those making polite conversation in the drawing-room heard the Czarina's terrible cry as her sister, ashen-faced, made haste to leave the hot mauve room. "I hope I never see you again! Never! Never!" It was left to Olga to take her aunt by the hand and lead her, blind with tears, to the apartments she had left so short a time before.

"Like a dog! She drove me away like a dog!" Ella kept saying, as they went down the marble corridors to the white and gold doors guarded, in honour of the Grand Duchess, by two of the Ethiopian attendants. But it was not Her Imperial Highness Elizabeth Feodorovna, nor the Mother Superior of a nursing sisterhood who fell sobbing on the velvet couch inside the doors. It was simply a woman, cruelly rejected by her sister, her nearest relative in Russia, for daring to protest against Rasputin and his sinister influence; for begging that sister to go to Livadia and stay there 'for her health's sake' at least until the spring.

"Aunt Ella, dear, please don't cry! It'll be all right in the morning, just you wait and see!" The Grand Duchess's maid brought sal volatile, and Olga signed to her to leave the room.

"I shan't be here in the morning. I shall go back to Petrograd by train tonight. There are twenty houses where I'll be made welcome—"

"Yes, yes, of course, but there *isn't* another train tonight . . . Yes, maybe, we could get a special, but it *is* late, and you're so tired, coming all the way from Moscow. Stay till the morning. Try to get some sleep."

Olga coaxed her aunt into taking off her habit, and helped her into a dressing-gown. It hardly seemed to belong to a convent life, being made of the finest embroidered lawn, and in it Ella looked still young and lovely when Olga loosened the gold hair so like her own. Even when her tears were dried with a handkerchief soaked in eau de cologne, Ella was too agitated to relax. She talked about the trains—a time-table—the connection to Moscow—her regret that Dmitri, who had lived in her house as a child, was far away at Mohilev—her anxiety about Marisha, who had a new love younger than herself—and so on, aimlessly, disjointedly, until after a long sigh she said:

"I suppose all this is my fault."

"But you were never fooled by Rasputin, Aunt Ella."

"I wasn't thinking about Rasputin. I was thinking that if I hadn't married your Uncle Sergei, Alix would never have come to Russia, or met Nicky."

"Oh come now, that's just silly," said Olga affectionately. "You might as well say mamma could have gone to visit Aunt Irene in Prussia, and married there. And she did stay, often, with Aunt Victoria in England, but she didn't marry an Englishman. She and papa met at your wedding, we all know that; only they would have fallen in love with each other wherever they met."

"Yes, but what I meant was, it was from me she learned to love our Orthodox faith. I found it beautiful and comforting when I came to Russia as a bride, but she went further, deeper into the mysticism which only Rasputin could satisfy. And then the *hating,* Olga! How she hated everyone who didn't bow down to her as the young empress—*that* she never learned from me—and yet I never had such a happy home as hers."

Olga sat uncomfortably silent, and her aunt went on:

"Couldn't you persuade her to go to Livadia, Olga? It's the only possible alternative to what may be in store for her, if your father abdicates."

Olga's fingers tightened on her aunt's hand. "Do you really think my father is going to abdicate?"

"If he's no longer competent to rule . . . if *she* continues to rule in his name . . . And some of our cousins hate her even more than she hates them. They want to have her shut up in a convent, if not in prison—unless Rasputin goes."

"Then Rasputin will have to go."

"That's what Dmitri says."

"Have you been discussing all this with Dmitri?"

"I haven't seen Dmitri for months—well, weeks," said his aunt in some confusion. ". . . You must forgive me, Olga dear, I've spoken to you much too frankly, but it's better you should know the truth. God knows, my only concern is for you and your dear sisters, and what is to become of you and little Alexis!"

"We'll be all right, aunt. And now you must really get some rest, it's nearly midnight. I'll come to you as soon as you send for me tomorrow morning."

She stooped to kiss her aunt good-night. But Ella kept hold of Olga's hand, and her grey eyes were inscrutable as she looked up at her niece and said:

"Dmitri thinks Alexis is too young to rule."

* * *

So that was one more tiny piece of the jigsaw puzzle presented by two people whose meeting and whose marriage had created such unusual problems for their children. Once, a younger Olga had thought of them only as papa and mamma, two people beyond all human questioning. Growing up, she had learned for herself their weakness and their strength, and now was learning more from other people. There was grandmamma, who had been afraid of the stiff German princess as a bride for her son, and Aunt Ella, who held herself responsible for Alix's religious fervour, and above all there was Dr. Botkin, who had revealed her dreadful legacy of haemophilia. Olga knew much, now, of what was driving this man and this woman towards their destiny. Before December was half over, the last piece of the puzzle came almost by chance into her hands.

It came when she was in a mood to seize at anything, any prospect of freedom from the dreariness which seemed to settle on the palace after Aunt Ella, icily calm, had given her blessing to the assembled Household and departed with a mounted escort to the station at Czarskoe Selo in the black darkness of the winter morning.

But before she discovered more of her father's past, outwardly simple but more enigmatic than her mother's, Olga had a brief message from Simon Hendrikov. She had learned before the end of October that he had come safely through the fighting near Kovel and was with a reserve battalion at Minsk, but that was a verbal message passed on by Dolly by telephone to the palace hospital. Now Dolly, greatly daring, brought his letter to the Winter Palace on one of Olga's committee days. There were hospital wards in the Winter Palace now, as well as the repositories for medical supplies, and a young nurse from the British Red Cross hospital had no great difficulty in passing the sentries.

There was no opportunity for a private word, for two of the Czarina's younger ladies-in-waiting were in the small room used as an office for the Soldiers' Families Relief Committee, but Dolly ventured to say:

"We were all hoping you would visit our little hospital yesterday, Madame. The Grand Duke Dmitri spent two hours in the wards, and everybody was so pleased!"

"I thought His Highness was at Mohilev."

"He told us he had forty-eight hours' leave."

"Ah well, when you had the Grand Duke Dmitri you didn't need me," said Olga. "But thank you very much for coming, Darya Karlovna." Dolly dimpled, and went away delighted. Olga, before she could read Simon's letter, reflected that Dmitri had undertaken a round trip of at least fifty-six hours to spend forty-eight in Petrograd, in his apartment with the hospital wards above, and wondered what pressing business or pleasure had brought him to the city.

Alone in the bedroom where she had laid her furs, the Grand Duchess opened Simon's letter. It was short and to the point.

My Princess,

We have now received orders to entrain for Petrograd, and will be at the Guards barracks until the middle of February. This means I can expect, by the duty roster, to be at Czarskoe Selo from then until the end of March.

I hope you will let me see you and be with you again. But there must be no more secret meetings. They are not fair to you. Give me the right to tell His Majesty that I love you. Once you said we were living in a changing world. Princesses have married commoners before now, even in the world we know. And my heart is yours always,

Simon

She memorised the words before she destroyed the single sheet of paper. They were very clear in her mind as she left the Winter Palace by the throne room of Peter the Great, and stopped to look at the red velvet throne under the draped canopy. It always seemed such a little throne for such an enormous man.

Now she had two alternatives, both seemingly impossible—to marry Simon Hendrikov, knowing her tainted blood, or to take the power in an army *coup d'état* and ascend that little, waiting throne.

She hoped all evening for a telephone call from Dmitri, which never came.

Her father's past rose before her unexpectedly, next day, when owing to an emergency change in Tatiana's hospital schedule Olga took her sister's place at a reception organised by the Refugee Committee.

"I admire your devotion, Olga Nicolaievna," said the lady-in-waiting, as they settled themselves in the limousine for the drive to Petrograd. "It's a presentation of purses, isn't it? Very tiring for you, especially after yesterday.".

"It's very disappointing for the people, not to have Tania," said Olga gaily. "Still, they do expect to see one of us, so I must go. I wonder when we'll be able to trust Anastasia with a Committee!"

She was fond of Countess Gendrikova, the youngest of her mother's ladies, and forced herself to laugh and talk on the way into the city. They were late, even by Russian standards, for the occasion, and apologising for Tatiana Olga had no time to glance at the list of those to be presented. The routine began, the names were called, the generous donors (they were nearly all women) came up to curtsey and kiss Olga's hand. She distributed a testimonial, a medal, sometimes both. It was very like a school prizegiving. The Malachite Room, where the ceremony took place, became unbearably hot.

"Madame Mathilde Kchessinskaia."

The dancer curtseyed to the ground, and lifted her vivacious face to Olga's with a smile.

"My thanks, madame, and my congratulations."

The prescribed words came mechanically, and Olga put the certificate and the medal into the little gloved hands. She listened to the citation, read aloud. Russia's *prima ballerina assoluta,* who had opened a hospital ward in her Petrograd residence and turned her dacha at Strelna into a convalescent home for the wounded, had recently undertaken a dancing tour across the empire from Reval to the Caspian Sea. All the fees for her share in the performances were in the purse now to be handed to Her Imperial Highness . . . At this point the eulogy was interrupted by applause.

"I'm one of your admirers, madame," said Olga. "I'd like to have a word with you after the ceremony. I want to hear more about your remarkable tour."

The ballerina curtseyed again and returned to her little gilt chair at the back of the hall. When she was brought to Olga in a small salon where tea was immediately served, the girl had recovered from her surprise, although she was still not sure of what she was going to say. It was quite impossible to say to Mala Kchessinskaia, at the very top of her profession, the adored for so many years of the Grand Duke Andrei, fulfilled both as an artist and as a woman, "Were you once, and are you still, my father's mistress?" She began to talk about the tour.

"How could you possibly go on stage, night after night, in

places like Tiflis and Baku, after travelling for hours in a crowded train? Didn't you get very tired?"

"Sometimes," Kchessinskaia smiled. "But I was lucky enough to have a wonderful new partner, who was a great support to me. Has Your Imperial Highness seen Vladimirov dance in Petrograd?"

"Did he appear in the tercentenary performance at the Maryinski?"

"Only in the ballet. He was understudying Fyodor Surov then. Vladimirov is very young, you know: he only graduated from the School in 1911—the summer I celebrated my twenty years on the imperial stage."

As she spoke, she touched an ornament pinned to her grey velvet dress—a diamond eagle pendant with a rose sapphire drop, the imperial gift which marked that twentieth anniversary. Looking at her, Olga could hardly believe that she was forty-four, the same age as the haggard, worn-out empress, for the ballerina, delicately built, had the complexion and the vitality of a much younger woman. Seen without the advantage of stage make up and lighting, she was no beauty; it was the piquancy and sparkle of her expression which gave her charm. It was not a face which concealed secrets, like so many faces at the court, and Olga was suddenly convinced that there was no truth in the rumours, so acceptable to the jealous Czarina, that this woman had taken bribes for placing orders with the army contractors.

She said, "You had no partner when I saw you dance at Krasnoe Selo, just before the declaration of war."

"In the mazurka? That's my favourite solo number. And—*A Life for the Czar* has always had a very special meaning for me."

There it was—the opening which Olga was too inexperienced to handle. And the dancer, as if sensing this, went on:

"I saw *you* that night, Madame, closer than I ever saw you before. Of course I remember you as a child, when the Empress Dowager used to bring you and your sisters to the matinées, but the imperial box at the Maryinski is a very long way from the stage! In that little theatre at Krasnoe I felt quite close to you when I was standing in the wings . . . You looked so lovely in your pink dress. I could see His Majesty was very proud of you."

"But it was you he looked for that night, madame. He saluted you at your dressing-room window, as we left the theatre."

With a little laugh, quite without the bitterness Olga knew

in her mother's laughter, Kchessinskaia said, "That window! It has rather special memories for both of us. Outside that window, in my first summer season at Krasnoe, your father used to stand and gossip with me before the performances. He was only the Czarevich then, of course: a young lieutenant in the cavalry."

"And after the performances?"

"Afterwards we became very good friends. I think he knew he could trust me, for he told me all about the beautiful princess he hoped to marry, in spite of the difficulties in their way . . . Those were happy summers at Krasnoe." She lifted one expressive hand in a dancer's gesture. "I have never seen him alone since his wedding day."

It was a finished, stage performance, and yet Olga knew instinctively that it was sincere. She also knew that beneath the smoothness, the sweet sympathy, there was a will of steel, that a passionate tigress breathed beneath the tame domestic cat. I bet *she* never felt like a mother to him, nor called him Little Boy Blue, was Olga's thought.

"There's a stretch of road on the Moscow highway," said Kchessinskaia, "that I can never pass without remembering our farewell. You know where the short cut to Volkhonski joins the high road, before the approach to Czarskoe Selo? That was where we said good-bye, twenty-three years ago . . . It's almost my only unhappy memory of our companionship."

"You were fortunate in your youth, madame."

"Yes, my friends and I were young together in happier times than these." The ballerina smiled at Olga, and she was not acting now. "Tell His Majesty that I shall always remember what he used to call me. *Radouchka*, bringer of joy."

16

WHAT BURST IN FIRE through the snow was the murder of Rasputin. The first intimation that the charlatan had reached the end of his course on earth came very quietly to the Alexander Palace at Czarskoe Selo. It was a beautiful December morning, with deep snow on the ground but clear blue skies. Alexis, brought home from Mohilev on Monsieur Gilliard's plea that lessons were being totally neglected at GHQ, recruited Anastasia as soon as their midday break from school work came round, and the pair of them had a lively snowball fight beside the frozen lake. Then, with the help of some of the gardeners, they planned the foundations of a snow mountain, "the biggest ever!" said Alexis. "Bigger than the one Cousin Dmitri built last winter for the little kids at Pavlovsk!"

"You never saw that one."

"No, but Olga told me all about it."

Mr. Gibbs, the Czarevich's other tutor, called Alexis indoors for an English lesson, and Anastasia sat down near her mother's table in the morning-room to sign 'OTMA' on some of the vast pile of Christmas cards which the sisters would send out.

"I thought you had a French essay to finish before luncheon," said her mother mildly. "Can't the cards wait until the afternoon?"

"I've got to see about the Christmas trees for the hospital in the afternoon, mamma. And the big one we always have in the *manège*."

It was all normal and cheerful enough. There was nothing in the tapping of Anna Virubova's walking sticks, as she limped across the parquet of the next room, to indicate that this was anything but her usual morning visit. But the sight of Ania's pale face, puffy with tears, and her bulging eyes, was a certain prelude to disaster.

"Ania, lovey, what has happened?" cried the Czarina. She tried to rise, and the loose pages of her writing pad were scattered on the floor.

"It's Father Grigori. Dearest, beloved Majesty, they telephoned to me from Petrograd. His bed hasn't been slept in. He didn't come home at all last night."

"Not come home? But you told me yourself he had agreed to go to supper with Felix Yusupov—"

"At the palace on the Moika—to meet Princess Irina—"

"Irina's in the country. Ania!" cried the Czarina, as the first hint of the terrible truth dawned upon her, "why didn't you tell me that before? If he was asked to meet Irina, then his enemies may have been preparing a trap for him—"

"I didn't think it mattered," whimpered her cringing friend. "I thought it would be all right, because Dmitri Pavlovich was going to be there too. I only warned our dear Father Grigori not to drink too much wine—"

"Too much wine!" The Czarina had struggled to her feet, and was clutching the back of her armchair. "They may have given him *poisoned* wine! Oh my God, what shall I do, what shall I do?"

"Dearest Majesty—"

"Be quiet, Ania," said Anastasia, "can't you see you've terrified my mother?" She put her young arm round the Czarina's trembling body. "Mamma, come and lie down. It'll be all right soon, they'll find Father Grigori any minute, he can't be very far away." The child hardly knew what she was saying. And the Czarina, deaf to comfort, whispered "Oh, my heart!" and collapsed between her armchair and the floor.

It was the first time the youngest Grand Duchess had ever been faced with such an emergency. She handled it quietly, pulling at the bellrope, sending two footmen running for Dr. Botkin and the Czarina's principal dresser, Madeleine, and got rid of Anna Virubova, while the Czarina was being carried unconscious to her bedroom, by ordering a sleigh to take her home. "You can do far more good in the Srednaia, Anna Alexandrovna," she said with a touch of Olga's decision. "Go back and start telephoning to everybody you can think of who might know where Father Grigori is now. Start by ringing up his housekeeper. And don't come back here until my mother sends for you."

"Would you like me to call the hospital, my dear?" said the lady-in-waiting on duty gently. "Don't you think one of your sisters should come home?"

"I'd like to wait for half an hour, Isa. You know, all this may be a false alarm. He may have stayed for breakfast at the Moika, and then gone for a sleigh ride into the country with Felix, it's such a glorious day."

"As you wish, Anastasia."

But before the half hour was over one of the chamberlains was bowing before Anastasia Nicolaievna, with a message that the Minister of the Interior desired to speak on the telephone with Her Imperial Majesty.

"I'll take the call myself." The main telephone of the palace was in the Czarina's mauve boudoir. The girl went to pick it up, and Baroness Isa, who followed her, was struck by the coolness of her greeting.

"This is the Grand Duchess Anastasia speaking, Monsieur Protopopov. Her Imperial Majesty is indisposed, and can't talk to you at present . . . No, I can't say when, her doctor is with her. You may give me the message. What? They discovered this *when*? . . . After Monsieur Purishkevich talked to the police?"

The baroness, watching, saw the girl's fingers curl into the palm of her free hand, and shook her head warningly at Dr. Botkin, who had come to say the Czarina had recovered from her fainting fit. They both waited until Anastasia laid down the telephone. But before either of them dared to speak she picked it up again and said to the palace operator:

"Please get me the Grand Duchess Tatiana at the hospital."

* * *

"I think we'd better all go back together," said Tatiana to her sisters fifteen minutes later.

"What, three of us come off the wards and all go panting home," said Olga, "just because Rasputin is lying blind drunk in some bath house, or bawling dirty songs in a cheap cabaret?"

"Felix wouldn't go to a public bath house any more than he'd go to a cheap cabaret."

"Don't you believe it! Felix hasn't reformed all that much. He's quite equal to a bit of fun when Irina's not at home."

"But he invited Father Grigori to *meet* Irina."

"Tania's right, Olga," said Marie. "We know he went away with Felix, because his people saw them leaving, and

Grigori Efimovich was all dressed up for the occasion. And you've heard what the Minister told Anastasia."

"All you've got to go on," said Olga argumentatively, "is that a policeman heard shots in the courtyard of Felix's house on the Moika and went to investigate. He saw this man Purishkevich, who shouted out, "We've shot Rasputin!" or "We've killed Rasputin!" or some such nonsense. So why didn't the police go inside and look for the body, if they believed what Purishkevich said was true?"

"Because Dmitri was indoors with Felix," said Tatiana patiently. "You know the police have no right to enter any house while a Grand Duke is there. Not without a special warrant, and perhaps not even then—papa would know."

"We've only the Minister's word for it that Dmitri *was* there," said Olga. "You two go home if you want to. I'm staying here till I come off duty at two o'clock."

She went home on foot across the parks, trudging through the snow in her fur-lined boots, with her head bent before the wind which had sprung up as the winter day turned to an early twilight. She usually went to the side door, or the garden entrance, but when she saw the line of motors in the great forecourt the Grand Duchess Olga passed between the great colonnades and halted on the threshold of a hall usually silent and empty. It was filled with men, nearly all in uniform, with a few women among them, courtiers who in the secluded life led by the imperial family were seen by them only at irregular intervals, but who had all emerged from their obscure if well-paid posts for this exceptional occasion. In the inner circle of their group was the Minister of the Interior, himself surrounded by men in frock coats, with leather portfolios under their arms, who appeared to be arguing with him and with each other.

Silence fell as Olga entered, and she was greeted by low bows and curtseys. The lady-in-waiting who had been with Anastasia earlier in the day came quickly to her side.

"How is my mother, Isa?" said Olga in a low voice.

"She is—very tired, Your Imperial Highness. Shall I announce—"

"No," said Olga. Then, raising her voice, she said to the Minister, "Are you holding a public meeting, Monsieur Protopopov?"

"N-no, Madame."

"Then be good enough to come with me."

The officers, saluting, made way to let them pass. Olga led the sweating Minister to an anteroom where the Czar's guests waited to be received in audience: a high-ceilinged room, with hunting trophies on the walls, and tables spread with uncut magazines.

"What was the meaning of that extraordinary scene?"

The bejewelled empresses in their satin décolletages, gazing from the portraits in the Crimson Hall, were no more commanding than the girl whose fur *shuba* was thrown back to reveal a nurse's dress, and Protopopov licked his lips.

"Madame, the murder of Grigori Efimovich has roused great excitement, here as in the city—"

"Murder? The police have found the body, then?"

"Not yet, but it can only be a matter of hours—"

"Then how do you know it's murder?"

"One of the miscreants has confessed, Madame."

"The Deputy, Purishkevich?"

Yes, Purishkevich. Who had talked too much, and who undeniably was drunk when the police reached the Yusupov palace. But whose story—repeated when he was sober—was that he and a doctor (doctor an unstable witness, had fainted early in the numerous attempts at murder)—

"The *numerous* attempts?"

"Alas, yes. These two men had joined Prince Felix Yusupov and the Grand Duke Dmitri in a plot to kill Grigori Efimovich Rasputin by administering poison. They invited him to one of the—er—intimate little suppers he was known to enjoy, in a—h'm—luxuriously furnished room, a cellar room, in the Yusupov palace. There was music, balalaika and gramophone music—"

"Never mind the entertainment, Minister."

"He drank poison in the wine, he ate poison in the cakes, and he *enjoyed* it!" burst out Protopopov. "Prince Felix shot him with the Grand Duke's Browning, and he rose to his feet with the bullets in his body as if he were rising from the dead! He staggered as far as the courtyard. They beat him with a club there, and even then he nearly reached the gate! It was Purishkevich, according to his own confession, who fired the shots which killed the holy man."

"So you have a full confession, but no body?"

"Exactly, Madame."

"And nothing to support a drunken exhibitionist's confession? No traces that murder was actually done?"

"There was a pool of blood in the courtyard of the palace. Prince Felix said he had shot a dog."

Olga's lips twitched. "Who knows?" she said. "Perhaps he had."

"Surely, Madame, there is no question of condoning—"

"One moment," she interrupted him coldly, "I understand why *you* are here: Her Majesty naturally required a full account from you in person. But who are these officials you appear to have brought with you? Are you holding a trial of the princes in their absence—and in the absence of the Czar?"

"Madame, I'm trying to save the princes from their folly!" cried the Minister. "These gentlemen are the legal advisers to my Ministry, part of the permanent secretariat, and three more from the cabinet of the Public Prosecutor. I asked them all to accompany me to Czarskoe Selo, to explain to Her Imperial Majesty that what she wanted done was legally impossible, totally against the laws of the Russian Empire—"

"What she wanted done?"

"She wanted Prince Felix and the Grand Duke Dmitri to be taken before a firing squad and shot."

Then he saw the girl's composure break, and heard her cry: "A summary execution! My God, have we *all* gone mad?"

There was indeed a double element of madness and of farce in what remained of the darkening day at the Alexander Palace. The farce was supplied by Anna Virubova, whom the Czarina insisted in bringing away from her own little house and installing in the rooms recently occupied by the Grand Duchess Elizabeth Feodorovna. "They will murder Ania too!" insisted the Czarina, and so the crippled woman arrived in a wheel-chair, escorted by her bewildered, elderly parents, and of course by the indispensable Sister Akulina. The private lift stuck between two floors with Sister Akulina and some of the baggage in it, and the holy woman's screams indicated very little trust in Providence, or in the palace electricians who got the lift in motion after an hour's delay. Madame Virubova herself, once she was certain of the imperial protection, had to be firmly told not to use the telephone, as she was jamming the little switchboard with her frantic calls to every place in Petrograd where Rasputin, alive or dead, might be. Tatiana told her again and again that the lines must be kept open for a call from Mohilev. Everybody hoped that the Czar would telephone, but he contented himself with sending a telegram saying he would return from GHQ as soon as possible.

Olga read the brief message over and over, and tried to find some meaning in it. Was her father, like his wife, grief-stricken at the disappearance of the Friend who had swayed his judgment and corrupted his intentions for so long? Or was he simply relieved? Would he return in time to save his young cousin and his niece's husband from the fate the Czarina had demanded for them both?

The only way to allay her madness was to issue a warrant committing them both to house arrest. Even when she was assured that this had been done the Czarina went from one excess of anger to another. "I could kill them! I could kill them with my own hands!" she kept repeating through the night, until Alexandra Feodorovna slept the sleep which only veronal could bring.

It was nearly midnight when Olga crept downstairs to her mother's mauve boudoir. She had been haunted all evening by the thought that while Felix Yusupov was held inside a palace protected by an outer wall, gates and a courtyard, where able-bodied servants were armed and ready to defend their master, Dmitri was alone in his apartment on the Neva embankment, with only his elderly valet and perhaps a soldier-servant to act as bodyguard. He could be taken out and killed at any time—if anyone could be found, or paid, to avenge Rasputin.

"I suppose I'll have to think of something else." Dmitri's words, as they stood beside the snow mountain, came back to Olga with new force. Worse still, she remembered what she had once said to him in the very room where he was now a prisoner: "If only we could get rid of Rasputin!" So many people must have spoken as she did, unthinkingly, but Dmitri and his friend *had* thought of something else, they *had* got rid of the tainted creature. And they might have to pay for it with their own lives.

At last she picked up the telephone and asked to be connected with the Grand Duke Paul. Dmitri's father, as the Czar's only surviving uncle, was not without influence in the Family, although since his return from banishment following a morganatic marriage he had taken little share in public affairs. He lived with his second wife and family in Czarskoe Selo. The telephone rang again and again in his beautiful home, but not so much as a footman answered. At last the palace operator said:

"Exchange says the telephone is out of order, Madame."

"Try to put me through to the Grand Duke Dmitri in the city, then."

Olga listened for the ringing tone in vain. There was a vibrant silence on the line, and then the sleepy voice reported:

"His Highness's telephone has been disconnected, please Madame."

"Thank you." That was it, then—Dmitri was held incommunicado, and beyond help.

Next morning, Olga waited only to hear that Rasputin's body had not been found, and went by motor to the hospital, in time to relieve a delighted young nurse of the last two hours of her night duty.

At the winter solstice it was still night at nine o'clock in the morning, and all the artificial lights were burning in the Catherine Palace when an orderly brought a message: Captain Hendrikov was on the telephone.

"Captain Hendrikov!" It was the name Olga had wished but hardly dared hope to hear. She ran through the long corridors where the great Catherine had walked in state, and ran, as Catherine never ran, upstairs three steps at a time.

"Simon!"

"Is it you, Princess?"

"Oh Simon darling, I'm so glad to hear your voice! Are you calling from Petrograd?"

"Yes, from the barracks. We came in yesterday afternoon. I know what's happened, Olga Nicolaievna; is there anything I can do to help?"

"I can't remember *when* anyone said that to me! Oh Simon, it's so wonderful to have you back! Tell me, is my cousin Kirill Vladimirovich in Petrograd?"

"The Grand Duke? No, he's still at Mohilev."

"Oh. I thought—but it doesn't matter now you're here. I'm so terribly worried about my other cousin—Dmitri."

She felt rather than marked a slight hesitation in Simon's reply. "His Highness is under house arrest, isn't he?"

"Yes, and I want him to be under guard as well." Olga explained the situation, and the disconnected telephones. She said she was afraid 'some of Rasputin's followers' might break in through the hospital wards on the upper floors of Dmitri's palace: of her real fear she dared not speak. "Could you get in touch with Dolly?" she pleaded. "She's living-in at the British Red Cross hospital now. She would know if *anything* has been done to make sure of Dmitri's safety. And if she says there aren't any soldiers there, couldn't you order a bodyguard yourself?"

"I'll go straight to the Palace Quay and find out what's happening, Princess."

After the babel of yesterday's conflicting voices, Simon's voice was steady and reassuring. Olga smiled.

"Is there much disturbance in the city?" she asked him.

"More like general rejoicing. They say the Kazanski church was crowded yesterday, everybody was lighting candles before the ikon of St. Dmitri, and it was the same thing at the church of Vladimir. I haven't been out of barracks yet, but my mother telephoned this morning, and she said most of the houses on the Fourth Line were illuminated last night. D'you remember the Fourth Line?"

"I remember everything. Oh Simon, please come soon!"

Simon Hendrikov laid down the telephone, despising himself for what was left unsaid. Would she have liked to hear that along with the candles round the ikons of St. Dmitri, simple folk were placing picture postcards of herself, the pictures in nurse's uniform which she had laughingly declared to be a libel? Dmitri and Olga, the ideal couple, the two most attractive members of the whole Family, were already paired off in the minds of those still loyal to the monarchy as a hope for the future. In the mess the night before, Simon's colonel had gone so far as to discuss the proposal, now an open secret, to declare the Czar unfit to rule and raise Alexis to the throne under the regency of the Grand Duke Nicholas Nicolaievich. "The best of both worlds, gentlemen!" the colonel had chuckled. "The Heir succeeds, and we get Nikolasha back again, to give us another victory like Erzurum!" There was no limit to the euphoria in the army on the night when the story of Rasputin's murder had spread all over Petrograd.

Alexis and Nikolasha made a strong combination, but would

it be as strong as Dmitri and Olga? Especially if she was fond of him, as her anxiety for the Grand Duke's safety clearly showed. Much as he loved her, Simon smiled at Olga's calm assurance that a newly promoted captain could fall out a bodyguard and march it off to protect a man under house arrest, all too likely soon to be on a charge of murder. It was not arrogance, it was the Romanov certainty that a bodyguard would always be forthcoming, and the irony was that this bodyguard was intended to protect the man Simon regarded as a serious rival.

Being free to leave the barracks, he went out through the ornate iron gates and looked for a droshki. There was not one to be seen, something unusual in that district, the heart of the garrison quarter, where the Tauride Palace stood. The imperial double eagle flag was drooping in the frozen air above the palace, and Simon wondered if the Deputies were in session, listening to Monsieur Purishkevich plead his right to parliamentary immunity for the murder of Rasputin. He crossed the bustling avenues to the embankment of the Neva.

There all was hushed under the snow. The wide river was frozen from bank to bank, and as happened every winter a number of people, shapeless and sexless in their heavy wraps, were taking short cuts from one shore to another along the footpaths on the icy surface. Above their heads the cathedral chimes were ringing *Gospodoi pomiloui*.

Simon walked on the river side of the embankment, saw two city policemen standing guard outside the Grand Duke Dmitri's residence, crossed the quay and passed outside the heavy door. There was a side gate, unguarded, opening on a courtyard where a British Red Cross ambulance was standing, and Simon walked straight in at the hospital entrance with no challenge from the white-haired porter, who rose from his stool and bowed as the young officer asked authoritatively for Darya Karlovna Hendrikova. He was invited to walk upstairs to the hospital floors.

"I don't think much of the Grand Duke's house arrest," he said to Dolly when their greetings were over, and told her why.

"Only two city policemen at the door?" she said, puzzled. "There were six when I came on duty at eight o'clock, and four on the side gate as well."

"They've been withdrawn, then. Exactly what the Grand Duchess was afraid of!"

He described Olga's anxiety, and Dolly shook her head. "If there *is* a break-in," she said, "there's nobody here to stop it. Simon, what are we going to do?"

"She asked me if the Grand Duke Kirill was in town. He's not, but if he were, I don't believe he'd lift a finger to help. I'm going to Czarskoe Selo to see the Grand Duke Paul!"

"Simon, you can't, not in that uniform!"

"In civilian clothes, then."

"Doesn't matter if you're out of uniform. You're a serving officer, couldn't you be court-martialled for interfering with the course of justice?"

"Justice!" said Simon. "But you're right, Dolly. Somebody else must take the message, only—who?"

"Somebody quite impartial. Outside the whole thing. And clever, able to speak Russian—"

"You wouldn't be thinking of your admirer, Plain Joe Calvert?"

"Joe would like to do it, but he'd quote at least three rules of the American Foreign Service saying why he shouldn't. No, but I know the man who'd go to the Grand Duke Paul, and make him act! Captain Allen, at the British Embassy."

"Would he be willing?"

"I think he would, for me."

* * *

The body of Rasputin was found on the morning of the third day. The amateur conspirators had flung it into a hole in the Neva, so badly weighted that it soon floated into the current, which washed it under the ice into one of the canals. The doctors who performed the autopsy found that Rasputin had survived poison, bullets and blows, and pronounced him dead by drowning.

By that time the Czar had returned from GHQ. By that time, too, the Grand Duke Paul had joined Dmitri in Petrograd, along with the distinguished officer who had been Dmitri's tutor, and other friends. Outside, patrols from His Majesty's Regiment, one of the special security regiments of the Household, guarded all the entrances to the palace where the Grand Duke was under house arrest.

The Czar did not interfere with these arrangements. Neither did he oppose his wife's desire to be solely responsible for the burial of the *staretz*, once 'Our Friend', and now canonised as 'Our Dear Martyr'. The body was taken to a resting-place on the way to Czarskoe Selo, prepared for the grave by Sister Akulina, and then, early in the morning of the fifth day after the murder, buried in a corner of the palace park. The service was short, the mourners few, but all the young Grand Duchesses were present with their parents.

Then the Czar made known the punishment of the two principal plotters. Nobody could touch Purishkevich, a member of the Duma, nor was Dr. Lazavert an important conspirator. But Prince Felix Yusupov was banished to his estates in Kursk province, and the Grand Duke Dmitri Pavlovich was also to be removed under guard from Petrograd, and posted to military duty at Kasvin on the Persian front.

"I won't have them shot, Alix, make up your mind to it," he told his wife, and to the older courtiers, who murmured discreetly that the sentences might be too severe, the Czar would only say, "I spared their lives, which is more than my father would have done. Let them be content with that!"

It was not until several days after her father's return that Olga was able to speak to him alone. She was admitted to his study just after Alexis emerged, rushing stormily past her and down the corridor, and the Czar was smiling when she entered the room.

"I hope you're in a gentler mood than Tiny," he said whimsically. "He's gone off furious with me because I didn't bring his new cat back from Mohilev."

"Is that Verushka? We've heard a good deal about Verushka since he came back himself."

"I can't keep track of all the names he gives them, and I didn't make matters any better by telling him that the little brute got out of her basket down at the station and was last seen wriggling away beneath a pile of railway sleepers."

"He really is cat crazy. I thought Zubrovka's kittens might have kept him happy: she had five, all in one litter."

"Still, it's wonderful to see him so bright and well," said the Czar. "Now, what can I do for you, my dear?"

"Father, I don't quite know how to begin."

The Czar's face changed. "I see," he said, "you've come to

add your voice to all the petitions I've had from the Family to pardon Felix and Dmitri Pavlovich."

"Not exactly."

"What then?"

Olga stood with her hands linked behind her back, as when she had recited Pushkin and Lermontov to her father not so many years before.

"I've come to beg you to commute the sentence on Dmitri," she said. "Leave him at Kasvin for two months or three, but not more, his health won't stand it. That's what makes his punishment so much harder than Felix Yusupov's. He'll have a very pleasant spring in Kursk, in his own house, with Irina and the little girl. But poor Dmitri isn't strong enough for the Caucasian front."

Nicholas II turned over a pile of letters on his desk. "That's the point his grandmamma makes," he said negligently. "Dmitri's weak chest. Considering that her own husband was assassinated in the evening of his days, I should have thought the Queen of Greece might have known better than plead for a murderer."

"I thought all the Family had written to plead for Dmitri."

"They did, here's their letter, with no fewer than sixteen signatures. Including even your dear Aunt Miechen's. Would you like to see what I've written across it?" He turned the document for Olga to read the words: *Nobody is allowed to commit murder.*

"But Dmitri swore to his father that he didn't fire a single shot!"

"And Dmitri's father would swear anything to me." The Czar drummed his fingers on his death. "Incidentally, my personal police sent me an odd report upon my uncle Paul. It seems that before Father Grigori's body was discovered, a man from the British Embassy visited him in haste and secrecy. Immediately after, Paul persuaded General Voieikov to double or triple the military guard on Dmitri."

"There *was* no military guard, the morning after he was arrested. Only two city policemen. Easy to overpower in an attempt to kidnap Dmitri."

"To kidnap him? Olga, how do you know all this?"

"I suspected it. And I sent a man I trust to find out what was going on at the Palace Quay."

"I believe I can almost guess his name. Was it Captain Hendrikov?"

"Yes."

"An officer of my Garde Equipage, asked by my daughter to interfere in an affair under the jurisdiction of the civil power. Did you put your request in writing to this man?"

"No, we were talking on the telephone."

"Good. Then I think I'll order an investigation by the young man's commanding officer, who *may* decide to proceed to a court-martial."

"I advise you to do nothing of the sort."

"You advise *me*?"

"Because if anybody tries to break Captain Hendrikov, I'll make it publicly known that the police guard on my cousin was withdrawn, was totally inadequate after the first few hours. And I have witnesses at the British Red Cross hospital who saw them marched away."

"On the orders of the Chief of Police, no doubt."

"Who takes his orders from the Minister of the Interior. And *he* takes his orders from my mother."

"Do you realise what you're saying, Olga?"

"Perfectly. If you'd been here that first night, you'd have known she'd stick at nothing to get revenge for Rasputin. It's entirely due to Simon and his British friend that Dmitri was alive next day. And perhaps—a little due to me."

The Czar lay back in his chair, his face was very pale. "Pour me a glass of water, please." She brought him the glass and he drank thirstily. The skin of his face was drawn and wrinkled, as if the man had been scorched by some fierce inner fire.

"Are you in love with Simon Hendrikov, Olga?"

"I've been in love with Simon for a long time."

"You know that nothing can possibly come of it?"

"But he loves me." She smiled. "I'm not asking for permission to marry him."

"It would never be granted. You, the Czar's daughter—"

"You gave my Aunt Olga permission to marry Colonel Koulikovski two months ago, after her divorce from Uncle Peter. And she was a Czar's daughter too."

"That was the outcome of a very long attachment, following

on an unfortunate first marriage. You can't say you've been forced into marriage against your will."

"As Aunt Olga was. You can call it what you like, father: 'a very long attachment' is as good a phrase as any; but the truth is that Aunt Olga, in the end, has done exactly what she wanted, she's made a new life with the man she loves. As Marisha hopes to do! As they all did, your uncles and cousins, when they married divorcées, or women not their equal in rank, or didn't marry their mistresses at all! Nikolasha, Kirill, Andrei, your Uncle Paul, my Uncle Misha—every one did just exactly as he pleased; and yet they can be sanctimonious about it like Boris, when he had the nerve to ask me to marry him, with Zina Rashevskaia actually living in his house! Why shouldn't I have a little happiness, with the man who loves me too?"

"But this is what your mamma has always said, 'Let the others behave badly if they must! It's *our* family the good Russian people take for their example!' And dear mamma and I *have* set an example of virtuous living, for which we can only give thanks as the time draws closer to our silver wedding. That'll be in 1919, Olga, not so far away now."

"But when you were a young man you did exactly what you pleased too, didn't you—when you were in love with Madame Kchessinskaia?"

The Czar started. "I've only loved one woman in my whole life," he said. "And that was the girl I married."

"I don't know that *that* makes it any better," said Olga. "—Oh, don't think I'm blaming you! I don't see how any man could resist Kchessinskaia, even now. I think she's adorable! She brought her dancing fees for the Refugees, when I was there, and we talked afterwards."

"About—old times?"

"Only about some happy times. The dressing-room window at the Krasnoe theatre, and a pet name you used to have for her—"

"Radouchka?"

"Bringer of joy," said Olga, and went to put her arms round her father's neck. "Oh, my poor father, I'm so glad you had some joy once!"

She could tell that the Czar was moved when he said, "What is it you want, my darling?"

"Some joy for me too."

"This young man?"

"If you would only allow him to be near us for a little while. He's true and loyal, father, you don't know how true! Whatever he did to protect Dmitri, he only did it to please me."

"I thought you came here to plead for Dmitri, and now you're pleading for Simon Hendrikov."

"But I do still ask you to forgive Dmitri! Oh, not at once, because my mother would be furious, and I know he can't come back to Petrograd. But take him away from that terrible Kasvin soon. Banish him to the Crimea if you must—"

"To enjoy the fine weather," said the Czar. "I wonder you don't ask me to turn Livadia over to him outright. No, Olga, I will not pardon Dmitri. You don't know what doom he and Felix may have brought upon us." He gently put Olga's clinging arms aside and took a letter from his desk. "A courier came in today from Mohilev, with all the mail which arrived after I left. This was among them—my last letter from Father Grigori. He must have written it just before he was trapped into going to that fatal supper party. Read it, and see what Dmitri and Felix have done to me and mine."

"A letter from Rasputin!"

Olga recognised the peasant's handwriting—sprawling, illiterate, unmistakable.

> "I write and leave this letter behind me at St. Petersburg. [Olga read aloud] I feel that I shall leave this life before the first of January.
>
> Czar of the land of Russia! If you hear the sound of the bell which tells you Grigori has been killed, you must know this:
>
> If your relatives have wrought my death, then no one of your family will remain alive for more than two years.
>
> They will be killed by the Russian people."

17

"WHAT FOOLS THEY ARE," said Mara Trenova, "to think the Russian people give a damn for the Grand Duke Dmitri."

She was standing at a window of the old Hotel du Nord in the great square opposite the Nicholas Station, which had been closed to the public since before midnight. It was now nearly two in the morning, and while she and her friends were perfectly capable of talking and drinking tea or anything else available until dawn, it was irritating to be confined to a hotel room by order of Nicholas the Bloody. The departure, under guard, of Dmitri to the Persian front had taken everybody by surprise. The Znamenia Square had been fenced off, the hotels and lodging houses in which the square abounded told to close their doors, and at one a.m. two companies of Cossacks had cantered in to police the approaches to the station.

'All this for one common or garden little royal murderer," said Smirnov at her elbow. "Our people didn't get the red carpet treatment when *they* took the road to exile."

There was a growl of assent, but at the same time there was a fascination in the spectacle of the vast square, completely empty but for the Cossacks riding round and round as if they were in the ring at the circus. The horses had to be kept moving, even with their blankets on, for the night was bitterly cold: 1917 had come in with blizzards and freezing temperatures which broke the records of most people's memory. The snow of the Znamenia Square had been flattened by many feet all day long, but there was always a new powdery carpeting which the wind blew up in eddies round the horses and their red-clad riders.

"What are they expecting us to do?" asked one of the six or seven men and women huddled together for warmth at the uncurtained window. "Rush out and stage a last-minute rescue?" There was a laugh, through which Mara heard the voice of

Sergiev telling Sasha to put another log into the stove. Sergiev was no longer a copyboy at the *Pravda.* As Jacob Levin had predicted, he was ambitious, and now he had Mitia for a slave at the office, and Sasha, in whose room they were meeting, to put his own logs on the fire. Sasha was a deserter, whose first-hand stories about the brutality of his officers and the starvation of the men had run for three underground issues of *Pravda,* which made the boy feel important; besides, he had money from his father to pay for the protection his new comrades in Petrograd were giving him.

"Tired, Mara?" Smirnov put his arm round the girl and pressed her strongly to his side.

"Yes, I am tired, Smirnov. It's been a long day."

"But worth it, now we can see the better days ahead."

"Oh, yes!"

"The cars are coming now," said someone. "We should have had binoculars."

"*Only* binoculars?" The ugly laugh came again. Smirnov, unobserved, sketched a playful little bite on Mara's neck, somewhere between her high collar and her hair. She gave him a side-glance of surprise. Her comrades disapproved of public endearments; their sexual drives were sublimated into politics for a good deal of the time, but Smirnov, a recruit from Georgia, had a reputation for adventures more lighthearted than the singleminded revolutionaries liked. It was something new for him to make advances to Mara Trenova, but she remembered that Smirnov, too, had a room in the hotel, and was probably hunting for a temporary bedfellow. She decided to go with him if he asked her: it was far too late, even when the police barriers were removed, to go back on foot to the Yamskaia through the snow.

Smirnov, with his healthy colour, tumbled black hair and black southern eyes, was at least more physically attractive than his fellow-Georgian, the bespectacled and bearded Agabagov, who was huddled next to Sasha on the dingy couch. It would be pleasant enough to share Smirnov's bed for one night, even in the Hotel du Nord, in a squalid room which would inevitably bring back memories of Jacob Levin. Mara resented her own bourgeois dislike of those memories, but she never admitted that her whole attitude to men and sex had been conditioned by Simon Hendrikov's rejection, Jacob Levin's brutality, and Joe Calvert's cool indifference into an aridity of flesh and spirit which made her almost incapable of physical satisfaction. She was Trenova, a good comrade, a good worker for the revolution, and that was all.

"There he is!"

There had been enough blowing on the frost which encrusted the double windows of Sasha's room to give everybody a good view of Dmitri's tall figure, in the grey Guards greatcoat, on the pavement between the two limousines. His father, nearly as tall as himself, got out of a car and stood beside him, accompanied by someone unrecognisable in furs.

"Who's the girl?"

"Probably that sister of his."

"Not your friend Olga, eh, Trenova?"

They saw the young Grand Duke's hand rise and fall, acknowledging the salute of the captain of the guard. He turned and walked between them under the overhanging roof of the station, and the rest of his party followed him into the darkness.

"And now for the private coupé, the champagne and chicken sandwiches, and then the bed made up with silken sheets," said one of the young women, named Sofie. "The show's over, dears. I wonder when they'll fall out the Cossacks, and let us all go home?"

"Don't go yet, comrades," said the deserter eagerly. "There's enough tea for all of us left in the samovar."

"We might as well go through the plans for our operation across the river," said Agabagov, and the others agreed. The dingy plush curtains were drawn again across the windows, and the group settled down around the stove. Operation 'Across the River' was the name for an intended raid on the beautiful house which the ballerina, Kchessinskaia, had built about ten years earlier, and which to the revolutionaries was one of the great symbols of Czarist corruption. Agabagov had suborned the dancer's housekeeper. She had already shown him over the house while her mistress was absent, and would open the doors to his commando when the day came. Mara listened to his greedy description of the Empire drawing-room hung with yellow silk, the conservatory, the larders, the cellar. The loot would be tremendous.

She herself was sitting on the floor with a cushion between her back and the wall, and a sketching block and pencil in her hands.

"Get some inspiration?" Sergiev growled.

"I think so. Show you later on."

She took out a pencil and began to sketch. Mara was not a trained commercial artist, but she had a talent for turning out line drawings in which the action was suggested by little stick-like figures, and these were adapted for propaganda by Efron, one of the men sitting on Sasha's bed and noisily drinking his tea through a precious cube of beet sugar held between his teeth. Efron was a professional. They were all professionals, dedicated Party members, regarding Trenova with the faint if indulgent suspicion she owed to her Social Revolutionary past. She knew now that she would never be in the front rank of the struggle, like Maria Spiridonova and Katarina Brechkovska, two of her SR heroines who were still alive after many years in the Czar's prisons. She was not considered suitable for direct action, although she had been issued with a Mauser pistol for self-defence when the revolution should begin. She knew she would never have the patience Brechskovska had shown until her arrest in spreading Marxist beliefs among the peasants and the pilgrims on their way to the holy city of Kiev. But she had a gift for the stinging phrase, the jingle, the slogan, although she acknowledged that she had not invented anything so good as the two simple slogans which the shock troops of the red daybreak would shout: "All Power to the People!" and "Bread! Peace! Freedom!"

"Show me," said Efron, sliding to the floor beside her. "H'm! Not bad!"

Mara had drawn four little sketches, in which the two limousines were shown as horse-drawn prison vans, with Dmitri standing between them. The hand which had been raised in salute was now seen clawing at a crown slipping from his head; in the last sketch he was trying to retrieve it from the gutter with a dripping sword.

"Can you do anything with that, Efron?"

"I'll get to work on it right away, and bring it round to the Yamskaia first thing in the morning for you to do the captions."

Mara was about to say "All right!" when her thigh was pinched between Smirnov's thumb and forefinger, and she changed the words to "Ten o'clock would be better, I'll be ready at ten."

Efron was still studying her sketches. "A strip of four, I think, like the others," he said. "I'm just wondering if we couldn't get a woman in here too. The sister—we haven't done anything on her."

"Or Olga again," suggested Smirnov. "Wasn't she supposed to be sweet on him at one time?"

"I thought so, when I saw them together after the *Poltava* launching," Mara said. There was no need to tell the comrades that on a day very soon after the *Poltava* launching she had seen with her own jealous eyes that the Grand Duchess Olga had fallen in love with Simon Hendrikov, and that he was deeply in love with her. There was no need to say anything at all, because the girl Sofie was squealing:

"Yes, do Olga, do her all over again! That Rasputin and Olga cartoon was the best you've ever done!"

"I must have another look at it," said Efron, and Sofie at once gave him a copy from her handbag. "I carry it around," she said, "People were *yelling* at it in the 'Bi-Ba-Bo' last night."

"Just an idea I had in a food queue," said Mara modestly. It was true that on the day Rasputin's body was found she had been in one of the endless bakery queues, trying to buy half a loaf of bread, and had heard one of the shawled women shuffling forward behind her telling her neighbour that the Czar's daughter Tatiana had been present at Rasputin's murder, dressed as a boy.

"What would she want to see a horrible thing like that for?" marvelled the neighbour, and the first woman explained:

"Because he raped her, see, in her own bed at the palace, when she was only twelve years old, and she wanted to be there to see 'em cut his balls off, that was why!"

From this promising beginning Mara and Efron had devised a strip of four images: one of Olga naked on a four-poster bed with crowns on the bedposts, with Rasputin crouching over her; and three showing the murder and the fictitious castration. In these, Olga was not merely dressed as a boy, she was wearing the uniform of the Chevalier Guards, with huge breasts bursting out of the tunic, and Dmitri in the same uniform was nuzzling her back. The strip, circulated underground, had had a huge success, and Mara had never confessed, even to herself, that she had substituted Olga for the Tatiana of the street woman's fantasy, because she remembered only too well the proud and lovely face, the eagerness of the girl who had wanted to be shown the Zabalkanski, and because she wanted to degrade that girl by every means in her power.

* * *

The four young sisters in their palace at Czarskoe Selo knew nothing of the slanders of the food queues, any more than they knew about Mara Trenova's cartoon strips or the series Sergiev was writing for an underground paper under the title of 'The Lovers of the Grand Duchesses'. The hunchback himself was impotent, but the wealth of scatological detail implied a vast experience, and the details were better understood by his readers than they could ever have been by the Czar's younger daughters, who thought 'taking a lover' meant becoming engaged to be married.

Marie, at least, used the word 'lover' for the man who made the first proposal for her hand. This was one consequence of the disastrous extension of the war to Rumania, where two German armies, invading the country by the Carpathian passes and the valley of the Danube, had ended a lightning war with the capture of Bucharest. The Rumanian court and government fled to Jassy, and Prince Carol, now the Crown Prince, travelled to Petrograd with the prime minister, Bratianu, to ask help from Russia as the long-term protector of the Slavs.

"But I never dreamed he would ask leave to marry *me!*" Marie marvelled, after an official dinner party at which she had listened with her usual sweetness and docility to Carol's account of the mountain fighting in his country. "Imagine having a lover, at my age!"

"Well, that's it, Mashka, you really are too young," said Tatiana reasonably. "That's just what papa said to Prince Carol."

"Lots of girls are married at seventeen," said Marie.

"But you don't mean you would even *think* of marrying Carol?" said Olga, and added tactfully, "even if he is a lot nicer than he used to be."

"Well, who *are* we going to marry, if we don't start marrying soon? I think Carol's very nice. I'd love to be in the mountains with them all, riding with the guns like his mother does, and bringing in the wounded under fire, and cooking their meals over charcoal braziers—"

"Being a heroine, in fact," said Anastasia slyly, and was

amazed when Marie, the target of so much of the family teasing, suddenly burst into tears and ran out of the room.

"Go after her, Imp, and apologise," said Olga. "You really hurt her feelings."

"Her nerves must be like fiddle strings," said the girl, repeating what she had heard someone say about the Czarina. But she obeyed, she was very fond of her sister Marie, and Olga, left alone, thought that what Marie really wanted was not the showy Balkan prince, nor even adventure with the troops alongside his courageous but theatrical mother Queen Marie: it was what drove so many girls into an early marriage—the desire to get away from home. If the ambitious Carol did eventually win a Romanov princess for his bride, it would be because Marie Nicolaievna was not determined, like the Olga of nearly three years ago, 'to live and die in Russia', but to lead the rough-and-tumble Balkan life which would suit her so much better than the tense silences of Czarskoe Selo.

They had all lived through the first weeks after the Rasputin murder in a state of shock. The Czarina, when she appeared among them, sat for long periods in her chair staring fixedly before her and saying nothing, but she spent most of her time in her mauve boudoir alone or with Alexis, with whom she invariably shared her meals, such as they were. She only roused herself to express passionate anger against her sister Ella, who had telegraphed to the Grand Duke Dmitri congratulating him on what she called his patriotic deed, but in truth she was no more separated in spirit from her sister than she was from her own four girls. The only one who could rouse her from her frozen grief was her own creation as Minister of the Interior, Monsieur Protopopov, who had taken up spiritualism, and presently announced to the Czarina that he was in touch, through the spirit world, with the martyred Rasputin.

The Czar's apathy was of a different sort. The Allied ambassadors who saw him during January 1917 found that his memory had almost completely gone, and that when talking his dark eyes moved aimlessly in a face so drawn and wrinkled as to be nearly unrecognisable. He sent for his brother Michael, who had done better in the Caucasus than anyone expected, and seemed to find some pleasure in going to tea with Michael at the palace of Gachina. He listened unmoved to the Duma President's reports of the shortage of food supplies in the armies and the cities, and the strikes in the great war factories—all of which, Rodzianko warned, was bound to end in revolution. He still declined to grant a workable constitution or a ministry responsible to the Duma.

Almost the only positive thing he did after punishing his cousin Dmitri and Felix Yusupov for the murder of Rasputin was to arrange for the posting of Captain Simon Hendrikov to Czarskoe Selo, and inform the Minister of the Palace that the Marine Guards officer was to have the entrée to his home. So now Olga had a 'lover' too, a young man who was actually allowed to take tea with her in one of the smaller salons of the guest wing—both of them comfortable but ungrateful beside the blazing pine logs while the blizzard howled across the park outside.

"I wish it was summer! I wish we could go for walks!" Olga sighed in the dusk of a February afternoon.

"I wish I could take you hundreds of miles away from here," said Simon.

"Where would you take me to? Your dacha?"

"We'd start at the dacha. But it wouldn't be winter—"

"Of course not, it would be summertime. With all the furniture exactly in the same place, and everything happening just as it did three years ago—except that we wouldn't have Mashka and Anastasia along."

"And we wouldn't have to go back to the *Standart,*" said Simon, falling in with her mood. "My God, I remember that night so well. Everybody felt honoured because His Majesty came to dinner in the mess, and I could hardly talk, let alone eat, because I thought you might have come on deck, and I was missing another chance to be with you."

Olga smiled. "I remember lying in a deck chair that evening, watching the stars come out, and wishing—"

"What did you wish, Princess?"

"For the world to be different, I suppose. We didn't know *how* different it was going to be. Let's go on pretending. Where'll we go to when we leave the dacha?"

Neither of them had seen much of the world outside Russia. They had to settle on Copenhagen, which they both knew, although Simon had explored the summer beaches and the winding oldworld streets while Olga had only lived at the palace of Amalienborg. "My grandmother wanted to take me back two years ago," said Olga. "I didn't see how we could possibly go."

"I haven't been in Copenhagen since my sister Betsy married, back in 1910."

"Granny's always ready to plan a trip. Her latest idea is to take us all off to the Crimea."

"Are we still pretending, Princess?"

"No, this is absolutely true. She was terribly upset about what happened to Dmitri, and now she's worried about my sisters and me. She says if mamma won't take us to Livadia, she'll open up her own palace at Ai Todor, so that all of us can have a winter holiday."

"Olga!" Simon seized her hand. "It's the best thing that could possibly happen. You must go!"

"But you said you were so happy, now that we're meeting every day—"

"I'd be happier still if I knew you were out of danger," said Simon grimly. "*Dushenka,* please believe me, it's the wisest thing to do. Surely when His Majesty goes back to Mohilev, you can persuade the Czarina to go south—perhaps only for a few weeks, until things are more settled in Petrograd—and take all of you with her?"

"You think it's important that my mother should go too?"

"Very."

"But she thinks her popularity has never been greater!" Olga answered him obliquely. "She gets hundreds of letters and telegrams every day, sympathising about Rasputin, and thanking her for all the good she does, and everything!"

"Ninety-five per cent of those messages are written at the Ministry of the Interior."

"You mean Protopopov . . . ?" She didn't flare up, she took it calmly; Simon saw with compassion that Olga Nicolaievna knew the truth as well as he did.

"I'd love to go to the Crimea," she said uncertainly, "it's so wonderful there in February. Think of the bougainvillaea, all rose and purple on our white walls, and the freesias and cyclamen growing wild over the terraces, down to the shore! And the hot sun at noon, instead of snowstorms and icy cold . . . But we couldn't go now, Simon. Not until the Allied Delegates have held their conference, and they haven't even left for Murmansk yet."

"There's always one thing more to stay for," said Simon Hendrikov. "Olga, for God's sake, don't let it be the one thing too many!"

"And don't you be so gloomy," she said with forced cheerfulness. "Even if Petrograd *is* badly disturbed, we're perfectly safe out here. We've got the Cossack Escort, the Marine Guards, the Railway Regiment, and His Majesty's Own Regiment all here for our protection: don't you think that's enough to look after five women and a boy?"

"If the regiments are loyal, yes."

"How can you possibly think they're disloyal?"

"How can you risk believing that they're not?"

* * *

Always one thing more. That was the sombre thought in Simon's mind when he rose that evening in the Marine Guards' mess to drink the health of His Imperial Majesty, and listened to the fervent exclamations of "God bless him!" repeated up and down the long, silver-laden table. Always one thing more to stay for, and of all fatuous things to take any risks for, the Inter-Allied Conference was certainly the worst. Even a junior officer, who knew nothing except how to fight on the Vistula or the Stohod, knew that the latest discussion between the Allied Powers was doomed to failure from the start.

Very probably the British delegation headed by Lord Milner, and the French, headed by the Minister for the Colonies, Gaston Doumergue, were quite aware that they had set out on a useless errand as they began on their Arctic voyage, round the North Cape and through the Kola Inlet to the town ambitiously called Port Romanov at the head of the new Murmansk railway. They found in it a sample of Russia at its worst, with heaps of stinking refuse and untidy piles of fir logs between the little wooden houses which looked like workmen's huts, and what was far worse, huge stockpiles of munitions rusting on the makeshift quays. The train into which they were ushered was the first to travel the new Murmansk railway from end to end. It took three days to reach Petrograd after a nine-hundred-mile journey along the single track, which was wretchedly ballasted and inclined, through the tundra and the frozen forests, and when the delegates arrived in Petrograd they found sporadic strikes in progress, and agitators openly haranguing the food queues even in main arteries such as the Liteini Prospekt. The official talks with their Russian colleagues degenerated into farce: who, they felt, could promise more aid to a country so obviously unable to help itself? The six million Russian losses were written off as an heroic but useless sacrifice by Allies who, in February 1917, had reason to fear their own countries would lose the World War—unless the one country missing, the one great Ally, should at last decide to take the field.

Meanwhile, of course, there were the usual empty celebrations. The delegates stayed at the Hotel Europa, and were lavishly entertained by society. The Grand Duchess Marie Pavlovna, 'Aunt Miechen' to her relatives, gave them a dinner so magnificent that the Empress Dowager telegraphed from Kiev, demanding at least equal splendour at the Alexander Palace, where the British, French, Italians and Rumanians were to be entertained on the last Saturday evening of their stay. She even gave some instructions about how Olga was to be dressed which aroused the Czarina's never long dormant jealousy.

"Such a fuss," she said, while three of her own six dressers were with the young Grand Duchess, "sending to the Treasury for the Empress Catherine's coronet! I'm surprised Granny didn't insist on the imperial crown."

"We all wish you felt able to meet the delegates yourself, mamma," said loyal Tatiana. "And papa must wish it most of all."

"But Olga's going to look simply lovely," said Marie. "Do you know she spent the whole afternoon reading notes about the guests, and memorising not only their names but what they look like in their photographs?"

"Taking a leaf out of Aunt Miechen's book, I suppose," sniffed the Czarina. "It really isn't necessary to remember these people's names; a smile and a bow are all they can expect."

"But you keep telling us we ought to talk," objected Anastasia.

"Not on state occasions . . . Olga, come in and let us all see you. Yes, you look very nice."

The younger girls were speechless as Olga came slowly towards them. She wore a court dress of white silk, revealing whiter shoulders, with the diamond necklace of her sixteenth birthday, and the red riband of the Order of St. Catherine. The little coronet the Empress Catherine had worn as the wife of the Czarevich, before the path to power opened out before her, was made of two separate bands of priceless rubies, set between diamonds, and crowned, as if it had been made for her, Olga Nicolaievna's golden hair.

"You're not wearing rouge, are you?"

"Oh mother, certainly not!"

"She's excited, that's all," said Anastasia. "Oh, how I wish I could be in the drawing-room when you walk in!"

"Yes, but it's all wrong," said the Czarina pettishly. "You're half in court dress and half out. You should be wearing a *kokoshnik* and a veil with the coronet, and you should have a train falling from your shoulders too."

"Trains aren't worn in wartime," said Olga. The sick woman's jealous pinpricks made no impression on a girl exultant at playing, for the first time, one of the leading roles on a state occasion, and confident in the beauty which she saw reflected, only half an hour later, in the admiring eyes of many men. She 'made the circle' with the Czar at eight o'clock, pacing in her white and diamonds through the great flower-filled reception rooms where fragrant wood burned in the porcelain stoves, and contriving to say something friendly and personal to each of the Allied statesmen. In that she succeeded better than the Czar, who confined himself to such banalities as "Is this your first visit to Russia?" and "Did you have a comfortable journey from Port Romanov?" His sombre eyes only brightened when as they sat down to a simple wartime dinner, served from the gold plate and priceless glass which had been in storage for years, he saw his daughter talking animatedly with the laughing guests who sat near her at the foot of the table. In his heart he acknowledged that her mother, as a hostess, had never even made anybody smile.

It was all over in a couple of hours. The State dinner was only a show-piece, not intended as an occasion for private talk, and carriages were ready to take the guests back to the station shortly after ten. The Czar and his daughter said the good-nights required by protocol, and by protocol were thanked: a French delegate, who had appreciated the champagne, was the only one to step out of line in the diplomatic circle and press an undiplomatic kiss on the Grand Duchess Olga's hand.

"*Mes hommages, Altesse!*" he said. "How well a crown becomes your lovely head!"

"*Je vous remercie, monsieur.*"

She walked pensively, alone, up the great staircase. Tatiana was still with their mother, and only the three dressers were waiting in the warm bedroom. Olga asked for a glass of water, and to be left alone for a quarter of an hour.

"Your Imperial Highness has a headache!" said the chief dresser, all solicitude.

"No, but I want a cigarette." She went as far as to light one while the women were in the room, and almost immediately threw it into the open stove. Cigarettes had no place in her brief magnificence; they belonged to the nurse's uniforms and the jersey coats of summer mornings, not to the coronet of the Empress Catherine. Olga sat down at her dressing-table, and saw a thousand sparks gleam, in the light of the chandeliers, from her necklace and the diadem. She put her hands up to the coronet and found it too securely fastened to be removed without help. It was still hers to wear for a few more minutes—the crown which, if she had listened to Dmitri, might, on a thousand to one chance, have been hers for life.

* * *

The Czarevich Alexis was bored and irritable. He wanted, more than anything in the world, to go back to GHQ at Mohilev, but his father lingered at Czarskoe Selo, procrastinating, still temporising with Rodzianko and all the others, even including his brother the Grand Duke Michael, who brought him warnings of famine and the outbreak of a general strike. He told Alexis that it might be some time before any train could take them back to Mohilev—"The snow is clogging the permanent way, Sunbeam," he said, "don't you know over a thousand railway engines are out of action?"

"I wish you wouldn't call me Sunbeam, you know I hate it. Nobody calls me Sunbeam at Mohilev! And the permanent way isn't clogged round Petrograd, Zilchik and I saw a lot of trains running yesterday."

"Well then, you had an interesting outing: didn't you enjoy it?"

"Not as much as I used to," said the boy. "I don't know

what's the matter with everybody these days. The people at the stations don't seem to want to talk to me any more! I bow, but they don't always bow back; they just stare, or look away."

"You've grown so tall, they probably don't recognise you." The Czar spoke abstractedly, but Monsieur Gilliard, who had observed his pupil's distress at the unfriendliness of the railway people, pointed out in private that the boy was really pining for companionship. The Swiss tutor went even further: he said that Alexis was too much with his mother, in her present state of health, for his own good.

"You're right, monsieur, we've been neglecting him," said the Czar, and the tutor permitted himself to laugh. There was no danger of Alexis being neglected in that palace, where his health had been the chief concern for years, but now, as he said, the boy was splendidly well, and he needed to play with boys of his own age, or older. The Czar agreed, and plans were made to invite a group of cadets from the military school in Petrograd for an afternoon of games in the snow at Czarskoe Selo.

It was the happiest and noisiest occasion at the palace for many a day. Alexis was enchanted to be with soldiers again, and although the soldiers were only boys of seventeen and eighteen they might well, on the next call-up, find themselves in the front line of the Russian Army. With the cadets he skated on the frozen lake (his hands crossed with Nagorny's) and played a fast and furious war-game with snowballs for ammunition. But the success of the afternoon was the snow mountain, now very high, and the lads went down in quick succession, braking their toboggans to a grinding halt and running round the base of the mountain to start again.

"Just look at Nagorny, waiting for Alexis at the foot like a mother hen with a duckling," said Olga, who with Simon by her side was among the score of spectators who had come out to look on. The sailor-servant never took his eyes off his charge, who was not allowed to come down the slide alone; as fast as Alexis reached the foot Nagorny picked him off the toboggan he shared with one of the cadets.

"Just look at the driver, he's as white as a snowman," said Simon, indicating the tall cadet who had steered Alexis down the snow mountain.

"He must have got well plastered with snowballs in the war-game," said Olga. The tall cadet was laughing, and very flushed. They saw him wipe his brow with a handkerchief as he took the toboggan from Nagorny and ran off to the starting place.

"Alexis Nicolaievich is having the time of his life."

"Yes, and it isn't over yet, they're going to have a wonderful tea as soon as it gets dark."

"Olga," said Simon in a changed voice, "here comes Her Majesty."

It was the first time he had set eyes on Alexandra Feodorovna for many months. He saw that she was haggard and pale, and there were traces of grey in the hair visible beneath her fur hat, but she was not permanently crippled, as rumour said she was. She carried a walking stick, but so did many of the ladies on that frosty day, and she was smiling at the boys as she talked easily with Monsieur Gilliard.

"I'm glad she's come out to see the fun," said Olga.

"Her Majesty is looking well," said Simon. "Have you spoken to her yet about going to the Crimea?"

"Oh, Simon, how you harp on that! One would think you were anxious to get rid of me."

"Of *you—dushenka*, girl of my heart—" He took her fur-clad arm so violently that Olga moved away and whispered, "Don't! People will see! And I must go in now, Simon. Tatiana and I are going to preside at the boys' tea. They're going to have blinis and plum cake, isn't that a nice mixture?"

"Blinis for *tea*?"

"Alexis always asks for blinis on a special occasion. I bet those boys are hungry enough now to eat a dozen each!"

So it seemed, when the cadets came ravenously into the dining-room prepared for them. The blinis were served smoking hot, delicious little pancakes of buckwheat flour with every possible accompaniment already on the table: saucers of sour cream, chopped onions, burbot roe from the Gulf of Finland, chopped hardboiled eggs, smetana, and for those with a sweet tooth, fresh butter and raspberry jam. There were pitchers of milk and light beer on the long table, set between platters of cut plum cake and other good things, and Olga and Tatiana offered tea with sugar and lemon.

There was only one boy who seemed to have no appetite, and

that was the tall cadet who had driven Alexis on the toboggan. He was still flushed, although the sports were over, and now his eyes seemed to be paining him, for he was blinking even in the soft candlelight. Alexis was sitting beside him, anxiously pressing him to eat.

"Olga," he said to his sister, as she came up to pour their tea, "this is my friend Peter Arkadeivich, and he says he isn't a bit hungry!"

"Perhaps he doesn't like blinis," suggested Olga, as the tall cadet leaped to his feet. "Would you rather have a meat patty, Peter Arkadeivich? I can't believe you're not hungry, after tobogganing all afternoon!"

"I beg Your Imperial Highness not to trouble," said the boy in a hoarse voice. "I do like blinis very much, and these are excellent. It's just that I'm so thirsty, if you please—"

"Then you must have some tea. Here's a cup, and when I've poured out for the others, I'll bring you more."

She moved on down the table, but she kept her eye on them, for Alexis was clearly delighted with his new friend, and chattering like a magpie. He ought to see more nice boys like these, she thought, and presently went back to sit between Peter Arkadeivich and the cadet on his other side, asking the friendly questions that were second nature to her, about their homes and families. Peter Arkadeivich had beautiful manners. He spoke to his sovereign's daughter clearly and concisely, as he was taught at military school, but he had to apologise more than once for coughing, and Olga said sympathetically:

"You've caught a little cold, haven't you, Peter Arkadeivich?"

"It's nothing, Your Imperial Highness."

"I'll tell them to mix a honey drink for you, and that'll make your throat more comfortable."

Alexis told Olga later on that Peter Arkadeivich (champion of the school sports last summer and a candidate for the artillery) thought his sister was terrific. He went to bed a happy boy, saying he wished every day could be like this one.

But the days which followed were like those his sister knew so well, with the Czar still fighting the Duma, and threatening to dissolve the session which had resumed after a short winter recess, and the President, Rodzianko, threatening more than once that each report he made at Czarskoe Selo might be the last.

The terrible winter conditions were still slowing up railway transport, and now nearly sixty thousand supply trucks were laid up at different stations on the routes to the front, but plans for the next offensive were going forward, and the tracks were open between Petrograd and Mohilev. The Czar prepared to return to GHQ. Characteristically, he took the same evasive action as in the summer of 1915, when he told Dmitri he would give up the idea of assuming the supreme command. This time he told Rodzianko that he would appear personally before the Duma on a given day, raising hopes that even at the eleventh hour he would agree to a constitutional ministry, and then, on the night before, he left his home and went back to Mohilev.

His farewells to his family were short and hurried. The Czarina, who dreaded the effects of their separation, was in tears, and Alexis was almost as distressed at being left behind.

"But you'll bring Verushka back with you next time, won't you, papa?"

"Who's Verushka—oh yes, the cat. All right, I will, if I remember."

"You've got to remember." Alexis kissed his father; he was not too big for kisses, although he was nearly as tall as the little Czar.

"Don't kiss me, father, I've got a streaming cold," said Olga from the background.

"Yes you have, poor ducky, and Tania too," said their father fondly. "Better have hot lemon drinks and spend tomorrow in bed."

"That's what we mean to do."

They were still in bed, and in a raging fever, when Simon Hendrikov came to the palace two evenings later, and asked, according to custom, for the honour of an audience with the Grand Duchess Olga.

He waited in the little salon, just long enough to begin feeling anxious, until Marie came to greet him in her forthright way.

"I'm awfully sorry, Simon Karlovich," she said, barely acknowledging his bow, "both my sisters are ill in bed. I can't even tell Olga you're here, because Dr. Botkin and mamma are with her now."

"Ill in bed? Good heavens, Marie Nicolaievna, what's the matter?"

"I'm afraid you'll laugh, Simon—they've both got measles."

"Laugh? I'm not laughing! Measles can be horribly uncomfortable for a grown-up person. Is Olga—are they both feeling miserable?"

"I'm afraid they are, just at present, and the worst is, Alexis seems to be coming down with it too."

"What absolutely rotten luck." He saw that Marie was pale and strained. "Haven't you all *had* measles?" he said angrily.

"Not us, we were far too well taken care of. But the doctors say the girls'll be much better by tomorrow; if you like to bring a little note next time you come, I'll see that Olga gets it."

"You're very kind, Marie Nicolaievna, but that's what I came to say: I won't be here tomorrow. I've been ordered to the Marine Guards barracks at Petrograd."

"Who ordered that?" the girl asked sharply.

"The commander of the Garde Equipage, the Grand Duke Kirill. He wants two companies detached from Czarskoe Selo."

"Because of the rioting that's started in the city?"

"I'm afraid so, yes. But don't tell your sister—yet."

"I won't, the doctors say they're to be kept very quiet. Good luck to you, Simon Karlovich, and come back soon!"

He kissed the girl's hand, and kept it for a moment in his own. "Give her my love," he said. "Poor Olga! How in the world did *they* contrive to catch the measles?"

"We know exactly how," said Marie Nicolaievna. "One of the cadets, a boy called Peter Arkadeivich, was coming down with it that day they were all playing with Alexis on the snow mountain."

18

IT WAS MARCH IN the western world; it was still February by the Russian calendar when the long-awaited revolution erupted in Petrograd.

Joe Calvert had a ringside seat for it, since during the early days he was often at the American Embassy in the Furshtatskaia, not far from the Tauride Palace where the Duma was in session. It was nearly a year since Ambassador Marye had asked for his recall for reasons of health—reasons not accepted by the Czar's government, which at once suspected an intended American affront. His successor, Ambassador David Francis, was a jovial gentleman of sixty-seven summers, who since his elderly wife had chosen to remain at home liked to surround himself with members of the Foreign Service, irrespective of rank, who could play a good game of poker. Mr. Francis had achieved fame in the United States as the organiser of the St. Louis Fair.

It was not a poker session which took Joe to the embassy on the day the shooting started in the streets. The career officers of his Service were meeting almost daily for an informal briefing session after the Washington cables and the local press digests were read, because for over a month it had been apparent that the United States was preparing to enter the war, and not by the road of conciliation. President Wilson had played his chosen role of mediator up to the hilt, and as lately as the New Year it seemed as if the Allies, with victory still far from their grasp, would have to accept his mediation and with it a compromise peace. Then the Germans, in one of their classic crises of dementia, had announced a policy of unrestricted submarine warfare as the only means of bringing Britain to her knees. Early in February the United States severed relations with the German government, and so, on President Wilson's appeal, did most of the Latin-American states. The Emperor Franz Josef had just died, and Gavrilo Princip, still in prison, was dying; as the Great War became a global war few remembered that it had begun with just two shots fired in a Sarajevo street.

The rioting which started the day before Simon Hendrikov, much against his will, was forced to leave Czarskoe Selo had pursued what was for Petrograd a normal course. The strikes in the war factories became a general strike, the tramcars stopped, the bridges were raised, and crowds of demonstrators were cleared by the military from the main thoroughfares. When Joe went to the Furshtatskaia for the briefing it seemed as if Ambassador Francis was preparing to go out, for his Russian driver was waiting with his team at the front door. The ambassador owned a Ford touring car, an object of great interest to the public, which was driven by his Negro valet and majordomo, Philip Jordan, but in the bitter winter weather he was using his sleigh. The horses were snorting and pawing a little under their warm blankets. In the grey day the American flags, worn in each bridle over the horse's outer ear, struck a note of lively colour. After the firing began the ambassador was persuaded to send the sleigh back to the stable and cancel the engagement he had made for lunch.

At the same time there was no real danger. Joe gave the Liteini Prospekt a wide berth, and took short cuts across the Gardens to his flat without seeing any incident, although a confused yelling and stampeding from the direction of the Nevski Prospekt suggested that the Cossacks had got the strikers on the run. Everything was normal in the Italianskaia, and he was mildly surprised when Varvara, not usually so attentive, pulled open the apartment door before he could take out his key.

"The master is here, *barin*," she said with a toothless smile, and Joe laughed. Captain Allen was still the master of the house to Varvara, and his tenant slapped him on the back as he rose rather stiffly from the basket chair beside the stove.

"Where've you come from this time, you old horse-thief?"

"From Murmansk, for my sins. Helping to shepherd our delegates aboard the minesweeper that's going to take them back to Aberdeen took a lot longer than I anticipated."

"Must have done," said Joe. "They left here quite a while ago."

"Their train broke down at Kem, with three hundred miles to go," said Dick. "That's when an interpreter really came in handy. I got stuck at Kem myself on the way back. What a dump! It was the last straw for the Allied delegates. They'd been told it was possible to haul over three thousand tons of war supplies daily, across the tundra; now they've seen for themselves it's barely possible to handle one."

"Well, have a drink," suggested Joe. "I don't need to ask Varvara if there's enough lunch for two, she always breaks out the emergency supplies when the master comes home. You staying long in Petrograd this time?"

"If I can get a room at the Moskva, but I hear it's choc-a-bloc with Siberian escapees and Social Dems. from Finland these days."

"You'd better bunk in here, if you don't mind the little room."

"Thanks, Joe, I'd like that. I'll pick up my stuff at the embassy—it'll only be for a day or two."

He studied the contents of his glass in silence. Joe had never seen him look wearier or more depressed, even after the knifing incident at 'The Red Sarafan'.

"What's the news from Washington?" Dick roused himself to say.

"Nothing special."

"H'm." Dick's mind seemed to go back to his last journey. "They used too much German POW labour for it," he said, and Joe knew he was talking about the Murmansk railway. "No wonder there's not a trestle bridge that can be trusted, from one end of the line to the other. If Nicholas knew what was good for him, he'd order Trepov to get his repair gangs on the job—and at the double."

"First they've got to make the trucks available, to bring in the war material."

"I wasn't thinking of the war material. I was thinking of the personal safety of the Romanovs. Murmansk's the only port open in the whole of Northern Russia, and they may need that perishing railway if they have to make a quick getaway."

"You think things are that bad?"

"Of course I do, and you do too. The strikes which German money paid for, and the rioting, and the scandals, were all planned months ago. Nicholas has thrown away all his chances, and the Duma won't be able to control the situation. Make no mistake about it, Joe—the revolution is about to begin."

"And then?"

"Then, even if President Wilson declares war tomorrow, it'll be too late for some nice kids out at Czarskoe Selo. And if they packed their bags tonight and arrived incognito at the British Embassy, we couldn't get them out through Finland now. It would have to be the Murmansk route, and I tell you—just one more freeze-up on the tundra, just one more hold-up at Kem, and you can write off the Romanov family as another casualty of the war."

"Let's hope things won't look quite so grim tomorrow."

But tomorrow, and the day after that, came and went, and half of Captain Allen's predictions were proved true. The Duma, now in constant session, rejected an imperial ukase from Mohilev ordering them to suspend their sittings. Instead, they sent Nicholas II their final advice to grant a constitution, adding, from the pen of Rodzianko, "Tomorrow it may be too late!" By the time the lethargic emperor at last gave his consent, it was too late. The troops refused to continue firing on the crowds. They threw away their rifles and embraced the workers who swarmed across the barricades made out of captured vehicles and uprooted trees. A soldier in one of the crack regiments shot an officer and roused his comrades to mutiny. One by one the finest regiments of Petrograd—the Transfiguration, in which the Czar himself was a colonel—the Volinski and all the others, now manned only by boys and the disaffected comb-outs from the replacement depots, broke ranks and went off singing to the Duma.

For many of them the rallying point was Preobrazhenskaia Ploshad, the great square of the Transfiguration Regiment, but almost as many made straight for the Tauride Gardens round the palace Catherine II had built for her lover, Prince Potemkin. The Americans, from their embassy windows, saw them stumbling and shouting down the Furshtatskaia. The military attaché identified the regiments by their insignia, for all were now marching under a new banner—the red flag.

"Here comes the Garde Equipage," he threw back over his shoulder. "And—my God, yes it is! the Grand Duke Kirill's right out there in front!"

"You're kidding!" But it was true, they all recognised the tall figure of the Czar's first cousin, Aunt Miechen's eldest son, marching under the red flag, with a red ribbon on his coat. He had been punished, years ago, for marrying without the Czar's permission: banished, deprived of his rank, estates and decorations, and even after the sentence of banishment was lifted, snubbed and humiliated at the imperial court. There was just the suspicion of a smile on his handsome face as he led his men towards the Duma. Now, aligned with the Czar's enemies, it was his turn to punish the Czar.

"I'm going to try and get inside the Duma," said Joe Calvert, grabbing his fur hat.

"Going to see the last act?" someone said.

"Or the curtain-raiser."

* * *

While the overture to the last act of the Imperial Duma was being played, all was peaceful at Czarskoe Selo.

The illness of the older girls and their brother had roused the Czarina from her torpor of grief for Rasputin. The maternal instinct, so very strong in her, revived with her children's need, and although trained nurses were at once brought from the palace hospital, it was their mother who bathed the girls tenderly and prepared the few sips of cooling drink Alexis was allowed. She put on the uniform with the red cross worn at the beginning of the war, and in fresh white limped from the girls' big bedroom to her son's little one, listening to Alexis cough, holding him up in his bouts of sickness and all the time terrified that some minor, internal blood vessel would break and precipitate catastrophe.

The Czar wrote sympathetically but abstractedly, saying it would be better if 'the chicks' all came down with measles together, and got it over.

"He wouldn't say that if he knew how ill poor Olga and Tania are," said Anastasia to Marie. "Dr. Botkin says it's far worse having measles after you're grown up."

"You and I are nearly grown up, Imp, so we must pray that we don't get it too," said Marie in a voice as frightened as she felt. "Because there's nobody else left now." Anastasia nodded, she knew exactly what her sister meant. No one really close to them was there to take charge in those days when courtier after courtier seemed to be called for urgent reasons to Petrograd, and then telephoned regrets that the train strike prevented his return. The two loyal ladies-in-waiting whom the girls knew as 'Nastinka' and 'Isa' could be counted on to come into service in their turn, and so could Mademoiselle Schneider, the Czarina's Reader, but the men left behind were old men, bound entirely by the traditions of a former age. The Czarina seemed not to notice the defections. One of her closest friends, Madame Dehn, a simple good-natured creature who had once gone on a pilgrimage with Rasputin, had come to visit her from Petrograd, and with Lili Dehn for confidante she seemed to feel the need of no one else, not even Anna Virubova. "And wouldn't you know Awful Ania would get measles too?" said Anastasia disgustedly.

"She probably thinks it's the sincerest form of flattery. You must never go into her bedroom, 'Stasia, remember that!"

"Mamma told me not to." The youngest Grand Duchess carried innumerable messages from the private apartments to Anna Virubova's sickroom in the guest wing, where the crippled woman was being nursed through the measles by Sister Akulina. "Thank you, darling," the Czarina said a dozen times a day. "What would I do without you? You're my legs!"

"I wish I were a brain, and not a pair of legs!" said Anastasia. "I wish Olga or Tania would get better, and tell us what to do! When I ask mamma about the troubles in the city, she tells me to go away and do a nice jig-saw puzzle; and yet she sits there crying and whispering to Lili, and burning papa's letters with her diaries in the boudoir stove!"

"I'm going to send for General Voeiekov." And Marie did so, much to the surprise of the Commandant of the Palace, who found the strong, gauche Grand Duchess suddenly invested with the dignity he remembered in her grandfather, Alexander III. Yes, he was bound to admit to Her Imperial Highness, there had been serious rioting in Petrograd, and in fact the Winter Palace and the Admiralty were being attacked, at that very moment, by disloyal troops, but two leading members of the Duma had gone to consult His Majesty at Mohilev, and reinforcements would soon be on their way from General Alexeiev's command to the capital.

"Is it true there have been mutinies in the Navy too?" said Marie.

Well, yes, there had been disturbances at Kronstadt, but there too the situation was well in hand.

"And at Helsingfors?" Marie persisted.

"There are no recent reports from Finland."

"Why not?"

"Madame, the telephone lines are down in the Grand Duchy."

"Surely the telephone lines can be repaired."

"It will certainly be done tomorrow, Your Imperial Highness."

The girls went upstairs to their room. Monsieur Gilliard was pacing up and down the gallery, he said the doctors thought Alexis was a little better. They all three looked out from one of the great windows across the snowy park, and saw the Cossacks of the Escort riding slowly, at the prescribed interval, along the boundary made by the nearest avenue.

"Ten o'clock, and all's well!" said Monsieur Gilliard. "Please God we'll have good news from Mohilev in the morning!"

"And please God all the sick ones will be feeling better," said Anastasia, so soberly that Marie caught at her hand when they were alone in their room.

"Are *you* all right, Anastasia? Do you want me to take your temperature?"

"Don't be silly, you're not on the ward now! I'm perfectly all right."

"Good, but I think we ought to gargle with permanganate, and drink some quinine and water before we go to bed."

"Will that keep us from having measles?"

"It's the only thing I can think of. And we simply mustn't be ill now!"

"Can't we have some tea as well?"

A scared maid from the old nursery wing brought them tea, and said she didn't know what had happened to the footmen. They sat up in bed in their white nightgowns to drink it, pleased by the unusual treat, and so concerned with the need to keep well that when they woke in the grey morning the Grand Duchesses said almost simultaneously "How do you feel?" and laughed with relief when the answer was "I feel fine!" But when they went in their dressing-gowns to whisper at their sisters' door, the nurse on duty shook her head. The usual adult complications had set in: Olga's eyes and Tatiana's ears were badly affected by the disease. There was no question of even peeping in at them that day.

It was Monday, the beginning of a new week, when with a little effective generalship there might still have been room for hope. But the Czar's message from Mohilev, when it came, was only an order that the riots in the capital should cease forthwith, and that order was impossible to carry out. General Khabalov was still holding the Winter Palace, but as no food had been provided for the loyal troops it was doubtful how long their loyalty would last. The experienced regiments ordered to reinforce the garrison of Czarskoe Selo were not within two hundred miles of their objective, for the revolutionaries had cut or blocked the railway line, and the roads were barricaded. As for the garrison itself, it was melting away. The mounted men were seen no more on the avenues: the Escort, the Railway Regiment, the Personal Regiment, the personal police were all on their way to Petrograd and the victorious Duma. Rodzianko himself, as a last gesture, telephoned to the Czarina, and with rough compassion told her: "When a house is on fire it's best to leave it. Pack your trunks, Madame, and go!" There were so many people in the President's room, so many hundreds more pushing and shouting in the corridors outside, that Rodzianko could hardly hear the answer of the woman he had mistrusted and opposed so long. And yet the low intense words registered, and came back to him later:

"My children are dangerously ill and can't be moved. I will never leave my children!"

The Marine Guards at this time were still on duty at the Alexander Palace, for the Grand Duke Kirill had not yet made up his mind to go over to the revolution. In the early dusk every man was mustered to guard the various entrances, and some light artillery mounted in the great forecourt after news was received that a rabble of soldiers and workers was on the way from Petrograd to take 'the German woman' prisoner. They came by train and trucks and stolen automobiles, many drunk, all singing and shouting, and were welcomed and given food by the Czarskoe Selo militia. By the late evening the beautiful mansions of the Czar's Village were lit by flaming torches as the mob caroused up and down the avenues. The power station was seized, and electricity cut off in the palace. The lifts stopped running, and only the strong arms of Madame Dehn and the grit of little Anastasia enabled the Czarina, lame and half fainting with anxiety for her husband, to climb the stair to the rooms where her ailing children lay.

But the Garde Equipage stood firm behind the closed gates, and the terrible cold, the eighteen degrees of frost which came with the darkness caused the mob to withdraw at last, and go off to fraternise with their new comrades in the militia barracks. Their yells died away and dissolved into singing in the distance.

"I must go out myself and thank our brave defenders," said Alexandra Feodorovna.

"I'll come with you, mamma," said Marie. "No, not you, 'Stasia, you've been sniffling a bit since tea time. Are you all right?"

"I'm fine," said Anastasia, hastily pocketing her handkerchief.

"Good, but stay indoors with Lili, we won't be long. Mamma, don't you think we might ask the Guards to come into the hall in relays, and give them all some tea?"

"I don't know, Mashka, we've never given them tea before."

"There's never been a night like this before," Marie said grimly. She slung a fur cape round her shoulders and went out, carefully supporting her mother down the icy steps. They went slowly along the lines, talking to the men, who were half frozen, and accepted the offer of tea with incredulous pleasure. Twice on the first trip, and twice on the half dozen walks she took between the courtyard and the gate, Marie's cape fell off into the snow, and every time it was picked up and carefully wrapped round her by some rough fellow with the ice of his own breath whitening his moustache.

Inside the hall Anastasia was in her element, presiding over the samovars, and directing the servants, such as were available, in passing tea and great slices of buttered bread to the men as they came in. Marie helped too; she had taken her exhausted mother back to Lili and her ladies, and then went outdoors and in, although her back was beginning to ache and her face and hands to burn in spite of the cold. She felt her fur hat very tight across her brow, but every time she raised her hand to ease it Marie realised her head was bare.

"Isn't this fun!" exulted Anastasia. "I've found some men who were on the *Standart* on our last cruise, look, those three over there. Do go and talk to them, Mashka, it's just like being on the yacht again!"

"I only wish Simon Karlovich was here."

"Poor Olga wouldn't like him to see her now, all over spots."

Marie laughed wearily. But she went to talk to the men from the happy *Standart* days, and to all the others who came so awkwardly into the palace of the Czar, until at midnight it was decided to stand down half the guard, and relieve the others in two hour rotas until midnight. The servants, without asking permission, had gone to bed; the two girls were left alone in the candlelit hall.

"Should we blow the candles out, Marie?"

"They'll burn down to their sockets by and by. Let's go and ask the night nurse how the others are. And then let's go to bed."

They looked at each other, both very flushed, shivering even in the warm hall. Then Marie said reluctantly:

"How do *you* feel now?"

"I feel absolutely awful."

"So do I."

* * *

The mounting of the guard at the Alexander Palace on that winter night was one of the last attempts to defend the Russian monarchy. By the time Marie and Anastasia woke early next morning, miserable in the onset of measles, their cousin the Grand Duke Kirill had ordered the remnants of the Garde Equipage back to another barracks near the Moika canal, from where he would presently lead them to the Duma. Others had preceded them there, for almost the whole cabinet, and many other leaders of the Czarist regime, had gone to the Tauride Palace on that wild Monday night to seek protection from the revolutionaries. Last of all came Protopopov, whining, cringing, disguised. He and his fellows were assured that the Imperial Duma did not shed blood, but this did not save them from imprisonment. They were all confined in due course in the fortress of St. Peter and St. Paul.

Next morning Joe Calvert found not an inch of space available in the public galleries of the Duma, where he had taken his unobtrusive seat so many times in the past. It seemed as if twenty separate meetings were taking place in the galleries alone, and as many more in every corridor as speeches and arguments, restrained for so long, broke out among the elected Deputies, the officers of the regiments which had gone over, and above all among the men who burst into the building waving the red flag and singing the *Marseillaise*. Pushed from one side of the Catherine Hall to the other, Joe was at least present for the eclipse of the old reliables of the Duma, men like Rodzianko and Prince Lvov who had struggled with the Czar's stubborn apathy for years. He saw them superseded, whatever their nominal functions were to be, by the brilliant young leader of the Social Revolutionaries, Alexander Kerensky.

Kerensky occupied the rostrum for hours that day. Slim and blond and only thirty-six, he poured his eloquence in torrents over the crowd. The beautiful voice which he had used to such effect as defence counsel in the great labour trials grew raucous as the day wore on, but the words never failed him. Alone, Kerensky stemmed the tide of hatred which flowed into the hall as it filled with armed soldiers, workmen, students, all dedicated to anarchy rather than a new form of government. The only concession he made to them—and he made it quickly and willingly—was the opening of the Budget Committee room to their leaders who, following Trotsky's example after Bloody Sunday in 1905, had made themselves into a Soviet of Soldiers' and Workers' Deputies.

It was in one of the eddies of the crowd which followed this announcement that Joe found himself side by side with Mara Trenova, who in her fur hat, her suit with the worn leather belt and her high boots looked not unlike a soldiers' Deputy herself.

"Hallo, Mara Ivanovna!" Joe managed to gasp. "Come to see the red dawn breaking?"

"It has broken at last, thank—thanks to a few brave men," she said. "Now the real work begins. Guchkov and Shulgin have left for GHQ, to persuade Nicholas Romanov to abdicate; we can go on from there tomorrow. All power to the people!"

"Sounds great," said Joe. He pulled her into a corner of the hall, where stacked arms and greatcoats made a slight protection against the swaying mass. "Only what they seem to be shouting is 'All power to the Soviet!' "

"It's the same thing," she assured him. "Kerensky himself helped to establish the Petrograd Soviet."

"And what d'you think of *him*?" Joe was tall enough to see Kerensky's fair head bobbing above the rostrum; the rest of a physically insignificant man was hidden from sight. But Mara followed the jerk of his chin.

"Kerensky? I used to meet him often at the Hendrikovs, when I was at school with Dolly."

"Yes, I know you did, I've met him there myself, but what d'you think of him now?"

"Too much war talk. He mustn't forget the desire of the workers for bread, peace and freedom!"

"I remember where you were very thrilled at the beginning of the war when he and his friends told the workers to defend their country first, and the revolution would come afterwards."

"Oh, at the beginning of the war!" she said impatiently. "Aren't six million Russian dead proof enough that we were willing to defend our country? Now it's surely time to put an end to the useless massacres! The workers want a government that'll make peace with Germany, and that's what Kerensky must be made to understand!"

"From what I've heard him say today, the new government would want to go on fighting, right alongside the Allies."

"Our Allies have made sacrifices too," said Mara. "They'll understand our position better than a neutral."

Joe bit his lip. It was the old sneer with which any Russian could win an argument about the war: America was neutral, an American couldn't understand. But before he could speak a young man with a black beard and spectacles pushed aside the pile of coats and weapons and seized Mara by the arm.

"We're going 'Across the River' now, Trenova!" he shouted above the din. "Don't you want to see the fun?"

"Oh I do, I do!" Joe Calvert heard her say, and without another look or word for him she was off, arm-in-arm with the bearded man and another of the same Georgian type, all three pushing their way somehow out of the Tauride Palace. Joe followed them within an hour. He had been there since eight o'clock that morning, and it was nearly eight at night, but only hunger and fatigue drew him from a scene where fresh orators harangued the crowds on every subject from taxation to illiteracy. He thought, as he had often thought on Madame Hendrikova's evenings, what amazing stamina the Russians had for talk.

In the Tauride Gardens behind the palace, once famous for their snow mountains, hundreds of men who had no hope of entering the building had made a kind of bivouac, with charcoal braziers burning on the snow, and even one or two field kitchens dispensing food of a sort. The stacked arms and the glint of bayonets made it seem as if an army on the march was camped round the Duma, and in fact a fair proportion of the army had come exulting from the surrender of the Winter Palace. Joe picked his way unchallenged through the mob. Once in the Furshtatskaia, only two blocks from the American Embassy, he drew in several gulps of the fresh icy air. The snow was falling in soft flakes on the almost empty street.

The last rumour he heard in the gardens—spluttered out by a soldier who insisted on kissing him and doing a little bear-dance in the snow—was that Nicholas II had abdicated.

It was not true then; the monarchy lasted one more day, during which the Soviet and the Duma hammered out a compromise for the creation of a provisional government. Then the Czar signed the instrument of abdication, exactly eleven days after his return to GHQ, and was taken back under close arrest to the palace where his wife was already a prisoner of the State.

* * *

Unless the end of March brought a severe snowstorm, as sometimes happened, the worst of the Russian winter appeared to be over within ten days of the Czar's abdication. The Fourth Line, as Joe Calvert walked along to call on the Hendrikovs, was lighted by fitful sunshine which gave a foretaste of the coming spring. The lime trees were still sheathed in ice, but snow had begun to slide off the roofs, and patches of black earth were appearing in the little city gardens.

Madame Hendrikova herself opened the door to him.

"Welcome, dear friend!" she said. "What a long time since you've been here! What incredible changes we have seen!"

"It seems like a long time to me," said Joe, hanging up his coat and hat. His Russian lessons had ended nearly six months earlier, and he had not seen Madame Hendrikova since. Even in the dim hall he could see that her hair was now quite grey, but she was as erect as ever, wearing a neat plaid silk blouse with a fountain-pen clipped to the breast pocket, and a wrist watch on a leather strap instead of the old silver fob she used to brandish at her tardy students. "I called the hospital," he said, "they told me Dolly was having the day off, so I thought—"

"You're very welcome, and Dolly will be glad to see you. She has another visitor today, someone you know—"

It was Captain Richard Allen. He was sitting at a table

already set for tea, between Dolly and her father, and seeming quite at home in the familiar living-room. His presence and Dolly's blush so disconcerted Joe that after he had greeted the professor and his daughter he could find nothing better to say to Dick than, "I didn't know you were back in Petrograd."

"I've been around. All well at the Italianskaia?"

"No damage done so far." And then the maid came in with the samovar, over which Dolly undertook to preside, giving Joe a chance to say quietly to her mother:

"I've been wondering about your son, madame. Dolly said you had a telephone call a week ago?"

"We haven't heard since then, but you know what the telephone's been like."

"He's still at the barracks on the Moika?"

"As far as we know." It was said with a glance at Professor Hendrikov, and Joe took the hint at once. He turned to Simon's father.

"Dolly's been telling me," he said, "that you played quite a part in the abdication of the Grand Duke Michael."

"Oh, I wouldn't say that, my dear boy," said the professor, brightening up, "I only provided what Dolly says I'm so fond of, namely pens, ink and paper."

"I'm not really clear as to how it all came about, sir."

"I don't believe the Grand—I mean Michael Alexandrovich, is quite clear on the matter himself. Of course it came as a great surprise to him."

"Because he must have thought if his brother did abdicate, the Czarevich Alexis would succeed."

"So everybody thought. But then there was the question of the child's health, and the father couldn't face a possible separation from the boy, so he named his brother as his successor on the throne." The professor coughed.

"But nobody really imagined Michael would wear the crown?"

"He, least of all! By good luck he was in Petrograd—with the Putiatins in the Millionnaia—and when he joined us he proved most willing to sign an act of abdication on his own behalf. I had to smile when Kerensky said to him, "Promise us not to consult your wife," and he said "Don't you worry, she's out at Gachina!" He knew, poor devil, that the Countess Brassova had been very ambitious to wear a crown."

"So you composed the abdication document?"

"Not I, no indeed! I literally did supply the paper from my writing case, but the statement was drawn up by my old friend Vladimir Nabokov, of the *Rech*. He was as quick and clever as always, it didn't take *him* long! And when Michael Alexandrovich signed his name, somehow we were all aware that the Romanov dynasty had come to an end, that there would never, in our new world, be any room for a pretender to a toppled throne. It was all over in five minutes, and Kerensky was extremely moved. He shook poor Michael warmly by the hand, and said 'Monseigneur, you're one of the noblest of men!' and all of us applauded. It was yet another triumph for Alexander Kerensky."

"And for you too, my worthy father," a new voice said.

"Simon!" cried Madame Hendrikova.

Perhaps he had come in very quietly, or perhaps they had all been riveted by Professor Hendrikov's story; however it was, Simon Hendrikov had arrived unnoticed, and was standing in the open door, with one shoulder against the jamb. He was in uniform, but the uniform looked as if he had slept in it for days, and the fur hat in his hand as if it had been rolling along the gutters. To four of the people present it seemed that he had been drinking; to Richard Allen, the one most competent to judge, Simon Hendrikov was one of the walking wounded, suffering from the internal bleeding of his own lost cause.

"Sorry if I startled you," said Simon between drawn-back lips. "I didn't want to interrupt father's gloat over the downfall of the Romanovs—or was it over the triumph of his own little genius, Alex Kerensky? Sorry if I turned up to remind you that there *are* still men living who haven't forgotten the oath of allegiance they took to His Majesty the Czar."

"My dear boy, don't exaggerate," said his mother, gathering her wits about her. "We're delighted to see you. We've all been wondering where you were—"

"You didn't have to worry," said her son. "I told you when I was allowed to telephone—one man, one call—that I wasn't far away. I've been confined to barracks all this while, with the rest of the Politically Suspect—that's what they're calling us now, Politically Suspect—me and about twenty more who had the wits to see what our great commander, Kirill Vladimirovich, was up to. Mind you, I had my suspicions, when they pulled some of us out of Czarskoe Selo! Kirill wanted to have us under lock and key in the Moika if we refused to join him on his great march to the Tauride. Under the red flag! Well, I've been spared that disgrace, never mind what it cost me—"

"Simon, do stop," said Dolly. "You're tired out, you're not yourself. Let me pour you a cup of tea—"

Simon looked at her owlishly. "That's where you're wrong, my dear sister," he said, "I never was more myself than I am at this moment. And I don't want tea. Buckets of tea! That's the great Russian prescription for every malady. Thank you, I had enough vodka to float the *Standart* on my way here."

"On your way from the Moika?"

"Who said anything about the Moika? I've been to Glinka Street. Wanted to see for myself if it was true what they were saying, that the red flag was flying from Kirill Vladimirovich's house. It was too. Bastard of hell! He broke his oath to his sovereign, and disgraced the whole Garde Equipage when he marched them off to the Duma to suck—"

"Take it easy, Simon," said Joe.

"Oh, you're there, are you?" said Simon as if he realised Joe's presence for the first time. "And Captain Allen, too; that's fine. I did you a good turn when Dolly and Joe picked you up in the Yamskaia, now it's up to you to do something for me."

"If I can," said Dick. Joe Calvert thought he was the only one able to listen to Simon without dismay or embarrassment: his pale eyes showed only an appraising interest.

But Simon had gone off on another tack.

"You know, I blame you for a lot of this," he said to his father. "You and your pet Kerensky. You had him here night after night, listening to him and buttering him up, and now, by God, he's Minister of Justice in the Provisional Government *and* a leading figure in the great Petrograd Soviet! How's that for a double turn? You and your lectures on the French Revolution! You thought I was too dumb to understand what you were getting at, didn't you? But Jesus, I could listen, I used to listen in this room night after night, to your seminars getting your views on Mirabeau and Danton, and all they did to overthrow the Bourbon tyrants, until a little man like Alex Kerensky thought *he* was Mirabeau—at the very least; now he thinks he's Bonaparte! That's what they call him when he goes raving and tearing through the Tauride, spouting speeches like the one I heard him make this afternoon. Napoleonchik, that's what they call him! Not Bonaparte, Napoleonchik! The pocket Napoleon!"

"As a matter of fact they call him Speedy," said Richard Allen.

Simon's jaw dropped. "They call him what?"

"Speedy. The police call him that. He moves around the town so fast, they can't keep up with him." Seeing that he had stopped Simon's tirade, he went on placidly, "My dear old chap, you said you needed help, and if I can I'll help you. Just tell me this: are you absent without leave from your quarters?"

"I've got a twenty-four hour pass."

"Of which you've already wasted some at Glinka Street and the Tauride. And also in several bars, of course. Now what do you want me to do?"

"It's something only father can do, not you," said Simon sulkily. "Father, I want you to go to Kerensky and arrange for my transfer into a Line regiment—any regiment that's serving at the front. On the Vistula, on the Stohod, anywhere. Kerensky wants to carry on the war against the Germans. So do I. I'm not going to break the oath I took to the Czar, not me."

Dick looked warningly at the shaken old professor, and said, "I think that can be arranged, perhaps tomorrow morning. After you've had a bath and food, and a good sleep."

"Ah!" said Simon, with the cunning of the partly sober, "I know what you want to do. You want to hustle me off to bed before I put my foot in it. Before I disgrace my dear papa, the great liberal historian, godfather of the Russian Revolution. Well, I'm not going to play your game, so don't you think it. I've got to have twenty-four hours for myself, no, not twenty-four left now, say twelve. Because first I'm going out to Czarskoe Selo to see my girl."

"What girl?" his mother asked, and Dolly began to cry.

Captain Allen's voice for the first time had a parade-ground rasp in it. "Don't be a damned fool," he said. "If you go out there in your present mood you'll get a bullet through your head."

"How'd you know?"

"Because I was there myself this morning," said Dick, and Joe wondered fleetingly in what disguise the Englishman had visited a palace now guarded in strength by the soldiers of the Soviet. As if he had read Joe's thoughts, Dick explained:

"I went in under a safe conduct, as a special messenger from the British Embassy."

"Did you—see any of them?" Simon got out.

"Certainly not. I had an interview with the new Commandant, Korovichenko, that was all. Their Majesties are both being held incommunicado at present, as prisoners of State, and the young people are still in their bedrooms, convalescing."

"But they're not prisoners?"

"Not officially, no. The two older girls are making a pretty good recovery from the measles, I was told. Alexis is better, Anastasia never was very ill, but unfortunately the Grand Duchess Marie is still lying between life and death. Apparently she was coming down with measles the night she went in and out to the Marine Guards in the courtyard, giving them tea and all that, and the chill she caught turned into pneumonia." Dick paused. "If it hadn't been for that, I really think they would have made a bolt for it at the last minute, but of course it would've been fatal even to take the poor girl out of bed."

"The Garde Equipage was in the courtyard!" said Simon. "And I wasn't there."

Professor Hendrikov cleared his throat. "Simon, my dear lad," he said, "we all respect your feelings. You've been closer to the imperial family than most of us, and naturally you're concerned about their fate. I'm sure they're in no danger, because Kerensky is in charge of them, and everything is settling down so fast. There can hardly have been a major revolution since recorded history began which was carried out with so little bloodshed or looting, apart from Madame Kchessinskaia's house, which was occupied and pillaged by some hotheads on the first night. And even that was only a symbolic act—"

"Sorry to disagree, professor," Dick Allen interrupted, "it hadn't anything to do with symbolism. I believe the taking of the Kchessinskaia house was ordered by somebody who hasn't arrived yet, to provide a command post for his future operations. It's very convenient for the Soviet's GHQ at the Finland Station—"

"You're thinking of Lenin," Joe Calvert stated rather than said.

"Oh, to hell with your symbolism and your Soviet!" Simon Hendrikov burst out again. "What I want to know is, what's going to happen to the imperial family? Will they be allowed to travel south under a trustworthy escort, and live quietly at Livadia?"

"Too easy," said Dick with the ghost of a smile. "Even Kerensky couldn't bring that about. What my ambassador is trying to arrange is their safe conduct to England, as soon as the children are well enough to travel. King George is waiting to receive them all, and the Germans are willing to give them some sort of a *laissez-passer.*"

"England!" said Simon, with something horribly like a sob. Dolly put her hand on his bowed head. "Oh, don't, my dear," she whispered. "You must try not to mind so much—if it's what would be best for *her.*"

19

OLGA'S CONVALESCENCE WAS a fume of dreams. She had suffered from nightmares during the worst days of her illness, nightmares in which they told her that her father was no longer Czar, that her mother was under arrest, and that their children were under lock and key in their palace home, and sometimes her dormant intelligence told her that those evil dreams were true. Very often, too, she had bad dreams about Simon Hendrikov. She saw him lying again in the charnel house of neglected wounded at Warsaw, or imagined him dead in the last stand of the Guards on the Stohod, and often, equally painfully, she was in his arms, on the verge of the act of love, and felt him torn from her body in the very moment of satisfaction. Sometimes, raging and frustrated, she heard him speak to her from behind the iron fences of the palace park, now made out of bayonets: he spoke the lines from *Young Lochinvar* which she had read to him on a summer day in the Fourth Line, or else he said, as he had said then, "I wanted to be alone with you, we're never alone!" That sent her back to Lermontov, and the poem which haunted her on the night long ago when Simon was on his way back to her in the hospital train, and she raised herself on her pillows, reciting:

I want to be alone with you,
   A moment quite alone,
The minutes left to me are few,
They say I'll soon be gone

and going on through the poem to the poignant lines:

And say I died, and for the Czar,
And say what fools the doctors are,
And that I shook you by the hand,
And spoke about my native land

until her mother, sitting by her bed, held her hands and said, "Hush, Olga, you're disturbing Tatiana!" To which Olga replied coherently, "But she can't hear a thing we say."

When her mother told her by daylight what had been only whispered in the darkness of her nightmare, that her father had abdicated and was coming home to them, the girl waited until she could ask one of the doctors for a piece of paper and wrote the news for Tatiana to read. *Father has abdicated*—in Olga's widely spaced writing, the fact seemed more brutal when the paper was held out to Tatiana's urgent hands and consternation spread across her lovely face. But once the truth was told there were no lapses into nightmare. A strong constitution reasserted itself, and it was only Olga's obstinate refusal to face a changed world which kept her dreaming through that strange convalescence, when one by one the doctors and nurses who had cared for them were allowed by the jailers to leave their palace prison, and were seen no more.

Olga's last defence against reality was to shelter behind the condition of her eyes. She was forbidden to read until she had completely recovered from all the side effects of measles, and bandages soaked in soothing lotion were tied over her inflamed eyelids. When the bandages were finally removed, she asked for a disfiguring green shade. She always wore it when her father came to sit with them.: it was too painful to look at his stunned and beaten face.

A spring day came when Olga's sense of fun returned, and she wrote on Tatiana's pad that they looked like two of the three wise monkeys—Hear no Evil and See no Evil, and was rewarded by hearing her sister laugh for the first time since their illness began. Ten minutes later the green shade had been thrown away, and Olga was looking critically at her own reflection in the mirror. Her hair had lost its sheen and her face its colour, but she felt strength coming back with every breath, and when Tatiana fell into a light doze Olga for the first time ventured outside their rooms to see the world.

At first sight it had only changed in one respect: there were no footmen on duty in the gallery. There was only Alexis, curled up in a window seat with Joy, and the boy and the dog hurled themselves into her arms like one being in their delight at seeing Olga again.

"You don't know how glad I am to see you, Olga," said Alexis, when the kissing and exclaiming were over. "You're the only person around here who ever gives me a straight answer to a straight question."

"That's a very serious thing to say."

"Well, but it's true! Zilchik used to tell me things, but now when I ask him anything important he tells me not to be inquisitive or go bothering mamma and papa. Look, I don't mean to bother them. But when I try to talk to mamma she only cries, and papa says he was born on the birthday of the long-suffering Job, and that's why everything went wrong."

"I don't think that was really why, Alexis."

"Nor do I. After all, how do we know papa was born on the same day as the long-suffering Job? There's nothing about it in the Bible."

"I think it tells about Job in the *Lives of the Saints*, or so papa once said."

"It's an awfully long time ago, but never mind. What I want to know is, who's going to be the next Czar of Russia?"

"The *next* Czar?"

The boy's face grew red. "Well, there's got to be a Czar, hasn't there? Papa told me he was too tired to carry on, and Uncle Misha was tired too, and nobody seems even to have thought of me!"

"They probably thought you were too young, Alexis."

"They might have asked me, anyway." He kicked the wood of the window seat. "But now Monsieur Kerensky says there's going to be an election soon, so perhaps I'll have another chance, what do you think?"

"I don't suppose they're planning to elect a Czar, whatever else they do. I think we have to face it, dear, people are tired of the Romanovs—"

"But *why*? What did *we* do that was so wrong? You and the other girls and me?"

If Olga had given her brother the straight answer he hoped to have from her, she would have said, 'We were born of the wrong parents, at the wrong time.' But she equivocated, like all the others, and said, "The Russian people are more tired of the war than they are of the Romanovs. Maybe when peace comes, they'll change their minds again."

"But we'll be living in England then."

"I'm sure we won't be in England all our lives, we're only going there on a long visit."

"That's good. But we won't be going in the *Standart*, I'm afraid."

"The *Standart* doesn't belong to us any more."

"That's what mamma said. It seems incredulous—incredible," said the boy. "I can't believe I'll never see my friends on board again, nor my regiments, nor the officers at the Stavka—" His lips quivered ominously.

"Come on, Alexis," said his sister bracingly, "let's not sit here moping and feeling sorry for ourselves. Do you know I haven't been out of doors for weeks? We'll go for a stroll in the garden, just as far as the lake and back—"

"If they let us," said Alexis doubtfully.

"Why shouldn't they?"

The brother and sister walked to the head of the great staircase. All was silent in the hall below. The King Charles, sensing a walk to come, rushed barking down the red-carpeted stairs.

"Get back, you Romanov scum! Get back to your own quarters!"

A soldier in a filthy uniform, with felt boots split at the uppers, had appeared from one of the side rooms where the Cossacks of the Escort had waited for their turn on duty. He was trailing his rifle by its sling. The spaniel frisked down the remaining steps and ran towards him, wagging its tail.

"Joy! Joy!" The little creature halted at its master's anxious call. The soldier raised his rifle and took aim at Joy.

"No!" screamed Olga, and "No, comrade, no!" cried Monsieur Gilliard, who had appeared in time to run downstairs, heedless of the rifle, expostulating in Russian so bad that even the soldier smiled. He pretended rage and stamped his foot, and used the weapon to wave them back upstairs. No one spoke until they were safely in the schoolroom with the door shut. Then the Swiss tutor turned on his pupil in the anger of a great relief.

"I've told you again and again, Alexis, you must never let Joy or Jimmy out without their leads."

"I forgot."

"That brute might have killed the dog," said Olga, shivering. "And we weren't doing anything, we were only going for a little walk."

"I've seen that fellow before. He's one of the Soviet soldiers, who don't allow us the slightest indulgence," said Monsieur Gilliard. "And my dear Olga Nicolaievna, we only go for walks when *they* permit it, and then under their escort. Just for the time being, just until Their Majesties and you get leave to go to England, we shall all have to remember that we're their prisoners."

It would have been less strange, the girls in their innocence occasionally said—after Marie had quite recovered, and Tatiana had got back most of her hearing—if they had been taken in to the city and locked up in one of the bastions of Peter and Paul, political prisoners, fed on bread and water, instead of sharing this world divided between home life and imprisonment. They were not State prisoners; this Monsieur Kerensky assured them on more than one of the flying visits which, living up to his nickname of Speedy, he paid to the former emperor and his family. As Minister of Justice in the Provisional Government, Kerensky had the sole responsibility for the Romanovs: as a famous defence lawyer he felt obliged to assert the liberties of some of his charges. The young ladies were held in protective custody only, and not subject to interrogation, he chivalrously said, even while he ordered the Czar to live apart from the Czarina, until an investigation was opened to determine if she had been in treasonable communication with the enemy. The husband and wife were permitted to have their meals together in the presence of guards, provided they only spoke Russian, which in spite of much tuition had never been Alexandra Feodorovna's forte. The Czarina was unexpectedly docile. She had been alarmed by the arrest of her two friends, Madame Dehn and Madame Virubova, although the former was released after a very brief imprisonment. Ania was in the fortress prison of Peter and Paul, a warning to others that the Provisional Government had its eye on the friends of Rasputin.

Gradually they all shook down together into a new way of living. They still had servants to wait on them, and food no worse than Alexandra's own menus, but they had no friends, for the brilliant court which the Czarina had affected to ignore had vanished at the first breath of revolution. Two very old men, two foreign tutors, four devoted ladies, made up the little circle which walked in the park, sawed wood, planted seeds as the days grew longer, in full view of the Soviet soldiers and those of their friends able to take the train trip from Petrograd to look at the Romanovs through the park fences as they might have looked at wild beasts in a zoo.

"I don't know how papa can do it," Olga confessed. "First clearing the snow away and then laying out a kitchen garden, with everybody staring and sneering, and those brutes in uniform trying to trip him up with the gardening tools, or yelling at him to go back if he moves ten paces beyond the bridge! Why can't he stay in the library, and work on his stamp collection? Dmitri said he was keen enough on that at GHQ."

"You know he's accustomed to a lot of exercise," said Tatiana. "He really hates to feel confined."

"Don't we all." Olga herself longed for the freedom of the park and the lilacs coming into bud by the wall of the Znamenia church, but she stayed indoors for much of the exercise time rather than face the mocking eyes outdoors. To the old church she did go one Sunday with her parents, to give thanks for Marie's recovery and pray for the success of the Russian army which Kerensky had launched in a new offensive against the Germans, but when she saw her father piously crossing himself at the name of the Provisional Government Olga turned her head away.

The darkness of Good Friday came, followed by the joy of Easter Sunday. Alexis was passionately eager that Easter should be as beautifully observed as ever, with all the drama of the Orthodox rites, the midnight mass and the clergy walking round the church with tapers in their hands in search of the vanished Christ. He wanted—they all wanted—to renew the joyful greeting, when the priest says to the people, "Christ is risen!" and the people answer, "He is risen indeed!" Alexis wanted the exciting presentation of the Easter eggs, and the friends and retainers streaming through the palace to exchange the resurrection kisses with the Little Father and his family.

"No Easter eggs this year, Treasure," his pale mother told him sadly.

"Why ever not?"

"Colonel Korovichenko won't allow us to order any."

"Then can't we get out some of the old ones and polish them up?"

"If you like. You can take some of the Fabergé eggs from my boudoir."

"Alexis is really thinking of the supper," said Anastasia. She was as gaily impudent as ever, having been less ill than her sisters, and only despairing that the attack of measles, from which Marie had risen as slim as a willow wand, had not melted one ounce from her own obstinate puppy fat.

"Who wouldn't think of the supper?" said the boy. "*Pashka* stuffed with preserved fruit, and lovely melted sugar dripping off the *kulich*—we'll have those, won't we, mamma?"

"If Colonel Korovichenko says we may."

But the Commandant had no patience with such bourgeois notions. The Romanovs were allowed to give one glass of wine to their servants as an Easter present, and even that meant a row with the soldiers' soviet, which having held a meeting to debate the point, demanded a glass of wine for every soldier too. Olga stayed upstairs in her room. She knew she was behaving badly, and she didn't care. If her family chose to act like saints and martyrs, turning the other cheek to their enemies on Easter Day, she admired them for it; she couldn't live up to their example. Olga Nicolaievna had been stripped of the title of Grand Duchess: she could not at once forget her imperial past; nor the fact that in this very palace only a year ago, and for all the years she could remember, a thousand courtiers, soldiers, guards had thronged the halls where now a few men in tattered uniforms argued over their right to a free glass of wine. She remembered the Crimson Hall on other Easters, when the uniforms of the whole Empire shone in a kaleidoscope of ostrich plumes, crimson caftans, Arab turbans and vermilion tunics, and white-gloved servants carried salvers laden with good things from one guest to another. She remembered the Easter eggs, the hundreds of eggs carved from amethyst, from gold, from opal, with the tiny toys inside which Fabergé made for the delight of little princesses. They had received just one egg on their first Easter as prisoners—an offering which the brave old Queen of Greece carried from Pavlovsk and handed through the grilles of the locked gates to a good-tempered guard.

It was not until after dark that another egg was brought, this time in a small square package with no address, but which one of her mother's dressers took straight to Olga.

"Madame, a man and a girl brought this gift to the gate half an hour ago. They insisted it was for you, and only you: the sentries accepted it and sent it in."

"The sentries did!" marvelled Olga. "They can't be Soviet sentries, then!"

"No, Madame, the *sovietski* troops were relieved at eight o'clock by men of the Sharpshooters Reserve. And they are—loyal."

"At least they're kind," amended Olga. "A man and a girl, you say. Have you any idea what they looked like?"

"A pretty girl, the soldier said. The man was older, rough, one of the 'dark people', as the saying goes."

"Thank you." For a wild moment she had hoped it was Dolly Hendrikova and Simon, but an older man, a peasant, hardly sounded like the Marine Guards officer she knew. But Olga's intuition was so far right that when the woman left her alone, and she opened the small package, the first wrapping inside the cardboard container was a note from Dolly.

"Your Imperial Highness," the schoolgirl scrawl began, "My brother has exchanged into a Line regiment and left for the western front. He bows to you and begs you to accept his Easter blessing. I bow respectfully to you and kiss your hand.—DKH."

Inside more wrapping paper was an Easter egg. It was the cheapest-looking egg Olga had ever seen, being made of satin in a crude shade of cherry red, with a huge 'XB' for 'Christ is risen' in diamanté ribbon writing on one side. It looked like the kind of egg sold in the Petrograd bazaar where she had never been allowed to go, the Gostinnoi Dvor. And inside, a paper folded between the two halves was more precious to Olga than all the jewelled Fabergé toys of the past, for it contained two lines in Simon's own handwriting:

Gone is the resurrection kiss,
But yet to come: you swore it me!

"He remembered that; how wonderful!" she said softly; and she remembered too, in the darkness of this sad Easter Sunday, the glowing morning of their reunion less than a year ago when Simon had come back from Odessa many weeks too late for Easter. She had teased him with the lines from Pushkin, with her hands on the breast of his tunic, and then she 'swore it him', that kiss, next year, on the Easter morning that would find her a prisoner and Simon on his way back to the front. And brave little Dolly had risked coming to the palace prison to bring his Easter message to the girl he loved! Olga went to bed in a mood between happiness and tears, with the paper folded underneath her pillow. It was not until the middle of the night, when there was no sound in the room but Tatiana's even breathing, that she awoke suddenly as if a voice had called her, and with a pang of purest terror recalled the whole of the verse which Russia's greatest poet had written:

> *Your beauty in the grave's abyss*
> *Has vanished, and your misery;*
> Gone is the resurrection kiss,
> But yet to come: you swore it me!

* * *

At Easter the former Czar seemed to have regained all his old fatalistic composure. He had convinced himself that the abdication signed at the request of nearly every general in his army had succeeded in its purpose, which was to avoid the horrors of civil war in Russia. The Provisional Government was carrying on the struggle against Germany, in accordance with the oath he had sworn in the Winter Palace, and he waited trustingly for them to arrange his transportation to a new life in England. "And at least," he said cheerfully to his family, "I've no beastly papers to sign now."

Even his wife was reconciled to a future in the land where so much of her childhood had been spent. In England, as a granddaughter of Queen Victoria, she had a position of her own, whereas she had been outraged at a well-meant suggestion by the Grand Duke Paul that the imperial family should take refuge in his villa on the outskirts of Paris. "Life in a suburb like Boulogne-sur-Seine!" she fumed. "Does Uncle Paul expect us to do our own housework and marketing?"

"I think that would be rather fun," said Marie.

"Can I go to boarding-school after we get to England, and play netball and hockey like the girls in our school stories?" said Anastasia.

"It's not so long since you wanted to have a grown-up dance," said Tatiana, whose hearing was improving every day.

"There's nobody to dance with now."

"They're not in much of a hurry to send us anywhere," said Olga. She felt that the guards were more aggressive, the people who watched them at exercise more insulting, and the Minister of Justice more vague about his plans for their future. Still—

"I've every confidence in Alexander Feodorovich Kerensky," said the former Czar. "He really is a most valuable man, with a sincere love of Russia. I only wish I'd met him sooner."

"Well, why didn't you?" The words trembled unspoken on Olga's tongue. Why didn't you go to the Duma, as they begged and begged you to do, and meet him there? Why didn't you grant a responsible ministry and a real constitution? Why did you have to get all of us into this horrible mess?

"It's the complacency that makes me sick," she said later on to Tatiana. "That, and the condescension. I believe papa still thinks of himself as the God-anointed monarch, who just *might* consent to speak to an elected Minister of Justice—"

"I take it, then, you won't be joining papa's history class this term?" said Tatiana, dryly for her.

"I don't much care for his own interpretation of history." And when the parents told the children what an interesting syllabus they had prepared, so that lessons need not fall behind this summer, Olga said curtly that at twenty-one she thought her education was completed, and would beg to be excused from her mother's lectures on religious systems and Monsieur Gilliard's extension course in French.

"But you ought to come to history," said Anastasia, after a few mornings when all the older persons in the diminished entourage had been pressed into service to give lessons to the younger. "Honestly, Alexis is a riot!"

"What does Alexis do?"

"Asks a lot of questions father doesn't want to answer. About Peter the Great and *his* son Alexis, and how Peter had him tortured to death rather than let him reign. And Alexander plotting to kill Paul I, so that he could be the Czar instead of his father, and, you know, all the Romanovs who got rid of anybody who came between them and the throne—"

"Professor Petrov used to give us very milk-and-water stuff compared with that."

"Or else Alexis is smarter than the rest of us," suggested

Anastasia. Olga said it was very likely. Under Anastasia's sharp eyes she refused to say what she really felt: that Alexis had found a way to show his fierce resentment at being dropped from the succession. Later she was sure of it, when she opened one or two of his history books to see if passages so critical of the Romanovs were really included in the text, and discovered that the fly-leaves had been torn out with large jagged tears which suggested temper.

"Prayer to God and service to the Czar will never be in vain" was what the child had taken as his motto and written in all his books. Did his disavowal, at least of 'service to the Czar' mean that Alexis had been completely disillusioned by his father's abdication? The only word of reproach Olga had ever heard him utter was a complaint that Nicholas had forgotten to bring the new cat, Verushka, home with him when he left Mohilev under arrest, as if the cat had become in his mind a substitute for the crown. That was a relapse into childhood, but the elaborate teasing about Romanovs who never reigned or were betrayed by their nearest and dearest, was vengeance on an adult plane. She almost felt relief, though of a painful sort, when the emerging adult came to her in tears next morning and threw himself into her arms like a baby, sobbing that the *sovietski* soldiers had killed all the collies—and the little fawns—and *Vanka!*

"Brutes! Beasts! Devils!" Vanka, that cleverest of all their pets, the circus donkey who would go to anyone for a sweet or a caress, who had trotted confidently up to the two-legged animal armed with a rifle in the very moment before the shot rang out! "Don't cry, Alexis, please don't cry!"

"But *why*, Olga? The baby deer hadn't done them any harm!"

"They were ours, that was enough. Here's my handkerchief—"

"What if they try to hurt Pussy and Zubrovka?"—with a sob.

"Cats are awfully good at looking after themselves, Alexis. But maybe it would be a good idea to let them live in the kitchens now, and they'd get more to eat. After all, you still have both the dogs—"

"And I'm never, never going to let Joy off his lead again."

Olga was very gentle with her brother for the rest of that day, and the gentle mood continued after he had gone to bed. She endured another reading aloud of *Through the Postern Gate*, and after the saga of Little Boy Blue and his motherly sweetheart had turned her parents' mind to the happy days at Walton-on-Thames, she even looked out some of the song albums bought at that time, and played accompaniments for her mother's singing. Alexandra Feodorovna had never had more than a pretty voice, and now it cracked and broke piteously in the upper register, but Nicholas leaned on the piano and looked at her as if she were lovely Alix of Hesse again, and he the Heir to the throne of All the Russias.

> If we must part, oh! why should it be now?
> Is this a dream? Then waking would be pain,
> Oh, do not wake me—
> Let me dream again!

"Beautiful, Sunny, beautiful! You wrote those words into my diary at Walton, do you remember?" said Nicholas, and to Tatiana there was something very touching in the way the grey-haired, grey-bearded man bent lovingly over his wife's hand. Then Marie asked for 'Abide with me', which she had always called 'Nurse Cavell's hymn' since it became known that the brave Englishwoman, shot by the Germans in 1915, had repeated the words along with the clergyman who visited her cell on the night before her execution. The poignant hymn sent most of the party upstairs in a subdued mood. But Olga, going to bed, sang "Do not wake me, let me dream again!" with a very sarcastic inflection, and said as she put the light out:

"Do you suppose those two are ever going to wake up to reality?"

20

REALITY WAS IN THE outside world, far from Czarskoe Selo, where President Woodrow Wilson took the plunge at last and declared war on Germany. Immediately, Ambassador Francis found himself one of most sought-after men in Petrograd. Until then he had been somewhat isolated in his embassy, playing poker with his staff or taking walks along the Neva with Madame de Cram, a charming lady met on shipboard; a few days after America entered the war Mr. Francis was so busy that he called at the consulate and asked for Vice-Consul Calvert to be seconded to the embassy on a temporary basis.

"They tell me he's the finest linguist at our disposal," said the old gentleman, lighting one of the cigars he smoked all day long. "Sure, we've got Russian interpreters on the payroll, but how do I know when they're tellin' me the truth? I need Calvert right beside me, at least until this here mission they've wished on us has come and gone. And don't tell me his consular duties are any more important than that; why, most of our commercial interests in Russia have been at a standstill since the war began."

"They won't be at a standstill for long," said the consul. "Not now we've entered on a war of resources, as Mr. Wilson told the Congress. 'Oil, steel, money, bread!' he said; but it's going to take a lot of American know-how to get them all to Russia."

"It's a mighty slender life-line, I'll allow." The elderly ambassador stood looking with young Joe and the older consul at the huge map of the Russian Empire stretched over nearly the whole of one wall in the consul's office. Over the vast land-mass, stretching from the Gulf of Finland to the Bering Sea, only the thin track of the Trans-Siberian railway extended all the way from east to west, with its Pacific terminal, reached through Manchurian territory, at Vladivostok.

"I think our declaration of war is going to teach the Russians to take a new look at their own maps," Joe ventured. "Everything's been geared to the capital for generations. Now

Vladivostok will come into the limelight, when our war material starts arriving there."

"Wonder what the Japs'll say to that," said the ambassador, chewing his cigar. For there, due west of Vladivostok, lay the little offshore island, the country of the silent ally which had declared war on Germany in August 1914, and never fired or heard a shot in anger since.

"Well, that's the President's headache," continued Mr. Francis, neither of the other men having broken the silence. "Japan, eh? Wonder if the Root Mission'll plan a little stopover in Tokio en route for Petrograd? We'll have to arrange the red carpet treatment for 'em in Vladivostok, that's for sure. Well, Consul Caldwell is a great little fixer, they tell me."

"And a first-rate officer," said the consul. "Trouble is, Mr. Ambassador, the Service is mighty thin on the ground in Russia. Caldwell in Vladivostok, Consul-General Maddin Summers in Moscow, some representation in places like Irkutsk, and that's about it."

"Which is another way of saying you don't want me to borrow Calvert. What do you say to it yourself, Joe? Like the idea of working at the embassy for the next few months?"

"I'm here to work, sir. There's just one thing—"

"Speak your mind, son," said Mr. Francis encouragingly.

"Now that we're in the war at last, I'd like to resign from the Service and join the army."

At which both the older men became eloquent. The waste of time, the waste of training, the waste of a valuable Russian language qualification were all set against a step which might land Joe Calvert in some job on an army post in a middle-western city instead of with the death or glory boys in France. "Give it till the Root Mission's been and gone, and then we'll talk again," said the ambassador. "I'm going to need all the young guys like you that I can get to handle old Elihu and the other members of his mission. The good old USA has voted a credit of $100 million to the Provisional Government, and Elihu Root is going to make damned sure we get our money's worth."

"But the Root Mission won't be here until June, Mr. Ambassador," objected Joe.

"I'll keep you busy in the meantime, son. You know Kerensky personally, don't you?"

"Not very well. But I've met him several times at a friend's house over the past few years."

"You've got the entrée to his office at the Tauride?"

"Well yes, sir."

"Bully for you," said Mr. Francis. "I hear they call him Speedy now. Okay, Joe, whenever you catch Speedy on the wing, you just pass on this piece of thinking: No fight, no dough. That's what Uncle Sam wants, action; and Kerensky'd better be prepared to deliver the goods."

Joe felt more reconciled with his conscience after that brief talk, and after a far from brief cable (prompted, he suspected, by the ambassador himself) from his uncle at the State Department, reminding him that his job in Petrograd was, as the senior Calvert biblically said, in the forefront of the battle. He felt free to move around more in the city, to see the effects of the first month of revolution, and indeed to enjoy some of the places where poetry and rhetoric now flourished as they had never done before.

Mara Trenova saw him come in to a café called the 'Vienna', with Dolly Hendrikova on his arm, and two other couples, the men obviously young Americans, sitting down with them at a candle-lit table not far from the piano. She felt a quick annoyance at being there with Efron, the cartoonist, in his rough clothes, and Smirnov, whose boredom was obvious to everyone who looked their way. Smirnov was about to throw her over; their affair had not lasted long. And Dolly seemed so pleased and happy! I was a fool to come to the 'Vienna' at all, Mara thought angrily. It's a rotten, black-market, bourgeois place.

I have lost my way
This is the wrong city and the wrong midnight

She had heard a very handsome young man called Boris Pasternak reciting his own verses in 'The Red Sarafan' only two nights before, and those lines had stuck, oddly, in the head of a young woman who had been sure of her way ever since her first talk with Professor Rostov in one of the little classrooms at the Xenia School. This was not the time to give way to depression, with the first battle won for democracy, and the second, the greater, nearly ready to begin! *Pravda* had come out of its cellar and was no longer an underground publication. With a new office on the

Moika, and a man called Molotov as editor, *Pravda* had given its first post-revolution issue away free and then sold an unbelievable one hundred thousand copies of the second. It was a useful, solid achievement, far more important in the long run than direct action, whether carried out with picric acid or a Mauser pistol.

It was humiliating to be concerned with the presence in the 'Vienna' of Dolly Hendrikova and Joe Calvert and their friends: concerned to the point of getting up and following them when they finished their drinks and left, looking at their watches, just as someone was about to recite Mayakovsky's fighting poem, "LISTEN, YOU SWINE!" Efron and Smirnov merely looked up and nodded as Mara left the table. She went out quietly, so as not to disturb the reciter, and loitered until Joe's party had collected their coats and fur hats. Then she followed them to the Nevski Prospekt and northwards. It was nearly ten o'clock, and as they had checked their watches she supposed they had an appointment for ten, no doubt in some Czarist stronghold, a mansion where an elaborate supper was set behind shuttered windows, and the guests, drinking champagne, would proceed to plan a rescue of the Romanovs. Mara realised that she was light-headed, though not from the glass of adulterated wine she had drunk in the 'Vienna'. Hunger was her trouble: it was some time now since the supplies at the Kchessinskaia house had come to an end, satisfying though it had been to raid the kitchens on the night the ballerina's venial housekeeper had turned over the place to Agabagov and his gang. It was even more satisfying to think of the owner of the house, Russia's one and only *prima ballerina assoluta*, flying for her life across the Alexander Bridge with an old shawl tied round her head like any of the cleaners at the Maryinsky Theatre. Imagine Kchessinskaia slinking along in the shadows, like the jealous woman whose fantasy of exposing a Czarist plot and handing over Joe and Dolly to the Soviet militia exploded as soon as Mara came into the glow of light outside the big cinema at the corner of the Morskaia. Light which revealed the American dream in all its global supremacy, shining on the letters above the entrance:

Douglas Fairbanks
in
THE AMERICANO

* * *

After that exposure of Dolly's frivolity (and not Dolly Hendrikova's alone, there was a long queue of people shambling in to see the American movie) Mara was determined to prove her own seriousness by attending a concert at the Maryinsky Theatre in aid of the victims of the revolution. It was difficult to get anyone to go with her, for Kerensky was to be the principal speaker, and her friends refused to take Kerensky seriously, but finally the girl Sofie, tired of dressing up in the contents of Kchessinskaia's wardrobes, good-naturedly agreed to make the effort. And when they got to the theatre even Sofie, nibbling sunflower seeds, was impressed by the sight of the imperial box, once draped with blue and gold in honour of the Family, now occupied by thirty old revolutionaries who only three weeks before had been confined in Schlüsselburg prison, or even further away in their long Siberian exile. For Mara Trenova it was a dream come true to see and hear Vera Figner, one of the founders of the People's Will assassination group, who had carried the explosives in at least one train attempt on the life of Alexander II, and Katarina Brechskovska, now a fat old lady clinging with exaggerated affection to Kerensky's arm.

"Comrade Brechskovska seems more excited about the American gold than our fallen comrades," Sofie scowled, and Mara found herself making lame excuses for the old women. Figner was sixty-five; age and imprisonment had destroyed her eloquence, and she stood on the Maryinsky stage like a mummy or a memorial to the past. But Mara's heart was full when Spiridonova came down to the footlights and held out her arms to the cheering audience. Spiridonova was still only thirty-one: it was ten years since she had shot and killed the brutal Luzhenovski, a leader of the repressions which followed Bloody Sunday, and with her burning eyes and big sulky mouth she represented a kind of perverse femininity which drew an unexpected response from Mara Trenova.

"You fancy her, don't you?" said Sofie shrewdly, and she laughed when Mara in her pedantic way began to recite all that the thin woman on the great stage, with her broad ugly face and dark hair parted in the middle, had done for the sacred cause of the revolution. "I still say you fancy her, and welcome!" she said scornfully. "All these SR fogies are dead on their feet, and they don't know it."

In her heart Mara admitted the girl was right. The show was dragging terribly. It had begun with the *Marseillaise*, played in the slow time preferred by the revolutionaries of 1917, and was to end with a funeral march no gayer than the lugubrious speeches of the returned exiles. Kerensky was billed as the star turn, but 'Speedy' was not on his best form that afternoon. He was visibly worn out by weeks of oratory, for he harangued mass audiences nightly as Robespierre harangued the Jacobins, and even his flow of ideas, his lyrical metaphors, had begun to sound flat. His voice was not helped by the acoustics of the great theatre, and he had fallen back on exaggerated gestures and grimaces to make his points. With his right hand stuck in the breast of his coat, his left sawing the air, he seemed with his contorted face to be trying to dominate his audience with something like Rasputin's hypnotic power.

He was not the great leader the revolutionaries had hoped for, but they had not much longer to wait for leadership: the great man was on his way.

Early in April the long and careful preparations made by Parvus, Keskuela and other agents operating between the German government and the Bolsheviks in Switzerland were completed, and Lenin and his followers set out to return to Russia. At the expense of Germany, they were to be transported across German territory in a sealed train and from the port of Sässnitz to Malmö in Sweden by ferry. The Swedes, having permitted German agents to operate in their country for years, made no objection to a continuation of the journey north to Haparanda, from which frontier post the group stepped on to Russian territory in the Grand Duchy of Finland. Lenin, who had opposed the war consistently since 1914, was the best investment the Germans ever made, and worth more to them in his own person than several armoured divisions.

If the neutral Swedes received the transit passengers calmly, the neutral Swiss gave them a noisy send-off from the main station at Zürich. The large supplies of sugar and chocolate laid in by the Bolsheviks were confiscated by customs men before the sealed train started, and as it drew out of the station a crowd of indignant Switzers bellowed "Goodbye spies! German spies! Don't come back!" The answer, from behind the shuttered windows came in the singing of the *Internationale,* which the Bolsheviks liked better than the *Marseillaise.*

There were only thirty-two persons in the party, which included Lenin's wife Krupskaia, and his mistress Inessa Armand, and the sound of their singing was soon drowned by the turning of the wheels and the engine's whistle as the train made for Germany. But the sound swelled to a roar, an animal yell of triumph, when seven days later another train drew into the Finland Station at Petrograd, and a crowd of thousands surged forward to cheer their returned hero, Vladimir Ilyich Lenin.

Most of them, like Mara Trenova, were seeing him for the first time. Years had gone by since he left Russia, where he had suffered imprisonment and Siberian exile, but as he climbed up to the roof of an armoured car outside the Finland Station, and was seen in the light of the torches, it seemed as if every man there knew Lenin's face by heart and for ever.

He was forty-seven years old, eleven years older than Kerensky, but physical exercise had kept his stocky figure agile, and as he stood on the armoured car with his hands in his overcoat pockets, smiling, he was the embodiment of a controlled sexual power very different from Kerensky's romantic force. His fur hat was pushed back on his head, revealing a big domed forehead, a craggy nose, and a chin adorned with a reddish-brown beard: there was something Mongolian about the whole cast of his face. His supporters yelled and swarmed around him. There had been a fresh fall of spring snow that morning, so that the Finland Station and the buildings round about were covered in white. Between the white roofs and the black mass of people stretched a sea of red flags, a leaping, living thicket of torchlight, and in the middle stood the dark figure on the armoured car which dominated the scene. Mara Trenova, pushed mercilessly forward by the movement of the crowd, saw that all round the car stood a double rank of Soviet soldiers with their fingers on the triggers of their rifles. With a pang of foreboding she saw that the people's leader was guarded as closely as any Czar.

When Lenin had kept them waiting long enough for anticipation to become so keen that even breathing was stilled, he raised his right hand in a smooth simple gesture to shoulder level, with the palm opened towards the throng. Broad, short-fingered and virile, that hand never moved as he spoke his opening words in a voice resonant but without passion, undramatic but totally assured—

"Dear comrades, soldiers, sailors, workers," said Lenin (and every man in the crowd knew that the words were spoken to himself alone) "the Russian revolution made by you has begun. It has opened a new epoch." The orchestrating hand moved once, and without rehearsal, in a spontaneous gesture, the red flags were lifted higher.

"All power to the Soviets! From here our prophetic words will spread across the land: Hail to the world Socialist revolution!"

21

WITH THE ARRIVAL OF Lenin, the fate of the Romanovs became a matter of grave concern to the Provisional Government. Some members of the Family had already slipped away from the revolutionaries, including the Empress Dowager and her daughters, who had reached their palaces in the Crimea, while others moved quietly on to their dachas in Finland. The most fortunate of them all now turned out to be the Grand Duke Dmitri, whose punishment had taken him safely out of the path of the revolution to the frontier of Persia. But the prisoners at Czarskoe Selo were the real problem, especially when the first plans for their departure were shattered by the British Cabinet.

"We shan't be going to England after all, my dears," said Nicholas to his daughters, trying to speak lightly, when Kerensky broke the news.

"But why, papa?"

"It seems we'd be most unwelcome guests. Mr. Lloyd George thinks the very sight of me would cause a general strike, and stop the war effort in all the factories and ports. And Ramsay MacDonald, that man Lenin's friend, has told the British I'm no better than a common murderer."

"What have they got to do with it?" said Tatiana indignantly. "The King is your cousin, you were to go to London as *his* guest—"

"That's a constitutional monarchy for you," said her father. "Poor Georgie has to bow to the will of his idiotic cabinet . . . Don't let's talk any more about it now, and don't say anything to poor mamma."

The girls saw that their parents' sense of rejection was acute; they had both been very fond of their English cousins. The first sense of hopelessness began to chill the spirits of them all.

One afternoon in early June the four sisters were sitting beside the lake, trying to ignore the stares and sometimes the jeers of the soldiers patrolling the bridge behind them. They were still pale and drained of energy, and although they had been under the public gaze all their lives, they were now morbidly sensitive about their appearance. The long bright hair of all four, so carefully brushed and tended, fell out in handfuls after the measles. On medical advice it had been cropped almost to the bone, and although the girls wore silk headscarves indoors and out, they all felt they were disfigured. When old Count Benckendorff, who still styled himself Grand Marshal of the Court, came looking for Olga, she nervously twitched the headscarf further across her brow.

"Your Imperial Highness," he said with a bow, "my profound apologies for disturbing you. A messenger is here from Monsieur Kerensky, with an urgent request that you will talk to him in private."

"A messenger from Alexander Feodorovich? Are you sure it's me he wants to see?"

"He asked for you, Madame, and there's no doubt he has the authority—" On a tiny salver, as if conjured from his pocket, the Count presented a note with the letterhead of the Ministry of Justice, and signed under a few lines of writing with the unmistakeable single name, Kerensky.

"Where have you put this man, Count Benckendorff?"

He was in the old waiting-room where Olga had questioned Protopopov after the murder of Rasputin. The room had not changed since that night; the heads of big game still stared beadily from the walls, and the magazines for the month of February had been laid out but not cut.

The envoy from Petrograd was studying a tapestry hanging above the empty fireplace. He swung round as Count Benckendorff ceremoniously announced "Her Imperial Highness the Grand Duchess Olga Nicolaievna," and acknowledged her titles with a slight smile and a slighter bow.

At the first glance, Olga thought it was Kerensky himself. The man before her had the same blond, crew-cut hair, the same aggressive nose, and the slender, supple build. But the features were more Slavic, and the voice, when the young man spoke, was more staccato than Kerensky's.

"Good-day to you, Citizeness Romanova," he said.

"You want to speak to me?" said Olga bluntly.

"In private, if you please, citizeness."

"You may leave us, Count Benckendorff."

"Happy to serve Your Imperial Highness," said the Marshal of the Court, with a vindictive glance at Kerensky's envoy. He laid the salver and the paper on a table near the door as he bowed himself out of Olga's presence.

"Be good enough to state your business," Olga said. "You have a message from the Minister of Justice?"

"Indirectly, yes. That is, Alexander Feodorovich knows the nature of my mission, and signed a gate pass admitting me to what I suppose we must still call a palace. I'm a member of the Petrograd Soviet of Soldiers and Workers, citizeness."

The words were rapidly spoken, but Olga had time to snatch at a fleeting resemblance, and an almost forgotten memory.

"Haven't I seen you before?" she said.

The Slavic features creased in a wider smile. "Ah, you're beginning to remember," said the man. "Try a little harder. Here in this very palace . . . in another kind of livery . . ." He pulled down his ill-fitting khaki tunic and drew himself up.

"I recognise you now," said Olga. "You're the footman who brought Rasputin to my rooms."

"And my name?"

"How should I remember your name?"

"You called me Ivan, very glibly, then. Of course we were all Ivan to you and the rest of the Romanovs, weren't we? Just another pair of hands, wearing white gloves in case a drop of honest sweat should ever touch you or your belongings . . . sixteen thousand of us there were in all your palaces—your obsequious slaves." He hissed the words at her, and Olga answered indifferently:

"I really never counted them. I wonder if there were many like you among what *we* called, and what fools we were, our faithful servants? You, who took a bribe from Rasputin, and money, I imagine, from the editors of the gutter press of Petrograd when you sold them the whole story—"

"I, whom you had thrown out of the palace, saying next time you would have me flogged—"

"If I'd had my wits about me I'd have had you shot."

The man in khaki and high boots burst out laughing. "Bravo, citizeness," he said. "You're true to your principles, anyway. I always told my comrades you had twenty times the guts of your father: with you on the throne our victory might have been postponed for years."

"Which is as good as admitting that when you were Ivan the footman you were already a member of the Bolsheviki, here in our home as an agent of your party?"

"Exactly"—with a bow. "Only you must call us the Communist party now, not Bolsheviki. That's the latest directive from our GHQ at the Kchessinskaia house, by order of Comrade Lenin himself."

"And afterwards? Did you go underground, as I believe the saying is, when you were rather forcibly removed from my service?"

"I returned to my mother's home in Switzerland, and continued to serve the Party there."

"And now you're back in Petrograd, a member of the Soviet. Why have you come here today? To gloat over us in our imprisonment? Or have you anything constructive to say?"

"What a girl you are!" said the young man admiringly. "Always forthright and to the point . . . I've never been accused of being a ladies' man, but I must say, if I were, you'd be the girl for me."

"You flatter me, Ivan. Or should I say Colonel? Are you a Soviet officer now?"

"Just a humble *apparatchik*, so far. But wouldn't you be more comfortable sitting down?"

"Thank you, I prefer to stand."

"Very well, now let us be serious. It must have been a severe blow to your pride, wasn't it, when your loving cousins in England declined the pleasure of your company? H'm? You don't want to answer that one, I see. Did you know that Comrade Trotsky, as soon as he arrived from Canada to join Lenin, began pressing for a State trial, a grand showpiece put on before the whole world, bringing your father and mother to justice on a charge of high treason?"

"I don't believe there will be such a trial, as long as Kerensky is Minister of Justice."

"He may not be at the Justice ministry for ever—or for long. But one thing is clear, and he has told you so himself: you and your sisters are not State prisoners. Three of you were war nurses. We'll stand on that record, and overlook the Romanov name."

"Am I supposed to express my gratitude?"

"It isn't necessary. Now!" His voice was sharp. "I've come to tell you something, important to you all. A message has been received from your aunt in England, through the British Ambassador, offering a permanent home to your sisters and yourself. Provided you can leave within a week, you're free to go."

"Leave in a week? B-but I don't understand," stammered Olga. "I mean, how can we? How would we travel? How could we even leave the country, the way things are?"

"It would be possible," the man said stolidly. "You could be escorted through Finland and then across the Gulf of Bothnia. One at a time, of course, because the four of you, travelling together, would probably be recognised, but you would meet in Stockholm and go on from there. You could be free and in London within a month from now."

Olga was silent. The idea was so unexpected, the plan so suspiciously easy, that she had no idea what to say. Except—

"Would my brother be allowed to leave with us?"

"No."

"Why not? He's only a child, and a delicate child too; what harm can he possibly do you in a foreign land?"

"He was born the Heir, and in a few years he could rally the monarchists around him anywhere. He's the representative of the legitimist principle—"

"While you and your friends represent the illegitimate principle?"

The pale boyish face flushed with anger. "Citizeness, you're throwing my birth in my teeth—"

"I know nothing whatever about your birth, and care less. I don't even know your name."

"My name is on the pass, you should have read it. But then you're very careless about names, Citizeness Romanova!"

"What do you mean by that?"

The voice which had been staccato suddenly became shrill. "What possessed you all to sign your names on the loving message we found in Rasputin's coffin?"

"*I* sign my name to a loving message—you must be crazy!"

"You went to his funeral."

"My mother was beside herself with grief. We didn't dare refuse."

"You knew his body was dug up and burned?"

"I heard about it later. It happened when I was ill."

"They found a holy picture, with your names on it, laid beneath his cheek."

Olga gave a long shuddering sigh. "A holy picture," she said. "Now I understand. There must be thousands of such pictures in existence, we used to sign them by the boxful for the troops. And somebody took one of them to put inside Rasputin's coffin. Sister Akulina!" she exclaimed, as recollection came. "She had charge of everything. She did it to compromise us . . . Was *she* one of your Party, too?"

"A very useful and experienced agent, citizeness."

Olga made a helpless gesture with her knotted hands. "So many traitors," she whispered, "everywhere we turned! And you were one of them! Why have you come here to help me, if you mean to help me? Or is this another trap, like Sister Akulina's?"

"No, it's not a trap, Olga Nicolaievna. It's a fair offer to give you a chance to save yourself. Because Kerensky seems to have sized up your parents pretty well. He thinks you'll never hear about the message from England, unless you hear it from our side."

"I suppose that's possible," she said, and sighed. "I know they think we must all stay together. Do they know already?"

"They'll hear about it when Kerensky comes tomorrow."

"Then I'll wait until the next day before I say anything to my sisters."

The man shrugged. "That's your affair," he said, "but don't delay too long." He turned to retrieve his cap from the stone mantel, and looked up at the tapestry.

"I remember that thing," he said, "from the days when I used to usher your father's visitors into this very room. Marie Antoinette and her children, isn't it?"

"Yes. It was copied from the Vigée-Lebrun picture, and presented to the Czarina by the French government."

"I understand the former Czarina had a great admiration for Marie Antoinette?"

"Only as a very unfortunate queen and woman."

"I needn't ask if you've read the works of Marx or Hegel, citizeness?"

"Not a word."

"Marx revised one of Hegel's statements in a very illuminating way. He pointed out that great events and personalities may well recur on the stage of history, but the second time they appear in farce, not tragedy. In other words, if Alexandra Feodorovna has ambitions to play the Queen of France, and die nobly on the guillotine—take care she doesn't drag the rest of you into the farce as well."

He moved towards the door, and Olga said reluctantly, "Thank you for coming."

"You can get in touch with me through Colonel Korochivenko." he said. "He'll know where to find me, as long as I'm in Petrograd."

"Are you going back to Switzerland?"

"No, but I'm expecting to be sent to Finland fairly soon." His hazel eyes gleamed. "I may be your escort from Helsingfors to Åbo one of these days. Make up your mind, Citizeness Romanova! And don't forget the old saying, 'It is later than you think'."

He sketched a salute with two fingers to the peak of his cap and went out quietly. Olga waited until the door closed behind him. Then she took Kerensky's *laissez-passer* from the salver and read his envoy's name:

Boris Heiden.

*   *   *

The thoughts of Karl Marx on farce and tragedy in history came back to Olga many times in the weeks that followed; never more vividly than on the night the Romanovs were taken away from the palace at Czarskoe Selo.

They were to go as a family. That had never been in question: the former Czar and Czarina had taken it for granted that their children would accompany them everywhere, and the latter had said vaguely, in answer to Olga's casual enquiry about an invitation from Aunt Victoria, that perhaps there *had* been some kindly idea of that sort, but of course papa and mamma could never let their chicks go to England alone. But before that it had been settled among the girls themselves, for the younger three hardly took time to consider Heiden's offer.

"I can never leave mamma," said Tatiana quietly, and Marie and Anastasia had protested a good deal less quietly that they couldn't possibly be parted from their parents and Alexis. "Unless any of us wants to go alone?" said Anastasia slyly. "Do you, Olga?"

"No, I'll stay."

"That's settled then. Hurrah! OTMA for ever!"

"And even if papa can't go to London now, "offered Tatiana, "things are much better here than they were at first, since Colonel Kobilinski became the palace commandant."

But when they were alone Tatiana said, "I don't want you to think I'm living with my head in the sand, Olga. There may be bad times ahead, worse than we've known yet, but I still think we ought to stick together. Whether we can make a go of it depends very much on you."

"Why on me?"

"Because you're the strongest and the cleverest of us all. But I don't know if you quite realise that from here on you and I have got to think of mamma and papa as if they were the children, and we the parents now. We have to make allowances for all the foolish things they say and do. And sometimes you're terribly impatient and sarcastic with them both."

"I don't see why they shouldn't hear the truth, once in a while."

"Could you keep it to 'once in a *great* while', my dear?"

"I'll try, Tatiana."

And she had tried, not always with success, during those blazing summer weeks when everything had gone wrong again. When the advance ordered by Kerensky, now prime minister and Minister for War, had failed miserably, as it was bound to fail when thirty-one Russian divisions, freed by government decree from any sort of discipline, had faced one hundred and sixty-four German divisions bound to knock Russia out of the war once and for all. When Lenin chose this moment to attempt a *coup d'état,* and blood ran again in the streets of Petrograd before the government won and the Communist leader fled to Finland. When the American missions arrived with their teams of experts, whose expertise was swiftly confounded by the total breakdown of what passed for technology in Russia. The former Czar's complacent comments on the 'liberal republic's' difficulties had been hard for a spirited girl to listen to in silence.

Nicholas seemed not quite to understand that it was because of the 'July Days', as the attempted Communist *coup* was called, that he and his family were sitting in the small hours of a stifling August morning in the Crimson Hall of their palace prison with their friends, servants, dogs and baggage disposed around them, waiting for orders to get aboard a train taking them to an unknown destination. Kerensky had had a bad scare in the July Days. He knew that Lenin had very nearly triumphed: that he had only been driven away because of the revelation that he had been in the pay of the Germans, something the average Russian was not yet prepared to stomach; but if Lenin came back, and next time, won? Then what would become of the ex-imperial family? Kerensky, and the select few he let into the secret, made plans to remove them to a place of safety.

"Only until the elections are over," Nicholas told his family. "Once the new Constituent Assembly is in session, Kerensky says we may return to Czarskoe Selo, probably in November."

"Where can they possibly take us, for a short stay of three months?" wondered his wife.

"I think it might be to some fine old Russian city like Kiev or Novgorod. Alexis, you and I'll be able to study history where it all happened."

"I'd rather go to Livadia," said the honest child.

"We're probably going further east than Novgorod, and we may be away for longer than three months," said Tatiana. "We've been told to take plenty of warm clothing with us."

"Kerensky knows what he's doing," said Nicholas confidently. "Travelling by rail, going east, the nearer we'll come to Vladivostok. Eh, chicks? How would you like to see Japan?"

But that had been before the farce began, the dismal farce now being enacted in the Crimson Hall. They had come downstairs at eleven p.m., the train was to leave at one, and now it was four o'clock in the morning, with everybody arguing and running to and fro, and the soldiers' soviet solemnly making speeches, and taking votes on what to do next. Their problem was the transport of the family's luggage, provisions and other belongings to the trucks waiting to take everything to the Alexandrovski Station: at the station the problem was getting the railwaymen to put the train on the line at all. Kerensky ran from the hall to the telephone and back again: he sent messengers to the station in staff cars, he conferred with the palace commandant until poor Colonel Kobilinski, who had been severely wounded earlier in the war, collapsed in an armchair and fell asleep with his mouth open. Alexis was asleep too, with his head on his mother's shoulder. He had been very lively early in the night, and very impressed when the priests from the Znamenia church came in chanting and bearing aloft the ikon of the Virgin of Znamenia to bless the travellers. But after a couple of hours, during which it seemed to his sisters that he never stopped fidgeting and stumbling over their feet, always with Joy's lead wound tightly round his wrist, the boy said, "I know it's a beautiful Russian custom to sit down with your friends and think kind wishes before going on a journey, but this is ridiculous!"

"Alexis is quite right," said Olga softly, as she watched sleep overtake him. "What fools we all look, sitting here hour after hour, and getting nowhere!"

"I like watching the soldiers," said Anastasia. "Some of them are funnier than the clowns at Cinizelli's circus."

"I hadn't thought of the circus. I was thinking *we* all look like the refugees at the Narva Gate, when Tatiana's committee ran a shelter there. With our bags and bundles, and our heads tied up in silk scarves like very grand *babushkas*—"

"You hate to go away, don't you, Olga?" said sympathetic Marie. She had Jimmy, the Pekinese, on her lap, along with one of the jewel boxes which they all carried.

"Yes, I'm sorry to be going." Olga said no more than that: there were no words to express her desolation at leaving the home they knew and loved the best, the hospital—now unvisited since their imprisonment began—where she had tried to serve, the wooded alleys and river banks where she had walked with Simon Hendrikov. Even the Crimson Hall was a reproach to her, with the Czarinas whom she had not dared to follow watching from the walls, and the young Queen Victoria looking down haughtily at the descendants who had lost their throne. The curtains had been left open, and daylight began to touch the sleeping faces, some stubbled, all grey with fatigue, and the empty tea glasses, the spat-out sunflower seeds on the floor of the great hall. Somebody said "Here comes Speedy!" as Kerensky rushed back from yet another argument on the telephone. There was a sudden rustle of movement, and the great entrance doors were pulled open. A voice said, "Now, Colonel Romanov!" and then they were on their way.

Tatiana had to run back at the last moment for the cushion from her mother's chair. It was a gift Alexandra cherished, having been filled with rose leaves by Tartar women for their empress, and the scent, still delicious, filled the motor car which took her to the station with her husband, Alexis, and Olga. The other girls crowded into a second car, and Kerensky headed the procession. It was nearly six o'clock and the sun had risen. They looked out eagerly at the familiar park, where the dew lay on the grass, but already they were at the open gates, and a cavalry company swung in behind the cars as they went through. All the way to the station the girls heard the familiar and now totally unreal clatter of a Sovereign's Escort.

One friend alone was there to greet them on the platform. This was General Tatischev, a former cavalry officer whom Nicholas had invited to accompany him as an ADC. Tatischev, now an elderly man with many civilian responsibilities, had not hesitated for a moment. "Give me enough time to pack my bag," he had said, and with his old army valise by his side he had waited stoically at the station through the long hours of the night. He gave immediate help in supervising the unloading of the baggage, while the Czar gleefully pointed out to his daughters that the train was flying the Japanese flag and carried the emblems of the Japanese Red Cross Mission. "I told you so!" he said cryptically. "I told you Kerensky knew what he was doing! Come, girlies, time to get into the train!"

The steps, of course, had been forgotten, and the coaches were extremely high. Alexandra Feodorovna's stiff limbs failed her, and she landed on her hands in the entrance to the coach. In darkness, she was carried inside a coupé and laid flat on the long seat. The girls scrambled in somehow, Nagorny lifted Alexis up out of his father's arms, and one by one the whole entourage was dragged aboard.

"Oh, poor mamma! Have you really hurt yourself?"

"My hands—"

"Feel her hands, Tatiana."

"They feel scratched, but I can't see. Open the window, Imp!"

"I can't, it's boarded up."

"Why are we in total darkness? Where's the light?" That was their father's voice, and then came Tatischev's, "I have matches, Sir."

The train started with a lurch, the match flared up. "There, mamma, it's not too bad," said Tatiana. "Your cushion saved you from a nasty graze. Marie, there's a little first-aid kit in my handbag."

"Let me take the matches, general," said Olga Nicolaievna. She knelt on the floor, as close to Tatiana as she dared, holding up the little flame in the darkness to which they had been translated from the bright day outside. The train gathered speed. They were on their way, protected by the flag of Japan. Whether their journey into the unknown would end in Japan or not, she had no means of telling. But Olga knew that the further east they went the closer they must come to the grim territory which lay between them and the Pacific Ocean. Like all the political exiles who had preceded them in chains and handcuffs, the Romanovs themselves were on their way to Siberia.

22

THE JULY DAYS WHICH were to alter radically the fate of the Romanovs began quietly for Joe Calvert. Joe's troubles had started earlier, and were to last longer, with the arrival of the USS *Buffalo* at Vladivostok in the month of June. She brought to Russia an Ambassador Extraordinary in the person of Senator Elihu Root, General Scott, the US Chief of Staff, and other distinguished Americans who all lived up to the prediction of Ambassador Francis in expecting the red carpet treatment, and got it.

Materially, the treatment was easy to provide. The former emperor's train was placed at the disposal of the Root Mission for their long journey to Petrograd on the Trans-Siberian Railway, and with their advisers, experts and escort the delegation filled the eight blue-painted coaches and overflowed into Alexandra Feodorovna's grey and lilac boudoir. In the capital Kerensky played host to them at the Winter Palace, where sumptuous suites were renovated to receive the Americans. There were not many great houses to which they could be invited, because those which had not been looted in the spring revolution were locked and shuttered, their owners far away, but the red carpets went down at the Astoria, the Europa and the Hotel de France, and Ambassador Francis kept open house at the Furshtatskaia.

That part of it, Joe conceded, was all right. There had been a flurry just before the Mission arrived, when all the press releases and set speeches had to be rewritten when it became known that President Wilson refused to allow the United States to be called an Ally; he insisted on the expression 'Associated Power', but there were plenty of people who could cope with that one, and also with the thirst of the special correspondents assigned by American newspapers to cover the mission to revolutionary Russia. What worried Joe, after what now seemed like the golden years of neutrality, was the in-fighting which started the moment the imperial train pulled into the Nicholas Station. He knew, of course, that they had their local troubles: Ambassador Francis was no favourite with the career officers of the Foreign Service, some of whom went so far as to declare that his close friend Madame de Cram was a German agent; but none of them had expected to be taken over so vigorously by the 'old Russia hands' accompanying Senator Root. General Judson, who had been an official observer in the Russo-Japanese War of 1905, and Arthur Bullard, the Secretary of the American Friends of Russian Freedom, who as a freelance had witnessed the political troubles of the same year, struck Joe as seasoned players to beware of when the chips were down, and he waited in trepidation for the fur to fly between the Russian railroad men of the Trans-Siberian and the Advisory Commission of Rail Experts headed by John F. Stevens.

One evening the Mission gave a farewell dinner to the Allies, with an invitation list so all-embracing that even Vice-Consul Calvert and Captain Richard Allen joined the company in the Malachite Hall.

"Very stout fellows, your delegates; not troubled at all by memories of the past," said Dick, as the two men walked away together.

"They *haven't* any memories of the past," said Joe. "The war began last sixth of April, don't you realise that?"

"Well, I do, old chap, but it didn't seem my place to say it. Jolly good dinner, jolly good speeches, any old how; one good thing about sitting down to dinner at six o'clock, you get the whole agony over before nine."

"With any luck they'll be gone the day after tomorrow."

"Expressing complete faith in the future of Russia."

"And leaving one hundred million US dollars behind them in the present," said Joe, stopping to light a cigarette. "Also a fragrant memory of Senator Root's opinion that the Russians are just an infant class in the art of being free, needing kindergarten material to teach them how to join the democratic community."

"Did he say all that?" said Dick admiringly. "No wonder you're looking a bit off-colour these days. Cheer up, Joe, at least they haven't started sending you propaganda material like the newsreel on the Battle of Arras I saw run off at our consulate today. Our new Department of Information must have odd ideas on what will make the new Russian army want to fight."

"Are you going to show it to the girls?" said Joe with a grin. He indicated a company of the new Women's Battalion of Death, swinging back across the bridge from a parade ground on the other side of the Neva. They were great strapping girls, sweating in heavy uniforms and high boots, and wearing black and red flashes on their sleeves. " 'Red for the revolution that shall not die, black for death rather than dishonour,' " quoted Joe. "Poetical fancy, isn't it?"

"You wouldn't call it poetical if you'd seen Mrs. Pankhurst taking the salute from 'em outside the Astoria," said Dick. "That's all we needed to complete the picture, a visit from the good old British suffragettes. Joe, I'd rather fight Spion Kop all over again than face the Battalion of Death; what do you say we walk over to the Island and see the Hendrikovs, and get the taste of a lot of things out of our mouths?"

"At this time of night?"

"It's barely half past nine; they'll be talking away for hours yet. Besides, Dolly has twenty-four hours off from hospital."

"You seem to follow Dolly's schedule pretty closely these days."

"Any objections?" The tone was so different from Dick Allen's usual sleepy acquiescence that Joe glanced at him in surprise. He shrugged instead of taking up the challenge. Dick and he were friends of three years' standing, but their friendship, so much interrupted by the Englishman's absences, had never progressed beyond a certain point. And three years of Joe's neutrality, of his guarded tongue, had made a barrier between them and complete confidence. They walked across the bridge in silence.

"Lights everywhere!" said Joe cheerfully, glancing up at the Hendrikovs' windows when they turned in to the Fourth Line. "Cousin Timofey must be in full cry tonight."

But the one who was crying was Dolly. They heard her sobs as they entered the front door, for once wide open, above the sound of agitated voices on the second floor. They looked at each other and dashed upstairs. On the landing they found Dolly, clutching an unknown young woman, also in tears. Two men they had never seen before, one in naval uniform, were trying to soothe them both.

"What the hell is the matter?" gasped Dick. "Dolly—your father—is anybody ill?"

"No, I don't think so—I don't know!" wailed Dolly. "We've had such a terrible fright. Three Red sailors came, and forced their way in . . . if it hadn't been for Commander Yakovlev I don't know what would have happened . . ."

"You hear, Mikhail?" cried the unknown young woman. "It'll be our turn next! If those roughs from Kronstadt can force their way into *this* house, you and I may be murdered in our beds tonight, and Mitia too! I'm leaving first thing in the morning, whatever you may do!"

"Why didn't the *dvornik* warn us, that's what he's paid for!" said Mikhail, presumably the lady's husband, and Joe, from long experience, realised that a typical Russian argument had only just begun. With a touch on Dolly's arm he slipped round the group and into the apartment.

The first thing he saw was the hatstand and the hall table, both lying on their sides. In the living-room the glassfronted bookcase had been smashed and emptied of the books, which had been soaked with oil from the hanging lamp, and there were knife slashes across the pictures and the upholstery of the various chairs. The windows were starred but not broken. Professor Hendrikov, very pale and breathing heavily, was lying on the sofa in his study, where, as in the hall, all the books had been toppled on the floor, and Madame Hendrikova, for once dishevelled, was holding smelling salts beneath his nose.

"What happened, for God's sake?" said Joe, and Madame Hendrikova tried to smile. "Some unwelcome visitors," she said. "Red sailors, very drunk . . . I'm so glad to have you here, dear Joe!"

"Dick's here, too. Shouldn't I get some brandy for the professor?"

"I don't suppose there's any left." It was true; Joe's quick investigation revealed nothing but the fine cut crystal decanters, smashed to pieces, in front of the sideboard's open doors.

"Where are the maids?" he called, and Madame Hendrikova answered, "There's only Lena, and she locked herself in the kitchen."

"Sensible girl." Joe hurried down the corridor and released the terrified Lett. "Go and help your mistress," he said, "the professor isn't well." But Joe's strong arm was needed to help the shaken old man to his room, and by that time Dolly, Dick, and the naval officer were back in the living-room with the front door closed.

"This is Commander Yakovlev, Joe Calvert," said Dick briefly. "I met him last time I was up at Murmansk, he's in the *Askelod.*"

The commander bowed. "I'm very glad I was able to help," he said. "I'm back on leave, and came to visit my cousins Dr. and Mrs. Martov (you saw them a few moments ago) just as Miss Hendrikova managed to escape from those ruffians and called out to me—"

"And he was *armed!*" said Dolly. "They were going to—they said they were going to burn down the house—"

They saw, they smelt the oil spilled across the books, and Commander Yakovlev nodded. He was, Joe noted, a pleasant-looking man, with a weather-beaten face and dark hair growing to a peak on his forehead. His uniform was well-worn but very spruce.

"Kronstadt!" he said deeply. "We think things are bad enough at Murmansk, but here—"

"Yes, but why this house and not another?" Richard Allen said. "Simple people, living very quietly, with nothing much worth looting—why pick on them?"

"I'm very much afraid it's because our son's an officer," said Madame Hendrikova, coming quietly back to the living-room. "At Kronstadt the hostility to the officer class is terrible."

"What, burn the flat down and probably the building along with it, just because your son was an officer in the Garde Equipage?" said Joe.

"Dolly, I'm very worried about your father," said Madame Hendrikova, evading the question. "I think we ought to get the doctor."

"I'll telephone, madame," said Joe, rising.

"They pulled the telephone out of the wall when they broke in. Lena will go, our doctor lives in the next Line. And now I must go back to sit with my husband, Commander Yakovlev: I don't know how to thank you for your rescue and protection."

The naval officer bowed over her hand. "If there is anything anyone can do, I know Madame Martov will be glad to help," he said. "I shall hope to have good news of Professor Hendrikov from her."

"Thank you." Dolly went to see him to the door, and Joe and Dick were left staring at each other.

"What a bloody awful mess," said Dick, stirring the broken glass and sodden paper with one foot.

"Don't worry about it, Dick," said Dolly, returning. "Lena and I will clean it up as soon as she comes back from the doctor's." She was very calm now, with red spots like rouge on her pale face, and she said, "Oh, do let's sit down!" with a sigh that showed her weakness in the relief from strain.

"Are *you* all right, Dolly?" said Joe. "Nobody seems to be concerned about you."

"Father was the only one they actually struck. Oh, but if it hadn't been for Commander Yakovlev—"

"He seems like an all right guy," said Joe.

"Were those men armed?" said Dick abruptly.

"Only with those knife things sailors carry. That's what they slashed the pictures with."

"Dirks. And Yakovlev's navy pistol was enough to scare them off?"

"Thank heaven, yes!"

Joe had found a bottle, overlooked in the back of the sideboard shelves. "I don't know what this is," he said, sniffing, "some sort of plum brandy, probably. You'd better drink some, Dolly, you look all in."

"And now perhaps Dolly will tell us the truth about this—incident," said Richard Allen gravely, when she had sipped from the bottle's metal cap. Dolly opened her eyes wide.

"You mean about why those wretches came?"

"It wasn't just because your brother's a serving officer at the front."

"It was mamma who said that, poor darling," Dolly said reluctantly. "You know how her generation are always trying to *pretend*! She heard what the soldiers said, we all did, even Commander Yakovlev—goodness knows, they were shouting at the pitch of their voices—but it was just too much for my mother to accept . . ."

"Was it something about Simon and the Grand Duchess Olga?" said Joe gently.

"Did you know too?"

"It wasn't hard to guess, when I saw him here just after the revolution."

"What those ruffians said was that we were enemies of the people and friends of the Romanov murderers," Dolly faltered. "They said this was the place where the Grand Duchess Olga met—met her secret—"

"Her secret lover," Dick finished it for her.

"Richard, how can you? I told you at Easter, when we went out to Czarskoe Selo with his gift to her, that it was just worship from afar! Poor Simon, how could it be anything else, with that wonderful girl?"

"But she did come here?" said Joe.

"Just once. And I was here too, for part of the time."

"How could those fellows know a thing like that?"

"Because somebody else was here as well," said Dolly, and her pretty face grew hard. "Mara Trenova. She betrayed them. And I could *kill* her for it!"

* * *

Mara Trenova, like Joe Calvert, had spent a harassing summer. There had been a great upheaval in the *Pravda* office, just at the moment of its renewed success, when a former bank robber called Joseph Stalin, more recently an exile in Siberia, had returned to Petrograd immediately after the revolution and proceeded to take over the paper. With Molotov out and Stalin in, there were the usual firings of lesser members of the staff, and among those who lost their jobs was the hunchback, Sergiev, who disappeared completely from his former haunts. Mara kept hers 'by the skin of her teeth', as Stalin told her—and she was more afraid of Stalin than of any terrorist met in the days of Jacob Levin—because the cartoons she and Efron worked on together had achieved a certain fame. Stalin even mentioned the cartoons to Lenin, when the great man visited the *Pravda* office, now reopened not far from the huge silent palace where Felix Yusupov and the Grand Duke Dmitri had lured Rasputin to his death.

"Good! Very good!" said Lenin, rubbing his hands and laughing his hard laugh. "We might be able to use something in this line in our cinema propaganda, by and by. That'll be the great medium of the future, don't you agree, Comrade What's-Your-Name—Trenova?"

"Yes, comrade." Mara had no views on the cinema, except

to feel annoyance at the American films which so many people who should have known better seemed to enjoy seeing, but she was prepared to be hypnotised by Vladimir Ilyich Lenin. Seen close, he was quite as impressive as the orator of the Finland Station, and much more so than Stalin, with his vulpine features and his thick moustache covering a brutal mouth. Lenin had a trick of closing one eye while he was preparing to summarise his opinion of a cartoon or an editorial, which gave his face a kindly, comical look: he used his face as he used his short, strong body, to express power and reliability. On this visit to *Pravda* the expressive face was smiling and conciliatory; he slapped Stalin on the back and praised him as a man of action. The demoniac power of the leader on the armoured car had been exchanged for a homespun comradeship which very nearly made Mara Trenova accept him as the hero she had waited to worship all her life.

Nearly, but not quite. For Mara's chronic jealousy was aroused by Lenin's companion, a woman who was said to be one of his few intimate friends, and high in the councils of what they were all trying to remember to call the Communist party. Her name was Alexandra Kollontai. Born, like so many of the revolutionaries, into an aristocratic family, she had become famous in her twenties as an agitator in the textile strikes of 1898, was exiled, had worked with Lenin for at least ten years. Mara Trenova hated her on sight, the mild little woman with soft blue eyes and hair just tinged with grey, whose eloquent and personal exposition of free love had earned her the name of the Red Rose of the Revolution.

"Is he sleeping with her?" she asked when the distinguished visitors had left, and the men in the newsroom laughed.

"Catch him! She says sex is like drinking a glass of water, have it or go without; he says keep all your strength for the world revolution. How'd *you* like that, Trenova?"

"She's got a handsome sailor about half her age, down-river in Kronstadt. Dybenko's got strength to serve the revolution, and the Red Rose too," said one of the reporters.

"Wouldn't mind a piece of her myself."

"I bet it's not all world revolution in the Kchessinskaia house. Not when they get going on the Grand Duke Andrei's champagne."

"There can't be much left for them. *We* had all we wanted

at the beginning, when *they* were still in Switzerland," said Mara.

"That's right, you were with Smirnov then, in the good old Agabagov days. Been there for supper lately, Trenova?"

No, and that was where the jealousy began, of course. But Lenin had praised her drawings, and Mara was stimulated to produce the best series since she had drawn Olga Nicolaievna in the arms of Rasputin. It showed Maria Bachkarova, the peasant woman who founded the Battalion of Death, leading her girls—enormous of buttock and breast—to the service at St. Isaac's cathedral when their standard was consecrated, and then the girls behind the lines, performing other services for Kerensky's soldiers. But immediately after that success came the failed *coup d'état*, when the machine-guns rattled again along the Nevski Prospekt, and Lenin, after haranguing his followers from the balcony of the Kchessinskaia house was forced, as his enemies said, to 'do his disappearing act again'. For Mara the worst aspect of the clash between government and Communists was a raid on the *Pravda* offices, and the total destruction of the printing presses by government troops. She was thrown out of work, and after a few weeks of desperation was thankful when Stalin offered her a job on the paper hastily vamped up to take *Pravda*'s place, and called *Rabochi Put, The Workers' Path.*

* * *

During the July Days Joe Calvert tried in vain to keep in touch with his friends in the Fourth Line. He soon realised that the three sailors who had planned to destroy Dolly's home were only the advance guard of a greater force from Kronstadt when he heard of the two destroyers which sailed up the Neva in support of Lenin, carrying Communist crews which terrorised the town. The sailors were finally overcome, and taken to the prison of Peter and Paul, but Kerensky, true to his belief that the Revolution must shed no blood, carried out no executions for mutiny, and the men were soon released. Like all the American staff Joe was kept close to his embassy during those anxious days, and when they ended the next crisis was the arrival of forty men representing the American Red Cross. They had been issued with army uniforms before sailing from San Francisco, and as they all had the assimilated rank of officers they at once became known to the Americans in Petrograd as The Haitian Army.

Once these worthies had been found hotel rooms and office space, embarking on a career of wrangling and dissension which beat all the quarrels of the Russians, Joe was able to telephone to Dolly Hendrikova at her little hospital to suggest a meeting.

"How's your father, Dolly? How are they both?"

"Much better, but mother was terribly anxious about papa last week. He could hear the firing, and the yelling from the Neva, and it upset him badly. But the doctor says he's able to travel now, and they're going to the dacha in a few days' time."

"Swell idea, and you're going too, I hope."

"Not right away."

"Oh, Dolly, you can't stay on your own in Petrograd!"

"I can't even *talk* any longer," she said in a whisper, "meet me in the Summer Garden, by the kiosk, at noon?"

"I'll be there."

It was a convenient meeting-place between her hospital and his embassy, and Joe reached it through almost empty streets. The tempo of Petrograd life had been grinding to a halt since the revolution, and now the cracks in the imperial façade were very obvious. The St. Petersburg of 1914 had turned into a neglected place, a vista of lifeless palaces beside a river foul with the refuse of three days of street fighting and oily with the miasma of a stifling summer.

The Fortress bells were ringing the '*Kol slaven*' as Joe reached the kiosk, which had nothing to sell but apples and a few children's toys, and saw Dolly coming towards him down one of the long unweeded avenues. He hurried to meet her, so fresh and neat in her Red Cross uniform, and they found a stone seat as far as possible from the children's playground, where a bush of fading lilac gave them the illusion of privacy. And there Dolly told him firmly that of course she couldn't give up the hospital, they were short-staffed as it was, and what about last summer, when papa and mamma had gone on holiday without her?

"This summer isn't last summer," said Joe grimly. "And you certainly can't be in that apartment, at any time, all by yourself."

"Oh no, the apartment's going to be closed up. And you know I've got about a dozen cousins and their wives and husbands, to go and stay with if I ever have another twenty-four hours off."

"I do know it, but what I hate is having you walking around the town alone. Good God, look at what happened last week!"

"Last week we were too busy with the civilian casualties to listen to the firing. Please don't fret, Joe! Mamma and papa are very willing for me to stay here, they want *somebody* to be waiting to welcome Simon when he comes back from the front."

If he comes back from the front. Joe and Dick Allen both believed that Captain Hendrikov's third campaign would be his last, but it did no good to say so: he only asked gently, "Have you any news at all?" and Dolly shook her head.

"Won't you get *any* leave to go to Finland? You had two weeks last year."

"I'm going to try to work right through to the end of November. After that, we'll see."

"What's so special about November?"

"If father can get a substitute to take his classes, we might spend the winter with my sister in Copenhagen."

Joe felt blank. He wanted her to be out of danger, but Copenhagen, after his three years in Russia, seemed to Joe Calvert to be in another world. He hardly heard what Dolly was saying, something about 'Richard' having advised Professor Hendrikov to transfer his account from the Imperial Bank of Russia to the Private Bank in Helsingfors, and deposit his securities there as well.

He hadn't meant to tell her what had been in his mind for months, for Vice-Consul Calvert, with nothing but his modest salary, had little to offer a girl; but there she was beside him, so pretty and engaging, and soon, perhaps, to be right out of his reach! He blurted out:

"I worry about you, Dolly, I can't help it, you're so little and cute, and you'll be all alone if—if Simon doesn't come back. Please give me the right to take care of you, then and for ever. I love you so much, and I'll try so hard to make you happy. Please say you'll marry me. Please!"

Her hazel eyes were fixed so trustingly on his, and her lips were parted as if to whisper Yes. Joe's arm was round her already, and when Dolly put her hand in his free hand he was sure it was all right. Her words, when they came, were like a douche of cold water in his face.

"Joe!" she said, "dear Joe! I've had a feeling you would ask me that some day, and I did so hope you wouldn't. Because

I hate to hurt you—and I've got to tell you, I don't think I could ever be your wife."

"Why not?"

"Because, deep down, I don't think you love me enough."

"Dolly!"

"Was that an awful thing to say? I didn't mean to be unkind. I know you're very, very fond of me, just as I'm fond of you. And *you're* so kind, Joe! If I were ever in any trouble I'd come running straight to you, and if I said Yes and we got married I think we *would* be happy together, 'right now', as you say. It's not 'right now' that scares me, it's the future."

"We would share the future, Dolly sweet—"

"Oh no we wouldn't, because I'm not really the right girl for you. You only think so because I'm *here*, and we've known each other for three years, and you've been a little bit in love with Russia all that time. I saw it happen to you, right at the beginning, and my mother saw it too. You were fascinated by St. Petersburg from the very first moment, and I suppose I'm a tiny part of Petersburg, so it wasn't too difficult to think yourself into being in love with me. But I'm not nearly clever enough for you, Joe. You've a brilliant career ahead of you, everybody says so—"

"Everybody?"

"All the people who've met you at our house, including Nabokov and Kerensky, and they're pretty good judges, don't you agree? And Richard thinks that some day you'll be the American ambassador to Russia—maybe twenty years from now—"

"What'll Russia be like by that time, I wonder?"

"I don't know, but when you come back to live in that great palace on the Furshtatskaia, you ought to have an American lady as Madam Ambassadress, not silly little Dolly Hendrikova from the Fourth Line, who wouldn't know what to say to the diplomatic corps—"

"Who would charm every man in the diplomatic corps."

Dolly shook her head. "It's no use," she said, "I'm not even clever enough to make you understand."

"I certainly don't understand why you're talking about an outside chance, that may or may not come up twenty years from now." Joe hesitated. There was something he didn't want to say, but it came out. "Are you turning me down because there's somebody else?"

Dolly grew pink and compressed her lips.

"Sometimes lately I wondered if it was Dick Allen."

"Please, Joe! I do like him very much—"

"You're twenty, and he's nearly forty—"

"I don't think age makes any difference."

"When did it start between you and him, Dolly?"

"I suppose—after we found him hurt that night in Mara's flat. He seemed so young then—changed somehow—"

"He can change into anything he wants to be," said Joe. "And he's a loner, has been all his life. I shouldn't think he'd ever want to settle down."

"How boring you make marriage sound!" said Dolly with a flash of temper, and Joe asked quickly, "Are you engaged to him?"

"Not officially."

"Then can I go on seeing you?"

"Of course you can! We'll meet at Cousin Timofey's, just like we used to do at home. And maybe I'll *be* at home quite soon again, when father and mother come back to settle the university thing. After all, they'll be less than fifty miles from Petrograd. It isn't as if they were going to Siberia!"

23

A FAMILY WHICH HAD gone to Siberia was scattered forlornly along the docks of a river port on a sultry August midnight, guarded by three hundred men of the Sharpshooters' Reserve.

Not only history but chance was now shaping the destiny of the Romanovs. The chance that Alexander Kerensky, as a child, had been impressed by a photograph of the governor's house in remote Tobolsk, an ancient town in the Ural region of Siberia, and as head of the Provisional Government decided that the Romanovs could spend the winter there before an attempt was made to get them away to Japan. He had no reports on the actual state of the governor's mansion, very dilapidated by 1917, nor apparently did it occur to him that a town two hundred miles from the railway line and accessible only by river steamer in summer, by a frozen dirt road in winter, was hardly a suitable base for an escape attempt.

It did occur to several members of the former Czar's party when they were ordered to leave the train at Tiumen. Until then, their spirits had been rising steadily. When they were clear of the environs of Petrograd, and the shutters were taken off the train windows, it was exhilarating to see the countryside again, and like old times to sit in the dining car, enjoying well-prepared meals, and see the villages go by. The windows were boarded up when the train stopped at a station, but that did not happen often in their four days of travel. One early morning they stopped so long at a place called Ekaterinburg that they began to think their journey would end there. But the train went on across the mountains, and soon Nicholas was able to show his boy the great pillar with 'Europe' on one side and 'Asia' on the other, and tell him, "Now you're really in Siberia!"

"You were one of the first people ever to travel on the Trans-Siberian railway, weren't you, papa?"

"I suppose I was, from west to east. I laid the first stone of the east–west line at Vladivostok in 1891. Long before I could persuade your dear mamma to marry me!"

"And then you went on to Japan, and a wicked Japanese tried to kill you."

"He did indeed. Dear Greek Georgie saved my life that day, and carried a scar on his own skull to prove it."

"If you had been killed, papa, would Uncle Misha have been the Czar?"

How he harps on that, thought Olga. But Nicholas replied tranquilly, "No, my next brother would have succeeded me. Poor fellow! You children never knew your Uncle George. He was an invalid, and had to live in the Caucasus. He died there when he was only twenty-seven."

"What was the matter with poor Uncle George? Did he have pains in all his joints, like I used to do, and was he carried about sometimes, instead of walking?"

"No, nothing like that. He had a lung complaint, that was why he had to live in a dry climate. The air of St. Petersburg didn't agree with him at all."

"I don't think it's agreed with us very well."

Tatiana changed the subject by asking Alexis if he remembered the Great Trans-Siberian Easter Egg which Fabergé had made for the Czar in 1900, and which ever since had been kept with other precious objects in a locked glass case. Alexis had sometimes been allowed to take it out and look at the tiny model of the imperial train which it contained, with gold carriages, a platinum engine and rubies for headlights. This, of course, led to a general discussion of whether the Trans-Siberian Easter Egg had been packed, and if so in which box or valise: in those early hours of their east-bound journey they were often agitated about treasures left behind. Meanwhile the Siberian landscape rolled on in all its vastness beyond the windows of the train, and now and then they caught a glimpse of the old Siberian highway, running slightly to the north of the modern railroad. It was the Chain Track, down which so many political prisoners had stumbled with their hands in fetters on their way to the mines or to Sakhalin.

In the old days there had always been two trains in the imperial convoy, one going ahead to make sure the line was neither mined nor bombed before the sovereigns went by. Now the Romanovs themselves were in the leading train, and the soldiers travelled with the baggage in the second, so that the family party could almost forget they were not on an excursion, perhaps to some town where they would be greeted as of old with the banners, the ikons and the chanted Te Deum. But awareness of captivity came back with a rush when they reached Tiumen, and were told their journey would continue by steamer to Tobolsk. There Colonel Kobilinski, in terror for the security of his prisoners if the local dockers staged a demonstration, ordered his soldiers to line the wharves and the decks of the steamer *Rus* on which they were all to embark. It was three o'clock in the morning before the last of the baggage was carried aboard.

Alexis and his mother went to their berths at once, the others stayed on deck to watch the scene on the dock. Eugene Kobilinski, short, dark and nervous, was here, there and everywhere, urging speed; the soldiers, who since the revolution had been permitted by an order introduced by the Petrograd Soviet to disobey any unacceptable form of military discipline, slouched and smoked and took as long over the job as they pleased. But at least there was no demonstration, perhaps because at that hour of the morning the Tiumen dockers were too tired to stage one; the *Rus* cast off her mooring ropes, blew her steam whistle, and departed.

After their broken night it was mid-morning before the party gathered on the first-class deck. In peace-time it had been the preserve of government officials en route for the far north, and the wealthy Siberian merchants who traded in fish, skins and furs, while the steerage was reserved for peasants, Kirghiz and Buriat tribesmen, and 'politicals' going to imprisonment in the Beresov district beyond Tobolsk. The latter had been guarded by armed Cossacks, carrying the deadly whip called the *nagaika*, while the Sharpshooters, lounging on the steerage deck with their tunics unbuttoned, seemed to be taking their duties lightly enough. But Alexis, exploring the steamer with Nagorny, reported that their rifles lay ready to their hands.

"Does anybody know when we dock at Tobolsk?" Olga asked, and her father himself said, "Not till tomorrow afternoon. About half past four, according to Colonel Kobilinski."

"It's a long way from Tiumen," said Marie.

"It's a long way from anywhere." There was nothing to be seen for hours of their voyage: nothing but the steppe on either bank, and the vast Siberian skies above, the horizon marked only by the receding line of the Ural mountains beyond which Europe lay. There was something hypnotic about the beat of the engines and the ripple of the Tobol river, something ominous about the silence of the few figures which could be seen from time to time as they approached a village. The last time they had made a river voyage together was on the Volga, during the tercentenary celebrations, when the peasants waded waist deep into the water to catch a glimpse of their Batiushka, the Little Father Czar. Nobody alluded to that triumphal voyage. Nobody so much as mentioned Rasputin when the *Rus* passed his native village, Povrovskoe. The former Czarina sat with her head bent over her embroidery, and the girls respected her silence. But everyone was remembering the dead man's prophecies, "You will visit my home, whether you want to or not," and that other, still more ominous, "If I die or you desert me, you will lose your crown and your son within six months." The boy was safe beside them, with Nagorny chasing him all over the boat, but the crown had gone in three months, not in six, and out of the brilliant court and Guard of the Czar of All the Russias the man who had worn the imperial crown had now only two gentlemen in attendance, his childhood playmate Prince Dolgoruki and the faithful Tatischev. Alexandra Feodorovna had with her the lady styled her Reader, Ekaterina Schneider, who began to teach her Russian at Harrogate, where as Princess Alix of Hesse she took a cure for rheumatism at the time of her engagement; and the young Countess Gendrikova. This was the court of Nicholas and Alexandra, on board the *Rus*, on their way to prison.

"I wonder if we're going to like this place," said Alexis doubtfully, when the steamer arrived at Tobolsk. The scene was strange, and perhaps frightening to a child, for the ancient town was situated on high bluffs above the waters'-meet where the Tobol river flowed into the mighty Irtysh. There was a roar from the falls and a sudden absence of sunlight, as the high cliffs threw their shadows over the *Rus* and her passengers. Or else Alexis was perceptive enough to feel what his elder sisters felt: that even when they were allowed to take a brisk walk away from the dock and along the towing path—a walk very welcome after nearly seven days in the train and boat—they were still in a place saturated by centuries of imprisonment.

Among the historic buildings which dominated the cliffs above the Irtysh was the Swedish Tower, built by the Swedes whom Peter the Great took prisoner at the battle of Poltava, and for two hundred years since Poltava the Romanovs had consigned their enemies to Tobolsk. The Dekabrists had been brought here in the reign of Nicholas I. The Poles who staged the Warsaw rising of 1863 had ended their days here. Now to Tobolsk came the man crowned as Nicholas II; the tables were turned; he and his were prisoners.

"I don't know if we're going to like Tobolsk," said Anastasia, as she and Alexis scampered ahead of the others down the towing path, "but I'm awfully glad we're going to live on the boat for a few days, aren't you?"

"Oh yes, I like the boat, and I've got to know some of the soldiers, too."

"Some of them are very nice."

"Eugene Stepanovich is nice, he really worries about us." For Colonel Kobilinski, before his charges were permitted to disembark, had made a horrified inspection of the governor's mansion which had looked so pleasant in a photograph, thirty years before. It was filthy. He ordered cleaning and renovating which would take at least a week.

For that one week, during which the *Rus* was still their home, the rather desperately gay, holiday feeling which they had all cultivated since leaving Czarskoe Selo prevailed among the Romanovs. Every excursion among the paths and fields beyond the bluffs was a treat; the sun shone, and the pallor of their confinement became a healthy tan; father and son found the river life as fascinating on the Irtysh as on the Dnieper in the days when the Czar was also the Commander-in-Chief. Marie talked tirelessly to the soldier escort, and was soon a mine of information on their homes and families. Alexandra Feodorovna remained aboard the *Rus*, always with somebody to keep her company: she never complained of her heart now, but the sciatica was growing worse, and she was often in great pain. It made her smile of thanks all the more touching when her children brought back tiny posies of Siberian flowers, growing so sparsely on the edge of the steppe, as long ago they had carried her the wild roses of the Crimea.

They could forget for hours at a time, in such surroundings, that they were in captivity. Every now and again they had a sharp reminder in a barked order or a scowling face, or as when Olga, throwing a tennis ball to Alexis, strayed unintentionally off the permitted path. They were playing near the river, and the boy threw the ball so straight and hard that his sister missed the catch, and had to go scrambling down the bank to bring the ball back. They were beginning to learn that even an old tennis ball was a treasure, that nothing must be lost, and she was laughing when she found it in the wet gravel; but then a heavy body jumped down the bank behind her, and one of the guards took Olga roughly by the arm. It was the first time any of them had touched her, and it was only by an effort that she caught back the words, "Take your hands off me!" She had learned already to smile ingratiatingly as she said:

"I was only picking up my brother's ball."

"You'll stay where we can see you if you know what's good for you." He gave her arm a shake. "Understand?"

"Yes, I understand. Will you let me go now, please?"

But the man kept her in his grasp until they had both clambered back to the footpath, and then he took the tennis ball away from her and put it in his pocket. "Too good an excuse, chasing after a thing like that," he growled. "Don't try to run away again, little sister."

"I wonder where he thinks we're going to run to," Olga said lightly to Alexis, a rather frightened spectator of the scene. She called to the girls, and they all sat in a ring to play guessing games, while the soldiers walked suspiciously up and down. But for the rest of that day she felt the heavy hand on her arm, and remembered the picture of Maslova in *Resurrection*—'After the Sentence', with the soldier starting the condemned woman on her way to prison and Siberia.

Their own prison, the governor's mansion, was ready for them at last. It was not a large house, so that all their companions except the faithful Gilliard were to sleep in another house across the street. Alexis had a small bedroom to himself, with Nagorny in a smaller one next door, but the sisters found they were expected to share a large corner room, in which four plain bedsteads had been placed.

"It's rather like a dormitory in one of your old school stories, Imp," said Olga as she looked around.

"Good idea, let's call it the OTMA dormitory," said Marie, who was always cheerful.

"The beds are softer than the ones at home," said Anastasia, bouncing on a spring mattress, and Tatiana, untying her silk headscarf, said, "Thank goodness! We won't have to wear these things indoors."

"We're almost presentable now." The four heads, the golden, the red-gold, the shades of brown, were clustered together in the dressing-table mirror, and Olga said, "I do believe you're going to have little curls, Mashka."

"So I am"—much gratified.

"Do you remember how shocked mamma was when you told her Marisha had bobbed her hair? We'll all have bobbed hair, by and by.'

"I don't think it quite makes up for measles."

"Let's go and see what it's like downstairs."

It was quite roomy, quite well furnished, and the commissar representing the Soviet, by name Makarov, seemed to have no objection to what Colonel Kobilinski had done to make his charges' lot more comfortable. There were no guards posted indoors. But almost immediately after their arrival a fence was erected all round the house and its neglected dusty grounds: not too high to prevent the Romanovs from seeing across it from their bedroom windows, but quite high enough to prevent any of the townspeople from seeing in. The hopes Nicholas had cherished of being allowed out on the steppe for an occasional day's shooting, were dashed at once. He took to sawing wood as a means of exercise.

By the time September came in, with cooler and thinner airs, they had settled down to some kind of routine. Lessons began again, and Alexis once more displayed remarkable dexterity in asking questions which had some bearing on their own fate, this time in English history. King John and Magna Carta, King Charles at war with his parliament, King James chased off his throne by the revolution of 1688—"I'd no idea he knew so much," marvelled Anastasia.

"Some of those stories were in the picture books they used to send from England. I do remember something about King Charles up an oak tree—"

"Don't mention it to Alexis, he hasn't discovered that one yet."

"I'll be glad when Mr. Gibbs gets here, and takes over the English history class from poor papa." For the English tutor, as devoted as his Swiss colleague, was following the Romanovs to Siberia, and hoped to reach them before the rivers froze. The last loyal member of their entourage, Baroness Buxhoeveden, whom they called Isa, had been operated on for appendicitis about the time they were removed from Czarskoe Selo, and could easily have made that an excuse for staying in Petrograd. She, too, was determined to reach Tobolsk as soon as she could get a travel permit.

Mr. Gibbs brought no reassuring news. General Dukhonin's offensive had been a failure, and under German attacks the Russian troops were deserting by whole companies. A general named Kornilov had attempted to establish a military dictatorship in Petrograd, and to defeat him Kerensky had to call in the help of the Soviet. Trotsky, who had remained in the capital when his leader fled to Finland, had organised a body of Red Guards who helped to defeat Kornilov, but remained under arms. It was the first overt threat of civil war in Russia.

The former Czar heard all this with his accustomed calm. But when he was alone with the men he regarded as his ADCs, he said for the first time that he was beginning to regret his abdication. He had been persuaded by unscrupulous men that it was necessary for the good of Russia, to spare Russia the horrors of civil war, and now since the July Days Russian had been fighting Russian, and what might not the future bring? He longed for news, and the shortage of reliable news was one of the severest trials in the governor's mansion as September slipped into October, and the only break in the monotony was the weekly outing to church on Sunday, with Alexandra Feodorovna pushed in a wheel-chair between a file of armed soldiers, while the citizens of Tobolsk stood on tiptoe behind them to see those who had been their rulers trudging through the autumn mud.

There was an erratic telegraph service between Tobolsk and Petrograd, and a still more erratic delivery of newspapers to the prisoners. Nicholas received a few belated copies of *The Times* which they all read until the paper was reduced to shreds, but the soldiers' soviet, after a long discussion, voted to suppress *The Times* unless every word was translated into Russian for their approval. After that the prisoners relied on the local paper, such as it was, and the local lending library, which supplied them with tattered copies of standard Russian novels. There was no censorship of the girls' reading now, and Olga read *Resurrection* again, from pages spattered with food stains and tobacco crumbs. She felt the same strange affinity with Katerina Maslova, tramping with the chain gang across Siberia, through towns whose names had a new significance: Tiumen, Omsk, Ekaterinburg.

"The cell in which Maslova was imprisoned was a long room twenty-one feet long and sixteen feet broad, occupied by fifteen persons." She had read that first in her pretty bedroom at the Alexander Palace. Now she and her sisters shared a room of almost exactly those dimensions. Should they be thankful that instead of fifteen they were only four?

The Czar, in his delightful way, read aloud to his family. They had to hear about Little Boy Blue again, while the girls bent their heads decorously over the drawn-thread work they were doing, on coarse local linen with silks brought from their home, to fashion into Christmas gifts. They had *The Rosary*, for Alexandra Feodorovna's sake, and *Greenmantle* for Alexis, who never tired of the adventures of Richard Hannay. They had read it earlier in the year, and Nicholas, in his simple way, was still amazed at the skill of 'the writer fellow' who had described the battle of Erzurum only a few months after the Grand Duke Nicholas had won it.

"I wish I knew if Nikolasha's had a chance to read it himself," he said, and his wife smiled indulgently at the once hated name.

"I wonder if anybody'll ever write a book about us," said Anastasia.

"*I* wish I had another book by John Buchan," said Alexis.

"I'll get you *The Thirty-nine Steps* some day," said Mr. Gibbs. "It's about Richard Hannay too."

"Oh, wonderful! And no girls messing about in it?"

"Not a girl," said the tutor, with a smile of apology at the four sisters.

"There's a girl in *Greenmantle*," said Anastasia. "Hilda von Einem. And she's in love with Sandy—"

"Yes, but they don't start *kissing*, and all that rot."

"No, because she's a villainess," said Marie seriously. "I like a book to have a real heroine, very beautiful, who does brave deeds."

"Oh, Mashka!" Olga said, "when will you ever realise that you're a heroine yourself?"

"*Me?*"

"That night at Czarskoe Selo," said Olga, "the last time with the Garde Equipage. When you went out and in, trying to help mamma even though you were feeling ill, and got pneumonia . . . You were ready to give your life for all of us that night. I call that being a real heroine."

"Like Nurse Cavell?"

"Exactly like Nurse Cavell."

Reading, and talking about the people in the stories, helped to pass the time, but they were all hungry for news of the real people who had once been their friends. Alexandra wrote faithfully to Anna Virubova, though without much hope that the letters would reach her. Madame Virubova had been removed from Petrograd by order of the Provisional Government, and was now in the great fortress prison of Sveaborg, outside Helsingfors, to which Kerensky had also consigned Badmaiev, the Tibetan wizard of the Rasputin days. But others were free, who might have written, and did not, to the sovereigns on whom they had once fawned, and it was not until the end of October that a letter came from the far distant Crimea with news of all the Family.

It was written by the Empress Dowager from her palace at Ai Todor, and after many loving messages and condolences the old lady continued in her usual debonair strain:

> " 'How I wish the dear girls were here with us in the Crimea' " [Nicholas read aloud] " 'The young people contrive to amuse themselves in spite of everything, and the autumn has been so fine that the beach parties go on until all hours by the light of bonfires and the moon.' That sounds very pleasant, doesn't it?"

"It doesn't exactly sound as if they were missing us," said Tatiana. "Please go on, papa."

> " 'Michael and that impossible wife of his are still at Gachina, and I hope she's proud now of all her liberal friends have done to destroy the monarchy. Sometimes poor Misha seems as far away from me as you, beloved Nicky, but at least they have left him some freedom of movement. I am glad to have both

my daughters close to me. Xenia is thankful to be able to see Felix and Irina—they, and little Irina, are well—and all her boys are as healthy and noisy as ever. Olga, needless to say, is very happy with her baby son.' "

Nicholas paused. "How old is my sister Olga?" he enquired.
"Thirty-five," said Marie. "Imagine Aunt Olga with a baby!"

" 'I don't know if you've heard the great news about Ducky and Kirill. They wisely left Petrograd and went to Finland, and after they reached their manor dear Ducky gave birth to a son and heir.' "

The Czar stopped again. "Now Ducky *must* be over forty," he observed.

"Forty-one," said his wife. "She and Kirill must be very happy to have a son at last."

"Everybody's having babies," said Anastasia.

"Except us," said Marie.

"Does granny say anything about Marisha?" said Tatiana.

"Marisha married Prince Putiatin soon after we left home," said Nicholas. "And Dmitri—what's this about Dmitri? Sometimes I can't read her writing.

" 'Dear Dmitri has behaved so loyally and nobly. The Provisional Government, so-called, sent him word that his exile was over and asked him to return to Petrograd. He replied that he was on the Persian front by the Czar's orders, and would respect them by staying there until the war is over.' "

"Very correct of Dmitri," commented Nicholas.

"Does Motherdear say anything about his health?" asked Alexandra.

"No, she goes on to another matter," said Nicholas with a twinkle in his eyes. "Listen to this, girls."

" 'The latest piece of gossip from Odessa, unconfirmed as yet, is that Carol of Rumania has entered into a morganatic marriage with a young person rejoicing in the name of Zizi Lambrino. One feels so much for that wild boy's parents, poor Missy of Rumania will be beside herself.' "

"There goes my only hope of matrimony," said Marie solemnly.

"We hadn't a chance, Mashka; the Zizis and the Zinas always win," said Olga with equal gravity. Suddenly they were all laughing wildly, even their mother, in an almost hysterical reaction to this glimpse of a world which was going on without them. But even though she laughed till she cried, and had to search for her handkerchief, Olga was impressed by her mother's quiet acceptance of so much good news about her old enemies. Kirill, who had betrayed her when he marched his men to the Duma under the red flag, Felix and Dmitri, the murderers of Rasputin, even Ducky, her much disliked former sister-in-law—all these were names which would once have roused her to passionate denunciations and contempt. "How good she's trying to be!" the girl thought, and she touched Alexandra's white hair with a spontaneous kiss before she kissed her hand and said goodnight.

Before many nights had passed the family's painfully achieved calm and hopefulness were shattered by news of the outside world brought them by a shaken and reluctant Kobilinski. He walked in as the whole household was having evening tea, for the younger children had been acting a little play, as they were fond of doing, and everyone available had been in the audience. The drawing-room was warm and cosy, the samovar was steaming, it was a pleasant Russian domestic scene.

"Sir," said Eugene Kobilinski, "I feel you ought to know that despatches have been received by telegraph from Petrograd. The news they convey is very—very disquieting."

"Well, out with it, man!"

"If these despatches are correct, there must have been a rising in the capital. Lenin is said to have returned, and the Red Guards hold the key points of the city. Kerensky is in flight. And the Winter Palace—the palace, Sir, when the message ended—was being shelled by a battle cruiser from Kronstadt, the *Aurora.*"

"Good God!"

It was an hour before the news, in all its implications, was thoroughly discussed. Kobilinski, desperately worried about the news Lenin's triumph would have upon his men, went to the guardroom but promised to remain within call. Nicholas was so sure that new telegrams would arrive before midnight, contradicting what they had already heard, that he and his wife were only willing to retire when their gentlemen volunteered to sit up for a couple of hours and pass on any news which might come in. The men settled down to play cards in the dining-room.

It was nearly one o'clock when Olga came downstairs in her stocking feet. As keyed up as anybody in the house, she had only partly undressed and was unable to go to sleep. When there was silence in the 'OTMA dormitory' she slipped out: the drawing-room stove would still be warm, and an hour with a book, beside a good oil lamp, might enable her to relax, might ease the appalling sense of their helplessness in this dead heart of the Siberian steppe. The moonlight was flooding cold into the hall.

She had almost reached the shelter of the warm room when the dining-room door was opened, and through the crack she heard General Tatischev's voice, decisive and resigned:

"Well, gentlemen, if Kerensky has really thrown in his hand the game is up. Personally I knew when I left Petrograd that I shouldn't come out of this alive. I only ask two things: not to be separated from the Czar . . . and to be allowed to die with him."

24

ON THE BLEAK, LATE autumn day after the cruiser *Aurora* came upriver from Kronstadt to anchor in the Neva off the Winter Palace, Joe Calvert woke up to discomfort in the shabby apartment on the Italianskaia. The heating in the building had not functioned for several days, and Varvara had apparently neglected to start the wood fire in the living-room stove. He went into the kitchen to complain, shivering in his dressing-gown, and found it empty. Joe damned the transport delays and the food queues where the old woman spent so much of her time, and prepared to make his own coffee. There was no water in the kitchen tap. There was no water in the bathroom taps either, and he was only able to shave by using some of the drinking water he kept in a glass pitcher. Fuming, and dabbing at his chin with a square of lint, Joe breakfasted off the remains of the water and two dry biscuits, and let himself out into the empty street. He hoped Varvara would have some decent food ready, and his bed made, by the time he went back to the apartment.

A day and a night passed before Joe Calvert returned to the Italianskaia, and he never saw or heard of Varvara again. She had been killed as she shuffled across the street on her way to work, knocked down, with her skull cracking against the kerb, by a Red Guard truck careering round a corner on its way to seize one of the telephone exchanges as part of the plan which Lenin and his henchmen had worked out to gain control of Petrograd. Joe, as he hurried through the public gardens, could hear the sound of shouting from the top of the Liteini Prospekt, and when he saw a dense crowd of men struggling round the Prospekt end of the Alexander Bridge he guessed that the troops or police, or both, had received orders to raise the bridges to prevent the workers crossing from the northern quarters into the centre of the city. He went no nearer than the corner of the Furshtatskaia to investigate, but made for the embassy door, in front of which several American cars were parked. He guessed that on a day when trouble was so obviously brewing many of the newcomers to Petrograd had left their own offices to gather at the one place where reliable news was likely to be had.

Vice-Consul Calvert found that, as he had expected, the handsome entrance hall was full of men with serious faces, and, as a pleasant surprise, that a cup of hot coffee was immediately available. It was not served in the usual embassy style, for the kitchen coffee-pots had been dumped on a marble-topped console table with a few cans of condensed milk, dripping stickily from raggedly punched holes, and the teacups had no saucers, but it was blessedly hot and stimulating after his cold-water breakfast. While he drank it one of the attachés told him that the Red Guards had control of the water supply and other public utilities, with all the railway stations. 'Looks like Lenin learned his lesson last July," the man said. "He's making sure of the key points before he tries another *putsch*."

"I thought Trotsky and Kamenev were masterminding the next operation."

"Sure, but Lenin will hog all the credit."

"Either way it's a pretty poor look-out for Mr. K."

The ambassador was not present. Only a few days earlier he had advised Washington that public sentiment was turning against the Bolsheviks, and more demonstrations were not to be expected—an error of judgment which probably accounted, Joe thought, for the sardonic smiles of some of the senior officers of the Foreign Service clustered round the coffee table. They were preserving a diplomatic silence. The man doing most of the talking was Raymond Robins of the American Red Cross, whom the embassy officials regarded as arrogant, tactless and high-handed to the last degree.

He was a striking-looking man in his early forties, with an actor's mobile face, strong features and jet black hair. In uniform as one of the 'colonels' of the Red Cross Mission, otherwise known as The Haitian Army, he had arrived in Petrograd just before the July Days, and so far had had no direct contact with Lenin, for whom he had developed an almost fanatical hero-worship. It was not a popular view-point at the American Embassy, and Joe felt relieved when the press attaché drew him, with his second cup of coffee in his hand, into one of the side rooms.

"Joe, I hate to ask you, but none of the Russian translators has shown up today, and the Governor's asking for the press digest. Could you bat out a few lines for him?"

"Sure. Glad to do it." Glad to have something to do, was what he meant, but the file of newspapers to work on was much smaller than usual.

"Looks as though the press is going out of business too," he said. "Where's Stalin's paper, *Rabochi Put*?"

"Mr. K. sent three companies of Cossacks yesterday, to close it down."

"And the Cossacks obeyed orders, did they?"

"They did yesterday. What they'll do today is anybody's guess."

There was really not much in the papers except a few communiqués from Mohilev, still the site of GHQ, and a list of additional foodstuffs to be rationed by the end of the week, but Joe Calvert was a two-finger typist, and the digest took longer than it need have done. He had just finished, straining his eyes after the electric light flickered and went out, when the press attaché came back and said briefly, "Governor wants you."

Ambassador Francis, who still liked to be called by the title he had held as Governor of Missouri, was making a gallant effort to look dignified and statesmanlike when Joe entered his room. For once he was not smoking a cigar. He wore a frock coat, which he called a Prince Albert, with immaculate white slips to his waistcoat, and a handsome gold watch chain spanned his considerable girth. But beneath the façade Joe saw a tired old man in a job too big for him, and thought compassionately that David R. Francis was finding Petrograd, 1917, a good deal more complicated than the St. Louis Fair. The Counsellor and the First Secretary, looking harassed, were also in the room.

"Mr. Calvert," the ambassador began, "you once told me you had the entrée to Kerensky's office at the Tauride. D'you happen to know your way around the Winter Palace?"

"Not exactly, sir. I was there at the Root Mission's farewell dinner last summer, when you and Mr. Kerensky were the guests of honour."

"In the Malachite Hall, yes, of course you were. And that's plenty good enough to be going on with. I'm going to send a little rescue party along to the Winter Palace right now, and I want you should go along with them in case they need an interpreter."

"To rescue the Ministers, sir?"

"Kerensky," said the Counsellor irritably. "Kerensky alone, of course. The Ministers will have to take their chance."

"Fact is," said Mr. Francis in a more kindly tone, "I've been in touch with Mr. Kerensky, off and on, this morning. He doesn't want to admit it, but it looks as if this city will fall to the Bolsheviks before midnight, and if they take the power the first thing they'll do is ask the Germans for an armistice."

Joe nodded. It was the old bogey, constantly in the minds of the Allies.

"Whereas if Kerensky takes off, and rallies what's left of the army at Pskov, he has a fair chance of saving the situation. The Soviet has no power outside Petrograd—none at all."

"Quite so, sir; but do you think he has any chance of getting through the city, past all the Bolshevik checkpoints, without being arrested, or even shot at sight?"

"He says he's willing to risk it. Thinks the shock element of seeing him appear may turn the trick. Now, before you leave, is there any angle you can think of which may be useful if he gets awkward at the last minute and refuses to go? You used to meet him socially, you said."

"I never knew him really well. But enough to know that he's a very proud man—well, conceited if you like—and I'm pretty sure he'll never accept protection under the American flag."

"He's not too proud to ride in an American car, I hope?"

"Very few Russians know one make of car from another. But he won't want to go down in history as having passed the Bolshevik checkpoints flying the Stars and Stripes."

"Something in that," conceded the ambassador. "But I don't see why he should kick at the flag, considering what he's costing the United States." He turned to the Counsellor. "Did you see Caldwell's last report from Vladivostok? Over half a million tons of American military stores lying on the wharves there, and not a single unit of the Asiatic Squadron to protect as much as a packing-case! I'm going to cable Washington to have the *Brooklyn* sent to Vladivostok, licketty-split, if Lenin comes to power . . . All right, Calvert, off you go, Captain Riggs can take you in his car. Use your own judgment about the flag."

Joe went back to the hall to collect his coat. The excitement seemed to be rising; not only had Raymond Robins reached his peroration and was quoting poetry, as he loved to do, but a much younger man with a Stetson hat on the back of his head had stolen half his audience, and was shouting:

"He's there! He's back! Lenin's at the Smolny, and he's holding them in the hollow of his hand! Damnedest thing you ever saw, Lenin with his beard off, and a wig over his big bald head. But that voice, you couldn't possibly mistake it, ever—"

"Excuse me, Mr. Reed," said Joe, pushing past the vehement young man.

"What's all the hurry, Calvert? Don't you want to come back to the Smolny with me and see democracy in action?" John Reed had an open, laughing face and a breezy, back-slapping manner. Joe Calvert thought of him as the poor man's Jack London.

"I've been watching democracy in action for the past three years, while you were cutting capers down in Mexico," he said. It was unlike Joe to be gratuitously disagreeable, but among the clashes of personality which distinguished the American community he had to admit that his clash with John Reed, a man of his own age and background, Harvard 1910, who had blossomed out as a Communist and a draft dodger, was as violent a clash as any. He ran down the steps furiously and jumped into the military attaché's car.

The struggle for the Alexander Bridge seemed to have ended with a strong force of Red Guards in command of the approach, and Joe looked up anxiously at the Grand Duke Dmitri's palace as they went by. He saw a Red Cross flag fluttering from the roof, but the British flag had gone, and his heart was gripped with a new fear for Dolly Hendrikova's safety. But there was no possibility of halting on the way to the Winter Palace; they went, as directed, to the Hermitage entrance, and after the minimum of explanation with the sentries, were told that the prime minister would join them as soon as possible. The Americans waited in an anteroom. In the hall beyond they could see women in uniform, and some of the boy cadets. It was not a very convincing force to repel a possible attack.

Kerensky ran downstairs with the speed which had earned

him his nickname, and came gaunt-faced and hollow-eyed to shake their hands. He was ready to go, and had a car of his own waiting. He told Joe he meant to go first to Pskov and then if necessary to Mohilev, while at the same time directing an operation to capture the wireless station at Czarskoe Selo, the most powerful in the whole of Russia. In the semi-military uniform he had affected since becoming Minister for War, Kerensky looked capable of doing all three things at once, and it was evident that he was living on his last reserves of nervous force. The departure did not take long. He said a brief good-bye to his staff, and got into his own car with Colonel Kuzmin, the commander of the Petrograd district, and an aide. The rest of the party piled into the car belonging to Captain Riggs, from which the owner ruefully removed the American flag.

"I guess that's the last I'll see of my automobile," said the soldier, looking rather bleakly after the procession as it drove away. "Think he's going to make it?"

"He might. Want to walk back through the square and see what's going on?"

"Okay."

The enormous square was only half full of people, and the huge blood-red palace showed no sign of life. Nobody came out on the balcony today, and Joe remembered how he had stood on the fringe of a vast throng of half a million people, cheering their Little Father, on the day when the Court was in and the People were out, on a summer Sunday of 1914. He listened absently to what his companion had to say of Kerensky's gall in sleeping in the Czar's bed in that palace, and driving in the Czar's own car.

Kerensky's reckless departure was successful. He passed all the Bolshevik checkpoints without hindrance, the Red Guards being apparently stunned by his audacity, and was on the highroad to Pskov before it was fairly realised that he had left the Winter Palace. And by the early evening the Palace Square was crowded again, with a crowd which had come not to cheer but to triumph: a crowd waiting for the signal of revolution, the single blank shell fired at the Winter Palace by the cruiser *Aurora* at nine o'clock that night. Then came the cannonading from across the Neva, as the batteries of the fortress of Peter and Paul attacked the palace with shell after shell. The firing was not very accurate but the effect on morale was enormous. The women, the rear-guard of the Battalion of Death, surrendered first and came out under promise of an amnesty; the boy soldiers held out a little longer. Finally, in the small hours of the morning, the Ministers of the Provisional Government accepted their defeat. When they came out under arrest, white-faced in the glare of the torches, the cheering crowd could be kept back no longer. They surged forward into the palace of the Romanovs, singing:

> Arise, ye prisoners of starvation!
> Arise, ye slaves of want and fear!

They knew that at last the Court was out and the People were in, and this time the People were there to stay.

There was little sleep that night for those who chose to remain in the American Embassy. The visitors of the morning drifted back to their hotels in the late afternoon, when the demonstrations seemed to be ending in a stalemate, but as the cloudy, rain-streaked daylight faded to an early darkness, Joe Calvert was among those who volunteered to stay in the building with the duty officers and the ambassador's household. Poker was a distraction in the early part of the evening. Then the firing began, just as they were all sitting down to a meal neither dinner nor supper, and the plates were pushed away as the Americans listened, and tried again and again to get news on the telephone which sometimes ceased to function for an hour at a time. The cadets of the military school were still holding out in their own building on Vassili Island, in the central post office, in the Astoria Hotel, and in the Engineers' Palace. By four in the morning the city seemed to be quiet. The exhausted men slept in armchairs and on couches, and only the US Marines posted outside the code and file room remained awake. It was still dark when someone shook Joe Calvert's shoulder and whispered, "Telephone for you—the British Embassy."

Half asleep, he stumbled to the telephone in the press attaché's room.

"Joe? Dick here. Thank God I've found you. I've been calling the flat for half an hour."

"Half an—say, what time is it?"

"Just on eight. Joe, I've got Dolly here, she spent the night in the embassy."

"Dolly? But what about the hospital?" He was dazed with fatigue and had a crick in his neck; none of this was making any sense.

"The Bolshies cleared them out when they were fighting for the bridge. Wanted to occupy Dmitri's palace, something symbolic I suppose. Lady Betty brought Dolly here because she'd nowhere else to go—"

"What about the wounded?" Joe was still trying to sort out the facts. Dolly at the British Embassy, he couldn't visualise it; Dolly under Dick's protection he could imagine only too well.

"The Red Guards put in their own medical orderlies. Now wake up, Joe, what I want you to do is get hold of a car and take Dolly over to the Italianskaia."

"What, back to the flat? She'll be a damn sight safer in your embassy."

"I doubt it," said Dick grimly. "I'm looking out of a window right now, and I see the Reds hauling field guns into Suvarov Square as hard as they can go. They mean to blast the cadets out of the Engineers' Palace, and I wouldn't be surprised if they had a bang at the embassy as well."

"Good God," said Joe, now fully awake, "I'll grab a car and be with you in ten minutes. How about you? Are you coming to the Italianskaia too?"

"Not likely," said Dick. "I'm off to the Smolny with General Knox. Those damn fool girls in the Women's Battalion are being held in some barracks instead of turned loose and sent home as they were promised. I don't know if we can stop a mass rape, but we'll do our damnedest to stop the order for a mass execution."

* * *

While exhausted men in the Allied embassies snatched a few hours of sleep after the surrender of the Winter Palace, the triumphant revolutionaries continued their marathon session at the Smolny Institute, the aristocratic girls' school taken over as their headquarters. In the beautiful white and gold hall where the Smolny girls had danced through the generations from the minuet to the mazurka, bearded and sweating men, some of them heavily armed, jostled for a place to see and hear the leaders of the Military Revolution Committee, and to bellow the magic formula, "All power to the Soviets!" The greatest ovation was reserved for Lenin, now named as chairman of the Council of People's Commissars.

The law-making started immediately, and went on through the daylight hours. Decrees to end the war by negotiation with the enemy, to end the private ownership of land, to abolish ranks and titles, to adopt the western calendar, followed each other in quick succession, the only approval necessary being the roars of satisfaction from the body of the hall. And with the law-making came the punishments; from the order to arrest Kerensky to the creation of People's Courts to try counter-revolutionaries and all the enemies of the Communist regime. The young cadets who surrendered during that day did so under an amnesty, like the women defenders of the palace, but many a body in cadet uniform was found in the canals for days to come. The women soldiers were more fortunate, for after the urgent appeal of General Knox they were set free.

There had been heavy street-fighting in Moscow, but by the time Joe Calvert drove back to the Italianskaia in the early evening Petrograd seemed orderly enough. A reduced tram service had been started, and some shops had opened for business, while the theatres announced performances as usual. Thankful for the lull, Joe ran the embassy Ford, which he had kept since morning, into the courtyard behind number 365. He took out the ignition key, went round to the front of the house and ran upstairs.

Dolly was badly scared when he brought her home in the morning, and he could do no more than strip his own bed, give her cold clean sheets and pillowcases, and beg her to get a few hours' rest, before he had to go back to his post of duty. But when he opened the front door that evening he smelt a savoury smell of cooking, and there was Dolly, coming flushed and smiling out of the kitchen with one of Varvara's coarse blue aprons tied over her own blue dress.

"Dolly! Are you all right?"

"Oh yes! I had such a lovely sleep, and now I'm getting supper ready!"

She looked so pretty, and it was a welcome such as he had never had to the bleak little flat. Joe took Dolly in his arms and kissed her heartily. She kissed him too, but they both knew they kissed as friends, not lovers, and he made no attempt to hold her back when she rushed into the kitchen and began stirring something in a saucepan with a long iron spoon. "What *are* you fixing?" he said, "it sure smells good."

"I found some canned meat and vegetables in your cupboard, enough for a good stew."

"Isn't the gas ring working?"

"The gas is still off, but I found a little spirit stove on the top shelf in the hall."

"Must be some of Dick's stuff, I never saw it before. And how about Varvara?"

"She didn't appear, but the maid in the next-door flat was so nice, Joe, she helped me to carry up the water."

"*Carry* the water?"

Dolly gaily explained that the water had been turned on at a standpipe in the courtyard for an hour that afternoon, and the tenants had filled buckets and jugs as long as they were able. There were two full pails in the bathroom and one in the kitchen, and it was drinkable; she would make tea by and by. Also, she had started up the stove in the living-room.

"You're a great little sport," said Joe, "I just hope you didn't get tired out. Put out your little heater for now and come and have a drink. Dick telephone?" he ended casually.

"The telephone's still out of order, Joe."

"It's been out all day." He had a quick wash in the bathroom basin, using about a pint of the precious water, and went back to the living-room, where he saw the table had been set for three.

"Do you remember how you used to order sherry cobblers?" Dolly asked, when he began to rummage in the depleted drinks cupboard.

"Do I not! I haven't even sherry, straight, to offer you, but how about a glass of cherry brandy? It's hardly an aperitif, but it certainly is warming."

"That would be very nice." He poured it, glad to see the bottle was nearly full, poured three fingers of rye for himself, and collapsed into the creaking basket chair.

"Poor Joe, are you exhausted?"

"It's been quite a day."

"And it—really—is all over?"

"Or it's just beginning." He wondered if she fully realised what the new revolution meant. She sat there looking into the open stove where the birch logs were crackling, so young and so composed, and she had made her shabby place of refuge into something so like a home that Joe Calvert was half prepared to fall in love with her again. He had not seen much of Dolly Hendrikova since their talk in the Summer Garden. She had turned him down so definitely, had made her preference so clear that day, that his pride forbade him to hunt after her when her parents went away to Finland. When they did meet, she was always sweet and friendly, but somehow not as open and appealing as she had been—as she was now, sitting by his fireside, and telling him eagerly about the excitement at the hospital and the great kindness of the ladies at the British Embassy.

"Dick and I really shanghaied you this morning, didn't we?" he said.

"Shanghaied?"

"Well, kidnapped. Carried you away to our own den. But we didn't mean you to turn into a maid of all work—"

"Getting supper ready isn't being a maid of all work—"

"It was a very sweet thing to do . . . Dolly, listen, I've still got the car, it's right here in the yard. Where would you like me to take you, after we've had something to eat? To your Cousin Timofey's?"

To his surprise Dolly blushed. "Richard didn't say anything about going to Timofey's," she said.

"*Richard* didn't—?"

"No. He wants to take me to Finland, tomorrow if he can. He doesn't think I ought to stay in Petrograd."

"I told you months ago you should have gone to Finland with your parents. And how does Dick propose to take you to Koivisto—by train?"

"He said by train."

"*If* he gets a travel permit, and that won't be tomorrow. The Bolsheviks have closed the main stations for the next few days."

Dolly was not listening to him, but to the sound of a key in the door. "That must be Richard now!" she said delightedly. "Shall I—"

"You must."

Joe listened for less than a minute to the sound of their greeting. The shy laugh, the deep voice saying her name, the movement of two bodies into a close embrace were not meant for his ears. He kicked the living-room door shut with one foot. Then he turned to the flawed mirror which hung beside the writing table and had a hard look at Vice-Consul Calvert, thin-faced and sallow, with his eyes reddened from the sleepless hours and even his brown hair dusty from the neglected streets of Petrograd. It wasn't a face to attract a girl, he thought, but then he remembered Dick's chameleon face with the round pale eyes, and wondered why it had to be Joe Calvert who was the odd man out.

* * *

He felt even more the odd man out an hour later, when leaving Dick and Dolly in the light and warmth of their little oasis in the desert of the city, he set out in the embassy Ford for the Fourth Line. There was one more small service he could render Dolly, and by doing it he would also give them time to discuss the plan of escape which Dick had very briefly outlined at the supper table. It sounded like a heavy risk to Joe, but with Dick in charge it was probably not more risky than the far shorter journey across Petrograd in an American car on a night when the Red Guards were in a mood to commandeer any and every form of transport. He took the back streets and the longest way round, approaching Vassili Island by the Nicholas Bridge, and there on the embankment of the Neva he was stopped by a Red patrol.

He presented his diplomatic passport, which only one of the six men gaping at the car was able to read, but the word *amerikanski* several times repeated seemed to impress them all. They let him pass without even pulling aside the mica flaps which served as windows for the car, and as Joe drove over the bridge in low gear he saw, looking back, that they were all moving off towards the big square where the Xenia School had stood. There was no patrol on the Island side, and no living creature visible. Only the body of a policeman, swinging from a lamp-post in the bitter wind, showed that the revolution had passed that way.

No lamps were lit on the Fourth Line, and Joe guessed that this was one of the areas where electricity had been cut off. He left his acetylene headlamps burning to show him the way to the familiar door. To his surprise it was open, and the hall and staircase yawned black before him. He had brought a flashlight, and by its pencil-thick beam Joe was able to insert Dolly's latchkey and try to open her father's door.

It was bolted top and bottom on the inside.

He dropped the latchkey in his pocket and felt for the gun which, by recent permission, all the American consuls were allowed to carry. With one hand closed round it, he raised the other to the electric bell, remembered that the power was cut, and knocked heavily on the panels. There was a faint shuffling movement inside the flat.

"Simon!" he said, with his lips close to the keyhole, "Simon! Is that you?" It might be a thief, or a whole gang of looters; with the gun in his hand he was ready to take a chance.

Then a voice, very hoarse but still recognisable, said "Who's there?"

"Joe Calvert."

"Are you alone?"

"Yes."

The bolts were dragged back, the chain rattled, and the beam from the flashlight revealed Simon's haggard face.

"Come in, quick!" was all he said, but he seized Joe's hand in a strong clasp, and when the door was made fast again he added, "There's a lamp in the kitchen. Come on!"

Joe followed Dolly's brother to the kitchen, where he had never been before, and by the light of a little oil lamp he saw a packet of Finnish flatbread lying open in a ring of crumbs on the deal table, and the rags of an army uniform upon the floor. He then saw that Simon was wearing a thick tweed suit, obviously made before the war and hanging loose, and a dark fisherman's jersey with a turtle neck.

"Is Dolly all right?" was the first thing he said.

"She's perfectly safe, we've got her at the Italianskaia right now."

Simon nodded. "What are you doing here, Joe?"

"I came to get some things she wants to take to Finland. But good God, Simon, where have you been? Dolly's been worried sick about you. The last time anybody heard of you was at the end of July—"

"I was wounded at Malodechno," the Russian said, in a tone of complete indifference, "and my arm went back on me as well. I couldn't write at all, Joe, and then they kept moving us about after the retreat."

"But three months, man! Where have you come from now?"

"I was discharged from hospital at Pskov at the weekend. Came on by train until the strike began, and then I got a lift in a truck as far as the Narva Gate. I walked from there."

"No wonder you're out on your feet. Come into the living-room and sit down."

There was oil in the big ceiling lamp which Professor Hendrikov had liked so much, and by its soft light Joe saw that Simon's eyes were unfocussed and glassy, his broad shoulders slumped as he sat down in the nearest chair. He had brought the packet of bread from the kitchen.

"This came from Koivisto," he said inconsequently. "Real Finnish flat bread. How did that get here?"

"Your mother probably left it behind when they were here at the end of September. Simon! You knew your parents were in Finland, didn't you?"

"Oh yes," he said in the same tone of indifference as he had used about his wound. "I had a long rigmarole about that from Dolly, I couldn't make head or tail of it. All about some drunks breaking in, and Commander Yakovlev coming to the rescue, and father—how is my father now?"

"Much better since they went to Finland. And Dolly's going there tomorrow, Simon, did you understand what I was telling you?"

"There won't be any trains running tomorrow."

"Dick Allen knows another way; he's going to take her. If you know what's good for you, you'll go along with them, and you won't stop going till you're all in Copenhagen."

"Just because Lenin and his gang have staged another revolution?"

"Exactly."

"Sorry, Joe, but I've got other plans."

"Such as?"

Simon had been turning the packet of flatbread in his hands. Now he placed it on the table with exaggerated care, as if food were an object for reverence, and said in the same dull way:

"I *was* going to the hospital to look for Dolly, but that's all right. So now I can go straight to the Yamskaia and have a word with Miss Trenova."

"With Mara? What the hell for?"

"According to Dolly, she was the one who sent the sailors here to wreck the place."

"That's never been proved to my satisfaction."

"You always did stick up for her."

"I don't, but you've got too much at risk to go charging off to that end of town. You're quite liable to be arrested as a counter-revolutionary. Besides," he was suddenly inspired to say, "she's probably still at the Smolny. She was there all last night, I heard; a fellow I know called John Reed was talking to her at four o'clock this morning. Leave her alone, there's a good old boy! Come straight back with me to Dolly, and have a square meal and a good night's sleep, and Dick will do his best to get you both away."

The unfocussed eyes wandered round the room, and Simon said irrelevantly, "It looks queer without the pictures and the books."

It was not only the books and pictures that were missing. The spaces on the wall where the still lifes had hung, and the vast canvas of the unmarried mother, the baby and the vodka bottle, showed how faded the wallpaper was, and the boarding over the splintered windows made the bare room look like a shelter for refugees. The warmth and grace of one Russian way of life, which Joe Calvert had enjoyed so much, had gone for ever.

He stood up. "I'm not going to hang around here, it's too damned dangerous." He was thinking of the open street door. and the possible checkpoints on the way back to the Italianskaia. "I wish you'd show me which is Dolly's room and help me find her things. She wants two wool dresses and her fur coat."

Simon got up obediently. But what he said had no bearing on his sister's clothes.

"Is it true the Czar and his family are at Tobolsk?"

"They've been at Tobolsk for nearly three months."

"And nobody's made any attempt to rescue them?"

"How could they, Simon? We all hoped against hope they'd be allowed to land in England, and when Ramsay MacDonald and Lloyd George queered that pitch they weren't so much removed to Tobolsk as just spirited away. I *have* heard of monarchist groups plotting a rescue, but I don't believe it's ever been tried."

"I see."

"That sort of thing wouldn't be in your future plans, would it?"

"I'll show you where Dolly's room is."

They packed a suitcase quickly by the light of the hand lamp, and Simon fetched a heavy civilian overcoat and some belongings of his own. Back in the living-room, pulling down the oil lamp to extinguish it, he said to Joe, "One good thing, there's hardly anything left for the looters. Or the squatters, whoever moves in first."

"One better thing, and it's thanks to Dick Allen, your father and mother transferred all their assets to Finland when they left. They won't arrive penniless in Copenhagen."

"I'd better check the drawers of my father's desk, in case he left any other papers, hadn't I?"

"Take the flashlight. There's no light in the study at all."

Simon closed the door between the two rooms. For Joe Calvert's benefit he went through the motions of pulling the drawers open noisily: they were empty, of course, and he had expected nothing less from his mother's efficiency. He only wanted to be in the study alone.

When he came back to the apartment, ravenous, filthy and exhausted, his only desires had been animal, to eat, to splash his face and hands with the last drops of water in the taps, and to get out of his tattered uniform. But the contact with Joe had roused him from that brutish state. His mind was alert to the luxury of thinking about Olga. In this room, where he now stood alone in total darkness, he had held her in his arms, had kissed her, had listened entranced to the confession of her love. She rose before him so vividly in the dark that he could almost see her golden hair and the lovely hollow of her cheek beneath the high Slavic bones and the dark blue eyes. He heard her voice again, reading *Young Lochinvar*, saying the lines he had learned by heart, and telling him:

" 'So faithful in love and so dauntless in war'—like you, Simon!"

He struck his strong left hand into the right which was almost useless now, as if he were taking a vow, and said to himself:

"*Dushenka moya!* I'll save you—if I can."

25

After she overheard General Tatischev's dry acceptance of the fact that their Siberian imprisonment might end in death, Olga passed through a period of deep depression. She was on the eve of her twenty-second birthday, and life was so strong in her that she refused to accept the fact of dying: what she feared as the first result of the Communist revolution was the staging of a State trial, probably in Moscow, of her father and mother. She knew that this had been one of Trotsky's aims from the moment he returned to Russia. But she betrayed her anxiety to no one, and her sisters' chief concern seemed to be the problem of keeping warm in a draughty house as the terrible cold of a Siberian winter closed down upon Tobolsk.

There was no immediate shortage of money, although the Provisional Government which paid their expenses had been swept away, and the political changes were not felt at once. Soviets were being formed all over Russia, and in the Ural region there were two very powerful Soviets at Ekaterinburg and Omsk, but Tobolsk, with its twenty-seven churches to twenty thousand inhabitants, remained the same God-fearing backwater it had been for so long. The onset of winter, coinciding with the revolution, cut the town off from all propaganda which could not be conveyed by telegraph.

The two representatives of the Petrograd Soviet who had replaced Makarov at the end of September were not Bolsheviks, but old-line Social Revolutionaries, and one of them, at least, was quite well disposed towards the Romanovs. They regarded it as part of their duty, however, to encourage political discussion among the soldiers assigned to guard the imperial prisoners, and Colonel Kobilinski found it increasingly difficult to assert his authority over the Sharpshooters. The units drawn from the 1st and 2nd Regiments became impassioned revolutionaries; the men from the 4th were goodnatured, and sometimes played games with the younger girls and Alexis.

Nicholas and his gentlemen spent hours every day in discussing each scrap of news that came their way. There were fruitless debates on the defeat of Kerensky, who had failed to lead the remnants of the army to the recapture of Petrograd, and was now in hiding. There were even longer debates on Lenin, whom the former Czar roundly denounced as a German agent, and the armistice he had concluded with Germany and Austria as the preliminary to a treaty of peace. Nicholas had never appeared more broken, even in the first days after his abdiciation, as when news of the armistice was received: the oath he swore in the Winter Palace, never to make peace while an enemy remained on Russian soil, was one he had taken as solemnly as his marriage vows. From the British, who had denied him a refuge, and the Americans he expected nothing, although their warships were keeping station outside the Arctic ports and Vladivostok. General Foch had already advised French intervention at Odessa, but more was probably to be hoped—said the former Commander-in-Chief gravely—from the new Volunteer Army which General Alexiev had at once begun to raise.

This was talk among men, confined to the dining-room; in the drawing-room Alexandra Feodorovna seldom alluded to politics now. She sat knitting thick woollen stockings for Alexis, who at every opportunity practised skiing up and down the yard, and her only complaint was the restriction of church services to one mass on Sunday mornings. But the evening prayers in which the whole family joined were a comfort, and Olga especially enjoyed the simplicity of these gatherings and the blending of the girl voices in hymns once intoned by the splendid Russian basses and baritones of the Orthodox church. She and the young lady-in-waiting, Countess Nastia Gendrikova, wrote some simple verses to supplement the old favourites. Sometimes a young deacon from the church where they were allowed to go on Sundays joined them to intone the evening liturgy, and after a time Olga noticed that Deacon Vasiliev often joined her father and the other gentlemen in the dining-room when the ladies wrapped their shawls round their shoulders and hurried upstairs to their glacial rooms. Alexis was usually in bed by that time, and under the ill-fitting door they could see the glimmer of the cherished lamp which always burned beneath his favourite ikon.

Olga watched the deacon; she watched her father's increasing cheerfulness and the return of something exalted and excited in her mother's face which reminded her of other days, and she decided to take counsel with Monsieur Gilliard. She knew him much better than the two Russians acting as ADCs to the man they still called the Czar; she also knew, for it had been thoroughly tested, the Swiss tutor's utter reliability. It was not easy in their cramped quarters for any two people to talk privately, but one morning at exercise time, when her father released Gilliard from work with the two-handed saw, Olga fell into step beside him and drew attention to her brother's increasing skill on skis.

"He hasn't got much room to practise in, poor fellow," said the Swiss.

"No, and yet he hardly ever complains. I've only once heard him say, 'Oh, if I could only take my skis outside the gates, just once, even for ten minutes!' Usually he's as patient as they are." She indicated Marie and Anastasia, who were taking turns at pushing each other on a swing rigged up not far from the wood pile.

"I wish Tatiana and you could find more outdoor pastimes."

"Well, we're a little old for swinging, don't you think? And so are *they*, of course. Eighteen and sixteen—they ought to have something better than a rotten old swing! Saddle horses. A motor car all their own. Lots of friends—" She sighed. "I hate the waste, for them."

"I hate the waste for all of you." He remembered the summer when Olga Nicolaievna was eighteen, that wonderful last summer before the war and the lovely girl who had enjoyed every moment of it. She looked much older now than twenty-two. Olga's hair had grown to the length of a short bob, not unbecoming, but it was an ashy blonde in colour, no longer living gold, and she looked pale and pinched as she huddled inside her thick cape.

"Dear Monsieur Gilliard," she said, "I've known you for such a long time, haven't I? Longer than any of the other friends who were brave enough to throw in their lot with ours—"

"You were barely ten when we started our French lessons. I remember Her Majesty bringing you and Tatiana into my classroom for the first time. I was very nervous and Tatiana was very shy, but you smiled and were ready to be friends, right from the start."

"I think you were more afraid of us than we were of you!

So, after twelve years, may I ask you a very important question?"

"Of course."

"You and Mr. Gibbs are free to come and go in the town—"

"With a military escort," the man put in.

"With an escort, yes. But you go to the shops, and the public library, you meet people. Tell me, do you ever hear, do you ever see the faintest sign, of any plan to rescue us, to set us free?"

"I wish to God I could say yes."

"So there's nothing to be expected from the townspeople. If any help comes, it must come from outside. But from where?"

"I've asked myself that a thousand times," the Swiss said between his teeth. "This is the right time for it, before the rivers freeze, and before the Bolsheviks take over Tobolsk as they took Ekaterinburg. Kobilinski's on our side, I know, and if the soldiers from the Fourth were on guard, it could be done. If only there were a few brave men outside to help us—"

"Have you ever heard my father speak of any?"

Monsieur Gilliard seemed to regret his outburst. He said, with his usual reserve, "His Majesty may discuss such matters with his ADCs, Olga Nicolaievna. Certainly not with me."

"But you've heard something? You sit with the ADCs in the evening, you have your meals together. You *must* know if there's something in the wind. Or have you given up hope, like General Tatischev? Do *you* think you'll never get out of here alive?"

"Has the general said that to you?"

"I've heard him say it, I don't know if he believes it. But you must tell me the truth, whatever it is, because I'm beginning to think our lives may depend on what's planned now."

"I've only heard one thing," her old friend said reluctantly, "and this His Majesty told me, just the other day: there are three hundred Russian officers at Tiumen, preparing to lead a force to Tobolsk to set us at liberty."

"Thank you," said Olga from her heart. "Only the other day, you say? Then perhaps there's still time for me to talk to father and mother. To find out what they're planning for us now."

"You won't betray my confidence, I hope?"

"Of course I won't."

So even in this tiny community of prisoners they were breathing the old infected court atmosphere of secrecy and intrigue. Olga said as much to Tatiana, when they snatched a moment to be alone together, and the elder sister told the younger of her fears.

"If they're planning some crack-brained scheme that'll turn the guards against us, we'll be separated and put into a *real* prison," said Olga grimly, and Tatiana for once agreed with her. "Three hundred of our officers in a little town like Tiumen, a likely story!" she said. "We must speak to papa tonight."

"Yes, but not a word about the three hundred. We can't give Zilchik away."

As it turned out, the young deacon stayed late at the mansion that night, and it was easy for Olga, when she and her sister followed their parents to their bedroom, to begin by saying:

"Father Vasiliev comes to say evening prayers for us nearly every night now, doesn't he?"

"I think I'll just look in and make sure that Baby is nicely tucked up," said Alexandra. She was wrapped in a long shawl, like both the girls, but a fleecy dressing-gown lay ready on the opened bed, and the room, hung with ikons and family portraits, was not without its comfort.

"Please, mamma, wait a minute, there's something we really want to ask you," said Tatiana, and the Czar, looking amused, asked if wasn't rather late to hold a family conference.

"We can't help wondering if Father Vasiliev is carrying messages—if he's in touch with any of our friends outside," said Olga. "If so, we think we ought to know about it."

"They've stumbled on our secret, Alix; I think we'll have to let them share it," said Nicholas. "We didn't want to raise your hopes until the time was ripe," he said to the girls. "But it soon will be. Three hundred brave men, officers of my army, are at Tiumen, preparing to come to our rescue. Your mamma has conferred a beautiful name on them: the Brotherhood of St. John of Tobolsk, and at her wish they've taken the swastika for their emblem."

He spoke in a low voice, and the high-flown name had to be repeated for Tatiana, whose hearing was still impaired.

"There are three hundred Reds on guard duty here alone, and other regiments in the town," said Olga. "I hardly think they'll stand by and let the Brotherhood whisk us away."

"A great many of the townsfolk have shown their loyalty, and all the clergy are on our side."

"Including Father Vasiliev, of course?"

"He's the chief local agent of the Brotherhood."

"Who's the agent in Tiumen?"

"Nicky dear, I think you've told them quite enough," said Alexandra Feodorovna. "We've been warned not to expect help until after Christmas—"

"Then the helpers will have to come by road," said Tatiana, "with the telegraph giving warning at every post station they go through."

"Who's financing the Brotherhood?" said Olga. It was another of the blunt practical questions her mother had always disliked.

"They can't very well reveal their sources," she said, "but Yaroshinski, who managed my hospital train, has undertaken to forward a large sum to Tiumen."

"I thought he was in prison," said Olga. "He was a confederate of Manuilov, whom Rodzianko had arrested. Oh mamma, what have you got yourself into this time?"

"I think Lieutenant Soloviev is a most trustworthy man," said Nicholas mildly, and Olga caught at the name.

"Is he the head of the organisation in Tiumen? Lieutenant Soloviev? What Soloviev is that? Not *Boris* Soloviev?"

"A trusted friend we used to meet at home," said her mother.

"In Anna Virubova's home, you mean," said Olga contemptuously. "I met him there once myself. Do you remember him, Tania?" she said, raising her voice. "He'd been in India, studying theosophy with Madame Blavatsky. Badmaiev brought him out to Czarskoe Selo, along with the Tea of Divine Grace and all the rest of the rubbish, and then to crown his career he married Grisha Rasputin's daughter. Rasputin's son-in-law, planning to rescue us! Oh, father!" she cried passionately, "how can you be fooled by such a story! How can you trust anyone connected with the man who did us so much harm before? I wouldn't go as far as the yard gate with Boris Soloviev, and I won't let the others, either! What he means to do is betray us to the Bolsheviks—"

Alexandra was weeping by this time, and protesting against the insult to the memory of Our Dear Martyr, while her husband made his accustomed reference to the long-suffering Job. But Olga stood her ground and got his promise—for what it was worth—to have no more transactions in secret with Tiumen.

"Not unless we all know about it," she said firmly, and Nicholas retorted, "Are *you* planning to set up a soviet, my girl?"

Whether the swastika brought bad luck to the Brotherhood, or whether the Brotherhood existed only in Soloviev's imagination, there was certainly no sign of an armed force on the frozen highway as the bitter winter days grew shorter, and the *Rus* came to her moorings for the last time until the spring. What did happen, with far-reaching consequences, was that on the Russian Christmas Day the young deacon, Vasiliev, publicly intoned the prayers for the long life and health of the imperial family, which had been forbidden to be sung in churches since the abdication.

It was the signal for the soldiers of the guard to begin a real harassment of their prisoners. This was not constant, because when the men of the 4th Sharpshooters were on duty there was always friendliness, but surly or friendly, there were now guards inside the house as well as out. The Czar was forbidden to wear epaulettes on the shoulders of his increasingly shabby uniforms. Letters were neither collected nor delivered, and the sense of isolation became acute. The brave lady-in-waiting who had risen from a hospital bed to join her imperial mistress at Tobolsk was not allowed to enter the governor's mansion at any time, and local people who had liked to leave little gifts for the prisoners were chased away with threats. Finally, the two Socialist Revolutionary commissars were recalled to Petrograd, and replaced by two Bolsheviks of a very different stamp.

The one ray of light in the gloom was the good health and good spirits of Alexis. He had had no recurrence of the bleeding since the nasal haemorrhage of two years back, and seemed to thrive in the winter weather. He was full of jokes and mystifications about the changing of the Russian calendar to western time, which took place in January, and announced that in 1918 they must all have two birthday parties, on the old date and the new. His own fourteenth birthday was due in August. "It's a long time to wait," he said.

As soon as the snow was really deep he clamoured for the building of a snow mountain bigger than any before, and one Monday morning, after a particularly heavy overnight snowfall, they all started work. It took days to get it as high as he wanted, for it was so cold that the water froze in the buckets before it could be poured on the rising slopes, but everybody helped—the tutors and Nagorny, and all the girls. The friendly soldiers of the 4th Regiment were smitten with the fever and carried water willingly. They too were eager for toboggan rides.

"Is it as high as the snow mountain Dmitri built for the little kids at Pavlovsk?" Alexis asked, when the mountain towered above the fence and the chute was smooth and ready for the toboggans.

"Oh, higher, I should think," said Olga. "He hadn't nearly as many people to help him as we have."

"But they were all free," said Alexis pensively. It was odd, his sister thought, how often he mentioned the snow mountain he had never seen, the slide built beside the Slavianka river on the winter day when Dmitri wanted to raise her to the throne. Imprisonment, and the ugly shadow of Rasputin which still lay across their lives, had so chilled the warm responses of Olga's body that the sexual memories of that afternoon, of Dmitri's kisses and his close embrace, had no longer any power to move her. All she retained of the snow mountain at Pavlovsk was her own prophetic cry, "Farewell, my youth!" She felt so strongly that her youth was over that when the new mountain was at last complete she was prepared to be a spectator with her father and the older men. It was only to please Alexis that she pulled herself up the ladder to the top of the toboggan run. But once on the platform, with the lively young faces looking up at her from the yard, and the novelty of a view into an unknown Tobolsk street, some of the excitement of life came back to Olga Nicolaievna. With a shout of "Here I come!" she launched herself down the icy track in a sparkling illusion of liberty.

26

WHEN RICHARD ALLEN USED the back stairs in the old house on the Italianskaia he was accustomed to knock a little warning on the door before he opened it with his own key. On the evening in late February when he went there for the last time he omitted the warning, slid the key in noiselessly, and signalled to the two trembling girls behind him to wait on the landing. Once inside, with the door closed behind him, he said experimentally, "Joe?"

Joe came out of the living-room at once. "Hallo!" he said. "Where have you been hiding yourself? Something up?"

"Are you alone, old man?"

"Absolutely."

Dick relaxed. "Thank God for that. One never knows from day to day, and I was afraid you'd have some Russians quartered on you."

"I'm still pleading diplomatic immunity. Well, don't stand there, come on in!"

"I'm on a job," said Dick gravely. "We've got visitors." He opened the door behind him. "Will you come in now, please?" Joe heard him say.

The two girls who came in were very young. When they were in the lighted room, and slowly taking off their heavy overcoats, Joe saw that the eldest was not more than sixteen, the younger her junior by perhaps two years—the youngest 'visitors' Dick Allen had ever brought to this place of refuge.

"This is the American friend I was telling you about," Dick said cheerfully. "Mr. Calvert. I'm sure he'll be glad to make you a cup of tea."

The elder girl whispered her thanks. Joe saw that they were both badly shaken, and drew forward two chairs to the stove.

"Come and sit down," he said. "You must be tired. Have you come a long way?"

"No," Dick answered for them, "but they've a long way to

go, and I must change my clothes before we start. Princess," he said to the girl, "will you and your sister try to rest for ten minutes, while I talk to Mr. Calvert? Then I'll explain to you exactly where we're going, and what I want you to do."

"We're in your hands, Captain Allen," she said. She had taken off her rough woollen cap, and fair hair as fine as floss silk fell round her shoulders. She put it back with one beautifully manicured hand.

"I don't have to ask you who they are," said Joe, as he followed Dick into the kitchen and filled the kettle from the water bucket. "I know. I saw them with their father and mother once, at an embassy reception."

"Yes, well, the Cheka arrested their father early this afternoon. He's in the Shpalernaia Street prison, and their ass of a mother wasted hours at Cheka headquarters trying to intercede for him before she came to the embassy and was put on to me. Now she wants the kids taken across the border. Fool of a woman—they should have left a year ago, but she hung on hoping to save their houses and their art collection, and now, of course, she can only think of life or death."

"She isn't going too?"

"Won't desert her husband in his hour of need. Won't realise that a Romanov prince hasn't a hope of going free until the day he walks out of his cell to face the firing squad—I've got to change."

He poured two glasses of vodka from the bottle in the kitchen cupboard and led the way to the little bedroom, which was glacially cold. Joe drank his at a gulp, he had taken to vodka at last, and the warmth spread gratefully through his body while he listened to Dick talk.

"I don't mind admitting this one's a bastard," said the Englishman, pulling some rough garments out of the wardrobe and taking off his jacket. "Those poor little devils are in a state of shock. They saw their father arrested, and the Cheka men rampaging through the house, and then their mother went into screaming hysterics which lasted for about an hour. It was her maid who kept her head. That's the maid's clothes the girls are wearing. Joe, have you got a car?"

"Every last car we had went off with the ambassador and his staff to Vologda."

"Oh, hell, I never thought of that. It would have been a help if you could have driven us to the Okhta station, like you did the night I took Dolly over. Well, there's nothing for it, we'll have to take the tram."

"You're going through the forest?"

"What else? I daren't risk crossing the ice with those two babies. They haven't got white clothing, and there's no time to get any; what's more, the moon is at the full. And too many escapees have lost their nerve when the arc lights from the Kronstadt forts are switched on. Besides, I'm getting a bit too old for the ice caper."

Dick had been changing his clothes as he talked. When he took up his untasted glass of vodka he was dressed as a Petrograd working man, in a heavy frieze coat reaching to his knees, and his trousers tucked into shabby knee-length boots. Like Joe, he drank his vodka at a gulp. "God, I'm tired!" he said.

"How long are you going to keep this racket up?"

"Oh, a little while longer, I expect. Now that the ambassador's gone back to London, some of us had better hang around."

"Isn't Dolly getting impatient to see you again?" Joe was rather proud of himself: he could say her name without the slightest pang.

Dick smiled, and when he smiled, in the dim light of a ten-watt lamp, he did look young again, as young as on the night when Dolly found him wounded, and looked at him with new eyes. "The wedding's fixed for June," he said.

"Congratulations! I suppose I have to say the best man won."

"You're a good sport, Joe. Now I must get back to my ewe lambs."

"Just a minute," said Joe Calvert. "When do you expect you'll be back from Finland?"

"Day after tomorrow, with any luck."

"I'll probably still be here."

"How d'you mean, probably?"

"I've been recalled," said Joe. "The cable came in yesterday. Recalled to Washington for re-posting. Proceed immediately, you know the sort of thing."

"Can't proceed immediately when you're leaving Russia. Exit permit, travel warrant, it all takes the devil of a time. You'll be here all right! We'll have a long yarn when I get back, Joe, and meantime congratulations to you too. I'll bet you're glad to be let off Vologda."

"Vologda sounds like a living death."

When Joe carried the tea into the living-room the two young girls seemed more at ease. There was even a little colour in their pale faces, and both listened attentively to what Dick Allen had to say.

"The princess asked me to take you to Imatra, to your aunt at the Valtio Hotel. That means a rather difficult route across the border, because as you know General Mannerheim is fighting the Reds in Finland, and the front in Karelia is what soldiers call 'fluid', and we don't want to run into any action. So there may be a delay here and there before we can cross the border."

"But the Germans aren't in Karelia, are they?" said the younger girl. She was pretty, Joe saw, and trying hard to be composed. "Papa was so worried when the fighting began again."

"No, the Germans aren't in Karelia. But they're not a hundred miles from Petrograd, which was one reason the princess entrusted you to me. Mr. Calvert's ambassador left Petrograd for that same reason, and went away to a little town called Vologda, on the Trans-Siberian railway. Now we're taking the train too, only we go north from the Okhta station, and it'll take us four hours to reach our destination. You may be able to sleep a little in the train."

"I feel as if I'd never sleep again," said the girl with a shudder.

"Now, when I knew we were going to take a trip together I sent a Russian friend of mine on ahead of us, and when we leave the train he'll have a sleigh and horses waiting. When you're alone with Ivan and me you can talk as much as you like, but try not to talk in the tram or in the train. Your voices might give you away, you see, and you'll have to keep your gloves on all the time. Try not to cry, try not to think. This is one big thing you can do for your mother, to put up with being tired as well as unhappy, and maybe hungry too, for a few hours between now and tomorrow morning, and then she'll know you're out of danger."

The girls had beautiful manners; they stood up at once when Dick said they must go, and thanked Joe for his 'very kind hospitality'. He wished them Godspeed, but he felt uneasy once they were gone. He had felt uneasy, in fact, ever since Dick

Allen said, "I don't mind admitting this one's a bastard."

* * *

The same feeling of unease had been with Dick Allen for the whole of his journey. It had all seemed to go smoothly enough in the north-bound train, where he was sure nobody suspected them to be other than a boorish, half-drunken workman and his two frightened daughters, and when they got to Grusino Ivan had been waiting there with the sleigh and the horse, himself bundled up in furs and with extra wraps for his passengers. Then they drove west towards the Finnish border, along the snowy back-roads Dick had come to know so well on his old fishing trips, while the two girls huddled together for warmth in the piercing cold. They were alone and unchallenged in the moonlit forests. But when they reached the first staging point on their route Dick's uneasiness became acute. The peasant, Igor, whose hut they always used, was surly; it was getting too risky, he grumbled even while he took their money, the Finns were fighting all up and down Lake Ladoga. He objected to turning out in the middle of the night to find the men who would take them along the next stage on the way to Imatra.

But he left on snowshoes, and the girls fell into an exhausted slumber. Dick watched them in the firelight of the peasant's hut. The little one, whose name was Ludmila, had cried herself to sleep in her sister's arms, and they were lying, curled up like two puppies, on the battered couch where Dolly Hendrikova had rested on the night he brought her along this road to safety. But Dolly had not been sleepy, she had chattered happily about their future plans, and she had kissed him—his Dolly, who had seen something in a battered old soldier she could love. He thought about the wedding in June and rose noiselessly to his feet. Ivan, who had been sitting on a stool by the fire, got up too.

"He's been away an hour longer than usual," said Dick in a low voice. "I hope he hasn't run into any trouble on the border."

"I've been worrying," the young man confessed. "I was beginning to think we should have carried straight on without him."

"The poor old nag was ready to founder, and I don't know the footpaths on the other side half as well as the guides do. Besides, the girls had to get some rest."

"I thought I heard his footsteps then."

"Look out, Ivan, and make sure it's him."

"It's him all right, and he's alone."

Dick slipped his revolver back into its holster, and gently aroused the girls. The peasant came in, as surly as before, but he had passed on the word to their friends across the border, who would be waiting with a sleigh on the far side of the river.

"You hear that, Princess Rita?" Dick said cheerfully to the older girl. "We've got to walk for an hour, I'm afraid, but it's easy going, and then you'll see a big black and white post, and when we're past it we'll be safe in the Grand Duchy."

It was not easy going, and they walked for nearly two hours before they came in sight of whatever safety there might be in a Finland torn by civil war. The girls stepped out bravely at first, but they began to stumble and lag behind, and the two men dared not raise their voices to urge them on. They took Rita and Ludmila by the arms, and pulled them along the forest paths, at some places deep in snow. They half carried them along the last mile to the frontier post, where a frozen river which marked the border glimmered in the light of the setting moon. To his huge relief Dick saw two men in white cloaks waiting on the far side.

Ludmila was terrified of the river. The ice would break, and they would all be drowned, she sobbed, and her sister, too, had reached the breaking point.

"It's no use, we'll have to carry them," said Dick. The two Finns had come down to the river bank, and were making urgent signs. They pushed back their white hoods, and Dick recognised two trusted guides. Suppressing a groan he lifted Ludmila up in his arms. The trudge through the snow had exhausted him as well as his charges, and the leg wounded in the Boer War, so long ago, felt as if it would give way beneath him. He was up to the knees in water as the ice cracked and broke beneath his weight.

"Come on, Ivan," he said between his teeth. He was afraid of letting Ludmila fall, and was thankful that the Finns in their high boots came more than half way to meet them. He gladly passed the weeping child into their arms.

"Where's the sleigh?" he demanded, as soon as they stood gasping on the Finnish bank.

"Just beyond the trees. Be quick, captain, we can't waste time. There's a Cheka patrol out on the border tonight—"

"A *Cheka* patrol?"

"So the foresters say. Can you walk, young lady, or must we carry you to the sleigh?"

"We can walk," said Rita bravely, and the other Finn seized a hand of each and began to hurry them up the bank and into the protecting trees.

"Halt, you over there! Halt or we fire!" The dreaded challenge rang down the frozen river; the moonlight shone on the black leather jackets of the special police emerging from the trees to the north.

"The patrol!" cried the remaining Finn. "Run for your lives!"

Dick Allen took a few steps, and fell. He scrambled up, his knee refused to bear him, and he jerked out his revolver and fired a few shots. He knew that it was useless, he was outnumbered ten to one, and the Cheka men were upon him. He raised his hands high above his head.

* * *

Joe Calvert made arrangements to leave Russia without a great deal of trouble. His exit permit was issued with only a day's delay, and at the cost of standing in line for nearly three hours at the Finland Station he had obtained a travel warrant and the possibility, though not the actual reservation, of a seat in a 'soft' coach in the train to Helsingfors. He packed his belongings into two valises, said his official goodbyes to the few Americans remaining in Petrograd, and was ready to leave Russia in a matter of hours.

He was very glad to go. The months since the revolution had been a terrible strain, as the 'Extraordinary Commission', the Cheka, established a police network far more efficient and brutal than the Czar's Okhrana, and hunger and disease took their toll of the civilian population. The seizure of all private assets, including safe deposit boxes, raised endless problems at the consulate, and at the embassy, while the ambassador remained in Petrograd, there had been constant friction.

Ambassador Francis made his position perfectly clear from the first. He thought Bolshevism 'a foul monster', and advocated America's early and violent opposition to it. 'Colonel' Raymond Robins, on the other hand, continued to admire Lenin and called Trotsky 'the greatest Jew since Christ'. Sometimes Joe Calvert thought he was the only man in the Furshtatskaia who had not made an inflammatory speech for or against the new Russian government, or threatened to 'take a poke' at one of his fellow-Americans.

It was beginning to grow dark, for the February afternoon was overcast, when he heard the familiar knock on the service door, and waited for the sound of Dick's latchkey. Instead of that the knock came again, and Joe felt a sudden alarm grip his body. He had no fear of a looting raid, for when the Kronstadt sailors put into action the new rule that all property belonged to the community, and came looking for furniture and bedding, they came right up the front stairs and threatened to break in the front door. Diplomatic status had not saved Joe from one such invasion. But this might be another kind of trap, and he began to sweat. The last thing he wanted was a run-in with the Bolshies, within a few hours of his going free.

He went to the back door and said, "Who's there?"

"A messenger from Dick. His friend Ivan."

Joe undid the bolts reluctantly. There was a dim shape on the service landing, a shape of furs and mufflers, and Joe caught the gleam of white teeth in a bearded face. The man slipped quickly past him into the flat.

In the feeble light of the living-room Joe saw an unmistakably Russian face, the face of a young man disfigured by an old scar and heavy recent abrasions, but smiling anxiously.

"Mr. Calvert? Please forgive me for coming without warning. Captain Allen told me some time ago how to get here. He wanted me to tell you if anything went wrong for him. And—I'm sorry to bring bad news—he is now in the hands of the Cheka."

Joe felt his very bones go soft, and he motioned to the newcomer to sit down. All he could say was, "When was this?"

"Just before first light, yesterday morning, on the Finnish border."

"*Yesterday* morning?"

"It took me all of thirty-six hours to get back to Petrograd. I wouldn't have got away at all, if it hadn't been for Dick."

"Just a minute." He fetched what was left of the vodka from the kitchen. It was the only stimulant he had to offer an obviously exhausted man.

"Where is he now?" he asked as he handed Ivan a glass.

"Thank you, this is good . . . He's at the Shpalernaia Street prison. You knew he was taking people across the border?"

"I knew something about it. I even heard him mention your name the last time he was here, if you're the Ivan who was to meet him some place up the line."

"That's right. I was one of the Russian group who worked with him. I—used to be an officer in the Garde Equipage."

"You'd better tell me the whole story," said Joe. He listened in silence, and at the end his only query was, "What do you think went wrong?"

Ivan shrugged. "It looks as if Igor's gone over to the other side. He probably alerted the Cheka patrol at the same time as he went to bring the Finnish guides. What puzzles me is what the Cheka men were doing so far away from Gorokhovia Street. We used to think of Rasputin when we said 'Gorokhovaia Street', now it means something worse."

"How do you know they took him to the Shpalernaia?"

"Two of our people here saw him being taken in."

"How did he look?"

"Badly beaten up."

"Okay," said Joe, getting to his feet. "So the thing to do is spring him, as fast as we can."

"If he's alive."

"They'll keep him alive, all right." To make him talk, of course, to give away the names of his group and their pathetic customers. "Four o'clock," he said, looking at his watch. "I'm going to the Smolny. You'd better go to the British Embassy and tell them what you've just told me."

"Dick always said nobody at the embassy could protect him if he ever got into trouble. And haven't they all gone back to England?"

"Ask for the naval attaché," said Joe. "He stayed on, and if anyone can help, he will. Now let's go through the details once again."

When he was sure the story was fixed in his brain, Joe poured the man called Ivan another small measure of vodka and put the rest into his travelling flask. Dick would need it if he were still alive to drink it, and Joe had heard of enough summary executions to know that this was open to doubt. As he shrugged himself into his fur-lined greatcoat he said to his exhausted visitor:

"Did you know a man called Simon Hendrikov in the Garde Equipage? You did? Any idea where he is now?"

"Still in Petrograd. I believe he hangs out round the Lavra quarter."

"I wish to God he'd gone with his family to Copenhagen."

"Is that where they are?"

"Thanks to Richard Allen."

* * *

Grey Petrograd was like a ghost town now, but at the end of its short avenue the Smolny Institute was ablaze with light. The sentries carried their rifles at port arms; the row of machine-guns which Joe remembered from his visits to the commercial section was protected by tarpaulins from the falling snow. He knew the drill: the challenge which came as soon as he walked up the steps beneath Quarenghi's eight white columns, under the pediment on which the red flag flew, and then the armed escort to a crowded guardroom. Joe told the duty officer that he wanted to see Comrade Mara Trenova, 'employed'—as he knew from something John Reed had once let drop—'in TEO, the theatrical section of the People's Commissariat for Education'. It sounded knowledgeable, and after the slow examination of his own papers Joe was allowed to fill up the endless forms in triplicate, while the soldiers breathing down his neck grunted their amazement that the *amerikanski* could write such a beautiful, running Cyrillic script. He completed each form with a flourish: 'Nature of business—cultural.'

Then he waited for half an hour, oppressed as always by the constant racket and tramping going on inside the Smolny, where comrades were addressing meetings, carpenters hammering away at new partitions, deputations arriving from Soviets outside the capital, and delegates from the different workers' unions coming in to present their fraternal greetings to the Commissars. Gradually his lungs adapted themselves to the odours of the Smolny, of soup made from horseflesh, clothes stiff with sweat and grime, and that other stench which proved that sanitation at the seat of power was no better than elsewhere. He was glad when a girl messenger wearing high boots and some sort of military uniform came to conduct him to the theatrical section of *Narkompros*, housed in a former classroom with some of the girls' desks left in, and a few matchboard partitions dividing it into cubicles. Mara Trenova's was slightly larger than the others. She leaned across a desk heaped with papers to offer him her cold hand.

"You're quite a stranger, Mr. Calvert; I hardly expected to receive *you* here," she said in a tone as dry as her skin and hair. She had a pencil stuck behind one ear.

"I only discovered the other day you'd gone to *Narkompros*," said Joe easily. "Last time I heard, you were working on a newspaper."

"*Rabochi Put*; yes, we survived Kerensky's last-ditch attempt to destroy us," she said with her bitter smile. "After the revolution the editor found me a cinema job in TEO."

"And how d'you like making movies?"

"I've got nothing to do with the actual production! I write scripts and continuity, and also I'm head of research for the whole theatrical section."

"I bet that keeps you busy," said Joe. "I saw your name on the credits for last week's show at the cinema in the Passage."

"Oh, you do go to see our films?" She actually blushed with pleasure. "I did the linking shots for that—between each scene, a Czarist emblem. A hand holding a pair of handcuffs or shaking a knout, just a simple symbol, but quite effective."

"Very effective, I thought."

"We have great plans for more truly cultural productions. Just at present, you understand, the need is for quite elementary propaganda films."

"Suited to your great mass audience," said Joe. He wondered how much longer he would have to spend on buttering her up, when Dick's life might hang on a matter of minutes, but he didn't dare rush her; he had always known Mara Trenova for an unbalanced creature, who responded well to praise. He was prepared to continue his praises of the rubbish which had replaced Douglas Fairbanks and William Farnum in the cinemas of the Nevski Prospekt, but Mara herself, as if recalled by the word 'cultural' to her own duties, looked at her watch and said,

"Well, what can I do for you, Joe? I take it this is an official visit?"

"It is and it isn't," said Joe. "It's an emergency." As briefly as possible he asked her to arrange for him to meet Vladimir Ilyich Lenin, to ask for clemency for Richard Allen, in the

Shpalernaia prison. Before he could finish, he felt her hand over his mouth, and the trembling of her body as she stood beside him.

"Are you mad to talk about the Cheka here? Are you crazy, to think I'll do your dirty work for you?"

Joe Calvert shook himself free. "I thought you liked Dick Allen," he said. "You helped him once, when he was knifed in 'The Red Sarafan'."

"That was quite different! I only knew him then as *your* friend—"

"He's still my friend, and he's the man Dolly Hendrikova is going to marry, one of these days—"

"Is that any reason I should help him to avoid punishment?"

"Considering what you did to the Hendrikovs—yes."

"What *I* did to the Hendrikovs?"

"The day you betrayed them to the Kronstadt sailors, for a cheap revenge on Simon and—Olga Romanova."

This time Mara put her finger to her own lips at the word Romanova. "That's the name one must never say," she whispered. "What do you mean about the Kronstadt sailors?"

He quickly described the wrecking of the flat, and Dolly's conviction that Mara had revealed the Grand Duchess Olga's visit to the terrorists.

"What a fool Dolly is," she said contemptuously. "I never told anybody about meeting—that girl—in the Fourth Line. But somebody else saw her then, and told his friends. The doorman!"

"Stepan? I sometimes wondered about that. But he disappeared after the July Days, and couldn't be questioned, by me or Dick either. And Dolly was so sure—"

"Stepan was one of us," said Mara. "He used to report on everybody in that building, and their visitors. I know it was a man called Yakovlev who had him dismissed from the job."

"A common spy, and one of 'you'," said Joe. "Oh, Mara, do you never feel ashamed?"

"Not when I think of the better world I'm helping to construct."

"The world of the Cheka and the Shpalernaia prison?"

"Or your world, in which I'm suspected of betraying people who were once my friends? My mother's friends?" Mara's voice softened. "Joe, you don't understand. I have no power, absolutely none, to go to Comrade Lenin to beg for an English spy—yes, a common spy, and one of *you*—because I would put myself under suspicion of sympathising with the counter-revolutionaries."

"I'm not asking you to beg for Dick. I'm asking you to get me an interview, that's all: I'll do the rest myself."

"I would have to put the request through at least two other people before it would reach his office, and even if he agreed to see you it might take a week—"

"So let's get started," he said, and Mara Trenova gave in.

"I'll send your name upstairs," she said, "but you won't get away with 'nature of business—cultural' when it's to do with *him*."

"Write this down," said Joe, for she had dipped a steel pen in the ink, "write 'the case of Captain Richard Allen, a British subject, unlawfully detained at the Shpalernaia prison'. That way, the cards are on the table!"

"Don't blame me if you find yourself in the Shpalernaia too." She sealed the sheet of paper and rang a table bell for a messenger. "You do realise it may be hours before you get an answer? I'm sorry I can't ask you to wait here, but I'll take you to the canteen and see you get a glass of tea, and I'll tell the upstairs messengers where you can be found. Will that do?"

Joe picked up her hand and kissed it. He felt grateful and angry and sorry for her, with her thin burned-out face, all at the same time.

"We don't go in for bourgeois manners here," she said.

"Mara, it may be bourgeois, but let me just say this: thank you for me, and thank you for Dick Allen too. He once said you hadn't made up your mind whether to be a saint or a revolutionary. I'm going to tell him you turned out to be a saint."

"Perhaps I was really meant to be a martyr."

* * *

Joe spent two hours in the canteen. It was crowded, but he was allowed to occupy a small table by himself. Aware that he was under surveillance by the four burly men at the next table, he did his best to look unconcerned, and not as if several trains of thought were simultaneously starting and clashing in his brain. Dick in prison and undergoing interrogation by the Cheka—

that was the overriding theme; but he had time to think of Dolly, who had depended on Joe Calvert as a help in trouble, and her brother Simon, who had talked so ardently about rescuing the Grand Duchess Olga from Tobolsk, and was hanging about in Petrograd, a down-and-out among the human refuse in the Lavra. The final worry was his own departure, for the train to Helsingfors left officially at ten, and as the hands of the canteen clock passed eight Joe began to wonder if he would be kept waiting until after ten o'clock, and then shown abruptly to the door.

It was eight-fifteen when they came for him, and as he was taken back to the guardroom where his fur hat and greatcoat had been locked away on his arrival, Joe was certain these items would now be returned to him as a preliminary to departure. This time, however, he was carefully searched, and he was glad that the gun he had carried during the revolution was in one of his suitcases at the flat. The envelope with his train ticket and other documents got the closest scrutiny before it was returned to him with his passport, and when the examining officer was satisfied that Joe was not carrying firearms, vitriol or a hand grenade he was told curtly that Comrade Lenin would see him now.

The upper floor of the Smolny, evidently reserved for top-ranking members of the Soviet, was even more crowded and bustling than the halls below. Men and women in and out of uniform were hurrying from room to room, always with piles of paper or leather pouches in their hands, and Joe, side-stepping to avoid a girl who came charging at him with a steel filing tray, was hit squarely in the face by a door, opening outwards, which some energetic official must have opened with a kick. One of his soldier escorts asked him, with a guffaw, if he were hurt. Joe, feeling blood oozing from a cut above his eye, made no reply.

They came to a door guarded by two sentries with fixed bayonets, who after a word with the escort permitted Joe to pass. He was admitted to Lenin's presence with one eye rapidly closing, and blood trickling down his cheek.

With the other eye, he could see that he was in a little room, sparsely furnished with a high wall desk, a small desk, now vacant, for a secretary, and a large table illuminated by a single cone of light coming from a green-shaded lamp swung low from the ceiling. It lit up the bald head, the great domed forehead, and the cold eyes of the new ruler of Russia, Vladimir Ilyich Lenin.

"Mr. Calvert—" Lenin began in English—"Good heavens, have you been fighting?"

"I had an argument with a door, coming along the corridor," said Joe. "One of your staff came out with the devil of a rush!"

Lenin smiled. "We're making a new nation," he said, "so naturally we're all in a hurry. But let me see if I can find something for that nasty cut. Do take a chair!"

He disappeared behind a partition which seemed to divide what had once been a much larger room, and Joe heard the murmur of a woman's voice. He knew that Lenin lived on the premises, in the simplest manner possible, with his wife Krupskaia. He remembered diplomatic complaints, in the old days, that the Czarina listened from a hidden balcony to the Czar's discussions with ambassadors and with his Ministers. Joe wondered if Krupskaia performed the same listening service for Lenin.

The chair which Lenin had indicated was too far from his work table for Joe to see clearly the papers in the open dossier lying on the bare top, but he could recognise, upside down, his own identity photograph and Dick's, each attached to a closely typed foolscap sheet. He held his handkerchief to the bleeding cut with a feeling of despair.

Lenin came back with a small piece of sticking plaster which looked as if it had been used before, and a glass of water. "This seems to be all we have by way of first aid," he said cheerfully. "You prefer your handkerchief? Very well. I'm sure they have some iodine downstairs." He sat down at the table and drew the dossier towards him. "Our records show you have a remarkable grasp of Russian, Mr. Calvert. My English is rusty, but I would prefer to use it during this interview."

"First let me say, sir," Joe began formally, "that I'm grateful to you for *giving* me the interview, especially at such short notice."

"It is rather unusual, isn't it?" said Lenin. "If this were Washington, do you think the President of the United States would make himself so readily available to, say, a young vice-consul of the French Republic?"

"New methods for new nations," Joe retorted. "I needn't apologise for my rank in the Foreign Service, Mr. Lenin. The proper person to wait upon you in this matter is His Excellency the British Ambassador."

"Who fled the country over a month ago. I believe a person from the embassy is here, bombarding Trotsky with requests for an interview. You showed better judgment in coming straight to me. I haven't met many Americans as yet. The last, or perhaps the first, to come with a similar petition to this room was your own ambassador, before he left for Vologda. A charming old gentleman, a hopeless amateur of course." Lenin tilted his chair back, and in a characteristic gesture, stuck his middle fingers in the armholes of his waistcoat. "I believe he was connected with what you call show business before he became ambassador?"

"He was at one time the Governor of Missouri, Mr. Lenin. And the petition, as you call it, he addressed to you on behalf of his Rumanian colleague was entirely successful."

"The Rumanian was being held on a technical charge, Mr. Calvert; deportation was a sufficient punishment in his case. Now you have come to plead for someone who under our new laws is a criminal—the counter-revolutionary, Richard Allen. Caught redhanded by the special police in the act of smuggling two members of the Romanov family across the frontier into Finland."

"Two girls in their teens, who never did any harm to anybody—"

"I'm sure you'd say the same of the former Czar's daughters, and no doubt Allen would try to get *them* across the border, if he could."

"That's a mere hypothesis, and in the present case, let me remind you, Captain Allen can plead diplomatic immunity to Russian jurisdiction. He ought not to be held in the Shpalernaia prison without a trial."

"He can no longer plead diplomatic immunity, Mr. Calvert. Allen is, and has been for years, a member of the British SIS—the Secret Intelligence Service. Since the revolution, he has ranked as the number three man in their apparatus in Russia. You know the organisation, I suppose?"

"I've heard of the SIS, and I know it exists solely in opposition to German Intelligence. We're still at war with Germany, Mr. Lenin! And so are you."

Lenin smiled. "The peace treaty will be signed within the next few days," he said.

"Which means that counting the troops withdrawn from Russia

since last September, Germany will be able to throw forty more divisions into her next attack on the Allies in the west."

"Which means, as I see it, the imperialist countries will be weakened, and the world revolution brought nearer, by a still greater slaughter."

Joe's whole head and face seemed to be throbbing. He pressed the handkerchief to the cut above his eye again. To his limited vision the figure of Lenin seemed to swell to a giant size. His reddish beard had grown again, and between the pointed beard and the heavy forehead his features were inscrutable. If the slaughter of tens of thousands meant so little to him, how could Joe Calvert persuade him to spare the life of one Englishman? He said desperately, "If you consider Richard Allen is a criminal—"

"A political criminal, Mr. Calvert; that's why he was arrested by the Cheka and not by the border guards."

"Very well. If you refuse to grant him clemency, or even to give him a fair trial, will you allow me to visit him tonight, in the Shpalernaia?"

Lenin glanced down at the page headed by Joe's identity photograph. "Tonight?" he said. "I thought you were leaving for Helsingfors at ten. You must be a very devoted friend of this man Allen! You shared a flat with him for several years?"

"He's been there, off and on, since his posting to Stockholm. You could say I shared his flat, but not his activities. I'm his friend."

"I've thought of a way to test your friendship," Lenin said. "I can't grant clemency to a counter-revolutionary and let him go free, but neither do I intend to stage a trial for a man like Richard Allen. The one who'll be brought to justice, for the whole world to see, is Nicholas Romanov. What I can do for the man Allen, and I will do it on one condition, is what I did in the case of the Rumanian diplomat: I'll order him to be deported."

Joe moistened his lips. "What's the condition?"

"I'm not a novel reader, Mr. Calvert. Fiction has always appeared to me to have nothing to do with the proletarian struggle. But when I was living in England I did read some novels by a so-called proletarian writer, Charles Dickens. One was called *A Tale of Two Cities*. Have you read it?"

"I have."

"Dickens was not a Marxist writer, naturally. He was a sloppy sentimentalist, like our would-be comrade in arms, Ramsay MacDonald. But one character has always stuck in my memory, though I really don't know why: the English lawyer who went to the Conciergerie prison, and took the place of his friend condemned to die by the guillotine."

"The whole point of the substitution being that Sydney Carton closely resembled the condemned man."

"Whereas you and your friend are quite unlike, and we mustn't strain the credulity of the warders at the Shpalernaia. Oh, and there was one other interesting point: the lawyer—Carton you call him? I'd forgotten that—was in love with his friend's wife. Is there any complication like that in your case?"

It was one of the flashes of insight which gave Lenin his demoniac power over the minds of men. Joe Calvert acknowledged it at the same time as he replied steadily, "Captain Allen is a bachelor like myself."

"I see. So what I propose is this: *we* rid ourselves of a reportedly unresponsive and intractable prisoner, and you do a service to your valued friend, on this condition: that he takes your place on the train tonight, travelling in your name, and keeps your identity until he crosses the Swedish border."

Joe's hand travelled instinctively to the wallet in his inside pocket, which contained the precious travel warrant. "And me?" he said hoarsely. "When can I apply for another permit to leave Russia?"

The big forehead was raised a fraction, the cone of light, so bright in the darkness, caught a gleam of amusement in the small merciless eyes.

"You, Mr. Calvert? I think we may want to keep you with us for a long time yet."

* * *

Less than six weeks from that talk in Lenin's cold, shadowy room, Joe Calvert was finishing dinner with his uncle in a brilliantly lit and overheated suite in the Biltmore Hotel in New York City.

The menu had been of his own choosing: shad roe, grilled steak and french fries, green salad with thousand-island dressing, and chocolate ice-cream. He had thought about it all the way across the Atlantic in a British ship with strict rationing and a captain extremely nervous about submarines.

"Gee whittakers, what a good dinner!" he said when the waiters had wheeled out the service table. His uncle answered, "You can do with a bit of feeding up!"

The senior Joseph Calvert belonged to the same lean and rangy type as his nephew, but even in his youth he had never been such a 'string bean', as he thought of the gaunt young man before him. The kid was twenty-nine, and looked forty, which might do him some good with the old fogeys at State, and certainly his London tailoring did his slimness credit. "You wait until tomorrow night and the spread your mother's getting ready for you. Poor Vinnie—I reckon she started planning it the moment she got the cable with your sailing date."

"I just wish I could speak to them this evening."

"All your dad's fault, he won't have the telephone in the house. Only thing I'm sorry about is, you weren't in Baltimore *last* night to hear the President's great fighting speech in the Armory."

The Sunday papers were scattered on the floor, stacks of them: the words of the President's peroration stared up at Joe from the front page of the *New York Times*:

> Germany has once more said that force, and force alone, shall decide whether justice and peace shall reign in the affairs of men. There is therefore but one response possible from us: Force to the utmost, Force without stint or limit, which shall make Right the law of the world.

"I've listened to an awful lot of great fighting speeches in the past four years," he said wearily.

"You'll feel better after a good night's sleep," his uncle said. "Let's have a highball and relax. Scotch? How much ice? Soda?"

"Just for the hell of it, I'm going to get me some fresh cold water from the spigot." Joe went into the bathroom, came back with his tie loosened, and sprawled in an oversprung, velvet armchair. "Good God," he said, "what luxury! The water runs, the can flushes, the towels are clean—in another minute I'll wake up and find I'm dreaming."

"You had it rough the past few months."

"Not as rough as some."

"Well, in any event, it's a great foundation for the future. (You haven't taken to cigars yet, I see.) And it's your future I came up to New York to discuss with you, because I don't want you *or* me to put a foot wrong when we get back to Foggy Bottom tomorrow morning. First off, I want to check through all the details as to how you got out of Russia. I'm seeing Secretary Lansing in the morning, and we ought to make sure that both our stories jibe."

"There's only one story, uncle. Tell it the way it happened."

"Right! You gave up your seat in the train to this Englishman, and the Reds brought him along in an ambulance. Two guys from the Red Cross had come to the station to tell you good-bye, and when you didn't show they checked around and found you were being held in protective custody at your apartment. Then they just about tore the town apart, and got through to old Dave Francis at Vologda, and at the end of a week the Reds let you get on the freedom train too. Is that about right?"

"Just about. It was Wellwood and Tasker who started it all, and the ambassador was first-rate too. But the one who really helped me to get away was Raymond Robins. All right, shake your head, I used to feel that way about him too—I thought he was some kind of a ham actor, and that was all. But he has the inside track with Trotsky, and he never let up on the kind of international scandal it would make, an American vice-consul in protective custody and all that, until finally they got sick of it at the Smolny and let me go. My guess is they were too busy celebrating their precious treaty with the Germans to bother about the likes of me."

"Brest-Litovsk, and a pack of trouble for the rest of us." Mr. Calvert shook his head. "But let's get back to you. My advice is, soft-pedal Robins when you tell your story. He's coming back next month, and my guess is he won't even be received by the President. Nobody takes him seriously now. As for Sissons, all that stuff he wrote about Lenin and the money he took from Germany is going into the inactive files, where nobody may read it for the next fifty years. Now you're as hot as a pistol, Joe. You did a great job in Russia, and everybody knows it, I've seen to that. I've arranged for you to meet Mr. Lansing, and Newton D. Baker, the Secretary of War. Talk about inside tracks—Secretary

Baker sure has the inside track with the President! A good interview with Mr. Baker, Joe, and you're all set for a really plum job at State—if you talk about the right people and the right things."

"As we say at the Smolny, keep your nose clean."

"How's that again?"

"I'm not sure I want a plum job at State. What did you have in mind?"

"The new Russian desk they're planning to set up in May."

"If I'm not posted back to Europe, I'm going to join the army. How do you think I felt last month in England, when the big attack was on? Our troops in action for the first time? All those German divisions released from Russia, so damned nearly breaking through? I was surprised the British girls didn't snow me under with white feathers—"

"Now take it easy, boy! Take it easy! Maybe I can fix up some sort of a deal with Newton D. Maybe—oh, hell, you kids are all the same! Can't I get it through your fool head that if you stay alive, and yes, okay, keep your nose clean, you just might end up an ambassador yourself?"

* * *

Mr. Calvert's exuberant view of his nephew's future did not seem to be shared by anyone in Washington. Joe reported to his immediate superior in the Foreign Service, was congratulated on five years of good work and told to take a three weeks' vacation before reporting for a language qualification exam. It was all very flat, and his interviews with the Secretary of State and the Secretary of War did not take long. Mr. Lansing was reserved and impatient, Mr. Baker relaxed and cheerful, but both men showed interest in only ten minutes of Joe's four years in Russia—the interview with Lenin. He was made to go over that word for word in the presence of stenographers.

Mr. Baker alone took the subject of the interview a little further, and asked what became of the Englishman, Captain Allen.

"He was badly beaten up in the Shpalernaia, sir; he's been recuperating in Copenhagen."

"Does he know he owes his liberty to you?"

"The British naval attaché was working closely with the

Red Cross men, that night at the Finland Station. He got in touch with Captain Allen later, and gave him a pretty good idea of what happened. I got a very nice letter from Captain Allen while I was in London, and one from his fiancée too."

"No more than you deserved! One more thing, Mr. Calvert: when you left Russia, it wasn't on a deportation order, was it?"

"Just as an ordinary traveller."

"So you weren't declared *persona non grata* by the Bolsheviks?"

"No, sir."

It was an odd little coda to his interview with the Secretary of War, but Joe forgot about it before the train pulled into Baltimore and he saw his father and mother on the platform. It was a very happy reunion, and though his mother of course shed tears and his father pump-handled his arm to a painful degree, they all settled down to each other very quickly, and five years seemed to be bridged even before they were ready for Mrs. Calvert's welcome-home supper. It turned into a kind of running buffet, for the neighbours drifted in and out all through the warm April evening, bringing young people whom Joe remembered as knickerbockered kids on bikes, or young married women with babies in their cribs at home whom he remembered as debutantes at the Bachelors' Cotillions. They were all delighted to have him back. Nobody was at all interested in Russia.

His father was interested in gardening, and in moving little flags on a map of the western battlefront, where General Foch and the Allies had succeeded, but only just, in containing Ludendorff. Mrs. Calvert was interested in the rationing which had been imposed in January—America's 'heatless, meatless, wheatless, sweetless days'—in movie stars like the Biograph Girl, now identified as Mary Pickford, and above all in President Wilson's second marriage to a charming widow. It was all very relaxing, and Joe felt no desire for wilder amusements. He had had an exhausting week of sex and drink in London.

Baltimore had changed very little in five years, and if Joe's old flames were married there was a new crop of 'belles' with delicious slurred voices, pretty faces, and shining bobbed hair. There were more automobiles parked in the pleasant suburban streets, and more telephone subscribers (although not Joe's father), but very little else that was modern: it was hard to believe in Baltimore that the nation was at war. When Joe went to Washington—and his uncle was in almost daily touch by telegram, setting up appointments for him with this or that official who had 'pull'—he was amazed at the swarming streets and office buildings, the pace and tempo of the capital. After Petrograd it took a bit of getting used to.

He was very glad to be out of Petrograd. He appreciated the comforts and the efficiency of his own country as never before. The Russians had got themselves into the devil of a mess, and it was not Joe Calvert's business to care how they got out of it. He considered all the loose ends of his Petrograd life to have been neatly tied up when he got Dick Allen's neck out of the noose and sent him off to Dolly, and no one was left there whom he regretted, or to regret him. Only it was curious how often, as the beautiful spring days went by, and the dogwood and fruit blossom flowered in the public gardens and by the ornamental waters of Washington, he found himself thinking of the city on the Neva—of the Fourth Line, and the smell of tar, salt and linden—even of the maddening, dirty, exciting corridors of the Smolny.

The men he met in Washington were vitally interested in Russia, but not in the Russia Joe Calvert had known so short a time before. The emphasis had shifted from Petrograd to Siberia. This was not because of the imprisonment of the Romanovs, for any Congressman knew that to evince the slightest sympathy for Nicholas the Bloody was a quick way to lose the Jewish vote, but because of a new development during the weekend when President Wilson made his 'Force to the utmost' speech against Germany: the beginning of Japanese armed intervention in Siberia.

It started very quietly. With an immensely valuable stockpile of Allied war material on the wharves at Vladivostok. With a few Allied warships in the harbour, keeping an eye on it. With a few 'incidents' between Communists and Asiatic shopkeepers, and a few brawls between seamen, nothing out of the ordinary in an ocean port. Then, on an April day, a few hundred Japanese Marines were set ashore "to protect Japanese property". It was a very small, token force, and there was no fighting, nothing to suggest any great international repercussions—

The same situation as at Sarajevo.

One day after he had been on home leave for two weeks,

Joe received a telegram from his uncle, summoning him to Washington: "come quickest," the message ran, "important news." Mr. Calvert's messages were always urgent, but Joe went off to the train in good spirits; he thought there might be word of his next posting. He found, as soon as he met his uncle, that Secretary Newton D. Baker had arranged for him to meet President Wilson at the White House.

Joe's first feeling was one of consternation, his second, that if he'd known he would have worn a different tie.

"I told you Newton D. was a great fixer," Mr. Calvert chuckled as they walked up Pennsylvania Avenue, "but I sure kept my fingers crossed yesterday. The Cabinet meeting was cancelled, and I thought maybe today's appointments would be cancelled too, after the President hurt his hand in that damned tank."

"Hurt his hand in a *tank*?"

"Yeah, that show tank they set up, something to do with the Liberty Bond drive, I guess. The injury wasn't mentioned in the press, but Mr. Wilson's hand was badly burned on some bearing, or something he was pulling himself up by, when he was inspecting the tank yesterday morning."

Joe stopped in his stride. "D'you think it was the work of terrorists?" he said.

"Terrorists? In *Washington*?"

"Well, uncle, why would any part of a stationary tank be hot enough to burn a person, unless there was a deliberate hook-up in the electrical system?"

"Nonsense, boy, it was an accident, Mr. Baker told me so himself. He was the only one who got to see the President after it happened." They walked on rapidly. "Terrorists, huh? Seems to me you spent too long in Petrograd."

Joe laughed. He remembered Dick Allen telling him long ago that he was getting Russian fever, like everybody else. When you hear a bang, you think it's a bomb. A show tank, wired up for the Presidential visit—it didn't sound like an accident.

"Now don't get started on terrorists," said Mr. Calvert crossly, as they parted at the gates of the White House. "Don't mention the Romanovs. Just answer the questions he puts to you—he's a great question and answer boy—and say, there's one sure-fire way to know if you've got his interest, it's when he puts the flowers on the floor. What flowers? The roses, or whatever, that the new Mrs. Wilson fixes in a bowl on his desk with her own hands. Fresh every morning, and of course he doesn't want to hurt her feelings, but what he likes is a bare desk, all the time. And when he's really interested in what you're saying, he sets the rose-bowl on the carpet and gets into his stride."

Except for the roses the desk was bare, with one folder on its polished surface. That was the only thing the large airy room of the President of the United States, Commander-in-Chief of the armed forces, had in common with the little room at Smolny, where Lenin believed himself to be making a new nation, and the man with the lean Scottish face who gave Joe a courteous greeting was Lenin's exact opposite in habit of mind and heritage. There were no soldiers with fixed bayonets outside President Wilson's door; nothing but the flag behind his chair and the Presidential seal to indicate his office, and yet Joe Calvert knew that in two months of his own thirtieth year, from the Smolny to the White House, he had travelled between the two poles of the world's power.

"I hope your hand is better, Sir," he said diffidently. When the President was seated the injured hand lay rather inertly on the desk top, expertly bandaged and taped with snowy lint.

"Much better today, but it's still throbbing a bit," said the President. "It was a silly thing to happen, all my own fault." He smiled. "The last time I saw you, Mr. Calvert, you were a sophomore at Princeton, trying out for the team."

Joe Calvert was sophisticated enough to know that the 'recollection' stunt was the one politicians pulled most often, implying not so much a good memory as a well-trained team of secretaries, and yet it always worked. He had only seen Woodrow Wilson on the public platform since he ceased to be the president of Princeton University: he had almost forgotten the younger, comparatively carefree man who had been such an impassioned, shouting, cheering supporter of Princeton football. "I didn't make the team, Sir," he said.

"Not that team, no; but you played well for our side in Russia. I've been reading your final report with great interest." He opened the folder, and Joe braced himself for the usual questions about his meeting with Lenin. But the President wasted no time in going over that ground: he had the written account before him, and that was enough. He started the question and answer conversation which Joe's uncle had warned him to expect.

What did Mr. Calvert know of General Alexeiev, the former Czar's Chief of Staff, who had led the first armed opposition to Bolshevism? Of Admiral Kolchak, a potential leader, who was on his way back to Russia via Peking? Of the Cossack Ataman, Kaledin, whom the Allies were backing in South Russia? Of the general called Skoropadski, who seemed to be siding with the Germans in their occupation of the Ukraine? Was there any hope that Kerensky might lead the fight again?

"I don't think so," said Joe. "He escaped to Finland in January, about the time the Communists murdered the Kadet leaders in their hospital beds. It was rumoured that he was back in Petrograd in disguise, but no reliable informant can swear to having seen him."

"Pity. We sunk a lot of dollars in Mr. Kerensky . . . You were in Finland yourself, of course, on the way home. What's your opinion of General Mannerheim?"

The President's line of questioning was perfectly clear to Joe. The Commander-in-Chief, who must hesitate to divert any part of the American war effort from the western front, was now being forced to consider military intervention in Russia. Mannerheim was the only White General who had really tackled the Red menace, on the smaller scale of his own land, and Joe Calvert said as much.

'He gave me lunch, Sir, in his railroad coach, and a safe conduct through his lines to Torneå-Haparanda. I could see he felt the civil war was as good as won then, even before von der Goltz brought in the Germans on his side."

"The British put Marines ashore at Murmansk last month, in case the Germans advanced that far north."

"I should say we've nothing to fear from a German advance through Finland as long as Mannerheim is in command. But what happens when he wins the war is anybody's guess. He's not the head of government, Mr. Svinhufvud is, and it was Svinhufvud who went to Berlin and came to an agreement with the Germans."

"Ye-es," the President drawled. "I haven't been given an appreciation of that aspect of the matter." He moved his bandaged hand and winced.

"Can I help you, Sir?"

"If you'd put this bowl of roses on the floor. Thank you." Mr. Wilson stretched his arms across the desk top and flexed the shoulders which bore so much responsibility. He asked Joe Calvert the key question:

"In your own view, is an Allied intervention in Russia likely to succeed?"

Joe looked rather desperately round the stately room. It was very quiet, except for the hum of a mower in the gardens of the White House. Mrs. Wilson's roses were so perfect that not a petal had fallen when Joe set them on the floor.

"Mr. President, I'm not a military expert, and I haven't been in Russia half as long as some other members of the Service—"

"Mr. Calvert, in the White House time is not measured by weeks or months or years, but by deep human experience. And I think your experience in Russia went very deep with you. Don't be afraid to speak your mind."

"Well then, frankly, I don't think a military intervention against the Communists is likely to work out. The Allies—the Associated Power would get no support from the Russian generals, because they're already quarrelling among themselves, and landing small forces at so many different points means no co-ordination. And then the Communists are certain to make a great appeal to patriotism. Yes, Sir, I know Lenin came to power on the peace plank, but he'll kick it over if the issue's big enough, and Trotsky just might turn out to be some kind of a military genius. He licked the Red Guards into shape fast enough; with new enemies to face I think he'd do the same with the Red Army."

"Ye-es," the President drawled again. "That's very clear. Thank you." He looked beyond Joe for a moment, out of the window, as if he were seeing as far as Vladivostok. Then, with a brief glance at the folder on his desk, he said, "I admired your persevering attendance at the Duma, Mr. Calvert. I read a digest of your letters to your uncle, occasionally; they became more vivid as you became more proficient in Russian. What took you to the gallery of the Tauride Palace, week after week?"

"I got interested in it, Sir."

"Yes. Well, as Mr. Lenin dissolved the Constituent Assembly

by force of arms when his own party failed to win the elections, I doubt if anyone will be going to the Tauride Palace for some time to come." He paused. "Mr. Calvert, I want you to go back to Russia in a few weeks' time."

"To Vologda, Sir?" It was a horrible thought. Back at Vologda on the Trans-Siberian railway, cooped up with that grumbling poker school of refugee ambassadors! He was reassured by President Wilson's smile.

"Mr. Baker thought you would do well at Vologda, say as assistant military attaché. Your English friend, Captain Allen, found that quite an elastic term! But we don't want to send you back by Petrograd. You could be very useful at Vladivostok, working with Mr. Caldwell, and as of the first of April you would have full consular rank."

"Thank you, Sir." The President stood up, and Joe did too. The interview was over. Against all his expectations, but perhaps not altogether against his hopes, he was being posted back to Russia.

"Mr. Baker told me of your wish to join the army, which does you credit, Mr. Calvert. We can't second a valuable man like you from the Foreign Service at the present time. But if things develop as we anticipate in Siberia, I think I can arrange for you to be commissioned," said the Commander-in-Chief.

27

AT THE SAME TIME as the American Cabinet was considering armed intervention in Siberia, Simon Hendrikov achieved his goal, and entered the vast province beyond the Ural mountains.

It had taken him nearly six months to get as far as Tiumen, within two hundred miles of his princess, after his strength had been carefully built up from a neglected wound, semi-starvation and exposure to the cold, until he was able to sustain the character assigned him by the leader in the most competent plot yet devised to rescue the imperial family.

Simon was travelling on the Trans-Siberian railway in the comparative luxury of what had once been a 'soft' coach for six, and was now occupied by only sixteen people, all provided with food packets and in some cases with flasks of cold tea as well. He was posing as a sackman, one of the black marketeers who left Petrograd with empty sacks and came back with bulging ones, sacks filled with food from the provinces where food was still obtainable, but Simon's sack was far from empty on the outward trip. It contained the uniform of a Red Guards officer, which he intended to wear after he was through Tiumen, and the body of the former owner was probably now polluting the Neva after having been tipped into the appropriately named Drainage Canal.

In the first frenzy of Lenin's revolution, when officers like Simon Hendrikov were liable to arrest on sight as counter-revolutionaries, he had gone to earth on the banks of the Drainage Canal at the point where it flowed into the Neva near the Lavra, the great complex of Alexander Nevski which contained eleven churches and four cemeteries, all of which had for many years offered a refuge to fugitives from justice. There, until the snows began late in November, he had slept in the Tikhvin cemetery, moving with other shadows like himself from the tombs of Tchaikovski and Glinka to the tomb of Dostoievski, and creeping out by day for a bowl of kasha or a patty and tea at the kind of eating shop where the down-and-outs of the Lavra went. When sleeping rough became impossible he found a bed of sorts in the attic of what had been a beautiful home on the Millionnaia, abandoned by its former owners, and now the resort of ex-officers like himself, anarchists who were misfits even in a Communist society, and professional thieves. The latter helped him to obtain forged papers and a forged labour book, without which he could neither obtain work nor leave the city.

Simon had realised, within a few days of his return to Petrograd, that he could never hope to go off alone to Tobolsk and, single-handed, carry off his princess from her Siberian prison. For that he needed funds and helpers. Some time after Christmas he learned from one of the vagrants of the Millionnaia that the former Grand Marshal of the Court, Count Benckendorff, had organised a supply line to the imperial family, whose own funds had run out since the fall of the Provisional Government. They had dismissed many of their servants, and were now actually in debt to the tradespeople of Tobolsk. He went to see the old gentleman, whom age and infirmity had prevented from accompanying the prisoners to Siberia, and learned that his stepson, Prince Dolgoruki, was the ADC in attendance on the Czar (as Benckendorff put it) and thus one of the chief links between him and the outside world. Simon also heard for the first time of the Brotherhood of St. John of Tobolsk, and eagerly asked to be told how to join them.

The Grand Marshal shook his head. "Be patient for a few more weeks, my dear Hendrikov," he said. "I've sent half a dozen young men like yourself to Tiumen, and so far not one of them has come back to give us an accurate report of any real attempt at a rescue or an escape. Wait until we know more of the facts." He sighed. "I'm not quite satisfied with our agent in Tiumen—Rasputin's son-in-law."

"I thought we'd heard the last of Rasputin," said Simon. "What's the son-in-law's name?"

"Soloviev. He seems genuine enough, but—I'm sending one more officer to Tiumen next week to size up the situation. Would you like to have a talk with him before he goes? Vassili Yakovlev is his name—he was in the ill-fated *Askelod*, at Murmansk."

"Commander Yakovlev?" said Simon, brightening. "I've met

him once or twice, and he did my family a very good turn last summer. Can I meet him here?"

"I would rather not," said Benckendorff. "I think the friends sheltering my wife and me will begin to object if too many young men are seen coming and going; we don't want to invite the attentions of the Cheka."

Eventually Simon and Yakovlev met in a *traktir* near the Warsaw Station, which was always full of people hoping to obtain travel warrants, so full that two men, one very shabby, talking in a corner, passed unnoticed. Yakovlev, in civilian clothes, looked healthy and prosperous. He was extremely guarded with the younger man, giving away no details about himself or his mission to Tiumen, but practically ordering Simon to "Get out of that thieves' kitchen on the Millionaia and get yourself back into condition. I can find you a job, if you've got a labour book. It won't be worth much, but you'll draw decent rations, and if you can hold it down for a month, I'll be here for another talk exactly four weeks from today."

"I'll hold it down." Simon was not so sure that he could, when he found out what the job was: medical orderly in a huge general hospital near the Baltiski Station. The building was nearly a hundred years old, and almost falling down, the wooden floors and walls were impossible to keep clean. Simon carried pails of water, emptied sluices, scrubbed the operating theatre and acted in emergencies as a stretcher bearer. He loathed the work, but he soon realised how well Yakovlev had placed him. The Baltiski General was a far better hideout than any abandoned house, especially since the dangerous state of the dark streets, where men were assaulted and even murdered for whatever they had in their pockets, had caused Trotsky to order the Red Guards to clean up the robbers' dens. Nobody questioned a diligent medical orderly, at a time when a typhus epidemic had begun to hit the city, largely as a result of the water shortage and the condition of the sewers. Also the rations, while coarse, were regular, and Simon's health improved in spite of the long hours, When he was given a big bowl of cabbage soup and a hunk of fresh bread for supper, he sat over the food in torpid animal pleasure. It was only in dreams that he remembered another hospital, where he had been a Palace Pet, with an empress and her lovely daughters at his own bedside.

When he kept his appointment with Yakovlev, he saw satisfaction in the other man's eyes, but Yakovlev said nothing but, "Wait for ten minutes and then follow me up to the Fontanka," before he drained his glass of tea and pushed his way out through the crowded *traktir*. Simon, as he obeyed, could see the man walking slowly, trim and well-knit in his decent overcoat and fur hat, up the long, dreary avenue which led to the Fontanka on its way to meet the Neva at Galerni Island. It was a dismal part of Petrograd, and in the steadily-falling snow there was no one to spy on the two when Simon caught up with Yakovlev on the embankment of the Fontanka Canal. There Yakovlev held out his hand.

"You've got back in shape, well done," he said briefly. "I thought you would, but I had to make dead sure. We don't want any weaklings in our operation."

"There *is* an operation, then?" said Simon eagerly. "Have you been to Tobolsk?"

"I didn't go as far as Tobolsk, because I didn't want anyone we may meet there to remember my face when we go in as a group." It was still a Romanov face, Simon thought, although Yakovlev was dark where most of the Romanovs were fair; but the look was there and made him think of Olga. "I've been to Tiumen," Yakovlev went on. "I met some of the incurable romantics who call themselves the Brotherhood of St. John and couldn't rescue a dog from a burning kennel, let alone the Czar of Russia."

"Did you hear how *he* is—how they are?"

"Well enough, but kept in very close confinement now. Living on army rations. Bullied by a real swine of a Commissar, Hokrianov, a former stoker. I only wish I'd had him in the *Askelod*."

"And Soloviev, Rasputin's son-in-law?"

"A fake and a charlatan, like Rasputin before him. Nearly all the money poor old Benckendorff collected for the imperial family has stuck to Lieutenant Soloviev's greasy paws. So now I'm sure of that, I mean to bypass Soloviev, and mount the rescue operation on my own. With hand-picked men. Do you still want to be one of them?"

"I do. I'll follow you, Yakovlev—I haven't forgotten what you did for my parents and my sister, that day in the Fourth Line."

Yakovlev smiled. "Can you ride, with that arm?"

"I don't see why not."

"Because we'll have to take them out by road, before the river traffic opens. And the Czarina's a liability; she can hardly move now, except in a wheel-chair."

"And the boy?"

"In splendid health."

"Well, then, the sooner the better, I should say."

"We'll have to wait to operate out of Moscow, after the government goes there next month."

"What's the government got to do with it?"

"I'm a government employee. Rather a valued one, I think." He smiled grimly at Simon's look of surprise. "You see, I handled the problem rather differently from you and all the death or glory boys. When I came on leave from Murmansk last summer I let it be known I was a convert to the gospel preached by our own ratings—who killed my Captain in the first revolution and shot the Admiral later on—and when the *Sovnarkom* took over, nobody sang the *Internationale* louder than Vassili Yakovlev. I've a nice berth at the Admiralty—Commissariat section, providing double rations and extra vodka for those swine down at Kronstadt, whom Trotsky called in my presence the fine flower of the Russian revolution."

"I couldn't do that," said Simon flatly.

"Do what?"

"Act a part like that, every day of my life."

"I don't suppose you could, Hendrikov; every man to his trade. By the way, my immediate superior at the Admiralty is Captain Gordienko. You may remember him as a petty officer in the *Standart*, back in '14."

"*Remember* him!" Simon remembered Gordienko, posted at the rail to help Alexis aboard, on the day the *Standart* started her last summer cruise, and how nearly he and the sailor, Derevenko, had let the child fall between them. Had that been a put-up job, like so many other things? "What makes me want to vomit," he said, "is to think how many traitors *they* had round about them, even among those they called their friends."

Yakovlev nodded, and the Romanov look was clear upon his face. "That's why I'm working for *Sovnarkom*, and cheering Comrade Lenin," he said. "They taught us some useful lessons in infiltration."

And that was why, on a night in April, a sackman with a Red Guard uniform in his sack struggled out of an overcrowded train at Tiumen.

* * *

Yakovlev was not to know that what had caused the closer confinement of the Romanovs, with increasing spites and deprivations, was their last great pleasure—the snow mountain.

The young people had enjoyed it for exactly a month before the day when their parents for the first time climbed up the ascent ladder and stood upon the platform at the top. It was no wonder the guards stared and muttered, for Alexandra Feodorovna had never been seen out of doors since the church privileges ended after Christmas, but it was a sunny March morning, and she was encouraged to hobble out of the house on her husband's arm.

There had been recent orders from Petrograd about the disposition of the guard which had brought the prisoners all the way from Czarskoe Selo. The unit of the 4th Regiment of Sharpshooters was to be withdrawn, and replaced by more politically reliable men, young troops from the neighbourhood of the capital, and on that pleasant March day they were to start the long trek back to the railroad at Tiumen. They had always been friendly to their prisoners, even kind, and the goodbyes in the yard—especially to Marie, their favourite—were cordial. Then Alexandra, who had snubbed so many aristocrats in her time, had the unlucky idea of climbing to the top of the snow mountain to wave to these humble men as they marched off.

She stood there, leaning on her husband's arm and Tatiana's, for long enough to see them go, and then to watch Alexis make one descent of the chute in Nagorny's clasp. The boy was so delighted to have his mother watching them that the fun on the snow mountain grew fast and furious as the afternoon wore on. Tea was a cheerful meal. Meantime, the soldiers' soviet was holding a meeting to discuss the unprecedented action of Citizeness Romanova.

Such discussions took a long time, for each one opened with a debate on the right to debate the matter in hand, and in this case there were two schools of thought, and everybody had to have his say. Some of the comrades thought Alexandra had climbed the mountain to signal to counter-revolutionaries mysteriously hidden in the street. Others believed she had exposed herself to the risk of assassination, for which her guards would of course be blamed. After a long, enjoyable evening of argument and speechification, the two schools united in a unanimous decision: the snow mountain must be destroyed.

Demolition work began next morning and went on all day. Picks were required, and a great deal of brute strength. The work had been well done, and it seemed as if a few of the toiling soldiers came to regret their decision, for some shame-faced looks were directed at Alexis and his younger sisters, standing disconsolate in the snow. Hokriakov, the Bolshevik Commissar, came out with his colleague Rodionov to gloat over the children's dismay. He was an ignorant and brutal man, with the vindictive mediocrity of many of those like him who had climbed to minor authority in the Party, and he enjoyed swaggering through the rooms of the Romanovs in the black leather jacket which had come to be recognised as the uniform of the Cheka.

He took up a heavy hammer to lend a hand in the work of destruction. No one was quite sure what happened, and certainly none of the children were anywhere near him, but the snow mountain had been sufficiently undermined for a large block of ice to slide forward unexpectedly and knock the hammer out of Hokriakov's hand. It fell on his foot, and the pain was sharp. Hokriakov hopped on the other foot, swearing.

Olga came forward from her place in the shelter of the stone entrance to the house.

"Let me have a look at that, Commissar," she said. "Your foot may be bleeding."

"So what would you like to do—rub salt in it?"

"Don't be ridiculous; come in and take your boot off," she said, with such authority that Hokriakov followed her into a little cloakroom beside the door, and with an oath took his high boot off. Olga gently removed a matted sock and studied a singularly unpleasant foot.

"It's a very bad bruise, and you may be lame for a day or two," she said. "Anastasia, be nice, and run to the kitchen for a basin of hot water."

"Isn't my foot clean enough for Your High-and-Mightiness?" growled the ex-stoker.

"I've seen dirtier feet in hospital," she told him. "We clean them up before we put the bandage on."

She washed the injured foot carefully, applied some ointment on a lint pad, and made the bandage fast. The Commissar, like Anastasia holding the first-aid box, looked on in silence.

"I never thought the day would come when I'd have a Romanov at *my* feet," he said with an attempt at swagger. But when Olga drew the sock on, and looked round for the boot, he took her chin into his powerful fingers and tilted her face up. The blonde hair fell in strands across her forehead, under the knitted cap she had not stopped to pull off, and the blue eyes were steadfast on his own. "You're not such a bad wench, Romanova, after all," he said, and added a word to which he was not accustomed—"Thanks."

"I hope you've all heard about the latest flirtation—Olga and the Commissar," said Anastasia when the family assembled for tea. There was a shout of laughter. The joke lasted the whole evening, for the evenings were sometimes terribly long. They tried to break the monotony with charades and little plays, Nicholas and Anastasia surprisingly good in a Chekov play, *The Bear*, and Alexis willing to play any part—even a girl's. But the fun had gone out of his days with the destruction of the snow mountain, and Joy was getting old now, and less willing to play in the icy yard. Olga invented a game called Happy Times, which sometimes amused him in the evening. Each person had to recall some time, or place, or meal which had been pleasant in the past, and the boy liked asking questions about the years before he was born, the games his sisters played then, the lessons they had learned.

"Was my christening a Happy Time, Olga?" he asked when they had gone through every court ceremonial she could remember.

"It was for me, because I was your godmother, and delighted to have a little court dress made specially for the occasion."

"And my godfathers were the whole Russian Army."

"Not exactly," said Nicholas quietly. "All the combatant soldiers in the war against Japan."

"Oh yes, that war. I don't expect anybody had as many godfathers as me, ever."

"No. But I'll tell you who didn't have a Happy Time," said Olga, "and that was the old lady who carried you to the font. She was so blind and lame they were afraid she'd drop you in and drown you. So she wore a pair of tennis shoes, with rubber soles, under a satin dress—"

"I bet everybody else thought she was crazy."

It was not easy to play Happy Times, when each day was so dark and so monotonous, and such news as reached them was increasingly bad. Not a word was heard of the old empress and her family in the Crimea, but it was said that the Grand Duchess Ella had been arrested in her own convent in Moscow, and the Grand Duke Michael taken from his palace at Gachina to house arrest at Perm. The only good news was of Dmitri, who when the Bolsheviks took power went from the Persian front to Teheran and a refuge in the British Legation. He had applied for a commission in the British Army. "Oh, good for Dmitri! Good for him!" cried Olga with some of her old exuberance when she knew that Dmitri, at least, was free.

Amazingly, their parents continued to bask in their fantasy of freedom. The Brotherhood of St. John must act soon, before the thaw set in and while the frozen rivers could still be crossed by vehicles; Our Dear Martyr's son-in-law had promised, and was sure to keep his word. The Soviet government was in Moscow now, and the Germans had sent an ambassador to Moscow, Count von Mirbach: there was a whisper that Mirbach, too, was trying to organise a rescue. "Well, really!" said Alexandra Feodorovna, "I must decline to take advantage of the Kaiser's kind arrangements! After what they've done to your father I'd rather die in Russia than be rescued by the Germans!"

"You're tempting Providence, mamma," said Olga.

"It's not as if we'd be going to *live* in Germany," coaxed Tatiana. "And honestly we do need somebody to help us out of here."

"Where shall we live, we've never discussed that," said Marie. "Mamma, you don't want to go to Paris, and we obviously can't go to London now. Why don't we plan to go to Copenhagen? The Danish cousins are good fun."

"They haven't lifted a finger to help us, any more than our English cousins have," said Alexandra bitterly. "One place I will *not* go to is Switzerland. Imagine living in Swiss hotels as ex-royalties, like the Serbs and the Greeks; imagine being snapshotted by tourists and interviewed for the American press!"

"I'd love to give interviews and allow my picture to be taken by anyone who wanted! I think Switzerland sounds like fun," said Anastasia to Olga, later.

"Switzerland sounds like heaven." Olga was growing frightened, though she never showed it. Instead of replacements from the Czarskoe Selo garrison, the new and augmented force at the mansion was composed of Red Guards from Omsk, a strongly Bolshevik town, who shouted obscenities and scratched filthy drawings on the fence, whenever the girls went into the yard. The Commissar had forgotten his brief gratitude, and egged them on. Olga felt that a ring of hate was slowly tightening round them, from which the Romanovs never would escape.

Poor Marie regretted, to the end of her life, that in a final dredging up of memories for Happy Times, she was the one who told Alexis about a summer journey when the four small girls were allowed to get out of the imperial train to picnic and play, and their play had taken the form of sliding down the grass of the railroad embankment on silver trays taken from the dining car. She told him how the courtiers had joined in, and how one old general had looked particularly silly, coasting along in gala uniform with all his medals, but Alexis cared nothing for the general: he wanted to try sliding on a tray himself. And perhaps because they had all, even Nagorny, begun to take his good health for granted, nobody was aware that Alexis had borrowed a tin tray from the kitchen and was about to use it as if the staircase was an indoor version of the snow mountain.

Until they heard the crash at the bottom of the stairs.

He was carried to his room and Nagorny undressed him, while Dr. Botkin stood ready to examine him for any bumps or lacerations. He had a bruise on his forehead, which was bleeding slightly, and a lump the size of a hen's egg on one knee—just the kind of damage an ordinary schoolboy might do to himself at any rough sport, and so his sisters bracingly told him, at the same time as they were telling him it was nearly bedtime anyway, and why didn't he have a supper tray in bed?

But before long the forced cheerfulness was at an end, the dark blue swellings made their appearance, and the dreadful haemophilia, always latent, declared itself again. The bruised blood seeped from the knee along the thigh, the leg cramped fast against the thin boyish body, and his mother, beside herself with grief and anxiety, was praying to the soul of Rasputin to intercede in heaven for her child.

It was the worst attack Alexis had suffered for six years. The time aboard the *Standart*, the time of the nasal haemorrhage, had been nothing like as bad as this. Dr. Botkin tried everything that had helped in the past, and even the Commissars, once they were sure the boy was not shamming, told him to draw on the local hospital for anything he might need. But there was nothing to be done, nothing but wait and hope that, as some physicians believed had happened without the prayers of Rasputin, the haemophilic bleeding would stop of its own accord. Later, the torture of leg irons might have to be imposed to release the locked limb from its rigid cramp against the body; in the meantime, with Dr. Botkin always reluctant to administer morphine, the poor boy's only release from pain was fainting.

He was very brave for the first two days, and then pain mastered him. They heard him crying and then screaming, high spasms of screaming, until finally, as his anguished sisters huddled in their cold room, they heard him sob:

"I want to die, mother! I can't bear such awful pain much longer! Mother, please, I want to die!"

It was the voice of an adult human being, in the grip of torment. But his mother's voice, hoarse with tears, soothed him with the words of his infancy:

"Hush, Baby, be agooweeone. Hush, my Sunbeam, mother's holding you fast. Sleep well and be agooweeone."

* * *

By the twenty-second of April the worst of the attack was over. Alexis was unable to stand, much less walk, and his old bedridden life began again, but he was out of pain. That was the day when a small troop of horse cantered up to the governor's mansion at Tobolsk, and Alexandra Feodorovna, smiling for the first time for many days, limped into the girls' room to tell them the rescuers were there at last.

"They're in the Red Guards uniform, but I *know* they're members of the Brotherhood!" she exulted. "Good Russian men—some of them mere boys. I haven't seen such kindly faces for a long time. Now they'll be in touch with us at once—"

"They'll stable their horses and have some food first, whoever they are," said Olga.

"And if they really are our rescuers," said Tatiana, to humour her mother, "don't you think we ought to start doing what we've often talked about—sew some of our jewels into the clothes we're going to wear?"

The selection of the garments and the jewels kept them occupied for an hour, while Alexis dozed in the next room, until a maid came to beg 'Her Imperial Majesty' to go downstairs. There, Kobilinski was waiting to present to both the Majesties an emissary from the Moscow Soviet, Special Commissar Vassili Yakovlev.

It hardly sounded like a rescuer, but the prisoners felt some degree of confidence in the well-built, well-spoken man in the dress of an ordinary seaman, who so obviously belonged to the world they had left behind. Over tea, he made social conversation, showing some knowledge of the theatre and the arts; he was extremely courteous to the girls. He only seemed disconcerted once, when on enquiring for the missing member of the family he was told that Alexis Nicolaievich had been seriously ill, and might be confined to bed for weeks. "I shall bring my own doctor to see him in the morning," he declared. Yes, he had a doctor, and a hundred and fifty men, fully armed with machine-guns, and a telegraph operator to keep him in direct touch with the Kremlin.

"He's a very pleasant fellow, but he's not a rescuer," said Nicholas, when the unexpected guest had gone.

"At least he's a Special Commissar," said Olga, determinedly cheerful. "I only hope he outranks Hokriakov, and sends away that horrible crowd from Omsk."

"I wonder what he came for," mused the Czar. "He reminds me of somebody, I don't know who."

The Special Commissar came back next day with an army doctor who visited Alexis, conferred with Dr. Botkin, and went away. The Romanovs were still completely in the dark about Yakovlev's mission ,and what the powers of a Special Commissar might be. These were revealed next day, and only to Colonel Kobilinski, after prolonged telegraphic exchanges with the Kremlin, but not until Commissar Yakovlev had had a few words with Comrade Hendrikov in the neglected saddle-room which was one of the outbuildings of the governor's mansion.

"It's no good, Simon, that poor kid can't be moved. Our man is certain of that, and his sisters must stay with him."

"Oh God, the kid again! The measles, and now this! Can't he be packed into a *tarantass*, with his mother?"

"The doctors told me jolting in a *tarantass* would be the death of him. Sounds a bit extreme, but that's what they said—"

"And I suppose there's no question of leaving him behind?"

"You know them better than that."

In the glow from a stable lantern, their only light, Simon's face was very pale. His head was aching, his heart torn with the strain of being so near to his princess and still unable to set her free. "So what are you going to do?" he said.

"I'm going to take the Czar and possibly the Czarina. I *must* leave with him, I've my orders from Sverdlov, and the Red Guards they sent along with us at the last minute know what those orders are. It's leave with him or be shot ourselves—there's no other alternative."

Simon jumped at the Czarina's name. "Then if Her Majesty goes," he said, "one of the Grand Duchesses must go with her. They'd never send a sick woman off on a trip like this without one of her daughters. For God's sake, Vassili Vaslevich, make sure the Grand Duchess Olga accompanies her mother!"

"It's because of her you're here, isn't it?"

"Did I make it obvious, when we were talking back in Petrograd?"

"Not at all. It was—something those ruffians from Kronstadt shouted, when I was hustling them downstairs after they broke into your father's flat."

"Dolly told me about that."

"Simon, I promise you, I'll do everything I can. But you know you gave me your word to follow me, and my first job's to get the Czar clear, to spare him the public trial Sverdlov and Lenin are setting up in Moscow. I've got to persuade those Reds they sent along with us that I've my orders to go east to Omsk, not west along the track to Moscow, and even if we get to Omsk we've still got half the Empire to cross before we're within sight of the Pacific. We have the guns and I'm prepared to stand and fight along the way if I must, but let's get out of Tobolsk without bloodshed. Agreed?"

"Agreed, if Olga Nicolaievna can go too."

Next day, it seemed as if she might. By that time Yakovlev had produced all his impressive authorisations from Moscow: the letters signed by Jacob Sverdlov, the President of the All-

Russian Congress of Soviets, whose rank in the Party was almost equal to Lenin's, threatening Colonel Kobilinski and all the men under his command with instant death if the Special Commissar's orders were not carried out. These orders were to take the entire Romanov family under escort to Moscow, and they represented months of acting a part, of intrigue in high places, of sheer bluff, by the one man who had the strength to plan, and so far to carry out his plan, the escape for the prisoners which Kerensky had vaguely visualised—along the clear track of the Trans-Siberian to Vladivostok and Japan.

Yakovlev's master plan had foundered on the building of the snow mountain, and its aftermath.

The order for the Czar to go to Moscow dissipated at a blow all the Christian resignation his wife had shown during more than a year in captivity. She raged as she had raged in the days of Rasputin—as if Kobilinski, Yakovlev, Nicholas himself, were the Ministers she made and unmade with a stroke of the pen in the months before Rasputin's murder. He should not go, she raved; and when Tatiana persuaded her that he *must* go, they were powerless to prevent it, she insisted in outspoken language that she must go as well. He had thrown away the crown, she cried, when he was all alone at Mohilev, and God knew what he might say or do or sign in Moscow if she were not by his side to prompt him and advise! Then she was told that she might go, with the Grand Duchess Olga to keep her company: the Czar might take Prince Dolgoruki or General Tatischev. She ordered Olga to prepare for the journey, and went to throw herself upon her son's bed, and clutch the weeping, bewildered Alexis to her breast.

For a few hours, while the preparations were going on, Simon Hendrikov thought the miracle had happened, and that he would hold Olga in his arms again. He felt light-headed at the very thought. He must have been light-headed in fact, for his face and hands were burning, and at the evening meal his tongue seemed thick in his mouth when he exchanged a few guarded words with the other members of Yakovlev's silent company. He even stumbled when he went up a rickety wooden stair to their temporary sleeping place to put his few possessions in an old valise. Everything was strapped up, they were all ready to go.

"But are *they* ready?" he said in an undertone to Yakovlev

in the deserted mess hall. "I thought we were going to leave before midnight."

They both listened to the soughing of the wind. It had the sound of spring, and they heard the drip of water from the eaves.

"The roads are going to be liquid mud," Yakovlev said. ". . . They had tea at half past ten, they said goodbye to everybody before half past eleven, and now it's nearly two. God *knows* what's causing the hold-up—"

"You can't hurry them, I learned that at Livadia—"

"Yes, but this isn't a holiday, it's a matter of life or death."

What was holding them up was Alexandra's last-minute decision that Olga should not be the daughter to accompany her to Moscow. "Olga's the eldest, and has the most authority with Colonel Kobilinski," she argued feverishly. "With Baby ill, she's the right one to take the responsibility. Olga and Tania, together, can manage the whole household and look after Baby too. Olga, what do you think yourself? Shouldn't Marie be the one to come with papa and me?"

"As you wish, mother; only the Commissar did say it should be me."

"As if it mattered!" her mother said impatiently. "He only meant one of you girls; any one. Papa and I alone will be expected to talk to this man Sverdlov and his confederates, neither you nor Prince Dolgoruki will be asked for your opinion. Marie, hurry and get ready to come with us. All the rest of you do what you can to help her."

It was after three when Prince Dolgoruki came out and said that 'Their Imperial Majesties' were ready to start the journey. The *tarantasses*, rough Siberian springless carts in which two passengers and a driver could travel in discomfort, had been waiting in the yard for hours. The horses were brought out and backed in between the shafts, the mounts of the escort were led out of the stable. There were nearly two hundred of them now, for a detachment of Colonel Kobilinski's men had insisted on riding rearguard: they were openly suspicious of the strangers from Moscow.

Simon sat his horse with the reins gathered up in his left hand; his right arm, like his head, felt numb. He saw the servants putting a mattress into one of the carts. That would be for the Czarina to lie down on, with Olga sitting by her side. He was glad to see the servants had brought rugs and blankets too.

The Czar came out, looking up at the troopers with a vague smile. He was to travel alone in one *tarantass* with Commissar Yakovlev. Then the Czarina came, and her husband and Prince Dolgoruki helped her to her place. The doorway was suddenly filled with people watching them depart.

There was no sound in the courtyard where the snow mountain had stood, and which was now churned into mud by the horses' hoofs, except the faint jingling of their harness. Simon saw a tall shape in a long fur coat, heavily veiled against the sleet, climb into the *tarantass* beside the Czarina. He thought of the moment when dawn broke over the steppe and he would see Olga's face again. He wondered at what point along their eastward journey it would be safe to reveal himself to her.

Yakovlev got into the *tarantass* beside the man he had taken out of his prison-house, and a sergeant gave the words of command. Simon wheeled his horse, and gave one look backward at the lighted door.

It was then he saw Olga—not, as he had believed, on her way to safety, but standing with another girl's arm round her, and her own hand lifted in farewell. The shawl fell back from her fair short hair, and Simon saw his princess, at the breadth of a filthy yard; and as her hand went to her mouth he knew that she had seen him too. His impulse, the strongest impulse of his life, was to dismount and run to her side, to seize her and hold her against them all. But the column was moving through the open gates, and someone snatched at his reins and pulled his horse back into line. He had time for one look at the face of his idol, still beautiful to him, and then the breadth of the world was between them once again.

* * *

It was Tatiana's practical good sense which saved Olga from complete collapse. Stunned by the glimpse of Simon, overjoyed that he had come to the very gates of her prison, she was yet more shaken by the knowledge that only her mother's incurable meddling had prevented her from being on the dark road south with Simon now. But Tatiana had not recognised Simon Hendrikov, and she immediately drew her sisters back into the warm house.

"We can't do anything more to help them now," she said. "We must go to bed and try to get some sleep, there's a lot to do tomorrow morning."

What there was to do occupied all the sisters fully. It consisted in looking through all the trunks in the attic, to which they had at last been allowed access on behalf of the travellers, and discovering how many of their garments and personal possessions had been looted. They had no summer dresses or light shoes at all, very little indeed but their heavy winter clothing, and spring was on its way. Hokriakov, challenged by Olga, told them their fancy clothes had been distributed among the workers whose need was greater than theirs.

"Do you think I believe that for a moment?" she said contemptuously. "Your soldiers stole our things and sold them to buy vodka." It was only the intervention of Colonel Kobilinski, whom she had asked to be present, which prevented the Commissar from striking her.

"Don't provoke them too far," said Tatiana uneasily. She was making lists of what remained to them, always a congenial employment for Tatiana, but she was nearly as much on edge as Olga. The news coming in of flooding rivers and highways washed away made it seem as if a confrontation in Moscow was not the worst danger to be feared for their parents and Marie. It was a great relief when a telegram from Marie announced their arrival at the railhead at Tiumen, but then silence fell again, and there was no word that they had reached Moscow. There was no news at all until Colonel Kobilinski's men came back.

The commandant asked to see Olga alone, and told her their strange story. First, they said, Commissar Yakovlev had said they were to travel to Moscow by way of Omsk. It was not the direct way but it was a possible way, and nobody had questioned the Special Commissar's decision.

"But he was taking them east instead of west," interrupted Olga.

"Exactly, and if he could have got Their Majesties through Omsk he might have got them safely through to the Pacific. But sixty miles west of the town the train was stopped by members of the Omsk Soviet, and Yakovlev ordered to go no further. He said he only took his orders from Moscow and insisted on going into Omsk to telephone."

"He was in constant touch with Moscow while he was here, I know."

"In touch with President Sverdlov, every day. Oh, he had the right credentials, no doubt of that! So he went off to Omsk, with a Red Guards officer who had fallen sick along the way, to put the man in hospital. But he couldn't get round Sverdlov this time. He came back to the train, where the local Soviet was mounting guard, and said Comrade Sverdlov had ordered him to deliver his prisoners to the Soviet at Ekaterinburg, east of Tiumen."

"And is that where they are now?"

"Presumably, but my men left them at Tiumen, and came back by road."

"What an extraordinary story," said Olga. "First east, then west, and nowhere near Moscow. Eugene Stepanovich, I *know*, I feel certain that Yakovlev planned a rescue attempt. What do you think went wrong?"

Kobilinski hesitated. "You know I'm no politician, Your Imperial Highness. But I'm inclined to think this man Yakovlev was double-crossed by Sverdlov—which means Lenin, of course. He obviously had their confidence up to a point, and as we know the German Ambassador has been bringing pressure to bear on the People's Commissars to get Their Majesties out of Tobolsk. So what was simpler than to let Yakovlev bring them away, and make sure he was intercepted, before he could move far in either direction, by one or other of the Ural Soviets?"

"That's just what frightens me," said Olga, for the ferocity of the Ural Soviets was notorious. "Oh, if they had been taken anywhere else than Ekaterinburg!"

Colonel Kobilinski tried to reassure her.

"Perhaps it's only a halt on the way to Moscow. We shall hear more in a day or two," he said.

What the terrified girls heard was that their parents and Marie were imprisoned in a house called the Ipatiev Dom, and that Prince Dolgoruki had been arrested and taken away, for no reason given, as soon as the train reached Ekaterinburg. Yakovlev sent a telegram to Colonel Kobilinski which might have been entitled 'Failure of a Mission', for it read:

Take the detachment with you

and depart
I have resigned
and I am not responsible
for any consequences

* * *

Across the steppes of Siberia summer followed winter in the course of one week, or so it seemed to the nomad tribes which resumed their wanderings, or to the townsfolk of Tobolsk watching the *Rus* cast off her moorings and set her course again down the mighty river.

In the governor's mansion all seasons were alike to the imprisoned. Alexis a little better, the rooms a little less icy, the snow in the yard all gone—these were the only perceptible differences. There was no longer any attempt at study, or acting plays, or the game of Happy Times. There was only an increasing fear of their jailers, whose severity increased with every day.

Colonel Kobilinski, heart-broken, was relieved of his command and ordered back to Petrograd. When he was gone the last check on the two Commissars was removed, and Hokriakov was ingenious in new harassments. One day he ordered the keys to be removed from all the doors, and the bedroom doors to be left ajar at all times. Often the girls awoke to hear the breathing of a soldier, standing still—more terrifying than a prowler—just inside their sleeping-room. The other Commissar, Rodionov, made a rule that none of the girls was to be seen at a window at any time; the sentries were given orders to fire if anyone was seen looking out.

Alexis was partly exempt from this ruling, because the Commissars allowed him to be wheeled to the window of his room and back again in his mother's old wheel-chair. They seemed to think that looking across the yard at the occasional passer-by would encourage him to start walking, but the fact was that although he wore the torturing leg brace for hours together, the child could hardly take a step alone. The news of his illness got out in the town, and although few of the citizens of Tobolsk came near the governor's mansion since the advent of the Red Guards from Omsk, one intrepid schoolboy was arrested in the act of climbing up to look over the stockade into the yard. His defence was that he wanted to see the poor little Czarevitch, who was so ill. He was taken out and shot.

Hokriakov had a congenial time cross-examining Alexis about a 'plot' between the two boys, and pointing out what happened to a boy who didn't obey the benevolent orders of the new revolutionary state. The former Heir to the Throne put an end to the scene with a good deal of dignity, by squaring his shoulders on the pillow and saying, "Go away, please, you're making my head ache." But he paid for it with a sleepless night, and his head was still aching next day. As he told Olga, he couldn't get that other boy out of his mind.

On a Sunday in May, two weeks after a sad, late Easter, when the doctors thought Alexis might be fit to be carried aboard the *Rus* in a few days, the two Commissars gave a final demonstration of their power. The priests and nuns who had been allowed to come on Sundays, to hold a service with the little household at an improvised altar in the drawing-room, were seized and stripped, on the grounds that they were carrying secret messages or firearms. The cries of the nuns and the coarse laughter of the soldiers conducting the search rang in the children's ears for hours, and when the time came for evening prayers the Commissars went on a new rampage. Through the house they went, tearing down the ikons from the bedroom walls and throwing them out of the windows with the valuable miniatures of her children which Alexandra had been forced to leave behind. Finally the ikon which had accompanied Alexis to the Stavka was wrenched off its hook and sent smashing into the hall with the lamp which had shone upon it all night long since the boy could remember anything at all. His sisters, herded into their bedroom by a grinning lout with a bayonet, heard Monsieur Gilliard remonstrating in his bad Russian, and Nagorny growling, and then the sound of one heavy blow. Who was the victim, they could only guess.

Tatiana and Anastasia undressed and fell asleep at last, while Olga lay down fully clothed upon her bed. She had kept some stubs of candle for emergencies, and by the light of one of them she studied Tatiana's lovely face and Anastasia's merry one, which looked older and more purposeful in sleep. She thought of Marie at Ekaterinburg, and not for the first time she blamed herself that she had not overridden their parents' selfishness and accepted

Boris Heiden's offer to get them all away to England while there was time. Or if, before the measles began, she had listened to Simon Hendrikov's advice to leave for the Crimea.

A faint scratching at the door, standing ajar, brought her off her bed in a moment. Nagorny or Gilliard—it had to be one or the other, and in the darkness she heard the sailor's voice.

"Your Imperial Highness!"

"Is it Alexis?"

"He's asking for you."

"I'll get a candle."

Shading it with her hand she crept out to the landing. In the faint light a bruise stood out upon Nagorny's cheek. Olga touched it very gently. The healthy blood had dried already, and the sailor dropped to his knees and kissed her hand. There was no sound in the house except the murmur of voices from the improvised guardroom at the door.

"What if they come upstairs?"

"They won't get past me if they do."

"No, no, you must warn me, we can't have any trouble. Stay by the door, Nagorny—please!"

Olga slipped inside her brother's room. By the candlelight she could see him sitting up in bed, with the dog Joy looking warily from his basket at the far side of the room. She set the stump of candle in its saucer on the bedside table, dropped on her knees, and slid her arm round the boy's thin shoulders. "You've brought a light, Olga," he murmered. "Oh, I'm so glad!"

"Sh-h, we mustn't talk too loud. What's the matter, darling—are you missing mamma?"

"You know I always miss her," he said reproachfully. "But—I got to feeling scared in the dark, without my ikon and my dear *lampadka*!"

"We heard them—taking it away, and we were all so sorry. But there's nothing to be scared about, Alexis; God doesn't need a lamp to see us by."

"You believe that, don't you, Olga?"

"Absolutely." She made her confession of faith with no sense that she was talking to a child. Alexis had taken another step forward into manhood; even his voice seemed deeper, and the planes of the man's face were coming through the childish curves. His hair had not been cut since his illness began, and it fell over his brow and ears, the colour of a bright copper penny.

"Well, that's what I wanted to ask you about," he said. "Do you think God's angry with me now?"

"Angry with *you*? But why?"

"Because when I was hurting so, after I fell downstairs, I kept telling mamma I wanted to die, I wanted to die, and it isn't true! I want to live, Olga! I *don't* want to die!"

"You mustn't talk like that, not now, when you're getting better all the time. Think, in just a few days we'll be out on the river again, on our way to father and mother and Marie, and Nagorny and you will sit on deck and watch everything that happens on the steamer—"

"I want to live, even if I'll never be the Czar."

Olga's head dropped on the pillow beside her brother's. Through tears, she heard him whisper, "And I meant to be such a good Czar, and go down in history—"

"Did you, Alexis?"

"I meant to grant a constitution, and have Monsieur Rodzianko for my prime minister, like they do in England, and tell him to build hospitals and schools, and never, never go to war—"

The child's dream, she saw, had been very strong. He must have been dreaming it in the days of Dmitri's fantasy of putting her upon the throne, the days when in her headstrong way she had indulged the fantasy, telling herself that she was not her brother's keeper, and that if her father abdicated she would do whatever was best for Russia . . . She saw now that the Empress Olga had never had a chance of reigning, any more than the Emperor Alexis: they were two leaves blown on the great gale of revolution which might some day sweep across the world.

"I wish you'd say something good to me now, like mamma does—"

"Oh, Alexis, I'm not nearly good enough myself."

"You're my godmother, you should be able to say *something*."

"Would you like us to say the Lord's Prayer together?"

"I've said it twice tonight already. Once with Nagorny, and once with Zilchik, after they took away my *lampadka*. Say some of that hymn you and Nastia made up, the one you wrote into that book mamma gave you at the New Year. The one about patience."

"I can't remember all of it, but I'll try." She heard Nagorny shift his position by the open door and knew that he was listening too.

> "Give patience, Lord, to us Thy children,
> In these dark, stormy days to bear
> The persecution of our people,
> The tortures falling to our share."

"Say about 'the hour of utmost dread'."

Olga went on:

> "Lord of the world, God of Creation,
> Give us Thy blessing through our prayer,
> Give peace of heart to us, O Master,
> This hour of utmost dread to bear."

Her arm was growing cramped beneath the boy's weight now, light though it was; she moved slightly, and settled him more deeply on his pillows.

"They're going to kill us, aren't they?" he said.

"Oh, Alexis!"

"Will it hurt very much? Olga, what'll it be like to die?"

She was going to whisper something about saying a prayer, something better than her poor verses, but then Olga found the inspiration, or the grace, to say:

"Do you remember when you were so ill in the train, that time coming back from Mohilev, and they couldn't let you lie down flat in bed? Nagorny held you in his arms the whole night long, didn't he?"

"Yes, they told me afterwards: all night long."

"I think when our time comes to die—when we're old, old men and women—it'll be just like that. Like being taken into very strong arms, and then held fast through the darkness."

She felt his breathing relax, and Alexis said drowsily, "Very strong arms, I like that. For all of us?"

"All of us."

"Then I won't mind—so—"

By the candle flame she saw the dark lashes sweep his cheek

as sleep descended. Very cautiously she took her arm away and blew out the light. Very gently she laid her forehead against one of the boy's long hands.

Am I my brother's keeper?

Yes.

28

WHEN THE GERMAN AMBASSADOR, whose help Alexandra Feodorovna had disdained, was shot dead in Moscow, it was the most discussed assassination—in Russia at least—since the now almost forgotten murders at Sarajevo. It started a series of reactions in the All-Russian Congress of Soviets, then in session in the new capital, and brought Lenin back to Petrograd for the first time since the seat of power shifted from the Smolny Institute to the Kremlin.

He was to speak in the Maly Theatre, and Mara Trenova saw the red flags going up round the railings of the Michael Square and in clusters at the windows of the Hotel Europa as she walked to work on a hot summer morning.

When the Smolny was dismantled the TEO had moved to temporary offices above a concert hall on a corner of the Nevski Prospekt not far from the Catherine Canal. The section was due to move to Moscow in September, but there were propaganda films in production and other projects to be completed before then, and the TEO was working at full strength. There was little time for comradely greetings as the members arrived and settled down to work, and Mara was not aware of any especial chill in the atmosphere as she hung up her jacket and knitted cap and went to her desk beside the window.

The premises were too small to be partitioned off, and several times during the morning, when Mara lifted her head from her work, she met the speculative gaze of the section chief, Ilya Korv, whose face was familiar wherever the new propaganda posters could be pasted up in Russia. He was a big fair man nearer fifty than forty, whose humorous, kindly expression and powerful shoulders made him a natural model for the Productive Peasant, the Punctual Traindriver, and other mythic heroes of the new Russia.

When the morning's work was nearly over he crossed the room and perched on a corner of Mara's desk. "You're down to see the rushes of the anti-Romanov picture at six o'clock, aren't you?" he began.

"Yes, *Coronets and Loving Hearts.* It's ready for subtitles, Maltsev said."

"Any outside assignment before that? No? Then I'd like you to investigate the children's theatre show we've had complaints about, over on Vassili Island. There's a performance at three o'clock."

"That's the animal show." Mara opened a letter file. " 'Subversive indoctrination . . . insults to Marxism and the heroes of the Winter Palace . . .'—that's pretty strong for poor old Rudov and his beasties!" She looked up with a smile, but Korv's grey eyes were cold. "We've had three different complaints from citizens living in the Maly Prospekt," he said. "There must be something in it. Come and have your soup with me and let's talk."

"All right." Mara went to get her cap and jacket. Her summer suit of dark green linen was three years old and needed pressing, but it had been of fairly good quality to start with, and she looked better dressed than most of the women workers in *Narkompros.* The customers in the National Kitchen across the Prospekt were noticeably shabby, and in the hot, close room their infrequently washed clothes and bodies gave off a disagreeable smell. Mara's appetite was gone before she and Ilya Korv, after standing in line for ten minutes, secured bowls of beet soup and hunks of black bread, and looked around for seats.

"Over here," said Korv, indicating two vacant stools at a table occupied by young soldiers of the new Red Army, sweating in their coarse grey uniforms. "Aren't we going to sit with the others?" she said, for there was no canteen at the temporary office, and most of the workers ate their midday meal at the National Kitchen.

"We're all right here." Korv smiled and nodded at the soldiers, who had stopped eating to stare at them. "Before I forget, I've got kind remembrances to give you, from an old friend of yours I saw in Moscow."

"Jacob Levin?"

"What put Levin into your head?"

"I saw his photograph in one of the Congress pictures. He was with the Presidium, only four seats away from Comrade Sverdlov—"

"Yes, he ranks high in the Moscow Soviet these days. But it wasn't Levin who sent his regards. It was Comrade Sergiev, who used to work with you on *Castle Comments.*"

"He was the copyboy on *Castle Comments*, when I was Levin's secretary."

"He's a war correspondent for *Pravda* now."

"I know, I've seen his by-line. Isn't it strange to be talking about war correspondents when only six months ago we were dedicated to eternal peace?"

Korv looked quickly at the soldiers. They had lost interest in the man and the girl and were deep in their own conversation. He said in a low voice, "We're at war because of the Czarist counter-revolutionaries and their foreign allies. The Japanese are landing troops by the thousand, the Czechs are fighting all along the Trans-Siberian. Comrade Lenin himself has said our first task must be the creation of a mighty Socialist army—"

"And words like 'motherland' and 'patriotism' are respectable again."

Ilya Korv sighed. "Out of your own mouth," he said. "Comrade Mara, this is what I wanted to talk to you about. We held a meeting last night, after you left the office, to discuss your sarcastic criticisms of our just resistance to the foreign aggressors. Your fellow-workers feel that you are introducing a subversive element into our group which must not be allowed to develop into open dissidence. By a majority vote, I was elected to warn you accordingly."

Mara's pale face had flushed an ugly red. "What about the minority vote?" she asked. "Was that in my favour?"

"On the contrary. The meeting was unanimous in its disapproval of your recent unco-operative attitude: the minority vote was for a public reprimand. What I am giving you, as privately as possible, is an official warning."

"A warning against what?"

"Comrade, listen to me. From the moment the Fifth Congress opened, according to every other member of the section, you championed the Social Revolutionary, Maria Spiridonova. Who consistently attacked Comrade Lenin in the vilest terms. I was there on the opening day, I heard her. She accused Lenin to his face of betraying the peasants and treachery to the nation in concluding peace with Germany. We know she sent Blumkin to kill the German Ambassador in the hopes that Germany would be goaded into resuming the war with us—"

"We also know that Trotsky sent a Lettish regiment and a detachment of armoured cars to surround the SR party headquarters—"

"Because the SRs were planning a *coup d'état* to take the power from the people's leaders, and frustrate all the hopes of our glorious revolution."

"You can't deny that Spiridonova has been absolutely consistent in her own beliefs," said Mara.

"Spiridonova's beliefs have landed her in jail."

"*What?*"

"She was arrested just before dawn this morning, and taken to prison in the Kremlin. Lenin will announce it in the Maly Theatre tonight . . . Don't you want your bread? You mustn't waste it."

She dumbly pushed the hunk of bread across the table. The soldiers were getting up to leave, and shouldering their rifles and their packs.

"Why are you telling me this about Spiridonova now?"

"For your own good. I know, we all know, how much you used to admire her, and it's true she was a good revolutionary in her day. But now Maria Spiridonova has been declared an enemy of the state, and if you say one more word in her defence, you'll be dismissed from the People's Commissariat for Education."

"I can get another job at *Pravda*, or *Rabochi Put*."

"Nobody can move from job to job at his own free will. You might be put to work with the 'mofectives'—the morally defective children. But more likely you'd be directed into a munition factory. Either way you'll have less time to spend at 'The Red Sarafan', where it's reported that you're seen far too often—"

"Surely I can do what I like in my off-duty hours?"

"There are no off-duty hours for a good servant of the state. Now, Comrade Mara!" (for Korv saw tears of anger in her eyes) "you *must* believe that I'm your friend. Last night I carried the majority with me when I proposed this warning should be given in private. I marked you for the children's assignment today so that you won't be in the office while you're so overwrought.

Stay in the park all afternoon and think calmly over what I've said. Clear your mind of all subversive thoughts, and come to the meeting in the Maly prepared to give a hero's welcome to Lenin."

Ilya Korv smiled, his poster smile, so natural, which brought out the laughter wrinkles at the corners of his eyes. One of his large hands, still calloused from his beginnings as a sheet metal operative at the great Putilov Works, closed over the girl's clasped hands. "Good comrades both?" he said.

"Good comrades . . . You're very kind, Korv. I wish I had met someone like you when I was young."

The man laughed. "How old are you, Comrade Mara?"

"Twenty-three."

"I'm more than twice your age." He patted her hands, and released them. "Poor child, you've missed your father."

* * *

Mara Trenova walked slowly away towards the Neva. Too stunned by the news from Moscow to be aware of the passers-by, she noted automatically that pictures of Lenin, clenched fist raised above cloth cap, were being pasted on the billboards which stood outside such overspill government offices as the TEO. Far down the Morskaia she saw the red flags at the windows of the old General Staff Headquarters. Just over the Police Bridge, outside the cinema, there were coloured posters called 'The Workers Fight Against Foreign Aggression!'—the model was Ilya Korv in a workman's shirt and trousers, his sleeves rolled up over his powerful forearms, with a hammer raised to strike.

The children's theatre accused of subversion was at some distance, in a shabby park on the Maly Prospekt in the centre of Vassili Island. It could be reached directly by the Sixteenth Line off the University Quay, but Mara had time to kill, and she instinctively headed towards the Fourth Line, which she knew so well. She passed the corner where she had stood to watch the Grand Duchess Olga pass, on her way from launching the *Poltava* three years earlier, and walked into the empty roadway to calculate the distance, as she had done then. Ten paces exactly from the pavement to the carriage. You couldn't hit a barn door at ten paces, said that ornament of the Presidium, Jacob Levin. You couldn't pull the trigger, could you now?

Each flat in the Fourth Line had been divided up for workers' families, and lines of family washing adorned most of the balconies. Across the middle of the street, strung between two tall lime trees, was a grimy banner, red lettering on white, announcing that 'The Rule of the Proletariat is the Death of the Bourgeois Horde!' It was a slogan now to be seen in every propaganda hall in Russia, and must have been displayed in the Fourth Line as part of the May Day celebrations. One end of the banner was attached to the tree outside what had been the Hendrikovs' living-room window.

Now who would have thought that Plain Joe Calvert, always so correct and cautious, would be the man to put his hand in the fire for the friend who had cut him out with Dolly Hendrikova? Mara had not forgotten Joe's brief appearance at the Smolny. It had brought her the fresh breath of a different way of life and a recollection of old times. From then, she dated the overt criticism of the regime which now threatened her with relegation to a *Rabfak* or the instruction of 'mofective' children, and her increasing disillusionment with Lenin. Lenin, so gossip said, had done a deal with Plain Joe Calvert and had been outwitted by the Americans. Lenin, who had sent Maria Spiridonova back to the prison where the Czar had kept her.

She came to the park at last. There was a sign above the gate picked out in electric light bulbs, meant to be switched on when electricity supplies permitted, which made one of the favourite Bolshevik statements: 'Children are the Flowers of Life.' So many bulbs were missing that the sign read Chi r n are t Flowe s of L e, and the flowers themselves looked pale and woefully undernourished as they went along the dusty path leading to the children's theatre.

It had been opened by an old star of the circus, long famous for his animal acts, in a tumbledown wooden hut which might once have held the gardeners' implements. Rudov himself, whom Mara remembered seeing as a child, was taking the money at the door, and for the price of admission—thirty kopecks only—she received, instead of a ticket, a small bag of carrots chopped in rings and a sprig of parsley. This, no doubt, was the 'counter-revolutionary waste of food' mentioned in one of the letters of complaint.

Inside the hut, Mara found herself one of the few adults present. The benches were crammed with children, keyed up

to an anticipation which broke into applause when a bear cub dressed in a blue smock climbed up to the stage and made them a courtly bow. Then he pulled a cord to display a curtain bearing the title of the show, which was 'Hares of All Lands, Unite!' and a hare appeared, holding up a book with wooden pages, entitled in huge letters *Das Kapital*.

This was the signal for the cub to pull a second curtain, revealing a stage set of the Winter Palace and the Palace Square. The palace was manned by an army of rabbits, wearing hats and holding rifles, whose sensitive noses twitched anxiously as they peered out of the windows at the empty square. The hare holding *Das Kapital* turned the wooden pages with a sound like a clapper, which was the signal for an army of twenty hares, hatless, to appear from the wings and storm the palace. They dragged in miniature cannon, which let off cannon balls; the rabbits replied with rifle fire from the windows. After much firing, and frantic cheering from the audience, the rabbits laid down their rifles and surrendered, and the victorious hares, having occupied the Winter Palace, raised the red flag from the roof. The bear cub repeated his performance with the curtains, and all the actors streamed into the auditorium to receive the carrots and parsley, and many caresses, from the hands of the delighted children.

The whole thing was over in about half an hour. Rudov told Mara it would be repeated twice more that day. The old clown spoke ingratiatingly, as he would never have done when he was one of the kings of the Russian circus, billed as The Inimitable Rudov; she suspected that he guessed from her workmanlike suit, and the heavy satchel slung from her shoulder, that she represented some sort of officialdom. "I hope the lady enjoyed herself?" he said anxiously, and spoke about his animals, and the patience required to train them. She congratulated him and walked away. There was a stone seat near the entrance where it was possible to write her notes.

It would have been so easy to send in the kind of report the letter-writing busybodies wanted, about the reduction of a great national event to the level of a circus trick, and so on—a report which would probably have added Rudov to the bursting population of the Shpalernaia prison. Instead, Mara began, "For thirty kopecks, the price of a cup of tea at a National Kitchen, the lucky children of Petrograd are able to see, at the

Rudov Theatre in the Vassili Park, a remarkable dual illustration of Pavlov's theory of conditioned reflexes and Meyerhold's principle of audience participation." That was the carrots and parsley, of course, but it would do the trick, it was just the sort of pompous rubbish to be acceptable at *Narkompros*. She wrote a full page of description and praise, omitting any reference to *Das Kapital*, and ending with the words, "This is a delightful entertainment for young people, and if there were more shows like it there would be fewer mofective children in Petrograd." She had to substitute 'Petrograd' for 'St. Petersburg' at the end of her report.

Later, after long wanderings through the park and the grass-grown streets of the Island, she returned to the empty TEO office and laid it on Ilya Korv's desk for him to read next morning. She had heard his voice when she passed the open door of the concert hall, and knew that he was there already, with Maltsev, the producer of a movie of which she knew nothing but the title. *Coronets and Loving Hearts*—it was an exposé of imperial vice, she had been told. If so, the title was far too complimentary.

About twenty people were scattered about the concert hall, which had been used for some time to show the rushes of TEO's propaganda films. *Coronets* began on time, with the symbols of Czarist oppression she herself had chosen coming up on the crawl sheet, over the credits: the knout, the handcuffs, the chained prisoners toiling across the snows of Siberia. Then came the opening shots of the four Grand Duchesses, dissolves from their photographs in court dress, taken together and separately. The photographs were completely out of date, having been taken before the war, so that Anastasia appeared as quite a small girl, but they made the point of elegance and luxury, complemented by a background of sofas with satin cushions, fur rugs, and vases full of exotic flowers. The two younger girls wore white ribbons in their flowing hair, and only Olga and Tatiana were wearing coronets. But when the film proper began it was clear that, if not the coronets, the 'loving hearts' were applicable to all four: it was simply a pornographic movie of the sexual promiscuity of the former Grand Duchesses.

Mara was sitting at one side of the room, at a table with a lamp just strong enough to light the page of her reporter's note-book. It made her conspicuous in the dark hall, and she saw one or two men turning to look at her, as if wondering what a young woman's reactions would be to the perversions on the screen. The producer had employed four actresses, each with a faint resemblance to one of the Grand Duchesses, and by a skilful use of make-up had made that resemblance more positive. It was quite clear who they were meant to be, and clarity was assured by repeated cuts to the original photographs. The effect of the total sexual commitment of the girls—shown copulating with grooms, footmen, sailors, guardsmen, inevitably with Rasputin and ultimately with animals—was greatly heightened by the contrast between the four innocent, girlish faces of the real photographs and the indiscriminate whoring on the screen.

When the lights went up at the end of twenty minutes there was a good deal of applause, but the clapping was slow and lazy, as if it came from lax hands; and the spectators rose and moved away with a curious, satiated lassitude. Ilya Korv's face, when he came up to Mara's table, was no longer the humorous kindly face of the Ideal Worker, but slack-lipped and moist with sweat.

"Strong stuff, eh, Trenova?" he said, and squeezed her arm. She shut her notebook hastily: she had written only a few words.

"It should have an excellent effect," she said primly, and some man guffawed in the background.

"I'll want your subtitles in the morning, Trenova," said the producer. "I want to rush a print straight to Ekaterinburg."

"We must arrange a showing in the House of Special Purpose," said Korv with a laugh. "Don't be late for the rally, Comrade Mara."

"What's the House of Special Purpose?" Mara asked.

"It's where Nicholas the Bloody and his brats are locked up at Ekaterinburg."

"Why do they call it that?"

"Use your imagination, Trenova!"

Korv turned away with his arm round Maslev's shoulders, and Mara was free to go to the dreadful lavatory and retch. She had eaten nothing since the soup, and her empty stomach was contorted by the spasms induced by utter disgust, shot through with the recognition of personal guilt. What she had seen on the screen was very little worse than the cartoon strip she herself had devised of Rasputin's violation of Olga; only the animation, and the inclusion of the younger girls, and above all the bestiality made it worse. And Lenin himself had called the cinema 'the great medium of the future'—Lenin, who had consigned those girls to a house whose sinister purpose was clear enough. He means to have them all killed in cold blood, she thought. As tomorrow he may order the execution of Spiridinova.

It was impossible to think of returning to her wretched home. She went instead, and as an act of defiance, to 'The Red Sarafan', where there was always company. But when she got there a young man was reciting a poem by Blok, and she sat down to listen:

Rancour, rancour to make one weep,
To make one's blood seethe in dismay,
Rancour sanctified, rancour black and deep,
Comrade, on this day—vigil keep!

A waitress lounged up to Mara's table and asked what she wanted to drink. It was this girl who was later to depose that 'Trenova had been drinking heavily', though in fact she only drank two vodkas at 'The Red Sarafan'. But Mara was not used to vodka, and the drinks went quickly to her head.

To bring all bourgeois to ruination
We'll fan a world-wide conflagration.
World conflagration, fed by blood,
Bless us, O Lord!

The performance was over; it had been a day of performances. Blok, and Hares of the World, and something she had to write sub-titles for. She opened her satchel and felt for her thick notebook. She had rammed it far down in the bag, upon the detritus of labour card, ration book, accreditations and identity papers, and all the TEO pamphlets she was obliged to carry. Mara rummaged in the darkness and came upon something cold and hard. It was the loaded Mauser she had carried through the two revolutions.

She laid the pistol on top of all the layers of papers and took out her notebook. The waitress, bringing the second vodka, saw that Mara Trenova was writing busily, like so many of the failed writers who used the ambience of 'The Red Sarafan' to bolster their misfit personalities. Nobody paid any attention when the scribbled page was crumpled up and dropped beneath the table. But it was retrieved and produced later as proof of her mental derangement: instead of sub-titles for 'a valuable cultural film' it was scribbled over with the words: "Bread, peace, freedom= Famine, war, oppression" followed by "Blood and rancour = Leninleninlenin."

Mara had promised to be in time for the rally, and she was. She went no further than the foyer of the Maly Theatre, where her press card, and her reporter's notebook, gave credibility to her statement that she was covering Comrade Lenin's arrival for the TEO. Ilya Korv and his whole section were already seated, and nobody challenged Mara Trenova's right to be there. A thin girl in a green suit, with an open satchel swinging from her shoulder, attracted nobody's attention.

Lenin, who had enough German blood to hate the feckless Russian unpunctuality, arrived on time. He stopped in the doorway of the Maly to greet the chairman of the Petrograd Soviet, who had organised the rally, between the evening sunlight in the Michael Square, filled with cheering people, and the bright foyer. He was about ten places away from the half-educated, bitter and frustrated girl whose hero worship had turned to rancorous disappointment in him and in the world. He was the perfect target whom her first owner, Jacob Levin, had trained and taunted her to kill, except that Levin had been thinking of the old Czar and not the new.

"You couldn't pull the trigger, could you now?"

She took the pistol from her open bag and snapped off the safety catch. It was heavy in her hand, too heavy, but there was no time to worry about that. She pulled the trigger at ten paces and saw blood streak out on Lenin's big bald head. Then the rain of blows upon her own head and body felled her to the ground.

* * *

When Mara Trenova fully recovered consciousness she knew that she was in the Fortress of St. Peter and St. Paul. She had become aware of that hours earlier, when the quarter chime of "Lord, have mercy upon us" began to penetrate her coma, and she even knew, from what the warders said as they dragged her back from her summary trial, that she was in the Trubetzkoi bastion.

It was the strongest place in the entire prison, reserved for the chief enemies of the state. The Dekabrists had preceded her here, and the assassins of Alexander II; Anna Virubova had spent months in the bastion, listening as Mara was listening to the sound of lapping water from the Neva running just under the level of the ventilators. To have achieved imprisonment in the Trubetzkoi must be accounted Mara Trenova's last success. She already knew from the charge read at her trial, indicting her for "the *attempted* murder of Vladimir Ilyich Lenin", that she had been in that, as in so much else, a failure. Bruised from head to foot by her beating, held up between two warders, she remembered little else of the summary court, except that her only words of defence had been "I am Ivan Trenov's daughter!" and that she had felt a cloudy, professional indignation that her name was being mispronounced Ternova.

The cell was in total darkness, broken only by a ray of light from the corridor, coming through the warders' spyhole. They had taken everything away from her except her stained and torn clothing, her satchel and the gun as a matter of course, and even her watch and her mother's wedding ring. But when she was able to lift her head from the pillow stuffed with seaweed, and sit up on the iron bed built, like the table, into the wall of her cell, Mara knew what time it was: the cathedral bells so far above her dungeon were chiming the midnight *Kol slaven*, 'How glorious is our Lord in Sion,' which none of Russia's new masters had yet thought to stop.

She felt her way to the iron washstand and splashed her face with the cold water she found there. She had a premonition, as the midnight chime brought the sound of movement all through the Trubetzkoi bastion, that she would never hear the cathedral chimes again. When the four armed men came in, carrying chains and lanterns, Mara felt only thankfulness that they were disposing of her quickly. There would not be another day of the terrible interrogation to make her name her accomplices in the 'plot'.

> I have lost my way
> This is the wrong city and the wrong midnight—

These were the only words Mara could recollect when she

was led out with a line of the condemned of that day, although one older woman seemed to be praying, and two men in the tattered remnants of the Horse Guards uniforms were muttering the words of the old national anthem. They were taken into a little yard in the heart of the fortress, with the blank wall of the Mint on the right and the Trubetzkoi bastion on the left, like a great squat blockhouse behind its palisade. Then she realised that facing them was a line of Red Guards armed with rifles, and like the other woman she began to scream and struggle, writhing in her chains. She was aware that someone was tying a cloth over her eyes, and in that darkness the words of the *kontakion*, which she had heard and mocked so often, came back to her and destroyed her illusion that she was dying a martyr's death:

All we go down to the dust
And weeping o'er the grave we make our song:

The rifles blazed out across the prison yard—

Alleluia! Alleluia! Alleluia!

29

WHILE LENIN WAS recovering from the shallow scalp wound received in the foyer of the Maly Theatre, it was announced that his would-be assassin, now executed, was a counter-revolutionary and White agent. Her name was variously given in the newspapers as Martha or Maria Ternova, an accomplice of the woman Spiridonova who had instigated the murder of the German Ambassador. On the principle of guilt by association, all 'Ternova's' former colleagues were assigned to other employment, in the war factories or the institutions for defective children.

By that time the Romanov family had been united for about six weeks, and the group left behind at Tobolsk had almost forgotten the nightmare of their journey to Ekaterinburg.

The trip downriver to Tiumen had been quite different from their first journey on the *Rus*. Alexis had to be carried aboard, and so far from moving about the ship or even sitting on deck to watch the passing scenery, he was locked in a cabin with Nagorny and made to stay there for the whole two days. Olga and her sisters were a little better off, because they had a new companion: Baroness 'Isa' Buxhoeveden, who courageously followed them to Tobolsk and then was forbidden to visit them, was at last allowed to join the sisters on their journey to Ekaterinburg. She had much to hear from them, and also much to tell of what she had gathered in Tobolsk. Commissar Yakovlev, forced to abandon his charges to the Ural Soviet, had courageously gone on to Moscow and confronted Sverdlov with an accusation of what he called contradictory orders. He had not been punished for his boldness, for he was seen drinking with Sverdlov that same night, but it was later given out that he had defected, and was fighting with the White Army raised by Admiral Kolchak.

Olga listened to this with interest and hope. It was clear from all Isa said that the townspeople of Tobolsk had taken Yakovlev at his face value as a Special Commissar, and the men who accompanied him had attracted no attention in the town.

If he had succeeded in joining the Whites, it was possible that Simon had done so too, and would at least be among his own kind; she was burning with impatience to see and question Marie. Meantime, Isa's courageous presence was a great help. She had not been crushed by imprisonment like Countess Gendrikova and Mademoiselle Schneider, and was able to cheer up these old friends. The gentlemen admired her, and as the *Rus* made her way downstream there was a spurt of renewed hope in the tiny court surrounding the former Grand Duchesses.

It was extinguished at Tiumen. There for the first time the three girls and Alexis were exposed to the fury of an angry crowd as they made their way, carrying as much of the luggage as they could, from the steamer to the train. Members of the local Soviet wanted to arrest them and try them for treason on the spot, and the squad of soldiers conducting them to Ekaterinburg had to push their way through the crowd with fixed bayonets. The Tiumen Reds had made sure that no luxuries nor even comforts would be provided in the grimy fourth-class carriages into which the Romanov party was pushed. The cushions they brought with them had to be laid along one wooden seat for Alexis, while the girls and Nagorny sat, uncomfortably close, on the opposite side.

The older ladies, with General Tatischev and the two tutors, were herded into another fourth-class carriage, and forbidden to talk to 'Nicholas the Bloody's youngsters'. Before the wood-burning train started its two hundred mile journey across the steppe their hearts were wrung to hear Alexis crying and asking for a drink of boiled water. There was none to be had, and no water in the lavatory: hot, hungry and miserably uncomfortable the boy and his sisters were slowly carried west.

"Ekaterinburg at last! Wake up, Alexis!" said Olga cheerfully, when the outskirts of the town were seen in the late afternoon of the second day. The boy had been dozing, with his head in Anastasia's lap; he sat up drowsily and rubbed his eyes.

"Will papa and mamma be at the station to meet us?" he asked. He was evidently thinking of Czarskoe Selo and the imperial comings and goings, with the station staff bowing, hats in hand, and the limousines waiting beside the neat flower-beds outside.

"Oh, I shouldn't think so. They'll be waiting at the Ipatiev House, all ready to give us a nice tea, I hope . . . What is it, Tania?"

Her sister was worriedly consulting one of her neatly written lists.

"What *I* hope is that we'll be able to have baths and change into fresh clothing," said Tatiana. "All the underwear was packed in the Vuitton trunk. And I'm nearly sure I saw it left behind on the platform at Tiumen."

"I bet those horrible people robbed us right and left," said Anastasia.

"Never mind, we know where the most important things of all are," said Olga, and the sisters exchanged glances. Every jewel they possessed had been carefully sewn into the hems and seams of the skirts and jackets they were wearing.

"We're stopping! But there isn't any platform! Oh, bother, they're taking us into the freight yard!" They were all talking at once, as the train shunted backwards and forwards, overshooting the points, so that baggage fell off the racks in all directions, until it came to a halt at last in the grimy locomotive yards outside the town of Ekaterinburg. A detachment of Red Guards, walking along the track, told the passengers roughly to get away from the windows and pull down the shades 'if you know what's good for you'.

"When may we get out?" Olga asked.

"When we say so, citizeness, and it won't be until the coast's clear. There's people in this town would like to tear you murderers limb from limb."

"I don't believe I ever killed anything bigger than a fly," said Anastasia in a small voice, after the patrol had gone by. "Oh, Olga, I do so want to be with papa and mamma and Marie!"

"We'll have to be patient a little while longer, sweetie." And all Olga could do was to set them an example, for their patience wore very thin as the long light evening turned at last to darkness, and still they remained in the locked coach, waiting for release. Nobody bothered to tell them that the inhabitants of Red Ekaterinburg had been roused against them, not only by the local Soviet, which was violently Bolshevik, but by the arrival of five hundred Kronstadt sailors, who had been drinking and terrorising the town for days. Nobody told them that fighting had broken out in Siberia between the Red Army and a large, well-disciplined body of Czech prisoners of war, big enough to form an army corps, who wanted to go back to Europe and fight the Germans but were perfectly willing to remain in Russia and fight the Reds. This new phase of the civil war had further enraged the people against their former Little Father the Czar, the man they held responsible for all their miseries.

His son and daughters were not allowed to leave the train until next morning. They plucked up hope when they saw a line of one-horse cabs, drawn by wretched animals, creeping into the freight yard, and Olga, risking a shout or even a shot, put her head out of the window to see what was happening.

"There's a soldier getting into the carriage where Isa and Nastia are," she reported. "Oh, I hope they're allowed to come and join us now!"

But the Red officer, accompanied by a suspicious Commissar of the local Soviet, was making other arrangements for the former ladies-in-waiting, and comparing a file of photographs in his hand with the anxious faces in front of him.

"Sophia Buxhoeveden, Pierre Gilliard, Sydney Gibbs. You, and you, and you. Take your stuff and get out of the train, you're free to go. Don't you understand me, citizeness? Go to any damned place you want to; you're no further concern of ours. Now the woman with the German name—you, Schneider—and Anastasia Gendrikova, and Tatischev, former general—you with the beard—you're under arrest. Leave your luggage, you won't be needing it again."

"Lieutenant," said the old general sturdily, as the horrified women began to cry, "I am entirely at your disposal. But these two ladies have done nothing to deserve arrest, any more than I have. Take me if you must, but let them go free."

The Commissar took Nastia's trembling chin in a hard grip. "This here's not a bad-looking lass," he said. "What would you do with yourself if I let you go, my dear?"

The gentle young countess drew herself up and said very clearly, "Serve my empress till the day I die!"

"Take them away."

The Romanovs were hustled from the train after the three prisoners were removed, and the three so inexplicably set free watched in horror as they saw Tatiana stumble and fall, trying to keep Jimmy the Pekinese in her arms and carry a heavy suitcase at the same time, and Anastasia, equally burdened, keeping tight hold of Joy the spaniel's lead. They heard the cry of execration which went up from the crowd mobbing the freight yards as the cabs drove away. They saw the suitcases and trunks taken from the baggage car and dragged along the ground, bursting open even before the crowd rushed in to loot them, snatching at clothes and boots and books indiscriminately, and literally tearing the fur coats apart. One packing case contained letters, no doubt treasonable, and therefore to be handed over to the Soviet for despatch to Moscow, but when all the letters were found to be in English interest waned, and they were scattered like confetti about the yard. A fine rain finally dampened the popular enthusiasm. The letters in Alexandra Feodorovna's clear, elegant penmanship were trodden deep into the mud. They were all letters she had written to her husband at the Stavka, and taken by him to Tobolsk, and on one, which fluttered in the Siberian wind longer than the others, could have been read the words:

> . . . the Czar rules and not the Duma! Please, my Nicky, Russia's saviour, be agooweeone and keep Stürmer and Protopopov, Our Friend advises it . . . and remember me loves oo, Little Boy Blue.

* * *

"Oh, my Olga, my first-born darling, my good, brave girl! I knew you'd take care of the others, and bring them safe to me!"

For once Alexandra's emotionalism did not jar on Olga, as she clasped the weeping, white-haired woman in her arms. For once she did not feel that Alexandra was the child, and she the mother, when after the long strain of the journey from Tobolsk she gave the burden back to the hands which first had ruled her life. In that greeting, that embrace, the mother and daughter were closer than ever before, and the frictions of the four war years were all but forgotten.

They were all tearful and emotional when the girls ran into the Ipatiev house, Nagorny following with Alexis in his arms, and it was not until he had been thoroughly kissed and cried over that the boy exclaimed,

"But where's Zilchik?"

"Yes, what have you done with them all?" said Nicholas cheerfully.

"Aren't they here already?" said Olga blankly. "We saw three of them going away with the soldiers."

"They'll be here any minute," said Marie.

"Or else they've been taken to another house," said Tatiana.

"Remember, they weren't allowed to live in our house at Tobolsk."
"Perhaps Nagorny can tell us something—"

But the sailor had been too occupied with 'His Imperial Highness' to pay any attention to the older ladies and gentlemen.

"We'll hear in the morning," said Tatiana firmly. She was determined not to let their reunion be spoiled by worry. But they never saw their friends again, for General Tatischev, the countess, and Miss Schneider, were taken to join Prince Dolgoruki in prison, and from there they were all taken to be shot. As for Monsieur Gilliard, he and the English tutor and Baroness 'Isa' lived at the freight yard for ten days, until they were thrown out of the town, sleeping in one stationary train after another, and by day visiting the British consul in an attempt to get help to the Romanov family. It was hopeless; there were ten thousand Soviet soldiers in Ekaterinburg.

But on the first night the family could keep up a pretence that everything was going to be all right, even though the newcomers quailed at the sight of the guards, indoor and outdoor, who occupied all the ground floor of the Ipatiev house. There was a cellar below that, so far unoccupied, and above were the five rooms allocated to the family, Dr. Botkin, and their few remaining servants. The windows were covered with whitewash, and a high stockade had been built right round the house.

"It's a real prison, isn't it?" said Olga to Marie. It was difficult to find privacy anywhere in five crowded rooms, and the four girls were once again to share a bedroom, but Tatiana and Anastasia were with their parents in their room, and Nagorny was putting Alexis to bed.

Marie shook her curly head. "It's pretty bad," she admitted. "You'll hate the Commissar, Avdiev—he's drunk half the time, and even when he's not he's so insulting! He comes in when we're eating, and takes food off our plates with his dirty hands, and says we must learn to share it with our betters—"

"Oh, horrors!"

"The guards are beastly too. They shout dirty words at us when we go out—"

"Oh, we *do* go out?"

"For an hour in the afternoon. But it's really pleasanter to stay indoors."

"I can imagine."

"Olga dear, you look so tired. Why don't you lie down for a little while?"

"Not when I've got you all to myself. Marie, tell me, darling, did you know Simon Karlovich was with Yakovlev's men?"

Marie looked quickly at the half-closed door. There was the usual soldier lurking in the hall.

"I've been wondering if *you* knew," she said. "I didn't dare to write."

"I saw him right at the end, just as you went away. Marie, when did *you* see him—or did he speak to you?"

"Yes, he did. It was at the last *isba* we stopped at before we got to Tiumen. It was morning, still very dark, and papa and mamma were indoors having coffee. I went out to the *tarantass* for something mamma wanted, and suddenly he was right there beside me, with the muffler, like they all wore, pulled away from his face. I knew him at once, but I didn't dare speak, there were so many of them around, so I just smiled. And Simon said, very quick and low, "Tell her I adore her, and I'll try again," and that was all.

"Oh, Marie, you darling! Oh, how marvellous to get his message! How I wonder where he is, and what he's doing now!"

Marie looked troubled. "Olga, I hate to tell you this, but Simon was left behind at Omsk. He got ill, he must have been ill that day outside Tiumen, because he was the one who was taken into Omsk when Yakovlev went in to telephone. And I'd got quite friendly with some of the soldiers by that time—they told me the man who went off in the car was coming down with typhus."

"With typhus—and all alone at Omsk! Marie, he may be *dead* by this time! Oh, Simon, I'll never see you again—" Olga burst into tears, and Marie stood aghast. In more than a year of imprisonment she had never seen her elder sister cry.

"Olga, please don't, you mustn't, or you'll set us all off, you know you will! Olga, you've been so brave, and stood up to everything—can't you just be happy with his message, and knowing he came all that way to see you, and that he wanted so much to try again?"

Olga held out her hand for a handkerchief. "I'm sorry, Marie," she said. ". . . I thought all the loving was knocked out of me. But I was wrong."

"At least you've known that a man loves you. We never did."

"Oh, Marie!" Olga's eyes were still full of tears. But she made a great effort; Marie was right, they mustn't all start crying on this happy evening of their reunion. She dried her eyes and combed her short fair hair. There had been no hope of a bath, of course, and the Vuitton trunk was certainly missing: she would have to put on a clean cotton dress over the garments she had travelled in.

"What wardrobes!" she said, trying to be natural, nodding at the built-in cupboards in the corners of the room. "Right up to the ceiling. We'll have to stand on your shoulders, Mashka, if we want to get at the top shelves."

"It's a queer house altogether, the Ipatiev Dom."

"I *thought* that was what they called it, you've all said so in your letters. But the man at the station called it something else—"

"Did he, Olga? It's called the Ipatiev House because a man called Ipatiev built it, they moved him out to put us in."

"Yes, but after we got out of the train I heard the commissar tell the cab driver to take us to the House of Special Purpose—have you ever heard it called that, Marie?"

"Sometimes."

"What do you suppose it means?"

"I'm afraid to ask."

* * *

Gradually and painfully, they settled down to life in the House of Special Purpose. They were all up and dressed by eight o'clock for an inspection by the Commissar, Avdiev, who drunk or sober insisted on a head count every morning. After that, with any luck, they were given black coffee and stale bread for breakfast, and occupied themselves as best they could until two in the afternoon, the appointed time for the main meal of the day. Sometimes it did not arrive till four or five, for although they had a cook and a kitchen boy in their own service, there was nothing to be cooked: the food was brought in from a Soviet communal kitchen, and sometimes sampled—or even spat in—by the guards. Nicholas and the girls walked up and down the yard in the afternoon, when their vision was extended to include the red flag flying on the roof of the house where they were imprisoned, and a cross surrounded by machine guns on the dome of the Church of the Ascension in a neighbouring square. They listened, sometimes gratefully, to the sounds of life and freedom going on all around them. Ekaterinburg was a busy place, a mining town built for the most part of wooden one story houses, but having in the centre the spacious homes, surrounded by gardens, of the men who had made fortunes in the gold and platinum mines of the Urals. The town was entirely in the hands of the Communists. The leading hotel, called the American House, was the headquarters of the Cheka, and it was a Cheka man, Jakob Yurovski, who presently replaced Avdiev in charge of the prisoners.

Whether Avdiev or Yurovski was the Commissar in charge, the guards themselves were equally intolerable. They were drawn from the local factory workers, bloodthirsty and rancorous to the last degree, and they persecuted their charges, the girls especially, by every means in their power. Olga and her sisters had become accustomed at Tobolsk to the men prowling round their rooms at night: at Ekaterinburg the orderly officer made the rounds of the house twice every hour during the night, and the other twelve men of the inner guard were free to come and go as they pleased through the family rooms. Here, too, there was a new humiliation: each prisoner had to be accompanied to the lavatory by a grinning and interested member of the guard. It was too much for Anastasia, who returned from the first such expedition in floods of tears.

"Imp, darling," Olga comforted her, "try not to think it matters. They're only animals, just poor resentful dogs, and you wouldn't mind Jimmy or Joy coming into the lavatory with you—would you?"

"A—dog wouldn't st-stare at you, and say such awful things—"

"I know, it's horrible, but just pretend they aren't there. Look through them, that's what I do! They're punishing us because we were born Romanov, all right, let's *be* Romanovs! Chin up, Anastasia! Each one from now on pretends she's Catherine the Great!"

It helped a little. They were OTMA again, a closed corporation, walking up and down the yard arm in arm, four abreast, ignoring the catcalls and obscenities of the men on duty. They took turns in amusing Alexis, whose spirits were very low. The faithful Nagorny was the first of their sad little company to go, for Nagorny struck a guard intending to steal a gold chain with images belonging to Alexis, and for that the penalty was death. They tried to keep it from Alexis, but he guessed, and Olga could only be thankful that their mother was there to pet and coax her 'Sunbeam', and assure him that his dear Nagorny was safe, safe for ever, having only gone ahead of them for a little while.

Olga saw with awe that Alexandra Feodorovna had come to terms with death. She was grateful whenever a priest of the Orthodox faith was allowed to come to them, and scrupulous in the forms of the morning and evening prayers, but the old religious fanaticism, the mystic longings Rasputin had known how to exploit, seemed to have dropped away. With a beautiful and inspiring serenity and faith she waited for whatever the future might bring. Her husband's ties to earth were stronger. He still believed in the possibility of a rescue, and at the end of June kept his family up and fully dressed for several nights, on the strength of a letter signed 'Officer' which the cook had smuggled in to him. It gave some explicit plans for an escape, but whether it was in earnest or a cruel hoax they never knew.

Olga felt this episode most cruelly, because it raised her hopes that Simon Hendrikov had come to Ekaterinburg and meant to try again. With half her mind she knew it was a fantasy, for if Simon was still alive he might well be in a Bolshevik prison, but she clung obstinately to her dream of Young Lochinvar and to the message he had whispered to Marie. When their father, after several wakeful nights, had to admit that no help was coming, she said sadly to her sister:

"It's no use, Mashka, it was just another wild idea, like the Brotherhood of St. John of Tobolsk. Nobody can get us out of here unless the Czech Legion can arrive in time. And they're still east of Tiumen, over three hundred miles away, even if they capture every station on the railway it may take them weeks to fight their way into Ekaterinburg. And where will we be when they come? Still here, doing our little bits of laundry in a bucket of dirty water? Or mending our clothes?"

"I think housework's fun," said Marie stoutly. If Olga was still the leader, Marie, just past her nineteenth birthday, had emerged as a girl of great character, as strong in personality as in her body. She was also very pretty, with her brown curls and huge blue eyes, and as she said, running her hands down her slim flanks, "there's one good thing about a prison diet—nobody'll ever call me Fat Little Bow-Wow again!" The soldiers never shouted at Marie, but they watched her as she swung up and down the yard with her hands in the pockets of her cotton dress, and sometimes they whispered together and licked their lips.

The time came when what Olga had begun to dread, took place. They were all asleep in the darkest hour of the night when their door was quietly opened and two soldiers came in, one with a dark lantern in his hand. They were drunk, but far from incapable, and they were even willing to parley with the frightened girls. The guards had drawn lots, they said, for who got the chance, and they had won; now they were going to take 'the two cute little young ones' down to the cellar.

"Just a moment." Olga had slung on her dressing-gown, while Tatiana, who had only heard half of what was muttered, put her arms round her younger sisters. Olga pushed the men out to the landing. From the mere fact that they were whispering and not shouting, she guessed that they were afraid of the commandant, just as she was afraid of her father hearing them and coming out to see what was wrong. That they were absolutely set on their vile purpose was quite apparent; one of them actually had his Nagan pistol in his hand as he told her in explicit terms that he meant to have a woman, and couldn't face his mates again unless he did.

"Yes, but not one of my sisters, they're very young, you'd frighten them," said Olga, and the one without the gun said the younger the better. He wanted the one with the curls, she swung her hips at the boys when she went by.

Olga braced herself against the door. "I won't let you interfere with any of my sisters, and that's flat," she said.

"Maybe you'd like to come with us yourself, you stuck-up old bitch?"

"If you force me to, I will."

The sudden raucous shout of laughter was like a blow. "Hark at her, Stepan, she's asking for it! Little sister, we'd have to be hard up to take on the likes of you! Better take a look at yourself in the mirror, you old crow!"

He tore the front of Olga's nightdress open, and spat between her breasts. At the same time the voice of the orderly officer, preparing to make his rounds, was heard calling from the hall.

"Coming, comrade!" "Just doing a night patrol, comrade!" The two men clattered downstairs without a backward look. And Olga stumbled down the corridor into the lavatory, ripped off the hem of her nightdress, poured water from the enamel jug on it and rubbed her defiled breast until the white skin was an angry red. Then she looked at herself in the cracked mirror. *Old* bitch, *old* crow—the stinging adjective had hit its mark. In this moment of utter humiliation, Olga saw that the thin, haggard face staring wildly back from the mirror was close to being the face of an old woman. A line from *Resurrection* came into her mind, the words of the woman taken prisoner to Siberia: "I had ceased to be a human being and had become a thing."

She went back to her sisters and calmed them. The men had been quite reasonable, she said, and she didn't think they would come back again. Nor did they, for within a few days all the men under Avdiev's command had gone along with himself, and Jacob Yurovski, the new commandant, kept a tighter discipline in the House of Special Purpose.

The inner guard Yurovski brought with him to the house were all men from the Cheka headquarters at the Amerikanski Dom. Some of them were Russians, but others were prisoners of war who had shown a special aptitude for police work, among them being at least one German. Others spoke a language which Alexandra Feodorovna thought she could identify as Magyar. All wore the black leather jackets of the Cheka, and went about their duties with a cold professionalism very different from the ranting of Avdiev's louts.

The outer guard, which numbered fifty, had been replaced, but the replacements were still local factory workers, and Yurovski himself had lived in Ekaterinburg, running a photographer's business, before he joined the Cheka. Bearded and bespectacled, he was possessed of a cold hate for the monarchy, hating with the special intensity of a Jew who believed that the Romanovs alone were responsible for the pogroms which had regularly swept through the villages and ghettos of Imperial Russia. He came to the House of Special Purpose at the moment of Mara Trenova's attempt on Lenin's life—an attempt which started off a real Red terror of cruelty and oppressions, and this wave of terrorism exactly suited the mood of Yurovski and of the Ural Soviet, which had never intended, once he was in their clutches, to let the former Czar leave Ekaterinburg alive.

The Romanovs, who were no longer allowed to read the newspapers, knew nothing about the campaign of ruthless repression which was filling the prisons and the scaffolds of Russia.

But they knew from the sounds beyond the stockade that there was much movement in the town, and one afternoon they actually heard a man shouting 'The Czechs are west of Tiumen!' before a guard ran up and herded them into the house. It was something to think about with fear and hope. They dreaded Yurovski's reaction if the Whites fought their way into Ekaterinburg. They watched his face when he came near them as if they could read the news of battle in his eyes.

The sixteenth of July began badly. They had no piano now, but they often sang Russian hymns after morning prayers, and one of the guards confessed afterwards that he had been touched to hear the fresh young voices lifted in 'The Cherubim's Song'. But this morning Marie suggested Nurse Cavell's hymn, still her favourite, and they all began to sing the English words:

Abide with me, fast falls the eventide,
The darkness deepens, Lord, with me abide.
When other helpers fail, and comforts flee—
Help of the helpless, O abide with me.

Almost before the first verse ended, Yurovski was in the living-room, icily telling them that to sing, as well as to speak, in any foreign language was absolutely forbidden, did they understand him? The girls nodded dispiritedly and went back to sew in the stifling bedroom. They had very few clothes left now, and those required constant mending.

At some time before the main meal of the day the little kitchen boy disappeared. The cook, whose only employment was brewing the coffee and warming up the tepid food sent in from the Soviet kitchen, came in wringing his hands to say the *sovietski* guards had taken the little boy away and he hadn't come back, what was to be done? Nothing, obviously. The fate of Nagorny was in all their minds, though it was hard to know what the kitchen boy, a meek little soul, could have done to offend the guards. They were now so small a company that the loss of even the least member left a gap. They still had the cook, a valet and a lady's maid for Alexandra Feodorovna, but Dr. Botkin was the only man left for Nicholas to talk to, and they had given up hoping to see the six good friends parted from them at the railway station. The girls and their father went out to the yard for exercise, and there unusual noises warned Nicholas that some pieces of light artillery, probably machine-guns, were being dragged into place against the stockade. The machine-guns on the roof of the church still pointed menacingly in their direction.

"Do you think it means the Czechs are coming near, papa?" asked Tatiana.

"I don't know, my dear, I wish I did."

"But you hope so, don't you?"

"I hardly know what to hope for, any more."

They were ordered to keep away from the stockade, and presently were herded indoors. It was still very hot inside the house. Supper was served, and the man who brought it from the communal kitchen said he knew nothing about the missing boy. Alexis began to worry about him and wonder if he had been shot like the poor boy in Tobolsk. To calm him, Dr. Botkin went upstairs and began to tell him stories, while his father and mother settled down silently to a game of bezique. Seeing them absorbed, Tatiana proposed to her sisters that they should go up to their room and talk.

"What's there to talk about?" yawned Olga.

"We could play Happy Times," said Anastasia. "We haven't played that for ages."

"I ought to mend the lace on my petticoat, it's beginning to rip."

"You're not supposed to strain your eyes, you know," said careful Tatiana.

"It's only nine o'clock, it'll be light enough to sew for an hour yet."

"Oh, come on, Olga, you can do that tomorrow," said Marie, and Olga gave in. They went upstairs and sat on their iron beds. Since the weather became so hot they were allowed to open their window at night, but as iron bars had been fixed across it since Yurovski came, their view was even more depressing than before. They played Favourite Meals as part of Happy Times, with Olga choosing the caviar which the Ural Cossacks brought every spring as a present to the Little Father, and Marie saying she'd always wanted to eat *zakuski* and drink vodka with the men. They played Favourite People, which was not a success, because their favourites were scattered far and wide, or dead, and then, after their parents came upstairs and whispered good-night at their door, they began in whispers themselves so as not to rouse Alexis, to play the Happiest Time of All.

"I wonder why we never thought of that before," said Olga. "Anastasia, you begin."

The girl, who had just passed her seventeenth birthday, pretended to be deep in reflection. "My long life!" she said lightly. "I think I've been happiest when we were acting. Even at Tobolsk, it was such fun acting with father in *The Bear*."

"You're far and away the best actress of us all," said Marie.

"I like pretending to be somebody I'm not. If we ever get away from here I'd like to be an actress, acting a scene in a prison, and knowing as soon as the curtain fell I would be free . . . Now you, Tania."

"My happiest time? I think it was when the English sailors came to Kronstadt, just before the war. We had such wonderful fun!"

"Olga?"

"Oh, I don't know. My first dance, I suppose. Do you remember that dance at Livadia?" She had said the first thing that came into her head, and a girl's first dance was a perfectly conventional choice. She was touched to see Tatiana's thin face light up as her sister said, "We all thought you looked beautiful that night, and so grown up! We leaned over the balcony and watched you opening the ball with Dmitri."

"We thought Dmitri was going to fall in love with you," said Anastasia shrewdly, and Olga said, "So did I!" She remembered a pale pink dress and a diamond necklace, and Dmitri's arm holding her lightly as they waltzed in the marble ballroom at Livadia.

"I never went to any ball, but I disgraced myself the first time I wore an evening dress and high heels at a dinner party," said Marie. "Do you remember that blue dress, and how I tripped and fell? And father looked round and said 'Of course—it's fat Marie!' Yes, you can all laugh—it was terrible! What I think were our happiest times were the cruises on the *Standart*, we always felt so—free. And then I loved going ashore for picnics, like that heavenly day in Finland, Olga, when we went to tea at Simon Karlovich's dacha."

Olga flashed her sister a quick look of gratitude. She said that just to please me, bless her, and let me know she hasn't forgotten about Simon, she thought. Oh, if I could have just one day, only one, with Simon, in Finland, in the woods!

It was still daylight when they went to bed, and the House of Special Purpose was ominously quiet. Olga, who had been sleeping badly, lay awake for a long time. Through the partly opened window, between the bars, she could see a few stars in the darkening summer blue. They made her think of the night aboard the *Standart*, after her visit to the dacha, when she had swung lazily in a cushioned hammock on the deck, and wondered if she was falling in love with Simon Hendrikov.

It was a gentle thought, and Olga was smiling when she fell asleep. It was only an hour later when her father came to wake them, saying they must rise and dress quickly, they had all been ordered to go downstairs. "All of us," he said, "the servants and Dr. Botkin too. Marie, go and help to dress Alexis. Just put a few things in one of the suitcases, they say we won't need much."

"What's happened, papa? Where are we going?"

"Yurovski wants to move us away from here for a few days. The Czechs have outflanked the city and are coming close; I suppose he's afraid of an attempt to rescue us."

He was obviously very excited and eager. The girls hastily put on the suits into which they had sewn their jewels, though it was too warm for jackets, and they decided to wear no hats. Anastasia took the Pekinese in her arms, and Alexis was carried out of his bedroom by his father, who declared that the boy's legs were growing too long for his poor old papa, and Dr. Botkin helped Alexandra Feodorovna, who clung painfully to the banister.

"Come this way," said Yurovski, waiting in the hall. "You'll have to wait a few minutes, the motors haven't arrived yet. My men are in the rooms on this floor, but you'll find some chairs in the cellar."

It was an empty room, not twenty feet square, lighted only by stable lanterns. The time was only a little past midnight, and there was still some light in the sky, which the lanterns seemed to turn to a deeper blue.

"What a queer place!"

"It doesn't seem to be used for anything."

"I was rather expecting to find some of our missing luggage, tucked away down here. Are you quite comfortable on that hard chair, mamma?"

"Joy! Joy!"

The boy's cry, which they had heard so often, reached Olga's ears too late for her, or any of them, to stop the spaniel. He had twitched his leash out of his master's lax grip, and ran in terror, a streak of brown and white, out of the cellar in the House of Special Purpose.

"You've been told again and again to keep him on his lead!"

"Oh, Anastasia, do go and find him and bring him back!" pleaded Alexis, nearly in tears.

"Thanks, I'd rather not. There are two men in the corridor with bayonets. It's all right, Alexis! He can't get out of the yard."

"He'll be waiting for us when we get into the motors," said Marie.

"I don't hear any motors. Oh, Olga, do you think they'll *hurt* him?"

"They're not hurting him at all, I can hear him barking. Move over this way a bit, Alexis, you're really too heavy for papa."

Olga sat down on the edge of a chair and took part of her brother's weight against her shoulder. It was only then that she saw the writing on the wall—two lines from Heine, written over the previous day's date, as if the German member of the Cheka had been down clearing out the cellar—

Balthasar was on that same night
Murdered by his slaves

There was hardly time for the words to sink in before the cellar door was flung wide open, and the Cheka men, headed by Yurovski, burst in with drawn revolvers in their hands.

She knew, with a great spasm of terror, that the hour of utmost dread had struck. She was aware that her mother had clutched her crucifix, that her father, with one arm round Alexis, was trying to rise and stammering "What are you—?" or "What do you—" at the same time as Yurovski choked out "Your friends are—you are guilty—" and then the shrieks and the revolver shots rang out together.

Olga flung herself across her brother. The first bullet caught her in the shoulder and spun her round. The second, in her chest, knocked her to the floor. They were falling, writhing, moaning all around her, and the men from the corridor, armed with rifles, were clubbing the dying girls with the rifle butts. The cellar reeked of fear and death. Then the last bullet struck her in the throat, a tide of blood poured from her mouth, and Olga was at peace.

30

SIMON HENDRIKOV REACHED Ekaterinburg on an autumn day, when the wind was whipping along the dusty streets, and leaden skies gave promise of an early winter.

Joe Calvert was waiting for him at the redbrick railway station. The freight yards beyond, where the Romanovs had been locked up for the whole of one night in May, were now filled with Allied armoured cars, and the passenger station was full of men dressed like Simon himself, in Russian uniform with a red and white badge representing the Lion of Bohemia.

"Simon, it's good to see you. You're looking well."

"So are you. I suppose I ought to call you Lieutenant Calvert now!"

"Don't kid me, captain. I'm embarrassed that my uniform's so new. I only got my release from the consular corps when the President decided to send an American Military Mission to the Czechs."

"So you said in your letter."

They were awkward with one another, making trite conversation, in this first meeting after so much had happened to them both. Joe Calvert said, to cover the awkwardness:

"I wish I'd known you were in Tiumen when I came west three weeks ago. It was a big surprise, when I got here, to read your name on the roster of Russian officers serving in the Czech Legion."

"I haven't been at Tiumen very long. I was at Omsk for more than two months, after the Czechs got me out of prison, and took me on the strength."

"You had a bad go of typhus before that, didn't you?"

"Yes. But as I couldn't have acted the part of a Red officer much longer, you could say the typhus saved my life. If I had any reason for living left."

"I've fixed a car," said Joe gently. "We have to pick it up at Czech HQ. You'll want to report in anyway, and then they'll arrange about your billet."

"No billet needed. I only got a short pass, and I'll have to go back to Tiumen on the night train."

"Tough going, but the trains are running better now. Up this way."

The Cheka had been flung out of the Amerikanski Dom when the Czech troops entered Ekaterinburg on the twenty-fifth of July, and it was now the headquarters of the Czech Legion in that area. There was only one way to get there, and that was up the long, hilly Liberty Street, past the House of Special Purpose, still conspicuous because of its stockade, and the white and green flag of the Independent Siberian Government flying where the red flag had flown. There were sentries posted at the gates, and Joe was not surprised when Simon identified the house at once. He stopped and said, "Is that the place?"

"Yes."

"Why the sentries?"

"Everything inside's been locked and sealed, until the full investigation can begin."

"Have *you* been inside?"

"Oh no. It was sealed off long before I got here. Mr. Gibbs and Monsieur Gilliard went in, right at the start—they had a whole lot of guts, those two—and Gibbs told me everything about it." He added gently, "You wouldn't want to see the cellar, Simon."

It was an odd thing to say, for the man was a soldier, who had seen death all around him for four long years. But the horror of the spattered cellar, where a hasty washing had not removed all the blood from the walls and floor, was surely something the man who had loved Olga could not bear to see.

"I don't want to see inside the house. I only want to see the place where they were buried." Simon moved on a few paces. "Was that the yard where they were let out for exercise?"

"I believe it was—it had to be. The Czarevich's little dog was found there, half-starved, when the Czech troops came in."

"Little Joy? The spaniel?"

"Yes, it was a King Charles. One of General Knox's ADCs is going to take it to England with him."

"I've seen Alexis playing with his dog a hundred times."

He thought of Joy gambolling at the foot of the snow mountain, climbing wet-pawed into the car where he sat with Olga by his side.

"Here we are at HQ," said Joe. While Simon was talking to the Czech commanding officer he lit a cigarette and strolled up and down the hall of the Amerikanski Dom, thinking about the ordeal immediately ahead. To say that Simon Hendrikov was looking well was a mere figure of speech: the man had had typhus fever, a spell in a Bolshevik prison before the Czechs took Omsk, and finally a crushing blow, and he showed it in his face and manner. But Joe was glad he had arranged for the young man to come to Ekaterinburg. He was only disturbed by what Simon had just said about the place where the Romanovs were buried.

The part of the forest to which they were bound was only one of the places in Siberia where the Bolsheviks had attempted to wipe the Romanovs from the face of the earth. After the murders at the House of Special Purpose, the Grand Duke Michael had been shot dead at Perm; at Alapaevsk the Czarina's sister, the Grand Duchess Elizabeth, had been killed with five Romanov princes, all of them flung living down a mine shaft; and others were in the Fortress of Peter and Paul awaiting execution. Ten thousand Russians had died in the Red terror: the British Embassy in Petrograd had been stormed and the naval attaché killed; in Moscow the Allied diplomats had to take shelter from the mob in the American consulate. All American citizens other than the military had been ordered to leave a country which had deliberately cut itself off from the world. All this was certainly known to Simon Hendrikov: there was one hideous special circumstance in the deaths of Olga and her family which he had just revealed he did not know.

Joe decided to take the bull by the horns. When Simon reappeared he drew him into a tiny anteroom, hardly bigger than a cupboard, where there was a brief chance of privacy.

"Simon," he said, "are you sure you want to go through with this? To take that drive, I mean?"

"That's what I came for, isn't it?"

"Sure it is. But there's one thing I'd better explain first. Out there at the Four Brothers—the Czar and his family aren't actually buried there—"

"But I thought that's where they were taken, afterwards—"

"Yes, they were *taken*, but then the bodies were destroyed, they weren't buried."

"How, destroyed?"

Joe told him the brutal truth. "They were dismembered at the site, and the remains were dissolved with sulphuric acid, and burned in a petrol bonfire."

Simon's square-cut face turned white. He swallowed a rush of bitter water to his mouth. It was clear that he had no words to express his horror. Joe went on, "It was the peasants from Koptiaki who broke the story first. They were coming into town with a mess of lake fish to sell, and they saw the cars, and the flames. They went back to the place later and found a lot of—objects, which helped in the identification."

"But there must have been *some* remains!"

"The bones are at the bottom of the mine shaft now, and the frost is setting in. There's nothing more to be done about it until the spring."

"But if no bodies were found maybe they aren't dead at all!" The hazel eyes lit up with hope, the fanatic hope which Joe had encountered in others who refused to believe the Romanovs were dead. "There was a story going the rounds in Omsk," Simon said, "that they'd been helped to escape and taken to a yacht in the White Sea, and that they're all on the yacht still, sailing round and round until the war is over—"

"Like the Flying Dutchman," said Joe sadly. "Don't wish that on them, whatever you do. Just try to accept that their troubles on earth are all over now."

"But Olga Nicolaievna, and her sisters, and the boy—their lives were only beginning."

Joe gripped his arm and piloted him out to the street. An army car was waiting, and beside it a Czech driver and his sergeant armed with a rifle snapped to attention and saluted as the two officers came out.

"Up the Koptiaki road, Jan," said Joe. "You know the place."

"Do we need an armed escort?" Simon asked. He spoke in French, and Joe answered in that language that there had been cases of Red snipers lurking in the woods and it was best to take no chances. The war between Russia and the west was only beginning; he had a notion that it might last in one form or another for the next fifty years. But—

"Simon," he said, "the war in Europe is as good as won.

Germany and Austria will sue for peace any day. Don't you think it's time you made some plans for the future?

"I haven't got a future now."

"My God, man, you're only—what is it—twenty-seven? You've a long life ahead of you. You'll recover from all this. When the Czech Legion goes home, to their new independent country, and I go back to my job in Vladivostok, I want you to come along with me. I'll get you a visa for the United States, and we'll work out some sort of job idea once you're there."

Simon actually laughed. "I don't know any job but soldiering," he said, "and I can't speak two words of English—"

"Learn it, then. Go *on* to England, if you like that idea better; Dolly and her husband will see you get a start. And you've got all the rest of your family in Copenhagen. You're not exactly alone in the world."

"Thanks, but talking about ideas, I don't like the idea of sponging on my relatives. Too many people have been doing that since the revolution . . . Joe, I appreciate you want to help me. But I'm quite satisfied with the job I'm doing now, fighting the Reds. If you people would send us more men and arms, we'd get it over all the sooner."

Joe shrugged his shoulders. It was the old cry, echoing through all the countries of the world since the murders at Sarajevo: More men! More guns! In Siberia Lieutenant Calvert was as much convinced as Plain Joe Calvert had been in Washington that Allied intervention in Russia could only make a desperate situation worse. But the President's military advisers had thought otherwise, and by the time the Japanese landed over seventy thousand men in Siberia, Mr. Wilson had been persuaded to order landings at Murmansk, Archangel and Vladivostok, of forces quite insufficient to their task in numbers and morale. Trotsky had responded to the challenge, as Joe had foreseen. He was making the Red Army into a great and disciplined fighting force.

The army car was slowing down as the road became a mere cart track, going deeper into the forest round Ekaterinburg. Yurovski and his gang had not brought the bodies of their victims, flung into the bottom of a truck, much more than ten miles out of town.

"Better stop here, Jan," said Joe in Russian. "We're liable to break a spring if we go much further. You two wait here till we come back."

He led Simon down a path to a clearing blackened by fire, where four pine trees stood sentinel above a disused iron mine working, with their bare trunks slashed and scarred like the saplings growing up around them.

"Is this the place?" said Simon. Instinctively he lowered his voice.

"This is the Four Brothers mine, Simon."

"They ought to call it the Four Sisters now." His face was suddenly convulsed. "But they'll be forgotten, all of them! They might as well never have lived, if it was only to end like this!"

"They won't be forgotten, not as long as decent Russians live."

"Ah!" said Simon Hendrikov, "and you've been telling me I should get out of Russia! Well, Olga didn't run away, and neither will I. I'll stay in Russia till the day I die, and fight her murderers."

Joe walked a few paces across the clearing. There were the marks of tyre tracks and spades, used for digging up the ground where many pathetic relics of the Romanovs had already been found. Simon seemed unwilling to put his foot on the burned patch, as if it truly was a grave. Joe heard the anguished voice behind him saying, "I never could do anything to help her . . . We had so little time together . . . but I loved her better than my life."

He waited a few minutes before he looked round. When he did so he saw Simon's lips moving, and supposed he was saying a prayer. But Simon was not praying. He was only repeating the words of the pledge he and Olga had once made to one another:

Gone is the resurrection kiss
But yet to come: you swore it me!

I swear it, Olga, he promised in his heart. He said aloud:

"Come, Joe, we must go back."

They walked back to the waiting car in silence. The skies were leaden over the Four Brothers, and soon the snow would come, to cover all.

ABOUT THE AUTHOR

Catherine Gavin is internationally known for her historical novels, three of which have been major American book club choices. Translated into nine foreign languages, her books include four novels now grouped as The Second Empire Quartet, set in the nineteenth century and ranging in scene from Finland to Mexico. In her new Great War series of novels, of which *The Snow Mountain* is the fourth and last book, Dr. Gavin reveals the knowledge of men and women under the stress of battle which she gained as a British war correspondent in World War II.

LOGIC OVERVIEW III—THE SEVEN STAGES OF SCIENTIFIC INVESTIGATION: THE SCIENTIFIC METHOD

(See Chapter 13)

1. Identify the problem
2. Devise preliminary hypotheses
3. Collect additional facts
4. Formulate a refined explanatory hypothesis
5. Deduce consequences from the refined hypothesis
6. Test the consequences deduced
7. Apply the theory

LOGIC OVERVIEW IV—MILL'S METHODS OF INDUCTIVE INFERENCE

(See Chapter 12)

1. **The Method of Agreement**: The one factor or circumstance that is *common* to all the cases of the phenomenon under investigation is likely to be the cause (or effect) of that phenomenon.

   A B C D occur together with w x y z.
   A E F G occur together with w t u v.
   Therefore A is the cause (or the effect) of w.

2. **The Method of Difference**: The one factor or circumstance whose *absence* or *presence distinguishes* all cases in which the phenomenon under investigation occurs from those cases in which it does not occur, is likely to be the cause, or part of the cause, of that phenomenon.

   A B C D occur together with w x y z.
   B C D occur together with x y z.
   Therefore A is the cause, or the effect, or an indispensable part of the cause of w.

3. **The Joint Method of Agreement and Difference**: The *combination*, in the same investigation, of the Method of Agreement and the Method of Difference.

   A B C — x y z. A B C — x y z.
   A D E — x t w. B C — y z.
   Therefore A is the effect, or the cause, or an indispensable part of the cause, of x.

4. **The Method of Residues**: When some portion of the phenomenon under examination is known to be the consequence of well-understood antecedent circumstances, we may infer that the *remainder* of that phenomenon is the effect of the remaining antecedents.

   A B C — x y z.
   B is known to be the cause of y.
   C is known to be the cause of z.
   Therefore A is the cause of x.

5. **The Method of Concomitant Variation**: When the variations in one phenomenon are highly *correlated* with the variation in another phenomenon, one of the two is likely to be the cause of the other, or they may be related as the products of some third factor causing both.

   A B C — x y z.
   A^+BC — x^+yz.
   Therefore A and x are causally connected.

INTRODUCTION TO LOGIC

INTRODUCTION TO LOGIC

THIRTEENTH EDITION

Irving M. Copi
University of Hawaii

Carl Cohen
University of Michigan

Upper Saddle River, New Jersey 07458

Library of Congress Cataloging-in-Publication Data

Copi, Irving M.
Introduction to logic / Irving M. Copi, Carl Cohen.—13th ed.
p. cm.
Includes bibliographical references and index.
ISBN-13: 978-0-13-614139-6
ISBN-10: 0-13-614139-0
1. Logic—Textbooks. I. Cohen, Carl, II. Title.
BC108.C69 2008
160—dc22

2007041752

Editor-in-Chief: Sarah Touborg
Project Manager (Editorial): Sarah Holle
Editorial Assistant: Carla Worner
Director of Marketing: Brandy Dawson
Marketing Manager: Sasha Anderson-Smith
Senior Managing Editor: Mary Rottino
Production Editor: Aptara/Kelly Ricci
Project Management Liaison: Joe Scordato
Operations Specialist: Cathleen Petersen
Senior Art Director: Pat Smythe
Interior and Cover Design: Ilze Lemesis
Cover Illustration/Photo: Tom Herzberg/SIS/Images.com
Illustrator (Interior): Aptara
Director, Image Resource Center: Melinda Patelli
Manager, Rights and Permissions: Zina Arabia
Manager, Visual Research: Beth Brenzel
Manager, Cover Visual Research & Permissions: Karen Sanatar
Image Permission Coordinator: Silvana Attanasio
Photo Researcher: Sheila Norman
Composition/Full-Service Management: Aptara
Printer/Binder: The Courier Companies
Cover Printer: Phoenix Color Corp.

Credits and acknowledgments borrowed from other sources and reproduced, with permission, in this textbook appear on appropriate pages within text.

Pearson Education LTD.
Pearson Education Australia PTY, Limited
Pearson Education Singapore, Pte. Ltd
Pearson Education North Asia Ltd
Pearson Education, Canada, Ltd
Pearson Educación de Mexico, S.A. de C.V.
Pearson Education—Japan
Pearson Education Malaysia, Pte. Ltd

10 9 8 7 6 5 4 3 2
Student ISBN 0-13-614139-0
978-0-13-614139-6

We dedicate this thirteenth edition of *Introduction to Logic* to the many thousands of students and their teachers, at hundreds of universities in the United States and around the world, who have relied on earlier editions of the book, and have greatly helped to improve it, over five decades.

In a Republican nation, whose citizens are to be led by persuasion and not by force, the art of reasoning becomes of the first importance.

—THOMAS JEFFERSON

Reason is the instrument on which we rightly depend when reliable judgments are needed. Nonrational instruments—habits and hunches and the like—are commonly employed, we know. But when circumstances are complicated, when our decisions affect our loved ones and ourselves gravely, when a great deal is at stake in passing judgment, we *reason* the matter out as best we can, because that is the most likely course to success.

There are rational methods, methods well tested and confirmed, for determining what is true. There are well-established techniques, rational techniques, for drawing new inferences from what we already know to be true. Our ignorance is vast, of course, and therefore we must often resort to some authority in reaching judgment—but the need for reason cannot be escaped even then, because we must decide as wisely as we can which authorities deserve our respect. In every serious intellectual pursuit we come ultimately to rely on reasoning, because there is nothing that can successfully replace it.

By nature we are endowed with powers of reasoning. Logic is the study of the uses of those powers. Intuitively, we may have long acted on sound principles, partly grasped. With care, we can bring these principles to the surface, formulate them precisely, and learn how to apply them with confidence to problems that may be solved by reason. In the study of logic we come first to recognize our own native capacities, and then to strengthen them through practice. The study of logic helps one to reason well by illuminating the principles of *correct* reasoning.

Whatever the sphere in which knowledge is sought—whether in science, or in politics, or in the conduct of our private lives—we use logic in reaching defensible conclusions. In the formal study of logic, with which this book is concerned, we learn how to acquire truths and how to evaluate competing claims for truth. Ideally, every college course should contribute to this end, yet we know that many do not. Much that is taught in college classes soon grows out of date. But the skills of accurate thinking never become obsolete, and the development of these skills lies squarely within the province of the study of logic. The study of logic helps us to identify arguments that are good, and to understand why they are good. The study of logic helps us to identify arguments that are bad, and to understand why they are bad. No study is more useful or more widely relevant to our serious concerns than this.

This considered assurance we give to our readers: A command of the fundamental principles of correct reasoning, which the study of this book promotes, will make a deeply satisfying, significant, and permanent contribution to one's intellectual life.

Preface to the Thirteenth Edition

Earlier editions of *Introduction to Logic* have been warmly received by our philosophical colleagues around the world. James Druley from Reedley College, Madera, CA, who was one of the reviewers of the twelfth edition wrote: "Several times, after reading a part of the text I have thought, 'That could not have been written any more insightfully or elegantly; that could not have been explained better.'" We are gratified by such kind words, of course, but we are not content. In this thirteenth edition we correct some inaccuracies, reformulate some dense passages, and introduce some new material. The essential structure and substance of the book have been retained, but for those who are familiar with earlier editions of the text we note here five major adjustments that we think will be helpful to both instructors and students.

First. The material in Part I has been compressed. Complexities in the identification of arguments are now more closely tied to the basic concepts introduced in Chapter 1, thus permitting Chapter 2 to be devoted entirely to the *analysis* of arguments. Discussion of the uses and misuses of language is now integrated with the examination of definitions, permitting the consolidation of two earlier chapters (3 and 4) into one. The account of informal fallacies (now Chapter 4) has been extended by including some fallacies that had been earlier passed over, with juicy illustrations taken from current controversies.

Second. The greatest change in this edition appears at the point where the construction of formal proofs of validity is first introduced, in what is now Chapter 9. Users of the book have impressed on us the need to make less formidable the tasks with which the introductory student is confronted at this juncture. The passage—from the first illustrations of formal proofs to exercise sets in which some rather complicated proofs are called for—was speedy, and for many it was frustrating. The intellectual *gradient* in this chapter has been reduced. The construction of proofs is explained and illustrated at gradually increasing levels of difficulty.

The illustrations used to this end are taken from the exercise sets that have long been relied on. However, it is also very convenient to preserve, for those and other exercises, the same numbering as was used in previous editions. Completely renumbering the exercises would prove disruptive for many.

Devising a formal proof can never be the mechanical procedure some students long for, of course, but with the path of deductive strategizing made somewhat smoother, the construction of proofs may become less puzzling and more fun. The introduction of formal proofs is now friendlier than it was, and has been expanded substantially.

Third. In Part III, where causal analyses are integrated into the discussion of hypotheses and their confirmation in science, the exposition has been reordered and tightened. Some historical materials thought by many to be tangential have been eliminated. This presentation (now Chapter 13) is shorter and more direct than it was, yet we have retained some of the classical illustrations of scientific method that are as beautiful as they are instructive. The scientific examples used here are taken mainly from research and discoveries of this decade.

Fourth. The treatment of footnotes has been changed. Notes of two kinds are distinguished. Some footnotes pertain to logical restrictions supposed by the text, or to the usage of terms in the text, or to other intellectual refinements that are properly tied to the material at that point in the text. These continue to appear, as they must, on the pages where those refinements are relevant. The majority of notes, however, supply references to articles, books, persons, speeches, research activities, and the like that readers may wish to investigate and are surely entitled to know. (The trove most commonly mined is *The New York Times,* a periodical from whose pages illustrative arguments and examples bubble perpetually.) Such references are not central to the study of logic itself. When placed on the text page they may encumber the exposition of logical concerns, and therefore they now appear as endnotes at the end of each chapter.

Fifth. Introduction to Logic in all of its editions has been rich with illustrative materials and exercises taken from events and controversies in real life, from history and some classical sources, but mainly from contemporary periodicals and books. We take pride in the fact that, as our reviewers have noted, those studying "Copi and Cohen" are inescapably introduced to a very wide range of intellectual concerns and thus learn more than logic. Exhibiting arguments and theories (good and bad) by illustrating them with genuine controversies in the world of college students, rather than illustrations concocted for the purpose, has been a notable feature of our book, and no small task to maintain. Logical theory is most fully grasped when it is vividly applied to contemporary human affairs. In this edition of *Introduction to Logic* we have added many fresh illustrations, replacing those more dated, along with some new arguments arising in connection with the lively issues of the first decade of the twenty-first century. In the selection of these illustrations and exercises we seek scrupulously to avoid partisanship. On all sides of controversial issues, good arguments, and bad ones, may appear. Support for one view or another in current controversy is not our proper business; the understanding and analysis of arguments is.

Two other changes deserve brief mention here. First, a comprehensive account of the syllogism, largely unaltered, is presented in the first chapters of Part II. However, we have changed the placement of what we call the *deduction* of the fifteen valid forms of the categorical syllogism. This deduction, unique and elegant, is very much in the spirit of analytical syllogistics, but it is not vital for a student's understanding of syllogisms and therefore it now appears as an Appendix to Chapter 6. There are no other such appendixes. Second, the ideal number of exercise solutions to provide is perennially in dispute; some instructors prefer more, some would include none at all. We have decided to retain, at the back of the book, solutions to selected exercises in Chapters 5, 6, 7, 8, 9, 10, and 14—but also to eliminate the long discursive solutions, which are much less widely relied on, for exercises in other chapters. This has made possible the more gradual and more detailed introduction to formal proofs of validity in the body of the book.

In this thirteenth edition of *Introduction to Logic* we aim to realize yet more fully the combination of accuracy, clarity, and penetration that has always been our objective. To this end we have relied on the support and advice of students and instructors who use the book and who are sensitive to its shortcomings. We conclude, therefore, with an earnest invitation to our readers to join us in advancing this never-ending project. Send us corrections as needed, and suggestions of every kind. Your contributions, warmly welcome, may be most conveniently addressed to Carl Cohen at **ccohen@umich.edu**. The experience and wisdom of the students and teachers who rely on *Introduction to Logic* have helped to make it the world's most widely used book in the study of logic. We receive your responses to it with respect and heartfelt gratitude.

Carl Cohen
The University of Michigan, Ann Arbor

To students of logic around the world who have given us perceptive guidance and loyal support, we express our heartfelt gratitude.

Among the many scholars who have contributed to the improvement of this thirteenth edition of *Introduction to Logic* there are some whose efforts have been particularly penetrating and long-continued. To them we convey most respectful thanks:

Prof. Benjamin Abellera, of the University of the District of Columbia
Prof. Keith Burgess-Jackson, of the University of Texas at Arlington
Prof. Daniel E. Flage, of James Madison University, Harrisonburg, Virginia
Prof. Joseph Gilbert, of the State University of New York at Brockport
Ms. Erika Malinoski, of the University of Michigan
Ms. Deborah Pugh, of Stanford, California
Mr. Chris Raabe, of Yakatut, Alaska
Mr. Paul Tang, of California State University, Long Beach

Contributors to this edition have been very numerous. College students, as well as instructors, have written to suggest improvements, to point out ambiguities or inaccuracies, to note typographical errors, to suggest useful illustrative materials. All receive our direct response, of course; but we take satisfaction in listing here also the names of some of those to whom we are indebted for contributions large and small to this thirteenth edition of *Introduction to Logic:*

Prof. John M. Abbarno, of D'Youville College, Buffalo, New York
Dr. Gerald Abrams, of the University of Michigan, Ann Arbor
Mr. Russell Alfonso, of the University of Hawaii, Honolulu
Mr. Wyatt Dean Ammon, of Hamline University, St. Paul, Minnesota
Mr. Jason Bates, of the University of Michigan, Ann Arbor
Ms. Amelia Bischof, of Ithaca College, Ithaca, New York
Prof. Jeffery Borrowdale, of Cuesta College, San Louis Obispo, California
Mr. Nicholas Bratton, of Seattle, Washington
Mr. Bryan Campbell, of Vanderbilt University, Nashville, Tennesee
Prof. Rebecca Carr, of George Washington University, Washington, D.C.
Prof. Sidney Chapman, of Richland College, Dallas, Texas
Prof. Zoe Close, of Grossmont College, El Cajon, California
Prof. William S. Cobb, of the University of Michigan, Ann Arbor
Prof. Malcolm S. Cohen, of the University of Michigan, Ann Arbor
Mr. Keith Coleman, of the University of Kansas, Lawrence
Mr. Joshua De Young, of the University of Michigan, Ann Arbor
Mr. Eric Dyer, of the University of Michigan, Ann Arbor
Prof. Elmer H. Duncan, of Baylor University, Waco, Texas
Mr. Kumar Eswaran, of Temple University, Philadelphia, Pennsylvania
Prof. Kevin Funchion, of Salem State College, Salem, Massachusetts
Ms. Elizabeth Gartner, of the University of Michigan, Ann Arbor
Prof. Faith Gielow, of Villanova University, Villanova, Pennsylvania
Mr. Anand Giridharadas, of Mumbai, India
Prof. Sidney Gospe, of the University of Washington, Seattle
Mr. Michael Graubert, of London, England
Dr. Robert A. Greene, of the University of Michigan, Ann Arbor

Mr. Joseph Grcic, of Indiana State University, Terre Haute, Indiana
Ms. Janice Grzankowski, of Cheektowaga, New York
Mr. Matthew Hampel, of the University of Michigan, Ann Arbor
Prof. Allan Hancock, of Cuesta College, San Louis Obispo, California
Prof. Warren Harbison, of Boise State University, Boise, Idaho
Mr. Abdul Halim B. Abdul Karim, of the National University of Singapore
Prof. Clare Swift Heiller, of Bakersfield College, Bakersfield, California
Prof. Jeremiah Joaquin, De La Salle University, Manila, Philippines
Prof. Royce Jones, of Illinois College, Jacksonville, Illinois
Prof. Gale Justin, California State University at Sacramento
Mr. Rory Kraft, Jr., of Michigan State University, East Lansing
Prof. Richard T. Lambert, of Carroll College, Helena, Montana
Mr. James Lipscomb, of Tarrytown, New York
Mr. Charles Lambros, of the State University of New York at Buffalo
Mr. Andrew LaZella, of Hamline University, St. Paul, Minnesota
Prof. Gerald W. Lilje, of Washington State University, Pullman
Ms. Linda Lorenz, of Ann Arbor, Michigan
Prof. E. M. Macierowski, of Benedictine College, Atchison, Kansas
Prof. Krishna Mallik, of Bentley College, Waltham, Massachusetts
Mr. Neil Manson, of the University of Aberdeen, United Kingdom
Prof. Edwin Martin, of North Carolina State University, Raleigh
Prof. Michael J. Matthis, of Kutztown University, Kutztown, Pennsylvania
Prof. George Mavrodes, of the University of Michigan, Ann Arbor
Prof. Leemon McHenry, of Wittenberg University, Springfield, Ohio
Mr. David A. Mihaila, of Honolulu, Hawaii
Prof. Richard W. Miller, of the University of Missouri at Rolla
Ms. Erin Moore, of Ohio State University, Columbus
Ms. Susan Moore, of Fairgrove, Michigan
Prof. Kippy Myers, of Freed-Hardeman University, Henderson, Tennessee
Mr. Michael North, of the University of Michigan, Ann Arbor
Prof. Sumer Pek, of the University of Michigan, Ann Arbor
Prof. Ray Perkins, Plymouth State College, Plymouth, New Hampshire
Prof. Howard Pospesel, of the University of Miami, Coral Gables, Florida
Mr. Robert Picciotto, of Gastonia, North Carolina
Mr. Wayne Praeder, of the U.S. Chess Federation
Prof. Dennis P. Quinn, of St. Vincent College, Latrobe, Pennsylvania
Mr. Nicholas Quiring, of the University of Michigan, Ann Arbor
Mr. Jay Rapaport, of the University of Michigan, Ann Arbor
Dr. Patrick Rarden, of Appalachian State University, Boone, North Carolina
Prof. Lee C. Rice, of Marquette University, Milwaukee, Wisconsin
Dr. Thomas Riggins, of New York University, New York City
Prof. Blaine B. Robinson, of the South Dakota School of Mines, Rapid City
Mr. Milton Schwartz, Esq., of New York, New York
Mr. Amit Sharma, of V. S. Niketan College, Kathmandu, Nepal
Prof. Emeritus Albert C. Shaw, of Rowan College, Glassboro, New Jersey
Prof. Edward Sherline, of the University of Wyoming, Laramie
Dr. Barbara M. Sloat, of the University of Michigan, Ann Arbor
Ms. Lauren Shubow, of the University of Michigan, Ann Arbor
Mr. Jason A. Sickler, of the University of North Dakota, Grand Forks
Ms. Stefanie Silverman, of the University of Michigan, Ann Arbor
Prof. Michael Slattery, of Villanova University, Villanova, Pennsylvania
Prof. James Stewart, of Bowling Green State University, Bowling Green, Ohio

Mr. Andrew Tardiff, of North Kingstown, Rhode Island
Mr. J. A. Van de Mortel, of Cerritos College, Norwalk, California
Mr. Chris Viger, of the University of Western Ontario
Mr. Roy Weatherford, of the University of South Florida, Tampa
Prof. Allen Weingarten, of Morristown, New Jersey
Prof. Warren Weinstein, of California State University at Long Beach
Prof. Philip H. Wiebe, of Trinity Western University, British Columbia, Canada
Mr. Michael Wingfield, of Lake Dallas, Texas
Mr. Isaiah Wunsch, of the University of Michigan, Ann Arbor

Two other groups deserve special mention. First, we express warm thanks to the twelve penetrating scholars, from around the country, each of whom submitted a meticulous review of the twelfth edition and made many very helpful suggestions for this edition. In alphabetical order they are:

Emil Badici, University of Florida, Gainesville, Florida
Stephen Barnes, Northwest Vista College, San Antonio, Texas
Teresa Britton, Eastern Illinois University, Charleston, Illinois
Jennifer Caseldine-Bracht, Indiana Univ.—Purdue Univ., Ft. Wayne, Indiana
James Druly, Reedley College, Madera Center, Madera, California
R. Valentine Dusek, University of New Hampshire, Durham, New Hampshire
David O'Connor, Seton Hall University, South Orange, New Jersey
David C. Ring, Orange Coast College, Costa Mesa, California
Rudy Saldana, Citrus College, Glendora, California
Mark L. Thomas, Blinn College, Bryan, Texas
David A. Truncellito, George Washington University, Washington, DC
Maria Zaccaria, Georgia Perimeter College, Dunwoody, Georgia

At the University of Michigan, in Ann Arbor, ten of my students lent their sharp eyes and keen minds in the continuing effort to eliminate errors from the text. They are: Tamara Andrade, Maximilian Bauer, Evan Blanchard, Benjamin Block, Meredith Crimp, Morgan Fett, Medeline Metzger, John Oltean, Meghan Urisko, and Cynthia Yuen. We are grateful for their loyal support.

Finally, we acknowledge the good will, unflagging energy, and keen intelligence of the entire editorial staff at Prentice Hall, the Project Manager, Sarah Holle, and the long-time contributor to this book, Carla Worner. We also note with pleasure the successful efforts of Kelly Ricci and her staff at Aptara, whose painstaking labors produced the handsome volume now in each reader's hands.

Carl Cohen
The University of Michigan, Ann Arbor

INTRODUCTION TO
LOGIC

Waterfall, by M. C. Escher, is all wrong. The water flows away, and going away comes closer; it flows downward, and going down it comes up, returning to the point from which it began. What can account for the plausible appearance of what we know to be impossible? The artist plays with the normal assumptions of our vision. The corner points of the central cube in this picture are connected in ways that cause us to perceive what is farthest away on the structure as closest, and to perceive its highest points as also its lowest. We are duped by Escher's artistry.

As perception may be tricked by a clever picture, our thinking may be tricked by a clever argument. There are principles that underlie good reasoning, but when we violate them we are likely to be misled—or by carelessness to mislead ourselves. In *Waterfall* we confront disorder in seeing, and then with scrutiny detect its cause. In the study of logic we confront many bad arguments, and then with scrutiny learn what makes them bad.

PART I

Logic and Language

"Come now, and let us reason together."

Isaiah 1:18

"All our lives we are giving and accepting reasons. Reasons are the coin we pay for the beliefs we hold."

Edith Watson Schipper

Basic Logical Concepts

1.1 What Logic Is

Logic is the study of the methods and principles used to distinguish correct from incorrect reasoning.

When we reason about any matter, we produce arguments to support our conclusions. Our arguments include reasons that we think justify our beliefs. However, not all reasons are good reasons. Therefore we may always ask, when we confront an argument: Does the conclusion reached *follow* from the premises assumed? To answer this question there are objective criteria; in the study of logic we seek to discover and apply those criteria.

Reasoning is not the only way in which we support an assertion we make or accept. We may appeal to authority or to emotion, which can be very persuasive and are appropriate in some contexts. We often rely, without reflection, simply on habits. But when we aim to make *judgments* that are to be relied on, their most solid foundation will be correct reasoning. Using the methods and techniques of logic—the subject matter of this book—we can distinguish reliably between sound and faulty reasoning.

1.2 Propositions and Arguments

We begin by examining more closely the most fundamental concepts in the study of logic, concepts presupposed in the paragraphs just above. In reasoning we construct and evaluate *arguments*; arguments are built with *propositions.* Although these concepts are apparently simple, they require careful analysis.

A. PROPOSITIONS

Propositions are the building blocks of our reasoning. A **proposition** asserts that something is the case. We may affirm a proposition, or deny it—but every proposition either asserts what really is the case, or it does not. Therefore every proposition is either true, or it is false.

There are many propositions about whose truth we are uncertain. "There is life on some other planet in our galaxy," for example, is a proposition that, so far as we now know, may be true or may be false. Its "truth value" is unknown. But this proposition, like every proposition, must be either true or false.

A question *asserts* nothing, and therefore it is not a proposition. "Do you know how to play chess?" is indeed a sentence, but that sentence makes no claim about the world. Neither is a command a proposition ("Come quickly!"), or an exclamation ("Oh my gosh!"). Questions, commands, and exclamations—unlike propositions—are neither true nor false.

When we assert some proposition, we do so using a sentence in some language. However, the proposition we assert is not identical to that sentence. This is evident because two different sentences, consisting of different words differently arranged, may have the same meaning and may be used to assert the very same proposition. For example, "Leslie won the election" and "The election was won by Leslie" are plainly two different sentences that make the same assertion.

Sentences are always parts of some language, but propositions are not tied to English or to any given language. The four sentences

It is raining.	(English)
Está lloviendo.	(Spanish)
Il pleut.	(French)
Es regnet.	(German)

are in different languages, but they have a single meaning; all four, using different words, may be uttered to assert the very same proposition. *Proposition* is the term we use to refer to what it is that declarative sentences are typically used to assert.

The term **statement** is not an exact synonym of *proposition*, but it is often used in logic in much the same sense. Some logicians prefer "statement" to "proposition," although the latter has been more commonly used in the history of logic. In this book we use both terms.

The very same sentence can be used to make very different statements (or to assert very different propositions), depending on the context in which it is expressed. For example, the sentence, "The largest state in the United States was once an independent republic," was at one time a true statement (or proposition) about Texas, but it is now a false statement about Alaska. The same words assert different propositions at different times.

Propositions may be *simple*, like those used in the preceding illustrations, but they may also be *compound*, containing other propositions within themselves. Consider the following proposition, from a recent account of the exploitation of the Amazon Basin in Brazil:

> The Amazon Basin produces roughly 20 percent of the Earth's oxygen, creates much of its own rainfall, and harbors many unknown species.[1]

This sentence asserts the conjunction of three propositions, concerning what the Amazon Basin produces, and what it creates, and what it harbors. The passage thus constitutes a *conjunctive* proposition. Asserting a conjunctive proposition is equivalent to asserting each of its component propositions separately.

Some compound propositions do not assert the truth of their components. In *disjunctive* (or *alternative*) *propositions*, no one of the components is asserted. Abraham Lincoln (in a message to Congress in December 1861) said, "Circuit courts are useful, or they are not useful." This disjunctive proposition is plainly true, but either one of its components might be false.

Other compound propositions that do not assert their components are *hypothetical* (or *conditional*) *propositions*. The eighteenth-century freethinker Francois Voltaire said, "If God did not exist, it would be necessary to invent him." Here, again, neither of the two components is asserted. The proposition that "God does not exist" is not asserted, nor is the proposition that "it is necessary to invent him." Only the "if–then" proposition is asserted by the hypothetical or conditional statement, and that compound statement might be true even if both of its components were false.

In logic, the internal structure of propositions is important. To evaluate an argument we need a full understanding of the propositions that appear in that argument. Propositions of many different kinds will be analyzed in this book.

B. ARGUMENTS

With propositions as building blocks, we construct *arguments.* In any argument we affirm one proposition on the basis of some other propositions. In doing this, an *inference* is drawn. **Inference** is a process that may tie together a cluster of propositions. Some inferences are *warranted* (or correct); others are not. The logician analyzes these clusters, examining the propositions with which the process begins and with which it ends, as well as the relations among these propositions. Such a cluster of propositions constitutes an *argument.* Arguments are the chief concern of logic.

Argument is a technical term in logic. It need not involve disagreement, or controversy. In logic, **argument** refers strictly to any group of propositions of which one is claimed to follow from the others, which are regarded as providing support for the truth of that one. For every possible inference there is a corresponding argument.

In writing or in speech, a passage will often contain several related propositions and yet contain no argument. An argument is not merely a collection of propositions; it is a cluster with a structure that captures or exhibits some inference. We describe this structure with the terms *conclusion* and *premise*. The **conclusion** of an argument is the proposition that is affirmed on the basis of the other propositions of the argument. Those other propositions, which are affirmed (or assumed) as providing support for the conclusion, are the **premises** of the argument.

We will encounter a vast range of arguments in this book—arguments of many different kinds, on many different topics. We will analyze arguments in politics, in ethics, in sports, in religion, in science, in law, and in everyday life. Those who defend these arguments, or who attack them, are usually aiming to establish the truth (or the falsity) of the conclusions drawn. As logicians, however, our interest is in the arguments as such. As agents or as citizens we may be deeply concerned about the truth or falsity of the conclusions drawn. But *as logicians* we put those interests aside. Our concerns will be chiefly two. First, we will be concerned about the *form* of an argument under consideration, to determine if that argument is *of a kind* that is likely to yield a warranted conclusion. Second, we will be concerned about the *quality* of the argument, to determine whether it *does in fact* yield a warranted conclusion.

Arguments vary greatly in the degree of their complexity. Some are very simple. Other arguments, as we will see, are quite intricate, sometimes because of the structure or formulation of the propositions they contain, sometimes because of the relations among the premises, and sometimes because of the relations between premises and conclusion.

The simplest kind of argument consists of one premise and a conclusion that is claimed to follow from it. Each may be stated in a separate sentence, as in the following argument that appears on a sticker affixed to biology textbooks in the state of Alabama:

> No one was present when life first appeared on earth. Therefore any statement about life's origins should be considered as theory, not fact.

Or both premise and conclusion may be stated within the same sentence, as in this argument arising out of recent advances in the science of human genetics:

> Since it turns out that all humans are descended from a small number of African ancestors in our recent evolutionary past, believing in profound differences between the races is as ridiculous as believing in a flat earth.[2]

The order in which premises and conclusion appear can also vary, but it is not critical in determining the quality of the argument. It is common for the conclusion of an argument to *precede* the statement of its premise or premises. On the day Babe Ruth hit his 700th home run (13 July 1934), the following argument appeared in the *New York Times:*

> A record that promises to endure for all time was attained on Navin Field today when Babe Ruth smashed his seven-hundredth home run in a lifetime career. It promises to live, first because few players in history have enjoyed the longevity on the diamond of the immortal Bambino, and, second, because only two other players in the history of baseball have hit more than 300 home runs.

This is an example of an argument whose two premises, each numbered, appear after the conclusion is stated. It is also an example of a very plausible argument whose conclusion is false.[3]

Even when premise and conclusion are united in one sentence, the conclusion of the argument may come first. The English utilitarian philosopher, Jeremy Bentham, presented this crisp argument:

> Every law is an evil, for every law is an infraction of liberty.[4]

Although this is only one short sentence, it is an argument because it contains two propositions, of which the first (every law is an evil) is the conclusion and the second (every law is an infraction of liberty) is the premise. However, no single proposition can be an argument, because an argument is made up of a group of propositions. Yet some propositions, because they are compound, do sound like arguments, and care must be taken to distinguish them from the arguments they resemble. Consider the following hypothetical proposition:

> If I did not want people to be agreeable, that would save me the trouble of liking them.

Neither the first nor the second component of this proposition is asserted. All that is asserted is that the former implies the latter, and both might well be false. No inference is drawn, no conclusion is claimed to be true. The great novelist Jane Austen wrote, in a letter:

> I do not want people to be very agreeable, as it saves me the trouble of liking them a great deal.[5]

In this case we do have an argument. The first proposition is asserted as a premise, and the second proposition is also asserted to follow from that premise as its conclusion. A hypothetical proposition may *look like* an argument, but it can never *be* an argument, and the two should not be confused.

These arguments of Jeremy Bentham and Jane Austen are short and simple; most arguments are longer and more complicated. Every argument, however, short or long, simple or complex, consists of a group of propositions of which one is the conclusion and the other(s) are the premises offered to support it.

Although every argument is a structured cluster of propositions, not every structured cluster of propositions is an argument. Consider this very recent account of global inequality:

> In the same world in which more than a billion people live at a level of affluence never previously known, roughly a billion other people struggle to survive on the purchasing power equivalent of less than one U.S. dollar per day. Most of the world's poorest people are undernourished, lack access to safe drinking water or even the most basic health services and cannot send their children to school. According to Unicef, more than 120 million children die every year—about 30,000 per day—from avoidable, poverty-related causes.[6]

This report is deeply troubling—but there is no argument here.

Reasoning is an art, as well as a science. It is something we *do*, as well as something we understand. Giving reasons for our beliefs comes naturally, but skill in the art of building arguments, and testing them, requires practice. One who has practiced and strengthened these skills is more likely to reason correctly than one who has never thought about the principles involved. Therefore we provide in this book very many opportunities for practice in the analysis of argument.

EXERCISES

Identify the premises and conclusions in the following passages.

EXAMPLE

1. A well-regulated militia being necessary to the security of a free state, the right of the people to keep and bear arms shall not be infringed.

—*The Constitution of the United States,* Amendment 2

SOLUTION

Premise: A well-regulated militia is necessary for the security of a free state.

Conclusion: The right of the people to keep and bear arms shall not be infringed.

2. What stops many people from photocopying a book and giving it to a pal is not integrity but logistics; it's easier and inexpensive to buy your friend a paperback copy.

—Randy Cohen, *The New York Times Magazine,* 26 March 2000

3. Thomas Aquinas argued that human intelligence is a gift from God and therefore "to apply human intelligence to understand the world is not an affront to God, but is pleasing to him."

—Recounted by Charles Murray in *Human Accomplishment* (New York: HarperCollins, 2003)

4. Sir Edmund Hillary is a hero, not because he was the first to climb Mount Everest, but because he never forgot the Sherpas who helped him achieve this impossible feat. He dedicated his life to helping build schools and hospitals for them.

—Patre S. Rajashekhar, "Mount Everest," *National Geographic*, September 2003

5. Standardized tests have a disparate racial and ethnic impact; white and Asian students score, on average, markedly higher than their black and Hispanic peers. This is true for fourth-grade tests, college entrance exams, and every other assessment on the books. If a racial gap is evidence of discrimination, then all tests discriminate.

—Abigail Thernstrom, "Testing, the Easy Target," *The New York Times*, 15 January 2000

6. Good sense is, of all things in the world, the most equally distributed, for everybody thinks himself so abundantly provided with it that even those most difficult to please in all other matters do not commonly desire more of it than they already possess.

—René Descartes, *A Discourse on Method*, 1637

7. When Noah Webster proposed a *Dictionary of the American Language*, his early 19th century critics presented the following argument against it: "Because any words new to the United States are either stupid or foreign, there is no such thing as the American language; there's just bad English."

—Jill Lepore, "Noah's Mark," *The New Yorker*, 6 November 2006

8. The death penalty is too costly. In New York State alone taxpayers spent more than $200 million in our state's failed death penalty experiment, with no one executed.

   In addition to being too costly, capital punishment is unfair in its application. The strongest reason remains the epidemic of exonerations of death row inmates upon post-conviction investigation, including ten New York inmates freed in the last 18 months from long sentences being served for murders or rapes they did not commit.

—L. Porter, "Costly, Flawed Justice," *The New York Times*, 26 March 2007

9. Houses are built to live in, not to look on; therefore, let use be preferred before uniformity.

—Francis Bacon, "Of Building," in *Essays*, 1597

10. To boycott a business or a city [as a protest] is not an act of violence, but it can cause economic harm to many people. The greater the economic impact of a boycott, the more impressive the statement it makes. At the same time, the economic consequences are likely to be shared by people who are innocent of any wrongdoing, and who can ill afford the loss of income: hotel workers, cab drivers, restauranteurs and merchants. The boycott weapon ought to be used sparingly, if for no other reason than the harm it can cause such bystanders.

—Alan Wolfe, "The Risky Power of the Academic Boycott," *The Chronicle of Higher Education*, 17 March 2000

11. Ethnic cleansing was viewed not so long ago as a legitimate tool of foreign policy. In the early part of the 20th century forced population shifts were not uncommon; multicultural empires crumbled and nationalism drove the formation of new, ethnically homogenous countries.

—Belinda Cooper, "Trading Places," *The New York Times Book Review*, 17 September 2006

12. If a jury is sufficiently unhappy with the government's case or the government's conduct, it can simply refuse to convict. This possibility puts powerful pressure on the state to behave properly. For this reason a jury is one of the most important protections of a democracy.

—Robert Precht, "Japan, the Jury," *The New York Times*, 1 December 2006

13. Without forests, orangutans cannot survive. They spend more than 95 percent of their time in the trees, which, along with vines and termites, provide more than 99 percent of their food. Their only habitat is formed by the tropical rain forests of Borneo and Sumatra.

—Birute Galdikas, "The Vanishing Man of the Forest," *The New York Times*, 6 January 2007

14. Omniscience and omnipotence are mutually incompatible. If God is omniscient, he must already know how he is going to intervene to change the course of history using his omnipotence. But that means he can't change his mind about his intervention, which means he is not omnipotent.

—Richard Dawkins, *The God Delusion* (New York: Houghton Mifflin, 2006)

15. Reason is the greatest enemy that faith has; it never comes to the aid of spiritual things, but more frequently than not struggles against the divine Word, treating with contempt all that emanates from God.

—Martin Luther, *Last Sermon in Wittenberg*, 17 January 1546

1.3 Recognizing Arguments

Before we can evaluate an argument, we must *recognize* it. We must be able to distinguish argumentative passages in writing or speech. Doing this assumes, of course, an understanding of the language of the passage. However, even with a thorough comprehension of the language, the identification of an argument can be problematic because of the peculiarities of its formulation. Even when we are confident that an argument is intended in some context, we may be unsure about which propositions are serving as its premises and which as its conclusion. As we have seen, that judgment cannot be made on the basis of the order in which the propositions appear. How then shall we proceed?

A. CONCLUSION INDICATORS AND PREMISE INDICATORS

One useful method depends on the appearance of certain common indicators, certain words or phrases that typically serve to signal the appearance of an argument's conclusion or of its premises. Here is a partial list of **conclusion indicators:**

therefore	for these reasons
hence	it follows that
so	I conclude that
accordingly	which shows that
in consequence	which means that
consequently	which entails that
proves that	which implies that
as a result	which allows us to infer that
for this reason	which points to the conclusion that
thus	we may infer

Other words or phrases typically serve to mark the premises of an argument and hence are called **premise indicators.** Usually, but not always, what follows any one of these will be the premise of some argument. Here is a partial list of premise indicators:

since	as indicated by
because	the reason is that
for	for the reason that
as	may be inferred from
follows from	may be derived from
as shown by	may be deduced from
inasmuch as	in view of the fact that

B. ARGUMENTS IN CONTEXT

The words and phrases we have listed may help to indicate the presence of an argument or identify its premises or conclusion, but such indicators do not necessarily appear. Sometimes it is just the meaning of the passage, or its setting, that indicates the presence of an argument. For example, during the intense controversy over the deployment of additional U.S. troops to Iraq in 2007, one critic of that deployment wrote:

> As we send our young men and women abroad to bring order to Iraq, many of its so-called leaders have abandoned their posts. We have given the Iraqis an opportunity to iron out their differences and they throw it back in our faces. Iraq does not deserve our help.[7]

No premise indicators or conclusion indicators are used here, yet the argument is clear. Indicators are also absent in the following argument, recently offered by a notorious atheist, whose premises and conclusions are unmistakable:

> Half the American population believes that the universe is 6,000 years old. They are wrong about this. Declaring them so is not "irreligious intolerance." It is intellectual honesty.[8]

Often, however, the force of an argument can be appreciated only when one understands the *context* in which that argument is presented. For example, the undergraduate admission system of the University of Michigan that gave a fixed number of extra points to all members of certain minority groups was held unconstitutional by the U.S. Supreme Court in *Gratz v. Bollinger* in 2003. Justice Ruth Bader Ginsburg dissented, defending the Michigan system with the following argument:

> Universities will seek to maintain their minority enrollment . . . whether or not they can do so in full candor. . . . [They] may resort to camouflage. If honesty is the best policy, surely Michigan's accurately described, fully disclosed College affirmative action program is preferable to achieving similar numbers through winks, nods, and disguises.[9]

This argument derives its force from the realization that universities had in fact long disguised their preferential admission programs to avoid attacks based on the equal protection clause of the 14th Amendment to the U.S. Constitution. Chief Justice William Rehnquist's response to Justice Ginsburg's argument is also intelligible only in the context of her defense of the preferential admission system. Rehnquist wrote:

> These observations are remarkable for two reasons. First, they suggest that universities—to whose academic judgment we are told we should defer—will pursue their affirmative action programs whether or not they violate the United States Constitution. Second, they recommend that these violations should be dealt with, not by requiring the Universities to obey the Constitution, but by changing the Constitution so that it conforms to the conduct of the universities.[10]

Rehnquist's reference to "changing the Constitution" must be understood in the light of the fact that the Michigan undergraduate admission system had been held unconstitutional. His reference to the pursuit of affirmative action programs "whether or not they violate the United States Constitution" can best be understood in the light of Ginsburg's earlier reference to the possible use of "winks, nods, and disguises."

The full force of argument and counterargument can be grasped, in most circumstances, only with an understanding of the *context* in which those arguments are presented. In real life, context is critical.[11]

C. PREMISES NOT IN DECLARATIVE FORM

It is not uncommon for the premises of an argument to be presented in the form of questions. But if questions assert nothing, and do not express propositions, how is this possible? On the surface they make no assertions; beneath the surface an interrogative sentence can serve as a premise when its question is **rhetorical**—that is, when it suggests or assumes an answer that is made to serve as the premise of an argument. The sentence may be interrogative even though its meaning is declarative.

This use of questions is sometimes obvious, as in a recent letter to The *New York Times* objecting to a new series of U.S. coins that will honor former presidential wives. The critic writes:

> I am irked by the new set of coins being issued. While some first ladies have influenced our country, should we bestow this honor on people who are unelected, whose only credential is having a prominent spouse?[12]

Plainly, the critic means to affirm the proposition that we should not bestow this honor on such people. He continues:

> Wouldn't honoring women who have served as governors, Supreme Court justices or legislators be a more fitting tribute to this nation's women than coins featuring "First Spouses"?[13]

This critic obviously believes that honoring such achievements would be a more fitting tribute, but he again expresses that proposition with a question. His letter also provides an illustration of the need to rely on context to interpret declarative statements that are actually made. The writer's report that he is "irked" by the new set of coins is no doubt true, but this statement is more than a mere description of his state of mind; he means to express the judgment that such a set of coins *ought not* be issued.

Using questions to express a premise is sometimes counterproductive, however, because it may invite answers (by the listener, or silently by the reader) that threaten the conclusion at which the argument aims. For example, the archbishop of the Anglican Church in Nigeria, who is an ardent opponent of homosexuality and views it as deeply sinful, argues thus:

> Why didn't God make a lion to be a man's companion? Why didn't He make a tree to be a man's companion? Or better still, why didn't He make another man to be a man's companion? So even from the creation story you can see that the mind of God, God's intention, is for man and woman to be together.[14]

Conclusions drawn about God's intentions, using as premises questions that invite a myriad of different responses, may be undermined by the answers they elicit.

Questions can serve most effectively as premises when the answers assumed really do seem to be clear and inescapable. In such cases the readers (or hearers) are led to provide the apparently evident answers for themselves, thus augmenting the persuasiveness of the argument. Here is an example: Some who find euthanasia morally unacceptable reject the defense of that practice as grounded in the right to self-determination possessed by the terminally ill patient. They argue as follows:

> If a right to euthanasia is grounded in self-determination, it cannot reasonably be limited to the terminally ill. If people have a right to die, why must they wait until they are actually dying before they are permitted to exercise that right?[15]

The question is forceful because its answer appears to be undeniable. It seems obvious that there is no good reason why, if people have a right to die grounded in self-determination, they must wait until they are dying to exercise that right. Hence (this critique concludes) the right to euthanasia, if there is one, cannot be limited to the terminally ill.*

*The argument has much merit, but from the perspective of its religious advocates, it may prove to be a two-edged sword.

Arguments that depend on rhetorical questions are always suspect. Because the question is neither true nor false, it may be serving as a device to suggest the truth of some proposition while avoiding responsibility for asserting it. That proposition is likely to be dubious, and it may in fact be false. To illustrate, in 2007 Arab leaders in Jerusalem expressed great anxiety about the safety of the Al-Aqsa mosque when the Israeli government began construction of a ramp leading to the platform (also sacred to the Jews) on which that very holy mosque is situated. In reviewing the situation an Israeli partisan asked, "Is it possible that Arab leaders are more interested in attacking Israel than protecting religious and cultural monuments?"[16] Well, yes, that is possible, of course—but it may not be true, and the question framed in this way is plainly intended to cause the reader to believe that Arab leaders were being duplicitous in voicing their concerns. Did the author *assert* that such duplicity lay behind the Arab objections? No, he didn't *say* that!

Gossip columnists thrive on suggestive questions. Celebrity tidbits commonly appear in the form, "Isn't it true that Jackie [Kennedy] stole Aristotle [Onassis] from her kid sister?"[17] and "Does Paris Hilton have any talent as an actress?" Accusers who protect themselves by framing their accusations in interrogative sentences may shield themselves from the indignant complaints of their target. "No," they may insist, "that is not what I said!"

It is wise policy to refrain from arguing with questions.

In some arguments the conclusion appears in the form of an imperative. The reason, or reasons, we ought to perform a given act are set forth as premises, and we are then directed to act in that way. Thus in Proverbs 4:7 we read:

> Wisdom is the principal thing; therefore get wisdom.

Here the second clause is a command, and a command, like a question, is neither true nor false and cannot express a proposition. Therefore, strictly speaking, it cannot be the conclusion of an argument. But it surely is meant to be the conclusion of an argument in this passage from Proverbs. How can we explain this apparent inconsistency? It is useful in many contexts to regard a command as no different from a proposition in which hearers (or readers) are told that they would be wise to act, or ought to act, in the manner specified in the command. Thus the conclusion of the argument in Proverbs may be rephrased as "Getting wisdom is what you should do." Assertions of this kind may be true or false, as most will agree. What difference there is between a command to do something and a statement that it should be done is an issue that need not be explored here. By ignoring that difference (if there really is one), we are able to deal uniformly with arguments whose conclusions are expressed in this form.

Reformulations of this kind can clarify the roles of an argument's constituent propositions. We seek to grasp the *substance* of what is being asserted, to understand what claims are serving to support what inferences, whatever their external forms. Some needed reformulations are merely grammatical. A proposition that functions as a premise may take the form of a phrase rather than a declarative sentence. This is well illustrated in the following argumentative passage, whose conclusion is a very sharp criticism of the United States.

> What is a failed state? It is one that fails to provide security for the population, to guarantee rights at home or abroad, or to maintain functioning democratic institutions. On this definition the United States is the world's biggest failed state.[18]

The second and third premises of this argument are compressed into phrases, but the propositions for which these phrases are shorthand are clear enough, and their critical role in the author's reasoning is evident.

D. UNSTATED PROPOSITIONS

Arguments are sometimes obscure because one (or more) of their constituent propositions is not stated but is assumed to be understood. An illustration will be helpful here. The chairman of the Department of Sociology at City College, CUNY, presents two strong but controversial arguments, in parallel, regarding the justifiability of the death penalty. The first premise of each argument is the hypothesis that the factual belief (of the proponent, or of the opponent, of the penalty) about what does in fact deter homicide is mistaken. The second premise of each argument, although entirely plausible, is not stated, leaving the reader the task of reconstructing it.

The first argument goes like this:

> If the proponent of the death penalty is incorrect in his belief that the [death] penalty deters homicide, then he is responsible for the execution of murderers who should not be executed.[19]

This argument relies on the unstated second premise that "No one should be executed to advance an objective that is not promoted by execution." Hence one who *mistakenly* believes that the objective (deterring murders) is achieved by executing those convicted is responsible for the execution of murderers who should not be executed.

The second argument goes like this:

> If the opponent of the death penalty is incorrect in his belief that the death penalty doesn't deter, he is responsible for the murder of innocent individuals who would not have been murdered if the death penalty had been invoked.[20]

This argument relies on the unstated second premise that "Protecting the lives of innocent individuals from murder justifies the execution of murderers if other murderers are then deterred by the fear of execution." Hence one who *mistakenly* believes that the death penalty does not deter murderers is responsible for the lives of innocents who are subsequently murdered.

In each of these arguments the assumed but unstated second premise is plausible. One might find both arguments persuasive—leaving open for empirical investigation the question of whether, in fact, the death penalty does deter murder. However, the force of each of the arguments depends on the truth of the unstated premise on which it relies.

A premise may be left unstated because the arguer supposes that it is unquestioned common knowledge. In the controversy over the cloning of human beings, one angry critic wrote:

> Human cloning—like abortion, contraception, pornography and euthanasia—is intrinsically evil and thus should never be allowed.[21]

This is plainly an argument, but part of it is missing. The argument relies on the very plausible but unstated premise that "what is intrinsically evil should never be allowed." Arguments in everyday discourse very often rely on some proposition that is understood but not stated. Such arguments are called **enthymemes.** We will examine them more closely later in this book.

The unstated premise on which an enthymeme relies may not be universally accepted; it may be uncertain or controversial. An arguer may deliberately refrain from formulating that critical premise, believing that by allowing it to remain tacit, the premise is shielded from attack. For example, medical research using embryonic stem cells (cells found in the human embryo that can develop into other types of cells and into most types of tissue) is highly controversial. One U.S. senator used the following enthymeme in attacking legislation that would permit government financing of such research:

> This research [involving the use of embryonic stem cells] is illegal, for this reason: The deliberate killing of a human embryo is an essential component of the contemplated research.[22]

The stated premise is true: Research of this kind is not possible without destroying the embryo. However, the conclusion that such research is illegal depends on the unstated premise that the killing of a human embryo is illegal—and *that* claim is very much in dispute.

The effectiveness of an enthymeme may depend on the hearer's knowledge that some proposition is false. To emphasize the falsity of some *other* proposition, a speaker may construct an argument in which the first premise is a hypothetical proposition of which the target is the antecedent (the "if" component), and the consequent (the "then" component) is a proposition known by everyone to be false. The unstated falsehood of this second component is the second premise of the enthymematic argument. The unstated falsehood of the first component is the conclusion of the argument. To illustrate, the distinguished political philosopher John Rawls admired Abraham Lincoln as the president who most appreciated the moral equality of human beings. Rawls frequently quoted Lincoln's enthymematic argument, "If slavery is not wrong, nothing is wrong." It is of course wildly false to say that nothing is wrong—from which it follows that it is equally false to say that slavery is not wrong.*

1.4 Arguments and Explanations

Passages that appear to be arguments are sometimes not arguments but *explanations.* The appearance of words that are common indicators—such as "because," "for," and "therefore"—cannot settle the matter, because those words are used in both explanations and arguments.† We need to know the intention of the author. Compare the following two passages:

1. Lay up for yourselves treasures in heaven, where neither moth nor rust consumes and where thieves do not break in and steal. For where your treasure is, there will your heart be also.

   —*Matt. 7:19*

2. Therefore is the name of it [the tower] called Babel; because the Lord did there confound the language of all the earth.

   —*Gen. 11:19*

The first passage is clearly an argument. Its conclusion, that one ought to lay up treasures in heaven, is supported by the premise (here marked by the word "for") that one's heart will be where one's treasure is laid up. The second passage, which uses the word "therefore" quite appropriately, is not an argument. It *explains* why the tower (whose construction is recounted in Genesis) is called Babel. The tower was given this name, we are told, because it is was the place where humankind, formerly speaking one language, became confounded by many languages.‡ The passage assumes that

*Samuel Freeman, "John Rawls, Friend and Teacher," *Chronicle of Higher Education,"* 13 December 2002. And Bruno Bettelheim, a survivor of the Nazi death camps at Dachau and Buchenwald (and a distinguished psychiatrist), wrote: "If all men are good, then there never was an Auschwitz."

†The premise indicator "since" often has a temporal sense as well. Thus, in the lyric of the famous old song, "Stormy Weather," the line "Since my man and I ain't together, keeps rainin' all the time," is deliberately ambiguous, and richly suggestive. (Music by Harold Arlen, words by Ted Roehler, 1933.)

‡The name "Babel" is derived from the Hebrew word meaning" to confound"—that is, to confuse by mixing up or lumping together in an indiscriminate manner.

the reader knows that the tower had that name; the intention is to explain why that name was given to it. The phrase, "Therefore is the name called Babel," is not a conclusion but a completion of the explanation of the naming. And the clause, "because the Lord did there confound the language of all the earth," is not a premise; it could not serve as a reason for believing that Babel was the name of the tower, because the fact that that *was* the name is known by those to whom the passage is addressed. In this context, "because" indicates that what follows will *explain* the giving of that name, Babel, to that tower.

These two passages illustrate the fact that superficially similar passages may have very different functions. Whether some passage is an argument or an explanation depends on the *purpose* to be served by it. If our aim is to establish the truth of some proposition, Q, and we offer some evidence, P, in support of Q, we may appropriately say "Q because P." In this case we are giving an argument *for* Q, and P is our premise. But suppose that Q is known to be true. In that case we don't have to give any reasons to support its truth, but we may wish to give an account of *why* it is true. Here also we may say "Q because P"—but in this case we are giving not an argument *for* Q, but an explanation *of* Q.

In responding to a query about the apparent color of quasars (celestial objects lying far beyond our galaxy), one scientist wrote:

> The most distant quasars look like intense points of infrared radiation. This is because space is scattered with hydrogen atoms (about two per cubic meter) that absorb blue light, and if you filter the blue from visible white light, red is what's left. On its multibillion-light-year journey to earth quasar light loses so much blue that only infrared remains.[23]

The author is not seeking to convince his reader that quasars have the apparent color they do, but rather giving the causes of this fact; he is explaining, not arguing.

However, it may be difficult at times to determine whether an author intends to be explaining some state of affairs, or to be arguing for some conclusion that is critical in that explanation. Here, for example, is a passage that may be interpreted in either way.

> I would like to highlight another property of water, unique but also vital to making life on Earth possible. As water cools, approaching its freezing point, its density suddenly decreases, reversing the usual "natural convection" patterns in which colder fluids sink. This reversal causes the coldest strata of water to rise to the top of an ocean or lake. These large bodies of water now freeze from the top down. Were it not for this unique property of water, the oceans and lakes would have long and completely frozen over from the bottom up with dire consequences for any life-sustaining liquid water on Earth.[24]

More than one conclusion may be inferred from the same premise, thus presenting two arguments. Similarly, more than one thing may be accounted for by the same fact, thus presenting two explanations. Here is an illustration:

> The *Oxford English Dictionary* is a historical dictionary, providing citations meant to show the evolution of every word, beginning with the earliest known usage. So a key task, and a popular sport for thousands of volunteer word aficionados, is antedating: finding earlier citations than those already known.[25]

That antedating is a key task for the makers of that dictionary is accounted for by the fact that the *Oxford English Dictionary* is a *historical* dictionary. This same fact about the dictionary explains why, for word aficionados, antedating is a popular sport.

If an author writes "Q because P," how can we tell whether he intends to explain or to persuade? We can ask: What is the status of Q in that context? Is Q a proposition whose truth needs to be established or confirmed? In that case, "because P" is probably offering a premise in its support; "Q because P" is in that instance an argument. Or is Q a proposition whose truth is known, or at least not in doubt in that context? In that case, "because P" is probably offering some account of why Q has come to be true; "Q because P" is in that instance an explanation.

In an explanation, one must distinguish *what* is being explained from what the explanation *is*. In the explanation from Genesis given at the beginning of this section, *what* is being explained is how the tower of Babel came to have that name; the explanation *is* that it was there that the Lord did confound the language of all the earth. In the astronomical example given subsequently, *what* is being explained is the fact that quasars appear to be red; the explanation *is* that as light travels from the very distant quasar to earth all the blue in that light is filtered out.

If we are sensitive to the context, we will usually be able to distinguish an explanation from an argument. However, there will always be some passages whose purpose is uncertain, and such passages may deserve to be given alternative, equally plausible "readings"—viewed as an argument when interpreted in one way and as an explanation when interpreted in another.

EXERCISES

Some of the following passages contain explanations, some contain arguments, and some may be interpreted as either an argument or an explanation. What is your judgment about the chief function of each passage? What would have to be the case for the passage in question to be an argument? To be an explanation? Where you find an argument, identify its premises and conclusion. Where you find an explanation, indicate what is being explained and what the explanation is.

EXAMPLE

1. Humans have varying skin colors as a consequence of the distance our ancestors lived from the Equator. It's all about sun. Skin color is what regulates our body's reaction to the sun and its rays. Dark skin evolved to protect the body from excessive sun rays. Light skin evolved when people migrated away from the Equator and needed to make vitamin D in their skin. To do that they had to lose pigment. Repeatedly over history, many people moved dark to light and light to dark. That shows that color is not a permanent trait.

   —Nina Jablonski, "The Story of Skin," *The New York Times*, 9 January 2007

SOLUTION

This is essentially an explanation. *What* is being explained is the fact that humans have varying skin colors. The explanation *is* that different skin colors evolved as humans came to live at different distances from the Equator and hence needed different degrees of protection from the rays of the sun. One might interpret the passage as an argument whose conclusion is that skin color is not a permanent trait of all humans. Under this interpretation, all the propositions preceding the final sentence of the passage serve as premises.

2. David Bernstein [in *Only One Place of Redress: African Americans, Labor Regulations and the Courts*, 2001] places labor laws at the center of the contemporary plight of black Americans. Many of these ostensibly neutral laws (e.g. licensing laws, minimum-wage laws, and collective bargaining laws) were either directly aimed at stymieing black economic and social advancement or, if not so aimed, were quickly turned to that use. A huge swath of the American labor market was handed over to labor unions from which blacks, with few exceptions, were totally excluded. The now longstanding gap between black and white unemployment rates dates precisely from the moment of government intervention on labor's behalf. In short (Bernstein argues) the victories of American labor were the undoing of American blacks.

   —Ken I. Kirsch, "Blacks and Labor—the Untold Story," *The Public Interest*, Summer 2002

3. Animals born without traits that led to reproduction died out, whereas the ones that reproduced the most succeeded in conveying their genes to posterity. Crudely speaking, sex feels good because over evolutionary time the animals that liked having sex created more offspring than the animals that didn't.

   —R. Thornhill and C. T. Palmer, "Why Men Rape," *The Sciences*, February 2000.

4. Changes are real. Now, changes are only possible in time, and therefore time must be something real.

—Immanuel Kant, *Critique of Pure Reason* (1781), "Transcendental Aesthetic," section II

5. The nursing shortage in the United States has turned into a full-blown crisis. Because fewer young people go into nursing, one third of registered nurses in the United States are now over 50 years of age, and that proportion is expected to rise to 40 percent over the next decade. Nurses currently practicing report high rates of job dissatisfaction, with one in five seriously considering leaving the profession within the next five years. . . . Hospitals routinely cancel or delay surgical cases because of a lack of nursing staff.

—Ronald Dworkin, "Where Have All the Nurses Gone?," *The Public Interest*, Summer 2002

6. To name causes for a state of affairs is not to excuse it. Things are justified or condemned by their consequences, not by their antecedents.

—John Dewey, "The Liberal College and Its Enemies," *The Independent*, 1924

7. One may be subject to laws made by another, but it is impossible to bind oneself in any matter which is the subject of one's own free exercise of will. . . . It follows of necessity that the king cannot be subject to his own laws. For this reason [royal] edicts and ordinances conclude with the formula, "for such is our good pleasure."

—Jean Bodin, *Six Books of the Commonwealth*, 1576

8. I like Wagner's music better than anybody's. It is so loud that one can talk the whole time without people hearing what one says.

—Oscar Wilde, *The Picture of Dorian Gray*, 1891

9. Three aspects of American society in recent decades make cheating more likely.

First, there is the rise of a market-drenched society, where monetary success is lauded above all else. Second, there is the decline of religious, communal, and family bonds and norms that encourage honesty. Finally, there is the absence of shame by those public figures who are caught in dishonest or immoral activities. No wonder so many young people see nothing wrong with cutting corners or worse.

—Howard Gardner, "More Likely to Cheat," *The New York Times*, 9 October 2003

10. Love looks not with the eyes but with the mind;
And therefore is wing'd Cupid painted blind.

—William Shakespeare, *A Midsummer Night's Dream*, act 1, scene 1

11. An article in *The New York Times*, "Why Humans and Their Fur Parted Ways," suggested that the fact that women have less body hair than men is somehow related to greater sexual selection pressure on women. A reader responded with the following letter:

> Here is an elaboration for which I have no evidence but it is consistent with what we think we know: sexual selection has probably strongly influenced numerous traits of both sexes.
>
> Youthful appearance is more important to men when selecting a mate than it is to women. The longer a woman can look young, the longer she will be sexually attractive and the more opportunities she will have to bear offspring with desirable men. Hairlessness advertises youth.
>
> Hence a greater sexual selection pressure on women to lose body hair.

—T. Doyle, "Less Is More," *The New York Times*, 26 August 2003

12. MAD, mutually assured destruction, was effective in deterring nuclear attack right through the cold war. Both sides had nuclear weapons. Neither side used them, because both sides knew the other would retaliate in kind. This will not work with a religious fanatic [like Mahmoud Ahmadinejad, President of the Islamic Republic of Iran]. For him, mutual assured destruction is not a deterrent, it is an inducement. We know already that Iran's leaders do not give a damn about killing their own people in great numbers. We have seen it again and again. In the final scenario, and this applies all the more strongly if they kill large numbers of their own people, they are doing them a favor. They are giving them a quick free pass to heaven and all its delights.

—Bernard Lewis, quoted in *Commentary*, June 2007

13. About a century ago, we discovered that planetary orbits are not stable in four or more dimensions, so if there were more than three space dimensions, planets would not orbit a sun long enough for life to originate. And in one or two space dimensions, neither blood flow nor large numbers of neuron connections can exist. Thus, interesting life can exist only in three dimensions.

—Gordon Kane, "Anthropic Questions," *Phi Kappa Phi Journal*, Fall 2002

14. Translators and interpreters who have helped United States troops and diplomats now want to resettle in the United States. They speak many strategically important languages of their region. The United States does not have an adequate number of interpreters and translators who are proficient in these languages. Therefore, we need them. Q.E.D.

—"Welcome the Translators," Oswald Werner
The New York Times, 3 November 2007

15. The Treasury Department's failure to design and issue paper currency that is readily distinguishable to blind and visually impaired individuals violates Section 504 of the Rehabilitation Act, which provides that no disabled person shall be "subjected to discrimination under any program or activity conducted by any Executive agency."

—Judge James Robertson, Federal District Court for the District of Columbia, *American Council of the Blind v. Sec. of the Treasury*, No. 02-0864 (2006)

16. Rightness [that is, acting so as to fulfill one's duty] never guarantees moral goodness. For an act may be the act which the agent thinks to be his duty, and yet be done from an indifferent or bad motive, and therefore be morally indifferent or bad.

—Sir W. David Ross, *Foundations of Ethics*, (Oxford: Oxford University Press, 1939)

17. Man did not invent the circle or the square or mathematics or the laws of physics. He discovered them. They are immutable and eternal laws that could only have been created by a supreme mind: God. And since we have the ability to make such discoveries, man's mind must possess an innate particle of the mind of God. To believe in God is not "beyond reason."

—J. Lenzi, "Darwin's God," *The New York Times Magazine*, 18 March 2007

18. Many of the celebratory rituals [of Christmas], as well as the timing of the holiday, have their origins outside of, and may predate, the Christian commemoration of the birth of Jesus. Those traditions, at their best, have much to do with celebrating human relationships and the enjoyment of the goods that this life has to offer. As an atheist I have no hesitation in embracing the holiday and joining with believers and nonbelievers alike to celebrate what we have in common.

—John Teehan, "A Holiday Season for Atheists, Too,"
The New York Times, 24 December 2006

19. All ethnic movements are two-edged swords. Beginning benignly, and sometimes necessary to repair injured collective psyches, they often end in tragedy, especially when they turn political, as illustrated by German history.

—Orlando Patterson, "A Meeting with Gerald Ford," *The New York Times*, 6 January 2007

20. That all who are happy, are equally happy, is not true. A peasant and a philosopher may be equally *satisfied*, but not equally *happy*. Happiness consists in the multiplicity of agreeable consciousness. A peasant has not the capacity for having equal happiness with a philosopher.

—Samuel Johnson, in Boswell's *Life of Johnson*, 1766

1.5 Deductive and Inductive Arguments

Every argument makes the claim that its premises provide grounds for the truth of its conclusion; that claim is the mark of an argument. However, there are two very different ways in which a conclusion may be supported by its premises, and thus there are two great classes of arguments: the *deductive* and the *inductive*. Understanding this distinction is essential in the study of logic.

A *deductive argument* makes the claim that its conclusion is supported by its premises *conclusively*. An *inductive argument*, in contrast, does not make such a claim. Therefore, if we judge that in some passage a claim for conclusiveness is being made, we treat the argument as deductive; if we judge that such a claim is not being made, we treat it as inductive. Because every argument either makes this claim of conclusiveness (explicitly or implicitly) or does not make it, every argument is either deductive or inductive.

When the claim is made that the premises of an argument (if true) provide incontrovertible grounds for the truth of its conclusion, that claim will be either correct or not correct. If it is correct, that argument is *valid*. If it is not correct (that is, if the premises when true fail to establish the conclusion irrefutably although claiming to do so), that argument is *invalid*.

For logicians the term *validity* is applicable only to deductive arguments. To say that a deductive argument is valid is to say that it is not possible for its conclusion to be false if its premises are true. Thus we define **validity** as follows: A deductive argument is *valid* when, if its premises are true, its conclusion *must* be true. In everyday speech, of course, the term *valid* is used much more loosely.

Although every deductive argument makes the claim that its premises guarantee the truth of its conclusion, not all deductive arguments live up to that claim. Deductive arguments that fail to do so are invalid.

Because every deductive argument either succeeds or does not succeed in achieving its objective, every deductive argument is either valid or invalid. This point is important: If a deductive argument is not valid, it must be invalid; if it is not invalid, it must be valid.

The central task of deductive logic (treated at length in Part II of this book) is to discriminate valid arguments from invalid ones. Over centuries, logicians devised powerful techniques to do this—but the traditional techniques for determining validity differ from those used by most modern logicians. The former, called *classical logic* and rooted in the analytical works of Aristotle, are explained in Chapters 6, 7, and 8 of this book. The techniques of *modern symbolic logic* are presented in detail in Chapters 9, 10, and 11. Logicians of the two schools differ in their methods and in their interpretations of some arguments, but ancients and moderns agree that the fundamental task of deductive logic is to develop the tools that enable us to distinguish arguments that are valid from those that are not.

The central task of inductive arguments is to ascertain the facts by which conduct may be guided directly, or on which other arguments may be built. Empirical investigations are undertaken—as in medicine, or social science, or astronomy—leading, when inductive techniques are applied appropriately, to factual conclusions, most often concerning cause-and-effect relationships of some importance.

A great variety of inductive techniques are examined in detail in Part III of this book, but an illustration of the inductive process will be helpful at this point to contrast induction with deduction. Medical investigators, using inductive methods, are anxious to learn the causes of disease, or the causes of the transmission of infectious diseases. Sexually transmitted diseases (STDs), such as acquired immune deficiency syndrome (AIDS), are of special concern because of their great seriousness and worldwide spread. Can we learn inductively how to reduce the spread of STDs? Yes, we can.

In 2006 the National Institutes of Health announced that large-scale studies of the spread of STDs in Kenya and Uganda (African countries in which the risk of HIV infection, commonly resulting in AIDS, is very high) was sharply lower among circumcised men than among those who were not circumcised. Circumcision is not a "magic bullet" for the treatment of disease, of course. But we did learn, by examining the experience of very many voluntary subjects (3000 in Uganda, 5000 in Kenya, divided into circumcised and uncircumcised groups) that a man's risk of contracting AIDS from heterosexual sex is *reduced by half* as a result of circumcision. The risk to women is also reduced by about 30 percent.*

*So great is the advantage of circumcision shown by these studies that they were stopped, on 13 December 2006, by the Data Safety and Monitoring Board of the National Institutes of Health, to be fair to all participants by announcing the probable risks of the two patterns of conduct.

These are discoveries (using the inductive method called *concomitant variation*, which is discussed in detail in Chapter 12) of very great importance. The causal connection between the absence of circumcision and the spread of STDs is not known with certainty, the way the conclusion of a deductive argument is known, but it is now known with a very high degree of probability.

Inductive arguments make weaker claims than those made by deductive arguments. Because their conclusions are never certain, the terms *validity* and *invalidity* do not apply to inductive arguments. We can evaluate inductive arguments, of course; appraising such arguments is a central task of scientists in every sphere. The higher the level of probability conferred on its conclusion by the premises of an inductive argument, the greater is the merit of that argument. We can say that inductive arguments may be "better" or "worse," "weaker" or "stronger," and so on. The argument constituted by the circumcision study is very strong, the probability of its conclusion very high. Even when the premises are all true, however, and provide strong support for the conclusion, that conclusion is not established with certainty. The entire theory of induction, techniques of analogical and causal reasoning, methods for appraising inductive arguments and for quantifying and calculating probabilities are presented at length in Chapters 11, 12, 13, and 14.

Because an inductive argument can yield no more than some degree of probability for its conclusion, it is always possible that additional information will strengthen or weaken it. Newly discovered facts may cause us to change our estimate of the probabilities, and thus may lead us to judge the argument to be better (or worse) than we had previously thought. In the world of inductive argument—even when the conclusion is judged to be very highly probable—*all* the evidence is never in. New discoveries may eventually disconfirm what was earlier believed, and therefore we never assert that an inductive conclusion is absolutely certain.

Deductive arguments, on the other hand, cannot become better or worse. They either succeed or they do not succeed in exhibiting a compelling relation between premises and conclusion. If a deductive argument is valid, *no* additional premises can possibly add to the strength of that argument. For example, if all humans are mortal and Socrates is human, we may conclude without reservation that Socrates is mortal—*and that conclusion will follow from those premises no matter what else may be true in the world, and no matter what other information may be discovered or added.* If we come to learn that Socrates is ugly, or that immortality is a burden, or that cows give milk, none of those findings nor any other findings can have any bearing on the validity of the original argument. The conclusion that follows with certainty from the premises of a deductive argument follows from any enlarged set of premises with the same certainty, regardless of the nature of the premises added. If an argument is valid, nothing in the world can make it more valid; if a conclusion is validly inferred from some set of premises, nothing can be added to that set to make that conclusion follow more strictly, or more validly.

This is not true of inductive arguments, however, for which the relationship claimed between premises and conclusion is much less strict and very different in kind. Consider the following inductive argument:

Most corporation lawyers are conservatives.
Miriam Graf is a corporation lawyer.
Therefore Miriam Graf is probably a conservative.

This is a fairly good inductive argument; its first premise is true, and if its second premise also is true, its conclusion is more likely to be true than false. But in this case (in contrast to the argument about Socrates' mortality), new premises added to the original pair might weaken or (depending on the content of those new premises) strengthen the original argument. Suppose we also learn that

Miriam Graf is an officer of the American Civil Liberties Union (ACLU).

and suppose we add the (true) premise that

Most officers of the ACLU are not conservatives.

Now the conclusion (that Miriam Graf is a conservative) no longer seems very probable; the original inductive argument has been greatly weakened by the presence of this additional information about Miriam Graf. Indeed, if the final premise were to be transformed into the universal proposition

No officers of the ACLU are conservatives.

the opposite of the original conclusion would then follow deductively—that is, validly—from the full set of premises affirmed.

On the other hand, suppose we enlarge the original set of premises by adding the following additional premise:

Miriam Graf has long been an officer of the National Rifle Association (NRA).

The original conclusion (that she is a conservative) would be supported by this enlarged set of premises with even greater likelihood than it was by the original set.

Inductive arguments do not always acknowledge explicitly that their conclusions are supported only with some degree of probability. On the other hand, the mere presence of the word "probability" in an argument gives no assurance that the argument is inductive. There are some strictly deductive arguments *about* probabilities themselves, in which the probability of a certain combination of events is deduced from the probabilities of other events.*

In sum, the distinction between induction and deduction rests on the nature of the claims made by the two types of arguments about the *relations* between their premises and their conclusions. Thus we characterize the two types of arguments as follows: A **deductive argument** is one whose conclusion is claimed to follow from its premises with absolute necessity, this necessity not being a matter of degree and not depending in any way on whatever else may be the case. In sharp contrast, an **inductive argument** is one whose conclusion is claimed to follow from its premises only with probability, this probability being a matter of degree and dependent on what else may be the case.

1.6 Validity and Truth

A deductive argument is valid when it is successful. Its validity refers to the relation between its propositions—between the set of propositions that serve as the premises and the one proposition that serves as the conclusion of that argument. If the conclusion follows with logical necessity from the premises, we say that the argument is valid. Therefore *validity can never apply to any single proposition by itself*, because the needed relation cannot possibly be found within any one proposition.

Truth and falsity, on the other hand, *are* attributes of individual propositions. A single statement that serves as a premise in an argument may be true; the statement that serves as its conclusion may be false. This conclusion might have been validly inferred, but to say that any conclusion (or any single premise) is itself valid or invalid makes no sense.

Truth is the attribute of a proposition that asserts what really is the case. When I assert that Lake Superior is the largest of the five Great Lakes, I assert what really is the case, what is true. If I had claimed that Lake Michigan is the largest of the Great Lakes my assertion would not be in accord with the real world; therefore it would be false. This contrast between validity and truth is important: *Truth and falsity are attributes of individual propositions or statements; validity and invalidity are attributes of arguments.*

Just as the concept of validity cannot apply to single propositions, the concept of truth cannot apply to arguments. Of the several propositions in an

---

*If, for example, we learn that the probability of three successive heads in three tosses of a coin is $1/8$, we may infer deductively that the probability of getting at least one tail in three tosses of a coin is $7/8$. Other illustrations of such arguments are given in Chapter 14.

argument, some (or all) may be true and some (or all) may be false. However, the argument as a whole is neither true nor false. Propositions, which are statements about the world, may be true or false; deductive arguments, which consist of inferences from one set of propositions to other propositions, may be valid or invalid.

The relations *between* true (or false) propositions and valid (or invalid) arguments are critical and complicated. Those relations lie at the heart of deductive logic. Part II of this book is devoted largely to examination of those complex relations, but a preliminary discussion of the relation between validity and truth is in order here.

We begin by emphasizing that an argument may be valid even if one or more of its premises is not true. Every argument makes a claim about the relation between its premises and the conclusion drawn from them; that relation may hold even if the premises turn out to be false or the truth of the premises is in dispute. This point was made dramatically by Abraham Lincoln in 1858 in one of his debates with Stephen Douglas. Lincoln was attacking the *Dred Scott* decision of the Supreme Court, which had held that slaves who had escaped into Northern states must be returned to their owners in the South. Lincoln said:

> I think it follows [from the *Dred Scott* decision] and submit to the consideration of men capable of arguing, whether as I state it in syllogistic form the argument has any fault in it:
>
> > Nothing in the Constitution or laws of any State can destroy a right distinctly and expressly affirmed in the Constitution of the United States.
> >
> > The right of property in a slave is distinctly and expressly affirmed in the Constitution of the United States.
> >
> > Therefore, nothing in the Constitution or laws of any State can destroy the right of property in a slave.
>
> I believe that no fault can be pointed out in that argument; assuming the truth of the premises, the conclusion, so far as I have capacity at all to understand it, follows inevitably. There is a fault in it as I think, but the fault is not in the reasoning; but the falsehood in fact is a fault of the premises. I believe that the right of property in a slave is *not* distinctly and expressly affirmed in the Constitution, and Judge Douglas thinks it is. I believe that the Supreme Court and the advocates of that decision [the *Dred Scott* decision] may search in vain for the place in the Constitution where the right of property in a slave is distinctly and expressly affirmed. I say, therefore, that I think one of the premises is not true in fact.[26]

The reasoning in the argument that Lincoln recapitulates and attacks is not faulty—but its second premise (that "the right of property in a slave is . . . affirmed in the Constitution") is plainly false. The conclusion has therefore not been established. Lincoln's logical point is correct and important: *An argument may be valid even when its conclusion and one or more of its premises are false.* The validity of an argument, we emphasize once again, depends only on the *relation* of the premises to the conclusion.

There are many possible combinations of true and false premises and conclusions in both valid and invalid arguments. Here follow seven illustrative arguments, each prefaced by the statement of the combination (or truth and validity) that it represents. With these illustrations (whose content is deliberately trivial) before us, we will be in a position to formulate some important principles concerning the relations between truth and validity.

I. Some *valid* arguments contain *only true* propositions—true premises and a true conclusion:

All mammals have lungs.
All whales are mammals.
Therefore all whales have lungs.

II. Some *valid* arguments contain *only false* propositions—false premises and a false conclusion:

All four-legged creatures have wings.
All spiders have four legs.
Therefore all spiders have wings.

This argument is valid because, if its premises were true, its conclusion would have to be true also—even though we know that in fact both the premises *and* the conclusion of this argument are false.

III. Some *invalid* arguments contain *only true* propositions—all their premises are true, and their conclusions are true as well:

If I owned all the gold in Fort Knox, then I would be wealthy.
I do not own all the gold in Fort Knox.
Therefore I am not wealthy.

The true conclusion of this argument does not follow from its true premises. This will be seen more clearly when the immediately following illustration is considered.

IV. Some *invalid* arguments contain *only true premises* and have a *false conclusion*. This is illustrated by an argument exactly like the previous one (III) in form, changed only enough to make the conclusion false.

If Bill Gates owned all the gold in Fort Knox, then Bill Gates would be wealthy.
Bill Gates does not own all the gold in Fort Knox.
Therefore Bill Gates is not wealthy.

The premises of this argument are true, but its conclusion is false. Such an argument cannot be valid because it is impossible for the premises of a valid argument to be true and its conclusion to be false.

V. Some *valid* arguments have *false premises and a true conclusion:*

All fishes are mammals.
All whales are fishes.
Therefore all whales are mammals.

The conclusion of this argument is true, as we know; moreover, it may be validly inferred from these two premises, both of which are wildly false.

VI. Some *invalid* arguments also have *false premises and a true conclusion:*

All mammals have wings.
All whales have wings.
Therefore all whales are mammals.

From Examples V and VI taken together, it is clear that we cannot tell from the fact that an argument has false premises and a true conclusion whether it is valid or invalid.

VII. Some *invalid* arguments, of course, contain *all false* propositions—false premises and a false conclusion:

All mammals have wings.
All whales have wings.
Therefore all mammals are whales.

These seven examples make it clear that there are valid arguments with false conclusions (Example II), as well as invalid arguments with true conclusions (Examples III and VI). Hence it is clear that *the truth or falsity of an argument's conclusion does not by itself determine the validity or invalidity of that argument.* Moreover, *the fact that an argument is valid does not guarantee the truth of its conclusion* (Example II).

Two tables (referring to the seven preceding examples) will make very clear the variety of possible combinations. The first table shows that *invalid* arguments can have every possible combination of true and false premises and conclusions:

Invalid Arguments		
	True Conclusion	**False Conclusion**
True Premises	Example III	Example IV
False Premises	Example VI	Example VII

The second table shows that *valid* arguments can have only three of those combinations of true and false premises and conclusions:

Valid Arguments		
	True Conclusion	**False Conclusion**
True Premises	Example I	—
False Premises	Example V	Example II

The one blank position in the second table exhibits a fundamental point: *If an argument is valid and its premises are true, we may be certain that its conclusion is true also.* To put it another way: *If an argument is valid and its conclusion is false, not all of its premises can be true.* Some perfectly valid arguments do have false conclusions, but any such argument must have at least one false premise.

When an argument is valid *and* all of its premises are true, we call it *sound.* The conclusion of a sound argument obviously must be true—and only a sound argument can establish the truth of its conclusion. If a deductive argument is not sound—that is, if the argument is not valid *or* if not all of its premises are true—it fails to establish the truth of its conclusion even if in fact the conclusion is true.

To test the truth or falsehood of premises is the task of science in general, because premises may deal with any subject matter at all. The logician is not (professionally) interested in the truth or falsehood of propositions so much as in the logical relations between them. By *logical relations between propositions* we mean those relations that determine the correctness or incorrectness of the arguments in which they occur. The task of determining the correctness or incorrectness of arguments falls squarely within the province of logic. The logician is interested in the correctness even of arguments whose premises may be false.

Why do we not confine ourselves to arguments with true premises, ignoring all others? Because the correctness of arguments whose premises are not known to be true may be of great importance. In science, for example, we verify theories by *deducing* testable consequences from uncertain theoretical premises—but we cannot know beforehand which theories are true. In everyday life also, we must often choose between alternative courses of action, first seeking to deduce the consequences of each. To avoid deceiving ourselves, we must reason correctly about the consequences of the alternatives, taking each as a premise. If we were interested only in arguments with true premises, we would not know which set of consequences to trace out until we knew which of the alternative premises was true. But if we knew which of the alternative premises was true, we would not need to reason about it at all, because our purpose was to help us decide which alternative premise to *make* true. To confine our attention to arguments with premises known to be true would therefore be self-defeating.

Effective methods for establishing the validity or invalidity of deductive arguments are presented and explained at length in Part II of this book.

EXERCISES

Construct a series of deductive arguments, on any subject of your choosing, each with only two premises, having the following characteristics:

1. A valid argument with one true premise, one false premise, and a false conclusion
2. A valid argument with one true premise, one false premise, and a true conclusion
3. An invalid argument with two true premises and a false conclusion
4. An invalid argument with two true premises and a true conclusion
5. A valid argument with two false premises and a true conclusion
6. An invalid argument with two false premises and a true conclusion
7. An invalid argument with one true premise, one false premise, and a true conclusion
8. A valid argument with two true premises and a true conclusion

SUMMARY

The most fundamental concepts of logic are introduced in this chapter.

In Section 1.1 we explained why logic is defined as the study of the methods and principles used to distinguish correct from incorrect reasoning.

In Section 1.2 we gave an account of propositions, which may be asserted or denied, and which are either true or false, and of arguments—the central concern of logicians—which are clusters of propositions of which one is the conclusion and the others are the premises offered in its support.

In Section 1.3 we discussed difficulties in the recognition of arguments, arising from the variety of ways in which the propositions they contain may be expressed, and sometimes even the absence of their express statement in arguments called enthymemes.

In Section 1.4 we discussed the differences between arguments and explanations, showing why this distinction often depends on the context, and the intent of the passage in that context.

In Section 1.5 we explained the fundamental difference between deductive arguments, whose conclusions may be certain (if the premises are true and the reasoning valid), and inductive arguments, aiming to establish matters of fact, whose conclusions may be very probable but are never certain.

In Section 1.6 we discussed validity and invalidity (which apply to deductive arguments) as contrasted with truth and falsity (which apply to propositions). We explored some of the key relations between validity and truth.

End Notes

[1]Scott Wallace, "Last of the Amazon," *National Geographic*, January 2007.

[2]David Hayden, "Thy Neighbor, Thy Self," *The New York Times*, 9 May 2000.

[3]Hank Aaron hit his 700th home run on 21 July 1973, thirty-nine years later.

[4]Jeremy Bentham, *Principles of Legislation*, 1802.

[5]To her sister, Cassandra, in a letter dated 24 December 1798.

[6]Peter Singer, "What Should a Billionaire Give—and What Should You?" *The New York Times Magazine*, December 17, 2006.

[7]Roger Woody, "Why Iraq's a Mess," *The New York Times*, 26 January 2007.

[8]Sam Harris, *Letter to a Christian Nation* (New York: Alfred A. Knopf, 2006).

[9]*Gratz v. Bollinger*, 539 U.S. 244 (2003).

[10]Ibid.

[11]If you are told that I am bringing a lobster home for dinner, you will have little doubt that I intend to eat it, not feed it.

[12]Irit R. Rasooly, "Faces on a Coin," *The New York Times*, 7 January 2007.

[13]Ibid.

[14]Archbishop Peter Akinola, quoted in *The New York Times*, 25 December 2006.

[15]Ramsey Colloquium of the Institute on Religion and Public Life, "Always to Care, Never to Kill," *The Wall Street Journal*, 17 November 1991.

[16]David Gelernter, "Ramping Up the Violence," *The Weekly Standard*, 26 February 2007.

[17]Lloyd Shearer, a famous Hollywood columnist, quoted in *The New York Times*, 27 May 2001.

[18]Noam Chomsky, *Failed States* (New York: Henry Holt, 2006).

[19]Steven Goldberg, "The Death Penalty," *The New York Times*, 20 December 2004.

[20]Ibid.

[21]"The Vote to Ban Human Cloning," *The New York Times*, 2 August 2001.

[22]Senator Sam Brownback, of Kansas, at a Senate hearing in April 2000, on a bill to permit such funding.

[23]Jeff Greenwald, "Brightness Visible," *The New York Times Magazine*, 14 May 2000.

[24]Joseph Bamberger, "Water's Inimitable Qualities," *The New York Times*, 17 July 2007.

[25]James Gleick, "Cyber-Neologoliferation," *The New York Times Magazine*, 5 November 2006.

[26]From *The Collected Works of Abraham Lincoln*, vol. 3, Roy P. Basler, editor (New Brunswick, NJ: Rutgers University Press, 1953).

Analyzing Arguments

2.1 Paraphrasing Arguments

Arguments in everyday life are often more complex—more tangled and less precise—than those given as illustrations in Chapter 1. Premises may be numerous and in topsy-turvy order; they may be formulated awkwardly, and they may be repeated using different words; even the meaning of premises may be unclear. To sort out the connections of premises and conclusions so as to evaluate an argument fairly, we need some analytical techniques.

The most common, and perhaps the most useful technique for analysis is *paraphrase*. We paraphrase an argument by setting forth its propositions in clear language and in logical order. This may require the reformulation of sentences, and therefore great care must be taken to ensure that the paraphrase put forward captures correctly and completely the argument that was to be analyzed.

The following argument, whose premises are confusingly intertwined, was part of the majority decision of the U.S. Supreme Court when, in 2003, it struck down as unconstitutional a Texas statute that had made it a crime for persons of the same sex to engage in certain forms of intimate sexual conduct. Justice Anthony Kennedy, writing for the majority, said this:

> The [present] case does involve two adults who, with full and mutual consent from each other, engaged in sexual practices common to a homosexual life style. The petitioners are entitled to respect for their private lives. The state cannot demean their existence or control their destiny by making their private sexual conduct a crime. Their right to liberty under the Due Process Clause [of the 14th Amendment to the U.S. Constitution] gives them the full right to engage in their conduct without intervention of the government. It is a

> premise of the Constitution that there is a realm of personal liberty which the government may not enter. The Texas statute furthers no legitimate state interest which can justify its intrusion into the personal and private life of the individual.[1]

Although the general thrust of this decision is clear, the structure of the argument, which is really a complex of distinct arguments, is not. We can clarify the whole by paraphrasing the decision of the Court as follows:

1. The Constitution of the United States guarantees a realm of personal liberty that includes the private, consensual sexual activity of adults.
2. The conduct of these petitioners was within that realm of liberty and they therefore had a full right, under the Constitution, to engage in the sexual conduct in question without government intervention.
3. The Texas statute intrudes, without justification, into the private lives of these petitioners, and demeans them, by making their protected, private sexual conduct a crime.
4. The Texas statute that criminalizes such conduct therefore wrongly denies the rights of these petitioners and must be struck down as unconstitutional.

In this case the paraphrase does no more than set forth clearly what the premises indubitably assert. Sometimes, however, paraphrasing can bring to the surface what was assumed in an argument but was not fully or clearly stated. For example, the great English mathematician, G. H. Hardy, argued thus: "Archimedes will be remembered when Aeschylus is forgotten, because languages die and mathematical ideas do not."[2] We may paraphrase this argument by spelling out its claims:

1. Languages die.
2. The plays of Aeschylus are written in a language.
3. So the work of Aeschylus will eventually die.
4. Mathematical ideas never die.
5. The work of Archimedes was with mathematical ideas.
6. So the work of Archimedes will never die.
7. Therefore Archimedes will be remembered when Aeschylus is forgotten.

This paraphrase enables us to distinguish and examine the premises and inferences compressed into Hardy's single sentence.

EXERCISES

Paraphrase each of the following passages, which may contain more than one argument.

1. The [Detroit] Pistons did not lose because of the lack of ability. They are an all-around better team. They lost because of the law of averages. They will beat the [San Antonio] Spurs every two times out of three. When you examine the NBA finals [of 2005], that is exactly how they lost the seventh (last game) because that would have been three out of three. The Spurs will beat the Pistons one out of three. It just so happens that, that one time was the final game, because the Pistons had already won two in a row

   —Maurice Williams, "Law of Averages Worked Against Detroit Pistons," *The Ann Arbor* (Michigan) *News*, 8 July 2005

2. Hundreds of thousands of recent college graduates today cannot express themselves with the written word. Why? Because universities have shortchanged them, offering strange literary theories, Marxism, feminism, deconstruction, and other oddities in the guise of writing courses.

   —Stanley Ridgeley, "College Students Can't Write?" *National Review Online*, 19 February 2003

3. Racially diverse nations tend to have lower levels of social support than homogenous ones. People don't feel as bound together when they are divided on ethnic lines and are less likely to embrace mutual support programs. You can have diversity or a big welfare state. It's hard to have both.

   —David Brooks (presenting the views of Seymour Lipset), "The American Way of Equality," *The New York Times*, 14 January 2007

4. Orlando Patterson claims that "freedom is a natural part of the human condition." Nothing could be further from the truth. If it were true, we could expect to find free societies spread throughout human history. We do not. Instead what we find are every sort of tyrannical government from time immemorial.

   —John Taylor, "Can Freedom Be Exported," *The New York Times*, 22 December 2006

5. *The New York Times* reported, on 30 May 2000, that some scientists were seeking a way to signal back in time. A critical reader responded thus:

> It seems obvious to me that scientists in the future will never find a way to signal back in time. If they were to do so, wouldn't we have heard from them by now?

—Ken Grunstra, "Reaching Back in Time,"
The New York Times, 6 June 2000

6. Nicholas Kristof equates the hunting of whales by Eskimos with the whaling habits of Japanese, Norwegians, and Icelanders. The harsh environment of the Inupiat [Eskimos] dictates their diet, so not even the most rabid antiwhaling activist can deny their inalienable right to survive. The Japanese and the European whale-hunting countries can choose the food they consume; they have no need to eat whales. It is not hypocritical to give a pass to the relatively primitive society of the Inupiat to hunt a strictly controlled number of whales for survival while chastising the modern societies that continue to hunt these magnificent mammals for no good reason.

—Joseph Turner, "Their Whale Meat, and Our Piety,"
The New York Times, 18 September 2003

7. Space contains such a huge supply of atoms that all eternity would not be enough time to count them and count the forces which drive the atoms into various places just as they have been driven together in this world. So we must realize that there are other worlds in other parts of the universe with races of different men and different animals.

—Lucretius, *De Rerum Natura,* First Century B.C.

8. If you marry without love, it does not mean you will not later come to love the person you marry. And if you marry the person you love, it does not mean that you will always love that person or have a successful marriage. The divorce rate is very low in many countries that have prearranged marriage. The divorce rate is very high in countries where people base their marriage decisions on love.

—Alex Hammoud, "I Take This Man, for Richer Only,"
The New York Times, 18 February 2000

9. Our entire tax system depends upon the vast majority of taxpayers who attempt to pay the taxes they owe having confidence that

they're being treated fairly and that their competitors and neighbors are also paying what is due. If the public concludes that the IRS cannot meet these basic expectations, the risk to the tax system will become very high, and the effects very difficult to reverse.

—David Cay Johnston, "Adding Auditors to Help IRS Catch Tax Cheaters," *The New York Times*, 13 February 2000

10. People and governments want to talk, talk, talk about racism and other forms of intolerance; we are obsessed with racial and ethnic issues. But we come to these issues wearing earplugs and blinders, and in a state of denial that absolves us of complicity in any of these hateful matters. Thus, the other guy is always wrong.

—Bob Herbert, "Doomed to Irrelevance," *The New York Times*, 6 November 2001

2.2 Diagramming Arguments

A second technique for the analysis of arguments is *diagramming*. With a diagram we can represent the structure of an argument graphically; the flow of premises and conclusions is displayed in a two-dimensional chart, or picture, on the page. A diagram is not needed for a simple argument, even though drawing one can enhance our understanding. When an argument is complex, with many premises entwined in various ways, a diagram can be exceedingly helpful.

To construct the diagram of an argument we must first number all the propositions it contains, in the order in which they appear, circling each number. Using arrows between the circled numbers, we can then construct a diagram that shows the relations of premises and conclusions without having to restate them. To convey the process of inference on the two-dimensional page, we adopt this convention: A conclusion always appears in the space *below* the premises that give it support; coordinate premises are put on the same horizontal level. In this way, an argument whose wording may be confusing can be set forth vividly in iconic form. The structure of the argument is displayed visually.[3]

Here follows a straightforward argument that may be readily diagrammed:

① There is no consensus among biologists that a fertilized cell is alive in a sense that an unfertilized egg or unused sperm is not. ② Nor is there a consensus about whether a group of cells without even a rudimentary nervous system is in any sense human. ③ Hence there are no compelling experimental data to decide the nebulous issue of when "human" life begins.[4]

The circled numbers serve to represent the propositions, so we can diagram the argument as follows:

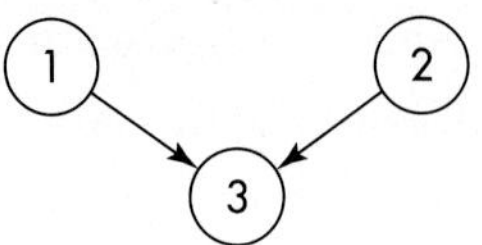

When the several premises of an argument are not all coordinate—that is, when some premises give direct support not to the conclusion but to other premises that support the conclusion—the diagram can show this quite clearly. Here is an argument illustrating this feature of diagramming:

> ① Football analysis is trickier than the baseball kind because ② football really is a team sport. ③ Unlike in baseball, all eleven guys on the field are involved in every play. ④ Who deserves the credit or blame is harder to know than it looks.[5]

The diagram looks like this:

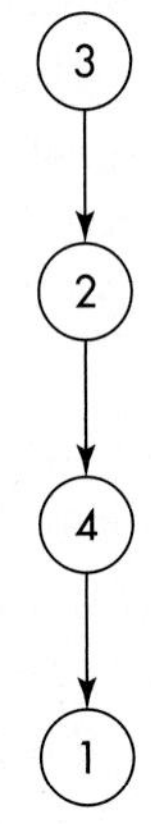

An alternative plausible interpretation of this argument can be represented by a different diagram:

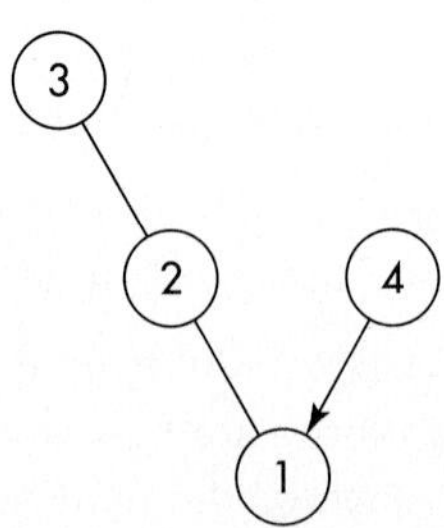

Another strength of diagrams is their ability to exhibit relations *between* the premises that may be critical to the argument. Each premise of an argument may support its conclusion separately, as in the arguments above. In some arguments, however, the premises support the conclusion only when they are considered *jointly*—and this is a feature of the reasoning that a diagram is well suited to display, by providing a visual representation of that connection. The following argument illustrates this:

> ① General Motors makes money (when it does) on new cars and on the financing of loans. ② Car dealers, by contrast, make most of their money on servicing old cars and selling used ones. ③ So car dealers can thrive even when the automaker languishes.[6]

By bracketing the premises in the diagram of this argument, we show that its premises give support only because they are *joined together,* thus:

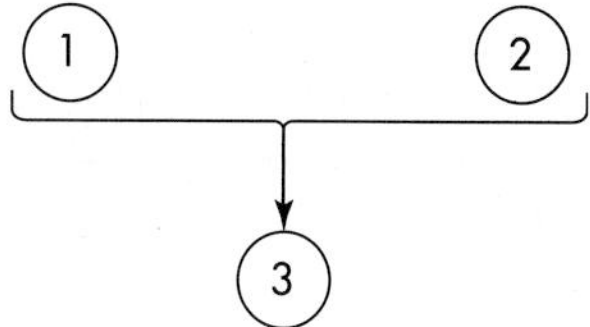

In this argument, neither premise supports the conclusion independently. It is the combination of the facts that General Motors makes most of its money in one way, while car dealers make most of their money in another way, that supports the conclusion that the latter may thrive while the former languishes.

Often we can *show* what we cannot as conveniently say. Diagrams are particularly useful when an argument's structure is complicated. Consider the following argument:

> ① Desert mountaintops make good sites for astronomy. ② Being high, they sit above a portion of the atmosphere, enabling a star's light to reach a telescope without having to swim through the entire depths of the atmosphere. ③ Being dry, the desert is also relatively cloud-free. ④ The merest veil of haze or cloud can render a sky useless for many astronomical measures.[7]

Proposition ① is plainly the conclusion of this argument, and the other three provide support for it—but they function differently in giving that support. Statement ② supports, by itself, the claim that mountaintops are good sites for telescopes. But statements ③ and ④ must work together to support the claim that *desert* mountaintops are good sites for telescopes. A diagram shows this neatly:

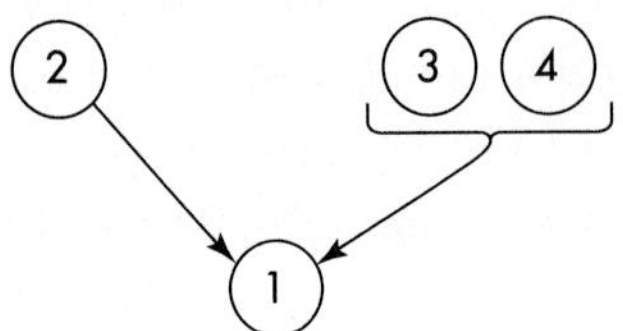

Some complications may be revealed more clearly using paraphrase. When an argument has a premise that is not stated explicitly, a paraphrase allows us to formulate the tacit premise and then add it to the list explicitly. A diagram requires the representation of the tacit premise in some way that indicates visually that it has been added (a broken circle around a number is commonly used), but even then the added premise remains to be precisely formulated. Thus the argument

> Since there are no certainties in the realm of politics, politics must be the arena for negotiation between different perspectives, with cautious moderation likely to be the best policy.[8]

is best clarified by a paraphrase in which its tacit premise and internal complexity is made explicit, thus:

1. There are no certainties in the realm of politics.
2. Where there are no certainties, those with different perspectives must negotiate their differences.
3. The best policy likely to emerge from such negotiation is one of cautious moderation.
4. Therefore politics is the realm for negotiation between different perspectives, with cautious moderation likely to be the best policy.

The number of arguments in a passage is determined, most logicians agree, by the number of conclusions it contains. If a passage contains two or more arguments, and a number of propositions whose relations are not obvious, a diagram may prove particularly useful in sorting things out. A passage in a letter from Karl Marx to Friedrich Engels illustrates this nicely:

> ① To hasten the social revolution in England is the most important object of the International Workingman's Association. ② The sole means of hastening it is to make Ireland independent. Hence ③ the task of the "International" is everywhere

> to put the conflict between England and Ireland in the foreground, and ④ everywhere to side openly with Ireland.[9]

There are two conclusions in this passage and hence two arguments. But both conclusions are inferred from the same two premises. A diagram exhibits this structure:

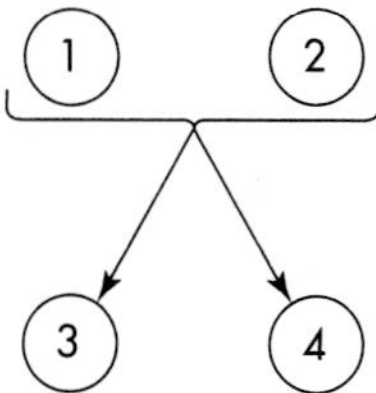

Two conclusions (and hence two arguments) may have a single stated premise. For example,

> Older women have less freedom to fight sexual harassment at their jobs or to leave a battering husband, because age discrimination means they won't easily find other ways of supporting themselves.[10]

The single premise here is that older women cannot easily find alternative ways to support themselves. The two conclusions supported by that premise are (a) that older women have less freedom to fight sexual harassment at their jobs, and (b) that older married women have less freedom to leave a battering husband. A *single argument* ordinarily means an argument with a single conclusion, regardless of how many premises are adduced in its support.

When there are two or more premises in an argument, or two or more arguments in a passage, the order of appearance of premises and conclusions may need to be clarified. The conclusion may be stated last, or first; it may sometimes be sandwiched between the premises offered in its support, as in the following passage:

> The real and original source of inspiration for the Muslim thinkers was the Quran and the sayings of the Holy Prophet. It is therefore clear that the Muslim philosophy was not a carbon copy of Greek thought, as it concerned itself primarily and specifically with those problems which originated from and had relevance to Muslims.[11]

Here the conclusion, that "Muslim philosophy was not a carbon copy of Greek thought," appears after the first premise of the argument and before the second.

The same proposition that serves as a conclusion in one argument may serve as premise in a different argument, just as the same person may be a commander in one context and a subordinate in another. This is well illustrated by a passage from the work of Thomas Aquinas. He argues:

> Human law is framed for the multitude of human beings.
>
> The majority of human beings are not perfect in virtue.
>
> Therefore human laws do not forbid all vices.[12]

The conclusion of this argument is used immediately thereafter as a premise in another, quite different argument:

> Vicious acts are contrary to acts of virtue.
>
> But human law does not prohibit all vices. . . .
>
> Therefore neither does it prescribe all acts of virtue.[13]

No special techniques are needed, to grasp these arguments of St. Thomas. But when the cascade of arguments is compressed, a paraphrase is helpful in showing the flow of reasoning. Consider the following passage:

> Because ① the greatest mitochondrial variations occurred in African people, scientists concluded that ② they had the longest evolutionary history, indicating ③ a probable African origin for modern humans.[14]

We might diagram the passage thus:

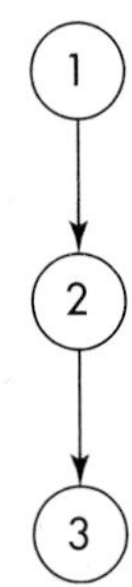

A paraphrase of this passage, although perhaps more clumsy, more fully exhibits the cascade of the two arguments that are compressed in it:

1. The more mitochondrial variation in a people, the longer its evolutionary history.
2. The greatest mitochondrial variations occur in African people.

Therefore African people have had the longest evolutionary history.

1. African people have had the longest evolutionary history.
2. Modern humans probably originated where people have had the longest evolutionary history.

Therefore modern humans probably originated in Africa.

These examples make it evident that the same proposition can serve as a premise, where it occurs as an assumption in an argument; or as a conclusion, where it is claimed to follow from other propositions assumed in an argument. "Premise" and "conclusion" are always *relative* terms.

Multiple arguments may be interwoven in patterns more complicated than cascades, and these will require careful analysis. The diagramming technique then becomes particularly useful. In John Locke's *Second Treatise of Government*, for example, two arguments are combined in the following passage:

> It is not necessary—no, nor so much as convenient—that the legislative should be always in being; but absolutely necessary that the executive power should, because there is not always need of new laws to be made, but always need of execution of the laws that are made.

The component propositions here may be numbered thus: ① It is not necessary or convenient that the legislative [branch of government] should be always in being; ② it is absolutely necessary that the executive power should be always in being; ③ there is not always need of new laws to be made; ④ there is always need of execution of the laws that are made. The diagram for this passage is

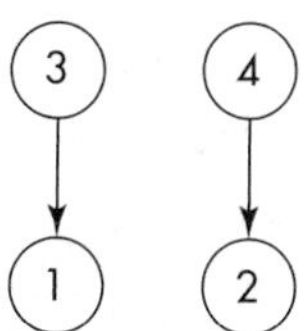

which shows that the conclusion of the second argument is stated between the conclusion and the premise of the first argument, and that the premise of the first argument is stated between the conclusion and the premise of the second argument. The diagram also shows that both conclusions are stated before their premises.

That very same diagram shows the logical structure of two related arguments of the Roman philosopher Seneca, in support of the deterrence theory of punishment. He wrote:

> ① No one punishes because a sin has been committed, ② but in order that a sin will not be committed. [For] ③ what has passed cannot be recalled, but ④ what lies in the future may be prevented.

That "no one punishes because a sin has been committed" is the conclusion of one argument; its premise is that "what has passed cannot be recalled." That "[we do punish] in order that a sin will not be committed" is the conclusion of a second argument, whose premise is that "what lies in the future may be prevented."

Diagramming and paraphrasing are both very useful tools with which we can analyze arguments so as to understand more fully the relations of premises to conclusions.

EXERCISES

A. Diagram each of the following passages, which may contain more than one argument.

EXAMPLE

1. In a recent attack upon the evils of suburban sprawl, the authors argue as follows:

> The dominant characteristic of sprawl is that each component of a community—housing, shopping centers, office parks, and civic institutions—is segregated, physically separated from the others, causing the residents of suburbia to spend an inordinate amount of time and money moving from one place to the next. And since nearly everyone drives alone, even a sparsely populated area can generate the traffic of a much larger traditional town.[15]

SOLUTION

① The dominant characteristic of sprawl is that each component of a community—housing, shopping centers, office parks, and civic institutions—is segregated, physically separated from the others, causing ② the residents of suburbia to spend an inordinate amount of time and money moving from one place to the next. And since ③ nearly everyone drives alone, ④ even a sparsely populated area can generate the traffic of a much larger traditional town.

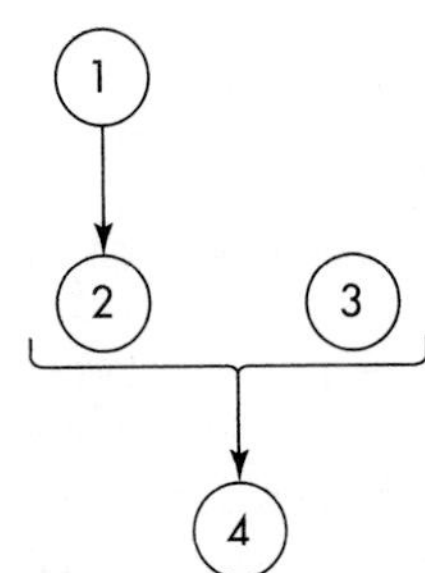

2. At any cost we must have filters on our Ypsilanti Township library computers. Pornography is a scourge on society at every level. Our public library must not be used to channel this filth to the people of the area.

—Rob. J. and Joan D. Pelkey,
The Ann Arbor (Michigan) *News*, 3 February 2004

3. At his best, Lyndon Johnson was one of the greatest of all American presidents. He did more for racial justice than any president since Abraham Lincoln. He built more social protections than anyone since Franklin Roosevelt. He was probably the greatest legislative politician in American history. He was also one of the most ambitious idealists. Johnson sought power to use it to accomplish great things.

—Alan Brinkley, "The Making of a War President,"
The New York Times Book Review, 20 August 2006

4. Married people are healthier and more economically stable than single people, and children of married people do better on a variety of indicators. Marriage is thus a socially responsible act. There ought to be some way of spreading the principle of support for marriage throughout the tax code.

—Anya Bernstein, "Marriage, Fairness and Taxes,"
The New York Times, 15 February 2000

5. The distinguished economist J. K. Galbraith long fought to expose and improve a society exhibiting "private opulence and public squalor." In his classic work, *The Affluent Society* (Boston: Houghton Mifflin, 1960), he argued as follows:

> Vacuum cleaners to insure clean houses are praiseworthy and essential in our standard of living. Street cleaners to insure clean streets are an unfortunate expense. Partly as a result, our houses are generally clean and our streets generally filthy.

6. Defending the adoption of the euro in place of the pound as the monetary unit of the United Kingdom, Prime Minister Tony Blair said this: "The argument is simple. We are part of Europe. It affects us directly and deeply. Therefore we should exercise leadership in order to change Europe in the direction we want."

—Reported by Alan Cowell in the *The New York Times*, 9 December 2001

7. California's "three strikes and you're out" law was enacted 10 years ago this month (March, 2004). Between 1994 and 2002, California's prison population grew by 34,724, while that of New York, a state without a "three strikes" law, grew by 315. Yet during that time period New York's violent crime rate dropped 20 percent more than California's. No better example exists of how the drop in crime cannot be attributed to draconian laws with catchy names.

—Vincent Schiraldi, "Punitive Crime Laws," *The New York Times*, 19 March 2004

8. No one means all he says, and yet very few say all they mean, for words are slippery and thought is viscous.

—Henry Adams, *The Education of Henry Adams* (1907)

9. The first impression becomes a self-fulfilling prophesy: we hear what we expect to hear. The interview is hopelessly biased in favor of the nice.

—Malcom Gladwell, "The New-Boy Network," *The New Yorker*, 29 May 2000

10. No government can ever guarantee that the small investor has an equal chance of winning. It is beyond dishonest to pretend that rules can be written to prevent future financial scandals. No set of regulations can insure fairness and transparency in the [securities] markets.

—Lester Thurow, "Government Can't Make the Market Fair," *The New York Times*, 23 July 2002

B. There may be one argument or more than one argument in each of the following passages. Paraphrase the premises and conclusions (or use diagrams if that is helpful) to analyze the arguments found in each passage.

EXAMPLE

1. An outstanding advantage of nuclear over fossil fuel energy is how easy it is to deal with the waste it produces. Burning fossil fuels produces 27,000 million tons of carbon dioxide yearly, enough to make, if solidified, a mountain nearly one mile high with a base twelve miles in circumference. The same quantity of energy produced from nuclear fission reactions would generate two million times less waste, and it would occupy a sixteen-meter cube. All of the high level waste produced in a year from a nuclear power station would occupy a space about a cubic meter in size and would fit safely in a concrete pit.

—James Lovelock, *The Revenge of Gaia: Earth's Climate Crisis and the Fate of Humanity* (New York: Basic Books, 2006)

SOLUTION

① An outstanding advantage of nuclear over fossil fuel energy is how easy it is to deal with the waste it produces. ② Burning fossil fuels produces 27,000 million tons of carbon dioxide yearly, enough to make, if solidified, a mountain nearly one mile high with a base twelve miles in circumference. ③ The same quantity of energy produced from nuclear fission reactions would generate two million times less waste, and it would occupy a sixteen-meter cube. ④ All of the high level waste produced in a year from a nuclear power station would occupy a space about a cubic meter in size and would fit safely in a concrete pit.

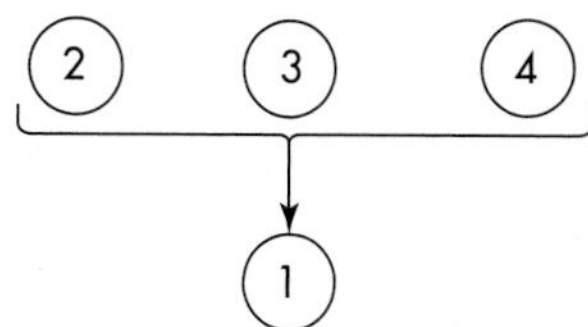

2. Why decry the wealth gap? First, inequality is correlated with political instability. Second, inequality is correlated with violent crime. Third, economic inequality is correlated with reduced life expectancy. A fourth reason? Simple justice. There is no moral justification for chief executives being paid hundreds of times more than ordinary employees.

—Richard Hutchinsons, "When the Rich Get Even Richer," *The New York Times*, 26 January 2000

3. Genes and proteins are discovered, not invented. Inventions are patentable, discoveries are not. Thus, protein patents are intrinsically flawed.

—Daniel Alroy, "Invention vs. Discovery," *The New York Times*, 29 March 2000

4. Ultimately, whaling's demise in Japan may have little to do with how majestic, smart, or endangered the mammals are, but a good deal to do with simple economics. A Japanese newspaper conducted a survey in Japan regarding the consumption of whale meat, and reported that of all the thousands of respondents, only 4 percent said that they actually ate whale meat at least sometimes. The newspaper then wrote this: "A growing number of Japanese don't want to eat whale meat. And if they won't eat it, they won't buy it. And if they won't buy it, say good-bye to Japanese whaling."

—Reported in *Asahi Shimbun*, April 2002

5. On the 18th of July, 2002, the *Consejo Juvenil Sionisto Argentino* (Young Zionists of Argentina) held a mass demonstration to promote widespread remembrance of the horror of the bombing of the Jewish Community Center in Buenos Aires, exactly eight years earlier. At this demonstration the Young Zionists carried a huge banner, which read: *"Sin memoria, no hay justicia. Sin justicia, no hay futuro."*

6. Back in 1884, Democratic nominee Grover Cleveland was confronted by the charge that he had fathered an out-of-wedlock child. While Republicans chanted, "Ma, Ma, where's my Pa," Cleveland conceded that he had been supporting the child. No excuses, no evasions. One of his supporters—one of the first spin doctors—gave this advice to voters:

   > Since Grover Cleveland has a terrific public record, but a blemished private life, and since his opponent, James G. Blaine, has a storybook private life but a checkered public record, why not put both where they perform best—return Blaine to private life, keep Cleveland in public life.

7. "Wars don't solve problems; it creates them," said an Oct. 8 letter about Iraq.

   World War II solved problems called Nazi Germany and militaristic Japan, and created alliances with the nations we crushed. The Revolutionary War solved the problem of taxation without representation, and created the United States of America. The Persian Gulf War solved the problem of the Iraqi invasion of Kuwait. The Civil War solved the problem of slavery.

   These wars created a better world. War is the only way to defeat evil enemies with whom there is no reasoning. It's either us or them. What creates true peace is victory.

   —Keith Kraska, "Necessary Wars," *The New York Times*, 15 October 2002

8. In the *Crito,* Plato presents the position of the Athenian community, personified as "the Laws," speaking to Socrates or to any citizen of the community who may contemplate deliberate disobedience to the state:

   > He who disobeys us is, as we maintain, thrice wrong; first, because in disobeying us he is disobeying his parents; secondly, because we are the authors of his education; thirdly, because he has made an agreement with us that he will duly obey our commands.

9. The reality is that money talks. Court officers, judges and juries treat private lawyers and their clients differently from those who cannot pay for representation. Just as better-dressed diners get prime tables

at a restaurant, human nature dictates better results for those who appear to have money.

—Desiree Buenzle, "Free Counsel and Fairness," *The New York Times*, 15 January 2007

10. The town of Kennesaw, GA passed a *mandatory gun ownership* law, in 1982, in response to a *handgun ban* passed in Morton Grove, IL. Kennesaw's crime rate dropped sharply, while Morton Grove's did not. Criminals, unsurprisingly, would rather break into a house where they aren't at risk of being shot. . . . Criminals are likely to suspect that towns with laws like these on the books will be unsympathetic to malefactors in general, and to conclude that they will do better elsewhere. To the extent that's true, we're likely to see other communities adopting similar laws so that criminals won't see them as attractive alternatives.

—Glenn Reynolds, "A Rifle in Every Pot," *The New York Times*, 16 January 2007

2.3 Complex Argumentative Passages

Some arguments are exceedingly complicated. Analyzing passages in which several arguments are interwoven, with some propositions serving as both premises and subconclusions while other propositions serve only as premises, and still others are repeated in different words, can be a challenge. The diagramming technique is certainly helpful, but there is no mechanical way to determine whether the diagram actually does represent the author's intent accurately. More than one plausible interpretation may be offered, and in that case more than one diagram can reasonably be used to show the logical structure of that passage.

To analyze fairly, we must strive to understand the flow of the author's reasoning, and to identify the role of each element in the passage as part of that flow. The examples that follow (in which component propositions have been numbered for purposes of analysis) show the ways in which we can set forth the connections between premises and conclusions. Only after that is done, when we have identified the arguments within a passage and the relations of those arguments, can we go about deciding whether the conclusions do indeed follow from the premises affirmed.

In the following set of arguments, the final conclusion of the passage appears in the very first statement, which is not unusual. Four premises directly support this conclusion; two of these are subconclusions, which in turn are supported, in different ways, by other premises affirmed in the passage:

① It is very unlikely that research using animals will be unnecessary or poorly done.
② Before an experiment using a vertebrate animal is carried out, the protocol

for that experiment must be reviewed by an institutional committee that includes a veterinarian and a member of the public, and ③ during the research the animal's health and care are monitored regularly. ④ Researchers need healthy animals for study in science and medicine, because ⑤ unhealthy animals could lead to erroneous results. This is a powerful incentive for ⑥ scientists to make certain that any animals they use are healthy and well nourished. Furthermore, ⑦ research involving animals is expensive, and because ⑧ funding is limited in science, ⑨ only high quality research is able to compete effectively for support.[16]

The following diagram shows the logical structure of this passage. To "read" the diagram we replace the numbers with the indicated propositions, beginning with those highest on the page and therefore earliest in the logical cascade. We thus follow each of the several paths of reasoning to the final conclusion.

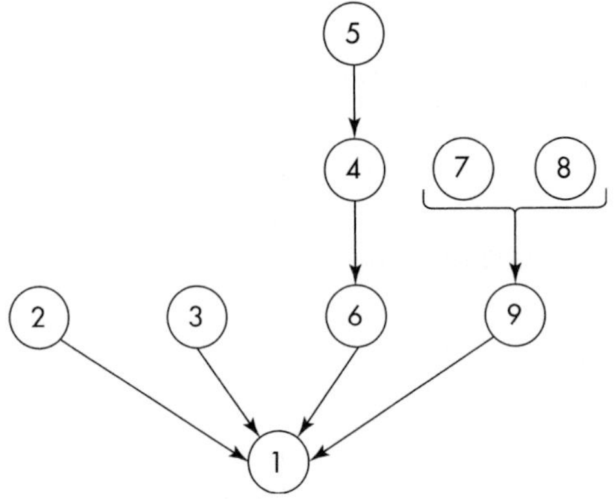

Repetition complicates the task of analysis. Individual propositions are sometimes repeated within an argument in differently worded sentences, sometimes for emphasis and at other times by oversight. The diagram reveals this because we can assign the same number to different formulations of the same proposition. The following passage, comprising three distinct arguments, exhibits this confusing duplication of propositions:

① The Big Bang theory is crumbling. . . . ② According to orthodox wisdom, the cosmos began with the Big Bang—an immense, perfectly symmetrical explosion 20 billion years ago. The problem is that ③ astronomers have confirmed by observation the existence of huge conglomerations of galaxies that are simply too big to have been formed in a mere 20 billion years. . . . Studies based on new data collected by satellite, and backed up by earlier ground surveys, show that ④ galaxies are clustered into vast ribbons that stretch billions of light years, and ⑤ are separated by voids hundreds of millions of light years across.

> Because ⑥ galaxies are observed to travel at only a small fraction of the speed of light, mathematics shows that ⑦ such large clumps of matter must have taken at least one hundred billion years to come together—five times as long as the time since the hypothetical Big Bang. . . . ③ Structures as big as those now seen can't be made in 20 billion years. . . . ② The Big Bang theorizes that matter was spread evenly through the universe. From this perfection, ③ there is no way for such vast clumps to have formed so quickly.[17]

In this passage the premises that report observational evidence, ④, ⑤, and ⑥, give reasons for ⑦, the great length of time that would have had to elapse since the Big Bang. This passage of time is used to support the subconclusion (formulated in three slightly different ways) that ③ structures as big as those now seen are too big to have been formed in that period of time. From that subconclusion, combined with ②, a short statement (formulated in two slightly different ways) of the original symmetry and spread that the Big Bang theory supposes, we infer the final conclusion of the passage, ①: that the Big Bang theory is crumbling—the proposition with which the passage begins. The following diagram shows this set of logical relations:

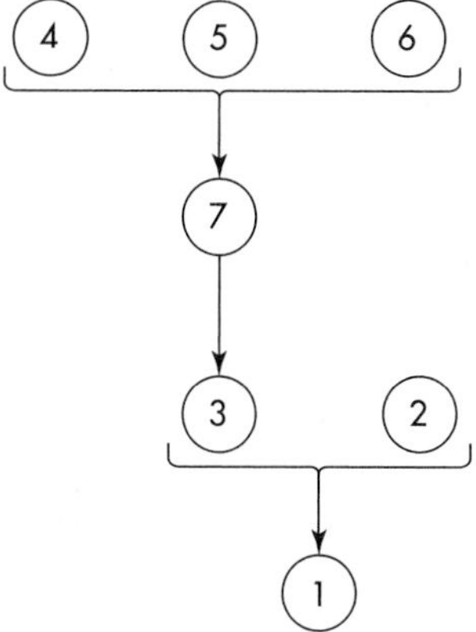

The fact that a premise may appear in compressed form, sometimes as a short noun phrase, must be borne in mind. In the following argument the phrase, "the scattering in the atmosphere" serves as a premise, ④, that may be reformulated as "the sun's energy is scattered in the atmosphere." This compression, along with repetition, makes it more difficult to analyze this argument:

> ① Solar-powered cars can never be anything but experimental devices. ② Solar power is too weak to power even a mini-car for daily use. ③ The solar power entering the atmosphere is about 1 kilowatt per square yard. Because of

> ④ the scattering in the atmosphere, and because ⑤ the sun shines half a day on the average at any place on earth, ⑥ average solar power received is 1/6 kilowatt, or 4 kilowatt hours a day. . . . Tests on full-size cars indicate that ⑦ 300,000 watt hours are required in a battery for an electric car to perform marginally satisfactorily. So, ⑧ 40 square yards of cells would be needed to charge the car batteries, about the size of the roof of a tractor-trailer. ① It is not undeveloped technologies that put solar power out of the running to be anything but a magnificently designed experimental car. It is cosmology.[18]

The first proposition in this passage, asserting that "solar powered cars can never be more than experimental," is the final conclusion. It is repeated in more elaborate form at the end of the passage, as a diagram of the passage shows:

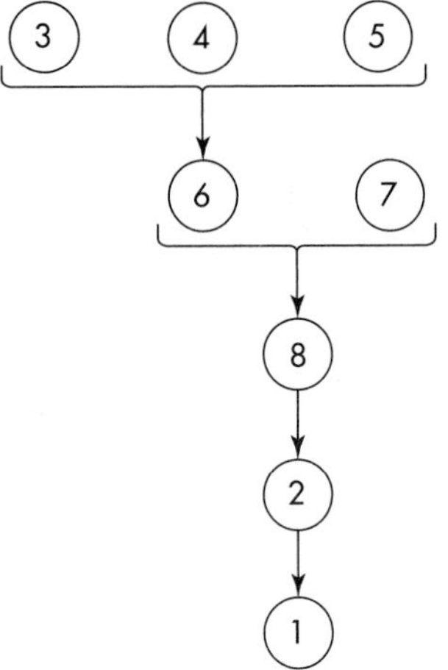

Complex argumentative passages can be entirely cogent. The following complex argument, for example, was offered by a distinguished editor in defense of her highly controversial editorial policy:

> The *Journal* [the *New England Journal of Medicine*] . . . has taken the position that ① it will not publish reports of unethical research, regardless of their scientific merit. . . . There are three reasons for our position. First, ② the policy of publishing only ethical research, if generally applied, would deter unethical work. ③ Publication is an important part of the reward system in medical research, and ④ investigators would not undertake unethical studies if they knew the results would not be published. Furthermore, ⑤ any other policy would tend to lead to more unethical work, because, as I have indicated, ⑥ such studies may be easier to carry out and thus ⑦ may give their practitioners a competitive edge. Second, ⑧ denying publication even when the ethical violations are minor

> protects the principle of the primacy of the research subject. ⑨ If small lapses were permitted we would become inured to them, and ⑩ this would lead to larger violations. And finally, ⑪; refusal to publish unethical work serves notice to society at large that even scientists do not consider science the primary measure of a civilization. ⑫ Knowledge, although important, may be less important to a decent society than the way it is obtained.[19]

Again, the final conclusion appears at the beginning of the passage, and the three major premises that support it directly, ②, ⑧, and ⑪, are themselves supported by various other premises arranged differently. However, each of the many propositions in the passage has a clear logical role in leading to the conclusion that the passage aims to justify: Reports of research done in unethical ways will not be published in the *New England Journal of Medicine*, regardless of their scientific merit. The following diagram shows the logical structure of this complicated but carefully reasoned passage:

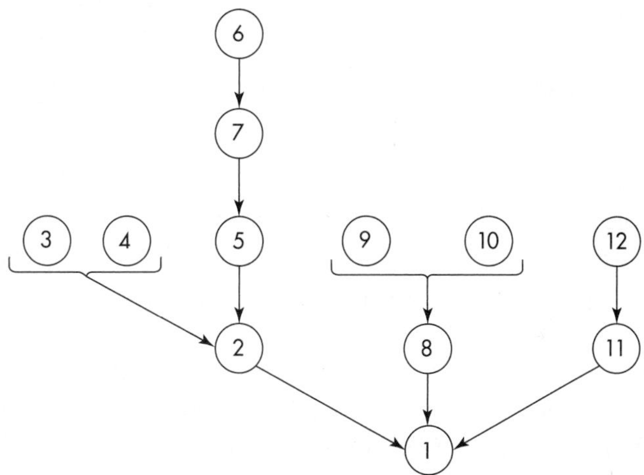

Arguments in newspaper editorials and letters-to-the-editor columns often fall short of this standard. They may include statements whose role is unclear; connections among the statements in the argument may be tangled or misstated; the flow of argument may be confused even in the mind of the author. Logical analysis, paraphrase supported by diagrams, can expose such deficiencies. By exhibiting the *structure* of a reasoning process, we can better see what its strengths and weaknesses may be. The aim and special province of logic is the evaluation of arguments, but successful evaluation presupposes a clear grasp of the structure of the argument in question.

EXERCISES

Each of the following famous passages, taken from classical literature and philosophy, comprises a set of arguments whose complicated interrelations are critical for the force of the whole. Construct for each the diagram that you would find most helpful in analyzing the flow of argument in that passage. More than one interpretation will be defensible.

1. A question arises: whether it be better [for a prince] to be loved than feared or feared than loved? One should wish to be both, but, because it is difficult to unite them in one person, it is much safer to be feared than loved, when, of the two, one must be dispensed with. Because this is to be asserted in general of men, that they are ungrateful, fickle, false, cowards, covetous. . . . and that prince who, relying entirely on their promises, has neglected other precautions, is ruined, because friendships that are obtained by payments may indeed be earned but they are not secured, and in time of need cannot be relied upon. Men have less scruple in offending one who is beloved than one who is feared, for love is preserved by the link of obligation which, owing to the baseness of men, is broken at every opportunity for their advantage; but fear preserves you by a dread of punishment which never fails.

   —Niccoló Machiavelli, *The Prince,* 1515

2. Democratic laws generally tend to promote the welfare of the greatest possible number; for they emanate from the majority of the citizens, who are subject to error, but who cannot have an interest opposed to their own advantage. The laws of an aristocracy tend, on the contrary, to concentrate wealth and power in the hands of the minority; because an aristocracy, by its very nature, constitutes a minority. It may therefore be asserted, as a general proposition, that the purpose of a democracy in its legislation is more useful to humanity than that of an aristocracy.

   —Alexis de Tocqueville, *Democracy in America,* 1835

3. ". . . . You appeared to be surprised when I told you, on our first meeting, that you had come from Afghanistan."

   "You were told, no doubt."

   "Nothing of the sort. I *knew* you came from Afghanistan. From long habit the train of thoughts ran so swiftly through my mind that I arrived at the conclusion without being conscious of intermediate steps. There were such steps, however. The train of reasoning ran, 'Here is a gentleman of medical type, but with the air of a military man. Clearly an army doctor, then. He has just come from the tropics, for his face is dark, and that is not the natural tint of his skin, for his wrists are fair. He has undergone hardship and sickness, as his haggard face says clearly. His left arm has been injured. He holds it in a stiff and unnatural manner. Where in the tropics could an English army doctor have seen much hardship and got his arm wounded? Clearly in Afghanistan.' The whole train of thought did not occupy a second. I then remarked that you came from Afghanistan, and you were astonished."

"It is simple enough as you explain it," I said, smiling.

—A. Conan Doyle, *A Study in Scarlet,* 1887

4. Nothing is demonstrable unless the contrary implies a contradiction. Nothing that is distinctly conceivable implies a contradiction. Whatever we conceive as existent, we can also conceive as nonexistent. There is no being, therefore, whose non-existence implies a contradiction. Consequently there is no being whose existence is demonstrable.

—David Hume, *Dialogues Concerning Natural Religion,* Part IX, 1779

CHALLENGE TO THE READER

In the *Ethics* (1677), Baruch Spinoza, one of the most influential of all modern thinkers, presents a deductive philosophical system in which the central conclusions—about God, about nature, and about human life and human freedom—are demonstrated in "geometrical" fashion. Here follows an example. Proposition 29 of the first book of the *Ethics* (there are five books in all) reads:

> In nature there is nothing contingent, but all things are determined from the necessity of the divine nature to exist and act in a certain manner.

Immediately after the statement of each proposition in the *Ethics* appears its proof. The proof of Prop. 29 (from which internal references to proofs given earlier in the same work have been omitted for the sake of clarity) appears immediately below. Analyze this proof, by constructing a diagram that shows the structure of the argument, or by paraphrasing it in a way that makes it clear and persuasive to a modern reader.

> Whatever is, is in God. But God cannot be called a contingent thing, for He exists necessarily and not contingently. Moreover, the modes of the divine nature [the creations which depend on, or have been created by, God immediately] have followed from it necessarily and not contingently. . . . But God is the cause of these modes not only in so far as they simply exist, but also in so far as they are considered as determined to any action. If they are not determined by God it is an impossibility and not a contingency that they should determine themselves; and, on the other hand, if they are determined by God it is an impossibility and not a contingency

> that they should render themselves indeterminate. Wherefore all things are determined from a necessity of the divine nature, not only to exist, but to exist and act in a certain manner, and there is nothing contingent.

2.4 Problems in Reasoning

In reasoning we advance from premises known (or affirmed for the purpose) to conclusions. We construct arguments of our own every day, in deciding how we shall act, in judging the conduct of others, in defending our moral or political convictions, and so on. Skill in devising good arguments (and in deciding whether a proffered argument is good) is of enormous value, and this skill can be improved with practice. Ancient games of reasoning, such as chess and go, exercise that skill, and there are some widely known commercial games (Clue and Mastermind are examples) that also have this merit.

Problems may be contrived which are designed to test and strengthen logical skills; some of these are presented in this section. Such problems are far neater than those that arise in real life, of course. But solving them may require extended reasoning in patterns not very different from those employed by a detective, a journalist, or a juror. Chains of inferences will be needed, in which subconclusions are used as premises in subsequent arguments. Finding the solution may require the creative recombination of information given earlier or discovered. Contrived problems can prove frustrating—but solving them, like every successful application of reasoning, is quite satisfying. In addition to being models for the employment of reason, logical games and puzzles are good fun. "The enjoyment of the doubtful," wrote the philosopher John Dewey, "is a mark of the educated mind."

One type of reasoning problem is the common brainteaser, in which, using only the clues provided, we must determine the names or other facts about certain specified characters. Here is a simple example:

> In a certain flight crew, the positions of pilot, copilot, and flight engineer are held by three persons, Allen, Brown, and Carr, though not necessarily in that order. The copilot, who is an only child, earns the least. Carr, who married Brown's sister, earns more than the pilot. What position does each of the three persons hold?

To solve such problems we look first for a sphere in which we have enough information to reach some conclusions going beyond what is given in the premises. In this case we know most about Carr: he is not the pilot, because he earns more than the pilot; and he is not the copilot because the copilot earns the least. By elimination we may infer that Carr must be the flight engineer. Using that subconclusion we can determine Brown's position. Brown is not the copilot because he has a sister and the copilot is an only child; he is not the flight engineer because Carr is. Brown must therefore be the pilot. Allen, the only one left, must therefore be the copilot.

When problems of this type become more complex, it is useful to construct a graphic display of the alternatives, called a *matrix*, which we fill in as we accumulate new information. The helpfulness of such a matrix will be seen in solving the following problem:

> Alonzo, Kurt, Rudolf, and Willard are four creative artists of great talent. One is a dancer, one is a painter, one is a singer, and one is a writer, though not necessarily in that order.
>
> 1. Alonzo and Rudolf were in the audience the night the singer made his debut on the concert stage.
> 2. Both Kurt and the writer have had their portraits painted from life by the painter.
> 3. The writer, whose biography of Willard was a best-seller, is planning to write a biography of Alonzo.
> 4. Alonzo has never heard of Rudolf.
>
> What is each man's artistic field?

To remember the facts asserted in these premises, as well as the subconclusions that may be inferred from them, would be a demanding task. Written notes could become a confusing clutter. We need a method for storing and exhibiting the information given and the intermediate conclusions drawn, keeping it all available for use as the number of inferences increases and the chain of arguments lengthens. The matrix we construct allows us to represent all the relevant possibilities and to record each inference drawn.

For this problem the matrix must display an array of the four persons (in four rows) and the four artistic professions (in four columns) that they hold. It would look like this:

	Dancer	Painter	Singer	Writer
Alonzo				
Kurt				
Rudolf				
Willard				

When we conclude that one of those individuals (named at the left of one of the rows) cannot be the artist whose profession is at the top of one of the columns, we write an N (for "No") in the box to the right of that person's name and in the column headed by that profession. We can immediately infer, from premise (1), that neither Alonzo nor Rudolph is the singer, so we place an N to the right of their names, in the third (singer) column. We can infer from premise (2) that Kurt is neither the painter nor the writer, so we enter an N to the right of his name in the second (painter) and the fourth (writer) columns. From premise (3) we see that the writer is neither Alonzo nor Willard, so we enter an N to the right of their names in the fourth column. The entries we have made thus far are all justified by the information given originally, and our matrix now looks like this:

	Dancer	Painter	Singer	Writer
Alonzo			N	N
Kurt		N		N
Rudolf			N	
Willard				N

From the information now clearly exhibited, we can conclude by elimination that Rudolf must be the writer, so we enter a Y (for "Yes") in the box to the right of Rudolf's name in the fourth (writer) column, and we place an N in the other boxes to the right of his name. The array now makes it evident that the painter must be either Alonzo or Willard, and we can eliminate Alonzo in this way: Rudolf had his portrait painted by the painter (from premise 2), and Alonzo has never heard of Rudolf (from premise 4)—therefore Alonzo cannot be the painter. So we enter an N to the right of Alonzo's name under column 2 (painter). We may conclude that Alonzo must be the dancer, so we enter a Y to the right of Alonzo's name in the first (dancer) column. In that same column we can now enter an N for both Kurt and Willard. The only possible category remaining for Kurt is singer, and therefore we enter a Y in that box for him, and an N in the singer column for Willard. By elimination, we conclude that Willard must be the painter and put a Y in the last empty box in the matrix. Our completed graphic display looks like this:

	Dancer	Painter	Singer	Writer
Alonzo	Y	N	N	N
Kurt	N	N	Y	N
Rudolf	N	N	N	Y
Willard	N	Y	N	N

Our matrix now filled in, the full solution is evident: Alonzo is the dancer; Kurt is the singer; Rudolf is the writer; Willard is the painter.

Some brainteasers of this kind, requiring solutions on several dimensions, are very challenging and almost impossible to solve without using a matrix.

In the real world, we are often called upon to reason from some present state of affairs to its causes, from what is to what was. Scientists—especially archeologists, geologists, astronomers, and physicians—commonly confront events or conditions whose origins are problematic. Reasoning that seeks to explain how things must have developed from what went before is called **retrograde analysis.** For example, to the amazement of astronomers, comet Hyakutake, streaking by the earth in 1996, was found to be emitting variable X-rays a hundred times stronger than anyone had ever predicted a comet might emit. A comet expert at the Max Planck Institute in Germany remarked, "We have our work cut out for us in explaining these data—but that's the kind of problem you love to have."

We do love to have them, and for that reason problems in retrograde analysis are often devised for amusement. In the real world, logical problems arise within a theoretical framework that is supplied by scientific or historical knowledge; but in contrived problems that framework must be provided by the problem itself. Some rules or laws must be set forth within which logical analysis can proceed. The chessboard is the setting for the most famous of all problems in retrograde analysis; the rules of chess provide the needed theoretical context. No skill in playing chess is required, but readers who are not familiar with the rules of chess may skip the illustration that follows.

Retrograde problems in chess commonly take this form: An arrangement of pieces on the chessboard is given; it was reached in a game of chess in which all the rules of the game were obeyed. What move, or series of moves, has just been completed? An example of such a problem follows. The diagram presents a position reached in an actual game of chess, all moves in that game having been made in accordance with the rules of chess. The black king has just moved.

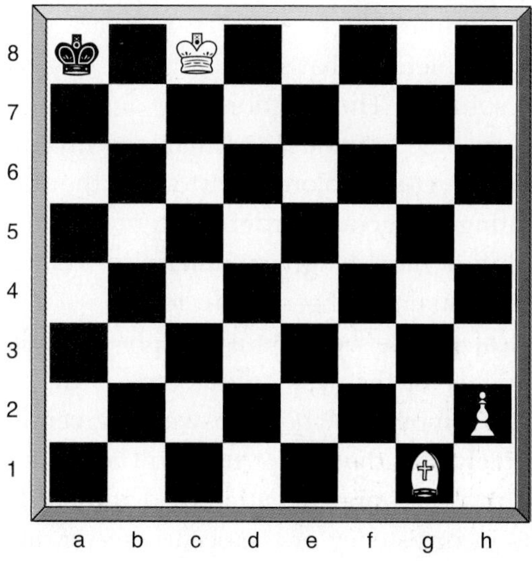

For the purpose of analysis, the rows are numbered from bottom to top, 1 to 8, and the columns are lettered from left to right, a to h. Each square on the board can then be identified by a unique letter–number combination: The black king is on a8, the white pawn on h2, and so on. The problem is this: The last move was made by black. What was that move? And what was white's move just before that? Can you reason out the solution before reading the next paragraph?

Solution: Because the two kings may never rest on adjacent squares, the black king could not have moved to its present position from b7 or from b8; therefore we may be certain that the black king has moved from a7, where it was in check.

That much is easily deduced. But what preceding white move could have put the black king in check? No move by the white bishop (on g1) could have done it, because there would have been no way for that bishop to move to that square, g1, without the black king having been in check with white to move. Therefore it must be that the check was *discovered* by the movement of a white piece that had been blocking the bishop's attack and was captured by the black king on its move to a8. What white piece could have been on that black diagonal and moved from there to the white square in the corner? Only a knight that had been on b6. We may therefore be certain that before black's last move (the black king from a7 to a8), white's last move was that of a white knight from b6 to a8.[20]

Problems of reasoning that confront us in the real world are rarely this tidy. Many real problems are not described accurately, and their misdescription may prove so misleading that no solution can be reached. In cases of that kind, some part or parts of the description of the problem need to be rejected or replaced. However, we cannot do this when we are seeking to solve logical puzzles of the sort presented here.

In the real world, moreover, even when they are described accurately, problems may be incomplete in that something not originally available may be essential for the solution. The solution may depend on some additional scientific discovery, or some previously unimagined invention or equipment, or the search of some as-yet-unexplored territory. In the statement of a logical puzzle, as in the writing of a good murder mystery, all the information that is sufficient for the solution must be given; otherwise we feel that the mystery writer, or the problem maker, has been unfair to us.

Finally, the logical puzzle presents a sharply formulated question (for example, which member of the artistic foursome is the singer? What were black's and white's last moves?) whose answer, if given and proved, solves the problem definitively. But that is not the form in which many real-world problems arise. Real problems are often identified, initially at least, only by the recognition of some inconsistency or the occurrence of an unusual event, or perhaps just by the feeling that something is amiss, rather than by a well-formed question seeking a clearly defined answer. In spite of these differences, contrived problems and puzzles are useful in strengthening our reasoning skills. And they are fun.

EXERCISES

The following problems require reasoning for their solution. To prove that an answer is correct requires an argument (often containing subsidiary arguments) whose premises are contained in the statement of the problem—and whose final conclusion is the answer to it. If the answer is correct, it is possible to construct a valid argument proving it. In working these problems, readers are urged to concern themselves not merely with discovering the answers but also with formulating arguments to prove that those answers are correct.

1. In a certain mythical community, politicians never tell the truth, and nonpoliticians always tell the truth. A stranger meets three natives and asks the first of them, "Are you a politician?" The first native answers the question. The second native then reports that the first native denied being a politician. The third native says that the first native *is* a politician.

How many of these three natives are politicians?

2. Of three prisoners in a certain jail, one had normal vision, the second had only one eye, and the third was totally blind. The jailor told the prisoners that, from three white hats and two red hats, he would select three and put them on the prisoners' heads. None could see what color hat he wore. The jailor offered freedom to the prisoner with normal vision if he could tell what color hat he wore. To prevent a lucky guess, the jailor threatened execution for any incorrect answer. The first prisoner could not tell what hat he wore. Next the jailor made the same offer to the one-eyed prisoner. The second prisoner could not tell what hat he wore either. The jailor did not bother making the offer to the blind prisoner, but he agreed to extend the same terms to that prisoner when he made the request. The blind prisoner said:

> I do not need to have my sight;
> From what my friends with eyes have said,
> I clearly see my hat is _____!

How did he know?

3. On a certain train, the crew consists of the brakeman, the fireman, and the engineer. Their names, listed alphabetically, are Jones, Robinson, and Smith. On the train are also three passengers with corresponding names, Mr. Jones, Mr. Robinson, and Mr. Smith. The following facts are known:

   a. Mr. Robinson lives in Detroit.

   b. The brakeman lives halfway between Detroit and Chicago.

   c. Mr. Jones earns exactly $40,000 a year.

   d. Smith once beat the fireman at billiards.

   e. The brakeman's next-door neighbor, one of the three passengers mentioned, earns exactly three times as much as the brakeman.

   f. The passenger living in Chicago has the same name as the brakeman.

   What is the engineer's name?

4. The employees of a small loan company are Mr. Black, Mr. White, Mrs. Coffee, Miss Ambrose, Mr. Kelly, and Miss Earnshaw. The positions they occupy are manager, assistant manager, cashier, stenographer, teller, and clerk, though not necessarily in that order. The assistant manager is the manager's grandson, the cashier is the stenographer's son-in-law, Mr. Black is a bachelor, Mr. White is twenty-two years old, Miss Ambrose is the teller's stepsister, and Mr. Kelly is the manager's neighbor.

   Who holds each position?

5. Benno Torelli, genial host at Miami's most exclusive nightclub, was shot and killed by a racketeer gang because he fell behind in his protection payments. After considerable effort on the part of the police, five suspects were brought before the district attorney, who asked them what they had to say for themselves. Each of them made three statements, two true and one false. Their statements were

   Lefty: I did not kill Torelli. I never owned a revolver in all my life. Spike did it.

   Red: I did not kill Torelli. I never owned a revolver. The others are all passing the buck.

   Dopey: I am innocent. I never saw Butch before. Spike is guilty.

Spike: I am innocent. Butch is the guilty one. Lefty did not tell the truth when he said I did it.

Butch: I did not kill Torelli. Red is the guilty one. Dopey and I are old pals.

Whodunnit?

6. Mr. Short, his sister, his son, and his daughter are fond of golf and often play together. The following statements are true of their foursome:

a. The best player's twin and the worst player are of the opposite sex.

b. The best player and the worst player are the same age.

Which one of the foursome is the best player?

7. Daniel Kilraine was killed on a lonely road, 2 miles from Pontiac, Michigan, at 3:30 A.M. on March 17 of last year. Otto, Curly, Slim, Mickey, and the Kid were arrested a week later in Detroit and questioned. Each of the five made four statements, three of which were true and one of which was false. One of these persons killed Kilraine.

Their statements were

Otto: I was in Chicago when Kilraine was murdered. I never killed anyone. The Kid is the guilty one. Mickey and I are pals.

Curly: I did not kill Kilraine. I never owned a revolver in my life. The Kid knows me. I was in Detroit the night of March 17.

Slim: Curly lied when he said he never owned a revolver. The murder was committed on St. Patrick's Day. Otto was in Chicago at this time. One of us is guilty.

Mickey: I did not kill Kilraine. The Kid has never been in Pontiac. I never saw Otto before. Curly was in Detroit with me on the night of March 17.

The Kid: I did not kill Kilraine. I have never been in Pontiac. I never saw Curly before. Otto erred when he said I am guilty.

Whodunnit?

8. Six balls confront you. Two are red; two are green; two are blue. You know that in each color pair, one ball is heavier than the other. You also know that all three of the heavier balls weigh the same, as do all three of the lighter balls. The six balls (call them R1, R2, G1, G2, B1, and B2) are otherwise indistinguishable. You have only a balance scale; if equal weights are placed on the two sides of your scale, they will balance; if unequal weights are placed on the two sides, the heavier side will go down. With no more than two weighings on that balance scale, how can you identify the heavier and the lighter balls in all three pairs?

9. In the same mythical community described in Exercise 1, a stranger meets three other natives and asks them, "How many of you are politicians?" The first native replies, "We are all politicians." The second native says, "No, just two of us are politicians." The third native then says, "That isn't true either."

   Is the third native a politician?

10. Imagine a room with four walls, with a nail placed in the center of each wall, as well as in the ceiling and floor, six nails in all. The nails are connected to each other by strings, each nail connected to every other nail by a separate string. These strings are of two colors, red or blue, and of no other color. All these strings obviously make many triangles, because any three nails may be considered the apexes of a triangle.

    Can the colors of the strings be distributed so that no one triangle has all three sides (strings) of the same color? If so, how? And if not, why not?

CHALLENGE TO THE READER

Here is a final reasoning problem whose solution requires the construction of a set of sustained arguments. It isn't easy—but solving it is well within your power and will give you great pleasure.

You are presented with a set of twelve metal balls, apparently identical in every respect: size, color, and so on. In fact, eleven of them are identical, but one of them is "odd": It differs from all the rest in weight only; it is either heavier, or lighter, than all the others. You are given a balance scale, on which the balls can be weighed against one another. If the same number of balls are put on each side of the balance, and the "odd" ball is on one side, that side will go down if the odd ball is heavier, or up if the odd ball is lighter; the two sides will balance if the odd ball is not among those weighed and the same number of balls are placed on each side. You are allowed three weighings only; any removal or addition of a ball constitutes a separate weighing.

Your challenge is this: Devise a set of *three* weighings that will enable you to identify the odd ball wherever it may lie in a random mixing of the twelve balls, *and* that will enable you to determine whether the odd ball is heavier or lighter than the rest.

SUMMARY

In this chapter we have discussed techniques for the analysis of arguments, and some of the difficulties confronted in that process.

In Section 2.1 we explained the paraphrasing of an argumentative passage, in which the essential propositions may be reworded (or supplied if they are assumed but missing), and in which premises and conclusions are put into most intelligible order.

In Section 2.2 we explained the diagramming of an argument, in which the propositions of an argument are represented by numbers, and the relations of the premises and conclusions are then exhibited graphically in two dimensions, by showing on a page the relations of those numbered propositions.

In Section 2.3 we discussed complex argumentative passages, in which the conclusions of subarguments may serve as premises for further arguments, and whose complete analysis generally requires an intricate diagram, or an extensive paraphrase.

In Section 2.4 we discussed contrived problems of reasoning, which often mirror the complexities confronted by many different kinds of investigation in real life, and whose solutions require the construction of extended sets of arguments and subarguments.

End Notes

[1]*Lawrence v. Texas*, 539 U.S. 558 (2003).

[2]G. H. Hardy, *A Mathematician's Apology* (Cambridge: Cambridge University Press, 1940).

[3]This technique was first developed and perfected decades ago by several distinguished logicians: Monroe C. Beardsley, in *Practical Logic* (Englewood Cliffs, NJ: Prentice Hall, 1950); Stephen N. Thomas, in *Practical Reasoning in Natural Language* (Englewod Cliffs, NJ: Prentice Hall, 1973); and Michael Scriven, in *Reasoning* (New York: McGraw-Hill, 1976). We follow their lead.

[4]John Blass "Stem Cell Research: When Does Life Begin?" *The New York Times*, 25 January 2007.

[5]Adam Gopnick, "The Unbeautiful Game," *The New Yorker*, 8 January 2007.

[6]James Surowieki, "Dealer's Choice," *The New Yorker*, 4 September 2006.

[7]Blanchard Hiatt, *University of Michigan Research News*, September 1979.

[8]Robert Alter, "Neocon or Not?" *The New York Times Book Review*, 25 June 2006.

[9]Karl Marx, Letter #141, 9 April 1870, in *Karl Marx and Friedrich Engels Correspondence*, 1846–1895 (New York: International Publishers, 1936).

[10]Boston Women's Health Book Collective, *Our Bodies, Our Selves* (New York: Simon & Schuster, 1984).

[11]C. A. Quadir, *Philosophy and Science in the Islamic World* (London: Croom Helm, 1988).

[12]Thomas Aquinas, *Summa Theologiae*, I, Question 96, Article 2, circa 1265.

[13]Ibid., Article 3.

[14]*Science*, 26 May 1995.

[15]Paraphrased in part from Andres Duany, Elizabeth Plater-Zyberk, and Jeff Speck, *Suburban Nation: The Rise of Sprawl and the Decline of the American Dream* (New York: North Point Press, 2000).

[16]*Science, Medicine, and Animals* (Washington, DC: National Academy of Sciences, 1991).

[17]Eric J. Lerner, "For Whom the Bang Tolls," *The New York Times*, 2 June 1991.

[18]Victor Wouk, "You Can't Drive Solar Cars to Work," *The New York Times*, 15 July 1991.

[19]Marcia Angell, "The Nazi Hypothermia Experiments and Unethical Research Today," *New England Journal of Medicine*, 17 May 1990.

[20]Readers who find retrograde analysis enjoyable will take delight in a collection of such problems, compiled by the logician Raymond Smullyan, and entitled *The Chess Mysteries of Sherlock Homes* (New York: Alfred A. Knopf, 1979).

Language and Definitions

3.1 Language Functions

We reason using language, manipulating propositions in a logical or *informative* spirit. But language is used in a great variety of ways, only some of which are informative. Without the intention to inform, we may *express* ourselves using language: "That's really great!" we may say; and the poet, overcome by the beauty of an ancient city, channels his emotions in writing these lines:

> Match me such marvel, save in Eastern clime—
> A rose-red city—"half as old as time.[1]

Of course, some expressive discourse also has informative content, and may express attitudes as well as beliefs.

> Grow old along with me!
> The best is yet to be,
> The last of life for which the first was made[2]

Moreover, some discourse is *directive,* with or without expressive or informative elements. It seeks to guide or to command. "Step on the scale, please," we may be told. Or we may receive this good advice:

> "Drive defensively. The cemetery is full of law-abiding citizens who had the right of way."

A mixture of functions is a natural feature of almost all our uses of language. We can see this in our own speech and writing. *Emotive* language may be used to advance our purposes in directing others: "That conduct is utterly disgusting!" says parent to child, expressing an attitude, seeking to direct behavior, and (with those same words) probably reporting a fact. We may say that language has three major functions:

1. *Informative*
2. *Expressive*
3. *Directive*

To these we may add less common types of use:

4. *Ceremonial* language (as when we say, "How do you do?" upon being introduced to a stranger), in which words may combine expressive and other functions; and
5. *Performative* language (as when we say, "I apologize for my foolish remark,"), in which words themselves serve, when spoken or written, to perform the function they announce. Other examples are "I congratulate you, . . ." "I accept your offer, . . ." and "I promise you that. . . ."

When we reason—affirm or deny propositions, formulate or evaluate arguments, and so on—it is the informative use of language that is our principal concern.

The *uses* of language must be distinguished from the *forms* of language. The several uses of language (informative, expressive, etc.) are implemented using different forms. Sentences (the units of our language that express complete thoughts) may be *declarative* in form, or *exclamatory*, or *imperative*, or *interrogative*. When we are reasoning, our sentences are usually declarative; when we are expressing emotion, our sentences (e. g., "That's fantastic!") are often exclamatory. When we are seeking to direct conduct our sentences (e.g., "Take off your pants!") are likely to be imperative in form. But there is no strict correlation between function and form.

We saw earlier that a premise may be affirmed by asking a rhetorical question, but attitudes also may be expressed using an interrogative form: (e.g., "What can you possibly mean by that?"). Similarly, a directive function may be served by reporting a fact in declarative mode, as when we cause a companion to move more quickly by saying, "Good heavens, it's late!"

It would be convenient if a given function were invariably executed using language in some specific grammatical form, but that is simply not the case: Language is too loose and its uses too variable to expect that. In determining the real function of a sentence, therefore, context is again critical.

In the informative mode, we distinguish between facts a sentence formulates and facts about the speaker who formulates them. If someone says, "War is always the wrong solution to international conflict," that may indeed be true, but it is also evidence of the *beliefs* of the person who utters that remark.

When someone says, "I strongly oppose our involvement in this war on moral grounds," that is a statement (probably true) about the speaker, but it also serves to express a judgment about the morality of the war under discussion. To open an argument with a statement of one's own views is by no means deceptive; it is one of the common ways in which judgment and biographical report are appropriately integrated.

However, the combination of functions is in some cases not appropriate, and the clash can create troubling controversy. Here is a famous example: Protesting the military draft during the Vietnam War, a young man was arrested in the Los Angeles County Courthouse for wearing a jacket on which a deliberate obscenity was emblazoned; he was convicted of "offensive conduct" under the California penal code. But the recognition of very natural tension that sometimes arises between the different functions of language led to his ultimate exculpation by the United States Supreme Court. Justice John Harlan wrote:

> [M]uch linguistic expression serves a dual communicative function: it conveys not only ideas capable of relatively precise, detached explication, but otherwise inexpressible emotions as well. In fact, words are often chosen as much for their emotive as their cognitive force. We cannot sanction the view that the Constitution, while solicitous of the cognitive content of individual speech, has little or no regard for that emotive function which, practically speaking, may often be the more important element of the message sought to be communicated. . . . and in the same vein, we cannot indulge the facile assumption that one can forbid particular words without also running a substantial risk of suppressing ideas in the process.[3]

Appellate courts can be very wise. Being sensitive to the flexibility of language and recognizing the different functions served by language in a given context are necessary precursors to the application of the logical analysis that is our central concern in this book.

In summary, the principal uses of language are three: informative, expressive, and directive; the grammatical forms of language are essentially four: declarative, interrogative, imperative, and exclamatory. There is no sure connection between the grammatical form of a passage and the use or uses its author intends. Language that serves any one of the three principal functions may take any one of the four grammatical forms.

EXERCISES

A. Which of the various functions of language are exemplified by each of the following passages?

1. Check the box on line 6a unless your parent (or someone else) can claim you as a dependent on his or her tax return.

—U.S. Internal Revenue Service, "Instructions," Form 1040, 2006

2. 'Twas brillig, and the slithy toves
Did gyre and gimble in the wabe;
All mimsy were the borogoves,
And the mome raths outgrabe.

—Lewis Carroll, *Through the Looking Glass*, 1871

3. What traveler among the ruins of Carthage, of Palmyra, Persepolis, or Rome, has not been stimulated to reflections on the transiency of kingdoms and men, and to sadness at the thought of a vigorous and rich life now departed. . . ?

—G. W. F. Hegel,
Lectures on the Philosophy of History, 1823

4. Moving due south from the center of Detroit, the first foreign country one encounters is not Cuba, nor is it Honduras or Nicaragua or any other Latin American nation; it is Canada.

5. I was a child and she was a child,
In this kingdom by the sea,
But we loved with a love that was more than love—
I and my Annabel Lee—

—Edgar Allan Poe, "Annabel Lee," 1849

6. Reject the weakness of missionaries who teach neither love nor brotherhood, but chiefly the virtues of private profit from capital, stolen from your land and labor. Africa awake, put on the beautiful robes of Pan-African Socialism!

—W. E. B. Dubois, "Pan-Africa," 1958

7. If I speak in the tongues of men and of angels, but have not love, I am a noisy gong or a clanging cymbal.

—I Cor. 13:1

8. I herewith notify you that at this date and through this document I resign the office of President of the Republic to which I was elected.

—President Fernando Collor De Mello,
in a letter to the Senate of Brazil, 29 December 1992

9. American life is a powerful solvent. It seems to neutralize every intellectual element, however tough and alien it may be, and to fuse it in the native good will, complacency, thoughtlessness, and optimism.

—George Santayana, *Character and Opinion in the United States*, 1934

10. The easternmost point of land in the United States—as well as the northernmost point and the westernmost point—is in Alaska.

B. What language functions are most probably *intended* to be served by each of the following passages?

1. There is no caste here. Our Constitution is color-blind, and neither knows nor tolerates classes among citizens. In respect of civil rights, all citizens are equal before the law. The humblest is the peer of the most powerful.

   —Justice John Harlan, dissenting in *Plessy v. Ferguson*, 163 U.S. 537, 1896

2. Judges do not know how to rehabilitate criminals—because no one knows.

   —Andrew Von Hirsch, *Doing Justice—The Choice of Punishment* (New York: Hill & Wang, 1976)

3. When tillage begins, other arts follow. The farmers therefore are the founders of human civilization.

   —Daniel Webster, "On Agriculture," 1840

4. The only thing necessary for the triumph of evil is for good men to do nothing.

   —Edmund Burke, letter to William Smith, 1795

5. They have no lawyers among them, for they consider them as a sort of people whose profession it is to disguise matters.

   —Sir Thomas More, *Utopia*, 1516

6. White society is deeply implicated in the ghetto. White institutions created it, white institutions maintain it, and white society condones it.

   —The National Commission on Civil Disorders (Kerner Commission), 1968

7. The bad workmen who form the majority of the operatives in many branches of industry are decidedly of the opinion that bad workmen ought to receive the same wages as good.

   —John Stuart Mill, *On Liberty*, 1859

8. War is the greatest plague that can afflict humanity; it destroys religion, it destroys states, it destroys families. Any scourge is preferable to it.

   —Martin Luther, *Table Talk*, 1566

9. Human history becomes more and more a race between education and catastrophe.

   —H. G. Wells, *The Outline of History*, 1920

10. The man who insists upon seeing with perfect clearness before he decides, never decides.

—Henri-Frederic Amiel, *Amiel's Journal*, 1885

11. Among other evils which being unarmed brings you, it causes you to be despised.

—Niccolò Machiavelli, *The Prince*, 1515

12. Eternal peace is a dream, and not even a beautiful one. War is a part of God's world order. In it are developed the noblest virtues of man: courage and abnegation, dutifulness and self-sacrifice. Without war the world would sink into materialism.

—Helmuth Von Moltke, 1892

13. Language! the blood of the soul, sir, into which our thoughts run, and out of which they grow.

—Oliver Wendell Holmes, *The Autocrat of the Breakfast-Table*, 1858

14. Over the past 133 years, more than 7,500 scientists, including social scientists, have been elected to the National Academy of Sciences. It appears that only three of them have been black.

—*The Journal of Blacks in Higher Education*, Summer 1996

15. A little philosophy inclineth man's mind to atheism; but depth in philosophy bringeth man's mind about to religion.

—Francis Bacon, *Essays*, 1601

16. You'll never have a quiet world until you knock the patriotism out of the human race.

—George Bernard Shaw, *O'Flaherty, V.C.*, 1915

17. If [he] does really think that there is no distinction between virtue and vice, why, sir, when he leaves our houses let us count our spoons.

—Samuel Johnson, 1763

18. Man scans with scrupulous care the character and pedigree of his horses, cattle, and dogs before he matches them; but when he comes to his own marriage he rarely, or never, takes any such care.

—Charles Darwin, *The Descent of Man*, 1871

19. The story of the whale swallowing Jonah, though a whale is large enough to do it, borders greatly on the marvelous; but it would have approached nearer to the idea of miracle if Jonah had swallowed the whale.

—Thomas Paine, *The Age of Reason*, 1796

20. The notion of race is the hydra-headed monster which stifles our most beautiful dreams before they are fairly dreamt, calling us away from the challenges of normal human interaction to a dissonance of suspicion and hatred in pursuit of a fantasy that never was.

—C. Eric Lincoln, *Coming Through the Fire* (Durham, NC: Duke University Press, 1996)

C. For the following passages, indicate what propositions they may be intended to assert, if any; what overt actions they may be intended to cause, if any; and what they may be regarded as providing evidence for about the speaker, if anything.

1. I will not accept if nominated and will not serve if elected.

—William Tecumseh Sherman, message to the Republican National Convention, 1884

2. The government in its wisdom considers ice a "food product." This means that Antarctica is one of the world's foremost food producers.

—George P. Will

3. Mankind has grown strong in eternal struggles and it will only perish through eternal peace.

—Adolf Hitler, *Mein Kampf*, 1925

4. Without music, earth is like a barren, incomplete house with the dwellers missing. Therefore the earliest Greek history and Biblical history, nay the history of every nation, begins with music.

—Ludwig Tieck, quoted in Paul Henry Lang, *Music in Western Civilization* (New York: W. W. Norton, 1941)

5. Research is fundamentally a state of mind involving continual reexamination of doctrines and axioms upon which current thought and action are based. It is, therefore, critical of existing practices.

—Theobald Smith, *American Journal of Medical Science*, 1929

6. I have tried sedulously not to laugh at the acts of man, nor to lament them, nor to detest them, but to understand them.

—Baruch Spinoza, *Tractatus Theologico-politicus*, 1670

7. Of what use is political liberty to those who have no bread? It is of value only to ambitious theorists and politicians.

—Jean-Paul Marat, *L' Ami du peuple*, 1789

8. While there is a lower class I am in it, while there is a criminal element I am of it, and while there is a soul in prison I am not free.

—Eugene Debs, 1918

9. If there were a nation of gods they would be governed democratically, but so perfect a government is not suitable to men.

—Jean-Jacques Rousseau, *The Social Contract*, 1762

10. There are three classes of citizens. The first are the rich, who are indolent and yet always crave more. The second are the poor, who have nothing, are full of envy, hate the rich, and are easily led by demagogues. Between the two extremes lie those who make the state secure and uphold the laws.

—Euripides, *The Suppliant Women*

11. I am convinced that turbulence as well as every other evil temper of this evil age belongs not to the lower but to the middle classes—those middle classes of whom in our folly we are so wont to boast.

—Lord Robert Cecil, *Diary in Australia*, 1852

12. God will see to it that war shall always recur, as a drastic medicine for ailing humanity.

—Heinrich Von Treitschke, *Politik*, 1916

13. I would rather that the people should wonder why I wasn't President than why I am.

—Salmon P. Chase, at the Republican National Convention, 1860

14. He [Benjamin Disraeli] is a self-made man, and worships his creator.

—John Bright, 1882

15. We hear about constitutional rights, free speech and the free press. Every time I hear these words I say to myself, "That man is a Red, that man is a Communist." You never heard a real American talk in that manner.

—Frank Hague, speech before the Jersey City Chamber of Commerce, 12 January 1938

16. Even a fool, when he holdeth his peace, is counted wise: And he that shutteth his lips is esteemed a man of understanding.

—Prov. 17:28

17. A word fitly spoken is like apples of gold in ornaments of silver.

—Prov. 25:11

18. I have sworn upon the altar of God eternal hostility against every form of tyranny over the mind of man.

—Thomas Jefferson, 1800

19. A free man thinks of nothing less than of death, and his wisdom is not a meditation upon death but upon life.

—Baruch Spinoza, *Ethics*, 1677

20. I have seen, and heard, much of Cockney impudence before now; but never expected to hear a coxcomb ask two hundred guineas for flinging a pot of paint in the public's face.

—John Ruskin, on Whistler's painting, "Nocturne in Black and Gold," 1878

3.2 Emotive Language, Neutral Language, and Disputes

Because a given sentence, or passage, can serve several functions—that is, for example, it can express feelings while reporting facts—the clever use of language can be deceptive or manipulative, and the careless use of language can lead to needless misunderstanding and dispute.

The words we use to covey *beliefs* may be neutral and exact, but they may also have (by accident or by design) an impact on the *attitudes* of our listeners. A rose by any other name would smell as sweet (as Shakespeare wrote), but our response to a flower is likely to be influenced if we are told, as it is handed to us, that it is commonly called "skunkweed." The negative attitudes that are commonly evoked by some words lead to the creation of *euphemisms* to replace them—gentle words for harsh realities. Janitors become "maintenance workers," and then "custodians." "Waiters" become "waitpersons," and then "servers,"—and so on.

The medical vocabulary dealing with human reproduction and elimination is neutral and not offensive, but the four-letter words that are vulgar synonyms of those medical terms are shocking to many because of the attitudes they evoke. There are "seven dirty words" that may not be used on the broadcast media in the United States—because they have unacceptable emotive meanings that are sharply distinguishable from their literal meanings.[4]

Emotionally colored language is appropriate in some contexts—in poetry for example—but it is highly inappropriate in other contexts—in survey research, for example. The responses to a survey will certainly depend in good measure on the words used in asking the questions. Whether we should avoid emotive language, or rely on it, depends on the purpose language is intended to serve in the context. If we aim to provide an unbiased report of facts, we undermine that objective if we use words that are heavily charged with emotional meaning. Sometimes, however, it is nearly impossible to avoid some emotive content—such as when those in conflict about the morality of abortion call themselves either "pro-life," or "pro-choice." In logic we generally strive for language that is, so far as possible, free of the distortion that emotive meanings introduce.

Playing on the emotions of readers and listeners is a central technique in the advertising industry. When the overriding aims are to persuade and sell, manipulating attitudes becomes a sophisticated professional art. Rhetorical tricks are also common in political campaigns, and the choice of words is critical. The best defense against trickery, for voters as for consumers, is an awareness of the real uses to which the language before us is being put. We must be on guard against those who use words to make the worse appear the better cause. "With words," said Benjamin Disraeli, "we govern men."

When parties are in dispute, the differences between them that lead to that dispute may be disagreements in beliefs about the facts, or disagreements in attitude about facts that are actually agreed upon. This uncertainty, and the confusion to which it can lead, may arise because the words being used in the dispute have very different emotive meanings. To illustrate this, imagine a dispute between X and Y about legislation authorizing the death penalty for murder. X and Y may agree or disagree about the facts: whether capital punishment really is an effective deterrent to murder. They may also agree or disagree about whether it is right for the state to execute criminals, whatever may be the facts about its deterrent effectiveness. So it is possible that they could agree about factual beliefs but disagree in their attitudes, or they might agree in their attitudes but disagree about their beliefs. It is also possible, of course, that they disagree both in attitude and in belief.

When we seek to resolve disputes that have both factual and emotional aspects, it is important to determine what really is at issue between the disputing parties. If the disagreement truly is one about whether the death penalty deters in fact, then resolution of the dispute will require, first of all, an effort to determine those facts objectively—although this may not be easy to do. If, on the other hand, the disagreement arises from conflicting convictions about the rightness of state-authorized executions, whether or not the death penalty deters, coming to agreement about the facts is likely to prove insufficient to resolve the dispute.

In many cases a disagreement in attitude about some event or possible outcome is rooted in a disagreement in some belief about facts; in other cases it is not. One of the greatest of all football coaches and one of the greatest of all writers on sports differed profoundly about the importance of winning. Wrote the journalist, Grantland Rice:

> For when the One Great Scorer comes
> To write against your name.
> He marks—not that you won or lost—
> But how you played the game.

Said the coach, Vince Lombardi:

> Winning isn't everything. It's the only thing.

Do you believe that this disagreement in attitude was rooted in a disagreement in belief?

Of course we do not reach agreement simply by recognizing the nature of the dispute. But until we recognize the real nature of a dispute, and the differing functions of the language used by the conflicting parties, it is unlikely that the resolution of differences can be achieved.

EXERCISES

Identify the kinds of agreement or disagreement most probably exhibited by the following pairs.

1. a. Answer a fool according to his folly,
Lest he be wise in his own conceit.

—Prov. 26:5

b. Answer not a fool according to his folly,
Lest thou also be like unto him.

—Prov. 26:4

2. a. Our country: in her intercourse with foreign nations may she always be in the right; but our country, right or wrong!

—Stephen Decatur, toast at a dinner in Norfolk, Virginia, April 1816

b. Our country, right or wrong. When right, to be kept right; when wrong, to be put right.

—Carl Schurz, speech in the U.S. Senate, January 1872

3. a. A bad peace is even worse than war.

—Tacitus, *Annals*

b. The most disadvantageous peace is better than the most just war.

—Desiderius Erasmus, *Adagia*, 1539

4. a. A stitch in time saves nine.
b. Better late than never.

5. a. Absence makes the heart grow fonder.
b. Out of sight, out of mind.

6. **a.** The race is not to the swift, nor the battle to the strong.

—Eccl. 9:11

b. But that's the way to bet.

—Jimmy the Greek

7. **a.** For that some should rule and others be ruled is a thing not only necessary, but expedient; from the hour of their birth, some are marked out for subjection, others for rule. . . . It is clear, then, that some men are by nature free, and others slaves, and that for these latter slavery is both expedient and right.

—Aristotle, *Politics*

b. If there are some who are slaves by nature, the reason is that men were made slaves against nature. Force made the first slaves, and slavery, by degrading and corrupting its victims, perpetuated their bondage.

—Jean-Jacques Rousseau, *The Social Contract*, 1762

8. **a.** War alone brings up to its highest tension all human energy and puts the stamp of nobility upon the peoples who have the courage to face it.

—Benito Mussolini, *Encyclopedia Italiana*, 1932

b. War crushes with bloody heel all justice, all happiness, all that is Godlike in man. In our age there can be no peace that is not honorable; there can be no war that is not dishonorable.

—Charles Sumner, *Addresses on War*, 1904

9. **a.** Next in importance to freedom and justice is popular education, without which neither freedom nor justice can be permanently maintained.

—James A. Garfield, 1880

b. Education is fatal to anyone with a spark of artistic feeling. Education should be confined to clerks, and even them it drives to drink. Will the world learn that we never learn anything that we did not know before?

—George Moore, *Confessions of a Young Man*, 1888

10. **a.** Belief in the existence of god is as groundless as it is useless. The world will never be happy until atheism is universal.

—J. O. La Mettrie, *L'Homme Machine*, 1865

b. Nearly all atheists on record have been men of extremely debauched and vile conduct.

—J. P. Smith, *Instructions on Christian Theology*

11. a. I know of no pursuit in which more real and important services can be rendered to any country than by improving its agriculture, its breed of useful animals, and other branches of a husbandsman's cares.

—George Washington, letter to John Sinclair

b. With the introduction of agriculture mankind entered upon a long period of meanness, misery, and madness, from which they are only now being freed by the beneficent operations of the machine.

—Bertrand Russell, *The Conquest of Happiness,* 1930

12. a. Whenever there is, in any country, uncultivated land and unemployed poor, it is clear that the laws of property have been so far extended as to violate natural right.

—Thomas Jefferson

b. Every man has by nature the right to possess property of his own. This is one of the chief points of distinction between man and the lower animals.

—Pope Leo XIII, *Rerum Novarum,* 1891

13. a. The right of revolution is an inherent one. When people are oppressed by their government, it is a natural right they enjoy to relieve themselves of the oppression, if they are strong enough, either by withdrawal from it, or by overthrowing it and substituting a government more acceptable.

—Ulysses S. Grant, *Personal Memoirs,* vol. 1

b. Inciting to revolution is treason, not only against man, but against God.

—Pope Leo XIII, *Immortale Dei,* 1885

14. a. Language is the armory of the human mind; and at once contains the trophies of its past, and the weapons of its future conquests.

—Samuel Taylor Coleridge

b. Language—human language—after all, is little better than the croak and cackle of fowls, and other utterances of brute nature—sometimes not so adequate.

—Nathaniel Hawthorne, *American Notebooks,* 1835

15. a. How does it become a man to behave towards the American government today? I answer, that he cannot without disgrace be associated with it.

—Henry David Thoreau, *An Essay on Civil Disobedience*, 1849

b. With all the imperfections of our present government, it is without comparison the best existing, or that ever did exist.

—Thomas Jefferson

3.3 Disputes and Ambiguity

Many disputes, whether about beliefs or about attitudes, are genuine. However, some disputes are merely verbal, arising only as a result of linguistic misunderstanding. The terms used by the disputing parties may have more than one meaning—they may be *ambiguous*—but such ambiguity may be unrecognized by the disputing parties. To uncover and to resolve verbal disagreements, ambiguities must be identified, and the alternative meanings of the critical terms in the dispute must be distinguished and clarified.

Disputes fall into three categories. The first is the *obviously genuine dispute.* If A roots for the Yankees, and B for the Red Sox, they are in genuine disagreement, although they disagree mainly in attitude. If C believes that Miami is south of Honolulu, and D denies this, they too are in genuine disagreement, but in this dispute about geographic facts a good map can settle the matter.

A second category is disputes in which the apparent conflict is not genuine and can be resolved by coming to agreement about how some word or phrase is to be understood. These may be called *merely verbal disputes.* F may hold that a tree falling in the wilderness with no person to hear it creates no sound, while G insists that a sound really is produced by the falling tree. If a "sound" is the outcome of a human auditory sensation, then F and G may agree that there was none; or if a "sound" is simply what is produced by vibrations in the air, then they may agree that a sound was indeed produced. Getting clear about what is meant by "sound" will resolve the disagreement, which was no more than verbal.

A third category, more slippery, is disputes that are *apparently verbal but really genuine.* A misunderstanding about the use of terms may be involved in such cases, but when that misunderstanding has been cleared up there remains a disagreement that goes beyond the meanings of the words. For example, should a film in which explicit sexual activity is depicted be considered "pornography"? J holds that its explicitness makes it pornographic and offensive; K holds that its beauty and sensitivity make it art and not pornography. Plainly they disagree about what "pornography" means—but after that ambiguity has been exposed, it is likely that the parties will still disagree in their judgment of that film. Whether the film is "pornographic" may be settled by a definition of that term, but a deeper disagreement is then likely to be exposed. The word "pornographic" plainly carries pejorative associations. J, who finds the film objectionable, understands the word "pornographic" in one way, while K, who approves of the film, uses the word "pornographic" differently. Does the sexually explicit content of the film make it objectionable and thus "pornographic"? J and K differ in their uses of the word, but for both of them the emotional meaning of the word is very negative; and they also differ about the criteria for the application of that negative word, "pornography."

In summary, when confronting a dispute that arises in discourse, we must first ask whether there is some ambiguity that can be eliminated by clarifying the alternative meanings in play. If there is, then we must ask whether clearing up that linguistic issue will resolve the matter. If it does, the dispute was indeed merely verbal. If it does not, the dispute was genuine, although it may have appeared to be merely verbal.

EXERCISES

A. Identify three disagreements in current political or social controversy that are of the three types described in this section: one that is genuine, one that is merely verbal, and one that is apparently verbal but really genuine. Explain the disagreements in each case.

B. Discuss each of the following disputes. If the dispute is obviously genuine, indicate each of the disputers' positions with respect to the proposition at issue. If it is merely verbal, resolve it by explaining the different senses attached by the disputers to the key word or phrase that is used ambiguously. If it is an apparently verbal dispute that is really genuine, locate the ambiguity and explain the real disagreement involved.

1. Daye: Pete Rose was the greatest hitter in the history of baseball. He got more hits than any other major league player.

Knight: No, Barry Bonds deserves that title. He hit more home runs than any other major league player.

2. Daye: Despite their great age, the plays of Sophocles are enormously relevant today. They deal with eternally recurring problems and values such as love and sacrifice, the conflict of generations, life and death—as central today as they were over two thousand years ago.

Knight: I don't agree with you at all. Sophocles has nothing to say about the pressing and immediate issues of our time:

inflation, unemployment, the population explosion, and the energy crisis. His plays have no relevance to today.

3. Daye: Bob Jones is certainly a wonderful father to his children. He provides a beautiful home in a fine neighborhood, buys them everything they need or want, and has made ample provision for their education.

Knight: I don't think Bob Jones is a good father at all. He is so busy getting and spending that he has no time to be with his children. They hardly know him except as somebody who pays the bills.

4. Daye: Amalgamated General Corporation's earnings were higher than ever last year, I see by reading their annual report.

Knight: No, their earnings were really much lower than in the preceding year, and they have been cited by the Securities and Exchange Commission for issuing a false and misleading report.

5. Daye: Business continues to be good for National Conglomerate, Inc. Their sales so far this year are 25 percent higher than they were at this time last year.

Knight: No, their business is not so good now. Their profits so far this year are 30 percent lower than they were last year at this time.

6. Daye: Ann is an excellent student. She takes a lively interest in everything and asks very intelligent questions in class.

Knight: Ann is one of the worst students I've ever seen. She never gets her assignments in on time.

7. Daye: Tom did it of his own free will. No pressure was brought to bear on him; no threats were made; no inducements were offered; there was no hint of force. He deliberated about it and made up his own mind.

Knight: That is impossible. Nobody has free will, because everything anyone does is inevitably determined by heredity and environment according to inexorable causal laws of nature.

8. Daye: Professor Graybeard is one of the most productive scholars at the university. The bibliography of his publications is longer than that of any of his colleagues.

Knight: I wouldn't call him a productive scholar. He is a great teacher, but he has never produced any new ideas or discoveries in his entire career.

9. **Daye:** Betty finally got rid of that old Chevy and bought herself a new car. She's driving a Buick now.

Knight: No, Betty didn't buy herself a new car. That Buick is a good three years old.

10. **Daye:** Dick finally got rid of that old Ford of his and bought himself a new car. He's driving a Pontiac now.

Knight: No, Dick didn't buy himself a new car. It's his roommate's new Pontiac that he's driving.

11. **Daye:** Helen lives a long way from campus. I walked out to see her the other day, and it took me nearly two hours to get there.

Knight: No, Helen doesn't live such a long way from campus. I drove her home last night, and we reached her place in less than ten minutes.

12. **Daye:** Senator Gray is a fine man and a genuine liberal. He votes for every progressive measure that comes before the legislature.

Knight: He is no liberal, in my opinion. The old skinflint contributes less money to worthy causes than any other man in his income bracket.

13. **Daye:** The University of Winnemac overemphasizes athletics, for it has the largest college stadium in the world and has constructed new sports buildings instead of badly needed classroom space.

Knight: No, the University of Winnemac does not overemphasize athletics. Its academic standards are very high, and it sponsors a wide range of extracurricular activities for students in addition to its athletic program.

14. **Daye:** It was in bad taste to serve roast beef at the banquet. There were Hindus present, and it is against their religion to eat beef.

Knight: Bad taste, nothing! That was the tastiest meal I've had in a long time. I think it was delicious!

15. **Daye:** Don't ask your wife about it. You ought to use your own judgment.

Knight: I will use my own judgment, and in my judgment, I should ask my wife.

3.4 Definitions and Their Uses

Good definitions are plainly very helpful in eliminating verbal disputes, but there are other uses of definition that are important in logic. Before distinguishing these uses, one feature of all definitions must be emphasized: Definitions are definitions of *symbols* (not of objects), because only symbols have the meanings that definitions may explain. To illustrate, we can define the word "chair" because it has meaning; but a chair itself we cannot define. We can sit on a chair, or paint it, or burn it, or describe it—but we cannot define it because an actual chair is not a symbol that has a meaning to be explained. Sometimes we say, misleadingly, that the thing is being defined; in fact, what we *define* are always *symbols*.

Two commonly used technical terms are useful in discussing definitions. The **definiendum** is the symbol being defined. The **definiens** is the symbol (or group of symbols) used to explain the meaning of the definiendum. Put otherwise, the definiendum is the term to be defined, the definiens is the definition of it. However, it would be a mistake to say that the definiens is the *meaning* of the definiendum—rather, it is another symbol (or group of symbols) that *has the same meaning* as the definiendum.

With this preface, we may say that definitions, depending on how they are used, are of five kinds: (1) stipulative, (2) lexical, (3) precising, (4) theoretical, and (5) persuasive. We shall consider each in turn:

A. STIPULATIVE DEFINITIONS

A definition that has a meaning that is deliberately assigned to some symbol is called a **stipulative definition.** One who introduces a new symbol is free to assign to it, or *stipulate,* whatever meaning she cares to. Even an old term put into a new context may have its meaning stipulated. Definitions of this sort are sometimes called *nominal.*

Why introduce a term by stipulation? Many reasons can justify doing so. It may simply be convenient; one word may stand for many words in a message. It may protect secrecy, if the sender and the receiver are the only persons who understand the stipulation. It may advance economy of expression. In the sciences, new symbols are often defined by stipulation to mean what has been meant by a long sequence of familiar words, thus saving time and increasing clarity. Many numbers that would be cumbersome to write out, for example, have been given names by stipulation: The number equal to a billion trillions (10^{21}) has been named a "zeta," and the number equal to a trillion trillions (10^{24}) is called a "yotta."[5]

Some stipulative definitions are introduced in science to free the investigator from the distractions of the emotive associations of more familiar terms. In modern psychology, for example, the word "intelligence" is widely replaced by Spearman's "*g* factor"—a term intended to convey the same descriptive meaning without any emotional baggage. Excitement and interest may also be provided by introducing a catchy new term, as when "black hole" was introduced to replace "gravitationally completely collapsed star."[6] The word "quark," now widely used in physics, was introduced by the physicist Murray Gell-Mann in 1963 to name a type of subatomic particle about which he had been theorizing.[7] In philosophy, Charles Sanders Pierce had long referred to his philosophy as "pragmatism," but when that word came to be used carelessly he stipulated that his views would henceforth be known as "pragmaticism"—a word that is ugly enough, he said, that no one would want to steal it!

A stipulative definition is neither true nor false; it is neither accurate nor inaccurate. A symbol defined by a stipulative definition did not have that meaning before it was given that meaning by the definition, so the definition cannot be a report of the term's meaning. For anyone who accepts the stipulative definition, the definiendum and the definiens have the *same* meaning; that is a consequence of the definition, not a fact asserted by it. *A stipulative definition is a proposal* (or a resolution or a request or an instruction) *to use the definiendum to mean what is meant by the definiens.* Such a definition is therefore directive rather than informative. Proposals may be rejected, requests refused, instructions disobeyed—but they can be neither true nor false.

Stipulative definitions may be evaluated as useful in advancing some purpose, or as useless because they are too complex or unclear, but they cannot resolve genuine disagreements. By reducing the emotive role of language, however, and by simplifying discourse, they can help to prevent fruitless conflict.

B. LEXICAL DEFINITIONS

Most often the term being defined has some established use. When the purpose of the definition is to explain that use, or to eliminate ambiguity, the definition is called lexical. A **lexical definition** reports a meaning the definiendum already has. That report may be correct, or incorrect—and therefore it is clear that a lexical definition may be either true or false. Thus the definition "the word 'bird' means any warm-blooded vertebrate with feathers" is true; that is a correct report of how the word "bird" is generally used by speakers of English. On the other hand, the definition "the word 'bird' means any two-footed mammal" is obviously false.

Mistakes in word usage are usually not so obvious. We may call muddy water "turgid" when we mean to say that it is "turbid"; the lexical definition of "turgid" is "swollen" or "pompous." Some mistakes are downright funny, as when Mrs. Malaprop, a comically misspeaking character of the Restoration dramatist Richard Sheridan, gives the order to "illiterate him . . . from your memory" or uses the phrase "as headstrong as an allegory on the banks of the Nile." Nor are such confusions always fictional. At a U.S. university not long ago, students defined "actuary" as "a home for birds," and the definition of "duodenum" was given as "a number system in base 2."[8] Whether they are funny or sad, these are mistakes—incorrect reports of how English-speaking people use these words.

Here lies the central difference between lexical and stipulative definitions: Truth or falsity may apply to the former but not the latter. In a stipulative definition the definiendum has no meaning apart from (or before) the definition that introduces it, so that the definition cannot be true or false. But the definiendum of a lexical definition does have a prior and independent meaning, and therefore its definition may be true, or false, depending on whether that meaning is reported correctly or incorrectly.

What we here call a *lexical* definition has been referred to by some as a "real" definition—to indicate that the definiendum really does have the meaning identified. However, the question of whether the definiendum names any real or actually existing thing has nothing to do with whether the definition is lexical or stipulative. The definition "the word 'unicorn' means an animal like a horse but having a single straight horn projecting from its forehead" surely is a lexical definition, and a correct one; its definiendum means exactly what is meant by the definiens—but the definiendum in this case does not name or denote any existing thing, because there are no unicorns.

A qualification must be made at this point. Some definitions are indeed simply mistaken, but some uses that depart from what is normal may be better described as unusual or unorthodox. Word usage is a statistical matter, subject to variation over time—and therefore we cannot always specify "the" correct meaning of a term, but must give an account of its various meanings, as determined by the uses it has in actual speech and writing.

Some lexicographers try to overcome this variability by referring to "best" usage or "correct" usage. This effort cannot fully succeed, however, because "best" usage is also an inexact matter, measured by the number of prominent authors and speakers whose uses of the given term are in accord with that definition. Literary and academic uses of words lag behind changes in a living language, so definitions that report meanings accepted by some intellectual aristocracy are likely to be out of date. What is unorthodox at a given time may soon become commonplace. So lexical definitions must not ignore the ways in which a term is used by great numbers of those who speak that language, because if lexical definitions are not true to actual usage, the reports they give will not be entirely correct. To take account of language growth, good dictionaries often indicate which meanings of words are "archaic" or "obsolete," and which meanings are "colloquial" or "slang."

With this qualification understood—that is, bearing in mind the variability of a living language—lexical definitions are in essence true or false, in the sense that they may be true to actual usage, or may fail to be true to it.

C. PRECISING DEFINITIONS

Some terms are ambiguous; some terms are vague. A term is *ambiguous* in a given context when it has more than one distinct meaning and the context does not make clear which meaning is intended. A term is *vague* when there are borderline cases to which the term might or might not apply. A word or a phrase—for example, "libel" or "freedom of speech"—may be both ambiguous and vague. **Precising definitions** are those used to eliminate ambiguity or vagueness.

Every term is vague to some degree, but excessive vagueness causes serious practical problems. This is particularly true in the law, where acts that are forbidden (or permitted) by some statute need to be sharply demarcated. For example, as this is being written the precise meaning of the Second Amendment to the U.S. Constitution is being disputed in the federal courts. The Amendment reads:

> "A well regulated militia, being necessary to the security of a free State, the right of the people to keep and bear Arms shall not be infringed."

Many U.S. states have passed laws that prohibit handguns, and that require even lawfully owned guns to be kept in the home, unloaded and disassembled. Some appellate courts have struck down such laws as infringing the right to "bear arms." If the Amendment refers only to military affairs, then the right to bear arms is a *civic* but not an *individual* right. If, on the other hand, the Amendment's reference to a militia indicates only the purpose of the Amendment, while the right guaranteed is that of an *individual* "to keep and bear arms," such laws are unconstitutional. A precising definition of the phrase "keep and bear arms" is surely needed, and is likely to be soon forthcoming from the Supreme Court of the United States.*

---

*In March 2007 a précising definition by the U.S. Supreme Court was made more likely when the Circuit Court of the District of Columbia decided the case of *Parker v. District of Columbia*, striking down some gun control laws as violations of the Second Amendment, viewed (in this decision) as being a guarantee of the right of *individuals* to keep and bear arms.

The vagueness of units of measurement in science is a serious problem. "Horsepower" for example, is commonly used in reporting the power of motors, but its vagueness invited commercial deception. To overcome that, a precise definition was needed. "One horsepower" is now defined precisely as "the power needed to raise a weight of 550 pounds by one foot in one second"—calculated to be equal to 745.7 watts.*

A meter is the internationally accepted unit of measure for distance. Originally it was defined, by stipulation, as one ten-millionth of the distance from one of the earth's poles to the equator, and this was represented by a pair of carefully inscribed scratches on a metal bar made of platinum-iridium, kept in a vault near Paris, France. However, scientific research required more precision. A "meter" is now defined, precisely, as "the distance light travels in one 299,792,458th of a second." Building on this, a "liter" is defined precisely as the volume of a cube having edges of 0.1 meter.

The vagueness of terms such as "horsepower" and "meter" cannot be eliminated by appealing to ordinary usage, because ordinary usage is not sufficiently exact. If it were, the terms would not have been vague. Therefore, borderline cases can be resolved only by going beyond the report of normal usage with the definition given. Such definitions are called *precising definitions*.

A precising definition differs from both lexical and stipulative definitions. It differs from stipulative definitions in that its definiendum is not a new term, but one whose usage is known, although unhappily vague. In constructing a precising definition, therefore, we are not free to assign to the definiendum any meaning we please. Established usage must be respected as far as possible, while making the known term more precise. Neither can a precising definition be a simple report, because it must go beyond established usage if the vagueness of the definiendum is to be reduced. How that is done—how the gaps in ordinary language are filled in—may indeed be a matter of outright stipulation.

Appellate court judges are often obliged to define some common terms more precisely. The definitions they provide are not mere stipulations, because even when the judges go beyond established usage, they will explain their reasons for the refinements being introduced. For example, unreasonable searches and seizures are forbidden by the Fourth Amendment of the U.S. Constitution, and evidence obtained though an unreasonable seizure is

*The power of one real horse—say, one weighing 600 kilograms (or 1323 pounds)—is much greater, estimated to be about equal to 18,000 watts! A 200-horsepower automobile, therefore, has approximately the power of ten real horses.

generally held to be inadmissible in court. But what *is* a "seizure"? Suppose a suspect, running from the police, throws away a packet of drugs, which is then confiscated. Have those drugs been seized? A precising definition was formulated by the U.S. Supreme Court to resolve this matter. A seizure, the Court concluded, must involve either the use of some physical force that restrains movement, or the assertion of authority (such as an order to stop) to which a subject yields. If the subject keeps running, no seizure has occurred; the packet of drugs he throws while running from the police therefore cannot be the product of an unreasonable seizure, and will be admissible as evidence.[9]

The precise definitions of terms can be very important in the world of commerce. For example, is a sport utility vehicle (SUV) a car or a light truck? The fuel economy standards applied to "light trucks" are more lenient than those applied to "cars," and therefore auto manufacturers must know the criteria that will be used by the U.S. Department of Transportation to define these categories precisely.[10]

If a law is so vague that a citizen cannot be expected to be sure when he is disobeying it, it may be struck down by a court. U.S. Supreme Court Justice Thurgood Marshall long ago explained the need for precising definitions in law:

> It is a basic principle of due process that an enactment is void for vagueness if its prohibitions are not clearly defined. Vague laws offend several important values. First . . . we insist that laws give the person of ordinary intelligence a reasonable opportunity to know what is prohibited, so that he may act accordingly. Vague laws may trap the innocent by not providing fair warning. Second, if arbitrary and discriminatory enforcement is to be prevented, law must provide explicit standards for those who apply them. A vague law impermissibly delegates basic policy matters to policemen, judges, and juries for resolution on an ad hoc and subjective basis, with the attendant dangers of arbitrary and discriminatory application. Third . . . where a vague statute abuts upon sensitive areas of basic First Amendment freedoms, it operates to inhibit the exercise of those freedoms. Uncertain meanings inevitably lead citizens to "steer far wider of the unlawful zone" than if the boundaries of the forbidden areas were clearly marked.[11]

This principle was applied in 1996 when a federal law making it illegal to transmit "indecent" or "patently offensive" materials on the Internet was struck down as impermissibly vague.[12] To avoid such uncertainties, legislatures often preface the operative portions of a statute with a section called "definitions," in which the precise meanings of key terms in that statute are spelled out. Similarly, in labor–management contracts, the terms setting forth the agreed-upon rules of the workplace will be very carefully defined. Precising definitions are conceptual instruments of wide importance.

D. THEORETICAL DEFINITIONS

In science, and in philosophy, definitions often serve as a compressed summary, or recapitulation, of some theory. Such definitions, when they are faulty, are criticized not so much because they are not precise as because they are not adequate—they do not correctly encapsulate the theory in question.

How, for example, should we define the word "planet"? For many years it was believed with little controversy, and all children were taught, that planets are simply bodies in orbit around the sun and that there are nine planets in the solar system—of which the smallest is Pluto, made of unusual stuff, with an unusual orbit, and most distant from the Sun. But other bodies, larger than Pluto and oddly shaped, have been recently discovered orbiting the sun. Are they also planets? Why not? Older definitions had become conceptually inadequate. An intense controversy within the International Astronomical Union (IAU), still not fully resolved, has recently resulted in a new definition of "planet," according to which there are only eight planets in our solar system. And now a new category, "dwarf planet" (for bodies such as Pluto, Ceres, and Eris) has been defined. Needed were definitions that would accommodate new discoveries as well as old, while maintaining a consistent and fully intelligible account of the entire system. Such definitions (not as simple as we might like) were adopted by the IAU in 2006. A planet is "a celestial body that, within the Solar System, (1) is in orbit around the Sun; and (2) has sufficient mass for its self-gravity to overcome rigid body forces so that it assumes a hydrostatic equilibrium (nearly round) shape; and (3) has cleared the neighborhood around its orbit.[13]

In such controversies it is not simply the use of some word, such as "planet," that is at issue. What is wanted is a comprehensive grasp of the theory in which that term is a key element. A definition that encapsulates this larger understanding we rightly call a *theoretical definition*.

In philosophy also, theoretical definitions are sought. When Socrates struggles to find the correct definition of "justice" in Plato's *Republic*, he is not simply seeking a set of words that can serve as a synonym for justice. When Spinoza, in the *Ethics*, seeks to define "bondage" and "freedom," he is not examining how people use those words, nor is he merely hoping to eliminate borderline cases. Neither lexical nor précising (and certainly not stipulative) definitions are the philosophical objectives. More deeply, philosophers commonly seek to develop an account of human virtues that will help us to understand these and other forms of right conduct.

The quest for theoretical definitions remains compelling. What is a "right"? Is health care a right? Do nonhuman animals have rights? How might we best define the term? Which nations truly manifest "democracy"? Is the fact that leaders are elected by popular vote sufficient to make a government democratic? If not, what other political institutions or patterns of citizen conduct characterize democratic communities? What is the most appropriate application of that term? Theoretical definitions are the *products* of our comprehensive understanding in some sphere.

E. PERSUASIVE DEFINITIONS

The four categories we have discussed so far are concerned chiefly with the informative use of language. But definitions are also used at times to express feelings as well, so as to influence the conduct of others. A definition put forward to resolve a dispute by influencing attitudes or stirring emotions may be called a **persuasive definition.**

Persuasive definitions are common in political argument. From the left we hear "socialism" defined as "democracy extended to the economic sphere." From the right we hear "capitalism" defined as "freedom in the economic sphere." The directive intent of the emotive language in these definitions is obvious—but emotive coloration may also be injected subtly into wording that purports to be a correct lexical definition, and that appears on the surface to be that. As we seek to distinguish good reasoning from bad, we must be on guard against *persuasive* definitions.

In summary, we have distinguished five ways in which definitions are used. Thus any definition may be categorized in accordance with its principal function:

Stipulative
Lexical
Precising
Theoretical
Persuasive

Of course, some definitions may serve more than one of these functions. A stipulative definition may be intended to influence hearers manipulatively. A lexical definition may be used objectively to make discussion of some matter more precise, and so on. Here, as everywhere in language, context is critical.

EXERCISES

A. Find examples of definitions that function in each of the five ways distinguished and explain, in each case, how the definition serves that purpose.

B. Discuss the following.

> Federal law imposes a five-year mandatory prison sentence on anyone who "uses or carries a firearm" in connection with a narcotics crime. In 1998 the U.S. Supreme Court faced this question: Does traveling in a car with a gun in a locked glove compartment or trunk—as opposed to carrying a gun on

one's person—satisfy the meaning of "carry" in that law? Justice Stephen Breyer argued that Congress intended the word in its ordinary, everyday meaning, without the artificial limitation that it be immediately accessible. Quoting *Robinson Crusoe* and *Moby Dick*, he pointed to the common use of "carry" to mean "convey in a vehicle." The mandatory sentence, he concluded, is thus properly imposed. Justice Ruth Bader Ginsburg found Breyer's literary evidence selective and unpersuasive; in response, she offered quotations from Rudyard Kipling, the TV series *M.A.S.H.*, and President Theodore Roosevelt's "Speak softly and carry a big stick" to show that "carry" is properly understood in the federal statute to mean "the gun at hand, ready for use as a weapon" [*Muscarello v. U.S.*, U.S. 96-1654 (1998)]. In this controversy, which side puts forward the better precising definition?

3.5 The Structure of Definitions: Extension and Intension

A definition states the *meaning* of a term. When we look closely at the literal (or descriptive) meaning of a term, however, we see that there are different *senses* in which that term has meaning. With those different senses distinguished (our object just below), we will also see that definitions may be grouped and understood not only on the basis of their functions (as in the preceding section), but in view of the way those definitions are built: their *structure*.

We focus on *general* terms—terms that are applicable to more than one object—which are of critical importance in reasoning. The word "planet" is a typical general term; it is applicable to a number of objects, and it applies in the same sense equally to Mercury, Venus, Earth, Mars, Jupiter, Saturn, Uranus, and Neptune.* What is meant by the word "planet" *is* (in one sense) that set of objects. The collection of planets constitutes the meaning of the term, its *extensional* meaning. If I say that all planets have elliptical orbits, part of what I assert is that Mars has an elliptical orbit, and another part is that Venus has an elliptical orbit, and so on. The *extension* of the general term "planet" consists of the objects to which the term may be correctly applied. The *extensional meaning* (also called the *denotative meaning*) of a general term is the collection of the objects that constitutes the **extension** (or *denotation*) of the term.

To understand the meaning of a general term is to know how to apply it correctly. But it is not necessary to know all of the objects to which it may be applied correctly in order to apply it correctly. All the objects within the extension of a given term have some *common attributes* or characteristics that lead us

*But not to Pluto! As explained in the preceding section, Pluto is now classified by the International Astronomical Union as a "dwarf planet."

to use the same term to denote them. If we know these attributes, we may know the meaning of a term in a different sense, without knowing its extension. In this second sense, *meaning* supposes some *criterion for deciding*, with respect to any given object, whether it falls within the extension of that term. This sense of meaning is called the *intensional meaning* (or, sometimes, *connotative meaning*) of the term. The set of attributes shared by all and only those objects to which a general term refers is called the **intension** (or *connotation*) of that term.

Every general term has *both* an *in*tensional (or connotative) meaning and an *ex*tensional (or denotative) meaning. Consider the general term "skyscraper." It applies correctly to *all buildings over a certain height;* that is its intension. The extension of the term "skyscraper" is the class of buildings that contains the Empire State Building in New York, the Sears Tower in Chicago, the Shanghai World Financial Center, the Petronas Twin Towers in Kuala Lumpur, and others also—that is, the collection of the objects to which the term applies.

The extension of a term (its membership) is determined by its intension. The intension of the term "equilateral triangle" is the attribute of being a plane figure enclosed by three straight lines of equal length. The extension of "equilateral triangle" is the class of all those objects, and only those objects, that have this attribute. Because any object that has this attribute must be a member of that class, we say that the term's intension *determines* its extension.

However, the reverse is not true: The extension of a term does *not* determine its intension. Consider "equiangular triangle," which has an intension different from that of "equilateral triangle." The intension of "equiangular triangle" is the attribute of being a plane figure enclosed by three straight lines that intersect each other to form equal angles. It is true, of course, that the extension of the term "equiangular triangle" is exactly the same as the extension of the term "equilateral triangle." So if we were to identify the extension of one of these terms, that would leave the intension of the class uncertain; intension is not determined by extension. Terms may have different intensions and the same extension; but terms with different extensions cannot possibly have the same intension.

When attributes are added to the intension of a term, we say that the intension increases. Begin with a general term such as "person." Add "living." Add "over twenty years old." Add "born in Mexico." With each such addition the intension increases; the intension of the term "Living person over twenty years old born in Mexico" is far greater than that of "person." So these terms are given here in order of *increasing* intension. However, increasing their intention *decreases* their extension. The number of living persons is much lower than that of persons, and the number of living persons over twenty years old is lower still, and so on.

One may be tempted to say that extension and intension always vary inversely, but in fact that is not the case. This is because there comes a point when increasing the intension of the term has no effect on its extension. Consider this series: "living person," "living person with a spinal column," "living person with a spinal column less than one thousand years old," "living person with a spinal column less than one thousand years old who has not read all the books in the Library of Congress." These terms are clearly in order of increasing intension, but the extension of each of them is exactly the same, not decreasing at all. So we can say that, if terms are arranged in order of increasing intension, their extensions will be in *nonincreasing* order. That is, if extensions vary, they will vary inversely with the intensions.

Note that the extensions of some terms are empty; there simply are no objects having the indicated attributes. In Greek mythology, Bellerophon killed the fire-breathing Chimera, a monster with a lion's head, a goat's body, and a serpent's tail. We fully understand the intension of the term Chimera, but it has no extension.

Some bad arguments play on the fact that meaning can refer to extension or to intension, while extension may be empty. For example:

> The word "God" is not meaningless; therefore it has a meaning. But by definition, the word "God" means a being who is all-powerful and supremely good. Therefore that all-powerful and supremely good being, God, must exist.

The word "God" is certainly not meaningless, and so there is an intension that is its meaning. But it does not follow from the fact that a term has an intension that it denotes any existent thing.* A contemporary critic has argued in similar fashion:

> Kitsch is the sign of vulgarity, sleaze, schlock, sentimentality, and bad faith that mark and mar our human condition. That is why utopia can be defined as a state of affairs in which the term has disappeared because it no longer has a referent.[14]

Here the writer has failed to distinguish between *meaning* and *referent*. Many valuable terms—those naming mythological creatures, for example—have no existing referent, no extension, but we do not want or expect such terms to disappear. Terms with intension but no extension are very useful. If utopia someday comes, we may wish to express our good fortune in having eliminated "kitsch" and "sleaze," but to do that we will need to be able to use those very words meaningfully.

---

*The useful distinction between intension and extension was introduced and emphasized by St. Anselm of Canterbury (1033–1109), who is best known for his "ontological argument"—to which the preceding fallacious argument has little resemblance.

We now use the distinction between intension and extension to explain some techniques for constructing definitions. Some definitions approach a general term by focusing on the class of *objects* to which the term refers. Some definitions approach a general term by focusing on the *attributes* that determine the class. Each approach, as we shall see, has advantages and disadvantages.

EXERCISES

A. Arrange each of the following groups of terms in order of increasing intension.

1. Animal, feline, lynx, mammal, vertebrate, wildcat.

2. Alcoholic beverage, beverage, champagne, fine white wine, white wine, wine.

3. Athlete, ball player, baseball player, fielder, infielder, shortstop.

4. Cheese, dairy product, Limburger, milk derivative, soft cheese, strong soft cheese.

5. Integer, number, positive integer, prime number, rational number, real number.

B. Divide the following list of terms into five groups of five terms each, arranged in order of increasing intension.

Aquatic animal, beast of burden, beverage, brandy, cognac, domestic animal, filly, fish, foal, game fish, horse, instrument, liquid, liquor, musical instrument, muskellunge, parallelogram, pike, polygon, quadrilateral, rectangle, square, Stradivarius, string instrument, violin.

A. EXTENSION AND DENOTATIVE DEFINITIONS

Denotative definitions employ techniques that identify the extension of the term being defined. The most obvious way to explain the extension of a term is to identify the objects denoted by it. This is one very effective technique, but it has serious limitations.

We saw in the preceding section that two terms with different intensions (e.g., "equilateral triangle" and "equiangular triangle") may have the same extension. Therefore, even if we could enumerate all the objects denoted by a general term, that would not distinguish it from another term that has the very same extension.

Of course it is usually impossible to enumerate all the objects in a class. The objects denoted by the term "star" are literally astronomical in number;

the objects denoted by the term "number" are infinitely many. For most general terms, complete enumeration is practically out of the question. Therefore denotative definitions are restricted to partial enumerations of the objects denoted—and this limitation gives rise to serious difficulties. The core of the problem is this: Partial enumeration of a class leaves the meaning of the general term very uncertain.

Any given object has a great many attributes and thus may be included in the extensions of a great many different general terms. Therefore, any object given as an example of a general term is likely to be an example of many general terms with very different intensions. If I give the example of the Empire State Building to explain the term "skyscraper," there are many other classes of things to which I could be referring. And even if we give two examples, or three, or four, the same problem arises. Suppose I list, along with the Empire State Building, the Chrysler Building, and the Trump Tower. What is the class I have in mind? It could be skyscrapers. But all these are also "great structures of the twentieth century," "expensive pieces of real estate in Manhattan," or "landmarks in New York City." And each of these general terms denotes objects not denoted by the others. So partial enumeration cannot distinguish among terms that have different extensions.

We may seek to overcome this problem by naming groups of members of the class as examples. This technique, definition by subclass, does sometimes make complete enumeration possible. Thus we might define "vertebrate" to mean "amphibians and birds and fishes and reptiles and mammals." The completeness of the list gives some psychological satisfaction—but the meaning of the term "vertebrate" has not been adequately specified by such a definition.

Instead of naming or describing the objects denoted by the term being defined, as ordinary denotative definitions do, we might try *pointing* at them. Such definitions are called **ostensive definitions** or *demonstrative definitions*. An example of an ostensive definition is that "the word 'desk' means *this*," accompanied by a gesture such as pointing a finger in the direction of a desk.

Ostensive definitions have all the limitations mentioned earlier, as well as some limitations peculiar to themselves. Gestures have a geographic limitation; one can only indicate what is visible. We cannot ostensively define the word "ocean" in an inland valley. More seriously, gestures are invariably ambiguous. To point to a desk is also to point to a part of it, and also to its color and its size and its shape and material, and so on—in fact, one points to everything that lies in the general direction of the desk, including the lamp or the wall behind it.

This ambiguity might sometimes be resolved by adding a descriptive phrase to the *definiens*, thus producing a **quasi-ostensive definition**—for example, "the word 'desk' means *this* article of furniture" accompanied by the appropriate gesture. But such an addition supposes the prior understanding of the phrase "article of furniture," which defeats the purpose that ostensive definitions have been claimed to serve, having been alleged by some to be the "primary" (or primitive) definitions, the way we first learn the meanings of words. In fact, however, we first learn language by observing and imitating, not by relying on definitions.

Beyond such difficulties, all denotative defintitions have this further inadequacy: They *cannot* define words that, although perfectly meaningful, do not denote anything at all. When we say that there are no unicorns we are asserting, meaningfully, that the term "unicorn" does not denote, that its extension is empty. Terms with no extension are very important, and this shows that techniques of definition that rely on extension cannot reach the heart of the matter. "Unicorn" has no extension, but the term is certainly not meaningless. If it were meaningless, it would also be meaningless to say, "There are no unicorns." But this statement we fully understand, and it is true. Meaning pertains more to intension than to extension; the real key to definition is intension.

EXERCISES

C. Define the following terms by example, enumerating three examples for each term.

1. actor
2. boxer
3. composer
4. dramatist
5. element
6. flower
7. general (officer)
8. harbor
9. inventor
10. poet

D. For each of the terms given in Exercise Set A, find a nonsynonymous general term that your three examples serve equally well to illustrate.

B. INTENSION AND INTENSIONAL DEFINITIONS*

The *intension* of a term, we have said, consists of the attributes shared by all the objects denoted by the term, and shared only by those objects. If the attributes that define the term "chair" are "being a single raised seat" and "having a back," then *every* chair is a single raised seat with a back, and *only* chairs are single raised seats with a back.

Even within this restriction, three different senses of intension must be distinguished: the subjective, the objective, and the conventional. The **subjective intension** of a word for a speaker is the set of all the attributes the speaker believes to be possessed by objects denoted by that word. This set varies from individual to individual, and even from time to time for the same individual, and thus cannot serve the purposes of definition. The public meanings of words, not their private interpretations, are the logician's concern. The **objective intension** of a word is the total set of characteristics shared by all the objects in the word's extension. Within the objective intension of the term "circle," therefore, is the attribute that a circle encloses a greater area than any other plane figure having an equal perimeter. However, this attribute of circles is one that many who use the word are completely unaware of. No one possesses the omniscience required to understand all the attributes shared by the objects denoted by general terms, and therefore objective intension cannot be the public meaning whose explanation we seek to give.

People do communicate with one another and therefore do understand the terms they use; hence there must be publicly available intensions that are neither subjective nor objective in the senses just explained. Terms have stable meanings because there is an implicit agreement to use the same criterion for deciding about any object whether it is part of the term's extension. What makes a thing a circle, in common discourse, is its being a closed plane curve, all points of which are equidistant from a point within called the center. It is by convention that this criterion is established, and this meaning is the **conventional intension** of the term "circle." This is the important sense of intension for purposes of definition: It is public but does not require omniscience to use. The word "intension" is normally taken to mean *conventional intension*, and that is our usage here.

---

*A term that is sometimes used instead of "intension" is "connotation"; intensional definitions are connotative definitions. We avoid the use of the word "connotation" here because, in everyday English, the *connotation* of a term is its total significance, including especially its emotive as well as its descriptive meaning. Because we are concerned here only with informative significance, we put the term "connotation" aside; this section therefore uses the terms "intension" and "intensional."

What are the techniques, using intension, for defining terms? Several methods are common. The simplest and most frequently used is that of providing another word, whose meaning is already understood, that has the same meaning as the word being defined. Two words with the same meaning are called synonyms, so a definition given in this way is called a **synonymous definition.** Dictionaries, especially smaller ones, rely heavily on this method of defining terms. Thus a dictionary may define "adage" as meaning "proverb"; "bashful" may be defined as "shy"; and so on. Synonymous definitions are particularly useful when it is the meanings of words in another language that call for explanation. The word *chat* means "cat" in French; *amigo* means "friend" in Spanish; and so on. One learns the vocabulary of a foreign language by studying definitions using synonyms.

This is a good method of defining terms; it is easy, efficient, and helpful. But it has very serious limitations. Many words have no exact synonym, and therefore synonymous definitions are often not fully accurate and may mislead. Translation from one language to another can never be perfectly faithful to the original, and often fails to catch its spirit or convey its depth. From this realization comes the Italian proverb, *"Traduttore, traditore"* ("Translator, traitor").

A more serious limitation of synonymous definitions is this: When the concept the word aims to convey is simply not understood, every synonym may be as puzzling to the reader or hearer as the definiendum itself. Synonyms are virtually useless, therefore, when the aim is to construct a precising or a theoretical definition.

One may seek to explain the intension of a term by tying the definiendum to some clearly describable set of actions or operations; doing that is giving the term what is called an **operational definition.**[15]

For example, in the wake of the success of Einstein's theory of relativity, space and time could no longer be defined in the abstract way that Newton had used. It was therefore proposed to define such terms "operationally," that is, by means of the operations actually undertaken when we measure distances and durations. An operational definition of a term states that the term is applied correctly to a given case if and only if the performance of specified operations in that case yields a specified result. The numerical value given for length can be defined operationally by referring to the results of a specified measuring procedure, and so on. Only public and repeatable operations are accepted in the definiens of an operational definition. Social scientists have also applied this technique. Some psychologists, for example, have sought to replace abstract definitions of "mind" and "sensation" by operational definitions that refer only to behavior or to physiological observations.

Of all the kinds of definition, the one that is most widely applicable is **definition by genus and difference.** This is the most important of all uses of the intension of general terms, and it is far and away the technique that is most commonly relied on in defining terms. We therefore devote the next and final section of this chapter to a detailed examination of definition by genus and difference, and the rules that properly guide its use.

The following table summarizes the kinds of definition by function (of which there are five), and the six techniques that depend on extension (three) and intension (three).

Five Types of Definition	
1. Stipulative	
2. Lexical	
3. Precising	
4. Theoretical	
5. Persuasive	
Six Techniques for Defining Terms	
A. Extensional Techniques	***B. Intensional Techniques***
1. Definitions by example	4. Synonymous definitions
2. Ostensive definitions	5. Operational definitions
3. Quasi-ostensive definitions	6. Definitions by genus and difference

EXERCISES

E. Give synonymous definitions for each of the following terms.

1. absurd
2. buffoon
3. cemetery
4. dictator
5. egotism
6. feast
7. garret
8. hasten
9. infant
10. jeopardy
11. kine
12. labyrinth
13. mendicant
14. novice
15. omen
16. panacea
17. quack
18. rostrum
19. scoundrel
20. tepee

3.6 Definition by Genus and Difference

Definition by genus and difference relies directly on the intension of the terms defined, and it does so in the most helpful way. In view of their exceedingly common use, we look very closely at definitions of this type.*

Earlier we referred to the attributes that define a class. Normally these attributes are complex—that is, they can be analyzed into two or more other attributes. This complexity and analyzability can be understood in terms of classes. Any class of things having members may have its membership divided into subclasses. For example, the class of all triangles can be divided into three nonempty subclasses: equilateral triangles, isosceles triangles, and scalene triangles. The class whose membership is thus divided into subclasses is called the *genus*, and the various subclasses are its *species*. As used here, the terms "genus" and "species" are *relative* terms, like "parent" and "offspring." The same persons may be parents in relation to their children, but also offspring in relation to their parents. Likewise, a class may be a genus in relation to its own subclasses, but also a species in relation to some larger class of which it is a subclass. Thus the class of all triangles is a genus relative to the species *scalene triangle* and a species relative to the genus *polygon*. The logician's use of the words "genus" and "species" as relative terms is different from the biologist's use of them as fixed or absolute terms, and the two uses should not be confused.

A *class* is a collection of entities having some common characteristic. Therefore all members of a given genus have some characteristic in common. All members of the genus polygon (for example) share the characteristic of being closed plane figures bounded by straight line segments. This genus may be divided into different species or subclasses, such that all the members of each subclass have some further attribute in common that is shared by no member of any other subclass. The genus polygon is divided into triangles, quadrilaterals, pentagons, hexagons, and so on. Each species of the genus polygon differs from all the rest. What differentiates members of the subclass *hexagon* from the members of all other subclasses is *having precisely six sides*. In general, all members of all species of a given genus share some attribute that makes them members of the genus, but the members of any one species share some further attribute that differentiates them from the members of every other species of that genus. The characteristic that serves to distinguish them is called the *specific difference*. Having six sides is the specific difference between the species hexagon and all other species of the genus polygon.

*Definitions by genus and difference are also called *analytical* definitions, or by their Latin name, definitions *per genus et differentia*.

Thus, we may say that the attribute of being a hexagon is analyzable into the attributes of (1) being a polygon and (2) having six sides. To someone who did not know the meaning of the word "hexagon" or of any synonym of it, but who did know the meanings of the words "polygon," "sides," and "six," the meaning of the word "hexagon" can be readily explained by means of a definition by genus and difference: The word "hexagon" means "a polygon having six sides."

Using the same technique, we can readily define "prime number": A prime number is any natural number greater than one that can be divided exactly, without remainder, only by itself or by one.

Two steps are required to define a term by genus and difference. First, a genus must be named—the genus of which the species designated by the definiendum is the subclass. Second, the specific difference must be named—the attribute that distinguishes the members of that species from members of all others species in that genus. In the definition of prime number just given, the genus is the class of natural numbers greater than one: 2, 3, 4, . . ., and so on; the specific difference is the quality of being divisible without remainder only by itself or by one: 2, 3, 5, 7, 11, . . ., and so on. Definitions by genus and difference can be very precise.

Two limitations of definitions by genus and difference deserve notice, although such definitions remain, nevertheless, exceedingly useful. First, the method is applicable only to terms whose attributes are complex in the sense indicated above. If there are any attributes that are absolutely *unanalyzable*, then the words with those intensions cannot be defined by genus and difference. The sensed qualities of the specific shades of a color have been thought by some to be simple and unanalyzable in this sense. Whether there really are such unanalyzable attributes remains an open question, but if there are, they limit the applicability of definition by genus and difference. Second, the technique is not applicable when the attributes of the term are universal. Words such as "being," "entity," "existent," and "object," cannot be defined by the method of genus and difference because the class of all entities (for example) is not a species of some broader genus. A universal class (if there is one) constitutes the very highest class, or *summum genus*, as it is called. The same limitation applies to words referring to ultimate metaphysical categories, such as "substance" or "attribute." Neither of these limitations, however, is a serious handicap in most contexts in which definitions are needed.

Constructing good definitions by genus and difference is by no means a simple task; it requires thoughtful selection of the most appropriate genus for the term in question, as well as identification of the most helpful specific difference for that term. In appraising proposed definitions by genus and difference, especially when they are intended as lexical, there are five good rules that have been traditionally laid down.

Rule 1: A definition should state the essential attributes of the species.

Earlier we distinguished the conventional intension of a term from the subjective intension and the objective intension. To define a term using, as its specific difference, some attribute that is not normally recognized as its attribute, even though it may be a part of that term's objective intension, would be a violation of the spirit of this rule. The rule itself might best be expressed, using our terminology, by saying that *a definition should state the conventional intension of the term being defined.*

The conventional intension of a term is not always an intrinsic characteristic of the things denoted by that term. It may concern the origin of those things, or relations of the members of the class defined to other things, or the uses to which the members of that class are normally put. Thus the term "Stradivarius violin," which denotes a number of violins, has as its conventional intension no actual physical characteristic but rather the attribute of being a violin made in the Cremona workshop of Antonio Stradivari. The essential attributes of "governors" or "senators" would not be any specific mental or physical features that differentiate them from other persons, but the special relations they have to other citizens. The use of shape, or material, as the specific difference of a class is usually an inferior way to construct a definition. It is not an essential attribute of a "shoe," for example, that it is made of leather; what is critical in its definition is the use to which it is put, as an outer covering for the foot.

Rule 2: A definition must not be circular.

If the definiendum itself appears in the definiens, the definition can explain the meaning of the term being defined only to those who already understand it. So if a definition is *circular* it must fail in its purpose, which is to explain the meaning of the definiendum.

A book on gambling contains this blatant violation of the rule: "A compulsive gambler is a person who gambles compulsively."[16] And a sophisticated scientist, writing in a medical journal, lapses into definitional circularity in this passage: "This review defines stress as a specific morphological, biochemical, physiological, and/or behavioral change experienced by an organism in response to a stressful event or stressor."[17]

As applied to definitions by genus and difference, avoiding circularity rules out the use, in the definiens, of any synonym of the definiendum. For example, there is no point in defining "lexicon" as "a compilation of words like a dictionary." If the synonym "dictionary" is assumed to be understood, one could as well give a straightforward synonymous definition of "lexicon" instead of resorting to the more powerful but more complicated technique of genus and difference. By the same token, antonyms of the definiendum are also ruled out.

Rule 3: A definition must be neither too broad nor too narrow.

This is an easy rule to understand, but it is often difficult to respect. We don't want the definiens to denote more things than are denoted by the definiendum, or fewer things either, of course. But mistakes are often made. When Plato's successors in the Academy at Athens settled on the definition of "man" as "featherless biped," their critic, Diogenes, plucked a chicken and threw it over the wall into the Academy. There was a featherless biped—but no man! The definiens was too broad. Legend has it that to narrow the definition of "man," the attribute "having broad nails" was added to the definiens.

Finding or constructing the definiens that has precisely the correct breadth is the task faced by the lexicographer, and it is often very challenging. But if Rule 1 has been fully observed, the essence of the *definiendum* stated in the definiens, this rule will have been obeyed, because the conventional intension of the term cannot be too broad or too narrow.

Rule 4: Ambiguous, obscure, or figurative language must not be used in a definition.

Ambiguous terms in the definiens obviously prevent the definition from performing its function of explaining the definiendum. Obscure terms also defeat that purpose, but obscurity is a relative matter. What is obscure to amateurs may be perfectly familiar to professionals. A "dynatron oscillator" does truly mean "a circuit that employs a negative-resistance volt-ampere curve to produce an alternating current." Although it may be obscure to the ordinary person, the language of this definiens is wholly intelligible to the students of electrical engineering for whom the definition was written; its technical nature is unavoidable. Obscure language in nontechnical definitions may result in an effort to explain the unknown using what is even more unknown. Dr. Samuel Johnson, in his great *Dictionary of the English Language* (1755), defined "net" as meaning "anything reticulated or decussated at equal distances with interstices between the intersections"—a good example of obscurity in definition.

Another sort of obscurity arises when the language of the definiens is metaphorical. Figurative language may convey a "feel" for the term being defined, but it cannot give a clear explanation of the term. We do not learn the meaning of the word "bread" if we are told only that it is "the staff of life." *The Devil's Dictionary* (1911), by Ambrose Bierce, is a collection of witty definitions, many of which have a cynical bite. Bierce defined "fib" as "a lie that has not cut its teeth," and "oratory" as "a conspiracy between speech and action to cheat the understanding." Entertaining and insightful such definitions may be, but serious explanations of the definiendums they are not.

Rule 5: A definition should not be negative when it can be affirmative.

What a term *does* mean, rather than what it does *not* mean, is what the definition seeks to provide. There are far too many things that the vast majority of terms do not mean; we are unlikely to cover them all in a definition. "A piece of furniture that is not a bed or a chair or a stool or a bench" does not define a couch; neither does it define a dresser. We need to identify the attributes that the definiendum has, rather than those it does not have.

Of course there are some terms that are essentially negative and therefore require negative definitions. The word "bald" means "the state of not having hair on one's head," and the word "orphan" means "a child who does not have parents." Sometimes affirmative and negative definitions are about equally useful; we may define a "drunkard" as "one who drinks excessively," but also as "one who is not temperate in drinking." In those cases in which negatives are used appropriately in specifying the essential attributes, the genus must first be mentioned affirmatively. Then, sometimes, the species can be characterized accurately by rejecting all other species of that genus. Only rarely are the species few enough to make this possible. If, for example, we define "scalene" triangle as "a triangle that is neither equilateral nor isosceles," we respect poorly the spirit of Rule 1—because it is the essential attribute that the class does possess, "having sides of unequal length," that best defines it. In general, affirmative definitions are much preferred over negative ones.

In summary, intensional definitions, and among them definitions by genus and difference especially, can serve any of the purpose for which definitions are sought. They may help to eliminate ambiguity, to reduce vagueness, to give theoretical explanation, and even to influence attitudes. They are also commonly used to increase and enrich the vocabulary of those to whom they are provided. For most purposes, intensional definitions are much superior to extensional definitions, and of all definitions that rely on intensions, those constructed by genus and difference are usually the most effective and most helpful.

EXERCISES

A. Construct definitions for the following terms (in the box on the left side) by matching the *definiendum* with an appropriate genus and difference (from the box on the right side.)

Definiendum		Definiens	
		Genus	*Difference*
1. banquet	11. lamb	1. offspring	1. female
2. boy	12. mare	2. horse	2. male
3. brother	13. midget	3. man	3. very large
4. child	14. mother	4. meal	4. very small
5. foal	15. pony	5. parent	5. young
6. daughter	16. ram	6. sheep	
7. ewe	17. sister	7. sibling	
8. father	18. snack	8. woman	
9. giant	19. son	9. person	
10. girl	20. stallion		

B. Criticize the following in terms of the rules for definition by genus and difference. After identifying the difficulty (or difficulties), state the rule (or rules) that are being violated. If the definition is either too narrow or too broad, explain why.

1. A genius is one who, with an innate capacity, affects for good or evil the lives of others.

—Jacqueline Du Pre, in *Jacqueline Du Pre: Her Life, Her Music, Her Legend* (Arcade Publishing, 1999)

2. Knowledge is true opinion.

—Plato, *Theaetetus*

3. Life is the art of drawing sufficient conclusions from insufficient premises.

—Samuel Butler, *Notebooks*

4. "Base" means that which serves as a base.

—Ch'eng Wei-Shih Lun, quoted in Fung Yu-Lan, *A History of Chinese Philosophy*, 1959

5. Alteration is combination of contradictorily opposed determinations in the existence of one and the same thing.

—Immanuel Kant, *Critique of Pure Reason*, 1787

6. Honesty is the habitual absence of the intent to deceive.

7. Hypocrisy is the homage that vice pays to virtue.

—François La Rochefoucauld, *Reflections*, 1665

8. The word *body*, in the most general acceptation, signifieth that which filleth, or occupieth some certain room, or imagined place; and dependeth not on the imagination, but is a real part of that we call the universe.

—Thomas Hobbes, *Leviathan*

9. Torture is "any act by which severe pain or suffering, whether physical or mental, is intentionally inflicted on a person for such purposes as obtaining from him or a third person information or a confession."

—United Nations Convention Against Torture, 1984

10. "Cause" means something that produces an effect.

11. War . . . is an act of violence intended to compel our opponent to fulfill our will.

—Carl Von Clausewitz, *On War*, 1911

12. A raincoat is an outer garment of plastic that repels water.

13. A hazard is anything that is dangerous.

—*Safety with Beef Cattle*, U.S. Occupational Safety and Health Administration, 1976

14. To sneeze [is] to emit wind audibly by the nose.

—Samuel Johnson, *Dictionary*, 1814

15. A bore is a person who talks when you want him to listen.

—Ambrose Bierce, 1906

16. Art is a human activity having for its purpose the transmission to others of the highest and best feelings to which men have risen.

—Leo Tolstoi, *What Is Art?*, 1897

17. Murder is when a person of sound memory and discretion unlawfully killeth any reasonable creature in being, and under the king's peace, with malice aforethought, either express or implied.

—Edward Coke, *Institutes*, 1684

18. A cloud is a large semi-transparent mass with a fleecy texture suspended in the atmosphere whose shape is subject to continual and kaleidoscopic change.

—U. T. Place, "Is Consciousness a Brain Process?" *The British Journal of Psychology*, February 1956

19. Freedom of choice: the human capacity to choose freely between two or more genuine alternatives or possibilities, such choosing being always limited both by the past and by the circumstances of the immediate present.

—Corliss Lamont, *Freedom of Choice Affirmed*, 1967

20. Health is a state of complete physical, mental, and social well-being and not merely the absence of disease or infirmity.

—Constitution of the World Health Organization, 1946

21. By analysis, we mean analyzing the contradictions in things.

—Mao Zedong, *Quotations from Chairman Mao*, 1966

22. Noise is any unwanted signal.

—Victor E. Ragosine, "Magnetic Recording," *Scientific American*, February 1970

23. To explain (explicate, *explicare*) is to strip reality of the appearances covering it like a veil, in order to see the bare reality itself.

—Pierre Duhem, *The Aim and Structure of Physical Theory*, 1991

24. The Master said, Yu, shall I teach you what knowledge is? When you know a thing, to recognize that you know it, and when you do not know a thing, to recognize that you do not know it. That is knowledge.

—Confucius, *The Analects*

25. I would define political correctness as a form of dogmatic relativism, intolerant of those, such as believers in "traditional values," whose positions are thought to depend on belief in objective truth.

—Philip E. Devine, *Proceedings of the American Philosophical Association*, June 1992

C. Discuss the following definitions.

1. Faith is the substance of things hoped for, the evidence of things not seen.

—Heb. 11:1

2. "Faith is when you believe something that you know ain't true."

—Definition attributed to a schoolboy by William James in "The Will to Believe," 1897

3. Faith may be defined briefly as an illogical belief in the occurrence of the improbable.

—H. L. Mencken, *Prejudice*, 1922

4. Poetry is simply the most beautiful, impressive, and widely effective mode of saying things.

—Matthew Arnold, 1865

5. Poetry is the record of the best and happiest moments of the happiest and best minds.

—Percy Bysshe Shelley, *The Defence of Poetry*, 1821

6. Dog, n. A kind of additional or subsidiary Deity designed to catch the overflow and surplus of the world's worship.

—Ambrose Bierce, *The Devil's Dictionary*, c. 1911

7. Conscience is an inner voice that warns us somebody is looking.

—H. L. Mencken, 1949

8. A bond is a legal contract for the future delivery of money.

—Alexandra Lebenthal, Lebenthal and Company, 2001

9. "The true," to put it very briefly, is only the expedient in the way of our thinking, just as "the right" is only the expedient in the way of our behaving.

—William James, "Pragmatism's Conception of Truth," 1907

10. To be conceited is to tend to boast of one's own excellences, to pity or ridicule the deficiencies of others, to daydream about imaginary triumphs, to reminisce about actual triumphs, to weary quickly of conversations which reflect unfavorably upon oneself, to lavish one's society upon distinguished persons and to economize in association with the undistinguished.

—Gilbert Ryle, *The Concept of Mind*, 1949

11. Economics is the science which treats of the phenomena arising out of the economic activities of men in society.

—J. M. Keynes, *Scope and Methods of Political Economy*, 1891

12. Justice is doing one's own business, and not being a busybody.

—Plato, *The Republic*

13. Legend has it that the distinguished economist, John Maynard Keynes, enjoyed referring to a university education as "the inculcation of the incomprehensible into the indifferent by the incompetent."

14. By good, I understand that which we certainly know is useful to us.

—Baruch Spinoza, *Ethics*, 1677

15. Political power, then, I take to be a right of making laws with penalties of death, and consequently all less penalties, for the regulating and preserving of property, and of employing the force of the community in the execution of such laws, and in defense of the commonwealth from foreign injury, and all this only for the public good.

—John Locke, *Essay Concerning Civil Government*, 1690

16. And what, then, is belief? It is the demi-cadence which closes a musical phrase in the symphony of our intellectual life.

—Charles Sanders Peirce, "How to Make Our Ideas Clear," 1878

17. Political power, properly so called, is merely the organized power of one class for oppressing another.

—Karl Marx and Friedrich Engels, *The Communist Manifesto*, 1847

18. Grief for the calamity of another is *pity*; and ariseth from the imagination that the like calamity may befall himself.

—Thomas Hobbes, *Leviathan*, 1651

19. We see that all men mean by justice that kind of state of character which makes people disposed to do what is just and makes them act justly and wish for what is just.

—Aristotle, *Nichomachean Ethics*

20. Inquiry is the controlled or directed transformation of an indeterminate situation into one that is so determinate in its constituent distinctions and relations as to convert the elements of the original situation into a unified whole.

—John Dewey, *Logic: The Theory of Inquiry*, 1938

21. A fanatic is one who can't change his mind and won't change the subject.

—Winston Churchill

22. Regret is the pain people feel when they compare what is with what might have been.

—Richard Gotti, "How Not to Regret Regret," *Bottom Line Personal*, 30 September 1992

23. Happiness is the satisfaction of all our desires, *extensively*, in respect of their manifoldness, *intensively*, in respect of their degree, and *potensively*, in respect of their duration.

—Immanuel Kant, *Critique of Pure Reason*, 1787

24. A tragedy is the imitation of an action that is serious and also, as having magnitude, complete in itself; in language with pleasurable accessories, each kind brought in separately in the parts of the work; in a dramatic, not in a narrative form; with incidents arousing pity and fear, wherewith to accomplish its catharsis of such emotions.

—Aristotle, *Poetics*

25. Propaganda is manipulation designed to lead you to a simplistic conclusion rather than a carefully considered one.

—Anthony Pratkanis, *The New York Times*, 27 October 1992

26. . . . the frequently celebrated female intuition . . . is after all only a faculty for observing tiny insignificant aspects of behavior and forming an empirical conclusion which cannot be syllogistically examined.

—Germaine Greer, *The Female Eunuch*, 1971

27. A fetish is a story masquerading as an object.

—Robert Stoller, "Observing the Erotic Imagination," 1985

28. Religion is a complete system of human communication (or a "form of life") showing in primarily "commissive," "behabitive," and "exercitive" modes how a community comports itself when it encounters an "untranscendable negation of . . . possibilities."

—Gerald James Larson, "Prolegomenon to a Theory of Religion," *Journal of the American Academy of Religion*, 1978

29. Robert Frost, the distinguished New England poet, used to define a liberal as someone who refuses to take his own side in an argument.

—"Dreaming of JFK," *The Economist*, 17 March 1984

30. The meaning of a word is what is explained by the explanation of the meaning.

—Ludwig Wittgenstein, *Philosophical Investigations*, 1953

SUMMARY

In this chapter we have been concerned with the uses of language, and with definitions.

In Section 3.1 we identified the three chief uses of language—the *informative*, the *expressive*, and the *directive*—and two less common uses—the *ceremonial* and the *performative*.

In Section 3.2 we discussed the emotive and the neutral meanings of words. Disputes, we explained, may arise from conflicting beliefs about facts, or from conflicting attitudes about facts whose truth may (or may not) be agreed on, and we emphasized the importance of the neutral uses of language in logical discourse.

In Section 3.3 we explained that ambiguous terms are those that have more than one distinct meaning in a given context. We distinguished three different kinds of disputes: those that are *genuine*, whether the conflict be about beliefs or attitudes; those that are *merely verbal*, arising from the unrecognized use of ambiguous terms, and those that are *genuine but appear on the surface to be verbal*, in which a real difference remains even after apparent ambiguity has been eliminated.

In Section 3.4 we began the discussion of definitions, distinguishing the definiendum (the symbol that is to be defined) from the definiens (the symbol or group of symbols used to explain the meaning of the definiendum). We distinguished five different kinds of definition based on their functions: (1) *stipulative definitions*, with which a meaning is assigned to a term (and hence which cannot be true or false); (2) *lexical definitions*, which report the meaning that the term already has (and hence can be true or false); (3) *precising definitions*, which aim is to eliminate vagueness or ambiguity; (4) *theoretical definitions*, which aim is to encapsulate our understanding of some intellectual sphere; and (5) *persuasive definitions*, which aim to influence conduct.

In Section 3.5 we explained the structure of definitions, first distinguishing the *extension* of a general term, the objects denoted by it, from its *intension*, the attributes shared by all and only the members of the class designated by that term. We explained three varieties of extensional definition: *definition by example*, in which we list, or give examples of the objects denoted by the term; *ostensive definitions*, in which we point to, or indicate by gesture the extension of the term being defined; and *semi-ostensive definitions*, in which the pointing or gesture is accompanied by a descriptive phrase whose meaning is assumed known.

We also distinguished three varieties of intensional definition: *synonymous definitions*, in which we provide another word whose meaning is already understood that has the same meaning as the word being defined; *operational definitions*, which state that a term is applied correctly to a given case if and only if the performance of specified operations in that case yields a specified result; and *definitions by genus and difference*, of which a full account is given in the following Section.

In Section 3.6 we closely examined definitions by genus and difference, in which we first name the genus of which the species designated by the definiendum is a subclass, and then name the attribute (or specific difference) that distinguishes the members of that species from members of all other species of that genus. We formulated and explained five rules for the construction of good definitions by genus and difference: (1) A definition should state essential attributes; (2) a definition must not be circular; (3) a definition must not be too broad or too narrow; (4) definitions should not rely on ambiguous, obscure, or figurative language; and (5) when possible, definitions should not be negative.

End Notes

[1]John Burgon, "Petra" (1845), on the ruins of Petra, now in Jordan.

[2]Robert Browning, "Rabbi Ben Ezra," 1864.

[3]*Cohen v. California*, 403 U.S. 15, at p. 26 (1971).

[4]By provision of the Federal Communications Decency Act. The reason those seven words are held not fit to broadcast is the reason they are not listed here. But the letters with which they begin are: S, P, F, C, C, M, and T.

[5]Defined stipulatively in 1991 by the *Conference generale des poids et mesures* (General Committee on Weights and Measures), the international body that governs in the realm of scientific units. At the other extreme, a billionth of a trillionth has been stipulatively named a "zepto," and a trillionth of a trillionth is called is called a "yocto." Perhaps the most famous of all stipulations was the arbitrary naming of the number 10^{100} (represented by the digit 1 followed by 100 zeros) as a "googol"—a name suggested by the 9-year-old nephew of the mathematician, Edward Kasner, when he was asked for a word that might appropriately represent a very large number. The name of the now-famous Internet search firm, Google, is a deliberate misspelling of this term.

[6]The term was introduced by Dr. John Archibald Wheeler at a 1967 meeting of the Institute for Space Studies in New York City.

[7]In James Joyce's novel *Finnegan's Wake*, the word "quark" appears in the line, "Three quarks for Muster Mark," but Dr. Gell-Mann reported that he had chosen this name for the particle before he had encountered it in that novel.

[8]See *The Chronicle of Higher Education*, 30 May 1993.

[9]*California v. Hoary D.*, 499 U.S. 621 (1991).

[10]D. Hakim, "Government May Alter Line Between a Car and Truck," *The New York Times*, 25 March 2003.

[11]*Greyned v. City of Rockford*, 408 U.S. 104 (1972).

[12]*American Civil Liberties Union v. Reno*, 929 Fed. Supp. 824 (1996).

[13]In a system other than our solar system, the new definition requires that the body be (1) in orbit around a star or stellar remnant; and (2) have a mass below the limiting mass for thermonuclear fusion of deuterium; and (3) be above the minimum mass/size requirement for planetary status in the solar system.

[14]John P. Sisk, "Art, Kitsch and Politics," *Commentary*, May 1988.

[15]The term *operational definition* was first used by the Nobel Prize-winning physicist P. W. Bridgeman in his 1927 book, *The Logic of Modern Physics*.

[16]Jay Livingston, *Compulsive Gamblers* (New York: Harper & Row, 1974), p. 2.

[17]W. H. Voge, "Stress—The Neglected Variable in Experimental Pharmacology and Toxicology," *Trends in Pharmacological Science*, January 1987.

Fallacies

4.1 What Is a Fallacy?

We all strive to reason correctly, so one of the central tasks of logic is to identify the ways in which we are tempted to reason *in*correctly. We reason incorrectly when the premises of an argument fail to support its conclusion, and argument of that sort may be called fallacious. So in a very general sense, any error in reasoning is a fallacy.

Logicians, however, commonly use the term "fallacy" more narrowly, to designate not *any* errors in reasoning, but *typical* errors—mistakes in reasoning that exhibit a pattern that can be identified and named. The great logician Gottlob Frege observed that it is one of the logician's tasks to "indicate the *pitfalls* laid by language in the way of the thinker." In this book we use the term in this way.

In this narrower sense, each fallacy is a *type* of incorrect argument. Of course, many different arguments may make an error of some given type, that is, it may exhibit the *same kind of mistake* in reasoning. Any argument that does exhibit that kind of mistake is said to *commit* that fallacy. The particular argument that commits some known fallacy is commonly said to *be* a fallacy, because it is an individual example of that typical mistake.

To illustrate, if one accepts the premise that all science is essentially materialistic and then goes on to argue that Karl Marx, a very influential philosopher of the nineteenth century who was certainly a materialist, must therefore have been scientific, one reasons badly. It may indeed be true that Marx was scientific (as he claimed to be), but it does not *follow* from the fact that he was a materialist (which he certainly was) that he was scientific. The bad reasoning here is fallacious. If every P is a Q, it does not follow from the fact that one is a

Q that he is a P. All dogs are mammals, but not every mammal is a dog. We identify here a *pattern* of mistake; it is a very common mistake that we will explore in detail in Chapter 8. Because that pattern of error, or fallacy, appears in many different contexts, we flag it, and we warn against it by giving it a name: "the fallacy of affirming the consequent." The argument concerning Karl Marx *is* a fallacy because it *commits* that fallacy, and the fallacy it commits is the fallacy of affirming the consequent.

In this illustration the mistake that has been made is called a *formal* fallacy; it is a pattern of mistake that appears in deductive arguments of a certain specifiable form. There are other formal fallacies, and we shall examine them in Chapter 8. Most fallacies, however, are not formal but *in*formal: They are patterns of mistake that are made in the everyday uses of language. Informal fallacies, which we examine very closely in this chapter, arise from confusions concerning the *content* of the language used. There is no limit to the variety of forms in which that content may appear, and thus informal fallacies are often more difficult to detect than formal ones. It is language that deceives us here; we may be tricked by inferences that seem plausible on the surface but are in fact not warranted. Such traps, the "pitfalls" that language sets, can be avoided if the *patterns* of those mistakes are well understood. We devote considerable attention to these informal fallacies—the kinds of mistakes made in everyday speaking and writing, and commonly encountered, for example, in the "letters to the editor" in daily newspapers. These are the logical mistakes that we will name and explain.

Because language is slippery and imprecise, we must be cautious in this enterprise. Of course we must be careful not to make the mistakes in question, but we must also be careful to refrain from accusing others of making mistakes when they do not really do so. If we encounter an argument that appears to be fallacious, we must ask ourselves what really was meant by terms being used. The accusation of fallacy is sometimes unjustly leveled at a passage intended by its author to make a point that the critic has missed—perhaps even to make a joke. As we identify and classify the patterns of mistake in spoken and written language, we must try to penetrate the language used. Our logical standards should be high, but our application of those standards to arguments in ordinary life should also be generous and fair.

4.2 Classification of Fallacies

Informal fallacies are numerous and can therefore be best understood if they are grouped into categories, each with clearly identifiable features. This classification of fallacies is a controversial matter in logic. There is no one correct taxonomy of fallacies. Logicians have proposed lists of fallacies that vary greatly in length; different sets have been specified, and different names have been given to both the sets and the individual fallacies. Any classification of the kind that will follow here is bound to be arbitrary in some degree. Our aim is to provide a comprehensive scheme within which the most common informal fallacies can be helpfully identified—and avoided.

The outline of this classification appears immediately below. After presenting it, we will examine each group, and each individual fallacy, in detail.

- **Fallacies of relevance.** Fallacies of relevance are the most numerous and the most frequently encountered. In these fallacies, *the premises of the argument are simply not relevant to the conclusion*. However, because they are made to appear to be relevant, they may deceive. We will distinguish and discuss:
  - R1: The appeal to emotion
  - R2: The red herring
  - R3: The straw man
  - R4: The attack on the person
  - R5: The appeal to force
  - R6: Missing the point (irrelevant conclusion)

- **Fallacies of defective induction.** In fallacies of defective deduction, which are also common, the mistake arises from the fact that *the premises of the argument*, although relevant to the conclusion, *are so weak and ineffective* that relying on them is a blunder. We will distinguish and discuss:
  - The argument from ignorance
  - The appeal to inappropriate authority
  - False cause
  - Hasty generalization

- **Fallacies of presumption.** In fallacies of presumption, *too much is assumed* in the premises. The inference to the conclusion depends mistakenly on these unwarranted assumptions. We will distinguish and discuss:
  - Accident
  - Complex question
  - Begging the question

- **Fallacies of ambiguity.** The incorrect reasoning in fallacies of ambiguity arises from the *equivocal use of words or phrases*. Some word or phrase in one part of the argument has a meaning different from that of the same word or phrase in another part of the argument. We will distinguish and discuss:
  - Equivocation
  - Amphiboly

- Accent
- Composition
- Division

Which of all these fallacies is actually committed by a specific passage is often disputable. The mistake that is made in a given argument might be construed in different ways and thus might reasonably be viewed as an instance of more than one fallacy. Once again, in the realm of natural language, context is critical, and much depends on reasonable interpretation.[1]

4.3 Fallacies of Relevance

Fallacies of relevance are bald mistakes; they might better be called fallacies of *irrelevance*, because they arise when there is no real connection between the premises and the conclusion of an argument. Because that connection is missing, the premises offered cannot possibly establish the truth of the conclusion drawn. Of course, the premises may still be *psychologically* relevant to the conclusion. The mistake arises when some emotive features of language are used to support the truth of a claim for which no objective reasons have been given. We use the modern names of these fallacies here, but many of them have traditional names as well (usually in Latin), which we will also note. Six fallacies of relevance are of principal interest.

R1. THE APPEAL TO EMOTION (ARGUMENT *AD POPULUM*)

The argument *ad populum* ("to the populace") is baldest of all fallacies, and yet it is one of the most common. It is the instrument on which every demagogue and propagandist relies—an appeal to the emotions of the audience. It is a fallacy because, instead of evidence and rational argument, the speaker (or writer) relies on expressive language and other devices calculated to excite enthusiasm for or against some cause. Patriotism is one common cause about which it is easy to stir emotions, and we know that terrible abuses and injustices have been perpetrated in the name of patriotism. The oratory of Adolph Hitler, whipping up the racist enthusiasms of his German listeners, is a classic example. Love of country is an honorable emotion, but the appeal to that emotion in order to manipulate and mislead one's audience is intellectually disreputable. "Patriotism," Samuel Johnson observed, "is the last refuge of a scoundrel."

The patriotic argument may be used when the national cause is good, and the argument's author is no scoundrel. An emotional defense of belief lacks intellectual merit, but the conclusion of that bad argument may perhaps be supportable by other premises of a more rational sort. Still, offered as the premises of an argument, sheer emotion is fallacious. On 23 March 1775 the Virginia House of Burgesses passed a resolution delivering Virginia's troops to the Revolutionary War. The House was spurred to adopt this resolution by an oration whose emotional content has rarely been exceeded. Patrick Henry concluded this famous speech with the following appeal:

> . . . if we mean not basely to abandon the noble struggle in which we have been so long engaged, and which we have pledged ourselves never to abandon until the glorious object of our contest shall be obtained—we must fight! I repeat it, sir, we must fight! An appeal to arms and to the God of hosts is all that is left to us. . . . There is no retreat but in submission and slavery! Our chains are forged! Their clanking may be heard on the plains of Boston! . . . . Is life so dear, or peace so sweet, as to be purchased at the price of chains and slavery? Forbid it, Almighty God! I know not what course others may take; but as for me, give me liberty or give me death!

It is reported that the crowd, upon hearing his speech, jumped up and shouted: "To arms! To arms!"

A qualification may be in order here. If the passions of the speaker are used to convince his listeners that some beliefs are true, the argument is indeed fallacious. But if the speaker and his listener are in complete agreement in their beliefs, and the speaker aims only to spur his listeners to act in support of those mutual beliefs, the emotion he exhibits may serve a useful purpose. There is a distinction to be drawn between emotions used improperly as premises in argument and emotions used reasonably as triggers for appropriate conduct. However, this distinction will always be problematic because, when the speaker succeeds in spurring to action, it may be said that he has relied on emotion to convince his audience of the truth of some claim—the claim that now is the time to act, or the claim that the way to act in pursuit of the common goal is his way. In controversy, in deciding what conduct is appropriate, the appeal to emotion is unavoidably troubling.

The heaviest reliance on arguments *ad populum* is to be found in commercial advertising, where its use has been elevated almost to the status of a fine art. The products advertised are associated, explicitly or slyly, with things that we yearn for or that excite us favorably. Breakfast cereal is associated with trim youthfulness, athletic prowess, and vibrant good health; whiskey is associated with luxury and achievement, and beer with high adventure; the automobile is associated with romance, riches, and sex. The men depicted using the advertised product are generally handsome and distinguished, the women sophisticated and charming—or hardly dressed at all. So clever and persistent are the ballyhoo artists of our time that we are all influenced to some degree, in spite of our resolution to resist. Almost every imaginable device may be used to command our attention, even to penetrate our subconscious thoughts. We are manipulated by relentless appeals to emotion of every kind.

Of course, the mere association of some product with an agreeable feeling or satisfying emotion is by itself no argument at all. But when such associations are systematically impressed on us, there usually is an argument *ad populum* lurking not far below the surface. It is suggested that the product—some beer perhaps, or some perfume, or some brand of jeans—*is* sexy, or is associated with wealth, or power, or some other admired characteristic, and therefore we, in purchasing it, will acquire some of that same merit.

One variety of this bad argument is particularly crass because it suggests no more than that one is well advised to buy (or join, or support, etc.) simply because that is what everyone else is doing. Some call this the "bandwagon fallacy," from the known phenomenon that, in an exciting campaign, many will be anxious to "jump on the bandwagon"—to do what others do because so many others are doing it. Brazen examples of this bandwagon fallacy are common in the public media; here, for example, are the exact words of a recent advertisement on ABC TV:

> Why are so many people attracted to the Pontiac Grand Prix? It could be that so many people are attracted to the Grand Prix because—so many people are attracted to the Grand Prix!

This is the essence of an appeal to the populace.

Playing on the emotions of the general population is pernicious in the context of public polling. Those who are conducting the poll, if they are unscrupulous, may frame questions in ways designed to get the responses they seek, by using words or phrases with known emotive impact. Or, if used without design but carelessly, some words may have an impact that will vitiate the poll results. In serious survey research, therefore, questions will be worded with the very greatest care, avoiding terms that are emotionally loaded, to preserve the integrity of the poll results. It is sometimes difficult to avoid all emotional taint. Many Americans support "affirmative action," viewing it as a policy designed to treat minorities fairly. But many Americans also oppose "racial preferences" in college admissions or in employment. The outcome of any random poll on this topic will depend critically on which set of words—"affirmative action" or "racial preference"—is used in the questions asked.

When results using different words conflict, it may be said that importantly different questions had been asked. Perhaps. This is a perennial problem in survey research. In *argument*, however, the logical point remains very important: A conclusion defended with premises that are directed mainly at emotions is a fallacious argument *ad populum*.

Another variety of the appeal to emotion that appears with great frequency is also often given its own name: argument *ad misericordiam*. The Latin word *misericordiam* literally means "merciful heart"; this fallacy is the emotional appeal to *pity*.*

Pity is often an admirable human response. Justice, it is wisely said, should be tempered with mercy. Surely there are many situations in which leniency in punishment is justified by the special circumstances of the offender. In such situations—in the sentencing phase of a trial, for example—the identification of those circumstances and the reasons they might apply to a criminal already convicted are appropriately put before the court. That is no fallacy. It would be a fallacy, however, if such considerations were registered in the effort to cause a jury to acquit a defendant who is indeed guilty of the acts with which he or she is charged. When the premises (or intimated premises) of an argument boil down to no more than an appeal to the merciful heart, the argument is plainly *ad populum*, and fallacious. What is special about this variety is only that the emotions appealed to are of a particular kind: generosity and mercy.

In civil suits, when attorneys are seeking compensatory damages for the injuries suffered by their clients, there is often an effort to rely implicitly on the appeal to pity. The cause of the injury may be described as a faceless and unfeeling corporate juggernaut; or the injured party may be presented as the helpless victim of an uncaring bureaucracy or an incompetent professional. The miseries of the client's continuing disability may be depicted in some heart-rending way. The injured plaintiff may make it a point to limp painfully into the courtroom. A study by the Harvard School of Public Health has pretty well proved that the appeal to pity really works. When doctors are sued for malpractice, this study shows, the size of the monetary award to successful plaintiffs depends much more on the nature of the disability they suffered than on whether it could be shown that the doctor accused had in fact done anything wrong.[2]

In criminal trials, the sympathies of the jury plainly have no bearing on the guilt or innocence of the accused, but an appeal to those sympathies may nevertheless be made. Such an appeal may be made obliquely. At his trial in Athens, Socrates referred with disdain to other defendants who had appeared before their juries accompanied by their children and families, seeking acquittal by evoking pity. Socrates continued:

> I, who am probably in danger of my life, will do none of these things. The contrast may occur to [each juror's] mind, and he may be set against me, and vote in anger

---

*Some logicians give special names to other clusters of fallacious emotional appeals. Thus one might also distinguish the appeal to envy (*ad invidiam*), the appeal to fear (*ad metum*), the appeal to hatred (*ad odium*), and the appeal to pride (*ad superbium*). In all of these, the underlying mistake is the argument's reliance on feelings as premises.

> because he is displeased at me on this account. Now if there be such a person among you—mind, I do not say that there is—to him I may fairly reply: My friend, I am a man, and like other men, a creature of flesh and blood, and not "of wood or stone" as Homer says; and I have a family, yes, and sons, O Athenians, three in number, one almost a man, and two others who are still young; and yet I will not bring any of them here to petition you for acquittal.[3]

There are many ways to pull heartstrings. Although it is often successful, the appeal to pity is an obvious fallacy, ridiculed in the story of the trial of a youth accused of the murder of his mother and father with an ax. Confronted with overwhelming proof of his guilt, his attorney pleads for leniency on the grounds that his client is now an orphan!

R2. THE RED HERRING

The *red herring* is a fallacious argument whose effectiveness lies in *distraction*. Attention is deflected; readers or listeners are drawn to some aspect of the topic under discussion by which they are led away from the issue that had been the focus of the discussion. They are urged to attend to some observation or some claim that may be associated with the topic, but that is not relevant to the truth of what had originally been in dispute. A red herring has been drawn across the track.

This fallacy has a fascinating history. The phrase is believed to have been derived from the practice of those who tried to save a fox being hunted by leaving a misleading trail of scent (a smoked herring is very smelly and does become dark red) that would be likely to distract or confuse the dogs in hot pursuit. In many contexts, any *deliberately misleading trail* is commonly called a red herring. Especially in literature, and above all in suspense or detective stories, it is not rare for some character or event to be introduced deliberately to mislead the investigators (and the readers) and thus to add to the excitement and complexity of the plot. An ulterior political motivation may be suggested, a sexual scandal may be intimated—whatever can put the reader off the track may serve as a red herring. In the very popular novel and film, *The DaVinci Code*,[4] one of the characters, a Catholic bishop, enters the plot in ways that very cleverly mislead. His name is the author's joke: Bishop Aringarosa—meaning "red herring" in Italian.*

Fallacious arguments use this technique in various ways. The opponents of an appropriate tax measure may call attention to a new and appealing way in which funds can be raised by state-sponsored gambling. A defense of the prosperity produced by an economic system may be deflected by vigorously condemning the economic inequality that system permits. Economic inequality

---

*And in the world of finance, a prospectus issued to attract investors in a company about to go public, which tells much about the company but not the price of its shares, is also called a red herring.

may well be excessive or unfair, but if most of the members of a community are reasonably well off, that fact is not disproved by the reality of the enormous gap between the moderate wealth of most and the great wealth of some.

The distinguished political columnist David Broder has observed that in recent discussions of U.S. foreign policy in the Middle East, it has been the policy of some to urge that a show of military strength is a necessary element of our international posture. As Broder points out, however, it is a "rhetorical trick" to respond, whenever there is criticism of military expansion, that "its critics are soft on terror."[5] A classical red herring.

Another recent example arose during debate in Congress over legislation originally designed to oblige corporations to protect the accumulated funds that had been set aside for the pensions of their employees. One legislator, apparently seeking to protect his corporate donors, entered the debate with the irrelevant point that there is a serious need for the provision of better advice to retired persons on the investment of their pensions. No doubt there is. But one commentator astutely observed, "What does this have to do with employers squandering their workers' retirement? It's a red herring. . . . Mr. Smith's herring replaces a major national scandal with a minor scandal, in an attractive rhetorical wrapping."[6]

Again: At Duke University in 2006, three student athletes were indicted for rape; the indictments were plainly unfounded and soon withdrawn. When the prosecutor was charged with misconduct in office, feelings at the university grew intense. One member of the Duke faculty, writing in the local newspaper, defended the prosecutor and some other faculty members who had supported him. In the course of this defense she argued that the real "social disaster" in the Duke rape case was that "18 percent of the American population lives below the poverty line," and that we do not have "national health care or affordable childcare." That herring was bright red.[7]

R3. THE STRAW MAN

It is very much easier to win a fight against a person made of straw than against one made of flesh and blood. If one argues against some view by presenting an opponent's position as one that is easily torn apart, the argument is fallacious, of course. Such an argument commits the fallacy of the *straw man*.

One may view this fallacy as a variety of the red herring, because it also introduces a distraction from the real dispute. In this case, however, the distraction is of a particular kind: It is an effort to shift the conflict from its original complexity into a different conflict, between parties other than those originally in dispute. So common is this variety of distraction that the pattern of argument that relies on it has long carried its own name: the straw man argument.

In controversies of a moral or a political nature, a successful argument almost invariably requires some reasonable and nuanced distinctions, and perhaps also some narrowly described exceptions. The extreme position in any dispute—the claim that conduct of a certain kind is *always* wrong, or *always* justified—is likely to be difficult if not impossible to defend. Therefore it is often a fallacious device to contend that what one aims to defeat is indefensible because it is categorical or absolute. Victory may be achieved over this fictitious opponent, but one will have destroyed only a straw man.

One who urges the enlargement of the authority of some central administration may be fallaciously accused of seeking to transform the state into a "big brother" whose reach will extend into every corner of citizens' private lives. Such a "big brother" is likely to be no more than a straw man. One who urges the devolution of authority from central to more local governments may be portrayed, with similar fallacy, as the enemy of an efficient and effective administration—and that, too, is likely to be a straw man. In general, straw man arguments often take the form of supposing that the position under attack adopts the most extreme view possible—that *every* act or policy of a certain kind is to be rejected. The argument is easy to win, but its premises are not relevant to the conclusion that was originally proposed. The straw man argument often presents a genuine objection or criticism, and the objection may be sound, but it is aimed at a new and irrelevant target.

Straw man arguments present a special risk to their proponents. If, in controversy, a critic depicts her opponents in a way that is clearly more extreme and more unreasonable than is justifiable in the light of what they had written or said, readers or members of the audience are likely to recognize the exaggeration and to respond in a way quite opposite to what was hoped for. Readers (or listeners) may sense the unreasonableness of the portrayal and be offended by the unfairness. Even further, the readers or listeners, recognizing the distortion, may be caused by its unfairness to move intellectually to the side of the party that has been misrepresented, formulating in their own minds the response that may justly be made to the fallacious attack. Neutral persons who were to be persuaded may be thus transformed, by unfair fallacious argument, into adversaries. Every fallacious argument presents some risk of this kind; the fallacy of the straw man invites it with special force.

R4. ARGUMENT AGAINST THE PERSON (ARGUMENT *AD HOMINEM*)

Of all the fallacies of irrelevance, the argument against the person, or *ad hominem*, is among the most pernicious. Such arguments are common, as many fallacies are. But these, in addition to being unfair to the adversary (as straw man arguments are also) are hurtful, often inflicting serious personal damage without any opportunity for the fallacy to be exposed or its author chastised.

The phrase *ad hominem* translates as "against the person." An *ad hominem* argument is one in which the thrust is directed, not at a conclusion, but at some person who defends the conclusion in dispute. This personalized attack might be conducted in either of two different ways, for which reason we distinguish two major forms of the argument *ad hominem:* the *abusive* and the *circumstantial.*

A. Argument *ad hominem,* Abusive

One is tempted, in heated argument, to disparage the character of one's opponents, to deny their intelligence or reasonableness, to question their understanding, or their seriousness, or even their integrity. But the character of an adversary is logically irrelevant to the truth or falsity of what that person asserts, or to the correctness of the reasoning employed. A proposal may be attacked as unworthy because it is supported by "radicals," or by "reactionaries," but such allegations, even when plausible, are not relevant to the merit of the proposal itself.

Personal abuse can be psychologically persuasive, however, because it may induce strong disapproval of some advocate, and by unjustifiable extension in the mind of the hearer, disapproval of what had been advocated. For example, Judge Constance Baker Motley, long active in the civil rights movement, defends affirmative action with an *ad hominem* attack on its critics. She writes:

> Those who resist [affirmative action programs] deny that they are racists, but the truth is that their real motivation is racism, a belief in the inherent inferiority of African-Americans and people of mixed racial backgrounds.[8]

However, the merits (or demerits) of arguments about affirmative action are not illuminated by denigrating the character of those who take the side one rejects.

Ad hominem abusive has many variations. The opponent may be reviled (and his claims held unworthy) because he is of a certain religious or political persuasion: a "Papist" or an "atheist," a member of the "radical right" or the "loony left," or the like. A conclusion may be condemned because it has been defended by persons believed to be of bad character, or because its advocate has been closely associated with those of bad character. Socrates was convicted of impiety partly because of his long association with persons known to have been disloyal to Athens and rapacious in conduct. And very recently, when Clyde Collins Snow was called a racist because of the conclusions he reached as a forensic scientist, he replied as follows:

> My work devoted to the investigation of the disappearance, torture, and extrajudicial execution of human rights victims in many countries has often made me the target of public criticism and official outrage. To date, however, none of my critics has called me a racist. Among my detractors have been apologists for the brutal military junta in Argentina, representatives of General Pinochet's military in Chile,

> the Guatemalan Defense Minister, and Serbian government spokesmen. Thus Mr. Goodman [Snow's accuser] finds himself in interesting company.[9]

The accusation of *guilt by association* is a common form of *ad hominem* abuse.

B. Argument *ad hominem,* Circumstantial

The circumstances of one who makes (or rejects) some claim have no more bearing on the truth of what is claimed than does his character. The mistake made in the *circumstantial* form of the *ad hominem* fallacy is to treat those personal circumstances as the premise of an opposing argument.

Thus it may be argued fallaciously that *consistency* obliges an opponent to accept (or reject) some conclusion merely because of that person's employment, or nationality, or political affiliation, or other circumstances. It may be unfairly suggested that a member of the clergy must accept a given proposition because its denial would be incompatible with the Scriptures. Or it may be claimed that political candidates must support a given policy because it is explicitly propounded in the platform of their party. Such argument is irrelevant to the *truth* of the proposition in question; it simply urges that some persons' circumstances require its acceptance. Hunters, accused of the needless slaughter of unoffending animals, sometimes reply by noting that their critics eat the flesh of harmless cattle. Such a reply is plainly *ad hominem:* The fact that the critic eats meat does not even begin to prove that it is right for the hunter to kill animals for amusement.

When the circumstances of the speaker are used not merely as grounds for attack—suggesting a foolish inconsistency or the like—but used rather in a plainly negative spirit, a special name is given to such *ad hominem* arguments. They are called by their traditional Latin name, *tu quoque*. This Latin expression does not translate simply, but it means, in essence, "You're another," or more loosely, "Look who's talking." The substance of the fallacy is to contend that you (the first party) are just as bad as I am, just as guilty of whatever it is that you complained about. But of course that response is not a refutation of the original complaint. It may be true that the first party is guilty of the conduct in question, but calling that guilt to attention does not support the innocence of the second party, which is the issue in the argument at hand.

An illustration will be helpful. A correspondent for CNN interviewed Osama bin Laden, leader of the terrorist organization Al Queda, some years ago in Afghanistan. The exchange went like this:

Cliff Arnett (CNN): The United States government says that you are still funding military training camps here in Afghanistan for militant, Islamic fighters and that you're a sponsor of international terrorism. . . . Are these accusations true?

Osama bin Laden: . . . At the time that they condemn any Muslim leader who calls for his rights, they receive the highest official of the Irish Republican Army at the White House as a political leader. Wherever we look we find the U.S. as the leader of terrorism and crime in the world. The U.S. does not consider it a terrorist act to throw atomic bombs at nations thousands of miles away. . . . The U.S. does not consider it terrorism when hundreds of thousands of our sons and brothers in Iraq die for lack of food or medicine. So there is no basis for what the U.S. says.[10]

How the United States conducts its international relations is rightly open to criticism—but whatever may be true about that behavior, attacking it is no response to the allegation of Al Queda terrorism. This is a classic *tu quoque*.

The circumstances of an opponent are not properly the issue in serious argument. It is the substance of what is claimed, or denied, that must be addressed. It is true that highlighting one's opponent's circumstances may prove rhetorically effective in winning assent, or in persuading others, but the effectiveness of this device does not make up for its error. Arguments of this kind are fallacious.

Circumstantial *ad hominem* arguments are sometimes used to suggest that the opponents' conclusion should be rejected because their judgment is warped, dictated by their special situation rather than by reasoning or evidence. However, an argument that is favorable to some group deserves discussion on its merits; it is fallacious to attack it simply on the ground that it is presented by a member of that group and is therefore self-serving. The arguments in favor of a protective tariff (for example) may be bad, but they are not bad because they are presented by a manufacturer who benefits from such tariffs.

One argument of this kind, called **poisoning the well,** is particularly perverse. The incident that gave rise to the name illustrates the argument forcefully. The British novelist and Protestant clergyman Charles Kingsley, attacking the famous Catholic intellectual John Henry Cardinal Newman, argued thus: Cardinal Newman's claims were not to be trusted because, as a Roman Catholic priest (Kingsley alleged), Newman's first loyalty was not to the truth. Newman countered that this *ad hominem* attack made it impossible for him, and indeed for all Catholics, to advance their arguments, because anything they might say to defend themselves would then be undermined by others' alleging that, after all, truth was not their first concern. Kingsley, said Cardinal Newman, had "poisoned the well of discourse."

Between the abusive and the circumstantial varieties of argument *ad hominem* there is a clear connection: The circumstantial may be regarded as a special case of the abusive. When a circumstantial *ad hominem* argument explicitly or implicitly charges the opponents with *inconsistency* (among their beliefs, or between what they profess and what they practice), that is clearly one kind of abuse. When a circumstantial *ad hominem* argument charges the opponents with a lack of trustworthiness by virtue of group membership, that is an accusation of *prejudice* in defense of self-interest and is clearly also an abuse.

An important qualification is called for at this point. *Ad hominem* arguments are fallacious (and often unfair to the adversary) because an attack against some person is generally not relevant to the objective merits of the argument that person has put forward. However, there are some circumstances in which it is indeed reasonable to raise doubts about some conclusion by *impeaching the testimony* of one who makes a claim that would (if true) support the conclusion in question. In courtroom proceedings, for example, it is acceptable, and often effective, to call a jury's attention to the unreliability of a witness, and by so doing to undermine the claims upheld by the testimony of that witness. This may be done by exhibiting contradictions in the testimony given, showing that at least some of what has been asserted must be false. It may be done by showing (not merely asserting) that the witness lied—an abusive but in this context appropriate counterargument. Testimony may also be undermined by exhibiting the great benefits that would accrue to the witness from the acceptance of his testimony—impeaching by circumstance. These are, strictly speaking, *ad hominem* considerations, and yet they are not fallacious because of the special context in which those assertions are being put forward, and because of the agreed-upon rules for the evaluation of conflicting witnesses.

Even in these special circumstances, an attack on the person of the witness does not establish the *falsehood* of what had been asserted. Revealing a pattern of past dishonesty or duplicity, or showing an inconsistency with testimony earlier given, may cast justifiable doubt on the reliability of the speaker, but the truth or falsity of the factual claim made can be established only with evidence that bears directly on that claim, and not merely on some person who denies or asserts it. In each case we must ask: Is the attack on the person relevant to the truth of what is at issue? When, as commonly occurs, the attack is *not* relevant to the merits of the claim, the *ad hominem* argument is indeed fallacious.

R5. THE APPEAL TO FORCE (ARGUMENT *AD BACULUM*)

It seems odd to suppose that one could hope to establish some proposition as true, or persuade some other person of its truth, by resorting to force. Threats or strong-arm methods to coerce one's opponents can hardly be considered arguments at all. Traditionally, a category of fallacies of this kind has been identified as the *appeal to force* or the argument *ad baculum* (the appeal *ad baculum* means literally appeal to the stick!), and it surely is clear that however expedient force may prove to be, it cannot replace rational methods of argument. "Might makes right" is not a subtle principle, and we all reject it.

The force threatened need not be physical, of course. In 2000, two professors of law at Boise State University published (in a law journal of the University of Denver) an article that was harshly critical of the Boise Cascade Corporation, one of the world's largest producers of paper and wood products. Subsequently, the university issued a formal "errata" notice that "this article has been retracted for its lack of scholarship and false content."

Why did the university retract the article? Did Boise Cascade threaten the university with a lawsuit? "Well," said the university's general counsel, "'threaten' is an interesting word. Let's just say they pointed out that the objections they raised did rise to the level of being actionable." The university, it turns out, had received a highlighted copy of the article in question from the general counsel of Boise Cascade, together with a letter saying, "I have been advised to proceed with litigation against Denver University if any of these highlighted areas are republished by Denver University in any form."[11]

There are some circumstances in which threats may be introduced with more subtlety, and in such circumstances we may say that something like an argument—a plainly fallacious argument, to be sure—has been presented. What is put forward may be a veiled threat, or a proposition that suggests some danger if the proposition in question is not given full assent. It may be that certain *behaviors* are of importance, whatever may be doubted or believed. To illustrate, when the U.S. attorney general in the administration of President Ronald Reagan was under strong attack in the press for misconduct, the White House chief of staff at the time, Howard Baker, opened one meeting of his staff by saying:

> The President continues to have confidence in the Attorney General and I have confidence in the Attorney General and you ought to have confidence in the Attorney General, because we work for the President and because that's the way things are. And if anyone has a different view of that, or any different motive, ambition, or intention, he can tell me about it because we're going to have to discuss your status.[12]

One might say that nobody is fooled by an argument of this sort; the threatened party may *behave* appropriately but need not, in the end, accept the *truth* of the conclusion being insisted on. To this it was answered, by representatives of twentieth-century Italian fascism, that real persuasion can come through many different instruments, of which reason is one and the blackjack is another. But once the opponent is truly persuaded, they held, the instrument of persuasion may be forgotten. That fascist view appears to guide many of the governments of the globe to this day; but the argument *ad baculum*—reliance on the club, or on the threat of force in any form—is by reason unacceptable. The appeal to force is the abandonment of reason.

R6. MISSING THE POINT (*IGNORATIO ELENCHI*)*

Among the fallacies of relevance, the final category to be identified is perhaps the most difficult to describe with precision. It arises when the argument goes awry—when, on close examination, there is a "disconnect" between the premises and the conclusion. The twist may on occasion be an instrument of deliberate deception, but more often the fallacy is the product of sloppy thinking, a confusion in reasoning that the author of the argument herself does not fully recognize, or grasp.

Aristotle, the first to give a systematic classification of the informal fallacies, explains the fallacy we call *missing the point*, or *ignoratio elenchi*, as a *mistake* that is made in seeking to refute another's argument. The Latin word *elenchi* is derived from a Greek word that means a disproof, or a refutation. An *ignoratio elenchi* is a *mistaken refutation*, one that goes haywire because the person presenting it does not fully understand the proposition in dispute. He refutes, or tries to refute, a claim other than that which was originally at issue. *He misses the point*.

As an example, suppose that one person emphasizes how important it is to increase funding for the public schools. His opponent responds by insisting that a child's education involves much more than schooling and gets underway long before her formal schooling begins. That assertion is entirely reasonable, of course, but it misses the point of what was said earlier. One party presents an argument for P, to alleviate the need for funds; his interlocutor counters with an irrelevant Q, about the importance of preschool education.

Or suppose that some very controversial amendment to the tax code is proposed—say, the elimination of inheritance taxes. Such taxes, it is argued, are not fair because the money in the estate of a deceased person was already taxed at the time it was earned—and therefore to tax it again upon the person's death is to tax the same funds twice. But, responds the supporter of the tax, inheritance taxes are imposed only on large estates that can well afford the tax; and furthermore (the advocate of the tax continues), our government needs that money. This response is an *ignoratio elenchi*. The inheritance tax may certainly be defended, but the size of estates taxed and the need for the resulting funds misses the point of the argument that had been put forward: the claim of unfair double taxation. Similarly, in a controversy over a new and very expensive

*A variety of alternative names have been applied to this category, including *irrelevant conclusion* and *mistaken refutation*.

weapons system for the military, criticized (let us suppose) for its doubtful practicality and enormous expense, the premises of an argument offered in support of the new weapons will miss the point if they do no more than underscore the pressing need for strong national defense. Objectives stated in general terms—national security, a balanced budget—are easy to endorse; the difficult questions in dispute are likely to be whether some particular proposed measure (a particular weapon system, a particular tax) will in fact promote the end sought, and whether it is likely to do so as effectively and efficiently as its alternatives. Bypassing the hard questions by emphasizing our agreement on easy generalizations about larger objectives commits the *ignoratio elenchi:* It misses the point.

There is a sense in which every fallacy of irrelevance is an *ignoratio elenchi,* because in all these fallacies there is a gap between the premises and the conclusion. Premises that are not relevant—red herrings, straw men, personal attacks—all miss the point. That is true. But we reserve this name for those fallacies of irrelevance that do not fit into other categories. The *ignoratio elenchi* is, we may say, a catchall class of fallacies: fallacies in which the premises simply fail to connect to the intended conclusion with the coherence that rational argument requires.

There is another expression with similar breadth and flexibility, the widely used phrase *non sequitur*. Its meaning is "does not follow": A *non sequitur* is an argument in which the conclusion simply does not follow from the premises. Thus every fallacy is, in that general sense, also a *non sequitur*. As a candidate for the presidency of the United States in 2000, George W. Bush indicated that he was planning to grant a reprieve (under his authority as the governor of Texas) to a man who had been convicted of murder and was scheduled for execution. Why, he was asked, did he telegraph his intention before announcing his formal decision? He replied:

> I believe this is a case where it's important for me to send a signal about what I may do because it's a case where we're dealing with a man's innocence or guilt.[13]

The term *non sequitur* is most commonly applied when the failure of the argument is obvious, when the gap between the premises and the conclusion is painfully wide. "A great, rough *non sequitur,*" Abraham Lincoln observed in a speech in 1854, "was sometimes twice as dangerous as a well polished fallacy."[14]

And yet there are times when what appears at first to be a *non sequitur* will be seen upon reflection not to be one. Consider this report of a historic "legal fiasco."

> The prisoner pleaded guilty. He then said he had made a mistake, and the judge allowed him to change his plea to not guilty. The case was tried. The jury acquitted. "Prisoner," said Mr. Justice Hawkins, "a few minutes ago you said you were a thief. Now the jury say you are a liar. Consequently you are discharged."[15]

OVERVIEW

Fallacies of Relevance

R1. The Appeal to Emotion (*ad populum*)

An informal fallacy committed when the support offered for some conclusion is an inappropriate appeal to the emotions—patriotism, pity, or the like—of the listeners.

R2. The Red Herring

An informal fallacy committed when some distraction is used to mislead and confuse.

R3. The Straw Man

An informal fallacy committed when the position of one's opponent is misrepresented and that distorted position is made the object of attack.

R4. Argument Against the Person (*ad hominem*)

An informal fallacy committed when, rather than attacking the substance of some position, one attacks the person of its advocate, either abusively or as a consequence of his or her special circumstances.

R5. Appeal to Force (*ad baculum*)

An informal fallacy committed when force, or the threat of force, is relied on to win consent.

R6. Missing the Point (*ignoratio elenchi*)

An informal fallacy committed when one refutes, not the thesis one's interlocutor is advancing, but some different thesis that one mistakenly imputes to him or her.

EXERCISES

A. Identify and explain the fallacies of relevance in the following passages.

1. If you can't blame the English language and your own is unforgivingly precise, blame the microphone. That was the route Jacques Chirac took after his nuclear remark about a nuclear Iran. "Having one or perhaps a second bomb a little later, well, that's not very dangerous," Mr. Chirac said with a shrug. The press was summoned back for a retake. "I should rather have paid attention to what I was saying and understood that perhaps I was on the record," Mr. Chirac offered, as if the record rather than the remark were the issue.

   —Stacy Schiff, "Slip Sliding Away," *The New York Times*, 2 February 2007

2. Nietzsche was personally more philosophical than his philosophy. His talk about power, harshness, and superb immorality was the hobby of a harmless young scholar and constitutional invalid.

—George Santayana, *Egotism in German Philosophy*, 1915

3. Like an armed warrior, like a plumed knight, James G. Blaine marched down the halls of the American Congress and threw his shining lances full and fair against the brazen foreheads of every defamer of his country and maligner of its honor.

For the Republican party to desert this gallant man now is worse than if an army should desert their general upon the field of battle.

—Robert G. Ingersoll, nominating speech at the Republican National Convention, 1876

4. However, it matters very little now what the king of England either says or does; he hath wickedly broken through every moral and human obligation, trampled nature and conscience beneath his feet, and by a steady and constitutional spirit of insolence and cruelty procured for himself an universal hatred.

—Thomas Paine, *Common Sense*, 1776

5. This embarrassing volume is an out-and-out partisan screed made up of illogical arguments, distorted and cherry-picked information, ridiculous generalizations and nutty asides. It's a nasty stewpot of intellectually untenable premises and irresponsible speculation that frequently reads like a "Saturday Night Live" parody of the crackpot right.

—Michiko Kakutani, "Dispatch from Gomorrah, Savaging the Cultural Left," *The New York Times*, 6 February 2007.

6. I was seven years old when the first election campaign which I can remember took place in my district. At that time we still had no political parties, so the announcement of this campaign was received with very little interest. But popular feeling ran high when it was disclosed that one of the candidates was "the Prince." There was no need to add Christian and surname to realize which Prince was meant. He was the owner of the great estate formed by the arbitrary occupation of the vast tracts of land reclaimed in the previous century from the Lake of Fucino. About eight thousand families (that is, the majority of the local population) are still employed today in cultivating the estate's fourteen thousand hectares. The Prince was deigning to solicit "his" families for their vote so that he could become their deputy in parliament. The agents of the estate, who were working for the Prince, talked in impeccably liberal phrases: "Naturally," said they, "naturally, no one

will be forced to vote for the Prince, that's understood; in the same way that no one, naturally, can force the Prince to allow people who don't vote for him to work on his land. This is the period of real liberty for everybody; you're free, and so is the Prince." The announcement of these "liberal" principles produced general and understandable consternation among the peasants. For, as may easily be guessed, the Prince was the most hated person in our part of the country.

—Ignazio Silone, *The God That Failed,* 1949

7. According to R. Grunberger, author of *A Social History of the Third Reich*, Nazi publishers used to send the following notice to German readers who let their subscriptions lapse: "Our paper certainly deserves the support of every German. We shall continue to forward copies of it to you, and hope that you will not want to expose yourself to unfortunate consequences in the case of cancellation."

8. In *While Europe Slept: How Radical Islam Is Destroying the West from Within* (2006), Bruce Bawer argues that "by appeasing a totalitarian [Muslim] ideology Europe is "imperiling its liberty." Political correctness, he writes, is keeping Europeans from defending themselves, resulting in "its self-destructive passivity, softness toward tyranny, its reflexive inclination to appease." A review of the book in *The Economist* observes that Mr. Bawer "weakens his argument by casting too wide a net," and another reviewer, Imam Fatih Alev, says of Bawer's view that "it is a constructed idea that there is this very severe difference between Western values and Muslim values."

—"Clash Between European and Islamic Views, in Books,"
The New York Times, 8 February 2007.

9. To know absolutely that there is no God one must have infinite knowledge. But to have infinite knowledge one would have to be God. It is impossible to be God and an atheist at the same time. Atheists cannot prove that God doesn't exist.

—"Argument Against Atheism,"
http://aaron_mp.tripod.com/id2.html (2007)

10. When we had got to this point in the argument, and everyone saw that the definition of justice had been completely upset, Thrasymachus, instead of replying to me, said: "Tell me, Socrates, have you got a nurse?"

"Why do you ask such a question," I said, "when you ought rather to be answering?"

"Because she leaves you to snivel, and never wipes your nose; she has not even taught you to know the shepherd from the sheep."

—Plato, *The Republic*

11. I also admit that there are people for whom even the reality of the external world [is] a grave problem. My answer is that I do not address *them*, but that I presuppose a minimum of reason in my readers.

—Paul Feyerabend, "Materialism and the Mind-Body Problem," *The Review of Metaphysics*, 1963

12. Clarence Darrow, renowned criminal trial lawyer, began one shrewd plea to a jury thus:

> You folks think we city people are all crooked, but we city people think you farmers are all crooked. There isn't one of you I'd trust in a horse trade, because you'd be sure to skin me. But when it comes to having sympathy with a person in trouble, I'd sooner trust you folks than city folks, because you come to know people better and get to be closer friends.

—Irving Stone, *Clarence Darrow for the Defense*, 1943

13. A national organization called In Defense of Animals registered protest, in 1996, against alleged cruelty to animals being sold live or slaughtered in Chinese markets in San Francisco. Patricia Briggs, who brought the complaint to the city's Animal Welfare Commission, said: "The time of the crustaceans is coming. You'd think people wouldn't care about lobsters, because they aren't cuddly and fuzzy and they have these vacant looks and they don't vocalize. But you'd be surprised how many people care." To which response was given by Astella Kung, proprietor of Ming Kee Game Birds, where fowl are sold live: "How about the homeless people? Why don't the animal people use their energy to care for those people? They have no homes! They are hungry!"

—"Cuisine Raises Debate on Cruelty and Culture," *The New York Times*, 26 August 1996

14. The U.S. Department of Agriculture operates a price support program for the benefit of tobacco producers; its regulations limit the amount of tobacco that can be grown, and thus keep the price of tobacco high. Those same producers fight against consumer health regulations. On what ground? One analyst observed:

> For the proponent of price support regulations to turn around and fight consumer-health regulations on the grounds that government regulation is unwarranted interference by big brother and bad for the economy is the kind of argument that makes rational people wince.

—A. L. Fritschler, *Smoking and Politics* (Englewoood Cliffs, NJ: Prentice-Hall, 1983)

15. During World War I, the British government deliberately inflamed the anti-German sentiments of the people with cartoons: one of these cartoons appears immediately below.

Source: Wilson, David (20th century). The Bridgeman Art Library International. Private Collection/The Bridgeman Art Library.

B. Each of the following passages may be plausibly criticized by some who conclude that it contains a fallacy, but each will be defended by some who deny that the argument is fallacious. Discuss the merits of each argument and explain why you conclude that it does or does not contain a fallacy of relevance.

1. The chairman of General Electric, Jack Welch, was challenged at a stockholder's meeting recently by a nun who argued that GE was responsible for the cleanup of the Hudson River where pollutants from GE's plants had for many years been allowed to collect. Welch flatly denied the company's responsibility, saying, "Sister, you have to stop this conversation. You owe it to God to be on the side of truth here."

   —Elizabeth Kolbert, "The River," *The New Yorker*, 4 December 2000

2. Gender feminism is notoriously impossible to falsify: it chews up and digests all counterevidence, transmuting it into confirming evidence.

The fact that most people, including most women, do not see the pervasive and tenacious system of male power only shows how thoroughly they have been socialized to perpetuate it. The more women who reject the gender feminist perspective, the more this proves them in thrall to the androcentric system. Nothing and no one can refute the hypothesis of the sex-gender system for those who . . . see it so clearly "everywhere."

—Christina Sommers,
Proceedings of the American Philosophical Association, June 1992

3. As the American Revolution began to appear likely, some Americans sought reconciliation with England; Thomas Paine opposed reconciliation bitterly. In *Common Sense* (1776), he wrote:

> . . . all those who espouse the doctrine of reconciliation may be included within the following descriptions. Interested men, who are not to be trusted, weak men who cannot see, prejudiced men who will not see, and a certain set of moderate men who think better of the European world than it deserves; and this last class, by an ill-judged deliberation, will be the cause of more calamities to this Continent than all the other three.

4. "But I observe," says Cleanthes, "with regard to you, Philo, and all speculative sceptics, that your doctrine and practice are as much at variance in the most abstruse points of theory as in the conduct of common life."

—David Hume, *Dialogues Concerning Natural Religion*, 1779

5. A press release from the National Education Association (NEA) begins with the following statement. "America's teachers see smaller classes as the most critical element in doing a better job, a survey by the NEA indicates." . . . But the NEA, of course, is interested in having as many teachers in the schools as possible. For example, in a 3,000-pupil school system with 30 pupils assigned to each class, the teaching staff would be approximately 100. But if class size were changed to 25 the total number of teachers would rise to 120. And in a time of shrinking enrollments, that is a way to keep teachers on the public payroll. . . .

It is unfortunate that an organization with the professional reputation the National Education Association enjoys should be so self-serving.

—Cynthia Parsons, *Christian Science Monitor Service*

6. I testify unto every man that heareth the words of the prophecy of this book. If any man shall add unto these things, God shall add unto him the plagues that are written in this book: And if any man shall take away from the words of the book of this prophecy, God shall take away his part out of the book of life, and out of the holy city and *from* the things which are written in this book.

—Rev. 22: 18–19

7. **Anytus:** "Socrates, I think that you are too ready to speak evil of men: and, if you will take my advice, I would recommend you to be careful. Perhaps there is no city in which it is not easier to do men harm than to do them good, and this is certainly the case at Athens, as I believe that you know."

—Plato, *Meno*

8. The Greek historian Thucydides, in his *History of the Peloponnesian War*, gave the following account of an Athenian's appeal to representatives of the small island of Melos, to join Athens in its war against Sparta:

   You know as well as we do that, in the logic of human nature, right only comes into question where there is a balance of power, while it is might that determines what the strong exhort and the weak concede . . . . Your strongest weapons are hopes yet unrealized, while the weapons in your hands are somewhat inadequate for holding out against the forces already arranged against you . . . . Reflect that you are taking a decision for your country, a country whose fate hangs upon a single decision right or wrong.

9. In that melancholy book, *The Future of an Illusion*, Dr. Freud, himself one of the last great theorists of the European capitalist class, has stated with simple clarity the impossibility of religious belief for the educated man of today.

—John Strachey,
The Coming Struggle for Power, 1933

10. The classic trap for any revolutionary is always "What's your alternative?" But even if you *could* provide the interrogator with a blueprint, this does not mean he would use it; in most cases he is not sincere in wanting to know.

—Shulamith Firestone,
The Dialectic of Sex: The Case for Feminist Revolution, 1970

4.4 Fallacies of Defective Induction

The premises of the fallacious arguments described in the preceding section are not relevant to the conclusions drawn. However, there are many fallacious arguments in which the premises are relevant and yet are wholly inadequate.

These we call *fallacies of defective induction*. What are asserted as premises simply do not serve as good reasons to reach the conclusion drawn.

D1. THE ARGUMENT FROM IGNORANCE (ARGUMENT *AD IGNORANTIAM*)

If some proposition has not yet been proved false, we are not entitled to conclude that it is true. The same point can be made in reverse: If some proposition has not yet been proved true, we are not entitled to conclude that it is false. Many true propositions have not yet been proved true, of course, just as many false propositions have not yet been proved false. The fact that we cannot now be confident rarely serves as a good reason to assert knowledge of falsity, or of truth. Such an inference is defective; the fallacy is called the *argument from ignorance*, or the argument *ad ignorantiam*. Ignorance sometimes obliges us to suspend judgment, assigning neither truth nor falsity to the proposition in doubt.

As a current illustration, the great abolitionist, Frederick Douglass, will soon have a memorial, now being built at the northwest corner of Central Park in New York City. Beneath an 8-foot statue of Douglass himself is planned a quilt in granite, an array of squares that are supposed, in legend, to be part of a secret code used along the Underground Railroad to aid slaves escaping from their southern owners. But prominent historians now agree that there never was such a code. There is no surviving example of such a quilt, and there is not a single mention of quilting codes in any diaries or memoirs from that period. The designer of the memorial, Algernon Miller, nevertheless insists that the quilt remain part of the memorial project. "No matter what anyone has to say," argues Miller, "they [his scholarly critics] weren't there in that particular moment." Not knowing that the legend is false, he concludes that we are justified in presuming it true.

The fallacious appeal to ignorance crops up in science when plausible claims are held to be false because evidence of their truth cannot be provided. There may be good reason for its absence: In archeology or in paleontology, for instance, that evidence may have been destroyed over time. In astronomy or in physics, the evidence desired may be so distant in space or in time that it is physically unobtainable. The fact that some desired evidence has not been gathered does not justify the conclusion that an otherwise plausible claim is false.

The argument from ignorance is particularly attractive to those who defend propositions that are very doubtful, even far-fetched. Pseudo-scientists who make unverifiable claims about psychic phenomena (for example, about telepathy, or about contact with the dead) may insist that the truth of their claims is supported by the fact that their critics have been unable to prove their falsehood.

An argument from ignorance was confronted by Galileo, whose newly invented telescope, early in the seventeenth century, plainly revealed the mountains and valleys of the moon. In his day, the "truth" that the moon was a perfect crystalline sphere was unquestioned; it had to be perfect because that was what Aristotle had taught. Confronted by the evidence the telescope revealed, Galileo's Aristotelian opponents responded with an argument that seemed irrefutable: Any apparent irregularities on the moon's surface are in fact filled in with a crystalline substance that is, of course, invisible! This hypothesis saved the moon's perfection, was in accord with what Aristotle had taught—and could not be proved false. This fallacy deserved ridicule. Galileo answered with an *argumentum ad ignorantiam* of his own, absurd enough to expose his critics: The moon is not a perfect sphere, he replied, because there are surely crystal mountains—invisible!—rising high from its surface. Because my theological critics cannot prove the claim false, we cannot conclude that such mountains are not there!

Whenever some great change is proposed, within an institution, or in society at large, those threatened by it are likely to attack with an argument from ignorance. How do we know it will work? How do we know that it is safe? We do not know; and without the knowledge that it is workable and safe, we must not adopt the change proposed. To prove workability or safety in advance, however, is often impossible. The objection sometimes takes the form of questions that suggest (but do not assert) the most horrific outcomes.

The fallacy can be a serious hindrance to progress. When the recombination of DNA, now an invaluable tool in medical science, first became possible in the 1970s, objections to further experimentation in that field were based largely on ignorance. All experiments with recombinant DNA should be stopped immediately, said one prominent scientist, who asked: "If Dr. Frankenstein must go on producing his little biological monsters . . . how can we be sure what would happen once the little beasts escaped from the laboratory?"[16] Another fearful scientist who sought to block these investigations made the appeal to ignorance explicitly:

> Can we predict the consequences? We are ignorant of the broad principles of evolution. . . . We simply do not know. We are ignorant of the various factors we currently perceive to participate in the evolutionary process. We are ignorant of the depth of security of our own environmental niche. . . . We do not know.[17]

What we do not know does not justify condemning the effort to learn. Fortunately, these appeals to ignorance were not successful in halting experimentation in a scientific realm whose value in saving and improving lives has proved, in the years since, to be incalculable.

Policy changes may be supported, as well as opposed, by an appeal to ignorance. When the federal government issued a waiver allowing Wisconsin to reduce the additional benefits it had been giving to welfare mothers for having more than one child, the governor of Wisconsin was asked if there was any evidence that unwed mothers were having additional children simply to gain the added income. His reply, *ad ignorantiam*, was this: "No, there isn't. There really isn't, but there is no evidence to the contrary, either."[18]

In some circumstances, of course, the fact that certain evidence or results have not been obtained, even after they have been actively sought in ways calculated to reveal them, may have substantial argumentative force. New drugs being tested for safety, for example, are commonly given to rodents or other animal subjects for prolonged periods; the absence of any toxic effect on the animals is taken to be evidence (although not conclusive evidence) that the drug is probably not toxic to humans. Consumer protection often relies on evidence of this kind. In circumstances like these we rely, not on ignorance, but on our knowledge, or conviction, that if the result we are concerned about were likely to arise, it would have arisen in some of the test cases. This use of the inability to prove something true supposes that investigators are highly skilled, and that they very probably would have uncovered the evidence sought had that been possible. Tragic mistakes sometimes are made in this sphere, but if the standard is set too high—if what is required is a conclusive proof of harmlessness that cannot ever be given—consumers will be denied what may prove to be valuable, even life-saving, medical therapies.

Similarly, when a security investigation yields no evidence of improper conduct by the persons investigated, it would be wrong to conclude that the investigation has left us ignorant. A thorough investigation will properly result in the persons being "cleared." *Not* to draw a conclusion, in some cases, is as much a breach of correct reasoning as it would be to draw a mistaken conclusion.

The appeal to ignorance is common and often appropriate in a criminal court, where an accused person, in U.S. jurisprudence and British common law, is presumed innocent until proved guilty. We adopt this principle because we recognize that the error of convicting the innocent is far more grave than that of acquitting the guilty—and thus the defense in a criminal case may legitimately claim that if the prosecution has not proved guilt beyond a reasonable doubt, the only verdict possible is not guilty. The U.S. Supreme Court strongly reaffirmed this standard of proof in these words:

> The reasonable-doubt standard . . . is a prime instrument for reducing the risk of convictions resting on factual error. The standard provides concrete substance for the presumption of innocence—that bedrock axiomatic and elementary principle whose enforcement lies at the foundation of the administration of our criminal law.[19]

However, *this* appeal to ignorance succeeds only when innocence must be assumed in the absence of proof to the contrary; in other contexts, such an appeal is indeed an argument *ad ignorantiam*.

D2. THE APPEAL TO INAPPROPRIATE AUTHORITY (ARGUMENT *AD VERECUNDIAM*)

In attempting to make up one's mind about some difficult or complicated question, it is entirely reasonable to be guided by the judgment of an acknowledged expert. When we argue that a given conclusion is correct on the ground that an expert authority has come to that judgment, we commit no fallacy. Indeed, such recourse to authority is necessary for most of us on very many matters. Of course, an expert's judgment constitutes no conclusive proof; experts disagree, and even in agreement they may err, but expert opinion surely is one reasonable way to support a conclusion.

The fallacy of the appeal to inappropriate authority (*ad verecundiam*) arises when the appeal is made to parties who have no *legitimate* claim to authority in the matter at hand. Thus, in an argument about morality, an appeal to the opinions of Darwin, a towering authority in biology, would be fallacious, as would be an appeal to the opinions of a great artist such as Picasso to settle an economic dispute.[20] Care must be taken in determining whose authority it is reasonable to rely on, and whose to reject. Although Picasso was not an economist, his judgment might plausibly be given some weight in a dispute pertaining to the economic value of an artistic masterpiece; and if the role of biology in moral questions were in dispute, Darwin might indeed be an appropriate authority.

The most blatant examples of misplaced appeals to authority appear in advertising "testimonials." We are urged to drive an automobile of a particular make because a famous golfer or tennis player affirms its superiority; we are urged to drink a beverage of a certain brand because some movie star or football coach expresses enthusiasm about it. Whenever the truth of some proposition is asserted on the basis of the authority of one who has no special competence in that sphere, the appeal to inappropriate authority is the fallacy committed.

This appears to be a simple-minded mistake that is easy to avoid, but there are circumstances in which the fallacious appeal is tempting, and therefore intellectually dangerous. Here are two examples: In the sphere of international relations, in which weapons and war unhappily play a major role, one opinion or another is commonly supported by appealing to those whose special competence lies in the technical design or construction of weapons. Physicists such as Robert Oppenheimer and Edward Teller, for example, may indeed have been competent to give authoritative judgments regarding how certain weapons can (or cannot) function, but their knowledge in this sphere did not give them special wisdom in determining broad political goals. An appeal to the strong judgment of a distinguished physicist as to the wisdom of ratifying some international treaty would be an argument *ad verecundiam*. Similarly, we admire the depth and insight of great fiction—say, in the novels of Alexander

Solzhenitsyn or Saul Bellow—but to resort to their judgment in determining the real culprit in some political dispute would be an appeal *ad verecundiam*.[21]

The argument *ad verecundiam* is an appeal to one who has no legitimate claim to authority. Even one who does have a legitimate claim to authority may well prove mistaken, of course, and we may later regret our choice of experts. But if the experts we chose deserved their reputation for knowledge, it was no fallacy to rely on them even if they erred. Our mistake becomes one of reasoning (a fallacy) when our conclusion is based on the verdict of an authority who has no rational claim to expertise in that matter.[22]

D3. FALSE CAUSE (ARGUMENT *NON CAUSA PRO CAUSA*)

It is obvious that any reasoning that relies on treating as the cause of some thing or event what is not really its cause must be seriously mistaken. But often we are tempted to suppose, or led to suppose, that we understand some specific cause-and-effect relation when in fact we do not. The nature of the connection between cause and effect, and how we determine whether such a connection is present, are central problems of inductive logic and scientific method, discussed in detail in Part III of this book. Presuming the reality of a causal connection that does not really exist is a common mistake; in Latin the mistake is called the fallacy of *non causa pro causa*; we call it simply the fallacy of **false cause.**

Whether the causal connection alleged is indeed mistaken may sometimes be a matter for dispute. Some college faculty members, it has been argued, grade leniently because they fear that rigorous grading will cause lowered evaluations of them by their students and damage to their careers. Gradual "grade inflation" is said to be the result of this fear. One college professor wrote this:

> Course evaluation forms [completed by students] are now required in many institutions, and salaries are influenced by the results. When I joined the University of Michigan 30 years ago, my salary was higher than that of any member of the anthropology department who is still active today. My standards for grading have not followed the trend toward inflation. Student complaints about grades have increased, and now my salary is at the bottom of the professorial list.[23]

Do you think the author of this passage commits the fallacy of false cause?

We sometimes mistakenly presume that one event is caused by another because it follows that other closely in time. In primitive cultures such mistakes were common; the sun would invariably reappear after an eclipse if the drums had been beaten in the darkness, but we know that it is absurd to suppose that the beating of the drums was the cause of the sun's reappearance. Mere temporal succession does not establish a causal connection. This variety of false cause is called the fallacy of ***post hoc ergo propter hoc***—"after the thing, therefore because of the thing."

Even very sophisticated people sometimes commit this fallacy. A few years ago, a critic ridiculed the reasoning of a U.S. Congressman this way:

> I'm getting tired of assertions like those of Rep. Ernest Istook, Jr.—"As prayer has gone out of the schools, guns, knives, drugs, and gangs have come in"—with the unsupported implication that there is some causal connection between these events. . . . We could just as well say, "After we threw God out of the schools, we put a man on the moon." Students may or may not need more faith, but Congress could certainly use more reason.[24]

Mistakes of this kind are widespread. Unusual weather conditions are blamed on some unrelated celestial phenomenon that happened to precede them; an infection really caused by a virus is thought to be caused by a chill wind, or wet feet, and so on. Perhaps no sphere is more vulnerable to this sort of argument than that of crimes and punishments. Typical is this remark in a letter to the *New York Times:*

> The death penalty in the United States has given us the highest crime rate and greatest number of prisoners per 100,000 population in the industrialized world.[25]

Post hoc ergo propter hoc is an easy fallacy to detect when it is blatant, but even the best of scientists and statesmen are occasionally misled by it.

False cause is also the fallacy committed when one mistakenly argues against some proposal on the ground that any change in a given direction is sure to lead to further changes in the same direction—and thus to grave consequences. Taking this step, it may be said, will put us on a slippery slope to disaster—and such reasoning is therefore called the fallacy of the *slippery slope.* Whether the feared consequences will indeed arise is not determined by the first step in a given direction; the suggestion that a change in that direction will trigger a catastrophic chain reaction is not generally warranted, although such argument is commonly invoked in defense of the status quo. What needs to be determined is what, in fact, probably will (or will not) cause the results feared.

Consider the following illustration. One common objection to the legalization of assisted suicide is that once formal permission has been given to medical doctors to act in a way that is of disputable morality, doctors will be led to engage in more and greater immorality of the same or similar type. The first leniency ought to be avoided, according to this argument, because it will leave us insecure on a slope so slippery that our first step down cannot be our last. To this argument one keen critic responded:

> The slippery slope argument, although influential, is hard to deal with rationally. It suggests that once we allow doctors to shorten the life of patients who request it, doctors could and would wantonly kill burdensome patients who do not want to die. This suggestion is not justified. . . .

> Physicians often prescribe drugs which, in doses greater than prescribed, would kill the patient. No one fears that the actual doses prescribed will lead to their use of lethal doses. No one objects to such prescriptions in fear of a "slippery slope." Authorizing physicians to assist in shortening the life of patients who request this assistance no more implies authority to shorten the life of patients who want to prolong it, than authority for surgery to remove the gall bladder implies authority to remove the patient's heart.[26]

The supposition that moving in a given direction, however prudently, is sure to produce the dreadful result of moving in the same direction to excess, is the fallacy of the slippery slope.

There are circumstances, of course, in which the first step in a new direction does establish a precedent that makes additional movement in that direction easier to achieve. This may be good or bad. Opposing new legislation that would punish crimes more severely if they were motivated by racial hatred, one critic writes:

> There should not be a separate category for hate crimes. A murder is a murder; a beating is a beating. We should prosecute people for the crimes they commit, not why they commit them. If we start to categorize crimes by their motivation, we start down a very slippery slope.[27]

Some arguments of this kind have merit, because precedent can affect subsequent decision making. The slippery slope is indeed a fallacy—but the mere allegation that that fallacy has been committed does not prove the argument in question faulty.

D4. HASTY GENERALIZATION

Throughout our lives, we rely on statements about how things generally are and how people generally behave. But general claims, although critical in reasoning, must be carefully scrutinized: The universality of their application ought never be accepted or assumed without justification. **Hasty generalization** is the fallacy we commit when we draw conclusions about *all* the persons or things in a given class on the basis of our knowledge about only one (or only a very few) of the members of that class. We all know of persons who have generalized mistakenly about certain companies or governments because of a single experience. Stereotypes about people who come from certain countries, or cultures, are widespread and commonly mistaken; hasty generalizations about foreign cultures can be downright nasty, and are good illustrations of the fallacious leap to broad generalization on the basis of very little evidence.

An anecdote or single instance may indeed be relevant support for a general rule or theory. But when it is treated as proof of that theory, the generalization is not well founded; the induction is defective. Here is an example: Eating deep-fried foods tends to raise one's cholesterol level. A single instance in which it does not do so is hardly sufficient to show that such foods are healthy. The owner of a "fish and chips" shop in England fallaciously defended the healthfulness of his deep-fried cookery with this argument:

> Take my son, Martyn. He's been eating fish and chips his whole life, and he just had a cholesterol test, and his level is below the national average. What better proof could there be than a fryer's son?[28]

Foods or drugs that are harmless in one context may be harmful in another. To move from a single case, or a very few cases, to a large-scale generalization about all or most cases, is fallacious reasoning, but it is common and often tempting. It is also called the **fallacy of converse accident** because it is the reverse of another common mistake, known as the *fallacy of accident*, in which generalizations are misused in another way. We turn to it next.

OVERVIEW

Fallacies of Defective Induction

D1. The Argument from Ignorance (*ad ignorantiam*)

An informal fallacy in which a conclusion is supported by an illegitimate appeal to ignorance, as when it is supposed that something is likely to be true because we cannot prove that it is false.

D2. The Appeal to Inappropriate Authority (*ad verecundiam*)

An informal fallacy in which the appeal to authority is illegitimate because the authority appealed to has no special claim to expertise on the matter in question.

D3. False Cause

An informal fallacy in which the mistake arises from accepting as the cause of an event what is not really its cause.

D4. Hasty Generalization

An informal fallacy in which a principle that is true of a particular case is applied, carelessly or deliberately, to the great run of cases.

4.5 Fallacies of Presumption

Some mistakes in everyday reasoning are the consequence of an *unjustified assumption*, often suggested by the way in which the argument is formulated. That suggestion may be deliberate, or the assumption may be only an oversight. In either case, the upshot is that the reader, the listener, and even the author of the passage may be led to assume the truth of some unproved and unwarranted proposition. When such dubious propositions, buried in the argument, are crucial for the support of the conclusion, the argument is bad and can be very misleading. Arguments that depend on such unwarranted leaps are called **fallacies of presumption.**

In fallacious arguments of this kind the premises may indeed be relevant to the conclusion drawn, but that relevance is likely to flow from the tacit supposition of what has not been given support and may even be unsupportable. The presumption often goes unnoticed. To expose such a fallacy it is therefore usually sufficient to call attention to the smuggled assumption, or supposition, and to its doubtfulness or its falsity. Three common fallacies are included in this category.

P1. ACCIDENT

Circumstances alter cases. A generalization that is true by and large may not apply in a given case (or to some subcategory of cases) for good reasons. The reasons the generalization does not apply in those cases have to do with the special circumstances, also called the "accidental" circumstances, of that case or those cases. If these accidental circumstances are ignored, and we assume that the generalization applies universally, we commit the **fallacy of accident.**

In the preceding section we explained the *fallacy of converse accident*, or *hasty generalization*, the mistake of moving carelessly or too quickly *to* a generalization that the evidence does not support. *Accident* is the fallacy that arises when we move carelessly or unjustifiably *from* a generalization to some particulars that it does not in fact cover.

Experience teaches us that even generalizations that are widely applicable and very useful are likely to have exceptions for which we must be on guard. For example, there is a general principle in law that hearsay evidence—statements made by a third party outside court—may not be accepted as evidence in court; this is the "hearsay rule," and it is a good rule. But when the person whose oral communications are reported is dead, or when the party reporting the hearsay in court does so in conflict with his own best interest, that rule may not apply. Indeed, there is hardly any rule or general principle that does not have plausible exceptions, and we are likely to argue fallaciously if we reason on the supposition that some rule applies universally.

P2. COMPLEX QUESTION

One of the most common fallacies of presumption is asking a question in such a way as to presuppose the truth of some conclusion that is buried in the question. The question itself is likely to be rhetorical, with no answer actually being sought. But putting the question seriously, thereby introducing its presupposition surreptitiously, often achieves the questioner's purpose—fallaciously.

Thus an essayist recently asked:

> With all of the hysteria, all of the fear, all of the phony science, could it be that man-made global warming is the greatest hoax ever perpetrated on the American people?[29]

Such a statement assumes that much of the evidence supporting global warming is unreliable or "phony." Or a homeowner might ask, regarding a proposed increase in the property tax, "How can you expect the majority of the voters, who rent but don't own property and don't have to pay the tax, to care if the tax burden of others is made even more unfair?"—assuming both that the burden of the proposed tax is unfair and that those who rent rather than own their own homes are not affected by tax increases on property. Because assumptions like these are not asserted openly, the questioners evade the need to defend them forthrightly.

The **complex question** is often a deceitful device. The speaker may pose some question, then answer it or strongly suggest the answer with the truth of the premise that had been buried in the question simply assumed. A letter writer asks, "If America's booming economy depends on people's using consumer credit beyond their means, thus creating poverty, do we really have a healthy economy?"[30] But the role and the results of consumer credit remain to be addressed.

One critic of research in genetics hides his assumptions in this question: "What are the consequences of reducing the world's gene pool to patented intellectual property, controlled by a handful of life-science corporations?"[31] The "consequences" asked about are never actually discussed; they are only a device with which the reader may be frightened by the assumptions of the question—that the world's gene pool is soon likely to be reduced to patented intellectual property, and that a handful of corporations will soon control that gene pool. Establishing the plausibility of such threats requires much more than asking questions designed to presuppose them.

The appearance of a question in an editorial or headline often has the purpose of suggesting the truth of the unstated assumptions on which it is built: "Judge Took Bribe?" This technique is a common mark of what is called "yellow journalism." And in debate, whenever a question is accompanied by the aggressive demand that it be answered "yes or no," there is reason to suspect that the question is "loaded"—that it is unfairly complex.

> Does the distinguished senator believe that the American public is really so naïve that they will endorse just any stopgap measure?

This "question,"of course, cannot be answered "Yes." It conceals several unchallenged assumptions: that what is proposed is a "stopgap" measure, that it is inadequate, and that the American public would reject it.

The mistake that underlies the fallacy of complex question also underlies a common problem in parliamentary procedure. Deliberative bodies sometimes confront a motion that, although not intended deceptively, is covertly complex. In such circumstances there is a need, before discussion, to simplify the issues confronting the body. This accounts for the privileged position, in parliamentary procedure governed by *Robert's Rules of Order* or similar manuals, of the motion to *divide the question*. For example, a motion that the body "postpone for one year" action on some controversial matter may wisely be divided into the questions of whether to postpone action, and *if* that is done, then to determine the length of the postponement. Some members may support the postponement itself yet find the one-year period intolerably long; if the opportunity to divide the question were not given priority, the body might be maneuvered into taking action on a motion that, because of its complexity, cannot be decided in a way that captures the true will of the body. A presiding officer, having the duty to promote a fully rational debate, may solicit the motion to divide the question before beginning the substantive discussion.

Egregious examples of the fallacy of the complex question arise in dialogue or cross-examination in which one party poses a question that is complex, a second party answers the question, and the first party then draws a fallacious inference for which that answer was the ground. For example:

Lawyer: The figures seem to indicate that your sales increased as a result of these misleading advertisements. Is that correct?

Witness: They did not!

Lawyer: But you do admit, then, that your advertising was misleading. How long have you been engaging in practices like these?

When a question is complex, and all of its presuppositions are to be denied, they must be denied individually. The denial of only one presupposition may lead to the assumption of the truth of the other. In law, this has been called "the negative pregnant." Here is an illustration from a notorious murder trial:

Q: Lizzie, did you not take an axe and whack your mother forty times, and then whack your father forty-one times when faced with the prospect of cold mutton stew?

A: Not true. We were to eat brussel sprouts fondue that day.

P3. BEGGING THE QUESTION *(PETITIO PRINCIPII)*

The fallacy called **begging the question** is widely misunderstood, partly because its name is misleading. It is in fact the mistake of assuming the truth of what one seeks to prove. The "question" in a formal debate is the issue that is in dispute; to "beg" the question is to ask, or to suppose, that the very matter in controversy be conceded. This is an argument with no merit at all, of course, and one who makes such an assumption commits a gross fallacy.

The Latin name of the fallacy, for which "begging the question" is the translation, is *petitio principii*, so each instance of it is called a *petitio*. One might think the fallacy would be so obvious that no one would ever commit it, but that is not the case. The logical mistake arises because it is obscured, even from its author, by the language used. Logician Richard Whately used this classic example of a deceptive *petitio*:

> To allow every man unbounded freedom of speech must always be, on the whole, advantageous to the state; for it is highly conducive to the interests of the community that each individual should enjoy a liberty, perfectly unlimited, of expressing his sentiments.[32]

This statement says only that freedom of speech is a good thing because it is a good thing—which is not much of an argument.

In the effort to establish the desired conclusion, an author may cast about, searching for premises that will do the trick. Of course, the conclusion itself, reformulated in other words, will do the trick very nicely. Another illustration, equally fallacious, is found in this claim by a sixteenth-century Chinese philosopher:

> There is no such thing as knowledge which cannot be carried into practice, for such knowledge is really no knowledge at all.[33]

This fallacy, like the fallacy of missing the point, is often a *mistake* that is not recognized by the author of the passage. The presumption that is the heart of the fallacy is buried in the verbiage of the premises, sometimes obscured by confusing or unrecognized synonyms. The arguments are **circular**—every *petitio* is a circular argument—but the circle that has been constructed may be large and confusing, and thus the logical mistake goes unseen.

It would be wrong to suppose that only silly authors make this mistake. Even powerful minds are on occasion snared by this fallacy as is illustrated by a highly controversial issue in the history of philosophy. Logicians have long sought to establish the reliability of inductive procedures by establishing the truth of what is called the *principle of induction*. This is the principle that the laws of nature will operate tomorrow as they operate today, that in basic ways nature is essentially uniform, and that therefore we may rely on past experience to guide our conduct in the future. "That the future will be essentially like the past" is the claim at issue, but this claim, never doubted in ordinary life, turns out to be very difficult to prove. Some thinkers have claimed that they could prove it by showing that, when we have in the past relied on the inductive principle, we have always found that this method has helped us to achieve our objectives. They ask, "Why conclude that the future will be like the past?" and answer, "Because it always has been like the past."

As David Hume pointed out, however, this common argument is a *petitio*—it begs the question. The point at issue is whether nature *will continue* to behave regularly. That it *has* done so in the past cannot serve as proof that it *will* do so in the future, unless one assumes the very principle that is here in question: that the future will be like the past. And so Hume, granting that in the past the future has been like the past, asked the telling question with which philosophers still tussle: How can we know that future futures will be like past futures? They *may* be so, of course, but we cannot *assume* that they will be for the sake of *proving* that they will.[34]

Because the name of this fallacy is widely misunderstood, that name is sometimes wrongly used to refer to a linguistic device that is not a fallacy, not even an argument of any kind, but merely a provocative observation. A claim "begs" the question (in this sense) when it *raises* some question or opens the door to some controversy. Thus a magazine headline may mistakenly read, "The President's decision to invade Iraq begs the question: What are the limits of the President's war-making authority?" This use of the phrase is simply a linguistic mistake. To "beg the question" is not to raise the issue, but to *assume* the truth of the conclusion sought.

Circular arguments are certainly fallacious, but the premises are not irrelevant to the conclusions drawn. They are relevant; indeed, they prove the conclusion, but they do so trivially—they end where they began. A *petitio principii* is always technically valid, but always worthless.

OVERVIEW

Fallacies of Presumption

P1. Accident

An informal fallacy in which a generalization is applied to individual cases that it does not govern.

P2. Complex Question

An informal fallacy in which a question is asked in such a way as to presuppose the truth of some proposition buried in the question.

P3. Begging the Question (*petitio principii*)

An informal fallacy in which the conclusion of an argument is stated or assumed in one of the premises.

EXERCISES

Identify and explain any fallacies of defective induction or of presumption in the following passages.

1. My generation was taught about the dangers of social diseases, how they were contracted, and the value of abstinence. Our schools did not teach us about contraception. They did not pass out condoms, as many of today's schools do. And not one of the girls in any of my classes, not even in college, became pregnant out of wedlock. It wasn't until people began teaching the children about contraceptives that our problems with pregnancy began.

   —Frank Webster, "No Sex Education, No Sex," *Insight*, 17 November 1997

2. A national mailing soliciting funds, by People for the Ethical Treatment of Animals (PETA), included a survey in which questions were to be answered "yes" or "no." Two of the questions asked were these:

   "Do you realize that the vast majority of painful animal experimentation has no relation at all to human survival or the elimination of disease?"

   "Are you aware that product testing on animals does *not* keep unsafe products off the market?"

3. If you want a life full of sexual pleasures, don't graduate from college. A study to be published next month in *American Demographics* magazine shows that people with the most education have the least amount of sex.

   —*The Chronicle of Higher Education*, 23 January 1998

4. There is no surprise in discovering that acupuncture can relieve pain and nausea. It will probably also be found to work on anxiety, insomnia, and itching, because these are all conditions in which placebos work. Acupuncture works by suggestion, a mechanism whose effects on humans are well known.

   The danger in using such placebo methods is that they will be applied by people inadequately trained in medicine in cases where essential preliminary work has not been done and where a correct diagnosis has not been established.

   —Fred Levit, M.D., "Acupuncture is Alchemy, Not Medicine," *The New York Times*, 12 November 1997

5. In a motion picture featuring the famous French comedian Sacha Guitry, three thieves are arguing over division of seven pearls worth a king's ransom. One of them hands two to the man on his right, then two to the man on his left. "I," he says, "will keep three." The man on his right says, "How come you keep three?" "Because I am the leader." "Oh. But how come you are the leader?" "Because I have more pearls."

6. ". . . I've always reckoned that looking at the new moon over your left shoulder is one of the carelessest and foolishest things a body can do. Old Hank Bunker done it once, and bragged about it; and in less than two years he got drunk and fell off of the shot tower, and spread himself out so that he was just a kind of a layer, as you may say; and they slid him edgeways between two barn doors for a coffin, and buried him so, so they say, but I didn't see it. Pap told me. But anyway it all come of looking at the moon that way, like a fool."

—Mark Twain, *The Adventures of Huckleberry Finn,* 1885

7. Former Senator Robert Packwood of Oregon became so angry at the state's leading newspaper, the Portland *Oregonian*, that in response to a request from that paper for a quote, he offered this: "Since I quit talking to the *Oregonian*, my business has prospered beyond all measure. I assume that my business has prospered because I don't talk to the Oregonian. Therefore I will continue that policy. Thanks."

—*The New York Times*, 7 February 1999

8. Mr. Farrakhan, the Black Muslim leader, citing the example of Israel, said black Americans should also be able to form a country of their own on the African continent, and said he plans to ask African leaders to "carve out a territory for all people in the diaspora." He said black Americans should also be granted dual citizenship by all African countries. "We want dual citizenship," he said, "and because we don't know where we came from, we want dual citizenship everywhere."

—Kenneth Noble, "U.S. Blacks and Africans Meet to Forge Stronger Ties," *The New York Times*, 27 May 1993

9. The French claim to be a nation of rebels. In fact their heyday of revolution is over. Twenty-first century France rebels against change, not for it. What typically happens is that a French government

decides to do something radical like, say, enable companies to fire service-sector workers who assault their customers. The unions see this as the first step on the road to slavery and call a national strike. After a week of posturing the government backs down and waiters and sales clerks go back to insulting customers just as they have done since time immemorial.

—S. Clarke, "No Sex, Please, We're French," *The New York Times*, 23 March 2007

10. Hiroyuki Suzuki was formerly a member of the Sakaume gumi, an independent crime family in Japan known for its role in gambling. Mr. Suzuki's wife Mariko broke her kneecap, and when Mariko went to church the next Sunday, the minister put his hands on her broken knee and pronounced it healed. She walked away from church that day. Mr. Suzuki regarded her religion as a silly waste of time—but he was fascinated by the recovery of her knee. "In gambling," he said, "you use dice. Dice are made from bone. If God could heal her bone, I figured he could probably assist my dice and make me the best dice thrower in all of Japan." Mr. Suzuki's gambling skills did improve, enabling him to pay off his debts. He now says his allegiance is to Jesus.

—Stephanie Strom, "He Watched over His Rackets," *The New York Times*, 22 June 1999

4.6 Fallacies of Ambiguity

The meaning of words or phrases may shift as a result of inattention, or may be deliberately manipulated within the course of an argument. A term may have one sense in a premise but quite a different sense in the conclusion. When the inference drawn depends on such changes it is, of course, fallacious. Mistakes of this kind are called **fallacies of ambiguity** or sometimes "sophisms." The deliberate use of such devices is usually crude and readily detected—but at times the ambiguity may be obscure, the error accidental, the fallacy subtle. Five varieties are distinguished here.

A1. EQUIVOCATION

Most words have more than one literal meaning, and most of the time we have no difficulty keeping those meanings separate by noting the context and using our good sense when reading and listening. Yet when we confuse the several meanings of a word or phrase—accidentally or deliberately—we are using the word equivocally. If we do that in the context of an argument, we commit the **fallacy of equivocation.**

Sometimes the equivocation is obvious and absurd and is used in a joking line or passage. Lewis Carroll's account of the adventures of Alice in *Through the Looking Glass* is replete with clever and amusing equivocations. One of them goes like this:

> "Who did you pass on the road?" the King went on, holding his hand out to the messenger for some hay.
>
> "Nobody," said the messenger.
>
> "Quite right," said the King; "this young lady saw him too. So of course Nobody walks slower than you."

The equivocation in this passage is in fact rather subtle. As it is first used here, the word "nobody" simply means "no person." But reference is then made using a pronoun ("him"), as though that word ("nobody") had *named* a person. And when subsequently the same word is capitalized and plainly used as a name ("Nobody"), it putatively names a person having a characteristic (not being passed on the road) derived from the first use of the word. Equivocation is sometimes the tool of wit—and Lewis Carroll was a very witty logician.*

Equivocal arguments are always fallacious, but they are not always silly or comic, as in the example discussed in the following excerpt:

> There is an ambiguity in the phrase "have faith in" that helps to make faith look respectable. When a man says that he has faith in the president he is assuming that it is obvious and known to everybody that there is a president, that the president exists, and he is asserting his confidence that the president will do good work on the whole. But, if a man says he has faith in telepathy, he does not mean that he is confident that telepathy will do good work on the whole, but that he believes that telepathy really occurs sometimes, that telepathy exists. Thus the phrase "to have faith in x" sometimes means to be confident that good work will be done by x, who is assumed or known to exist, but at other times means to believe that x exists. Which does it mean in the phrase "have faith in God"? It means ambiguously both; and the self-evidence of what it means in the one sense recommends what it means in the other sense. If there is a perfectly powerful and good god it is self-evidently reasonable to believe that he will do good. In this sense "have faith in God" is a reasonable exhortation. But it insinuates the other sense, namely "believe that

---

*This passage very probably inspired David Powers, who formally changed his name to Absolutely Nobody and ran as an independent candidate for lieutenant governor of the state of Oregon. His campaign slogan was "Hi, I'm Absolutely Nobody. Vote for me." In the general election of 1992, he drew 7 percent of the vote.

there is a perfectly powerful and good god, no matter what the evidence." Thus the reasonableness of trusting God if he exists is used to make it seem also reasonable to believe that he exists.[35]

One kind of equivocation deserves special mention. This is the mistake that arises from the misuse of "relative" terms, which have different meanings in different contexts. For example, the word "tall" is a relative word; a tall man and a tall building are in quite different categories. A tall man is one who is taller than most men, a tall building is one that is taller than most buildings. Certain forms of argument that are valid for nonrelative terms break down when relative terms are substituted for them. The argument "an elephant is an animal; therefore a gray elephant is a gray animal" is perfectly valid. The word "gray" is a nonrelative term. But the argument "an elephant is an animal; therefore a small elephant is a small animal" is ridiculous. The point here is that "small" is a relative term: A small elephant is a very large animal. The fallacy is one of equivocation with regard to the relative term "small." Not all equivocation on relative terms is so obvious, however. The word "good" is a relative term and is frequently equivocated on when it is argued, for example, that so-and-so is a good general and would therefore be a good president, or that someone is a good scholar and is therefore likely to be a good teacher.

A2. AMPHIBOLY

The **fallacy of amphiboly** occurs when one is arguing from premises whose formulations are ambiguous because of their grammatical construction. The word "amphiboly" is derived from the Greek, its meaning in essence being "two in a lump," or the "doubleness" of a lump. A statement is amphibolous when its meaning is indeterminate because of the loose or awkward way in which its words are combined. An amphibolous statement may be true in one interpretation and false in another. When it is stated as premise with the interpretation that makes it true, and a conclusion is drawn from it on the interpretation that makes it false, then the fallacy of amphiboly has been committed.

In guiding electoral politics, amphiboly can mislead as well as confuse. During the 1990s, while he sat in the U.S. House of Representatives as a Democrat from California, Tony Coelho is reported to have said: "Women prefer Democrats to men." Amphibolous statements make dangerous premises—but they are seldom encountered in serious discourse.

What grammarians call "dangling" participles and phrases often present amphiboly of a striking sort, as in "The farmer blew out his brains after taking affectionate farewell of his family with a shotgun." And tidbits in the *New Yorker* make acid fun of writers and editors who overlook careless amphiboly:

> Dr. Salick donated, along with his wife, Gloria, $4.5 million to Queens College for the center.
>
> *Gloria is tax-deductible.*[36]

A3. ACCENT

We have seen that shifting the meaning of some term in an argument may result in a fallacy of ambiguity. Most commonly that shift is an equivocation, as noted earlier. Sometimes, however, the shift is the result of a change in *emphasis* on a single word or phrase, whose meaning does not change. When the premise of an argument relies on one possible emphasis, but a conclusion drawn from it relies on the meaning of the same words emphasized differently, the **fallacy of accent** has been committed.

This fallacy can be very serious, and in argument it can be very damaging. But its name seems innocuous. This is due, in part, to the origin of the name in the classification of fallacies first presented by Aristotle.[37] It happens that in the Greek language of Aristotle's day, some words spelled identically had different meanings depending on the way in which they were pronounced, or accented. And those different meanings could result in a deceptive argument, appropriately called a fallacy of accent. In English today there are not very many cases in which changing the accent in a word changes the meaning of the word. Three of the most common are *in*crease and in*crease*, *in*sult and in*sult*, *re*cord and re*cord*. These pairs of words accented differently mean different parts of speech—one member of each pair is a noun, the other a verb—and thus it is unlikely that fallacious argument would now arise from those differently accented words.

Over the centuries, however, while the Aristotelian name has been retained, it has come to be applied to a much wider category, which includes the misleading uses of *emphasis* in various forms and the use of meanings deliberately taken out of context. We are greatly stretching the name "accent" that Aristotle used. If we could overcome the weight of tradition, we might wisely rename the argument that misleads in this way "the fallacy of emphasis."

Consider, as an illustration, the different meanings that can be given to the statement

We should not speak ill of our friends.

When the sentence is read without any special stress on one of its words, this injunction is surely one with which we would all agree. But, if the sentence is read with stress on the word "friends," we might understand it to suggest that speaking ill of those who are *not* our friends is not precluded. Such an injunction is no longer acceptable as a moral rule. Or suppose we stress the word "speak" in this sentence. Then it might suggest that whereas nasty speech is to be avoided, one may *work* ill even on one's friends—a very troubling conclusion. If the word "we" is emphasized, the suggestion arises that the injunction applies to *us* but not to *others*. And so on. The various arguments that emerge are plainly the outcome of the deliberate manipulation of emphasis; the sentence can be used to achieve assorted fallacious ambiguities. How is the sentence to be rightly understood? That depends on its context, of course. Often, a phrase or a passage can be understood correctly only when its context is known, because that context makes clear the sense in which the words are intended.

Therefore the fallacy of accent may be construed broadly to include the distortion produced by pulling a quoted passage out of its context, putting it in another context, and there drawing a conclusion that could never have been drawn in the original context. Quoting out of context is sometimes done with deliberate craftiness. In the presidential election campaign of 1996 the Democratic vice-presidential candidate, Al Gore, was quoted by a Republican press aide as having said that "there is no proven link between smoking and lung cancer." Those were indeed Mr. Gore's exact words, uttered during a television interview in 1992. But they were only part of a sentence. In that interview, Mr. Gore's full statement was that some tobacco company scientists "*will claim with a straight face that* there is no proven link between smoking and lung cancer. . . . But the weight of the evidence accepted by the overwhelming preponderance of scientists is, yes, smoking does cause lung cancer."[38]

The omission of the words "will claim with a straight face" and of Gore's express conviction that cancer is caused by smoking, unfairly reversed the sense of the passage from which the quotation was pulled. The argument suggested by the abbreviated quotation, having the apparent conclusion that Mr. Gore seriously doubts the causal link between smoking and cancer, is an egregious example of the fallacy of accent.

Deliberate distortion of this kind is not rare. A biography by Thomas DiLorenzo, purporting to show that Abraham Lincoln was not the advocate of human equality he is widely thought to have been, quotes words of Lincoln that appear to mock the principle that "all men are created equal." Lincoln is quoted thus: "I am sorry to say that I have never seen two men of whom it is true. But I must admit I never saw the Siamese Twins, and therefore will not dogmatically say that no man ever saw a proof of this sage aphorism." DiLorenzo then remarks that such mockery contrasts sharply with the "seductive words of the Gettysburg Address, eleven years later, in which he purported to rededicate the nation to the notion that all men are created equal."[39] But DiLorenzo fails to report that those quoted words were in fact Lincoln's account of the view of an unnamed Virginia clergyman, a view he goes on immediately to reject, saying that it "sounds strangely in republican America." DiLorenzo's failure to report the context of the words quoted renders his argument fallacious and disreputable.

Advertising often relies on the same device. A theater critic who says of a new play that it is far from the funniest appearing on Broadway this year may find herself quoted in an ad for the play: "Funniest appearing on Broadway this year!" To avoid such distortions, and the fallacies of accent that are built on them, the responsible writer must be scrupulously accurate in quotation, always indicating whether italics were in the original, indicating (with dots) whether passages have been omitted, and so on.

Physical manipulation of print or pictures is commonly used to mislead deliberately through accent. Sensational words appear in large letters in the headlines of newspaper reports, deliberately suggesting mistaken conclusions to those who glance hastily at them. Later in the report the headline is likely to be qualified by other words in much smaller letters. To avoid being tricked, by news reports or in contracts, one is well advised to give careful attention to "the small print." In political propaganda the misleading choice of a sensational heading or the use of a clipped photograph, in what purports to be a factual report, will use accent shrewdly so as to encourage the drawing of conclusions known by the propagandist to be false. An account that may not be an outright lie may yet distort by accent in ways that are deliberately manipulative or dishonest.

Such practices are hardly rare in advertising. A remarkably low price often appears in very large letters, followed by "and up" in tiny print. Wonderful bargains in airplane fares are followed by an asterisk, with a distant footnote explaining that the price is available only three months in advance for flights on Thursdays following a full moon, or that there may be other "applicable restrictions." Costly items with well-known brand names are advertised at very low prices, with a small note elsewhere in the ad that "prices listed are for limited quantities in stock." Readers are drawn into the store but are likely to be unable to make the purchase at the advertised price. Accented passages, by themselves, are not strictly fallacies; they become embedded in fallacies when one interpretation of a phrase, flowing from its accent, is relied on to suggest a conclusion (for example, that the plane ticket or brand item can be purchased at the listed price) that is very doubtful when account is taken of the misleading accent.

Even the literal truth can be used, by manipulating its placement, so to deceive with accent. Disgusted with his first mate, who was repeatedly inebriated while on duty, the captain of a ship noted in the ship's log, almost every day, "The mate was drunk today." The angry mate took his revenge. Keeping the log himself on a day when the captain was ill, the mate recorded, "The captain was sober today."

A4. COMPOSITION

The term **fallacy of composition** is applied to both of two closely related types of mistaken argument. The first may be described as *reasoning fallaciously from the attributes of the parts of a whole to the attributes of the whole itself*. A flagrant example is to argue that, because every part of a certain machine is light in weight, the machine "as a whole" is light in weight. The error here is manifest when we recognize that a very heavy machine may consist of a very large number of lightweight parts. Not all examples of fallacious composition are so obvious, however. Some are misleading. One may hear it seriously argued that, because each scene of a certain play is a model of artistic perfection, the play as a whole is artistically perfect. This is as much a fallacy of composition as to argue that, because every ship is ready for battle, the whole fleet must be ready for battle.

The other type of composition fallacy is strictly parallel to that just described. Here, the fallacy is *reasoning from attributes of the individual elements or members of a collection to attributes of the collection or totality of those elements*. For example, it would be fallacious to argue that because a bus uses more gasoline than an automobile, all buses use more gasoline than all automobiles. This version of the fallacy of composition turns on a confusion between the "distributive" and the "collective" use of general terms. Thus, although college students may enroll in no more than six different classes each semester, it is also true that college students enroll in hundreds of different classes each semester. This verbal conflict is easily resolved. It may be true of college students, distributively, that each may enroll in no more than six classes each semester. We call this a *distributive* use of the term "college students," because we are speaking of college students taken *singly*. But it is true of college students, taken collectively, that they enroll in hundreds of different classes each semester. This is a *collective* use of the term "college students," in that we are speaking of college students all together, as a totality. Thus, buses, distributively, use more gasoline than automobiles, but collectively, automobiles use more gasoline than buses, because there are so many more of them.

This second kind of composition fallacy may be defined as the invalid inference that what may truly be predicated of a term distributively may also be truly predicated of the term collectively. Thus, the atomic bombs dropped during World War II did more damage than did the ordinary bombs dropped—but only distributively. The matter is exactly reversed when the two kinds of bombs are considered collectively, because so many more conventional bombs were dropped than atomic ones. Ignoring this distinction in an argument permits the fallacy of composition.

These two varieties of composition, though parallel, are really distinct because of the difference between a mere collection of elements and a whole constructed out of those elements. Thus, a mere collection of parts is no machine; a mere collection of bricks is neither a house nor a wall. A whole, such as a machine, a house, or a wall, has its parts organized or arranged in certain definite ways. And because organized wholes and mere collections are distinct, so are the two versions of the composition fallacy, one proceeding invalidly to wholes from their parts, the other proceeding invalidly to collections from their members or elements.

A5. DIVISION

The **fallacy of division** is simply the reverse of the fallacy of composition. In it the same confusion is present, but the inference proceeds in the opposite direction. As in the case of composition, two varieties of the fallacy of division may be distinguished. The first kind of division consists of *arguing fallaciously that what is true of a whole must also be true of its parts*. To argue that, because a certain corporation is very important and Mr. Doe is an official of that corporation, therefore Mr. Doe is very important, is to commit the fallacy of division. This first variety of the division fallacy is committed in any such argument, as in moving from the premise that a certain machine is heavy, or complicated, or valuable, to the conclusion that this or any other part of the machine must be heavy, or complicated, or valuable. To argue that a student must have a large room because the room is located in a large dormitory would be still another instance of the first kind of fallacy of division.

The second type of division fallacy is committed *when one argues from the attributes of a collection of elements to the attributes of the elements themselves*. To argue that, because university students study medicine, law, engineering, dentistry, and architecture, therefore each, or even any, university student studies medicine, law, engineering, dentistry, and architecture is to commit the second kind of division fallacy. It is true that university students, collectively, study all these various subjects, but it is false that university students, distributively, do so. Instances of this fallacy of division often look like valid arguments, for what is true of a class distributively is certainly true of each and every member. Thus the argument

Dogs are carnivorous.

Afghan hounds are dogs.

Therefore Afghan hounds are carnivorous.

is perfectly valid. Closely resembling this argument is another,

Dogs are frequently encountered in the streets.

Afghan hounds are dogs.

Therefore Afghan hounds are frequently encountered in the streets.

which is invalid, committing the fallacy of division. Some instances of division are obviously jokes, as when the classical example of valid argumentation,

Humans are mortal.

Socrates is a human.

Therefore Socrates is mortal.

is parodied by the fallacious

American Indians are disappearing.

That man is an American Indian.

Therefore that man is disappearing.

The old riddle, "Why do white sheep eat more than black ones?" turns on the confusion involved in the fallacy of division for the answer: "Because there are more of them," treats collectively what seemed to be referred to distributively in the question.

The fallacy of division, which springs from a kind of ambiguity, resembles the fallacy of accident (discussed in Section 4.5), which springs from unwarranted presumption. Likewise, the fallacy of composition, also flowing from ambiguity, resembles the hasty generalization we call "converse accident." But these likenesses are superficial. An explanation of the differences between the two pairs of fallacies will be helpful in grasping the errors committed in all four.

If we infer, from looking at one or two parts of a large machine, that because they happen to be well designed, every one of the machine's many parts is well designed, we commit the fallacy of converse accident or hasty generalization, for what is true about one or two parts may not be true of all. If we examine every single part and find that each is carefully made, and from that finding infer that the entire machine is carefully made, we also reason fallaciously, because however carefully the parts were produced, they may have been *assembled* awkwardly or carelessly. Here the fallacy is one of composition. In converse accident, one argues that some atypical members of a class have a specified attribute, and therefore that all members of the class, distributively, have that attribute; in composition, one argues that, because each and every member of the class has that attribute, the class *itself* (collectively) has that attribute. The difference is great. In converse accident, all predications are distributive, whereas in the composition fallacy, the mistaken inference is from distributive to collective predication.

Similarly, division and accident are two distinct fallacies; their superficial resemblance hides the same kind of underlying difference. In division, we argue (mistakenly) that, because the class itself has a given attribute, each of its members also has it. Thus, it is the fallacy of division to conclude that, because an army as a whole is nearly invincible, each of its units is nearly invincible. In accident, we argue (also mistakenly) that, because some rule applies in general, there are no special circumstances in which it might not apply. Thus, we commit the fallacy of accident when we insist that a person should be fined for ignoring a "No Swimming" sign when jumping into the water to rescue someone from drowning.

OVERVIEW

Fallacies of Ambiguity

A1. Equivocation

An informal fallacy in which two or more meanings of the same word or phrase have been confused.

A2. Amphiboly

An informal fallacy arising from the loose, awkward, or mistaken way in which words are combined, leading to alternative possible meanings of a statement.

A3. Accent

An informal fallacy committed when a term or phrase has a meaning in the conclusion of an argument different from its meaning in one of the premises, the difference arising chiefly from a change in emphasis given to the words used.

A4. Composition

An informal fallacy in which an inference is mistakenly drawn from the attributes of the parts of a whole to the attributes of the whole itself.

A5. Division

An informal fallacy in which a mistaken inference is drawn from the attributes of a whole to the attributes of the parts of the whole.

Unlike accident and converse accident, composition and division are fallacies of *ambiguity*, resulting from the multiple meanings of terms. Wherever the words or phrases used may mean one thing in one part of the argument and another thing in another part, and those different meanings are deliberately or accidentally confounded, we can expect the argument to be fallacious.

EXERCISES

A. Identify and explain the fallacies of ambiguity that appear in the following passages.

1. . . . the universe is spherical in form . . . because all the constituent parts of the universe, that is the sun, moon, and the planets, appear in this form.

—Nicolaus Copernicus, *The New Idea of the Universe*, 1514

2. Robert Toombs is reputed to have said, just before the Civil War, "We could lick those Yankees with cornstalks." When he was asked after the war what had gone wrong, he is reputed to have said, "It's very simple. Those damn Yankees refused to fight with cornstalks."

—E. J. Kahn, Jr., "Profiles (Georgia),"
The New Yorker, 13 February 1978

3. To press forward with a properly ordered wage structure in each industry is the first condition for curbing competitive bargaining; but there is no reason why the process should stop there. What is good for each industry can hardly be bad for the economy as a whole.

—Edmond Kelly, *Twentieth Century Socialism*, 1910

4. No man will take counsel, but every man will take money: therefore money is better than counsel.

—Jonathan Swift

5. I've looked everywhere in this area for an instruction book on how to play the concertina without success. (Mrs. F. M., Myrtle Beach, S.C., *Charlotte Observer*)

You need no instructions. Just plunge ahead boldly.

—*The New Yorker*, 21 February 1977

6. . . . each person's happiness is a good to that person, and the general happiness, therefore, a good to the aggregate of all persons.

—John Stuart Mill, *Utilitarianism*, 1861

7. If the man who "turnips!" cries
   Cry not when his father dies,
   'Tis a proof that he had rather
   Have a turnip than his father.

—Hester L. Piozzi, *Anecdotes of Samuel Johnson*, 1932

8. Fallaci wrote her: "You are a bad journalist because you are a bad woman."

—Elizabeth Peer, "The Fallaci Papers," *Newsweek*, 1 December 1980

9. A Worm-eating Warbler was discovered by Hazel Miller in Concord, while walking along the branch of a tree, singing, and in good view. (*New Hampshire Audubon Quarterly*)

   That's our Hazel—surefooted, happy, and with just a touch of the exhibitionist.

—*The New Yorker*, 2 July 1979

10. The basis of logic is the syllogism, consisting of a major and a minor premise and a conclusion—thus:

    Major Premise: Sixty men can do a piece of work sixty times as quickly as one man;

    Minor Premise: One man can dig a post-hole in sixty seconds; therefore—*Conclusion:* Sixty men can dig a post-hole in one second.

    This may be called the syllogism arithmetical, in which, by combining logic and mathematics, we obtain a double certainty and are twice blessed.

—Ambrose Bierce, *The Devil's Dictionary*, 1911

B. Each of the following passages may be plausibly criticized by some who conclude that it contains a fallacy, but each may be defended by some who deny that the argument is fallacious. Discuss the merits of the argument in each passage, and explain why you conclude that it does (or does not) contain a fallacy.

1. Seeing that eye and hand and foot and every one of our members has some obvious function, must we not believe that in like manner a human being has a function over and above these particular functions?

—Aristotle, *Nicomachean Ethics*

2. All phenomena in the universe are saturated with moral values. And, therefore, we can come to assert that the universe for the Chinese is a moral universe.

—T. H. Fang, *The Chinese View of Life*, 1956

3. The only proof capable of being given that an object is visible, is that people actually see it. The only proof that a sound is audible, is that people hear it: and so of the other sources of our experience. In like manner, I apprehend, the sole evidence it is possible to produce that anything is desirable, is that people actually desire it.

—John Stuart Mill, *Utilitarianism,* 1863

4. Thomas Carlyle said of Walt Whitman that he thinks he is a big poet because he comes from a big country.

—Alfred Kazin, "The Haunted Chamber," *The New Republic*, 23 June 1986

5. Mr. Levy boasts many excellent *bona fides* for the job [of Chancellor of the New York City Public Schools]. But there is one bothersome fact: His two children attend an elite private school on Manhattan's Upper East Side. Mr. Levy . . . should put his daughter and son in the public schools. I do not begrudge any parent the right to enroll a child in a private school. My wife and I considered several private schools before sending our children to a public school in Manhattan. Mr. Levy is essentially declaring the public schools unfit for his own children.

—Samuel G. Freedman, "Public Leaders, Private Schools," *The New York Times*, 15 April 2000

C. Identify and explain the fallacies of relevance or defective induction, or presumption, or ambiguity as they occur in the following passages. Explain why, in the case of some, it may be plausibly argued that what appears at first to be a fallacy is not when the argument is interpreted correctly.

1. John Angus Smith, approaching an undercover agent, offered to trade his firearm, an automatic, for two ounces of cocaine that he planned to sell at a profit. Upon being apprehended, Smith was charged with "using" a firearm "during and in relation to . . . a drug trafficking crime." Ordinarily conviction under this statute would result in a prison sentence of five years; however, if the firearm, as in this case, is "a machine gun or other automatic weapon" the mandatory sentence is 30 years. Smith was convicted and sentenced to 30 years in prison. The case was appealed to the U.S. Supreme Court.

   Justice Antonin Scalia argued that, although Smith certainly did intend to trade his gun for drugs, that was not the sense of "using" intended by the statute. "In the search for statutory meaning we give nontechnical terms their ordinary meanings . . . to speak of 'using a firearm' is to speak of using it for its distinctive purpose, as a weapon." If asked whether you use a cane, he pointed out, the question asks whether you walk with a cane, not whether you display "your grandfather's silver-handled walking stick in the hall."

Justice Sandra Day O'Connor retorted that we may do more than walk with a cane. "The most infamous use of a cane in American history had nothing to do with walking at all—the caning (in 1856) of Senator Charles Sumner in the United States Senate."

Justice Scalia rejoined that the majority of the Court "does not appear to grasp the distinction between how a word can be used and how it is ordinarily used. . . . I think it perfectly obvious, for example, that the falsity requirement for a perjury conviction would not be satisfied if a witness answered 'No' to a prosecutor's enquiry whether he had ever 'used a firearm' even though he had once sold his grandfather's Enfield rifle to a collector."

Justice O'Connor prevailed; Smith's conviction was affirmed.

—*John Angus Smith v. United States*, 508 U.S. 223, 1 June 1993

2. *Time Magazine* book critic Lev Grossman was "quite taken aback" in the summer of 2006 when he saw a full-page newspaper advertisement for Charles Frazier's novel, *Thirteen Moons*, that included a one-word quotation attributed to *Time*. Grossman had written, "Frazier works on an epic scale, but his genius is in the detail." The one-word quotation by which he was struck was "Genius."

—Henry Alford, "Genius!," *The New York Times Review of Books*, 29 April 2007

3. In the Miss Universe Contest of 1994, Miss Alabama was asked: If you could live forever, would you? And why? She answered:

> I would not live forever, because we should not live forever, because if we were supposed to live forever, then we would live forever, but we cannot live forever, which is why I would not live forever.

4. Order is indispensable to justice because justice can be achieved only by means of a social and legal order.

—Ernest Van Den Haag, *Punishing Criminals*, 1975

5. The Inquisition must have been justified and beneficial, if whole peoples invoked and defended it, if men of the loftiest souls founded and created it severally and impartially, and its very adversaries applied it on their own account, pyre answering to pyre.

—Benedetto Croce, *Philosophy of the Practical*, 1935

6. The following advertisement for a great metropolitan newspaper appears very widely in Pennsylvania:

> In Philadelphia nearly everybody reads the *Bulletin*.

7. . . . since it is impossible for an animal or plant to be indefinitely big or small, neither can its parts be such, or the whole will be the same.

—Aristotle, *Physics*

8. For the benefit of those representatives who have not been here before this year, it may be useful to explain that the item before the General Assembly is that hardy perennial called the "Soviet item." It is purely a propaganda proposition, not introduced with a serious purpose of serious action, but solely as a peg on which to hang a number of speeches with a view to getting them into the press of the world. This is considered by some to be very clever politics. Others, among whom the present speaker wishes to be included, consider it an inadequate response to the challenge of the hour.

—Henry Cabot Lodge, speech to the United Nations General Assembly, 30 November 1953

9. The war-mongering character of all this flood of propaganda in the United States is admitted even by the American press. Such provocative and slanderous aims clearly inspired today's speech by the United States Representative, consisting only of impudent slander against the Soviet Union, to answer which would be beneath our dignity. The heroic epic of Stalingrad is impervious to libel. The Soviet people in the battles at Stalingrad saved the world from the fascist plague and that great victory which decided the fate of the world is remembered with recognition and gratitude by all humanity. Only men dead to all shame could try to cast aspersions on the shining memory of the heroes of that battle.

—Anatole M. Baranovsky, speech to the United Nations General Assembly, 30 November 1953

10. Prof. Leon Kass reports a notable response to an assignment he had given students at the University of Chicago. Compose an essay, he asked, about a memorable meal you have eaten. One student wrote as follows:

> I had once eaten lunch with my uncle and my uncle's friend. His friend had once eaten lunch with Albert Einstein. Albert Einstein was once a man of great spirituality. Therefore, by the law of the syllogism, I had once eaten lunch with God.

—Leon Kass, *The Hungry Soul: Eating and the Perfecting of Our Nature* (New York: The Free Press, 1995)

11. Consider genetically engineered fish. Scientists hope that fish that contain new growth hormones will grow bigger and faster than

normal fish. Other scientists are developing fish that could be introduced into cold, northern waters, where they cannot now survive. The intention is to boost fish production for food. The economic benefits may be obvious, but not the risks. Does this make the risks reasonable?

—Edward Bruggemann, "Genetic Engineering Needs Strict Regulation," *The New York Times*, 24 March 1992

12. The multiverse theory actually injects the concept of a transcendent Creator at almost every level of its logical structure. Gods and worlds, creators and creatures, lie embedded in each other, forming an infinite regress in unbounded space.

This *reductio ad absurdum* of the multiverse theory reveals what a very slippery slope it is indeed. Since Copernicus, our view of the universe has enlarged by a factor of a billion billion. The cosmic vista stretches one hundred billion trillion miles in all directions—that's a 1 with 23 zeros. Now we are being urged to accept that even this vast region is just a miniscule fragment of the whole.

—Paul Davies, "A Brief History of the Multiverse," *The New York Times*, 12 April 2003

13. When Copernicus argued that the Ptolemaic astronomy (holding that the celestial bodies all revolved around the earth) should be replaced by a theory holding that the earth (along with all the other planets) revolved around the sun, he was ridiculed by many of the scientists of his day, including one of the greatest astronomers of that time, Clavius, who wrote in 1581:

> Both [Copernicus and Ptolemy] are in agreement with the observed phenomena. But Copernicus's arguments contain a great many principles that are absurd. He assumed, for instance, that the earth is moving with a triple motion . . . [but] according to the philosophers a simple body like the earth can have only a simple motion. . . . Therefore it seems to me that Ptolemy's geocentric doctrine must be preferred to Copernicus's doctrine.

14. All of us cannot be famous, because all of us cannot be well known.

—Jesse Jackson, quoted in *The New Yorker*, 12 March 1984

15. The God that holds you over the pit of hell, much as one holds a spider or some loathsome insect over the fire, abhors you, and is dreadfully provoked; his wrath towards you burns like fire; he looks upon you as worthy of nothing else but to be cast into the fire; you are ten thousand times so abominable in his eyes as the most hateful and venomous serpent is in ours. You have offended him infinitely more than a stubborn rebel did his prince; and yet it is nothing but his hand that holds you from falling into the fire every moment.

—Jonathan Edwards, "The Pit of Hell," 1741

16. Mysticism is one of the great forces of the world's history. For religion is nearly the most important thing in the world, and religion never remains for long altogether untouched by mysticism.

—John Mctaggart, Ellis Mctaggart, "Mysticism," *Philosophical Studies,* 1934

17. If science wishes to argue that we cannot know what was going on in [the gorilla] Binti's head when she acted as she did, science must also acknowledge that it cannot prove that nothing was going on. It is because of our irresolvable ignorance, as much as fellow-feeling, that we should give animals the benefit of doubt and treat them with the respect we accord ourselves.

—Martin Rowe and Mia Macdonald, "Let's Give Animals Respect They Deserve," *The New York Times,* 26 August 1996

18. If we want to know whether a state is brave we must look to its army, not because the soldiers are the only brave people in the community, but because it is only through their conduct that the courage or cowardice of the community can be manifested.

—Richard L. Nettleship, *Lectures on the Republic of Plato,* 1937

19. Whether we are to live in a future state, as it is the most important question which can possibly be asked, so it is the most intelligible one which can be expressed in language.

—Joseph Butler, "Of Personal Identity," 1736

20. Which is more useful, the Sun or the Moon? The Moon is more useful since it gives us light during the night, when it is dark, whereas the Sun shines only in the daytime, when it is light anyway.

—George Gamow (inscribed in the entry hall of the Hayden Planetarium, New York City)

SUMMARY

A fallacy is a type of argument that may seem to be correct, but that proves on examination not to be so. In this chapter we have grouped the major informal fallacies under four headings: (1) fallacies of relevance, (2) fallacies of defective induction, (3) fallacies of presumption, and (4) fallacies of ambiguity. Within each group we have named, explained, and illustrated the most common kinds of reasoning mistakes.

1. FALLACIES OF RELEVANCE

R1. Appeal to the Populace (*ad populum*): When correct reasoning is replaced by devices calculated to elicit emotional and nonrational support for the conclusion urged.

R2. The Red Herring: When correct reasoning is manipulated by the introduction of some event or character that *deliberately misleads* the audience and thus hinders rational inference.

R3. The Straw Man: When correct reasoning is undermined by the *deliberate misrepresentation* of the opponent's position.

R4. The Attack on the Person (*ad hominem*): When correct reasoning about some issue is replaced by an attack upon the *character or special circumstances* of the opponent.

R5. The Appeal to Force (*ad baculum*): When reasoning is replaced by *threats* in the effort to win support or assent.

R6. Missing the Point (*ignoratio elenchi*): When correct reasoning is replaced by the mistaken refutation of a position that was not really at issue.

2. FALLACIES OF DEFECTIVE INDUCTION

In fallacies of defective induction, the premises may be relevant to the conclusion, but they are far too weak to support the conclusion. Four major fallacies are as follows.

D1. Appeal to Ignorance (*ad ignorantiam*): When it is argued that a proposition is true on the ground that it has not been proved false, or when it is argued that a proposition is false because it has not been proved true.

D2. Appeal to Inappropriate Authority (*ad verecundiam*): When the premises of an argument appeal to the judgment of some person or persons who have no legitimate claim to authority in the matter at hand.

D3. False Cause: When one treats as the cause of a thing that which is not really the cause of that thing, often relying (as in the subtype *post hoc ergo propter hoc*) merely on the close temporal succession of two events.

D4. Hasty Generalization (*converse accident*): When one moves carelessly or too quickly from one or a very few instances to a broad or universal claim.

3. FALLACIES OF PRESUMPTION

In fallacies of presumption, the mistake in argument arises from relying on some proposition that is assumed to be true but is without warrant and is false or dubious. Three major fallacies are as follows.

P1. Accident: When one mistakenly applies a generalization to an individual case that it does not properly govern.

P2. Complex Question: When one argues by asking a question in such a way as to presuppose the truth of some assumption buried in that question.

P3. Begging the Question (*petitio principii*): When one assumes in the premises of an argument the truth of what one seeks to establish in the conclusion of that same argument.

4. FALLACIES OF AMBIGUITY

In fallacies of ambiguity, the mistakes in argument arise as a result of the shift in the meaning of words or phrases, from the meanings that they have in the premises to different meanings that they have in the conclusion. Five major fallacies are as follows.

A1. Equivocation: When the same word or phrase is used with two or more meanings, deliberately or accidentally, in formulating an argument.

A2. Amphiboly: When one of the statements in an argument has more than one plausible meaning, because of the loose or awkward way in which the words in that statement have been combined.

A3. Accent: When a shift of meaning arises within an argument as a consequence of changes in the emphasis given to its words or parts.

A4. Composition: This fallacy is committed (a) when one reasons mistakenly from the attributes of a part to the attributes of the whole, or (b) when one reasons mistakenly from the attributes of an individual member of some collection to the attributes of the totality of that collection.

A5. Division: This fallacy is committed (a) when one reasons mistakenly from the attributes of a whole to the attributes of one of its parts, or (b) when one reasons mistakenly from the attributes of a totality of some collection of entities to the attributes of the individual entities within that collection.

End Notes

[1]For a discussion of the methods of classifying fallacies, see Howard Kahane, "The Nature and Classification of Fallacies," in *Informal Logic*, edited by J. A. Blair and R. J. Johnson (Inverness, CA: Edgepress, 1980). For a more extensive theoretical treatment of fallacies, see C. L. Hamblin, *Fallacies* (London: Methuen, 1970); and J. Woods and D. Walton, *Argument: the Logic of the Fallacies* (Scarborough, Ont.: McGraw-Hill Ryerson, 1982). For a more detailed listing of the varieties of fallacies, see W. W. Fernside and W. B. Holther, *Fallacy: The Counterfeit of Argument* (Englewood Cliffs, NJ: Prentice-Hall, 1959), who name and illustrate fifty-one different fallacies; or D. H. Fischer, *Historians' Fallacies* (New York: Harper & Row, 1979), who distinguishes 112 different fallacies.

[2]Reported in *The New England Journal of Medicine*, 26 December 1996.

[3]Plato, *Apology*, 34; Jowett translation.

[4]Dan Brown, *The DaVinci Code* (New York: Random House, 2003).

[5]David Broder, "Deciding What to Do in Iraq Requires Thought, Not Gut Instinct," *The Washington Post*, 12 January 2007.

[6]www.Figarospeech.com, 19 March 2006.

[7]*The News & Observer*, Raleigh, NC, 5 January 2007.

[8]Constance Baker Motley, *Equal Justice Under Law* (New York: Farrar, Strauss & Giroux, 2001).

[9]Clyde Collins Snow, "'Kind' Racism," *The Sciences*, June 1997.

[10]Interview with Osama bin Laden, CNN, March 1997.

[11]Peter Monaghan, "A Journal Article Is Expunged and Its Authors Cry Foul," *The Chronicle of Higher Education*, 8 December 2000.

[12]"White House Orders Silence on Meese," *The Washington Post*, 29 April 1988.

[13]"Bush Expected to Grant a Stay of Execution," *The New York Times*, 1 June 2000.

[14]*The Collected Works of Abraham Lincoln*, R. P. Basler, editor (New Brunswick, NJ: Rutgers University Press, 1953), Vol. 2, p. 283.

[15]Stephen Tumim, *Great Legal Fiascos* (London, Arthur Barker, 1985).

[16]Erwin Chargaff, in a famous letter to the editor of *Science*, *Science*, vol. 192, p. 938, 1976.

[17]Robert Sinsheimer, "Troubled Dawn for Genetic Engineering," *New Scientist*, vol. 168, p. 148, 1975.

[18]"Wisconsin to Cut Welfare," *Ann Arbor News*, 11 April 1992.

[19]Justice William Brennan, writing for the Court, *In re Winship*, 397 U.S. 358, 1970.

[20]Fulton J. Sheen, a well-known Catholic bishop, remarked that it would be as fatuous for Albert Einstein to make judgments about God as it would be for Sheen to make judgments about relativity theory. "Both of us," Sheen wrote, "would be talking about something we know nothing about." Cited by Laurence A. Marschall, in *The Sciences*, August 2000.

[21]The Latin name was originated by John Locke, whose criticism was directed chiefly at those who think that citing learned authorities is enough to win any argument, who think it "a breach of modesty for others to derogate any way from it, and question authority," and who "style it impudence in anyone who shall stand out against them." That argument Locke named *ad verecundiam*—literally, an appeal to the *modesty* of those who might be so bold as to oppose authority (J. Locke, *An Essay Concerning Human Understanding*, 1690).

[22]For an extended and penetrating analysis of the argument *ad verecundiam*, see Jim Mackenzie, "Authority," *Journal of Philosophy of Education* 22 (1988).

[23]C. Loring Brace, "Faculty Is Powerless," *The New York Times*, 24 February 1998.

[24]Douglas E. McNeil, "School Prayer Fallacy," *The New York Times*, 10 June 1998. And some suggested that the 1954 insertion of the words "under God" into the Pledge of Allegiance was the cause of the host of social ills that followed! See Peter Steinfels. "Beliefs," *The New York Times*, 25 October 2003.

[25]I. Harvey, "Death Penalty Ethics," *The New York Times*, 13 February 1996.

[26]Ernest van den Haag, "Make Mine Hemlock," *National Review*, 12 June 1995.

[27]Zev Simpser, "A Murder Is a Murder," *The New York Times*, 3 May 2002.

[28]John Bedder, reported in "Fried and Salty, Yessir, Matey, but Truly English," *The New York Times*, 9 March 1993.

[29]Elizabeth Kolbert, "Talk of the Town," *The New Yorker*, 17 November 2003.

[30]Barbara Commins, "The Slide into Poverty," *The New York Times*, 10 September 2000.

[31]Jeremy Rifkin, "Issues in Genetic Research," *The Chronicle of Higher Education*, 3 July 1998.

[32]In his treatise, "Logic," which appeared in the *Encyclopaedia Metropolitana* (London, 1828).

[33]Weng Shou-Jen, *Record of Instructions* (c. 1518).

[34]See David Hume, "Sceptical Doubts Concerning the Operations of the Understanding," in *An Enquiry Concerning Human Understanding*, sec. 4 (1747).

[35]Richard Robinson, *An Atheist's Values* (Oxford: Oxford University Press, 1964), p. 121.

[36]*The New Yorker*, 3 March 2003.

[37]In the work whose title is generally given as *On Sophistical Refutations*.

[38]*The New York Times*, 18 June 1996.

[39]Thomas DiLorenzo, *The Real Lincoln: A New Look at Abraham Lincoln, His Agenda, and an Unnecessary War* (Prima Publishing, 2002).

Belvedere, by M.C. Escher, depicts a structure in which the relations of the base to the middle and upper portions are not rational; the pillars seem to connect the parts, but do so in ways that make no sense when closely examined. One pillar, resting on the railing at the rear, appears to support the upper story in front; two other pillars, which rise from the balustrade at the top of the front staircase, appear to support the upper portion of the building at its very rear! No such structure could ever stand.

A deductive argument rests upon premises that serve as its foundation. To succeed, its parts must be held firmly in place by the reasoning that connects those premises to all that is built upon them. If the deductive inferences are solid and reliable at every point, the argument may stand. But if any proposition in the argument is asserted on the basis of other propositions that cannot bear its weight, the argument will collapse as *Belvedere* would collapse. The architect studies the links that can make a building secure; the logician studies the links that can make a deductive argument valid.

PART II

Deduction

For as one may feel sure that a chain will hold when he is assured that each separate link is of good material and that it clasps the two neighboring links, namely, the one preceding and the one following it, so we may be sure of the accuracy of the reasoning when the matter is good, that is to say, when nothing doubtful enters into it, and when the form consists in a perpetual concatenation of truths which allows of no gap.

—*Gottfried Leibniz*

Categorical Propositions

5.1 The Theory of Deduction

We turn now to analysis of the structure of arguments. Preceding chapters have dealt mainly with the language in which arguments are formulated. In this and succeeding chapters we explore and explain the relations between the premises of an argument and its conclusion.

All of Part II of this book is devoted to **deductive arguments.** A deductive argument is one whose premises are claimed to provide conclusive grounds for the truth of its conclusion. If that claim is correct—that is, if the premises of the argument really do assure the truth of its conclusion with necessity—that deductive argument is **valid.** Every deductive argument either does what it claims, or it does not; therefore, every deductive argument is either valid or invalid. If it is valid, it is impossible for its premises to be true without its conclusion also being true.

The theory of deduction aims to explain the relations of premises and conclusion in valid arguments. It also aims to provide techniques for the appraisal of deductive arguments, that is, for discriminating between valid and invalid deductions. To accomplish this, two large bodies of theory have been developed. The first is called **classical logic** or **Aristotelian logic,** after the Greek philosopher who initiated this study. The second is called **modern logic** or **modern symbolic logic,** developed mainly during the twentieth century. Classical logic is the topic of this and the following two chapters (Chapters 5, 6, and 7); modern symbolic logic is the topic of Chapters 8, 9, and 10.

Aristotle (384–322 B.C.) was one of the towering intellects of the ancient world. After studying for twenty years in Plato's Academy, he became tutor to Alexander the Great; later he founded his own school, the Lyceum, where he contributed substantially to nearly every field of human knowledge. His great treatises on reasoning were gathered together after his death and came to be called the *Organon*, meaning literally the "instrument," the fundamental tool of knowledge.

The word *logic* did not acquire its modern meaning until the second century A.D., but the subject matter of logic was long understood to be the matters treated in Aristotle's seminal *Organon*. Aristotelian logic has been the foundation of rational analysis for thousands of years. Over the course of those centuries it has been very greatly refined: its notation has been much improved, its principles have been carefully formulated, its intricate structure has been completed. This great system of classical logic, set forth in this and the next two chapters, remains an intellectual tool of enormous power, as beautiful as it is penetrating.

5.2 Classes and Categorical Propositions

Classical logic deals mainly with arguments based on the relations of classes of objects to one another. By a **class** we mean a collection of all objects that have some specified characteristic in common.* Everyone can see immediately that two classes can be related in at least the following three ways:

1. All of one class may be included in all of another class. Thus the class of all dogs is *wholly included* (or wholly contained) in the class of all mammals.
2. Some, but not all, of the members of one class may be included in another class. Thus the class of all athletes is *partially included* (or partially contained) in the class of all females.
3. Two classes may have no members in common. Thus the class of all triangles and the class of all circles may be said to *exclude* one another.

These three relations may be applied to classes, or categories, of every sort. In a deductive argument we present propositions that state the relations between one category and some other category. The propositions with which such arguments are formulated are therefore called **categorical propositions.**

*The concept of classes was introduced briefly in Chapter 3, in explaining definitions based on the intension of terms.

Categorical propositions are the fundamental elements, the building blocks of argument, in the classical account of deductive logic. Consider the argument

> No athletes are vegetarians.
>
> All football players are athletes.
>
> Therefore no football players are vegetarians.

This argument contains three categorical propositions. We may dispute the truth of its premises, of course, but the relations of the classes expressed in these propositions yields an argument that is certainly valid: If those premises are true, that conclusion *must* be true. And it is plain that each of the premises is indeed categorical; that is, *each premise affirms, or denies, that some class S is included in some other class P, in whole or in part*. In this illustrative argument the three categorical propositions are about the class of all athletes, the class of all vegetarians, and the class of all football players.

The critical first step in developing a theory of deduction based on classes, therefore, is to identify the kinds of categorical propositions and to explore the relations among them.

5.3 The Four Kinds of Categorical Propositions

There are four and only four kinds of **standard-form categorical propositions.** Here are examples of each of the four kinds:

1. All politicians are liars.
2. No politicians are liars.
3. Some politicians are liars.
4. Some politicians are not liars.

We will examine each of these kinds in turn.

1. **Universal affirmative propositions.** In these we assert that *the whole of one class is included or contained in another class.* "All politicians are liars" is an example; it asserts that every member of one class, the class of politicians, is a member of another class, the class of liars. Any universal affirmative proposition can be written schematically as

   All *S* is *P*.

   where the letters *S* and *P* represent the *subject* and *predicate* terms, respectively. Such a proposition *affirms* that the relation of class *inclusion* holds between the two classes and says that the inclusion is complete, or *universal*. All members of *S* are said to be also members of *P*. Propositions in this standard form are called *universal affirmative propositions*. They are also called **A** *propositions*.

Categorical propositions are often represented with diagrams, using two interlocking circles to stand for the two classes involved. These are called **Venn diagrams,** named after the English logician and mathematician, John Venn (1824–1923), who invented them. Later we will explore these diagrams more fully, and we will find that such diagrams are exceedingly helpful in appraising the validity of deductive arguments. For the present we use these diagrams only to exhibit graphically the sense of each categorical proposition.

We label one circle *S*, for subject class, and the other circle *P*, for predicate class. The diagram for the **A** proposition, which asserts that all *S* is *P*, shows that portion of *S* which is outside of *P* shaded out, indicating that there are no members of *S* that are not members of *P*. So the **A** proposition is diagrammed thus:

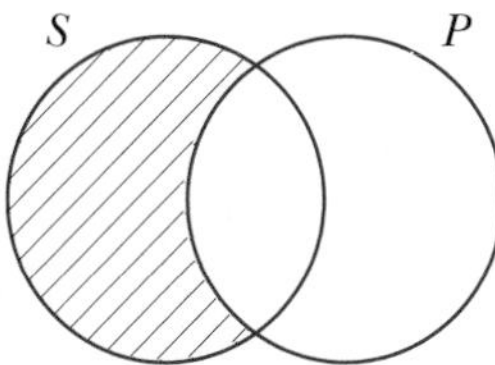

All *S* is *P*.

2. **Universal negative propositions.** The second example above, "No politicians are liars," is a proposition in which it is denied, universally, that any member of the class of politicians is a member of the class of liars. It asserts that the subject class, *S*, is wholly excluded from the predicate class, *P*. Schematically, categorical propositions of this kind can be written as

No *S* is *P*.

where again *S* and *P* represent the subject and predicate terms. This kind of proposition *denies* the relation of *inclusion* between the two terms, and denies it *universally*. It tells us that no members of *S* are members of *P*. Propositions in this standard form are called *universal negative propositions*. They are also called **E** propositions.

The diagram for the **E** proposition will exhibit this mutual exclusion by having the overlapping portion of the two circles representing the classes *S* and *P* shaded out. So the **E** proposition is diagrammed thus:

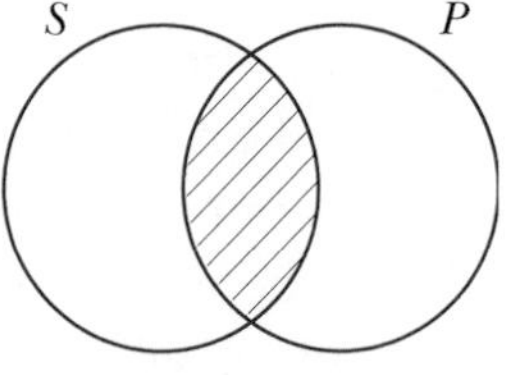

No *S* is *P*.

3. **Particular affirmative propositions.** The third example above, "Some politicians are liars," affirms that some members of the class of all politicians are members of the class of all liars. But it does not affirm this of politicians universally. Only some particular politician or politicians are said to be liars. This proposition does not affirm or deny anything about the class of all politicians; it makes no pronouncements about that entire class. Nor does it say that some politicians are not liars, although in some contexts it may be taken to suggest that. The literal and exact interpretation of this proposition is the assertion that the class of politicians and the class of liars *have some member or members in common*. That is what we understand this standard form proposition to mean.

"Some" is an indefinite term. Does it mean "at least one," or "at least two," or "at least several"? Or how many? Context might affect our understanding of the term as it is used in everyday speech, but logicians, for the sake of definiteness, interpret "some" to mean "*at least one*." A particular affirmative proposition may be written schematically as

Some *S* is *P*.

which says that at least one member of the class designated by the subject term *S* is also a member of the class designated by the predicate term *P*. The proposition *affirms* that the relation of class *inclusion* holds, but does not affirm it of the first class universally but only partially, that is, it is affirmed of some *particular* member, or members, of the first class. Propositions in this standard form are called *particular affirmative propositions*. They are also called **I** propositions.

The diagram for the **I** proposition indicates that there is at least one member of *S* that is also a member of *P* by placing an *x* in the region in which the two circles overlap. So the **I** proposition is diagrammed thus:

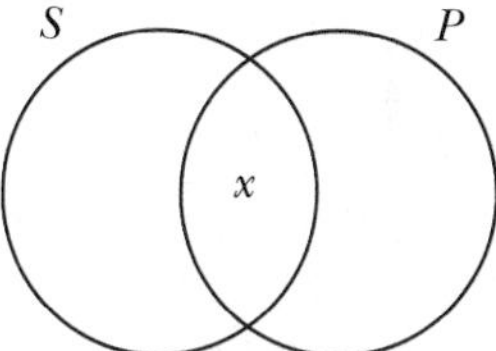

Some *S* is *P*.

4. **Particular negative propositions.** The fourth example above, "Some politicians are not liars," like the third, does not refer to politicians universally, but only to *some* member or members of that class; it is *particular*. Unlike the third example, however, it does not affirm the inclusion of some member or members of the first class in the second class; this is precisely what is *denied*. It is written schematically as

Some *S* is not *P*.

which says that at least one member of the class designated by the subject term *S* is excluded from the whole of the class designated by the predicate term *P*. The denial is not universal. Propositions in this standard form are called *particular negative propositions*. They are also called **O** propositions.

The diagram for the **O** proposition indicates that there is at least one member of *S* that is not a member of *P* by placing an *x* in the region of *S* that is outside of *P*. So the **O** proposition is diagrammed thus:

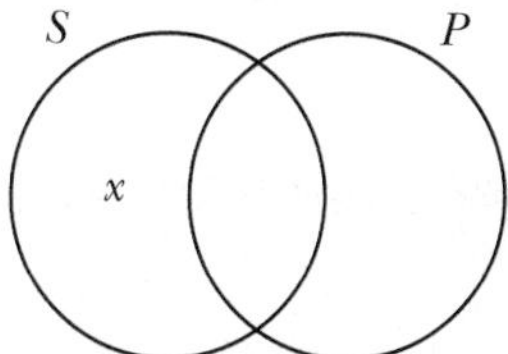

Some *S* is not *P*.

The examples we have used in this section employ classes that are simply named: politicians, liars, vegetarians, athletes, and so on. But subject and predicate terms in standard-form propositions can be more complicated. Thus, for example, the proposition "All candidates for the position are persons of honor and integrity" has the phrase "candidates for the position" as its subject term and the phrase "persons of honor and integrity" as its predicate term. Subject and predicate terms can become more intricate still, but in each of the four standard forms a relation is expressed between a subject class and a predicate class. These four—**A, E, I,** and **O** propositions—are the building blocks of deductive arguments.

This analysis of categorical propositions appears to be simple and straightforward, but the discovery of the fundamental role of these propositions, and the exhibition of their relations to one another, was a great step in the systematic development of logic. It was one of Aristotle's permanent contributions to human knowledge. Its apparent simplicity is deceptive. On this foundation—classes of objects and the relations among those classes—logicians have erected, over the course of centuries, a highly sophisticated system for the analysis of deductive argument. This system, whose subtlety and penetration mark it as one of the greatest of intellectual achievements, we now explore in the following three steps:

A. In the remainder of this chapter we examine the features of standard-form categorical propositions more deeply, explaining their relations to one another. We show what inferences may be drawn *directly* from these categorical propositions. A good deal of deductive reasoning, we will see, can be mastered with no more than a thorough grasp of **A, E, I,** and **O** propositions and their interconnections.

B. In the next chapter, we explain *syllogisms*—the arguments that are commonly constructed using standard-form categorical propositions. We explore the realm of syllogisms, in which every valid argument form is uniquely characterized and given its own name. And we develop powerful techniques for determining the validity (or invalidity) of syllogisms.

C. In Chapter 7 we integrate syllogistic reasoning and the language of argument in everyday life. We identify some limitations of reasoning based on this foundation, but we also glimpse the penetration and wide applicability that this foundation makes possible.

OVERVIEW

Standard-Form Categorical Propositions

Proposition Form	Name and Type	Example
All *S* is *P*.	**A** Universal affirmative	All lawyers are wealthy people.
No *S* is *P*.	**E** Universal negative	No criminals are good citizens.
Some *S* is *P*.	**I** Particular affirmative	Some chemicals are poisons.
Some *S* is not *P*.	**O** Particular negative	Some insects are not pests.

EXERCISES

Identify the subject and predicate terms in, and name the form of, each of the following propositions.

***1.** Some historians are extremely gifted writers whose works read like first-rate novels.

2. No athletes who have ever accepted pay for participating in sports are amateurs.

3. No dogs that are without pedigrees are candidates for blue ribbons in official dog shows sponsored by the American Kennel Club.

4. All satellites that are currently in orbits less than ten thousand miles high are very delicate devices that cost many thousands of dollars to manufacture.

***5.** Some members of families that are rich and famous are not persons of either wealth or distinction.

6. Some paintings produced by artists who are universally recognized as masters are not works of genuine merit that either are or deserve to be preserved in museums and made available to the public.

7. All drivers of automobiles that are not safe are desperadoes who threaten the lives of their fellows.

8. Some politicians who could not be elected to the most minor positions are appointed officials in our government today.

9. Some drugs that are very effective when properly administered are not safe remedies that all medicine cabinets should contain.

***10.** No people who have not themselves done creative work in the arts are responsible critics on whose judgment we can rely.

5.4 Quality, Quantity, and Distribution

A. QUALITY

Every standard-form categorical proposition either affirms, or denies, some class relation, as we have seen. If the proposition affirms some class inclusion, whether complete or partial, its quality is *affirmative*. So the **A** proposition, "All *S* is *P*," and the **I** proposition, "Some *S* is *P*," are both affirmative in quality. Their letter names, **A** and **I**, are thought to come from the Latin word, "**A**ff**I**rmo," meaning, "I affirm." If the proposition denies class inclusion, whether complete or partial, its quality is *negative*. So the **E** proposition, "No *S* is *P*," and the **O** proposition, "Some *S* is not *P*," are both negative in quality. Their letter names, **E** and **O**, are thought to come from the Latin word, "n**E**g**O**," meaning "I deny." Every categorical proposition has one quality or the other, affirmative or negative.

B. QUANTITY

Every standard-form categorical proposition has some class as its subject. If the proposition refers to all members of the class designated by its subject term, its quantity is *universal*. So the **A** proposition, "All *S* is *P*," and the **E** proposition, "No *S* is *P*," are both universal in quantity. If the proposition refers only to some members of the class designated by its subject term, its quantity is *particular*. So the **I** proposition, "Some *S* is *P*," and the **O** proposition, "Some *S* is not *P*," are both particular in quantity.

The quantity of a standard-form categorical proposition is revealed by the word with which it begins, either "all," "no," or "some." "All" and "no" indicate that the proposition is universal; "some" indicates that the proposition is particular. The word "no" serves also, in the case of the **E** proposition, to indicate its negative quality, as we have seen.

Because every standard-form categorical proposition must be either affirmative or negative, and must be either universal or particular, the four names uniquely describe each one of the four standard forms by indicating its quantity and its quality: universal affirmative (**A**), particular affirmative (**I**), universal negative (**E**), particular negative (**O**).

C. GENERAL SCHEMA OF STANDARD-FORM CATEGORICAL PROPOSITIONS

Between the subject and predicate terms of every standard-form categorical proposition occurs some form of the verb "to be." This verb (accompanied by "not" in the case of the **O** proposition) serves to connect the subject and predicate terms and is called the **copula.** Writing the four propositions schematically, as we did earlier (All *S* is *P*, Some *S* is *P*, etc.), only the words "is" and "is not" appear; but (depending on context) other forms of the verb "to be" may be appropriate. We may change the tense (for example, "Some Roman emperors were monsters" or "Some soldiers will not be heroes"), or change to the plural form of the verb (for example, "All squares are rectangles"). In these examples, "were" and "are" and "will not be" serve as copulas. However, the general skeleton of a standard-form categorical proposition always consists of just four parts: first the quantifier, then the subject term, next the copula, and finally the predicate term. The schema may be written as

Quantifier (subject term) copula (predicate term).

D. DISTRIBUTION

Categorical propositions are regarded as being about classes, the classes of objects designated by the subject and predicate terms. We have seen that a proposition may refer to classes in different ways; it may refer to *all* members of a class or refer to only *some* members of that class. Thus the proposition, "All senators are citizens," refers to, or is about, *all* senators, but it does not refer to all citizens. That proposition does not affirm that every citizen is a senator, but it does not deny it either. Every **A** proposition is thus seen to refer to all members of the class designated by its subject term, *S*, but does *not* refer to all members of the class designated by its predicate term, *P*.

To characterize the ways in which terms can occur in categorical propositions, we introduce the technical term **distribution.** A proposition distributes a term if it refers to all members of the class designated by that term. In **A, E, I,** and **O** propositions, the terms that are distributed vary, as follows.

In the A proposition (e.g., "All senators are citizens"): In this proposition, "senators" is distributed, but "citizens" is not. In **A** propositions (universal affirmatives) the subject term is distributed, but the predicate term is undistributed.

In the E proposition (e.g., "No athletes are vegetarians"): The subject term, "athletes," is distributed, because the whole class of athletes is said to be excluded from the class of vegetarians. But in asserting that the whole class of athletes is excluded from the class of vegetarians, it is also asserted that the whole class of vegetarians is excluded from the class of athletes. Of each and every vegetarian, the proposition says that he or she is not an athlete. Unlike an **A** proposition, therefore, an **E** proposition refers to all members of the class designated by its predicate term, and therefore also distributes its predicate term. **E** propositions (universal negatives) distribute both their subject and their predicate terms.

In the I proposition (e.g., "Some soldiers are cowards"): No assertion is made about all soldiers in this proposition, and no assertion is made about all cowards either. It says nothing about each and every soldier, and nothing about each and every coward. Neither class is wholly included, or wholly excluded, from the other. In **I** propositions (particular affirmatives) both subject and predicate terms are not distributed.

In the O proposition (e.g., "Some horses are not thoroughbreds"): Nothing is said about all horses. The proposition refers to some members of the class designated by the subject term; it says that of this part of the class of horses that it is excluded from the class of all thoroughbreds. But they are excluded from the *whole* of the latter class. Given the particular horses referred to, the proposition says that each and every member of the class of thoroughbreds is *not* one of those particular horses. When something is said to be excluded from a class, the whole of the class is referred to, just as, when a person is excluded from a country, all parts of that country are forbidden to that person. In **O** propositions (particular negatives) the subject term is not distributed, but the predicate term is distributed.

We thus see that universal propositions, both affirmative and negative, distribute their subject terms, whereas particular propositions, whether affirmative or negative, do not distribute their subject terms. Thus the *quantity* of any standard-form categorical proposition determines whether its *subject* term is distributed or undistributed. We likewise see that affirmative propositions, whether universal or particular, do not distribute their predicate terms, whereas negative propositions, both universal and particular, do distribute their predicate terms. Thus the *quality* of a standard-form categorical proposition determines whether its predicate term is distributed or undistributed.

In summary, the **A** proposition distributes only its subject term; the **E** proposition distributes both its subject and predicate terms; and the **I** proposition distributes neither its subject nor its predicate term; and the **O** proposition distributes only its predicate term.

Which terms are distributed by which standard-form categorical propositions will become very important when we turn to the evaluation of syllogisms. The following diagram presents all these distributions graphically, and may be useful in helping you to remember which propositions distribute which of their terms.

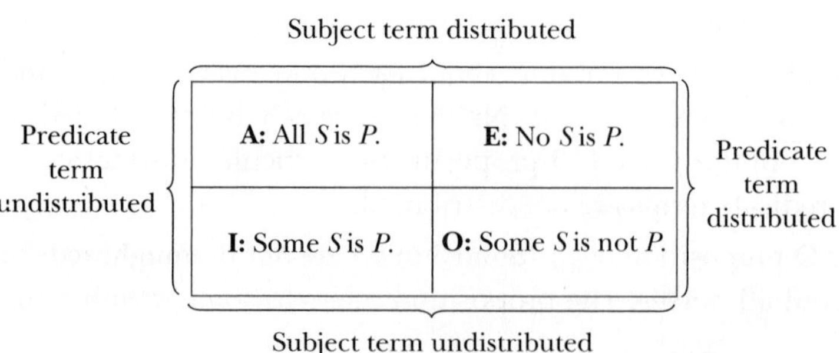

VISUAL LOGIC

The A proposition: All bananas are fruits.

This **A** proposition asserts that *every* member of the class of bananas (the subject class) is also a member of the class of fruits (the predicate class). When a term refers to every member of a class, we say that it is *distributed*. *In an* **A** *proposition, the subject term is always distributed.* But the **A** proposition does not refer to every member of the predicate class; this example does not assert that all fruits are bananas; it says nothing about every fruit. *In an* **A** *proposition, the predicate term is not distributed.*

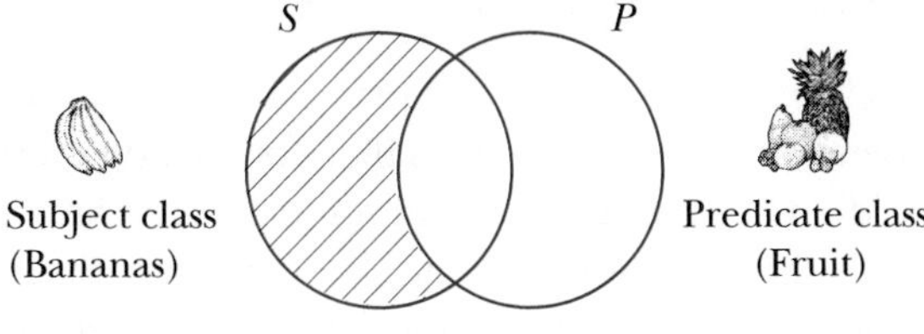

All *S* is *P*.

The E proposition: No bananas are fruits.

This **E** proposition asserts that *every* member of the class of bananas is *outside* the class of fruits. The *subject* term, "bananas," is plainly distributed. But because bananas are excluded from the entire class of fruits, this proposition refers to every member of the *predicate* class as well, because it plainly says that *no* fruit is a banana. *In an* **E** *proposition, both the subject term and the predicate term are distributed.*

Note that the concept of distribution has nothing to do with truth or falsity. This example proposition is certainly false—but, as in every **E** proposition, both of its terms are distributed.

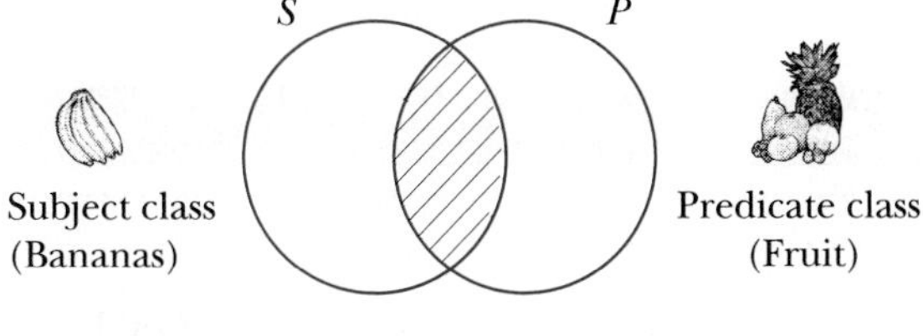

No *S* is *P*.

The I proposition: Some bananas are fruits.

The word "some" in this **I** proposition tells us that at least one member of the class designated by the subject term, "bananas," is also a member of the class designated by the predicate term, "fruits"—but this proposition makes no

(Continued)

claim about the subject class as a whole. Therefore, in this proposition, as in every **I** proposition, the subject term is not distributed. Nor does this proposition say anything about every member for the class of fruits (we are told only that there is at least one member of the class of bananas in it), so the predicate is not distributed either. *In an* **I** *proposition, neither the subject term nor the predicate term is distributed.*

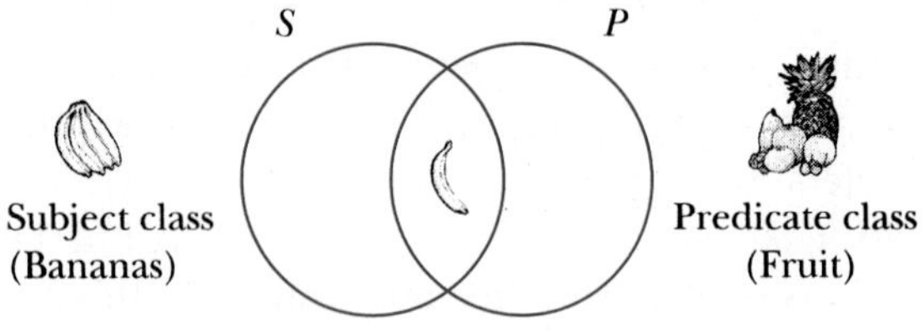

Some *S* is *P*.

The O proposition: Some bananas are not fruits.

The word "some" again tells us that this proposition is not about all members of the class of bananas; the *subject* term is therefore not distributed. But because we are told, in this proposition, that some bananas are not fruits, we are told something about the entire predicate class—namely, that the entire class of fruits does not have one of those subject bananas among them. *In an* **O** *proposition, the predicate term is distributed but the subject term is not distributed.*

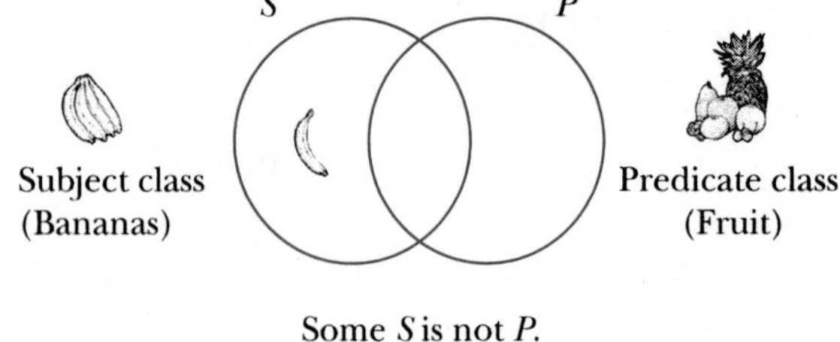

Some *S* is not *P*.

We conclude this section with a table that presents all the critical information about each of the four standard-form categorical propositions:

OVERVIEW

Quantity, Quality, and Distribution

Proposition	Letter Name	Quantity	Quality	Distributes
All *S* is *P*.	**A**	Universal	Affirmative	*S* only
No *S* is *P*.	**E**	Universal	Negative	*S* and *P*
Some *S* is *P*.	**I**	Particular	Affirmative	Neither
Some *S* is not *P*.	**O**	Particular	Negative	*P* only

EXERCISES

Name the quality and quantity of each of the following propositions, and state whether their subject and predicate terms are distributed or undistributed.

*1. Some presidential candidates will be sadly disappointed people.

2. All those who died in Nazi concentration camps were victims of a cruel and irrational tyranny.

3. Some recently identified unstable elements were not entirely accidental discoveries.

4. Some members of the military-industrial complex are mild-mannered people to whom violence is abhorrent.

*5. No leader of the feminist movement is a major business executive.

6. All hard-line advocates of law and order at any cost are people who will be remembered, if at all, only for having failed to understand the major social pressures of the twenty-first century.

7. Some recent rulings of the Supreme Court were politically motivated decisions that flouted the entire history of U.S. legal practice.

8. No harmful pesticides or chemical defoliants were genuine contributions to the long-range agricultural goals of the nation.

9. Some advocates of major political, social, and economic reforms are not responsible people who have a stake in maintaining the status quo.

*10. All new labor-saving devices are major threats to the trade union movement.

5.5 The Traditional Square of Opposition

The preceeding analysis of categorical propositions enables us to exhibit the relations among those propositions, which in turn provide solid grounds for a great deal of the reasoning we do in everyday life. We need one more technical term: *opposition*. Standard-form categorical propositions having the same subject terms and the same predicate terms may (obviously) differ from each other in quality, or in quantity, or in both. Any such kind of differing has been traditionally called **opposition.** This term is used even when there is no apparent disagreement between the propositions. The various kinds of opposition are correlated with some very important truth relations, as follows.

A. CONTRADICTORIES

Two propositions are **contradictories** if one is the denial or negation of the other—that is, if they cannot both be true and cannot both be false. Two standard-form categorical propositions that have the same subject and predicate terms but differ from each other in *both* quantity and quality are contradictories.

Thus the **A** proposition, "All judges are lawyers," and the **O** proposition, "Some judges are not lawyers," are clearly contradictories. They are opposed in both quality (one affirms, the other denies) and quantity (one refers to all, and the other to some). Of the pair, exactly one is true and exactly one is false. They cannot both be true; they cannot both be false.

Similarly, the **E** proposition, "No politicians are idealists," and the **I** proposition, "Some politicians are idealists," are opposed in both quantity and quality, and they too are contradictories.

In summary: **A** and **O** propositions are contradictories: "All *S* is *P*" is contradicted by "Some *S* is not *P*." **E** and **I** propositions are also contradictories: "No *S* is *P*" is contradicted by "Some *S* is *P*."

B. CONTRARIES

Two propositions are said to be **contraries** if they cannot both be true—that is, if the truth of one entails the falsity of the other. Thus, "Texas will win the coming game with Oklahoma," and "Oklahoma will win the coming game with Texas," are contraries. If either of these propositions (referring to the same game, of course) is true, then the other must be false. But these two propositions are not contradictories, because can game could be a draw and then both would be false. Contraries cannot both be true, but, unlike contradictories, they can both be false.

The traditional account of categorical propositions held that universal propositions (**A** and **E**) having the same subject and predicate terms but differing in quality (one affirming, the other denying) were contraries. Thus it was said that an **A** proposition, "All poets are dreamers," and its corresponding **E** proposition, "No poets are dreamers," cannot both be true—but they can both be false and may be regarded as contraries.*

*This Aristotelian interpretation has some troubling consequences that will be discussed in Section 5.7.

One difficulty with this Aristotelian account arises if either the **A** proposition or the **E** proposition is necessarily true—that is, if either is a logical or mathematical truth, such as "All squares are rectangles," or "No squares are circles." In such a case, the claim that the **A** proposition and the **E** proposition are contraries cannot be correct, because a necessarily true proposition cannot possibly be false and so cannot have a contrary, because contraries are two propositions that can both be false. Propositions that are neither necessarily true nor necessarily false are said to be **contingent.** So the reply to this difficulty is that the present interpretation assumes (not unreasonably) that the propositions in question are contingent, in which case the claim that **A** and **E** propositions having the same subject and predicate terms are contraries may be correct. For the remainder of this chapter, we therefore make the assumption that the propositions involved are contingent.

C. SUBCONTRARIES

Two propositions are said to be **subcontraries** if they cannot both be false, although they may both be true.

The traditional account held that particular propositions (**I** and **O**) having the same subject and predicate terms but differing in quality (one affirming the other denying) are subcontraries. It was said that the **I** proposition, "Some diamonds are precious stones," and the **O** proposition, "Some diamonds are not precious stones," could both be true—but they could not both be false and therefore must be regarded as subcontraries.

A difficulty similar to the one noted above arises here too. If either the **I** or the **O** proposition is necessarily false (for example, "Some squares are circles" or "Some squares are not rectangles"), it cannot have a subcontrary, because subcontraries are two propositions that can both be true. But if both the **I** and the **O** are contingent propositions, they can both be true, and as we noted in connection with contraries just above, we shall assume for the remainder of this chapter that they are contingent.

D. SUBALTERNATION

When two propositions have the same subject and the same predicate terms, and agree in quality (both affirming or both denying) but differ in quantity (one universal, the other particular), they are called *corresponding propositions.* This is also a form of "opposition" as that term has traditionally been used. Thus the **A** proposition, "All spiders are eight-legged animals," has a corresponding **I** proposition, "Some spiders are eight-legged animals." Likewise, the **E** proposition, "No whales are fishes," has a corresponding **O** proposition,

"Some whales are not fishes." This opposition between a universal proposition and its corresponding particular proposition is known as **subalternation.** In any such pair of corresponding propositions, the universal proposition is called the *superaltern*, and the particular is called the the *subaltern*.

In subalternation (in the classical analysis), the superaltern implies the truth of the subaltern. Thus, from the universal affirmative, "All birds have feathers," the corresponding particular affirmative, "Some birds have feathers," was held to follow. From the universal negative, "No whales are fishes," the corresponding particular, "Some whales are not fishes," was likewise held to follow. But of course the implication does not hold from the particular to the universal, from the subaltern to the superaltern. From the proposition, "Some animals are cats," it is obvious that we cannot infer that "All animals are cats." And it would be absurd to infer from "Some animals are not cats" that "No animals are cats."

E. THE SQUARE OF OPPOSITION

There are thus four ways in which propositions may be "opposed"—as *contradictories, contraries, subcontraries,* and as *sub-* and *superalterns*. These are represented using an important and widely used diagram called the **square of opposition,** which is reproduced as Figure 5-1.

Relations exhibited by this square of opposition were believed to provide the logical basis for validating certain elementary forms of argument. To explain these, we must first distinguish between **immediate inferences** and **mediate inferences.**

When we draw a conclusion from one or more premises, some inference must be involved. That inference is said to be *mediate* when more than one

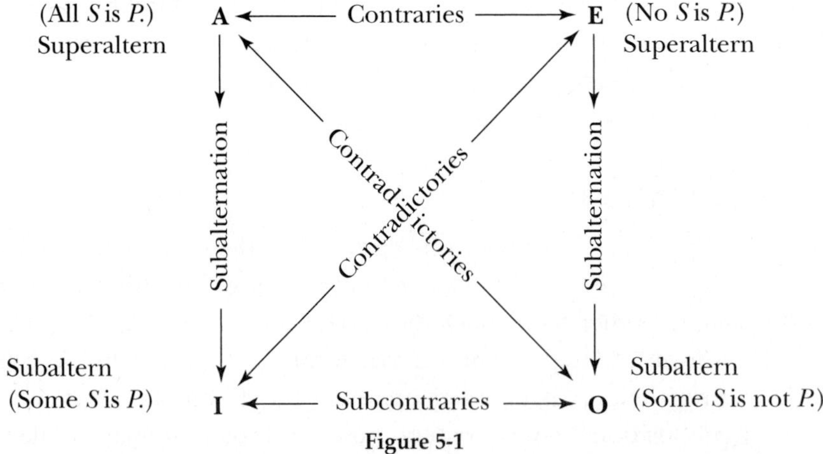

Figure 5-1

premise is relied on (as in a syllogism), because the conclusion is drawn from the first premise through the mediation of the second. However, when a conclusion is drawn from only one premise there is no such mediation, and the inference is said to be *immediate*.

A number of very useful immediate inferences may be readily drawn from the information embedded in the traditional square of opposition. Here are some examples:

- If an **A** proposition is the premise, then (according to the square of opposition) one can validly infer that the corresponding **O** proposition (that is, the **O** proposition with the same subject and predicate terms) is false.
- If an **A** proposition is the premise, then the corresponding **I** proposition is true.
- If an **I** proposition is the premise, its corresponding **E** proposition, which contradicts it, must be false.

Given the truth, or the falsehood, of any one of the four standard-form categorical propositions, the truth or falsehood of some or all of the others can be inferred immediately. A considerable number of immediate inferences are based on the traditional square of opposition; we list them here:

A is given as true:	**E** is false; **I** is true; **O** is false.
E is given as true:	**A** is false; **I** is false; **O** is true.
I is given as true:	**E** is false; **A** and **O** are undetermined.
O is given as true:	**A** is false; **E** and **I** are undetermined.
A is given as false:	**O** is true; **E** and **I** are undetermined.
E is given as false:	**I** is true; **A** and **O** are undetermined.
I is given as false:	**A** is false; **E** is true; **O** is true.
O is given as false:	**A** is true; **E** is false; **I** is true.*

*A proposition is undermined if its truth or falsity is not determined—fixed—by the truth or falsity of any other proposition. In another sense, a proposition is undetermined if one does not know that it is true and one also does not know that it is false. If it is given that an **A** proposition is undetermined, in either sense, we may infer that its contradictory **O** proposition must be undetermined in that same sense. For if that **O** proposition were known to be true, the **A** proposition contradicting it would be known to be false; and if that **O** proposition were known to be false, the **A** proposition contradicting it would be known to be true. The same reasoning applies to the other standard-form propositions. In general, if any of the four categorical propositions is given as undetermined in either sense, its contradictory must be undetermined in the same sense.

EXERCISES

A. If we assume that the first proposition in each of the following sets is true, what can we affirm about the truth or falsehood of the remaining propositions in each set? B. If we assume that the first proposition in each set is false, what can we affirm?

*1. **a.** All successful executives are intelligent people.
b. No successful executives are intelligent people.
c. Some successful executives are intelligent people.
d. Some successful executives are not intelligent people.

2. **a.** No animals with horns are carnivores.
b. Some animals with horns are carnivores.
c. Some animals with horns are not carnivores.
d. All animals with horns are carnivores.

3. **a.** Some uranium isotopes are highly unstable substances.
b. Some uranium isotopes are not highly unstable substances.
c. All uranium isotopes are highly unstable substances.
d. No uranium isotopes are highly unstable substances.

4. **a.** Some college professors are not entertaining lecturers.
b. All college professors are entertaining lecturers.
c. No college professors are entertaining lecturers.
d. Some college professors are entertaining lecturers.

5.6 Further Immediate Inferences

Three other important kinds of immediate inference are not associated directly with the square of opposition: *Conversion*, *Obversion*, and *Contraposition*. These we now explain:

A. CONVERSION

Conversion is an inference that proceeds by interchanging the subject and predicate terms of the proposition. "No men are angels" converts to "No angels are men," and these propositions may be validly inferred from one another. Similarly, "Some women are writers" and "Some writers are women" are logically equivalent, and by conversion either can be validly inferred from the other. Conversion is perfectly valid for all **E** propositions and for all **I** propositions. One standard-form categorical proposition is therefore said to be the **converse** of another when we derive it by simply interchanging the subject and predicate terms of that other proposition. The proposition from which it is derived is called the **convertend.** Thus, "No idealists are politicians" is the converse of "No politicians are idealists," which is its convertend.

The conversion of an **O** proposition is not, in general, valid. The **O** proposition, "Some animals are not dogs," is plainly true; its converse is the proposition, "Some dogs are not animals," which is plainly false. An **O** proposition and its converse are not, in general, logically equivalent.

The **A** proposition presents a special problem here. Of course, the converse of an **A** proposition does not in general follow from its convertend. From "All dogs are animals" we certainly may not infer that "All animals are dogs." Traditional logic recognized this, of course, but asserted, nevertheless, that something *like* conversion was valid for **A** propositions. On the traditional square of opposition, one could validly infer from the **A** proposition, "All dogs are animals," its subaltern **I** proposition, "Some dogs are animals." The **A** proposition says something about all members of the subject class (dogs), the **I** proposition makes a more limited claim, about only some of the members of that class. In general, it was held that one could infer "Some *S* is *P*" from "All *S* is *P*." And, as we saw earlier, an **I** proposition may be converted validly; if some dogs are animals, then some animals are dogs.

So, if we are given the **A** proposition that "All dogs are animals," we first infer that "Some dogs are animals" by subalternation, and from that subaltern we can by conversion validly infer that "Some animals are dogs." Hence, by a combination of subalternation and conversion, we advance validly from "All *S* is *P*" to "Some *P* is *S*." This pattern of inference, called *conversion by limitation* (or *conversion per accidens*) proceeds by interchanging subject and predicate terms and changing the quantity of the proposition from universal to particular. This type of conversion will be considered further in the next section.

In all conversions, the converse of a given proposition contains exactly the same subject and predicate terms as the convertend, their order being reversed, and always has the same quality (of affirmation or denial). A complete picture of this immediate inference as traditionally understood is given by the following table:

OVERVIEW

Valid Conversions

Convertend	Converse
A: All *S* is *P*.	**I:** Some *P* is *S*. (by limitation)
E: No *S* is *P*.	**E:** No *P* is *S*.
I: Some *S* is *P*.	**I:** Some *P* is *S*.
O: Some *S* is not *P*.	(conversion not valid)

B. CLASSES AND CLASS COMPLEMENTS

To explain other types of immediate inference we must examine more closely the concept of a "class" and explain what is meant by the *complement of a class.* Any class, we have said, is the collection of all objects that have a certain common attribute, which we may refer to as the "class-defining characteristic." The class of all humans is the collection of all things that have the characteristic of being human; its class-defining characteristic is the attribute of being human. The class-defining characteristic need not be a "simple" attribute; any attribute may determine a class. For example, the complex attribute of being left-handed and red-headed and a student determines a class—the class of all left-handed, red-headed students.

Every class has, associated with it, a **complementary class**, or **complement**, which is the collection of all things that do not belong to the original class. The complement of the class of all people is the class of all things that are *not* people. The class-defining characteristic of that complementary class is the (negative) attribute of not being a person. The complement of the class of all people contains no people, but it contains everything else: shoes and ships and sealing wax and cabbages—but no kings, because kings are people. It is often convenient to speak of the complement of the class of all persons as the "class of all nonpersons." The complement of the class designated by the term *S* is then designated by the term *non-S*; we may speak of the term *non-S* as being the complement of the term *S*.*

The word *complement* is thus used in two senses. In one sense it is the complement of a class, in the other it is the complement of a term. These are different but very closely connected. One term is the (term) complement of another just in case the first term designates the (class) complement of the class designated by the second term.

Note that a class is the (class) complement of its own complement. Likewise, a term is the (term) complement of its own complement. A sort of "double negative" rule is involved here, to avoid strings of "non's" prefixed to a term. Thus, the complement of the term "voter" is "nonvoter," but the complement of "nonvoter" should be written simply as "voter" rather than as "nonnonvoter."

One must be careful not to mistake contrary terms for complementary terms. "Coward" and "hero" are contraries, because no person can be both a coward and a hero. But we must not identify "cowards" with "nonheroes" because not everyone, and certainly not everything, need be one or the other.

---

*Sometimes we reason using what is called the *relative complement of a class*, its complement within some other class. For example, within the class of "children of mine" there is a subclass, "daughters of mine," whose relative complement is another subclass, "children of mine who are not daughters," or "sons of mine." But obversions, and other immediate inferences, rely on the absolute complement of classes, as defined above.

Likewise, the complement of the term "winner" is not "loser" but "nonwinner," for although not everything, or even everyone, is either a winner or a loser, absolutely everything is either a winner or a nonwinner.

C. OBVERSION

Obversion is an immediate inference that is easy to explain once the concept of a term complement is understood. To obvert a proposition, we change its quality (affirmative to negative or negative to affirmative) and replace the predicate term with its complement. However, the subject term remains unchanged, and so does the quantity of the proposition being obverted. For example, the **A** proposition, "All residents are voters," has as its obverse the **E** proposition, "No residents are nonvoters." These two are logically equivalent propositions, and either may be validly inferred from the other.

Obversion is a valid immediate inference when applied to *any* standard-form categorical proposition:

- The **E** proposition, "No umpires are partisans," has as its obverse the logically equivalent **A** proposition, "All umpires are nonpartisans."
- The **I** proposition, "Some metals are conductors," has as its obverse the **O** proposition, "Some metals are not nonconductors."
- The **O** proposition, "Some nations were not belligerents," has as its obverse the **I** proposition, "Some nations were nonbelligerents."

The proposition serving as premise for the obversion is called the **obvertend;** the conclusion of the inference is called the **obverse.** Every standard-form categorical proposition is logically equivalent to its obverse, so obversion is a valid form of immediate inference for all standard-form categorical propositions. To obtain the obverse of any proposition, we leave the quantity (universal or particular) and the subject term unchanged; we change the quality of the proposition and replace the predicate term with its complement. The following table gives a complete picture of all valid obversions:

OVERVIEW

Obversions

Obvertend	Obverse
A: All *S* is *P*.	**E**: No *S* is non-*P*.
E: No *S* is *P*.	**A**: All *S* is non-*P*.
I: Some *S* is *P*.	**O**: Some *S* is not non-*P*.
O: Some *S* is not *P*.	**I**: Some *S* is non-*P*.

D. CONTRAPOSITION

A third type of immediate inference, **contraposition,** can be reduced to the first two, conversion and obversion. To form the **contrapositive** of a given proposition, we replace its subject term with the complement of its predicate term, and we replace its predicate term with the complement of its subject term. Neither the quality nor the quantity of the original proposition is changed, so the contrapositive of an **A** proposition is an **A** proposition, the contrapositive of an **O** proposition is an **O** proposition, and so forth.

For example, the contrapositive of the **A** proposition, "All members are voters," is the **A** proposition, "All nonvoters are nonmembers." These are logically equivalent propositions, as will be evident on reflection. Contraposition is plainly a valid form of immediate inference when applied to **A** propositions. It really introduces nothing new, because we can get from any **A** proposition to its contrapositive by first obverting it, next applying conversion, and then applying obversion again. Beginning with "All *S* is *P*," we obvert it to obtain "No *S* is non-*P*," which converts validly to "No non-*P* is *S*," whose obverse is "All non-*P* is non-*S*." The contrapositive of any **A** proposition is the obverse of the converse of the obverse of that proposition.

Contraposition is a valid form of immediate inference when applied to **O** propositions also, although its conclusion may be awkward to express. The contrapositive of the **O** proposition, "Some students are not idealists," is the somewhat cumbersome **O** proposition, "Some nonidealists are not nonstudents," which is logically equivalent to its premise. This also can be shown to be the outcome of first obverting, then converting, then obverting again. "Some *S* is not *P*" obverts to "Some *S* is non-*P*," which converts to "Some non-*P* is *S*," which obverts to "Some non-*P* is not non-*S*."

For **I** propositions, however, contraposition is not, in general, a valid form of inference. The true **I** proposition, "Some citizens are nonlegislators," has as its contrapositive the false proposition, "Some legislators are noncitizens." The reason for this invalidity becomes evident when we try to derive the contrapositive of the **I** proposition by successively obverting, converting, and obverting. The obverse of the original **I** proposition, "Some *S* is *P*," is the **O** proposition, "Some *S* is not non-*P*," but (as we saw earlier) the converse of an **O** proposition does not generally follow validly from it.

In the case of **E** propositions, the contrapositive does not follow validly from the original, as can be seen when, if we begin with the true proposition, "No wrestlers are weaklings," we get, as its contrapositive, the obviously false proposition, "No nonweaklings are nonwrestlers." The reason for this invalidity we will see, again, if we attempt to derive it by successive obversion, conversion, and obversion. If we begin with the **E** proposition, "No *S* is *P*," and obvert it, we obtain the **A** proposition, "All *S* is non-*P*"—which in general cannot be validly converted *except by limitation*. If we do then convert it by limitation to obtain "Some non-*P* is *S*," we can obvert this to obtain "Some non-*P* is not non-*S*." This outcome we may call the *contrapositive by limitation*—and this too we will consider further in the next section.

Contraposition by limitation, in which we infer an **O** proposition from an **E** proposition (for example, we infer "Some non-*P* is not non-*S*" from "No *S* is *P*"), has the same peculiarity as conversion by limitation, on which it depends. Because a particular proposition is inferred from a universal proposition, the resulting contrapositive cannot have the *same* meaning, and cannot be logically equivalent to the proposition that was the original premise. On the other hand, the contrapositive of an **A** proposition is an **A** proposition, and the contrapositive of an **O** proposition is an **O** proposition, and in each of these cases the contrapositive and the premise from which it is derived are equivalent.

Contraposition is thus seen to be valid only when applied to **A** and **O** propositions. It is not valid at all for **I** propositions, and it is valid for **E** propositions only by limitation. The complete picture is exhibited in the following table:

OVERVIEW

Contraposition

Premise	Contrapositive
A: All *S* is *P*.	**A**: All non-*P* is non-*S*.
E: No *S* is *P*.	**O**: Some non-*P* is not non-*S*. (by limitation)
I: Some *S* is *P*.	(contraposition not valid)
O: Some *S* is not-*P*.	**O**: Some non-*P* is not non-*S*.

Questions about the relations between propositions can often be answered by exploring the various immediate inferences that can be drawn from one or the other of them. For example, given that the proposition, "All surgeons are physicians," is true, what can we know about the truth or falsehood of the proposition, "No nonsurgeons are nonphysicians?" Does this problematic proposition—or its contradictory or contrary—follow validly from the one given as true? To answer we proceed as follows: From what we are given, "All surgeons are physicians," we can validly infer its contrapositive, "All nonphysicians are nonsurgeons." From this, using conversion by limitation (valid according to the traditional view), we can derive "Some nonsurgeons are nonphysicians." But this is the contradictory of the proposition in question

("No nonsurgeons are nonphysicians"), which is thus no longer problematic but known to be false.

In the very first chapter of this book we noted that a valid argument whose premises are true *must* have a true conclusion, but also that a valid argument whose premises are false *can* have a true conclusion. Thus, from the false premise, "All animals are cats," the true proposition, "Some animals are cats," follows by subalternation. And from the false proposition, "All parents are students," conversion by limitation yields the true proposition, "Some students are parents." Therefore, if a proposition is given to be false, and the question is raised about the truth or falsehood of some *other*, related proposition, the recommended procedure is to begin drawing immediate inferences from either (1) the contradictory of the proposition known to be false, or (2) the problematic proposition itself. The contradictory of a false proposition must be true, and all valid inferences from that will also be true propositions. And if we follow the other course and are able to show that the problematic proposition implies the proposition that is given is false, we know that it must itself be false. Here follows a table in which the forms of immediateinference—conversion, obversion, and contraposition—are fully displayed:

OVERVIEW

Immediate Inferences: Conversion, Obversion, Contraposition

Conversion

Convertend	**Converse**
A: All *S* is *P*.	**I**: Some *P* is *S*. (by limitation)
E: No *S* is *P*.	**E**: No *P* is *S*.
I: Some *S* is *P*.	**I**: Some *P* is *S*.
O: Some *S* is not *P*.	(conversion not valid)

Obversion

Obvertend	**Obverse**
A: All *S* is *P*.	**E**: No *S* is non-*P*.
E: No *S* is *P*.	**A**: All *S* is non-*P*.
I: Some *S* is *P*.	**O**: Some *S* is not non-*P*.
O: Some *S* is not *P*.	**I**: Some *S* is non-*P*.

Contraposition

Premise	**Contrapositive**
A: All *S* is *P*.	**A**: All non-*P* is non-*S*.

E: No S is P.	O: Some non-P is not non-S. (by limitation)
I: Some S is P.	(contraposition not valid)
O: Some S is not P.	O: Some non-P is not non-S.

EXERCISES

A. State the converses of the following propositions, and indicate which of them are equivalent to the given propositions.

*1. No people who are considerate of others are reckless drivers who pay no attention to traffic regulations.

2. All graduates of West Point are commissioned officers in the U.S. Army.

3. Some European cars are overpriced and underpowered automobiles.

4. No reptiles are warm-blooded animals.

*5. Some professional wrestlers are elderly persons who are incapable of doing an honest day's work.

B. State the obverses of the following propositions.

*1. Some college athletes are professionals.

2. No organic compounds are metals.

3. Some clergy are not abstainers.

4. No geniuses are conformists.

*5. All objects suitable for boat anchors are objects that weigh at least fifteen pounds.

C. State the contrapositives of the following propositions and indicate which of them are equivalent to the given propositions.

*1. All journalists are pessimists.

2. Some soldiers are not officers.

3. All scholars are nondegenerates.

4. All things weighing less than fifty pounds are objects not more than four feet high.

*5. Some noncitizens are not nonresidents.

D. If "All socialists are pacifists" is true, what may be inferred about the truth or falsehood of the following propositions? That is, which can be known to be true, which can be known to be false, and which are undetermined?

*1. Some nonpacifists are not nonsocialists.
2. No socialists are nonpacifists.
3. All nonsocialists are nonpacifists.
4. No nonpacifists are socialists.
*5. No nonsocialists are nonpacifists.
6. All nonpacifists are nonsocialists.
7. No pacifists are nonsocialists.
8. Some socialists are not pacifists.
9. All pacifists are socialists.
*10. Some nonpacifists are socialists.

E. If "No scientists are philosophers" is true, what may be inferred about the truth or falsehood of the following propositions? That is, which can be known to be true, which can be known to be false, and which are undetermined?

*1. No nonphilosophers are scientists.
2. Some nonphilosophers are not nonscientists.
3. All nonscientists are nonphilosophers.
4. No scientists are nonphilosophers.
*5. No nonscientists are nonphilosophers.
6. All philosophers are scientists.
7. Some nonphilosophers are scientists.
8. All nonphilosophers are nonscientists.
9. Some scientists are not philosophers.
*10. No philosophers are nonscientists.

F. If "Some saints were martyrs" is true, what may be inferred about the truth or falsehood of the following propositions? That is, which can be known to be true, which can be known to be false, and which are undetermined?

*1. All saints were martyrs.
2. All saints were nonmartyrs.
3. Some martyrs were saints.
4. No saints were martyrs.
*5. All martyrs were nonsaints.
6. Some nonmartyrs were saints.

7. Some saints were not nonmartyrs.
8. No martyrs were saints.
9. Some nonsaints were martyrs.
*10. Some martyrs were nonsaints.
11. Some saints were not martyrs.
12. Some martyrs were not saints.
13. No saints were nonmartyrs.
14. No nonsaints were martyrs.
*15. Some martyrs were not nonsaints.

G. If "Some merchants are not pirates" is true, what may be inferred about the truth or falsehood of the following propositions? That is, which can be known to be true, which can be known to be false, and which are undetermined?

*1. No pirates are merchants.
2. No merchants are nonpirates.
3. Some merchants are nonpirates.
4. All nonmerchants are pirates.
*5. Some nonmerchants are nonpirates.
6. All merchants are pirates.
7. No nonmerchants are pirates.
8. No pirates are nonmerchants.
9. All nonpirates are nonmerchants.
*10. Some nonpirates are not nonmerchants.
11. Some nonpirates are merchants.
12. No nonpirates are merchants.
13. Some pirates are merchants.
14. No merchants are nonpirates.
*15. No merchants are pirates.

5.7 Existential Import and the Interpretation of Categorical Propositions

Categorical propositions are the building blocks of arguments, and our aim throughout is to analyze and evaluate arguments. To do this we must be able to diagram and symbolize the **A**, **E**, **I**, and **O** propositions. But before we can do that we must confront and resolve a deep logical problem—one that has been a source of controversy for literally thousands of years. In this section we explain this problem, and we provide a resolution on which a coherent analysis of syllogisms may be developed.

The issues here, as we shall see, are far from simple, but the analysis of syllogisms in succeeding chapters does not require that the complications of this controversy be mastered. It does require that the interpretation of categorical propositions that emerges from the resolution of the controversy be understood. This is commonly called the **Boolean interpretation** of categorical propositions—named after George Boole (1815–1864), an English mathematician whose contributions to logical theory played a key role in the later development of the modern computer. So if the outcome of the following discussion—summarized in the final two paragraphs of this section on pages 210–211 is fully grasped, the intervening pages of this section may be safely bypassed.

To understand the problem, and the Boolean outcome with which we emerge, it must be seen that some propositions have existential import, and some do not. A proposition is said to have **existential import** if it typically is uttered to assert the existence of objects of some kind. Why should this seemingly abstruse matter be of concern to the student of logic? Because the correctness of the reasoning in many arguments is directly affected by whether the propositions of which those arguments are built do, or do not, have existential import. We must arrive at a clear and consistent interpretation of categorical propositions in order to determine with confidence what may be rightly inferred from them, and to guard against incorrect inferences that are sometimes drawn from them.

We begin with **I** and **O** propositions, which surely do have existential import. Thus the **I** proposition, "Some soldiers are heroes," says that there exists at least one soldier who is a hero. And the **O** proposition, "Some dogs are not companions," says that there exists at least one dog that is not a companion. Particular propositions, **I** and **O** propositions, plainly *do* assert that the classes designated by their subject terms (for example, soldiers and dogs) are not empty—the class of soldiers, and the class of dogs (if the examples given here are true), each has at least one member.*

---

*A few propositions appear to be exceptions. "Some ghosts appear in Shakespeare's plays" and "Some Greek gods are described in the *Iliad*" are particular propositions that are certainly true even though there are neither ghosts nor Greek gods. However, it is the formulation that misleads in such cases. These statements do not themselves affirm the existence of ghosts or Greek gods; they say only that there are certain other propositions that are affirmed or implied in Shakespeare's plays and in the *Iliad*. The propositions of Shakespeare and Homer may not be true, but it is certainly true that their writings contain or imply those propositions. And that is all that is affirmed by these apparent exceptions, which arise chiefly in literary or mythological contexts. **I** and **O** propositions do have existential import.

VISUAL LOGIC

Aristotle v. Boole on Interpreting Categorical Propositions

Source: © Topham/The Image Works

There are two rival interpretations of categorical propositions: the Aristotelian, which is traditional, and the Boolean, which is modern.

In the interpretation of the ancient Greek philosopher Aristotle, the truth of a universal proposition ("All leprechauns wear little green hats," or "No frogs are poisonous") implies the truth of its corresponding particular proposition ("Some leprechauns wear little green hats" or "Some frogs are not poisonous").

In contrast, George Boole, a nineteenth-century English mathematician, argued that we cannot infer the truth of the particular proposition from the truth of its corresponding universal proposition, because (as both sides agree) every particular proposition asserts the existence of its subject class; if some frogs are not poisonous, there must be at least one frog. But if the universal proposition permits us to infer the corresponding particular proposition, then "All leprechauns wear little green hats" would permit us to infer that some leprechauns do, and that would imply that there really are leprechauns!

So, in the modern or Boolean interpretation, a universal proposition (an **A** or an **E** proposition) must be understood to assert only that "If there is such a thing as a leprechaun, it wears a little green hat," and "If there is such a thing as a frog, it is not poisonous."

Source: © Topham/The Image Works

If this is so, however, if **I** and **O** propositions have existential import (as no one would wish to deny), wherein lies the problem? The problem arises from the *consequences* of this fact, which are very awkward. Earlier we saw that an **I** proposition follows validly from its corresponding **A** proposition by subalternation. That is, from "All spiders are eight-legged animals," we infer validly that some spiders are eight-legged animals. And similarly, we said that an **O** proposition follows validly from its corresponding **E** proposition. But if **I** and

O propositions have existential import, and they follow validly from their corresponding **A** and **E** propositions, then **A** and **E** propositions must *also* have existential import, because a proposition with existential import cannot be derived validly from another that does not have such import.*

This consequence creates a very serious problem. We know that **A** and **O** propositions, on the traditional square of opposition, are contradictories. "All Danes speak English" is contradicted by "Some Danes do not speak English." Contradictories cannot both be true, because one of the pair must be false; nor can they both be false, because one of the pair must be true. But *if* corresponding **A** and **O** propositions do have existential import, as we concluded in the paragraph just above, then both contradictories *could* be false! To illustrate, the **A** proposition, "All inhabitants of Mars are blond," and its corresponding **O** proposition, "Some inhabitants of Mars are not blond," are contradictories; if they have existential import—that is, if we interpret them as asserting that there *are* inhabitants of Mars—then both these propositions are false if Mars has no inhabitants. And, of course, we do know that Mars has no inhabitants; the class of its inhabitants is empty, so both of the propositions in the example are false. But if they are both false, they *cannot be contradictories!*

Something seems to have gone wrong with the traditional square of opposition in cases of this kind. If the traditional square is correct when it tells us that **A** and **E** propositions validly imply their corresponding **I** and **O** propositions, then the square is not correct when it tells us that corresponding **A** and **O** propositions are contradictories. And in that case, the square is also mistaken in holding that the corresponding **I** and **O** propositions are subcontraries.

What is to be done? Can the traditional square of opposition be rescued? Yes, it can, but the price is high. We could rehabilitate the traditional square of opposition by introducing the notion of a *presupposition*. Much earlier (in Section 4.5), we observed that some complex questions are properly answered "yes" or "no" only if the answer to a prior question has been presupposed. "Did you spend the money you stole?" can be reasonably answered "yes" or "no" only if the presupposition that you stole some money is granted. Now, to rescue the square of opposition, we might insist that *all* propositions—that is, the four standard-form categorical propositions **A, E, I,** and **O**—presuppose (in the sense indicated above) that the classes to which they refer do have

*There is another way to show that the existential import of **A** and **E** propositions must follow from that of **I** and **O** propositions, on the traditional square of opposition. In the case of the **A** proposition, we could show it by relying on the (traditionally assumed) validity of conversion by limitation; in the case of the **E** proposition, we could show it by relying on the (traditionally assumed) validity of contraposition by limitation. The result is always the same as that reached above: On the traditional square of opposition, if **I** and **O** propositions have existential import, **A** and **E** propositions must also have existential import.

members; they are not empty. That is, questions about the truth or falsehood of propositions, and about the logical relations holding among them, are admissible and may be reasonably answered (in this interpretation) only if we presuppose that they never refer to empty classes. In this way, we may save all of the relationships set forth in the traditional square of opposition: **A** and **E** will remain contraries, **I** and **O** will remain subcontraries, subalterns will follow validly from their superalterns, and **A** and **O** will remain contradictories, as will **I** and **E.** To achieve this result, however, we must pay by making the blanket presupposition that all classes designated by our terms (and the complements of these classes) do have members—are not empty.*

Well, why not do just that? This existential presupposition is both necessary and sufficient to rescue Aristotelian logic. It is, moreover, a presupposition in full accord with the ordinary use of modern languages such as English in very many cases. If you are told, "All the apples in the barrel are Delicious," and you find when you look into the barrel that it is empty, what can you say? You would probably not say that the claim is false, or true, but would instead point out that there *are* no apples in the barrel. You would thus be explaining that the speaker had made a mistake, that in this case the existential presupposition (that there exist apples in the barrel) was false. And the fact that we would respond in this corrective fashion shows that we do understand, and do generally accept, the existential presupposition of propositions that are ordinarily uttered.

Unfortunately, this blanket existential presupposition, introduced to rescue the traditional square of opposition, imposes intellectual penalties that are too heavy to bear. There are very good reasons *not* to do it. Here are three such reasons.

First, this rescue preserves the traditional relations among **A, E, I,** and **O** propositions, but only at the cost of reducing their power to formulate assertions that we may need to formulate. If we invariably presuppose that the class designated has members, *we will never be able to formulate the proposition that denies that it has members!* And such denials may sometimes be very important and must surely be made intelligible.

Second, even ordinary usage of language is not in complete accord with this blanket presupposition. *Sometimes what we say does not suppose that there are*

*Phillip H. Wiebe argues that Aristotelian logic does not require the assumption that the class designated by the complement of the subject term be nonempty. See "Existential Assumptions for Aristotelian Logic," *Journal of Philosophical Research* 16 (1990–1991): 321–328. But Aristotelian logic certainly does require the assumption that at least the classes designated by the other three terms (the subject term, the predicate term, and the complement of the predicate term) are not empty—and this existential assumption gives rise to all the difficulties noted in the remarks that follow.

members in the classes we are talking about. If you say, for example, "All trespassers will be prosecuted," far from presupposing that the class of trespassers has members, you will ordinarily be intending to ensure that the class will become and remain empty!

Third, in science, and in other theoretical spheres, *we often wish to reason without making any presuppositions about existence.* Newton's first law of motion, for example, asserts that certain things are true about bodies that are not acted on by any external forces: They remain at rest, or they continue their straight-line motion. The law may be true; a physicist may wish to express and defend it without wanting to presuppose that there actually are any bodies that are not acted on by external forces.

Objections of this kind make the blanket existential presupposition unacceptable for modern logicians. The Aristotelian interpretation of categorical propositions, long thought to be correct, must be abandoned, and a more modern interpretation employed.

In modern logic it is not assumed that the classes to which categorical propositions refer always have members. The modern interpretation that explicitly rejects this assumption is called, as we noted earlier, Boolean.* We adopt the Boolean interpretation of categorical propositions in all that follows. This has important logical consequences. Therefore we set forth now what this Boolean interpretation of categorical propositions entails.

1. In some respects, the traditional interpretation is not upset. **I** *and* **O** *propositions continue to have existential import in the Boolean interpretation,* so the proposition "Some *S* is *P*" is false if the class *S* is empty, and the proposition "Some *S* is not-*P*" is likewise false if the class *S* is empty.
2. It also remains true in this interpretation that *the universal propositions,* **A** *and* **E**, *are the contradictories of the particular propositions,* **O** *and* **I**. That is, the proposition "All men are mortal" does contradict the proposition "Some men are not mortal," and the proposition "No gods are mortal" does contradict the proposition "Some gods are mortal."
3. All this is entirely coherent because, in the Boolean interpretation, *universal propositions are interpreted as having no existential import.* So even when the *S* class is empty, the proposition "All *S* is *P*" can be true, as can the proposition "No *S* is *P*." For example, the propositions "All unicorns have horns" and "No unicorns have wings" may both be true, even if

*Bertrand Russell, another of the founders of modern symbolic logic, also advanced this approach in a famous essay entitled "The Existential Import of Propositions," in *Mind*, July 1905, and referred to it there as "Peano's interpretation" of propositions, after Guiseppe Peano, a great Italian mathematician of the early twentieth century.

there are no unicorns. But if there are no unicorns, the **I** proposition, "Some unicorns have horns," is false, as is the **O** proposition, "Some unicorns do not have wings."

4. Sometimes, in ordinary discourse, we utter a universal proposition with which we do intend to assert existence. *The Boolean interpretation permits this to be expressed,* but doing so requires two propositions, one existential in force but particular, the other universal but not existential in force.
5. Some very important changes result from our adoption of the Boolean interpretation. *Corresponding* **A** *and* **E** *propositions can both be true and are therefore not contraries*. This may seem paradoxical and will be explained in detail later, in Sections 10.2 and 10.3. For the present it will suffice to say that, in the Boolean interpretation, "All unicorns have wings" is taken to assert that "If there is a unicorn, then it has wings," and "No unicorns have wings" is taken to assert that "If there is a unicorn, it does not have wings." And both of these "if. . . then" propositions can be true if indeed there are no unicorns.
6. In like manner, in the Boolean interpretation, corresponding **I** and **O** propositions, because they do have existential import, can both be false if the subject class is empty. So *corresponding* **I** *and* **O** *propositions are not subcontraries.*
7. In the Boolean interpretation, *subalternation*—inferring an **I** proposition from its corresponding **A**, and an **O** proposition from its corresponding **E**—*is not generally valid.* This is because, plainly, one may not validly infer a proposition that has existential import from one that does not.
8. The Boolean interpretation *preserves* some immediate inferences: *conversion for* **E** *and for* **I** *propositions* is preserved; *contraposition for* **A** *and for* **O** *propositions* is preserved; *obversion for any proposition* is preserved. But conversion by limitation, and contraposition by limitation, are not generally valid.
9. The traditional square of opposition, in the Boolean interpretation, is transformed in the following general way: *Relations along the sides of the square are undone, but the diagonal, contradictory relations remain in force.*

In short, the blanket existential presupposition is rejected by modern logicians. It is a mistake, we hold, to *assume* that a class has members if it is not asserted explicitly that it does. Any argument that relies on this mistaken assumption is said to commit the fallacy of existential assumption, or more briefly, the **existential fallacy.** With this Boolean interpretation clearly in mind, we are now in a position to set forth a powerful system for the symbolizing and diagramming of standard-form categorical syllogisms.

EXERCISES

In the preceding discussion of existential import, it was shown why, in the Boolean interpretation of propositions adopted in this book, some inferences, which traditionally were thought to be valid, mistakenly assume that certain classes have members; these inferences commit the existential fallacy and are not valid. This existential fallacy is committed in each of the following arguments; explain the point at which, in each argument, the mistaken existential assumption is made.

EXAMPLE

A. (1) No mathematician is one who has squared the circle.
therefore, (2) No one who has squared the circle is a mathematician;
therefore, (3) All who have squared the circle are nonmathematicians;
therefore, (4) Some nonmathematician is one who has squared the circle.

SOLUTION

Step (3) to step (4) is invalid. The inference at this point is conversion by limitation (that is, from *All S is P* to *Some P is S*), which was acceptable in the traditional interpretation but is invalid in the Boolean interpretation. This step relies on an inference from a universal proposition to a particular proposition, but the preceding discussion has shown that the classes in a universal proposition cannot be assumed to have members, whereas the classes in a particular proposition do have members. Thus the invalid passage from (3) to (4) permits the inference that the predicate class in (4) is not empty, and therefore that there *is* someone who has squared the circle! In inferring (4) from (3), one commits the existential fallacy.

B. (1) No citizen is one who has succeeded in accomplishing the impossible;
therefore, (2) No one who has succeeded in accomplishing the impossible is a citizen;
therefore, (3) All who have succeeded in accomplishing the impossible are noncitizens;
therefore, (4) Some who have succeeded in accomplishing the impossible are noncitizens;
therefore, (5) Some noncitizen is one who has succeeded in accomplishing the impossible.

C. (1) No acrobat is one who can lift himself by his own bootstraps;
therefore, (2) No one who can lift himself by his own bootstraps is an acrobat;
therefore, (3) Someone who can lift himself by his own bootstraps is not an acrobat. (From which it follows that there is at least one being who can lift himself by his own bootstraps.)

D. (1) It is true that: No unicorns are animals found in the Bronx Zoo;
therefore, (2) It is false that: All unicorns are animals found in the Bronx Zoo;
therefore (3) It is true that: Some unicorns are not animals found in the Bronx Zoo. (From which it follows that there exists at least one unicorn.)

*E. (1) It is false that: Some mermaids are members of college sororities;
therefore (2) It is true that: Some mermaids are not members of college sororities. (From which it follows that there exists at least one mermaid.)

5.8 Symbolism and Diagrams for Categorical Propositions

Because the Boolean interpretation of categorical propositions depends heavily on the notion of an empty class, it is convenient to have a special symbol to represent it. The zero symbol, 0, is used for this purpose. To say that the class designated by the term S has no members, we write an equals sign between S and 0. Thus the equation $S = 0$ says that there are no S's, or that S has no members.

To say that the class designated by S does have members is to deny that S is empty. To assert that there are S's is to deny the proposition symbolized by $S = 0$. We symbolize that denial by drawing a slanting line through the equals sign. Thus the inequality $S \neq 0$ says that there are S's, by denying that S is empty.

Standard-form categorical propositions refer to two classes, so the equations that represent them are somewhat more complicated. Where each of two classes is already designated by a symbol, the class of all things that belong to both of them can be represented by juxtaposing the symbols for the two original classes. For example, if the letter S designates the class of all satires and the letter *P* designates the class of all poems, then the class of all things that are both satires and poems is represented by the symbol *SP*, which thus designates the class of all satirical poems (or poetic satires). The common part or common membership of two classes is called the *product* or *intersection* of the two classes. The *product* of two classes is the class of all things that belong to both of them. The product of the class of all Americans and the class of all composers is the class of all American composers. (One must be on one's guard against certain oddities of the English language here. For example, the product of the class of all Spaniards and the class of all dancers is not the class of all Spanish dancers, for a Spanish dancer is not a dancer who is Spanish, but any person who performs Spanish dances. Similarly, with abstract painters, English majors, antique dealers, and so on.)

This new notation permits us to symbolize **E** and **I** propositions as equations and inequalities. The **E** proposition, "No *S* is *P*," says that no members of the class *S* are members of the class *P*; that is, there are no things that belong to both classes. This can be rephrased by saying that the product of the two classes is empty, which is symbolized by the equation $SP = 0$. The **I** proposition, "Some *S* is *P*," says that at least one member of *S* is also a member of *P*. This means that the product of the classes *S* and *P* is not empty and is symbolized by the inequality $SP \neq 0$.

To symbolize **A** and **O** propositions, it is convenient to introduce a new method of representing class complements. The complement of a class is the collection or class of all things that do not belong to the original class, as explained in Section 5.6. The complement of the class of all soldiers is the class of all things that are not soldiers—the class of all nonsoldiers. Where the letter *S* symbolizes the class of all soldiers, we symbolize the class of all nonsoldiers by $\bar{S}$ (read "S bar"), the symbol for the original class with a bar above it. The **A** proposition, "All *S* is *P*," says that all members of the class *S* are also members of the class *P*; that is, that there are no members of the class *S* that are not members of P or (by obversion) that "No *S* is non-*P*." This, like any other **E** proposition, says that the product of the classes designated by its subject and predicate terms is empty. It is symbolized by the equation $S\bar{P} = 0$. The **O** proposition, "Some *S* is not *P*," obverts to the logically equivalent **I** proposition, "Some *S* is non-*P*," which is symbolized by the inequality $S\bar{P} \neq 0$.

In their symbolic formulations, the interrelations among the four standard-form categorical propositions appear very clearly. It is obvious that the **A** and **O** propositions are contradictories when they are symbolized as $S\bar{P} = 0$ and $S\bar{P} \neq 0$, and it is equally obvious that the **E** and **I** propositions, $SP = 0$ and $SP \neq 0$, are contradictories. The *Boolean square of opposition* may be represented as shown in Figure 5-2.

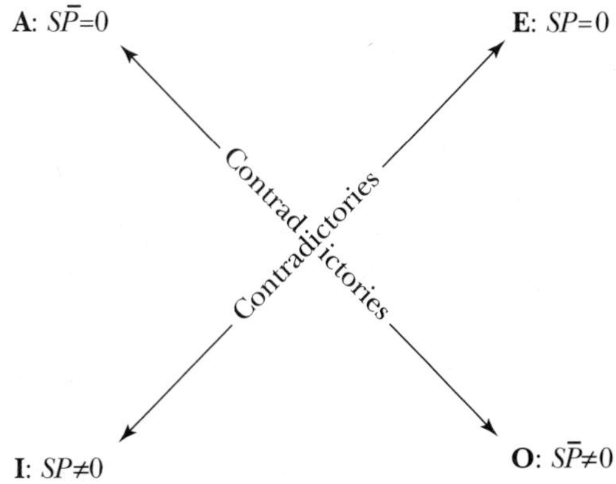

Figure 5-2 The Boolean Square of Opposition

OVERVIEW

Symbolic Representation of Categorical Propositions

Form	Proposition	Symbolic Representation	Explanation
A	All *S* is *P*.	$S\bar{P} = 0$	The class of things that are both *S* and non-*P* is empty.
E	No *S* is *P*.	$SP = 0$	The class of things that are both *S* and *P* is empty.
I	Some *S* is *P*.	$SP \neq 0$	The class of things that are both *S* and *P* is not empty. (*SP* has at least one member.)
O	Some *S* is not *P*.	$S\bar{P} \neq 0$	The class of things that are both *S* and non-*P* is not empty. ($S\bar{P}$ has at least one member.)

The notation shown in the table is useful, for example, in representing the relationship among contradictories in the Boolean square of opposition.

When first explaining the four types of standard-form categorical propositions, in Section 5.3, we represented the relations of the classes in those propositions graphically with intersecting circles, labeled *S* and *P*. Now we carry that process of diagramming categorical propositions somewhat further, enriching our notation in ways that will facilitate the analysis to follow. We begin by representing any class with an unmarked circle, labeled with the term that designates that class. The class *S* is diagrammed with a simple circle, as shown in Figure 5-3.

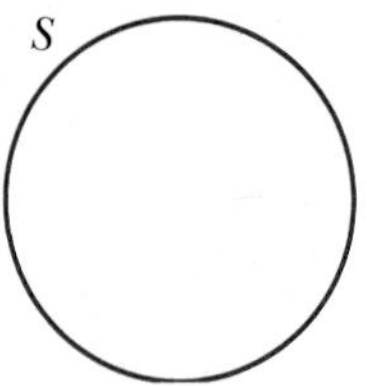

Figure 5-3

The diagram in Figure 5-3 is of a class, not a proposition. It represents the class *S*, but it says nothing about it. To diagram the proposition that *S* has no members, or that there are no *S*'s, we shade all of the interior of the circle representing *S*, indicating in this way that it contains nothing and is empty. To diagram the proposition that there are *S*'s, which we interpret as saying that there is at least one member of *S*, we place an *x* anywhere in the interior of the circle representing *S*, indicating in this way that there is something inside it, that it is not empty. Thus the two propositions, "There are no *S*'s," and "There are *S*'s," are represented by the two diagrams in Figure 5-4.

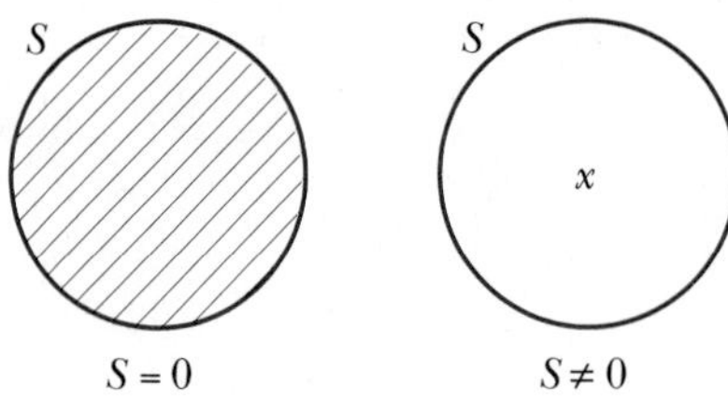

Figure 5-4

Note that the circle that diagrams the class *S* will also, in effect, diagram the class $\bar{S}$, for just as the interior of the circle represents all members of *S*, so the exterior of the circle represents all members of $\bar{S}$.

To diagram a standard-form categorical proposition, as explained in Section 5.3, two circles are required. Figure 5-5 shows a pair of intersecting circles, which we may use as the skeleton, or framework, for diagramming any standard-form categorical proposition whose subject terms are abbreviated by *S* and *P*.

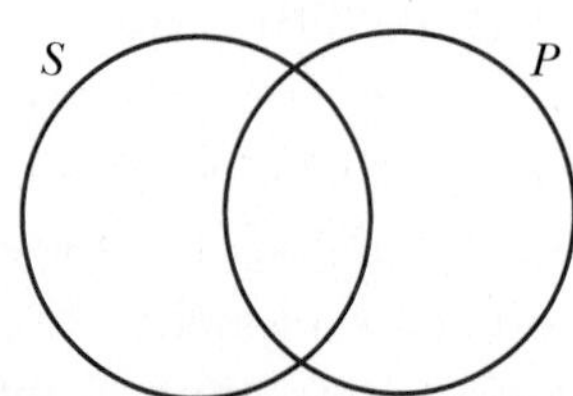

Figure 5-5

Figure 5-5 diagrams the two classes of *S* and *P* but diagrams no proposition concerning them. It does not affirm that either or both have members, nor does it deny that they have. As a matter of fact, there are more than two classes diagrammed by the two intersecting circles. The part of the circle labeled *S* that does not overlap the circle labeled *P* diagrams all *S*'s that are not *P*'s and can be thought of as representing the product of the classes *S* and $\bar{P}$. We may label it $S\bar{P}$. The overlapping part of the two circles represents the product of the classes *S* and *P*, and diagrams all things belonging to both of them. It is labeled *SP*. The part of the circle labeled *P* that does not overlap the circle labeled *S* diagrams all *P*'s that are not *S*'s, and represents the product of the class $\bar{S}$ and *P*. It is labeled $\bar{S}P$. Finally, the part of the diagram external to both circles represents all things that are neither in *S* nor in *P*; it diagrams the fourth class $\overline{SP}$, so labeled. With these labels inserted, Figure 5-5 becomes Figure 5-6.

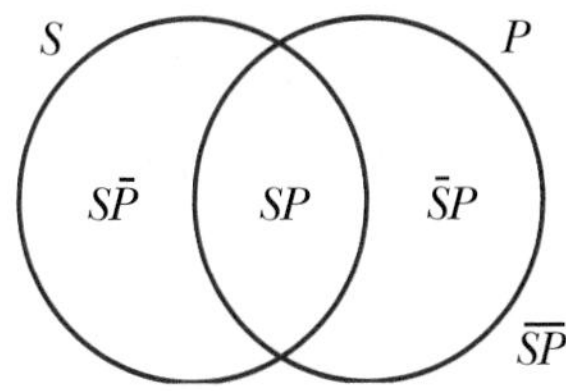

Figure 5-6

Figure 5-6 can be interpreted in terms of the several different classes determined by the class of all Spaniards (*S*) and the class of all painters (*P*). *SP* is the product of these two classes, containing all those things and only those things that belong to both of them. Every member of *SP* must be a member of both *S* and *P*; every member must be both a Spaniard and a painter. This product class *SP* is the class of all Spanish painters, which contains, among others, Velásquez and Goya. $S\bar{P}$ is the product of the first class and the complement of the second, containing all those things and only those things that belong to the class *S* but not to the class *P*. It is the class of all Spaniards who are not painters, all Spanish nonpainters, and it will contain neither Velásquez nor Goya, but it will include both the novelist Cervantes and the dictator Franco, among many others. $\bar{S}P$ is the product of the second class and the complement of the first, and is the class of all painters who are not Spaniards. This class $\bar{S}P$ of all non-Spanish painters includes, among others, both the Dutch painter Rembrandt and the American painter Georgia O'Keeffe. Finally, $\overline{SP}$ is the product of the complements of the two original classes. It contains all those things and only those things that are neither Spaniards nor painters. It is a very large class indeed, containing not merely English admirals and Swiss mountain climbers, but such things as the Mississippi River and Mount

Everest. All these classes are diagrammed in Figure 5-6, where the letters *S* and *P* are interpreted as in this paragraph.

Diagrams of this kind, as noted earlier, are called *Venn diagrams* after John Venn, the English logician who introduced this notation. When, in such diagrams, the several areas are labeled, but not marked in any other way, they represent *classes* only. Figure 5-6 illustrates this. It does not represent any proposition. In such a diagram, if a circle or part of a circle is blank, that signifies nothing—neither that there are, nor that there are not, members of the class represented by that space.

With certain additions, however, Venn diagrams can be used to represent *propositions* as well as classes. By shading out some spaces, or by inserting *x*'s in various parts of the picture, we can accurately diagram any one of the four standard-form categorical propositions. Because Venn diagrams (with appropriate markings) represent categorical propositions so fully and so graphically, these diagrams have become one of the most powerful and most widely used instruments for the appraisal of syllogistic arguments. Let us consider how each of the four basic categorical propositions can be represented using this technique.

To diagram the **A** proposition, "All *S* is *P*," symbolized by $S\bar{P} = 0$, we simply shade out the part of the diagram that represents the class $S\bar{P}$, thus indicating that it has no members or is empty. To diagram the **E** proposition, "No *S* is *P*," symbolized by $SP = 0$, we shade out the part of the diagram that represents the class *SP*, to indicate that it is empty. To diagram the **I** proposition, "Some *S* is *P*," symbolized by $SP \neq 0$, we insert an *x* into the part of the diagram that represents the class *SP*. This insertion indicates that the class product is not empty but has at least one member. Finally, for the **O** proposition, "Some *S* is not *P*," symbolized by $S\bar{P} \neq 0$, we insert an *x* into the part of the diagram that represents the class $S\bar{P}$, to indicate that it is not empty but has at least one member. Placed side by side, diagrams for the four standard-form categorical propositions display their different meanings very clearly, as shown in Figure 5-7.

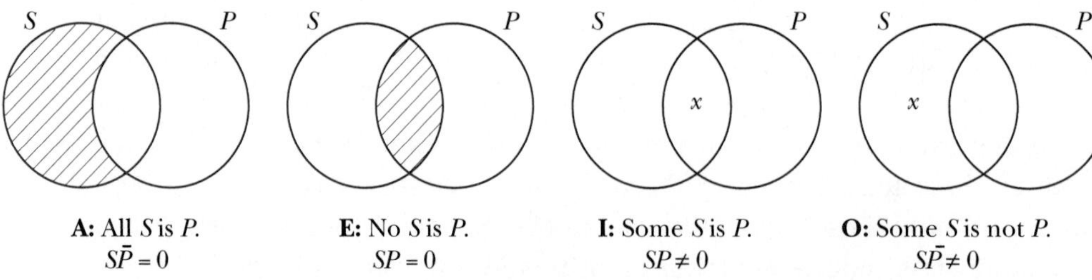

Figure 5-7

We have constructed diagrammatic representations for "No S is P" and "Some S is P," and because these are logically equivalent to their converses, "No P is S" and "Some P is S," the diagrams for the latter have already been shown. To diagram the **A** proposition, "All P is S," symbolized by $P\bar{S} = 0$ within the same framework, we must shade out the part of the diagram that represents the class $P\bar{S}$. It should be obvious that the class $P\bar{S}$ is the same as the class $\bar{S}P$—if not immediately, then by recognizing that every object that belongs to the class of all painters and the class of all non-Spaniards must (also) belong to the class of all non-Spaniards and the class of all painters—all painting non-Spaniards are non-Spanish painters, and vice versa. And to diagram the **O** proposition, "Some P is not S," symbolized by $P\bar{S} \neq 0$, we insert an x into the part of the diagram that represents the class $P\bar{S}$ (= $\bar{S}P$). Diagrams for these propositions then appear as shown in Figure 5-8.

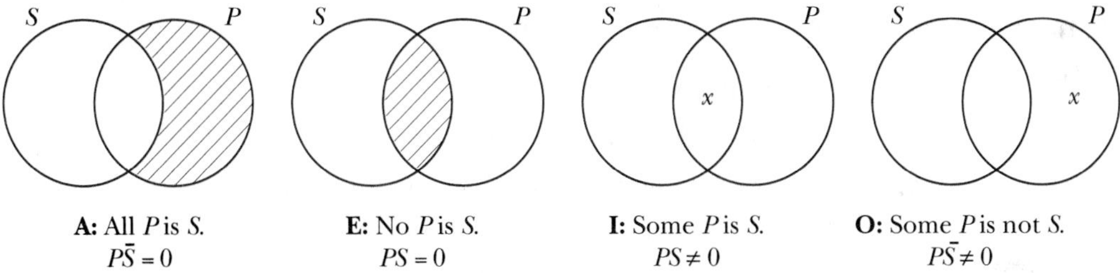

Figure 5-8

This further adequacy of the two-circle diagrams is mentioned because in the next chapter it will be important to be able to use a given pair of overlapping circles with given labels—say, S and M—to diagram any standard-form categorical proposition containing S and M as its terms, regardless of the order in which they occur in it.

The Venn diagrams constitute an *iconic* representation of the standard-form categorical propositions, in which spatial inclusions and exclusions correspond to the nonspatial inclusions and exclusions of classes. They provide an exceptionally clear method of notation. They also provide the basis for the simplest and most direct method of testing the validity of categorical syllogisms, as will be explained in Chapter 6.

EXERCISES

Express each of the following propositions as equalities or inequalities, representing each class by the first letter of the English term designating it, and symbolizing the proposition by means of a Venn diagram.

EXAMPLE

1. Some sculptors are painters.

SOLUTION

$SP \neq 0$

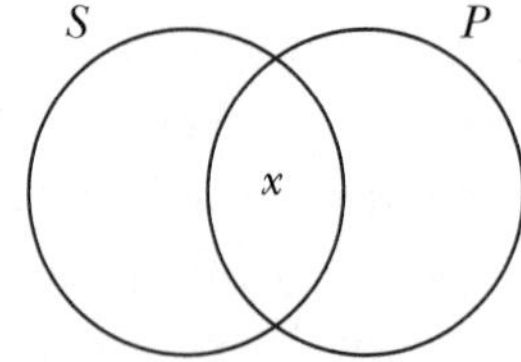

2. No peddlers are millionaires.
3. All merchants are speculators.
4. Some musicians are not pianists.

*5. No shopkeepers are members.

6. Some political leaders of high reputation are scoundrels.
7. All physicians licensed to practice in this state are medical school graduates who have passed special qualifying examinations.
8. Some stockbrokers who advise their customers about making investments are not partners in companies whose securities they recommend.
9. All puritans who reject all useless pleasure are strangers to much that makes life worth living.

*10. No modern paintings are photographic likenesses of their objects.

11. Some student activists are middle-aged men and women striving to recapture their lost youth.
12. All medieval scholars were pious monks living in monasteries.
13. Some state employees are not public-spirited citizens.
14. No magistrates subject to election and recall will be punitive tyrants.

*15. Some patients exhibiting all the symptoms of schizophrenia have bipolar disorder.

16. Some passengers on large jet airplanes are not satisfied customers.
17. Some priests are militant advocates of radical social change.
18. Some stalwart defenders of the existing order are not members of a political party.
19. No pipelines laid across foreign territories are safe investments.

*20. All pornographic films are menaces to civilization and decency.

SUMMARY

This chapter has introduced and explained the basic elements of classical, or Aristotelian, deductive logic, as distinguished from modern symbolic logic. (See Section 5.1.)

In Section 5.2 we introduced the concept of classes, on which traditional logic is built, and the categorical propositions that express relations between classes.

In Section 5.3 we explained the four basic standard-form categorical propositions:

A: universal affirmative

E: universal negative

I: particular affirmative

O: particular negative

In Section 5.4 we discussed various features of these standard-form categorical propositions: their quality (affirmative or negative) and their quantity (universal or particular). We also explained why different terms are distributed or undistributed, in each of the four basic kinds of propositions.

In Section 5.5 we explored the kinds of opposition arising among the several standard-form categorical propositions: what it means for propositions to be contradictories, or contraries, or subcontraries, or sub- and superalterns of one another. We showed how these relations are exhibited on the traditional square of opposition, and explained the immediate inferences that can be drawn from them.

In Section 5.6 we examined other kinds of immediate inferences that are based on categorical propositions: conversion, obversion, and contraposition.

In Section 5.7 we explored the controversial issue of existential import, showing that the traditional square of opposition can be retained only if we make a blanket assumption that the classes to which the subjects of propositions refer always do have some members—an assumption that modern logicians are unwilling to make. We then explained the interpretation of propositions to be adopted throughout this book, called Boolean, which retains much, but not all, of the traditional square of opposition while rejecting the blanket assumption of nonempty classes. In this Boolean interpretation, we explained that particular propositions (**I** and **O** propositions) are interpreted as having existential import, whereas universal propositions (**A** and **E** propositions) are interpreted as not having such import. We carefully detailed the consequences of adopting this interpretation of propositions.

In Section 5.8 we returned to the use of Venn diagrams, using intersecting circles to represent classes. We showed how, with additional markings, Venn diagrams may also be used to represent categorical propositions.

This chapter has provided the tools we will need to analyze categorical syllogisms, of which standard-form propositions are the essential building blocks.

Categorical Syllogisms

6.1 Standard-Form Categorical Syllogisms

We are now in a position to use categorical propositions in more extended reasoning. Arguments that rely on **A, E, I,** and **O** propositions commonly have two categorical propositions as premises and one categorical proposition as a conclusion. Such arguments are called *syllogisms;* a **syllogism** is, in general, a deductive argument in which a conclusion is inferred from two premises.

The syllogisms with which we are concerned here are called *categorical* because they are arguments based on the relations of classes, or categories—relations that are expressed by the categorical propositions with which we are familiar. More formally, we define a **categorical syllogism** as a deductive argument consisting of three categorical propositions that together contain exactly three terms, each of which occurs in exactly two of the constituent propositions.

Syllogisms are very common, very clear, and readily testable. The system of categorical syllogisms that we will explore is powerful and deep. The seventeenth-century philosopher and mathematician Gottfried Leibniz said, of the invention of the form of syllogisms, that it was "one of the most beautiful and also one of the most important made by the human mind." Syllogisms are the workhorse arguments with which deductive logic, as traditionally practiced, has been made effective in writing and in controversy.

It will be convenient to have an example to use as we discuss the parts and features of the syllogism. Here is a valid standard-form categorical syllogism that we shall use as illustrative:

No heroes are cowards.

Some soldiers are cowards.

Therefore some soldiers are not heroes.

To analyze such an argument accurately, it needs to be in *standard form*. A **categorical syllogism** is said to be in standard form (as the above sample is) when two things are true of it: (1) its premises and its conclusion are all standard-form categorical propositions (**A, E, I,** or **O**); and (2) those propositions are arranged in a specified *standard order*. The importance of this standard form will become evident when we turn to the task of testing the validity of syllogisms.

To explain the order of the premises that is required to put any syllogism into standard form, we need the *logical names* of the *premises* of the syllogism, and the names of the *terms* of the syllogism, and we must understand why those names—very useful and very important—are assigned to them. This is the next essential step in our analysis of categorical syllogisms.*

A. TERMS OF THE SYLLOGISM: MAJOR, MINOR, AND MIDDLE

The three categorical propositions in our example argument above contain exactly three terms: *heroes, soldiers,* and *cowards*. To identify the terms by name, we look to the conclusion of the syllogism, which of course contains exactly two terms. The conclusion in our sample is an **O** proposition, "Some soldiers are not heroes." The term that occurs as the *predicate* of the conclusion ("heroes," in this case) is called the **major term** of the syllogism. The term that occurs as the *subject* of the conclusion ("soldiers" in this case) is called the **minor term** of the syllogism. The third term of the syllogism ("cowards" in this case), which never occurs in the conclusion but always appears in both premises, is called the **middle term.**

The premises of a syllogism also have names. Each premise is named after the term that appears in it. The major term and the minor term must each occur in a different premise. The premise containing the major term is called the **major premise.** In the example, "heroes" is the major term, so the premise containing "heroes"—"No heroes are cowards"—is the major premise. It is the major premise not because it appears first, but only because it is the premise that contains the major term; it would be the major premise no matter in what order the premises were written.

The premise containing the minor term is called the **minor premise.** In the example, "soldiers" is the minor term, so the premise containing "soldiers"—"Some soldiers are cowards"—is the minor premise. It is the minor premise not because of its position, but because it is the premise that contains the minor term.

---

*In this chapter, for the sake of brevity we will refer to categorical syllogisms simply as "syllogisms," even though there are other kinds of syllogisms that will be discussed in later chapters.

OVERVIEW

The Parts of a Standard-Form Categorical Syllogism

Major Term	The predicate term of the conclusion.
Minor Term	The subject term of the conclusion.
Middle Term	The term that appears in both premises but not in the conclusion.
Major Premise	The premise containing the major term.
Minor Premise	The premise containing the minor term.

A syllogism is in standard form, we said, when its premises are arranged in a specified standard order. Now we can state that order: *In a standard-form syllogism, the major premise is always stated first, the minor premise second, and the conclusion last.* The reason for the importance of this order will soon become clear.

B. THE MOOD OF THE SYLLOGISM

Every syllogism has a mood. The **mood** of a syllogism is determined by the types (**A, E, I,** or **O**) of standard-form categorical propositions it contains. The mood of the syllogism is therefore represented by three letters, and those three letters are always given in standard-form order. That is, the first letter names the type of the syllogism's major premise; the second letter names the type of the syllogism's minor premise; the third letter names the type of the syllogism's conclusion. In our example syllogism, the major premise ("No heroes are cowards") is an **E** proposition; the minor premise ("Some soldiers are cowards") is an **I** proposition; the conclusion ("Some soldiers are not heroes") is an **O** proposition. Therefore the mood of this syllogism is **EIO.**

C. THE FIGURE OF THE SYLLOGISM

The mood of a standard-form syllogism is not enough, by itself, to characterize its logical form. This can be shown by comparing two syllogisms, A and B, with the same mood, which are logically very different.

A.

Major Term (great scientists) **Middle Term** (college graduates)
All great scientists are college graduates.
Minor Term (professional athletes) **Middle Term** (college graduates)
Some professional athletes are college graduates.
Minor Term (professional athletes) **Major Term** (great scientists)
Therefore some professional athletes are great scientists.

B.

Middle Term (artists) **Major Term** (egotists)
All artists are egotists.
Middle Term (artists) **Minor Term** (paupers)
Some artists are paupers.
Minor Term (paupers) **Major Term** (egotists)
Therefore some paupers are egotists.

Both of these are of mood **AII,** but one of them is valid and the other is not. The difference in their forms can be shown most clearly if we display their logical "skeletons" by abbreviating the minor terms as *S* (subject of the conclusion), the major terms as *P* (predicate of the conclusion), and the middle terms as *M*. Using the three-dot symbol "∴" for "therefore," we get these skeletons:

A. All *P* is *M*.	B. All *M* is *P*.
Some *S* is *M*.	Some *M* is *S*.
∴ Some *S* is *P*.	∴ Some *S* is *P*.

These are very different. In the one labeled A, the middle term, *M*, is the predicate term of both premises; but in the one labeled B, the middle term, *M*, is the subject term of both premises. Syllogism B will be seen to be a valid argument; syllogism A, on the other hand, is invalid.

These examples show that although the form of a syllogism is partially described by its mood (**AII** in both of these cases), syllogisms that have the same mood may differ importantly in their forms, depending on the relative positions of their middle terms. To describe the form of a syllogism completely we must state its *mood* (the three letters of its three propositions) *and* its *figure*—where by **figure** we mean the position of the middle term in its premises.

Syllogisms can have four—and only four—possible different figures:

1. The middle term may be the subject term of the major premise and the predicate term of the minor premise; or
2. The middle term may be the predicate term of both premises; or
3. The middle term may be the subject term of both premises; or
4. The middle term may be the predicate term of the major premise and the subject term of the minor premise.

These different possible positions of the middle term constitute the first, second, third, and fourth figures, respectively. Every syllogism must have one or another of these four figures. The characters of these figures may be visualized more readily when the figures are schematized as in the following array, in which reference to mood is suppressed and the quantifiers and copulas are not shown—but the relative positions of the terms of the syllogism are brought out:

M — *P*	*P* — *M*	*M* — *P*	*P* — *M*
S — *M*	*S* — *M*	*M* — *S*	*M* — *S*
∴ *S* — *P*	∴ *S* — *P*	∴ *S* — *P*	∴ *S* — *P*
First Figure	Second Figure	Third Figure	Fourth Figure

Any standard-form syllogism is completely described when we specify its mood and its figure. The syllogism we have been using as an example is in the second figure; "cowards," the middle term, is the predicate term of both premises. Its mood, as we pointed out, is **EIO.** So it is completely described as being a syllogism of the form **EIO–2.** It is a valid syllogism, as we noted; every valid syllogistic form, as we shall see, has it own name. The name of this form, **EIO–2,** is ***Festino.*** We say of this syllogism that it is "in *Festino.*"

Here is another example:

No *M* is *P*

All *S* is *M*

∴ No *S* is *P*

This syllogism is in the first figure (its middle term is the subject of the major premise and the predicate of the minor premise); its mood is **EAE.** So we may characterize it completely as **EAE–1,** a form whose unique name is ***Celarent.*** Any syllogism of this form is "in *Celarent,*" just as any syllogism of the earlier form is "in *Festino.*" And because *Celarent* (**EAE–1**) and *Festino* (**EIO–2**) are known to be *valid* forms, we may conclude that whenever we encounter an argument in one of these forms, it too is valid.

With these analytical tools we can identify every possible categorical syllogism by mood and figure. If we were to list all the possible moods, beginning with **AAA, AAE, AAI, AAO, AEA, AEE,** . . ., and so on, continuing until every possibility had been named, we would eventually (upon reaching **OOO**) have enumerated sixty-four possible moods. Each mood can occur in each of the four figures; $4 \times 64 = 256$. It is certain, therefore, that there are exactly 256 distinct forms that standard-form syllogisms may assume.

Of these 256 possible forms, as we shall see, only a few are valid forms. And each of those valid forms has a unique name, as will be explained.

EXERCISES

Rewrite each of the following syllogisms in standard form, and name its mood and figure. (*Procedure:* first, identify the conclusion; second, note its predicate term, which is the major term of the syllogism; third, identify the major premise, which is the premise containing the major term; fourth, verify that the other premise is the minor premise by checking to see that it contains the minor term, which is the subject term of the conclusion; fifth, rewrite the argument in standard form—major premise first, minor premise second, conclusion last; sixth, name the mood and figure of the syllogism.)

EXAMPLE

1. No nuclear-powered submarines are commercial vessels, so no warships are commercial vessels, because all nuclear-powered submarines are warships.

SOLUTION

Step 1. The conclusion is "No warships are commercial vessels."

Step 2. "Commercial vessels" is the predicate term of this conclusion and is therefore the major term of the syllogism.

Step 3. The major premise, the premise that contains this term, is "No nuclear-powered submarines are commercial vessels."

Step 4. The remaining premise, "All nuclear-powered submarines are warships," is indeed the minor premise, because it does contain the subject term of the conclusion, "warships."

Step 5. In standard form this syllogism is written thus:

No nuclear-powered submarines are commercial vessels.
All nuclear-powered submarines are warships.
Therefore no warships are commercial vessels.

Step 6. The three propositions in this syllogism are, in order, **E, A,** and **E.** The middle term, "nuclear-powered submarines," is the subject term of both premises, so the syllogism is in the *third* figure. The mood and figure of the syllogism therefore are **EAE–3.**

2. Some evergreens are objects of worship, because all fir trees are evergreens, and some objects of worship are fir trees.

3. All artificial satellites are important scientific achievements; therefore some important scientific achievements are not U.S. inventions, inasmuch as some artificial satellites are not U.S. inventions.

4. No television stars are certified public accountants, but all certified public accountants are people of good business sense; it follows that no television stars are people of good business sense.

*5. Some conservatives are not advocates of high tariff rates, because all advocates of high tariff rates are Republicans, and some Republicans are not conservatives.

6. All CD players are delicate mechanisms, but no delicate mechanisms are suitable toys for children; consequently, no CD players are suitable toys for children.

7. All juvenile delinquents are maladjusted individuals, and some juvenile delinquents are products of broken homes; hence some maladjusted individuals are products of broken homes.

8. No stubborn individuals who never admit a mistake are good teachers, so, because some well-informed people are stubborn individuals who never admit a mistake, some good teachers are not well-informed people.

9. All proteins are organic compounds, hence all enzymes are proteins, as all enzymes are organic compounds.

*10. No sports cars are vehicles intended to be driven at moderate speeds, but all automobiles designed for family use are vehicles intended to be driven at moderate speeds, from which it follows that no sports cars are automobiles designed for family use.

6.2 The Formal Nature of Syllogistic Argument

In all deductive logic we aim to discriminate valid arguments from invalid ones; in classical logic this becomes the task of discriminating valid syllogisms from invalid ones. It is reasonable to assume that the constituent propositions of a syllogism are all contingent—that is, that no one of those propositions is necessarily true, or necessarily false. Under this assumption, the validity or invalidity of any syllogism depends entirely on its *form*. Validity and invalidity are completely independent of the specific content of the argument or its subject matter. Thus any syllogism of the form **AAA–1**

All *M* is *P*

<u>All *S* is *M*</u>

∴ All *S* is *P*

is valid, regardless of its subject matter. The name of this syllogism's form is ***Barbara;*** no matter what terms are substituted for the letters *S*, *P*, and *M*, the resulting argument, "in *Barbara*," will always be valid. If we substitute "Athenians" and "humans" for *S* and *P*, and "Greeks" for *M*, we obtain this valid argument:

All Greeks are humans.

<u>All Athenians are Greeks.</u>

∴ All Athenians are humans.

And if we substitute the terms "soaps," "water-soluble substances," and "sodium salts" for the letters *S*, *P*, and *M* in the same form, we obtain

All sodium salts are water-soluble substances.

All soaps are sodium salts.

Therefore all soaps are water-soluble substances.

which also is valid.

A valid syllogism is a formally valid argument—valid by virtue of its form alone. This implies that if a given syllogism is valid, *any other syllogism of the same form will also be valid.* And if a syllogism is invalid, *any other syllogism of the same form will also be invalid.** The common recognition of this fact is attested to by the frequent use of "logical analogies" in argumentation. Suppose that we are presented with the argument

All liberals are proponents of national health insurance.

Some members of the administration are proponents of national health insurance.

Therefore some members of the administration are liberals.

and felt (justifiably) that, regardless of the truth or falsehood of its constituent propositions, the argument is invalid. The best way to expose its fallacious character is to construct another argument that has exactly the same form but whose invalidity is immediately apparent. We might seek to expose the given argument by replying: You might as well argue that

All rabbits are very fast runners.

Some horses are very fast runners.

Therefore some horses are rabbits.

We might continue: You cannot seriously defend this argument, because here there is no question about the facts. The premises are known to be true and the conclusion is known to be false. Your argument is of the same

*We assume, as noted above, that the constituent propositions are themselves contingent, that is, neither logically true (e.g., "All easy chairs are chairs") nor logically false (e.g., "Some easy chairs are not chairs"). The reason for the assumption is this: If it contained either a logically false premise or a logically true conclusion, then the argument would be valid regardless of its syllogistic form—valid in that it would be logically impossible for its premises to be true and its conclusion false. We also assume that the only logical relations among the terms of the syllogism are those asserted or entailed by its premises. The point of these restrictions is to limit our considerations in this chapter and the next to syllogistic arguments alone and to exclude other kinds of arguments whose validity turns on more complex logical considerations that are not appropriate to introduce at this place.

pattern as this analogous one about horses and rabbits. This one is invalid—so *your* argument is invalid. This is an excellent method of arguing; the logical analogy is one of the most powerful weapons that can be used in debate.

Underlying the method of logical analogy is the fact that the validity or invalidity of such arguments as the categorical syllogism is a purely formal matter. Any fallacious argument can be proved to be invalid by finding a second argument that has exactly the same form and is known to be invalid by the fact that its premises are known to be true while its conclusion is known to be false. (It should be remembered that an invalid argument may very well have a true conclusion—that an argument is invalid simply means that its conclusion is not logically implied or necessitated by its premises.)

This method of testing the validity of arguments has serious limitations, however. Sometimes a logical analogy is difficult to "think up" on the spur of the moment. And there are far too many invalid forms of syllogistic argument (well over two hundred!) for us to prepare and remember refuting analogies of each of them in advance. Moreover, although being able to think of a logical analogy with true premises and false conclusion proves its form to be invalid, *not* being able to think of one does not prove the form valid, for it may merely reflect the limitations of our thinking. There may be an invalidating analogy even though we are not able to think of it. A more effective method of establishing the formal validity or invalidity of syllogisms is required. The explanation of effective methods of testing syllogisms is the object of the remaining sections of this chapter.

EXERCISES

Refute any of the following arguments that are invalid by the method of constructing logical analogies.

EXAMPLE

1. All business executives are active opponents of increased corporation taxes, for all active opponents of increased corporation taxes are members of the chamber of commerce, and all members of the chamber of commerce are business executives.

SOLUTION

One possible refuting analogy is this: All bipeds are astronauts, for all astronauts are humans and all humans are bipeds.

2. No medicines that can be purchased without a doctor's prescription are habit-forming drugs, so some narcotics are not habit-forming drugs, because some narcotics are medicines that can be purchased without a doctor's prescription.

3. No Republicans are Democrats, so some Democrats are wealthy stockbrokers, because some wealthy stockbrokers are not Republicans.

4. No college graduates are persons having an IQ of less than 70, but all persons who have an IQ of less than 70 are morons, so no college graduates are morons.

***5.** All fireproof buildings are structures that can be insured at special rates, so some structures that can be insured at special rates are not wooden houses, because no wooden houses are fireproof buildings.

6. All blue-chip securities are safe investments, so some stocks that pay a generous dividend are safe investments, because some blue-chip securities are stocks that pay a generous dividend.

7. Some pediatricians are not specialists in surgery, so some general practitioners are not pediatricians, because some general practitioners are not specialists in surgery.

8. No intellectuals are successful politicians, because no shy and retiring people are successful politicians, and some intellectuals are shy and retiring people.

9. All trade union executives are labor leaders, so some labor leaders are conservatives in politics, because some conservatives in politics are trade union executives.

***10.** All new automobiles are economical means of transportation, and all new automobiles are status symbols; therefore some economical means of transportation are status symbols.

6.3 Venn Diagram Technique for Testing Syllogisms

In Chapter 5 we explained the use of two-circle Venn diagrams to represent standard-form categorical propositions. In order to test a categorical syllogism using Venn diagrams, one must first represent both of its premises in one diagram. That requires drawing *three* overlapping circles, for the two premises of a standard-form syllogism contain three different terms—minor term, major term, and middle term—which we abbreviate as *S*, *P*, and *M*, respectively.

We first draw two circles, just as we did to diagram a single proposition, and then we draw a third circle beneath, overlapping both of the first two. We label the three circles S, P, and M, in that order. Just as one circle labeled S diagrammed both the class S and the class $\bar{S}$, and as two overlapping circles labeled S and P diagrammed four classes (SP, $S\bar{P}$, $\bar{S}P$, and $\bar{S}\bar{P}$), three overlapping circles, labeled S, P, and M, diagram eight classes: $S\bar{P}\bar{M}$, $SP\bar{M}$, $\bar{S}P\bar{M}$, $S\bar{P}M$, SPM, $\bar{S}PM$, $\bar{S}\bar{P}M$, and $\bar{S}\bar{P}\bar{M}$. These are represented by the eight parts into which the three circles divide the plane, as shown in Figure 6-1.

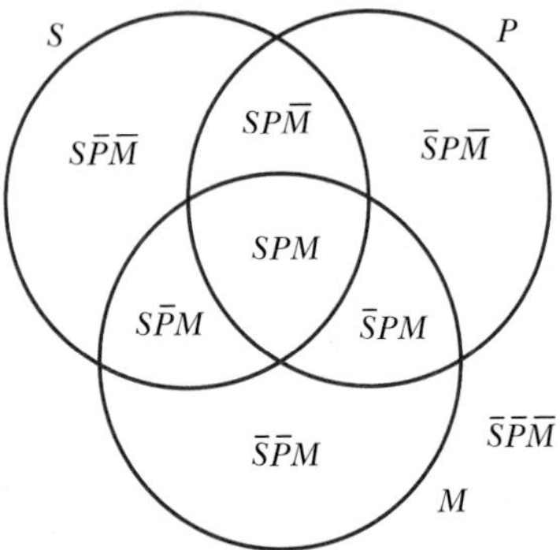

Figure 6-1

Figure 6-1 can be interpreted, for example, in terms of the various different classes determined by the class of all Swedes (S), the class of all peasants (P), and the class of all musicians (M). SPM is the product of these three classes, which is the class of all Swedish peasant musicians. $SP\bar{M}$ is the product of the first two and the complement of the third, which is the class of all Swedish peasants who are not musicians. $S\bar{P}M$ is the product of the first and third and the complement of the second: the class of all Swedish musicians who are not peasants. $S\bar{P}\bar{M}$ is the product of the first and the complement of the others: the class of all Swedes who are neither peasants nor musicians. Next, $\bar{S}PM$ is the product of the second and third classes with the complement of the first: the class of all peasant musicians who are not Swedes. $\bar{S}P\bar{M}$ is the product of the second class with the complements of the other two: the class of all peasants who are neither Swedes nor musicians. $\bar{S}\bar{P}M$ is the product of the third class and the complements of the first two: the class of all musicians who are neither Swedes nor peasants. Finally, $\bar{S}\bar{P}\bar{M}$ is the product of the complements of the three original classes: the class of all things that are neither Swedes nor peasants nor musicians.

If we focus our attention on just the two circles labeled P and M, it is clear that by shading out, or by inserting an x, we can diagram any standard-form categorical proposition whose two terms are P and M, regardless of which is the subject term and which is the predicate. Thus, to diagram the proposition "All M is P" ($M\bar{P} = 0$), we shade out all of M that is not contained

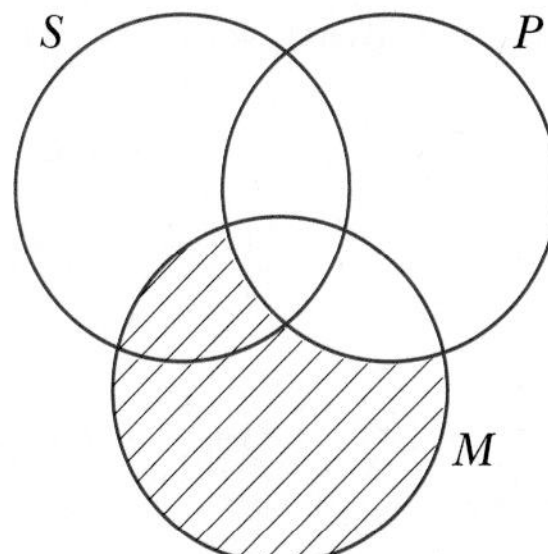

Figure 6-2

in (or overlapped by) *P*. This area, it is seen, includes both the portions labeled $S\bar{P}M$ and $\bar{S}\bar{P}M$. The diagram then becomes Figure 6-2.

If we focus our attention on just the two circles *S* and *M*, by shading out, or by inserting an *x*, we can diagram any standard-form categorical proposition whose terms are *S* and *M*, regardless of the order in which they appear in it. To diagram the proposition "All *S* is *M*" ($S\bar{M} = 0$), we shade out all of *S* that is not contained in (or overlapped by) *M*. This area, it is seen, includes both the portions labeled $S\bar{P}\bar{M}$ and $SP\bar{M}$. The diagram for this proposition will appear as Figure 6-3.

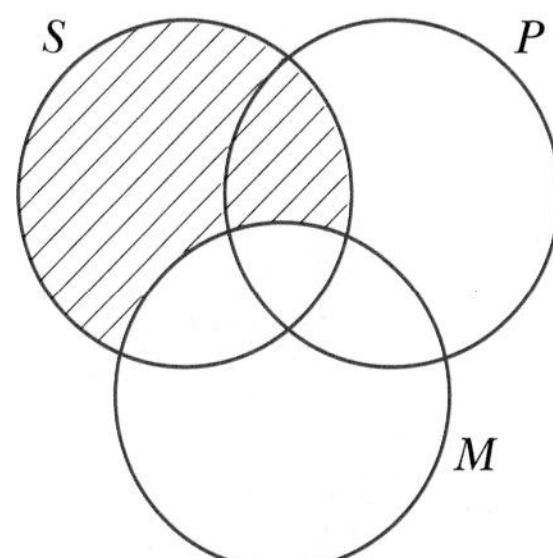

Figure 6-3

The advantage of using three overlapping circles is that it allows us to diagram two propositions together—on the condition, of course, that only three different terms occur in them. Thus diagramming both "All *M* is *P*" and "All *S* is *M*" at the same time gives us Figure 6-4.

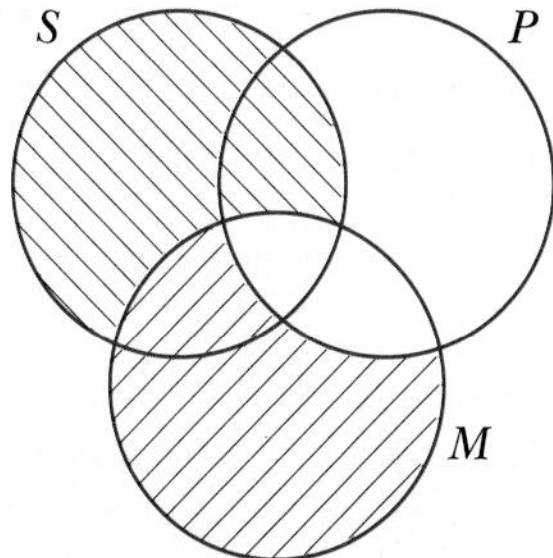

Figure 6-4

This is the diagram for both premises of the syllogism **AAA–1:**

All *M* is *P*.

<u>All *S* is *M*.</u>

∴ All *S* is *P*.

This syllogism is valid if and only if the two premises imply or entail the conclusion—that is, if together they say what is said by the conclusion. Consequently, diagramming the premises of a valid argument should suffice to diagram its conclusion also, with no further marking of the circles needed. To diagram the conclusion "All *S* is *P*" is to shade out both the portion labeled $S\bar{P}\overline{M}$ and the portion labeled $S\bar{P}M$. Inspecting the diagram that represents the two premises, we see that it also diagrams the conclusion. And from this we can conclude that **AAA–1** is a valid syllogism.*

Let us now apply the Venn diagram test to an obviously invalid syllogism, one containing three **A** propositions in the second figure:

All dogs are mammals.

<u>All cats are mammals.</u>

Therefore all cats are dogs.

Diagramming both premises gives us Figure 6-5.

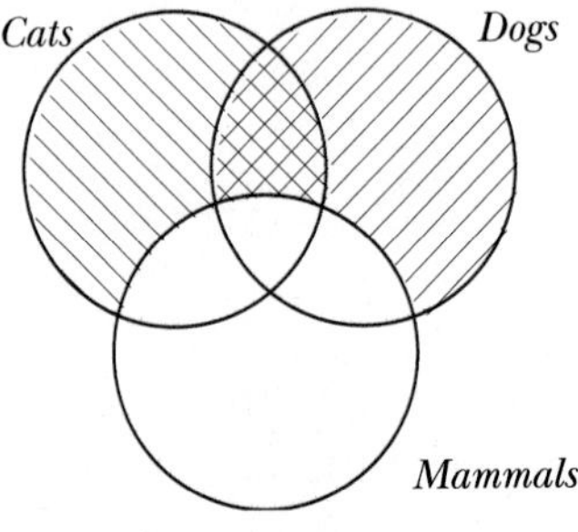

Figure 6-5

In this diagram, where *S* designates the class of all cats, *P* the class of all dogs, and *M* the class of all mammals, the portions $S\bar{P}\overline{M}$, $SP\overline{M}$, and $\bar{S}P\overline{M}$, have been

*The mood of this syllogism is **AAA** because it consists of three **A** propositions; it is in the first figure because its middle term is the subject of its major premise and the predicate of its minor premise. Any syllogism of this valid form, **AAA–1**, is called (as noted earlier) a syllogism in Barbara. The names of other valid syllogisms will be given in Section 6.5.

shaded out. But the conclusion has not been diagrammed, because the part $S\bar{P}M$ has been left unshaded, and to diagram the conclusion *both* $S\bar{P}\bar{M}$ and $S\bar{P}M$ must be shaded. Thus we see that diagramming both the premises of a syllogism of form **AAA–2** does *not* suffice to diagram its conclusion, which proves that the conclusion says something more than is said by the premises, which shows that the premises do not imply the conclusion. An argument whose premises do not imply its conclusion is invalid, so our diagram proves that the given syllogism is invalid. (It proves, in fact, that *any* syllogism of the form **AAA–2** is invalid.)

When we use a Venn diagram to test a syllogism with one universal premise and one particular premise, it is important to *diagram the universal premise first*. Thus, in testing the **AII–3** syllogism,

All artists are egotists.
Some artists are paupers.
Therefore some paupers are egotists.

we should diagram the universal premise, "All artists are egotists," before inserting an x to diagram the particular premise, "Some artists are paupers." Properly diagrammed, the syllogism looks like Figure 6-6.

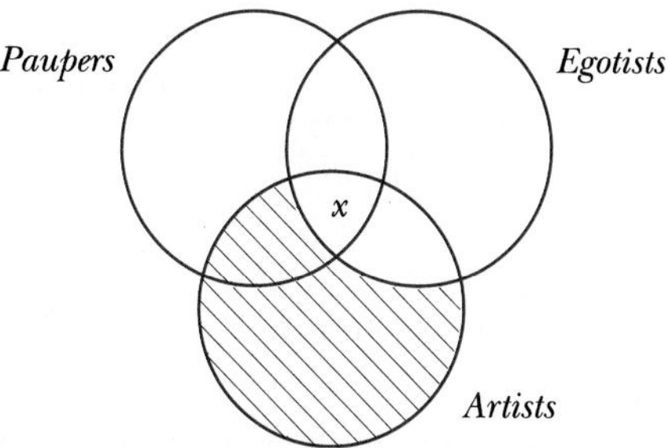

Figure 6-6

Had we tried to diagram the particular premise first, before the region $S\bar{P}M$ was shaded out along with $\bar{S}\bar{P}M$ in diagramming the universal premise, we would not have known whether to insert an x in SPM or in $S\bar{P}M$ or in both. And had we put it in $S\bar{P}M$ or on the line separating it from SPM, the subsequent shading of $S\bar{P}M$ would have obscured the information the diagram was intended to exhibit. Now that the information contained in the premises has been inserted into the diagram, we can examine it to see whether the conclusion already has been diagrammed. If the conclusion, "Some paupers are egotists," has been diagrammed, there will be an x somewhere in the overlapping part of the circles labeled "Paupers" and "Egotists." This overlapping part consists of both of the regions $SP\overline{M}$ and SPM, which together constitute SP. There is an *x* in the region SPM, so there *is* an *x* in the overlapping part SP. What the conclusion of the syllogism says has already been diagrammed by the diagramming of its premises; therefore the syllogism is valid.

Let us consider still another example, the discussion of which will bring out another important point about the use of Venn diagrams. Let's say we are testing the argument

> All great scientists are college graduates.
> Some professional athletes are college graduates.
> Therefore some professional athletes are great scientists.

After diagramming the universal premise first (Figure 6-7) by shading out both regions $SP\overline{M}$ and $\overline{S}P\overline{M}$,

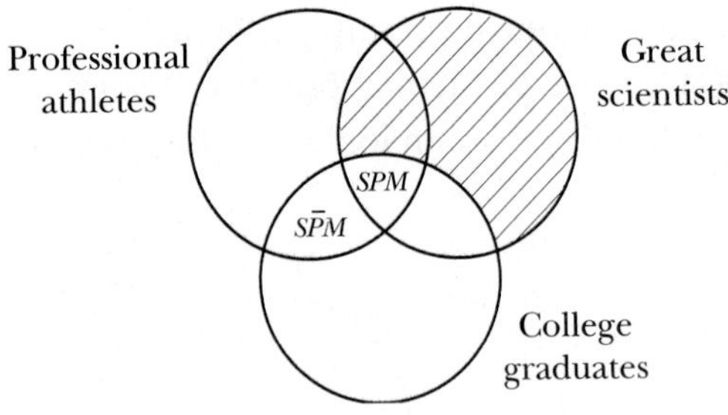

Figure 6-7

we may still be puzzled about where to put the *x* needed in order to diagram the particular premise. That premise is "Some professional athletes are college graduates," so an *x* must be inserted somewhere in the overlapping part of the two circles labeled "Professional athletes" and "College graduates." That overlapping part, however, contains two regions, SPM and $S\overline{P}M$. In which of these should we put an *x*? The premises do not tell us, and if we make an arbitrary decision to place it in one rather than the other, we would be inserting more information into the diagram than the premises warrant—which would spoil the diagram's use as a test for validity. Placing *x*'s in each of them would also go beyond what the premises assert. Yet by placing an *x* on the line that divides the overlapping region SM into the two parts SPM and $S\overline{P}M$, we can diagram exactly what the second premise asserts without adding anything to it. Placing an *x* on the line between two regions indicates that there is something that belongs in one of them, but does not indicate which one. The completed diagram of both premises thus looks like Figure 6-8.

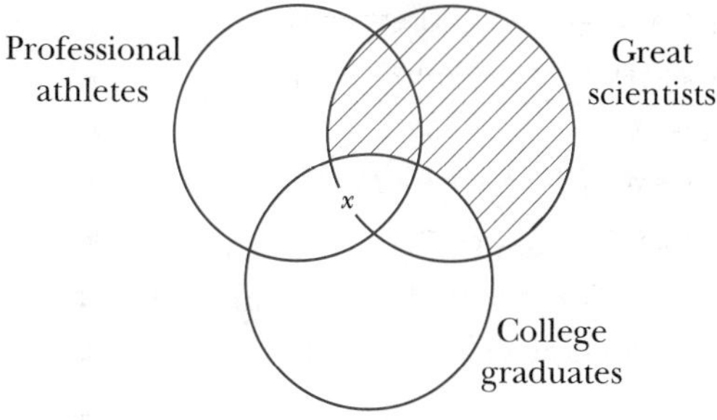

Figure 6-8

When we inspect this diagram of the premises to see whether the conclusion of the syllogism has already been diagrammed in it, we find that it has not. For the conclusion, "Some professional athletes are great scientists," to be diagrammed, an x must appear in the overlapping part of the two upper circles, either in $SP\overline{M}$ or in SPM. The first of these is shaded out and certainly contains no x. The diagram does not show an x in SPM either. True, there must be a member of *either* SPM or $S\bar{P}M$, but the diagram does not tell us that it is in the former rather than the latter and so, for all the premises tell us, the conclusion may be false. We do not know that the conclusion *is* false, only that it is not asserted or implied by the premises. The latter is enough, however, to let us know that the argument is invalid. The diagram suffices to show not only that the given syllogism is invalid, but that *all* syllogisms of the form **AII–2** are invalid.

The general technique of using Venn diagrams to test the validity of any standard-form syllogism may be summarized as follows. First, label the circles of a three-circle Venn diagram with the syllogism's three terms. Next, diagram both premises, diagramming the universal one first if there is one universal and one particular, being careful in diagramming a particular proposition to put an x on a line if the premises do not determine on which side of the line it should go. Finally, inspect the diagram to see whether the diagram of the premises contains a diagram of the conclusion: If it does, the syllogism is valid; if it does not, the syllogism is invalid.

What is the theoretical rationale for using Venn diagrams to distinguish valid from invalid syllogisms? The answer to this question divides into two parts. The first part has to do with the formal nature of syllogistic argument as explained in Section 6.2. It was shown there that one legitimate test of the validity or invalidity of a syllogism is to establish the validity or invalidity of a different syllogism that has exactly the same form. This technique is basic to the use of Venn diagrams.

The explanation of *how* the diagrams serve this purpose constitutes the second part of the answer to our question. Ordinarily, a syllogism will be about classes of objects that are not all present, such as the class of all musicians,

VISUAL LOGIC

Where do I place the x in a Venn diagram?

In the Venn diagram representing a categorical syllogism, the three terms of the syllogism (*S*ubject term, *P*redicate term, and *M*iddle term) are represented by three interlocking circles labeled *S*, *P*, and *M*.

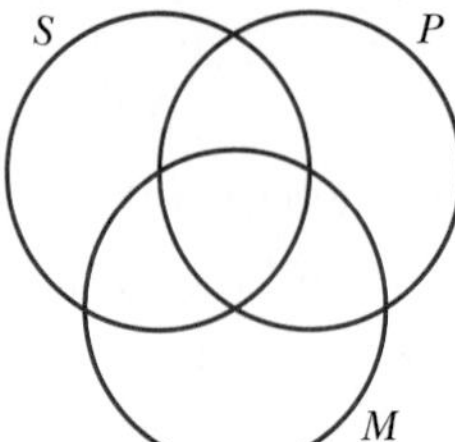

Diagram of three circles, *S*, *P*, and *M*, with nothing else showing

When one of the premises of a syllogism calls for an *x* to be placed on a line in such a Venn diagram, we may ask: Which line? And why? Answer: The *x* is always placed *on the line of the circle designating the class not mentioned in that premise.*

Example: Suppose you are given as premise, "Some *S* is *M*." You may not be able to determine whether the *x* representing that "some" is a *P* or is not a *P*—so the *x* goes on the line of the *P* circle, thus:

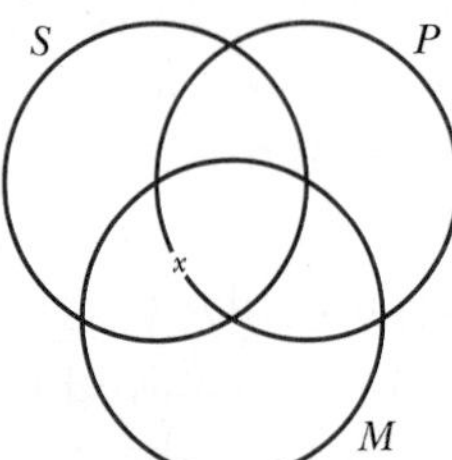

Diagram of three circles with *x* on the *P* circle

Another example: Suppose you are given as premise, "Some *M* is not *P*." You may not be able to determine whether the *M* that is not *P* is an *S* or is not an *S*—so the *x* goes on the line of the *S* circle, thus:

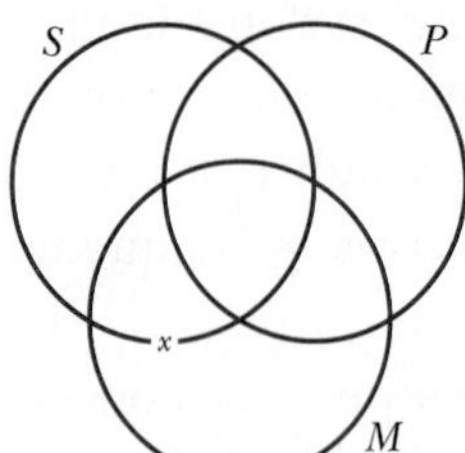

Diagram of three circles with *x* on the *S* circle

or great scientists, or sodium salts. The relations of inclusion or exclusion among such classes may be reasoned about and may be empirically discoverable in the course of scientific investigation. But they certainly are not open to direct inspection, because not all members of the classes involved are ever present at one time to be inspected. We can, however, examine situations of our own making, in which the only classes concerned contain by their very definitions only things that are present and open to direct inspection. And we can argue syllogistically about such situations of our own making. Venn diagrams are devices for expressing standard-form categorical propositions, but they also are situations of our own making, patterns of graphite or ink on paper, or lines of chalk on blackboards. And the propositions they express can be interpreted as referring to the diagrams themselves. An example can help to make this clear. Suppose we have a particular syllogism whose terms denote various kinds of people who are successful, interested in their work, and able to concentrate, and who may be scattered widely over all parts of the world:

> All successful people are people who are keenly interested in their work.
>
> No people who are keenly interested in their work are people whose attention is easily distracted when they are working.
>
> Therefore no people whose attention is easily distracted when they are working are successful people.

Its form is **AEE–4**, and it may be schematized as

> All *P* is *M*.
>
> No *M* is *S*.
>
> ∴ No *S* is *P*.

We may test it by constructing the Venn diagram shown in Figure 6-9, in which regions $SP\bar{M}$ and $\bar{S}P\bar{M}$ are shaded out to express the first premise, and $S\bar{P}M$ and SPM are shaded out to express the second premise.

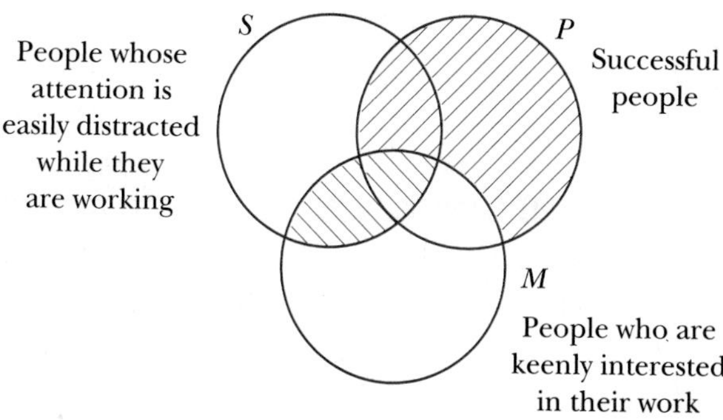

Figure 6-9

Examining Figure 6-9, we find that *SP* (which consists of the regions *SPM* and $SP\overline{M}$) has been shaded out, so the syllogism's conclusion has already been diagrammed. How does this tell us that the given syllogism is valid? This syllogism concerns large classes of remote objects: There are many people whose attention is easily distracted while they are working, and they are scattered far and wide. However, we can construct a syllogism of the same form that involves objects that are immediately present and directly available for our inspection. These objects are the points within the unshaded portions of the circles labeled *S*, *P*, and *M* in our Venn diagram. Here is the new syllogism:

> All points within the unshaded part of the circle labeled *P* are points within the unshaded part of the circle labeled *M*.
>
> No points within the unshaded part of the circle labeled *M* are points within the unshaded part of the circle labeled *S*.
>
> Therefore no points within the unshaded part of the circle labeled *S* are points within the unshaded part of the circle labeled *P*.

This new syllogism refers to nothing remote; it is about the parts of a situation we ourselves have created: the Venn diagram we have drawn. All the parts and all the possibilities of inclusion and exclusion among these classes are immediately present to us and directly open to inspection. We can literally *see* all the possibilities here, and know that because all the points of *P* are also points of *M*, and because *M* and *S* have no points in common, *S* and *P* cannot possibly have any points in common. Because the new syllogism refers only to classes of points in the diagram, it can be literally *seen* to be valid by looking at the things it talks about. The original syllogism about classes of people has exactly the same form as this second one, so we are assured by the formal nature of syllogistic argument that the original syllogism is also valid. The explanation is exactly the same for Venn diagram proofs of the invalidity of invalid syllogisms; there, too, we test the original syllogism indirectly by testing directly a second syllogism that has exactly the same form and referring to the diagram that exhibits that form.

EXERCISES

A. Write out each of the following syllogistic forms, using *S* and *P* as the subject and predicate terms of the conclusion, and *M* as the middle term. (Refer to the chart of the four syllogistic figures, if necessary, on p. 227.) Then test the validity of each syllogistic form using a Venn diagram.

EXAMPLE

1. AEE–1

SOLUTION

We are told that this syllogism is in the first figure, and therefore the middle term, *M*, is the subject term of the major premise and the predicate term of the minor premise. (See chart on p. 228.) The conclusion of the syllogism is an **E** proposition and therefore reads: No *S* is *P*. The first (major) premise (which contains the predicate term of the conclusion) is an **A** proposition, and therefore reads: All *M* is *P*. The second (minor) premise (which contains the subject term of the conclusion) is an **E** proposition and therefore reads: No *S* is *M*. This syllogism therefore reads as follows:

All *M* is *P*.
No *S* is *M*.
Therefore no *S* is *P*.

Tested by means of a Venn diagram, as in Figure 6-10, this syllogism is shown to be invalid.

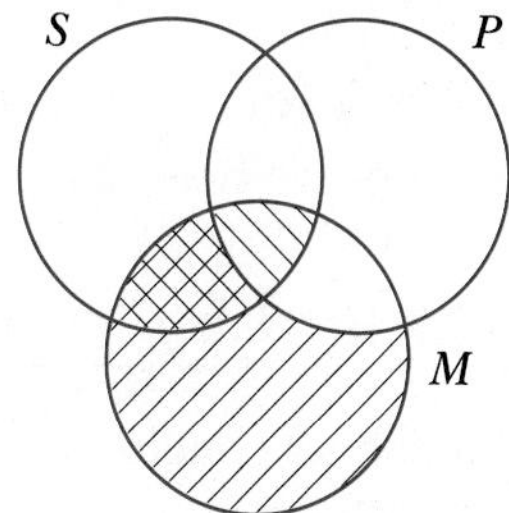

Figure 6-10

2. EIO–2 **3. OAO–3**
4. AOO–4 ***5. EIO–4**
6. OAO–2 **7. AOO–1**
8. EAE–3 **9. EIO–3**
***10. IAI–4** **11. AOO–3**
12. EAE–1 **13. IAI–1**
14. OAO–4 ***15. EIO–1**

B. Put each of the following syllogisms into standard form, name its mood and figure, and test its validity using a Venn diagram.

***1.** Some reformers are fanatics, so some idealists are fanatics, because all reformers are idealists.

2. Some philosophers are mathematicians; hence some scientists are philosophers, because all scientists are mathematicians.

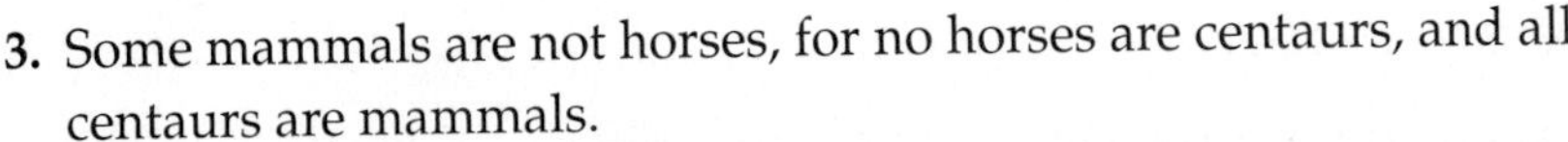

3. Some mammals are not horses, for no horses are centaurs, and all centaurs are mammals.

4. Some neurotics are not parasites, but all criminals are parasites; it follows that some neurotics are not criminals.

*5. All underwater craft are submarines; therefore no submarines are pleasure vessels, because no pleasure vessels are underwater craft.

6. No criminals were pioneers, for all criminals are unsavory persons, and no pioneers were unsavory persons.

7. No musicians are astronauts; all musicians are baseball fans; consequently, no astronauts are baseball fans.

8. Some Christians are not Methodists, for some Christians are not Protestants, and some Protestants are not Methodists.

9. No people whose primary interest is in winning elections are true liberals, and all active politicians are people whose primary interest is in winning elections, which entails that no true liberals are active politicians.

*10. No weaklings are labor leaders, because no weaklings are true liberals, and all labor leaders are true liberals.

6.4 Syllogistic Rules and Syllogistic Fallacies

A syllogism may fail to establish its conclusion in many different ways. To help avoid common errors we set forth rules—six of them—to guide the reasoner; any given standard-form syllogism can be evaluated by observing whether any one of these rules has been violated. Mastering the rules by which syllogisms may be evaluated also enriches our understanding of the syllogism itself; it helps us to see how syllogisms work, and to see why they fail to work if the rules are broken.

A violation of any one of these rules is a mistake, and it renders the syllogism invalid. Because it is a mistake of that special *kind*, we call it a fallacy; and because it is a mistake in the *form* of the argument, we call it a *formal fallacy* (to be contrasted with the *informal* fallacies described in Chapter 4). In reasoning with syllogisms, one must scrupulously avoid the fallacies that violations of the rules invariably yield. Each of these formal fallacies has a traditional name, explained below.

Rule 1. Avoid four terms.

A valid standard-form categorical syllogism must contain exactly three terms, each of which is used in the same sense throughout the argument.

In every categorical syllogism, the conclusion asserts a relationship between two terms, the subject (minor term) and the predicate (major term). Such a conclusion can be justified only if the premises assert the relationship of each of those two terms to the same third term (middle term). If the premises fail to do this consistently, the needed connection of the two terms in the conclusion cannot be established, and the argument fails. So every valid categorical syllogism must involve three terms—no more and no less. If more than three terms are involved, the syllogism is invalid. The fallacy thus committed is called the **fallacy of four terms.**

The mistake that commonly underlies this fallacy is equivocation, using one word or phrase with two different meanings. Most often it is the middle term whose meaning is thus shifted, in one direction to connect it with the minor term, in a different direction to connect it with the major term. In doing this the two terms of the conclusion are connected with two different terms (rather than with the same middle term), and so the relationship asserted by the conclusion is not established.*

When the expression *"categorical syllogism"* was defined at the beginning of this chapter, we noted that by its nature every syllogism must have three and only three terms.† So this rule ("Avoid four terms") may be regarded as a reminder to make sure that the argument being appraised really is a categorical syllogism.

Rule 2. Distribute the middle term in at least one premise.

A term is "distributed" in a proposition when (as was explained in Section 5.4) the proposition refers to **all** *members of the class designated by that term. If the middle term is not distributed in at least one premise, the connection required by the conclusion cannot be made.*

Historian Barbara Tuchman (in *The Proud Tower*, New York: Macmillan, 1966) observed that many early critics of anarchism relied on the following "unconscious syllogism":

All Russians were revolutionists.

All anarchists were revolutionists.

Therefore, all anarchists were Russians.

This syllogism is plainly invalid. Its mistake is that it asserts a connection between anarchists and Russians by relying on the links between each of those classes and the class of revolutionists—but revolutionists is an *un*distributed term in both of the premises. The first premise does not refer to all revolutionists,

---

*Because it is the middle term that is most often manipulated, this fallacy is sometimes called "the fallacy of the ambiguous middle." However, this name is not generally applicable, because one (or more) of the other terms may have its meaning shifted as well. Ambiguities may result in as many as five or six different terms being involved, but the mistake retains its traditional name: the fallacy of four terms.

†The term *syllogism* is sometimes defined more broadly than it has been in this book. The informal fallacy of equivocation, explained and warned against in Chapter 4, may arise in many different argumentative contexts, of course.

and neither does the second. Revolutionists is the middle term in this argument, and if the middle term is not distributed in at least one premise of a syllogism, that syllogism cannot be valid. The fallacy this syllogism commits is called the **fallacy of the undistributed middle.**

What underlies this rule is the need to *link* the minor and the major terms. If they are to be linked by the middle term, either the subject or the predicate of the conclusion must be related to the *whole* of the class designated by the middle term. If that is not so, it is possible that each of the terms in the conclusion may be connected to a different part of the middle term, and not necessarily connected with each other.

This is precisely what happens in the syllogism given in the preceding example. The Russians are included in a *part* of the class of revolutionists (by the first premise), and the anarchists are included in a *part* of the class of revolutionists (by the second premise)—but *different* parts of this class (the middle term of the syllogism) may be involved, and so the middle term does not successfully link the minor and major terms of the syllogism. In a valid syllogism, *the middle term must be distributed in at least one premise.*

Rule 3. Any term distributed in the conclusion must be distributed in the premises.

> *To refer to* **all** *members of a class is to say more about that class than is said when only* **some** *of its members are referred to. Therefore, when the conclusion of a syllogism distributes a term that was undistributed in the premises, it says more about that term than the premises did. But a valid argument is one whose premises logically entail its conclusion, and for that to be true the conclusion must not assert any more than is asserted in the premises. A term that is distributed in the conclusion but is not distributed in the premises is therefore a sure mark that the conclusion has gone beyond its premises and has reached too far. The fallacy is that of* **illicit process.**

The conclusion may overreach with respect to either the minor term (its subject), or the major term (its predicate). So there are two different forms of illicit process, and different names have been given to the two formal fallacies involved. They are

Illicit process of the major term (an **illicit major**).
Illicit process of the minor term (an **illicit minor**).

To illustrate an illicit process of the major term, consider this syllogism:

All dogs are mammals.
<u>No cats are dogs.</u>
Therefore no cats are mammals.

The reasoning is obviously bad, but where is the mistake? The mistake is in the conclusion's assertion about *all* mammals, saying that all of them fall outside the class of cats. Bear in mind that an **A** proposition distributes its subject term but does not distribute its predicate term. Hence the premises make no assertion about *all* mammals—so the conclusion illicitly goes beyond what the premises assert. Because "mammals" is the major term in this syllogism, the fallacy here is that of an illicit major.

To illustrate illicit process of the minor term, consider this syllogism:

All traditionally religious people are fundamentalists.

All traditionally religious people are opponents of abortion.

Therefore all opponents of abortion are fundamentalists.

Again we sense quickly that something is wrong with this argument, and what is wrong is this: The conclusion makes an assertion about *all* opponents of abortion, but the premises make no such assertion; they say nothing about *all* abortion opponents. So the conclusion here goes illicitly beyond what the premises warrant. And in this case "opponents of abortion" is the minor term, so the fallacy is that of an illicit minor.

Rule 4. Avoid two negative premises.

*Any negative proposition (**E** or **O**) denies class inclusion; it asserts that some or all of one class is excluded from the whole of the other class. Two premises asserting such exclusion cannot yield the linkage that the conclusion asserts, and therefore cannot yield a valid argument. The mistake is named the* **fallacy of exclusive premises.**

Understanding the mistake identified here requires some reflection. Suppose we label the minor, major, and middle terms of the syllogism *S*, *P*, and *M*, respectively. What can two negative premises tell us about the relations of these three terms? They can tell us that *S* (the subject of the conclusion) is wholly or partially excluded from all or part of *M* (the middle term), and that *P* (the predicate of the conclusion) is wholly or partially excluded from all or part of *M*. However, any one of these relations may very well be established no matter how *S* and *P* are related. The negative premises cannot tell us that *S* and *P* are related by inclusion or by exclusion, partial or complete. Two negative premises (where *M* is a term in each) simply cannot justify the assertion of *any* relationship whatever between *S* and *P*. Therefore, if both premises of a syllogism are negative, the argument must be invalid.

Rule 5. If either premise is negative, the conclusion must be negative.

If the conclusion is affirmative—that is, if it asserts that one of the two classes, S or P, is wholly or partly contained in the other—it can only be inferred from premises that assert the existence of a third class that contains the first and is itself contained in the second. However, class inclusion can be stated only by affirmative propositions. Therefore, an affirmative conclusion can follow validly only from two affirmative premises. The mistake here is called the **fallacy of drawing an affirmative conclusion from a negative premise.**

If an affirmative conclusion requires two affirmative premises, as has just been shown, we can know with certainty that if either of the premises is negative, the conclusion must also be negative, or the argument is not valid.

Unlike some of the fallacies identified here, this fallacy is not common, because any argument that draws an affirmative conclusion from negative premises will be instantly recognized as highly implausible. Even an illustration of the mistake will appear strained:

No poets are accountants.
Some artists are poets.

Therefore some artists are accountants.

Immediately it will be seen that the *ex*clusion of poets and accountants, asserted by the first premise of this syllogism, cannot justify *any* valid inference regarding the *in*clusion of artists and accountants.

Rule 6. From two universal premises no particular conclusion may be drawn.
*In the Boolean interpretation of categorical propositions (explained in Section 5.7), universal propositions (**A** and **E**) have no existential import, but particular propositions (**I** and **O**) do have such import. Wherever the Boolean interpretation is supposed, as in this book, a rule is needed that precludes passage from premises that have no existential import to a conclusion that does have such import.*

This final rule is not needed in the traditional or Aristotelian account of the categorical syllogism, because that traditional account paid no attention to the problem of existential import. However, when existential import is carefully considered, it will be clear that if the premises of an argument do not assert the existence of anything at all, the conclusion will be unwarranted when, from it, the existence of some thing may be inferred. The mistake is called the **existential fallacy.**

Here is an example of a syllogism that commits this fallacy:

All household pets are domestic animals.
No unicorns are domestic animals.

Therefore some unicorns are not household pets.

If the conclusion of this argument were the universal proposition, "No unicorns are household pets," the syllogism would be perfectly valid for all. And because, under the traditional interpretation, existential import may be inferred from universal as well as from particular propositions, it would not be problematic (in that traditional view) to say that the conclusion in the example given here is simply a "weaker" version of the conclusion we all agree is validly drawn.

In our Boolean view, however, the conclusion of the example ("Some unicorns are not household pets"), because it is a particular proposition, is not just "weaker," it is very different. It is an **O** proposition, a particular proposition, and thus has an existential import that the **E** proposition ("No unicorns are household pets") cannot have. Reasoning that is acceptable under the traditional view is therefore unacceptable under the Boolean view because, from the Boolean perspective, that reasoning commits the existential fallacy—a mistake that cannot be made under the traditional interpretation.*

The six rules given here are intended to apply only to standard-form categorical syllogisms. In this realm they provide an adequate test for the validity of any argument. If a standard-form categorical syllogism violates any one of these rules, it is invalid; if it conforms to all of these rules, it is valid.

OVERVIEW

Syllogistic Rules and Fallacies

Rule	Associated Fallacy
1. Avoid four terms.	Four terms
2. Distribute the middle term in at least one premise.	Undistributed middle
3. Any term distributed in the conclusion must be distributed in the premises.	Illicit process of the major term (illicit major); Illicit process of the minor term (illicit minor)
4. Avoid two negative premises.	Exclusive premises
5. If either premise is negative, the conclusion must be negative.	Drawing an affirmative conclusion from a negative premise
6. No particular conclusion may be drawn from two universal premises.	Existential fallacy

*Another interesting consequence of the difference between the traditional and the Boolean interpretation of categorical propositions is this: In the traditional view there is a need for a rule that states the converse of Rule 5 ("If either premise is negative, the conclusion must be negative"). The converse states simply that "If the conclusion of a valid syllogism is negative, at least one premise must be negative." And that is indisputable, because if the conclusion is negative, it denies inclusion. But affirmative premises assert inclusion. Therefore affirmative premises cannot entail a negative conclusion. This corollary is unnecessary in the Boolean interpretation because the rule precluding the existential fallacy (Rule 6) will, in the presence of the other rules, suffice to invalidate any syllogism with affirmative premises and a negative conclusion.

FLOWCHART FOR APPLYING THE SIX SYLLOGISTIC RULES

The following chart captures the process for working through the six rules of validity for categorical syllogisms.

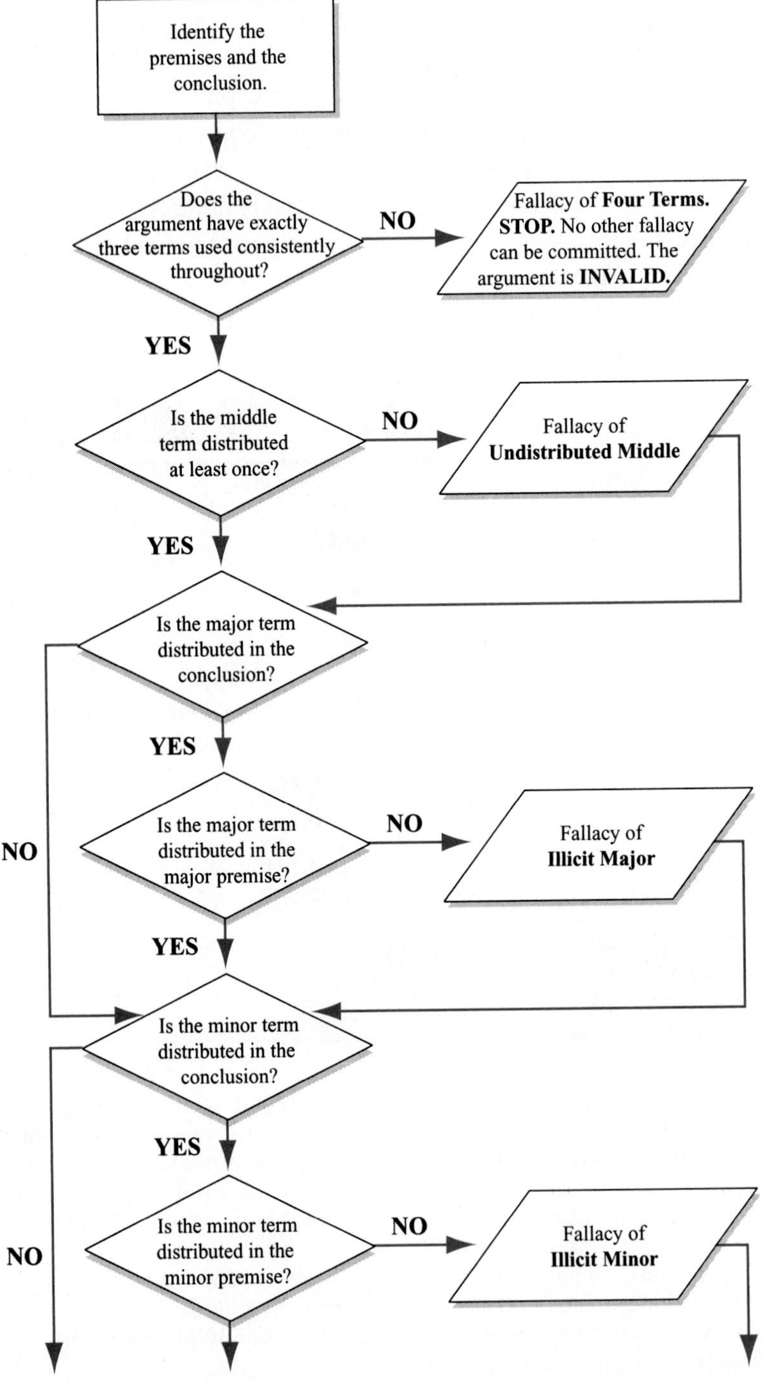

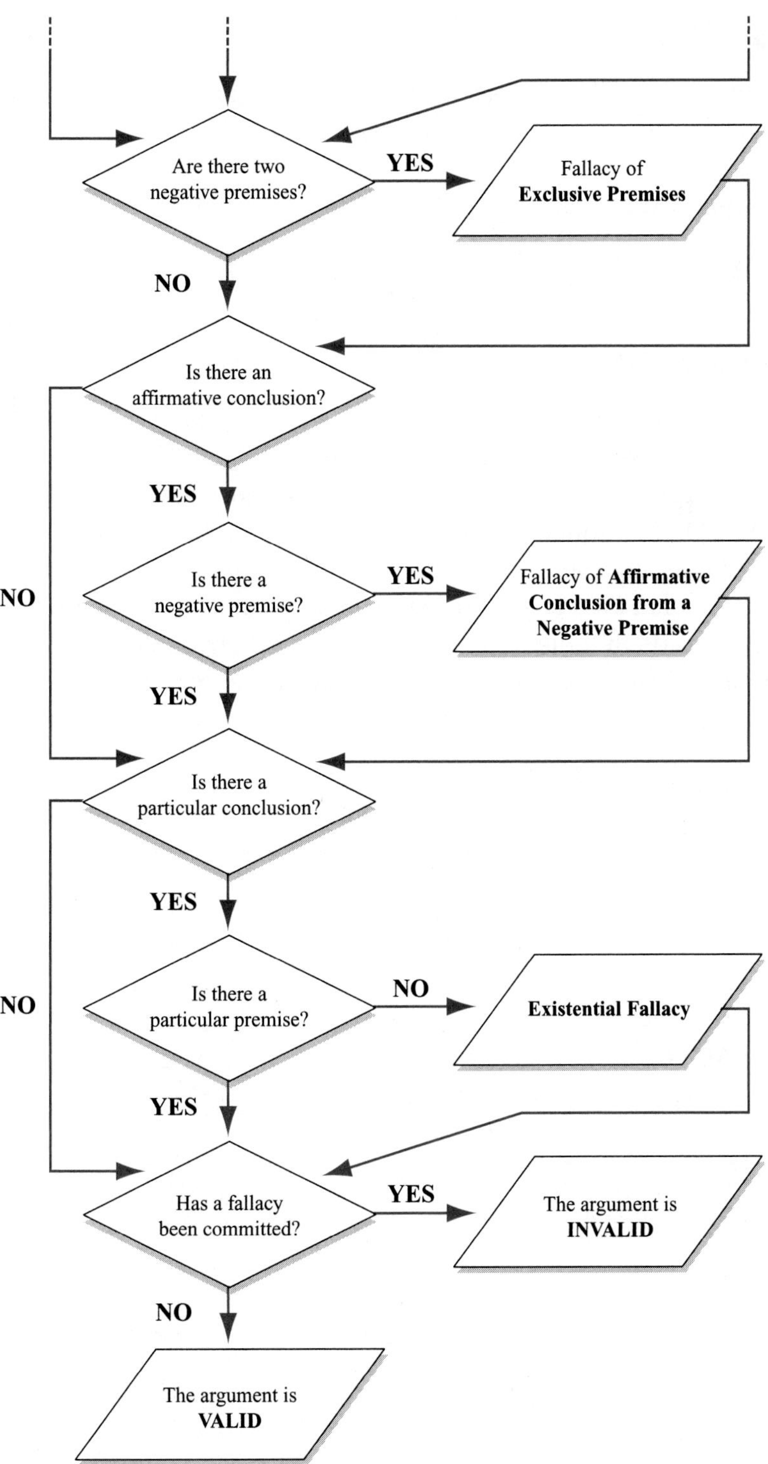

Adapted from Daniel E. Flage, *Essentials of Logic*, 2e (Englewood Cliffs, NJ: Prentice Hall, 1995)

EXERCISES

A. Identify the rule that is broken by invalid syllogisms of the following forms, and name the fallacy that each commits.

EXAMPLE

1. **AAA–2**

SOLUTION

Any syllogism in the second figure has the middle term as predicate of both the major and the minor premise. Thus any syllogism consisting of three **A** propositions, in the second figure, must read: All *P* is *M*; all *S* is *M*; therefore all *S* is *P*. *M* is not distributed in either of the premises in that form, and therefore it cannot validly be inferred from such premises that all *S* is *P*. Thus every syllogism of the form **AAA–2** violates the rule that the middle term must be distributed in at least one premise, thereby committing the fallacy of the undistributed middle.

2. **EAA–1**

3. **IAO–3**

4. **OEO–4**

*5. **AAA–3**

6. **IAI–2**

7. **OAA–3**

8. **EAO–4**

9. **OAI–3**

*10. **IEO–1**

11. **EAO–3**

12. **AII–2**

13. **EEE–1**

14. **OAO–2**

*15. **IAA–3**

B. Identify the rule that is broken by any of the following syllogisms that are invalid, and name the fallacy that is committed.

EXAMPLE

1. All textbooks are books intended for careful study.

Some reference books are books intended for careful study.

Therefore some reference books are textbooks.

SOLUTION

In this syllogism, "textbooks" is the major term (the predicate of the conclusion) and "reference books" is the minor term (the subject of the conclusion). "Books intended for careful study" is therefore the middle term, and it appears as the predicate of both premises. In neither of the premises is this middle term distributed, so the syllogism violates the rule that the middle term must be distributed in at least one premise, thereby committing the fallacy of the undistributed middle.

2. All criminal actions are wicked deeds.

All prosecutions for murder are criminal actions.

Therefore all prosecutions for murder are wicked deeds.

3. No tragic actors are idiots.

Some comedians are not idiots.

Therefore some comedians are not tragic actors.

4. Some parrots are not pests.

All parrots are pets.

Therefore no pets are pests.

***5.** All perpetual motion devices are 100 percent efficient machines.

All 100 percent efficient machines are machines with frictionless bearings.

Therefore some machines with frictionless bearings are perpetual motion devices.

6. Some good actors are not powerful athletes.

All professional wrestlers are powerful athletes.

Therefore all professional wrestlers are good actors.

7. Some diamonds are precious stones.

Some carbon compounds are not diamonds.

Therefore some carbon compounds are not precious stones.

8. Some diamonds are not precious stones.
Some carbon compounds are diamonds.
Therefore some carbon compounds are not precious stones.

9. All people who are most hungry are people who eat most.
All people who eat least are people who are most hungry.
Therefore all people who eat least are people who eat most.

***10.** Some spaniels are not good hunters.
All spaniels are gentle dogs.
Therefore no gentle dogs are good hunters.

C. Identify the rule that is broken by any of the following syllogisms that are invalid, and name the fallacy that is committed.

EXAMPLE

1. All chocolate eclairs are fattening foods, because all chocolate eclairs are rich desserts, and some fattening foods are not rich desserts.

SOLUTION

In this syllogism the conclusion is affirmative ("all chocolate eclairs are fattening foods"), while one of the premises is negative ("some fattening foods are not rich desserts"). The syllogism therefore is invalid, violating the rule that if either premise is negative the conclusion must also be negative, thereby committing the fallacy of affirmative conclusion from a negative premise.

2. All inventors are people who see new patterns in familiar things, so all inventors are eccentrics, because all eccentrics are people who see new patterns in familiar things.

3. Some snakes are not dangerous animals, but all snakes are reptiles, therefore some dangerous animals are not reptiles.

4. Some foods that contain iron are toxic substances, for all fish containing mercury are foods that contain iron, and all fish containing mercury are toxic substances.

***5.** All opponents of basic economic and political changes are outspoken critics of the liberal leaders of Congress, and all right-wing extremists are opponents of basic economic and political changes. It follows that all outspoken critics of the liberal leaders of Congress are right-wing extremists.

6. No writers of lewd and sensational articles are honest and decent citizens, but some journalists are not writers of lewd and sensational articles; consequently, some journalists are honest and decent citizens.

7. All supporters of popular government are democrats, so all supporters of popular government are opponents of the Republican Party, inasmuch as all Democrats are opponents of the Republican Party.
8. No coal-tar derivatives are nourishing foods, because all artificial dyes are coal-tar derivatives, and no artificial dyes are nourishing foods.
9. No coal-tar derivatives are nourishing foods, because no coal-tar derivatives are natural grain products, and all natural grain products are nourishing foods.

*10. All people who live in London are people who drink tea, and all people who drink tea are people who like it. We may conclude, then, that all people who live in London are people who like it.

6.5 Exposition of the Fifteen Valid Forms of the Categorical Syllogism

The *mood* of a syllogism is its character as determined by the forms (**A, E, I,** or **O**) of the three propositions it contains. There are sixty-four possible moods of the categorical syllogism; that is, sixty-four possible sets of three propositions: **AAA, AAI, AAE,** and so on, to . . . **EOO, OOO.**

The *figure* of a syllogism is its logical shape, as determined by the position of the middle term in its premises. So there are four possible figures, which can be most clearly grasped if one has in mind a chart, or iconic representation, of the four possibilities, as exhibited in the Overview table:

OVERVIEW

The Four Figures

	First Figure	Second Figure	Third Figure	Fourth Figure
Schematic Representation	M – P S – M ∴S – P	P – M S – M ∴S – P	M – P M – S ∴S – P	P – M M – S ∴S – P
Description	The middle term is the subject of the major premise and the predicate of the minor premise.	The middle term is the predicate of both major and minor premises.	The middle term is the subject of both the major and minor premises.	The middle term is the predicate of the major premise and the subject of the minor premise.

It will be seen that:

- In the first figure the middle term is the subject of the major premise and the predicate of the minor premise;
- In the second figure the middle term is the predicate of both premises;
- In the third figure the middle term is the subject of both premises;
- In the fourth figure the middle term is the predicate of the major premise and the subject of the minor premise.

Each of the sixty-four moods can appear in each of the four figures. The mood and figure of a given syllogism, taken together, uniquely determine the logical form of that syllogism. Therefore there are (as noted earlier) exactly 256 (64×4) possible forms of the standard-form categorical syllogism.

The vast majority of these forms are not valid. We can eliminate every form that violates one or more of the syllogistic rules set forth in the preceding section. The forms that remain after this elimination are the only valid forms of the categorical syllogism. Of the 256 possible forms, there are exactly fifteen forms that cannot be eliminated and thus are valid.*

To advance the mastery of syllogistics, classical logicians gave a unique name to every valid syllogism, each characterized completely by mood and figure. Understanding this small set of valid forms, and knowing the name of each, is very useful when putting syllogistic reasoning to work. Each name, carefully devised, contained three vowels representing (in standard-form order: major premise, minor premise, conclusion) the mood of the syllogism named. Where there are valid syllogisms of a given mood but in different figures, a unique name was assigned to each. Thus, for example, a syllogism of the mood **EAE** in the first figure was named *Celarent*, whereas

---

*It should be borne in mind that we adopt here the Boolean interpretation of categorical propositions, according to which universal propositions (**A** and **E** propositions) do not have existential import. The classical interpretation of categorical propositions, according to which all the classes to which propositions refer do have members, makes acceptable some inferences that are found here to be invalid. Under that older interpretation, for example, it is plausible to infer the subaltern from its corresponding superaltern—to infer an **I** proposition from its corresponding **A** proposition, and an **O** proposition from its corresponding **E** proposition. This makes plausible the claim that there are other valid syllogisms (so-called weakened syllogisms) that are not considered valid here. Compelling reasons for the rejection of that older interpretation (and hence the justification of our stricter standards for valid syllogisms) were given at some length in Section 5.7.

a syllogism of the mood **EAE** in the second figure, also valid, was named *Cesare.**

These names had (and still have) a very practical purpose: If one knows that only certain combinations of mood and figure are valid, and can recognize by name those valid arguments, the merit of any syllogism in a given figure, or of a given mood, can be determined almost immediately. For example, the mood **AOO** is valid only in the second figure. That unique form (**AOO–2**) is known as ***Baroko.***† One who is familiar with *Baroko* and able to discern it readily may be confident that a syllogism of this mood presented in any other figure may be rejected as invalid.

The standard form of the categorical syllogism is the key to the system. A neat and efficient method of identifying the few valid syllogisms from among the many possible syllogisms is at hand, but it depends on the assumption that the propositions of the syllogism in question either are in (or can be put into) standard order—major premise, minor premise, then conclusion. The unique identification of each valid syllogism relies on the specification of its mood, and its mood is determined by the letters characterizing its three constituent propositions *in that standard order*. If the premises of a valid syllogism were to be set forth in a different order, then that syllogism would remain valid, of course; the Venn diagram technique can prove this. But much would be lost. Our ability to identify syllogisms uniquely, and with that identification our ability to comprehend the forms

*The principles that governed the construction of those traditional names, the selection and placement of consonants as well as vowels, were quite sophisticated. Some of these conventions relate to the place of the weakened syllogisms noted just above and are therefore not acceptable in the Boolean interpretation we adopt. Some other conventions remain acceptable. For example, the letter **s** that follows the vowel **e** indicates that when that **E** proposition is converted *simpliciter*, or simply (as all **E** propositions will convert), then that syllogism reduces to, or is transformed into, another syllogism of the same mood in the first figure, which is viewed as the most basic figure. To illustrate, *Festino*, in the second figure, reduces, when its major premise is converted simply, to *Ferio*; and *Cesare*, in the second figure, reduces to *Celarent*, and so on. The possibility of these and other reductions explains why the names of groups of syllogisms begin with the same consonant. The intricate details of the classical naming system need not be fully recounted here.

†Here is an example of *Baroko*:

> All good mathematicians have creative intellects.
>
> Some scholars do not have creative intellects.
>
> Therefore some scholars are not good mathematicians.

With practice one comes to recognize the *cadence* of the different valid forms.

of those syllogisms fully and to test their validity crisply, all rely on their being in standard form.*

Classical logicians studied these forms closely, and they became fully familiar with their structure and their logical "feel." This elegant system, finely honed, enabled reasoners confronting syllogisms in speech or in texts to recognize immediately those that were valid, and to detect with confidence those that were not. For centuries it was common practice to defend the solidity of reasoning in progress by giving the names of the forms of the valid syllogisms being relied on. The ability to provide these identifications even in the midst of heated oral disputes was considered a mark of learning and acumen, and it gave evidence that the chain of deductive reasoning being relied on was indeed unbroken. Once the theory of the syllogism has been fully mastered, this practical skill can be developed with profit and pleasure.

Syllogistic reasoning was so very widely employed, and so highly regarded as the most essential tool of scholarly argument, that the logical treatises of its original and greatest master, Aristotle, were venerated for more than a thousand years. His analytical account of the syllogism still carries the simple name that conveys respect and awe: the *Organon*, the *Instrument*.†

As students of this remarkable logical system, our proficiency in syllogistics may be only moderate—but we will nevertheless find it useful to have before us a synoptic account of all the valid syllogisms. These fifteen valid syllogisms (under the Boolean interpretation) may be divided by figure into four groups:‡

---

*The burdensome consequences of ignoring standard form have been eloquently underscored by Keith Burgess-Jackson in his unpublished essay, "Why Standard Form Matters," October 2003.

†Valid syllogisms are powerful weapons in controversy, but the effectiveness of those weapons depends, of course, on the truth of the premises. A great theologian, defiant in battling scholars who resisted his reform of the Church, wrote: "They may attack me with an army of six hundred syllogisms. . ." (Erasmus, *The Praise of Folly*, 1511).

‡In the older tradition, in which reasoning from universal premises to particular conclusions was believed to be correct, the number of valid syllogisms (each uniquely named) was of course more than fifteen. To illustrate, if an **I** proposition may be inferred from its corresponding **A** proposition (as we think mistaken), the valid syllogism known as *Barbara* (**AAA–1**) will have a putatively valid "weakened" sister, *Barbari* (**AAI–1**); and if an **O** proposition may be inferred from its corresponding **E** proposition (as we think mistaken), the valid syllogism known as *Camestres* (**AEE–2**) will have a putatively valid "weakened" brother, *Camestrop* (**AEO–2**).

OVERVIEW

The Fifteen Valid Forms of the Standard-Form Categorical Syllogism

In the first figure (in which the middle term is the subject of the major premise and the predicate of the minor premise):

1. **AAA–1** ***Barbara***
2. **EAE–1** ***Celarent***
3. **AII–1** ***Darii***
4. **EIO–1** ***Ferio***

In the second figure (in which the middle term is the predicate of both premises):

5. **AEE–2** ***Camestres***
6. **EAE–2** ***Cesare***
7. **AOO–2** ***Baroko***
8. **EIO–2** ***Festino***

In the third figure (in which the middle term is the subject of both premises):

9. **AII–3** ***Datisi***
10. **IAI–3** ***Disamis***
11. **EIO–3** ***Ferison***
12. **OAO–3** ***Bokardo***

In the fourth figure (in which the middle term is the predicate of the major premise and the subject of the minor premise):

13. **AEE–4** ***Camenes***
14. **IAI–4** ***Dimaris***
15. **EIO–4** ***Fresison***

EXERCISES

A. At the conclusion of Section 6.3, in exercise group B (on pp. 243–244), ten syllogisms were to be tested using Venn diagrams. Of these ten syllogisms, numbers 1, 4, 6, 9, and 10 are valid. What is the *name* of each of these five valid syllogisms?

EXAMPLE

Number 1 is **IAI–3** (*Disamis*).

APPENDIX
Deduction of the Fifteen Valid Forms of the Categorical Syllogism

In Section 6.5 the fifteen valid forms of the categorical syllogism were identified and precisely characterized. The unique name of each syllogism is also given there—a name assigned in view of its unique combination of mood and figure. The summary account of these fifteen syllogisms appears in the Overview immediately preceding.

It is possible to *prove* that these, and only these, are the valid forms of the categorical syllogism. This proof—*the deduction of the valid forms of the categorical syllogism*—is presented as an appendix, rather than in the body of the chapter, because mastering it is not essential for the student of logic. However, understanding it can give one a deeper appreciation of the *system* of syllogistics. And for those who derive satisfaction from the intricacies of analytical syllogistics, thinking through this deduction will be a pleasing, if somewhat arduous challenge.

We emphasize that if the chief aims of study are to recognize, understand, and apply the valid forms of the syllogism, as exhibited in Section 6.5, this appendix may be bypassed.

The deduction of the fifteen valid syllogisms is not easy to follow. Those who pursue it must keep two things very clearly in mind: (1) The *rules of the syllogism,* six basic rules set forth in Section 6.4, are the essential tools of the deduction; and (2) The *four figures of the syllogism,* as depicted in the Overview in Section 6.5 (p. 255) are referred to repeatedly as the rules are invoked.

We have seen that there are 256 *possible* forms of the syllogism, sixty-four moods (or combinations of the four categorical propositions) in each of the four figures. The deduction of the fifteen valid syllogisms proceeds by *eliminating* the syllogisms that violate one of the basic rules and that thus cannot be valid.

The conclusion of every syllogism is a categorical proposition, either **A,** or **E,** or **I,** or **O.** We begin by dividing all the possible syllogistic forms into four groups, each group having a conclusion with a different form (**A, E, I,** or **O**). Every syllogism must of course fall into one of these four groups. Taking each of the four groups in turn, we ask what characteristics a valid syllogism with such a conclusion must possess. That is, we ask what forms are *excluded* by one or more of the syllogistic rules if the conclusion is an **A** proposition, and if the conclusion is an **E** proposition, and so on.

After excluding all those invalid syllogisms, only the valid syllogisms remain. To assist in visualization, we note in the margin as we proceed the moods and figures, and the names, of the fifteen valid categorical syllogisms.

Case 1: If the conclusion of the syllogism is an A proposition

Barbara
The traditional name for the valid syllogism with the mood and figure **AAA–1**

In this case, neither premise can be an **E** or an **O** proposition, because if either premise is negative, the conclusion must be negative (Rule 5). Therefore the two premises must be **I** or **A** propositions. The minor premise cannot be an **I** proposition because the minor term (the subject of the conclusion, which is an **A**) is distributed in the conclusion, and therefore if the minor premise were an **I** proposition, a term would be distributed in the conclusion that is not distributed in the premises, violating Rule 3. The two premises, major and minor, cannot be **I** and **A,** because if they were, either the distributed subject of the conclusion would not be distributed in the premise, violating Rule 3, or the middle term of the syllogism would not be distributed in either premise, violating Rule 2. So the two premises (if the conclusion is an **A**) must both be **A** as well, which means that the only possible valid mood is **AAA.** But in the second figure **AAA** again results in the middle term being distributed in neither premise; and in both the third figure and the fourth figure **AAA** results in a term being distributed in the conclusion that is not distributed in the premise in which it appears. Therefore, if the conclusion of the syllogism is an **A** proposition, the only valid form it can take is **AAA** in the first figure. This valid form, **AAA–1,** is the syllogism traditionally given the name *Barbara.*

Summary of Case 1: If the syllogism has an **A** conclusion, there is only one possibly valid form: **AAA–1**—*Barbara.*

Case 2: If the conclusion of the syllogism is an **E** proposition

Camestres
The traditional name for the valid syllogism with the mood and figure **AEE–2**

Camenes
The traditional name for the valid syllogism with the mood and figure **AEE–4**

Celarent
The traditional name for the valid syllogism with the mood and figure **EAE–1**

Both the subject and the predicate of an **E** proposition are distributed, and therefore all three terms in the premises of a syllogism having such a conclusion must be distributed, and this is possible only if one of the premises is also an **E.** Both premises cannot be **E** propositions, because two negative premises are never allowed (Rule 4), and the other premise cannot be an **O** proposition because then both premises would also be negative. Nor can the other premise be an **I** proposition, for if it were, a term distributed in the conclusion would then not be distributed in the premise, violating Rule 3. So the other premise must be an **A,** and the two premises must be either **AE** or **EA.** The only possible moods (if the conclusion of the syllogism is an **E** proposition) are therefore **AEE** and **EAE.**

If the mood is **AEE,** it cannot be either in the first figure or in the third figure, because in either of those cases a term distributed in the conclusion would then not be distributed in the premises. Therefore, the mood **AEE** is possibly valid only in the second figure, **AEE–2** (traditionally called *Camestres*), or in the fourth figure, **AEE–4** (traditionally called *Camenes*). And if the mood is **EAE,** it cannot be in the third figure or in the fourth figure, because again that would mean that a term distributed in the conclusion would not be distributed in the premises, which leaves as valid only the first

Cesare
The traditional name for the valid syllogism with the mood and figure **EAE–2**

figure, **EAE–1** (traditionally called *Celarent*), and the second figure, **EAE–2** (traditionally called *Cesare.*)

Summary of Case 2: If the syllogism has an **E** conclusion, there are only four possibly valid forms: **AEE–2, AEE–4, EAE–1**, and **EAE–2**—*Camestres, Camenes, Celarent*, and *Cesare*, respectively.

Darii
The traditional name for the valid syllogism with the mood and figure **AII–1**

Datisi
The traditional name for the valid syllogism with the mood and figure **AII–3**

Disamis
The traditional name for the valid syllogism with the mood and figure **IAI–3**

Dimaris
The traditional name for the valid syllogism with the mood and figure **IAI–4**

Case 3: If the conclusion is an **I** proposition

In this case, neither premise can be an **E** or an **O**, because if either premise is negative, the conclusion must be negative. The two premises cannot both be **A,** because a syllogism with a particular conclusion cannot have two universal premises (Rule 6). Neither can both premises be **I,** because the middle term must be distributed in at least one premise (Rule 2). So the premises must be either **AI** or **IA,** and therefore the only possible moods with an **I** conclusion are **AII** and **IAI.**

AII is not possibly valid in the second figure or in the fourth figure because the middle term must be distributed in at least one premise. The only valid forms remaining for the mood **AII,** therefore, are **AII–1** (traditionally called *Darii*) and **AII–3** (traditionally called *Datisi*). If the mood is **IAI,** it cannot be **IAI–1** or **IAI–2,** because they also would violate the rule that requires the middle term to be distributed in at least one premise. This leaves as valid only **IAI–3** (traditionally called *Disamis*), and **IAI–4** (traditionally called *Dimaris*).

Summary of Case 3: If the syllogism has an **I** conclusion, there are only four possibly valid forms: **AII–1, AII–3, IAI–3**, and **IAI–4**—*Darii, Datisi, Disamis*, and *Dimaris*, respectively.

Baroko
The traditional name for the valid syllogism with the mood and figure **AOO–2**

Ferio
The traditional name for the valid syllogism with the mood and figure **EIO–1**

Case 4: If the conclusion is an O proposition

In this case, the major premise cannot be an **I** proposition, because any term distributed in the conclusion must be distributed in the premises. So the major premise must be either an **A** or an **E** or an **O** proposition.

Suppose the major premise is an **A.** In that case, the minor premise cannot be either an **A** or an **E,** because two universal premises are not permitted when the conclusion (an **O**) is particular. Neither can the minor premise then be an **I,** because if it were, either the middle term would not be distributed at all (a violation of Rule 2), or a term distributed in the conclusion would not be distributed in the premises. So, if the major premise is an **A,** the minor premise has to be an **O,** yielding the mood **AOO.** In the fourth figure, **AOO** cannot possibly be valid, because in that case the middle term would not be distributed, and in the first figure and the third figure **AOO** cannot possibly be valid either, because that would result in terms being distributed in the conclusion that were not distributed in the premises. For the mood **AOO,** the only possibly valid form remaining, if the major premise is an **A,** is therefore in the second figure, **AOO–2** (traditionally called *Baroko*).

Now suppose (if the conclusion is an **O**) that the major premise is an **E.** In that case, the minor premise cannot be either an **E** or an **O,** because two negative premises are not permitted. Nor can the minor premise be an **A,** because two universal premises are precluded if the conclusion is particular (Rule 6). This leaves only the mood **EIO**—and this mood is valid in all four figures, traditionally known as *Ferio* **(EIO–1)**, *Festino* **(EIO–2)**, *Ferison* **(EIO–3)**, and *Fresison* **(EIO–4).**

Festino
The traditional name for the valid syllogism with the mood and figure **EIO–2**

Ferison
The traditional name for the valid syllogism with the mood and figure **EIO–3**

Fresison
The traditional name for the valid syllogism with the mood and figure **EIO–4**

Finally, suppose (if the conclusion is an **O**) that the major premise is also an **O** proposition. Then, again, the minor premise cannot be an **E** or an **O,** because two negative premises are forbidden. And the minor premise cannot be an **I,** because then the middle term would not be distributed, or a term that is distributed in the conclusion would not be distributed in the premises. Therefore, if the major premise is an **O,** the minor premise must be an **A,** and the mood must be **OAO**. But **OAO–1** is eliminated, because in that case the middle term would not be distributed. **OAO–2** and **OAO–4** are also eliminated, because in both a term distributed in the conclusion would then not be distributed in the premises. This leaves as valid only **OAO–3** (traditionally known as *Bokardo*).

Bokardo
The traditional name for the valid syllogism with the mood and figure **OAO–3**

Summary of Case 4: If the syllogism has an **O** conclusion, there are only six possibly valid forms: **AOO–2, EIO–1, EIO–2, EIO–3, EIO–4,** and **OAO–3**—*Baroko, Ferio, Festino, Ferison, Fresison,* and *Bokardo.*

This analysis has demonstrated, by elimination, that there are exactly fifteen valid forms of the categorical syllogism: one if the conclusion is an **A** proposition, four if the conclusion is an **E** proposition, four if the conclusion is an **I** proposition, and six if the conclusion is an **O** proposition. Of these fifteen valid forms, four are in the first figure, four are in the second figure, four are in the third figure, and three are in the fourth figure. This completes the deduction of the fifteen valid forms of the standard-form categorical syllogism.

EXERCISES

For students who enjoy the complexities of analytical syllogistics, here follow some theoretical questions whose answers can all be derived from the systematic application of the six rules of the syllogism set forth in Section 6.4. Answering these questions will be much easier if you have fully grasped the deduction of the fifteen valid syllogistic forms presented in this appendix.

EXAMPLE

1. Can any standard-form categorical syllogism be valid that contains exactly three terms, each of which is distributed in both of its occurrences?

SOLUTION

No, such a syllogism cannot be valid. If each of the three terms were distributed in both of its occurrences, all three of its propositions would have to be **E** propositions, and the mood of the syllogism would thus be **EEE,** which violates Rule 4, which forbids two negative premises.

2. In what mood or moods, if any, can a first-figure standard-form categorical syllogism with a particular conclusion be valid?
3. In what figure or figures, if any, can the premises of a valid standard-form categorical syllogism distribute both major and minor terms?
4. In what figure or figures, if any, can a valid standard-form categorical syllogism have two particular premises?

*5. In what figure or figures, if any, can a valid standard-form categorical syllogism have only one term distributed, and that one only once?

6. In what mood or moods, if any, can a valid standard-form categorical syllogism have just two terms distributed, each one twice?
7. In what mood or moods, if any, can a valid standard-form categorical syllogism have two affirmative premises and a negative conclusion?
8. In what figure or figures, if any, can a valid standard-form categorical syllogism have a particular premise and a universal conclusion?
9. In what mood or moods, if any, can a second figure standard-form categorical syllogism with a universal conclusion be valid?

*10. In what figure or figures, if any, can a valid standard-form categorical syllogism have its middle term distributed in both premises?

11. Can a valid standard-form categorical syllogism have a term distributed in a premise that appears undistributed in the conclusion?

SUMMARY

In this chapter we have examined the standard-form categorical syllogism: its elements, its forms, its validity, and the rules governing its proper use.

In Section 6.1, the major, minor, and middle terms of a syllogism were identified:

- **Major term:** the predicate of the conclusion
- **Minor term:** the subject of the conclusion
- **Middle term:** the third term appearing in both premises but not in the conclusion.

We identified major and minor premises as those containing the major and minor terms, respectively. We specified that a categorical syllogism is in standard form when its propositions appear in precisely this order: major premise first, minor premise second, and conclusion last.

We also explained in Section 6.1 how the mood and figure of a syllogism are determined.

The mood of a syllogism is determined by the three letters identifying the types of its three propositions, **A, E, I,** or **O.** There are sixty-four possible different moods.

The figure of a syllogism is determined by the position of the middle term in its premises. The four possible figures are described and named thus:

- **First figure:** The middle term is the subject term of the major premise and the predicate term of the minor premise.
  Schematically: *M–P, S–M*, therefore *S–P*.
- **Second figure:** The middle term is the predicate term of both premises.
  Schematically: *P–M, S–M*, therefore *S–P*.
- **Third figure:** The middle term is the subject term of both premises.
  Schematically: *M–P, M–S*, therefore *S–P*.
- **Fourth figure:** The middle term is the predicate term of the major premise and the subject term of the minor premise.
  Schematically: *P–M, M–S*, therefore *S–P*.

In Section 6.2, we explained how the mood and figure of a standard-form categorical syllogism jointly determine its logical form. Because each of the sixty-four moods may appear in all four figures, there are exactly 256 standard-form categorical syllogisms, of which only a few are valid.

In Section 6.3, we explained the Venn diagram technique for testing the validity of syllogisms, using overlapping circles appropriately marked or shaded to exhibit the meaning of the premises.

In Section 6.4, we explained the six essential rules for standard-form syllogisms and named the fallacy that results when each of these rules is broken:

- **Rule 1.** A standard-form categorical syllogism must contain exactly three terms, each of which is used in the same sense throughout the argument.
  Violation: Fallacy of four terms.

- **Rule 2.** In a valid standard-form categorical syllogism, the middle term must be distributed in at least one premise.
Violation: Fallacy of undistributed middle.
- **Rule 3.** In a valid standard-form categorical syllogism, if either term is distributed in the conclusion, then it must be distributed in the premises.
Violation: Fallacy of the illicit major, or fallacy of the illicit minor.
- **Rule 4.** No standard-form categorical syllogism having two negative premises is valid.
Violation: Fallacy of exclusive premises.
- **Rule 5.** If either premise of a valid standard-form categorical syllogism is negative, the conclusion must be negative.
Violation: Fallacy of drawing an affirmative conclusion from a negative premise.
- **Rule 6.** No valid standard-form categorical syllogism with a particular conclusion can have two universal premises.
Violation: Existential fallacy.

In Section 6.5, we presented an exposition of the fifteen valid forms of the categorical syllogism, identifying their moods and figures, and explaining their traditional Latin names:

AAA–1 (*Barbara*); **EAE–1** (*Celarent*); **AII–1** (*Darii*); **EIO–1** (*Ferio*); **AEE–2** (*Camestres*); **EAE–2** (*Cesare*); **AOO–2** (*Baroko*); **EIO–2** (*Festino*); **AII–3** (*Datisi*); **IAI–3** (*Disamis*); **EIO–3** (*Ferison*); **OAO–3** (*Bokardo*); **AEE–4** (*Camenes*); **IAI–4** (*Dimaris*); **EIO–4** (*Fresison*).

In the Appendix to Chapter 6 (which may be omitted), we presented the deduction of the fifteen valid forms of the categorical syllogism, demonstrating, through a process of elimination, that only those fifteen forms can avoid all violations of the six basic rules of the syllogism.

Syllogisms in Ordinary Language

7.1 Syllogistic Arguments

In ordinary discourse the arguments we encounter rarely appear as neatly packaged, standard-form categorical syllogisms. So the syllogistic arguments that arise in everyday speech cannot always be readily tested. They can be tested, however, if we *put* them into standard form—and we can generally do that by reformulating their constituent propositions. The term **syllogistic argument** refers to any argument that either *is* a standard-form categorical syllogism or that *can be reformulated as* a standard-form categorical syllogism without any loss or change of meaning.

We want to test the validity of syllogistic arguments. If they are fallacious or misleading, that will be most easily detected, as Immanuel Kant pointed out, when they are set out in correct syllogistic form. The process of reformulation is therefore important because the effective tests discussed in Chapter 6—Venn diagrams and the rules for categorical syllogisms—cannot be applied directly until the syllogism is in standard form. Putting it into standard form is called **reduction (or translation) to standard form.** When we reformulate (or reduce) a loosely put argument that appears in ordinary language into a classical syllogism, the resulting argument is called a **standard-form translation** of the original argument. Effecting this reformulation can present some difficulties.

We already know the tests for validity (Venn diagrams and the rules for syllogisms). What we need, to evaluate syllogistic arguments using these tests, are techniques for *translating* syllogistic arguments from their loose forms into standard form. With these techniques in hand, we can first *translate* the argument into standard form, and then *test* that argument using the Venn diagram method or the syllogistic rules.

To describe the various techniques for reduction to standard form, we begin by noting the kinds of problems that create the need for them—that is, by noting different ways in which a syllogistic argument in ordinary language may *deviate* from a standard-form categorical argument. Understanding those deviations, we can proceed to counteract them.

First deviation. The premises and conclusion of an argument in ordinary language may appear in an *order* that is not the order of the standard-form syllogism. This difficulty is easily remedied by reordering the premises: The major premise is put first, the minor premise second, and the conclusion third. (Recall that the major premise is the premise that contains the term that is the predicate term of the conclusion, whereas the minor premise contains the term that is the subject term of the conclusion.)

Second deviation. A standard-form categorical syllogism always has exactly three terms. The premises of an argument in ordinary language may appear to involve *more than three terms*—but that appearance may be deceptive. If the number of terms can be reduced to three without loss of meaning, the reduction to standard form may be successful.

Third deviation. The *component propositions* of the syllogistic argument in ordinary language *may not all be standard-form propositions.* This deviation is very common, but if the components can be converted into standard-form propositions without loss of meaning, the reduction to standard form may be successful.

To cope with the second and third of these deviant patterns, there are known techniques, which we now explain.

7.2 Reducing the Number of Terms to Three

A valid syllogism must have exactly three terms. If more than three terms seem to be involved in an argument of apparently syllogistic form, it may be possible to translate the argument into a standard-form categorical syllogism that is equivalent to it but that contains only three terms and is perfectly valid. How can that be done?

One way is by *eliminating synonyms*. A synonym of one of the terms in the syllogism is not really a fourth term, but only another way of referring to one of the three classes involved. So we begin by eliminating synonyms, if any appear. For example, the following syllogistic argument appears to contain six terms:

No wealthy persons are vagrants.

All lawyers are rich people.

Therefore no attorneys are tramps.

However, "wealthy" and "rich" are synonyms, as are "lawyer" and "attorney," and also "vagrant" and "tramp." If the synonyms are eliminated, the argument becomes

No wealthy persons are vagrants.

All lawyers are wealthy persons.

Therefore no lawyers are vagrants.

This argument in standard form, **EAE–1** (*Celarent*), is plainly valid.

A second way to reduce the number of terms to three is by *eliminating class complements*, a concept explained in Section 5.6. We illustrate this using the following syllogistic argument, whose propositions are standard-form categorical propositions:

All mammals are warm-blooded animals.

No lizards are warm-blooded animals.

Therefore all lizards are nonmammals.

On the surface, this argument appears to be invalid, because it seems to have four terms—and it also draws an affirmative conclusion from a negative premise, which breaks one of the rules of the syllogism.

This argument, however, is in fact perfectly valid when it is translated into standard form. We can reduce the number of terms to three, because two of the terms in it ("mammals" and "nonmammals") are complements of one another. So, by obverting the conclusion (to *obvert* a proposition, we change its quality and replace the predicate term by its complement), we get "No lizards are mammals." Using this valid immediate inference, we derive the following standard-form translation of the original argument:

All mammals are warm-blooded animals.

No lizards are warm-blooded animals.

Therefore no lizards are mammals.

which is logically equivalent to the original because it has identically the same premises and a logically equivalent conclusion. This standard-form translation conforms to all the syllogistic rules and thus is known to be valid. Its form is **AEE–2** (*Camestres*).

There may be more than one translation of a syllogistic argument into standard form, but if any one of those translations yields a valid syllogism, all the others must be valid as well. Thus, for example, the preceding illustrative argument can also be reduced to standard form in a different (but logically equivalent) way. This time we leave the conclusion unchanged and work with the premises. We take the contrapositive of the first premise, and we obvert the second premise. We then get:

All non(warm-blooded animals) are nonmammals.

All lizards are non(warm-blooded animals).

Therefore all lizards are nonmammals.

This is also a valid translation; its form is **AAA–1** (*Barbara*), and it conforms to all the rules of the syllogism.

Any syllogistic argument that appears to contain four terms can be reduced to standard form (that is, can be translated into a logically equivalent standard-form categorical syllogism) if one of its terms is the complement of one of the other three. Likewise, reduction from an argument with five terms is possible if two of its terms are complements of other terms in the argument; and even arguments with as many as six terms may be reduced to standard form if three of those terms are complements of other terms in the argument. The key to such reductions is to use the valid immediate inferences discussed in Chapter 5: conversion, obversion, and contraposition.

More than one immediate inference may be needed to reduce the argument to standard form. Consider this example:

No nonresidents are citizens.

All noncitizens are nonvoters.

Therefore all voters are residents.

The argument has six terms, but it is in fact valid, and that can be shown by reducing it to standard form, which can be done in more than one way. Perhaps the most natural reduction is to convert and then obvert the first premise. This yields "All citizens are residents." Then take the contrapositive of the second premise, which yields "All voters are citizens." The argument is then in standard form:

All citizens are residents.

All voters are citizens.

Therefore all voters are residents.

The middle term ("citizens") is the subject term of the major premise and the predicate term of the minor premise, so the syllogism is in the first figure. Its three propositions are universal affirmatives. This is a syllogism in *Barbara*, **AAA–1**, and it is plainly valid.

EXERCISES

Translate the following syllogistic arguments into standard form, and test their validity by using either Venn diagrams or the syllogistic rules set forth in Chapter 6.

EXAMPLE

1. Some preachers are persons of unfailing vigor. No preachers are non-intellectuals. Therefore some intellectuals are persons of unfailing vigor.

SOLUTION

This argument may be translated into: Some preachers are persons of unfailing vigor. (Some *P* is *V*.) All preachers are intellectuals. (By obversion: All *P* is *I*.) Therefore some intellectuals are persons of unfailing vigor. (Some *I* is *V*.) Shown on a Venn diagram, this syllogism is seen to be valid:

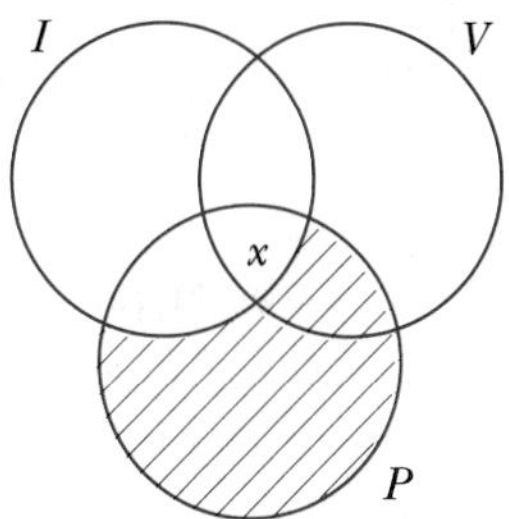

2. Some metals are rare and costly substances, but no welder's materials are nonmetals; hence some welder's materials are rare and costly substances.

3. Some Asian nations were nonbelligerents, because all belligerents were allies either of Germany or Britain, and some Asian nations were not allies of either Germany or Britain.

4. Some nondrinkers are athletes, because no drinkers are persons in perfect physical condition, and some people in perfect physical condition are not nonathletes.

***5.** All things inflammable are unsafe things, so all things that are safe are nonexplosives, because all explosives are flammable things.

6. All worldly goods are changeable things, for no worldly goods are things immaterial, and no material things are unchangeable things.

7. All those who are neither members nor guests of members are those who are excluded; therefore no nonconformists are either members or guests of members, for all those who are included are conformists.

8. All mortals are imperfect beings, and no humans are immortals, whence it follows that all perfect beings are nonhumans.

9. All things present are nonirritants; therefore no irritants are invisible objects, because all visible objects are absent things.

*10. All useful things are objects no more than six feet long, because all difficult things to store are useless things, and no objects over six feet long are easy things to store.

7.3 Translating Categorical Propositions into Standard Form

We noted in Section 7.1 that syllogistic arguments in ordinary language may deviate from standard-form categorical syllogisms not only because they may appear to contain more than three terms (as discussed in Section 7.2), but also because the component propositions of the syllogism in ordinary language may not all be standard-form propositions. **A, E, I,** and **O** propositions are clearly somewhat stilted, and many syllogistic arguments in everyday life contain nonstandard-form propositions. To reduce these arguments to standard form requires that their constituent propositions be translated into standard form.

It would be very convenient if there were some neat list of rules that we could use to effect such translations. Unfortunately, ordinary language is too rich and too multiform to permit the compilation of such a set of rules. Different sorts of transformation are called for in different settings, and to know what is called for we must, in every case, understand fully the given nonstandard-form proposition that needs to be reformulated. If we understand the proposition, we can reformulate it without losing or changing its meaning.

Although no complete set of rules can be given, we can describe a number of well-tested methods for translating nonstandard propositions of different sorts. These methods—we will present nine of them in this section—must be regarded as guides rather than rules; they are *techniques* with which nonstandard-form propositions of certain describable kinds can be reformulated into standard-form propositions that may serve as constituents of syllogistic arguments.

I. Singular Propositions. Some propositions affirm or deny that a specific individual or object belongs to a given class—for example, "Socrates is a philosopher," and "This table is not an antique." These are called **singular propositions.** Such propositions do not affirm or deny the inclusion of one class in another (as standard-form propositions do), but we can nevertheless *interpret* a singular proposition as a proposition dealing with classes and their interrelations. We do this in the following way.

To every individual object there corresponds a unique **unit class** (one-membered class) whose only member is that object itself. Then, to assert that an object *s* belongs to a class *P* is logically equivalent to asserting that the unit class *S* containing just that object *s* is wholly included in the class *P*. And to assert that an object *s* does *not* belong to a class *P* is logically equivalent to asserting that the unit class *S* containing just that object *s* is wholly excluded from the class *P*.

It is customary to make this interpretation automatically, without any notational adjustment. Thus it is customary to take any affirmative singular proposition of the form "*s* is *P*" as if it were already expressed as the logically equivalent **A** proposition, "All *S* is *P*," and we similarly understand any negative singular proposition "*s* is not *P*" as an alternative formulation of the logically equivalent **E** proposition, "No *S* is *P*"—in each case understanding *S* to designate the unit class whose only member is the object *s*. Thus no explicit translations are provided for singular propositions; traditionally they have been classified as **A** and **E** propositions as they stand. As Kant remarked, "Logicians are justified in saying that, in the employment of judgments in syllogisms, singular judgments can be treated like those that are universal."[1]

The situation, however, is not quite so simple. Bear in mind that particular propositions have existential import, but universal propositions do not. Using this Boolean interpretation (for reasons explained in Section 5.7), we find that if singular propositions are treated mechanically as **A** and **E** propositions in syllogistic arguments, and we check the validity of those arguments using Venn diagrams or the rules set forth in Chapter 6, serious difficulties arise.

In some cases, obviously valid two-premise arguments containing singular propositions translate into valid categorical syllogisms, such as when

All *H* is *M*.	goes into the obviously valid	All *H* is *M*.
s is an *H*.	**AAA–1** categorical syllogism in *Barbara*	All *S* is *H*.
∴ *s* is an *M*.		∴ All *S* is *M*.

In other cases, however, obviously valid two-premise arguments containing singular propositions translate into categorical syllogisms that are *invalid*, such as when

s is *M*.	goes into the invalid	All *S* is *M*.
s is *H*.	**AAI–3** categorical syllogism	All *S* is *H*.
∴ Some *H* is *M*.		∴ All *H* is *M*.

which commits the existential fallacy, violating Rule 6.

On the other hand, if we translate singular propositions into particular propositions, there is the same kind of difficulty. In some cases, obviously valid two-premise arguments containing singular propositions translate into *valid* categorical syllogisms, such as when

All *H* is *M*.	goes into the obviously valid	All *H* is *M*.
s is an *H*.	**AII–1** categorical syllogism in *Darii*	Some *S* is *H*.
∴ s is an *M*.		∴ Some *S* is *M*.

In other cases, however, obviously valid two-premise arguments containing singular propositions translate into categorical syllogisms that are *invalid*, such as when

s is *M*.	goes into the invalid	Some *S* is *M*.
s is *H*.	**III–3** categorical syllogism	Some *S* is *H*.
∴ Some *H* is *M*.		∴ Some *H* is *M*.

which commits the fallacy of the undistributed middle, violating Rule 2.

The difficulty arises from the fact that a singular proposition contains more information than is contained in any single one of the four standard-form categorical propositions. If "*s* is *P*" is construed as "All *S* is *P*," then what is lost is the existential import of the singular proposition, the fact that *S* is not empty. But if "*s* is *P*" is construed as "Some *S* is *P*," then what is lost is the universal aspect of the singular proposition, which distributes its subject term, the fact that *all S* is *P*.

The solution to the difficulty is to construe singular propositions as conjunctions of standard-form categorical propositions. An affirmative singular proposition is equivalent to the conjunction of the related **A** and **I** categorical propositions. Thus "*s* is *P*" is equivalent to "All *S* is *P*" *and* "Some *S* is *P*." A negative singular proposition is equivalent to the conjunction of the related **E** and **O** categorical propositions. Thus "*s* is not *P*" is equivalent to "No *S* is *P*" *and* "Some *S* is not *P*." Venn dia-

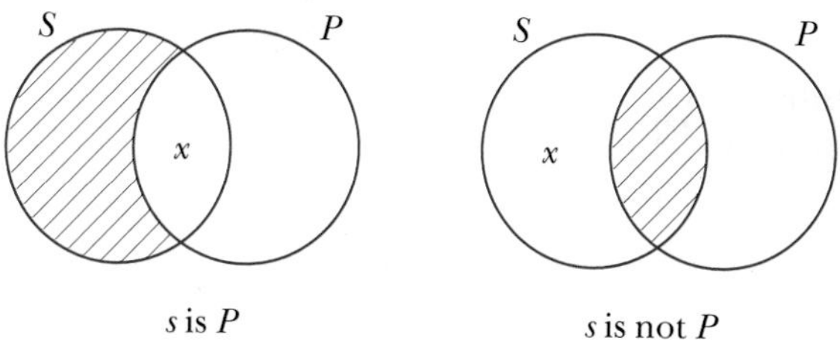

Figure 7-1

grams for affirmative and negative singular propositions are shown in Figure 7-1.

In applying the syllogistic rules to evaluate a syllogistic argument containing singular propositions, we must take account of *all* the information contained in those singular propositions, both distribution and existential import.

If we keep in mind the existential import of singular propositions when we invoke the syllogistic rules or apply Venn diagrams to test the validity of syllogistic arguments, it is acceptable practice to regard singular propositions as universal (**A** or **E**) propositions.

II. Categorical Propositions That Have Adjectives or Adjectival Phrases as Predicates, Rather than Substantives or Class Terms. For example, "Some flowers are beautiful" and "No warships are available for active duty" are categorical propositions, and yet they must be translated into standard-form categorical propositions; they deviate from standard form only in that their predicates, "beautiful" and "available for active duty," designate *attributes* rather than classes. However, every attribute *determines* a class, the class of things having that attribute, so every such proposition corresponds to a logically equivalent proposition that is in standard form. The two examples cited correspond to the **I** and **E** propositions "Some flowers are beauties" and "No warships are things available for active duty." When a categorical proposition is in standard form except that it has an adjectival predicate instead of a predicate term, the translation into standard form is made by replacing the adjectival predicate with a term designating the class of all objects of which the adjective may truly be predicated.

III. Categorical Propositions Whose Main Verbs Are Other than the Standard-Form Copula "To Be." Examples of this very common type are "All people seek recognition" and "Some people drink Greek wine." The usual method of translating such a statement into standard form is to regard all of it, except the subject term and the quantifier, as naming a class-defining characteristic. Those words can then be replaced by a term designating the class determined by that class-defining characteristic and may be linked to the subject with a standard copula. Thus the two examples given translate into the standard-form categorical propositions, "All people are seekers of recognition" and "Some people are Greek-wine drinkers."

IV. **Statements in Which the Standard-Form Ingredients Are All Present But Not Arranged in Standard-Form Order.** Two examples are "Racehorses are all thoroughbreds" and "All is well that ends well." In such cases, we first decide which is the subject term and then rearrange the words to express a standard-form categorical proposition. Such translations are usually quite straightforward. It is clear that the two preceding statements translate into the **A** propositions "All racehorses are thoroughbreds" and "All things that end well are things that are well."

V. **Categorical Propositions Whose Quantities Are Indicated by Words Other than the Standard-Form Quantifiers "All," "No," and "Some."** Statements beginning with the words "every" and "any" are easily translated. The propositions "Every dog has its day" and "Any contribution will be appreciated" reduce to "All dogs are creatures that have their days" and "All contributions are things that are appreciated." Similar to "every" and "any" are "everything" and "anything." Paralleling these, but clearly restricted to classes of persons, are "everyone," "anyone," "whoever," "whosoever," "who," "one who," and the like. These should present no difficulty.

The grammatical particles "a" and "an" may also serve to indicate quantity, but whether they are being used to mean "all" or "some" depends largely on the context. Thus "A bat is a mammal" and "An elephant is a pachyderm" are reasonably interpreted as meaning "All bats are mammals" and "All elephants are pachyderms." But "A bat flew in the window" and "An elephant escaped" quite clearly do not refer to all bats or all elephants; they are properly reduced to "Some bats are creatures that flew in the window" and "Some elephants are creatures that escaped."

The particle "the" may be used to refer either to a particular individual or to all the members of a class. There is little danger of ambiguity here, for such a statement as "The whale is a mammal" translates in almost any context into the **A** proposition "All whales are mammals," whereas the singular proposition "The first president was a military hero" is already in standard form as an **A** proposition (a singular proposition having existential import) as discussed in the first subparagraph of this section.[2]

Although affirmative statements beginning with "every" and "any" are translated into "All *S* is *P*," negative statements beginning with "not every" and "not any" are quite different. Their translations are much less obvious and require great care. Thus, for example, "Not every *S* is *P*" means that *some S is not P*, whereas "Not any *S* is *P*" means that *no S* is *P*.

VI. **Exclusive Propositions.** Categorical propositions involving the words "only" or "none but" are often called **exclusive propositions,** because in general they assert that the predicate applies exclusively to the subject named. Examples of such usages are "Only citizens can vote" and "None but the brave deserve the fair." The first translates into the standard-form categorical proposition, "All those who can vote are citizens," and the second into the standard-form categorical proposition, "All those who deserve the fair are those who are brave." Propositions beginning with "only" or "none but" usually translate into **A** propositions using this general rule: Reverse the subject and the predicate, and replace the "only" with "all." Thus "Only *S* is *P*" and "None but *S*'s are *P*'s" are usually understood to express "All *P* is *S*."

There are some contexts in which "only" and "none but" are used to convey some further meaning. "Only *S* is *P*" or "None but *S*'s are *P*'s" may suggest either that "All *S* is *P*" or that "Some *S* is *P*." This is not always the case, however. Where context helps to determine meaning, attention must be paid to it, of course. But in the absence of such additional information, the translations first suggested are adequate.

VII. **Categorical Propositions That Contain No Words to Indicate Quantity.** Two examples are "Dogs are carnivorous" and "Children are present." Where there is no quantifier, what the sentence is intended to express may be doubtful. We may be able to determine its meaning only by examining the context in which it occurs, and that examination usually will clear up our doubts. In the first example it is very probable that "Dogs are carnivorous" refers to *all* dogs, and is to be translated as "All dogs are carnivores." In the second example, on the other hand, it is plain that only *some* children are referred to, and thus the standard-form translation of "Children are present" is "Some children are beings who are present."

VIII. **Propositions That Do Not Resemble Standard-Form Categorical Propositions But Can Be Translated Into Standard Form.** Some examples are "Not all children believe in Santa Claus," "There are white elephants," "There are no pink elephants," and "Nothing is both round and square." On reflection, these propositions will be seen to be logically equivalent to, and therefore to translate into, the following standard-form propositions: "Some children are not believers in Santa Claus,"

"Some elephants are white things," "No elephants are pink things," and "No round objects are square objects."

IX. Exceptive Propositions. Some examples of **exceptive propositions** are "All except employees are eligible," "All but employees are eligible," and "Employees alone are not eligible." Translating exceptive propositions into standard form is somewhat complicated, because propositions of this kind (much like singular propositions) make *two* assertions rather than one. Each of the logically equivalent examples just given asserts not merely that *all nonemployees are eligible* but also (in the usual context) that *no employees are eligible*. Where "employees" is abbreviated to *S* and "eligible persons" to *P*, these two propositions can be written as "All non-*S* is *P*" and "No *S* is *P*." These are clearly independent and together assert that *S* and *P* are complementary classes.

Each of these exceptive propositions is *compound* and therefore cannot be translated into a single standard-form categorical proposition. Rather, each must be translated into an explicit conjunction of two standard-form categoricals. Thus the three illustrative propositions about eligibility translate identically into "All nonemployees are eligible persons, and no employees are eligible persons."

It should be noted that some arguments depend for their validity on numerical or quasi-numerical information that cannot be put into standard form. Such arguments may have constituent propositions that mention quantity more specifically than standard-form propositions do, usually by the use of quantifiers such as "one," "two," "three," "many," "a few," "most," and so on. When such specific quantitative information is critical to the validity of the argument in which it is mentioned, the argument itself is *asyllogistic* and therefore requires a more complicated analysis than that provided by the simple theory of the categorical syllogism. Yet some quasi-numerical quantifiers occur in arguments that do lend themselves to syllogistic analysis. These include "almost all," "not quite all," "all but a few," and "almost everyone." Propositions in which these phrases appear as quantifiers may be treated like the explicitly exceptive propositions just described. Thus the following exceptive propositions with quasi-numerical quantifiers are also compound: "Almost all students were at the dance," "Not quite all students were at the dance," "All but a few students were at the dance," and "Only some students were at the dance." Each of these *affirms* that *some students were at the dance* and *denies* that *all students were at the dance*. The quasi-numerical information they present is irrelevant from the point of view of syllogistic inference, and all are translated as "Some students are persons who were at the dance, and some students are not persons who were at the dance."

Because exceptive propositions are not categorical propositions but conjunctions, arguments containing them are not syllogistic arguments as we are using that term. But they may nevertheless be susceptible to syllogistic analysis and appraisal. How an argument containing an exceptive proposition should be tested depends on the exceptive proposition's position in the argument. If it is a premise, then the argument may have to be given two separate tests. For example, consider the argument:

Everyone who saw the game was at the dance.

Not quite all the students were at the dance.

So some students didn't see the game.

Its first premise and its conclusion are categorical propositions, which are easily translated into standard form. Its second premise, however, is an exceptive proposition, not simple but compound. To discover whether its premises imply its conclusion, first test the syllogism composed of the first premise of the given argument, the first half of its second premise, and its conclusion. In standard form, we have

All persons who saw the game are persons who were at the dance.

Some students are persons who were at the dance.

Therefore some students are not persons who saw the game.

The standard-form categorical syllogism is of form **AIO–2** and commits the fallacy of the undistributed middle, violating Rule 2. However, the original argument is not yet proved to be invalid, because the syllogism just tested contains only part of the premises of the original argument. We now have to test the categorical syllogism composed of the first premise and the conclusion of the original argument together with the second half of the second premise. In standard form we then get a very different argument:

All persons who saw the game are persons who were at the dance.

Some students are not persons who were at the dance.

Therefore some students are not persons who saw the game.

This is a standard-form categorical syllogism in *Baroko*, **AOO–2**, and it is easily shown to be valid. Hence the original argument is valid, because the conclusion is the same, and the premises of the original argument *include* the premises of this valid standard-form syllogism. Thus, to test the validity of an argument, one of whose premises is an exceptive proposition, may require testing two different standard-form categorical syllogisms.

If the premises of an argument are both categorical propositions, and its conclusion is exceptive, then we know it to be invalid, for although the two categorical premises may imply one or the other half of the compound conclusion, they cannot imply them both. Finally, if an argument contains exceptive propositions as both premises and conclusion, all possible syllogisms constructable out of the original argument may have to be tested to determine its validity. Enough has been explained to enable the student to cope with such situations.

It is important to acquire facility in translating the many varieties of non-standard-form propositions into standard form, because the tests of validity that we have developed—Venn diagrams and the syllogistic rules—can be applied directly only to standard-form categorical syllogisms.

EXERCISES

Translate the following into standard-form categorical propositions.

EXAMPLE

1. Roses are fragrant.

SOLUTION

Standard-form translation: All roses are fragrant things.

2. Orchids are not fragrant.

3. Many a person has lived to regret a misspent youth.

4. Not everyone worth meeting is worth having as a friend.

***5.** If it's a Junko, it's the best that money can buy.

6. If it isn't a real beer, it isn't a Bud.

7. Nothing is both safe and exciting.

8. Only brave people have ever won the Congressional Medal of Honor.

9. Good counselors are not universally appreciated.

***10.** He sees not his shadow who faces the sun.

11. To hear her sing is an inspiration.

12. He who takes the sword shall perish by the sword.

13. Only members can use the front door.

14. Nobody doesn't like Sara Lee.

***15.** The Young Turks support no candidate of the Old Guard.

16. All styles are good, except the tiresome.

17. They also serve who only stand and wait.

18. Happy indeed is she who knows her own limitations.

19. A thing of beauty is a joy forever.

*20. He prayeth well who loveth well.

21. All that glitters is not gold.

22. None think the great unhappy but the great.

23. He jests at scars that never felt a wound.

24. Whatsoever a man soweth, that shall he also reap.

*25. A soft answer turneth away wrath.

7.4 Uniform Translation

For a syllogistic argument to be testable, it must be expressed in propositions that together contain exactly three terms. Sometimes this aim is difficult to accomplish and requires a more subtle approach than those suggested in the preceding sections. Consider the proposition, "The poor always you have with you." It clearly does not assert that *all* the poor are with you, or even that *some* (particular) poor are *always* with you. There are alternative methods of reducing this proposition to standard form, but one perfectly natural route is by way of the key word "always." This word means "at all times" and suggests the standard-form categorical proposition, "All times are times when you have the poor with you." The word "times," which appears in both the subject and the predicate terms, may be regarded as a **parameter,** an auxiliary symbol that is helpful in expressing the original assertion in standard form.

Care should be taken not to introduce and use parameters in a mechanical, unthinking fashion. One must be guided always by an understanding of the proposition to be translated. Thus the proposition, "Smith always wins at billiards," pretty clearly does not assert that Smith is incessantly, at all times, winning at billiards! It is more reasonable to interpret it as meaning that Smith wins at billiards whenever he plays. And so understood, it translates directly into "All times when Smith plays billiards are times when Smith wins at billiards."

Not all parameters need be temporal. To translate some propositions into standard form, the words "places" and "cases" can be introduced as parameters. Thus "Where there is no vision the people perish" and "Jones loses a sale whenever he is late" translate into "All places where there is no vision are places where the people perish" and "All cases in which Jones is late are cases in which Jones loses a sale."

The introduction of parameters often is requisite for the **uniform translation** of all three constituent propositions of a syllogistic argument into standard form. Because a categorical syllogism contains exactly three terms, to test a syllogistic argument we must translate its constituent propositions into standard-form categorical propositions that contain just three terms. The elimination of synonyms and the applications of conversion, obversion, and contraposition have already been discussed in Section 7.2. However, for many syllogistic arguments, the number of terms cannot be reduced to three either by eliminating synonyms or by applying conversion, obversion, or contraposition. Here uniform translation requires the introduction of a parameter—the *same* parameter—into all three of the constituent propositions. Consider the following argument:

> Soiled paper plates are scattered only where careless people have picnicked.
>
> There are soiled paper plates scattered about here.
>
> Therefore careless people must have been picnicking here.

This argument is perfectly valid, but before it can be proved valid by our diagrams or rules, its premises and conclusion must be translated into standard-form categorical propositions involving only three terms. The second premise and the conclusion may be translated most naturally into "Some soiled paper plates are things that are scattered about here" and "Some careless people are those who have been picnicking here," but these two statements contain four different terms. To reduce the argument to standard form, we begin with the first premise, which requires a parameter for its standard-form expression, and then we use the same parameter in translating the second premise and the conclusion into standard form. The word "where" in the first premise suggests that the parameter "places" can be used. If this parameter is used to obtain uniform standard-form translations of all three propositions, the argument translates into:

> All places where soiled paper plates are scattered are places where careless people have picnicked.
>
> This place is a place where soiled paper plates are scattered.
>
> Therefore this place is a place where careless people have picnicked.

This standard-form categorical syllogism is in *Barbara* with mood and figure **AAA–1** and has already been proved valid.

The notion of standardizing expressions through the use of a parameter is not an altogether easy one to grasp, but some syllogistic arguments cannot be translated into standard-form categorical syllogisms by any other method. Another example may help to make clear the technique involved. Let us take the argument:

> The hounds bay wherever a fox has passed, so the fox must have taken another path, because the hounds are quiet.

First, we must understand what is asserted in the given argument. We may take the statement that the hounds are quiet as asserting that the hounds are not baying here and now. This step is part of the necessary process of eliminating synonyms, because the first assertion makes explicit reference to the baying of hounds. And in the same manner we may understand the conclusion that the fox must have taken another path as asserting that the fox did not pass here. The word "wherever" in the first assertion should suggest that the parameter "places" can be used in its translation. The standard-form translation thus arrived at is

All places where a fox has passed are places where the hounds bay.

This place is not a place where the hounds bay.

Therefore this place is not a place where a fox has passed.

This standard-form categorical syllogism is in *Camestres*, with mood and figure **AEE–2,** and its validity is easy to establish.

EXERCISES

A. Translate the following propositions into standard form, using parameters where necessary.

EXAMPLE

1. He groans whenever he is reminded of his loss.

SOLUTION

Standard-form translation: All times when he is reminded of his loss are times when he groans.

2. She never drives her car to work.

3. He walks where he chooses.

4. He always orders the most expensive item on the menu.

***5.** She does not give her opinion unless she is asked to do so.

6. She tries to sell life insurance wherever she may happen to be.

7. His face gets red when he gets angry.

8. If he is asked to say a few words, he talks for hours.

9. Error of opinion may be tolerated where reason is left free to combat it.

***10.** People are never so likely to settle a question rightly as when they discuss it freely.

B. For each of the following arguments:

- **a.** Translate the argument into standard form.
- **b.** Name the mood and figure of its standard-form translation.
- **c.** Test its validity using a Venn diagram. If it is valid, give its traditional name.
- **d.** If it is invalid, name the fallacy it commits.

EXAMPLE

1. Since all knowledge comes from sensory impressions and since there's no sensory impression of substance itself, it follows logically that there is no knowledge of substance.

—Robert M. Pirsig, *Zen and the Art of Motorcycle Maintenance* (New York: Bantam, 1975)

SOLUTION

a. Standard-form translation:

No things derived from sensory impressions are items of knowledge of substance itself.

All items of knowledge are things derived from sensory impressions.

Therefore, no items of knowledge are items of knowledge of substance itself.

b. Mood and figure: **EAE–1**

c. Valid; *Celarent*

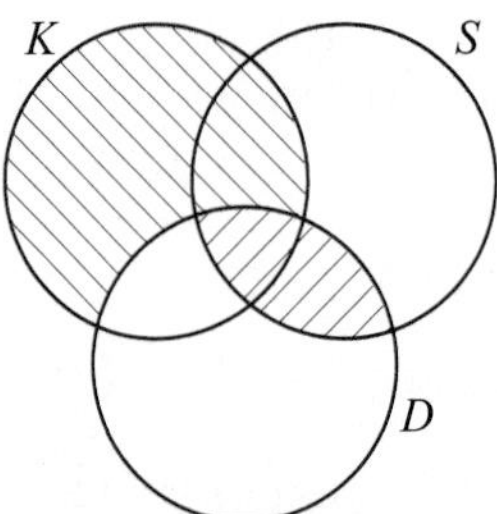

2. . . . no names come in contradictory pairs; but all predicables come in contradictory pairs; therefore no name is a predicable.

—Peter Thomas Geach, *Reference and Generality* (Ithaca, NY: Cornell University Press, 1980)

3. Barcelona Traction was unable to pay interest on its debts; bankrupt companies are unable to pay interest on their debts; therefore, Barcelona Traction must be bankrupt.

—John Brooks, "Annals of Finance," *The New Yorker*, 28 May 1979

4. Extremism in defense of liberty, or virtue, or whatever is *always* a vice—because extremism is but another name for fanaticism which is a vice by definition.

—Irving Kristol, "The Environmentalist Crusade," *The Wall Street Journal*, 16 December 1974

***5.** All syllogisms having two negative premises are invalid. Some valid syllogisms are sound. Therefore some unsound arguments are syllogisms having two negative premises.

6. Not all is gold that glitters, for some base metals glitter, and gold is not a base metal.

7. Where there's smoke there's fire, so there's no fire in the basement, because there's no smoke there.

8. It seems that mercy cannot be attributed to God. For mercy is a kind of sorrow, as Damascene says. But there is no sorrow in God; and therefore there is no mercy in Him.

—Thomas Aquinas, *Summa Theologiae*, I, question 21, art. 3

9. . . . because intense heat is nothing else but a particular kind of painful sensation; and pain cannot exist but in a perceiving being; it follows that no intense heat can really exist in an unperceiving corporeal substance.

—George Berkeley, *Three Dialogues Between Hylas and Philonous, in Opposition to Sceptics and Atheists*, 1713

***10.** Only those who ignore the facts are likely to be mistaken. No one who is truly objective is likely to be mistaken. Hence no one who ignores the facts is truly objective.

11. All bridge players are people. All people think. Therefore all bridge players think.

—Oswald and James Jacoby, "Jacoby on Bridge," Syndicated Column, 5 November 1966

12. Whenever I'm in trouble, I pray. And since I'm always in trouble, there is not a day when I don't pray.

—Isaac Bashevis Singer, interview in *The New York Times*

13. The after-image is not in physical space. The brain-process is. So the after-image is not a brain-process.

—J. J. C. Smart, "Sensations and Brain Processes," *Philosophical Review*, April 1959

14. It must have rained lately, because the fish are not biting, and fish never bite after a rain.

***15.** . . . it is obvious that irrationals are uninteresting to engineers, since they are concerned only with approximations, and all approximations are rational.

—G. H. Hardy, *A Mathematician's Apology* (Cambridge: Cambridge University Press, 1940)

16. Since to fight against neighbors is an evil, and to fight against the Thebans is to fight against neighbors, it is clear that to fight against the Thebans is an evil.

—Aristotle, *Prior Analytics*

17. According to Aristotle, none of the products of Nature are due to chance. His proof is this: That which is due to chance does not reappear constantly nor frequently, but all products of Nature reappear either constantly or at least frequently.

—Moses Maimonides, *The Guide for the Perplexed*, 1180

18. Not all who have jobs are temperate in their drinking. Only debtors drink to excess. So not all the unemployed are in debt.

19. It will be a good game tomorrow, for the conference title is at stake, and no title contest is ever dull.

***20.** Bill didn't go to work this morning, because he wore a sweater, and he never wears a sweater to work.

21. Cynthia must have complimented Henry, because he is cheerful whenever Cynthia compliments him, and he's cheerful now.

22. There must be a strike at the factory, for there is a picket line there, and pickets are present only at strikes.

23. Epidemiology is not merely the study of epidemics of infectious disease; it is the broad examination of the rates and patterns of disease in the community. By almost any standard drug abuse can be regarded as a disease; accordingly it can be profitably investigated by the methods of epidemiology.

—"Science and the Citizen," *Scientific American*, February 1975

24. Since morals, therefore, have an influence on the actions and affections, it follows, that they cannot be deriv'd from reason; and that because reason alone, as we have already prov'd, can never have any such influence.

—David Hume, *A Treatise of Human Nature*, 1739

***25.** All valid syllogisms distribute their middle terms in at least one premise, so this syllogism must be valid, for it distributes its middle term in at least one premise.

26. No valid syllogisms have two negative premises. No syllogisms on this page are invalid. Therefore no syllogisms on this page have two negative premises.

27. Good poll numbers raise money. Good press gets you good poll numbers. Good press gets you money.

—an advisor to Elizabeth Dole, during her campaign for the Republican presidential nomination, quoted in *The New York Times*, 15 April 2000

28. There are plants growing here, and since vegetation requires water, water must be present.

29. No one present is out of work. No members are absent. Therefore all members are employed.

***30.** The competition is stiff, for there is a great deal of money involved, and there is never easy competition where much money is at stake.

31. There are handsome men, but only man is vile, so it is false that nothing is both vile and handsome.

32. What is simple cannot be separated from itself. The soul is simple; therefore, it cannot be separated from itself.

—Duns Scotus, *Oxford Commentary on the Sentences of Peter Lombard*, 1302

33. Although he complains whenever he is sick, his health is excellent, so he won't complain.

34. We. . . define a metaphysical sentence as a sentence which purports to express a genuine proposition, but does, in fact, express neither a tautology nor an empirical hypothesis. And as tautologies and empirical hypotheses form the entire class of significant propositions, we are justified in concluding that all metaphysical assertions are nonsensical.

—Alfred J. Ayer, *Language, Truth, and Logic*, 1936

***35.** This syllogism is valid, for all invalid syllogisms commit an illicit process, and this syllogism commits no illicit process.

7.5 Enthymemes

Syllogistic arguments occur frequently, but their premises and conclusions are not always stated explicitly. Often only part of the argument is expressed, the rest being "understood." Thus one may justify the conclusion that "Jones is a citizen" by mentioning only the one premise, "Jones is a native-born American." As stated, the argument is incomplete, but the missing premise is easily supplied from knowledge of the Constitution of the United States. If the missing premise were stated, the completed argument would appear as

All native-born Americans are citizens.

Jones is a native-born American.

Therefore Jones is a citizen.

Stated in full, the argument is a categorical syllogism of form **AAA–1,** *Barbara*, and is perfectly valid. An argument that is stated incompletely, part being "understood" or only "in the mind," is called an **enthymeme.** An incompletely stated argument is characterized as being *enthymematic*.

In everyday discourse, and even in science, many inferences are expressed enthymematically. The reason is easy to understand. A large body of propositions can be presumed to be common knowledge, and many speakers and writers save themselves trouble by not repeating well-known and perhaps trivially true propositions that their hearers or readers can perfectly well be expected to supply for themselves. Moreover, it is not at all unusual for an argument to be *rhetorically* more powerful and persuasive when stated enthymematically than when enunciated in complete detail. As Aristotle wrote in his *Rhetoric*, "Speeches that . . . rely on enthymemes excite the louder applause."

Because an enthymeme is incomplete, its omitted parts must be taken into account when testing its validity. Without the missing premise, the inference is invalid. However, when the unexpressed premise is easily supplied, in all fairness it ought to be included as part of the argument when one is appraising it. In such a case, one assumes that the maker of the argument did have more in mind than was stated explicitly. In most cases there is no difficulty in supplying the tacit premise that the speaker (or writer) intended but did not express. Thus, for example, as he explains the solution to the mystery in "The Adventure of Silver Blaze," Sherlock Holmes formulates an argument of which one critical premise is left unstated yet is very plainly supposed:

> A dog was kept in the stalls, and yet, though someone had been in and fetched out a horse, the dog had not barked. . . . Obviously the visitor was someone whom the dog knew well.

We all understand very well what is tacit here, that the dog would have barked had the visitor been a stranger. In fairness to the author, Arthur Conan Doyle, that premise must be seen as part of Holmes's argument.

In supplying a suppressed premise, a cardinal principle is that the proposition must be one that speakers can safely presume their hearers to accept as true. Thus it would be foolish to suggest taking the conclusion itself as a suppressed premise, for if the arguer could have expected the auditors to accept that proposition as a premise, without proof, it would have been idle to present it to them as the conclusion of an argument.

Any kind of argument can be expressed enthymematically, but the kinds of enthymemes that have been most extensively studied are incompletely expressed syllogistic arguments. We confine our attention to these in the remainder of this section. Enthymemes traditionally have been divided into different *orders*, according to which part of the syllogism is left unexpressed. A **first-order enthymeme** is one in which the syllogism's major premise is not stated. The preceding example is of the first order. A **second-order enthymeme** is one in which only the major premise and the conclusion are stated, the minor premise being suppressed. An example of this type is "All students are opposed to the new regulations, so all sophomores are opposed to them." Here the minor premise is easily supplied, being the obviously true proposition, "All sophomores are students." A **third-order enthymeme** is one in which both premises are stated, but the conclusion is left unexpressed. An example of this type is the following:

> Our ideas reach no farther than our experience: we have no experience of divine attributes and operations: I need not conclude my syllogism: you can draw the inference yourself.[3]

Two steps are involved in testing an enthymeme for validity: The first is to supply the missing part of the argument, the second is to test the resulting syllogism. Formulating the unstated proposition fairly may require sensitivity to the context and an understanding of the intentions of the speaker. Consider the following argument: "No true Christian is vain, but some churchgoers are vain." It is the conclusion that remains unstated, so this is plainly a third-order syllogism. What *is* the intended conclusion? If the speaker intends to imply only that "Some churchgoers are not true Christians," the argument is valid (**EIO–2,** *Festino*). However, if the speaker's intention is to establish that "Some true Christians are not churchgoers," the enthymeme is invalid (**IEO–2**), because in that case the fallacy of illicit process of the major term is committed.

Usually, the context indicates unambiguously what the unstated proposition is. For example, in a U.S. Supreme Court opinion in which federal legislation regulating intrastate violence motivated by gender (the Violence Against Women Act) was held unconstitutional, the critical argument of the majority was expressed thus:

> Gender-motivated crimes of violence are not, in any sense of the phrase, economic activity. . . . Thus far in our nation's history our cases have upheld Commerce Clause regulation of intrastate activity only where that activity is economic in nature.[4]

The proposition that is understood but not stated in this argument is assuredly its conclusion: that gender-motivated crimes of violence may not be regulated by Congress under the long-existing precedent of Supreme Court cases.

To test this third-order enthymeme, we reformulate the argument so that its premises and (tacit) conclusion are in standard form. The major premise (the premise containing the predicate of the conclusion) is stated first; then mood and figure are identified:

> *Major premise:* All activities that may be regulated by Congress under the precedent of Supreme Court cases are economic activities.
>
> *Minor premise:* No intrastate gender-motivated crimes of violence are economic activities.
>
> *Conclusion* (unstated but clearly indicated by the context): No intrastate gender-motivated crimes of violence are activities that may be regulated by Congress under the precedent of Supreme Court cases.

The mood of this syllogism is **AEE;** it is in the second figure because the middle term is the predicate of both premises. Its form is therefore *Camestres*, a valid syllogistic argument.

In some cases a third-order enthymeme may seem to be invalid without regard to context—for example, when both premises are negative, or when both premises are particular propositions, or when their common term is undistributed. In such cases, no syllogistic conclusion could follow validly, and hence such enthymemes are invalid in any context.

If it is one of the premises of the argument that is missing, it may be possible to make the argument valid only by adding a premise that is highly implausible—and pointing this out is certainly a legitimate criticism of an enthymematic argument. An even more crushing criticism, of course, would be to show that no additional premise, however implausible, can transform the enthymeme into a valid categorical syllogism.

The difference between enthymemes and normal syllogisms is essentially rhetorical, not logical. No new logical principles need be introduced in dealing with enthymemes, and they must be tested, ultimately, by the same methods that apply to standard-form categorical syllogisms.

EXERCISES

For each of the following enthymematic arguments:

a. Formulate the plausible premise or conclusion, if any, that is missing but understood.

b. Write the argument in standard form, including the missing premise or conclusion needed to make the completed argument valid—if possible—using parameters if necessary.

c. Name the order of the enthymeme.

d. If the argument is not valid even with the understood premise included, name the fallacy that it commits.

EXAMPLE

1. Transgenic animals are manmade and as such are patentable.

—Alan E. Smith, cited in *Genetic Engineering* (San Diego, CA: Greenhaven Press, 1990)

SOLUTION

a. The premise understood but not stated here is that whatever is manmade is patentable.

b. Standard-form translation:

All manmade things are patentable things.

<u>All transgenic animals are manmade things.</u>

Therefore, all transgenic animals are patentable things.

c. The enthymeme is first-order, because the premise taken as understood is the major premise of the completed argument.

d. This is a valid syllogism of the form **AAA–1,** *Barbara.*

2. Abraham Beame. . . campaigned for mayor—as has been mentioned in recent weeks more often and with more irony than he might have wished—on the slogan "If you don't know the buck, you don't know the job—and Abe knows the buck."

—*The New Yorker*, 26 August 1974

3. Although these textbooks purport to be a universal guide to learning of great worth and importance—there is a single clue that points to another direction. In the six years I taught in city and country schools, no one ever stole a textbook.

—W. Ron Jones, *Changing Education*, Winter 1974

4. As a matter of fact, man, like woman, is flesh, therefore passive, the plaything of his hormones and of the species, the restless prey of his desires.

—Simone De Beauvior, *The Second Sex*, 1949

***5.** You never lose respect for a man who is a vicious competitor, and you never hate a man you respect.

—Pancho Gonzalez, former U.S. tennis champion

6. . . . I am an Idealist, since I believe that all that exists is spiritual.

—John McTaggart Ellis McTaggart, *Philosophical Studies*, 1922

7. And why not become a perfect anthropomorphite? Why not assert the deity or deities to be corporeal, and to have eyes, a nose, mouth, ears, etc.? Epicurus maintained that no man had ever seen reason but in a human figure; therefore, the gods must have a human figure. And this argument, which is deservedly so much ridiculed by Cicero, becomes, according to you, solid and philosophical.

—David Hume, *Dialogues Concerning Natural Religion*, part V, 1779

8. Small countries tend to remember history especially well, since it often turns out badly for them.

—Marc Falcoff, "Semper Fidel," *The New Republic*, 3 July 1989

9. It must have rained lately, because the fish just aren't biting.

***10.** It is not likely that the lies, misstatements, and omissions in President Carter's book are the result of ignorance. They must be the result, therefore, of malevolence.

—Facts and Logic About the Middle East, www.factsandlogic.org (2007)

11. No enthymemes are complete, so this argument is incomplete.

12. The chairman of the Student Conduct Legislative Council [at Stanford] argued that free speech rights extend only to victimized minorities, since the white majority does not need such protections.

—Nat Hentoff, "Stanford and the Speech Police," *The Washington Post*, 30 July 1990

13. Only demonstrative proof should be able to make you abandon the theory of the Creation; but such a proof does not exist in Nature.

—Moses Maimonides, *The Guide for the Perplexed*, 1180

14. It is probably true that the least destructive nuclear weapons are the most dangerous, because they make it easier for a nuclear war to begin.

—Freeman Dyson, "Reflections: Weapons and Hope," *The New Yorker*, 6 February 1984

***15.** Man tends to increase at a greater rate than his means of subsistence; consequently he is occasionally subject to a severe struggle for existence.

—Charles Darwin, *The Descent of Man*, 1871

16. No internal combustion engines are free from pollution; but no internal combustion engine is completely efficient. You may draw your own conclusion.

17. A nation without a conscience is a nation without a soul. A nation without a soul is a nation that cannot live.

—Winston Churchill

18. Liberty means responsibility. That is why most men dread it.

—George Bernard Shaw, *Maxims for Revolutionists*, 1903

19. Who controls the past controls the future. Who controls the present controls the past.

—George Orwell, 1984

***20.** Productivity is desirable because it betters the condition of the vast majority of the people.

—Stephen Miller, "Adam Smith and the Commercial Republic," *The Public Interest*, Fall 1980

21. Advertisements perform a vital function in almost any society, for they help to bring buyers and sellers together.

—Burton M. Leiser, *Liberty, Justice, and Morals*, 1986

22. Logic is a matter of profound human importance precisely because it is empirically founded and experimentally applied.

—John Dewey, *Reconstruction in Philosophy*, 1920

23. *Iphigeneia at Aulis* is a tragedy because it demonstrates inexorably how human character, with its itch to be admired, combines with the malice of heaven to produce wars which no one in his right mind would want and which turn out to be utterly disastrous for everybody.

—George E. Dimock, Jr., Introduction to *Iphigeneia at Aulis* by Euripides, 1992

24. . . . the law does not expressly permit suicide, and what it does not expressly permit it forbids.

—Aristotle, *Nichomachean Ethics*

***25.** The man who says that all things come to pass by necessity cannot criticize one who denies that all things come to pass by necessity: for he admits that this too happens of necessity.

—Epicurus, Fragment XL, Vatican Collection

7.6 Sorites

Sometimes a single categorical syllogism will not suffice to account for our ability to draw a desired conclusion from a group of premises. Thus, from the premises

All diplomats are tactful.

Some government officials are diplomats.

All government officials are people in public life.

one cannot draw the conclusion

Some people in public life are tactful.

using a *single* syllogistic inference. Yet the indicated conclusion is entailed by the stated premises. To derive it requires two syllogisms rather than one. A stepwise process of argumentation must be resorted to, in which each step is a separate categorical syllogism. When stated explicitly, the required argument is

All diplomats are tactful individuals.

Some government officials are diplomats.

Therefore some government officials are tactful individuals.

All government officials are people in public life.

Therefore some people in public life are tactful individuals.

This argument is not a syllogism but a *chain* of categorical syllogisms, connected by the conclusion of the first, which is a premise of the second. This chain has only two links, but more extended arguments may consist of a greater number. Because a chain is no stronger than its weakest link, an argument of this type is valid if, and only if, all of its constituent syllogisms are valid.

Where such an argument is expressed enthymematically, with only the premises and the final conclusion stated, it is called a **sorites*** (pronounced sō-rī´-tēz). Sorites may have three, four, or *any* number of premises. Some are very lengthy indeed. The following example is drawn from the *Monadology* of the philosopher Gottfried Leibniz:

> The human soul is a thing whose activity is thinking. A thing whose activity is thinking is one whose activity is immediately apprehended, and without any representation of parts therein. A thing whose activity is immediately apprehended without any representation of parts therein is a thing whose activity does not contain parts. A thing whose activity does not contain parts is one whose activity is not motion. A thing whose activity is not motion is not a body. What is not a body is not in space. What is not in space is insusceptible of motion. What is insusceptible of motion is indissoluble (for dissolution is a movement of parts). What is indissoluble is incorruptible. What is incorruptible is immortal. Therefore the human soul is immortal.

*From the Greek, soros, meaning heap or pile; a sorites is a pile of syllogisms.

This sorites contains ten premises! Any sorites may be tested by making its intermediate conclusions or steps explicit, then testing separately the various categorical syllogisms thus obtained. If we ignore the possibility that an equivocation is present, then the validity of Leibniz's sorites is easily verified.

It is convenient to note here, in connection with the exercises at the end of this section, that a sorites is in standard form when all of its propositions are in standard form, when each term occurs exactly twice, and when every proposition (except the last) has a term in common with the proposition that immediately follows it. Thus one standard-form translation of Lewis Carroll's sorites

(1) Every one who is sane can do Logic.

(2) No lunatics are fit to serve on a jury.

<u>(3) None of your sons can do Logic.</u>

Therefore none of your sons is fit to serve on a jury.

is

(2) All persons fit to serve on a jury are sane persons.

(1′) All sane persons are persons who can do Logic.

<u>(3′) No sons of yours are persons who can do Logic.</u>

Therefore no sons of yours are persons fit to serve on a jury.

One can test it by stating the suppressed subconclusion explicitly and then testing the resulting categorical syllogisms.

EXERCISES

A. Translate the following sorites into standard form, and test their validity.[5]

EXAMPLE

1. (1) Babies are illogical.

(2) Nobody is despised who can manage a crocodile.

<u>(3) Illogical persons are despised.</u>

Therefore babies cannot manage crocodiles.

SOLUTION

Standard-form translation:

(1′) All babies are illogical persons.

(2′) All illogical persons are despised persons.

<u>(3′) No persons who can manage crocodiles are despised persons.</u>

Therefore, no babies are persons who can manage crocodiles.

This sorites consists of two syllogisms, as follows:

All *I* is *D*.	No *M* is *D*.
All *B* is *I*.	All *B* is *D*.
Therefore all *B* is *D*.	Therefore no *B* is *M*.

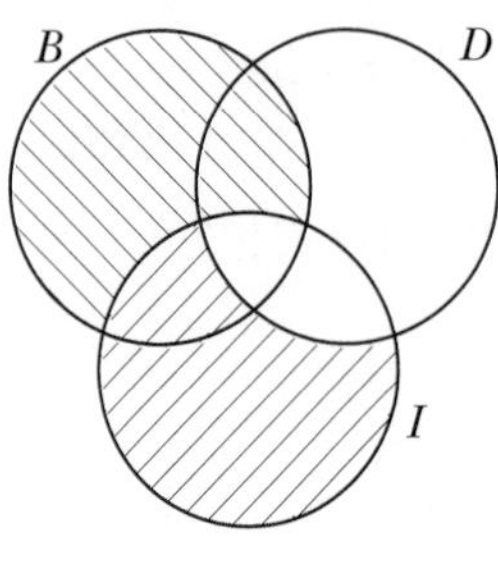

Valid, Barbara

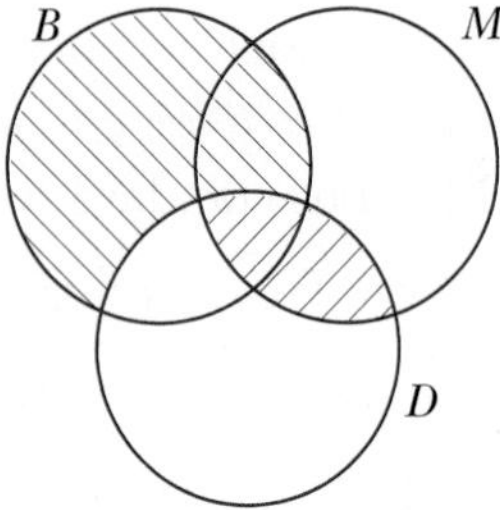

Valid, Cesare

2. (1) No experienced person is incompetent.

(2) Jenkins is always blundering.

(3) No competent person is always blundering.

Therefore Jenkins is inexperienced.

3. (1) The only books in this library that I do not recommend for reading are unhealthy in tone.

(2) The bound books are all well written.

(3) All the romances are healthy in tone.

(4) I do not recommend that you read any of the unbound books.

Therefore all the romances in this library are well written.

4. (1) Only profound scholars can be dons at Oxford.

(2) No insensitive souls are great lovers of music.

(3) No one whose soul is not sensitive can be a Don Juan.

(4) There are no profound scholars who are not great lovers of music.

Therefore all Oxford dons are Don Juans.

***5.** (1) No interesting poems are unpopular among people of real taste.

(2) No modern poetry is free from affectation.

(3) All your poems are on the subject of soap bubbles.

(4) No affected poetry is popular among people of real taste.

(5) Only a modern poem would be on the subject of soap bubbles.

Therefore all your poems are uninteresting.

6. (1) None but writers are poets.

(2) Only military officers are astronauts.

(3) Whoever contributes to the new magazine is a poet.

<u>(4) Nobody is both a military officer and a writer.</u>

Therefore not one astronaut is a contributor to the new magazine.

B. Each of the following sets of propositions can serve as premises for a valid sorites. For each, find the conclusion and establish that the argument is valid.

***1.** (1) No one reads the *Times* unless he is well educated.

(2) No hedgehogs can read.

(3) Those who cannot read are not well educated.

2. (1) All puddings are nice.

(2) This dish is a pudding.

(3) No nice things are wholesome.

3. (1) The only articles of food that my doctor allows me are such as are not very rich.

(2) Nothing that agrees with me is unsuitable for supper.

(3) Wedding cake is always very rich.

(4) My doctor allows me all articles of food that are suitable for supper.

4. (1) All my daughters are slim.

(2) No child of mine is healthy who takes no exercise.

(3) All gluttons who are children of mine are fat.

(4) No son of mine takes any exercise.

***5.** (1) When I work a logic example without grumbling, you may be sure it is one that I can understand.

(2) These sorites are not arranged in regular order, like the examples I am used to.

(3) No easy example ever makes my head ache.

(4) I can't understand examples that are not arranged in regular order, like those I am used to.

(5) I never grumble at an example, unless it gives me a headache.

7.7 Disjunctive and Hypothetical Syllogisms

Propositions are *categorical* when they affirm or deny the inclusion or exclusion of categories or classes. Syllogisms, arguments consisting of two premises and a conclusion, are called categorical when the propositions they contain are categorical. Up to this point our analysis has been of categorical syllogisms only. However, a syllogism may contain propositions that are not categorical. Such cases are not called categorical syllogisms but are instead named on the basis of the kind of propositions they contain. Here we look briefly at some other kinds of propositions and the syllogisms to which they give rise.

The categorical propositions with which we are familiar are *simple* in the sense that they have a single component, which affirms or denies some class relation. In contrast, some propositions are *compound*, in that they contain more than one component, each of which is itself some other proposition.

Consider first the *disjunctive* (or alternative) proposition. An example is "She was driven either by stupidity or by arrogance." Its two components are "she was driven by stupidity" and "she was driven by arrogance." The disjunctive proposition contains those two component propositions, which are called its *disjuncts*. The disjunctive proposition does not categorically affirm the truth of either one of its disjuncts, but says that at least one of them is true, allowing for the possibility that both may be true.

If we have a disjunction as one premise, and as another premise the denial or contradictory of one its two disjuncts, then we can validly infer that the other disjunct in that disjunction is true. Any argument of this form is a valid **disjunctive syllogism.** A letter writer, critical of a woman nominated for high office by President George W. Bush, wrote:

> In trying to cover up her own illegal peccadillo or stonewall her way out of it, she was driven either by stupidity or arrogance. She's obviously not stupid; her plight must result, then, from her arrogance.[6]

As we use the term in this section, not every disjunctive syllogism is valid. The argument

> She was either arrogant or stupid.
>
> She was arrogant.
>
> Therefore she was not stupid.

is an example of what may be called an invalid disjunctive syllogism. We readily see that, even if the premise were true, she may have been arrogant *and* stupid. The truth of one disjunct of a disjunction does not imply the falsehood of the other disjunct, because both disjuncts of a disjunction can be true. We have a valid disjunctive syllogism, therefore, only where the categorical premise contradicts one disjunct of the disjunctive premise and the conclusion affirms the other disjunct of the disjunctive premise.

An objection might be raised at this point, based on such an argument as the following:

Either Smith is in New York or Smith is in Paris.

Smith is in New York.

Therefore Smith is not in Paris.

Here the categorical premise affirms one disjunct of the stated disjunction, and the conclusion contradicts the other disjunct, yet the conclusion seems to follow validly. Closer analysis shows, however, that the stated disjunction plays no role in the argument. The conclusion follows enthymematically from the second, categorical premise, with the unexpressed additional premise being the obviously true proposition that "Smith cannot be both in New York and in Paris," which can be stated in disjunctive form as

Either Smith is not in New York or Smith is not in Paris.

When this tacit premise is supplied and the superfluous original disjunction is discarded, the resulting argument is easily seen to be a valid disjunctive syllogism. The apparent exception is not really an exception, and the objection is groundless.

The second kind of compound proposition we consider is the *conditional* (or *hypothetical*) proposition, an example of which is "If the first native is a politician, then the first native lies." A conditional proposition contains two component propositions: The one following the "if" is the *antecedent*, and the one following the "then" is the *consequent*. A syllogism that contains conditional propositions exclusively is called a **pure hypothetical syllogism;** for example,

If the first native is a politician, then he lies.

If he lies, then he denies being a politician.

Therefore if the first native is a politician, then he denies being a politician.

In this argument it can be observed that the first premise and the conclusion have the same antecedent, that the second premise and the conclusion have the same consequent, and that the consequent of the first premise is the same as the antecedent of the second premise. It should be clear that any pure hypothetical syllogism whose premises and conclusion have their component parts so related is a valid argument.

A syllogism that has one conditional premise and one categorical premise is called a **mixed hypothetical syllogism.** Two valid forms of the mixed hypothetical syllogism have been given special names. The first is illustrated by

> If the second native told the truth, then only one native is a politician.
>
> The second native told the truth.
>
> Therefore only one native is a politician.

Here the categorical premise affirms the antecedent of the conditional premise, and the conclusion affirms its consequent. Any argument of this form is valid and is said to be in the *affirmative mood* or ***modus ponens*** (from the Latin *ponere,* meaning "to affirm"). One must not confuse the valid form *modus ponens* with the clearly invalid form displayed by the following argument:

> If Bacon wrote *Hamlet*, then Bacon was a great writer.
>
> Bacon was a great writer.
>
> Therefore Bacon wrote *Hamlet*.

This argument differs from *modus ponens* in that its categorical premise affirms the consequent, rather than the antecedent, of the conditional premise. Any argument of this form is said to commit the **fallacy of affirming the consequent.**

The other valid form of mixed hypothetical syllogism is illustrated by:

> If the one-eyed prisoner saw two red hats, then he could tell the color of the hat on his own head.
>
> The one-eyed prisoner could not tell the color of the hat on his own head.
>
> Therefore the one-eyed prisoner did not see two red hats.

Here the categorical premise denies the consequent of the conditional premise, and the conclusion denies its antecedent. Any argument of this form is valid and is said to be in the form ***modus tollens*** (from the Latin *tollere,* meaning "to deny"). One must not confuse the valid form *modus tollens* with the clearly invalid form displayed by the following argument:

> If Carl embezzled the college funds, then Carl is guilty of a felony.
>
> Carl did not embezzle the college funds.
>
> Therefore Carl is not guilty of a felony.

This argument differs from *modus tollens* in that its categorical premise denies the antecedent, rather than the consequent, of the conditional premise. Any argument of this form is said to commit the **fallacy of denying the antecedent.**

OVERVIEW

Principal Kinds of Syllogisms

1. **Categorical syllogisms,** which contain only categorical propositions affirming or denying the inclusion or exclusion of categories. Example:

   All *M* is *P*.

   All *S* is *M*.

   Therefore all *S* is *P*.

2. **Disjunctive syllogisms,** which contain a compound, disjunctive (or alternative) premise asserting the truth of at least one of two alternatives, and a premise that asserts the falsity of one of those alternatives. Example:

   Either *P* is true or *Q* is true.

   P is not true.

   Therefore *Q* is true.

3. **Hypothetical syllogisms,** which contain one or more compound, hypothetical (or conditional) propositions, affirming that if one of its components (the antecedent) is true then the other of its components (the consequent) is true. Two subtypes are distinguished:

   A. **Pure hypothetical syllogisms** contain conditional propositions only. Example:

      If *P* is true, then *Q* is true.

      If *Q* is true, then *R* is true.

      Therefore if *P* is true, then *R* is true.

   B. **Mixed hypothetical syllogisms** contain both a conditional premise and a categorical premise.

      If the categorical premise affirms the truth of the antecedent of the conditional premise, and the consequent of that conditional premise is the conclusion of the argument, the form is valid and is called *modus ponens*. Example:

      If *P* is true, then *Q* is true.

      P is true.

      Therefore *Q* is true.

      If the categorical premise affirms the falsity of the consequent of the conditional premise, and the falsity of the antecedent of that

(Continued)

conditional premise is the conclusion of the argument, the form is valid and is called *modus tollens*. Example:

If *P* is true, then Q is true.

Q is false.

Therefore *P* is false.

EXERCISES

Identify the form and discuss the validity or invalidity of each of the following arguments.

EXAMPLE

1. If a man could not have done otherwise than he in fact did, then he is not responsible for his action. But if determinism is true, it is true of every action that the agent could not have done otherwise. Therefore, if determinism is true, no one is ever responsible for what he does.

—Winston Nesbit and Stewart Candlish, "Determinism and the Ability to Do Otherwise," *Mind*, July 1978

SOLUTION

This is a pure hypothetical syllogism. Valid.

2. Men, it is assumed, act in economic matters only in response to pecuniary compensation or to force. Force in the modern society is largely, although by no means completely, obsolete. So only pecuniary compensation remains of importance.

—John Kenneth Galbraith, *The New Industrial State*, (Boston: Houghton Mifflin, 1967)

3. If each man had a definite set of rules of conduct by which he regulated his life he would be no better than a machine. But there are no such rules, so men cannot be machines.

—A. M. Turing, "Computing Machinery and Intelligence," *Mind*, vol. 59, 1950

4. If the second native told the truth, then the first native denied being a politician. If the third native told the truth, then the first native denied

being a politician. Therefore if the second native told the truth, then the third native told the truth.

***5.** If the one-eyed prisoner does not know the color of the hat on his own head, then the blind prisoner cannot have on a red hat. The one-eyed prisoner does not know the color of the hat on his own head. Therefore the blind prisoner cannot have on a red hat.

6. If all three prisoners have on white hats, then the one-eyed prisoner does not know the color of the hat on his own head. The one-eyed prisoner does not know the color of the hat on his own head. Therefore all three prisoners have on white hats.

7. The stranger is either a knave or a fool. The stranger is a knave. Therefore the stranger is no fool.

8. If the first native is a politician, then the third native tells the truth. If the third native tells the truth, then the third native is not a politician. Therefore if the first native is a politician, then the third native is not a politician.

9. Mankind, he said, judging by their neglect of him, have never, as I think, at all understood the power of Love. For if they had understood him they would surely have built noble temples and altars, and offered solemn sacrifices in his honor; but this is not done.

—Plato, *Symposium*

***10.** I have already said that he must have gone to King's Pyland or to Capleton. He is not at King's Pyland, therefore he is at Capleton.

—Arthur Conan Doyle, *The Adventure of Silver Blaze*

11. If then, it is agreed that things are either the result of coincidence or for an end, and that these cannot be the result of coincidence or spontaneity, it follows that they must be for an end.

—Aristotle, *Physics*

12. There is no case known (neither is it, indeed, possible) in which a thing is found to be the efficient cause of itself; for in such a case it would be prior to itself, which is impossible.

—Thomas Aquinas, *Summa Theologiae*, I, question 2, art. 3

13. Either wealth is an evil or wealth is a good; but wealth is not an evil; therefore wealth is a good.

—Sextus Empiricus, *Against the Logicians*, second century A.D.

14. I *do* know that this pencil exists; but I could not know this, if Hume's principles were true; *therefore*, Hume's principles, one or both of them, are false.

—G. E. Moore, *Some Main Problems of Philosophy* (New York: Allen & Unwin, 1953)

***15.** It is clear that we mean something, and something different in each case, by such words [as *substance, cause, change*, etc.]. If we did not we could not use them consistently, and it is obvious that on the whole we do consistently apply and withhold such names.

—C. D. Broad, *Scientific Thought*, 1923

16. If number were an idea, then arithmetic would be psychology. But arithmetic is no more psychology than, say, astronomy is. Astronomy is concerned, not with ideas of the planets, but with the planets themselves, and by the same token the objects of arithmetic are not ideas either.

—Gottlob Frege, *The Foundations of Arithmetic*, 1893

17. . . . If a mental state is to be identical with a physical state, the two must share all properties in common. But there is one property, spatial localizability, that is not so shared; that is, physical states and events are located in space, whereas mental events and states are not. Hence, mental events and states are different from physical ones.

—Jaegwon Kim, "On the Psycho-Physical Identity Theory," *American Philosophical Quarterly*, 1966

18. When we regard a man as morally responsible for an act, we regard him as a legitimate object of moral praise or blame in respect of it. But it seems plain that a man cannot be a legitimate object of moral praise or blame for an act unless in willing the act he is in some important sense a "free" agent. Evidently free will in some sense, therefore, is a precondition of moral responsibility.

—C. Arthur Campbell, *In Defence of Free Will*, 1938

19. In spite of the popularity of the finite-world picture, however, it is open to a devastating objection. In being finite the world must have a limiting boundary, such as Aristotle's outermost sphere. That is impossible, because a boundary can only separate one part of space from another. This objection was put forward by the Greeks, reappeared in the scientific skepticism of the early Renaissance and probably occurs to any schoolchild who thinks about it today. If one accepts the objection, one must conclude that the universe is infinite.

—J. J. Callahan, "The Curvature of Space in a Finite Universe," *Scientific American*, August 1976

*20. Total pacifism might be a good principle if everyone were to follow it. But not everyone does, so it isn't.

—Gilbert Harman, *The Nature of Morality*, 1977

7.8 The Dilemma

The **dilemma** is a common form of argument in ordinary language. It is, in essence, an argumentative device in which syllogisms on the same topic are combined, sometimes with devastating effect. Each of the constituent syllogisms may be quite ordinary, and therefore the dilemma is not of special importance from a strictly logical point of view. But the premises of the syllogisms so combined are formulated disjunctively, and devised in a way designed to trap the opponent by forcing him to accept one or the other of the disjuncts. Thus the opponent is forced to accept the truth of the conclusion of one or the other of the syllogisms combined. When this is done successfully, the dilemma can prove to be a powerful instrument of persuasion.

We say somewhat loosely that a person is "in" a dilemma (or "impaled on the horns of a dilemma") when that person must choose between two alternatives, both of which are bad or unpleasant. The dilemma is a form of argument intended to put one's opponent in just that kind of position. In debate, one uses a dilemma to offer alternative positions to one's adversary, from which a choice must be made, and then to prove that no matter which choice is made, the adversary is committed to an unacceptable conclusion.

The distinguished physicist Richard Feynman, recounting his experiences in the 1986 investigation of the catastrophic explosion of the *Challenger* space shuttle, was caustic in his criticism of mismanagement by administrators in the National Aeronautics and Space Administration (NASA). He said:

> Every time we talked to higher level managers, they kept saying they didn't know anything about the problems below them. . . . Either the group at the top didn't know, in which case they should have known, or they did know, in which case they were lying to us.[7]

An attack of this kind is designed to push the adversaries (in this case the NASA administrators) into a corner and there annihilate them. The only explicitly stated premise of the argument is a disjunction, but one of the disjuncts must obviously be true; Either they knew or they didn't know about the problems below them. And whichever disjunct is chosen, the result for the adversary is very bad. The conclusion of a dilemma can itself be a disjunction (for example, "Either the NASA administrators did not know what they should have known, or they lied") in which case we call the dilemma a

complex dilemma. But the conclusion may also be a categorical proposition, in which case we call it **simple dilemma.**

A dilemma need not always have an unpleasant conclusion. An example of one with a happy conclusion is provided by the following simple dilemma:

> If the blest in heaven have no desires, they will be perfectly content; so they will be also if their desires are fully gratified; but either they will have no desires, or have them fully gratified; therefore they will be perfectly content.

The premises of a dilemma need not be stated in any special order; the disjunctive premise that offers the alternatives may either precede or follow the other. And the consequences of those alternatives may be stated in a conjunctive proposition or in two separate propositions. An argument in dilemma form is often expressed enthymematically; that is, its conclusion generally is thought to be so obvious that it scarcely needs to be spelled out. This is well illustrated in a passage from a letter of President Abraham Lincoln, defending the Emancipation Proclamation that freed the slaves of the Confederacy:

> But the proclamation, as law, either is valid, or is not valid. If it is not valid, it needs no retraction, If it is valid, it cannot be retracted, any more than the dead can be brought to life.[8]

Three ways of evading or refuting the conclusion of a dilemma have been given special names, all relating to the fact that a dilemma has two (or more) "horns." These three ways of defeating a dilemma are known as "going (or escaping) between the horns," "taking (or grasping) it by the horns," and "rebutting it by means of a counterdilemma." Note that these are not ways to prove the dilemma invalid; rather, they are ways in which one seeks to avoid its conclusion without challenging the formal validity of the argument.

One escapes between the horns of a dilemma by rejecting its disjunctive premise. This method is often the easiest way to evade the conclusion of a dilemma, for unless one half of the disjunction is the explicit contradictory of the other, the disjunction may very well be false. For example, one justification sometimes offered for giving grades to students is that recognizing good work will stimulate the students to study harder. Students may criticize this theory using the following dilemma:

> If students are fond of learning, they need no stimulus, and if they dislike learning, no stimulus will be of any avail. But any student is either fond of learning or dislikes it. Therefore a stimulus is either needless or of no avail.

This argument is formally valid, but we can evade its conclusion by *going between the horns*. The disjunctive premise is false, for students have all kinds of attitudes toward learning: Some may be fond of it, many dislike it, and many are indifferent. For that third group a stimulus may be both needed and of some avail. Going between the horns does not prove the conclusion to be false but shows merely that the argument does not provide adequate grounds for accepting that conclusion.

When the disjunctive premise is unassailable, as when the alternatives exhaust the possibilities, it is impossible to escape between the horns. Another method of evading the conclusion must be sought. One such method is to *grasp the dilemma by the horns*, which involves rejecting the premise that is a conjunction. To deny a conjunction, we need only deny one of its parts. When we grasp the dilemma by the horns, we attempt to show that at least one of the conditionals is false. The dilemma just above, attacking the use of grades in school, relies on the conditional "If students are fond of learning, they need no stimulus." The proponent of grading may grasp this dilemma by the horns and argue that even students who are fond of learning may sometimes need stimulus, and that the additional stimulus provided by grades promotes careful study by even the most diligent students. There may be good response to this, of course—but the original dilemma has been grasped firmly by the horns.

Rebutting a dilemma by means of a counterdilemma is the most ingenious method of all, but it is seldom cogent, for reasons that will appear presently. To rebut a given dilemma in this way, one constructs another dilemma whose conclusion is opposed to the conclusion of the original. *Any* counterdilemma may be used in rebuttal, but ideally it should be built up out of the same ingredients (categorical propositions) that the original dilemma contained.

A classical example of this elegant kind of rebuttal concerns the legendary argument of an Athenian mother attempting to persuade her son not to enter politics:

> If you say what is just, men will hate you; and if you say what is unjust, the gods will hate you; but you must either say the one or the other; therefore you will be hated.

Her son rebutted that dilemma with the following one:

> If I say what is just, the gods will love me; and if I say what is unjust, men will love me. I must say either the one or the other. Therefore I shall be loved!

In public discussion, where the dilemma is one of the strongest weapons of controversy, the use of a rebuttal of this kind, which derives an opposite conclusion from almost the same premises, is a mark of great rhetorical skill. But if we examine the dilemma and rebutting counterdilemma more closely, we see that their conclusions are not as opposed as they might at first have seemed.

The conclusion of the first dilemma is that the son will be hated (by men or by the gods), whereas that of the rebutting dilemma is that the son will be loved (by the gods or by men). But these two conclusions are perfectly compatible.

The rebutting counterdilemma serves merely to establish a conclusion different from that of the original. Both conclusions may very well be true together, so no refutation has been accomplished. But in the heat of controversy analysis is unwelcome, and if such a rebuttal occurred in a public debate, the average audience might agree that the rebuttal was an effective reply to the original argument.

That this sort of rebuttal does not refute the argument but only directs attention to a different aspect of the same situation is perhaps more clearly shown in the case of the following dilemma, advanced by an "optimist":

> If I work, I earn money, and if I am idle, I enjoy myself. Either I work or I am idle. Therefore either I earn money or I enjoy myself.

A "pessimist" might offer the following counterdilemma:

> If I work, I don't enjoy myself, and if I am idle, I don't earn money. Either I work or I am idle. Therefore either I don't earn money or I don't enjoy myself.

These conclusions represent merely different ways of viewing the same facts; they do not constitute a disagreement over what the facts are.

No discussion of dilemmas would be complete unless it mentioned the celebrated lawsuit between Protagoras and Euathlus. Protagoras, a teacher who lived in Greece during the fifth century B.C., specialized in teaching the art of pleading before juries. Euathlus wanted to become a lawyer, but not being able to pay the required tuition, he made an arrangement according to which Protagoras would teach him but not receive payment until Euathlus won his first case. When Euathlus finished his course of study, he delayed going into practice. Tired of waiting for his money, Protagoras brought suit against his former pupil for the tuition money that was owed. Unmindful of the adage that the lawyer who tries his own case has a fool for a client, Euathlus decided to plead his own case in court. When the trial began, Protagoras presented his side of the case in a crushing dilemma:

> If Euathlus loses this case, then he must pay me (by the judgment of the court); if he wins this case, then he must pay me (by the terms of the contract). He must either lose or win this case. Therefore Euathlus must pay me.

The situation looked bad for Euathlus, but he had learned well the art of rhetoric. He offered the court the following counterdilemma in rebuttal:

> If I win this case, I shall not have to pay Protagoras (by the judgment of the court); if I lose this case, I shall not have to pay Protagoras (by the terms of the contract, for then I shall not yet have won my first case). I must either win or lose this case. Therefore I do not have to pay Protagoras![9]

Had you been the judge, how would you have decided?

Note that the conclusion of Euathlus's rebutting dilemma is *not* compatible with the conclusion of Protagoras's original dilemma. One conclusion is the explicit denial of the other. However, it is rare that a counterdilemma stands in this relation to the dilemma against which it is directed. When it does, the premises involved are themselves inconsistent, and it is this implicit contradiction that the two dilemmas make explicit.

EXERCISES

Discuss the various arguments that might be offered to refute each of the following.

EXAMPLE

1. If we interfere with the publication of false and harmful doctrines, we shall be guilty of suppressing the liberties of others, whereas if we do not interfere with the publication of such doctrines, we run the risk of losing our own liberties. We must either interfere or not interfere with the publication of false and harmful doctrines. Hence we must either be guilty of suppressing the liberties of others or else run the risk of losing our own liberties.

SOLUTION

It is impossible to go between the horns. It is possible to grasp it by either horn, arguing either (a) that liberties do not properly include the right to publish false and harmful doctrines or (b) that we run no risk of losing our own liberties if we vigorously oppose false and harmful doctrines with true and helpful ones. And it could plausibly be rebutted (but not refuted) by the use of its ingredients to prove that "we must either be guiltless of suppressing the liberties of others or else run no risk of losing our own liberties."

2. If you tell me what I already understand, you do not enlarge my understanding, whereas if you tell me something that I do not understand, then your remarks are unintelligible to me. Whatever you tell me must be either something I already understand or something that I do not understand. Hence whatever you say either does not enlarge my understanding or else is unintelligible to me.

3. If the conclusion of a deductive argument goes beyond the premises, then the argument is invalid, while if the conclusion of a deductive argument does not go beyond the premises, then the argument brings nothing new to light. The conclusion of a deductive argument must either go beyond the premises or not go beyond them. Therefore either deductive arguments are invalid or they bring nothing new to light.

4. If a deductive argument is invalid, it is without value, whereas a deductive argument that brings nothing new to light is also without value. Either deductive arguments are invalid or they bring nothing new to light. Therefore deductive arguments are without value.

***5.** If the general had been loyal, he would have obeyed his orders, and if he had been intelligent, he would have understood them. The general either disobeyed his orders or else he did not understand them. Therefore the general must have been either disloyal or unintelligent.

6. If he was disloyal, then his dismissal was justified, and if he was unintelligent, then his dismissal was justified. He was either disloyal or unintelligent. Therefore his dismissal was justified.

7. If the several nations keep the peace, the United Nations is unnecessary, while if the several nations go to war, the United Nations will have been unsuccessful in its purpose of preventing war. Now, either the several nations keep the peace or they go to war. Hence the United Nations is unnecessary or unsuccessful.

8. If people are good, laws are not needed to prevent wrongdoing, whereas if people are bad, laws will not succeed in preventing wrongdoing. People are either good or bad. Therefore either laws are not needed to prevent wrongdoing or laws will not succeed in preventing wrongdoing.

9. Archbishop Morton, Chancellor under Henry VII, was famous for his method of extracting "contributions" to the king's purse. A person who lived extravagantly was forced to make a large contribution, because it was obvious that he could afford it. Someone who lived modestly was forced to make a large contribution because it was clear that he must have saved a lot of money on living expenses. Whichever way he turned he was said to be "caught on Morton's fork."

—Dorothy Hayden, *Winning Declarer Play* (New York: Harper & Row, 1969)

***10.** All political action aims at either preservation or change. When desiring to preserve, we wish to prevent a change to the worse; when desiring to change, we wish to bring about something better. All political action is then guided by some thought of better and worse.

—Leo Strauss, *What Is Political Philosophy?*, 1959

11. If a thing moves, it moves either in the place where it is or in that where it is not; but it moves neither in the place where it is (for it remains therein) nor in that where it is not (for it does not exist therein); therefore nothing moves.

—Sextus Empiricus, *Against the Physicists*

12. And what a life should I lead, at my age, wandering from city to city, ever changing my place of exile, and always being driven out! For I am quite sure that wherever I go, there, as here, the young men will flock to me; and if I drive them away, their elders will drive me out at their request; and if I let them come, their fathers and friends will drive me out for their sakes.

—Plato, *Apology*

13. If Socrates died, he died either when he was living or when he was dead. But he did not die while living; for assuredly he was living, and as living he had not died. Nor did he die when he was dead, for then he would be twice dead. Therefore Socrates did not die.

—Sextus Empiricus, *Against the Physicists*

14. Inevitably, the use of the placebo involved built-in contradictions. A good patient–doctor relationship is essential to the process, but what happens to that relationship when one of the partners conceals important information from the other? If the doctor tells the truth, he destroys the base on which the placebo rests. If he doesn't tell the truth, he jeopardizes a relationship built on trust.

—Norman Cousins, *Anatomy of an Illness*

***15.** The decision of the Supreme Court in *U.S. v. Nixon* (1974), handed down the first day of the Judiciary Committee's final debate, was critical. If the President defied the order, he would be impeached. If he obeyed the order, it was increasingly apparent, he would be impeached on the evidence.

—Victoria Schuck, "Watergate," *The Key Reporter*, Winter 1975–1976

16. If we are to have peace, we must not encourage the competitive spirit, whereas if we are to make progress, we must encourage the competitive spirit. We must either encourage or not encourage the competitive spirit. Therefore we shall either have no peace or make no progress.

17. The argument under the present head may be put into a very concise form, which appears altogether conclusive. Either the mode in which the federal government is to be constructed will render it sufficiently dependent on the people, or it will not. On the first supposition, it will be restrained by that dependence from forming schemes obnoxious to their constituents. On the other supposition, it will not possess the confidence of the people, and its schemes of usurpation will be easily defeated by the State governments, who will be supported by the people.

—James Madison, *The Federalist Papers*, no. 46, 1788

18. . . . a man cannot enquire either about that which he knows, or about that which he does not know; for if he knows, he has no need to enquire; and if not, he cannot; for he does not know the very subject about which he is to enquire.

—Plato, *Meno*

19. We tell clients to try to go through the entire first interview without even mentioning money. If you ask for a salary that is too high, the employer concludes that he can't afford you. If you ask for one that is too low, you're essentially saying, "I'm not competent enough to handle the job that you're offering."

—James Challenger, "What to Do—and Not to Do—When Job Hunting," *U.S. News & World Report*, 6 August 1984

***20.** "Pascal's wager" is justifiably famous in the history of religion and also of betting. Pascal was arguing that agnostics—people unsure of God's existence—are best off betting that He does exist. If He does but you end up living as an unbeliever, then you could be condemned to spend eternity in the flames of Hell. If, on the other hand, He doesn't exist but you live as a believer, you suffer no corresponding penalty for being in error. Obviously, then, bettors on God start out with a big edge.

—Daniel Seligman, "Keeping Up," *Fortune*, 7 January 1985

SUMMARY

In this chapter we have examined syllogistic argument as it is used in ordinary language, exhibiting the different guises in which syllogisms appear and showing how they may be best understood, used, and evaluated.

In Section 7.1, we explained the need for techniques to translate syllogistic arguments of any form into standard form, and we identified the ways in which syllogistic arguments may deviate from standard-form categorical syllogisms.

In Section 7.2, we explained how syllogisms in ordinary language appearing to have more than three terms may sometimes have the number of terms in them appropriately reduced to three—by elimination of synonyms, and by elimination of complementary classes.

In Section 7.3, we explained how the propositions of a syllogistic argument, when not in standard form, may be translated into standard form so as to allow the syllogism to be tested either by Venn diagrams or by use of the rules governing syllogisms. Nonstandard propositions of nine different kinds were examined, and the methods for translating each kind were explained and illustrated:

1. Singular propositions
2. Propositions having adjectives as predicates
3. Propositions having main verbs other than the copula "to be"
4. Statements having standard-form ingredients, but not in standard-form order
5. Propositions having quantifiers other than "all," "no," and "some"
6. Exclusive propositions, using "only" or "none but"
7. Propositions without words indicating quantity
8. Propositions not resembling standard-form propositions at all
9. Exceptive propositions, using "all except" or similar expressions

In Section 7.4, we explained how the uniform translation of propositions into standard form, essential for testing, may be assisted by the use of parameters.

In Sections 7.5 and 7.6, we explained enthymemes, syllogistic arguments in which one of the constituent propositions has been suppressed, and sorites, in which a chain of syllogisms may be compressed into a cluster of linked propositions.

In Section 7.7, we explained syllogisms other than categorical: disjunctive syllogisms and hypothetical syllogisms, so called because they contain disjunctive or hypothetical premises.

In Section 7.8, we discussed the rhetorical use of dilemmas, disjunctive arguments that give to the adversary a choice of alternatives neither of which is acceptable. We explained and illustrated the three possible patterns of rhetorical response: going between the horns of the dilemma, grasping the dilemma by its horns, or devising a counterdilemma.

End Notes

[1]Immanuel Kant, *Critique of Pure Reason*, 1787, The Analytic of Concepts, chap. 1, sec. 2. More than a century later, Bertrand Russell presented a very different interpretation of singular propositions and universal propositions, and he later argued (in *My Philosophical Development*, 1959) that logic "cannot get far" until the two forms are seen to be "completely different" because the one (the singular) attributes a predicate to a named subject, while the other (the universal) expresses a relation between two predicates. Russell's interpretation had by that time become central to the theory of quantification in modern symbolic logic, discussed at length below, in Chapter 10; Kant's observation pertained to the use of singular propositions in traditional syllogisms, which he knew to be very powerful logical instruments.

[2]In some contexts the article "the" is deliberately omitted to achieve desired ambiguity. When United Nations Resolution 242 was adopted, calling for the return of "territory" captured by Israel in the Six-Day War in 1967, it was formally agreed that the English version of the Resolution would be authoritative, because the Resolution when expressed in French would require the definite article (*le territoire*), of which the English translation is "the territory," meaning *all* the territory captured, which is precisely what the agreed-upon English version carefully refrains from saying. The omission of the definite article in English can be logically significant.

[3]David Hume, *Dialogues Concerning Natural Religion*, part 2 (1779).

[4]*U.S. v. Morrison*, 529 U.S. 598 (2000).

[5]All the following exercises, except 4 and 6 under A, are taken, with little or no modification, from Lewis Carroll's *Symbolic Logic* (New York: C. N. Potter, 1977).

[6]Peter Bertocci, "Plight Must Come from Arrogance,"*Ann Arbor* (Mich.) *News*, 19 January 2001.

[7]James Gleick, *Genius: The Life and Science of Richard Feynman* (New York: Pantheon Books, 1992).

[8]Letter to James C. Conkling, 26 August 1863.

[9]E. P. Northrop, *Riddles in Mathematics: A Book of Paradoxes* (Melbourne, FL: Krieger Publishing, 1975).

Symbolic Logic

8.1 Modern Logic and Its Symbolic Language

We seek a full understanding of deductive reasoning. For this we need a general theory of deduction. A general theory of deduction will have two objectives: (1) to explain the relations between premises and conclusions in deductive arguments, and (2) to provide techniques for discriminating between valid and invalid deductions. Two great bodies of logical theory have sought to achieve these ends. The first, called classical (or Aristotelian) logic, was examined in Chapters 5 through 7. The second, called modern (or modern symbolic) logic, is the subject in this and the following two chapters.

Although these two great bodies of theory have similar aims, they proceed in very different ways. Modern logic does not build on the system of syllogisms discussed in preceding chapters. It does not begin with the analysis of categorical propositions. It does seek to discriminate valid from invalid arguments, although it does so using very different concepts and techniques. Therefore we must now begin afresh, developing a modern logical system that deals with some of the very same issues dealt with by traditional logic—and does so even more effectively.

Modern logic begins by first identifying the fundamental logical *connectives* on which deductive argument depends. Using these connectives, a general account of such arguments is given, and methods for testing the validity of arguments are developed.

This analysis of deduction requires an artificial symbolic language. In a natural language—English or any other—there are peculiarities that make exact logical analysis difficult: Words may be vague or equivocal, the construction of arguments may be ambiguous, metaphors and idioms may confuse or mislead, emotional appeals may distract—problems discussed in Part I of this book. These difficulties can be largely overcome with an artificial language in which logical relations can be formulated with precision. The most fundamental elements of this modern symbolic language will be introduced in this chapter.

Symbols greatly facilitate our thinking about arguments. They enable us to get to the heart of an argument, exhibiting its essential nature and putting aside what is not essential. Moreover, with symbols we can perform some logical operations almost mechanically, with the eye, which might otherwise demand great effort. It may seem paradoxical, but a symbolic language therefore helps us to accomplish some intellectual tasks without having to think too much.*

Classical logicians did understand the enormous value of symbols in analysis. Aristotle used symbols as variables in his own analyses, and the refined system of Aristotelian syllogistics uses symbols in very sophisticated ways, as the preceding chapters have shown. However, much real progress has been made, mainly during the twentieth century, in devising and using logical symbols more effectively.

The modern symbolism with which deduction is analyzed differs greatly from the classical. The relations of classes of things are not central for modern logicians as they were for Aristotle and his followers. Instead, logicians look now to the internal structure of propositions and arguments, and to the logical links—very few in number—that are critical in all deductive argument. Modern symbolic logic is therefore not encumbered, as Aristotelian logic was, by the need to transform deductive arguments into syllogistic form, an often laborious task explained in the immediately preceding chapter.

The system of modern logic we now begin to explore is in some ways less elegant than analytical syllogistics, but it is more powerful. There are forms of deductive argument that syllogistics cannot adequately address. Using the approach taken by modern logic with its more versatile symbolic language, we can pursue the aims of deductive analysis directly and we can penetrate more deeply. The logical symbols we shall now explore permit more complete and more efficient achievement of the central aim of deductive logic: discriminating between valid and invalid arguments.

---

*The Arabic numerals we use today (1, 2, 3, . . .) illustrate the advantages of an improved symbolic language. They replaced cumbersome Roman numerals (i, ii, iii, . . .), which are very difficult to manipulate. To multiply 113 by 9 is easy; to multiply CXIII by IX is not so easy. Even the Romans, some scholars contend, were obliged to find ways to symbolize numbers more efficiently.

8.2 The Symbols for Conjunction, Negation, and Disjunction

In this chapter we shall be concerned with relatively simple arguments such as:

> The blind prisoner has a red hat or the blind prisoner has a white hat.
>
> The blind prisoner does not have a red hat.
>
> Therefore the blind prisoner has a white hat.

and

> If Mr. Robinson is the brakeman's next-door neighbor, then Mr. Robinson lives halfway between Detroit and Chicago.
>
> Mr. Robinson does not live halfway between Detroit and Chicago.
>
> Therefore Mr. Robinson is not the brakeman's next-door neighbor.

Every argument of this general type contains at least one compound statement. In studying such arguments we divide all statements into two general categories, simple and compound. A **simple statement** does not contain any other statement as a component. For example, "Charlie's neat" is a simple statement. A **compound statement** does contain another statement as a component. For example, "Charlie's neat and Charlie's sweet" is a compound statement, because it contains two simple statements as components. Of course, the components of a compound statement may themselves be compound.*

---

*In formulating definitions and principles in logic, one must be very precise. What appears simple often proves more complicated than had been supposed. The notion of a "component of a statement" is a good illustration of this need for caution.

One might suppose that a *component* of a statement is simply a part of a statement that is itself a statement. But this account does not define the term with enough precision, because one statement may be a *part* of a larger statement and yet not be a *component* of it in the strict sense. For example, consider the statement: "The man who shot Lincoln was an actor." Plainly the last four words of this statement are a part of it, and could indeed be regarded as a statement; it is either true or it is false that Lincoln was an actor. But the statement that "Lincoln was an actor," although undoubtedly a part of the larger statement, is not a *component* of that larger statement.

We can explain this by noting that, for part of a statement to be a component of that statement, two conditions must be satisfied: (1) The part must be a statement in its own right; *and* (2) If the part is replaced in the larger statement by any other statement, the result of that replacement must be meaningful—it must make sense.

The first of these conditions is satisfied in the Lincoln example, but the second is not. Suppose the part "Lincoln was an actor" is replaced by "there are lions in Africa." The result of this replacement is nonsense: "The man who shot there are lions in Africa." The term *component* is not a difficult one to understand, but—like all logical terms—it must be defined accurately and applied carefully.

A. CONJUNCTION

There are several types of compound statements, each requiring its own logical notation. The first type of compound statement we consider is the *conjunction*. We can form the **conjunction** of two statements by placing the word "and" between them; the two statements so combined are called **conjuncts.** Thus the compound statement, "Charlie's neat and Charlie's sweet" is a conjunction whose first conjunct is "Charlie's neat" and whose second conjunct is "Charlie's sweet."

The word "and" is a short and convenient word, but it has other uses besides connecting statements. For example, the statement, "Lincoln and Grant were contemporaries" is *not* a conjunction, but a simple statement expressing a relationship. To have a unique symbol whose only function is to connect statements conjunctively, we introduce the **dot** "•" as our symbol for conjunction. Thus the previous conjunction can be written as "Charlie's neat • Charlie's sweet." More generally, where p and q are any two statements whatever, their conjunction is written $p \bullet q$.

We know that every statement is either true or false. Therefore we say that every statement has a **truth value,** where the truth value of a true statement is *true,* and the truth value of a false statement is *false*. Using this concept, we can divide compound statements into two distinct categories, according to whether the truth value of the compound statement is determined wholly by the truth values of its components, or is determined by anything other than the truth values of its components.

We apply this distinction to conjunctions. The truth value of the conjunction of two statements is determined wholly and entirely by the truth values of its two conjuncts. If both its conjuncts are true, the conjunction is true; otherwise it is false. For this reason a conjunction is said to be a **truth-functional compound statement,** and its conjuncts are said to be **truth-functional components** of it.

Not every compound statement is truth-functional. For example, the truth value of the compound statement, "Othello believes that Desdemona loves Cassio," is not in any way determined by the truth value of its component simple statement, "Desdemona loves Cassio," because it could be true that Othello believes that Desdemona loves Cassio, regardless of whether she does or not. So the component, "Desdemona loves Cassio," is not a truth-functional component of the statement, "Othello believes that Desdemona loves Cassio," and the statement itself is not a truth-functional compound statement.

For our present purposes we define a **component of a compound statement** as being a **truth-functional component** if, when the component is replaced in the compound by any different statements having the same truth value as each other, the different compound statements produced by those replacements also have the same truth values as each other. And now we define a **compound statement** as being a **truth-functional compound statement** if all of its components are truth-functional components of it.[1]

We shall be concerned only with those compound statements that are truth-functionally compound. In the remainder of this book, therefore, we shall use the term *simple statement* to refer to any statement that is not truth-functionally compound.

A conjunction is a truth-functional compound statement, so our dot symbol is a **truth-functional connective.** Given any two statements, p and q, there are only four possible sets of truth values they can have. These four possible cases, and the truth value of the conjunction in each, can be displayed as follows:

Where p is true and q is true, $p \bullet q$ is true.
Where p is true and q is false, $p \bullet q$ is false.
Where p is false and q is true, $p \bullet q$ is false.
Where p is false and q is false, $p \bullet q$ is false.

If we represent the truth values "true" and "false" by the capital letters **T** and **F**, the determination of the truth value of a conjunction by the truth values of its conjuncts can be represented more compactly and more clearly by means of a **truth table:**

p	q	p • q
T	T	T
T	F	F
F	T	F
F	F	F

This truth table can be taken as defining the dot symbol, because it explains what truth values are assumed by $p \bullet q$ in every possible case.

We abbreviate simple statements by capital letters, generally using for this purpose a letter that will help us remember which statement it abbreviates. Thus we may abbreviate "Charlie's neat and Charlie's sweet" as $N \bullet S$. Some conjunctions, both of whose conjuncts have the same subject term—for example, "Byron was a great poet and Byron was a great adventurer"—are more briefly and perhaps more naturally stated in English by placing the "and" between the predicate terms and not repeating the subject term, as in "Byron was a great poet and a great adventurer." For our purposes, we regard the latter as formulating the same statement as the former and symbolize either one as $P \bullet A$. If both conjuncts of a conjunction have the same predicate term, as in "Lewis was a famous explorer and Clark was a famous explorer," again the conjunction is usually stated in English by placing the "and" between the subject terms and not repeating the predicate, as in "Lewis and Clark were famous explorers." Either formulation is symbolized as $L \bullet C$.

As shown by the truth table defining the dot symbol, a conjunction is true if and only if both of its conjuncts are true. The word "and" has another use in which it signifies not *mere* (truth-functional) conjunction but has the sense of "and subsequently," meaning temporal succession. Thus the statement, "Jones entered the country at New York and went straight to Chicago," is significant and might be true, whereas "Jones went straight to Chicago and entered the country at New York" is hardly intelligible. And there is quite a difference between "He took off his shoes and got into bed" and "He got into bed and took off his shoes."* Such examples show the desirability of having a special symbol with an exclusively truth-functional conjunctive use.

Note that the English words "but," "yet," "also," "still," "although," "however," "moreover," "nevertheless," and so on, and even the comma and the semicolon, can also be used to conjoin two statements into a single compound statement, and in their conjunctive sense they can all be represented by the dot symbol.

B. NEGATION

The **negation** (or *contradictory* or *denial*) of a statement in English is often formed by the insertion of a "not" in the original statement. Alternatively, one can express the negation of a statement in English by prefixing to it the phrase "it is false that" or "it is not the case that." It is customary to use the symbol "~," called a **curl** or a **tilde,** to form the negation of a statement. Thus, where *M* symbolizes the statement "All humans are mortal," the various statements "Not all humans are mortal," "Some humans are not mortal," "It is false that all humans are mortal," and "It is not the case that all humans are mortal" are all symbolized as $\sim M$. More generally, where *p* is any statement whatever, its negation is written $\sim p$. It is obvious that the curl is a truth-functional operator. The negation of any true statement is false, and the negation of any false

---

*In *The Victoria Advocate*, Victoria, Texas, 27 October 1990, appeared the following report: "Ramiro Ramirez Garza, of the 2700 block of Leary Lane, was arrested by police as he was threatening to commit suicide and flee to Mexico."

statement is true. This fact can be presented very simply and clearly by means of a truth table:

p	$\sim p$
T	F
F	T

This truth table may be regarded as the definition of the negation "~" symbol.

C. DISJUNCTION

The **disjunction** (or *alternation*) of two statements is formed in English by inserting the word "or" between them. The two component statements so combined are called *disjuncts* (or *alternatives*).

The English word "or" is ambiguous, having two related but distinguishable meanings. One of them is exemplified in the statement, "Premiums will be waived in the event of sickness or unemployment." The intention here is obviously that premiums are waived not only for sick persons and for unemployed persons, but also for persons who are *both* sick *and* unemployed. This sense of the word "or" is called *weak* or *inclusive*. An **inclusive disjunction** is true if one or the other or both disjuncts are true; only if both disjuncts are false is their inclusive disjunction false. The inclusive "or" has the sense of "either, possibly both." Where precision is at a premium, as in contracts and other legal documents, this sense is made explicit by the use of the phrase "and/or."

The word "or" is also used in a *strong* or *exclusive* sense, in which the meaning is not "at least one" but "at least one and at most one." Where a restaurant lists "salad or dessert" on its dinner menu, it is clearly meant that, for the stated price of the meal, the diner may have one or the other *but not both*. Where precision is at a premium and the exclusive sense of "or" is intended, the phrase "but not both" is often added.

We interpret the inclusive disjunction of two statements as an assertion that at least one of the statements is true, and we interpret their **exclusive disjunction** as an assertion that at least one of the statements is true but not both are true. Note that the two kinds of disjunction have a part of their meanings in common. This partial common meaning, that at least one of the disjuncts is true, is the *whole* meaning of the inclusive "or" and a *part* of the meaning of the exclusive "or."

Although disjunctions are stated ambiguously in English, they are unambiguous in Latin. Latin has two different words corresponding to the two different senses of the English word "or." The Latin word *vel* signifies weak or inclusive disjunction, and the Latin word *aut* corresponds to the word "or" in its strong or exclusive sense. It is customary to use the initial letter of the word *vel* to stand for "or" in its weak, inclusive sense. Where p and q are any two statements whatever, their weak or inclusive disjunction is written $p \vee q$. Our symbol for inclusive disjunction, called a **wedge** (or, less frequently, a *vee*) is also a truth-functional connective. A weak disjunction is false only if both of its disjuncts are false. We may regard the wedge as being defined by the following truth table:

p	q	$p \vee q$
T	T	T
T	F	T
F	T	T
F	F	F

The first specimen argument presented in this section was a *disjunctive syllogism*.*

The blind prisoner has a red hat or the blind prisoner has a white hat.
The blind prisoner does not have a red hat.
Therefore the blind prisoner has a white hat.

Its form is characterized by saying that its first premise is a disjunction; its second premise is the negation of the first disjunct of the first premise; and its conclusion is the same as the second disjunct of the first premise. It is evident that the disjunctive syllogism, so defined, is valid on either interpretation of the word "or"; that is, regardless of whether an inclusive or exclusive disjunction is intended. The typical valid argument that has a disjunction for a premise is, like the disjunctive syllogism, valid on either interpretation of the word "or," so a simplification may be effected by translating the English word "or" into our logical symbol "$\vee$"—*regardless of which meaning of the English word "or" is intended.* In general, only a close examination of the context, or an explicit questioning of the speaker or writer, can reveal which sense of "or" is intended. This problem, often impossible to resolve, can be avoided if we agree to treat *any* occurrence of the word "or" as inclusive. On the other hand, if it is stated explicitly that the disjunction is intended to be exclusive, by means of the added phrase "but not both," for example, we have the symbolic machinery to formulate that additional sense, as will be shown directly.

Where both disjuncts have either the same subject term or the same predicate term, it is often natural to compress the formulation of their disjunction in English by placing the "or" so that there is no need to repeat the common part of the two disjuncts. Thus, "Either Smith is the owner or Smith is the manager" might equally well be stated as "Smith is either the owner or the manager,"

*A *syllogism* is a deductive argument consisting of two premises and a conclusion. The term *disjunctive syllogism* is being used in a narrower sense here than it was in Chapter 7.

and either one is properly symbolized as $O \vee M$. And "Either Red is guilty or Butch is guilty" may be stated as "Either Red or Butch is guilty"; either one may be symbolized as $R \vee B$.

The word "unless" is often used to form the disjunction of two statements. Thus, "You will do poorly on the exam unless you study" is correctly symbolized as $P \vee S$. The reason is that we use "unless" to mean that if one proposition is not true, the other is or will be true. The preceding sentence can be understood to mean, "If you don't study, you will do poorly on the exam"—and that is the thrust of the disjunction, because it asserts that one of the disjuncts is true, and hence that if one of them is false, the other must be true. Of course, you may study *and* do poorly on the exam.

The word "unless" is sometimes used to convey more information; it may mean (depending on context) that one or the other proposition is true but that not both are true. That is, "unless" may be intended as an exclusive disjunction. Thus it was noted by Ted Turner that global warming will put New York under water in one hundred years, and "will be the biggest catastrophe the world has ever seen—unless we have nuclear war."[2] Here the speaker did mean that at least one of the two disjuncts is true, but of course they cannot both be true. Other uses of "unless" are ambiguous. When we say, "The picnic will be held unless it rains," we surely do mean that the picnic will be held if it does not rain. But do we mean that it will not be held if it does rain? That may be uncertain. It is wise policy to treat every disjunction as weak or inclusive *unless* it is certain than an exclusive disjunction is meant. "Unless" is best symbolized simply with the wedge ($\vee$).

D. PUNCTUATION

In English, punctuation is absolutely required if complicated statements are to be clear. A great many different punctuation marks are used, without which many sentences would be highly ambiguous. For example, quite different meanings attach to "The teacher says John is a fool" when it is given different punctuations. Other sentences require punctuation for their very intelligibility, as, for example, "Jill where Jack had had had had had had had had had had the teacher's approval." Punctuation is equally necessary in mathematics. In the absence of a special convention, no number is uniquely denoted by $2 \times 3 + 5$, although when it is made clear how its constituents are to be grouped, it denotes either 11 or 16: the first when punctuated $(2 \times 3) + 5$, the second when punctuated $2 \times (3 + 5)$. To avoid ambiguity, and to make meaning clear, punctuation marks in mathematics appear in the form of parentheses, ( ), which are used to group individual symbols; brackets, [ ], which are used to group expressions that include parentheses; and braces, { }, which are used to group expressions that include brackets.

In the language of symbolic logic those same punctuation marks—parentheses, brackets, and braces—are equally essential, because in logic compound statements are themselves often compounded together into more complicated ones. Thus $p \bullet q \vee r$ is ambiguous: it might mean the conjunction of p with the disjunction of q with r, or it might mean the disjunction whose first disjunct is the conjunction of p and q and whose second disjunct is r. We distinguish between these two different senses by punctuating the given formula as $p \bullet (q \vee r)$ or else as $(p \bullet q) \vee r$. That the different ways of punctuating the original formula do make a difference can be seen by considering the case in which p is false and q and r are both true. In this case the second punctuated formula is true (because its second disjunct is true), whereas the first one is false (because its first conjunct is false). Here the difference in punctuation makes all the difference between truth and falsehood, for different punctuations can assign different truth values to the ambiguous $p \bullet q \vee r$.

The word "either" has a variety of different meanings and uses in English. It has conjunctive force in the sentence, "There is danger on either side." More often it is used to introduce the first disjunct in a disjunction, as in "Either the blind prisoner has a red hat or the blind prisoner has a white hat." There it contributes to the rhetorical balance of the sentence, but it does not affect its meaning. Perhaps the most important use of the word "either" is to punctuate a compound statement. Thus the sentence

> The organization will meet on Thursday and Anand will be elected or the election will be postponed.

is ambiguous. This ambiguity can be resolved in one direction by placing the word "either" at its beginning, or in the other direction by inserting the word "either" before the name "Anand." Such punctuation is effected in our symbolic language by parentheses. The ambiguous formula $p \bullet q \vee r$ discussed in the preceding paragraph corresponds to the ambiguous sentence just examined. The two different punctuations of the formula correspond to the two different punctuations of the sentence effected by the two different insertions of the word "either."

The negation of a disjunction is often formed by use of the phrase "neither—nor." Thus the statement, "Either Fillmore or Harding was the greatest U.S. president," can be contradicted by the statement, "Neither Fillmore nor Harding was the greatest U.S. president." The disjunction would be symbolized as $F \vee H$, and its negation as either $\sim(F \vee H)$ or as $(\sim F) \bullet (\sim H)$. (The logical equivalence of these two symbolic formulas will be discussed in Section 8.9.) It should be clear that to deny a disjunction stating that one or another statement is true requires that both be stated to be false.

The word "both" in English has a very important role in logical punctuation, and it deserves the most careful attention. When we say "Both Jamal and Derek are not . . ." we are saying, as noted just above, that "Neither Jamal nor Derek is . . ."; we are applying the negation to each of them. But when we say "Jamal and Derek are not both . . .," we are saying something very different; we are applying the negation to the pair of them taken together, saying that "it is not the case that they are both . . .". This difference is very substantial. Entirely different meanings arise when the word "both" is placed differently in the English sentence. Consider the great difference between the meanings of

Jamal and Derek will not both be elected.

and

Jamal and Derek will both not be elected.

The first denies the conjunction $J \bullet D$ and may be symbolized as $\sim(J \bullet D)$. The second says that each one of the two will not be elected, and is symbolized as $\sim(J) \bullet \sim(D)$. Merely changing the *position* of the two words "both" and "not" alters the logical force of what is asserted.

Of course, the word "both" does not always have this role; sometimes we use it only to add emphasis. When we say that "Both Lewis and Clark were great explorers," we use the word only to state more emphatically what is said by "Lewis and Clark were great explorers." When the task is logical analysis, the punctuational role of "both" must be very carefully determined.

In the interest of brevity—that is, to decrease the number of parentheses required—it is convenient to establish the convention that *in any formula, the negation symbol will be understood to apply to the smallest statement that the punctuation permits*. Without this convention, the formula $\sim p \vee q$ is ambiguous, meaning either $(\sim p) \vee q$, or $\sim(p \vee q)$. By our convention we take it to mean the first of these alternatives, for the curl *can* (and therefore by our convention *does*) apply to the first component, p, rather than to the larger formula $p \vee q$.

Given a set of punctuation marks for our symbolic language, it is possible to write not just conjunctions, negations, and weak disjunctions in it, but exclusive disjunctions as well. The exclusive disjunction of p and q asserts that at least one of them is true but not both are true, which is written as $(p \vee q) \bullet \sim(p \bullet q)$.

The truth value of any compound statement constructed from simple statements using only the truth-functional connectives—dot, curl, and wedge—is completely determined by the truth or falsehood of its component simple statements. If we know the truth values of simple statements, the truth value of any truth-functional compound of them is easily calculated. In working with such compound statements we always begin with their inmost components and work outward. For example, if A and B are true statements and X and Y are false statements, we calculate the truth value of the compound statement $\sim[\sim(A \bullet X) \bullet (Y \vee \sim B)]$ as follows. Because X is false, the conjunction $A \bullet X$ is false, and so its negation $\sim(A \bullet X)$ is true. B is true, so its negation $\sim B$ is false, and because Y is also false, the disjunction of Y with $\sim B$, $Y \vee \sim B$, is false. The bracketed formula $[\sim(A \bullet X) \bullet (Y \vee \sim B)]$ is the conjunction of a true with a false statement and is therefore false. Hence its negation, which is the entire statement, is true. Such a stepwise procedure always enables us to determine the truth value of a compound statement from the truth values of its components.

In some circumstances we may be able to determine the truth value of a truth-functional compound statement even if we cannot determine the truth or falsehood of one or more of its component simple statements. We do this by first calculating the truth value of the compound statement on the assumption that a given simple component is true, and then by calculating the truth value of the compound statement on the assumption that the same simple component is false, doing the same for each component whose truth value is unknown. If both calculations yield the *same* truth value for the compound statement in question, we have determined the truth value of the compound statement without having to determine the truth value of its components, because we know that the truth value of any component cannot be other than true or false.

OVERVIEW

Punctuation in Symbolic Notation

The statement

I will study hard and pass the exam or fail

is ambiguous. It could mean "I will study hard and pass the exam or I will fail the exam" or "I will study hard and I will either pass the exam or fail it."

The symbolic notation

$$S \bullet P \vee F$$

is similiarly ambiguous. Parentheses resolve the ambiguity. In place of "I will study hard and pass the exam or I will fail the exam," we get

$$(S \bullet P) \vee F$$

and in place of "I will study hard and I will either pass the exam or fail it," we get

$$S \bullet (P \vee F)$$

EXERCISES

A. Using the truth table definitions of the dot, the wedge, and the curl, determine which of the following statements are true.

***1.** Rome is the capital of Italy v Rome is the capital of Spain.

2. ~(London is the capital of England • Stockholm is the capital of Norway).

3. ~London is the capital of England • ~Stockholm is the capital of Norway.

4. ~(Rome is the capital of Spain v Paris is the capital of France).

***5.** ~Rome is the capital of Spain v ~Paris is the capital of France.

6. London is the capital of England v ~London is the capital of England.

7. Stockholm is the capital of Norway • ~Stockholm is the capital of Norway.

8. (Paris is the capital of France • Rome is the capital of Spain) v (Paris is the capital of France • ~Rome is the capital of Spain).

9. (London is the capital of England v Stockholm is the capital of Norway) • (~Rome is the capital of Italy • ~Stockholm is the capital of Norway).

***10.** Rome is the capital of Spain v ~(Paris is the capital of France • Rome is the capital of Spain).

11. Rome is the capital of Italy • ~(Paris is the capital of France v Rome is the capital of Spain).

12. ~(~Paris is the capital of France • ~Stockholm is the capital of Norway).

13. ~[~(~Rome is the capital of Spain v ~Paris is the capital of France) v ~(~Paris is the capital of France v Stockholm is the capital of Norway)].

14. ~[~(~London is the capital of England • Rome is the capital of Spain) • ~(Rome is the capital of Spain • ~Rome is the capital of Spain)].

***15.** ~[~(Stockholm is the capital of Norway v Paris is the capital of France) v ~(~London is the capital of England • Rome is the capital of Spain)].

16. Rome is the capital of Spain v (~London is the capital of England v London is the capital of England).

17. Paris is the capital of France • ~(Paris is the capital of France • Rome is the capital of Spain).

18. London is the capital of England • ~(Rome is the capital of Italy • Rome is the capital of Italy).

19. (Stockholm is the capital of Norway v ~Paris is the capital of France) v ~(~Stockholm is the capital of Norway • ~London is the capital of England).

*20. (Paris is the capital of France v ~Rome is the capital of Spain) v ~(~Paris is the capital of France • ~Rome is the capital of Spain).

21. ~[~(Rome is the capital of Spain • Stockholm is the capital of Norway) v ~(~Paris is the capital of France v ~Rome is the capital of Spain)].

22. ~[~(London is the capital of England • Paris is the capital of France) v ~(~Stockholm is the capital of Norway v ~Paris is the capital of France)].

23. ~[(~Paris is the capital of France v Rome is the capital of Italy) • ~(~Rome is the capital of Italy v Stockholm is the capital of Norway)].

24. ~[(~Rome is the capital of Spain v Stockholm is the capital of Norway) • ~(~Stockholm is the capital of Norway v Paris is the capital of France)].

*25. ~[(~London is the capital of England • Paris is the capital of France) v ~(~Paris is the capital of France • Rome is the capital of Spain)].

B. If *A*, *B*, and *C* are true statements and *X*, *Y*, and *Z* are false statements, which of the following are true?

*1. ~*A* v *B*

2. ~*B* v *X*

3. ~*Y* v *C*

4. ~*Z* v *X*

*5. (*A* • *X*) v (*B* • *Y*)

6. (*B* • *C*) v (*Y* • *Z*)

7. ~(*C* • *Y*) v (*A* • *Z*)

8. ~(*A* • *B*) v (*X* • *Y*)

9. ~(*X* • *Z*) v (*B* • *C*)

*10. ~(*X* • ~*Y*) v (*B* • ~*C*)

11. (*A* v *X*) • (*Y* v *B*)

12. (*B* v *C*) • (*Y* v *Z*)

13. (*X* v *Y*) • (*X* v *Z*)

14. ~(*A* v *Y*) • (*B* v *X*)

*15. ~(*X* v *Z*) • (~*X* v *Z*)

16. ~(*A* v *C*) v ~(*X* • ~*Y*)

17. ~(*B* v *Z*) • ~(*X* v ~*Y*)

18. ~[(*A* v ~*C*) v (*C* v ~*A*)]

19. ~[(*B* • *C*) • ~(*C* • *B*)]

*20. ~[(*A* • *B*) v ~(*B* • *A*)]

21. [*A* v (*B* v *C*)] • ~[(*A* v *B*) v *C*]

22. [*X* v (*Y* • *Z*)] v ~[(*X* v *Y*) • (*X* v *Z*)]

23. $[A \bullet (B \vee C)] \bullet \sim[(A \bullet B) \vee (A \bullet C)]$

24. $\sim\{[(\sim A \bullet B) \bullet (\sim X \bullet Z)] \bullet \sim[(A \bullet \sim B) \vee \sim(\sim Y \bullet \sim Z)]\}$

*25. $\sim\{\sim[(B \bullet \sim C) \vee (Y \bullet \sim Z)] \bullet [(\sim B \vee X) \vee (B \vee \sim Y)]\}$

C. If *A* and *B* are known to be true and *X* and *Y* are known to be false, but the truth values of *P* and *Q* are not known, of which of the following statements can you determine the truth values?

*1. $A \vee P$

2. $Q \bullet X$

3. $Q \vee \sim X$

4. $\sim B \bullet P$

*5. $P \vee \sim P$

6. $\sim P \vee (Q \vee P)$

7. $Q \bullet \sim Q$

8. $P \bullet (\sim P \vee X)$

9. $\sim(P \bullet Q) \vee P$

*10. $\sim Q \bullet [(P \vee Q) \bullet \sim P]$

11. $(P \vee Q) \bullet \sim(Q \vee P)$

12. $(P \bullet Q) \bullet (\sim P \vee \sim Q)$

13. $\sim P \vee [\sim Q \vee (P \bullet Q)]$

14. $P \vee \sim(\sim A \vee X)$

*15. $P \bullet [\sim(P \vee Q) \vee \sim P]$

16. $\sim(P \bullet Q) \vee (Q \bullet P)$

17. $\sim[\sim(\sim P \vee Q) \vee P] \vee P$

18. $(\sim P \vee Q) \bullet \sim[\sim P \vee (P \bullet Q)]$

19. $(\sim A \vee P) \bullet (\sim P \vee Y)$

*20. $\sim[P \vee (B \bullet Y)] \vee [(P \vee B) \bullet (P \vee Y)]$

21. $[P \vee (Q \bullet A)] \bullet \sim[(P \vee Q) \bullet (P \vee A)]$

22. $[P \vee (Q \bullet X)] \bullet \sim[(P \vee Q) \bullet (P \vee X)]$

23. $\sim[\sim P \vee (\sim Q \vee X)] \vee [\sim(\sim P \vee Q) \vee (\sim P \vee X)]$

24. $\sim[\sim P \vee (\sim Q \vee A)] \vee [\sim(\sim P \vee Q) \vee (\sim P \vee A)]$

*25. $\sim[(P \bullet Q) \vee (Q \bullet \sim P)] \bullet \sim[(P \bullet \sim Q) \vee (\sim Q \bullet \sim P)]$

D. Using the letters *E*, *I*, *J*, *L*, and *S* to abbreviate the simple statements, "Egypt's food shortage worsens," "Iran raises the price of oil," "Jordan requests more U.S. aid," "Libya raises the price of oil," and "Saudi Arabia buys five hundred more warplanes," symbolize these statements.

*1. Iran raises the price of oil but Libya does not raise the price of oil.

2. Either Iran or Libya raises the price of oil.

3. Iran and Libya both raise the price of oil.

4. Iran and Libya do not both raise the price of oil.

*5. Iran and Libya both do not raise the price of oil.

6. Iran or Libya raises the price of oil but they do not both do so.

7. Saudi Arabia buys five hundred more warplanes and either Iran raises the price of oil or Jordan requests more U.S. aid.

8. Either Saudi Arabia buys five hundred more warplanes and Iran raises the price of oil or Jordan requests more U.S. aid.

9. It is not the case that Egypt's food shortage worsens, and Jordan requests more U.S. aid.

*10. It is not the case that either Egypt's food shortage worsens or Jordan requests more U.S. aid.

11. Either it is not the case that Egypt's food shortage worsens or Jordan requests more U.S. aid.

12. It is not the case that both Egypt's food shortage worsens and Jordan requests more U.S. aid.

13. Jordan requests more U.S. aid unless Saudi Arabia buys five hundred more warplanes.

14. Unless Egypt's food shortage worsens, Libya raises the price of oil.

*15. Iran won't raise the price of oil unless Libya does so.

16. Unless both Iran and Libya raise the price of oil neither of them does.

17. Libya raises the price of oil and Egypt's food shortage worsens.

18. It is not the case that neither Iran nor Libya raises the price of oil.

19. Egypt's food shortage worsens and Jordan requests more U.S. aid, unless both Iran and Libya do not raise the price of oil.

*20. Either Iran raises the price of oil and Egypt's food shortage worsens, or it is not the case both that Jordan requests more U.S. aid and that Saudi Arabia buys five hundred more warplanes.

21. Either Egypt's food shortage worsens and Saudi Arabia buys five hundred more warplanes, or either Jordan requests more U.S. aid or Libya raises the price of oil.

22. Saudi Arabia buys five hundred more warplanes, and either Jordan requests more U.S. aid or both Libya and Iran raise the price of oil.

23. Either Egypt's food shortage worsens or Jordan requests more U.S. aid, but neither Libya nor Iran raises the price of oil.

24. Egypt's food shortage worsens, but Saudi Arabia buys five hundred more warplanes and Libya raises the price of oil.

***25.** Libya raises the price of oil and Egypt's food shortage worsens; however, Saudi Arabia buys five hundred more warplanes and Jordan requests more U.S. aid.

8.3 Conditional Statements and Material Implication

Where two statements are combined by placing the word "if" before the first and inserting the word "then" between them, the resulting compound statement is a **conditional** statement (also called a *hypothetical*, an *implication*, or an *implicative statement*). In a conditional statement the component statement that follows the "if" is called the **antecedent** (or the *implicans* or—rarely—the *protasis*), and the component statement that follows the "then" is the **consequent** (or the *implicate* or—rarely—the *apodosis*). For example, "If Mr. Jones is the brakeman's next-door neighbor, then Mr. Jones earns exactly three times as much as the brakeman" is a conditional statement in which "Mr. Jones is the brakeman's next-door neighbor" is the antecedent and "Mr. Jones earns exactly three times as much as the brakeman" is the consequent.

A conditional statement asserts that in any case in which its antecedent is true, its consequent is also true. It does not assert that its antecedent is true, but only that *if* its antecedent is true, then its consequent is also true. It does not assert that its consequent is true, but only that its consequent is true *if* its antecedent is true. The essential meaning of a conditional statement is the *relationship* asserted to hold between the antecedent and the consequent, in that order. To understand the meaning of a conditional statement, then, we must understand what the relationship of implication is.

Implication plausibly appears to have more than one meaning. We found it useful to distinguish different senses of the word "or" before introducing a special logical symbol to correspond exactly to a single one of the meanings of the English word. Had we not done so, the ambiguity of the English would have infected our logical symbolism and prevented it from achieving the clarity and precision aimed at. It will be equally useful to distinguish the different senses of "implies" or "if–then" before we introduce a special logical symbol in this connection.

Consider the following four conditional statements, each of which seems to assert a different type of implication, and to each of which corresponds a different sense of "if–then":

A. If all humans are mortal and Socrates is a human, then Socrates is mortal.

B. If Leslie is a bachelor, then Leslie is unmarried.

C. If this piece of blue litmus paper is placed in acid, then this piece of blue litmus paper will turn red.

D. If State loses the homecoming game, then I'll eat my hat.

Even a casual inspection of these four conditional statements reveals that they are of quite different types. The consequent of **A** follows *logically* from its antecedent, whereas the consequent of **B** follows from its antecedent by the very *definition* of the term "bachelor," which means unmarried man. The consequent of **C** does not follow from its antecedent either by logic alone or by the definition of its terms; the connection must be discovered empirically, because the implication stated here is *causal*. Finally, the consequent of **D** does not follow from its antecedent either by logic or by definition, nor is there any causal law involved. Statement **D** reports a *decision* of the speaker to behave in the specified way under the specified circumstances.

These four conditional statements are different in that each asserts a different type of implication between its antecedent and its consequent. But they are not completely different; all assert types of implication. Is there any identifiable common meaning, any partial meaning that is common to these admittedly different types of implication, although perhaps not the whole or complete meaning of any one of them?

The search for a common partial meaning takes on added significance when we recall our procedure in working out a symbolic representation for the English word "or." In that case, we proceeded as follows. First, we emphasized the difference between the two senses of the word, contrasting inclusive with exclusive disjunction. The inclusive disjunction of two statements was observed to mean that at least one of the statements is true, and the exclusive disjunction of two statements was observed to mean that at least one of the statements is true but not both are true. Second, we noted that these two types of disjunction had a common *partial* meaning. This partial common meaning, that at least one of the disjuncts is true, was seen to be the *whole* meaning of the weak, inclusive "or," and a *part* of the meaning of the strong, exclusive "or." We then introduced the special symbol "v" to represent this common partial meaning (which is the entire meaning of "or" in its inclusive sense). Third, we noted that the symbol representing the common partial meaning is an adequate translation of either sense of the word "or" for the purpose of retaining the disjunctive syllogism as a valid form of argument. It was admitted that translating an exclusive "or" into the symbol "v" ignores and loses part of the word's meaning. But the part of its meaning that is preserved by this translation is all that is needed for the disjunctive syllogism to remain a valid form of argument. Because the disjunctive syllogism is typical of arguments involving disjunction, with which we are concerned here, this partial translation of the word "or," which may abstract from its "full" or "complete" meaning in some cases, is wholly adequate for our present purposes.

Now we wish to proceed in the same way, this time in connection with the English phrase "if–then." The first part is already accomplished: We have already emphasized the differences among four senses of the "if–then" phrase, corresponding to four different types of implication. We are now ready for the second step, which is to discover a sense that is at least a part of the meaning of all four types of implication.

We approach this problem by asking: What circumstances suffice to establish the falsehood of a given conditional statement? Under what circumstances should we agree that the conditional statement

> If this piece of blue litmus paper is placed in that acid solution, then this piece of blue litmus paper will turn red.

is *false?* It is important to realize that this conditional does not assert that any blue litmus paper is actually placed in the solution, or that any litmus paper actually turns red. It asserts merely that *if* this piece of blue litmus paper is placed in the solution, *then* this piece of blue litmus paper will turn red. It is proved false if this piece of blue litmus paper is actually placed in the solution and does not turn red. The acid test, so to speak, of the falsehood of a conditional statement is available when its antecedent is true, because if its consequent is false while its antecedent is true, the conditional itself is thereby proved false.

Any conditional statement, "If p, then q," is known to be false if the conjunction $p \bullet {\sim}q$ is known to be true—that is, if its antecedent is true and its consequent is false. For a conditional to be true, then, the indicated conjunction must be false; that is, its negation ${\sim}(p \bullet {\sim}q)$ must be true. In other words, for any conditional, "If p then q," to be true, ${\sim}(p \bullet {\sim}q)$, the negation of the conjunction of its antecedent with the negation of its consequent, must also be true. We may then regard ${\sim}(p \bullet {\sim}q)$ as a part of the meaning of "If p then q."

Every conditional statement means to deny that its antecedent is true and its consequent false, but this need not be the whole of its meaning. A conditional such as **A** on page 331 also asserts a logical connection between its antecedent and consequent, as **B** asserts a definitional connection, **C** a causal connection, and **D** a decisional connection. No matter what type of implication is asserted by a conditional statement, *part* of its meaning is the negation of the conjunction of its antecedent with the negation of its consequent.

We now introduce a special symbol to represent this common partial meaning of the "if–then" phrase. We define the new symbol "$\supset$," called a

horseshoe, by taking $p \supset q$ as an abbreviation of $\sim(p \bullet \sim q)$. The exact significance of the $\supset$ symbol can be indicated by means of a truth table:

p	q	$\sim q$	$p \bullet \sim q$	$\sim(p \bullet \sim q)$	$p \supset q$
T	T	F	F	T	T
T	F	T	T	F	F
F	T	F	F	T	T
F	F	T	F	T	T

Here the first two columns are the guide columns; they simply lay out all possible combinations of truth and falsehood for p and q. The third column is filled in by reference to the second, the fourth by reference to the first and third, the fifth by reference to the fourth, and the sixth is identical to the fifth by definition.

The symbol $\supset$ is not to be regarded as denoting *the* meaning of "if–then," or standing for *the* relation of implication. That would be impossible, for there is no single meaning of "if–then"; there are several meanings. There is no unique relation of implication to be thus represented; there are several different implication relations. Nor is the symbol $\supset$ to be regarded as somehow standing for *all* the meanings of "if–then." These are all different, and any attempt to abbreviate all of them by a single logical symbol would render that symbol ambiguous—as ambiguous as the English phrase "if–then" or the English word "implication." The symbol $\supset$ is completely unambiguous. What $p \supset q$ abbreviates is $\sim(p \bullet \sim q)$, whose meaning is included in the meanings of each of the various kinds of implications considered but does not constitute the entire meaning of any of them.

We can regard the symbol $\supset$ as representing another kind of implication, and it will be expedient to do so, because a convenient way to read $p \supset q$ is "If p, then q." But it is not the same kind of implication as any of those mentioned earlier. It is called **material implication** by logicians. In giving it a special name, we admit that it is a special notion, not to be confused with other, more usual, types of implication.

Not all conditional statements in English need assert one of the four types of implication previously considered. Material implication constitutes a fifth type that may be asserted in ordinary discourse. Consider the remark, "If Hitler was a military genius, then I'm a monkey's uncle." It is quite clear that it does not assert logical, definitional, or causal implication. It cannot represent a decisional implication, because it scarcely lies in the speaker's power to make the consequent true. No "real connection," whether logical, definitional, or causal, obtains between antecedent and consequent here. A conditional of this sort is often used as an emphatic or humorous method of denying its antecedent. The consequent of such a conditional is usually a statement that is obviously or ludicrously false. And because no true conditional can have both its antecedent true and its consequent false, to affirm such a conditional amounts to denying that its antecedent is true. The full meaning of the present conditional seems to be the denial that "Hitler was a military genius" is true when "I'm a monkey's uncle" is false. And because the latter is so obviously false, the conditional must be understood to deny the former.

The point here is that no "real connection" between antecedent and consequent is suggested by a material implication. All it asserts is that, as a matter of fact, it is not the case that the antecedent is true when the consequent is false. Note that the material implication symbol is a truth-functional connective, like the symbols for conjunction and disjunction. As such, it is defined by the truth table:

p	q	$p \supset q$
T	T	T
T	F	F
F	T	T
F	F	T

As thus defined by the truth table, the symbol $\supset$ has some features that may at first appear odd: The assertion that a false antecedent materially implies a true consequent is true; and the assertion that a false antecedent materially implies a false consequent is also true. This apparent strangeness can be dissipated in part by the following considerations. Because the number 2 is smaller than the number 4 (a fact notated symbolically as $2 < 4$), it follows that *any* number smaller than 2 is smaller than 4. The conditional formula

If $x < 2$, then $x < 4$.

is true for any number x whatsoever. If we focus on the numbers 1, 3, and 4, and replace the number variable x in the preceding conditional formula by each of them in turn, we can make the following observations. In

If $1 < 2$, then $1 < 4$.

both antecedent and consequent are true, and of course the conditional is true. In

If $3 < 2$, then $3 < 4$.

the antecedent is false and the consequent is true, and of course the conditional is again true. In

If $4 < 2$, then $4 < 4$.

VISUAL LOGIC

Material Implication

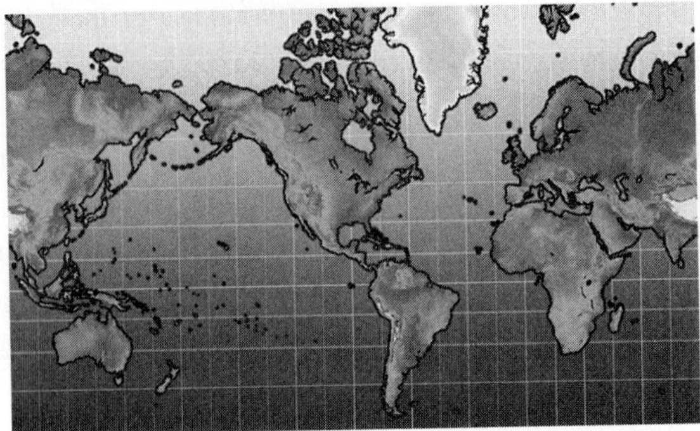

Source: Photodisc/Getty Images

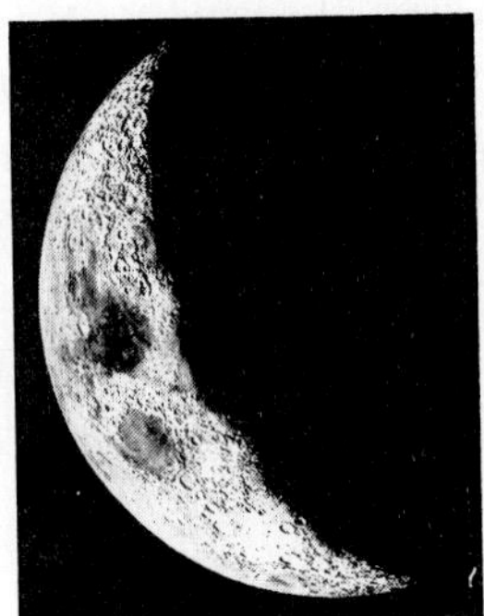

Source: Photodisc/Getty Images

If the world is flat, then the moon is made of green cheese.

This proposition, in the form $F \supset G$, is a material implication. A material implication is true when the antecedent (the "if" clause) is false. Therefore a material implication is true when the antecedent is false and the consequent is also false, as in this illustrative proposition.

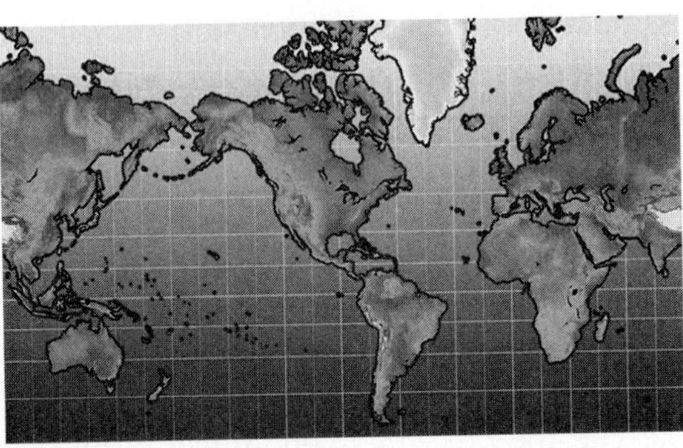

Source: Photodisc/Getty Images

Source: Photodisc/Getty Images

If the world is flat, the moon is round.

This proposition, in the similar form $F \supset R$, is also a material implication. A material implication is true when the antecedent (the "if" clause) is false. Therefore a material implication is true when the antecedent is false and the consequent is true, as in this illustrative proposition.

A material implication is false only if the antecedent is true and the consequent is false. Therefore a material implication is true whenever the antecedent is false, whether the consequent is false or true.

both antecedent and consequent are false, but the conditional remains true. These three cases correspond to the first, third, and fourth rows of the table defining the symbol ⊃. So it is not particularly remarkable or surprising that a conditional should be true when both antecedent and consequent are true, when the antecedent is false and the consequent is true, or when antecedent and consequent are both false. Of course, there is no number that is smaller than 2 but not smaller than 4; that is, there is no true conditional statement with a true antecedent and a false consequent. This is exactly what the defining truth table for ⊃ lays down.

Now we propose to translate any occurrence of the "if–then" phrase into our logical symbol ⊃. This proposal means that in translating conditional statements into our symbolism, we treat them all as merely material implications. Of course, most conditional statements assert more than that a merely material implication holds between their antecedents and consequents. So our proposal amounts to suggesting that we ignore, or put aside, or "abstract from," part of the meaning of a conditional statement when we translate it into our symbolic language. How can this proposal be justified?

The previous proposal to translate both inclusive and exclusive disjunctions by means of the symbol ∨ was justified on the grounds that the validity of the disjunctive syllogism was preserved even if the additional meaning that attaches to the exclusive "or" was ignored. Our present proposal to translate all conditional statements into the merely material implication symbolized by ⊃ may be justified in exactly the same way. Many arguments contain conditional statements of various different kinds, but the validity of all valid arguments of the general type with which we will be concerned is preserved even if the additional meanings of their conditional statements are ignored. This remains to be proved, of course, and will occupy our attention in the next section.

Conditional statements can be formulated in a variety of ways. The statement

> If he has a good lawyer, then he will be acquitted.

can equally well be stated without the use of the word "then" as

> If he has a good lawyer, he will be acquitted.

The order of the antecedent and consequent can be reversed, provided that the "if" still directly precedes the antecedent, as

> He will be acquitted if he has a good lawyer.

It should be clear that, in any of the examples just given, the word "if" can be replaced by such phrases as "in case," "provided that," "given that," or "on condition that," without any change in meaning. Minor adjustments in the phrasings of antecedent and consequent permit such alternative phrasings of the same conditional as

> That he has a good lawyer implies that he will be acquitted.

or

> His having a good lawyer entails his acquittal.

A shift from active to passive voice accompanies a reversal of order of antecedent and consequent, yielding the logically equivalent

> His being acquitted is implied (or entailed) by his having a good lawyer.

Any of these is symbolized as $L \supset A$.

The notions of necessary and sufficient conditions provide other formulations of conditional statements. For any specified event, many circumstances are necessary for it to occur. Thus, for a normal car to run, it is necessary that there be fuel in its tank, its spark plugs properly adjusted, its oil pump working, and so on. So if the event occurs, every one of the conditions necessary for its occurrence must have been fulfilled. Hence to say

> That there is fuel in its tank is a necessary condition for the car to run.

can equally well be stated as

> The car runs only if there is fuel in its tank.

which is another way of saying that

> If the car runs then there is fuel in its tank.

Any of these is symbolized as $R \supset F$. In general, "q is a *necessary condition* for p" is symbolized as $p \supset q$. And, likewise, "p *only if* q" is also symbolized a $p \supset q$.

For a specified situation there may be many alternative circumstances, any one of which is sufficient to produce that situation. For a purse to contain more than a dollar, for example, it is sufficient for it to contain five quarters, or eleven dimes, or twenty-one nickels, and so on. If any one of these circumstances obtains, the specified situation will be realized. Hence, to say "That the purse contains five quarters is a sufficient condition for it to contain more than a dollar" is to say "If the purse contains five quarters then it contains more than a dollar." In general, "p is a *sufficient condition* for q" is symbolized as $p \supset q$.

To illustrate, recruiters for the Wall Street investment firm Goldman, Sachs (where annual bonuses are commonly in the millions) grill potential employees repeatedly. Those who survive the grilling are invited to the firm's offices for a full day of interviews, culminating in a dinner with senior

Goldman executives. As reported recently, "Agile brains and near-perfect grades are necessary but not sufficient conditions for being hired. Just as important is fitting in."[3]

If p is a sufficient condition for q, we have $p \supset q$, and q must be a necessary condition for p. If p is a necessary condition for q, we have $q \supset p$, and q must be a sufficient condition for p. Hence, if p is necessary *and* sufficient for q, then q is sufficient *and* necessary for p.

Not every statement containing the word "if" is a conditional. None of the following statements is a conditional: "There is food in the refrigerator if you want some," "Your table is ready, if you please," "There is a message for you if you're interested," "The meeting will be held even if no permit is obtained." The presence or absence of particular words is never decisive. In every case, one must understand what a given sentence means, and then restate that meaning in a symbolic formula.

EXERCISES

A. If A, B, and C are true statements and X, Y, and Z are false statements, determine which of the following are true, using the truth tables for the horseshoe, the dot, the wedge, and the curl.

***1.** $A \supset B$

2. $A \supset X$

3. $B \supset Y$

4. $Y \supset Z$

***5.** $(A \supset B) \supset Z$

6. $(X \supset Y) \supset Z$

7. $(A \supset B) \supset C$

8. $(X \supset Y) \supset C$

9. $A \supset (B \supset Z)$

***10.** $X \supset (Y \supset Z)$

11. $[(A \supset B) \supset C] \supset Z$

12. $[(A \supset X) \supset Y] \supset Z$

13. $[A \supset (X \supset Y)] \supset C$

14. $[A \supset (B \supset Y)] \supset X$

***15.** $[(X \supset Z) \supset C] \supset Y$

16. $[(Y \supset B) \supset Y] \supset Y$

17. $[(A \supset Y) \supset B] \supset Z$

18. $[(A \bullet X) \supset C] \supset [(A \supset C) \supset X]$

19. $[(A \bullet X) \supset C] \supset [(A \supset X) \supset C]$

***20.** $[(A \bullet X) \supset Y] \supset [(X \supset A) \supset (A \supset Y)]$

21. $[(A \bullet X) \vee ({\sim}A \bullet {\sim}X)] \supset [(A \supset X) \bullet (X \supset A)]$

22. $\{[A \supset (B \supset C)] \supset [(A \bullet B) \supset C]\} \supset [(Y \supset B) \supset (C \supset Z)]$

23. $\{[(X \supset Y) \supset Z] \supset [Z \supset (X \supset Y)]\} \supset [(X \supset Z) \supset Y]$

24. $[(A \bullet X) \supset Y] \supset [(A \supset X) \bullet (A \supset Y)]$

***25.** $[A \supset (X \bullet Y)] \supset [(A \supset X) \vee (A \supset Y)]$

B. If A and B are known to be true, and X and Y are known to be false, but the truth values of P and Q are not known, of which of the following statements can you determine the truth values?

*1. $P \supset A$

2. $X \supset Q$

3. $(Q \supset A) \supset X$

4. $(P \bullet A) \supset B$

*5. $(P \supset P) \supset X$

6. $(X \supset Q) \supset X$

7. $X \supset (Q \supset X)$

8. $(P \bullet X) \supset Y$

9. $[P \supset (Q \supset P)] \supset Y$

*10. $(Q \supset Q) \supset (A \supset X)$

11. $(P \supset X) \supset (X \supset P)$

12. $(P \supset A) \supset (B \supset X)$

13. $(X \supset P) \supset (B \supset Y)$

14. $[(P \supset B) \supset B] \supset B$

*15. $[(X \supset Q) \supset Q] \supset Q$

16. $(P \supset X) \supset ({\sim}X \supset {\sim}P)$

17. $(X \supset P) \supset ({\sim}X \supset Y)$

18. $(P \supset A) \supset (A \supset {\sim}B)$

19. $(P \supset Q) \supset (P \supset Q)$

*20. $(P \supset {\sim}{\sim}P) \supset (A \supset {\sim}B)$

21. ${\sim}(A \bullet P) \supset ({\sim}A \vee {\sim}P)$

22. ${\sim}(P \bullet X) \supset {\sim}(P \vee {\sim}X)$

23. ${\sim}(X \vee Q) \supset ({\sim}X \bullet {\sim}Q)$

24. $[P \supset (A \vee X)] \supset [(P \supset A) \supset X]$

*25. $[Q \vee (B \bullet Y)] \supset [(Q \vee B) \bullet (Q \vee Y)]$

C. Symbolize the following, using capital letters to abbreviate the simple statements involved.

*1. If Argentina mobilizes then if Brazil protests to the UN then Chile will call for a meeting of all the Latin American states.

2. If Argentina mobilizes then either Brazil will protest to the UN or Chile will call for a meeting of all the Latin American states.

3. If Argentina mobilizes then Brazil will protest to the UN and Chile will call for a meeting of all the Latin American states.

4. If Argentina mobilizes then Brazil will protest to the UN, and Chile will call for a meeting of all the Latin American states.

*5. If Argentina mobilizes and Brazil protests to the UN then Chile will call for a meeting of all the Latin American states.

6. If either Argentina mobilizes or Brazil protests to the UN then Chile will call for a meeting of all the Latin American states.

7. Either Argentina will mobilize or if Brazil protests to the UN then Chile will call for a meeting of all the Latin American states.

8. If Argentina does not mobilize then either Brazil will not protest to the UN or Chile will not call for a meeting of all the Latin American states.

9. If Argentina does not mobilize then neither will Brazil protest to the UN nor will Chile call for a meeting of all the Latin American states.

***10.** It is not the case that if Argentina mobilizes then both Brazil will protest to the UN and Chile will call for a meeting of all the Latin American states.

11. If it is not the case that Argentina mobilizes then Brazil will not protest to the UN, and Chile will call for a meeting of all the Latin American states.

12. Brazil will protest to the UN if Argentina mobilizes.

13. Brazil will protest to the UN only if Argentina mobilizes.

14. Chile will call for a meeting of all the Latin American states only if both Argentina mobilizes and Brazil protests to the UN.

***15.** Brazil will protest to the UN only if either Argentina mobilizes or Chile calls for a meeting of all the Latin American states.

16. Argentina will mobilize if either Brazil protests to the UN or Chile calls for a meeting of all the Latin American states.

17. Brazil will protest to the UN unless Chile calls for a meeting of all the Latin American states.

18. If Argentina mobilizes, then Brazil will protest to the UN unless Chile calls for a meeting of all the Latin American states.

19. Brazil will not protest to the UN unless Argentina mobilizes.

***20.** Unless Chile calls for a meeting of all the Latin American states, Brazil will protest to the UN.

21. Argentina's mobilizing is a sufficient condition for Brazil to protest to the UN.

22. Argentina's mobilizing is a necessary condition for Chile to call for a meeting of all the Latin American states.

23. If Argentina mobilizes and Brazil protests to the UN, then both Chile and the Dominican Republic will call for a meeting of all the Latin American states.

24. If Argentina mobilizes and Brazil protests to the UN, then either Chile or the Dominican Republic will call for a meeting of all the Latin American states.

***25.** If neither Chile nor the Dominican Republic calls for a meeting of all the Latin American states, then Brazil will not protest to the UN unless Argentina mobilizes.

8.4 Argument Forms and Refutation by Logical Analogy

The central task of deductive logic, we have said, is discriminating valid arguments from invalid ones. If the premises of a valid argument are true (we explained in the very first chapter), its conclusion *must* be true. If the conclusion of a valid argument is false, at least one of the premises must be false. In short, the premises of a valid argument give *incontrovertible proof* of the conclusion drawn.

This informal account of validity must now be made more precise. To do this we introduce the concept of an *argument form*. Consider the following two arguments, which plainly have the *same* logical form. Suppose we are presented with the first of these arguments:

If Bacon wrote the plays attributed to Shakespeare, then Bacon was a great writer.

Bacon was a great writer.

Therefore Bacon wrote the plays attributed to Shakespeare.

We may agree with the premises but disagree with the conclusion, judging the argument to be invalid. One way of proving invalidity is by the method of logical analogy. "You might as well argue," we could retort, "that

If Washington was assassinated, then Washington is dead.

Washington is dead.

Therefore Washington was assassinated.

And you cannot seriously defend this argument," we would continue, "because here the premises are known to be true and the conclusion is known to be false. This argument is obviously invalid; your argument is of the *same form*, so yours is also invalid." This type of refutation is very effective.

This method of **refutation by logical analogy** points the way to an excellent general technique for testing arguments. To prove the invalidity of an argument, it suffices to formulate another argument that (1) has exactly the same form as the first and (2) has true premises and a false conclusion. This method is based on the fact that validity and invalidity are purely *formal* characteristics of arguments, which is to say that any two arguments that have exactly the same form are either both valid or both invalid, regardless of any differences in the subject matter with which they are concerned.*

---

*Here we assume that the simple statements involved are neither logically true (e.g., "All chairs are chairs") nor logically false (e.g., "Some chairs are nonchairs"). We also assume that the only logical relations among the simple statements involved are those asserted or entailed by the premises. The point of these restrictions is to limit our considerations, in this chapter and the next, to truth-functional arguments alone, and to exclude other kinds of arguments whose validity turns on more complex logical considerations that are not appropriately introduced at this point.

A given argument exhibits its form very clearly when the simple statements that appear in it are abbreviated by capital letters. Thus we may abbreviate the statements, "Bacon wrote the plays attributed to Shakespeare," "Bacon was a great writer," "Washington was assassinated," and "Washington is dead," by the letters *B*, *G*, *A*, and *D*, respectively, and using the familiar three-dot symbol "∴" for "therefore," we may symbolize the two preceding arguments as

$B \supset G$ $\qquad\qquad$ $A \supset D$

G $\qquad$ and $\qquad$ D

$\therefore B$ $\qquad\qquad$ $\therefore A$

So written, their common form is easily seen.

To discuss forms of arguments rather than particular arguments having those forms, we need some method of symbolizing argument forms themselves. To achieve such a method, we introduce the notion of a **variable.** In the preceding sections we used capital letters to symbolize particular simple statements. To avoid confusion, we use small, or lowercase, letters from the middle part of the alphabet, *p*, *q*, *r*, s, . . ., as *statement variables*. A **statement variable,** as we shall use the term, is simply a letter for which, or in place of which, a statement may be substituted. Compound statements as well as simple statements may be substituted for statement variables.

We define an **argument form** as any array of symbols containing statement variables but no statements, such that when statements are substituted for the statement variables—the same statement being substituted for the same statement variable throughout—the result is an argument. For definiteness, we establish the convention that in any argument form, *p* shall be the first statement variable that occurs in it, *q* shall be the second, *r* the third, and so on. Thus the expression

$p \supset q$

q

$\therefore p$

is an argument form, for when the statements *B* and *G* are substituted for the statement variables *p* and *q*, respectively, the result is the first argument in this section. If the statements *A* and *D* are substituted for the variables *p* and *q*, the result is the second argument. Any argument that results from the substitution of statements for statement variables in an argument form is called a **substitution instance** of that argument form. It is clear that any substitution instance of an argument form may be said to have that form, and that any argument that has a certain form is a substitution instance of that form.

For any argument there are usually several argument forms that have the given argument as a substitution instance. For example, the first argument of this section,

$B \supset G$

G

$\therefore B$

is a substitution instance of each of the four argument forms

$p \supset q$	$p \supset q$	$p \supset q$	p
q	r	r	q
$\therefore p$	$\therefore p$	$\therefore s$	$\therefore r$

Thus we obtain the given argument by substituting B for p and G for q in the first argument form; by substituting B for p and G for both q and r in the second; B for both p and s and G for both q and r in the third; and $B \supset G$ for p, G for q, and B for r in the fourth. Of these four argument forms, the first corresponds more closely to the structure of the given argument than do the others. It does so because the given argument results from the first argument form by substituting a different simple statement for each different statement variable in it. We call the first argument form the *specific form* of the given argument. Our definition of the specific form of a given argument is the following: If an argument is produced by substituting consistently a different simple statement for each different statement variable in an argument form, that argument form is the **specific form of that argument.** For any given argument, there is a unique argument form that is the specific form of that argument.

EXERCISES

Here follows a group of arguments (Group **A,** lettered **a–o**) and a group of argument forms (Group **B,** numbered **1–24**). For each of the arguments (in Group **A**), indicate which of the argument forms (in Group **B**), if any, have the given argument as a *substitution instance.* In addition, for each given argument (in Group **A**), indicate which of the argument forms (in Group **B**), if any, is the *specific form* of that argument.

EXAMPLES

Argument **a** in Group **A:** Examining all the argument forms in Group **B,** we find that the only one of which Argument **a** is a *substitution instance* is Number **3.** Number **3** *is* also the *specific form* of Argument **a.**

Argument **j** in Group **A:** Examining all the argument forms in Group **B,** we find that Argument **j** is a *substitution instance* of *both* Number **6** and Number **23.** But *only* Number **23** is the *specific form* of Argument **j.**

Argument **m** in Group **A:** Examining all the argument forms in Group **B,** we find that Argument **m** is a *substitution instance* of *both* Number **3** and Number **24.** But there is *no* argument form in Group **B** that is the *specific form* of Argument **m.**

Group A—Arguments

a. $A \bullet B$
$\therefore A$

b. $C \supset D$
$\therefore C \supset (C \bullet D)$

c. E
$\therefore E \vee F$

d. $G \supset H$
$\sim H$
$\therefore \sim G$

***e.** I
J
$\therefore I \bullet J$

f. $(K \supset L) \bullet (M \supset N)$
$K \vee M$
$\therefore L \vee N$

g. $O \supset P$
$\sim O$
$\therefore \sim P$

h. $Q \supset R$
$Q \supset S$
$\therefore R \vee S$

i. $T \supset U$
$U \supset V$
$\therefore V \supset T$

j. $(W \bullet X) \supset (Y \bullet Z)$
$\therefore (W \bullet X) \supset [(W \bullet X) \bullet (Y \bullet Z)]$

k. $A \supset B$
$\therefore (A \supset B) \vee C$

l. $(D \vee E) \bullet \sim F$
$\therefore D \vee E$

m. $[G \supset (G \bullet H)] \bullet [H \supset (H \bullet G)]$
$\therefore G \supset (G \bullet H)$

n. $(I \vee J) \supset (I \bullet J)$
$\sim (I \vee J)$
$\therefore \sim (I \bullet J)$

***o.** $(K \supset L) \bullet (M \supset N)$
$\therefore K \supset L$

Group B—Argument Forms

***1.** $p \supset q$
$\therefore \sim q \supset \sim p$

2. $p \supset q$
$\therefore \sim p \supset \sim q$

3. $p \bullet q$
$\therefore p$

4. p
$\therefore p \vee q$

***5.** p
$\therefore p \supset q$

6. $p \supset q$
$\therefore p \supset (p \bullet q)$

7. $(p \vee q) \supset (p \bullet q)$
$\therefore (p \supset q) \bullet (q \supset p)$

8. $p \supset q$
$\sim p$
$\therefore \sim q$

9. $p \supset q$
$\sim q$
$\therefore \sim p$

***10.** p
q
$\therefore p \bullet q$

11. $p \supset q$
$p \supset r$
$\therefore q \vee r$

12. $p \supset q$
$q \supset r$
$\therefore r \supset p$

13. $p \supset (q \supset r)$
$p \supset q$
$\therefore p \supset r$

14. $p \supset (q \bullet r)$
$(q \vee r) \supset \sim p$
$\therefore \sim p$

*15. $p \supset (q \supset r)$
$q \supset (p \supset r)$
$\therefore (p \vee q) \supset r$

16. $(p \supset q) \bullet (r \supset s)$
$p \vee r$
$\therefore q \vee s$

17. $(p \supset q) \bullet (r \supset s)$
$\sim q \vee \sim s$
$\therefore \sim p \vee \sim s$

18. $p \supset (q \supset r)$
$q \supset (r \supset s)$
$\therefore p \supset s$

19. $p \supset (q \supset r)$
$(q \supset r) \supset s$
$\therefore p \supset s$

*20. $(p \supset q) \bullet [(p \bullet q) \supset r]$
$p \supset (r \supset s)$
$\therefore p \supset s$

21. $(p \vee q) \supset (p \bullet q)$
$\sim(p \vee q)$
$\therefore \sim(p \bullet q)$

22. $(p \vee q) \supset (p \bullet q)$
$(p \bullet q)$
$\therefore p \vee q$

23. $(p \bullet q) \supset (r \bullet s)$
$\therefore (p \bullet q) \supset [(p \bullet q) \bullet (r \bullet s)]$

24. $(p \supset q) \bullet (r \supset s)$
$\therefore p \supset q$

8.5 The Precise Meaning of "Invalid" and "Valid"

We are now in a position to address with precision the central questions of deductive logic:

1. *What precisely is meant* by saying that an argument form is invalid, or valid?
2. *How do we decide* whether a deductive argument form is invalid, or valid?

The first of these questions is answered in this section, the second in the following section.

We proceed by using the technique of refutation by logical analogy.* If the specific form of a given argument has any substitution instance whose premises are true and whose conclusion is false, then the given argument is invalid. We may define the term **invalid** as applied to argument forms as follows: *An argument form is invalid if and only if it has at least one substitution instance with true premises and a false conclusion.* Refutation by logical analogy is based on the fact that any argument whose specific form is an *invalid argument form* is an invalid argument. Any argument form that is not invalid must be **valid.** Hence *an argument form is valid if and only if it has no substitution instances with true premises and a false conclusion.* And because validity is a formal notion, an argument is valid if and only if the specific form of that argument is a *valid argument form.*

A given argument is proved invalid if a refuting analogy can be found for it, but "thinking up" such refuting analogies may not always be easy. Happily, it is not necessary, because for arguments of this type there is a simpler, purely

*Just as in analyzing the categorical syllogism; we discuss refutation by logical analogy in Section 6.2.

mechanical test based on the same principle. Given any argument, we test the specific form of that argument, because its validity or invalidity determines the validity or invalidity of the argument.

8.6 Testing Argument Validity Using Truth Tables

Knowing exactly what it means to say that an argument is valid, or invalid, we can now devise a method for *testing* the validity of every truth-functional argument. Our method, using a truth table, is very simple and very powerful. It is simply an application of the analysis of argument forms just given.

To test an argument form, we examine all possible substitution instances of it to see if any one of them has true premises and a false conclusion. Of course any argument form has an infinite number of substitution instances, but we need not worry about having to examine them one at a time. We are interested only in the truth or falsehood of their premises and conclusions, so we need consider only the truth values involved. The arguments that concern us here contain only simple statements and compound statements that are built up out of simple statements using the truth-functional connectives symbolized by the dot, curl, wedge, and horseshoe. Hence we obtain all possible substitution instances whose premises and conclusions have different truth values by examining all possible different arrangements of truth values for the statements that can be substituted for the different statement variables in the argument form to be tested.

When an argument form contains just two different statement variables, *p* and *q*, all of its substitution instances are the result of either substituting true statements for both *p* and *q*, or a true statement for *p* and a false one for *q*, or a false one for *p* and a true one for *q*, or false statements for both *p* and *q*. These different cases are assembled most conveniently in the form of a truth table. To decide the validity of the argument form

$p \supset q$

q

$\therefore p$

we construct the following truth table:

p	q	p ⊃ q
T	T	T
T	F	F
F	T	T
F	F	T

Each row of this table represents a whole class of substitution instances. The **T**'s and **F**'s in the two initial or guide columns represent the truth values of the statements substituted for the variables p and q in the argument form. We fill in the third column by referring back to the initial or guide columns and the definition of the horseshoe symbol. The third column heading is the first "premise" of the argument form, the second column is the second "premise" and the first column is the "conclusion." In examining this truth table, we find that in the third row there are **T**'s under both premises and an **F** under the conclusion, which indicates that there is at least one substitution instance of this argument form that has true premises and a false conclusion. This row suffices to show that the argument form is invalid. Any argument of this specific form (that is, any argument the specific argument form of which is the given argument form) is said to commit the fallacy of affirming the consequent, since its second premise affirms the consequent of its conditional first premise.

Truth tables, although simple in concept, are powerful tools. In using them to establish the validity or the invalidity of an argument form, it is critically important that the table first be constructed correctly. To construct the truth table correctly, there must be a guide column for each statement variable in the argument form, p, q, r, and so on. The array must exhibit all the possible combinations of the truth and falsity of all these variables, so there must be a number of horizontal rows sufficient to do this: four rows if there are two variables, eight rows if there are three variables, and so on. And there must be an additional vertical column for each of the premises and for the conclusion, and also a column for each of the symbolic expressions out of which the premises and conclusion are built. The construction of a truth table in this fashion is essentially a mechanical task; it requires only careful counting and the careful placement of **T**'s and **F**'s in the appropriate columns, all governed by our understanding of the several truth-functional connectives—the dot, the wedge, the horseshoe—and the circumstances under which each truth-functional compound is true and the circumstances under which it is false.

Once the table has been constructed and the completed array is before us, it is essential to *read* it correctly, that is, to use it correctly to make the appraisal of the argument form in question. We must note carefully which columns are those representing the premises of the argument being tested, and which column represents the conclusion of that argument. In testing the argument just above, which we found to be invalid, we noted that it was the second and third columns of the truth table that represent the premises, while the conclusion was represented by the first (leftmost) column. Depending on which argument form we are testing, and the order in which we have placed the columns as the table was built, it is possible for the premises and the conclusion to appear in any order at the top of the table. Their position to the right or to the left is not significant; we, who use the table, must understand which column represents what, and we must understand what we are in search of. *Is there any one case,* we ask ourselves, *any single row in which all the premises are true and the conclusion false*? If there is such a row, the argument form is invalid; if there is no such row, the argument form must be valid. After the full array has been neatly and accurately set forth, great care in reading the truth table accurately is of the utmost importance.

8.7 Some Common Argument Forms

A. COMMON VALID FORMS

Some valid argument forms are exceedingly common and may be intuitively understood. These may now be precisely identified. They should be recognized wherever they appear, and they may be called by their widely accepted names: (1) **Disjunctive Syllogism,** (2) ***Modus Ponens,*** (3) ***Modus Tollens,*** and, (4) **Hypothetical Syllogism.**

Disjunctive Syllogism

One of the simplest argument forms relies on the fact that in every true disjunction, at least one of the disjuncts must be true. Therefore, if one of them is false, the other must be true. Arguments in this form are exceedingly common. When a candidate for a high appointed office was forced to withdraw her candidacy because of a tax violation involving one of her employees, a critic wrote: "In trying to cover up her illegal alien peccadillo, or stonewall her way out of it, she was driven either by stupidity or arrogance. She's obviously not stupid; her plight must result, then, from her arrogance."[4]

We symbolize the Disjunctive Syllogism as

$p \vee q$

$\sim p$

$\therefore q$

And to show its validity we construct the following truth table:

p	q	$p \vee q$	$\sim p$
T	T	T	F
T	F	T	F
F	T	T	T
F	F	F	T

Here, too, the initial or guide columns exhibit all possible different truth values of statements that may be substituted for the variables p and q. We fill in the third column by referring back to the first two, and the fourth by reference to the first alone. Now the third row is the only one in which T's appear under both premises (the third and fourth columns), and there a T also appears under the conclusion (the second column). The truth table thus shows that the argument form has no substitution instance having true premises and a false conclusion, and thereby proves the validity of the argument form being tested.*

Here, as always, it is essential that the truth table be *read* accurately; the column representing the conclusion (second from the left) and the columns representing the premises (third and fourth from the left) must be carefully identified. Only by using those three columns correctly can we reliably determine the validity (or invalidity) of the argument form in question. Note that the very same truth table could be used to test the validity of a very different argument form, one whose premises are represented by the second and third columns and whose conclusion is represented by the fourth column. That argument form, as we can see from the top row of the table, is invalid. The truth-table technique provides a completely mechanical method for testing the validity of any argument of the general type considered here.

We are now in a position to justify our proposal to translate any occurrence of the "if–then" phrase into our material implication symbol "$\supset$". In section 8.3, the claim was made that all valid arguments of the general type with which we are concerned here that involve "if–then" statements remain valid when those statements are interpreted as affirming merely material implications. Truth tables can be used to substantiate this claim, and will justify our translation of "if–then" into the horseshoe symbol.

Modus Ponens

The simplest type of intuitively valid argument involving a conditional statement is illustrated by the argument:

> If the second native told the truth, then only one native is a politician.
>
> The second native told the truth.
>
> Therefore only one native is a politician.

*As used in this chapter, the term *Disjunctive Syllogism* is the name of an elementary argument form, here proved valid. This form is always valid, of course, and therefore, in modern logic, "Disjunctive Syllogism" always refers to an elementary argument form that is valid. In traditional logic, however, the term "disjunctive syllogism" is used more broadly, to refer to any syllogism that contains a disjunctive premise; some such syllogisms may of course be invalid. One must be clear whether the expression is being used in the broader or the narrower sense. Here we use it in the narrower sense.

The specific form of this argument, known as *Modus Ponens* ("the method of putting, or affirming") is

$p \supset q$

p

$\therefore q$

and is proved valid by the following truth table:

p	q	$p \supset q$
T	T	T
T	F	F
F	T	T
F	F	T

Here the two premises are represented by the third and first columns, and the conclusion is represented by the second. Only the first row represents substitution instances in which both premises are true, and the **T** in the second column shows that in these arguments the conclusion is true also. This truth table establishes the validity of any argument of the form *modus ponens*.

Modus Tollens

If a conditional statement is true, then if the consequent is false, the antecedent must also be false. The argument form that relies on this is very commonly used to establish the falsehood of some proposition under attack. To illustrate, a distinguished rabbi, insisting that the Book of Genesis was never meant to be a scientific treatise, presented this crisp argument:

> A literal reading of Genesis would lead one to conclude that the world is less than 6,000 years old and that the Grand Canyon could have been carved by the global flood 4,500 years ago. Since this is impossible, a literal reading of Genesis must be wrong.[5]

The argument may be symbolized as

$p \supset q$

$\sim q$

$\therefore \sim p$

The validity of this argument form, called *Modus Tollens* ("the method of taking away or denying"), may be shown by the following truth table:

p	q	$p \supset q$	$\sim q$	$\sim p$
T	T	T	F	F
T	F	F	T	F
F	T	T	F	T
F	F	T	T	T

Here again, there is no substitution instance, no line, on which the premises, $p \supset q$ and $\sim q$, are both true and the conclusion, $\sim p$, is false.

Hypothetical Syllogism

Another common type of intuitively valid argument contains only conditional statements. Here is an example:

If the first native is a politician, then the first native lies.

If the first native lies, then the first native denies being a politician.

Therefore if the first native is a politician, then the first native denies being a politician.

The specific form of this argument is

$p \supset q$

$q \supset r$

$\therefore p \supset r$

This argument, called a **Hypothetical Syllogism,*** contains three distinct statement variables, so the truth table must have three initial (or guide) columns and requires eight rows to list all possible substitution instances. Besides the initial columns, three additional columns are needed: two for the premises, the third for the conclusion. The table is

p	q	r	$p \supset q$	$q \supset r$	$p \supset r$
T	T	T	T	T	T
T	T	F	T	F	F
T	F	T	F	T	T
T	F	F	F	T	F
F	T	T	T	T	T
F	T	F	T	F	T
F	F	T	T	T	T
F	F	F	T	T	T

*Called a *pure hypothetical syllogism* in Chapter 7.

In constructing it, we fill in the fourth column by referring back to the first and second, the fifth by reference to the second and third, and the sixth by reference to the first and third. Examining the completed table, we observe that the premises are true only in the first, fifth, seventh, and eighth rows, and that in all of these the conclusion is also true. This truth table establishes the validity of the argument form and proves that the Hypothetical Syllogism remains valid when its conditional statements are translated by means of the horseshoe symbol.

Enough examples have been provided to illustrate the proper use of the truth-table technique for testing arguments. And perhaps enough have been given to show that the validity of any valid argument involving conditional statements is preserved when its conditionals are translated into merely material implications. Any doubts that remain can be allayed by the reader's translating and testing similar examples.

As more complicated argument forms are considered, larger truth tables are required to test them, because a separate initial or guide column is required for each different statement variable in the argument form. Only two are required for a form with just two variables, and that table will have four rows. But three initial columns are required for a form with three variables, such as the hypothetical syllogism, and such truth tables have eight rows. To test the validity of an argument form such as that of the *Constructive Dilemma*,

$(p \supset q) \bullet (r \supset s)$

$p \vee r$

$\therefore q \vee s$

which contains four distinct statement variables, a truth table with four initial columns and sixteen rows is required. In general, to test an argument form containing n distinct statement variables we need a truth table with n initial columns and 2^n rows.

B. COMMON INVALID FORMS

Two invalid argument forms deserve special notice because they superficially resemble valid forms and therefore often tempt careless writers or readers. The *fallacy of affirming the consequent*, discussed also in Section 7.7, is symbolized as

$p \supset q$

q

$\therefore p$

Although the shape of this form is something like that of *modus ponens*, the two argument forms are very different, and this form is not valid. It is well illustrated in a "bogus syllogism" about the dictatorial president of Iraq, the late Saddam Hussein. Here is that syllogism (as recounted in 2005 by Orlando Patterson), whose invalidity does indeed render it bogus: "If one is a terrorist one is a tyrant who hates freedom. Saddam Hussein is a tyrant who hates freedom. Therefore Saddam Hussein is a terrorist."[6] Let us suppose that the hypothetical first premise is true, and that the second premise describing Saddam Hussein is also true. But that second premise affirms (about Saddam Hussein as one tyrant) only the *consequent* of the preceding hypothetical. The argument plainly commits the fallacy of affirming the consequent.

Another invalid form, called the *fallacy of denying the antecedent*, has a shape somewhat like that of *modus tollens* and may be symbolized as

$p \supset q$

$\sim p$

$\therefore \sim q$

An example of this fallacy is the campaign slogan used by a candidate for mayor of New York City some years ago: "If you don't know the buck, you don't know the job—and Abe knows the buck." The unstated conclusion to which the voter was deliberately tempted was that "Abe knows the job"—a proposition that does not follow from the stated premises.

Both of these common fallacies may readily be shown to be invalid by means of truth tables. In each case there is one line of the truth table in which the premises of these fallacious arguments are all true, but the conclusion is false.

C. SUBSTITUTION INSTANCES AND SPECIFIC FORMS

A given argument can be a substitution instance of several different argument forms, as we noted earlier when defining argument form. Hence the valid disjunctive syllogism examined on page 317, which may be symbolized as

$R \vee W$

$\sim R$

$\therefore W$

is a substitution instance of the valid argument form

$p \vee q$

$\sim p$

$\therefore q$

and is *also* a substitution instance of the *in*valid argument form

p

q

$\therefore r$

It is obvious, in this last form, that from two premises, p and q, we cannot validly infer r. So it is clear that an invalid argument form can have a valid argument *or* an invalid argument as a substitution instance. Therefore, in determining whether any given argument is valid, *we must look to the specific form of the argument* in question. Only the specific form of the argument reveals the full logical structure of that argument, and because it does, we know that if the specific form of an argument is valid, the argument itself must be valid.

In the illustration just given, we see an argument ($R \vee W$, $\sim R$, $\therefore W$), and two argument forms of which that argument could be a substitution instance. The first of these argument forms ($p \vee q$, $\sim p$, $\therefore q$) is valid, and because that form is the *specific* form of the given argument, its validity establishes that the given argument is valid. The second of these argument forms is invalid, but because it is *not* the specific form of the given argument, it cannot be used to show that the given argument is invalid.

This point should be emphasized: An argument form that is valid can have only valid arguments as substitution instances. That is, all of the substitution instances of a valid form *must* be valid. This is proved by the truth-table proof of validity for the valid argument form, which shows that there is no possible substitution instance of a valid form that has true premises and a false conclusion.

EXERCISES

A. Use truth tables to prove the validity or invalidity of each of the argument forms in section 8.4, Group B, pages 345–346.

B. Use truth tables to determine the validity or invalidity of each of the following arguments.

***1.** $(A \vee B) \supset (A \bullet B)$
$A \vee B$
$\therefore A \bullet B$

2. $(C \vee D) \supset (C \bullet D)$
$C \bullet D$
$\therefore C \vee D$

3. $E \supset F$
$F \supset E$
$\therefore E \vee F$

4. $(G \vee H) \supset (G \bullet H)$
$\sim(G \bullet H)$
$\therefore \sim(G \vee H)$

***5.** $(I \vee J) \supset (I \bullet J)$
$\sim(I \vee J)$
$\therefore \sim(I \bullet J)$

6. $K \vee L$
K
$\therefore \sim L$

7. $M \vee (N \bullet \sim N)$
   M
   $\therefore \sim(N \bullet \sim N)$

8. $(O \vee P) \supset Q$
   $Q \supset (O \bullet P)$
   $\therefore (O \vee P) \supset (O \bullet P)$

9. $(R \vee S) \supset T$
   $T \supset (R \bullet S)$
   $\therefore (R \bullet S) \supset (R \vee S)$

*10. $U \supset (V \vee W)$
   $(V \bullet W) \supset \sim U$
   $\therefore \sim U$

C. Use truth tables to determine the validity or invalidity of the following arguments.

*1. If Angola achieves stability, then both Botswana and Chad will adopt more liberal policies. But Botswana will not adopt a more liberal policy. Therefore Angola will not achieve stability.

2. If Denmark refuses to join the European Community, then, if Estonia remains in the Russian sphere of influence, then Finland will reject a free trade policy. Estonia will remain in the Russian sphere of influence. So if Denmark refuses to join the European community, then Finland will reject a free trade policy.

3. If Greece strengthens its democratic institutions, then Hungary will pursue a more independent policy. If Greece strengthens its democratic institutions, then the Italian government will feel less threatened. Hence, if Hungary pursues a more independent policy, the Italian government will feel less threatened.

4. If Japan continues to increase the export of automobiles, then either Korea or Laos will suffer economic decline. Korea will not suffer economic decline. It follows that if Japan continues to increase the export of automobiles, then Laos will suffer economic decline.

*5. If Montana suffers a severe drought, then, if Nevada has its normal light rainfall, Oregon's water supply will be greatly reduced. Nevada does have its normal light rainfall. So if Oregon's water supply is greatly reduced, then Montana suffers a severe drought.

6. If equality of opportunity is to be achieved, then those people previously disadvantaged should now be given special opportunities. If those people previously disadvantaged should now be given special opportunities, then some people receive preferential treatment. If some people receive preferential treatment, then equality of opportunity is not to be achieved. Therefore equality of opportunity is not to be achieved.

7. If terrorists' demands are met, then lawlessness will be rewarded. If terrorists' demands are not met, then innocent hostages will be

murdered. So either lawlessness will be rewarded or innocent hostages will be murdered.

8. If people are entirely rational, then either all of a person's actions can be predicted in advance or the universe is essentially deterministic. Not all of a person's actions can be predicted in advance. Thus, if the universe is not essentially deterministic, then people are not entirely rational.

9. If oil consumption continues to grow, then either oil imports will increase or domestic oil reserves will be depleted. If oil imports increase and domestic oil reserves are depleted, then the nation eventually will go bankrupt. Therefore, if oil consumption continues to grow, then the nation eventually will go bankrupt.

*10. If oil consumption continues to grow, then oil imports will increase and domestic oil reserves will be depleted. If either oil imports increase or domestic oil reserves are depleted, then the nation will soon be bankrupt. Therefore, if oil consumption continues to grow, then the nation will soon be bankrupt.

8.8 Statement Forms and Material Equivalence

A. STATEMENT FORMS AND STATEMENTS

We now make explicit a notion that was tacitly assumed in the preceding section, the notion of a *statement form*. There is an exact parallel between the relation of argument to argument form, on the one hand, and the relation of statement to statement form, on the other. The definition of a statement form makes this evident: A **statement form** is any sequence of symbols containing statement variables but no statements, such that when statements are substituted for the statement variables—the same statement being substituted for the same statement variable throughout—the result is a statement. Thus $p \vee q$ is a statement form, because when statements are substituted for the variables p and q, a statement results. The resulting statement is a disjunction, so $p \vee q$ is called a **disjunctive statement form.** Analogously, $p \bullet q$ and $p \supset q$ are called *conjunctive* and *conditional statement forms*, and $\sim p$ is called a *negation form* or *denial form*. Just as any argument of a certain form is said to be a substitution instance of that argument form, so any statement of a certain form is said to be a *substitution instance* of that statement form. And just as we distinguished the *specific form* of a given argument, so we distinguish the **specific form** of a given statement as that statement form from which the statement results by substituting consistently a different simple statement for each different statement variable. Thus $p \vee q$ is the *specific form* of the statement, "The blind prisoner has a red hat or the blind prisoner has a white hat."

B. TAUTOLOGOUS, CONTRADICTORY, AND CONTINGENT STATEMENT FORMS

The statement, "Lincoln was assassinated" (symbolized as *L*), and the statement, "Either Lincoln was assassinated or else he wasn't" (symbolized as $L \vee \sim L$), are both obviously true. But, we would say, they are true "in different ways" or have "different kinds" of truth. Similarly, the statement, "Washington was assassinated" (symbolized as *W*), and the statement "Washington was both assassinated and not assassinated" (symbolized as $W \bullet \sim W$), are both plainly false—but they also are false "in different ways" or have "different kinds" of falsehood. These differences in the "kinds" of truth or of falsehood are important and very great.

That the statement *L* is true, and that the statement *W* is false, are historical facts—facts about the way events did happen. There is no logical necessity about them. Events might have occurred differently, and therefore the truth values of such statements as *L* and *W* must be discovered by an empirical study of history. But the statement $L \vee \sim L$, although true, is not a truth of history. There is logical necessity here: Events could not have been such as to make it false, and its truth can be known independently of any particular empirical investigation. The statement $L \vee \sim L$ is a logical truth, a formal truth, true in virtue of its form alone. It is a substitution instance of a statement form all of whose substitution instances are true statements.

A statement form that has only true substitution instances is called a *tautologous statement form*, or a **tautology.** To show that the statement form $p \vee \sim p$ is a tautology, we construct the following truth table:

p	$\sim p$	$p \vee \sim p$
T	F	T
F	T	T

There is only one initial or guide column to this truth table, because the form we are considering contains only one statement variable. Consequently, there are only two rows, which represent all possible substitution instances. There are only **T**'s in the column under the statement form in question, and this fact shows that all of its substitution instances are true. Any statement that is a substitution instance of a tautologous statement form is true in virtue of its form, and is itself said to be tautologous, or a tautology.

A statement form that has only false substitution instances is said to be **self-contradictory,** or a **contradiction,** and is logically false. The statement form $p \bullet \sim p$

is self-contradictory, because only **F**'s occur under it in its truth table, signifying that all of its substitution instances are false. Any statement, such as $W \bullet {\sim}W$, which is a substitution instance of a self-contradictory statement form, is false in virtue of its form and is itself said to be self-contradictory, or a contradiction.

Statement forms that have both true and false statements among their substitution instances are called **contingent statement forms.** Any statement whose specific form is contingent is called a "*contingent statement*."* Thus p, ${\sim}p$, $p \bullet q$, $p \vee q$, and $p \supset q$ are all contingent statement forms. And such statements as L, ${\sim}L$, $L \bullet W$, $L \vee W$, and $L \supset W$ are contingent statements, because their truth values are dependent or contingent on their contents rather than on their forms alone.

Not all statement forms are so obviously tautological or self-contradictory or contingent as the simple examples cited. For example, the statement form $[(p \supset q) \supset p] \supset p$ is not at all obvious, though its truth table will show it to be a tautology. It even has a special name, *Peirce's law*.

C. MATERIAL EQUIVALENCE

Material equivalence is a truth-functional connective, just as disjunction and material implication are truth-functional connectives. The truth value of any truth-functional connective, as explained earlier, depends on (is a function of) the truth or falsity of the statements it connects. Thus, we say that the disjunction of A and B is true if either A is true or B is true or if they are both true. **Material equivalence** is the truth-functional connective that asserts that the statements it connects have the *same* truth value. Two statements that are equivalent in truth value, therefore, are materially equivalent. One straightforward definition is this: Two statements are *materially equivalent* when they are both true, or both false.

Just as the symbol for disjunction is the wedge, and the symbol for material implication is the horseshoe, there is also a special symbol for material equivalence, the three-bar sign "≡." And just as we gave truth-table definitions for the wedge and the horseshoe, we can do so for the three-bar sign, or **tribar.** Here is the truth table for material equivalence, "≡":

p	q	$p \equiv q$
T	T	T
T	F	F
F	T	F
F	F	T

*It will be recalled that we are assuming here that no simple statements are either logically true or logically false. Only contingent simple statements are admitted here. See footnote, on page 342.

Any two true statements materially imply one another; that is a consequence of the meaning of material implication. And any two false statements also materially imply one another. Therefore any two statements that are materially equivalent must imply one another, because they are either both true or both false.

Any two statements, A and B, that are materially equivalent imply one another, so we may infer from their material equivalence that B is true *if* A is true, and also that B is true *only if* A is true. Because both of these relations are entailed by material equivalence, we can read the three-bar sign, $\equiv$, to say *"if and only if."*

In everyday discourse we use this logical relation only occasionally. I will go to the championship game, one may say, if and only if I can acquire a ticket. I will go *if* I do acquire a ticket, but I can go *only if* I acquire a ticket. So my going to the game, and my acquiring a ticket to the game, are materially equivalent.

Every implication is a *conditional* statement, as we noted earlier. Two statements, A and B, that are materially equivalent entail the truth of the conditional $A \supset B$, and also entail the truth of the conditional $B \supset A$. Because the implication goes both ways when material equivalence holds, a statement of the form $A \equiv B$ is often called a **biconditional.**

There are four truth-functional connectives on which deductive arguments commonly depend: *conjunction, disjunction, material implication,* and *material equivalence*. Our discussion of the four is now complete.

OVERVIEW

The Four Truth-Functional Connectives

Truth-Functional Connective	Symbol (Name of Symbol)	Proposition Type	Names of Components of Propositions of That Type	Example
And	• (dot)	Conjunction	Conjuncts	Carol is mean and Bob sings the blues. $C \bullet B$
Or	∨ (wedge)	Disjunction	Disjuncts	Carol is mean **or** Tyrell is a music lover. $C \vee T$
If . . . then	⊃ (horseshoe)	Conditional	Antecedent, Consequent	**If** Bob sings the blues, **then** Myrna gets moody. $B \supset M$
If and only if	≡ (tribar)	Biconditional	Components	Myrna gets moody **if and only if** Bob sings the blues. $M \equiv B$

Note: "Not" is not a connective, but is a truth-function operator, so it is omitted here.

D. ARGUMENTS, CONDITIONAL STATEMENTS, AND TAUTOLOGIES

To every argument there corresponds a conditional statement whose antecedent is the conjunction of the argument's premises and whose consequent is the argument's conclusion. Thus, an argument having the form of *Modus Ponens,*

$p \supset q$

p

$\therefore q$

may be expressed as a conditional statement of the form $[(p \supset q) \bullet p] \supset q$. If the argument expressed as a conditional has a valid argument form, then its conclusion must in every case follow from its premises, and therefore the conditional statement of it may be shown on a truth table to be a tautology. That is, the statement that the conjunction of the premises implies the conclusion will (if the argument is valid) have all and only true instances.

Truth tables are powerful devices for the evaluation of arguments. An argument form is valid if and only if its truth table has a **T** under the conclusion in every row in which there are **T**'s under all of its premises. This follows from the precise meaning of *validity*. Now, if the conditional statement expressing that argument form is made the heading of one column of the truth table, an **F** can occur in that column only in a row in which there are **T**'s under all the premises and an **F** under the conclusion. But there will be no such row if the argument is valid. Hence only **T**'s will occur under a conditional statement that corresponds to a valid argument, and that conditional statement *must* be a tautology. We may therefore say that an argument form is valid if, and only if, its expression in the form of a conditional statement (of which the antecedent is the conjunction of the premises of the given argument form, and the consequent is the conclusion of the given argument form) is a tautology.

For every *invalid* argument of the truth-functional variety, however, the corresponding conditional statement will not be a tautology. The statement that the conjunction of its premises implies its conclusion is (for an invalid argument) either contingent or contradictory.

EXERCISES

A. For each statement in the left-hand column, indicate which, if any, of the statement forms in the right-hand column have the given statement as a substitution instance, and indicate which, if any, is the specific form of the given statement.

1. $A \vee B$
2. $C \bullet {\sim}D$
3. ${\sim}E \supset (F \bullet G)$
4. $H \supset (I \bullet J)$
*5. $(K \bullet L) \vee (M \bullet N)$
6. $(O \vee P) \supset (P \bullet Q)$
7. $(R \supset S) \vee (T \bullet {\sim}U)$
8. $V \supset (W \vee {\sim}W)$
9. $[(X \supset Y) \supset X] \supset X$
*10. $Z \equiv {\sim}{\sim}Z$

a. $p \bullet q$
b. $p \supset q$
c. $p \vee q$
d. $p \bullet {\sim}q$
e. $p \equiv q$
f. $(p \supset q) \vee (r \bullet s)$
g. $[(p \supset q) \supset r] \supset s$
h. $[(p \supset q) \supset p] \supset p$
i. $(p \bullet q) \vee (r \bullet s)$
j. $p \supset (q \vee {\sim}r)$

B. Use truth tables to characterize the following statement forms as tautologous, self-contradictory, or contingent.

*1. $[p \supset (p \supset q)] \supset q$
2. $p \supset [(p \supset q) \supset q]$
3. $(p \bullet q) \bullet (p \supset {\sim}q)$
4. $p \supset [{\sim}p \supset (q \vee {\sim}q)]$
*5. $p \supset [p \supset (q \bullet {\sim}q)]$
6. $(p \supset p) \supset (q \bullet {\sim}q)$
7. $[p \supset (q \supset r)] \supset [(p \supset q) \supset (p \supset r)]$
8. $[p \supset (q \supset p)] \supset [(q \supset q) \supset {\sim}(r \supset r)]$
9. $\{[(p \supset q) \bullet (r \supset s)] \bullet (p \vee r)\} \supset (q \vee s)$
10. $\{[(p \supset q) \bullet (r \supset s)] \bullet (q \vee s)\} \supset (p \vee r)$

C. Use truth tables to decide which of the following biconditionals are tautologies.

*1. $(p \supset q) \equiv ({\sim}q \supset {\sim}p)$
2. $(p \supset q) \equiv ({\sim}p \supset {\sim}q)$
3. $[(p \supset q) \supset r] \equiv [(q \supset p) \supset r]$
4. $[p \supset (q \supset r)] \equiv [q \supset (p \supset r)]$
*5. $p \equiv [p \bullet (p \vee q)]$
6. $p \equiv [p \vee (p \bullet q)]$
7. $p \equiv [p \bullet (p \supset q)]$
8. $p \equiv [p \bullet (q \supset p)]$
9. $p \equiv [p \vee (p \supset q)]$
*10. $(p \supset q) \equiv [(p \vee q) \equiv q]$
11. $p \equiv [p \vee (q \bullet {\sim}q)]$
12. $p \equiv [p \bullet (q \bullet {\sim}q)]$
13. $p \equiv [p \bullet (q \vee {\sim}q)]$
14. $p \equiv [p \vee (q \vee {\sim}q)]$
*15. $[p \bullet (q \vee r)] \equiv [(p \bullet q) \vee (p \bullet r)]$
16. $[p \bullet (q \vee r)] \equiv [(p \vee q) \bullet (p \vee r)]$
17. $[p \vee (q \bullet r)] \equiv [(p \bullet q) \vee (p \bullet r)]$
18. $[p \vee (q \bullet r)] \equiv [(p \vee q) \bullet (p \vee r)]$
19. $[(p \bullet q) \supset r] \equiv [p \supset (q \supset r)]$
*20. $[(p \supset q) \bullet (q \supset p)] \equiv [(p \bullet q) \vee ({\sim}p \bullet {\sim}q)]$

8.9 Logical Equivalence

At this point we introduce a new relation, important and very useful, but not a connective, and somewhat more complicated than any of the truth-functional connectives just discussed.

Statements are materially equivalent when they have the same truth value. Because two materially equivalent statements are either both true, or both false, we can readily see that they must (materially) imply one another, because a false antecedent (materially) implies any statement, and a true consequent is (materially) implied by any statement. We may therefore read the three-bar sign, $\equiv$, as "if and only if."

However, statements that are materially equivalent most certainly cannot be substituted for one another. Knowing that they are materially equivalent, we know only that their truth values are the same. The statements, "Jupiter is larger than the Earth" and "Tokyo is the capital of Japan," are materially equivalent because they are both true, but we obviously cannot replace one with the other. Similarly, the statements, "All spiders are poisonous" and "No spiders are poisonous," are materially equivalent simply because they are both false, and they certainly cannot replace one another!

There are many circumstances, however, in which we must express the relationship that does permit mutual replacement. Two statements can be equivalent in a sense much stronger than that of material equivalence; they may be equivalent in *meaning* as well as having the same truth value. If they do have the same meaning, any proposition that incorporates one of them can just as well incorporate the other; there will not be—there cannot be—any case in which one of these statements is true while the other is false. Statements that are equivalent in this very strong sense are called *logically equivalent*.

Of course, any two statements that are logically equivalent are materially equivalent as well, for they obviously have the same truth value. Indeed, if two statements are logically equivalent, they are materially equivalent under *all* circumstances—and this explains the short but powerful definition of **logical equivalence:** *Two statements are logically equivalent if the statement of their material equivalence is a tautology.* That is, the statement that they have the same truth value is itself necessarily true. And this is why, to express this very strong logical relationship, we use the three-bar symbol with a small **T** immediately above it, $\overset{T}{\equiv}$, indicating that the logical relationship is of such a nature that the material equivalence of the two statements is a tautology. And because material equivalence is a biconditional (the two statements implying one another), we may think of this symbol of logical equivalence, $\overset{T}{\equiv}$, as expressing a tautological biconditional.

Some simple logical equivalences that are very commonly used will make this relation, and its great power, very clear. It is a commonplace that p and $\sim\sim p$ mean the same thing; "he is aware of that difficulty" and "he is not unaware of that difficulty" are two statements with the same content. In substance, either of these expressions may be replaced by the other because they both say the same thing. This principle of **double negation,** whose truth is obvious to all, may be exhibited in a truth table, where the material equivalence of two statement forms is shown to be a tautology:

p	$\sim p$	$\sim\sim p$	$p \overset{T}{\equiv} \sim\sim p$
T	F	T	T
F	T	F	T

This truth table proves that p and $\sim\sim p$ are *logically equivalent*. This very useful logical equivalence, double negation, is symbolized as

$$p \overset{T}{\equiv} \sim\sim p$$

The difference between *material equivalence* on the one hand and *logical equivalence* on the other hand is very great and very important. The former is a truth-functional connective, $\equiv$, which may be true or false depending only on the truth or falsity of the elements it connects. But the latter, logical equivalence, $\overset{T}{\equiv}$, is not a mere connective, and it expresses a relation between two statements that is not truth-functional. Two statements are logically equivalent only when it is absolutely impossible for them to have different truth values. But if they *always* have the same truth value, logically equivalent statements must have the same meaning, and in that case they may be substituted for one another in any truth-functional context without changing the truth value of that context. By contrast, two statements are materially equivalent if they merely *happen* to have the same truth value, even if there are no factual connections between them. Statements that are merely materially equivalent certainly may not be substituted for one another!

There are two well-known logical equivalences (that is, logically true biconditionals) of great importance because they express the interrelations among conjunction and disjunction, and their negations. Let us examine these two logical equivalences more closely.

First, what will serve to deny that a disjunction is true? Any disjunction $p \vee q$ asserts no more than that at least one of its two disjuncts is true. One cannot contradict it by asserting that at least one is false; we must (to deny it) assert that both disjuncts are false. Therefore, asserting the *negation of the disjunction* $(p \vee q)$ is logically equivalent to asserting the *conjunction of the negations of p and of q*. To show this in a truth table, we may formulate the biconditional, $\sim(p \vee q) \equiv (\sim p \bullet \sim q)$, place it at the top of its own column, and examine its truth value under all circumstances, that is, in each row.

p	q	p ∨ q	~(p ∨ q)	~p	~q	~p • ~q	~(p ∨ q) ≡ (~p • ~q)
T	T	T	F	F	F	F	T
T	F	T	F	F	T	F	T
F	T	T	F	T	F	F	T
F	F	F	T	T	T	T	T

Of course we see that, whatever the truth values of p and of q, this biconditional must always be true. It is a tautology. Because the statement of that material equivalence *is* a tautology, we conclude that the two statements are logically equivalent. We have proved that

$$\sim(p \vee q) \overset{T}{\equiv} (\sim p \bullet \sim q)$$

Similarly, asserting the conjunction of p and q asserts that both are true, so to contradict this assertion we need merely assert that at least one is false. Thus, asserting the negation of the conjunction, $(p \bullet q)$, is logically equivalent to asserting the disjunction of the negations of p and of q. In symbols, the biconditional, $\sim(p \bullet q) \equiv (\sim p \vee \sim q)$ may be shown, in a truth table, to be a tautology. Such a table proves that

$$\sim(p \bullet q) \overset{T}{\equiv} (\sim p \vee \sim q)$$

These two tautologous biconditionals, or logical equivalences, are known as De Morgan's theorems, because they were formally stated by the mathematician and logician Augustus De Morgan (1806–1871). **De Morgan's theorems** can be formulated in English thus:

a. The negation of the disjunction of two statements is logically equivalent to the conjunction of the negations of the two statements;

and

b. The negation of the conjunction of two statements is logically equivalent to the disjunction of the negations of the two statements.

These theorems of De Morgan are exceedingly useful.

Another important logical equivalence is very helpful when we seek to manipulate truth-functional connectives. Material implication, ⊃, was defined in Section 8.3) as an abbreviated way of saying $\sim(p \bullet \sim q)$. That is, "p materially implies q" simply means, by definition, that it is not the case that p is true while q is false. In this definition we see that the *definiens*, $\sim(p \bullet \sim q)$, is the denial of a conjunction. And by De Morgan's theorem we know that any such denial is logically equivalent to the disjunction of the denials of the conjuncts; that is, we know that $\sim(p \bullet \sim q)$ is logically equivalent to $(\sim p \vee \sim\sim q)$; and this expression in turn, applying the principle of double negation, is logically equivalent to $\sim p \vee q$. Logically equivalent expressions mean the same thing, and therefore the original *definiens* of the horseshoe, $\sim(p \bullet \sim q)$, may be replaced with no change of meaning by the simpler expression $\sim p \vee q$. This gives us a very useful definition of material implication: $p \supset q$ *is logically equivalent to* $\sim p \vee q$. In symbols we write:

$$(p \supset q) \stackrel{T}{\equiv} (\sim p \vee q)$$

This definition of material implication is widely relied on in the formulation of logical statements and the analysis of arguments. Manipulation is often essential, and manipulation is more efficient when the statements we are working with have the same central connective. With the simple definition of the horseshoe we have just established, $(p \supset q) \stackrel{T}{\equiv} (\sim p \vee q)$, statements in which the horseshoe is the connective can be conveniently replaced by statements in which the wedge is the connective; and likewise, statements in disjunctive form may be readily replaced by statements in implicative form. When we seek to present a formal proof of the validity of deductive arguments, replacements of this kind are very useful indeed.

Before going on to the methods of testing for validity and invalidity in the next section, it is worthwhile to pause for a more thorough consideration of the meaning of material implication. Implication is central in argument but, as we noted earlier, the word "implies" is highly ambiguous. *Material* implication, on which we rely in this analysis, is only one sense of that word, although it is a very important sense, of course. The definition of material implication explained just above makes it clear that when we say, in this important sense, that "p implies q," we are saying no more than that "either q is true or p is false."

Asserting the "if–then" relation in this sense has consequences that may *seem* paradoxical. For in this sense we can say, *correctly*, "If a statement is true, then it is implied by any statement whatever." Because it is true that the earth is round, it follows that "The moon is made of green cheese implies that the earth is round." This appears to be very curious, especially because it also follows that "The moon is *not* made of green cheese implies that the earth is round." Our precise understanding of material implication also entitles us to say, *correctly*, "If a statement is false, then it implies any statement whatever." Because it is false that the moon is made of green cheese, it follows that "The moon is made of green cheese implies that the earth is round;" and this is the more curious when we realize that it also follows that "The moon is made of green cheese implies that the earth is *not* round."

Why do these true statements seem so curious? It is because we recognize that the shape of the earth and the cheesiness of the moon are utterly irrelevant to each other. As we normally use the word "implies," a statement cannot imply some other statement, false or true, to which it is utterly irrelevant. That is the case when "implies" is used in most of its everyday senses. And yet those "paradoxical" statements in the preceding paragraph are indeed true, and not really problematic at all, because they use the word "implies" in the logical sense of "material implication." The precise meaning of material implication we have made very clear; we understand that to say p materially implies q is only to say that either p is false or q is true.

What needs to be borne in mind is this: *Meaning*—subject matter—is strictly irrelevant to material implication. *Material implication is a truth function*. Only the truth and falsity of the antecedent and the consequent, not their content, are relevant here. There is nothing paradoxical in stating that any disjunction is true that contains one true disjunct. Well, when we say that "The moon is made of green cheese (materially) implies that the earth is round," we know that to be logically equivalent to saying "Either the moon is not made of green cheese or the earth is round"—a disjunction that is most certainly true. And any disjunction we may confront in which "The moon is not made of green cheese" is the first disjunct will certainly be true, no matter what the second disjunct asserts. So, yes, "The moon is made of green cheese (materially) implies that the earth is square" because that is logically equivalent to "The moon is not made of green cheese or the earth is square." A false statement materially implies any statement whatever. A true statement is materially implied by any statement whatever.

Every occurrence of "if–then" should be treated, we have said, as a material implication, and represented with the horseshoe, $\supset$. The justification of this practice, its logical expediency, is the fact that doing so preserves the validity of all valid arguments of the type with which we are concerned in this part of our logical studies. Other symbolizations have been proposed, adequate to other types of implication, but they belong to more advanced parts of logic, beyond the scope of this book.

8.10 The Three "Laws of Thought"

Some early thinkers, after having defined logic as "the science of the laws of thought," went on to assert that there are exactly three *basic* laws of thought, laws so fundamental that obedience to them is both the necessary and the sufficient condition of correct thinking. These three have traditionally been called:

- The **principle of identity.** This principle asserts that *if any statement is true, then it is true.* Using our notation we may rephrase it by saying that the principle of identity asserts that every statement of the form $p \supset p$ must be true, that every such statement is a tautology.
- The **principle of noncontradiction.** This principle asserts that *no statement can be both true and false.* Using our notation we may rephrase it by saying that the principle of noncontradiction asserts that every statement of the form $p \bullet {\sim}p$ must be false, that every such statement is self-contradictory.
- The **principle of excluded middle.** This principle asserts that *every statement is either true or false.* Using our notation we may rephrase it by saying that the principle of excluded middle asserts that every statement of the form $p \vee {\sim}p$ must be true, that every such statement is a tautology.

It is obvious that these three principles are indeed true—logically true—but the claim that they deserve privileged status as the most fundamental laws of thought is doubtful. The first (identity) and the third (excluded middle) are tautologies, but there are many other tautologous forms whose truth is equally certain. And the second (noncontradiction) is by no means the only self-contradictory form of statement.

We do use these principles in completing truth tables. In the initial columns of each row of a table we place either a **T** or an **F**, being guided by the principle of excluded middle. Nowhere do we put both **T** and **F**, being guided by the principle of noncontradiction. And once having put a **T** under a symbol in a given row, then (being guided by the principle of identity) when we encounter that symbol in other columns of that row, we regard it as still being assigned a **T**. So we could regard the three laws of thought as principles governing the construction of truth tables.

Nevertheless, in regarding the entire system of deductive logic, these three principles are no more important or fruitful than many others. Indeed, there are tautologies that are more fruitful than they for purposes of deduction, and in that sense more important than these three. A more extended treatment of this point lies beyond the scope of this book.[7]

Some thinkers, believing themselves to have devised a new and different logic, have claimed that these three principles are in fact not true, and that obedience to them has been needlessly confining. But these criticisms have been based on misunderstandings.

The principle of identity has been attacked on the ground that things change, and are always changing. Thus, for example, statements that were true of the United States when it consisted of the thirteen original states are no longer true of the United States today, which has fifty states. But this does not undermine the principle of identity. The sentence, "There are only thirteen states in the United States," is incomplete, an elliptical formulation of the statement that "There were only thirteen states in the United States *in 1790*"—and that statement is as true today as it was in 1790. When we confine our attention to complete, nonelliptical formulations of propositions, we see that their truth (or falsity) does not change over time. The principle of identity is true, and it does not interfere with our recognition of continuing change.

The principle of noncontradiction has been attacked by Hegelians and Marxists on the grounds that genuine contradiction is everywhere pervasive, that the world is replete with the inevitable conflict of contradictory forces. That there are conflicting forces in the real word is true, of course—but to call these conflicting forces "contradictory" is a loose and misleading use of that term. Labor unions and the private owners of industrial plants may indeed find themselves in conflict—but neither the owner nor the union is the "negation" or the "denial" or the "contradictory" of the other. The principle of noncontradiction, understood in the straightforward sense in which it is intended by logicians, is unobjectionable and perfectly true.

The principle of excluded middle has been the object of much criticism, on the grounds that it leads to a "two-valued orientation," which implies that things in the world must be either "white or black," and which thereby hinders the realization of compromise and less than absolute gradations. This objection also arises from misunderstanding. Of course the statement "This is black" cannot be jointly true with the statement "This is white"—where "this" refers to exactly the same thing. But although these two statements cannot both be true, they can both be false. "This" may be neither black nor white; the two statements are *contraries*, not contradictory. The contradictory of the statement "This is white" is the statement "It is not the case that this is white" and (if "white" is used in precisely the same sense in both of these statements) one of them must be true and the other false. The principle of excluded middle is inescapable.

All three of these "laws of thought" are unobjectionable—so long as they are applied to statements containing unambiguous, nonelliptical, and precise terms. They may not deserve the honorific status assigned to them by some philosophers,* but they are indubitably true.

---

*Plato appealed explicitly to the principle of noncontradiction in Book IV of his *Republic* (at nos. 436 and 439); Aristotle discussed all three of these principles in Books IV and XI of his *Metaphysics*. Of the principle of noncontradiction, Aristotle wrote: "That the same attribute cannot at the same time belong and not belong to the same subject and in the same respect" is a principle "which everyone must have who understands anything that is," and which "everyone must already have when he comes to a special study." It is, he concluded, "the most certain of all principles."

SUMMARY

This chapter has presented the fundamental concepts of modern symbolic logic.

In Section 8.1, we explained the general approach of modern symbolic logic, and its need for an artificial symbolic language.

In Section 8.2, we introduced and defined the symbols for negation (the curl: ~); and for the truth-functional connectives of conjunction (the dot: •) and disjunction (the wedge: ∨). We also explained logical punctuation.

In Section 8.3, we discussed the different senses of implication, and defined the truth-functional connective material implication (the horseshoe: ⊃).

In Section 8.4, we explained the formal structure of arguments, defined argument forms, and explained other concepts essential in analyzing deductive arguments.

In Section 8.5, we gave a precise account of valid and invalid argument forms.

In Section 8.6, we explained the truth-table method of testing the validity of argument forms.

In Section 8.7, we identified and described a few very common argument forms, some valid and some invalid.

In Section 8.8, we explained the formal structure of statements and defined essential terms for dealing with statement forms. We introduced tautologous, contradictory, and contingent statement forms, and defined a fourth truth-functional connective, material equivalence (three bars: ≡).

In Section 8.9, we introduced and defined a powerful new relation, logical equivalence, using the symbol $\stackrel{T}{\equiv}$. We explained why statements that are logically equivalent may be substituted for one another, while statements that are merely materially equivalent cannot replace one another. We introduced several logical equivalences of special importance: De Morgan's theorems, the principle of double negation, and the definition of material implication.

In Section 8.10, we discussed certain logical equivalences that have been thought by many to be fundamental in all reasoning: the principle of identity, the principle of noncontradiction, and the principle of the excluded middle.

End Notes

[1]Somewhat more complicated definitions have been proposed by David H. Sanford in "What Is a Truth Functional Component?" *Logique et Analyse* 14 (1970): 483–486.

[2]Ted Turner, quoted in *The New Yorker*, 30 April 2001.

[3]"The Firm" *The New Yorker*, 8 March 1999.

[4]Peter J. Bertocci, "Chavez' Plight Must Come from Arrogance," *The New York Times*, 19 January 2001.

[5]Rabbi Ammiel Hirsch, "Grand Canyon," *The New York Times*, 10 October 2005.

[6]Orlando Patterson, "The Speech Misheard Round the World," *The New York Times*, 22 January 2005. Mr. Patterson's wording of the syllogism is very slightly different but has exactly the same logical force.

[7]For further discussion of these matters, the interested reader can consult I. M. Copi and J. A. Gould, eds., *Readings on Logic*, 2d ed. (New York: Macmillan, 1972), part 2; and I. M. Copi and J. A. Gould, eds., *Contemporary Philosophical Logic* (New York: St. Martin's Press, 1978), part 8.

Methods of Deduction

9.1 Formal Proof of Validity

In theory, truth tables are adequate to test the validity of any argument of the general type we have considered. In practice, however, they become unwieldy as the number of component statements increases. A more efficient method of establishing the validity of an extended argument is to deduce its conclusion from its premises by a sequence of elementary arguments, each of which is known to be valid. This technique accords fairly well with ordinary methods of argumentation.

Consider, for example, the following argument:

If Anderson was nominated, then she went to Boston.

If she went to Boston, then she campaigned there.

If she campaigned there, she met Douglas.

Anderson did not meet Douglas.

Either Anderson was nominated or someone more eligible was selected.

Therefore someone more eligible was selected.

The validity of this argument may be intuitively obvious, but let us consider the matter of proof. The discussion will be facilitated by translating the argument into symbolism as

$A \supset B$

$B \supset C$

$C \supset D$

$\sim D$

$A \vee E$

$\therefore E$

To establish the validity of this argument by means of a truth table requires a table with thirty-two rows, because five different simple statements are involved. We can prove the argument valid by deducing its conclusion instead using a sequence of just four elementary valid arguments. From the first two premises, $A \supset B$ and $B \supset C$, we validly infer that $A \supset C$ as a Hypothetical Syllogism. From $A \supset C$ and the third premise, $C \supset D$, we validly infer that $A \supset D$ as another Hypothetical Syllogism. From $A \supset D$ and the fourth premise, $\sim D$, we validly infer that $\sim A$ by *Modus Tollens*. And from $\sim A$ and the fifth premise, $A \vee E$, as a Disjunctive Syllogism we validly infer E, the conclusion of the original argument. That the conclusion can be deduced from the five premises of the original argument by four elementary valid arguments proves the original argument to be valid. Here the elementary valid argument forms Hypothetical Syllogism (H.S.), *Modus Tollens* (M.T.), and Disjunctive Syllogism (D.S.) are used as **rules of inference** in accordance with which conclusions are validly inferred or deduced from premises.

This method of deriving the conclusion of a deductive argument—using rules of inference successively to prove the validity of the argument—is as reliable as the truth-table method discussed in Chapter 8, if the rules are used with meticulous care. But it improves on the truth-table method in two ways: It is vastly more efficient, as has just been shown; and it enables us to follow the flow of the reasoning process from the premises to the conclusion and is therefore much more intuitive and more illuminating. The method is often called **natural deduction.** Using natural deduction, we can provide a *formal proof* of the validity of an argument that is valid.

A *formal proof of validity* is given by writing the premises and the statements that we deduce from them in a single column, and setting off in another column, to the right of each such statement, its "justification," or the reason we give for including it in the proof. It is convenient to list all the premises first and to write the conclusion either on a separate line, or slightly to one side and separated by a diagonal line from the premises. If all the statements in the column are numbered, the "justification" for each statement consists of the numbers of the preceding statements from which it is inferred, together with the abbreviation for the rule of inference by which it follows from them. The formal proof of the example argument is written as

1.	$A \supset B$	
2.	$B \supset C$	
3.	$C \supset D$	
4.	$\sim D$	
5.	$A \vee E$	
	$\therefore E$	
6.	$A \supset C$	1, 2, H.S.
7.	$A \supset D$	6, 3, H.S.
8.	$\sim A$	7, 4, M.T.
9.	E	5, 8, D.S.

We define a **formal proof of validity** of a given argument as a *sequence of statements, each of which is either a premise of that argument or follows from preceding statements of the sequence by an elementary valid argument, such that the last statement in the sequence is the conclusion of the argument whose validity is being proved.*

We define an **elementary valid argument** as *any argument that is a substitution instance of an elementary valid argument form.* Note that *any* substitution instance of an elementary valid argument form is an elementary valid argument. Thus the argument

$(A \bullet B) \supset [C \equiv (D \vee E)]$

$A \bullet B$

$\therefore C \equiv (D \vee E)$

is an elementary valid argument because it is a substitution instance of the elementary valid argument form *Modus Ponens* (M.P.). It results from

$p \supset q$

p

$\therefore q$

by substituting $A \bullet B$ for p and $C \equiv (D \vee E)$ for q, and it is therefore of that form even though *modus ponens* is not *the specific form* of the given argument.

Modus Ponens is a very elementary valid argument form indeed, but what *other* valid argument forms are considered to be rules of inference? We begin with a list of just nine rules of inference that can be used in constructing formal proofs of validity. With their aid, formal proofs of validity can be constructed for a wide range of more complicated arguments. The names provided are for the most part standard, and the use of their abbreviations permits formal proofs to be set down with a minimum of writing.

9.2 The Elementary Valid Argument Forms

Our object is to build a set of logical rules—rules of inference—with which we can prove the validity of deductive arguments if they are valid. We began with a few elementary valid argument forms that have already been introduced—*Modus Ponens,* for example, and Disjunctive Syllogism. These are indeed simple and common. But we need a set of rules that is more powerful. The rules of inference may be thought of as a logical toolbox, from which the tools may be taken, as needed, to prove validity. What else is needed for our toolbox? How shall we expand the list of rules of inference?

The needed rules of inference consist of two sets, each set containing rules of a different kind. The first is a set of elementary valid argument forms. The second set consists of a small group of elementary logical equivalences. In this section we discuss only the elementary valid argument forms.

To this point we have become acquainted with four elementary valid argument forms:

1. *Modus Ponens (M.P.)*

$p \supset q$
p
$\therefore p$

2. *Modus Tollens (M.T.)*

$p \supset q$
$\sim q$
$\therefore \sim p$

3. Hypothetical Syllogism (H.S.)

$p \supset q$
$q \supset r$
$\therefore p \supset r$

4. Disjunctive Syllogism (D.S.).

$p \vee q$
$\sim p$
$\therefore q$

For an effective logical toolbox we need to add five more. Let us examine these additional argument forms—each of which is valid and can be readily proved valid using a truth table.

5. Rule 5 is called **Constructive Dilemma** (C.D.) It is symbolized as

$(p \supset q) \bullet (r \supset s)$

$p \vee r$

$\therefore q \vee s$

In general, a dilemma is an argument in which one of two alternatives must be chosen. In this argument form the alternatives are two conditional propositions,

$p \supset q$ and $r \supset s$. We know from *Modus Ponens* that if we are given $p \supset q$ and p, we may infer q; and if we are given $r \supset s$ and r, we may infer s. Therefore it is clear that if we are given *both* $p \supset q$, and $r \supset s$, and *either* p or r (that is, either of the antecedents), we may infer validly either q or s (that is, one or the other of the consequents.) Constructive Dilemma is, in effect, a combination of two arguments in *Modus Ponens* form, and it is most certainly valid, as a truth table can make evident. We add Constructive Dilemma (C.D.) to our tool box.

6. Absorption (Abs.)

$p \supset q$

$\therefore p \supset (p \bullet q)$

Any proposition p always implies itself, of course. Therefore, if we know that $p \supset q$, we may validly infer that p implies both itself and q. That is all that Absorption says. Why (one may ask) do we need so elementary a rule? The need for it will become clearer as we go on; in short, we need it because it will be very convenient, even essential at times, to carry the p across the horseshoe. In effect, Absorption makes the principle of identity, one of the basic logical principles discussed in Section 8.10, always available for our use. We add Absorption (Abs.) to our logical toolbox.

The next two elementary valid argument forms are intuitively very easy to grasp if we understand the logical connectives explained earlier.

7. Simplification (Simp.)

$p \bullet q$

$\therefore p$

says only that if two propositions, p and q, are true when they are conjoined $(p \bullet q)$, we may validly infer that one of them, p, is true by itself. We simplify the expression before us; we "pull" p from the conjunction and stand it on its own. Because we are given that $p \bullet q$, we know that both p and q must be true; we may therefore know with certainty that p is true.

What about q? Isn't q true for exactly the same reason? Yes, it is. Then why does the elementary argument form, Simplification, conclude only that p is true? The reason is that we want to keep our toolbox uncluttered. The rules of inference must always be applied *exactly* as they appear. We surely need a rule that will enable us to take conjunctions apart, but we do not need two such rules; one will suffice. When we may need to "pull" some q from a conjunction we will be able to put it where p is now, and then use only the one rule, Simplification, which we add to our toolbox.

8. Conjunction (Conj.)

p

q

$\therefore p \bullet q$

says only that if two propositions, *p,* and *q,* are known to be true, we can put them together into one conjunctive expression, $p \bullet q$. We may conjoin them. If they are true separately, they must also be true when they are conjoined. And in this case the order presents no problem, because we may always treat the one we seek to put on the left as *p,* and the other as *q.* That *joint* truth is what a conjunction asserts. We add Conjunction (Conj.) to our logical toolbox.

The last of the nine elementary valid argument forms is also a straightforward consequence of the meaning of the logical connectives—in this case, disjunction.

9. Addition (Add.)

p

$\therefore p \vee q$

We know that any disjunction must be true if either of its disjuncts is true. That is, $p \vee q$ is true if *p* is true, or if *q* is true, or if they are both true. That is what disjunction means. It obviously follows from this that if we know that some proposition, *p,* is true, we also know that *either* it is true or some other—any other!—proposition is true. So we can construct a disjunction, $p \vee q$, using the one proposition known to be true as *p,* and adding to it (in the logical, disjunctive sense) any proposition we care to. We call this logical addition. The additional proposition, *q,* is not conjoined to *p;* it is used with *p* to build a disjunction that we may know with certainty to be true because one of the disjuncts, *p,* is known to be true. And the disjunction we thus build will be true *no matter what that added proposition asserts*—no matter how absurd or wildly false it may be! We know that Michigan is north of Florida. Therefore we know that either Michigan is north of Florida *or* the moon is made of green cheese! Indeed, we know that either Michigan is north of Florida *or* $2 + 2 = 5$. The truth or falsity of the added proposition does not affect the truth of the disjunction we build, because that disjunction is made certainly true by the truth of the disjunct with which we began. Therefore, if we are given *p* as true, we may validly infer *for any q whatever* that $p \vee q$. This principle, Addition (Add.), we add to our logical toolbox.

Our set of nine elementary valid argument forms is now complete.

All nine of these argument forms are very plainly valid. Any one of them whose validity we may doubt can be readily proved to be valid using a truth table. Each of them is simple and intuitively clear; as a set we will find them powerful as we go on to construct formal proofs for the validity of more extended arguments.

OVERVIEW

Rules of Inferences: Elementary Valid Argument Forms

Name	Abbreviation	Form
1. *Modus Ponens*	M.P.	$p \supset q$ p $\therefore q$
2. *Modus Tollens*	M.T.	$p \supset q$ $\sim q$ $\therefore \sim p$
3. Hypothetical Syllogism	H.S.	$p \supset q$ $q \supset r$ $\therefore p \supset r$
4. Disjunctive Syllogism	D.S.	$p \vee q$ $\sim p$ $\therefore q$
5. Constructive Dilemma	C.D.	$(p \supset q) \bullet (r \supset s)$ $p \vee r$ $\therefore q \vee s$
6. Absorption	Abs.	$p \supset q$ $\therefore p \supset (p \bullet q)$
7. Simplification	Simp.	$p \bullet q$ $\therefore p$
8. Conjunction	Conj.	p q $\therefore p \bullet q$
9. Addition	Add.	p $\therefore p \vee q$

Two features of these elementary arguments must be emphasized. First, *they must be applied with exactitude.* An argument that one proves valid using *Modus Ponens* must have that exact form: $p \supset q$, p, therefore q. Each statement variable must be replaced by some statement (simple or compound) consistently and accurately. Thus, for example, if we are given $(C \vee D) \supset (J \vee K)$ and $(C \vee D)$, we may infer $(J \vee K)$ by *Modus Ponens.* But we may not infer $(K \vee J)$ by *Modus*

Ponens, even though it may be true. The elementary argument form must be fitted *precisely* to the argument with which we are working. No shortcut—no fudging of any kind—is permitted, because we seek to know with certainty that the outcome of our reasoning is valid, and that can be known only if we can demonstrate that *every link in the chain of our reasoning is absolutely solid.*

Second, these elementary valid arguments must be applied to *the entire lines* of the larger argument with which we are working. Thus, for example, if we are give $[(X \bullet Y) \supset Z] \bullet T$, we cannot validly infer X by Simplification. X is one of the conjuncts of a conjunction, but that conjunction is part of a more complex expression. X may not be true even if that more complex expression is true. We are given only that *if* X and Y are both true, then Z is true. Simplification applies only to the entire line, which must be a conjunction; its conclusion is the left side (and only the left side) of that conjunction. So, from this same line, $[(X \bullet Y) \supset Z)] \bullet T$, we may validly infer $(X \bullet Y) \supset Z$ by Simplification. But we may not infer T by Simplification, even though it may be true.

Formal proofs in deductive logic have crushing power, but they possess that power only because, when they are correct, there can be not the slightest doubt of the validity of each inference drawn. The tiniest gap destroys the power of the whole.

The nine elementary valid argument forms we have given should be committed to memory. They must be always readily in mind as we go on to construct formal proofs. Only if we comprehend these elementary argument forms fully, and can apply them immediately and accurately, may we expect to succeed in devising formal proofs of the validity of more extended arguments.

EXERCISES

Here follow a set of twenty elementary valid arguments. They are valid because each of them is exactly in the form of one of the nine elementary valid argument forms. For each of them, state the rule of inference by which its conclusion follows from its premise or premises.

EXAMPLE

1. $(A \bullet B) \supset C$

$\therefore (A \bullet B) \supset [(A \bullet B) \bullet C]$

SOLUTION

Absorption. If $(A \bullet B)$ replaces p, and C replaces q, this argument is seen to be exactly in the form $p \supset q$, therefore $p \supset (p \bullet q)$.

***1.** $(A \bullet B) \supset C$

$\therefore (A \bullet B) \supset [(A \bullet B) \bullet C]$

2. $(D \vee E) \bullet (F \vee G)$

$\therefore D \vee E$

3. $H \supset I$

$\therefore (H \supset I) \vee (H \supset {\sim}I)$

4. ${\sim}(J \bullet K) \bullet (L \supset {\sim}M)$

$\therefore {\sim}(J \bullet K)$

***5.** $[N \supset (O \bullet P)] \bullet [Q \supset (O \bullet R)]$

$N \vee Q$

$\therefore (O \bullet P) \vee (O \bullet R)$

6. $(X \vee Y) \supset {\sim}(Z \bullet {\sim}A)$

${\sim}{\sim}(Z \bullet {\sim}A)$

$\therefore {\sim}(X \vee Y)$

7. $(S \equiv T) \vee [(U \bullet V) \vee (U \bullet W)]$

${\sim}(S \equiv T)$

$\therefore (U \bullet V) \vee (U \bullet W)$

8. ${\sim}(B \bullet C) \supset (D \vee E)$

${\sim}(B \bullet C)$

$\therefore D \vee E$

9. $(F \equiv G) \supset {\sim}(G \bullet {\sim}F)$

${\sim}(G \bullet {\sim}F) \supset (G \supset F)$

$\therefore (F \equiv G) \supset (G \supset F)$

***10.** ${\sim}(H \bullet {\sim}I) \supset (H \supset I)$

$(I \equiv H) \supset {\sim}(H \bullet {\sim}I)$

$\therefore (I \equiv H) \supset (H \supset I)$

11. $(A \supset B) \supset (C \vee D)$

$A \supset B$

$\therefore C \vee D$

12. $[E \supset (F \equiv {\sim}G)] \vee (C \vee D)$

${\sim}[E \supset (F \equiv {\sim}G)]$

$\therefore C \vee D$

13. $(C \vee D) \supset [(J \vee K) \supset (J \bullet K)]$

${\sim}[(J \vee K) \supset (J \bullet K)]$

$\therefore {\sim}(C \vee D)$

14. ${\sim}[L \supset (M \supset N)] \supset {\sim}(C \vee D)$

${\sim}[L \supset (M \supset N)]$

$\therefore {\sim}(C \vee D)$

***15.** $(J \supset K) \bullet (K \supset L)$

$L \supset M$

$\therefore [(J \supset K) \bullet (K \supset L)] \bullet (L \supset M)$

16. $N \supset (O \vee P)$

$Q \supset (O \vee R)$

$\therefore [Q \supset (O \vee R)] \bullet [N \supset (O \vee P)]$

17. $(S \supset T) \supset (U \supset V)$

$\therefore (S \supset T) \supset [(S \supset T) \bullet (U \supset V)]$

18. $(W \bullet {\sim}X) \equiv (Y \supset Z)$

$\therefore [(W \bullet {\sim}X) \equiv (Y \supset Z)] \vee (X \equiv {\sim}Z)$

19. $[(H \bullet {\sim}I) \supset C] \bullet [(I \bullet {\sim}H) \supset D]$

$(H \bullet {\sim}I) \vee (I \bullet {\sim}H)$

$\therefore C \vee D$

***20.** $[(O \supset P) \supset Q] \supset {\sim}(C \vee D)$

$(C \vee D) \supset [(O \supset P) \supset Q]$

$\therefore (C \vee D) \supset {\sim}(C \vee D)$

9.3 Formal Proofs of Validity Exhibited

We have defined a formal proof of validity for a given argument as a sequence of statements, each of which is either a premise of that argument or follows from preceding statements of the sequence by an elementary valid argument, such that the last statement in the sequence is the conclusion of the argument whose validity is being proved. Our task will be to build such sequences, to prove the validity of arguments with which we are confronted.

Doing this can be a challenge. Before attempting to construct such sequences, it will be helpful to become familiar with the look and character of formal proofs. In this section we examine a number of complete formal proofs, to see how they work and to get a "feel" for constructing them.

Our first step is not to devise such proofs, but to understand and appreciate them. A sequence of statements is put before us in each case. Every statement in that sequence will be either a premise, or will follow from preceding statements in the sequence using one of the elementary valid argument forms—just as in the illustration that was presented in Section 9.1. When we confront such a proof, but the rule of inference that justifies each step in the proof is not given, we know (having been told that these are completed proofs) that every line in the proof that is not itself a premise can be deduced from the preceding lines. To understand those deductions, the nine elementary valid argument forms must be kept in mind.

Let us look at some proofs that exhibit this admirable solidity. Our first example is Exercise 1 in the set of exercises on pages 382–383.

EXAMPLE 1

1. $A \bullet B$
2. $(A \vee C) \supset D$

   $\therefore A \bullet D$
3. A
4. $A \vee C$
5. D
6. $A \bullet D$

The first two lines of this proof are seen to be premises, because they appear before the "therefore" symbol (∴); what appears immediately to the right of that symbol is the conclusion of this argument, $A \bullet D$. The very last line of the sequence is (as it must be if the formal proof is correct) that same conclusion, $A \bullet D$. What about the steps between the premises and the conclusion? Line 3, A, we can deduce from line 1, $A \bullet B$, by Simplification. So we put, to the right of line 3, the line number from which it comes and the rule by which it is inferred from that line, "1, Simp." Line 4 is $A \vee C$. How can that be inferred from the lines above it? We can*not* infer it from line 2 by Simplification. But we can infer it from line 3, A, by Addition. Addition tells us that if p is true, then $p \vee q$ is true, whatever q may be. Using that logical pattern precisely, we may infer from A that $A \vee C$ is true. To the right of line 4 we therefore put "3, Add." Line 5 is D. D appears in line 2 as the consequent of a conditional statement $(A \vee C) \supset D$. We proved on line 4 that $A \vee C$ is true; now, using *Modus Ponens,* we combine this with the conditional on line 2 to prove D. To the right of line 5 we therefore write "2, 4, M.P." *A* has been proved true (on line 3) and *D* has been proved true (on line 5). We may therefore validly conjoin them, which is what line 6 asserts: $A \bullet D$. To the right of line 6 we therefore write "3, 5, Conj." This line, $A \bullet D$, is the conclusion of the argument, and it is therefore the last statement in the sequence of statements that constitutes this proof. The proof, which had been presented to us complete, has thus been "fleshed out" by specifying the justification of each step within it.

In this example, and the exercises that follow, every line of each proof can be justified by using one of the elementary valid argument forms in our logical toolbox. No other inferences of any kind are permitted, however plausible they may seem. When we had occasion to refer to an argument form that has two premises (e.g., M.P. or D.S.), we indicated first, in the justification, the numbers of the lines used, *in the order in which they appear in the elementary valid form*. Thus, line 5 in Example 1 is justified by 2, 4, M.P.

To become proficient in the construction of formal proofs, we must become fully familiar with the shape and rhythm of the nine elementary argument forms—the first nine of the rules of inference that we will be using extensively.

EXERCISES

Each of the following exercises presents a flawless formal proof of validity for the indicated argument. For each, state the justification for each numbered line that is not a premise.

1.
1. $A \bullet B$
2. $(A \vee C) \supset D$
   $\therefore A \bullet D$
3. A
4. $A \vee C$
5. D
6. $A \bullet D$

2.
1. $(E \vee F) \bullet (G \vee H)$
2. $(E \supset G) \bullet (F \supset H)$
3. $\sim G$
   $\therefore H$
4. $E \vee F$
5. $G \vee H$
6. H

3.
1. $I \supset J$
2. $J \supset K$
3. $L \supset M$
4. $I \vee L$
   $\therefore K \vee M$
5. $I \supset K$
6. $(I \supset K) \bullet (L \supset M)$
7. $K \vee M$

4.
1. $N \supset O$
2. $(N \bullet O) \supset P$
3. $\sim(N \bullet P)$
   $\therefore \sim N$
4. $N \supset (N \bullet O)$
5. $N \supset P$
6. $N \supset (N \bullet P)$
7. $\sim N$

*5. 1. $Q \supset R$
2. $\sim S \supset (T \supset U)$
3. $S \lor (Q \lor T)$
4. $\sim S$
$\therefore R \lor U$
5. $T \supset U$
6. $(Q \supset R) \bullet (T \supset U)$
7. $Q \lor T$
8. $R \lor U$

6. 1. $W \supset X$
2. $(W \supset Y) \supset (Z \lor X)$
3. $(W \bullet X) \supset Y$
4. $\sim Z$
$\therefore X$
5. $W \supset (W \bullet X)$
6. $W \supset Y$
7. $Z \lor X$
8. X

7. 1. $(A \lor B) \supset C$
2. $(C \lor B) \supset [A \supset (D \equiv E)]$
3. $A \bullet D$
$\therefore D \equiv E$
4. A
5. $A \lor B$
6. C
7. $C \lor B$
8. $A \supset (D \equiv E)$
9. $D \equiv E$

8. 1. $F \supset \sim G$
2. $\sim F \supset (H \supset \sim G)$
3. $(\sim I \lor \sim H) \supset \sim\sim G$
4. $\sim I$
$\therefore \sim H$
5. $\sim I \lor \sim H$
6. $\sim\sim G$
7. $\sim F$
8. $H \supset \sim G$
9. $\sim H$

9. 1. $I \supset J$
2. $I \lor (\sim\sim K \bullet \sim\sim J)$
3. $L \supset \sim K$
4. $\sim(I \bullet J)$
$\therefore \sim L \lor \sim J$
5. $\supset (I \bullet J)$
6. $\sim I$
7. $\sim\sim K \bullet \sim\sim J$
8. $\sim\sim K$
9. $\sim L$
10. $\sim L \lor \sim J$

*10. 1. $(L \supset M) \supset (N \equiv O)$
2. $(P \supset \sim Q) \supset (M \equiv \sim Q)$
3. $\{[(P \supset \sim Q) \lor (R \equiv S)] \bullet$
$(N \lor O)\} \supset [(R \equiv S) \supset (L \supset M)]$
4. $(P \supset \sim Q) \lor (R \equiv S)$
5. $N \lor O$
$\therefore (M \equiv \sim Q) \lor (N \equiv O)$
6. $[(P \supset \sim Q) \lor (R \equiv S)] \bullet (N \lor O)$
7. $(R \equiv S) \supset (L \supset M)$
8. $(R \equiv S) \supset (N \equiv O)$
9. $[(P \supset \sim Q) \supset (M \equiv \sim Q)] \bullet$
$[(R \equiv S) \supset (N \equiv O)]$
10. $(M \equiv \sim Q) \lor (N \equiv O)$

9.4 Constructing Formal Proofs of Validity

We turn now to one of the central tasks of deductive logic: proving formally that valid arguments really are valid. In the preceding sections we examined formal proofs that needed only to be supplemented by the justifications of the steps taken. From this point, however, we confront arguments whose formal proofs must be constructed. This is an easy task for many arguments, a more challenging task for some. But whether the proof needed is short and simple, or long and complex, the rules of inference are in every case our instruments. Success requires *mastery* of these rules. Having the list of rules before one will probably not be sufficient. One must be able to call on the rules "from within" as the proofs are being devised. The ability to do this will grow rapidly with practice, and yields many satisfactions.

We begin by constructing proofs for simple arguments. The only rules needed (or available for our use) are the nine elementary valid argument forms with which we have been working. This limitation we will later overcome, but even with only these nine rules in our logical toolbox, very many arguments can be formally proved valid. We begin with arguments that require, in addition to the premises, no more than two additional statements.

We will look first at two examples, the first two in the set of exercises on pages 385–386.

First example: Consider the argument:

1. A

B

$\therefore (A \vee C) \bullet B$

The conclusion of this argument $(A \vee C) \bullet B$ is a conjunction; we see immediately that the second conjunct, B, is readily at hand as a premise in line 2. All that is now needed is the statement of the disjunction, $(A \vee C)$, which may then be conjoined with B to complete the proof. $(A \vee C)$ is easily obtained from the premise A, in line 1; we simply add C using the rule Addition, which tells us that to any given p we may add (disjunctively) any q whatever. In this example we have been told that A is true, so we may infer by this rule that $A \vee C$ must be true. The third line of this proof is "3. A $\vee$ C, 1, Add." In line 4 we can conjoin this disjunction (line 3) with the premise B (line 2): "4. $(A \vee C) \cdot B$, 3, 2, Conj." This final line of the sequence is the conclusion of the argument being proved. The formal proof is complete.

Here is a second example of an argument whose formal proof requires only two additional lines in the sequence:

2. $D \supset E$

$D \bullet F$

$\therefore E$

The conclusion of this argument, E, is the consequent of the conditional statement $D \supset E$, which is given as the first premise. We know that we will be able to infer the truth of E by *Modus Ponens* if we can establish the truth of *D*. We can establish the truth of *D*, of course, by Simplification from the second premise, *D* • *F*. So the complete formal proof consists of the following four lines:

1. *D* ⊃ *E*
2. *D* • *F* /∴ *E*
3. *D* 2, Simp.
4. *E* 1, 3, M.P.

In each of these examples, and in all the exercises immediately following, a formal proof for each argument may be constructed by adding just two additional statements. This will be an easy task *if the nine elementary valid argument forms are clearly in mind*. Bear in mind that the final line in the sequence of each proof is always the conclusion of the argument being proved.

EXERCISES

1. *A*
   B
   ∴ (*A* v *C*) • *B*

2. *D* ⊃ *E*
   D • *F*
   ∴ *E*

3. *G*
   H
   (*G* • *H*) v *I*

4. *J* ⊃ *K*
   J
   ∴ *K* v *L*

*5. *M* v *N*
   ~*M* • ~*O*
   ∴ *N*

6. *P* • *Q*
   R
   ∴ *P* • *R*

7. *S* ⊃ *T*
   ~*T* • ~*U*
   ∴ ~*S*

8. *V* v *W*
   ~*V*
   ∴ *W* v *X*

9. *Y* ⊃ *Z*
   Y
   ∴ *Y* • *Z*

*10. *A* ⊃ *B*
   (*A* • *B*) ⊃ *C*
   ∴ *A* ⊃ *C*

11. *D* ⊃ *E*
   (*E* ⊃ *F*) • (*F* ⊃ *D*)
   ∴ *D* ⊃ *F*

12. (*G* ⊃ *H*) • (*I* ⊃ *J*)
   G
   ∴ *H* v *J*

13. ~(*K* • *L*)
   K ⊃ *L*
   ∴ ~*K*

14. (*M* ⊃ *N*) • (*M* ⊃ *O*)
   N ⊃ *O*
   ∴ *M* ⊃ *O*

*15. (*P* ⊃ *Q*) • (*R* ⊃ *S*)
   (*P* v *R*) • (*Q* v *R*)
   ∴ *Q* v *S*

16. (*T* ⊃ *U*) • (*T* ⊃ *V*)
   T
   ∴ *U* v *V*

17. $(W \vee X) \supset Y$
W
$\therefore Y$

18. $(Z \bullet A) \supset (B \bullet C)$
$Z \supset A$
$\therefore Z \supset (B \bullet C)$

19. $D \supset E$
$[D \supset (D \bullet E)] \supset (F \supset \sim G)$
$\therefore F \supset \sim G$

***20.** $(\sim H \vee I) \vee J$
$\sim(\sim H \vee I)$
$\therefore J \vee \sim H$

21. $(K \supset L) \supset M$
$\sim M \bullet \sim(L \supset K)$
$\therefore \sim(K \supset L)$

22. $(N \supset O) \supset (P \supset Q)$
$[P \supset (N \supset O)] \bullet [N \supset (P \supset Q)]$
$\therefore P \supset (P \supset Q)$

23. $R \supset S$
$S \supset (S \bullet R)$
$\therefore [R \supset (R \bullet S)] \bullet [S \supset (S \bullet R)]$

24. $[T \supset (U \vee V)] \bullet [U \supset (T \vee V)]$
$(T \vee U) \bullet (U \vee V)$
$\therefore (U \vee V) \vee (T \vee V)$

***25.** $(W \bullet X) \supset (Y \bullet Z)$
$\sim[(W \bullet X) \bullet (Y \bullet Z)]$
$\therefore \sim(W \bullet X)$

26. $A \supset B$
$A \vee C$
$C \supset D$
$\therefore B \vee D$

27. $(E \bullet F) \vee (G \supset H)$
$I \supset G$
$\sim(E \bullet F)$
$\therefore I \supset H$

28. $J \vee \sim K$
$K \vee (L \supset J)$
$\sim J$
$\therefore L \supset J$

29. $(M \supset N) \bullet (O \supset P)$
$N \supset P$
$(N \supset P) \supset (M \vee O)$
$\therefore N \vee P$

***30.** $Q \supset (R \vee S)$
$(T \bullet U) \supset R$
$(R \vee S) \supset (T \bullet U)$
$\therefore Q \supset R$

9.5 Constructing More Extended Formal Proofs

Arguments whose formal proof requires only two additional statements are quite simple. We now advance to construct formal proofs of the validity of more complex arguments. However, the process will be the same: The target for the final statement of the sequence will always be the conclusion of the argument, and the rules of inference will always be our only logical tools.

Let us look closely at an example—the first exercise of Set A on page 387, an argument whose proof requires three additional statements:

1. $A \vee (B \supset A)$
$\sim A \bullet C$
$\therefore \sim B$

In devising the proof of this argument (as in most cases), we need some plan of action, some strategy with which we can progress, using our rules, toward the conclusion sought. Here that conclusion is ~*B*. We ask ourselves: Where in the premises does *B* appear? Only as the antecedent of the hypothetical (*B* ⊃ *A*), which is a component of the first premise. How might ~*B* be derived? Using *Modus Tollens,* we can infer it from *B* ⊃ *A* if we can establish that hypothetical separately and also establish ~*A*. Both of those needed steps can be readily accomplished. ~*A* is inferred from line 2 by Simplification:

3. ~*A* 2, Simp.

We can then apply ~*A* to line 1, using Disjunctive Syllogism to infer (*B* ⊃ *A*):

4. (*B* ⊃ *A*) 1, 3, D.S.

The proof may then be completed using *Modus Tollens* on lines 4 and 3:

5. ~*B* 4, 3, M.T.

The strategy used in this argument is readily devised. In the case of some proofs, devising the needed strategy will not be so simple, but it is almost always helpful to ask: What statement(s) will enable one to infer the conclusion? And what statement(s) will enable one to infer *that*? And so on, moving backward from the conclusion toward the premises given.

EXERCISES

A. For each of the following arguments, it is possible to provide a formal proof of validity by adding just three statements to the premises. Writing these out, carefully and accurately, will strengthen your command of the rules of inference, a needed preparation for the construction of proofs that are more extended and more complex.

1. *A* ∨ (*B* ⊃ *A*)
~*A* • *C*
∴ ~*B*

2. (*D* ∨ *E*) ⊃ (*F* • *G*)
D
∴ *F*

3. (*H* ⊃ *I*) • (*H* ⊃ *J*)
H • (*I* ∨ *J*)
∴ *I* ∨ *J*

4. (*K* • *L*) ⊃ *M*
K ⊃ *L*
∴ *K* ⊃ [(*K* • *L*) • *M*]

***5.** *N* ⊃ [(*N* • *O*) ⊃ *P*]
N • *O*
∴ *P*

6. *Q* ⊃ *R*
R ⊃ *S*
~*S*
∴ ~*Q* • ~*R*

7. *T* ⊃ *U*
V ∨ ~*U*
~*V* • ~*W*
∴ ~*T*

8. ~*X* ⊃ *Y*
Z ⊃ *X*
~*X*
∴ *Y* • ~*Z*

9. (A ∨ B) ⊃ ~C
C ∨ D
A
∴ D

***10.** E ∨ ~F
F ∨ (E ∨ G)
~E
∴ G

11. (H ⊃ I) • (J ⊃ K)
K ∨ H
~K
∴ I

12. L ∨ (M ⊃ N)
~L ⊃ (N ⊃ O)
~L
∴ M ⊃ O

13. (P ⊃ Q) • (Q ⊃ P)
R ⊃ S
P ∨ R
∴ Q ∨ S

14. (T ⊃ U) • (V ⊃ W)
(U ⊃ X) • (W ⊃ Y)
T
∴ X ∨ Y

***15.** (Z • A) ⊃ B
B ⊃ A
(B • A) ⊃ (A • B)
∴ (Z • A) ⊃ (A • B)

Formal proofs most often require more than two or three lines to be added to the premises. Some are very lengthy. Whatever their length, however, the same process and the same strategic techniques are called for in devising the needed proofs. In this section we rely entirely on the nine elementary valid argument forms that serve as our rules of inference.

As we begin to construct longer and more complicated proofs, let us look closely at an example of such proofs—the first exercise of Set B on page 389. It is not difficult, but it is more extended than those we have worked with so far.

1. A ⊃ B
A ∨ (C • D)
~B • ~E
∴ C

The strategy needed for the proof of this argument is not hard to see: To obtain C we must break apart the premise in line 2; to do that we will need ~*A*; to establish ~*A* we will need to apply *Modus Tollens* to line 1 using ~*B*. Therefore we continue the sequence with the fourth line of the proof by applying Simplification to line 3:

1. A ⊃ B
2. A ∨ (C • D)
3. ~B • ~E /∴ C
4. ~B 3, Simp.

Using line 4 we can obtain ~*A* from line 1:

5. ~*A* 1, 4, M.T.

With ~*A* established we can break line 2 apart, as we had planned, using D.S.:

6. *C* • *D* 2, 5, D.S.

The conclusion may be pulled readily from the sixth line by Simplification.

7. *C* 6, Simp.

Seven lines (including the premises) are required for this formal proof. Some proofs require very many more lines than this, but the object and the method remain always the same.

It sometimes happens, as one is devising a formal proof, that a statement is correctly inferred and added to the numbered sequence but turns out not to be needed; a solid proof may be given without using that statement. In such a case it is usually best to rewrite the proof, eliminating the unneeded statement. However, if the unneeded statement is retained, and the proof remains accurately constructed using other statements correctly inferred, the inclusion of the unneeded statement (although perhaps inelegant) does not render the proof incorrect. Logicians tend to prefer shorter proofs, proofs that move to the conclusion as directly as the rules of inference permit. But if, as one is constructing a more complicated proof, it becomes apparent that some much earlier statement(s) has been needlessly inferred, it may be more efficient to allow such statement(s) to remain in place, using (as one goes forward) the more extended numbering that that inclusion makes necessary. *Logical solidity* is the critical objective. A solid formal proof, one in which *each step is correctly derived and the conclusion is correctly linked to the premises by an unbroken chain of arguments using the rules of inference correctly,* remains a proof—even if it is not as crisp and elegant as some other proof that could be devised.

EXERCISES

B. For each of the following arguments, a formal proof of validity can be constructed without great difficulty, although some of the proofs may require a sequence of eight or nine lines (including premises) for their completion.

1. *A* ⊃ *B*
A ∨ (*C* • *D*)
~*B* • ~*E*
∴ *C*

2. (*F* ⊃ *G*) • (*H* ⊃ *I*)
J ⊃ *K*
(*F* ∨ *J*) • (*H* ∨ *L*)
∴ *G* ∨ *K*

3. (~*M* • ~*N*) ⊃ (*O* ⊃ *N*)
N ⊃ *M*
~*M*
∴ ~*O*

4. (*K* ∨ *L*) ⊃ (*M* ∨ *N*)
(*M* ∨ *N*) ⊃ (*O* • *P*)
K
∴ *O*

***5.** $(Q \supset R) \bullet (S \supset T)$
$(U \supset V) \bullet (W \supset X)$
$Q \vee U$
$\therefore R \vee V$

6. $W \supset X$
$(W \bullet X) \supset Y$
$(W \bullet Y) \supset Z$
$\therefore W \supset Z$

7. $A \supset B$
$C \supset D$
$A \vee C$
$\therefore (A \bullet B) \vee (C \bullet D)$

8. $(E \vee F) \supset (G \bullet H)$
$(G \vee H) \supset I$
E
$\therefore I$

9. $J \supset K$
$K \vee L$
$(L \bullet {\sim}J) \supset (M \bullet {\sim}J)$
${\sim}K$
$\therefore M$

***10.** $(N \vee O) \supset P$
$(P \vee Q) \supset R$
$Q \vee N$
${\sim}Q$
$\therefore R$

In the study of logic, our aim is to evaluate arguments in a natural language, such as English. When an argument in everyday discourse confronts us, we can prove it to be valid (if it really is valid) by first translating the statements (from English, or from any other natural language) into our symbolic language, and then constructing a formal proof of that symbolic translation. The symbolic version of the argument may reveal that the argument is, in fact, more simple (or possibly more complex) than one had supposed on first hearing or reading it. Consider the following example (the first in the set of exercises that immediately follow):

1. If either Gertrude or Herbert wins, then both Jens and Kenneth lose. Gertrude wins. Therefore Jens loses. (*G*—Gertrude wins; *H*—Herbert wins; *J*—Jens loses; *K*—Kenneth loses.)

Abbreviations for each statement are provided in this context because, without them, those involved in the discussion of these arguments would be likely to employ various abbreviations, making communication difficult. Using the abbreviations suggested greatly facilitates discussion.

Translated from the English into symbolic notation, this first argument appears as

1. $(G \vee H) \supset (J \bullet K)$
2. G $/\therefore J$

The formal proof of this argument is short and straightforward:

3. $G \vee H$ 2, Add.
4. $J \bullet K$ 1, 3, M. P.
5. J 4, Simp.

EXERCISES

C. Each of the following arguments in English may be similarly translated, and for each, a formal proof of validity (using only the nine elementary valid argument forms as rules of inference) may be constructed. These proofs vary in length, some requiring a sequence of thirteen statements (including the premises) to complete the formal proofs. The suggested abbreviations should be used for the sake of clarity. Bear in mind that, as one proceeds to produce a formal proof of an argument presented in a natural language, it is of the utmost importance that *the translation into symbolic notation of the statements appearing discursively in the argument be perfectly accurate;* if it is not, one will be working with an argument that is *different* from the original one, and in that case any proof devised will be useless, being not applicable to the original argument.

1. If either Gertrude or Herbert wins, then both Jens and Kenneth lose. Gertrude wins. Therefore Jens loses. (*G*—Gertrude wins; *H*—Herbert wins; *J*—Jens loses; *K*—Kenneth loses.)

2. If Adriana joins, then the club's social prestige will rise; and if Boris joins, then the club's financial position will be more secure. Either Adriana or Boris will join. If the club's social prestige rises, then Boris will join; and if the club's financial position becomes more secure, then Wilson will join. Therefore either Boris or Wilson will join. (*A*—Adriana joins; *S*—The club's social prestige rises; *B*—Boris joins; *F*—The club's financial position is more secure; *W*—Wilson joins.)

3. If Brown received the message, then she took the plane; and if she took the plane, then she will not be late for the meeting. If the message was incorrectly addressed, then Brown will be late for the meeting. Either Brown received the message or the message was incorrectly addressed. Therefore either Brown took the plane or she will be late for the meeting. (*R*—Brown received the message; *P*—Brown took the plane; *L*—Brown will be late for the meeting; *T*—The message was incorrectly addressed.)

4. If Nihar buys the lot, then an office building will be constructed; whereas if Payton buys the lot, then it will be quickly sold again. If Rivers buys the lot, then a store will be constructed; and if a store is constructed, then Thompson will offer to lease it. Either Nihar or Rivers will buy the lot. Therefore either an office building or a store will be constructed. (*N*—Nihar buys the lot; *O*—An office building will be constructed; *P*—Payton buys the lot; *Q*—The lot will be quickly sold again; *R*—Rivers buys the lot; *S*—A store will be constructed; *T*—Thompson will offer to lease it.)

***5.** If rain continues, then the river rises. If rain continues and the river rises, then the bridge will wash out. If the continuation of rain would cause the bridge to wash out, then a single road is not sufficient for the town. Either a single road is sufficient for the town or the traffic engineers have made a mistake. Therefore the traffic engineers have made a mistake. (*C*—Rain continues; *R*—The river rises; *B*—The bridge washes out; *S*—A single road is sufficient for the town; *M*—The traffic engineers have made a mistake.)

6. If Jonas goes to the meeting, then a complete report will be made; but if Jonas does not go to the meeting, then a special election will be required. If a complete report is made, then an investigation will be launched. If Jonas's going to the meeting implies that a complete report will be made, and the making of a complete report implies that an investigation will be launched, then either Jonas goes to the meeting and an investigation is launched or Jonas does not go to the meeting and no investigation is launched. If Jonas goes to the meeting and an investigation is launched, then some members will have to stand trial. But if Jonas does not go to the meeting and no investigation is launched, then the organization will disintegrate very rapidly. Therefore either some members will have to stand trial or the organization will disintegrate very rapidly. (*J*—Jonas goes to the meeting; *R*—A complete report is made; *E*—A special election is required; *I*—An investigation is launched; *T*—Some members have to stand trial; *D*—The organization disintegrates very rapidly.)

7. If Ann is present, then Bill is present. If Ann and Bill are both present, then either Charles or Doris will be elected. If either Charles or Doris is elected, then Elmer does not really dominate the club. If Ann's presence implies that Elmer does not really dominate the club, then Florence will be the new president. So Florence will be the new president. (*A*—Ann is present; *B*—Bill is present; *C*—Charles will be elected; *D*—Doris will be elected; *E*—Elmer really dominates the club; *F*—Florence will be the new president.)

8. If Mr. Jones is the manager's next-door neighbor, then Mr. Jones's annual earnings are exactly divisible by 3. If Mr. Jones's annual earnings are exactly divisible by 3, then $40,000 is exactly divisible by 3. But $40,000 is not exactly divisible by 3. If Mr. Robinson is the manager's next-door neighbor, then Mr. Robinson lives halfway between Detroit and Chicago. If Mr. Robinson lives in Detroit, then he does not live halfway between Detroit and Chicago. Mr. Robinson lives in Detroit. If Mr. Jones is not the manager's next-door neighbor, then either Mr. Robinson or Mr. Smith is the manager's next-door neighbor. Therefore Mr. Smith is the manager's next-door neighbor. (*J*—Mr. Jones is the manager's next-door neighbor; *E*—Mr. Jones's annual earnings are exactly divisible by 3; *T*—$40,000 is exactly divisible by 3; *R*—Mr. Robinson is the manager's next-door neighbor; *H*—Mr. Robinson lives halfway between Detroit and Chicago; *D*—Mr. Robinson lives in Detroit; *S*—Mr. Smith is the manager's next-door neighbor.)

9. If Mr. Smith is the manager's next-door neighbor, then Mr. Smith lives halfway between Detroit and Chicago. If Mr. Smith lives halfway between Detroit and Chicago, then he does not live in Chicago. Mr. Smith is the manager's next-door neighbor. If Mr. Robinson lives in Detroit, then he does not live in Chicago. Mr. Robinson lives in Detroit. Mr. Smith lives in Chicago or else either Mr. Robinson or Mr. Jones lives in Chicago. If Mr. Jones lives in Chicago, then the manager is Jones. Therefore the manager is Jones. (*S*—Mr. Smith is the manager's next-door neighbor; *W*—Mr. Smith lives halfway between Detroit and Chicago; *L*—Mr. Smith lives in Chicago; *D*—Mr. Robinson lives in Detroit; *I*—Mr. Robinson lives in Chicago; *C*—Mr. Jones lives in Chicago; *B*—The manager is Jones.)

***10.** If Smith once beat the editor at billiards, then Smith is not the editor. Smith once beat the editor at billiards. If the manager is Jones, then Jones is not the editor. The manager is Jones. If Smith is not the editor and Jones is not the editor, then Robinson is the editor. If the manager is Jones and Robinson is the editor, then Smith is the publisher. Therefore Smith is the publisher. (*O*—Smith once beat the editor at billiards; *M*—Smith is the editor; *B*—The manager is Jones; *N*—Jones is the editor; *F*—Robinson is the editor; *G*—Smith is the publisher.)

9.6 Expanding the Rules of Inference: Replacement Rules

The nine elementary valid argument forms with which we have been working are powerful tools of inference, but they are not powerful enough. There are very many valid truth-functional arguments whose validity cannot be proved using only the nine rules thus far developed. We need to expand the set of rules, to increase the power of our logical toolbox.

To illustrate the problem, consider the following simple argument, which is plainly valid:

> If you travel directly from Chicago to Los Angeles, you must cross the Mississippi River. If you travel only along the Atlantic seaboard, you will not cross the Mississippi River. Therefore if you travel directly from Chicago to Los Angeles, you will not travel only along the Atlantic seaboard.

Translated into symbolic notation, this argument appears as

$D \supset C$

$A \supset {\sim}C$

$/\therefore D \supset {\sim}A$

This conclusion certainly does follow from the given premises. But, try as we may, there is no way to prove that it is valid using only the elementary valid argument forms. Our logical toolbox is not fully adequate.

What is missing? Chiefly, what is missing is the ability to replace one statement by another that is logically equivalent to it. We need to be able to put, in place of any given statement, any other statement whose meaning is exactly the same as that of the statement being replaced. And we need rules that identify legitimate replacements precisely.

Such rules are available to us. Recall that the only compound statements that concern us here (as we noted in Section 8.2) are *truth-functional* compound statements, and in a truth-functional compound statement, if we replace any component by another statement having the same truth value, the truth value of the compound statement remains unchanged. Therefore we may accept as an additional principle of inference what may be called the general **rule of replacement**—a rule that permits us to infer from any statement the result of replacing any component of that statement by any other statement that is *logically equivalent* to the component replaced.

The correctness of such replacements is intuitively obvious. To illustrate, the principle of *Double Negation* (D.N.) asserts that p is logically equivalent to ${\sim}{\sim}p$. Using the rule of replacement we may say, correctly, that from the statement $A \supset {\sim}{\sim}B$, any one of the following statements may be validly inferred:

$A \supset B$,

${\sim}{\sim}A \supset {\sim}{\sim}B$,

${\sim}{\sim}(A \supset {\sim}{\sim}B)$, and even

$A \supset {\sim}{\sim}{\sim}{\sim}B$.

When we put any one of these in place of $A \supset {\sim}{\sim}B$, we do no more than exchange one statement for another that is its logical equivalent.

This rule of replacement is a powerful enrichment of our rules of inference. In its general form, however, its application is problematic because its content is not definite; we are not always sure what statements are indeed logically equivalent to some other statements, and thus (if we have the rule only in its general form) we may be unsure whether that rule applies in a given case. To overcome this problem in a way that makes the rule of replacement applicable with indubitable accuracy, we make the rule *definite* by listing *ten specific logical equivalences* to which the rule of replacement may certainly be applied. Each of these equivalences—they are all logically true biconditionals—will serve as a separate rule of inference. We list the ten logical equivalences here, as ten rules, and we number them consecutively to follow the first nine rules of inference already set forth in the preceding sections of this chapter.

OVERVIEW

The Rules of Replacement: Logically Equivalent Expressions

Any of the following logically equivalent expressions may replace each other wherever they occur.

Name	Abbreviation	Form
10. De Morgan's theorems	De M.	$\sim(p \bullet q) \overset{T}{\equiv} (\sim p \vee \sim q)$
		$\sim(p \vee q) \overset{T}{\equiv} (\sim p \bullet \sim q)$
11. Commutation	Com.	$(p \vee q) \overset{T}{\equiv} (q \vee p)$
		$(p \bullet q) \overset{T}{\equiv} (q \bullet p)$
12. Association	Assoc.	$[p \vee (q \vee r)] \overset{T}{\equiv} [(p \vee q) \vee r]$
		$[p \bullet (q \bullet r)] \overset{T}{\equiv} [(p \bullet q) \bullet r]$
13. Distribution	Dist.	$[p \bullet (q \vee r)] \overset{T}{\equiv} [(p \bullet q) \vee (p \bullet r)]$
		$[p \vee (q \bullet r)] \overset{T}{\equiv} [(p \vee q) \bullet (p \vee r)]$
14. Double Negation	D.N.	$p \overset{T}{\equiv} \sim\sim p$
15. Transposition	Trans.	$(p \supset q) \overset{T}{\equiv} (\sim q \supset \sim p)$
16. Material Implication	Impl.	$(p \supset q) \overset{T}{\equiv} (\sim p \vee q)$
17. Material Equivalence	Equiv.	$(p \equiv q) \overset{T}{\equiv} [(p \supset q) \bullet (q \supset p)]$
		$(p \equiv q) \overset{T}{\equiv} [(p \bullet q) \vee (\sim p \bullet \sim q)]$
18. Exportation	Exp.	$[(p \bullet q) \supset r] \overset{T}{\equiv} [p \supset (q \supset r)]$
19. Tautology	Taut.	$p \overset{T}{\equiv} (p \vee p)$
		$p \overset{T}{\equiv} (p \bullet p)$

Let us now examine each of these ten logical equivalences. We will use them frequently and will rely on them in constructing formal proofs of validity, and therefore we must grasp their force as deeply, and control them as fully, as we do the nine elementary valid argument forms. We take these ten in order, giving for each the name, the abbreviation commonly used for it, and its exact logical form(s).

10. De Morgan's Theorems **De M.** $\sim(p \bullet q) \overset{T}{\equiv} (\sim p \vee \sim q)$

$\sim(p \vee q) \overset{T}{\equiv} (\sim p \bullet \sim q)$

This logical equivalence was explained in detail in Section 8.9. De Morgan's theorems have two variants. One variant asserts that when we deny that two propositions are *both* true, that is logically equivalent to asserting that either one of them is false, or the other one is false, or they are both false. (The negation of a conjunction is logically equivalent to the disjunction of the negation of the conjuncts.) The second variant of De Morgan's theorems asserts that when we deny that *either* of two propositions is true, that is logically equivalent to asserting that both of them are false. (The negation of a disjunction is logically equivalent to the conjunction of the negations of the disjuncts.)

These two biconditionals are tautologies, of course. That is, the expression of the material equivalence of the two sides of each is *always* true, and thus can have no false substitution instance. All ten of the logical equivalences now being recognized as rules of inference are tautological biconditionals in exactly this sense.

11. Commutation **Com.** $(p \vee q) \overset{T}{\equiv} (q \vee p)$

$(p \bullet q) \overset{T}{\equiv} (q \bullet p)$

These two equivalences simply assert that the *order* of statement of the elements of a conjunction, or of a disjunction, does not matter. We are always permitted to turn them around, to *commute* them, because, whichever order happens to appear, the meanings remain exactly the same.

Recall that Rule 7, Simplification, permitted us to pull p from the conjunction $p \bullet q$, but not q. Now, with Commutation, we can always replace $p \bullet q$ with $q \bullet p$—so that, with Simplification and Commutation both at hand, we can readily establish the truth of each of the conjuncts in any conjunction we know to be true.

12. Association **Assoc.** $[p \vee (q \vee r)] \overset{T}{\equiv} [(p \vee q) \vee r]$

$[p \bullet (q \bullet r)] \overset{T}{\equiv} [(p \bullet q) \bullet r]$

These two equivalences do no more than allow us to group statements differently. If we know three different statements to be true, to assert that p is true along with q and r clumped, is logically equivalent to asserting that p and q clumped is true along with r. Equivalence also holds if the three are grouped as disjuncts: p or the disjunction of $q \vee r$, is a grouping logically equivalent to the disjunction $p \vee q$, or r.

13. Distribution **Dist.** $[p \bullet (q \vee r)] \overset{T}{\equiv} [(p \bullet q) \vee (p \bullet r)]$

$[p \vee (q \bullet r)] \overset{T}{\equiv} [(p \vee q) \bullet (p \vee r)]$

Of all the rules permitting replacement, this one may be the least obvious—but it too is a tautology, of course. Its also has two variants. The first variant asserts merely that the *conjunction* of one statement with the disjunction of two other statements is logically equivalent to either the disjunction of the first with the second or the disjunction of the first with the third. The second variant asserts merely that the *disjunction* of one statement with the conjunction of two others is logically equivalent to the conjunction of the disjunction of the first and the second and the disjunction of the first and the third. The rule is named *Distribution* because it *distributes* the first element of the three, exhibiting its logical connections with each of the other two statements separately.

14. Double Negation **D.N.** $p \overset{T}{\equiv} {\sim}{\sim}p$

Intuitively clear to everyone, this rule simply asserts that any statement is logically equivalent to the negation of the negation of that statement.

15. Transposition **Trans.** $(p \supset q) \overset{T}{\equiv} ({\sim}q \supset {\sim}p)$

This logical equivalence permits us to turn any conditional statement around. We know that if any conditional statement is true, then if its consequent is false its antecedent must also be false. Therefore any conditional statement is logically equivalent to the conditional statement asserting that the negation of its consequent implies the negation of its antecedent.

16. Material Implication **Impl.** $(p \supset q) \overset{T}{\equiv} ({\sim}p \vee q)$

This logical equivalence does no more than formulate the definition of material implication explained in Section 8.9 as a replacement that can serve as a rule of inference. There we saw that $p \supset q$ simply means that either the antecedent, p, is false or the consequent, q, is true.

As we go on to construct formal proofs, this definition of material implication will become very important, because it is often easier to manipulate or combine two statements if they have the same basic form—that is, if they are both in disjunctive form, or if they are both in implicative form. If one is in disjunctive form and the other is in implicative form, we can, using this rule, transform one of them into the form of the other. This will be very convenient.

17. Material Equivalence **Equiv.** $(p \equiv q) \overset{T}{\equiv} [(p \cdot q) \vee ({\sim}p \cdot {\sim}q)]$

$(p \equiv q) \overset{T}{\equiv} [(p \supset q) \cdot (q \supset p)]$

The two variants of this rule simply assert the two essential meanings of material equivalence, explained in detail in Section 8.8. There we explained that two statements are materially equivalent if they both have the same truth value; therefore (first variant) the assertion of their material equivalence (with the tribar, ≡) is logically equivalent to asserting that they are both true, or that they are both false. We also explained at that point that if two statements are both true, they must materially imply one another, and likewise if they are both false, they must materially imply one another; therefore (second variant) the statement that they are materially equivalent is *logically* equivalent to the statement that they imply one another.

18. Exportation **Exp.** $[(p \bullet q) \supset r] \overset{T}{\equiv} [p \supset (q \supset r)]$

This replacement rule states a logical biconditional that is intuitively clear upon reflection: If one asserts that two propositions conjoined are known to imply a third, that is logically equivalent to asserting that if one of those two propositions is known to be true, then the truth of the other must imply the truth of the third. Like all the others, this logical equivalence may be readily confirmed using a truth table.

19. Tautology **Taut.** $p \overset{T}{\equiv} (p \vee p)$

$p \overset{T}{\equiv} (p \bullet p)$

The two variants of this last rule are patently obvious but very useful. They say simply that any statement is logically equivalent to the disjunction of itself with itself, and that any statement is logically equivalent to the conjunction of itself with itself. It sometimes happens that, as the outcome of a series of inferences, we learn that either the proposition we seek to establish is true *or* that it is true. From this disjunction we may readily infer (using this rule) that the proposition in question is true. The same applies to the conjunction of a statement with itself.

It should be noted that the word "tautology" is used in three different senses. It can mean (1) a *statement form* all of whose substitution instances are true; in this sense the statement form $(p \supset q) \supset [p \supset (p \supset q)]$ is a tautology. It can mean (2) a *statement*—for example, $(A \supset B) \supset [A \supset (A \supset B)]$ whose specific form is a tautology in sense (1). And it can mean (3) *the particular logical equivalence* we have just introduced, number 19 in our list of rules of inference.

As we look back on these ten rules, we should be clear about what it is they make possible. They are not rules of "substitution" as that term is correctly used; we *substitute* statements for statement variables, as when we say that $A \supset B$ is a substitution instance of the expression $p \supset q$. In such operations we may substitute *any* statement for any statement variable so long as it is substituted for *every other* occurrence of that statement variable. But when these listed rules of replacement are applied, we exchange, or *replace*, a component of one statement *only by a statement that we know (by one of these ten rules) to be logically equivalent to that component.* For example, by transposition we may replace $A \supset B$ by $\sim B \supset \sim A$. And these rules permit us to replace one occurrence of that component without having to replace any other occurrence of it.

EXERCISES

The following set of arguments involves, in each case, one step only, in which one of the ten logical equivalences set forth in this section has been employed. Here are two examples, the first two in the exercise set immediately following.

EXAMPLE 1

$(A \supset B) \bullet (C \supset D)$

$\therefore (A \supset B) \bullet (\sim D \supset \sim C)$

SOLUTION

The conclusion of this simple argument is exactly like its premise, except for the fact that the second conjunct in the premise, $(C \supset D)$, has been replaced by the logically equivalent expression $(\sim D \supset \sim C)$. That replacement is plainly justified by the rule we call Transposition (Trans.):

$$[(p \supset q) \overset{T}{\equiv} (\sim q \supset \sim p)$$

EXAMPLE 2

$(E \supset F) \bullet (G \supset \sim H)$

$(\sim E \vee F) \bullet (G \supset \sim H)$

SOLUTION

In this case the conclusion differs from the premise only in the fact that the conditional statement $(E \supset F)$ has been replaced, as first conjunct, by the disjunctive statement $(\sim E \vee F)$. The rule permitting such a replacement, Material Implication (Impl.), has the form

$$(p \supset q) \overset{T}{\equiv} (\sim p \vee q)$$

For each of the following one-step arguments, state the one rule of inference by which its conclusion follows from its premise.

1. $(A \supset B) \bullet (C \supset D)$

$\therefore (A \supset B) \bullet (\sim D \supset \sim C)$

2. $(E \supset F) \bullet (G \supset \sim H)$

$\therefore (\sim E \vee F) \bullet (G \supset \sim H)$

3. $[I \supset (J \supset K)] \bullet (J \supset \sim I)$

$\therefore [(I \bullet J) \supset K] \bullet (J \supset \sim I)$

4. $[L \supset (M \vee N)] \vee [L \supset (M \vee N)]$

$\therefore L \supset (M \vee N)$

***5.** $O \supset [(P \supset Q) \bullet (Q \supset P)]$

$\therefore O \supset (P \equiv Q)$

6. $\sim(R \vee S) \supset (\sim R \vee \sim S)$

$\therefore (\sim R \bullet \sim S) \supset (\sim R \vee \sim S)$

7. $(T \vee \sim U) \bullet [(W \bullet \sim V) \supset \sim T]$
$\therefore (T \vee \sim U) \bullet [W \supset (\sim V \supset \sim T)]$

8. $(X \vee Y) \bullet (\sim X \vee \sim Y)$
$\therefore [(X \vee Y) \bullet \sim X] \vee [(X \vee Y) \bullet \sim Y]$

9. $Z \supset (A \supset B)$
$\therefore Z \supset (\sim\sim A \supset B)$

***10.** $[C \bullet (D \bullet \sim E)] \bullet [(C \bullet D) \bullet \sim E]$
$\therefore [(C \bullet D) \bullet \sim E] \bullet [(C \bullet D) \bullet \sim E]$

11. $(\sim F \vee G) \bullet (F \supset G)$
$\therefore (F \supset G) \bullet (F \supset G)$

12. $(H \supset \sim I) \supset (\sim I \supset \sim J)$
$\therefore (H \supset \sim I) \supset (J \supset I)$

13. $(\sim K \supset L) \supset (\sim M \vee \sim N)$
$\therefore (\sim K \supset L) \supset \sim(M \bullet N)$

14. $[(\sim O \vee P) \vee \sim Q] \bullet [\sim O \vee (P \vee \sim Q)]$
$\therefore [\sim O \vee (P \vee \sim Q)] \bullet [\sim O \vee (P \vee \sim Q)]$

***15.** $[(R \vee \sim S) \bullet \sim T] \vee [(R \vee \sim S) \bullet U]$
$\therefore (R \vee \sim S) \bullet (\sim T \vee U)$

16. $[V \supset \sim(W \vee X)] \supset (Y \vee Z)$
$\therefore \{[V \supset \sim(W \vee X)] \bullet [V \supset \sim(W \vee X)]\} \supset (Y \vee Z)$

17. $[(\sim A \bullet B) \bullet (C \vee D)] \vee [\sim(\sim A \bullet B) \bullet \sim(C \vee D)]$
$\therefore (\sim A \bullet B) \equiv (C \vee D)$

18. $[\sim E \vee (\sim\sim F \supset G)] \bullet [\sim E \vee (F \supset G)]$
$\therefore [\sim E \vee (F \supset G)] \bullet [\sim E \vee (F \supset G)]$

19. $[H \bullet (I \vee J)] \vee [H \bullet (K \supset \sim L)]$
$\therefore H \bullet [(I \vee J) \vee (K \supset \sim L)]$

***20.** $(\sim M \vee \sim N) \supset (O \supset \sim\sim P)$
$\therefore \sim(M \bullet N) \supset (O \supset \sim\sim P)$

9.7 The System of Natural Deduction

The nineteen rules of inference that have been set forth (nine elementary argument forms and ten logical equivalences) are all the rules that are needed in truth-functional logic. It is a *complete* system of natural deduction.* This means that, using this set of rules, which is compact and readily mastered, one can construct a formal proof of validity for *any* valid truth functional argument.[1]

Two seeming flaws of this list of nineteen rules deserve attention. First. The set is somewhat *redundant*, in the sense that these nineteen do not constitute

*This kind of completeness of a set of rules can be proved. One method of proving such completeness may be found in I. M. Copi, *Symbolic Logic*, 5th ed. (New York: Macmillan, 1979), chap. 8.

the bare minimum that would suffice for the construction of formal proofs of validity for extended arguments. To illustrate this we might note that *Modus Tollens* could be dropped from the list without any real weakening of our proof apparatus, because any line that depends on that rule can be justified by appealing instead to other rules in our list. Suppose, for example, we know that $A \supset D$ is true, and that $\sim D$ is true, and suppose we want to deduce that $\sim A$ is true. *Modus Tollens* allows us to do that directly. But if *Modus Tollens* were not included in the list of rules, we would still have no trouble deducing $\sim A$ from $A \supset D$ and $\sim D$; we would simply need to insert the intermediate line, $\sim D \supset \sim A$, which follows from $A \supset D$ by Transposition (Trans.), then obtain $\sim A$ from $\sim D \supset \sim A$ by *Modus Ponens* (M.P.). We keep *Modus Tollens* in the list because it is such a commonly used and intuitively obvious rule of inference. Others among the nineteen rules are redundant in this same sense.

Second, the list of nineteen rules may also be said to be *deficient* in one sense. Because the set of rules is short, there are some arguments that, although they are simple and intuitively valid, require several steps to prove. To illustrate this point, consider the argument

$A \vee B$

$\sim B$

$/\therefore A$

which is obviously valid. Its form, equally valid, is

$p \vee q$

$\sim q$

$/\therefore p$

But this elementary argument form has not been included as a rule of inference. No single rule of inference will serve in this case, so we must construct the proof using two rules of inference, commuting the first premise, and then applying Disjunctive Syllogism, thus:

1.	$A \vee B$	
2.	$\sim B$	$/\therefore A$
3.	$B \vee A$	1, Com.
4.	A	3, 2, D.S.

One may complain that the system is in this way clumsy, at times obliging a slow and tortuous path to a proof that ought to be easy and direct. But, there is good reason for this clumsiness. We certainly want a set of rules that is complete, as this set is. But we also want a set of rules that is short and easily mastered. We could add rules to our set—additional equivalences, or additional valid argument forms—but with each such addition our logical toolbox would become more congested and more difficult to command. We could delete some rules (e.g., *Modus Tollens,* as noted above), but with each such deletion the set, although smaller, would become even more clumsy, requiring extended proofs for very simple arguments. Long experience has taught that this set of nineteen rules serves as an ideal compromise: a list of rules of inference that is short enough to master fully, yet long enough to do all that one may need to do with reasonable efficiency.

There is an important difference between the first nine and the last ten rules of inference. *The first nine rules can be applied only to whole lines of a proof.* Thus, in a formal proof of validity, the statement A can be inferred from the statement $A \bullet B$ by Simplification only if $A \bullet B$ constitutes a whole line. It is obvious that A cannot be inferred validly either from $(A \bullet B) \supset C$ or from $C \supset (A \bullet B)$, because the latter two statements can be true while A is false. And the statement $A \supset C$ does not follow from the statement $(A \bullet B) \supset C$ by Simplification or by any other rule of inference. It does not follow at all, for if A is true and B and C are both false, $(A \bullet B) \supset C$ is true but $A \supset C$ is false. Again, although $A \vee B$ follows from A by Addition, we cannot infer $(A \vee B) \supset C$ from $A \supset C$ by Addition or by any other rule of inference. For if A and C are both false and B is true, $A \supset C$ is true but $(A \vee B) \supset C$ is false. On the other hand, *any of the last ten rules can be applied either to whole lines or to parts of lines.* Not only can the statement $A \supset (B \supset C)$ be inferred from the whole line $(A \bullet B) \supset C$ by Exportation, but from the line $[(A \bullet B) \supset C] \vee D$ we can infer $[A \supset (B \supset C)] \vee D$ by Exportation. By replacement, logically equivalent expressions can replace each other wherever they occur, even where they do not constitute whole lines of a proof. But the first nine rules of inference can be used only with whole lines of a proof serving as premises.

The notion of *formal proof* is an *effective* notion, which means that it can be decided quite mechanically, in a finite number of steps, whether or not a given sequence of statements constitutes a formal proof (with reference to a given list of rules of inference). No thinking is required, either in the sense of thinking about what the statements in the sequence "mean" or in the sense of using logical intuition to check any step's validity. Only two things are required. The first is the ability to see that a statement occurring in one place is precisely the same as a statement occurring in another, for we must be able to check that some statements in the proof are premises of the argument being proved valid and that the last statement in the proof is the conclusion of that argument. The second thing that is required is the ability to see whether a given statement has a certain pattern—that is, to see if it is a substitution instance of a given statement form.

Thus, any question about whether the numbered sequence of statements on page 401 is a formal proof of validity can easily be settled in a completely mechanical fashion. That lines 1 and 2 are the premises and line 4 is the conclusion of the given argument is obvious on inspection. That 3 follows from preceding lines by one of the given rules of inference can be decided in a finite number of steps—even where the notation "1, Com." is not written at the side. The explanatory notation in the second column is a help and should always be included, but it is not, strictly speaking, a necessary part of the proof itself. At every line, there are only finitely many preceding lines and only finitely many rules of inference or reference forms to be consulted. Although it is time-consuming, it can be verified by inspection and comparison of shapes that 3 does not follow from 1 and 2 by *modus ponens*, or by *modus tollens*, or by a hypothetical syllogism, . . . and so on, until in following this procedure we come to the question of whether 3 follows from 1 by the principle of commutation, and there we see, simply by looking at the forms, that it does. In the same way, the legitimacy of *any* statement in *any* formal proof can be tested in a finite number of steps, none of which involves anything more than comparing forms or shapes.

To preserve this effectiveness, we require that only one step be taken at a time. One might be tempted to shorten a proof by combining steps, but the space and time saved are negligible. More important is the effectiveness we achieve by taking each step by means of one single rule of inference.

Although a formal proof of validity is effective in the sense that it can be mechanically decided of any given sequence whether it is a proof, *constructing* a formal proof is not an effective procedure. In this respect, formal proofs differ from truth tables. The making of truth tables is completely mechanical: given any argument of the sort with which we are now concerned, we can always construct a truth table to test its validity by following the simple rules of procedure set forth in Chapter 8. But we have no effective or mechanical rules for the construction of formal proofs. Here we must think or "figure out" where to begin and how to proceed. Nevertheless, proving an argument valid by constructing a formal proof of its validity is much easier than the purely mechanical construction of a truth table with perhaps hundreds or even thousands of rows.

Although we have no purely mechanical rules for constructing formal proofs, some rough-and-ready rules of thumb or hints on procedure may be suggested. The first is simply to begin deducing conclusions from the given premises by the given rules of inference. As more and more of these subconclusions become available as premises for further deductions, the greater is the likelihood of being able to see how to deduce the conclusion of the argument to be proved valid. Another hint is to try to eliminate statements that occur in the premises but not in the conclusion. Such elimination can proceed, of course, only in accordance with the rules of inference, but the rules contain many techniques for eliminating statements. Simplification is such a rule, whereby the right-hand conjunct can be dropped from a whole line that is a conjunction. And Commutation is a rule that permits switching the left-hand conjunct of a conjunction over to the right-hand side, from which it can be dropped by Simplification. The "middle" term q can be eliminated by a Hypothetical Syllogism given two statements of the patterns $p \supset q$ and $q \supset r$. Distribution is a useful rule for transforming a disjunction of the pattern $p \vee (q \bullet r)$ into the conjunction $(p \vee q) \bullet (p \vee r)$, whose right-hand conjunct can then be eliminated by Simplification. Another rule of thumb is to introduce by means of Addition a statement that occurs in the conclusion but not in any premise. Yet another method, often very productive, is to work backward from the conclusion by looking for some statement or statements from which it can be deduced, and then trying to deduce those intermediate statements from the premises. There is, however, no substitute for practice as a method of acquiring facility in the construction of formal proofs.

9.8 Constructing Formal Proofs Using the Nineteen Rules of Inference

Having now a set of nineteen rules at our disposition, rather than just nine, the task of constructing formal proofs becomes somewhat more complicated. The objective remains the same, of course, but the process of devising the proof involves inspection of a larger intellectual toolbox. The unbroken logical chain that we devise, leading ultimately to the conclusion, may now include steps justified by either an elementary valid argument form or a logical equivalence. Any given proof is likely to employ rules of both kinds. The balance or order of their use is determined only by the logical need encountered as we implement the strategy that leads to the consummation of the proof.

Following is a set of flawless formal proofs, each of which relies on rules of both kinds. To become accustomed to the use of the full set of rules, we examine each of these proofs to determine what rule has been used to justify each step in that proof, noting that justification to right of each line. We begin with two examples.

EXAMPLE 1

1. **1.** $A \supset B$

2. $C \supset \sim B$

$\therefore A \supset \sim C$

3. $\sim\sim B \supset \sim C$

4. $B \supset \sim C$

5. $A \supset \sim C$

OVERVIEW

The Rules of Inference

Nineteen rules of inference are specified for use in constructing formal proofs of validity. They are as follows:

Elementary Valid Argument Form	Logically Equivalent Expressions
1. ***Modus Ponens*** (M.P.) $p \supset q, p, \therefore q$	**10. De Morgan's theorems** (De M.) $\sim(p \bullet q) \overset{T}{\equiv} (\sim p \vee \sim q)$ $\sim(p \vee q) \overset{T}{\equiv} (\sim p \bullet \sim q)$
2. ***Modus Tollens*** (M.T.) $p \supset q, \sim q, \therefore \sim p$	**11. Commutation** (Com.) $(p \vee q) \overset{T}{\equiv} (q \vee p)$ $(p \bullet q) \overset{T}{\equiv} (q \bullet p)$
3. Hypothetical Syllogism (H.S.) $p \supset q, q \supset r, \therefore p \supset r$	**12. Association** (Assoc.) $[p \vee (q \vee r)] \overset{T}{\equiv} [(p \vee q) \vee r]$ $[p \bullet (q \bullet r)] \overset{T}{\equiv} [(p \bullet q) \bullet r]$
4. Disjunctive Syllogism (D.S.) $p \vee q, \sim p, \therefore q$	**13. Distribution** (Dist.) $[p \bullet (q \vee r)] \overset{T}{\equiv} [(p \bullet q) \vee (p \bullet r)]$ $[p \vee (q \bullet r)] \overset{T}{\equiv} [(p \vee q) \bullet (p \vee r)]$
5. Constructive Dilemma (C.D.) $(p \supset q) \bullet (r \supset s), p \vee r, \therefore q \vee s$	**14. Double Negation** (D.N.) $p \overset{T}{\equiv} \sim\sim p$
6. Absorption (Abs.) $p \supset q, \therefore p \supset (p \bullet q)$	**15. Transposition** (Trans.) $(p \supset q) \overset{T}{\equiv} (\sim q \supset \sim p)$
7. Simplification (Simp.) $p \bullet q, \therefore p$	**16. Material Implication** (Impl.) $(p \supset q) \overset{T}{\equiv} (\sim p \vee q)$
8. Conjunction (Conj.) $p, q, \therefore p \bullet q$	**17. Material Equivalence** (Equiv.) $(p \equiv q) \overset{T}{\equiv} [(p \supset q) \bullet (q \supset p)]$ $(p \equiv q) \overset{T}{\equiv} [(p \bullet q) \vee (\sim p \bullet \sim q)]$
9. Addition (Add.) $p, \therefore p \vee q$	**18. Exportation** (Exp.) $[(p \bullet q) \supset r] \overset{T}{\equiv} [p \supset (q \supset r)]$
	19. Tautology (Taut.) $p \overset{T}{\equiv} (p \vee p)$ $p \overset{T}{\equiv} (p \bullet p)$

SOLUTION

Line 3 is simply line 2 transposed; we write beside line 3: 2, Trans.
Line 4 is simply line 3 with ~~*B* replaced by *B*; so we write beside line 4: 3, D.N.
Line 5 applies the Hypothetical Syllogism argument form to lines 1 and 4. We write beside line 5: 1, 4, H. S.

EXAMPLE 2

2. **1.** $(D \bullet E) \supset F$
2. $(D \supset F) \supset G$
$\therefore E \supset G$
3. $(E \bullet D) \supset F$
4. $E \supset (D \supset F)$
5. $E \supset G$

SOLUTION

Line 3 merely commutes $(D \bullet E)$ from line 1; we write: 1, Com.
Line 4 applies Exportation to line 3; we write: 3, Exp.
Line 5 applies Hypothetical Syllogism to lines 4 and 2; we write; 4, 2, H.S.

EXERCISES

A. For each numbered line (that is not a premise) in each of the formal proofs that follow below, state the rule of inference that justifies it.

1. **1.** $A \supset B$
2. $C \supset \sim B$
$\therefore A \supset \sim C$
3. $\sim\sim B \supset \sim C$
4. $B \supset \sim C$
5. $A \supset \sim C$

2. **1.** $(D \bullet E) \supset F$
2. $(D \supset F) \supset G$
$\therefore E \supset G$
3. $(E \bullet D) \supset F$
4. $E \supset (D \supset F)$
5. $E \supset G$

3. **1.** $(H \vee I) \supset [J \bullet (K \bullet L)]$
2. I
$\therefore J \bullet K$
3. $I \vee H$
4. $H \vee I$
5. $J \bullet (K \bullet L)$
6. $(J \bullet K) \bullet L$
7. $J \bullet K$

4. **1.** $(M \vee N) \supset (O \bullet P)$
2. $\sim O$
$\therefore \sim M$
3. $\sim O \vee \sim P$
4. $\sim(O \bullet P)$
5. $\sim(M \vee N)$
6. $\sim M \bullet \sim N$
7. $\sim M$

***5.**
1. $(Q \vee {\sim}R) \vee S$
2. ${\sim}Q \vee (R \bullet {\sim}Q)$
$\therefore R \supset S$
3. $({\sim}Q \vee R) \bullet ({\sim}Q \vee {\sim}Q)$
4. $({\sim}Q \vee {\sim}Q) \bullet ({\sim}Q \vee R)$
5. ${\sim}Q \vee {\sim}Q$
6. ${\sim}Q$
7. $Q \vee ({\sim}R \vee S)$
8. ${\sim}R \vee S$
9. $R \supset S$

6.
1. $T \bullet (U \vee V)$
2. $T \supset [U \supset (W \bullet X)]$
3. $(T \bullet V) \supset {\sim}(W \vee X)$
$\therefore W \equiv X$
4. $(T \bullet U) \supset (W \bullet X)$
5. $(T \bullet V) \supset ({\sim}W \bullet {\sim}X)$
6. $[(T \bullet U) \supset (W \bullet X)] \bullet$
$[(T \bullet V) \supset ({\sim}W \bullet {\sim}X)]$
7. $(T \bullet U) \vee (T \bullet V)$
8. $(W \bullet X) \vee ({\sim}W \bullet {\sim}X)$
9. $W \equiv X$

7.
1. $Y \supset Z$
2. $Z \supset [Y \supset (R \vee S)]$
3. $R \equiv S$
4. ${\sim}(R \bullet S)$
$\therefore {\sim}Y$
5. $(R \bullet S) \vee ({\sim}R \bullet {\sim}S)$
6. ${\sim}R \bullet {\sim}S$
7. ${\sim}(R \vee S)$
8. $Y \supset [Y \supset (R \vee S)]$
9. $(Y \bullet Y) \supset (R \vee S)$
10. $Y \supset (R \vee S)$
11. ${\sim}Y$

8.
1. $A \supset B$
2. $B \supset C$
3. $C \supset A$
4. $A \supset {\sim}C$
$\therefore {\sim}A \bullet {\sim}C$
5. $A \supset C$
6. $(A \supset C) \bullet (C \supset A)$
7. $A \equiv C$
8. $(A \bullet C) \vee ({\sim}A \bullet {\sim}C)$
9. ${\sim}A \vee {\sim}C$
10. ${\sim}(A \bullet C)$
11. ${\sim}A \bullet {\sim}C$

9.
1. $(D \bullet E) \supset {\sim}F$
2. $F \vee (G \bullet H)$
3. $D \equiv E$
$\therefore D \supset G$
4. $(D \supset E) \bullet (E \supset D)$
5. $D \supset E$
6. $D \supset (D \bullet E)$
7. $D \supset {\sim}F$
8. $(F \vee G) \bullet (F \vee H)$
9. $F \vee G$
10. ${\sim}{\sim}F \vee G$
11. ${\sim}F \supset G$
12. $D \supset G$

***10.**
1. $(I \vee {\sim}{\sim}J) \bullet K$
2. $[{\sim}L \supset {\sim}(K \bullet J)] \bullet$
$[K \supset (I \supset {\sim}M)]$
$\therefore {\sim}(M \bullet {\sim}L)$
3. $[(K \bullet J) \supset L] \bullet$
$[K \supset (I \supset {\sim}M)]$
4. $[(K \bullet J) \supset L] \bullet$
$[(K \bullet I) \supset {\sim}M]$
5. $(I \vee J) \bullet K$
6. $K \bullet (I \vee J)$
7. $(K \bullet I) \vee (K \bullet J)$
8. $(K \bullet J) \vee (K \bullet I)$
9. $L \vee {\sim}M$
10. ${\sim}M \vee L$
11. ${\sim}M \vee {\sim}{\sim}L$
12. ${\sim}(M \bullet {\sim}L)$

We now advance to the construction of formal proofs using the full set of rules of inference. We begin with simple arguments, whose proofs require only two statements added to the premises. Each of those statements, of course, may be justified by either an elementary valid argument form or by one of the rules of replacement. We begin with two examples, the first two exercises of Set **B**, immediately following.

EXAMPLE 1

1. $A \supset \sim A$

$\therefore \sim A$

SOLUTION

The first step in this proof, obviously, must manipulate the single premise. What can we do with it that will be helpful? If we apply Material Implication (Impl.), we will obtain a statement, $\sim A \vee \sim A$, to which we can apply the valid argument form Tautology (Taut.), and that will yield the conclusion we seek. So the proof is

1. $A \supset \sim A$

$\therefore \sim A$

2. $\sim A \vee \sim A$ 1, Impl.
3. $\sim A$ 2, Taut.

EXAMPLE 2

2. $B \bullet (C \bullet D)$

$\therefore C \bullet (D \bullet B)$

SOLUTION

In this proof we need only rearrange the statements, all of which are given as true. In the first step we can commute the main conjunction of the first premise, which will yield $(C \bullet D) \bullet B$. Then we need only regroup the three statements by Association. So the proof is

1. $B \bullet (C \bullet D)$

$\therefore C \bullet (D \bullet B)$

2. $(C \bullet D) \bullet B$ 1, Com.
3. $C \bullet (D \bullet B)$ 2, Assoc.

In this proof, as in all formal proofs, the last line of the sequence we construct *is* the conclusion we are aiming to deduce.

EXERCISES

B. For each of the following arguments, adding just two statements to the premises will produce a formal proof of its validity. Construct a formal proof for each of these arguments.

In these formal proofs, and in all the proofs to follow in later sections, note to the right of each line the rule of inference that justifies that line of the proof. It is most convenient if the justification specifies first the number of the line (or lines) being used, and then the name (abbreviated) of the rule of inference that has been applied to those numbered lines.

1. $A \supset \sim A$
$\therefore \sim A$

2. $B \bullet (C \bullet D)$
$\therefore C \bullet (D \bullet B)$

3. E
$\therefore (E \vee F) \bullet (E \vee G)$

4. $H \vee (I \bullet J)$
$\therefore H \vee I$

***5.** $\sim K \vee (L \supset M)$
$\therefore (K \bullet L) \supset M$

6. $(N \bullet O) \supset P$
$\therefore (N \bullet O) \supset [N \bullet (O \bullet P)]$

7. $Q \supset [R \supset (S \supset T)]$
$Q \supset (Q \bullet R)$
$\therefore Q \supset (S \supset T)$

8. $U \supset \sim V$
V
$\therefore \sim U$

9. $W \supset X$
$\sim Y \supset \sim X$
$\therefore W \supset Y$

***10.** $Z \supset A$
$\sim A \vee B$
$\therefore Z \supset B$

11. $C \supset \sim D$
$\sim E \supset D$
$\therefore C \supset \sim\sim E$

12. $F \equiv G$
$\sim(F \bullet G)$
$\therefore \sim F \bullet \sim G$

13. $H \supset (I \bullet J)$
$I \supset (J \supset K)$
$\therefore H \supset K$

14. $(L \supset M) \bullet (N \supset M)$
$L \vee N$
$\therefore M$

***15.** $(O \vee P) \supset (Q \vee R)$
$P \vee O$
$\therefore Q \vee R$

16. $(S \bullet T) \vee (U \bullet V)$
$\sim S \vee \sim T$
$\therefore U \bullet V$

17. $(W \bullet X) \supset Y$
$(X \supset Y) \supset Z$
$\therefore W \supset Z$

18. $(A \vee B) \supset (C \vee D)$
$\sim C \bullet \sim D$
$\therefore \sim(A \vee B)$

19. $(E \bullet F) \supset (G \bullet H)$
$F \bullet E$
$\therefore G \bullet H$

***20.** $I \supset [J \vee (K \vee L)]$
$\sim[(J \vee K) \vee L]$
$\therefore \sim I$

21. $(M \supset N) \bullet (\sim O \vee P)$
$M \vee O$
$\therefore N \vee P$

22. $(\sim Q \supset \sim R) \bullet (\sim S \supset \sim T)$
$\sim\sim(\sim Q \vee \sim S)$
$\therefore \sim R \vee \sim T$

23. $\sim[(U \supset V) \bullet (V \supset U)]$
$(W \equiv X) \supset (U \equiv V)$
$\therefore \sim(W \equiv X)$

24. $(Y \supset Z) \bullet (Z \supset Y)$
$\therefore (Y \bullet Z) \vee (\sim Y \bullet \sim Z)$

***25.** $A \vee B$
$C \vee D$
$\therefore [(A \vee B) \bullet C] \vee [(A \vee B) \bullet D]$

26. $[(E \vee F) \bullet (G \vee H)] \supset (F \bullet I)$
$(G \vee H) \bullet (E \vee F)$
$\therefore F \bullet I$

27. $(J \bullet K) \supset [(L \bullet M) \vee (N \bullet O)]$
$\sim(L \bullet M) \bullet \sim(N \bullet O)$
$\therefore \sim(J \bullet K)$

28. $(P \supset Q) \supset [(R \vee S) \bullet (T \equiv U)]$
$(R \vee S) \supset [(T \equiv U) \supset Q]$
$\therefore (P \supset Q) \supset Q$

29. $[V \bullet (W \vee X)] \supset (Y \supset Z)$
$\sim(Y \supset Z) \vee (\sim W \equiv A)$
$\therefore [V \bullet (W \vee X)] \supset (\sim W \equiv A)$

***30.** $\sim[(B \supset \sim C) \bullet (\sim C \supset B)]$
$(D \bullet E) \supset (B \equiv \sim C)$
$\therefore \sim(D \bullet E)$

As we advance to arguments whose formal proofs require three lines added to the premises, it becomes important to devise a strategy for determining the needed sequence. Most such arguments remain fairly simple, but the path to the proof may sometimes be less than obvious. Again we begin with two examples, the first two exercises of Set **C**, which follows the examples.

EXAMPLE 1

1. $\sim A \supset A$
$\therefore A$

SOLUTION

We have only one premise with which to work. It is often fruitful to convert conditional statements into disjunctive statements. Doing that with line 1 (using Impl.) will yield $\sim\sim A$ as the first of the disjuncts; that component may be readily replaced with *A;* then, applying the argument form Tautology will give us what we aim for. The proof is

1. $\sim A \supset A$

$\therefore A$

2. $\sim\sim A \vee A$ — 1, Impl.

3. $A \vee A$ — 2, D.N.

4. A — 3, Taut.

EXAMPLE 2

1. ~B v (C • D)

   B ⊃ C

SOLUTION

The single premise in this argument contains the statement *D*. We need a proof whose conclusion is *B* ⊃ *C*, and therefore we must somehow eliminate that *D*. How can we do that? We can break apart the statement (*C* • *D*) by *distributing* the statement ~*B*. Distribution asserts, in one of its variants, that [*p* v (*q* • *r*)] $\overset{T}{\equiv}$ [(*p* v *q*) • (*p* v *r*)]. Applied to line 1, that replacement will yield (~*B* v C) • (~*B* v *D*). These two expressions are just conjoined, so by simplification we may extract (~*B* v C). This statement may be replaced, using Impl., by *B* ⊃ *C*, which is the conclusion sought. The proof is

1. ~B v (C • D)	
∴ B ⊃ C	
2. (~B v C) • (~B v D)	1, Dist.
3. ~B v C	2, Simp.
4. B ⊃ C	3, Impl.

EXERCISES

C. For each of the following arguments, a formal proof may be constructed by adding just three statements to the premises. Construct a formal proof of validity for each of them.

1. ~A ⊃ A
   ∴ A

2. ~B v (C • D)
   ∴ B ⊃ C

3. E v (F • G)
   ∴ E v G

4. H • (I • J)
   ∴ J • (I • H)

*5. [(K v L) v M] v N
   ∴ (N v K) v (L v M)

6. O ⊃ P
   P ⊃ ~P
   ∴ ~O

7. Q ⊃ (R ⊃ S)
   Q ⊃ R
   ∴ Q ⊃ S

8. T ⊃ U
   ~(U v V)
   ∴ ~T

9. W • (X v Y)
   ~W v ~X
   ∴ W • Y

*10. (Z v A) v B
   ~A
   ∴ Z v B

11. $(C \vee D) \supset (E \bullet F)$
$D \vee C$
$\therefore E$

12. $G \supset H$
$H \supset G$
$\therefore (G \bullet H) \vee (\sim G \bullet \sim H)$

13. $(I \supset J) \bullet (K \supset L)$
$I \vee (K \bullet M)$
$\therefore J \vee L$

14. $(N \bullet O) \supset P$
$(\sim P \supset \sim O) \supset Q$
$\therefore N \supset Q$

***15.** $[R \supset (S \supset T)] \bullet [(R \bullet T) \supset U]$
$R \bullet (S \vee T)$
$\therefore T \vee U$

Formal proofs of validity sometimes require many steps or lines in the needed sequence. We will find that certain *patterns* of inference are encountered repeatedly in longer proofs. It is wise to become familiar with these recurring patterns.

This may be nicely illustrated using the first two exercises of Set **D,** which follows immediately below. First, suppose that a given statement, *A,* is known to be false. The next stage of the proof may require that we prove that some different statement, say *B,* is implied by the truth of the statement that we know is false. This can be easily proved, and the pattern is not uncommon. Put formally, how may we infer $A \supset B$ from $\sim A$? Let us examine the argument.

EXAMPLE 1

1. $\sim A$

$\therefore A \supset B$

SOLUTION

If $\sim A$ is known to be true, as here, then *A* must be false. A false statement materially implies any other statement. So $A \supset B$ must be true, whatever *B* may assert, if we know that $\sim A$ is true. In this case, $\sim A$ is given as premise; we only need to add the desired *B* and then apply Implication. The proof of the argument (or the proof segment, when it is a part of some longer proof) is

1. $\sim A$

$\therefore A \supset B$

2. $\sim A \vee B$ 1, Add.

3. $A \supset B$ 2, Impl.

EXAMPLE 2

1. C

$\therefore D \supset C$

This pattern arises very frequently. The truth of some statement *C* is known. In this case it is given as a premise; in some longer proof we might have established its truth at some other point in the sequence. We know that a true statement is materially implied by any statement whatever. Therefore any statement we choose, *D*, must imply *C*. Put formally, how may we infer $D \supset C$ from *C*?

SOLUTION

D does not appear in the premise but it does appear in the conclusion, so we must somehow get *D* into the sequence of steps. We could simply add *D*, but that won't succeed—because after commuting that disjunction, and replacing it, using Impl., with a conditional, we wind up with $\sim D \supset C$, which is certainly not the conclusion we were after. We want $D \supset C$. To obtain this needed result we must, in the very first step, add $\sim D$ rather than *D*. This we certainly may do, because Addition permits us to add disjunctively any statement whatever to a statement we know to be true. Then, applying Com. and Impl. will give us what we seek. The formal proof of the argument in this case (or the proof segment, when it occurs as part of a longer proof) is

1. C
   $\therefore D \supset C$
2. $C \vee \sim D$ 1, Add.
3. $\sim D \vee C$ 2, Com.
4. $D \supset C$ 3, Impl.

EXERCISES

D. Each of the following exercises immediately below exhibits a commonly recurring pattern. Constructing the formal proof in each case will take some ingenuity, and (in a few cases) the proof will require eight or nine lines. However, most of these proofs will present little difficulty, and devising the strategies needed to produce them is excellent practice. Construct a formal proof for each of the following arguments.

1. $\sim A$
   $\therefore A \supset B$

2. C
   $\therefore D \supset C$

3. $E \supset (F \supset G)$
   $\therefore F \supset (E \supset G)$

4. $H \supset (I \bullet J)$
   $\therefore H \supset I$

***5.** $K \supset L$
   $\therefore K \supset (L \vee M)$

6. $N \supset O$
   $\therefore (N \bullet P) \supset O$

7. $(Q \vee R) \supset S$
   $\therefore Q \supset S$

8. $T \supset U$
   $T \supset V$
   $\therefore T \supset (U \bullet V)$

9. $W \supset X$
   $Y \supset X$
   $\therefore (W \vee Y) \supset X$

*10. $Z \supset A$
   $Z \vee A$
   $\therefore A$

When, after substantial practice, one has become well familiar with the nineteen rules of inference, and is comfortable in applying them, it is time to tackle formal proofs that are longer and more convoluted. The three sets of exercises that follow will present some challenges, but devising these formal proofs will be a source of genuine satisfaction. The great mathematician, G. H. Hardy, long ago observed that there is a natural and widespread thirst for intellectual "kick"—and that "nothing else has quite the kick" that solving logical problems has.

Arguments in a natural language, as in the last two sets, need no further explanation. After translating them into symbolic notation, using the suggested abbreviations, the procedure for constructing the proofs is no different from that used when we begin with an argument formulated in symbols. Before adventuring further in the realm of logical proofs, it will be helpful to examine, from Exercise Set **E**, two examples of the kinds of formal proofs we will be dealing with from this point forward.

The arguments presented in all these sets of exercises are valid. Therefore, because the system of nineteen rules we have devised is known to be complete, we may be certain that a formal proof for each one of those arguments can be constructed. But the path from the premises to the conclusion may be far from obvious. In each case, some plan of action must be devised as one goes forward.

We illustrate the need for a plan of attack, and the way in which such a plan may be devised, by examining very closely two of the exercises—the first and the last—in Set **E**, which follows on pages 416–417.

EXAMPLE 1

1. $A \supset \sim B$
   $\sim(C \bullet \sim A)$
   $\therefore C \supset \sim B$

SOLUTION

In this argument the conclusion unites a statement that appears in the second premise, *C*, with a statement that appears in the first premise, ~*B*.

How shall we effect that unification? The first premise is a conditional whose consequent, ~*B*, is also the consequent of the conclusion. The second premise contains the negation of the antecedent of the first premise, ~*A*. If we can manipulate the second premise so as to emerge with *C* ⊃ *A*, we can achieve the needed unification with H.S. We can do that. If we apply De M. to the second premise we will get a disjunction that, when replaced by a conditional using Impl., will be one short step away from the conditional needed. The formal proof is

1. *A* ⊃ ~*B*
2. ~(*C* • ~*A*)
   ∴ *C* ⊃ ~*B*
3. ~*C* v ~~*A* — 2, De M.
4. *C* ⊃ ~~*A* — 3, Impl.
5. *C* ⊃ *A* — 4, D.N.
6. *C* ⊃ ~*B* — 5, 1, H.S.

Note that in this proof, as in many, a somewhat different sequence can be devised that leads to the same successful result. Line 3 is a needed first step. But we could have kept the disjunction on line 4, at that point only replacing ~~*A* by *A*:

4. ~*C* v *A*	3, D.N.	Replacement of this by a conditional is then needed.
5. *C* ⊃ *A*	4, Impl.	H.S. will then again concludes the proof:
6. *C* ⊃ ~*B*	5, 1, H.S.	

The difference between the two sequences, in this case, is chiefly one of order. Sometimes there are alternative proofs using quite different strategies altogether.

Let us examine, as our final explication of the detail of formal proofs, one of the longer arguments in Set **E**, exercise 20, in which devising the strategy needed is more challenging.

EXAMPLE 2

20. (*R* v *S*) ⊃ (*T* • *U*)
~*R* ⊃ (*V* ⊃ ~*V*)
~*T*
∴ ~*V*

The conclusion we seek, ~*V*, appears only in the second of three premises, and even there it is buried in a longer compound statement. How may we prove it? We notice that the consequent of the second premise (*V* ⊃ ~*V*) is a conditional that, if replaced by a disjunction, yields ~*V* v ~*V*, which in turn yields ~*V* independently, by Taut. Might we obtain (*V* ⊃ ~*V*) by M.P.? For that we need ~*R*. *R* appears in the first premise, as part of a disjunction; if we can obtain the negation of that disjunction, we may derive ~*R*. To obtain the negation of that disjunction we need the negation of the consequent of the first premise, so M.T. may be applied. It can be seen that the negation of that consequent (*T* • *U*) should be available, because the third premise asserts ~*T*, and if ~*T* is true, than (*T* • *U*) surely is false. How may we show this? We look at the negation that we seek: ~(*T* • *U*). This is logically equivalent to ~*T* v ~*U*. We can establish ~*T* v ~*U* simply by adding ~*U* to ~*T*. All the elements of the plan are before us; we need only put them into a logical sequence that is watertight. This is not at all difficult once the strategy has been devised. We begin by building the negation of the consequent of the first premise, then derive the negation of the antecedent of that premise, then obtain ~*R*. With ~*R* we establish (*V* ⊃ ~*V*) by M.P., and the conclusion we want to prove is at hand. The actual lines of the formal proof are

1. (*R* v *S*) ⊃ (*T* • *U*)		
2. ~*R* ⊃ (*V* ⊃ ~*V*)		
3. ~*T*		
∴ ~*V*		
4. ~*T* v ~*U*	3, Add.	
5. ~(*T* • *U*)	4, De M.	
6. ~(*R* v *S*)	1, 5, M. T.	
7. ~*R* • ~*S*	6, De M.	
8. ~*R*	7, Simp.	
9. *V* ⊃ ~*V*	2, 8, M.P.	
10. ~*V* v ~*V*	9, Impl.	
11. ~*V*	10, Taut.	Q.E.D.

At the conclusion of a proof it is traditional practice to place the letters Q.E.D.—a minor exhibition of pride in the form of an acronym for the Latin expression, *Quod erat demonstrandum*—What was to be demonstrated.

EXERCISES

E. Construct a formal proof of validity for each of the following arguments.

1. *A* ⊃ ~*B*
   ~(*C* • ~*A*)
   ∴ *C* ⊃ ~*B*

2. (*D* • ~*E*) ⊃ *F*
   ~(*E* v *F*)
   ∴ ~*D*

3. (*G* ⊃ ~*H*) ⊃ *I*
   ~(*G* • *H*)
   ∴ *I* v ~*H*

4. (*J* v *K*) ⊃ ~*L*
   L
   ∴ ~*J*

***5.** $[(M \bullet N) \bullet O] \supset P$
$Q \supset [(O \bullet M) \bullet N]$
$\therefore \sim Q \vee P$

6. $R \vee (S \bullet \sim T)$
$(R \vee S) \supset (U \vee \sim T)$
$\therefore T \supset U$

7. $(\sim V \supset W) \bullet (X \supset W)$
$\sim(\sim X \bullet V)$
$\therefore W$

8. $[(Y \bullet Z) \supset A] \bullet [(Y \bullet B) \supset C]$
$(B \vee Z) \bullet Y$
$\therefore A \vee C$

9. $\sim D \supset (\sim E \supset \sim F)$
$\sim(F \bullet \sim D) \supset \sim G$
$\therefore G \supset E$

***10.** $[H \vee (I \vee J)] \supset (K \supset J)$
$L \supset [I \vee (J \vee H)]$
$\therefore (L \bullet K) \supset J$

11. $M \supset N$
$M \supset (N \supset O)$
$\therefore M \supset O$

12. $(P \supset Q) \bullet (P \vee R)$
$(R \supset S) \bullet (R \vee P)$
$\therefore Q \vee S$

13. $T \supset (U \bullet V)$
$(U \vee V) \supset W$
$\therefore T \supset W$

14. $(X \vee Y) \supset (X \bullet Y)$
$\sim(X \vee Y)$
$\therefore \sim(X \bullet Y)$

***15.** $(Z \supset Z) \supset (A \supset A)$
$(A \supset A) \supset (Z \supset Z)$
$\therefore A \supset A$

16. $\sim B \vee [(C \supset D) \bullet (E \supset D)]$
$B \bullet (C \vee E)$
$\therefore D$

17. $\sim F \vee \sim[\sim(G \bullet H) \bullet (G \vee H)]$
$(G \supset H) \supset [(H \supset G) \supset I]$
$\therefore F \supset (F \bullet I)$

18. $J \vee (\sim J \bullet K)$
$J \supset L$
$\therefore (L \bullet J) \equiv J$

19. $(M \supset N) \bullet (O \supset P)$
$\sim N \vee \sim P$
$\sim(M \bullet O) \supset Q$
$\therefore Q$

***20.** $(R \vee S) \supset (T \bullet U)$
$\sim R \supset (V \supset \sim V)$
$\sim T$
$\therefore \sim V$

F. Construct a formal proof of validity for each of the following arguments, in each case using the suggested notation.

***1.** Either the manager didn't notice the change or else he approves of it. He noticed it all right. So he must approve of it. *(N, A)*

2. The oxygen in the tube either combined with the filament to form an oxide or else it vanished completely. The oxygen in the tube could not have vanished completely. Therefore the oxygen in the tube combined with the filament to form an oxide. *(C, V)*

3. If a political leader who sees her former opinions to be wrong does not alter her course, she is guilty of deceit; and if she does alter her course, she is open to a charge of inconsistency. She either alters her course or she doesn't. Therefore either she is guilty of deceit or else she is open to a charge of inconsistency. *(A, D, I)*

4. It is not the case that she either forgot or wasn't able to finish. Therefore she was able to finish. *(F, A)*

***5.** If the litmus paper turns red, then the solution is acid. Hence if the litmus paper turns red, then either the solution is acid or something is wrong somewhere. *(R, A, W)*

6. She can have many friends only if she respects them as individuals. If she respects them as individuals, then she cannot expect them all to behave alike. She does have many friends. Therefore she does not expect them all to behave alike. *(F, R, E)*

7. If the victim had money in his pockets, then robbery wasn't the motive for the crime. But robbery or vengeance was the motive for the crime. The victim had money in his pockets. Therefore vengeance must have been the motive for the crime. *(M, R, V)*

8. Napoleon is to be condemned if he usurped power that was not rightfully his own. Either Napoleon was a legitimate monarch or else he usurped power that was not rightfully his own. Napoleon was not a legitimate monarch. So Napoleon is to be condemned. *(C, U, L)*

9. If we extend further credit on the Wilkins account, they will have a moral obligation to accept our bid on their next project. We can figure a more generous margin of profit in preparing our estimates if they have a moral obligation to accept our bid on their next project. Figuring a more generous margin of profit in preparing our estimates will cause our general financial condition to improve considerably. Hence a considerable improvement in our general financial condition will follow from our extension of further credit on the Wilkins account. *(C, M, P, I)*

***10.** If the laws are good and their enforcement is strict, then crime will diminish. If strict enforcement of laws will make crime diminish, then our problem is a practical one. The laws are good. Therefore our problem is a practical one. *(G, S, D, P)*

11. Had Roman citizenship guaranteed civil liberties, then Roman citizens would have enjoyed religious freedom. Had Roman citizens enjoyed religious freedom, there would have been no persecution of the early Christians. But the early Christians were persecuted. Hence Roman citizenship could not have guaranteed civil liberties. *(G, F, P)*

12. If the first disjunct of a disjunction is true, the disjunction as a whole is true. Therefore if both the first and second disjuncts of the disjunction are true, then the disjunction as a whole is true. *(F, W, S)*

13. If the new courthouse is to be conveniently located, it will have to be situated in the heart of the city; and if it is to be adequate to its function, it will have to be built large enough to house all the city offices. If the new courthouse is situated in the heart of the city and is built large enough to house all the city offices, then its cost will run to over $10 million. Its cost cannot exceed $10 million. Therefore either the new courthouse will have an inconvenient location or it will be inadequate to its function. (*C, H, A, L, O*)

14. Jalana will come if she gets the message, provided that she is still interested. Although she didn't come, she is still interested. Therefore she didn't get the message. (*C, M, I*)

*15. If the Mosaic account of the cosmogony (the account of the creation in Genesis) is strictly correct, the sun was not created until the fourth day. And if the sun was not created until the fourth day, it could not have been the cause of the alternation of day and night for the first three days. But either the word "day" is used in Scripture in a different sense from that in which it is commonly accepted now or else the sun must have been the cause of the alternation of day and night for the first three days. Hence it follows that either the Mosaic account of the cosmogony is not strictly correct or else the word "day" is used in Scripture in a different sense from that in which it is commonly accepted now. (*M, C, A, D*)

16. If the teller or the cashier had pushed the alarm button, the vault would have locked automatically, and the police would have arrived within three minutes. Had the police arrived within three minutes, the robbers' car would have been overtaken. But the robbers' car was not overtaken. Therefore the teller did not push the alarm button. (*T, C, V, P, O*)

17. If people are always guided by their sense of duty, they must forgo the enjoyment of many pleasures; and if they are always guided by their desire for pleasure, they must often neglect their duty. People are either always guided by their sense of duty or always guided by their desire for pleasure. If people are always guided by their sense of duty, they do not often neglect their duty; and if they are always guided by their desire for pleasure, they do not forgo the enjoyment of many pleasures. Therefore people must forgo the enjoyment of many pleasures if and only if they do not often neglect their duty. (*D, F, P, N*)

18. Although world population is increasing, agricultural production is declining and manufacturing output remains constant. If agricultural production declines and world population increases, then either new food sources will become available or else there will be a radical redistribution of food resources in the world unless human nutritional requirements diminish. No new food sources will become available, yet neither will family planning be encouraged nor will human nutritional requirements diminish. Therefore there will be a radical redistribution of food resources in the world. (*W, A, M, N, R, H, P*)

19. Either the robber came in the door, or else the crime was an inside one and one of the servants is implicated. The robber could come in the door only if the latch had been raised from the inside; but one of the servants is surely implicated if the latch was raised from the inside. Therefore one of the servants is implicated. (*D, I, S, L*)

***20.** If I pay my tuition, I won't have any money left. I'll buy a computer only if I have money. I won't learn to program computers unless I buy a computer. But if I don't pay tuition, I can't enroll in classes; and if I don't enroll in classes I certainly won't buy a computer. I must either pay my tuition or not pay my tuition. So I surely will not learn to program computers! (*P, M, C, L, E*)

G. The five arguments that follow are also valid, and a proof of the validity of each of them is called for. However, these proofs will be somewhat more difficult to construct than those in earlier exercises, and students who find themselves stymied from time to time ought not become discouraged. What may appear difficult on first appraisal may come to seem much less difficult with continuing efforts. Familiarity with the nineteen rules of inference, and repeated practice in applying those rules, are the keys to the construction of these proofs.

1. If you study the humanities, then you will develop an understanding of people, and if you study the sciences, then you will develop an understanding of the world about you. So if you study either the humanities or the sciences, then you will develop an understanding either of people or of the world about you. (*H, P, S, W*)

2. If you study the humanities then you will develop an understanding of people, and if you study the sciences then you will develop an understanding of the world about you. So if you study both the humanities and the sciences, you will develop an understanding both of people and of the world about you. (*H, P, S, W*)

3. If you have free will, then your actions are not determined by any antecedent events. If you have free will, then if your actions are not determined by any antecedent events, then your actions cannot be predicted. If your actions are not determined by any antecedent events, then if your actions cannot be predicted then the consequences of your actions cannot be predicted. Therefore if you have free will, then the consequences of your actions cannot be predicted. (*F, A, P, C*)

4. Socrates was a great philosopher. Therefore either Socrates was happily married or else he wasn't. (*G, H*)

***5.** If either Socrates was happily married or else he wasn't, then Socrates was a great philosopher. Therefore Socrates was a great philosopher. (*H, G*)

9.9 Proof of Invalidity

For an invalid argument there is, of course, no formal proof of validity. But if we fail to discover a formal proof of validity for a given argument, this failure does not prove that the argument is invalid and that no such proof can be constructed. It may mean only that we have not tried hard enough. Our inability to find a proof of validity may be caused by the fact that the argument is not valid, but it may be caused instead by our own lack of ingenuity—as a consequence of the noneffective character of the process of proof construction. Not being able to construct a formal proof of its validity does not prove an argument to be invalid. What *does* constitute a proof that a given argument is invalid?

The method about to be described is closely related to the truth-table method, although it is a great deal shorter. It will be helpful to recall how an invalid argument form is proved invalid by a truth table. If a single case (row) can be found in which truth values are assigned to the statement variables in such a way that the premises are made true and the conclusion false, then the argument form is invalid. If we can somehow make an assignment of truth values to the simple component statements of an argument that will make its premises true and its conclusion false, then making that assignment will suffice to prove the argument invalid. To make such an assignment is, in effect, what the truth table does. If we can make such an assignment of truth values without actually constructing the whole truth table, much work will be eliminated.

Consider this argument:

If the governor favors public housing, then she is in favor of restricting the scope of private enterprise.

If the governor were a socialist, then she would be in favor of restricting the scope of private enterprise.

Therefore if the governor favors public housing, then she is a socialist.

It is symbolized as

$F \supset R$

$S \supset R$

$\therefore F \supset S$

and we can prove it invalid without having to construct a complete truth table. First we ask, "What assignment of truth values is required to make the conclusion false?" It is clear that a conditional is false only if its antecedent is true and its consequent false. Hence assigning the truth value "true" to F and "false" to S will make the conclusion $F \supset S$ false. Now if the truth value "true" is assigned to R, both premises are made true, because a conditional is true whenever its consequent is true. We can say, then, that if the truth value "true" is assigned to F and to R, and the truth value "false" is assigned to S, the argument will have true premises and a false conclusion and is thus proved to be invalid.

This method of proving invalidity is an alternative to the truth-table method of proof. The two methods are closely related, however, and the essential connection between them should be noticed. In effect, what we did when we made the indicated assignment of truth values was to construct one row of the given argument's truth table. The relationship can perhaps be seen more clearly when the truth-value assignments are written out horizontally:

F	R	S	$F \supset R$	$S \supset R$	$F \supset S$
True	True	False	True	True	False

in which configuration they constitute one row (the second) of the truth table for the given argument. *An argument is proved invalid by displaying at least one row of its truth table in which all its premises are true but its conclusion is false.* Consequently, we need not examine *all* rows of its truth table to discover an argument's invalidity: discovering a single row in which its premises are all true and its conclusion false will suffice. This method of proving invalidity is a method of constructing such a row without having to construct the entire truth table.*

The present method is shorter than writing out an entire truth table, and the amount of time and work saved is proportionally greater for arguments involving a greater number of component simple statements. For arguments

*The whole truth table (were we to construct it) would of course test the validity of the *specific form* of the argument in question. If it can be shown that the specific form of an argument is invalid, we may infer that the argument having that specific form is an invalid argument. The method described here differs only in that truth values here are assigned directly to premises and conclusion; nonetheless, the relation between this method and the truth-table method applied in Chapter 8 is very close.

with a considerable number of premises, or with premises of considerable complexity, the needed assignment of truth values may not be so easy to make. There is no mechanical method of proceeding, but some hints may prove helpful.

It is most efficient to proceed by assigning those values seen immediately to be essential if invalidity is to be proved. Thus, any premise that simply asserts the truth of some statement *S* suggests the immediate assignment of **T** to *S* (or **F** if the falsehood of *S* was asserted as premise), because we know that all the premises must be made true. The same principle applies to the statements in the conclusion, except that the assignments of truth values there must make the conclusion false. Thus a conclusion of the form $A \supset B$ suggests the immediate assignment of **T** to *A* and **F** to *B*, and a conclusion in the form $A \vee B$ suggests the immediate assignment of **F** to *A* and **F** to *B*, because only those assignments could result in a proof of invalidity.

Whether one ought to begin by seeking to make the premises true or by seeking to make the conclusion false depends on the structure of the propositions; usually it is best to begin wherever assignments can be made with greatest confidence. Of course, there will be many circumstances in which the first assignments have to be arbitrary and tentative. A certain amount of trial and error is likely to be needed. Even so, this method of proving invalidity is almost always shorter and easier than writing out a complete truth table.

EXERCISES

Prove the invalidity of each of the following by the method of assigning truth values.

***1.** $A \supset B$
$C \supset D$
$A \vee D$
$\therefore B \vee C$

2. $\sim(E \bullet F)$
$(\sim E \bullet \sim F) \supset (G \bullet H)$
$H \supset G$
$\therefore G$

3. $I \vee \sim J$
$\sim(\sim K \bullet L)$
$\sim(\sim I \bullet \sim L)$
$\therefore \sim J \supset K$

4. $M \supset (N \vee O)$
$N \supset (P \vee Q)$
$Q \supset R$
$\sim(R \vee P)$
$\therefore \sim M$

***5.** $S \supset (T \supset U)$
$V \supset (W \supset X)$
$T \supset (V \bullet W)$
$\sim(T \bullet X)$
$\therefore S \equiv U$

6. $A \equiv (B \vee C)$
$B \equiv (C \vee A)$
$C \equiv (A \vee B)$
$\sim A$
$\therefore B \vee C$

7. D ⊃ (E v F)
   G ⊃ (H v I)
   ~E ⊃ (I v J)
   (I ⊃ G) • (~H ⊃ ~G)
   ~J
   ∴ D ⊃ (G v I)

8. K ⊃ (L • M)
   (L ⊃ N) v ~K
   O ⊃ (P v ~N)
   (~P v Q) • ~Q
   (R v ~P) v ~M
   ∴ K ⊃ R

9. (S ⊃ T) • (T ⊃ S)
   (U • T) v (~T • ~U)
   (U v V) v (S v T)
   ~U ⊃ (W • X)
   (V ⊃ ~S) • (~V ⊃ ~Y)
   X ⊃ (~Y ⊃ ~X)
   (U v S) • (V v Z)
   ∴ X • Z

*10. A ⊃ (B ⊃ ~C)
   (D ⊃ B) • (E ⊃ A)
   F v C
   G ⊃ ~H
   (I ⊃ G) • (H ⊃ J)
   I ≡ ~D
   (B ⊃ H) • (~H ⊃ D)
   ∴ E ≡ F

9.10 Inconsistency

An argument is proved invalid if truth values can be assigned to make all of its premises true and its conclusion false. If a deductive argument is not invalid, it must be valid. So, if truth values *cannot* be assigned to make the premises true and the conclusion false, then the argument must be valid. This follows from the definition of validity, but it has this curious consequence: Any argument whose premises are inconsistent must be valid.

In the following argument, for example, the premises appear to be totally irrelevant to the conclusion:

If the airplane had engine trouble, it would have landed at Bend.

If the airplane did not have engine trouble, it would have landed at Creswell.

The airplane did not land at either Bend or Creswell.

Therefore the airplane must have landed in Denver.

Here is its symbolic translation:

A ⊃ B

~A ⊃ C

~(B v C)

∴ D

Any attempt to assign truth values to its component simple statements in such a way as to make the conclusion false and the premises all true is doomed to failure. Even if we ignore the conclusion and attend only to the premises, we find that there is no way to assign truth values to their components such that the premises will all be true. No truth-value assignment can make them all true because they are inconsistent with one another. Their conjunction is self-contradictory, being a substitution instance of a self-contradictory statement form. If we were to construct a truth table for this argument, we would find that in every row at least one of the premises is false. Because there is no row in which the premises are all true, there is no row in which the premises are all true and the conclusion false. Hence the truth table for this argument would establish that it is in fact valid. And, of course, we can also provide a formal proof of its validity:

1. $A \supset B$	
2. $\sim A \supset C$	
3. $\sim(B \vee C)$ / $\therefore D$	
4. $\sim B \bullet \sim C$	3, De. M.
5. $\sim B$	4, Simp.
6. $\sim A$	1,5, M.T.
7. C	2,6, M.P.
8. $\sim C \bullet \sim B$	4, Com
9. $\sim C$	8, Simp.
10. $C \vee D$	7, Add.
11. D	10, 9, D.S.

In this proof, lines 1 though 9 are devoted to making explicit the inconsistency that is implicitly contained in the premises. That inconsistency emerges clearly in line 7 (which asserts C) and line 9 (which asserts ~C). Once this explicit contradiction has been expressed, the conclusion follows swiftly using Add. and D.S.

Thus we see that if a set of premises is inconsistent, those premises will validly yield any conclusion, no matter how irrelevant. The essence of the matter is more simply shown with the following outrageous argument, whose openly inconsistent premises allow us to infer—validly!—an irrelevant and absurd conclusion.

Today is Sunday.

Today is not Sunday.

Therefore the moon is made of green cheese.

In symbols we have

1. S

2. $\sim S$ / $\therefore M$

And the formal proof of its validity is almost immediately obvious:

3. $S \vee M$ 1, Add.

4. M 3, 2, D.S.

Of course, an argument that is valid because its premises are inconsistent cannot possibly be *sound*—for if the premises are inconsistent with each other, they cannot possibly be all true. By such an argument, therefore, it is not possible to establish any conclusion to be true, because we know that at least one of the premises must be false.

How can such meager premises make any argument in which they occur valid? The premises of a valid argument imply its conclusion not merely in the sense of "material" implication, but *logically*, or strictly. In a valid argument it is logically impossible for the premises to be true when the conclusion is false—and this is the situation that obtains when it is logically impossible for the premises to be true, putting the conclusion aside. What we have shown is this: *Any argument with inconsistent premises is valid, regardless of what its conclusion may be.* Its validity may be established by a truth table, or as we saw above by a formal proof, in which the contradiction is first formally expressed (for example, S and $\sim S$), the desired conclusion is then added to one side of the contradiction (for example, $S \vee M$), and that desired conclusion (for example, M) is then inferred by Disjunctive Syllogism using the other side of the contradiction (for example, $\sim S$).

This discussion helps to explain why consistency is prized so highly. One reason is that inconsistent statements cannot both be true. In a courtroom, therefore, cross-examination often aims to bring a hostile witness to contradict himself. If a witness makes inconsistent assertions, all that he says cannot be true, and his credibility is seriously undermined. When it has been once established that a witness has lied under oath (or is perhaps thoroughly confused), no testimony of that witness can be fully trusted. Lawyers say: *Falsus in unum, falsus in omnibus*; untrustworthy in one thing, untrustworthy in all.

Another, deeper reason why inconsistency is so repugnant is that—as we have seen—any and every conclusion follows logically from inconsistent statements taken as premises. Inconsistent statements are not "meaningless"; their trouble is just the opposite. They mean too much. They mean everything, in the sense of *implying* everything. And if *everything* is asserted, half of what is asserted is surely *false*, because every statement has a denial.

We are thus provided with an answer to the old riddle: What happens when an irresistible force meets an immovable object? The situation described by the riddle involves a contradiction. An irresistible force can meet an immovable object only if both exist; there must be an irresistible force and there must also be an immovable object. But if there is an irresistible force, there can be no immovable object. Let us make the contradiction explicit: There is an immovable object, and there is no immovable object. From these inconsistent premises, *any* conclusion may validly be inferred. So the correct answer to the question, "What happens when an irresistible force meets an immovable object?" is "Everything!"

Inconsistency, devastating when found among the premises of an argument, can be highly amusing. Everett Dirksen, leader of the Republican Party in the U.S. Senate for a decade in the twentieth century, enjoyed describing himself as "a man of fixed and unbending principles, the first of which is to be flexible at all times."[2] When an internal contradiction, not recognized by a speaker, yields unseen absurdity, we call the statement an "Irish Bull." Writes the schoolboy, for example, "The climate of the Australian interior is so bad that the inhabitants don't live there any more." Yogi Berra, famous for his Irish Bulls, observed that a certain restaurant, once very popular, had become "so crowded that nobody goes there any more." And, said he, "When you see a fork in the road, take it."

Sets of propositions that are internally inconsistent cannot all be true, as a matter of logic. But human beings are not always logical and do utter, and sometimes may even believe, two propositions that contradict one another. This may seem difficult to do, but we are told by Lewis Carroll, a very reliable authority in such matters, that the White Queen in *Alice in Wonderland* made a regular practice of believing six impossible things before breakfast!

EXERCISES

A. For each of the following, either construct a formal proof of validity or prove invalidity by the method of assigning truth values to the simple statements involved.

***1.** $(A \supset B) \bullet (C \supset D)$
$\therefore (A \bullet C) \supset (B \vee D)$

2. $(E \supset F) \bullet (G \supset H)$
$\therefore (E \vee G) \supset (F \bullet H)$

3. $I \supset (J \vee K)$
$(J \bullet K) \supset L$
$\therefore I \supset L$

4. $M \supset (N \bullet O)$
$(N \vee O) \supset P$
$\therefore M \supset P$

***5.** $[(X \bullet Y) \bullet Z] \supset A$
$(Z \supset A) \supset (B \supset C)$
B
$\therefore X \supset C$

6. $[(D \vee E) \bullet F] \supset G$
$(F \supset G) \supset (H \supset I)$
H
$\therefore D \supset I$

7. $(J \bullet K) \supset (L \supset M)$
$N \supset {\sim}M$
${\sim}(K \supset {\sim}N)$
${\sim}(J \supset {\sim}L)$
$\therefore {\sim}J$

8. $(O \bullet P) \supset (Q \supset R)$
$S \supset {\sim}R$
${\sim}(P \supset {\sim}S)$
${\sim}(O \supset Q)$
$\therefore {\sim}O$

9. $T \supset (U \bullet V)$
$U \supset (W \bullet X)$
$(T \supset W) \supset (Y \equiv Z)$
$(T \supset U) \supset \sim Y$
$\sim Y \supset (\sim Z \supset X)$
$\therefore X$

***10.** $A \supset (B \bullet C)$
$B \supset (D \bullet E)$
$(A \supset D) \supset (F \equiv G)$
$A \supset (B \supset \sim F)$
$\sim F \supset (\sim G \supset E)$
$\therefore E$

B. For each of the following, either construct a formal proof of validity or prove invalidity by the method of assigning truth values to the simple statements involved. In each case, use the notation in parentheses.

***1.** If the linguistics investigators are correct, then if more than one dialect was present in ancient Greece, then different tribes came down at different times from the north. If different tribes came down at different times from the north, they must have come from the Danube River valley. But archaeological excavations would have revealed traces of different tribes there if different tribes had come down at different times from the north, and archaeological excavations have revealed no such traces there. Hence if more than one dialect was present in ancient Greece, then the linguistics investigators are not correct. *(C, M, D, V, A)*

2. If there are the ordinary symptoms of a cold and the patient has a high temperature, then if there are tiny spots on his skin, he has measles. Of course the patient cannot have measles if his record shows that he has had them before. The patient does have a high temperature and his record shows that he has had measles before. Besides the ordinary symptoms of a cold, there are tiny spots on his skin. I conclude that the patient has a viral infection. *(O, T, S, M, R, V)*

3. If God were willing to prevent evil, but unable to do so, he would be impotent; if he were able to prevent evil, but unwilling to do so, he would be malevolent. Evil can exist only if God is either unwilling or unable to prevent it. There is evil. If God exists, he is neither impotent nor malevolent. Therefore God does not exist. *(W, A, I, M, E, G)*

4. If I buy a new car this spring or have my old car fixed, then I'll get up to Canada this summer and stop off in Duluth. I'll visit my parents if I stop off in Duluth. If I visit my parents, they'll insist on my spending the summer with them. If they insist on my spending the summer with them, I'll be there till autumn. But if I stay there till autumn, then I won't get to Canada after all! So I won't have my old car fixed. *(N, F, C, D, V, I, A)*

*5. If Salome is intelligent and studies hard, then she will get good grades and pass her courses. If Salome studies hard but lacks intelligence, then her efforts will be appreciated; and if her efforts are appreciated, then she will pass her courses. If Salome is intelligent, then she studies hard. Therefore Salome will pass her courses. *(I, S, G, P, A)*

6. If there is a single norm for greatness of poetry, then Milton and Edgar Guest cannot both be great poets. If either Pope or Dryden is regarded as a great poet, then Wordsworth is certainly no great poet; but if Wordsworth is no great poet, then neither is Keats nor Shelley. But after all, even though Edgar Guest is not, Dryden and Keats are both great poets. Hence there is no single norm for greatness of poetry. (*N, M, G, P, D, W, K, S*)

7. If the butler were present, he would have been seen; and if he had been seen, he would have been questioned. If he had been questioned, he would have replied; and if he had replied, he would have been heard. But the butler was not heard. If the butler was neither seen nor heard, then he must have been on duty; and if he was on duty, he must have been present. Therefore the butler was questioned. *(P, S, Q, R, H, D)*

8. If the butler told the truth, then the window was closed when he entered the room; and if the gardener told the truth, then the automatic sprinkler system was not operating on the evening of the murder. If the butler and the gardener are both lying, then a conspiracy must exist to protect someone in the house and there would have been a little pool of water on the floor just inside the window. We know that the window could not have been closed when the butler entered the room. There was a little pool of water on the floor just inside the window. So if there is a conspiracy to protect someone in the house, then the gardener did not tell the truth. *(B, W, G, S, C, P)*

9. Their chief would leave the country if she feared capture, and she would not leave the country unless she feared capture. If she feared capture and left the country, then the enemy's espionage network would be demoralized and powerless to harm us. If she did not fear capture and remained in the country, it would mean that she was ignorant of our own agents' work. If she is really ignorant of our agents' work, then our agents can consolidate their positions within the enemy's organization; and if our agents can consolidate their positions there, they will render the enemy's espionage network powerless to harm us. Therefore the enemy's espionage network will be powerless to harm us. *(L, F, D, P, I, C)*

*10. If the investigators of extrasensory perception are regarded as honest, then considerable evidence for extrasensory perception must be admitted; and the doctrine of clairvoyance must be considered seriously if extrasensory perception is tentatively accepted as a fact. If considerable evidence for extrasensory perception is admitted, then it must be tentatively accepted as a fact and an effort must be made to explain it. The doctrine of clairvoyance must be considered seriously if we are prepared to take seriously that class of phenomena called occult; and if we are prepared to take seriously that class of phenomena called occult, a new respect must be paid to mediums. If we pursue the matter further, then if a new respect must be paid to mediums, we must take seriously their claims to communicate with the dead. We do pursue the matter further, but still we are practically committed to believing in ghosts if we take seriously the mediums' claims to communicate with the dead. Hence if the investigators of extrasensory perception are regarded as honest, we are practically committed to believing in ghosts. *(H, A, C, F, E, O, M, P, D, G)*

11. If we buy a lot, then we will build a house. If we buy a lot, then if we build a house we will buy furniture. If we build a house, then if we buy furniture we will buy dishes. Therefore if we buy a lot, we will buy dishes. *(L, H, F, D)*

12. If your prices are low, then your sales will be high, and if you sell quality merchandise, then your customers will be satisfied. So if your prices are low and you sell quality merchandise, then your sales will be high and your customers satisfied. *(L, H, Q, S)*

13. If your prices are low, then your sales will be high, and if you sell quality merchandise, then your customers will be satisfied. So if either your prices are low or you sell quality merchandise, then either your sales will be high or your customers will be satisfied. *(L, H, Q, S)*

14. If Jordan joins the alliance, then either Algeria or Syria boycotts it. If Kuwait joins the alliance, then either Syria or Iraq boycotts it. Syria does not boycott it. Therefore if neither Algeria nor Iraq boycotts it, then neither Jordan nor Kuwait joins the alliance. *(J, A, S, K, I)*

*15. If either Jordan or Algeria joins the alliance, then if either Syria or Kuwait boycotts it, then although Iraq does not boycott it, Yemen boycotts it. If either Iraq or Morocco does not boycott it, then Egypt will join the alliance. Therefore if Jordan joins the alliance, then if Syria boycotts it, then Egypt will join the alliance. *(J, A, S, K, I, Y, M, E)*

C. If any truth-functional argument is valid, we have the tools to prove it valid; and if it is invalid, we have the tools to prove it invalid. Prove each of the following arguments valid or invalid. These proofs will be more difficult to construct than in preceding exercises, but they will offer greater satisfaction.

1. If the president cuts Social Security benefit payments, he will lose the support of the senior citizens; and if he cuts defense spending, he will lose the support of the conservatives. If the president loses the support of either the senior citizens or the conservatives, then his influence in the Senate will diminish. But his influence in the Senate will not diminish. Therefore the president will not cut either Social Security benefits or defense spending. *(B, S, D, C, I)*

2. If inflation continues, then interest rates will remain high. If inflation continues, then if interest rates remain high then business activity will decrease. If interest rates remain high, then if business activity decreases then unemployment will rise. So if unemployment rises, then inflation will continue. *(I, H, D, U)*

3. If taxes are reduced, then inflation will rise, but if the budget is balanced, then unemployment will increase. If the president keeps his campaign promises, then either taxes are reduced or the budget is balanced. Therefore if the president keeps his campaign promises, then either inflation will rise or unemployment will increase. *(T, I, B, U, K)*

4. Weather predicting is an exact science. Therefore either it will rain tomorrow or it won't. *(W, R)*

***5.** If either it will rain tomorrow or it won't rain tomorrow, then weather predicting is an exact science. Therefore weather predicting is an exact science. *(R, W)*

9.11 Indirect Proof of Validity

Contradictory statements cannot both be true. Therefore, a statement added to the premises that makes it possible to deduce a contradiction must entail a falsehood. This gives rise to another method of proving validity. Suppose we *assume* (for the purposes of the proof only) the *denial* of what is to be proved. And suppose, using that assumption, we can derive a contradiction. That contradiction will show that when we denied what was to be proved we were brought to absurdity. We will have established the desired conclusion *indirectly*, with a proof by *reductio ad absurdum*.

An *indirect proof of validity* is written out by stating as an additional assumed premise the negation of the conclusion. If we can derive an explicit contradiction from the set of premises thus augmented, the argument with which we began must be valid. The method is illustrated with the following argument:

1. $A \supset (B \bullet C)$
2. $(B \lor D) \supset E$
3. $D \lor A$

   $\therefore E$

In the very next line we make explicit our assumption (for the purpose of the indirect proof) of the denial of the conclusion.

4.	$\sim E$	I.P. (Indirect proof)

With the now enlarged set of premises we can, using the established rules of inference, bring out an explicit contradiction, thus:

5.	$\sim(B \lor D)$	2, 4, M.T.
6.	$\sim B \bullet \sim D$	5, De M.
7.	$\sim D \bullet \sim B$	6, Com.
8.	$\sim D$	7, Simp.
9.	A	3, 8, D.S.
10.	$B \bullet C$	1, 9, M.P.
11.	B	10, Simp.
12.	$\sim B$	6, Simp.
13.	$B \bullet \sim B$	11, 12, Conj.

The last line of the proof is an explicit contradiction, which is a demonstration of the absurdity to which we were led by assuming $\sim E$ in line 4. This contradiction, formally and explicitly expressed in the last line, exhibits the absurdity and completes the proof.

This method of indirect proof strengthens our machinery for testing arguments by making it possible, in some circumstances, to prove validity more quickly than would be possible without it. We can illustrate this by first constructing a direct formal proof of the validity of an argument, and then demonstrating the validity of that same argument using an indirect proof. In the following example, the proof without the *reductio ad absurdum* is on the left and requires fifteen steps; the proof using the *reductio ad absurdum* is on the right and requires only eight steps. An exclamation point (!) is used to indicate that a given step is derived after the assumption advancing the indirect proof had been made.

1. (H ⊃ I) • (J ⊃ K)
2. (I v K) ⊃ L
3. ~L

∴ ~(H v J)

4. ~(I v K)	2, 3, M. T.	4! ~~(H v J)	I. P. (Indirect Proof)
5. ~I • ~K	4, De M.	5! H v J	4, D. N.
6. ~I	5, Simp.	6! I v K	1, 5, C. D.
7. H ⊃ I	1, Simp.	7! L	2, 6, M. P.
8. ~H	7, 6, M. T.	8! L • ~L	7, 3, Conj.
9. (J ⊃ K) • (H ⊃ I)	1, Com.		
10. J ⊃ K	9, Simp.		
11. ~K • ~I	5, Com.		
12. ~K	11, Simp.		
13. ~J	10, 12, M. T.		
14. ~H • ~J	8, 13, Conj.		
15. ~(H v J)	14, De M.		

EXERCISES

A. For each of the following arguments, construct an indirect proof of validity.

1. 1. A v (B • C)
2. A ⊃ C
∴ C

2. 1. (G v H) ⊃ ~G
∴ ~G

3. 1. (D v E) ⊃ (F ⊃ G)
2. (~G v H) ⊃ (D • F)
∴ G

4. 1. (M v N) ⊃ (O • P)
2. (O v Q) ⊃ (~R • S)
3. (R v T) ⊃ (M • U)
∴ ~R

***5.** 1. D ⊃ (Z ⊃ Y)
2. Z ⊃ (Y ⊃ ~Z)
∴ ~D v ~Z

6. 1. (O v P) ⊃ (D • E)
2. (E v L) ⊃ (Q v ~D)
3. (Q v Z) ⊃ ~(O • E)
∴ ~O

7. 1. (F v G) ⊃ (D • E)
2. (E v H) ⊃ Q
3. (F v H)
∴ Q

8. 1. B ⊃ [(O v ~O) ⊃ (T v U)]
2. U ⊃ ~(G v ~G)
∴ B ⊃ T

B. For each of the following two arguments, construct an indirect proof of validity.

1. If a sharp fall in the prime rate of interest produces a rally in the stock market, then inflation is sure to come soon. But if a drop in the money supply produces a sharp fall in the prime rate of interest, then early inflation is equally certain. So inflation will soon be upon us. *(F, R, I, D)*

2. If precipitation levels remain unchanged and global warming intensifies, ocean levels will rise and some ocean ports will be inundated. But ocean ports will not be inundated if global warming intensifies. Therefore either precipitation levels will not remain unchanged or global warming will not intensify. *(L, G, O, P, D)*

C. For the following argument, construct both (a) a direct formal proof of validity and (b) an indirect proof of validity. Compare the lengths of the two proofs.

1. (V ⊃ ~W) • (X ⊃ Y)
2. (~W ⊃ Z) • (Y ⊃ ~A)
3. (Z ⊃ ~B) • (~A ⊃ C)
4. V • X

∴ ~B • C

9.12 Shorter Truth-Table Technique

There is still another method of testing the validity of arguments. We have seen how an argument may be proved *invalid* by assigning truth values to its component simple statements in such a way as to make all its premises true and its conclusion false. It is of course impossible to make such assignments if the argument is valid. So we can prove the *validity* of an argument by showing that *no such set of truth values can be assigned*. We do this by showing that its premises can be made true, and its conclusion false, only by assigning truth values *inconsistently*—that is, only with an assignment of values such that some component statement is assigned both a **T** and an **F**. In other words, if the truth value **T** is assigned to each premise of a valid argument, and the truth value **F** is assigned to its conclusion, this will necessitate assigning both **T** and **F** to some component statement—which is, of course, a contradiction. Here again we use the general method of *reductio ad absurdum*.

For example, we can very quickly prove the validity of the argument

(A ∨ B) ⊃ (C • D)

(D ∨ E) ⊃ G

∴ A ⊃ G

by first assigning **T** to each premise and **F** to the conclusion. But assigning **F** to the conclusion requires that **T** be assigned to *A* and **F** be assigned to *G*. Because **T** is assigned to *A*, the antecedent of the first premise is true, and because the premise as a whole has been assigned **T**, its consequent must be true also—so **T** must be assigned to both *C* and *D*. Because **T** is assigned to *D*, the antecedent of the second premise is true, and because the premise as a whole has been assigned **T**, its consequent must also be true, so **T** must be assigned to *G*. But we have already been forced to assign **F** to *G*, in order to make the conclusion false. Hence the argument would be invalid only if the statement *G* were both false and true, which is obviously impossible. Proving the validity of an argument with this "shorter truth-table technique" is one version of the use of *reductio ad absurdum*, reducing to the absurd—but instead of using the rules of inference, it uses truth-value assignments.

This *reductio ad absurdum* method of assigning truth values is often the quickest method of testing arguments, but it is more readily applied in some arguments than in others, depending on the kinds of propositions involved. Its easiest application is when **F** is assigned to a disjunction (in which case both of the disjuncts must be assigned **F**) or **T** to a conjunction (in which case both of the conjuncts must be assigned **T**). When assignments to simple statements are thus forced, the absurdity (if there is one) is quickly exposed. But where the method calls for **T** to be assigned to a disjunction, we cannot be sure which disjunct is true; and where **F** must be assigned to a conjunction, we cannot be sure which conjunct is false; in such cases we must make various "trial assignments," which slows the process and diminishes the advantage of this method. However, it remains the case that the *reductio ad absurdum* method of proof is often the most efficient means in testing the validity of a deductive argument.

EXERCISES

A. Use the *reductio ad absurdum* method of assigning truth values (the shorter truth-table technique) to determine the validity or invalidity of the arguments in Exercise Set B, on pages 355–356.

B. Do the same for the arguments in Exercise Set C, on pages 356–357.

SUMMARY

In this chapter we explained various methods with which the validity, and the invalidity, of deductive arguments may be proved.

In Section 9.1 we introduced and explained the notion of a formal proof of validity, and we listed the first nine rules of inference with which formal proofs may be constructed.

In Section 9.2 we examined in detail the elementary valid argument forms that constitute the first nine rules of inference, and illustrated their use in simple arguments.

In Section 9.3 we illustrated the ways in which the elementary valid argument forms can be used to build formal proofs of validty.

In Section 9.4 we began the process of constructing formal proofs of validity, using only the first nine rules of inference.

In Section 9.5 we illustrated the ways in which the first nine rules of inference can be used to construct more extended formal proofs of validity.

In Section 9.6 we introduced the general rule of replacement, and expanded the rules of inference by adding ten logical equivalences, each of which permits the replacement of one logical expression by another having exactly the same meaning.

In Section 9.7 we discussed the features of the system of natural deduction that contains nineteen rules of inference.

In Section 9.8 we began the enterprise of building formal proofs of validity using all nineteen rules of inference: nine elementary valid argument forms, and ten logical equivalences permitting replacement.

In Section 9.9 we explained the method of proving invalidity when deductive arguments are not valid.

In Section 9.10 we discussed inconsistency, explaining why any argument with inconsistent premises cannot be sound, but will be valid.

In Section 9.11 we explained and illustrated indirect proof of validity.

In Section 9.12 we explained and illustrated the shorter truth-table technique for proving validity.

End Notes

[1]See also John A. Winnie, "The Completeness of Copi's System of Natural Deduction," *Notre Dame Journal of Formal Logic* 11 (July 1970), pp. 379–382.

[2]Recounted by George Will, in *Newsweek*, 27 October 2003.

Quantification Theory

10.1 The Need for Quantification

Many valid deductive arguments cannot be tested using the logical techniques of the preceding two chapters. Therefore we must now enhance our analytical tools. We do this with *quantification*, a twentieth century development chiefly credited to Gottlob Frege (1848–1945), a great German logician and the founder of modern logic. His discovery of quantification has been called the deepest single technical advance ever made in logic.

To understand how quantification increases the power of logical analysis, we must recognize the limitations of the methods we have developed so far. The preceding chapters have shown that we can test deductive arguments effectively—but only arguments of one certain type, those whose validity depends entirely on the ways in which simple statements are truth-functionally combined into compound statements. Applying elementary argument forms and the rule of replacement, we draw inferences that permit us to discriminate valid from invalid arguments of that type. This we have done extensively.

When we confront arguments built of propositions that are *not* compound, however, those techniques are not adequate; they cannot *reach* the critical elements in the reasoning process. Consider, for example, the ancient argument

All humans are mortal.

Socrates is human.

Therefore Socrates is mortal.*

*It was to arguments of this type that the classical or Aristotelian logic was primarily devoted, as described in Chapters 5 and 6. Those traditional methods, however, do not possess the generality or power of the newer symbolic logic and cannot be extended to cover all deductive arguments of the kinds we are likely to confront.

This argument is obviously valid. But using the methods so far, introduced we can only symbolize it as

A

H

$\therefore M$

and on this analysis it appears to be invalid. What is wrong here? The difficulty arises from the fact that the validity of this argument, which is intuitively clear, depends on the *inner logical structure* of its premises, and that inner structure cannot be revealed by the system of symbolizing statements that we have developed thus far. The symbolization immediately above, plainly too blunt, is the best we can do without quantifiers. That is because the propositions in this valid argument are not compound, and the techniques presented thus far, which are designed to deal with compound statements, cannot deal adequately with noncompound statements. A method is needed with which noncompound statements can be described and symbolized in such a way that their inner logical structure will be revealed. The theory of **quantification** provides that method.

Quantification enables us to interpret noncompound premises as compound statements, without loss of meaning. With that interpretation we can then use all the elementary argument forms and the rule of replacement (as we have done with compound statements), drawing inferences and proving validity or invalidity—after which the compound conclusion reached may be transformed (again using quantification) back into the noncompound form with which we began. This technique adds very greatly to the power of our analytical machinery.

The methods of deduction developed earlier remain fundamental; quantifiers do not alter the rules of inference in any way. What has gone before may be called the *logic of propositions*. We now proceed, using some additional symbolization, to apply these rules of inference more widely, in what is called the *logic of predicates*. The inner structure of propositions, the relations of subjects and predicates, is brought to the surface and made accessible by *quantifiers*. Introducing this symbolization is the next essential step.

10.2 Singular Propositions

We begin with the simplest kind of noncompound statement, illustrated by the second premise of the illustrative argument above, "Socrates is human." Statements of this kind have traditionally been called *singular propositions*. An

affirmative singular proposition asserts that a particular individual has some specified attribute. *Socrates* is the subject term in the present example (as ordinary grammar and traditional logic both agree), and *human* is the predicate term. The subject term denotes a particular individual; the predicate term designates some attribute that individual is said to have.

The same subject term, obviously, can occur in different singular propositions. We may assert that "Socrates is mortal," or "Socrates is fat," or "Socrates is wise," or "Socrates is beautiful." Of these assertions, some are true (the first and the third), and some are false (the second and fourth.)* Similarly, the very same predicate term can occur in different singular propositions. The term *human* is a predicate that appears in each of the following: "Aristotle is human," "Brazil is human," "Chicago is human," and "O'Keeffe is human"—of which the first and fourth are true, while the second and third are false.

An "individual" in this symbolism can refer not only to persons, but to any individual *thing*, such as a country, a book, a city, or anything of which an *attribute* (such as human or heavy) can be predicated. Attributes do not have to be adjectives (such as "mortal" or "wise") as in our examples thus far, but can also be nouns (such as "a human"). In grammar the distinction between adjective and noun is important, of course, but in this context it is not significant. We do not need to distinguish between "Socrates is mortal" and "Socrates is a mortal." Predicates can also be verbs, as in "Aristotle writes," which can be expressed alternatively as "Aristotle is a writer." The critical first step is to distinguish between the subject and the predicate terms, between the individuals and the attributes they may be said to have. We next introduce two different kinds of symbols for referring to *individuals* and to *attributes*.

To denote individuals we use (following a very widely adopted convention) small, or lowercase letters, from *a* through *w*. These symbols are **individual constants.** In any particular context in which they may occur, each will designate one particular individual throughout the whole of that context. It is usually convenient to denote an individual by the first letter of its (or his or her) name. We may use the letter *s* to denote Socrates, *a* to denote Aristotle, *b* to denote Brazil, *c* to denote Chicago, and so forth.

*Here we follow the custom of ignoring the time factor, and use the verb "is" in the tenseless sense of "is, will be, or has been." Where considerations of time change are crucial, the somewhat more complicated symbolism of the logic of relations is required for an adequate treatment.

We use capital letters to symbolize attributes that individuals may have, and again it is convenient to use the first letter of the attribute referred to: *H* for human, *M* for mortal, *F* for fat, *W* for wise, and so forth.

We can now symbolize a singular proposition. By writing an attribute symbol immediately to the left of an individual symbol, we symbolize the singular proposition affirming that the individual named has the attribute specified. Thus the singular proposition, "Socrates is human," will be symbolized simply as *Hs*. And, of course, *Ha* symbolizes "Aristotle is human," *Hb* symbolizes "Brazil is human," *Hc* symbolizes "Chicago is human," and so forth.

It is important to note the pattern that is common to these terms. Each begins with the same attribute symbol, *H*, and is followed by a symbol for some individual, *s* or *a* or *b* or *c*, and so forth. We could write the pattern as "*H*—" where the dash to the right of the predicate symbol is a place marker for some individual symbol. This pattern we symbolize as *Hx*. We use *Hx* [sometimes written as *H(x)*] to symbolize the common pattern of all singular propositions that attribute "being human" to some individual. The letter *x* is called an **individual variable**—it is simply a place marker, indicating where the various individual letters *a* through *w* (the individual constants) may be written. When one of those constants does appear in place of *x*, we have a singular proposition. The letter *x* is available to serve as the variable because, by convention, *a* through *w* are the only letters we allow to serve as individual constants.

Let us examine the symbol *Hx* more closely. It is called a *propositional function*. We define a **propositional function** as an expression that (1) contains an individual variable and (2) becomes a statement when an individual constant is substituted for the individual variable.* So a propositional function is not itself a proposition, although it can become one by substitution. Individual constants may be thought of as the proper names of individuals. Any singular proposition is a substitution instance of a propositional function; it is the result of substituting some individual constant for the individual variable in that propositional function.

A propositional function normally has some true substitution instances and some false substitution instances. If *H* symbolizes human, *s* symbolizes Socrates, and *c* symbolizes Chicago, then *Hs* is true and *Hc* is false. With the substitution made, what confronts us is a proposition; before the substitution is made, we have only the propositional *function*. There are an unlimited number of such propositional functions, of course: *Hx*, and *Mx*, and *Bx*, and *Fx*,

*Some writers regard "propositional functions" as the meanings of such expressions, but here we define them to be the expressions themselves.

and *Wx*, and so on. We call these propositional functions *simple predicates*, to distinguish them from more complex propositional functions to be introduced in following sections. A **simple predicate** is a propositional function that has some true and some false substitution instances, each of which is an affirmative singular proposition.

10.3 Universal and Existential Quantifiers

A singular proposition affirms that some individual thing has a given predicate, so it is the substitution instance of some propositional function. If the predicate is *M* for mortal, or *B* for beautiful, we have the simple predicates *Mx* or *Bx*, which assert humanity or beauty of nothing in particular. If we substitute Socrates for the variable *x*, we get singular propositions, "Socrates is mortal," or "Socrates is beautiful." But we might wish to assert that the attribute in question is possessed by more than a single individual. We might wish to say that "Everything is mortal," or that "Something is beautiful." These expressions contain predicate terms, but they are not singular propositions because they do not refer specifically to any particular individuals. These are *general* propositions.

Let us look closely at the first of these general propositions, "Everything is mortal." It may be expressed in various ways that are logically equivalent. We could express it by saying "All things are mortal." Or we could express it by saying:

Given any individual thing whatever, it is mortal.

In this latter formulation the word "it" is a relative pronoun that refers back to the word "thing" that precedes it. We can use the letter *x*, our individual variable, in place of both the pronoun and its antecedent. So we can rewrite the first general proposition as

Given any *x*, *x* is mortal.

Or, using the notation for predicates we introduced in the preceding section, we may write

Given any *x*, *Mx*.

We know that *Mx* is a propositional function, not a proposition. But here, in this last formulation, we have an expression that *contains Mx*, and that clearly *is* a proposition. The phrase "Given any *x*" is customarily symbolized by "(*x*)," which is called the **universal quantifier.** That first general proposition may now be completely symbolized as

(*x*) *Mx*

which says, with great penetration, "Everything is mortal."

This analysis shows that we can convert a propositional function into a proposition not only by *substitution*, but also by *generalization*, or *quantification*.

Consider now the second general proposition we had entertained: "Something is beautiful." This may also be expressed as

There is at least one thing that is beautiful.

In this latter formulation, the word "that" is a relative pronoun referring back to the word "thing." Using our individual variable x once again in place of both the pronoun "that" and its antecedent "thing," we may rewrite the second general proposition as

There is at least one x such that x is beautiful.

Or, using the notation for predicates, we may write

There is at least one x such that Bx.

Once again we see that, although Bx is a propositional function and not a proposition, we have here an expression that contains Bx that *is* a proposition. The phrase "there is at least one x such that" is customarily symbolized by "$(\exists x)$" which is called the **existential quantifier.** Thus the second general proposition may be completely symbolized as

$(\exists x)\ Bx$

which says, with great penetration, "Something is beautiful."

Thus we see that propositions may be formed from propositional functions either by **instantiation,** that is, by substituting an individual constant for its individual variable, or by **generalization,** that is, by placing a universal or existential quantifier before it.

Now consider: The *universal* quantification of a propositional function, $(x)Mx$, is true if and only if *all* its substitution instances are true; that is what universality means here. It is also clear that the *existential* quantification of a propositional function, $(\exists x)Mx$, is true if and only if it has *at least one* true substitution instance. Let us assume (what no one would deny) that there exists at least one individual. Under this very weak assumption, every propositional function must have at least one substitution instance, an instance that may or may not be true. But it is certain that, under this assumption, if the *universal* quantification of a propositional function is true, then the *existential* quantification of it must also be true. That is, if every x is M, then, if there exists at least one thing, that thing is M.

Up to this point, only affirmative singular propositions have been given as substitution instances of propositional functions. Mx (x is mortal) is a propositional function. Ms is an instance of it, an affirmative singular proposition that says "Socrates is mortal." But not all propositions are affirmative. One may deny that Socrates is mortal, saying $\sim Ms$, "Socrates is not mortal." If Ms is a substitution instance of Mx, then $\sim Ms$ may be regarded as a substitution instance of the propositional function $\sim Mx$. And thus we may enlarge our conception of propositional functions, beyond the simple predicates introduced in the preceding section, to permit them to contain the negation symbol, "~."

With the negation symbol at our disposal, we may now enrich our understanding of quantification as follows. We begin with the general proposition

Nothing is perfect.

which we can paraphrase as

Everything is imperfect.

which in turn may be written as

Given any individual thing whatever, it is not perfect.

which can be rewritten as

Given any *x*, *x* is not perfect.

If P symbolizes the attribute of being perfect, we can use the notation just developed (the quantifier and the negation sign) to express this proposition ("Nothing is perfect.") as $(x) \sim Px$.

Now we are in a position to list and illustrate a series of important connections between universal and existential quantification.

First, the (universal) general proposition "Everything is mortal" is *denied* by the (existential) general proposition "Something is not mortal." Using symbols, we may say that $(x)Mx$ is denied by $(\exists x) \sim Mx$. Because each of these is the denial of the other, we may certainly say (prefacing the one with a negation symbol) that the biconditional

$$\sim(x)Mx \overset{T}{\equiv} (\exists x) \sim Mx$$

is necessarily, logically true.

Second, "Everything is mortal" expresses exactly what is expressed by "There is nothing that is not mortal"—which may be formulated as another biconditional, also logically true:

$$\sim(x)Mx \overset{T}{\equiv} \sim(\exists x) \sim Mx$$

Third, it is clear that the (universal) general proposition, "Nothing is mortal," is *denied* by the (existential) general proposition, "Something is mortal." In symbols we say that $(x) \sim Mx$ is denied by $(\exists x)Mx$. And because each of these is the denial of the other, we may certainly say (again prefacing the one with a negation symbol) that the biconditional

$$\sim(x)\sim Mx \overset{T}{\equiv} (\exists x)Mx$$

is necessarily, logically true.

And fourth, "Everything is not mortal" expresses exactly what is expressed by "There is nothing that is mortal"—which may be formulated as a logically true biconditional:

$(x){\sim}Mx \overset{\mathrm{T}}{\equiv} {\sim}(\exists x)Mx$

These four logically true biconditionals set forth the interrelations of universal and existential quantifiers. We may replace any proposition in which the quantifier is prefaced by a negation sign (using these logically true biconditionals) with another logically equivalent proposition in which the quantifier is not prefaced by a negation sign. We list these four biconditionals again, now replacing the illustrative predicate *M* (for mortal) with the symbol Φ (the Greek letter *phi*), which will stand for *any* simple predicate whatsoever.

$[(x)\Phi x] \overset{\mathrm{T}}{\equiv} [{\sim}(\exists x){\sim}\Phi x]$

$[(\exists x)\Phi x] \overset{\mathrm{T}}{\equiv} [{\sim}(x){\sim}\Phi x]$

$[(x){\sim}\Phi x] \overset{\mathrm{T}}{\equiv} [{\sim}(\exists x)\Phi x]$

$[(\exists x){\sim}\Phi x] \overset{\mathrm{T}}{\equiv} [{\sim}(x)\Phi x]$

Graphically, the general connections between universal and existential quantification can be described in terms of the square array shown in Figure 10-1.

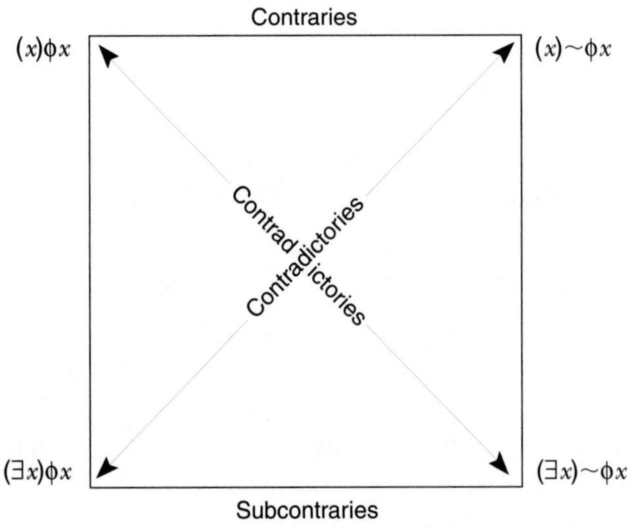

Figure 10-1

Continuing to assume the existence of at least one individual, we can say, referring to this square, that:

1. The two top propositions are *contraries;* that is, they may both be false but they cannot both be true.
2. The two bottom propositions are *subcontraries;* that is, they may both be true but they cannot both be false.
3. Propositions that are at opposite ends of the diagonals are *contradictories,* of which one must be true and the other must be false.
4. On each side of the square, the truth of the lower proposition is implied by the truth of the proposition directly above it.

10.4 Traditional Subject–Predicate Propositions

Using the existential and universal quantifiers, and with an understanding of the square of opposition in Figure 10-1, we are now in a position to analyze (and to use accurately in reasoning) the four types of general propositions that have been traditionally emphasized in the study of logic. The standard illustrations of these four types are the following:

All humans are mortal.	(universal affirmative: A)
No humans are mortal.	(universal negative: E)
Some humans are mortal.	(particular affirmative: I)
Some humans are not mortal.	(particular negative: O)

Each of these types is commonly referred to by its letter: the two affirmative propositions, **A** and **I** (from the Latin *affirmo,* I affirm); and the two negative propositions, **E** and **O** (from the Latin *nego,* I deny).*

In symbolizing these propositions by means of quantifiers, we are led to a further enlargement of our conception of a propositional function. Turning first to the **A** proposition, "All humans are mortal," we proceed by means of successive paraphrasings, beginning with

Given any individual thing whatever, if it is human then it is mortal.

The two instances of the relative pronoun "it" clearly refer back to their common antecedent, the word "thing." As in the early part of the preceding

*An account of the traditional analysis of these four types of propositions was presented in Chapter 5.

section, because those three words have the same (indefinite) reference, they can be replaced by the letter x and the proposition rewritten as

Given any x, if x is human then x is mortal.

Now using our previously introduced notation for "if–then," we can rewrite the preceding as

Given any x, x is human ⊃ x is mortal.

Finally, using our now-familiar notation for propositional functions and quantifiers, the original **A** proposition is expressed as

$(x)(Hx \supset Mx)$

In our symbolic translation, the **A** proposition appears as the universal quantification of a new kind of propositional function. The expression $Hx \supset Mx$ is a propositional function that has as its substitution instances neither affirmative nor negative singular propositions, but conditional statements whose antecedents and consequents are singular propositions that have the same subject term. Among the substitution instances of the propositional function $Hx \supset Mx$ are the conditional statements $Ha \supset Ma$, $Hb \supset Mb$, $Hc \supset Mc$, $Hd \supset Md$, and so on.

There are also propositional functions whose substitution instances are conjunctions of singular propositions that have the same subject terms. Thus the conjunctions $Ha \bullet Ma$, $Hb \bullet Mb$, $Hc \bullet Mc$, $Hd \bullet Md$, and so on, are substitution instances of the propositional function $Hx \bullet Mx$. There are also propositional functions such as $Wx \vee Bx$, whose substitution instances are disjunctions such as $Wa \vee Ba$ and $Wb \vee Bb$. In fact, any truth-functionally compound statement whose simple component statements are singular propositions that all have the same subject term may be regarded as a substitution instance of a propositional function containing some or all of the various truth-functional connectives: dot, wedge, horseshoe, three-bar equivalence, and curl, in addition to the simple predicates Ax, Bx, Cx, Dx, ... In our translation of the **A** proposition as $(x)(Hx \supset Mx)$, the parentheses serve as punctuation marks. They indicate that the universal quantifier (x) "applies to" or "has within its scope" the entire (complex) propositional function $Hx \supset Mx$.

Before going on to discuss the other traditional forms of categorical propositions, it should be observed that our symbolic formula $(x)(Hx \supset Mx)$ translates not only the standard-form proposition, "All *H*'s are *M*'s," but any other English sentence that has the same meaning. When, for example, a character in Henrik Ibsen's play, *Love's Comedy, says,* "A friend married is a friend lost," that is just another way of saying, "All friends who marry are friends who are lost." There are many ways, in English, of saying the same thing.

Here is a list, not exhaustive, of different ways in which we commonly express universal affirmative propositions in English:

H's are *M*'s.

An *H* is an *M*.

Every *H* is *M*.

Each *H* is *M*.

Any *H* is *M*.

No *H*'s are not *M*.

Everything that is *H* is *M*.

Anything that is *H* is *M*.

If anything is *H*, it is *M*.

If something is *H*, it is *M*.

Whatever is *H* is *M*.

H's are all *M*'s.

Only *M*'s are *H*'s.

None but *M*'s are *H*'s.

Nothing is an *H* unless it is an *M*.

Nothing is an *H* but not an *M*.

To evaluate an argument we must understand the language in which the propositions of that argument are expressed. Some English idioms are a little misleading, using a temporal term when no reference to time is intended. Thus the proposition, "*H*'s are always *M*'s," is ordinarily understood to mean simply that *all H*'s are *M*'s. Again, the same meaning may be expressed by the use of abstract nouns: "Humanity implies (or entails) mortality" is correctly symbolized as an **A** proposition. That the language of symbolic logic has a single expression for the common meaning of a considerable number of English sentences may be regarded as an advantage of symbolic logic over English for cognitive or informative purposes—although admittedly a disadvantage from the point of view of rhetorical power or poetic expressiveness.

Quantification of the A Proposition

The **A** proposition, "All humans are mortal," asserts that if anything is a human, then it is mortal. In other words, for any given thing *x*, if *x* is a human, *then x* is mortal. Substituting the horseshoe symbol for "if–then," we get

Given any x, x is human $\supset$ x is mortal.

In the notation for propositional functions and quantifiers this becomes

$(x)\ [Hx \supset Mx]$

Quantification of the E Proposition

The **E** proposition, "No humans are mortals," asserts that if anything is human, then it is not mortal. In other words, for any given thing *x*, *if* *x* is a human, *then* *x* is not mortal. Substituting the horseshoe symbol for "if–then," we get:

Given any x, x is a human ⊃ x is not mortal.

In the notation for propositional functions and quantifiers, this becomes

$(x)\ [Hx \supset {\sim}Mx]$

This symbolic translation expresses not only the traditional **E** form in English, but also such diverse ways of saying the same thing as "There are no *H*'s that are *M*," "Nothing is both an *H* and an *M*," and "*H*'s are never *M*."

Quantification of the I Proposition

The **I** proposition, "Some humans are mortal," asserts that there is at least one thing that is a human *and* is mortal. In other words, there is at least one *x* such that *x* is a human *and* *x* is mortal. Substituting the dot symbol for conjunction, we get

There is at least one x such that x is a human • x is mortal.

In the notation for propositional functions and quantifiers, this becomes

$(\exists x)\ [Hx \bullet Mx]$

Quantification of the O Proposition

The **O** proposition, "Some humans are not mortal," asserts that there is at least one thing that is a human and is not mortal. In other words, there is at least one *x* such that *x* is human *and* *x* is not mortal. Substituting the dot symbol for conjunction we get

There is a least one x such that x is a human • x is not mortal.

In the notation for propositional functions and quantifiers, this becomes

$(\exists x)\ [Hx \bullet {\sim}Mx]$

Where the Greek letters *phi* (Φ) and *psi* (Ψ) are used to represent any predicates whatever, the four general subject–predicate propositions of traditional logic may be represented in a square array as shown in Figure 10-2.

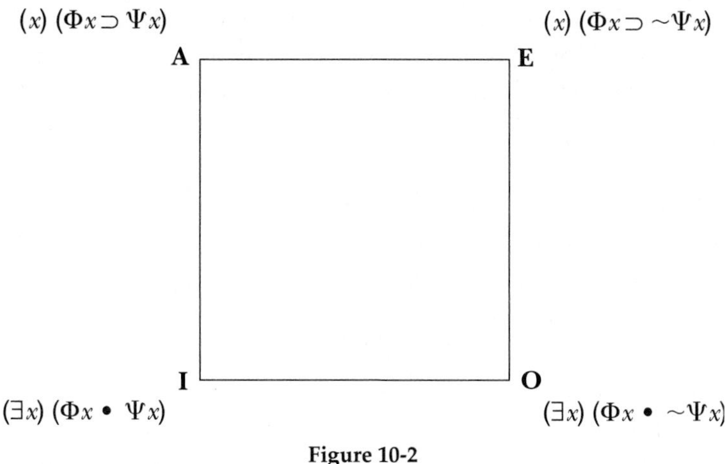

Figure 10-2

Of these four, the **A** and the **O** are contradictories, each being the denial of the other; **E** and **I** are also contradictories.

It might be thought that an **I** proposition follows from its corresponding **A** proposition, and an **O** from its corresponding **E,** but this is not so. An **A** proposition may very well be true while its corresponding **I** proposition is false. Where Φx is a propositional function that has no true substitution instances, then no matter what kinds of substitution instances the propositional function Ψx may have, the universal quantification of the (complex) propositional function $\Phi x \supset \Psi x$ will be true. For example, consider the propositional function, "*x* is a centaur," which we abbreviate as *Cx*. Because there are no centaurs, every substitution instance of *Cx* is false, that is, *Ca, Cb, Cc, . . . ,* are all false. Hence every substitution instance of the complex propositional function $Cx \supset Bx$ will be a conditional statement whose antecedent is false. The substitution instances $Ca \supset Ba$, $Cb \supset Bb$, $Cc \supset Bc$, . . . , are therefore all true, because any conditional statement asserting a material implication must be true if its antecedent is false. Because all its substitution instances are true, the universal quantification of the propositional function $Cx \supset Bx$, which is the **A** proposition $(x)(Cx \supset Bx)$, is true. But the corresponding **I** proposition $(\exists x)(Cx \bullet Bx)$ is false, because the propositional function $Cx \bullet Bx$ has no true substitution instances. That $Cx \bullet Bx$ has no true substitution instances follows from the fact that *Cx* has no true substitution instances. The various substitution instances of $Cx \bullet Bx$ are $Ca \bullet Ba$, $Cb \bullet Bb$, $Cc \bullet Bc$, . . . , each of which is a conjunction whose first conjunct is false, because *Ca, Cb, Cc, . . . ,* are all false. Because all its substitution instances are false, the existential quantification of the propositional function $Cx \bullet Bx$, which is the **I** proposition $(\exists x)(Cx \bullet Bx)$, is false. Hence an **A** proposition may be true while its corresponding **I** proposition is false.

This analysis shows also why an **E** proposition may be true while its corresponding **O** proposition is false. If we replace the propositional function *Bx* by the propositional function ~*Bx* in the preceding discussion, then $(x)(Cx \supset \sim Bx)$ may be true while $(\exists x)(Cx \bullet \sim Bx)$ will be false because, of course, there are no centaurs.

The key to the matter is this: **A** propositions and **E** propositions do not assert or suppose that anything exists; they assert only that (*if* one thing *then* another) is the case. But **I** propositions and **O** propositions do suppose that some things exist; they assert that (this *and* the other) is the case. The existential quantifier in **I** and **O** propositions makes a critical difference. It would plainly be a mistake to infer the existence of anything from a proposition that does not assert or suppose the existence of anything.

If we make the general assumption that there exists at least one individual, then $(x)(Cx \supset Bx)$ does imply $(\exists x)(Cx \supset Bx)$. But the latter is not an **I** proposition. The **I** proposition, "Some centaurs are beautiful," is symbolized as $(\exists x)(Cx \bullet Bx)$, which says that there is at least one centaur that is beautiful. But what is symbolized as $(\exists x)(Cx \supset Bx)$ can be rendered in English as "There is at least one thing such that, if it is a centaur, then it is beautiful." It does not say that there is a centaur, but only that there is an individual that is either not a centaur or is beautiful. This proposition would be false in only two possible cases: first, if there were no individuals at all; and second, if all individuals were centaurs and none of them was beautiful. We rule out the first case by making the explicit (and obviously true) assumption that there is at least one individual in the universe. And the second case is so extremely implausible that any proposition of the form $(\exists x)(\Phi x \supset \Psi x)$ is bound to be quite trivial, in contrast to the significant **I** form $(\exists x)(\Phi x \bullet \Psi x)$. The foregoing should make clear that, although in English the **A** and **I** propositions "All humans are mortal" and "Some humans are mortal" differ only in their initial words, "all" and "some," their difference in meaning is not confined to the matter of universal versus existential quantification, but goes deeper than that. The propositional functions quantified to yield **A** and **I** propositions are not just differently quantified; they are different propositional functions, one containing "⊃," the other "•." In other words, **A** and **I** propositions are not as much alike as they appear in English. Their differences are brought out very clearly in the notation of propositional functions and *quantifiers*.

For purposes of logical manipulation we can work best with formulas in which the negation sign, if one appears at all, applies only to simple predicates. So we will want to replace formulas in ways that have this result. This we can do quite readily. We know from the rule of replacement established in Chapter 9 that we are always entitled to replace an expression by another that is logically equivalent to it; and we have at our disposal four logical equivalences (listed in Section 10.3) in which each of the propositions in which the quantifier is negated is shown equivalent to another proposition in which the negation sign applies directly to the predicates. Using the rules of inference with which we have long been familiar, we can shift negation signs so that, in the end, they no longer apply to compound expressions but apply only to simple predicates. Thus, for example, the formula

$$\sim(\exists x)(Fx \bullet \sim Gx)$$

can be successively rewritten. First, when we apply the third logical equivalence given on page 444, it is transformed into

$$(x) \sim(Fx \bullet \sim Gx)$$

Then when we apply De Morgan's theorem, it becomes

$$(x)(\sim Fx \vee \sim\sim Gx)$$

Next, the principle of Double Negation gives us

$$(x)(\sim Fx \vee Gx)$$

And finally, when we invoke the definition of Material Implication, the original formula is rewritten as the **A** proposition

$$(x)(Fx \supset Gx)$$

We call a formula in which negation signs apply only to simple predicates a **normal-form formula.**

Before turning to the topic of inferences involving noncompound statements, the reader should acquire some practice in translating noncompound statements from English into logical symbolism. The English language has so many irregular and idiomatic constructions that there can be no simple rules for translating an English sentence into logical notation. What is required in each case is that the meaning of the sentence be understood and then restated in terms of propositional functions and quantifiers.

EXERCISES

A. Translate each of the following into the logical notation of propositional functions and quantifiers, in each case using the abbreviations suggested and making each formula begin with a quantifier, not with a negation symbol.

EXAMPLE

1. No beast is without some touch of pity. (*Bx*: *x* is a beast; *Px*: *x* has some touch of pity.)

SOLUTION

$(x)(Bx \supset Px)$

2. Sparrows are not mammals. (*Sx*: *x* is a sparrow; *Mx*: *x* is a mammal.)
3. Reporters are present. (*Rx*: *x* is a reporter; *Px*: *x* is present.)
4. Nurses are always considerate. (*Nx*: *x* is a nurse; *Cx*: *x* is considerate.)

*5. Diplomats are not always rich. (*Dx*: *x* is a diplomat; *Rx*: *x* is rich.)

6. "To swim is to be a penguin." (*Sx*: *x* swims; *Px*: *x* is a penguin.)
—Christina Slagar, curator, Monterey Bay Aquarium, 17 January 2003
7. No boy scout ever cheats. (*Bx*: *x* is a boy scout; *Cx*: *x* cheats.)
8. Only licensed physicians can charge for medical treatment. (*Lx*: *x* is a licensed physician; *Cx*: *x* can charge for medical treatment.)
9. Snake bites are sometimes fatal. (*Sx*: *x* is a snake bite; *Fx*: *x* is fatal.)

*10. The common cold is never fatal. (*Cx*: *x* is a common cold; *Fx*: *x* is fatal.)

11. A child pointed his finger at the emperor. (*Cx*: *x* is a child; *Px*: *x* pointed his finger at the emperor.)
12. Not all children pointed their fingers at the emperor. (*Cx*: *x* is a child; *Px*: *x* pointed his finger at the emperor.)
13. All that glitters is not gold. (*Gx*: *x* glitters; *Ax*: *x* is gold.)
14. None but the brave deserve the fair. (*Bx*: *x* is brave; *Dx*: *x* deserves the fair.)

*15. Only citizens of the United States can vote in U.S. elections. (*Cx*: *x* is a citizen of the United States; *Vx*: *x* can vote in U.S. elections.)

16. Citizens of the United States can vote only in U.S. elections. (*Ex*: *x* is an election in which citizens of the United States can vote; *Ux*: *x* is a U.S. election.)
17. Not every applicant was hired. (*Ax*: *x* is an applicant; *Hx*: *x* was hired.)
18. Not any applicant was hired. (*Ax*: *x* is an applicant; *Hx*: *x* was hired.)
19. Nothing of importance was said. (*Lx*: *x* is of importance; *Sx*: *x* was said.)

*20. They have the right to criticize who have a heart to help. (*Cx*: *x* has the right to criticize; *Hx*: *x* has a heart to help.)

B. Translate each of the following into the logical notation of propositional functions and quantifiers, in each case making the formula begin with a quantifier, *not* with a negation symbol.

1. Nothing is attained in war except by calculation.

—Napoleon Bonaparte

2. No one doesn't believe in laws of nature.

—Donna Haraway, *The Chronicle of Higher Education*, 28 June 1996

3. He only earns his freedom and existence who daily conquers them anew.

—Johann Wolfgang Von Goethe, *Faust*, Part II

4. No man is thoroughly miserable unless he be condemned to live in Ireland.

—Jonathan Swift

***5.** Not everything good is safe, and not everything dangerous is bad.

—David Brooks, in *The Weekly Standard*, 18 August 1997

6. There isn't any business we can't improve.

—Advertising slogan, Ernst and Young, Accountants

7. A problem well stated is a problem half solved.

—Charles Kettering, former research director for General Motors

8. There's not a single witch or wizard who went bad who wasn't in Slytherin.

—J. K. Rowling, in *Harry Potter and the Sorcerer's Stone*

9. Everybody doesn't like something, but nobody doesn't like Willie Nelson.

—Steve Dollar, Cox News Service

***10.** No man but a blockhead ever wrote except for money.

—Samuel Johnson

C. For each of the following, find a normal-form formula that is logically equivalent to the given one.

***1.** $\sim(x)(Ax \supset Bx)$

2. $\sim(x)(Cx \supset \sim Dx)$

3. $\sim(\exists x)(Ex \bullet Fx)$

4. $\sim(\exists x)(Gx \bullet \sim Hx)$

***5.** $\sim(x)(\sim Ix \vee Jx)$

6. $\sim(x)(\sim Kx \vee \sim Lx)$

7. $\sim(\exists x)[\sim(Mx \vee Nx)]$

8. $\sim(\exists x)[\sim(Ox \vee \sim Px)]$

9. $\sim(\exists x)[\sim(\sim Qx \vee Rx)]$

***10.** $\sim(x)[\sim(Sx \bullet \sim Tx)]$

11. $\sim(x)[\sim(\sim Ux \bullet \sim Vx)]$

12. $\sim(\exists x)[\sim(\sim Wx \vee Xx)]$

10.5 Proving Validity

In order to construct formal proofs of validity for arguments whose validity turns on the inner structures of noncompound statements that occur in them, we must expand our list of rules of inference. Only four additional rules are required, and they will be introduced in connection with arguments for which they are needed.

Consider the first argument we discussed in this chapter: "All humans are mortal. Socrates is human. Therefore Socrates is mortal." It is symbolized as

$(x)(Hx \supset Mx)$

Hs

$\therefore Ms$

The first premise affirms the truth of the universal quantification of the propositional function $Hx \supset Mx$. Because the universal quantification of a propositional function is true if and only if all of its substitution instances are true, from the first premise we can infer any desired substitution instance of the propositional function $Hx \supset Mx$. In particular, we can infer the substitution instance $Hs \supset Ms$.

From that and the second premise Hs, the conclusion Ms follows directly by *modus ponens*.

If we add to our list of rules of inference the principle that *any substitution instance of a propositional function can validly be inferred from its universal quantification*, then we can give a formal proof of the validity of the given argument by reference to the expanded list of elementary valid argument forms. This new rule of inference is the principle of **Universal Instantiation*** and is abbreviated as U.I. Using the Greek letter *nu* (ν) to represent any individual symbol whatever, we state the new rule as

UI: $\dfrac{(x)(\Phi x)}{\therefore \Phi \nu}$ (where ν is any individual symbol)

A formal proof of validity may now be written as

1. $(x)(Hx \supset Mx)$

2. Hs

$\therefore Ms$

3. $Hs \supset Ms$ 1, U.I.

4. Ms 3,2, M.P.

---

*This rule, and the three following, are variants of rules for natural deduction that were devised independently by Gerhard Gentzen and Stanislaw Jaskowski in 1934.

The addition of U.I. strengthens our proof apparatus considerably, but more is required. The need for additional rules governing quantification arises in connection with arguments such as "All humans are mortal. All Greeks are human. Therefore all Greeks are mortal." The symbolic translation of this argument is

$(x)(Hx \supset Mx)$

$(x)(Gx \supset Hx)$

$\therefore (x)(Gx \supset Mx)$

Here both premises and conclusion are general propositions rather than singular ones, universal quantifications of propositional functions rather than substitution instances of them. From the two premises, by U.I., we may validly infer the following pairs of conditional statements:

$$\begin{Bmatrix} Ga \supset Ha \\ Ha \supset Ma \end{Bmatrix} \quad \begin{Bmatrix} Gb \supset Hb \\ Hb \supset Mb \end{Bmatrix} \quad \begin{Bmatrix} Gc \supset Hc \\ Hc \supset Mc \end{Bmatrix} \quad \begin{Bmatrix} Gd \supset Hd \\ Hd \supset Md \end{Bmatrix} \ldots$$

and by successive uses of the principle of the hypothetical syllogism we may validly infer the conclusions:

$Ga \supset Ma, Gb \supset Mb, Gc \supset Mc, Gd \supset Md, \ldots$

If $a, b, c, d, \ldots$, were all the individuals that exist, it would follow that from the truth of the premises one could validly infer the truth of all substitution instances of the propositional function $Gx \supset Mx$. The universal quantification of a propositional function is true if and only if all its substitution instances are true, so we can go on to infer the truth of $(x)(Gx \supset Mx)$, which is the conclusion of the given argument.

The preceding paragraph may be thought of as containing an *informal* proof of the validity of the given argument, in which the principle of the hypothetical syllogism and two principles governing quantification are appealed to. But it describes indefinitely long sequences of statements: the lists of all substitution instances of the two propositional functions quantified universally in the premises, and the list of all substitution instances of the propositional function whose universal quantification is the conclusion. A *formal* proof cannot contain such indefinitely, perhaps even infinitely, long sequences of statements, so some method must be sought for expressing those indefinitely long sequences in some finite, definite fashion.

A method for doing this is suggested by a common technique of elementary mathematics. A geometer, seeking to prove that *all* triangles possess a certain attribute, may begin with the words "Let *ABC* be any arbitrarily selected triangle." Then the geometer begins to reason about the triangle *ABC*, and establishes that it has the attribute in question. From this she concludes that *all* triangles have that attribute. Now what justifies her final conclusion? Granted of the particular triangle *ABC* that *it* has the attribute, why does it follow that *all* triangles do? The answer to this question is easily given. If no assumption other than its triangularity is made about the triangle *ABC*, then the symbol "*ABC*" can be taken as denoting any triangle one pleases. Then the geometer's argument establishes that *any* triangle has the attribute in question, and if *any* triangle has it, then *all* triangles do. We now introduce a notation analogous to the geometer's in talking about "any arbitrarily selected triangle *ABC*." This will avoid the pretense of listing an indefinite or infinite number of substitution instances of a propositional function, for instead we shall talk about *any* substitution instance of the propositional function.

We shall use the (hitherto unused) lowercase letter y to denote any arbitrarily selected individual. We shall use it in a way similar to that in which the geometer used the letters *ABC*. Because the truth of *any* substitution instance of a propositional function follows from its universal quantification, we can infer the substitution instance that results from replacing x by y, where y denotes "any arbitrarily selected" individual. Thus we may begin our formal proof of the validity of the given argument as follows:

1.	$(x)(Hx \supset Mx)$	
2.	$(x)(Gx \supset Hx)$	
	$\therefore (x)(Gx \supset Mx)$	
3.	$Hy \supset My$	1, U.I.
4.	$Gy \supset Hy$	2, U.I.
5.	$Gy \supset My$	4,3, H.S.

From the premises we have deduced the statement $Gy \supset My$, which in effect, because y denotes "any arbitrarily selected individual," asserts the truth of *any* substitution instance of the propositional function $Gx \supset Mx$. Because *any* substitution instance is true, all substitution instances must be true, and hence the universal quantification of that propositional function is true also. We may add this principle to our list of rules of inference, stating it as follows: *From the substitution instance of a propositional function with respect to the name of any arbitrarily selected individual, one can validly infer the universal quantification of that propositional function.* This new principle permits us to *generalize,* that is, to go from a special substitution instance to a generalized or universally quantified expression, so we refer to it as the principle of **Universal Generalization** and abbreviate it as U.G. It is stated as

U.G.: Φy
$\therefore (x)(\Phi x)$ (where y denotes "any arbitrarily selected individual")

The sixth and final line of the formal proof already begun may now be written (and justified) as

6. $(x)(Gx \supset Mx)$ 5, U.G.

Let us review the preceding discussion. In the geometer's proof, the only assumption made about *ABC* is that it is a triangle; hence what is proved true of *ABC* is proved true of *any* triangle. In our proof, the only assumption made about *y* is that it is an individual; hence what is proved true of *y* is proved true of *any* individual. The symbol *y* is an individual symbol, but it is a very special one. Typically it is introduced into a proof by using U.I., and only the presence of *y* permits the use of U.G.

Here is another valid argument, the demonstration of whose validity requires the use of U.G. as well as U.I.: "No humans are perfect. All Greeks are humans. Therefore no Greeks are perfect.* The formal proof of its validity is:

1. $(x)(Hx \supset {\sim}Px)$
2. $(x)(Gx \supset Hx)$
   $\therefore (x)(Gx \supset {\sim}Px)$
3. $Hy \supset {\sim}Py$ 1, U.I.
4. $Gy \supset Hy$ 2, U.I.
5. $Gy \supset {\sim}Py$ 4,3, H.S.
6. $(x)(Gx \supset {\sim}Px)$ 5, U.G.

There may seem to be some artificiality about the preceding. It may be urged that distinguishing carefully between $(x)(\Phi x)$ and Φy, so that they are not treated as identical but must be inferred from each other by U.I. and U.G., is to insist on a distinction without a difference. But there certainly is a *formal* difference between them. The statement $(x)(Hx \supset Mx)$ is a noncompound statement, whereas $Hy \supset My$ is compound, being a conditional. From the two noncompound statements $(x)(Gx \supset Hx)$ and $(x)(Hx \supset Mx)$, no relevant inference can be drawn by means of the original list of nineteen rules of inference. But from the compound statements $Gy \supset Hy$ and $Hy \supset My$, the indicated conclusion $Gy \supset My$ follows by a hypothetical syllogism. The principle of U.I. is used to get from noncompound statements, to which our earlier rules of inference do not

*This is an appropriate point to observe that, for arguments of some kinds, the traditional syllogistic analysis can establish validity as efficiently as modern quantified logic. A classical logician would quickly identify this syllogism as having the mood **EAE** in the first figure—necessarily of the form *Celarent*, and therefore immediately seen to be valid. See Section 6.5 for a summary exposition of the valid standard-form categorical syllogisms.

usefully apply, to compound statements, to which they *can* be applied to derive the desired conclusion. The quantification principles thus augment our logical apparatus to make it capable of validating arguments essentially involving noncompound (generalized) propositions as well as the other (simpler) kind of argument discussed in earlier chapters. On the other hand, in spite of this formal difference, there must be a logical equivalence between $(x)(\Phi x)$ and Φy, or the rules U.I. and U.G. would not be valid. Both the difference and the logical equivalence are important for our purpose of validating arguments by reference to a list of rules of inference. The addition of U.I. and U.G. to our list strengthens it considerably.

The list must be expanded further when we turn to arguments that involve existential propositions. A convenient example with which to begin is "All criminals are vicious. Some humans are criminals. Therefore some humans are vicious." It is symbolized as

$(x)(Cx \supset Vx)$

$(\exists x)(Hx \bullet Cx)$

$\therefore (\exists x)(Hx \bullet Vx)$

The existential quantification of a propositional function is true if and only if it has at least one true substitution instance. Hence whatever attribute may be designated by Φ, $(\exists x)(\Phi x)$ says that there is at least one individual that has the attribute Φ. If an individual constant (other than the special symbol y) is used nowhere earlier in the context, we may use it to denote either the individual that has the attribute Φ, or some one of the individuals that have Φ if there are several. Knowing that there is such an individual, say, a, we know that Φa is a true substitution instance of the propositional function Φx. Hence we add to our list of rules of inference this principle: *From the existential quantification of a propositional function, we may infer the truth of its substitution instance with respect to any individual constant (other than y) that occurs nowhere earlier in that context.* The new rule of inference is the principle of **Existential Instantiation** and is abbreviated as "E.I." It is stated as:

E.I.: $(\exists x)(\Phi x)$ / $\therefore \Phi v$ [where v is any individual constant (other than y) having no previous occurrence in the context]

Granted the additional rule of inference E.I., we may begin a demonstration of the validity of the stated argument:

1. $(x)(Cx \supset Vx)$

2. $(\exists x)(Hx \bullet Cx)$

$\therefore (\exists x)(Hx \bullet Vx)$

3. $Ha \bullet Ca$ 2, E.I.
4. $Ca \supset Va$ 1, U.I.
5. $Ca \bullet Ha$ 3, Com.
6. Ca 5, Simp.
7. Va 4,6, M.P.
8. Ha 3, Simp.
9. $Ha \bullet Va$ 8,7, Conj.

Thus far we have deduced $Ha \bullet Va$, which is a substitution instance of the propositional function whose existential quantification is asserted by the conclusion. Because the existential quantification of a propositional function is true if and only if it has at least one true substitution instance, we add to our list of rules of inference the principle that *from any true substitution instance of a propositional function we may validly infer the existential quantification of that propositional function.* This fourth and final rule of inference is the principle of **Existential Generalization,** abbreviated as E.G. and stated as

E.G.: $\Phi\nu$ / $\therefore (\exists x)(\Phi x)$ (where ν is any individual symbol)

The tenth and final line of the demonstration already begun may now be written (and justified) as

10. $(\exists x)(Hx \bullet Vx)$ 9, E.G.

The need for the indicated restriction on the use of E.I. can be seen by considering the obviously invalid argument, "Some alligators are kept in captivity. Some birds are kept in captivity. Therefore some alligators are birds." If we failed to heed the restriction on E.I. that a substitution instance of a propositional function inferred by E.I. from the existential quantification of that propositional function can contain only an individual symbol (other than y) *that has no previous occurrence in the context,* then we might proceed to construct a "proof" of validity for this invalid argument. Such an erroneous "proof" might proceed as follows:

1. $(\exists x)(Ax \bullet Cx)$.
2. $(\exists x)(Bx \bullet Cx)$
   $\therefore (\exists x)(Ax \bullet Bx)$
3. $Aa \bullet Ca$ 1, E.I.
4. $Ba \bullet Ca$ 2, E.I. *(wrong!)*
5. Aa 3, Simp.
6. Ba 4, Simp.
7. $Aa \bullet Ba$ 5,6, Conj.
8. $(\exists x)(Ax \bullet Bx)$ 7, E.G.

The error in this "proof" occurs at line 4. From the second premise $(\exists x)(Bx \bullet Cx)$, we know that there is at least one thing that is both a bird and kept in captivity. *If* we were free to assign it the name *a* in line 4, we could, of course, assert $Ba \bullet Ca$. But we are not free to make any such assignment of *a*, for it has already been preempted in line 3 to serve as name for an alligator that is kept in captivity. To avoid errors of this sort, we must obey the indicated restriction whenever we use E.I. The preceding discussion should make clear that in any demonstration requiring the use of both E.I. and U.I., E.I. should always be used first.

For more complicated modes of argumentation, especially those that involve relations, certain additional restrictions must be placed on our four quantification rules. But for arguments of the present sort, traditionally called *categorical syllogisms*, the present restrictions are sufficient to prevent mistakes.

OVERVIEW

Rules of Inference: Quantification

Name	Abbreviation	Form	Effect
Universal Instantiation	U.I.	$(x)(\Phi x)$ $\therefore \Phi \nu$ (where ν is any individual symbol)	Any substitution instance of a propositional function can be validly inferred from its universal quantification.
Universal Generalization	U.G.	Φy $\therefore (x)(\Phi x)$ (where *y* denotes "any arbitrarily selected individual")	From the substitution instance of a propositional function with respect to the name of any arbitrarily selected individual, one may validly infer the universal quantification of that propositional function.
Existential Instantiation	E.I.	$(\exists x)(\Phi x)$ $\therefore \Phi \nu$ (where ν is any individual constant, other than *y*, having no previous occurrence in the context)	From the existential quantification of a propositional function, we may infer the truth of its substitution instance with respect to any individual constant (other than *y*) that occurs nowhere earlier in the context.
Existential Generalization	E.G.	$\Phi \nu$ $\therefore (\exists x)(\Phi x)$ (where ν is any individual constant)	From any true substitution instance of a propositional function, we may validly infer the existential quantification of that propositional function.

EXERCISES

A. Construct a formal proof of validity for each of the following arguments.

EXAMPLE

1. (x)(Ax ⊃ ~Bx)
   (∃x)(Cx • Ax)
   ∴ (∃x)(Cx • ~Bx)

SOLUTION

The conclusion of this argument is an existentially quantified statement. Plainly, the last step will therefore be the application of E.G. To obtain the line needed, we will first have to instantiate the premises, applying E.I. to the second premise and U.I. to the first premise. The restriction on the use of E.I. makes it essential that we apply E.I. *before* we apply U.I., so that we may use the same individual constant, say *a*, for both. The proof looks like this:

1. (x)(Ax ⊃ ~Bx)	
2. (∃x)(Cx • Ax)	
∴ (∃x)(Cx • ~Bx)	
3. Ca • Aa	2, E.I.
4. Aa ⊃ ~Ba	1, U.I.
5. Aa • Ca	3, Com.
6. Aa	5, Simp.
7. ~Ba	4,6, M.P.
8. Ca	3, Simp.
9. Ca • ~Ba	8,7, Conj.
10. (∃x)(Cx • ~Bx)	9, E.G.

1. $(x)(Ax \supset {\sim}Bx)$

2. $(x)(Dx \supset {\sim}Ex)$
$(x)(Fx \supset Ex)$
$\therefore (x)(Fx \supset {\sim}Dx)$

3. $(x)(Gx \supset Hx)$
$(x)(Ix \supset {\sim}Hx)$
$\therefore (x)(Ix \supset {\sim}Gx)$

4. $(\exists x)(Jx \cdot Kx)$
$(x)(Jx \supset Lx)$
$\therefore (\exists x)(Lx \cdot Kx)$

*5. $(x)(Mx \supset Nx)$
$(\exists x)(Mx \cdot Ox)$
$\therefore (\exists x)(Ox \cdot Nx)$

6. $(\exists x)(Px \cdot {\sim}Qx)$
$(x)(Px \supset Rx)$
$\therefore (\exists x)(Rx \cdot {\sim}Qx)$

7. $(x)(Sx \supset {\sim}Tx)$
$(\exists x)(Sx \cdot Ux)$
$\therefore (\exists x)(Ux \cdot {\sim}Tx)$

8. $(x)(Vx \supset Wx)$
$(x)(Wx \supset {\sim}Xx)$
$\therefore (x)(Xx \supset {\sim}Vx)$

9. $(\exists x)(Yx \cdot Zx)$
$(x)(Zx \supset Ax)$
$\therefore (\exists x)(Ax \cdot Yx)$

*10. $(x)(Bx \supset {\sim}Cx)$
$(\exists x)(Cx \cdot Dx)$
$\therefore (\exists x)(Dx \cdot {\sim}Bx)$

11. $(x)(Fx \supset Gx)$
$(\exists x)(Fx \cdot {\sim}Gx)$
$\therefore (\exists x)(Gx \cdot {\sim}Fx)$

B. Construct a formal proof of validity for each of the following arguments, in each case using the suggested notations.

*1. No athletes are bookworms. Carol is a bookworm. Therefore Carol is not an athlete. (*Ax*, *Bx*, *c*)

2. All dancers are exuberant. Some fencers are not exuberant. Therefore some fencers are not dancers. (*Dx*, *Ex*, *Fx*)

3. No gamblers are happy. Some idealists are happy. Therefore some idealists are not gamblers. (*Gx*, *Hx*, *Ix*)

4. All jesters are knaves. No knaves are lucky. Therefore no jesters are lucky. (*Jx*, *Kx*, *Lx*)

*5. All mountaineers are neighborly. Some outlaws are mountaineers. Therefore some outlaws are neighborly. (*Mx*, *Nx*, *Ox*)

6. Only pacifists are Quakers. There are religious Quakers. Therefore pacifists are sometimes religious. (*Px*, *Qx*, *Rx*)

7. To be a swindler is to be a thief. None but the underprivileged are thieves. Therefore swindlers are always underprivileged. (*Sx*, *Tx*, *Ux*)

8. No violinists are not wealthy. There are no wealthy xylophonists. Therefore violinists are never xylophonists. (*Vx*, *Wx*, *Xx*)

9. None but the brave deserve the fair. Only soldiers are brave. Therefore the fair are deserved only by soldiers. (*Dx*: *x* deserves the fair; *Bx*: *x* is brave; *Sx*: *x* is a soldier)

*10. Everyone that asketh receiveth. Simon receiveth not. Therefore Simon asketh not. *(Ax, Rx, s)*

10.6 Proving Invalidity

To prove the invalidity of an argument involving quantifiers, we can use the method of refutation by logical analogy. For example, the argument, "All conservatives are opponents of the administration; some delegates are opponents of the administration; therefore some delegates are conservatives," is proved invalid by the analogy, "All cats are animals; some dogs are animals; therefore some dogs are cats;" which is obviously invalid, because its premises are known to be true and its conclusion known to be false. Such analogies, however, are not always easy to devise. Some more effective method of proving invalidity is desirable.

In Chapter 9 we developed a method of proving invalidity for arguments involving truth-functional compound statements. That method consisted of making truth-value assignments to the component simple statements in arguments, in such a way as to make the premises true and the conclusions false. That method can be adapted for arguments involving quantifiers. The adaptation involves our general assumption that there is at least one individual. For an argument involving quantifiers to be valid, it must be impossible for its premises to be true and its conclusion false as long as there is at least one individual.

The general assumption that there is at least one individual is satisfied if there is exactly one individual, or exactly two individuals, or exactly three individuals, or . . . . If any one of these assumptions about the exact number of individuals is made, there is an equivalence between general propositions and truth-functional compounds of singular propositions. If there is exactly one individual, say *a*, then

$$(x)(\Phi x) \stackrel{T}{\equiv} \Phi a \stackrel{T}{\equiv} (\exists x)(\Phi x)$$

If there are exactly two individuals, say *a* and *b*, then

$$(x)(\Phi x) \stackrel{T}{\equiv} [\Phi a \bullet \Phi b] \quad \text{and} \quad (\exists x)(\Phi x) \stackrel{T}{\equiv} [\Phi a \vee \Phi b]$$

If there are exactly three individuals, say *a*, *b*, and *c*, then

$$(x)(\Phi x) \stackrel{T}{\equiv} [\Phi a \bullet \Phi b \bullet \Phi c] \quad \text{and} \quad (\exists x)(\Phi x) \stackrel{T}{\equiv} [\Phi a \vee \Phi b \vee \Phi c]$$

In general, if there are exactly *n* individuals, say *a*, *b*, *c*, ... *n*, then

$$(x)(\Phi x) \stackrel{T}{\equiv} [\Phi a \bullet \Phi b \bullet \Phi c \bullet \ldots \bullet \Phi n] \quad \text{and}$$

$$(\exists x)(\Phi x) \stackrel{T}{\equiv} [\Phi a \vee \Phi b \vee \Phi c \vee \ldots \Phi n]$$

These biconditionals are true as a consequence of our definitions of the universal and existential quantifiers. No use is made here of the four quantification rules explained in Section 10.5

An argument involving quantifiers is valid if, *and only if*, it is valid no matter how many individuals there are, provided there is at least one. So an argument involving quantifiers is proved invalid if there is a possible universe or *model* containing at least one individual such that the argument's premises are true and its conclusion false *of that model*. Consider the argument, "All mercenaries are undependable. No guerrillas are mercenaries. Therefore no guerrillas are undependable." It may be symbolized as

$(x)(Mx \supset Ux)$

$(x)(Gx \supset {\sim}Mx)$

$\therefore (x)(Gx \supset {\sim}Ux)$

If there is exactly one individual, say *a*, this argument is logically equivalent to

$Ma \supset Ua$

$Ga \supset {\sim}Ma$

$\therefore Ga \supset {\sim}Ua$

The latter can be proved invalid by assigning the truth value *true* to *Ga* and *Ua* and *false* to *Ma*. (This assignment of truth values is a shorthand way of describing the *model* in question as containing only the one individual, *a*, which is a guerrilla and undependable but is not a mercenary.) Hence the original argument is not valid for a model containing exactly one individual, and it is therefore *invalid*. Similarly, we can prove the invalidity of the first argument mentioned in this section (on p. 462) by describing a model containing exactly one individual, *a*, so that *Aa* and *Da* are assigned *truth* and *Ca* is assigned *falsehood*.*

Some arguments, for example,

$(\exists x)Fx$

$\therefore (x)Fx$

*Here we assume that the simple predicates *Ax*, *Bx*, *Cx*, *Dx*, . . . , occurring in our propositions are neither necessary, that is, logically true of all individuals (for example, *x* is identical with itself), nor impossible, that is, logically false of all individuals (for example, *x* is different from itself). We also assume that the only logical relations among the simple predicates involved are those asserted or logically implied by the premises. The point of these restrictions is to permit us to assign truth values arbitrarily to the substitution instances of these simple predicates without any inconsistency—for of course, a correct description of any model must be consistent.

may be valid for any model in which there is exactly one individual, but invalid for a model containing two or more individuals. Such arguments must also count as invalid, because a valid argument must be valid regardless of how many individuals there are, so long as there is at least one. Another example of this kind of argument is "All collies are affectionate. Some collies are watchdogs. Therefore all watchdogs are affectionate." Its symbolic translation is

$(x)(Cx \supset Ax)$

$(\exists x)(Cx \bullet Wx)$

$\therefore (x)(Wx \supset Ax)$

For a model containing exactly one individual, *a*, it is logically equivalent to

$Ca \supset Aa$

$Ca \bullet Wa$

$\therefore Wa \supset Aa$

which is valid. But for a model containing two individuals, *a* and *b*, it is logically equivalent to

$(Ca \supset Aa) \bullet (Cb \supset Ab)$

$(Ca \bullet Wa) \vee (Cb \bullet Wb)$

$\therefore (Wa \supset Aa) \bullet (Wb \supset Ab)$

which is proved invalid by assigning *truth* to *Ca*, *Aa*, *Wa*, *Wb*, and *falsehood* to *Cb* and *Ab*. Hence the original argument is not valid for a model containing exactly two individuals, and it is therefore *invalid*. For any invalid argument of this general type, it is possible to describe a model containing some definite number of individuals for which its logically equivalent truth-functional argument can be proved invalid by the method of assigning truth values.

It should be emphasized again: In moving from a given argument involving general propositions to a truth-functional argument (one that is logically equivalent to the given argument for a specified model), no use is made of our four quantification rules. Instead, each statement of the truth-functional argument is logically equivalent to the corresponding general proposition of the given argument, and that logical equivalence is shown by the biconditionals formulated earlier in this section on page 463, whose logical truth for the model in question follows from the very definitions of the universal and existential quantifiers.

The procedure for proving the invalidity of an argument containing general propositions is the following. First, consider a one-element model containing only the individual *a*. Then, write out the logically equivalent truth-functional argument for that model, which is obtained by moving from each general proposition (quantified propositional function) of the original argument to the substitution instance of that propositional function with respect to *a*. If the truth-functional argument can be proved invalid by assigning truth values to its component simple statements, that suffices to prove the original argument invalid. If that cannot be done, next consider a two-element model containing the individuals *a* and *b*. In order to obtain the logically equivalent truth-functional argument for this larger model, one can simply join to each original substitution instance with respect to *a* to a new substitution instance of the same propositional function with respect to *b*. This "joining" must be in accord with the logical equivalences stated on page 463; that is, where the original argument contains a *universally* quantified propositional function, $(x)(\Phi x)$, the new substitution instance Φb is combined with the first substitution instance *a* by *conjunction* ("•"); but where the original argument contains an *existentially* quantified propositional function $(\exists x)(\Phi x)$, the new substitution instance Φb is combined with the first substitution instance Φa by *disjunction* ("∨"). The preceding example illustrates this procedure. If the new truth-functional argument can be proved invalid by assigning truth values to its component simple statements, that suffices to prove the original argument invalid. If that cannot be done, next consider a three-element model containing the individuals *a*, *b*, and *c*. And so on. None of the exercises in this book requires a model containing more than three elements.

EXERCISES

In the following exercises, no model containing more than two elements is required.

A. Prove the invalidity of the following:

EXAMPLE

1. (∃x)(Ax • Bx)
   (∃x)(Cx • Bx)
   ∴ (x)(Cx ⊃ ~Ax)

SOLUTION

We first construct a model (or possible universe) containing exactly one individual, ⓐ. We then exhibit the logically equivalent propositions in that model. Thus,

(∃x)(Ax • Bx) (∃x)(Cx • Bx) ∴ (x)(Cx ⊃ ~Ax)	logically equivalent in ⓐ to	Aa • Ba Ca • Ba ∴ Ca ⊃ ~Aa

We may prove the argument invalid in this model by assigning truth values as follows:

Aa	*Ba*	*Ca*
T	T	T

Because the argument has been proved invalid in this model, the argument has been proved invalid.

1. $(\exists x)(Ax \bullet Bx)$
$(\exists x)(Cx \bullet Bx)$
$\therefore (x)(Cx \supset {\sim}Ax)$

2. $(x)(Dx \supset {\sim}Ex)$
$(x)(Ex \supset Fx)$
$\therefore (x)(Fx \supset {\sim}Dx)$

3. $(x)(Gx \supset Hx)$
$(x)(Gx \supset Ix)$
$\therefore (x)(Ix \supset Hx)$

4. $(\exists x)(Jx \bullet Kx)$
$(\exists x)(Kx \bullet Lx)$
$\therefore (\exists x)(Lx \bullet Jx)$

***5.** $(\exists x)(Mx \bullet Nx)$
$(\exists x)(Mx \bullet Ox)$
$\therefore (x)(Ox \supset Nx)$

6. $(x)(Px \supset {\sim}Qx)$
$(x)(Px \supset {\sim}Rx)$
$\therefore (x)(Rx \supset {\sim}Qx)$

7. $(x)(Sx \supset {\sim}Tx)$
$(x)(Tx \supset Ux)$
$\therefore (\exists x)(Ux \bullet {\sim}Sx)$

8. $(\exists x)(Vx \bullet {\sim}Wx)$
$(\exists x)(Wx \bullet {\sim}Xx)$
$\therefore (\exists x)(Xx \bullet {\sim}Vx)$

9. $(\exists x)(Yx \bullet Zx)$
$(\exists x)(Ax \bullet Zx)$
$\therefore (\exists x)(Ax \bullet {\sim}Yx)$

***10.** $(\exists x)(Bx \bullet {\sim}Cx)$
$(x)(Dx \supset {\sim}Cx)$
$\therefore (x)(Dx \supset Bx)$

B. Prove the invalidity of the following, in each case using the suggested notation.

***1.** All anarchists are bearded. All communists are bearded. Therefore all anarchists are communists. *(Ax, Bx, Cx)*

2. No diplomats are extremists. Some fanatics are extremists. Therefore some diplomats are not fanatics. *(Dx, Ex, Fx)*

3. All generals are handsome. Some intellectuals are handsome. Therefore some generals are intellectuals. *(Gx, Hx, Ix)*

4. Some journalists are not kibitzers. Some kibitzers are not lucky. Therefore some journalists are not lucky. *(Jx, Kx, Lx)*

***5.** Some malcontents are noisy. Some officials are not noisy. Therefore no officials are malcontents. *(Mx, Nx, Ox)*

6. Some physicians are quacks. Some quacks are not responsible. Therefore some physicians are not responsible. *(Px, Qx, Rx)*

7. Some politicians are leaders. Some leaders are not orators. Therefore some orators are not politicians. *(Px, Lx, Ox)*

8. None but the brave deserve the fair. Every soldier is brave. Therefore none but soldiers deserve the fair. (*Dx: x* deserves the fair; *Bx: x* is brave; *Sx: x* is a soldier)

9. If anything is metallic, then it is breakable. There are breakable ornaments. Therefore there are metallic ornaments. *(Mx, Bx, Ox)*

***10.** Only students are members. Only members are welcome. Therefore all students are welcome. *(Sx, Mx, Wx)*

10.7 Asyllogistic Inference

All the arguments considered in the preceding two sections were of the form traditionally called *categorical syllogisms.* These consist of two premises and a conclusion, each of which is analyzable either as a singular proposition or as one of the **A, E, I,** or **O** varieties. We turn now to the problem of evaluating somewhat more complicated arguments. These require no greater logical apparatus than has already been developed, yet they are **asyllogistic arguments**; that is, they cannot be reduced to standard-form categorical syllogisms, and therefore evaluating them requires a more powerful logic than was traditionally used in testing categorical syllogisms.

In this section we are still concerned with general propositions, formed by quantifying propositional functions that contain only a single individual variable. In the categorical syllogism, the only kinds of propositional functions quantified were of the forms $\Phi x \supset \Psi x$, $\Phi x \supset {\sim}\Psi x$, $\Phi x \bullet x$, and $\Phi x \bullet {\sim}\Psi x$. Now we shall be quantifying propositional functions with more complicated internal structures. An example will help make this clear. Consider the argument

Hotels are both expensive and depressing.

Some hotels are shabby.

Therefore some expensive things are shabby.

This argument, for all its obvious validity, is not amenable to the traditional sort of analysis. True enough, it could be expressed in terms of **A** and **I** propositions by using the symbols *Hx, Bx, Sx,* and *Ex* to abbreviate the propositional functions "*x* is a hotel," "*x* is both expensive and depressing," "*x* is shabby," and "*x* is expensive," respectively.* Using these abbreviations, we might propose to symbolize the given argument as

$(x)(Hx \supset Bx)$

$(\exists x)(Hx \bullet Sx)$

$\therefore (\exists x)(Ex \bullet Sx)$

---

*This would, however, violate the restriction stated in the footnote on page 464.

Forcing the argument into the straitjacket of the traditional **A** and **I** forms in this way obscures its validity. The argument just given in symbols is invalid, although the original argument is perfectly valid. A notation restricted to categorical propositions here obscures the logical connection between *Bx* and *Ex*. A more adequate analysis is obtained by using *Hx, Sx,* and *Ex,* as explained, plus *Dx* as an abbreviation for "*x* is depressing." By using these symbols, the original argument can be translated as

1. $(x)[Hx \supset (Ex \bullet Dx)]$

2. $(\exists x)(Hx \bullet Sx)$

$\therefore (\exists x)(Ex \bullet Sx)$

Thus symbolized, a demonstration of its validity is easily constructed. One such demonstration proceeds as follows:

3. $Hw \bullet Sw$	2, E.I.
4. $Hw \supset (Ew \bullet Dw)$	1, U.I.
5. Hw	3, Simp.
6. $Ew \bullet Dw$	4,5, M.P.
7. Ew	6, Simp.
8. $Sw \bullet Hw$	3, Com.
9. Sw	8, Simp.
10. $Ew \bullet Sw$	7,9, Conj.
11. $(\exists x)(Ex \bullet Sx)$	10, E.G.

In symbolizing general propositions that result from quantifying more complicated propositional functions, care must be taken not to be misled by the deceptiveness of ordinary English. One cannot translate from English into our logical notation by following any formal or mechanical rules. In every case, *one must understand the meaning of the English sentence, and then symbolize that meaning in terms of propositional functions and quantifiers.*

Three locutions of ordinary English that are sometimes troublesome are the following. First, note that a statement such as "All athletes are either very strong or very quick" is *not* a disjunction, although it contains the connective "or." It definitely does *not* have the same meaning as "Either all athletes are very strong or all athletes are very quick." The former is properly symbolized—using obvious abbreviations—as

$$(x)[Ax \supset (Sx \vee Qx)]$$

whereas the latter is symbolized as

$$(x)(Ax \supset Sx) \vee (x)(Ax \supset Qx)$$

Second, note that a statement such as "Oysters and clams are delicious"—while it *can* be stated as the conjunction of two general propositions, "Oysters are delicious and clams are delicious"—also can be stated as a single noncompound general proposition; in which case the word "and" is properly symbolized by the "$\vee$" rather than by the "$\bullet$." The stated proposition is symbolized as

$$(x)[(Ox \vee Cx) \supset Dx]$$

not as

$$(x)[(Ox \bullet Cx) \supset Dx]$$

For to say that oysters and clams are delicious is to say that anything is delicious that is *either* an oyster *or* a clam, *not* to say that anything is delicious that is *both* an oyster *and* a clam.

Third, what are called *exceptive* propositions require very careful attention. Such propositions—for example, "All except previous winners are eligible"—may be treated as the conjunction of two general propositions. Using the example just given, we might reasonably understand the proposition to assert both that previous winners are not eligible, *and* that those who are not previous winners are eligible. It is symbolized as:

$$(x)(Px \supset \sim Ex) \bullet (x)(\sim Px \supset Ex)$$

The same exceptive proposition may also be translated as a noncompound general proposition that is the universal quantification of a propositional function containing the symbol for material equivalence "$\equiv$," a biconditional, and symbolized thus

$$(x)(Ex \equiv \sim Px)$$

which can also be rendered in English as "Anyone is eligible if and only if that person is not a previous winner." In general, exceptive propositions are most conveniently regarded as quantified biconditionals.

Whether a proposition is in fact exceptive is sometimes difficult to determine. A recent controversy requiring resolution by a federal court panel illustrates this contextual difficulty. The Census Act, a law that establishes the rules for the conduct of the national census every ten years, contains the following passage:

> Sec. 195. Except for the determination of population for purposes of apportionment of Representatives in Congress among the several States, the Secretary [of Commerce] shall, if he considers it feasible, authorize the use of the statistical method known as "sampling" in carrying out the provisions of this title.

For the 2000 census, which did determine population for the purposes of apportionment, the Census Bureau sought to use the sampling technique, and was sued by the House of Representatives, which claimed that the passage quoted here prohibits sampling in such a census. The Bureau defended its plan, contending that the passage authorizes the use of sampling in some contexts, but in apportionment contexts leaves the matter undetermined. Which interpretation of that exceptive provision in the statute is correct?

The court found the House position correct, writing:

> Consider the directive "except for my grandmother's wedding dress, you shall take the contents of my closet to the cleaners." It is . . . likely that the granddaughter would be upset if the recipient of her directive were to take the wedding dress to the cleaners and subsequently argue that she had left this decision to his discretion. The reason for this result . . . is because of our background knowledge concerning wedding dresses: We know they are extraordinarily fragile and of deep sentimental value to family members. We therefore would not expect that a decision to take [that] dress to the cleaners would be purely discretionary.
>
> The apportionment of Congressional representatives among the states is the wedding dress in the closet. . . . The apportionment function is the "sole constitutional function of the decennial enumeration." The manner in which it is conducted may impact not only the distribution of representatives among the states, but also the balance of political power within the House. . . . This court finds that the Census Act prohibits the use of statistical sampling to determine the population for the purpose of apportionment of representatives among the states. . . .*

The exceptive proposition in this statute is thus to be understood as asserting the conjunction of two propositions: (1) that the use of sampling is not permitted in the context of apportionment, and (2) that in all other contexts sampling is discretionary. A controversial sentence in exceptive form must be interpreted in its context.

In Section 10.5, our list of rules of inference was expanded by four, and we showed that the expanded list was sufficient to demonstrate the validity of categorical syllogisms when they are valid. And we have just seen that the same expanded list suffices to establish the validity of asyllogistic arguments of the type described. Now we may observe that, just as the expanded list was sufficient to establish *validity* in asyllogistic arguments, so also the method of proving syllogisms invalid (explained in Section 10.6) by describing possible nonempty

---

*Decided by a specially appointed Voting Rights Act panel of three judges on 24 August 1998.

universes, or models, is sufficient to prove the *invalidity* of asyllogistic arguments of the present type as well. The following asyllogistic argument,

> Managers and superintendents are either competent workers or relatives of the owner.
>
> Anyone who dares to complain must be either a superintendent or a relative of the owner.
>
> Managers and foremen alone are competent workers.
>
> Someone did dare to complain.
>
> Therefore some superintendent is a relative of the owner.

may be symbolized as

$(x)[(Mx \vee Sx) \supset (Cx \vee Rx)]$

$(x)[Dx \supset (Sx \vee Rx)]$

$(x)(Mx \equiv Cx)$

$(\exists x)\, Dx$

$\therefore (\exists x)(Sx \bullet Rx)$

and we can prove it invalid by describing a possible universe or model containing the single individual *a* and assigning the truth value *true* to *Ca*, *Da*, *Fa*, *Ra*, and the truth value *false* to *Sa*.

EXERCISES

A. Translate the following statements into logical symbolism, in each case using the abbreviations suggested.

EXAMPLE

1. Apples and oranges are delicious and nutritious. *(Ax, Ox, Dx, Nx)*

SOLUTION

The meaning of this proposition clearly is that if anything is *either* an apple or an orange it is *both* delicious and nutritious. Hence it is symbolized as

$(x)[(Ax \vee Ox) \supset (Dx \bullet Nx)]$

2. Some foods are edible only if they are cooked. *(Fx, Ex, Cx)*
3. No car is safe unless it has good brakes. *(Cx, Sx, Bx)*

4. Any tall man is attractive if he is dark and handsome. (*Tx*, *Mx*, *Ax*, *Dx*, *Hx*)

*5. A gladiator wins if and only if he is lucky. (*Gx*, *Wx*, *Lx*)

6. A boxer who wins if and only if he is lucky is not skillful. (*Bx*, *Wx*, *Lx*, *Sx*)

7. Not all people who are wealthy are both educated and cultured. (*Px*, *Wx*, *Ex*, *Cx*)

8. Not all tools that are cheap are either soft or breakable. (*Tx*, *Cx*, *Sx*, *Bx*)

9. Any person is a coward who deserts. (*Px*, *Cx*, *Dx*)

*10. To achieve success, one must work hard if one goes into business, or study continuously if one enters a profession. (*Ax*: *x* achieves success; *Wx*: *x* works hard; *Bx*: *x* goes into business; *Sx*: *x* studies continuously; *Px*: *x* enters a profession)

11. An old European joke goes like this: In America, everything is permitted that is not forbidden. In Germany, everything is forbidden that is not permitted. In France, everything is permitted even if it's forbidden. In Russia, everything is forbidden even if it's permitted. (*Ax*: *x* is in America; *Gx*: *x* is in Germany; *Fx*: *x* is in France; *Rx*: *x* is in Russia; *Px*: *x* is permitted; *Nx*: *x* is forbidden)

B. For each of the following, either construct a formal proof of validity or prove it invalid. If it is to be proved invalid, a model containing as many as three elements may be required.

*1. $(x)[(Ax \vee Bx) \supset (Cx \bullet Dx)]$

$\therefore (x)(Bx \supset Cx)$

2. $(\exists x)\{(Ex \bullet Fx) \bullet [(Ex \vee Fx) \supset (Gx \bullet Hx)]\}$

$\therefore (x)(Ex \supset Hx)$

3. $(x)\{[Ix \supset (Jx \bullet {\sim}Kx)] \bullet [Jx \supset (Ix \supset Kx)]\}$

$(\exists x)[(Ix \bullet Jx) \bullet {\sim}Lx]$

$\therefore (\exists x)(Kx \bullet Lx)$

4. $(x)[(Mx \bullet Nx) \supset (Ox \vee Px)]$

$(x)[(Ox \bullet Px) \supset (Qx \vee Rx)]$

$\therefore (x)[(Mx \vee Ox) \supset Rx]$

*5. $(\exists x)(Sx \bullet Tx)$

$(\exists x)(Ux \bullet {\sim}Sx)$

$(\exists x)(Vx \bullet {\sim}Tx)$

$\therefore (\exists x)(Ux \bullet Vx)$

6. $(x)[Wx \supset (Xx \supset Yx)]$
$(\exists x)[Xx \bullet (Zx \bullet \sim Ax)]$
$(x)[(Wx \supset Yx) \supset (Bx \supset Ax)]$
$\therefore (\exists x)(Zx \bullet \sim Bx)$

7. $(\exists x)[Cx \bullet \sim (Dx \supset Ex)]$
$(x)[(Cx \bullet Dx) \supset Fx]$
$(\exists x)[Ex \bullet \sim (Dx \supset Cx)]$
$(x)(Gx \supset Cx)$
$\therefore (\exists x)(Gx \bullet \sim Fx)$

8. $(x)(Hx \supset Ix)$
$(x)[(Hx \bullet Ix) \supset Jx]$
$(x)[\sim Kx \supset (Hx \vee Ix)]$
$(x)[(Jx \vee \sim Jx) \supset (Ix \supset Hx)]$
$\therefore (x)(Jx \vee Kx)$

9. $(x)\{(Lx \vee Mx) \supset \{[(Nx \bullet Ox) \vee Px] \supset Qx\}\}$
$(\exists x)(Mx \bullet \sim Lx)$
$(x)\{[(Ox \supset Qx) \bullet \sim Rx] \supset Mx\}$
$(\exists x)(Lx \bullet \sim Mx)$
$\therefore (\exists x)(Nx \supset Rx)$

***10.** $(x)[(Sx \vee Tx) \supset \sim (Ux \vee Vx)]$
$(\exists x)(Sx \bullet \sim Wx)$
$(\exists x)(Tx \bullet \sim Xx)$
$(x)(\sim Wx \supset Xx)$
$\therefore (\exists x)(Ux \bullet \sim Vx)$

C. For each of the following, either construct a formal proof of its validity or prove it invalid, in each case using the suggested notation.

***1.** Acids and bases are chemicals. Vinegar is an acid. Therefore vinegar is a chemical. (Ax, Bx, Cx, Vx)

2. Teachers are either enthusiastic or unsuccessful. Teachers are not all unsuccessful. Therefore there are enthusiastic teachers. (Tx, Ex, Ux)

3. Argon compounds and sodium compounds are either oily or volatile. Not all sodium compounds are oily. Therefore some argon compounds are volatile. (Ax, Sx, Ox, Vx)

4. No employee who is either slovenly or discourteous can be promoted. Therefore no discourteous employee can be promoted. (Ex, Sx, Dx, Px)

*5. No employer who is either inconsiderate or tyrannical can be successful. Some employers are inconsiderate. There are tyrannical employers. Therefore no employer can be successful. *(Ex, Ix, Tx, Sx)*

6. There is nothing made of gold that is not expensive. No weapons are made of silver. Not all weapons are expensive. Therefore not everything is made of gold or silver. *(Gx, Ex, Wx, Sx)*

7. There is nothing made of tin that is not cheap. No rings are made of lead. Not everything is either tin or lead. Therefore not all rings are cheap. *(Tx, Cx, Rx, Lx)*

8. Some prize fighters are aggressive but not intelligent. All prize fighters wear gloves. Prize fighters are not all aggressive. Any slugger is aggressive. Therefore not every slugger wears gloves. *(Px, Ax, Ix, Gx, Sx)*

9. Some photographers are skillful but not imaginative. Only artists are photographers. Photographers are not all skillful. Any journeyman is skillful. Therefore not every artist is a journeyman. *(Px, Sx, Ix, Ax, Jx)*

*10. A book is interesting only if it is well written. A book is well written only if it is interesting. Therefore any book is both interesting and well written if it is either interesting or well written. *(Bx, Ix, Wx)*

D. Do the same (as in Set C) for each of the following.

*1. All citizens who are not traitors are present. All officials are citizens. Some officials are not present. Therefore there are traitors. *(Cx, Tx, Px, Ox)*

2. Doctors and lawyers are professional people. Professional people and executives are respected. Therefore doctors are respected. *(Dx, Lx, Px, Ex, Rx)*

3. Only lawyers and politicians are members. Some members are not college graduates. Therefore some lawyers are not college graduates. *(Lx, Px, Mx, Cx)*

4. All cut-rate items are either shopworn or out of date. Nothing shopworn is worth buying. Some cut-rate items are worth buying. Therefore some cut-rate items are out of date. *(Cx, Sx, Ox, Wx)*

*5. Some diamonds are used for adornment. Only things worn as jewels or applied as cosmetics are used for adornment. Diamonds are never applied as cosmetics. Nothing worn as a jewel is properly used if it has an industrial application. Some diamonds have industrial applications. Therefore some diamonds are not properly used. *(Dx, Ax, Jx, Cx, Px, Ix)*

6. No candidate who is either endorsed by labor or opposed by the *Tribune* can carry the farm vote. No one can be elected who does not carry the farm vote. Therefore no candidate endorsed by labor can be elected. (*Cx*, *Lx*, *Ox*, *Fx*, *Ex*)

7. No metal is friable that has been properly tempered. No brass is properly tempered unless it is given an oil immersion. Some of the ash trays on the shelf are brass. Everything on the shelf is friable. Brass is a metal. Therefore some of the ash trays were not given an oil immersion. (*Mx*: *x* is metal; *Fx*: *x* is friable; *Tx*: *x* is properly tempered; *Bx*: *x* is brass; *Ox*: *x* is given an oil immersion; *Ax*: *x* is an ash tray; *Sx*: *x* is on the shelf)

8. Anyone on the committee who knew the nominee would vote for the nominee if free to do so. Everyone on the committee was free to vote for the nominee except those who were either instructed not to by the party caucus or had pledged support to someone else. Everyone on the committee knew the nominee. No one who knew the nominee had pledged support to anyone else. Not everyone on the committee voted for the nominee. Therefore the party caucus had instructed some members of the committee not to vote for the nominee. (*Cx*: *x* is on the committee; *Kx*: *x* knows the nominee; *Vx*: *x* votes for the nominee; *Fx*: *x* is free to vote for the nominee; *Ix*: *x* is instructed by the party caucus not to vote for the nominee; *Px*: *x* had pledged support to someone else)

9. All logicians are deep thinkers and effective writers. To write effectively, one must be economical if one's audience is general, and comprehensive if one's audience is technical. No deep thinker has a technical audience if he has the ability to reach a general audience. Some logicians are comprehensive rather than economical. Therefore not all logicians have the ability to reach a general audience. (*Lx*: *x* is a logician; *Dx*: *x* is a deep thinker; *Wx*: *x* is an effective writer; *Ex*: *x* is economical; *Gx*: *x*'s audience is general; *Cx*: *x* is comprehensive; *Tx*: *x*'s audience is technical; *Ax*: *x* has the ability to reach a general audience)

*10. Some criminal robbed the Russell mansion. Whoever robbed the Russell mansion either had an accomplice among the servants or had to break in. To break in, one would either have to smash the door or pick the lock. Only an expert locksmith could have picked the lock. Had anyone smashed the door, he would have been heard. Nobody was heard. If the criminal who robbed the Russell mansion managed to fool the guard, he must have been a convincing actor. No one could rob the Russell mansion unless he fooled the guard. No criminal could be both an expert locksmith and a convincing actor. Therefore some criminal had an accomplice among the servants. (*Cx*: *x* is a criminal; *Rx*: *x* robbed the Russell mansion; *Sx*: *x* had an accomplice among the servants; *Bx*: *x* broke in; *Dx*: *x* smashed the door; *Px*: *x* picked the lock; *Lx*: *x* is an expert locksmith; *Hx*: *x* was heard; *Fx*: *x* fooled the guard; *Ax*: *x* is a convincing actor)

11. If anything is expensive it is both valuable and rare. Whatever is valuable is both desirable and expensive. Therefore if anything is either valuable or expensive then it must be both valuable and expensive. (*Ex*: *x* is expensive; *Vx*: *x* is valuable; *Rx*: *x* is rare; *Dx*: *x* is desirable)

12. Figs and grapes are healthful. Nothing healthful is either illaudable or jejune. Some grapes are jejune and knurly. Some figs are not knurly. Therefore some figs are illaudable. (*Fx*: *x* is a fig; *Gx*: *x* is a grape; *Hx*: *x* is healthful; *Ix*: *x* is illaudable; *Jx*: *x* is jejune; *Kx*: *x* is knurly)

13. Figs and grapes are healthful. Nothing healthful is both illaudable and jejune. Some grapes are jejune and knurly. Some figs are not knurly. Therefore some figs are not illaudable. (*Fx*: *x* is a fig; *Gx*: *x* is a grape; *Hx*: *x* is healthful; *Ix*: *x* is illaudable; *Jx*: *x* is jejune; *Kx*: *x* is knurly)

14. Gold is valuable. Rings are ornaments. Therefore gold rings are valuable ornaments. (*Gx*: *x* is gold; *Vx*: *x* is valuable; *Rx*: *x* is a ring; *Ox*: *x* is an ornament)

***15.** Oranges are sweet. Lemons are tart. Therefore oranges and lemons are sweet or tart. (*Ox*: *x* is an orange; *Sx*: *x* is sweet; *Lx*: *x* is a lemon; *Tx*: *x* is tart)

16. Socrates is mortal. Therefore everything is either mortal or not mortal. (*s*: Socrates; *Mx*: *x* is mortal)

SUMMARY

In Section 10.1, we explained that the analytical techniques of the previous chapters are not adequate to deal with arguments whose validity depends on the inner logical structure of noncompound propositions. We described quantification in general terms as a theory that, with some additional symbolization, enables us to exhibit this inner structure and thereby greatly enhances our analytical powers.

In Section 10.2, we explained singular propositions and introduced the symbols for an individual variable x, for individual constants (lowercase letters a through w), and for attributes (capital letters). We introduced the concept of a propositional function, an expression that contains an individual variable and becomes a statement when an individual constant is substituted for the individual variable. A proposition may thus be obtained from a propositional function by the process of instantiation.

In Section 10.3, we explained how propositions also can be obtained from propositional functions by means of generalization, that is, by the use of quantifiers such as "everything," "nothing," and "some." We introduced the universal quantifier (x), meaning "given any x," and the existential quantifier $(\exists x)$, meaning "there is at least one x such that." On a square of opposition, we showed the relations between universal and existential quantification.

In Section 10.4, we showed how each of the four main types of general propositions,

- **A:** universal affirmative propositions
- **E:** universal negative propositions
- **I:** particular affirmative propositions
- **O:** particular negative propositions

is correctly symbolized by propositional functions and quantifiers. We also explained the modern interpretation of the relations of **A, E, I,** and **O** propositions.

In Section 10.5, we expanded the list of rules of inference, adding four additional rules:

- Universal Instantiation, U.I.
- Universal Generalization, U.G.
- Existential Instantiation, E.I.
- Existential Generalization, E.G.

and showed how, by using these and the other nineteen rules set forth earlier, we can construct a formal proof of validity of deductive arguments that depend on the inner structure of noncompound propositions.

In Section 10.6, we explained how the method of refutation by logical analogy can be used to prove the invalidity of arguments involving quantifiers by creating a model, or possible universe, containing exactly one, or exactly two, or exactly three (etc.) individuals and the restatement of the constituent propositions of an argument in that possible universe. An argument involving quantifiers is proved invalid if we can exhibit a possible universe containing at least one individual, such that the argument's premises are true and its conclusion is false in that universe.

In Section 10.7, we explained how we can symbolize and evaluate asyllogistic arguments, those containing propositions not reducible to **A, E, I,** and **O** propositions, or singular propositions. We noted the complexity of exceptive propositions and other propositions whose logical meaning must first be understood and then rendered accurately with propositional functions and quantifiers.

Some point of view is assumed in all our perceptions. In looking at a picture the viewer craves some unambiguous perspective. The coherent representation of things (artists learned long ago) calls for a single vanishing point with which the horizontal lines of the picture are laid out. *Relativity*, by M. C. Escher, exhibits the perplexing result when that coherence is missing. There is no single point of view in this picture; the ceiling for one is the floor for another. Which way is up? Three perspectives throw all into confusion.

Knowledge also supposes some steady context, some accepted theory or shared perspective within which explanations can cohere. But the quest for new knowledge brings new perspectives that, because they are sometimes inconsistent with what had been long supposed, confuse and perplex us. New theories replace the old; what we had thought were facts become suppositions, possibly false. Inductive inquiry is not as dizzy as the world in Escher's *Relativity*, but his picture is a provocative reminder of the uncertainty of what we think we know.

PART III

Induction

The contrary of every matter of fact is still possible, because it can never imply a contradiction, and is conceived by the mind with the same facility and distinctness, as if ever so conformable to reality. That the sun will not rise tomorrow is no less intelligible a proposition, and implies no more contradiction than the affirmation, that it will rise. . . . It may, therefore, be a subject worthy of curiosity, to enquire what is the nature of that evidence which assures us of any real existence and matter of fact, beyond the present testimony of our senses, or the records of our memory.

David Hume

Analogical Reasoning

11.1 Induction and Deduction Revisited

Arguments are built on premises that are believed, or assumed, to be true. Some premises we establish by deductive arguments that have preceded, but very many of the premises on which we must rely cannot be established by deduction. Our reasoning process usually begins with the accepted truth of some "matters of fact," in David Hume's phrase. To establish matters of fact we must rely on reasoning that is *inductive.*

Induction thus provides the starting points—the foundation—for the reasoning that concerns us most. We reason to establish truths in our everyday lives, to learn facts about our society, to understand the natural world. Deduction is certainly powerful in enabling us to move from known (or assumed) propositions to other propositions that those premises entail, but in the search for truths with which our reasoning must begin, it is insufficient.

The inductive arguments with which we establish matters of fact differ fundamentally from the deductive arguments that were the concern in Part II of this book. One essential contrast between the two families of argument (noted much earlier in our discussion of basic logical concepts, Section 1.5) lies in the relation of the premises to the conclusion in the arguments of the two great families. In *deductive arguments,* the claim is made that conclusions follow with certainty from their premises. That claim is appropriate because any deductive argument, if it is good, brings to light in its conclusion what was already buried in its premises. The relation between premises and conclusion, in deduction, is one of *logical necessity.* In every deductive argument, if it is valid and if its premises are true, its conclusion *must* be true.

In *inductive arguments*—the concerns of this chapter and those that follow—the relations between premises and conclusion are not those of logical necessity. The claim of certainty is not made. The terms *valid* and *invalid* simply do not apply. This does not mean that inductive arguments are always weak; sometimes they are very strong indeed, and fully deserve our confidence.

Scientists now assert without reservation (for example) that smoking is a cause of cancer. This is true, but it is a truth that cannot be known with the demonstrative certainty of a valid syllogism. If *p or q* is true, and *not p* is true, we may conclude that *q* must be the case, beyond all doubt. It is a truth we establish as an inescapable consequence of the relations of the concepts involved. Empirical truths—about the consequences of smoking, or the causes of cancer, and all others of that sort—cannot satisfy the standard of deductive certainty. By that standard, as one distinguished medical investigator observes, "no one will ever be able to prove that smoking causes cancer, or that anything causes anything."[1]

In the realm of induction, as we seek new knowledge of facts about the world, nothing is beyond all doubt. We must rely on arguments that support their conclusions only as *probable*, or probably true. Some such arguments are of only moderate worth; others are very powerful, as we shall see. The strengths and weaknesses of inductive arguments, and the techniques for the evaluation of such arguments, are the focus of Part III of this book.

Arguments grounded on *analogies*, aiming to establish particular conclusions, are examined first, in this chapter. Arguments that go beyond particulars, aiming to establish generally applicable *causal laws*, are examined in the following chapter. The uses of hypotheses and their confirmation in developing *scientific theories* follows in Chapter 13; and we conclude, in Chapter 14, with an analysis of the concept of *probability* itself, the conceptual instrument with which inductive conclusions are commonly expressed.

11.2 Argument by Analogy

The most common type of inductive argument relies on *analogy*. If I report that I got very good service from a computer of a certain make and model, you may infer that a new computer of the same make and model will serve you well. That conclusion has some degree of probability, but the argument is far from compelling. When a new book is called to my attention and I infer that I will enjoy reading it because I have read and enjoyed other books by the same author, I may have my confidence in that author strengthened when I read the book—or I may be disappointed. Analogy is the common ground of our every day inferences from past experience to what the future will hold.

Here follow two more carefully formulated analogical arguments. The first concludes, on the basis of what we commonly think to be prudent and fair, that it would be prudent and fair to adopt now a major change in public policy:

> Some people look on preemployment testing of teachers as unfair—a kind of double jeopardy. "Teachers are already college graduates," they say. "Why should they be tested?" That's easy. Lawyers are college graduates and graduates of professional school, too, but they have to take a bar exam. And a number

of other professions ask prospective members to prove that they know their stuff by taking and passing examinations: accountants, actuaries, doctors, architects. There is no reason why teachers shouldn't be required to do this too.[2]

The second illustration is an argument—entirely plausible when first presented two centuries ago—whose conclusion is very probably false:

> We may observe a very great similitude between this earth which we inhabit, and the other planets, Saturn, Jupiter, Mars, Venus, and Mercury. They all revolve around the sun, as the earth does, although at different distances and in different periods. They borrow all their light from the sun, as the earth does. Several of them are known to revolve around their axis like the earth, and by that means, must have a like succession of day and night. Some of them have moons, that serve to give them light in the absence of the sun, as our moon does to us. They are all, in their motions, subject to the same law of gravitation, as the earth is. From all this similitude, it is not unreasonable to think that those planets may, like our earth, be the habitation of various orders of living creatures. There is some probability in this conclusion from analogy.[3]

Neither these arguments, nor those everyday inferences we draw about computers and books and the like, are demonstratively valid. Their conclusions are not claimed to follow from their premises with logical necessity, and they obviously do not follow with certainty. What is appropriate for judging the employability of lawyers and doctors may not be appropriate for judging the employability of teachers. The earth is very likely to be the only inhabited planet in our solar system. Your new computer may prove unsuitable for the work you do, and I may find my favorite author's latest book intolerably dull. In all such arguments it is plainly possible—logically possible—that although the premises are true, the conclusions are false. Arguments by analogy are not to be classified as either valid or invalid; probability is all that is claimed for them.

In addition to their use in arguments, analogies are very often used nonargumentatively, for the purpose of lively description. The literary uses of analogy in metaphor and simile are tremendously helpful to the writer who strives to create a vivid picture in the reader's mind. In the continuing controversy in the United States over immigration, for example, one writer expressed his views with a forceful analogy:

> I'm a third-generation American. I don't know all the legal details about how my grandparents got here. But I do know that they worked very hard, paid their taxes, and raised a son who served his country. Americans being against immigration is like a house being against its bricks.[4]

Analogy is also used in explanation, when something that may not be familiar to the reader is made somewhat more intelligible by being compared to something else, presumably more familiar, to which it has certain similarities. When

Analogies—But No Arguments

Nonargumentative analogies are commonly encountered in the writing of high school students—and some of these are quite funny. We pause for a chuckle:

1. She grew on him like she was a colony of *E. coli* and he was room-temperature Canadian beef.
2. McMurphy fell 12 stories, hitting the pavement like a Hefty bag filled with vegetable soup.
3. Her hair glistened in the rain, like a nose hair after a sneeze.
4. Even in his last years, Grandpappy had a mind like a steel trap, only one that had been left out so long it had rusted shut.
5. He was deeply in love. When she spoke he thought he heard bells, like a garbage truck backing up.
6. She had a deep, throaty, genuine laugh, like that sound a dog makes just before it throws up.
7. His thoughts tumbled in his head, making and breaking alliances like underpants in a dryer without Cling Free.
8. The hailstones leaped from the pavement, just like maggots when you fry them in hot grease.
9. The ballerina rose gracefully *en pointe* and extended one slender leg behind her, like a dog at a fire hydrant.
10. She walked into my office like a centipede with 98 missing legs.

www.qwertyed.com/q_pages.

Eric Lander, the director of the Genome Center at the Massachusetts Institute of Technology sought to explain the huge eventual impact of the Human Genome Project, analogy was one of the devices he used to enhance the understanding of those unfamiliar with genetic research:

> The genome project is wholly analogous to the creation of the periodic table in chemistry. Just as Mendeleev's arrangement of the chemical elements in the periodic table made coherent a previously unrelated mass of data, so the tens of thousands of genes in present-day organisms will all turn out to be made from combinations of a much smaller number of simpler genetic modules or elements, the primordial genes, so to speak.[5]

The use of analogies in description and explanation is not the same as their use in argument, though in some cases it may not be easy to decide which use is intended. *But* whether used argumentatively or otherwise, analogy is not difficult to define. To draw an **analogy** between two or more entities is to indicate one or more respects in which they are similar.

This definition explains what an analogy is, but there is still the problem of characterizing an *argument* by analogy. Let us analyze the structure of a particular analogical argument, using a very simple example. Consider the argument that a new car whose purchase I am now contemplating will be very satisfactory because my old car, of the same make and model, has long given very satisfactory service. The two entities that are said to be similar are two cars. Three points of analogy are involved, three respects in which the two entites are said to resemble each other: first, in being cars; second, in being of the same make and model; and third, in serving me well.

The three points of analogy do not play identical roles in the argument, however. The first two occur in the premises, whereas the third occurs both in the premises and in the conclusion. The given argument may be described as having premises that assert, first, that two things are similar in two respects, and second, that one of those things has a further characteristic, from which the conclusion is drawn that the other thing also has that further characteristic.

Analogical argument is one of the most fundamental tools of appellate courts. The inference in the case before the court is shown to be very much like some other inference drawn previously, and if it was clearly correct in that earlier case, it is held to be correct in this one too. In 2004, the U.S. Supreme Court decided unanimously a case requiring the interpretation of the Sixth Amendment of the U.S. Constitution, which gives to every criminal defendant the right "to be confronted with the witnesses against him." Does this forbid the use, at a defendant's trial, of testimony from a witness who is not available for cross-examination, even if the trial judge believes that testimony to be reliable? Yes, said Justice Antonin Scalia, delivering the opinion of the Court, it does. The right to cross-examine adverse witnesses was firmly established in the English common law at the time our Constitution was adopted. Justice Scalia's subsequent analogy epitomizes the argument of the Court:

> Admitting statements deemed reliable by a judge is fundamentally at odds with the right of confrontation. Dispensing with confrontation because testimony is obviously reliable is akin to dispensing with a jury trial because a defendant is obviously guilty. This is not what the Sixth Amendment prescribes."[6]

Analogical argument is also common in political controversy. Sometimes the analogy is effective, sometimes it is far-fetched. The threat of global warming, and the need of our country to respond concretely to that threat, was argued heatedly before the Congress of the United States, in 2007, by former presidential candidate Al Gore, who described the danger as a "planetary emergency." Against those who thought him to be exaggerating the dangers, he then argued:

> The planet has a fever. If your baby has a fever you go to the doctor. If the doctor says you need to intervene here, you don't say "I read a science-fiction novel that says it's not a problem." You take action.[7]

Not every analogical argument need concern exactly two things or exactly three different characteristics, of course. Thus the argument presented earlier, suggesting that other planets in our solar system may well be inhabited, draws analogies among six things (the then-known planets) in some eight respects. Apart from these numerical differences, however, all analogical arguments have the same general structure or pattern. Every **analogical argument** *proceeds from the similarity of two or more things in one or more respects to the similarity of those things in some further respect*. Schematically, where *a*, *b*, *c*, and *d* are any entities and *P*, *Q*, and *R* are any attributes or "respects," an analogical argument may be represented as having the form

a, *b*, *c*, *d* all have the attributes *P* and *Q*.
a, *b*, *c* all have the attribute *R*.
Therefore *d* probably has the attribute *R*.

In identifying, and especially in appraising, analogical arguments, it may be found helpful to recast them into this form.

EXERCISES

All of the following passages contain analogies. Distinguish those that contain analogical arguments from those that make nonargumentative uses of analogy.

EXAMPLE

1. A Man ought no more to value himself for being wiser than a Woman, if he owes his Advantage to a better Education, than he ought to boast of his Courage for beating a Man when his hands were bound.

—Mary Astell, *An Essay in Defence of the Female Sex*, 1721

SOLUTION

This is an analogical argument. The analogy drawn here is between beating a man when his hands are bound and being wiser than a woman as a consequence of a better education, one party having an enormous advantage in both cases. In the first case, it is plain that one with such an advantage ought not to boast of his courage; in the second case (this argument concludes), it is equally inappropriate for one with such an advantage to boast of his relative wisdom.

2. "I'm not anti-Semitic, I'm just anti-Zionist" is the equivalent of "I'm not anti-American, I just think the United States shouldn't exist."

—Benjamin Netanyahu, *A Place Among the Nations*, (New York: Bantam Books, 1993)

3. Instead of investing in the future, we throw money away on absurd luxuries, finance corrupt and hostile oil-rich countries, pollute our atmosphere and increase our trade deficit. Sort of like driving a Hummer to the shopping mall.

—Eric Buckvar, "A Wasteful Society," *The New York Times,* 23 March 2007

4. The British are less rigid about punctuation and related matters, such as footnote and bibliographic form, than Americans are. An Englishwoman, lecturing Americans on semicolons is a little like an American lecturing the French on sauces.

—Louis Menand, "Bad Comma," *The New Yorker,* 28 June 2004

5. Studies show that girls get better grades in high school and college than boys—yet only about 35 percent of National Merit Scholarship winners are girls. The Executive Director of FairTest contends that the "inequity is due solely to gender bias in the test used to select eligible students." But the spokeswoman for the National Merit Scholarship Corporation, Elaine Detweiler, replies "We don't really know why girls do worse on the exams. To blame the test for the difference between how boys and girls perform is like blaming a yardstick that boys are taller than girls."

—"Merit Test Defended," *The Los Angeles Times,* 26 May 1993

6. The famous chemist and biologist Justus von Liebig dismissed the germ theory with a shrug of the shoulders, regarding Pasteur's view that microbes could cause fermentation as ridiculous and naive as the opinion of a child "who would explain the rapidity of the Rhine current by attributing it to the violent movement of the many millwheels at Maintz."

—René Dubos, *Pasteur and Modern Science* (New York: Da Capo Press, 1988)

7. Talking about Christianity without saying anything about sin is like discussing gardening without saying anything about weeds.

—The Rev. Lord Soper, quoted in *The New York Times,* 24 December 1998

8. Men and women may have different reproductive strategies, but neither can be considered inferior or superior to the other, any more than a bird's wings can be considered superior or inferior to a fish's fins.

—David M. Buss, "Where Is Fancy Bred? In the Genes or in the Head?" *The New York Times,* 1 June 1999

9. "This is a matter of national spirit," said Marjorie Wilson, coordinator of the Kangaroo Protection Cooperative, an Australian wildlife

group. "We believe here that we have enough meat in this country to satisfy people without them having to eat their national symbol. You Americans don't cook your bald eagles, do you?"

—"Battling over a National Symbol," *The New York Times*, 10 July 1995

10. One sure thing is that melting sea ice cannot be implicated in the coastal flooding that many global warming models have projected. Just as melting ice cubes do not cause a glass of water to overflow, melting sea ice does not increase oceanic volume. Any future rise in sea level would result from glaciers melting on land.

—Walter Gibbs, "Research Predicts Summer Doom for Northern Icecap," *The New York Times*, 11 July 2000

11. Thomas Henry Huxley, Charles Darwin's nineteenth-century disciple, presented this analogy: "Consciousness would appear to be related to the mechanism of the body simply as a collateral product of its working and to be completely without any power of modifying that working, as the steam whistle which accompanies the work of a locomotive is without influence upon its machinery."

12. The Elgin Marbles—17 figures and 56 panels that once decorated the Parthenon, on the Acropolis in Athens—were taken from the Parthenon in 1801 by Thomas Bruce, the seventh Earl of Elgin, and brought to the British Museum, in London. The Greeks say that he stole them; the British say that they were properly acquired, by purchase. Some Britons urged that the Marbles be returned to Greece in time for the Olympic Games to be held in Athens in 2004. Said one of the leaders of the Labor Party: "The Parthenon without the Elgin Marbles is like a smile missing a tooth."

13. The Feminists decided to examine the institution of marriage as it is set up by law in order to find out whether or not it did operate in women's favor. It became increasingly clear to us that the institution of marriage "protects" women in the same way that the institution of slavery was said to "protect" blacks—that is, that the word "protection" in this case is simply a euphemism for oppression.

—Sheila Cronan, "Marriage," in Anne Koedt, Ellen Levine, and Anita Rapone, eds., *Radical Feminism* (New York: Quadrangle Books, 1976)

14. Wittgenstein used to compare thinking with swimming: just as in swimming our bodies have a natural tendency to float on the surface so that it requires great physical exertion to plunge to the bottom, so in thinking it requires great mental exertion to force our minds away from the superficial, down into the depth of a philosophical problem.

—George Pitcher, *The Philosophy of Wittgenstein* (Englewood Cliffs, NJ: 1964)

15. A person without a goal is like a computer without a program. And that's an ugly piece of furniture.

—Steve Danish, "Getting a Life," *The New York Times*, March 1998

16. The quest for usable energy from fusion involves the use of interlocked magnetic fields to contain very hot (180 million degrees Fahrenheit) and highly compressed (to a density 20 times that of lead) electrically charged plasma (a kind of gas) within a vacuum chamber. The plasma must never touch the solid walls of its container, for if it does it instantly loses its heat and can never be coaxed into undergoing fusion. One scientific report put the problem this way:

Everything depends on keeping the plasma's magnetic bottle tightly stoppered . . . [but] confining a dollop of super-hot compressed plasma has proved to be harder than compressing and shaping a blob of jelly using only rubber bands. Each clever idea of the plasma physicists for solving this problem has been matched by a new challenge.

—Malcolm W. Browne, "Reviving the Quest to Tame the Energy of the Stars," *The New York Times*, 8 June 1999

17. It is important that we make clear at this point what definition is and what can be attained by means of it. It seems frequently to be credited with a creative power; but all it accomplishes is that something is marked out in sharp relief and designated by a name. Just as the geographer does not create a sea when he draws boundary lines and says: the part of the ocean's surface bounded by these lines I am going to call the Yellow Sea, so too the mathematician cannot really create anything by his defining.

—Gottlob Frege, *The Basic Laws of Arithmetic*, 1893

18. Children in school are like children at the doctor's. He can talk himself blue in the face about how much good his medicine is going to do them; all they think of is how much it will hurt or how bad it will taste. Given their own way, they would have none of it.

So the valiant and resolute band of travelers I thought I was leading toward a much hoped-for destination turned out instead to be more like convicts in a chain gang, forced under threat of punishment to move along a rough path leading nobody knew where and down which they could see hardly more than a few steps ahead. School feels like this to children: it is a place where *they* make you go and where *they* tell you to do things and where *they* try to make your life unpleasant if you don't do them or don't do them right.

—John Holt, *How Children Fail* (New York: Delta/Lawrence, 1964)

19. I simply can't imagine the world will ever be normal again for us. I do talk about "after the war," but it's as if I were talking about a castle in the air, something that can never come true.

I see the eight of us in the Annex as if we were a patch of blue sky surrounded by menacing black clouds. The perfectly round spot on which we're standing is still safe, but the clouds are moving in on us, and the ring between us and the approaching danger is being pulled tighter and tighter. We're surrounded by darkness and danger, and in our desperate search for a way out we keep bumping into each other. We look at the fighting down below and the peace and beauty up above. In the meantime, we've been cut off by the dark mass of clouds, so that we can go neither up nor down. It looms before us like an impenetrable wall, trying to crush us, but not yet able to. I can only cry out and implore, "Oh, ring, ring, open wide and let us out!"

—Anne Frank, from *The Diary of a Young Girl*, 8 November 1943

20. Unfortunately, the diary [of H. L. Mencken] reveals a man who was shockingly anti-Semitic and racist, to the point where his stature as a giant of American letters may be in danger. . . . I would draw a comparison with Richard Wagner, a virulent anti-Semite. One can still listen to Wagner's operas and appreciate their artistic beauty. The work is separated from the man. Or is it?

—Gwinn Owens, "Mencken—Getting a Bum Rap?"
The New York Times, 13 December 1989

11.3 Appraising Analogical Arguments

Some analogical arguments are much more cogent than others. Although no argument by analogy can be deductively valid, some such arguments yield conclusions that are very probably true, whereas others are very weak indeed. Analogical arguments are evaluated as better or worse depending on the degree of probability with which, relying on the premises they put forward, their conclusions may be affirmed.

Two commonplace examples will help to exhibit the features of analogical arguments that make them better or worse. Suppose you choose to purchase a given pair of shoes because other pairs like it have given you satisfaction in the past; and suppose you select a dog of a given breed because other dogs of that same breed have exhibited the characteristics that you prize. In both cases, analogical arguments have been relied on. To appraise the strength of these sample arguments, and indeed all analogical arguments, six criteria may be distinguished.

1. **Number of entities.** If my past experience with shoes of a certain kind is limited to only one pair that I wore and liked, I will be disappointed although not surprised by an apparently similar pair that I find flawed in unexpected ways. But if I have repeatedly purchased shoes just like those, I may reasonably suppose that the next pair will be as good as the ones worn earlier. Several experiences of the same kind with an item of just that sort will support the conclusion—that the purchase will be satisfying—much more than will a single instance. Each instance may be thought of as an additional entity, and the *number* of entities is the first criterion in evaluating an analogical argument.

   In general, *the larger the number of entities*—that is, cases in our past experience—*the stronger the argument*. But there is no simple ratio between that number and the probability of the conclusion. Six happy experiences with golden retrievers, intelligent and sweet-tempered dogs, will lead one to conclude that the next golden retriever will also be intelligent and sweet-tempered. However, the conclusion of an analogical argument that has six instances in its premises will not be exactly three times as probable as a similar argument that has two such instances in its premises. Increasing the number of entities is important, but so are other factors.
2. **Variety of the instances in the premises.** If my previous purchases of those good shoes had been from both a department store and a specialty store, and had been made both in New York and in California, by both mail order and direct sale, I may be confident that it is the shoes themselves and not their seller that accounts for my satisfaction. If my previous golden retrievers were both males and females, acquired both as puppies from breeders and as adults from the humane society, I may be more confident that it is their breed—not their sex or age or source—that accounts for my earlier satisfaction.

   We understand this criterion intuitively: *The more dissimilar the instances mentioned only in the premises of the analogical argument, the stronger is the argument.*
3. **Number of similar respects.** Among the instances in the premises there may have been various similarities: perhaps the shoes were of the same style, had the same price, were made of the same sort of leather; perhaps the dogs were of the same breed, came from the same breeder at the same age, and so on. All the respects in which the instances in the premises are

like one another, and also like the instance in the conclusion, increase the probability that the instance in the conclusion will have that further attribute at which the argument is aimed—giving great satisfaction in the case of the new shoes, being of a sweet disposition in the case of a new dog.

This criterion also is rooted in common sense: *The greater the number of respects in which the entity in the conclusion is similar to the entities in the premises, the more probable is that conclusion.* Again, of course, there is no simple numerical ratio between that conclusion and the number of similar respects identified.

4. **Relevance.** As important as the *number* of respects shared is the *kind* of respects in which the instances in the premises are like the instance in the conclusion. If the new pair of shoes, like the previous pairs, is purchased on a Tuesday, that is a likeness that will have no bearing on the satisfaction they give; but if the new pair, like all the previous pairs, had the same manufacturer, that will count heavily. *Respects add to the force of the argument when they are relevant* (as style of shoe, and price, and material surely are)—*and a single highly relevant factor contributes more to the argument than a host of irrelevant similarities.*

There will sometimes be disagreement about which attributes really are relevant in establishing the likelihood of our conclusion, but the *meaning* of relevance itself is not in dispute. One attribute is relevant to another when it is connected to that other, when there is some kind of *causal relation* between them. That is why identifying causal connections of one kind or another is critical in analogical arguments, and why establishing such connections is often crucial in determining the admissibility of evidence, as relevant or irrelevant, in a court of law.

Analogical arguments can be probable whether they go from cause to effect or from effect to cause. They can even be probable when the attribute in the premise is neither the cause nor the effect of the conclusion's attribute, provided both are the effect of the same cause. A doctor, noting the presence of a certain symptom in her patient, may predict another symptom accurately not because either symptom is the cause of the other, but because they are jointly caused by the same disorder. The color of a manufactured product is most often irrelevant to function, but it may serve as a relevant respect in an argument when that color is very unusual, and shared by the entities in the premises and the conclusion. The color itself may contribute nothing to the function of the product, but it may serve in argument if it is known to be an attribute of the manufacturing process of a unique producer.

The causal connections that are the key to the evaluation of analogical arguments can be discovered only empirically, by observation and experiment. The general theory of empirical investigation is the central concern of inductive logic, and will be discussed at length in the chapters that follow.

5. **Disanalogies.** A **disanalogy** is a point of difference, a respect in which the case we are reasoning about in our conclusion is distinguishable from the cases on which the argument is based. Returning to the example of the shoes, if the pair we plan to buy looks like those we had owned earlier, but is in fact much cheaper and made by a different company, those disanalogies will give us reason to doubt the satisfaction they will provide.

What was said earlier about relevance is also important here. Disanalogies undermine analogical arguments when the points of difference identified are relevant—causally connected to the outcome we are seeking. Investors often purchase shares of a stock mutual fund on the basis of its successful "track record," reasoning that because earlier purchases resulted in capital appreciation, a future purchase will do so as well. However, if we learn that the person who managed the fund during the period of its profitability has just been replaced, we confront a disanalogy that substantially reduces the strength of that analogical argument.

Disanalogies weaken analogical arguments. They are therefore commonly employed in *attacking* an analogical argument. As critics, we may try to show that the case in the conclusion is different in important ways from the earlier cases, and that what was true of them is not likely to be true of the present case. In the law, where the uses of analogy are pervasive, some earlier case or cases are often offered to a court as a precedent for deciding the case at hand. The argument is analogical. Opposing counsel will seek to *distinguish* the case at hand from the earlier cases; that is, counsel will seek to show that because there is some critical difference between the facts in the case at hand and the facts in those earlier cases, they do not serve as good precedents in the present matter. If the differences are great—if the disanalogy is indeed critical—that may demolish the analogical argument that had been put forward.

Because disanalogies are the primary weapon against an analogical argument, whatever can ward off any potential disanalogies will strengthen the argument. This explains why variety among the instances in the premises adds force to an argument. The more the instances in the premises vary from one to another, the less likely it is that a critic will be able to point to some disanalogy between all of them and the conclusion that will weaken the argument. To illustrate, suppose that Kim Kumar comes to a university as a first-year student; ten others from her secondary school have successfully completed studies at the same university.

We may argue analogically that in view of her secondary school preparation, she is likely to succeed as well. If all those other students from her school were similar to one another in some respect that bears on college study but differ from Kim in that respect, that disanalogy will undermine the argument for Kim's success. However, if we learn that the ten successful predecessors varied among themselves in many ways—in economic background, in family relations, in religious affiliation, and so on—those differences among them ward off such potential disanalogies. The argument for Kim's success is fortified—as we saw earlier—if the other students from her school serving as premises in the argument do not resemble each other closely, but exhibit substantial variety.

A confusion must be avoided: The principle that disanalogies weaken analogical arguments is to be contrasted with the principle that differences among the premises strengthen such arguments. In the former, the differences are between the instances in the premises and the instance in the conclusion; in the latter, differences are among the instances in the premises only. A disanalogy is a difference between the cases with which we have experience and the case about which a conclusion is being drawn. That conclusion (we may say in presenting the disanalogy as refutation) is not warranted because circumstances in the critical case are not similar to circumstances in earlier cases. The analogy is said to be "strained" or "does not hold." But when we point to dissimilarities among the premises we are strengthening the argument by saying, in effect, that the analogy has wide force, that it holds in cases like this and in other cases, and that therefore the respects in which the instances in the premises vary are not relevant to the matter with which the conclusion is concerned.

In summary, disanalogies undermine an analogical argument; dissimilarities among the premises reinforce it. And both considerations are tied to the question of relevance: Disanalogies tend to show that there are relevant respects in which the case in the conclusion differs from those in the premises; dissimilarities among the premises tend to show that other factors, which might have been thought causally relevant to the attribute of interest, are not really relevant at all.

Note that the very first criterion identified, pertaining to the *number* of entities among which the analogy is said to hold, is also linked to relevance. The greater the number of instances appealed to, the greater is the number of dissimilarities likely to obtain among them. Increasing the number of entities is therefore desirable, but as the number of entities increases, the impact of each additional case is reduced. The dissimilarity it may provide is more likely to have been provided by earlier instances, in which case it will add little or nothing to the protection of the conclusion from damaging disanalogies.

6. **Claim that the conclusion makes.** Every argument makes the claim that its premises give reasons to accept its conclusion. It is easy to see that the more one claims, the greater the burden of sustaining that claim, and that is obviously true for every analogical argument. The *modesty of the conclusion relative to the premises* is critical in determining the merit of the inference.

   If my friend gets 30 miles to the gallon from his new car, I may infer that, were I to acquire a car of the same make and model, I would get at least 20 miles to the gallon; that conclusion is modest and therefore very probable. Were my conclusion much bolder—say, that I would get at least 29 miles to the gallon—it would be less well supported by the evidence I have. In general, *the more modest the claim, the less burden is placed on the premises and the stronger the argument; the bolder the claim, the greater is the burden on the premises and the weaker the argument.*

   An analogical argument is strengthened by reducing the claim made on the basis of the premises affirmed, or by retaining the claim unchanged while supporting it with additional or more powerful premises. Likewise, an analogical argument is weakened if its conclusion is made bolder while its premises remain unchanged, or if the claim remains unchanged while the evidence in its support is found to exhibit greater frailty.

EXERCISES

A. For each of the following arguments by analogy, six additional premises are suggested. For each of these alternative premises, decide whether its addition would make the resulting argument more or less probable. Identify the criterion of appraisal that justifies this judgment, and explain how that criterion applies to the given case.

EXAMPLE

1. An investor has purchased one hundred shares of oil stock every December for the past five years. In every case the value of the stock has appreciated by about 15 percent a year, and it has paid regular dividends of about 8 percent a year on the price at which she bought it. This December she decides to buy another hundred shares of oil stock, reasoning that she will probably receive modest earnings while watching the value of her new purchase increase over the years.

   a. Suppose that she had always purchased stock in eastern oil companies before, and plans to purchase stock in an eastern oil company this year too.

b. Suppose that she had purchased oil stocks every December for the past fifteen years, instead of for only five years.
c. Suppose that the oil stocks previously purchased had gone up by 30 percent a year, instead of only 15 percent.
d. Suppose that her previous purchases of oil stock had been in foreign companies as well as in eastern, southern, and western U.S. oil companies.
e. Suppose she learns that OPEC has decided to meet every month instead of every six months.
f. Suppose she discovers that tobacco stocks have just raised their dividend payments.

SOLUTION

a. More probable. *Number of similar respects.* The change provides an additional respect in which the instance in the conclusion is the same as those in the premises.
b. More probable. *Number of entities.* With this change the number of entities in the premisses is substantially increased.
c. More probable. *Claim made by the conclusion.* With this change in the premises, the conclusion, although unchanged, is now, relatively speaking, substantially more modest.
d. More probable. *Variety among the premises.* With this change, the dissimilarity among the instances in the premises is clearly established.
e. Less probable. *Disanalogy.* With this change in the premises, a significant difference between the instance in the conclusion and the instances in the premises is introduced.
f. Neither. *Relevance.* It is unlikely that the dividends paid by tobacco companies would have any impact on the profitability of oil companies or the price of their shares.

2. A faithful alumnus, heartened by State's winning its last four football games, decides to bet his money that State will win its next game, too.

a. Suppose that since the last game, State's outstanding quarterback was injured in practice and hospitalized for the remainder of the season.
b. Suppose that two of the last four games were played away, and that two of them were home games.
c. Suppose that, just before the game, it is announced that a member of State's Chemistry Department has been awarded a Nobel Prize.

d. Suppose that State had won its last *six* games rather than only four of them.
e. Suppose that it has rained hard during each of the four preceding games, and that rain is forecast for next Saturday too.
f. Suppose that each of the last four games was won by a margin of at least four touchdowns.

3. Although she was bored by the last few foreign films she saw, Charlene agrees to go to see another one this evening, fully expecting to be bored again.

   a. Suppose that Charlene also was bored by the last few American movies she saw.
   b. Suppose that the star of this evening's film has recently been accused of bigamy.
   c. Suppose that the last few foreign films that Charlene saw were Italian, and that tonight's film is Italian as well.
   d. Suppose that Charlene was so bored by the other foreign films that she actually fell asleep during the performance.
   e. Suppose that the last few foreign films she saw included an Italian, a French, an English, and a Swedish film.
   f. Suppose that tonight's film is a mystery, whereas all of those she saw before were comedies.

4. Bill has taken three history courses and found them very stimulating and valuable, so he signs up for another one, confidently expecting that it too will be worthwhile.

   a. Suppose that his previous history courses were in ancient history, modern European history, and U.S. history.
   b. Suppose that his previous history courses had all been taught by the same professor scheduled to teach the present one.
   c. Suppose that his previous history courses had all been taught by Professor Smith, and the present one is taught by Professor Jones.
   d. Suppose that Bill had found his three previous history courses to be the most exciting intellectual experiences of his life.
   e. Suppose that his previous history courses had all met at 9 A.M., and that the present one is also scheduled to meet at 9 A.M.
   f. Suppose that, in addition to the three history courses he took previously, Bill had also taken and enjoyed courses in anthropology, economics, political science, and sociology.

5. Dr. Brown has stayed at the Queen's Hotel every fall for the past six years on her annual visit to New York, and she has been quite satisfied with her accommodations there. On her visit to New York this fall, Dr. Brown goes again to the Queen's Hotel, confidently expecting to enjoy her stay there again.

   a. Suppose that when she stayed at the Queen's Hotel before, she had occupied a single room twice, shared a double room twice, and twice occupied a suite.
   b. Suppose that last spring a new manager had been put in charge of the Queen's Hotel.
   c. Suppose that she had occupied a suite on all of her previous trips and is assigned a suite this time as well.
   d. Suppose that on her previous trips she had come to New York by train, but this time she flew.
   e. Suppose that, when she stayed at the Queen's Hotel before, her quarters had been the most luxurious she had ever known.
   f. Suppose that she had stayed at the Queen's Hotel three times a year for the past six years.

B. Analyze the structure of the analogical arguments in the following passages, and evaluate them in terms of the six criteria that have been explained.

1. If you cut up a large diamond into little bits, it will entirely lose the value it had as a whole; as an army divided up into small bodies of soldiers loses all its strength. So a great intellect sinks to the level of an ordinary one, as soon as it is interrupted and disturbed, its attention distracted and drawn off from the matter in hand: for its superiority depends upon its power of concentration—of bringing all its strength to bear upon one theme, in the same way as a concave mirror collects into one point all the rays of light that strike upon it.

   —Arthur Schopenhauer, "On Noise," 1851

2. It would be the height of hypocrisy if Pete Rose, one of baseball's star players, were allowed back into baseball and elected to the Hall of Fame after finally admitting that he placed bets on his team and other teams and lied about it. In coming to a decision about Rose, the Baseball Commissioner should remember that Olympic athletes who have been caught using performance-enhancing drugs are stripped permanently of their titles and medals.

   —Frank Ulrich, *The New York Times*, 8 January 2004

3. Look round the world: contemplate the whole and every part of it: you will find it to be nothing but one great machine, subdivided into an infinite number of lesser machines, which again admit of subdivisions, to a degree beyond what human senses and faculties can trace and explain. All these various machines, and even their most minute parts, are adjusted to each other with an accuracy which ravishes into admiration all men who have ever contemplated them. The curious adapting of means to ends, throughout all nature, resembles exactly, though it much exceeds, the production of human contrivance, of human design, thought, wisdom, and intelligence. Since therefore the effects resemble each other, we are led to infer, by all the rules of analogy, that the causes also resemble; and that the Author of Nature is somewhat similar to the mind of men; though possessed of much larger faculties, proportioned to the grandeur of the work, which he has executed. By this argument *a posteriori*, and by this argument alone, do we prove at once the existence of a Deity, and his similarity to human mind and intelligence.

—David Hume, *Dialogues Concerning Natural Religion*, 1779

4. The philosopher Metrodorus of Chios, who lived in the fourth century B.C., was greatly interested in the heavenly bodies. He wrote: "To consider the Earth as the only populated world in infinite space is as absurd as to assert that in an entire field of millet, only one grain will grow."

5. To the casual observer porpoises and sharks are kinds of fish. They are streamlined, good swimmers, and live in the sea. To the zoologist who examines these animals more closely, the shark has gills, cold blood, and scales; the porpoise has lungs, warm blood, and hair. The porpoise is fundamentally more like man than like the shark and belongs, with man, to the mammals—a group that nurses its young with milk. Having decided that the porpoise is a mammal, the zoologist can, without further examination, predict that the animal will have a four-chambered heart, bones of a particular type, and a certain general pattern of nerves and blood vessels. Without using a microscope the zoologist can say with reasonable confidence that the red blood cells in the blood of the porpoise will lack nuclei. This ability to generalize about animal structure depends upon a system for organizing the vast amount of knowledge about animals.

—Ralph Buchsbaum, *Animals without Backbones*
(Chicago: University Chicago Press, 1961)

6. The body is the substance of the soul; the soul is the functioning of the body. . . . The relationship of the soul to its substance is like that

of sharpness to a knife, while the relationship of the body to its functioning is like that of a knife to sharpness. What is called sharpness is not the same as the knife, and what is called the knife is not the same as sharpness. Nevertheless, there can be no knife if the sharpness is discarded, nor sharpness if the knife is discarded. I have never heard of sharpness surviving if the knife is destroyed, so how can it be admitted that the soul can remain if the body is annihilated?

—Fan Chen, *Essay on the Extinction of the Soul,*
in Fung Yu-Lan, *A History of Chinese Philosophy,* 1934

7. If a single cell, under appropriate conditions, becomes a person in the space of a few years, there can surely be no difficulty in understanding how, under appropriate conditions, a cell may, in the course of untold millions of years, give origin to the human race.

—Herbert Spencer, *Principles of Biology,* 1864

8. An electron is no more (and no less) hypothetical than a star. Nowadays we count electrons one by one in a Geiger counter, as we count the stars one by one on a photographic plate. In what sense can an electron be called more unobservable than a star? I am not sure whether I ought to say that I have seen an electron; but I have just the same doubt whether I have seen a star. If I have seen one, I have seen the other. I have seen a small disc of light surrounded by diffraction rings which has not the least resemblance to what a star is supposed to be; but the name "star" is given to the object in the physical world which some hundreds of years ago started a chain of causation which has resulted in this particular light-pattern. Similarly in a Wilson expansion chamber I have seen a trail not in the least resembling what an electron is supposed to be; but the name "electron" is given to the object in the physical world which has caused this trail to appear. How can it possibly be maintained that a hypothesis is introduced in one case and not in the other?

—Arthur Eddington, *New Pathways in Science,* 1939

9. Just as the bottom of a bucket containing water is pressed more heavily by the weight of the water when it is full than when it is half empty, and the more heavily the deeper the water is, similarly the high places of the earth, such as the summits of mountains, are less heavily pressed than the lowlands are by the weight of the mass of the air. This is because there is more air above the lowlands than above the mountain tops; for all the air along a mountain side presses upon the lowlands but not upon the summit, being above the one but below the other.

—Blaise Pascal, *Treatise on the Weight of the Mass of the Air,* 1653

10. Suppose that someone tells me that he has had a tooth extracted without an anaesthetic, and I express my sympathy, and suppose that I am then asked, "How do you know that it hurt him?" I might reasonably reply, "Well, I know that it would hurt me. I have been to the dentist and know how painful it is to have a tooth stopped [filled] without an anaesthetic, let alone taken out. And he has the same sort of nervous system as I have. I infer, therefore, that in these conditions he felt considerable pain, just as I should myself."

—Alfred J. Ayer, "One's Knowledge of Other Minds," *Theoria*, 1953

11. Now if we survey the universe, so far as it falls under our knowledge, it bears a great resemblance to an animal or organized body and seems actuated with a like principle of life and motion. A continual circulation of matter in it produces no disorder: a continual waste in every part is incessantly repaired; the closest sympathy is perceived throughout the entire system: and each part or member, in performing its proper offices, operates both to its own preservation and to that of the whole. The world, therefore, I infer, is an animal, and the Deity is the *soul* of the world, actuating it, and actuated by it.

—David Hume, *Dialogues Concerning Natural Religion*, 1779

12. One cannot require that everything shall be defined, any more than one can require that a chemist shall decompose every substance. What is simple cannot be decomposed, and what is logically simple cannot have a proper definition.

—Gottlob Frege, "On Concept and Object," 1892

13. Most endangered or threatened species in the United States find suitable habitat on private land, and the destruction of habitat is widely recognized as the leading cause of extinctions. For these reasons, protecting wildlife without regulating the use of private land has been compared by biologists to playing the piano with just the black keys.

—John H. Cushman, Jr., "Environmentalists Gain a Victory," *The New York Times*, 30 June 1995

14. Opposing legislation that would restrict handgun ownership in the United Kingdom, the husband of Queen Elizabeth II reasoned as follows:

> Look, if a cricketer, for instance, suddenly decided to go into a school and batter a lot of people to death with a cricket bat, which he could do very easily, are you going to ban cricket bats?

—Prince Philip, the Duke of Edinburgh, in an interview on the BBC, 19 December 1996

15. . . . The simplest form of the theological argument from design [was] once well known under the name "Paley's watch." Paley's form of it was just this: "If we found by chance a watch or other piece of intricate mechanism we should infer that it had been made by someone. But all around us we do find intricate pieces of natural mechanism, and the processes of the universe are seen to move together in complex relations; we should therefore infer that these too have a Maker."

—B. A. D. Williams, "Metaphysical Arguments," in D. F. Pears, ed., *The Nature of Metaphysics* (New York: Macmillan, 1957)

11.4 Refutation by Logical Analogy

"You should say what you mean," [said the March Hare, reproving Alice sharply.]

"I do," Alice hastily replied; "at least—at least I mean what I say—that's the same thing, you know."

"Not the same thing a bit!" said the Hatter. "Why, you might just as well say that 'I see what I eat' is the same thing as 'I eat what I see'!"

"You might just as well say," added the March Hare, "that 'I like what I get' is the same thing as 'I get what I like'!"

"You might just as well say," added the Dormouse, which seemed to be talking in its sleep, "that 'I breathe when I sleep' is the same thing as 'I sleep when I breathe'!"

"It *is* the same thing with you," said the Hatter, and here the conversation dropped.

—Lewis Carroll, *Alice's Adventures in Wonderland*

The Hare, the Hatter, and the Dormouse all seek to refute Alice's claim—that meaning what you say is the same as saying what you mean—by using a *logical analogy*. The form of an argument, as distinct from its particular content, is the most important aspect of that argument from a logical point of view. Therefore, we often seek to demonstrate the weakness of a given argument by stating another argument, known to be erroneous, that has the same logical form.

In the realm of deduction, a refuting analogy for a given argument is an argument that has the same form as the given argument but whose premises are known to be true and whose conclusion is known to be false. The refuting analogy is therefore known to be invalid, and the argument under attack, because it has the same form, is thus shown to be invalid as well. This is the same principle that underlies the testing of categorical syllogisms explained in Section 6.2, and it also underlies the repeated emphasis on the centrality of logical form, as explained in Section 8.4.

In the realm of inductive argument, our present concern, the technique of *refutation by logical analogy* can also be used to great effect. Scientific, political, or economic arguments, not purporting to be deductive, may be countered by presenting other arguments that have very similar designs, whose conclusions are known to be false or are generally believed to be improbable. Inductive arguments differ fundamentally from deductive arguments in the character of the support claimed to be given to the conclusion by the premises. All arguments, however, inductive as well as deductive, may be said to have some underlying form or pattern. If, when confronted by an inductive argument we wish to attack, we can present another inductive argument that has essentially the same form but is clearly flawed and whose conclusion is very doubtful, we throw similar doubt on the conclusion of the argument being examined.

Consider the following illustration. In two highly controversial cases before the U.S. Supreme Court in 2007,[8] the central issue was the constitutionality of the consideration of race by school boards in the assignment of students to public schools. In an editorial, the *New York Times* supported the race-conscious systems as fair, and called the objections to it "an assault on local school control." A prominent critic of the race-based systems wrote a critical response to that editorial, within which appeared the following passage:

> You argue that the race-based system "is applied to students of all races" and "does not advantage or disadvantage any particular racial group." But, of course, the same argument might have been made in defense of miscegenation statutes, which forbade blacks from marrying whites as well as whites from marrying blacks.[9]

The technique of refutation by logical analogy is here very keenly exemplified; the focus is on the *form* of the two arguments. The argument under attack has the same form as that of another argument whose unsatisfactoriness is now universally understood. We surely would not say that miscegenation statues are acceptable because they apply equally to all races. Some policies involving the use of race by the state are not acceptable (the critic argues) even when it is true that no particular racial group is disadvantaged by that use. By highlighting such unacceptability in some well-known settings (regulations governing marriage), he strikes a sharp blow against the argument in this setting that relies on the claim that no particular racial group is disadvantaged by the race-based policy under attack.

The presentation of a refutation by logical analogy is often signaled by the appearance of some revealing phrase: "You might just as well say," or some other words having that same sense. In the example just given, the telltale phrase is "the same argument might have been made. . . ." In another context, the argument that because Islamic culture had been brought to the country of Chad from without, it is no more than an Islamic overlay, is attacked with the refuting analogy of a scholar who introduces the refutation with a slightly different set of words: "One could as sensibly say that France has only a Christian overlay."[10]

When the point of the refuting analogy is manifest, no introductory phrases may be needed. The former governor of Mississippi, Kirk Fordice, argued that "It is a simple fact that the United States is a Christian nation" because "Christianity is the predominant religion in America." Journalist Michael Kinsley, with whom Fordice was debating on television, responded with these telling analogies: "Women are a majority in this country. Does that make us a female country? Or does it make us a white country because most people in this country are white?"[11]

A careless effort to refute an argument with an analogy can backfire when the allegedly refuting argument differs importantly from the target argument in ways that tend to reinforce the one that is under attack. This is illustrated by a recent exchange on the highly controversial topic of global warming. Newspaper columnist John Tierney raised some serious questions about the wisdom of immediate large-scale efforts to combat an apparent but uncertain climate trend.[12] A critic, Ray Sten, responded in this way:

> John Tierney suggests that we not worry much about climate change because its consequences are uncertain and far in the future, and in the meantime somebody may discover a technological quick fix. That's like telling a smoker not to worry because it's not certain whether he'll develop cancer, and besides, a cure may have been found by then. Call me a worry wart, but I'd quit smoking.[13]

The immediate and large-scale steps whose wisdom Tierney questions are thus likened to quitting smoking. There is, however, an important contrast between those two. Quitting has no economic costs (and even some economic benefits), while industrial changes designed to cut greenhouse gases by reducing the use of fossil fuels will probably be very costly. In presenting an analogy intended to refute Tierney, Mr. Stern (whose position on global warming may well be correct) undermines his cause by indirectly calling attention to the costs of the change he seeks to advance.

Here, to conclude, is a letter to the editor from Jeff Weaver, published in *The Ann Arbor (Mich.) News* in July 2005:

> I find it amusing that anyone would be offended by the name or appearance of a team mascot. But apparently there are people who are devastated that there are schools with team names such as the Hurons, Chippewas, Braves, Chiefs, Seminoles, etc.
>
> I sympathize with their plight. I would also suggest that we change the name of the Pioneers of Ann Arbor Pioneer High School. My forefathers were pioneers and I'm sure they would be devastated that a school adopted their name as a team mascot. That name and mascot are a direct slap against my people.

> While we are at it, we had better change the names of the Cowboys, Fighting Irish, Celtics, Hoosiers, Sooners, Boilermakers, Packers, Aggies, Oilers, Mountaineers, Friars, Patriots, Volunteers and Tar Heels, to name a few, because I'm sure those names are equally demeaning and degrading to those groups as well. . . .

Refutation by analogy when well designed can be exceedingly effective. If the argument presented as a refuting analogy is plainly rotten, and it does indeed have the same form as that of the argument under attack, that target argument must be seriously wounded.

EXERCISES

Each of the following is intended to be a refutation by logical analogy. Identify the argument being refuted in each and the refuting analogy, and decide whether they do indeed have the same argument form.

1. Steve Brill, founder of Court TV, has no doubt that cameras belong in the courtroom, and answers some critics in the following way: "Some lawyers and judges say that TV coverage makes the system look bad. They confuse the messenger with the message. If press coverage of something makes it look bad, that is a reason to have the press coverage. That criticism is like saying that because journalists were allowed to be with the troops in Vietnam, the Vietnam War was ruined."

   —Steve Brill, "Trial: A Starting Place for Reform," *Ann Arbor (Mich.) News,* 12 June 1995

2. The whole history of bolshevism, both before and after the October revolution, is full of instances of maneuvering, temporizing and compromising with other parties, bourgeois parties included! To carry on a war for the overthrow of the international bourgeoisie, a war which is a hundred times more difficult, prolonged and complicated than the most stubborn of ordinary wars between states, and to refuse beforehand to maneuver, to utilize the conflict of interests (even though temporary) among one's enemies, to refuse to temporize and compromise with possible (even though transitory, unstable, vacillating and conditional) allies—is this not ridiculous in the extreme? Is it not as though, when making a difficult ascent of an unexplored and hitherto inaccessible mountain, we were to refuse beforehand ever to move in zigzags, ever to retrace our steps, ever to abandon the course once selected to try others?

   —V. I. Lenin, *"Left Wing" Communism: An Infantile Disorder,* 1920

3. The distinguished naturalist E. O. Wilson argues that humans are no more than a biological species of a certain physical composition,

and that the human mind can have no characteristics attributable to nonphysical causes. This claim can no longer be disputed. "Virtually all contemporary scientists and philosophers expert on the subject agree [he writes] that the mind, which comprises consciousness and rational process, is the brain at work. . . . The brain and its satellite glands have now been probed to the point where no particular site remains that can reasonably be supposed to harbor a nonphysical mind.[14] Stephen Barr presented the following counterargument in the form of a logical analogy: "This [Wilson's argument quoted above] is on a par with Nikita Krushshev's announcement [aiming to support atheism] that Yuri Gagarin, the first human visitor to space, had failed to locate God. Does Wilson suppose that if there were an immaterial component to the mind it would show up in a brain scan?"[15]

4. The argument against new highways is given forceful statement by three distinguished urban planners: the authors write: "The only long term solutions to traffic are public transit and coordinated land use." New highways, they argue, bring "induced traffic." So building more highways will only cause more traffic congestion, not less.[16]

A highly critical reviewer responds to this argument as follows: "This is nonsense. . . . Long lines at a grocery store would not prompt anyone to say, "Well, we can't build any more grocery stores. That would only bring out more customers." Building more highways wouldn't lure cars. The cars come anyway."[17]

5. America's supply of timber has been increasing for decades, and the nation's forests have three times more wood today than in 1920. "We're not running out of wood, so why do we worry so much about recycling paper?" asks Jerry Taylor, the director of natural research studies at the Cato Institute. "Paper is an agricultural product, made from trees grown specifically for paper production. Acting to conserve trees by recycling paper is like acting to conserve cornstalks by cutting back on corn consumption."

—John Tierney, "Recycling Is Garbage,"
The New York Times Magazine, 30 June 1996

6. In 1996, heated controversy arose between the states of New Jersey and New York over formal possession of Ellis Island, located at the mouth of the Hudson River near the New Jersey shore, a tiny speck of land on which so many tens of thousands of immigrants to the United States first touched American soil. An essay defending New York's claim to the historic island appeared in the *New York Times* on

23 July 1996. The following letter appeared in the same newspaper four days later:

> Clyde Haberman is right that almost every immigrant who passed through Ellis Island was bound for New York, not New Jersey. But this fact does not determine where the island is. A significant number of passengers arriving at Newark International Airport are also on their way to New York, but it would be hard to argue that New York thus has a claim on the airport. Cincinnati International Airport is in Covington, Kentucky, and presumably, few travelers are on their way to sparsely populated northern Kentucky. Would Mr. Haberman suggest that the airport belongs to Ohio?

7. Edward Rothstein suggests that poverty and injustice cannot be considered among the root causes of Islamic terrorism because Osama bin Laden is a multimillionaire. By that logic, slavery could not have caused the Civil War because Abraham Lincoln was not a slave.

—Corey Robin, "The Root Causes of Terror," *The New York Times*, 17 November 2001

8. Each of the multitude of universes may have different laws of nature. Or different values of quantities that determine how they behave, such as the speed of light. Some may be suitable for life, and some may not. All those suitable for life may have life develop. Sometimes life will evolve only into dinosaurs rather than something more intelligent. We cannot attach any meaning to the fact that a life form which could ask anthropic questions [questions about the properties that are essential for intelligent life] did develop in at least one universe. It is very much like a lottery. If you win the lottery, you may feel very grateful, but someone had to win, and no one selected who that was, except randomly. Just because a universe has a unique set of laws and parameters should not lead one to wonder whether that set was designed.

—Gordon Kane, "Anthropic Questions," *Phi Kappa Phi Forum*, Fall 2002

9. Artificial human minds will never be made (we are told) because "artificial intelligence investigation is based on advanced solidstate physics, whereas the humble human brain is a viable semiliquid system!" That is no more reassuring than the suggestion that automobiles could never replace horses because they are made of metal, while the humble horse is a viable organic system with legs of flesh and bone.

—Michael D. Rohr, *The New York Times*, 27 March 1998

Courtesy of King Features Syndicate.

10. Modern political rhetoric [Ronald Dworkin argues] "is now extremely repetitive," and a good bit of it could be dispensed with—by law. "Every European democracy does this," the world's most highly regarded legal philosopher points out, "and Europeans are amazed that we do not."

Europeans are also amazed that we bathe as frequently as we do. What the hell kind of argument is that?

—David Tell, "Silencing Free Speech in the Name of Reform," *The Weekly Standard,* 25 November 1996

SUMMARY

In this chapter we began the analysis of induction. Section 11.1 reviewed the fundamental distinction between deductive arguments, which claim certainty for their conclusions, and inductive arguments, which make no such claim. The terms *validity* and *invalidity* do not apply to inductive arguments, whose conclusions can only have some degree of probability of being true.

In Section 11.2 we explained argument by analogy. An analogy is a likeness or comparison; we draw an analogy when we indicate one or more respects in which two or more entities are similar. An argument by analogy is an argument whose premises assert the similarity of two or more entities in one or more respects, and whose conclusion is that those entities are similar in some further respect. Its conclusion, like that of every inductive argument, can be no more than probable.

In Section 11.3 we explained six criteria used in determining whether the premises of an analogical argument render its conclusion more or less probable. These criteria are

1. The *number of entities* between which the analogy is said to hold
2. The *variety, or degree of dissimilarity,* among those entities or instances mentioned only in the premises
3. The *number of respects* in which the entities involved are said to be analogous
4. The *relevance* of the respects mentioned in the premises to the further respect mentioned in the conclusion
5. The *number and importance of disanalogies* between the instances mentioned only in the premises and the instance mentioned in the conclusion
6. The *modesty (or boldness)* of the conclusion relative to the premises

In Section 11.4 we explained refutation by logical analogy. To show that a given argument (whether inductive or deductive) is mistaken, one effective method is to present another argument, which is plainly mistaken, and whose form is the same as that of the argument under attack.

End Notes

[1]Bert Vogelstein, "So, Smoking Causes Cancer: This Is News?" *The New York Times,* 27 October 1996.

[2]Albert Shanker, "Testing Teachers," *The New York Times,* 8 January 1995.

[3]Thomas Reid, *Essays on the Intellectual Powers of Man,* Essay 1, 1785.

[4]Andrew Massimino, "Building a Country," *The New York Times,* 5 June 2006.

[5]Eric Lander, quoted in an interview in the *The New York Times,* 10 September 1996.

[6]*Crawford v. Washington,* 541 U.S. 36 (2004).

[7]F. Barringer and A. Revkin, "A Few Spitballs Greet Professor Gore," *The Ann Arbor (Mich.) News,* 22 March 2007.

[8]*Parents Involved in Community Schools v. Seattle School District No. 1* (No. 05-908); and *Crystal D. Meredith, Custodial Parent v. Jefferson County (KY) Board of Education* (No. 05-915)

[9]Roger Clegg, "An Issue for the Court: Diversity in Our Schools," *The New York Times,* 11 December 2006.

[10]Bassam Abed, in a letter to *The New York Times,* 26 June 1988.

[11]"Evangelical Update," *The New York Times*, 21 November 1992.

[12]John Tierney, "Findings," *The New York Times*, 13 February 2007.

[13]Ray Sten, "Debating Climate Change," *The New York Times*, 20 February 2007.

[14]E.O. Wilson, *Consilience* (New York-Alfred A. Knopf, 1998), p. 99.

[15]S. N. Barr, "Mindless Science," *The Weekly Standard*, 6 April 1998.

[16]A. Duany, E. Plater-Zyberk, and J. Speck, *Suburban Nation: The Rise of Sprawl and the Decline of the American Dream* (New York: North Point, 2000).

[17]F. Barnes, "Suburban Beauty: Why Sprawl Works," *The Weekly Standard*, 22 May 2000.

Causal Reasoning

12.1 Cause and Effect

Induction goes far beyond analogical arguments. When we know, or think we know, that one thing is the *cause* of another, or the *effect* of another, we can reason from cause to effect, or from effect to cause. If the supposed relations between cause and effect have been correctly established, the reasoning based on those relations is very powerful.

Causal reasoning is also of the very greatest practical importance. Our ability to control our environment, to live successfully and to achieve our purposes, depends critically on our knowledge of causal connections. To cure some disease, for example, physicians must know its cause—and of course they must learn the effects (including the side effects) of the drugs they administer.

In every sphere in which we take action and seek to achieve some result, the relation of cause and effect is fundamental. David Hume, one of the keenest of all thinkers in this arena, wrote:

> All reasonings concerning matter of fact seem to be founded on the relation of *Cause and Effect*. By means of that relation alone we can go beyond the evidence of our memory and senses. If you were to ask a man, why he believes any matter of fact, which is absent; for instance, that his friend is in the country, or in France; he would give you a reason; and this reason would be some other fact; as a letter received from him, or the knowledge of his former resolutions and promises. A man finding a watch or any other machine in a desert island, would conclude that there had once been men in that island. All our reasonings concerning fact are of the same nature. . . . If we would satisfy ourselves, therefore, concerning the nature of that evidence, which assures us of matters of fact, we must enquire how we arrive at the knowledge of cause and effect."[1]

The methods by which we arrive at such knowledge are the central concern of this chapter. This matter is complicated, however, by the fact that there are several different meanings of the word "cause." Therefore we begin by distinguishing these meanings from one another.

Things do not just happen. Events take place *under certain conditions,* and it is an axiom in the study of nature that to understand the world in which we live we must seek to learn the conditions under which events do or do not happen. It is customary to distinguish between the *necessary* and the *sufficient* conditions for the occurrence of an event.

A **necessary condition** for the occurrence of a specified event is a circumstance in whose *absence* the event *cannot* occur. For example, the presence of oxygen is a necessary condition for combustion to occur. If combustion occurs, then oxygen must have been present, because in the absence of oxygen there can be no combustion.

A **sufficient condition** for the occurrence of an event is a circumstance in whose *presence* the event *must* occur. The presence of oxygen is a necessary condition for combustion, as we noted, but it is not a sufficient condition for combustion to occur—because it is obvious that oxygen can be present without combustion occurring. For almost any substance, however, there is some range of temperature such that being in that range of temperature in the presence of oxygen is a sufficient condition for the combustion of that substance. So it is clear that for the occurrence of an event there may be several necessary conditions—and all of those necessary conditions must be included in the sufficient condition of that event.

Now the word "cause" is used (with respect to some event) sometimes to mean "the necessary condition of that event," and sometimes to mean "the sufficient condition of that event." It is most often used in the sense of necessary condition when the problem at hand is the *elimination* of some undesirable phenomenon. To eliminate it, one need only find some condition that is necessary to the existence of that phenomenon, and then eliminate that condition. What virus or bacterium is the cause of a certain illness? The physician cures the illness by administering a drug that will destroy those germs. The germs are said to be the *cause* of the disease in that they are a *necessary condition* for it—because in their absence the disease cannot occur.

However, the word "cause" is also commonly used to mean *sufficient condition*—especially when we are interested in the *production* of something desired, rather than the elimination of something undesirable. The metallurgist aims to discover what will produce greater strength in metal alloys, and when it is found that a certain process of mixed heating and cooling has that desired result, we say that such a process is the *cause* of the stronger alloy. It is correct to use the word "cause" in the one sense (necessary condition), or in the other (sufficient condition), but one should be clear about which of those meanings is intended.

Closely related to *sufficient condition* is another sense of the word "cause"—when a given phenomenon *tends* to have a causative role in the production of certain outcomes. For example, it is indeed correct to say that "smoking causes lung cancer," even though smoking cigarettes may long continue without having cancer as its result. And smoking is certainly not a necessary condition of lung cancer, because many such cancers arise in the total absence of smoking. But smoking cigarettes, in conjunction with very common biological circumstances, so frequently plays a role in the development of lung cancer that we think it correct to report that smoking is a "cause" of cancer.

This points to yet another common use of the term word "cause"—cause as the one factor that was critical in the occurrence of some phenomenon. An insurance company sends investigators to determine the cause of a mysterious fire. The investigators are likely to lose their jobs if they report that it was the presence of oxygen in the atmosphere that was the fire's cause—and yet of course it was (in the sense of necessary condition), for had there been no oxygen present there would have been no fire. Nor is the sufficient condition of the fire of interest to the company, for if the investigators reported that, although they had proof the fire was deliberately ignited by the policyholder, they had not yet been able to learn *all* the necessary conditions of the fire and therefore had not yet determined its full cause, they would certainly lose their jobs! What the company was seeking to discover was the incident or action that, in the presence of those conditions that usually prevail, *made the difference* between the occurrence and nonoccurrence of the fire.

In the real world, a huge man, forcibly resisting arrest, died shortly after having been beaten into submission by police officers in Cincinnati, Ohio, in November 2003. The county coroner investigating the death held it to be a "homicide," carefully noting that hostile or malign intent is not implied by that word. "Absent the struggle," the coroner said, "Mr. Jones would not have died at that precise moment in time, and the struggle therefore is the primary cause of his death."[2] This sense of cause as "critical factor" is common and useful.

And there are subdivisions of this third sense of cause. When there is a causal sequence—a chain of events in which *A* causes *B*, *B* causes *C*, *C* causes *D*, and *D* causes *E*—we may regard the outcome, *E*, as the effect of any one of those preceding events. The death described above (symbolized by *E*) was caused by the struggle, the struggle (*D*) was caused by the resistance, the resistance (*C*) was caused by the arrest, the arrest (*B*) was caused by some violation of law (*A*), and so on. We distinguish between the **remote cause** and the **proximate cause** of *E*. The proximate cause is the event closest to it in the chain of events. The death, *E*, is the result of the proximate cause of the struggle, *D*; the others are remote: *A* more remote than *B*, *B* more remote than *C*, and so on.

Persons who leave school before the age of 16 are five times more likely to die from a heart attack as are university graduates; and the death rate within one year of a heart attack is 3.5 percent for college graduates but 20 percent for those with fewer than eight years of formal schooling.[3] But a college education is not the proximate cause of good health, nor is ignorance the proximate cause of disease. A poor education is a link in the causal chain, often resulting in a less adequate understanding of the disease process and thus a failure to make the lifestyle changes needed to promote better medical outcomes. So it is commonly and correctly observed that poverty, affecting education almost universally, is one of the "root causes" of poor health—not its proximate cause, of course—but a remote cause that needs uprooting.

The several different senses of the word "cause" need to be distinguished. We can legitimately infer cause from effect only when by *cause* we mean *necessary condition*. And we can infer effect from cause only when by *cause* we mean *sufficient condition*. When inferences are drawn both from cause to effect and from effect to cause, the word "cause" must be used in the sense of **necessary and sufficient condition**—the cause regarded as the sufficient condition of the event and that sufficient condition regarded as the conjunction of all its necessary conditions. No single definition of *cause* conforms to all the different (and reasonable) uses of that word.

12.2 Causal Laws and the Uniformity of Nature

Every use of the word "cause," whether in everyday life, or in science, involves or presupposes the doctrine that cause and effect are uniformly connected. We will allow that some particular circumstance was the cause of some particular effect only if we agree that any other circumstance of that type will (if the attendant circumstances are sufficiently similar) cause another effect of the same kind as the first. In other words, similar causes produce similar effects. As we use the word "cause," part of its meaning is that every occurrence of a cause producing some effect is an *instance* or *example* of the general causal law that such circumstances are always accompanied by such phenomena. If it can be shown that in another situation, after an occurrence of that supposed cause, the supposed effect did *not* occur, we will relinquish the belief that the one is the cause of the other.

Because every assertion that a particular circumstance was the cause of a particular phenomenon implies the existence of some causal law, every assertion of causal connection contains a critical element of *generality*. A **causal law**, as we use the term, asserts that a circumstance of such-and-such kind is invariably attended by a phenomenon of a specified kind, no matter where or when it occurs.

How can we come to know such general truths? The causal relation is not purely logical or deductive; as David Hume emphasized, it cannot be discovered by any *a priori* reasoning.* Causal laws can be discovered only empirically, *a posteriori,* by an appeal to experience. But our experiences are always of *particular* circumstances, *particular* phenomena, and *particular* sequences of them. We may observe several instances of a circumstance (call it C), and every instance that we observe may be accompanied by an instance of a certain kind of phenomenon (call it *P*). But we will have experienced only some of the instances of C in the world, and our observations can therefore show us only that some cases of *C* are attended by *P.* Yet our aim is to establish a general, causal relation. How are we to get from the particulars we experience to the general proposition that *all* cases of *C* are attended by *P*—which is involved in saying that *C causes P?*

12.3 Induction by Simple Enumeration

When we assert that all cases of *C* are attended by *P*—that is, when we affirm a general causal relation—we have gone beyond analogy. The process of arriving at universal propositions from the particular facts of experience is called **inductive generalization.** Suppose we dip blue litmus paper into acid and it turns red. Suppose we do this three times, or ten times, always with the same result. What conclusion do we draw? By *analogy* we may draw a *particular* conclusion about what will happen to the color of the next piece of litmus paper we dip in acid—the fourth or the eleventh. Or we may draw a general conclusion about what will happen to *every* piece of blue litmus paper when it is dipped in acid. If we do the latter, it is an *inductive generalization* with which our argument concludes.

When the premises of an argument report a number of instances in which two attributes (or circumstances, or phenomena) occur together, we may infer

*Hume wrote: "But to convince us that all the laws of nature, and all the operations of bodies without exception, are known only by experience, the following reflections may, perhaps, suffice. Were any object presented to us, and were we required to pronounce concerning the effect, which will result from it, without consulting past observation, after what manner, I beseech you, must the mind proceed in this operation? It must invent or imagine some event, which it ascribes to the object as its effect; and it is plain that this invention must be entirely arbitrary. The mind can never possibly find the effect in the supposed cause, by the most accurate scrutiny and examination. For the effect is totally different from the cause, and consequently can never be discovered in it. . . . A stone or piece of metal raised into the air, and left without any support, immediately falls; but to consider the matter *a priori,* is there anything we can discover in this situation which can beget the idea of a downward, rather than an upward, or any other motion, in the stone or metal? . . . In vain, therefore, should we pretend to determine any single event, or infer any cause or effect, without the assistance of observation and experience" (*An Enquiry Concerning Human Understanding,* 1748, sec. IV).

by analogy that some particular instance of one attribute will also exhibit the other attribute. By inductive generalization we might infer that every instance of the one attribute will also be an instance of the other. Inductive generalization of the form

> Instance 1 of phenomenon *E* is accompanied by circumstance *C*.
>
> Instance 2 of phenomenon *E* is accompanied by circumstance *C*.
>
> Instance 3 of phenomenon *E* is accompanied by circumstance *C*.
>
> ---
>
> Therefore every instance of phenomenon *E* is accompanied by circumstance *C*.

is an **induction by simple enumeration.** An induction by simple enumeration is very similar to an argument by analogy, differing only in having a more general conclusion.

Simple enumeration is often used in establishing causal connections. Where a number of instances of a phenomenon are invariably accompanied by a certain type of circumstance, it is only natural to infer the existence of a causal relationship between them. Since the circumstance of dipping blue litmus paper in acid is accompanied in all observed instances by the phenomenon of the paper turning red, we infer by simple enumeration that dipping blue litmus paper in acid is the cause of its turning red. The analogical character of such an argument is quite apparent.

Because of the great similarity between argument by simple enumeration and argument by analogy, similar criteria for appraisal apply to both. Some arguments by simple enumeration may establish their conclusions with a higher degree of probability than others. The greater the number of instances appealed to, the greater is the probability of the conclusion. The various instances or cases of phenomenon E accompanied by circumstance C are often called *confirming instances* of the causal law asserting that C causes E. The greater the number of confirming instances, the greater is the probability of the causal law—other things being equal. Thus the first criterion for analogical arguments also applies directly to arguments by simple enumeration.

In a historical report, simple enumeration can provide persuasive grounds for inferring a causal relationship. To illustrate, legislative acts designed to savage some individual or group temporarily out of favor, called bills of attainder, are known to endanger their advocates when the pendulum of political power swings. The accuser today becomes the victim tomorrow. Condemning such a bill of attainder (aimed at Thomas Osborne, Earl of Danbury) in the British House of Lords, the Earl of Carnarvon drove the point home in 1678 with the following enumeration:

> My Lords, I understand . . . not a little of our English history, from which I have learnt the mischiefs of prosecutions such as these, and the ill fate of the prosecutors.

> I shall go no further back than the latter end of Queen Elizabeth's reign, at which time the Earl of Essex was run down by Sir Walter Raleigh, and your Lordships well know what became of Sir Walter Raleigh. My Lord Bacon, he ran down Sir Walter Raleigh, and your Lordships know what became of my Lord Bacon. The Duke of Buckingham, he ran down my Lord Bacon, and your Lordships know what happened to the Duke of Buckingham. Sir Thomas Wentworth, afterwards Earl of Strafford, ran down the Duke of Buckingham, and you all know what became of him. Sir Harry Vane, he ran down the Earl of Strafford, and your Lordships know what became of Sir Harry Vane. Chancellor Hyde, he ran down Sir Harry Vane, and your Lordships know what became of the Chancellor. Sir Thomas Osborne, now Earl of Danby, ran down Chancellor Hyde.
>
> What will now become of the Earl of Danby, your Lordships best can tell. But let me see that man that dare run the Earl of Danby down, and we shall soon see what will become of him.[4]

Rhetorically effective though this recounting of instances may be, it does not provide a trustworthy argument. The conclusion, that there is a causal connection between malicious accusation and subsequent destruction, appeals to six confirming instances—but the very nature of those instances prevents them from distinguishing between confirming instances of a genuine causal law and mere historical accidents.

The heart of the difficulty is this: The method of simple enumeration takes no account—*can* take no account—of exceptions to the causal law being suggested. Any alleged causal law may be overthrown by a single negative case, for any one disconfirming instance shows that what had been proposed as a "law" was not truly general. Exceptions *disprove* the rule—for an exception (or "negative instance") is either one in which the alleged cause is found and is not followed by the alleged effect (in this historical case, a bill of attainder whose author did not suffer a like fate), or one in which the effect is encountered while the alleged cause is absent—where (using our earlier schema) C is present without E, or E is present without C. In an argument by simple enumeration there is no place for either of these; the only legitimate premises in such an argument are reports of instances in which *both* the alleged cause and the alleged effect are present.

Four hundred years ago Sir Francis Bacon, in *The Advancement of Learning* (1605), clearly identified the shortcomings of induction by simple enumeration. He wrote: "The induction that proceeds by simple enumeration is childish;* its conclusions are precarious, and exposed to peril from a contradictory instance; and it generally reaches decision on too small a number of facts, and on those only that are on hand."

It is thus a grave weakness of simple enumeration arguments that, if we confine ourselves to them exclusively, we will not look for, and are therefore unlikely even to notice, the negative or disconfirming instances that might otherwise be found. For this reason, despite their fruitfulness and value in *suggesting* causal laws, inductions by simple enumeration are not at all suitable for *testing* causal laws. Yet such testing is essential; to accomplish it we must rely upon other types of inductive arguments—and to these we turn now.

12.4 Methods of Causal Analysis

The classic formulation of the methods central to all induction were given in the nineteenth century by John Stuart Mill (in *A System of Logic,* 1843). His systematic account of these methods has led logicians to refer to them as Mill's methods of inductive inference. The techniques themselves—five are commonly distinguished—were certainly not invented by him, nor should they be thought of as merely a product of nineteenth-century thought. On the contrary, these are universal tools of scientific investigation. The names Mill gave to them are still in use, as are Mill's precise formulations of what he called the "canons of induction." These techniques of investigation are permanently useful. Present-day accounts of discoveries in the biological, social, and physical sciences commonly report the methodology used as one or another variant (or combination) of these five techniques of inductive inference called **Mill's methods:** They are

1. The method of agreement
2. The method of difference
3. The joint method of agreement and difference

---

*Induction by simple enumeration can mislead even the learned. The author of an account of the creation of the Oxford English Dictionary [*The Professor and the Madman*] reported his faithful belief in a curious causal claim: "Ever since I was 4 years old, I have said "White Rabbits" at the very first moment of waking on every single first day of every single month that has passed. My mother, tucking me into bed one night, told me to do it, to bring good fortune; and since I have enjoyed fair good fortune for all of my subsequent days I have assumed that the acceptance of this moderate and harmless habit has had something to do with it, and so has reinforced my need to keep up the practice. . . . No fewer than 696 times I have maintained what has been a quite unvarying routine . . . when my eyes have snapped open with the first streaks of daylight, I have always uttered "White Rabbits."

—Simon Winchester, "Oh Dear, Too Late for the White Rabbits," *The New York Times*, 7 October 2006

4. The method of residues
5. The method of concomitant variation

We will examine each of these in turn, presenting Mill's classic statement of each (with one exception), followed by explication and illustration. These are the techniques on which science does and will rely in the search for causal laws.

A. THE METHOD OF AGREEMENT

John Stuart Mill wrote:

> If two or more instances of the phenomenon under investigation have only one circumstance in common, the circumstance in which alone all the instances agree, is the cause (or effect) of the given phenomenon.

This method goes beyond simple enumeration in that it seeks not only to discover the repeated conjunction of cause with effect, but also to identify the *only* circumstance, the *one* circumstance, that is invariably associated with the effect, or phenomenon, in which we are interested. This is an essential, and exceedingly common, tool of scientific inquiry. In searching for the cause of some deadly epidemic, for example, or in searching for the cause of some geological phenomenon, the epidemiologist or geologist will seek out the special circumstances that in every instance attend that result. In what way, they ask, do apparently differing sets of circumstances *agree,* where that result is produced?

Imagine, among the residents of some residence hall, a rash of stomach upsets, whose cause we must learn. The first line of inquiry naturally will be: What food or foods were eaten by *all* those who fell ill? Foods that were eaten by some but not all of those afflicted are not likely to be the cause of the outbreak; we want to know what circumstance can be found to be *common* to every case of the illness. Of course, what turns out to be common may not be a food; it may be the use of some infected utensil, or proximity to some noxious effluent, or other circumstance. But only when some circumstance is found in which *all* the cases of the illness agree are we on the way to the solution of the problem.

Schematically, the **method of agreement** may be represented as follows, where capital letters represent circumstances and lowercase letters denote phenomena:

A B C D occur together with *w x y z*.

A E F G occur together with *w t u v*.

Therefore *A* is the cause (or the effect) of *w*.

This method is particularly useful in identifying a *kind* of phenomenon, or a *range* of circumstances, whose investigation holds scientific promise. In molecular genetics, for example, the search for the causes of some inherited disease can be greatly narrowed down using the method of agreement. Is there a common factor among families in which some specific disorder is prevalent? By examining the genetic makeup of such families, then closing in on those genetic factors that are found in such families but are not found commonly in others, the chromosome (and sometimes the site on that chromosome) where the inherited defect lies may be identified. This has proved a very effective method in tracing the cause of some diseases.

Similarly, the fluoridation of water in developed areas around the globe was the consequence of the discovery, more than half a century ago, that in cities where the rates of dental decay were unusually low, the one circumstance in common was an unusually high level of fluorine in the water supply. To confirm the causal connection, two cities of comparable size along the Hudson River—Newburgh and Kingston, New York—were closely studied in the 1940s; Newburgh's water was treated with fluoride, Kingston's had no fluoride. The statistics proved remarkable: Children in Newburgh showed a *70 percent reduction in cavities* by the time they reached 14 years of age—and yet there were no differences between the two cities in rates of cancer, birth defects, or heart disease. The full explanation of this prevention of cavities could not be given at that time, but enough was known to justify the fluoridation of municipal water systems.

The method is widely powerful. A very promising development in the effort to help smokers break their addiction to nicotine was the discovery, reported in *Science* in 2007, that in a small number of persons who had suffered an injury to a particular region of their brains called the *insula,* the desire to smoke was immediately lost! Something in the insula appears to be a critical element in addiction. When statistical analyses of the data were completed, said a lead investigator from the University of Southern California, "it turned out that the likelihood of quitting smoking with ease after insula damage was 136 times higher than for damage anywhere else in the brain." A neuroscientist from the National Institute of Drug Abuse was enthusiastic: "To have any kind of variable produce this rate of quitting smoking is remarkable, to have it associated with a particular brain region is fantastic."[5] Thus, for addiction researchers, who are eager to apply the method of agreement to nicotine addiction, a major question has now become: "Can we learn to de-activate the insula?"[6]

In short, whenever we find *a single circumstance common to all instances* of a given phenomenon, we may rightly conclude that we have located at least the region of its cause.

The method of agreement has serious limitations, however. Looking chiefly to confirming instances, the method by itself is often insufficient to identify the cause being sought. The data available are seldom so conveniently arranged as to permit the identification of one circumstance common to all cases. And when inquiry reveals more than one circumstance common to all cases, this technique alone cannot evaluate those alternative possibilities.

Although the presence of agreement between circumstance and phenomenon is often inconclusive, the *absence* of agreement may help us to determine what is *not* the cause of a phenomenon of interest. The method of agreement is in essence eliminative; it points to the fact that circumstances arising in some of the cases, but not all of the cases, of the phenomenon in which we are interested, are not likely to be its cause. Those who argue against an alleged causal relation, therefore, are likely to call attention to the absence of uniform agreement, inferring that the alleged cause can be neither the sufficient condition nor the necessary condition of that phenomenon.

After we have learned all that the method of agreement can teach, other inductive methods capable of greater refinement in the search for causes are sure to be required.

EXERCISES

Analyze each of the following scientific reports, explaining how the pattern of the method of agreement is manifested by each. Discuss, in each case, the limitations of the method of agreement as applied to that quest for a causal connection.

1. Contaminated scallions, chopped up raw in salsa that was served free to every table at a Chi-Chi's restaurant in western Pennsylvania, almost certainly caused the large outbreak of hepatitis A in the region, the Centers for Disease Control and Prevention said yesterday. Bunches of scallions (green onions) were stored together in large buckets for five days or more with the ice they had been shipped in from Mexico. As a result, even if only some bunches were tainted with the hepatitis virus when they were delivered, it would have quickly spread to all the other scallions—the ice water in the bucket becoming "hepatitis soup." The scallions were later rinsed, chopped, refrigerated for two more days, and then added to the salsa which was made in 40-quart batches and kept refrigerated for up to three days. The outbreak, which has killed three people and made 575 other Chi-Chi's patrons sick, is the nation's biggest outbreak of hepatitis A from one source. Hepatitis A is spread by fecal matter from infected people, particularly those who fail to wash their hands after using the restroom. The virus does not multiply outside the body, but it can survive in food.

Hepatitis A is a common childhood disease in Mexico, and children commonly work on the scallion farms there; sewage-contaminated water could also have been the culprit, whether used to irrigate the scallions, or wash them, or make the ice used in shipping. How the scallions became contaminated is not known.

—"Government Makes It Official: Blame Scallions for Outbreak," *The New York Times*, 22 November 2003

2. Researchers at the University of California at Irvine have theorized that listening to Mozart's piano music significantly improves performance on intelligence tests. Dr. Frances H. Rauscher and her colleagues reported:

   We performed an experiment in which students were each given three sets of standard IQ spatial reasoning tasks; each task was preceded by 10 minutes of

   1. listening to Mozart's Sonata for Two Pianos in D major, K. 488; or
   2. listening to a relaxation tape; or
   3. silence.

   Performance was improved for those tasks immediately following the first condition compared to the second two.

   Test scores rose an average of 8 or 9 points following the Mozart sonata. Some of the students had reported that they liked Mozart, and some that they did not, but there were no measurable differences attributable to varying tastes. "We are testing a neurobiological model of brain function with these experiments," Dr. Rauscher said, "and we hypothesize that these patterns may be common in certain activities—chess, mathematics, and certain kinds of music. . . . Listening to such music may stimulate neural pathways important to cognition."

   —Frances H. Rauscher, Gordon L. Shaw, Katherine N. Ky, "Music and Spatial Task Performance," *Nature*, 14 October 1993

3. Medical researchers have concluded not only that the timing of sexual intercourse in relation to ovulation strongly influences the chance of conception, but that conception occurs *only* when intercourse takes place during a specifiable period in the menstrual cycle. The researchers summarized their findings thus:

   We recruited 221 healthy women who were planning to become pregnant. At the same time the women stopped using birth control methods, they began collecting daily urine specimens and keeping daily records of whether they had sexual intercourse. We measured estrogen and progesterone metabolites in urine to estimate the day of ovulation.

   In a total of 625 menstrual cycles for which the dates of ovulation could be estimated, 192 pregnancies were initiated. . . . Two thirds (n = 129) ended in live births. Conception occurred only when intercourse took place during a six-day period that ended on the estimated day of ovulation. The probability of conception ranged from 0.10 when intercourse occurred five days before ovulation to 0.33 when it occurred on the day of ovulation itself.

Conclusion: Among healthy women trying to conceive, nearly all pregnancies can be attributed to intercourse during a six-day period ending on the day of ovulation.

—Allen J. Wilcox, Clarice R. Weinberg, Donna D. Baird, "Timing of Sexual Intercourse in Relation to Ovulation," *The New England Journal of Medicine*, 7 December 1995

4. A large extended family in the town of Cartago, Costa Rica, has long suffered an unusual affliction—an incurable form of genetically caused deafness. Children born into the family have a 50 percent chance of developing the disease, and learn their fate at about the age of ten, when those who have inherited a genetic mutation find that they are beginning to lose their hearing. Scientists from the University of Washington have recently traced the cause of the family's affliction to a previously unknown gene, named the diaphanous gene, that helps operate the delicate hair cells in the inner ear that respond to sound vibrations.

This gene has a single mutation appearing in the Costa Rican family, whose founder arrived in Cartago from Spain in 1713, and who suffered from this form of deafness—as have half his descendants in the eight generations since. Many in the family remain in Cartago because the family's hereditary deafness is well-known and accepted there. With only a single family to be studied, and thus very few genetic differences to work with, pinpointing the gene took six years. The critical mutation involved just one of the 3,800 chemical letters that constitute the gene's DNA.

—Reported in *Science*, 14 November 1997

5. Researchers from the National Cancer Institute announced that they have found a number of genetic markers shared by gay brothers, indicating that homosexuality has genetic roots. The investigators, reporting in *Science*, 16 July 1993, have found that out of 40 pairs of gay brothers examined in their study, 33 pairs shared certain DNA sequences on their X chromosome, the chromosome men inherit only from their mothers. The implicit reasoning of this report is that, if brothers who have specific DNA sequences in common are both gay, these sequences can be considered genetic markers for homosexuality.

6. The relation between male circumcision and HIV infection has been a concern of the British medical journal, *Lancet*, for many years. Before the turn of this century investigators studying that relation wrote, in

> *Lancet*, that studies going back as far as 1989 showed a very greatly increased risk of HIV-1 infection for men who are not circumcised. The epidemiological and biological evidence that links the two, they later wrote, "has become compelling." Very recent studies in Kenya and Uganda have produced evidence that is even more compelling. In 2006, trials in those countries conducted by the U.S. National Institutes of Health were *stopped* because the results were so clear! It appeared that circumcision reduces a man's risk of contracting AIDS from heterosexual sex by about half, and therefore U.S. officials concluded that it would have been unethical to continue without offering circumcision to all 8000 men in the trials. The final figures, reevaluated and published in *Lancet* on 23 February 2007, are even more striking. They suggest that *circumcision reduces a man's risk of contracting AIDS by as much as 65 percent*. Dr. Anthony Fauci, of the National Institute of Allergy and Infectious Diseases, was emphatic: "Look. This is a one-time, permanent intervention that's safe when done under appropriate medical conditions. If we had an AIDS vaccine that was performing as well as this, it would be the talk of the town."

B. THE METHOD OF DIFFERENCE

John Stuart Mill wrote:

> If an instance in which the phenomenon under investigation occurs and an instance in which it does not occur, have every circumstance in common save one, that one occurring only in the former, the circumstance in which alone the two instances differ, is the effect, or the cause, or an indispensable part of the cause, of the phenomenon.

This pattern focuses not on what is common among those cases in which the effect is produced, but on what is *different* between those cases in which the effect is produced and those in which it is not. If we had learned, when investigating that rash of stomach upsets described earlier, that all those who had become ill had eaten the canned pears for dessert, but that the pears had been eaten by none of those who did not become ill, we would be fairly confident that the cause of the illness had been identified.

The difference between the *method of difference* and the method of agreement is highlighted in a recent report about the role of the hormone testosterone in the aggressive conduct of males.

> Among many species, testes are mothballed most of the year, kicking into action and pouring out testosterone only during a very circumscribed mating season—precisely the time when male–male aggression soars. Impressive though they seem, these data are only correlative—[reporting only] testosterone found on the scene repeatedly when aggression has occurred.

> The proof comes with the knife, the performance of what is euphemistically known as a subtraction experiment. Remove the source of the testosterone in species after species, and levels of aggression plummet. Reinstate normal testosterone levels afterward with injections of synthetic testosterone and aggression returns.
>
> The subtraction and replacement paradigm gives damning proof that this hormone is involved in aggression.[7]

Testosterone makes the critical difference, clearly, but the author of this report is careful not to assert that testosterone is *the cause* of male aggression. More accurately, the report states that testosterone is surely *involved* in aggression. As Mill would put it, the hormone is *an indispensable part of the cause* of male aggression. Wherever we can identify a single factor that makes the critical difference when all else remains normal—the factor that eliminates the phenomenon in question when we remove it, or the factor that produces the phenomenon in question when we introduce it—we will pretty surely have identified the cause, or an indispensable part of the cause, of the phenomenon we are investigating.

Schematically, where again capital letters denote circumstances and lowercase letters denote phenomena, the **method of difference** may be represented as follows:

A B C D occur together with *w x y z*.

B C D occur together with *x y z*.

Therefore *A* is the cause, or the effect, or an indispensable part of the cause of *w*.

The method of difference is of central importance in scientific investigations of almost every kind. One vivid illustration of its use is the ongoing investigation by medical researchers into the effects of particular proteins suspected as being implicated in the development of certain diseases. Whether the substance under investigation really is the cause (or an indispensable part of the cause) can only be determined when we create an experimental environment in which that substance has been eliminated. Investigators sometimes are able to do just that—not in humans, of course, but in mice which are subject to the same disease, from whom the gene that is known to produce the suspect protein is deleted. Animals so treated are then inbred, creating populations of what are called "knockout mice," precious in the world of contemporary medical research, in which the process relevant to the disease in question can be studied in an animal exactly like other animals subject to that disease, *except for the critical difference created by the knockout*, the absence of the substance hypothesized as cause. Such studies have resulted in some remarkable medical advances.

To illustrate, using knockout mice, scientists have been able to identify the gene that causes inflammation—swelling, redness, and pain. The gene *MIP-1 alpha*, present in mice and in humans, was suspected of producing the protein that begins the process of inflammation. Pathologists at the University of North Carolina at Chapel Hill bred mice that *lacked* the gene *MIP-1 alpha*, and then infected those mice, and also a control group of normal mice, with viruses known to cause influenza and other diseases. The normal mice did develop extreme inflammation as expected, but mice lacking the *MIP-1 alpha* gene had only slight inflammation. This is one big step toward the development of drugs that will allow humans to fight viral infections without painful and damaging inflammation.[8]

A famous and very dramatic illustration of the method of difference is provided by the following account of experiments confirming the true cause of yellow fever, long one of the great plagues of human kind. The experiments described here were conducted by U.S. Army doctors Walter Reed, James Carroll, and Jesse W. Lazear in November 1900. Earlier that year Dr. Carroll had contracted yellow fever by deliberately allowing himself to be bitten by an infected mosquito in another experiment; soon after, Dr. Lazear died of yellow fever, and the camp in which the following experiments took place was named for him:

> Experiments were devised to show that yellow fever was transmitted by the mosquito alone, all other reasonable opportunities for being infected being excluded. A small building was erected, all windows and doors and every other possible opening being absolutely mosquito-proof. A wire mosquito screen divided the room into two spaces. In one of these spaces fifteen mosquitoes, which had fed on yellow fever patients, were liberated. A nonimmune volunteer entered the room with the mosquitoes and was bitten by seven mosquitoes. Four days later, he suffered an attack of yellow fever. Two other nonimmune men slept for thirteen nights in the mosquito-free room without disturbances of any sort.
>
> To show that the disease was transmitted by the mosquito and not through the excreta of yellow fever patients or anything which had come in contact with them, another house was constructed and made mosquito-proof. For 20 days, this house was occupied by three nonimmunes, after the clothing, bedding and eating utensils and other vessels soiled with the discharge, blood and vomitus of yellow fever patients had been placed in it. The bed clothing which they used had been brought from the beds of the patients who had died of yellow fever, without being subjected to washing or any other treatment to remove anything with which it might have been soiled. The experiment was twice repeated by other nonimmune volunteers. During the entire period all the men who occupied the house were strictly quarantined and protected from mosquitoes. None of those exposed to these experiments contracted yellow fever. That they were not immune was subsequently shown, since four of them became infected either by mosquito bites or the injection of blood from yellow fever patients.[9]

That portion of the experiment described in the first paragraph above very deliberately created a single important difference between the subjects in the two carefully enclosed spaces: the presence of mosquitoes that had fed on yellow fever patients in the one space, the absence of such mosquitoes in the other.

That portion of the experiment described in the second paragraph above deliberately created a second use of the method of difference, in which the only significant difference between two groups of subjects, both of whom had submitted to very close contact with yellow fever victims, was the exposure of some of them to infected mosquito bites or infected blood. Absent that circumstance, no infection arose.

Science seeks causal laws. In the never-ending efforts to confirm or to disconfirm hypothesized causal connections, the method of difference is pervasive and powerful.

EXERCISES

Analyze each of the following reports, explaining the ways in which the method of difference has been applied in the investigations recounted. Discuss the strengths and weaknesses of the method of difference as it is used in each case.

1. How critical is sleep to memory? Researchers at two universities, separately, conducted experiments in 2003 designed to determine how sleep affects our ability to remember. College-age people were trained to perform certain tasks and then tested to see how much they recalled in confronting such tasks after either a night's sleep or several hours awake. "We all have the experience of going to sleep with a question and waking up with the solution," observed one of the investigators, Prof. Danial Margoliash, of the University of Chicago. But does the sleep really help?

It does, markedly. Not just as a matter of re-charge, but, the investigators found, because sleep *rescues* memories by storing and consolidating them deep in the brain's circuitry. At the University of Chicago, subjects trained to understand murky speech on a voice synthesizer could regularly understand more words after a night of sleep than matched counterparts who were tested just hours after the training with no intervening sleep. And at the Harvard Medical School, one hundred subjects were trained to perform certain finger-tapping sequences that they were later asked, at various intervals, to repeat. The process of memory consolidation required one or two nights of sleep—after which the performance of the subjects improved substantially.

— Reported in *Nature*, 9 October 2003

2. The heavy use of salt is widely suspected by experts to be the cause of an epidemic of high blood pressure and many deaths from heart disease around the world. But how prove that salt is the culprit? There are "natural experiments" in which isolated jungle or farming communities are introduced to modern civilization, move to cities, adopt high-salt diets, and commonly develop high blood pressure. But such evidence is inconclusive because many important factors change together; new stresses and many dietary changes accompany the increase in salt. How can the causal effects of salt by itself be tested?

Dr. Derek Denton, of the University of Melbourne, selected a group of normal chimpanzees, a species biologically very close to humans, in which to conduct the needed trials. A group of chimpanzees in Gabon, with normal blood pressure, were first studied in their natural state. The group was then divided in half, with one half receiving gradually increasing amounts of salt in their diet for twenty months. Normal blood pressure in a chimpanzee is 110/70. In Dr. Denton's experiment, the animals' blood pressure commonly rose as high as 150/90, and in some individuals much higher. But among animals in the control group, who received no additional salt, blood pressure did not rise. Six months after the extra salt was withdrawn from their diet, all the chimpanzees in the experimental group had the same low blood pressure they had enjoyed before the experiment. Because there was no other change in the lifestyle of those animals, the investigators concluded that changes in salt consumption caused the changes in blood pressure.

—D. Denton et al., "The Effect of Increased Salt Intake on Blood Pressure of Chimpanzees," *Nature*, October 1995

3. Does Louisiana hot sauce, the principal ingredient of the spicy New Orleans cocktail sauce commonly served with raw shellfish, kill certain bacteria found in raw oysters and clams? The answer appears to be yes. Bacteria of an infectious and sometimes fatal kind—*Vibrio vulnificus*—are found in 5 to 10 percent of raw shellfish on the market. Dr. Charles V. Sanders and his research team, from Louisiana State University Medical Center in New Orleans, added Louisiana hot sauce to cultures of *Vibrio* growing in test tubes; the sauce, even when greatly diluted, killed *V. vulnificus* in five minutes or less. "I couldn't believe what happened," Dr. Sanders said, admitting that he still eats raw oysters, "but only with plenty of hot sauce."

—Reported to the Interscience Conference on Antimicrobial Agents, New Orleans, October 1993

4. In Lithuania, rear-end auto collisions happen as they do in the rest of the world; bumpers crumple, tempers flare. But drivers there do

not seem to suffer the complaints so common in the United States, the headaches and lingering neck pains known as "whiplash syndrome." Dr. Harald Schrader and colleagues from University Hospital in Trondheim, Norway, without disclosing the purpose of their study, gave health questionnaires to 202 Lithuanian drivers whose cars had been struck from behind one to three years earlier in accidents of varying severity. The drivers' reports of their symptoms were compared to the reports of a control group (of the same size, same ages, and same home towns) of drivers who had not been in an accident. Thirty-five percent of the accident victims reported neck pain, but so did 33 percent of the controls; 53 percent of those who had been in an accident had headaches, but so did 50 percent of those in the control group. The researchers concluded: "No one in the study group had disabling or persistent symptoms as a result of the car accident."

What, then, can account for the explosion of whiplash cases elsewhere in the world? Drivers in the Lithuanian study did not carry personal injury insurance at the time of the study, and people there very infrequently sue one another. Most medical bills are paid by the government, and at the time of the study there were no claims to be filed, no money to be won, and nothing to be gained from a diagnosis of chronic whiplash. Chronic whiplash syndrome, the Norwegian researchers concluded, "has little validity."

—Harald Schrader et al., "Natural Evolution of Late Whiplash Syndrome Outside the Medicolegal Context," *The Lancet,* 4 May 1996

5. To determine the role of specific genes, mice are bred in which certain genes have been deleted, called "knockout mice." When normal mice are placed in a lighted room, with dark corners, they go immediately to the dark. In one recent experiment the mice, upon entering the dark, encounter a mild electric shock, and very quickly learn to stay away from those dark regions. Mice who lack a gene called *Ras-GRF* learn to be wary just as quickly as do normal mice. But, unlike normal mice, the knockout mice throw caution to the winds the next day, and chance the dark corners again and yet again. It appears that the *Ras-GRF* gene—probably very much like the analogous gene in humans—plays a critical role in the ability of the mice to remember fear. This gene is almost certainly crucial for the survival of mammals.

—Reported in *Nature,* December 1997

6. Here is some reassuring news for those whose career plans are slightly behind schedule: It turns out that peaking too early may kill you.

That's the finding of Stuart J. H. McCann, a professor of psychology at the University College of Cape Breton in Nova Scotia.

McCann's research concerns what he calls the "precocity-longevity hypothesis." McCann analyzed the lives of 1,672 U.S. governors who served between 1789 and 1978 and found that those who were elected at relatively tender ages generally died earlier than their less precocious counterparts. Even when he controlled for the year that the governors were born, or how long they served, and what state they governed, the pattern held. No matter how he sliced the data, or ran the regressions, or accounted for various statistical biases, the story remained the same: governors elected to office at younger ages tended to have shorter lives.

And what holds for state executives seems also to hold for other young achievers. McCann also analyzed smaller but more diverse sets of accomplished people—including American and French presidents, Canadian and British prime ministers, Nobel Laureates, signers of the Declaration of Independence, Academy Award winners, and seven centuries of Roman Catholic pontiffs. Again he found that "those who climb to the loftiest peaks in the shortest time also die younger. For the eminent, and perhaps for all, an early rise may lead to an early fall."

—*Personality and Social Psychology Bulletin*, February 2003

7. Cholera, caused by a water-borne bacterium ingested by drinking contaminated water, is a dreadful disease; pandemics of cholera in the 19th century killed tens of thousands. The accepted view, that it was caused by breathing a filthy miasma, was doubted by John Snow, a founding member of the London Epidemiological Society. When a terrible cholera epidemic struck London in 1848-49, Snow hypothesized that bad water, from urban wells and from the Thames River, was the villain. Some water companies drew their water from within the tidal section of the Thames, where the city's sewage was also dumped, thus providing their customers with excrement-contaminated drinking water. It stank, so some of the intake pipes were shifted to points above the tideway. In 1854 cholera returned with even greater horror. Snow identified two water companies, one of which had moved its intake to a point above the tidal region of the river, the other still supplying a fecal cocktail; his data from these two districts showed a strong connection between cholera mortality and water source. Snow also identified a particular well, on Broad Street, and plotted cholera mortality house by house in the area of that well—the number of dead increasing sharply with proximity to the Broad Street pump—while a

> few streets away on Warwick Street there were no cholera deaths at all. Just across from the Broad Street pump was the Poland Street Workhouse, whose wretched inmates remained healthy—the workhouse had its own well. The workers of the Lion Brewery, close to the pump on Broad Street, also had its own well; its workers did not contract cholera—they drank mainly malt liquor. The outbreak ended when Snow persuaded the authorities to *remove the handle from the Broad Street pump.* There is today a replica of the handleless pump outside a nearby pub named in honor of John Snow.
>
> Steven Shapin, "Sick City," *The New Yorker,* 6 November 2006

C. THE JOINT METHOD OF AGREEMENT AND DIFFERENCE

Although Mill believed that the **joint method of agreement and difference** was an additional and separate technique, it is best understood as the combined use of the method of agreement and the method of difference in the same investigation. It can be represented schematically (capital letters again denoting circumstances, lowercase letters denoting phenomena) as follows:

A B C—x y z.	*A B C—x y z.*
A D E—x t w.	*B C—y z.*

Therefore *A* is the effect, or the cause, or an indispensable part of the cause, of *x*.

Because each of the two methods (agreement schematized above on the left, difference schematized on the right) affords some probability to the conclusion, their joint use affords a higher probability to that conclusion. In many scientific investigations this combination serves as an extremely powerful pattern of inductive inference.

A notable advance in medicine provides an illustration of the power of the joint method. Hepatitis A is a liver infection that afflicted tens of thousands of Americans; it spread widely among children, chiefly through contaminated food or water, and was sometimes deadly. How might it be prevented? The ideal solution, of course, would be an effective vaccine. However, an enormous difficulty faced those who would test any vaccine for hepatitis A: It was very hard to predict where outbreaks of the infection would occur, and therefore it was usually not possible to select experimental subjects in ways that would yield reliable results. This difficulty was finally overcome in the following way.

A potential vaccine was tested in a community of Hasidic Jews, Kiryas Joel, in Orange County, New York, a community that was highly unusual in that it was plagued by yearly epidemics of this infection. Almost no one escaped hepatitis A in Kiryas Joel, and nearly 70 percent of the community members had been infected by the time they are nineteen years old. Dr. Alan

Werzberger, of the Kiryas Joel Institute of Medicine, and his colleagues recruited 1037 children in that community, ages two to sixteen, who had not been exposed to the hepatitis A virus, as determined by a lack of antibodies to the virus in their blood. Half of them (519) received a single dose of the new vaccine, and among those vaccinated children not a single case of hepatitis A was reported. Of the 518 children who received dummy injections, 25 became infected with hepatitis A soon after. The vaccine for hepatitis A had been found.[10]

Liver specialists in Boston and Washington greeted this study with admiration, calling it "a great breakthrough" and a "major medical advance." What is the pattern of inference on which this achievement relied? Both the method of agreement and the method of difference were employed, as is common in medical investigations. Among all those young residents of the community who became immune to hepatitis A, there was only one relevent circumstance *in common:* All the immunes had received the new vaccine. By itself, this strongly tended to show that the vaccine did cause that immunity. The method of difference supported this conclusion overwhelmingly: The circumstances of those who did become immune and those who did not were essentially alike *in every respect except one,* the administration of the vaccine to the immune residents.

The testing of new drugs or procedures is often conducted in what are called "double-arm" trials, one group receiving the new treatment while the other group does not, after which (in suitable cases) there may be a carefully executed crossover, in a second phase, in which those who originally did not receive the treatment do so, and those who originally did receive the treatment do not. The application of the joint method of agreement and difference underlies such investigations, which are common and exceedingly productive.

EXERCISES

Analyze each of the following reports, explaining the way in which the method of agreement and the method of difference have been jointly applied, and identifying the special force, if any, of their combination.

1. Pain can be agonizing, but it serves a useful function: It teaches people and animals to avoid dangers, and forces them to attend to wounds. Strangely, there are a very few people who never feel pain; they remain unaware of having suffered significant injuries.

One family in northern Pakistan has several such members. One, a ten-year old boy, became famous for giving street performances in which he put knives through his arms and walked on hot coals.

Tissue damage would result, but no discomfort. Geneticist C. G. Woods of Cambridge University searched for the cause of this remarkable inability to feel pain. Eventually he zeroed in on mutations in a gene, *SCN9A*, which codes for the channel through which sodium enters pain-sensing cells, critical to the pain signal. Testing with electric current, he could open and close sodium channels on some cells—but he could not open the sodium channels on those mutant cells. Said Woods, "This shows that rare diseases can still be of great importance because of the insights they give into biological processes."

A Yale University neurologist, Stephen Waxman, observes that if researchers could craft a drug that can make these channels inactive, as they are in the Pakistani family members, millions of people worldwide who suffer from chronic pain would be wonderfully served.

—Reported in *Nature*, 14 December 2006

2. A deadly heart ailment affecting about 1 million African American men—familial ameloyd cardiomyopathy—and another that afflicts older men of all ethnicities, are known to be caused by an abnormally folded protein that builds up in the organism. Transthyretin protein, made in the liver, has four subunits. A mutation in the gene that makes two of those subunits results in the instability of the protein, its misfolding, and eventually in death. That this is indeed the cause of the ailments was shown by the fact that a liver transplant, providing a healthy version of the critical gene, can result in cure—but often that correction comes too late to stymie the misfolding that did the damage.

A strange twist of nature, reported in *Science* in January 2003 by Dr. Jeffrey Kelly, of the Scripps Research Institute in San Diego, provided the clues to a therapy that can thwart the misfolding process. Because diseases of this kind are quite common in Portugal, families there are screened to see who has the mutated gene and is therefore at risk. One very large family was identified whose members had the mutated gene and yet never did contract the disease. It turned out that in this family, a second gene that made the other two subunits of the protein had undergone its own mutation, suppressing or reversing the disease process. Members of that family carried a cure to an inherited disease in their own genes.

Dr. Kelly found that as a result of this further mutation the disease was prevented by the erection of a kind of barrier between the normal and the abnormal protein states. Then, by screening libraries of small molecules, he located several that, already approved by the Food and

Drug Administration for other purposes, could mimic the effect of the second mutation, successful reversing the misfolded protein in animals.

3. Sixteen-year-old David Merrill, of Suffolk, Virginia, hypothesized that the loud sounds of hard-rock music have a bad effect on its devoted fans. He tested the theory on mice. Seventy-two mice were divided into three groups of 24, the first to be exposed to hard-rock music, the second to music by Mozart, and the third to no music at all. After becoming accustomed to their environments, but before being exposed to the music, Merrill tested all the mice in a maze, which took them an average of 10 minutes to complete. Then the groups were exposed to the music for 10 hours a day.

With repeated testing the control-group mice *reduced* their time in the maze by an average of 5 minutes. Those exposed to Mozart reduced their time by 8.5 minutes. The hard-rock mice *increased* their time in the maze by 20 minutes.

Merrill also reported that when, in an earlier attempt, he had allowed all the mice to live together, the project had to be cut short because, unlike the Mozart-listening mice, the hard-rock-listening mice killed other mice.

—Reported in *Insight*, 8 September 1997

4. Scientists have long known that severely restricting the number of calories that mice and other organisms consume lengthens their life span. Animals on low-calorie diets typically have abnormally cool body temperatures. Does low temperature, in itself, result in longer life? The answer is yes.

Bruno Conti, of the Scripps Research Institute in La Jolla, California, genetically engineered mice to have a faulty sense of body temperature. The alteration reduced the animals' temperatures by 0.03 to 0.05°C below normal; they were given as much food as they wanted, maintaining their normal weight. The low-temperature mice lived about 15 percent longer than normal mice did.

—Reported in *Science*, 3 November 2006

5. At a social gathering of eighty-five faculty members, graduate students, and staff workers in the Department of Food Science at the University of Illinois in Urbana-Champaign, the partygoers served themselves ice cream. They did not know they were also the subjects of an experiment. Half the participants were given 17-ounce bowls, and half 34-ounce bowls. In addition, half were given 2-ounce spoons to scoop out their ice cream, and half were given 3-ounce serving spoons.

With larger spoons, people served themselves 14.5 percent more, and with a larger bowl they heaped on 31 percent more. With both large spoon and large bowl these nutrition experts helped themselves to 56.8 percent more ice cream that those who used the smaller utensils. And all but three ate every bit of the ice cream they took. Smaller platters and smaller utensils may be the key to a successful diet.

—Reported by Brian Wansink in *The American Journal of Preventive Medicine,* September 2006

D. THE METHOD OF RESIDUES

John Stuart Mill wrote:

> Subduct from any phenomenon such part as is known by previous inductions to be the effect of certain antecedents, and the residue of the phenomenon is the effect of the remaining antecedents.

The first three methods seem to suppose that we can eliminate or produce the cause (or effect) of some phenomenon in its entirety, as indeed we sometimes can. In many contexts, however, we can only deduce the causal effect of some phenomenon by observing the *change* that it makes in a set of circumstances whose cause is already understood in part.

This method, focusing on *residues,* is well illustrated by the very simple device used to weigh truck cargos. The weight of the truck when empty is known. To determine the weight of the cargo, the entire truck is weighed with its cargo—and the weight of the cargo is then known to be the weight of the whole minus the weight of the truck. The known "antecedent," in Mill's phrase, is the recorded weight of the empty truck that must be subtracted from the reading on the scale; the cause of the difference between that reading and the known antecedent is obviously attributable to the remaining "antecedents"—that is, to the cargo itself.

Schematically, the **method of residues** can be represented as follows:

A B C—*x y z.*

B is known to be the cause of *y.*

C is known to be the cause of *z.*

Therefore *A* is the cause of *x.*

A splendid illustration of the effectiveness of the method of residues is provided by one of the great chapters in the history of astronomy, the discovery of the planet Neptune:

> In 1821, Bouvard of Paris published tables of the motions of a number of planets, including Uranus. In preparing the latter he had found great difficulty in making an orbit calculated on the basis of positions obtained in the years after 1800

agree with one calculated from observations taken in the years immediately following discovery. He finally disregarded the older observations entirely and based his tables on the newer observations. In a few years, however, the positions calculated from the tables disagreed with the observed positions of the planet and by 1844 the discrepancy amounted to 2 minutes of arc. Since all the other known planets agreed in their motions with those calculated for them, the discrepancy in the case of Uranus aroused much discussion.

In 1845, Leverrier, then a young man, attacked the problem. He checked Bouvard's calculations and found them essentially correct. Thereupon he felt that the only satisfactory explanation of the trouble lay in the presence of a planet somewhere beyond Uranus which was disturbing its motion. By the middle of 1846 he had finished his calculations. In September he wrote to Galle at Berlin and requested the latter to look for a new planet in a certain region of the sky for which some new star charts had just been prepared in Germany but of which Leverrier apparently had not as yet obtained copies. On the twenty-third of September Galle started the search and in less than an hour he found an object which was not on the chart. By the next night it had moved appreciably and the new planet, subsequently named Neptune, was discovered within 1° of the predicted place. This discovery ranks among the greatest achievements of mathematical astronomy.[11]

The phenomenon under investigation here is the movement of Uranus. A great part of that phenomenon, the orbit of Uranus around the sun, was well understood at the time. Observations of Uranus approximated this calculated orbit but exhibited a puzzling residue, some perturbation of what had been calculated, for which further explanation was needed. An additional "antecedent"—that is, an additional existing factor that would account for the perturbation—was hypothesized to be another (undiscovered) planet whose gravity would, together with what was already known about the orbit of Uranus, explain that residue. Once hypothesized, that new planet, Neptune, was very quickly found.

The method of residues differs from the other methods in that it can be used with the examination of only one case, whereas the others require the examination of at least two cases. And the method of residues, unlike the others, appears to depend on antecedently established causal laws, while the other methods (as Mill formulated them) do not. The method of residues is nevertheless an inductive, not a deductive, method (as some have suggested), because it yields conclusions that are only probable and cannot be *validly deduced* from their premises. An additional premise or two might transform an inference by the method of residues into a valid deductive argument, but that can be said for other inductive methods as well.

EXERCISES

Analyze each of the following arguments in terms of "antecedents" and "phenomena" to show how they follow the pattern of the method of residues.

1. For nineteen years space scientists, astronomers, and physicists have been puzzled by what appears to be a mysterious force pulling spacecraft in the direction of the sun. It was first noticed when the trajectories of two outward bound and very distant spacecraft (Pioneer 10 and 11, launched in 1972 and 1973) were carefully analyzed. The trajectories of two later probes (Galileo, launched toward Jupiter in 1989, and Ulysses, launched into polar orbit around the sun) have exhibited the same peculiarities: They give evidence of a weak force that perturbs their directions and velocities. This force was discovered by adding up the effects of all other known forces acting on the spacecraft and finding that something unexplained was left over.

   This force is apparently slowing the outward progress of the spacecraft speeding away from or around the sun—but in contrast to the force of gravity, the strength of this mystery force does not decline proportionally to the inverse square of a spacecraft's distance from the sun, but instead at a linear rate, which makes it very unlikely that the mystery force is a gravitational effect of the sun.

   Calculations were made using two independent methods, and data of different types, taking into account possible errors in the software and the hardware used in the measurements. A host of other possible errors were investigated and accounted for—and after ruling all of these out, a team of physicists from the Los Alamos National Laboratory announced that the mystery remained. This means that some hitherto unknown phenomenon may be at work—what physicists excitedly call "new physics."

   —Reported in *Physical Review Letters*, September 1998

2. In H. Davies' experiments on the decomposition of water by galvanism, it was found that besides the two components of water, oxygen and hydrogen, an acid and an alkali were developed at opposite poles of the machine. Since the theory of the analysis of water did not give reason to expect these products, their presence constituted a problem. Some chemists thought that electricity had the power of producing these substances of itself. Davies conjectured that there might be some hidden cause for this part of the effect—the glass might suffer decomposition, or some foreign matter might be in the water. He then proceeded to investigate whether or not the diminution or total elimination of possible causes would change or eliminate the effect in question. Substituting gold vessels for glass ones, he found no change in the effect and concluded that glass was not the cause. Using distilled water, he found a decrease in the quantity of acid and alkali involved, yet

enough remained to show that the cause was still in operation. He inferred that impurity of the water was not the sole cause, but was a concurrent cause. He then suspected that perspiration from the hands might be the cause, as it would contain salt which would decompose into acid and alkali under electricity. By avoiding such contact, he reduced the quantity of the effect still further, till only slight traces remained. These might be due to some impurity of the atmosphere decomposed by the electricity. An experiment determined this to be the case. The machine was put under an exhaust receiver and when it was thus secured from atmospheric influences, no acid or alkali was produced.

—G. Gore, *The Art of Scientific Discovery*, 1878

3. Satellite observations collected between 1992 and 2001 suggest that the upper surface of the Larsen C ice shelf, in Antarctica, dropped as much as 27 cm per year during that period. About a quarter of that shrinkage, or 7 cm, may have resulted from snow packing down into denser material called firn. Uncertainties about such factors as the height of the ocean tides, and the salinity of water beneath the ice shelf would account for no more than a small fraction of the remaining loss of height above water.

Therefore, concluded Andrew Shepherd, a glaciologist at the University of Cambridge in England, as much as 20 cm per year of the upper surface's drop must stem from melting. Nine-tenths of any mass of floating ice lies below the water's surface, suggesting that the Larsen C ice shelf is thinning by as much as 2 m each year.

The likely cause of this thinning is relatively warm water beneath the shelf. Even a very small temperature increase in the water below an ice shelf can make a big difference in the melting rate of the overlying ice. Larsen C is stable, and isn't shedding more icebergs than normal, Shepherd reported, but at its current rate of thinning, Larsen C could reach 200 m in thickness (the thickness at which other ice shelves have disintegrated) and therefore be susceptible to disintegration in 70 years—but if the waters in the region continue to warm, the demise of Larsen C could occur even sooner.

—Reported in *Science News*, 1 November 2003

4. Analyzing more than forty years of weather data, climatologists at the National Oceanic and Atmospheric Administration in Boulder, Colorado, recently found that the daily temperature range—the difference between the daytime maximum and the nighttime minimum temperatures—at 660 weather stations in the continental United States fluctuates in a very puzzling manner: the variation of the temperature range over the course of a week, in some regions, does not line up with any natural cycles that can be detected.

The average temperature range for the weekends (Saturday, Sunday, and Monday) varied from the average temperature range for weekdays (Tuesday, Wednesday, Thursday, and Friday)! Fluctuations in the daily range can be caused by natural factors; storm systems moving across an area, for example, can cause such fluctuation—but there are no natural factors known to fall consistently on certain days of the week.

The precise cause of this extraordinary pattern is not clear. However, contend the researchers (Piers M. deF. Forster and Susan Solomon), the only possible explanation for this weekend/weekday disparity is *human* activity and the atmospheric pollutants such activity creates.

—Reported in *Proceedings of the National Academy of Sciences*, 30 September 2003

5. It is no longer open to discussion that air has weight. It is common knowledge that a balloon is heavier when inflated than when empty, which is proof enough. For if the air were light, the more the balloon was inflated, the lighter the whole would be, since there would be more air in it. But since, on the contrary, when more air is put in, the whole becomes heavier, it follows that each part has a weight of its own, and consequently that the air has weight.

—Blaise Pascal, *Treatise on the Weight of the Mass of the Air*, 1653

E. THE METHOD OF CONCOMITANT VARIATION

The four methods discussed so far are all *eliminative* in nature. By eliminating some possible cause or causes of a given phenomenon, they support some other causal account hypothesized. The method of agreement eliminates as possible causes those circumstances in whose absence the phenomenon can nevertheless occur; the method of difference permits the elimination of some possible causes by removing an antecedent factor shown to be critical; the joint method is eliminative in both of these ways; and the method of residues seeks to eliminate as possible causes those circumstances whose effects have already been established by previous inductions.

However, in many situations, no one of these methods is applicable, because they involve circumstances that cannot possibly be eliminated. This is often the case in economics, in physics, in medicine, and wherever the general increase or decrease of one factor results in a concomitant increase or decrease of another—the complete elimination of either factor not being feasible.

John Stuart Mill wrote:

> Whatever phenomenon varies in any manner whenever another phenomenon varies in some particular manner is either a cause or an effect of that phenomenon or is connected with it through some fact of causation.

Concomitant variation is critical to the study of the causal impact of certain foods, for example. We cannot eliminate disease, no matter the diet; we can rarely eliminate foods of certain kinds from the diets of large populations. But we can note the effect of increasing or decreasing the intake of certain foods on the frequency of certain diseases in specified populations. One investigation of this kind examined the frequency of heart attacks compared to the frequency with which fish had been eaten by those in the study. The inductive conclusion was striking: Eating one fish meal a week reduced the risk of heart attack by 50 percent; eating just two fish meals a month reduced the risk of heart attack by 30 percent. Within some limits there appears to be a marked concomitant variation between cardiac arrests and the use of fish in the diet.[12]

Using plus and minus signs to indicate the greater or lesser degree to which a varying phenomenon is present in a given situation, the **method of concomitant variation** can be schematized as:

A B C – *x y z*.

A+ *B C* – *x*+ *y z*.

Therefore *A* and *x* are causally connected.

This method is very widely used. A farmer establishes that there is a causal connection between the application of fertilizer to the soil and the size of the crop by applying different amounts to different parts of a field, then noting the concomitant variation between the amounts of the additive and the yield. A merchant seeks to verify the efficacy of advertising of different kinds by running varied advertisements at varying intervals, then noting the concomitant increase or decrease of business during some of those periods.

Concomitant variation is exemplified in the search for the causes of divorce and of other important decisions among families. Of course the cause of any particular divorce will lie in the special circumstances of that marriage and that family, but there are conditions that tend generally to contribute to the breakup of families, and concomitant variation is useful in learning what these are. Analysis of data from the U.S. Census Bureau reveals that, in every decade since the 1940s, and in every region of the country, couples who were the parents of only girls divorced more often than couples who were the parents of only boys. It happened among whites and among blacks, among those with only high school diplomas and among those with college degrees. Parents with an only child who is a girl are 6 percent more likely to split up than parents of a single boy. The gap rises to 8 percent for parents of two girls versus parents of two boys, 10 percent for families with three girls, and 13 percent if there are four girls. Thousands upon thousands of U.S. divorces appear to stem partly from the number of girls in the family.

The age-old favoring of boys, overt and common in China, India, and other developing countries, is more subtle in the United States, but it remains a widespread factor in the dynamics of U.S. family life. Parents invest more in their sons, spending, when their families include a boy, an average of an additional $600 a year on housing. Fathers increase their workweeks after the birth of the first family child of either sex—but increase it by more than two hours if the child is a boy, less than one hour if it is a girl. These patterns of concomitant variation make it plain that parents have a preference for boys—a preference that will have increasingly important consequences when the technology for the selection of the sex of a baby, already known and reliable, becomes more widely available.[13]

When the increase of one phenomenon parallels the increase of another, we say that the phenomena vary *directly* with each other. However, the method permits the use of variation "in any manner," and we may also infer a causal connection when the phenomena vary *inversely*—the increase of one leading to the decrease of another. Thus economists often say that, other things remaining roughly stable, in an unregulated market an increase of the supply of some good (say, crude oil) will result in a concomitant decrease in its price. That relation does appear to be genuinely concomitant: When international tension threatens to reduce the available supply of crude oil, we note that the price of the oil almost invariably rises.

Some concomitant variations are entirely coincidental, of course. Care must be taken not to infer a causal connection from patterns of occurrence that are wholly fortuitous. But some variations that appear to be coincidental, or are otherwise puzzling, may have an obscure causal explanation. It has been shown that there is a high correlation between the number of storks found nesting in English villages and the number of babies born in each of those villages—the more storks, the more babies. Surely it is not possible that . . . . No, it's not. Villages with high birth rates have more newly married couples, and therefore have more newly constructed houses. Storks, it turns out, prefer to nest beside chimneys that have not been used previously by other storks.[14] Tracing the causal chains of phenomena that vary concomitantly, we may find links in common, which is what Mill meant when he said that the phenomena may be "connected . . . through some fact of causation."

Because the method of concomitant variation permits us to adduce, as evidence, changes in the *degree* to which circumstances and phenomena are present, it greatly strengthens our set of inductive techniques. It is a *quantitative* method of inductive inference, those earlier discussed being essentially qualitative. The use of concomitant variation therefore presupposes the existence of some method of measuring or estimating, even if only roughly, the degrees to which phenomena vary.

EXERCISES

Analyze each of the following arguments in terms of the variation of the "phenomena" to show how they follow the pattern of the method of concomitant variation.

1. The notion that poverty and mental illness are intertwined is not new—but finding evidence that one begets the other has often proved difficult. New research, which coincided with the opening of a new gambling casino on an Indian reservation, appears to strengthen that link, strongly suggesting that lifting children out of poverty (as casino income did in many cases) tends to diminish some (but not all) psychiatric symptoms.

   A study published in the *Journal of the American Medical Association* in October 2003 tracked 1420 children, ages 9 to 13, in rural North Carolina, very many of whom lived on a Cherokee Indian reservation. During the study a casino that had been opened on the reservation began distributing some of its profits to tribal families, the payments reaching about $6000 per year by 2001. The researchers found that the rate of psychiatric symptoms among the children who had risen from poverty dropped steadily; those children were less inclined to temper tantrums, stealing, bullying, and vandalism—common symptoms of oppositional defiant disorders.

   Children whose families rose above the poverty threshold showed a 40 percent decrease in behavioral symptoms. The rate of such behaviors, after four years, dropped to the same levels found among children whose families had never been poor. But the casino payments had no effect on children whose families were nevertheless unable to rise from poverty, or on those children whose families had not been poor to begin with.

   The economic change had a significant effect on only a fraction of the children followed. This, it was hypothesized, was a consequence of the fact that, although all the families that received the payment received the same amount of money, the payments resulted in lifting only 14 percent of those families above the poverty line which, in 2002, was $14,348 for a family of three. The study suggests, said Dr. Arline Geronimus, of the University of Michigan, that poverty puts stress on families, which can increase the likelihood that children will develop behavioral problems.

2. In Finland, heart attacks occur more frequently in the eastern part of the country than in the western and southern parts. Researchers seeking to explain these differences concluded that they "cannot be explained by individual lifestyle or by genetic factors." How, then, can they be explained? A study led by Dr. Anne Kousa, of the Geological Survey of Finland, examined heart attacks that occurred in 18,946 men, ages 35 to 74, in three different years. The researchers then correlated the incidence of heart attack in these populations with the level of water hardness—as measured by the presence of minerals in the water—in their communities. The study found that the degree of water hardness correlated directly with a lowered risk of heart attack. Drinking water rich in minerals appears to play a role in reducing heart disease.

— *Journal of Epidemiology and Community Health,* January 2004

3. When it comes to love, sex, and friendship, do birds of a feather flock together? Or is it more important that opposites attract? Dr. Claus Wedekind, of Bern University in Switzerland, hypothesized that body odor might signal that its owner had desirable immune genes—called MHC genes—that would help offspring to fight off diseases. He devised an experiment to see if human body odor correlated with MHC genes and if people could tell.

He and his team collected DNA samples for 49 female and 44 male university students. He asked the men to wear cotton T-shirts on two successive nights, to keep the shirt in a plastic bag, to use perfume-free detergents and soaps, and to avoid smelly rooms, smell-producing foods, and activities like smoking and sex that create odors. Meanwhile, the women were given a nasal spray to protect their nasal membranes from infection, and each received a copy of the Patrick Susskind novel *Perfume* to make them more conscious of odors.

When the T-shirts were collected, the women were asked to give ratings, for intensity, pleasantness, and sexiness, to three T-shirts from men with similar MHC genes, and three from men with dissimilar MHC genes, not knowing which was which.

Women who were dissimilar to a particular male's MHC perceived his odor as more pleasant than did women whose MHC was similar to the test man. Odors of men with dissimilar MHC reminded the women of their own mates or former mates twice as often as did the odors of men with similar MHC.

However, if a woman was taking oral contraceptives, which partly mimic pregnancy, this predilection was reversed, and they gave higher rating to men with similar MHC. "The Pill effect really surprised me," said Dr. Wedekind.

—*Proceedings* of the Royal Society of London, 1995

4. Stanley Coren sought to plumb the connections between sleeplessness and accidents. To do that he focused on the yearly shift to daylight time in eastern North America when (because clocks are moved forward one hour) most people lose an hour of sleep. He compared the number of accidents then with the number on normal days, and found that on the day after the time change, in Canada, there was an 8 percent increase in accidents. Then, examining the day after the return to standard time, when people gain an hour of sleep, he found a corresponding decrease in accidents. "What we're looking at," says the Director of the Human Chronobiology Laboratory at the University of Pittsburgh, commenting upon Soren's results, "is national jet lag."

—S. Coren, *Sleep Thieves* (New York: The Free Press, 1996)

5. Prof. Kathleen Vohs reports that two groups of college students were asked to read out loud from "a boring book on the biographies of scientists." One of the groups was obliged to wear fake expressions of delight and interest, while the other group was allowed to read the same texts naturally. Each group was afterward given a sum of money to spend on an assortment of goods, or to save. Those who had been faking delight spent 62 percent more than those who had not. Similarly, a group of students writing down their thoughts without restraint spent very much less that a similar group obliged while writing to avoid all thoughts about white bears. The more self-restraint that a person expends to control one impulse, it appears, the less self-restraint is available to control others.

—Reported in *The Journal of Consumer Research,* March 2007

6. Potassium in the urine is known to reflect potassium intake from the diet. At the Prosserman Center for Health Research in Toronto, Dr. Andrew Mente and colleagues analyzed urinary potassium as a useful clinical marker of a healthy diet. They collected urine samples from hundreds of patients and separately calculated the quality of their diets. The results were striking: as urinary potassium increased there was a steady and significant increase in diet quality score, as well as a steady decrease in body mass, blood pressure and heart rate. "This urinary marker," said Dr. Mente, "is a simple, objective, universally available measure of diet quality."

—*Urology/Nephrology News,* 20 November 2006

7. Whenever the U.S. says things that make a military conflict with Iran seem more likely, the price of oil rises, strengthening Iran's regime rather than weakening it. The more we talk about curbing Iranian

power, the more difficult it gets. . . . So cooling down the martial rhetoric, even if we plan to take military action eventually, would likely bring oil prices down, making Iran weaker. . . . Lower oil prices won't, by themselves, topple the mullahs in Iran. But it's significant that, historically, when oil prices have been low, Iranian reformers have been ascendant and radicals relatively subdued, and vice versa when prices have been high. Talking tough may look like a good way of demonstrating U.S. resolve, but when tough talk makes our opponent richer and stronger we may accomplish more by saying less.

—James Surowieki, "Troubled Waters over Oil,"
The New Yorker, 19 February 2007

OVERVIEW

Five Methods of Inductive Inference

1. **The method of agreement.** The one factor or circumstance that is *common* to all the cases of the phenomenon under investigation is likely to be the cause (or effect) of that phenomenon.

2. **The method of difference.** The one factor or circumstance whose absence or presence *distinguishes* all cases in which the phenomenon under investigation occurs from those cases in which it does not occur, is likely to be the cause, or part of the cause, of that phenomenon.

3. **The joint method of agreement and difference.** Although perhaps not a separate method, *the combination,* in the same investigation, *of the method of agreement and the method of difference* gives substantial probability to the inductive conclusion.

4. **The method of residues.** When some portion of the phenomenon under examination is known to be the consequence of well-understood antecedent circumstances, we may infer that *the remainder of that phenomenon is the effect of the remaining antecedents.*

5. **The method of concomitant variation.** *When the variations in one phenomenon are highly correlated with the variations in another phenomenon,* one of the two is likely to be the cause of the other, or they may be related as the products of some third factor causing both.

These are the inductive methods frequently called **Mill's methods,** most commonly used by scientists in their investigation of causal laws.

12.5 Limitations of Inductive Techniques

What do the methods explained in the preceding sections actually do for us? John Stuart Mill believed that they were instruments with which we may *discover* causal connections, and also that they were canons with which causal connections may be *proved*. On both counts he overestimated their power. Inductive techniques are indeed of very great importance, but their role in science is more limited than Mill supposed.

One substantial difficulty arises from the fact that, in formulating these methods, Mill made the assumption that one can identify cases "having *only* one circumstance in common" or other cases "having *every* circumstance in common save one." But these expressions must not be taken literally; any two objects will have many circumstances in common however different they may appear; and no two things can ever differ in only one respect—one will be farther to the north, one will be closer to the sun, and so on. Nor could we even examine all possible circumstances to determine if they differ in only one way. What the scientist has in mind as he applies these techniques are not all circumstances, but the sets of *relevant* circumstances—whether there is only one relevant circumstance in common, or all relevant circumstances save one in common. That is, we apply the methods to the circumstances that have some bearing on the causal connection in question.

Which are those circumstances? We cannot learn which factors are relevant using the methods alone. In order to use the methods we must come to the context in which they are to be applied with some analysis of causal factors already in mind. The caricature of the "scientific drinker" illustrates this difficulty: He drinks Scotch and soda one night, bourbon and soda the next night, and on the following nights brandy and soda, then rum and soda, then gin and soda. What is the *cause* of his intoxication? Repeatedly inebriated, he swears never to touch soda again!

This scientific drinker did apply the method of agreement in accordance with the rules—but his doing so was to no avail because the factors that really are relevant in those antecedent circumstances had not been identified and therefore could not be manipulated. Had *alcohol* been specified as one of the factors common to all the cases, it would have been possible to eliminate soda very quickly, of course, using the method of difference.

The heroic investigation of the causes of yellow fever, discussed earlier in connection with the method of difference, confirmed the conclusion that the fever is spread by the bite of an infected mosquito. We know that *now,* just as we know now that it is alcohol and not soda that causes drunkenness. But the yellow fever experiments required insight and imagination as well as courage;

the notion that the fever was spread by mosquitoes was originally thought to be silly, or absurd, or was not thought of at all. Circumstances in the real world do not come wearing tags marked "relevant" or "irrelevant." The testing of mosquito bites as cause required some earlier sorting of possibly relevant factors, to which the inductive methods might then be applied. With that prior analysis in hand, the methods can prove exceedingly helpful—but the methods by themselves, without some hypotheses in the background, are not *sufficient* instruments for scientific discovery.

Nor can the methods by themselves constitute rules for *proof*. Their application proceeds always on the basis of some antecedent hypotheses about causal factors, as noted just above, and because all circumstances cannot have been considered, attention will be confined to those believed to be the possible causes in question. However, this judgment regarding which circumstances are to be investigated may prove to have been in error. Medical scientists, for a very long time, did not consider dirty hands even as *possible* agents of infection, and so could not identify such dirtiness as the cause of disease.* Investigation is stymied when the investigators fail to break down the circumstances before them into the appropriate elements, elements that cannot be known in advance. Because the analyses presupposed by the application of the methods may be incorrect, or inadequate, the inferences based on those analyses may also prove to be mistaken. This dependence of induction on the merit of the underlying hypotheses shows that inductive techniques cannot by themselves provide the proof of causation that Mill had hoped for.

Yet another problem should be borne in mind: The application of inductive methods always depends on *observed* correlations, and even when the observations have been made accurately, they may be incomplete and therefore deceptive. The greater the number of observations, the greater is the likelihood that the correlation we observe is the manifestation of a genuine causal law—but no matter how great that number is, we cannot infer with certainty a causal connection among instances that have not yet been observed.

---

*The failure of physicians to wash their hands (because they did not understand how infectious diseases were spread) resulted in untold misery and uncounted deaths over centuries, especially from puerperal (or childbed) fever, which was carried on the hands of doctors from mother to mother, until the proof of that disastrous causal connection was given by the Hungarian physician Ignac Semmelweis, in the middle of the nineteenth century. See Sherwin B. Nuland, *The Doctors' Plague* (New York: W. W. Norton, 2003).

These limitations illuminate once again the great gulf between deduction and induction. A valid deductive inference constitutes a proof, or demonstration, but every inductive inference is, at best, highly probable and never demonstrative. Therefore Mill's claim that his canons are "methods of proof" must be rejected, along with the claim that they are "*the* methods of discovery."

Nevertheless, the techniques explained in this chapter are central in much of science and are very powerful. Because it is impossible for investigators to take *all* circumstances into account, the application of the methods must always suppose one or more causal *hypotheses* about the circumstances under investigation. Being unsure which factor(s) are the cause(s) of the phenomenon under investigation, we often formulate alternative hypotheses and subject each to testing. What the five methods of induction, being mainly eliminative in nature, enable us to determine is this: *If* some specified analysis of the antecedent circumstances is correct, one of these factors cannot be (or must be) the cause (or part of the cause) of the phenomenon in question. This may be deduced, and the deduction may be valid, but the soundness of that argument will always depend on the correctness of the antecedent analysis that had been supposed.

The methods of induction are splendid, but they can yield reliable results only when the hypothesis that they seek to confirm (or falsify) does identify correctly the circumstances that are causally relevant. The methods permit the *deduction* of those results only when that hypothesis has been assumed as a *premise* in the argument. The nature of the power these methods give us may now be seen. They are not paths for discovery; they are not rules for proof. *They are instruments for testing hypotheses.* The statements of these inductive techniques, taken together, describe the general method of controlled experiment, which is a common and indispensable tool in all of modern science.

So important is the role of hypotheses in systematic empirical investigations that the enterprise of devising and testing hypotheses may be regarded as *the* method of science—to which we turn in the next chapter.

EXERCISES

Analyze each of the following investigations, or arguments, and indicate which of the methods of causal reasoning—Mill's methods—are being used in each of them.

1. Teens who lose their virginity earlier than their peers are more likely to shoplift, destroy property, or sell drugs than their virgin counterparts, according to a recent national study of 7000 teenagers. Those who had sex early were 20 percent more likely to engage in delinquent acts one

year later compared to those whose first sexual experience occurred at the average age for their school. Those who waited longer than average to have sex had delinquency rates 50 percent lower a year later compared to average teens. Waiting appears to have a protective effect. "We're not finding that sex itself leads to delinquency; sex itself is not always a problem behavior," writes co-author and Ohio State sociologist Stacy Armour. However, "the timing of sexual initiation does matter. Kids go off on a different trajectory if they're having sex early."

—Reported in *The Journal of Youth and Adolescence,* February 2007

2. Strong evidence has been presented that a diet low in folic acid [a trace vitamin in the B complex] during pregnancy increases the chances of giving birth to a premature baby of lower than normal birth weight. Dr. Theresa Scholl [of the University of Medicine and Dentistry of New Jersey] studied the outcomes of pregnancy for 832 women from the inner city of Camden, N.J., to determine the influence of dietary and supplementary consumption of folic acid. "We found that the women who consumed less than 240 micrograms per day of folic acid had about a two to threefold greater risk of preterm delivery and low birth weight," she said. She reported that even small increases in the women's serum folic acid concentrations by the 28th week decreased the odds of preterm delivery as well as the chance of having a baby of low birth weight. Of the 219 women in the low-folic-acid category (receiving less than 240 micrograms a day), 44 had preterm, low birth weight infants. "The risks declined in direct relationship to increased serum levels of folic acid, showing that low intake is a risk factor throughout pregnancy," Dr. Scholl concluded.

—T. O. Scholl, et al., "Dietary and Serum Folate: Their Influence on the Outcome of Pregnancy," *American Journal of Clinical Nutrition,* April 1996

3. The sequence of DNA units in the genome of humans and in that of chimpanzees is 98.8 percent identical; humans and chimps shared a joint ancestor as recently as five million years ago. Relatively few genes, therefore, must define the essence of humanity, and biologists have long supposed that if they could identify genes that have *changed* in the evolutionary advance leading from that joint ancestor, they would better understand the genetic basis of how people differ from chimpanzees, and hence what makes humans human.

   This project received a significant boost in 2001 when a large London family with barely intelligible speech was found to have mutations in a gene called FOXP2. Chimpanzees also have an FOXP2 gene, but theirs is significantly different from ours. The human version shows signs of accelerated evolutionary change in the last 100,000 years, which suggests that the gene acquired a new function that helped to make human speech possible.

—Reported by Dr. Michelle Cargill of Celera Diagnostics, Alameda, CA, and Dr. Andrew Clark, of Cornell, in *Science,* 11 December 2003

4. A simple, inexpensive and surprisingly powerful combination of treatments that all but wiped out malaria in a group of HIV-positive children in a recent study in Uganda was described at a very recent medical conference in Los Angeles. The combination—taking one inexpensive antibiotic pill each day and sleeping under an insecticide-treated mosquito net—*reduced the incidence of malaria by 97 percent* compared with a control group. The study, conducted by Dr. Anne Gasasira of Makerere University in Kampala, Uganda, found that among 561 healthy children who were not HIV-infected and who did not take the antibiotic and sleep under bed nets, there were 356 episodes of malaria. This compared with 4 episodes among 300 children who were known to be HIV-infected and received both treatments. "The findings were shockingly dramatic," said Dr. Elaine Abrams, a professor of pediatrics and epidemiology at Columbia University.

—Reported at the *14th Conference on Retroviruses and Opportunistic Infections,* Los Angeles, 28 February 2007

5. Some theories arise from anecdotal evidence that is difficult to confirm. In *The Left-Hander Syndrome* (New York: Bantam Books, 1992), Stanley Coren sought to evaluate the common belief that left-handed persons die sooner than right-handers. But death certificates or other public records very rarely mention the hand preferred by the deceased. What could serve as a reliable data source with which that hypothesis could be tested? Coren searched baseball records, noting which hand baseball pitchers threw with, and then recording their ages at death. Right-handed pitchers, he found, lived on average nine months longer than lefties. Then, in a follow-up study, he and a colleague telephoned the relatives of people named on death certificates in two California counties, to ask which hand the deceased favored. Right-handed people (that study found) lived an average of nine years longer than lefties.

6. It has long been recognized that taller adults hold jobs of higher status and, on average, earn more than other workers. A large number of hypotheses have been put forward to explain the association between height and earnings. In developed countries, researchers have emphasized factors such as self esteem, social dominance, and discrimination. In this paper, we offer a simpler explanation: On average, taller people earn more because they are smarter. As early as age 3—before schooling has had a chance to play a role—and throughout childhood, taller children perform significantly better on cognitive tests. The correlation between height in childhood and adulthood is approximately 0.7 for both men and women, so that tall children are much more likely to become tall adults. As adults, taller individuals are more likely to select into higher paying occupations that require more advanced verbal and numerical skills and greater intelligence, for which they earn handsome returns. Using four data sets from the US and the UK, we find that the height premium in adult earnings can be explained by childhood scores on cognitive tests. Furthermore, we show that taller adults select into occupations that have higher cognitive skill requirements and lower physical skill demands.

—Anne Case and Christina Paxson, "Stature and Status: Height, Ability, and Labor Market Outcomes," *National Bureau of Economic Research,* Working Paper No. 12466, August 2006

7. Does the position of the arm, when blood pressure is being checked, make any difference? Researchers at the University of California at San Diego, using automated cuffs, took six readings from one hundred emergency room patients whose problems did not involve their circulatory systems. Their blood pressure was measured standing, sitting, and lying down; in each position it was measured with the arm straight out from the body and with the arm held at the side. They found that the position of the arm had a bigger effect on the readings than the position of the body. When the arm was parallel to the body readings were higher by as much as 14 millimeters of mercury. Dr. David A. Guss, one of the authors of the study, said that no single position was more accurate, "the most important thing is to use a consistent position from measurement to measurement."

—From the *Annals of Internal Medicine,* reported in *The New York Times,* 6 January 2004

8. Near the end of the Middle Ages, a few theologians (the "scientists" of that time) persuaded a king of France to give them permission for an

experiment that had been forbidden by the Roman Catholic Church. They were allowed to weigh the soul of a criminal by measuring him both before and after his hanging. As usually happens with academics, they came up with a definite result: the soul weighed about an ounce and a half.

—John Lukacs, "Atom Smasher Is Super Nonsense," *The New York Times*, 17 June 1993

9. Undoubtedly the outstanding point of departure of industrial social psychology was the series of studies performed in the Hawthorne plant of the Western Electric Company, starting in 1927. These were conducted by three Harvard professors, Elton Mayo, F. J. Roethlisberger, and T. N. Whitehead, and by W. J. Dickson of Western Electric. The original aim of the studies was to obtain concrete data on the effects of illumination, temperature, rest periods, hours of work, wage rate, etc., upon production. A group of six girls, average workers, were chosen for the experiment; their task was the assembly of telephone relays. Almost from the beginning, unexpected results appeared: The production rate kept going up whether rest periods and hours were increased or decreased! In each experimental period, whatever its conditions, output was higher than in the preceding one. The answer seemed to lie in a number of subtle social factors.

. . . As Homans summarizes it, the increase in the girls' output rate "could not be related to any change in their conditions of work, whether experimentally induced or not. It could, however, be related to what can only be spoken of as the development of an organized social group in a peculiar and effective relation with its supervisors."

—S. Stansfeld Sargent and Robert C. Williamson, *Social Psychology*, 1966

10. Does noise have an adverse effect on those subjected involuntarily to it? When the airport at Munich, Germany, moved, researchers from the University of Hamburg, the University of Gavle in Sweden, and Cornell University took that rare opportunity to conduct a prospective study on the effects of noise, measuring the performance of students near the old airport and near the new one, before and after the move. The reading skills of students in both groups were tested, along with short-term and long-term memory, as reported in the journal *Psychological Science*, in October 2002. After the move, improvements in memory and reading were found among students near the old airport, while among students living near the new airport, reading skills and memory performance declined.

High levels of noise do interfere with learning and development, those researchers concluded—but the brighter side of their findings was this: Most of the learning damage done by noise appeared to reverse itself when the noise was removed.

11. The mood changes that many people experience during the shorter days of winter have a physiological basis in the brain, according to a study reported in the British medical journal, *The Lancet*, in January 2003. One hundred healthy volunteers, ages 18 to 79, allowed researchers to draw blood samples, at different times of the year, from their jugular veins, to get blood as close to the brain as possible. The researchers then correlated levels of brain chemicals, especially seratonin, with the weather data—temperature, air pressure, rainfall, and sunlight—at the times of blood collection. Only sunlight had causal impact; seratonin levels were found to be lowest in the three months of winter, but varied depending on the brightness of the day. "Our findings [the researchers wrote] are further evidence for the notion that changes in release of seratonin by the brain underlie mood seasonality and seasonal affective disorder."

12. Prof. Norbert Schwartz, of the University of Michigan, conducted the following experiment. He tested the attitudes of people who had just used a University of Michigan copying machine in which, for some subjects, he had planted a dime which they found, while for others there was no windfall dime. After using the copier, subjects were asked how happy they were about life. Those who had found a dime were consistently more upbeat about "their lives as a whole," and about the economy and many other matters. "We found," said Prof. Schwartz, "that a dime can make you happy for about twenty minutes. Then the mood wears off."

—N. Schwartz, *Well Being: Foundations of Hedonic Psychology* (New York: Russell Sage Foundation, 1999)

13. The largest and longest-running study of American child care has found that keeping a preschooler in a day care center for a year or more increased the likelihood that the child would become disruptive in class—and that this effect persisted through the sixth grade. Every year spent in such centers for at least 10 hours per week was associated with a 1 per cent higher score on a standardized assessment of problem behaviors completed by teachers. Parents' guidance, and their genes, had the strongest influence on how children behaved—but this finding about the impact of day care centers held up regardless of the

child's sex, or family income, and regardless of the quality of the day care center.

—National Institute of Child Health and Human Development, "Early Child Care and Youth Development," 26 March 2007

14. Speed kills. A report from the Insurance Institute for Highway Safety, issued in November of 2003, concluded that increased speed limits on Interstate highways led to nearly 1,900 additional deaths in 22 states from 1996 to 1999. The report is based, oddly, on a study by the Transport Safety Authority of New Zealand, working in the United States, which showed that, when the Federal cap on speed limits was placed at 65 mph the number of deaths on U.S. highways decreased. But almost immediately after the repeal of that Federal cap on speed limits the number of deaths in the states that did not retain the 65 mph limit increased markedly, while the number of deaths in those states that retained the 65 mph limit did not increase. Drivers in states with higher speed limits, the study showed, drive faster, and where the driving is faster the number of traffic fatalities goes up.

—"Study Links Higher Speed Limits to Deaths" *The New York Times*, 24 November 2003

15. A 16-year study followed 8,867 non-smoking male professionals with normal body weight who participated in vigorous daily exercise and ate a healthy diet. Those who drank one-half to two normal servings of wine, beer, or hard liquor a day had a 41 to 62 percent reduction of heart attack risk compared with those who drank no alcohol at all. It seems clear that in moderate quantities alcoholic drinks reduce the likelihood of heart attack. This effect is found not only in those with heart disease. The lead author of the study writes: "Even in the lowest risk people, we still find a lower risk associated with moderate drinking."

—Kenneth Mukamal, "Alcohol Consumption and Risk for Coronary Heart Disease in Men with Healthy Lifestyles," *Archives of Internal Medicine*, 23 October 2006

16. For heart patients, "noetic" intervention, like prayer, and therapy relying on music, imagery and touch (MIT), is defined as "an intangible healing influence brought about without the use of a drug, device, or surgical procedure." 748 patients with coronary heart disease who were to undergo percutaneous coronary intervention (a type of stenting procedure), or elective cardiac catheterization, were enrolled at one of nine study sites between 1999 and 2002. To test the efficacy of noetic intervention, patients were randomized into four groups: one group (189 patients) received both offsite intercessory prayer and MIT therapy; a second group (182 patients) received intercessory prayer only; a third group (185 patients) received MIT therapy only; the fourth group (192 patients) received neither the intercessory prayer nor the MIT therapy. The interventional heart procedures were conducted according to each institution's standards practice, with a six-month period of follow-up. The prayer portion was double blinded, meaning that the patients and their care team did not know which patients were receiving intercessory prayer. The prayer groups for the study were located throughout the world and included Buddhist, Muslim, Jewish and many Christian denominations. 89 percent of the patients in this study also knew of someone praying for them outside of the study protocol.

As reported by the Duke University Medical Center, the researchers found no significant difference among the four treatment groups. Distant prayer and the bedside use of music, imagery and touch did not have a significant effect upon the primary clinical outcome of these patients undergoing medical interventions.

—"First Multicenter Trial of Intercessory Prayer," *The Lancet*, 16 July 2005

17. The impulse to share does not come naturally to one who is thinking about money. Psychologists found that subconscious reminders of money prompted people to become more independent in their work, and less likely to seek help from others or to provide it. In one experiment 52 undergraduates unscrambled sets of jumbled phrases; one group untangled phrases that were often about money, like "high salary paying," while another solved word puzzles that did not refer to money. Researchers then had the students work on a difficult abstract puzzle and offered to give help if they wanted it. Those who had been thinking about money worked on the problem by themselves an average of more than 70% longer than the others. Students "primed" to have money on their minds, while clearly self-reliant, were less likely than peers who had not been so primed to lend assistance, twice as slow to help another confused student, and about twice as stingy when asked to donate money to help needy students.

—Kathleen Vohs, Nicole Mead, and Miranda Goode, "The Psychological Consequences of Money," *Science*, 17 November 2006

SUMMARY

In this chapter we have examined the concept of cause, the nature of causal connections, and the methods used to establish causal laws.

In Section 12.1, we examined various meanings of "cause."

In Section 12.2, we explained the supposition of the uniformity of nature, and the generality of causal laws.

In Section 12.3, we discussed induction by simple enumeration.

In Section 12.4, we recounted and illustrated the principal techniques of inductive inference, called Mill's methods, explaining their essentially eliminative nature. These five methods are

1. The method of agreement
2. The method of difference
3. The joint method of agreement and difference
4. The method of residues
5. The method of concomitant variation

In Section 12.5, we explained the limitations and the strengths of these inductive techniques, concluding that, although they cannot do all that John Stuart Mill had claimed for them, they are profoundly important as the intellectual instruments with which scientific hypotheses are confirmed or disconfirmed.

End Notes

[1]David Hume, *An Enquiry Concerning Human Understanding* (1748), sec. IV.

[2]J. Dao, "Coroner in Cincinnati Rules Man's Struggle Led to Death," *The New York Times*, 4 December 2003.

[3]Reported by Connor O'Shea of the Duke University Medical Center, at the meetings of the European Society of Cardiology in August 2000.

[4]See Zachariah Chafee, Jr. *Three Human Rights in the Constitution of 1787* (1952).

[5]Dr. Steven Grant, quoted in *Science News*, 27 January 2007.

[6]Here quoting Dr. Nora Volkow, director of the National Institute of Drug Abuse, quoted by Benedict Carey, "In Clue to Addictive Behavior, A Brain Injury Halts Smoking," *The New York Times*, 26 January 2007.

[7]Robert Sapolsky, "Testosterone Rules," *Discover*, March 1997.

[8]D. N. Cook *et al.*, "Requirement of *MIP-1 alpha* for an Inflammatory Response to Viral Infection," *Science*, 15 September 1995.

[9]Paul Henle and William K. Frankena, *Exercises in Elementary Logic* (1940).

[10]A. Werzberger et al., "A Controlled Trial of a Formalin-Inactivated Hepatitis A Vaccine in Healthy Children," *The New England Journal of Medicine*, 13 August 1992.

[11]Edward Arthur Fath, *The Elements of Astronomy* (New York: McGraw-Hill, 1926), p. 170.

[12]D. S. Siscovick et al., "Dietary Intake and Cell Membrane Levels of Long-Chain *n*-3 Polyunsaturated Fatty Acids and the Risk of Primary Cardiac Arrest," *Journal of the American Medical Association*, 1 November 1995.

[13]The source of these data is the U.S. Census Bureau; the analysts are Gordon B. Dahl of the University of Rochester and Enrico Moretti of the University of California at Los Angeles, reporting online in *Slate*, in October 2003.

[14]J. L. Casti, *Searching for Certainty* (New York: William Morrow, 1991).

Science and Hypothesis

13

13.1 Scientific Explanation

We study the world scientifically to learn the truth about it. However, individual truths do not take us very far; a mere collection of facts no more constitutes a science than a collection of stones constitutes a house. The aim of science is to discover general truths (chiefly in the form of causal connections like those discussed in the preceding chapter) with which the facts we encounter can be *explained.*

What is an explanation? Every explanation gives an account, a set of statements from which the thing to be explained can be logically inferred. The best account will be the one that most reduces the problematic aspects of what was to be explained. Such an account will comprise a coherent set of general truths, or a theory. To explain some serious disease, for example, we need a coherent account of what causes that disease and how it can be treated. Is the presence or absence of some particular substance the key to the disorder? The theory explaining diabetes, for example, is a coherent account of the use of sugars by the human body and the central role, in that use, of a protein hormone called *insulin*, produced by certain special cells within the body. According to this theory, it is a deficiency of insulin (or the inability the body to use the insulin it produces) that explains the resulting disorder in the absorption of sugars from the blood. An account of this kind (here greatly oversimplified, of course) gives a scientific explanation of this serious disease. Patients suffer from diabetes *because* of their insulin deficiency.

When we say "*Q* because *P*," that may express either an explanation or an argument. It expresses an argument when we are inferring the conclusion, *Q*, from the premises, *P*. It expresses an explanation when, facing the *fact* of *Q*, our reasoning moves back from that fact to discover the circumstances that led to it. Diabetes—excess sugar in the blood—is a cruel fact in the lives of many patients. We *explain* their diabetes by calling attention to the insulin deficiency that has that result. The account of the interrelated set of circumstances in which the insulin deficiency, *P,* accounts for the sugar excess, *Q,* is thus an *explanation* of that disease.

A good explanation must offer truths that are *relevant* to the fact explained. If I seek to explain my being late to work on some occasion by calling attention to the rising birth rate in Brazil, the fact thus introduced may be correct, but it is not relevant, and it therefore cannot be a satisfactory explanation of my absence, the event in question. In this trivial example it is a single event for which an explanation is sought. In science we seek explanations that are not only true, and relevant, but also general. The explanations we aim for will provide an understanding of all the events of some given *kind*—say, all the occurrences of diabetes, for example.

The more facts for which a scientific theory accounts, the more powerful it is. Some theories are magnificent in their range and power. Here, for example, is a short statement of Isaac Newton's law of universal gravitation:

> Every particle of matter in the universe attracts every other particle with a force that is directly proportional to the product of the masses of the particles and inversely proportional to the square of the distance between them.

An explanation may be relevant and general, and yet not scientific. The regular motions of the planets were long thought to be accounted for by the "intelligence" that was held to reside in each planet. In some cultures, disease is "explained" as the work of an evil spirit that has invaded the body. These are certainly *un*scientific accounts, although the explanations they offer are general and also are relevant to the facts of interest. What, then, distinguishes genuinely scientific from unscientific explanations?

There are two chief differences. The first is *attitude.* An unscientific explanation is presented dogmatically; the account that it gives is regarded as being unquestionably true and not improvable. The opinions of Aristotle were accepted for centuries as the ultimate authority on matters of fact. Aristotle himself appears to have been open-minded, but his views were adopted by some medieval scholars in a rigid and unscientific spirit.* In contrast, the attitude of a serious scientist is undogmatic; explanations are put forward provisionally; hypotheses may be thought highly probable, but they are regarded as subject to alteration in the light of the evidence.

The vocabulary of science is sometimes misleading on this point. When what is first suggested as a "hypothesis" is well confirmed, its status may be elevated to that of a "theory"; after universal acceptance, it may be further

---

*One of the scholars to whom Galileo offered his telescope to view the newly discovered moons of Jupiter declined to look, expressing his certainty that no real moons could possibly be seen because no mention of them could be found in Aristotle's treatise on astronomy!

elevated to that of a "law." However, the use of these terms is not consistent. Newton's discovery is still called the "law of gravitation," while Einstein's contribution, which improved and superseded it, is referred to as the "theory of relativity." Whatever the terms used, the attitude of genuine scientists is not dogmatic. The general propositions of science are all in essence hypotheses, never absolutely certain.

The second difference concerns the *basis* for accepting the account in question. In science a hypothesis is worthy of acceptance only to the extent that there is good evidence for it. An unscientific belief may be held independently of what we should regard as evidence in its favor; the explanation is taken as simply true—perhaps because "everyone knows" that it is so, or perhaps because it is thought to have been revealed from on high. There is no reliable test of such claims, whereas in genuine science the claims for truth can be tested, and those tests lie in our experience. Thus we say that genuine science is *empirical.*

To say that a hypothesis is testable is at least to say that some prediction made on the basis of that hypothesis may confirm or disconfirm it. Science demands evidence. But, of course, the evidence accumulated that could confirm the hypothesis in question can never be complete, as we have earlier emphasized; *all* the evidence is never in hand. Therefore, even when that supporting evidence is very strong some doubt must remain, and certainty is unattainable. On the negative side, however, if the evidence shows indisputably that the predictions made on the basis of that hypothesis are false, our confidence that the hypothesis must be rejected may be total. Although we cannot complete the verification of a hypothesis, we can, with closure, establish that it has been falsified. For reasons of this kind, some philosophers have held that to say of a scientific hypothesis that it is testable is also to say that it is, at least in principle, falsifiable.

The test of truth may be direct or indirect. To determine whether it is raining outside, I need only glance out the window. However, the general propositions offered as explanatory hypotheses are not directly testable. If my lateness at work had been explained by my claim about some traffic accident, my employer, if suspicious, might test that explanation indirectly by seeking the police accident report. An indirect test deduces, from the proposition to be tested (for example, that I was involved in an accident), some other proposition (for example, that an accident report had been submitted) capable of being tested directly. If that deduced proposition is false, the explanation that implied it must be false. If the deduced proposition is true, that provides some evidence (but not conclusive evidence) that the explanation is true, having been indirectly confirmed.

Indirect testing is never certain. It always relies on some additional premises, such as the premise that accidents of the sort I described to my employer are invariably reported to the police. But the accident report that should have been submitted in my case may not have been, so its absence does not *prove* my explanation false. And even the truth of some added premises does not render my explanation *certain*—although the successful testing of the conclusion deduced (the reality of the accident report, in this example) does corroborate the premises from which it was deduced.

Even an unscientific explanation has *some* evidence in its favor, namely, the very fact it is held to explain. The unscientific theory that the planets are inhabited by "intelligences" that cause them to move in their observed orbits can claim, as evidence, the fact that the planets do move in those orbits. However, the great difference between that hypothesis and the reliable astronomical explanation of planetary movement lies in this: For the unscientific hypothesis there is no other directly testable proposition that can be deduced from it. Any scientific explanation of a given phenomenon, on the other hand, will have directly testable propositions deducible from it *other than the proposition stating the fact to be explained*. This is what we mean when we say that an explanation is *empirically verifiable*, and such verifiability is the most essential mark of a scientific explanation.*

13.2 Scientific Inquiry: Hypothesis and Confirmation

We seek scientific explanations that are correct, and whose correctness may be empirically verified. How can we obtain these explanations? No formulas for doing science can be given, but there are stages, or distinct phases, in most scientific investigations. By identifying and describing seven such stages we may come to understand more fully how good science advances.

A. IDENTIFYING THE PROBLEM

Scientific investigation begins with a problem of some kind. By *problem* is meant only some fact, or group of facts, for which no acceptable explanation is at that time available. The sociologist confronts a puzzling trend in work or play; what accounts for it? The medical investigator confronts a puzzling disease; what causes it? The economist observes different patterns of spending or saving; what explains the variations? Some problems are quite sharply identified, as when a detective confronts a specific crime and asks: Who is the perpetrator? Some problems may arise from a gap in current understanding.

*This general conception of "scientific explanation" rightly applies outside the realm of what is normally thought of as the sciences, such as physics or psychology. Thus, the explanation of an event such as my lateness to work as a consequence of a traffic accident, in being indirectly testable in various ways, is in this wide sense "scientific."

Eratosthenes, librarian at Alexandria in the third century, believed correctly that the earth was a sphere, but its size was unknown. His problem was to determine the circumference of the sphere we call earth. Reflective thinking—whether in sociology or medicine or law enforcement or physics, or any other realm—is *problem-solving* activity, as John Dewey and other modern philosophers have repeatedly emphasized. The recognition of some problem is the trigger for the science that ensues.

B. DEVISING PRELIMINARY HYPOTHESES

Preliminary speculation is the second step—some very tentative explanation of the problem identified. Long before a full solution is in sight, some theorizing is needed to indicate the kind of evidence needed, and perhaps to indicate where such evidence might best be sought. The detective examines the scene of the crime, interviews suspects, seeks clues. The physician examines the patient, records data, notes irregularities. Bare facts are accumulated; they become usable clues or revealing symptoms only when they are fitted into some coherent pattern, even if that pattern is speculative and incomplete. To illustrate, Thomas Malthus had shown, in "An Essay on the Principle of Population" (1798), that the tendency of population to grow faster than the food supply keeps most people at the edge of starvation. Charles Darwin, reading this while speculating about the origin of species many years later, hit upon an exceedingly fruitful notion. He wrote:

> It at once struck me that under these circumstances favourable variations would tend to be preserved, and unfavourable ones to be destroyed. . . . Here then I had at last got a theory by which to work" (*Autobiography, 1881*).

There are too many possibly relevant facts, too much data in the world, for the scientist to collect them all. The most thorough investigator must select some facts for further study and put other facts aside as not relevant. If the earth is a sphere, the rays of the sun will fall (at any given time) upon different points of that sphere at different angles. Might geometry help us to calculate the size of the earth? The outline of a theory is essential because without that the investigator cannot decide which facts, from the totality of facts, to select and pursue. However incomplete or tentative, a preliminary hypothesis of some kind is needed before serious inquiry can get underway.

C. COLLECTING ADDITIONAL FACTS

The preliminary hypothesis serves to guide the search for relevant facts. As a preliminary matter, the patient is thought to have some infection, and that hypothesis puts the physician on the trail of certain kinds of data that are normally associated with infection: temperature irregularities, patterns of inflammation, and the like. The preliminary supposition that the crime was committed by a member of the household will cause the detective to inquire into the conduct of persons residing there, and so on. If the angle with which the sun's rays strike the earth must differ at different points on the earth's surface, one must seek, in order to apply geometric principles, at least one point at which the sun is known to be *directly* overhead at a given time. Where might that be?

The second and third steps are not fully separable, of course; in real life they are interconnected and mutually suggestive. New facts found may cause an adjustment of the preliminary hypothesis; that adjustment may lead to facts earlier not noted. The process of gathering evidence by using the preliminary hypothesis merges with the process of refining that hypothesis, leading to new findings, and so on and on.

D. FORMULATING THE EXPLANATORY HYPOTHESIS

Eventually, the investigator—the scientist, or detective, or ordinary person—may come to believe that all the facts needed for solving the original problem are in hand. The task then becomes that of assembling the pieces of the puzzle in a way that makes sense of the whole. If that synthesis is successful, a hypothesis will emerge that accounts for all the data—the original set of facts that gave rise to the problem, as well as the additional facts to which earlier hypotheses had pointed. A surge in unemployment is explained by some larger theory of the labor market. The patient is found to be suffering from an identifiable infectious agent known to manifest the symptoms noted in this patient's condition. An identifiable member of the household is charged by the state as the perpetrator of the crime and the case against him is formulated.

There is no mechanical way to find some overarching theory. The actual discovery, or invention, of a successful explanatory hypothesis is a process of creation, in which imagination as well as knowledge is involved. That is why those who make important scientific discoveries are so widely honored and so much admired.

What *is* the circumference of the globe? Eratosthenes learned that in the Egyptian town of Syene (now called Aswan), the sun's rays shine directly down a deep well at a given time on a particular day each year. At that same time he could measure the sun's shadows (and therefore the angle of its rays) in Alexandria; he found that the rays there deviated from the vertical by 7°. That is about one-fiftieth of the 360° of the sphere's circumference. The distance between Syene and Alexandria was known. The circumference of the entire sphere of earth must therefore be about fifty times that distance. Eratosthenes' subsequent calculation of the earth's circumference ("250,000 *stadia*") is believed (we are unsure of the length of a *stadium*) to have an error of less than 5 percent. He had no way to confirm that calculation, but it was impressive science for his time. Truly great scientists—such as Einstein or Newton—are understandably viewed as creative geniuses.

E. DEDUCING FURTHER CONSEQUENCES

A good explanatory hypothesis will be fruitful; that is, it will explain not only the facts that provoked the inquiry but many other facts as well. It is likely to suggest some facts that had not even been thought of earlier. Verification of these additional facts may strongly confirm (but, of course, cannot prove with certainty) the hypothesis that led to them.

To illustrate, the cosmological theory known as the *Big Bang* hypothesizes that the present universe began with one singular explosive event. The initial fireball would have been smooth and homogenous, lacking structure. But the universe today exhibits a great deal of structure; its visible matter is clumped into galaxies, clusters of galaxies, and so on. If the Big Bang theory is correct, the seeds of the present structure of the universe must in principle be identifiable. We need to be able to look back in time—and by observing the most distant objects in an expanding universe, astronomers actually can, in effect, look back in time, since the light being received must have left its sources billions of years ago. If, in these observations, early structures were not detectable by the most sensitive instruments, the Big Bang theory would be seriously undermined. But if such structure *is* detectable, the Big Bang theory would be significantly confirmed.

F. TESTING THE CONSEQUENCES

Critical for the evaluation of every explanatory hypothesis is the accuracy of its predictions. Can the facts to which the theory points be ascertained? Often they can. If there were structure in the universe early in its expansion, as the Big Bang theory predicts, there would have to be irregularities, unevenness, that may be found in background radiation and traced to that early time. Happily, it is possible to measure that background radiation and thus to determine now, indirectly, that there were structural irregularities very shortly after the supposed Big Bang. To detect those predicted radiation irregularities, a special satellite was designed—the Cosmic Background Explorer (COBE). Using this satellite, the predicted irregularities have indeed been detected, giving very important confirmatory evidence for the truth of the Big Bang hypothesis.

Consider prediction in another context. In biology we may come to formulate the hypothesis that a particular protein is produced in mammals as a reaction to a particular enzyme, and that that enzyme is produced under the direction of a specifically identified gene. From this hypothesis we may deduce the further consequence that when that gene is absent there will be an absence, or a deficiency, of the protein in question.

To test that hypothesis we construct an experiment in which the effect of the identified gene may be measured. This can sometimes be done by breeding mice in which the critical gene has been deleted—"knockout mice." If, in such mice, the enzyme in question and the protein associated with it are indeed also absent, our hypothesis will have been strongly confirmed.* Much information that proves very valuable in medicine is acquired in just this way. We devise the experiment to determine whether what we thought to be true (if such-and-such were the case) really *is* true. And to do that we must often *construct* the very special circumstances in which such-and-such has been made the case. "An experiment," as the great physicist Max Planck said, "is a question that science poses to Nature; a measurement is the recording of Nature's answer."

It is not always feasible to construct the circumstances needed to perform a test. We must then seek the circumstances needed for testing in some natural setting. That was the case in the effort to test the general theory of relativity.† Einstein's theory proposed that gravitation is not a force (as Newton had thought) but a curved field in the space–time continuum, created by the presence of mass. This might be proved (or disproved), Einstein suggested, by measuring the deflection of starlight as it traveled close by the mass of the sun; the starlight needed would be visible only during a total eclipse of the sun. The testing of this prediction had to await the solar eclipse of 1919, when the sun would be silhouetted against the Hyades star cluster, for which the positions were known exactly. During that eclipse, physicist Sir Arthur Eddington stationed himself on a island off the western coast of Africa; another group of British scientists went to Brazil. The two teams measured accurately the apparent position of several of the stars in the cluster; their measurements plainly showed that light from these stars was indeed bent as it grazed the sun, and that it was bent by the exact amount of Einstein's prediction. The general theory of relativity had been very solidly confirmed.

---

*Testing of this kind relies on what we called the method of difference in Chapter 12. The many methods discussed there (Mill's methods) are intellectual tools used to confirm (or disconfirm) hypotheses.

†"The Foundation of the General Theory of Relativity" was published in 1916, in *Annalen der Physik*.

This theory showed that space, time, and gravity are so entwined that to speak sensibly about one there must be reference to the others. Einstein struggled to go further, to develop a theory in which all of nature's forces are merged into one single, overarching theory. In this effort neither he, nor anyone else, has yet succeeded.

A new approach—to construct a complete and unified theory of natural forces called string theory—now has many adherents. It offers a theoretical account that may unify gravity, quantum mechanics, and nature's other forces, and solve some earlier mathematical problems as well. String theory, which is based on a new conception of matter's fundamental constituents, is free of mathematical contradictions but it has not yet been confirmed.

What predictions does string theory make that might confirm it by experimental test? It may become possible to confirm the theory's predictions regarding new kinds of particles; it may become possible to test the prediction that highly energetic particle collisions will produce microscopic black holes. As this is being written, a gigantic particle accelerator, the Large Hadron Collider, is being built in Geneva, Switzerland, and is scheduled to begin operation in 2008. In a few years we may have empirical evidence to confirm the explanations given by string theory, or to disconfirm them.*

Evolutionary theory, as presented by Darwin in *The Origin of Species* (1859) and by very many of his successors, is now almost universally accepted as a correct explanation of the development of species of animals and plants. Predictions that can test this theory prospectively (rather than retrospectively) are difficult to devise because the natural selection hypothesized seems to require the passage of many generations. Very recently, a Harvard professor of evolutionary biology, Jonathan Losos, devised an experiment that makes speedy testing feasible. On some tiny cays in the Bahamas, where the brown lizard *Anolis sagrei* lives free of predators and reproduces rapidly, he introduced a predator whose activity would quickly result in the development (in those islands as compared to other, similar islands left unperturbed) of a lizard population with longer legs, much better suited to running away. Selective forces operated as expected; long legs came to predominate. The *Anolis* lizard when continually preyed upon climbs into trees and bushes, where short legs are much more advantageous. The further

*Some scientists contend that string theory makes no predictions whose testing will truly confirm or disconfirm it. See L. Smolin, *The Trouble with Physics,* (Boston: Houghton Mifflin, 2006); and P. Woit, *Not Even Wrong: The Failure of String Theory* (New York, Basic Books, 2006). It may be that the theory makes predictions that are testable in principle, but not testable in practice given current technological limitations. This heated controversy is likely to continue.

prediction was that natural selection would produce a reversal and that short legs would eventually predominate—and six months later that prediction also was confirmed. Evolution has been first manipulated and then deliberately reversed. Said Prof. Losos:

> Evolutionary biology is often caricatured as incompatible with controlled experimentation. Recent work has shown, however, that evolutionary biology can be studied on short time scales and that predictions about it can be tested experimentally. We predicted, and then demonstrated, a reversal in the direction of natural selection acting on limb length in a population of lizards. We did a controlled, replicable experiment in nature. It illustrates that evolutionary biology at its heart is no different from any other science.[1]

G. APPLYING THE THEORY

We aim first of all to explain the phenomena we encounter, but we also aim to *control* those phenomena to our advantage. The theories of Newton and Einstein and their successors play a central role not only in our understanding of celestial phenomena, they are also critical in our actual exploration of the solar system, and outer space beyond. Nuclear fusion is now well understood as a process; we seek to apply this understanding in producing energy on a scale we can control. Disease and disorder are understood as never before, incorporating the well-tested explanations of genetic theory and our grasp of the human genome; now we seek to put this understanding to use in clinical medicine by eliminating genetic disorders, and even by regenerating organic tissue. In this twenty-first century it is probably biological science, more than any other, whose explanations will enhance the quality and the length of ordinary human lives.

Good practice in every sphere must be guided by good theory. Good theory must pass the test of empirical verification. Theory and practice are not two realms; they are equally critical aspects of every genuinely scientific undertaking. More than two centuries ago, Immanuel Kant wrote a penetrating little book explaining why it makes no good sense to say, "that may be right in theory but it won't work in practice."[2] What is right in theory *does* work in practice. And for everything that does work in practice we may reasonably hope to discover the explanatory theory that underlies its success.

13.3 Evaluating Scientific Explanations

The same phenomenon may receive different explanations, all scientific in the sense we have described, and yet some of them may not be true. Conflicting explanations of some physical or economic phenomenon may be offered. In a criminal investigation we may hypothesize that the perpetrator was X, or was

Y. More than one hypothesis may account for the facts neatly, but not all can be true. How shall we choose among alternative scientific explanations?

Let us assume that all the alternatives are relevant and testable. How ought we determine which of the available hypotheses is the best? There are standards—going beyond relevance and testability—to which acceptable hypotheses may be expected to conform. Three criteria are most commonly used in judging the merit of competing hypotheses.

1. ***Compatibility* with previously well-established hypotheses.** Science aims at achieving a *system* of explanatory hypotheses. A satisfactory system must be internally consistent, of course. A satisfactory explanatory system cannot contain contradictory elements; if it did, the full set of propositions could not possibly be true. We progress by gradually expanding hypotheses to comprehend more and more facts, but each new hypothesis brought into the set must be compatible with those already confirmed.

   Sometimes the expansion involves only one new hypothesis, as when the aberrations in the orbit of Uranus were explained by the hypothesis that there was some other planet, uncharted at that time, whose mass was creating the aberrations. That supposition was perfectly consistent with the main body of astronomical theory at the time. A search for the mysterious object resulted in the discovery of the planet Neptune in 1846. The theory that led to that discovery *fit* very nicely with all the other theories concerning planetary movements generally accepted at that time.

   Although theoretical knowledge grows gradually, it does not always grow by adding just one new hypothesis after another in orderly fashion. Clumps of theory may be introduced; new hypotheses that are flatly inconsistent with older theories sometimes replace their predecessors outright, rather than being fitted in with them. Einstein's theory of relativity was of that sort: It shattered many of the preconceptions of the older, Newtonian theory of gravitation. In another branch of physics, it was discovered that radium atoms undergo spontaneous disintegration, and this well-confirmed fact was simply inconsistent with an older principle that matter could neither be created nor destroyed. To maintain a consistent set of hypotheses, the older principle had to be relinquished.

   The consistency of the set of scientific theories in a given field is thus achieved in different ways. However, apart from those cases in which some revolutionary theory upsets long-established principles, the first criterion for an acceptable new hypothesis is that it retain the existing consistency, be compatible with what is already known, or be reasonably believed.

When old and new collide, the established scientific theories will not be abandoned quickly in favor of some that are shinier or more trendy. The older body of theory will be adjusted to accommodate the new if that is possible. Large-scale change will be resisted. Einstein himself always insisted that his own work was a modification of Newton's, not a rejection of it. The principle of the conservation of matter was modified by being absorbed into the more comprehensive principle of the conservation of mass–energy. An established theory has the support that it does because it explains a considerable mass of data, so it cannot be dethroned by some new hypothesis unless the new hypothesis accounts for the same facts as well as (or better than) the older one, and accounts for other known facts also.

Science advances as its theories give more comprehensive explanations, more adequate accounts of the world we encounter. When inconsistencies arise, the greater age of one hypothesis does not automatically prove it correct. If the older view has been extensively confirmed, presumption will support it. When the newer, competing view has also received extensive confirmation, mere age and priority cease to be relevant. We must then decide between the competitors on the basis of something we learn about the observable facts. The ultimate court of appeal is always experience.

2. ***Predictive power.*** As we have seen, every scientific hypothesis must be testable, and testability requires that some observable fact or facts must be deducible from it. Alternative hypotheses will differ in the nature and extent of their predictions, and we seek the theoretical explanation that has the greater predictive power.

To illustrate, the behaviors of bodies near the surface of the earth were explained by Galileo Galilei (1564–1642) with his laws of falling bodies. The behaviors of bodies far off in the solar system were explained at about that same time by the German astronomer Johannes Kepler (1571–1630), who formulated the laws of planetary motion. Using the data that had been collected by Denmark's Tycho Brahe, Kepler could account for the motions of the planets on the basis of the elliptical orbits they travel around the sun. Galileo gave a theoretically powerful account of the various phenomena of terrestrial mechanics. Kepler gave a theoretically powerful account of celestial mechanics. But the two accounts were isolated from one another. Their unification was needed; it came with Isaac Newton's theory of universal gravitation, and his three laws of motion. All the phenomena explained by Galileo and by Kepler, and many more facts besides, were explained by Newton's account of universal gravitation.

A fact that can be deduced from a given hypothesis is said to be explained by it, and may also be said to be *predicted* by it. Newton's theories had enormous predictive power. The greater the predictive power of any hypothesis, the better it contributes to our understanding of the phenomena with which it is concerned.

Earlier we described the great predictive power of Einstein's general theory of relativity, which accounts for the admiration given to it and to its creator. We also pointed out that his enterprise—the development of an overarching theory of natural forces—is held by some to approach success now in the form of what is called string theory; some predictions of great interest are claimed to be deducible from this theory. If those predictions are one day confirmed, the predictive power of string theory will elevate it to a position of the very first importance in physics and cosmology.

However, the criterion of predictive power also has a negative side. If the hypothesis predicts what does not take place, or is in some other way shown to be inconsistent with well-attested observations, that hypothesis has been *falsified,* and must be rejected. A meaningful scientific hypothesis must be at least falsifiable—that is, we must know what would or might show it to be false. If there is no set of observable outcomes that will lead us to conclude that the hypothesis is false, we may seriously doubt if the hypothesis has any predictive power whatever.

Suppose we confront two different hypotheses, both of which fully explain some set of facts, both of which are testable, and both of which are compatible with the body of already established scientific theory. In such a case, it may be possible to devise a crucial experiment to decide between the conflicting theories. If the first hypothesis entails that, under a given set of circumstances, a specified result will occur, and the second entails that it will not, we may decide between the competitors by observing the presence or absence of that predicted result. Its appearance falsifies the second hypothesis; its nonappearance falsifies the first.

The experiment described earlier, in which the general theory of relativity was tested by making exact measurements of the starlight that passed closely by the mass of sun, was crucial in just this way. The theory of Newton and the theory of Einstein cannot both be correct. If the bending of the light is as Einstein's theory predicted, the Newtonian view is disconfirmed; if the bending of light is not observed, the general theory of relativity is disconfirmed. With good cameras, very careful observers, and a solar eclipse in which the three bodies (sun, moon, and earth) were correctly lined up, the crucial experiment might be made. Those ideal circumstances arose on 29 May 1919. Photographs proved that Einstein was right; we do live in a curved, four-dimensional space–time continuum. Einstein became a worldwide sensation overnight.

3. ***Simplicity.*** Two rival hypotheses may fit equally well with established theory, and they may also have predictive power that is roughly equal. In such circumstances we are likely to favor the simpler of the two. The conflict between the Ptolemaic (earth-centered) and the Copernican (sun-centered) theories of celestial motion was like that. Both fit well with earlier theory, and they predicted celestial movements about equally well. Both hypotheses relied on a clumsy (and as we now know mistaken) device, hypothesized epicycles (smaller circles of movement on the larger orbits), in order to explain some well-established astronomical observations. But the Copernican system relied on many fewer such epicycles and was therefore much simpler. This greater simplicity contributed substantially to its acceptance by later astronomers.

   Simplicity seems to be a "natural" criterion to invoke. In ordinary life also, we are inclined to accept the simplest theory that fits all the facts. Two theories about a crime may be presented at a trial; the verdict is likely to be given—perhaps ought to be given—in favor of the hypothesis that seems simpler, more natural.

   "Simplicity," however, is a tricky notion. That one of the competing theories will involve a smaller number of some troubling entity (such as the epicycles in the case of Copernican astronomy) is a rare situation. Each of two theories may be simpler than the other in different ways. One may rely on a smaller number of entities, while the other may rely on simpler mathematical equations. Even "naturalness" may prove to be deceptive. Many find it more "natural" to believe that the earth, which does not seem to be moving, really is not moving, and that the sun, which appears to move around us, is doing just that. The lesson here is that simplicity is a criterion that is difficult to formulate and not always easy to apply.

Progress in science is never easy and rarely straightforward. No one supposes that simply by applying the seven steps of the hypothetico-deductive method (recounted in Section 13.2) to some problem will lead to its solution. Correct explanatory hypotheses are often obscure, and may require very elaborate theoretical machinery. Devising a final, presumably correct theory may be exceedingly difficult. Far from being mechanical, the process commonly requires, in addition to laborious observation and measurement, insight and creative imagination.

When some hypothesis already in hand is widely believed to explain the phenomena in question, a replacement for it encounters very high hurdles.

The new hypothesis is likely to encounter ridicule and disdain. The new hypothesis is very probably inconsistent with some previously accepted theory, and the established view always has the upper hand. A crucial experiment, of the sort described earlier in the case of the general theory of relativity, is possible only in rare circumstances.

Contemporary physics faces a major conflict of just this kind. Between its two most powerful general theories there is an apparent conflict that cannot presently be resolved. The general theory of relativity is well confirmed. From its laws (describing gravity and how it shapes space and time), it is an apparently inevitable consequence that some collapsing, massive stars will form "black holes" from which escape would require a speed faster than light, which is impossible. The laws of quantum mechanics are also well confirmed, and they entail that information cannot ever be permanently lost, even if drawn into a black hole. Therefore, either there is some property of space and time, not now understood, that can account for the retention of that information, or there is some lawlessness in physics that can account for the permanent loss of that information. One of the two theories must need at least an amendment, but we do not yet know which one, and we do not have the means to construct an experiment that would enable us to decide between them.*

Confronted by such conflicts we will seek to apply the criteria of good scientific explanations we set forth earlier: Which of the competing theories is *simpler?* Which of the two has greater *compatibility* with previously established hypotheses? And, above all, which has the greater explanatory or *predictive power?* So long as definitive answers to these questions are lacking, the intellectual controversy is likely to continue unresolved.

It does happen in the history of scientific progress that such conflicts are sometimes resolved. There is no better way to exhibit the methods of science, and to exemplify the application of the criteria described here, than by recounting the observational confirmation by Galileo of the heliocentric account

---

*A hypothetical experiment has been proposed: Throw a volume of the *Encyclopedia Britannica* into a black hole. Will the information it contains be forever lost? Or is such a total loss impossible? A wager, light-hearted but serious, between two distinguished Cal Tech physicists has been placed on the outcome. Prof. Kip Thorne bets on relativity, whose equations describe space and time and predict that from the singularity of a black hole there could *never* be any recovery. Prof. John Preskill bets on quantum mechanics, whose equations precisely describe the lives of miniscule elementary particles and predict that the information can never be *totally* lost. The stakes of the wager are a set of encyclopedias, but payoff is unlikely to come soon. Their equally distinguised colleague, Prof. Stephen Hawking of Cambridge University, originally opined that "it could go either way," but has changed his mind, stating that black holes probably do not destroy information after all. [*Science News*, 25 September 2004]

of the solar system—and the resulting replacement of the geocentric account that had been accepted as true for more than a thousand years.

By the early 1600s, the movement of the planets against the backdrop of the fixed stars had been so carefully studied that their apparent movements were quite accurately predictable. The moon, also much studied, was believed by theologians to be a perfect sphere. The heavenly bodies, deemed flawless in shape and movement, were widely believed to travel in perfect circles around the Earth, which was the center of the world God had created. By 1609, Galileo had devised a telescope with 20-power magnification, its chief uses being thought at first to be maritime, or as a spyglass that could provide military advantage. With this instrument he observed the heavens, almost by accident, in January 1610. On the 7th of that month he began a long letter, reporting in detail his observations of the moon and other bodies. He wrote:

> I have observed with one of my telescopes. . . the face of the moon, which I have been able to see very near. . . . [W]hat is there can be discerned with great distinctness, and in fact it is seen that the moon is most evidently not at all of an even, smooth and regular surface, as a great many people believe of it and of the other heavenly bodies, but on the contrary it is rough and unequal. In short, it is shown to be such that sane reasoning cannot conclude otherwise than that it is full of prominences and cavities similar, but much larger, to the mountains and valleys spread over the Earth's surface.[3]

To save the hypothesis that the moon was indeed a perfect sphere, and thus to retain the coherence of the theological account of the heavenly bodies of which that perfection was one element, some of Galileo's critics later proposed the hypothesis—outrageously *ad hoc*—that the apparent cavities and irregularities on the surface of the moon were, in fact, filled in by a celestial substance that was flawless and crystalline, and thus invisible through Galileo's telescope!

More than the moon was examined by Galileo. His letter continued:

> And besides the observations of the Moon. . . many fixed stars are seen with the telescope that are not [otherwise] discerned; and only this evening I have seen Jupiter accompanied by three fixed stars, totally invisible [to the naked eye] by their smallness, and the configuration was in this form:[4]

At that point Galileo inserted a sketch that appears here as Figure 13-1, showing the three stars in a straight line, two to the east and one to the west of Jupiter; he reported that they did not extend more than one degree of longitude, but since at that time he supposed them to be fixed stars, their distances from Jupiter and from one another were indicated only very roughly.

On the following day, 8 January 1610, "led by I know not what," Galileo happened to observe Jupiter once again; the earlier positions of those "fixed

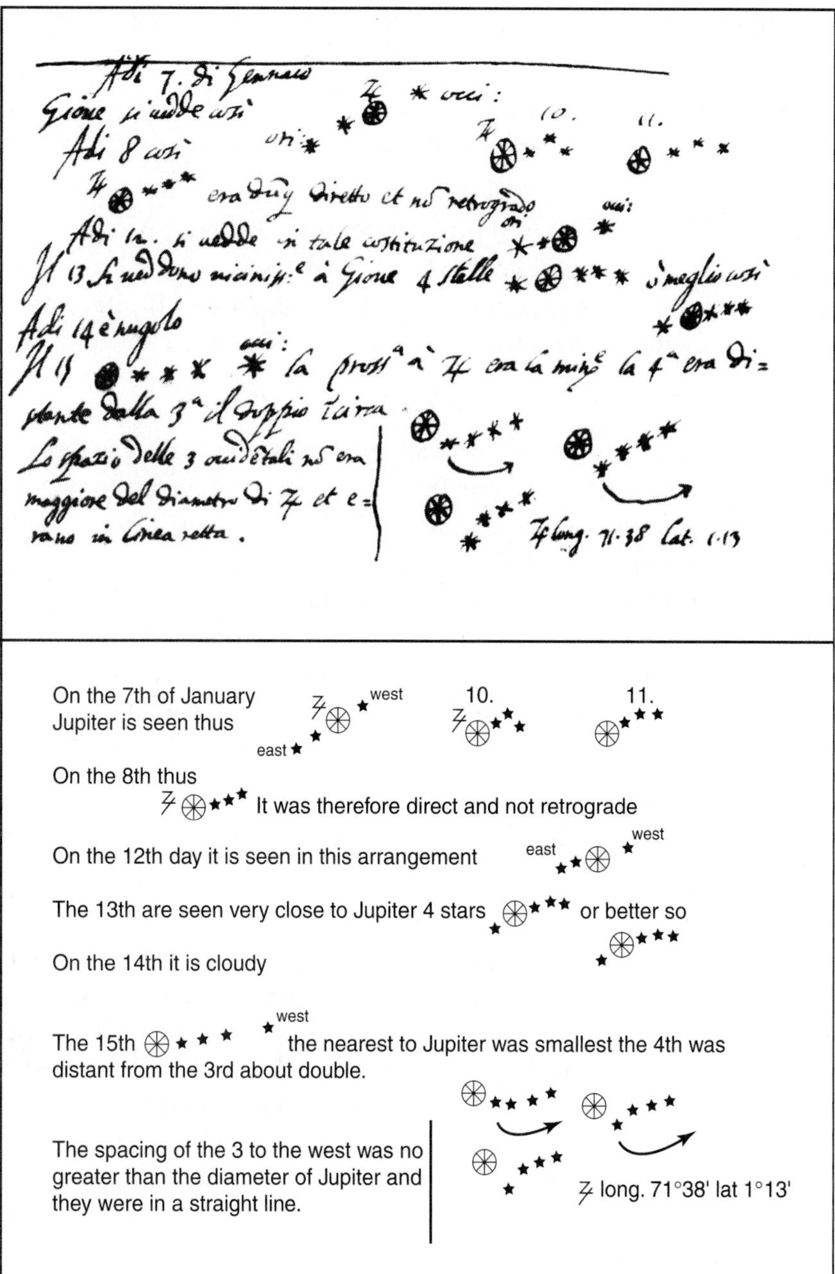

Figure 13-1 A photograph of the letter begun by Galileo on 7 January 1610, on which is recorded his first monumental observations of the four major satellites of Jupiter, thus confirming the Copernican account of the movement of the celestial bodies. The letter itself was to be sent to the Doge in Venice, with a telescope that Galileo intended to present him. On a draft of that letter which he happened to have in hand, Galileo made the critical notes of his observations, which appear on the bottom half of the sheet. The translation of the bottom half into English appears below. *Courtesy of the Special Collections Library, University of Michigan.*

stars" had fortunately been written down. His letter remained unsent; at the bottom of the sheet he wrote the following note:

> On the 8th thus: [he inserts a sketch showing Jupiter and three stars now closer to one another and nearly equidistant from one another, and *all three to the west of Jupiter!*]

This created a serious theoretical problem for Galileo, because at this time the assumption that the newly discovered stars were fixed had not been seriously doubted. Therefore their appearance on the other side of Jupiter had to be accounted for by Jupiter's movements. On the 8th he added the note:

> It [Jupiter's movement] was therefore direct and not retrograde.

If, on the 8th, Jupiter was to the east of all three stars, and the day before Jupiter had been to the west of two of them, Jupiter must have moved, and moved in a way that was *contrary* to reliable astronomical calculations! One can imagine Galileo's agitation as he waited for the observations of the following night; could his direct observations and his calculations remain so sharply inconsistent? On the 9th it was too cloudy to observe, but on the 10th, Jupiter apparently had moved back to the west, now apparently obscuring the third star, and the other two were again observed to the east of the planet! On 11 January a similar pattern was observed, but on this night Galileo later wrote:

> The star nearer Jupiter was half the size of the other, and very close to the other, whereas the other evenings all three of the said stars appeared of equal size and equally far apart.

Clearly, something had to give. From the accepted theories and beliefs a prediction confidently could be drawn, a deduction concerning the movements of Jupiter, which—if those three new stars were fixed, and Galileo's observations were accurate—did not take place. One could save the belief that those new stars were fixed by somehow revamping the entire set of astronomical calculations, but these were not in serious doubt; or, one could challenge the accuracy of Galileo's observations—which is what some of his critics later sought to do, calling his telescope an instrument of the devil. Galileo himself had no doubt about what he had seen, and he grasped quickly which element in the set of accepted hypotheses had to be relinquished, to the great distress of his dogmatic opponents. His note on the observation of the 11th continued:

> . . . from which it appears that around Jupiter there are three moving stars invisible to everyone to this time.

And these three moving stars, he later wrote,

> . . . revolved round Jupiter in the same manner as Venus and Mercury revolved round the sun.

The observations of the following nights confirmed this revolutionary conclusion, which, together with his earlier observations of the moon, cast serious doubt on the account of celestial bodies that had been widely and dogmatically affirmed for many centuries.

On 13 January 1610, Galileo observed a fourth "star," and the four major satellites of Jupiter had been discovered. These observations provided very strong confirmation of the Copernican hypothesis—an account of the celestial bodies that was difficult to reconcile with the established theological doctrine of Galileo's time. Many moons of Jupiter have been discovered since, but these four moons—Ganymede, Io, Europa, and Callisto—are appropriately called "the Galilean satellites." On a clear night, when Jupiter is visible in the sky, the revolutions of the Galilean satellites around the planet may be readily confirmed with no more than an ordinary pair of binoculars.

The ultimate success of the Copernican account of the solar system was due not merely to its greater simplicity, but to its correctness, made manifest in the much larger body of facts it was able to account for, and the remarkable predictions deducible from the theory that were very soon confirmed beyond reasonable doubt.

13.4 Classification as Hypothesis

It is a mistake to suppose that hypotheses are important only in the advanced sciences, such as physics and chemistry, but play no role in the so-called descriptive sciences, such as botany or history. In fact, description itself is based on, or embodies, hypotheses. Hypotheses are as critical to the various systems of classification in biology as they are to interpretation in history, and as they are to all knowledge in the social sciences.

In the science of history the importance of hypotheses is easily shown. Many historians seek explanations of past events that can account for them, and that can be confirmed by other recorded events. For some it is some larger purpose or pattern, religious or naturalistic, that explains the entire course of recorded history. For others, who reject such cosmic designs, the study of the past nevertheless reveals some historical laws that explain some past sequences and can then be used to predict some future events. Both of these two groups conceive of history as a theoretical science, not one that is merely descriptive; for both the role of hypothesis is central to the historian's enterprise.

A third group sets a more modest goal. For them the task of historians is simply to chronicle the past, to present an accurate description of past events in chronological order. Their concern is with the facts themselves, rather than with theories about the facts, so it might seem that they have no need of hypotheses.

However, past events are not so easily chronicled as this view would have us believe. The past itself simply is not available for this kind of bare description. What *is* available are records of the past, and traces of the past. We have government archives, epic poems, the writings of earlier historians, the artifacts unearthed by archeological excavations, and so on. It is from a great variety of facts like these that historians must infer the nature of the past events they aim to describe. They cannot do this without some hypotheses. Not all hypotheses are general; some are particular, and with particular hypotheses historians seek to convert the data at hand into evidence for their account of the events in question.

Historians are detectives on a grand scale. Their methods are the same, and their difficulties too. The evidence is scanty, and much of it has been destroyed by intervening wars or natural disasters. False or misleading clues throw detectives off the scent, and similarly, many existing "records" are falsifications of the past, perhaps unintentional, such as the writings of earlier, uncritical historians. The methods of science must be used by good detectives and good historians both, and even those historians who seek to limit themselves to the bare description of past events must work from some hypotheses. They are theorists in spite of themselves.

Biologists are in a more favorable position. The facts with which they deal are present and available for inspection. To describe the flora and fauna of a region, biologists are not obliged to draw elaborate inferences, as historians are, because they can perceive the data directly. Their descriptions are not casual or random, but highly systematic. They *classify* plants and animals, and do not merely describe them. But classification and description are, at bottom, the same process. To describe an animal as carnivorous is to classify it as a carnivore; to classify it as a reptile is to describe it as reptilian. To describe any object as having a certain attribute is to classify it as a member of the class of objects having that attribute.

Scientific **classification** involves not merely a single division of objects into groups, but further subdivision of each group into subgroups and subclasses, and so on. Classification is also the tool of our inquiry when we play "Twenty Questions"—but it is in fact a nearly universal tool, because it answers an almost universal need. Primitive people needed to sort the poisonous from the edible, the dangerous from the harmless, and so forth. We all draw distinctions, and we do so more meticulously with respect to the matters that chiefly concern us. The farmer's vegetables he will classify with greatest care, while treating all the flowers, in which he has no interest, as weeds. The florist will give delicate care to the classification of flowers, but may treat all the farmer's crops merely as "produce."

Two basic motives lead us to classify things. One is practical, the other theoretical. In any library, with many thousands of volumes, books could not be found if they were not shelved according to some system of classification. The larger the number of objects with which we deal, the greater is the need to classify them. In museums, libraries, large department stores, this practical need is plain.

The theoretical object of classification is less obvious. Alternative schemes of classification are neither true nor false. Objects may be described in different ways, from different points of view. The system of classification adopted will depend on the purpose or interest of the classifier. A librarian will classify books according to their subject matter; a bookbinder according to the material of their leaves and bindings, a bibliophile by date of publication and perhaps by rarity; a shipper by weight and size—and there will be other schemes of classification as well.

What is the special interest of scientists, leading them to prefer one scheme of classification over another? The scientist seeks knowledge, not merely of this or that particular fact, but of the general laws to which the facts conform, and of their causal interrelations. One scheme of classification is better than another, from the scientific point of view, to the extent that it is more fruitful in suggesting scientific laws, and more helpful in the formulation of explanatory hypotheses.

The theoretical, or scientific motivation for classifying objects is the desire to increase our knowledge of them, to achieve insight into their attributes, their similarities and differences, and their interrelations. Classification with a narrowly practical purpose—dangerous and harmless, or flying and swimming—will not much advance that understanding. The rattlesnake and the wild boar will go into one class, the grass snake and the domestic pig into the other; the bats and the birds will go into one class, the whales and the fishes in another. But snakes and boars are profoundly different, whereas whales and bats are profoundly like one another. Being warm-blooded or not, bearing young alive or laying eggs, are much more important characteristics than dangerousness on which to base a system of classification.

A characteristic is important when it indicates the presence of other characteristics. When an attribute is causally connected with many other attributes, it can serve in the framing of a greater number of causal laws, and of more general explanatory hypotheses. That classification scheme is best which is based on the most important characteristics of the objects to be classified. We cannot know in advance which these are, because we cannot know in advance the causal connections we aim to learn. So scientists classify *hypothetically*. Different classification schemes are tried, with the understanding that later they may be improved on or rejected. Later investigations may reveal other characteristics that are involved in a greater number of causal laws and explanatory hypotheses, and we will then revise the classification scheme so as to base our categories on it.

It is true that classification tends to be more important in the early or less developed stages of a science, but it need not diminish in importance as that science develops. Taxonomy is a legitimate, important, and still growing branch of biology, in which earlier systems of classification have been abandoned in favor of others that prove more productive. And some classificatory tools—such as the periodic table of the elements—remain valuable to the chemist.

Hypotheses in history are illuminated by these biological considerations. Historians, too, focus on what they find to be most important in increasing our understanding of past events. Life is too short to permit the description of past events in *complete* detail, so every description by a historian must be selective, recording only some of its features. How may that selection be made? Of course historians want to focus on what is important, ignoring the insignificant. Historians, like biologists and other scientists, regard those aspects of events as important that enter most widely into the formulation of causal laws and explanatory hypotheses—always subject to correction in the light of further research, of course. Early historians emphasized the political and military aspects of events, ignoring other attributes we now think to be important. The turn to economic and social attributes brought enormous changes in the work and the products of historians; today we go beyond economic and social issues to attend to cultural and other characteristics that are now thought to be causally related to a maximum number of others. And so the decision to focus on one rather than another set of attributes embodies some hypothesis about which characteristics really are important. Some such hypotheses are required before historians can even begin to do any systematic describing of the past. It is this *hypothetical* character of classification and description that leads us to regard hypothesis as the all-pervasive method of scientific inquiry.

EXERCISES

In each of the following passages,

a. What data are to be explained?

b. What hypotheses are proposed to explain them?

c. Evaluate the hypotheses in terms of the criteria presented in Section 13.3, pages 569–572.

1. In an unusual logjam of contradictory claims, a revolutionary new model of the universe, as a soccer ball, arrived on astronomers' desks in October of 2003—at least slightly deflated.

Based on an analysis of maps of the Big Bang, Dr. Jeffrey Weeks and colleagues, from Canton, NY, suggest that space is a kind of 12-sided hall of mirrors, in which the illusion of infinity is created by looking out and seeing multiple copies of the same stars.

If his model is correct, Dr. Weeks said, it would rule out one variant of the Big Bang theory that asserts that our own observable universe is just a bubble among others in a realm of vastly larger extent. "It means we can just about see the whole universe now." Dr. Weeks said.

Other astronomers, led by Dr. David Spergel of Princeton, said that their analysis of the same data had probably already ruled out the soccer-ball universe. The two groups of scientists, who have been in intense communication in recent days, disagree about whether the soccer ball universe has been refuted. But they all agree that what is amazing about this debate is that the controversy will actually be settled soon, underscoring the power of modern data to resolve issues that were once considered almost metaphysical.

In the scientific journal *Nature* Dr. Weeks wrote: "Since antiquity our ancestors have wondered whether our universe is finite or infinite. Now, after more than two millennia of speculation, observational data might finally settle this ancient question."

Dr. Weeks and his colleagues propose that the universe is 12-sided, a dodecahedron. The waves appearing in a radio map of the universe when it was very young indicate, he argues, that if you go far enough in one direction you would find yourself back where you started, like a cursor disappearing off the left side of a computer screen and reappearing on the right. Thus when cosmic radiation intersects the edges of the universe it would make identical circles on opposite sides of the sky—six pairs of circles, 35 degrees in diameter, in the case of Dr. Weeks' dodecahedron.

Dr. Max Tegmark, a cosmologist at the University of Pennsylvania, observed: "What's nice is that this is so testable. It's the truth or it's dead. The data are actually already out there; it's just a question of sifting through them. We ought to have seen those circles." So far the circles have not showed up. "Is space infinite or is it not?" Dr. Tegmark asked. "This is what got Giordano Bruno burned at the stake!"

—Reported in *Nature,* 9 October 2003

2. Population clusters—groups of persons who are found to buy the same things, get their entertainment from the same sources, exhibit similar voting patterns, and generally behave in quite similar ways—are of

growing interest. Michael J. Weiss has distinguished some 62 of these clusters, which he calls "distinctive lifestyle types." He also names them, and highlights some of their peculiarities.

In the *Towns and Gowns* cluster, for example, tequila is far more popular than elsewhere, and twice as many people watch the soap opera "Another World" there than do people elsewhere. In the *Military Quarters* cluster people are four times as likely to watch the TV show "Hard Copy" as the average American. Among the young, middle-class Americans in suburbia, furniture refinishing, downhill skiing, and cats are abnormally popular, while chess and tractor pulls are abnormally unpopular.

Lifestyle clusters are found useful by businesses seeking customers, by candidates seeking votes, by nonprofit organizations seeking new contributors, and so on. What may appear trivial can be very revealing. In Washington, DC, Weiss observes, "there is a fault line between the fans of Brie cheese, who tend to hold down executive jobs and write the laws, and those of Kraft Velveeta, who maintain the service economy." He asks: "What prompts some of us to eat Brie and others to devour Velveeta cheese?"

—Michael J. Weiss, *The Clustered World* (Boston: Little, Brown, 2000)

3. Monkeypox, a viral disease related to smallpox but less infectious and less deadly, was detected for the first time in the Americas in 2003. At least 20 cases have been reported, in three Midwestern states, Wisconsin, Illinois and Indiana, according to the Centers for Disease Control and Prevention.

The patients ranged in age from 4 to 48, and became ill between May 15th and June 3, 2003. All had direct or close contact with ill prairie dogs, which have become common household pets, and which might have caught monkeypox from another species, possibly Gambian giant pouched rats, which are imported as pets from West or Central Africa, where the disease had long occurred. Monkeypox in Africa is carried mainly by squirrels but is named after monkeys because it often kills them.

Several patients in the American outbreak work for veterinarians or pet stores that sold prairie dogs and Gambian rats. By quickly identifying the animals that can be infected with monkeypox, health officials hope to eliminate them before the disease becomes endemic in the Americas.

—Reported in the *The New York Times*, 9 June 2003

4. A small study of heart-disease patients testing a hypothesis so improbable that its principal investigator says he gave it a one-in-10,000 chance of succeeding has found that just a few treatments with an experimental drug, developed by Esperion Therapeutics of Ann Arbor, Michigan, reversed what may be the equivalent of years worth of plaque in coronary arteries.

Forty-seven heart attack patients were randomly assigned to be infused with either a concentration of a substance that mimics high density lipoprotein (or HDL, the substance that removes cholesterol from arteries) or to be infused with an inactive saline solution, which served as a control.

After 5 weekly infusions those who got the experimental drug had a 4.2 percent decrease in the volume of plaque in their coronary arteries, while those who had saline infusions had, if anything, a slight increase in their plaque.

"Until now," said Dr. Steven Nissen, a cardiologist at the Cleveland Clinic who directed the study, "the paradigm has been to prevent disease by lowering bad cholesterol (LDL). If you get the bad cholesterol low enough, the plaques don't build up in the artery walls. This experiment says you can also *remove* the disease in the wall of the artery."

—Reported in the *Journal of the American Medical Association*, 5 November 2003

5. Boy babies tend to be about 100 grams heavier on average than girl babies, but it has never been explained, until recently, why that is so. Investigators were unsure whether the increased weight was to be explained by the fact that mothers of boys took in more energy, or because (when the fetus was male) those mothers used the energy taken in more efficiently.

Dr. Rulla M. Tamimi, of the Harvard School of Public Health, sought to resolve this uncertainty by measuring the intake of calories. During the second trimester of their pregnancy, 244 women in Boston were asked to record their dietary intake in full detail. The data collected were later correlated with the resultant births. Women carrying boys, Dr. Tamimi found, took in (as carbohydrates, fats, or proteins) about 10 percent more calories than women carrying girls. It is intake, and not efficiency of use, that makes the difference.

But what accounts for that difference of intake? Dr. Tamimi speculated that it may be triggered by some signal from the testosterone given off by the male fetuses.

—Reported in the *British Medical Journal*, June 2003

6. Humans, apes, and dolphins are highly social animals with large brains; they have been shown to be aware of themselves by recognizing themselves in a mirror. Most animals pay very little attention to their reflections in a mirror. Elephants are like humans in being large-brained and empathic, but they don't share a common ancestor with humans the way apes do. Might they also recognize an image of themselves?

   Yes, they do. Elephants at the Bronx Zoo, in New York City, inspected themselves with their trunks while staring at their reflections in a huge mirror. One of the elephants (but only one) completed the highest level of self-recognition, called the "mark test." Researchers placed a white X above one eye of each elephant. After approaching the mirror, this elephant touched the mark with her trunk 12 times in 90 seconds—confirmation that she believed that what she saw in the mirror was indeed herself.

   —Reported by Diana Reiss, of the Wildlife Conservation Society and Columbia University, in *Proceedings of the National Academy of Sciences*, November 7, 2006

7. The Nobel Prize for chemistry for 2003 was shared by Dr. Peter Agre, who encountered a new protein by serendipity. He had been studying a particular protein found in blood when he found another protein contaminating his sample. Trying to develop an antibody that would hook on to the protein he was studying, Dr. Agre found that the antibody hooked on to the contaminating protein instead—which turned out to be one of the most abundant proteins found in blood samples, although no one had identified it before.

   But what did it do? He looked for similar proteins and found some—whose functions also were not known—in the roots of plants. The situation grew "curiouser and curiouser" Dr. Agre said. Finally he tried testing whether the new protein could be a water channel. That such channels might exist had been suggested long ago—but diffusion had then seemed to explain water movement, and specific channels had never been discovered.

   To test the water channel hypothesis, Dr. Agre added the gene that produced the mystery protein to the eggs of frogs. The modified eggs, placed in fresh water, quickly swelled and burst, strongly confirming that theory. "The eggs exploded like popcorn," Dr. Agre said. The newly discovered proteins, called "aquaporins," little wider than a water molecule, have recently been found also in human kidneys, where water is extracted from urine and recycled.

"This really fell into our laps," Dr. Agre said when his Nobel Prize was announced. "Being lucky is an important ingredient in scientific success."

8. Early in the eighteenth century Edmund Halley asked: "Why is the sky dark at night?" This apparently naive question is not easy to answer, because if the universe had the simplest imaginable structure on the largest possible scale, the background radiation of the sky would be intense. Imagine a static infinite universe, that is, a universe of infinite size in which the stars and galaxies are stationary with respect to one another. A line of sight in any direction will ultimately cross the surface of a star, and the sky should appear to be made up of overlapping stellar disks. The apparent brightness of a star's surface is independent of its distance, so that everywhere the sky should be as bright as the surface of an average star. Since the sun is an average star, the entire sky, day and night, should be about as bright as the surface of the sun. The fact that it is not was later characterized as Olbers' paradox (after the eighteenth-century German astronomer Heinrich Olbers). The paradox applies not only to starlight but also to all other regions of the electromagnetic spectrum. It indicates that there is something fundamentally wrong with the model of a static infinite universe, but it does not specify what.

—Adrian Webster, "The Cosmic Radiation Background," *Scientific American,* August 1974

9. Swedish researchers, collaborating with colleagues in South Africa, found that dung beetles active during the day detect polarity patterns in sunlight and rely on those patterns to find their way out of great masses of elephant dung. Dr. Marie Dacke, of the University of Lund, noticed subsequently that on moonlit nights one beetle species worked (rolling dung) particularly late. Could they have been relying upon the polarization of moonlight?

Researchers set up polarizing filters to shift the moonbeams—and sure enough, the African beetle, *Scarabaeus zambesianus* changed direction to compensate. When the polarization of the moonlight under the filter was rotated by 90 degrees, they found that beetles under that filter deviated from their course by almost exactly 90 degrees. "This is the first proof," writes Dr. Dacke in her report in *Nature* of 3 July 2003, "that any animal can use polarized moonlight for orientation."

10. For centuries (since the 1500s in Scandinavia) people have puzzled over lemmings, northern rodents whose populations surge and crash so quickly and so regularly that they inspired an enduring myth: that lemmings commit mass suicide when their numbers grow too large, pitching themselves off cliffs to their deaths in a foamy sea.

Scientists debunked that notion decades ago, but have never been certain what causes the rapid boom-and-bust population cycles—a mystery in ecology that has been hotly debated. "There have been several dozen hypotheses," said Dr. Oliver Gilg, an ecologist at the University of Helsinki in Finland, "and scientists were sticking so closely to their hypotheses that they were almost killing each other." But Dr. Gilg, the author of a recent study published in the journal *Science,* provides a single hypothesis that his team of researchers claims provides the entire explanation.

The rapid population cycles have nothing to do with self-annihilation, they contend, but everything to do with hungry predators. After 15 years of research they have discovered that the actions of four predator species—snowy owls, arctic foxes, seabirds called long-tailed skuas, and the weasel-like stoats—account for the four-year cycles during which lemming populations rapidly explode, and then nearly disappear. After creating a model based only on those four predators, they found that the model predicted precisely the numerical fluctuation of lemming populations in nature.

—Reported in *Science,* 31 October 2003

SUMMARY

In this chapter we explored the principles that underlie the methods of science.

In Section 13.1, we distinguished scientific from unscientific explanations, the former being always hypothetical and empirically verifiable, the latter dogmatic in spirit and not testable by propositions that can be deduced from them.

In Section 13.2, we examined the method of science, relying on the confirmation of hypotheses. We identified the seven stages that may be distinguished in any scientific inquiry:

1. The identification of some problem
2. The construction of some preliminary hypothesis
3. The collection of additional data in the light of that preliminary hypothesis
4. The formulation of a fully explanatory hypothesis supported by the data collected
5. The deduction of further consequences from the explanatory hypothesis
6. The testing of the consequences deduced

7. The application of the theory developed

In Section 13.3, we explored the evaluation of alternative scientific hypotheses. We identified criteria with which we might choose between competing hypotheses:

1. The compatibility of a theory with the body of theory previously established
2. The degree of predictive or explanatory power that a new theory manifests
3. The relative simplicity of competing theories

We illustrated these criteria with events in the history of science—most notably, the replacement of the geocentric (or Ptolemaic) theory of the solar system with the heliocentric (or Copernican) theory, confirmed by the remarkable observations of Galileo Galilei.

In Section 13.4, we discussed classification, an intellectual instrument that is greatly valued in the social and biological sciences as well as in the physical sciences, noting that every classificatory scheme suggests general truths and invites the formation of explanatory hypotheses.

End Notes

[1]D. Biello, "Island Lizards Morph in Evolutionary Experiment," *Scientific American*, 17 November 2006.

[2]*On the Old Saying: "That Might Be Right in Theory"* [*Uber den Gemeinspruch: Das mag in der Theorie richtig sein*], 1793, translated by E. B. Ashton (Philadelphia: University of Pennsylvania Press, 1974).

[3]This letter, dated 7 January 1610, apparently was written over a period of many days. It, and other notes taken by Galileo during these momentous days, are discussed in detail in Jean Meeus, "Galileo's First Records of Jupiter's Satellites," *Sky and Telescope*, February 1964; in Stillman Drake, "Galileo's First Telescopic Observations," *Journal of the History of Astronomy*, 1976, p. 153; and in Dale P. Cruikshank and David Morrison, "The Galilean Satellites of Jupiter," *Scientific American*, May 1976. A photocopy of the original sketch Galileo made to record his observations, his notes appearing on it in Italian, is reproduced in Figure 13-1, through the courtesy of the library of the University of Michigan, Ann Arbor, in whose rare-book room that precious manuscript is held.

[4]That Galileo began this letter on 7 January 1610 is clear; the exact days of that month on which he continued it, with sketches and notes, is a matter about which scholars disagree.

Probability

14.1 Alternative Conceptions of Probability

Probability is the central evaluative concept in all inductive logic. The theory of probability, as the American philosopher Charles Sanders Pierce put it, "is simply the science of logic quantitatively treated." The mathematical applications of this theory go far beyond the concerns of this book, but it is fitting to conclude our treatment of inductive logic with an analysis of the concept of probability and a brief account of its practical applications.

Scientific theories, and the causal laws that they encompass, can be no more than probable. Inductive arguments, even at their very best, fall short of the certainty that attaches to valid deductive arguments. We assign to theories, or to hypotheses of any sort, a *degree* of probability expressed discursively. As one example, we may assert, on the evidence we now have, that it is "highly probable" that Einstein's theory of relativity is correct. And as another example, although we cannot be certain that there is no life on other planets in our solar system, we can say that the probability of any theory that entails such life, in the light of what we know about these planets, is very low. We do not normally assign a numerical value to the probability of theories in this sense.

However, we can and do assign numbers to the probability of events in many contexts. The number we assign to the probability of an event is called the *numerical coefficient of probability,* and that number may be very useful. How can such numbers be reliably assigned? To answer this question we must distinguish two additional senses in which the concept of "probability" is used:

1. The *a priori* conception of probability
2. The relative frequency conception of probability

We use the first of these when we toss a coin and suppose that the probability that it will show heads is ½. We use the second of these when we say that the probability that an American woman of age 25 will live at least one additional year is .971. Games of chance—dice and cards—gave rise to the investigation of probability in the first sense,* the uses of mortality statistics gave rise to the investigation of probability in the second sense,† in both cases during the seventeenth century. The calculations in the two cases were of different kinds, leading eventually to the two different interpretations of the coefficient of probability. Both are important.

The ***a priori* theory of probability** asks, in effect, what a rational person ought to believe about some event under consideration, and assigns a number between 0 and 1 to represent the degree of belief that is rational. If we are completely convinced that the event will take place, we assign the number 1. If we believe that the event cannot possibly happen, our belief that it will happen is assigned the number 0. When we are unsure, the number assigned will be between 0 and 1. Probability is predicated of an event according to the degree to which one rationally believes that that event will occur. Probability is predicated of a proposition according to the degree to which a completely rational person would believe it.

How (in this theory) do we determine rationally, when we are unsure, what number between 0 and 1 ought to be assigned? We are unsure, in the classical view, because our knowledge is partial; if we knew everything about a coin being flipped, we could confidently predict its trajectory and its final resting position. But there is an enormous amount about that coin and its flip that we do not and cannot know. What we mainly know is this: The coin has two sides, and we have no reason to believe it more likely that it will come to rest on one side than on the other. So we consider all the possible outcomes that are (so far as we know) equally probable; in the case of a flipped coin there are two—heads and tails. Of the two, heads is only one. The probability of heads is therefore one over two, ½, and this number, .5, is said to be the probability of the event in question.

Similarly, when a deck of randomly shuffled cards is about to be dealt, they will come off the deck in exactly the sequence they are in, determined by the outcome of the preceding shuffle, which we do not know. We know only that there are 13 cards of each suit (out of a total of 52 in the deck) and therefore the probability that the first card dealt will be a spade is 13/52 or exactly ¼.

This is called the *a priori theory of probability* because we make the numerical assignment, ¼, before we run any trials with that deck of cards. If the deck is regular and the shuffle was fair, we think it is not necessary to take a sample, but only to consider the antecedent conditions: 13 spades, 52 cards,

*Pierre de Fermat (1608–1665) and Blaise Pascal, both distinguished mathematicians, reflected upon probabilities when corresponding about the proper division of the stakes when a game of chance had been interrupted.

†Captain John Graunt published (in 1662) calculations concerning what could be inferred from death records that had been kept in London from 1592.

and an honest deal. Any one card (as far as we know) has as much chance as any other of being dealt first.

In general, to compute the probability of an event's occurring in given circumstances, we divide the number of ways it can occur by the total number of possible outcomes of those circumstances, provided that there is no reason to believe that any one of those possible outcomes is more likely than any other. The probability of an event, in the *a priori* theory of probability, is thus expressed by a fraction, whose denominator is the number of equipossible outcomes and whose numerator is the number of outcomes that will successfully yield the event in question. Such numerical assignments ("successes over possibilities") are rational, convenient, and very useful.

There is an alternative view of probability. In this view the probability assigned to an event must depend on the *relative frequency* with which the event takes place. Earlier we suggested that the probability of a 25-year-old American woman living at least one additional year is .971. This can be learned only by examining the entire class of 25-year-old American women, and determining how many of them do indeed live, or have lived, at least one additional year. Only *after* we learn the mortality rates for that class of women can we make the numerical assignment.

We distinguish, in this theory, the *reference class* (25-year-old American women, in the example given) and the *attribute* of interest (living at least one additional year, in this example.) The probability assigned is the measure of the relative frequency with which the members of the class exhibit the attribute in question. In this theory also, probability is expressed as a fraction (and also often expressed in decimal form), but the denominator is in this case the number of members in the reference class and the numerator is the number of class members that have the desired attribute. If the number of male automobile drivers in California between the ages of 16 and 24 is y, and the number of such drivers who are involved in an automobile accident in the course of a year is x, the probability of an accident among such drivers in any given year we assign as x/y. The reference class here is the set of drivers described in certain ways, and the attribute is the fact of involvement in an automobile accident within some specified period. "Rational belief" is not at issue here. In the relative frequency theory of probability, probability is defined as *the relative frequency with which members of a class exhibit a specified attribute.*

Note that in both theories the probabilities assigned are relative to the evidence available. For the relative frequency theory this is obvious: The probability of a given attribute must vary with the reference class chosen for the computation. If the male automobile drivers in the reference class are between the ages of 36 and 44, the relative frequency of accidents will be lower; drivers in that range have, in fact, fewer accidents, and hence the computed probability of an accident will be lower. If the reference class consisted of females rather than males, that would again change the coefficient of probability. Probability is relative to the evidence.

This is also true in the *a priori* theory of probability. An event can be assigned a probability only on the basis of the evidence available to the person making the assignment. After all, a person's "rational belief" may change with changes in the knowledge that person possesses. For example, suppose that two people are watching a deck of cards being shuffled, and one of them happens to see, because of the dealer's slip, that the top card is black, but not its suit. The second observer sees nothing but the shuffle. If asked to estimate the probability of the first card's being a spade, the first observer will assign the probability ½, because he knows that there are 26 black cards, of which half are spades. The second observer will assign the probability ¼, because he knows only that there are 13 spades in the deck of 52 cards. Different probabilities are assigned by the two observers to the same event. Neither has made a mistake; both have assigned the correct probability relative to the evidence available to each—even if the card turns out to be a club. No event has any probability in and of itself, in this view, and therefore, with different sets of evidence, the probabilities may well vary.

These two accounts of probability—the relative frequency account and the *a priori* account—are in fundamental agreement in holding that probability is relative to the evidence. They are also in agreement in holding that a numerical assignment of probability can usually be made for a given event. It is possible to reinterpret the number assigned on the *a priori* theory as being a "shortcut" estimate of relative frequency. Thus the probability that a flipped coin, if it is fair, will show heads when it comes to rest may be calculated as a relative frequency; it will be the relative frequency with which the coin does show heads when it is randomly flipped a thousand, or ten thousand times. As the number of random flips increases (supposing the coin truly balanced), the fraction representing the relative frequency of heads will approach .5 more and more closely. We may call .5 the *limit of the relative frequency* of that event. In the light of such possible reinterpretation of numerical assignments, some theorists hold that the relative frequency theory is the more fundamental of the two. It is also true, however, that in a great many contexts the *a priori* theory is the simpler and more convenient theory to employ; we will rely chiefly on the latter as we go forward.

14.2 The Probability Calculus

The probability of single events, as we have seen, can often be determined. Knowing (or assuming) these, we can go on to calculate the probability of some complex event—an event that may be regarded as a whole of which its component single events are parts. To illustrate, the probability of drawing a spade from a shuffled deck of cards is ¼, as we have seen, relying on the *a priori* theory of probability. What, then, is the probability of drawing *two spades in succession* from a deck of playing cards? Drawing the first spade is the first component; drawing the second spade is the second; drawing two spades in succession is the complex event whose probability we may want to calculate. When it is known how the component events are related to each other, the probabilities of the complex event can be calculated from the probabilities of its components.

The **calculus of probability** is the branch of mathematics that permits such calculation. Here we explore only its elementary outline. Knowing the likelihood of certain outcomes in our everyday lives can be important; application of the probability calculus, therefore, can be extremely helpful. Mastery of its basic theorems is one of the most useful products of the study of logic.

The probability calculus can be most easily explained in terms of games of chance—dice, cards, and the like—because the artificially restricted universe created by the rules of such games makes possible the straightforward application of probability theorems. In this exposition, the *a priori* theory of probability is used, but all of these results can, with a minimum of reinterpretation, be expressed and justified in terms of the relative frequency theory as well.

Two elementary theorems will be discussed.

A. With the first we can calculate the probability of a complex event consisting of the *joint occurrences* of its components: the probability of two events both happening, or all the events of a specified set happening.

B. With the second we can calculate the probability of a complex event consisting of *alternative occurrences:* the probability that at least one (or more) of a given set of alternative events will occur. We take these in turn.

A. PROBABILITY OF JOINT OCCURRENCES

Suppose we wish to learn the probability of getting two heads in two flips of a coin. Call these two components *a* and *b;* there is a very simple theorem that enables us to compute the probability of *both a and b.* It is called the **product theorem,** and it involves merely multiplying the two fractions representing the probabilities of the component events. There are four distinct possible outcomes when two coins are tossed. These may be shown most clearly in a table:

First Coin	*Second Coin*
H	H
H	T
T	H
T	T

There is no reason to expect any one of these four cases more than another, so we regard them as equipossible. The case (two heads) about which we are asking occurs in only one of the four equipossible events, so the probability of getting two heads in two flips of a coins is $\frac{1}{4}$. We can *calculate* this directly: The joint occurrence of two heads is equal to the probability of getting a head on the first flip ($\frac{1}{2}$) multiplied by the probability of getting a head on the second flip ($\frac{1}{2}$), or $\frac{1}{2} \times \frac{1}{2} = \frac{1}{4}$. However, this simple multiplication succeeds only when the two events are **independent events**—that is, when the occurrence of the one does not affect the probability of the occurrence of the other.

The product theorem for independent events asserts that the probability of the joint occurrence of two independent events is equal to the product of their separate probabilities. It is written as

$$P(a \text{ and } b) = P(a) \times P(b)$$

where $P(a)$ and $P(b)$ are the separate probabilities of the two events, and $P(a$ and $b)$ designates the probability of their joint occurrence.

Applied to another case, what is the probability of getting 12 when rolling two dice? Two dice will show twelve points only if each of them shows six points. Each die has six sides, any one of which is as likely to be face up after a roll as any other. When a is the event of the first die showing 6, $P(a) = \frac{1}{6}$. And when b is the event of the second die showing 6, $P(b) = \frac{1}{6}$. The complex event of the two dice showing 12 is constituted by the joint occurrence of a and b. By the product theorem, $P(a \text{ and } b) = \frac{1}{6} \times \frac{1}{6} = \frac{1}{36}$, which is the probability of getting a 12 on one roll of two dice. The same result is shown if we lay out, in a table, all the separate equipossible outcomes of the roll of two dice. There are 36 possible outcomes, and only one of them is favorable to getting 12.

We do not need to restrict ourselves to two components. The product theorem may be *generalized* to cover the joint occurrence of any number of independent events. If we draw a card from a shuffled deck, replace it and draw again, replace it again and draw a third time, the likelihood of getting a spade in each drawing is not affected by success or failure in the other drawings. The probability of getting a spade in any one drawing is $\frac{13}{52}$, or $\frac{1}{4}$. The probability of getting three spades in three drawings, if the card is replaced after each drawing, is $\frac{1}{4} \times \frac{1}{4} \times \frac{1}{4} = \frac{1}{64}$. The general product theorem thus allows us to compute the probability of the joint occurrence of any number of independent events.

But suppose the events are not independent? Suppose that success in one case has an effect on the probability of success in another case? The examples thus far need take no account of any relationship among the component events. And yet component events may be related in ways that require more careful calculation. Consider a revised version of the example just given. Suppose we seek the probability of drawing three successive spades from a shuffled deck, *but the cards withdrawn are not replaced.* If each card drawn is not returned to the deck before the next drawing, the outcomes of the earlier drawings *do* have an effect on the outcomes of the later drawings.

If the first card drawn is a spade, then for the second draw there are only 12 spades left among a total of 51 cards, whereas if the first card is *not* a spade, then there are 13 spades left among 51 cards. Where a is the event of drawing a spade from the deck and not replacing it, and b is the event of drawing another spade from among the remaining cards, the probability of b, that is, $P(b \text{ if } a)$, is $12/51$ or $4/17$. And if both a and b occur, the third draw will be made from a deck of 50 cards containing only 11 spades. If c is this last event, then $P(c \text{ if both } a \text{ and } b)$ is $11/50$. Thus, the probability that all three are spades, if three cards are drawn from a deck and not replaced, is, according to the product theorem, $13/52 \times 12/51 \times 11/50$, or $11/850$. This is *less* than the probability of getting three spades in three draws when the cards drawn are replaced before drawing again, which was to be expected, because replacing a spade increases the probability of getting a spade on the next draw.

The general product theorem can be applied to real-world problems of consequence, as in the following true account. A California teenager, afflicted with chronic leukemia that would soon kill her if untreated, could be saved only if a donor with matching bone marrow were found. When all efforts to locate such a donor failed, her parents decided to try to have another child, hoping that a successful bone-marrow transplant might then be possible. But the girl's father first had to have his vasectomy reversed, for which there was only a 50 percent (.5) chance of success. And if that were successful, the mother, 45 years old at the time, would have only a .73 chance of becoming pregnant. And if she did become pregnant, there was only a one-in-four chance (.25) that the baby's marrow would match that of the afflicted daughter. And if there were such a match, there would still be only a .7 chance that the leukemia patient would live through the needed chemotherapy and bone-marrow transplant.

The probability of a successful outcome was seen at the outset to be low, but not hopelessly low. The vasectomy was successfully reversed, and the mother did become pregnant—after which prospects improved. It turned out that the baby did possess matching bone marrow. Then, in 1992, the arduous bone-marrow-transplant procedure was begun. It proved to be a complete success.* What was the probability of this happy outcome at the time of the parents' original decision to pursue it?

---

*Anissa Ayala, the patient, was married a year after the successful transplant; the sister who saved her life, Marissa Ayala, was a flower girl at her wedding. Details of this case were reported in *Life* magazine, December 1993.

EXERCISES

EXAMPLE

1. What is the probability of getting three aces in three successive draws from a deck of cards:

   a. If each card drawn is replaced before the next drawing is made?

   b. If the cards drawn are not replaced?

SOLUTION

a. If each card drawn *is replaced* before the next drawing is made, the component events have absolutely no effect on one another and are therefore *independent*. In this case, $P(a \text{ and } b \text{ and } c) = P(a) \times P(b) \times P(c)$. There are 52 cards in the deck, of which four are aces. So the probability of drawing the first ace, $P(a)$, is $\frac{4}{52}$, or $\frac{1}{13}$. The probability of drawing the second ace, $P(b)$, is likewise $\frac{1}{13}$, as is the probability of drawing the third ace, $P(c)$. So the probability of the joint occurrence of a and b and c is $\frac{1}{13} \times \frac{1}{13} \times \frac{1}{13}$, or $\frac{1}{2,197}$.

b. If the cards drawn are *not replaced*, the component events are *dependent*, not independent. The formula is $P(a \text{ and } b \text{ and } c) = P(a) \times P(b \text{ if } a) \times P(c \text{ if } a \text{ and } b)$. In this case, the probability of drawing the first ace, $P(a)$, remains $\frac{4}{52}$, or $\frac{1}{13}$. But the probability of drawing a second ace if the first card drawn was an ace, $P(b \text{ if } a)$, is $\frac{3}{51}$, or $\frac{1}{17}$. And the probability of drawing a third ace if the first two cards drawn were aces, $P(c \text{ if } a \text{ and } b)$, is $\frac{2}{50}$, or $\frac{1}{25}$. The probability of the joint occurrence of these three dependent events is therefore $\frac{1}{13} \times \frac{1}{17} \times \frac{1}{25}$, or $\frac{1}{5,525}$.

The probability of getting three successive aces in the second case is much lower than in the first, as one might expect, because without replacement the chances of getting an ace in each successive drawing are reduced by success in the preceding drawing.

2. What is the probability of getting tails every time in three tosses of a coin?

3. An urn contains 27 white balls and 40 black balls. What is the probability of getting four black balls in four successive drawings:

   a. If each ball drawn is replaced before making the next drawing?

   b. If the balls are not replaced?

4. What is the probability of rolling three dice so the total number of points that appear on their top faces is 3, three times in a row?

*5. Four men whose houses are built around a square spend an evening celebrating in the center of the square. At the end of the celebration each staggers off to one of the houses, no two going to the same house. What is the probability that each one reached his own house?

6. A dentist has her office in a building with five entrances, all equally accessible. Three patients arrive at her office at the same time. What is the probability that they all entered the building by the same door?

7. On 25 October 2003, at the Santa Anita Racetrack in Arcadia, California, Mr. Graham Stone, from Rapid City, South Dakota, won a single bet in which he had picked the winner of *six successive races*! Mr. Stone had never visited a racetrack; racing fans across the nation were stunned. The winning horses, and the odds of each horse winning, as determined just before the race in which it ran, were as follows:

Winning Horse	Odds
1. Six Perfections	5–1
2. Cajun Beat	22–1
3. Islington	3–1
4. Action This Day	26–1
5. High Chaparral	5–1
6. Pleasantly Perfect	14–1

Mr. Stone's wager cost $8; his payoff was $2,687,661.60.

The odds against such good fortune (or handicapping skill?), we might say in casual conversation, are "a million to one." Mr. Stone's payoff was at a rate far below that. Did he deserve a million-to-one payoff? How would you justify your answer?

8. In each of two closets there are three cartons. Five of the cartons contain canned vegetables. The other carton contains canned fruits: ten cans of pears, eight cans of peaches, and six cans of fruit cocktail. Each can of fruit cocktail contains 300 chunks of fruit of approximately equal size, of which three are cherries. If a child goes into one of the closets, unpacks one of the cartons, opens a can and eats two pieces of its contents, what is the probability that two cherries will be eaten?

9. A player at draw poker holds the seven of spades and the eight, nine, ten, and ace of diamonds. Aware that all the other players are drawing three cards, he figures that any hand he could win with a flush he

could also win with a straight. For which should he draw? (A *straight* consists of any five cards in numerical sequence; a *flush* consists of any five cards all of the same suit.)

***10.** Four students decide they need an extra day to cram for a Monday exam. They leave town for the weekend, returning Tuesday. Producing dated receipts for hotel and other expenses, they explain that their car suffered a flat tire, and that they did not have a spare.

The professor agrees to give them a make-up exam in the form of a single written question. The students take their seats in separate corners of the exam room, silently crowing over their deceptive triumph—until the professor writes the question on the blackboard: "Which tire?"

Assuming that the students had not agreed in advance on the identification of the tire in their story, what is the probability that all four students will identify the same tire?

B. PROBABILITY OF ALTERNATIVE OCCURRENCES

Sometimes we ask: What is the probability of the occurrence of *at least one* of some set of events, their alternative occurrence? This we can calculate if we know or can estimate the probability of each of the component events. The theorem we use is called the **addition theorem.**

For example, one might ask: What is the probability of drawing, from a shuffled deck of cards, *either* a spade *or* a club? Of course the probability of getting either of these outcomes will be greater than the probability of getting one of them, and certainly greater than the probability of getting the two of them jointly. In many cases, like this one, the probability of their alternative occurrence is simply the *sum* of the probability of the components. The probability of drawing a spade is ¼; the probability of drawing a club is ¼; the probability of drawing either a spade or a club is ¼ + ¼ = ½. When the question concerns joint occurrence, we multiply; when the question concerns alternative occurrence, we add.

In the example just above, the two component events are *mutually exclusive;* if one of them happens, the other cannot. If we draw a spade, we cannot draw a club, and vice versa. So the addition theorem, when events are mutually exclusive, is straightforward and simple:

$$P(a \text{ or } b) = P(a) + P(b)$$

This may be generalized to any number of alternatives, *a* or *b*, or *c* or. . . . If all the alternatives are mutually exclusive, the probability of one or another of them taking places is the sum of the probabilities of all of them.

Sometimes we may need to apply both the addition theorem and the product theorem. To illustrate, in the game of poker, a flush (five cards of the same suit) is a very strong hand. What is the probability of such a draw? We calculate first the probability of getting five cards in one given suit—say, spades. That is a joint occurrence, five component events that are certainly not independent, because each spade dealt reduces the probability of getting the next spade. Using the product theorem for dependent probabilities, we get

$$\frac{13}{52} \times \frac{12}{51} \times \frac{11}{50} \times \frac{10}{49} \times \frac{9}{48} = \frac{33}{66{,}640}$$

The same probability applies to a flush in hearts, or diamonds, or clubs. These four different flushes are mutually exclusive alternatives, so the probability of being dealt *any* flush is the sum of them: 33/66,640 + 33/66,640 + 33/66,640 + 33/66,640 = 33/16,660, a little less than .002. No wonder a flush is usually a winning hand.

Alternative events are often *not mutually exclusive,* and when they are not, the calculation becomes more complicated. Consider first an easy case: What is the probability of getting *at least* one head in two flips of a coin? The two components (getting a head on the first flip, or getting one on the second flip) are certainly not mutually exclusive; both could happen. If we simply add their probabilities, we get ½ + ½ = 1, or certainty—and we know that the outcome we are interested in is not certain! This shows that the addition theorem is not directly applicable when the component events are not mutually exclusive. But we can use it *indirectly,* in either of two ways.

First, we can break down the set of favorable cases into mutually exclusive events and then simply add those probabilities. In the coin example, there are three favorable events: head–tail, tail–head, and head–head. The probability of each (calculated using the product theorem) is ¼. The probability of getting at least one of those three mutually exclusive events (using the addition theorem) is the sum of the three: ¾, or .75.

There is another way to reach the same result. We know that no outcome can be both favorable and unfavorable. Therefore the probability of the alternative complex we are asking about will be equal to the probability that not one of the component alternatives occurs, *subtracted from 1.* In the coin example, the only unfavorable outcome is tail–tail. The probability of tail–tail is ¼; hence the probability of a head on *at least one* flip is 1 − ¼ = ¾, or .75, again. Using the notation $\bar{a}$ to designate an event that is *un*favorable to a, we can formulate the theorem for alternative events, where the component events are not mutually exclusive, in this way:

$$P(a) = 1 - P(\bar{a})$$

The probability of an event's occurrence is equal to 1, minus the probability that that event will not occur.*

Sometimes the first method is simpler, sometimes the second. The two methods may be compared using the following illustration: Suppose we have two urns, the first containing two white balls and four black balls, the second containing three white balls and nine black balls. If one ball is drawn at random from each urn, what is the probability of drawing *at least one white ball*? Using the first method we divide the favorable cases into three mutually exclusive alternatives and then sum them: (1) a white ball from the first urn and a black ball from the second ($2/6 \times 9/12 = 1/4$); (2) a black ball from the first urn and a white ball from the second ($4/6 \times 3/12 = 1/6$); and (3) a white ball from both urns ($2/6 \times 3/12 = 1/12$). These being mutually exclusive we can simply add $1/4 + 1/6 + 1/12 = 1/2$. That sum is the probability of drawing at least one white ball. Using the second method we determine the probability of failing, which is the probability of drawing a black ball from both urns: $4/6 \times 9/12$, and subtract that from 1. $1 - 1/2 = 1/2$. The two methods yield the same result, of course.

Application of the probability calculus sometimes leads to a result that, although correct, differs from what we might anticipate after a casual consideration of the facts given. Such a result is called *counterintuitive*. When a problem's solution is counterintuitive, one may be led to judge probability mistakenly, and such "natural" mistakes encourage, at carnivals and elsewhere, the following wager. Three dice are to be thrown; the operator of the gambling booth offers to bet you even money (risk one dollar, and get that dollar back plus one more if you win) that no one of the three dice will show a one. There are six faces on each of the dice, each with a different number; you get three chances for an ace; superficially, this looks like a fair game.

In fact it is *not* a fair game, and hefty profits are reaped by swindlers who capitalize on that counterintuitive reality. The game would be fair only if the appearance of any given number on one of the three dice precludes its appearance on either of the other two dice. That is plainly not true. The unwary player is misled by mistakenly (and subconsciously) supposing mutual exclusivity. Of course, the numbers are not mutually exclusive; some throws will result in the same number appearing on two or three of the dice. The attempt to identify and count all of the possible outcomes, and then to count the

*The reasoning that underlies this formulation of the theorem for alternative occurrences is as follows. The probability coefficient assigned to an event that is certain to occur is 1. For every event it is certain that either it occurs or it does not; a or $\bar{a}$; must be true. Therefore, $P(a \text{ or } \bar{a}) = 1$. Obviously, a and $\bar{a}$; are mutually exclusive, so the probability of one or the other is equal to the sum of their probabilities, that is, $P(a \text{ or } \bar{a}) = P(a) + P(\bar{a})$. So $P(a) + P(\bar{a}) = 1$. By moving $P(\bar{a})$ to the other side of the equation and changing its sign, we get $P(a) = 1 - P(\bar{a})$.

outcomes in which at least one ace appears, quickly becomes frustrating. Because the appearance of any given number does not exclude the appearance of that same number on the remaining dice, the game truly is a swindle—and this becomes evident when the chances of winning are calculated by first determining the probability of *losing* and subtracting that from 1. The probability of any single *non*-ace (a 2, or 3, or 4, or 5, or 6) showing up is $5/6$. The probability of losing is that of getting three non-aces, which (because the dice are independent of one another) is $5/6 \times 5/6 \times 5/6$, which equals $125/216$, or .579! The probability of the player throwing at least one ace, therefore, is $1 - 125/216 = 91/216$, which is .421. This is a gambling game to pass up.

Let us now attempt to work out a moderately complicated problem in probability. The game of craps is played with two dice. The *shooter*, who rolls the dice, wins if a 7 or an 11 turns up on the first roll, but loses if a 2, or 3, or 12 turns up on the first roll. If one of the remaining numbers, 4, 5, 6, 8, 9, or 10, turns up on the first roll, the shooter continues to roll the dice until either that same number turns up again, in which case the shooter wins, or a 7 appears, in which case the shooter loses. Craps is widely believed to be a "fair" game, that is, a game in which the shooter has an even chance of winning. Is this true? Let us calculate the probability that the shooter will win at craps.

To do this, we must first obtain the probabilities that the various numbers will occur. There are 36 different equipossible ways for two dice to fall. Only one of these ways will show a 2, so the probability here is $1/36$. Only one of these ways will show a 12, so here the probability is also $1/36$. There are two ways to throw a 3: 1–2 and 2–1, so the probability of a 3 is $2/36$. Similarly, the probability of getting an 11 is $2/36$. There are three ways to throw a 4: 1–3, 2–2, and 3–1, so the probability of a 4 is $3/36$. Similarly, the probability of getting a 10 is $3/36$. There are four ways to roll a 5 (1–4, 2–3, 3–2, and 4–1), so its probability is $4/36$, and this is also the probability of getting a 9. A 6 can be obtained in any one of five ways (1–5, 2–4, 3–3, 4–2, and 5–1), so the probability of getting a 6 is $5/36$, and the same probability exists for an 8. There are six different combinations that yield 7 (1–6, 2–5, 3–4, 4–3, 5–2, 6–1), so the probability of rolling a 7 is $6/36$.

The probability that the shooter will win on the first roll is the sum of the probability that a 7 will turn up and the probability that an 11 will turn up, which is $6/36 + 2/36 = 8/36$, or $2/9$. The probability of losing on the first roll is the sum of the probabilities of getting a 2, a 3, and a 12, which is $1/36 + 2/36 + 1/36 = 4/36$, or $1/9$. The shooter is twice as likely to win on the first roll as to lose on the first roll; however, the shooter is most likely not to do either on the first roll, but to get a 4, 5, 6, 8, 9, or 10. If one of these six numbers is thrown, the shooter is obliged to continue rolling the dice until that number is rolled again, in which case the shooter wins, or until a 7 comes up, which is a losing case. Those cases in which neither the number first thrown nor a 7 occurs can be ignored, for they are not decisive. Suppose the shooter gets a 4 on the first roll. The next *decisive* roll will show either a 4 or a 7. In a decisive roll, the equipossible cases are the three combinations that make up a 4 (1–3, 2–2, 3–1) and the six combinations that make up a 7. The probability of throwing a second 4 is therefore $\frac{3}{9}$. The probability of getting a 4 on the first roll was $\frac{3}{36}$, so the probability of winning by throwing a 4 on the first roll and then getting another 4 before a 7 occurs is $\frac{3}{36} \times \frac{3}{9} = \frac{1}{36}$. Similarly, the probability of the shooter winning by throwing a 10 on the first roll and then getting another 10 before a 7 occurs is also $\frac{3}{36} \times \frac{3}{9} = \frac{1}{36}$.

By the same line of reasoning, we can find the probability of the shooter winning by throwing a 5 on the first roll and then getting another 5 before throwing a 7. In this case, there are 10 equipossible cases for the decisive roll:

OVERVIEW

The Product Theorem

To calculate the probability of the *joint occurrence* of two or more events:

A. If the events (say, *a* and *b*) are *independent*, the probability of their joint occurrence is the simple product of their probabilities:

$P(a \text{ and b}) = P(a) \times P(b)$

B. If the events (say, *a* and *b* and *c*, etc.) are *not independent*, the probability of their joint occurrence is the probability of the first event times the probability of the second event if the first occurred, times the probability of the third event if the first and the second occurred, etc:

$P(a \text{ and } b \text{ and } c) = P(a) \times P(b \text{ if } a) \times P(c \text{ if both } a \text{ and } b)$

The Addition Theorem

To calculate the probability of the *alternative occurrence* of two or more events:

A. If the events (say *a* or *b*) are *mutually exclusive*, the probability of at least one of them occurring is the simple addition of their probabilities:

$P(a \text{ or } b) = P(a) + P(b)$

B. If the events (say *a* or *b* or *c*) are *not mutually exclusive*, the probability of at least one of them occurring may be determined by either

1. Analyzing the favorable cases into mutually exclusive events and summing the probabilities of those successful events; or
2. Determining the probability that no one of the alternative events will occur, and then subtracting that probability from 1.

the four ways to make a 5 (1–4, 2–3, 3–2, 4–1) and the six ways to make a 7. The probability of winning with a 5 is therefore $\frac{4}{36} \times \frac{4}{10} = \frac{2}{45}$. The probability of winning with a 9 is also $\frac{2}{45}$. The number 6 is still more likely to occur on the first roll, its probability being $\frac{5}{36}$. And it is more likely than the others mentioned to occur a second time before a 7 appears, the probability here being $\frac{5}{11}$. So the probability of winning with a 6 is $\frac{5}{36} \times \frac{5}{11} = \frac{25}{396}$. And again, likewise, the probability of winning with an 8 is $\frac{25}{396}$.

There are eight different ways for the shooter to win: if a 7 or 11 is thrown on the first roll, or if one of the six numbers 4, 5, 6, 8, 9, or 10 is thrown on the first roll *and* again before a 7. These ways are all exclusive; so the total probability of the shooter's winning is the sum of the probabilities of the alternative ways in which winning is possible, and this is $\frac{6}{36} + \frac{2}{36} + \frac{1}{36} + \frac{2}{45} + \frac{25}{396} + \frac{25}{396} + \frac{2}{45} + \frac{1}{36} = \frac{244}{495}$. Expressed as a decimal fraction this is .493. This shows that in a crap game the shooter has *less* than an even chance of winning—only slightly less, to be sure, but still less than .5.

EXERCISES

B. ***1.** Calculate the shooter's chances of winning in a crap game by the second method; that is, compute the chances of his losing, and subtract it from 1.

2. In drawing three cards in succession from a standard deck, what is the probability of getting at least one spade (a) if each card is replaced before making the next drawing? (b) if the cards drawn are not replaced?

3. What is the probability of getting at least one head in three tosses of a coin?

4. If three balls are selected at random from an urn containing 5 red, 10 white, and 15 blue balls, what is the probability that they will all be the same color (a) if each ball is replaced before the next one is withdrawn? (b) if the balls selected are not replaced?

***5.** If someone offers to bet you even money that you will not throw either an ace or a six on either of two successive throws of a die, should you accept the wager?

6. In a group of 30 students randomly gathered in a classroom, what is the probability that no two of those students will have the same birthday; that is, what is the probability that there will be no duplication of the same date of birth, ignoring the year and attending only to the month and the day of the month? How many students would need to be in the group in order for the probability of such a duplication to be approximately .5?

7. If the probability that a man of 25 will survive his 50th birthday is .742, and the probability that a woman of 22 will survive her 47th birthday is .801, and such a man and woman marry, what is the probability (a) that at least one of them lives at least another 25 years? (b) that only one of them lives at least another 25 years?

8. One partly filled case contains two bottles of orange juice, four bottles of cola, and four bottles of beer; another partly filled case contains three bottles of orange juice, seven colas, and two beers. A case is opened at random and a bottle selected at random from it. What is the probability that it contains a nonalcoholic drink? Had all the bottles been in one case, what is the probability that a bottle selected at random from it would contain a nonalcoholic drink?

9. A player in a draw-poker game is dealt three jacks and two small odd cards. He discards the latter and draws two cards. What is the probability that he improves his hand on the draw? (One way to improve it is to draw another jack to make four-of-a-kind; the other way to improve it is to draw any pair to make a full house.)

CHALLENGE TO THE READER

The following problem has been a source of some controversy among probability theorists. Is the correct solution counterintuitive?

***10.** Remove all cards except aces and kings from a deck, so that only eight cards remain, of which four are aces and four are kings. From this abbreviated deck, deal two cards to a friend. If she looks at her cards and announces (truthfully) that her hand contains an ace, what is the probability that both her cards are aces? If she announces instead that one of her cards is the ace of spades, what is the probability then that both her cards are aces? Are these two probabilities the same?*

14.3 Probability in Everyday Life

In placing bets or making investments, it is important to consider not only the probability of winning or receiving a return, but also *how much* can be won on the bet or returned on the investment. These two considerations, *safety* and

*For some discussion of this problem, see L. E. Rose, "Countering a Counter-Intuitive Probability," *Philosophy of Science* 39 (1972): 523–524; A. I. Dale, "On a Problem in Conditional Probability," *Philosophy of Science* 41 (1974): 204–206; R. Faber, "Re-Encountering a Counter-Intuitive Probability," *Philosophy of Science* 43 (1976): 283–285; and S. Goldberg, "Copi's Conditional Probability Problem," *Philosophy of Science* 43 (1976): 286–289.

productivity, often clash; greater potential returns usually entail greater risks. The safest investment may not be the best one to make, nor may the investment that promises the greatest return *if* it succeeds. The need to reconcile safety and maximum return confronts us not only in gambling and investing, but also in choosing among alternatives in education, employment, and other spheres of life. We would like to know whether the investment—of money or of time and energy—is "worth it"—that is, whether that wager on the future is wise, all things considered. The future cannot be known, but the probabilities may be estimated. When one is attempting to compare investments, or bets, or "chancy" decisions of any kind, the concept of *expectation value* is a powerful tool to use.

Expectation value can best be explained in the context of wagers whose outcomes have known probabilities. Any bet—say, an even-money bet of $1 that heads will appear on the toss of a coin—should be thought of as a purchase; the money is spent when the bet has been made. The dollar wagered is the price of the purchase; it buys some *expectation*. If heads appears, the bettor receives a return of two dollars (one his own, the other his winnings); if tails appears, the bettor receives a $0 return. There are only two possible outcomes of this wager, a head or a tail; the probability of each is known to be $\frac{1}{2}$; and there is a specified return ($2, or $0) associated with each outcome. We multiply the return yielded on each possible outcome by the probability of that outcome's being realized; the sum of all such products is the **expectation value** of the bet or investment. The expectation value of a one-dollar bet that heads will turn up when a fair coin is tossed is thus equal to $(\frac{1}{2} \times \$2) + (\frac{1}{2} \times \$0)$, which is $1. In this case, as we know, the "odds" are even—which means that the expectation value of the purchase was equal to the purchase price.

This is not always the case. We seek investments in which the expectation value purchased will prove greater than the cost of our investment. We want the odds to be in our favor. Yet often we are tempted by wagers for which the expectation value is less, sometimes much less, than the price of the gamble.

The disparity between the price and the expectation value of a bet can be readily seen in a raffle, in which the purchase of a ticket offers a small chance at a large return. How much the raffle ticket is really worth depends on how small the chance is *and* how large the return is. Suppose that the return, if we win it, is an automobile worth $20,000, and the price of the raffle ticket is $1. If 20,000 raffle tickets are sold, of which we buy one, the probability of our winning is $\frac{1}{20{,}000}$. The chances of winning are thus very small, but the return if we win is very large. In this hypothetical case, the expectation value of the raffle ticket is $(\frac{1}{20{,}000} \times \$20{,}000) + (\frac{19{,}999}{20{,}000} \times \$0)$, or precisely $1, the purchase price of the ticket. The usual purpose of a raffle, however, is to raise money for some worthy cause, and that can happen only if more money is collected from ticket sales than is paid out in prizes. Therefore many more than 20,000 tickets—perhaps 40,000 or 80,000 or 100,000—will be sold. Suppose that 40,000 tickets are sold. The expectation value of our $1 ticket then will be ($\frac{1}{40{,}000}$ × $20,000) + ($\frac{39{,}999}{40{,}000}$ × $0), or 50 cents. If 80,000 tickets are sold, the expectation value of the $1 ticket will be reduced to 25 cents, and so on. We may be confident that the expectation value of any raffle ticket we are asked to buy will be substantially less than the amount we are asked to pay for it.

Lotteries are very popular because of the very large prizes that may be won. States and countries conduct lotteries because every ticket purchased buys an expectation value equal to only a fraction of the ticket's price; those who run the lottery retain the difference, reaping huge profits.

The Michigan lottery, played by more than two-thirds of the citizens of that state, is typical. Different bets are offered. In one game, called the "Daily 3," the player may choose (in a "straight bet") any three-digit number from 000 to 999. After all bets are placed, a number is drawn at random and announced by the state; a player who has purchased a $1 straight-bet ticket on that winning number wins a prize of $500. The probability that the correct three digits in the correct order have been selected is 1 in 1000; the expectation value of a $1 "Daily 3" straight-bet ticket is therefore $\frac{1}{1000}$ × $500 + $\frac{999}{1000}$ × $0, or 50 cents.*

Lotteries and raffles are examples of great disparity between the price and the expectation value of the gambler's purchase. Sometimes the disparity is small, but the number of purchasers nevertheless ensures the profitability of the sale, as in gambling casinos, where every normal bet is one in which the purchase price is greater than the expectation value bought. In the preceding section we determined, using the product theorem and the addition theorem of the calculus of probability, that the dice game called craps is one in which the shooter's chance of winning is .493—just a little less than even. But that game is widely and mistakenly believed to offer the shooting player an even chance. Betting on the shooter in craps, at even money, is therefore a leading attraction in gambling casinos. But every such bet of $1 is a purchase of expectation value equal to (.493 × $2) + (.507 × $0), which is 98.6 cents. The difference of approximately a penny and a half may seem trivial, but because casinos receive that advantage (and other even greater advantages on other wagers) in thousands of bets made each day on the dice tables, they are very profitable enterprises. In the gambling fraternity, those who regularly bet on the shooter to win at craps

*However imprudent a wager on the "Daily 3" may be, it is a very popular lottery—so popular that it is now run twice a day, midday and evening. One may infer that either those who purchase such lottery tickets have not thought through the expected value of their wagers, or that such wagering offers them satisfactions independent of the money value of their bets.

are called paradoxically "right bettors," and among professional gamblers it is commonly said that "all right bettors die broke."

The concept of *expectation value* is of practical use in helping to decide how to save (or invest) money most wisely. Banks pay differing rates of interest on accounts of different kinds. Let us assume that the alternative bank accounts among which we choose are all government-insured, and that therefore there is no chance of a loss of the principal. At the end of a full year, the expectation value of each $1000 savings investment, at 5 percent simple interest, is ($1000 [the principal that we know will be returned]) + (.05 × $1000), or $1050 in all. To complete the calculation, this return must be multiplied by the probability of our getting it—but here we assume, because the account is insured, that our getting it is certain, so we merely multiply by 1, or 100/100. If the rate of interest is 6 percent, the insured return will be $1060, and so on. The expectation value purchased in such savings accounts is indeed greater than the deposit, the purchase price, but to get that interest income we must give up the use of our money for some period of time. The bank pays us for its use during that time because, of course, it plans to invest that money at yet higher rates of return.

Safety and productivity are considerations that are always in tension. If we are prepared to sacrifice a very small degree of safety for our savings, we may achieve a modest increase in the rate of return. For example, with that $1000 we may purchase a corporate bond, perhaps paying 8 or even 10 percent interest, in effect lending our money to the company issuing the bond. The yield on our corporate bond may be double that of a bank savings account, but we will be running the risk—small but real—that the corporation issuing the bond will be unable to make payment when the loan we made to them falls due. In calculating the expectation value of such a bond, say at 10 percent, the amount to be returned to the investor of $1000 is determined in precisely the same way in which we calculated the yield on a savings account. First we calculate the return, if we get it: ($1000 [the principal]) + (10% × $1000 [the interest]), or $1100 total return. But in this case the probability of our getting that return is not 100/100; it may be very high, but it is not certain. The fraction by which that $1100 return therefore must be multiplied is the probability, as best we can estimate it, that the corporation will be financially sound when its bond is due for payment. If we think this probability is very high—say, .99—we may conclude that the purchase of the corporate bond at 10 percent offers an expectation value ($1089) greater than that of the insured bank account at 5 percent ($1050), and is therefore a wiser investment. Here is the comparison in detail:

Insured bank account at 5 percent simple interest for 1 year:

Return = (principal + interest) = ($1000 + $50) = $1050

Probability of return (assumed) = 1

Expectation value of investment in this bank account:

(\$1050 × 1 = \$1050) + (\$0 × 0 = \$0) or \$1050 *total*

Corporate bond at 10 percent interest, at the end of 1 year:

Return if we get it = (principal + interest) = (\$1000 + \$100) = \$1100

Probability of return (estimated) = .99

Expectation value of investment in this corporate bond:

(\$1100 × .99 = \$1089) + (\$0 × .01 = \$0) or \$1089 *total*

However, if we conclude that the company to which we would be lending the money is not absolutely reliable, our estimated probability of ultimate return will drop, say, to .95, and the expectation value will also drop:

Corporate bond at 10 percent interest, at the end of 1 year:

Return if we get it = (principal + interest) = (\$1000 + \$100) = \$1100

Probability of return (new estimate) = .95

Expectation value of investment in this corporate bond:

(\$1100 × .95 = \$1045) + (\$0 × .05 = \$0) or \$1045 *total*

If this last estimate reflects our evaluation of the company selling the bond, then we will judge the bank account, paying a lower rate of interest with much greater safety, the wiser investment.

Interest rates on bonds or on bank accounts fluctuate, of course, depending on the current rate of inflation and other factors, but the interest paid on a commercial bond is always higher than that paid on an insured bank account *because* the risk of the bond is greater; that is, the probability of its anticipated return is lower. And the greater the known risk, the higher the interest rate must go to attract investors. Expectation value, in financial markets as everywhere, must take into consideration both probability (risk) and outcome (return).

When the soundness of a company enters our calculation of the expectation value of an investment in it, we must make some probability assumptions. Explicitly or implicitly, we estimate the fractions that we then think best represent the likelihoods of the possible outcomes foreseen. These are the fractions by which the returns that we anticipate in the event of these outcomes must be multiplied, before we sum the products. All such predictions are necessarily speculative, and all the outcomes calculated are therefore uncertain, of course.

When we can determine the approximate value of a given return *if* we achieve it, calculations of the kind here described enable us to determine what probability those outcomes *need* to have (given present evidence) so that our investment now will prove worthwhile. Many decisions in financial matters, and also many choices in ordinary life, depend (if they are to be rational) on such estimates of probability and the resultant expected value. The calculus of probability may have application whenever we must gamble on the future.

There is no gambling system that can evade the rigor of the probability calculus. It is sometimes argued, for example, that in a game in which there are even-money stakes to be awarded on the basis of approximately equiprobable alternatives (such as tossing a coin, or betting black versus red on a roulette wheel), one can be *sure to win* by making the same bet consistently—always heads, or always the same color—and doubling the amount of money wagered after each loss. Thus, if I bet $1 on heads, and tails shows, then I should bet $2 on heads the next time, and if tails shows again, my third bet, also on heads, should be $4, and so on. One cannot fail to win by following this procedure, some suppose, because extended runs (of tails, or of the color I don't bet on) are highly improbable.* And anyway, it is said, the longest run must *sometime* end, and when it does, the person who has regularly doubled the bet will always be money ahead.

Wonderful! Why need anyone work for a living, when we can all adopt this apparently foolproof system of winning at the gaming table? Let us ignore the fact that most gaming houses put an upper limit on the size of the wager they will accept, a limit that may block the application of the doubling system. What is the real fallacy contained in this doubling prescription? A long run of tails, say, is almost certain to end sooner or later, but it may end later rather than sooner. So an adverse run may last long enough to exhaust any finite amount of money the bettor has to wager. To be certain of being able to continue doubling the bet each time, no matter how long the adverse run may continue or how large the losses are that the run has imposed, the bettor would have to begin with an infinite amount of money. And, of course, a player with an infinite amount of money could not possibly win—in the sense of increasing his wealth.

Finally, there is a dangerous fallacy, in wagering or in investing, that an understanding of the calculus of probability may help us to avoid. The inevitable failure of the doubling technique underscores the truth that the probability of getting a head (or a tail) on the next toss of a fair coin cannot be affected by the outcomes of preceding tosses; each toss is an independent event. Therefore it is a foolish mistake to conclude, in flipping a coin, that because heads have appeared ten times in a row, tails is "due"—or to suppose

*In fact, a long random sequence of heads and tails (or reds and blacks on a roulette wheel, etc.) will include extended runs of one result (tails, or reds, etc.) with much greater frequency than is commonly supposed. A run of a dozen heads in a row—requiring a bet of $2048 on the 12th bet if one wagers steadily on tails in a doubling series that began with $1—is very far from rare. And after a run of twelve, of course, the chances of a thirteenth tail is ½!

that because certain digits have appeared frequently among winning lottery numbers that those digits are "hot." One who bets, or invests, on the supposition that some future event is made more probable, or less probable, by the frequency of the occurrence of independent events that have preceded it commits a blunder so common that it has been given a mocking name: "the gambler's fallacy."

On the other hand, if some mechanical device produces certain outcomes more frequently than others in a long-repeated pattern, one might conclude that the device is not designed (or is not functioning) as one supposed to yield outcomes that are equipossible. The dice may be loaded. Or a roulette wheel (if the ball very frequently stops at the same section of the wheel) may not be balanced properly. The *a priori* theory of probability ("successes over outcomes") is rationally applied when we are confident that the denominator of the fraction, the set of all outcomes, is a set of genuinely equipossible events. However, accumulated evidence may eventually cause one to conclude that the members of that set are not equipossible. At that point we may be well advised to revert to the frequency theory of probability, reasoning that the likelihood of certain outcomes is the fraction that represents the limit of the frequency with which that smaller set of outcomes has appeared. Whether we ought to apply the *a priori* theory or the relative frequency theory must depend on the evidence we have gathered and on our understanding of the calculus of probability as applied to that context.

EXERCISES

***1.** In the Virginia lottery in 1992, six numbers were drawn at random from 44 numbers; the winner needed to select all six, in any order. Each ticket (with one such combination) cost $1. The total number of possible six-number combinations was 7,059,052. One week in February of that year, the jackpot in the Virginia lottery had risen to $27 million. (a) What was the expectation value of each ticket in the Virginia lottery that week?

These unusual circumstances led an Australian gambling syndicate to try to buy all of the tickets in the Virginia lottery that week. They fell short, but they were able to acquire some 5 million of the available six-number combinations. (b) What was the expectation value of their $5-million purchase? (Yes, the Aussies won!)

2. At most crap tables in gambling houses, the house will give odds of 6 to 1 against rolling a 4 the "hard way," that is, with a pair of 2's as contrasted with a 3 and a 1, which is the "easy way." A bet made on a "hard way" 4 wins if a pair of 2's show before either a 7 is rolled or a 4 is made the "easy way"; otherwise it loses. What is the expectation purchased by a $1 bet on a "hard-way" 4?

3. If the odds in craps are 8 to 1 against rolling an 8 the "hard way" (that is, with two 4's), what is the expectation purchased by a $1 bet on a "hard-way" 8?

4. What expectation does a person with $15 have who bets on heads, beginning with a $1 bet, and uses the doubling technique, if the bettor resolves to play just four times and quit?

***5.** Anthrax is a disease that is nearly always deadly to cows and other animals. The nineteenth-century French veterinarian Louvrier devised a treatment for anthrax that was later shown to be totally without merit. His alleged "cure" was tried on two cows, selected at random from four cows that had received a powerful dose of anthrax microbes. Of the two he treated, one died and one recovered; of the two he left untreated, one died and one recovered. The reasons for recovery were unknown. Had Louvrier tested his "cure" on the two cows that happened to live, his treatment would have received impressive but spurious confirmation. What was the probability of Louvrier choosing, for his test, just those two cows that chanced to live?

6. On the basis of past performance, the probability that the favorite will win the Bellevue Handicap is .46, while there is a probability of only .1 that a certain dark horse will win. If the favorite pays even money, and the odds offered are 8 to 1 against the dark horse, which is the better bet?

7. If $100 invested in the preferred stock of a certain company will yield a return of $110 with a probability of .85, whereas the probability is only .67 that the same amount invested in common stock will yield a return of $140, which is the better investment?

8. The probability of being killed by a stroke of lightening, calculated using the frequency theory of probability, is approximately 1 in 3 million. That is about 58 times greater than was the probability of winning the jackpot ($390 million) in the Mega Millions lottery in the United States in March of 2007. In that lottery the chances of buying a successful ticket were 1 in 175, 711, 536. One of two winning tickets was in fact purchased by a Canadian truck driver. If he had known the size of the jackpot, and that it would be divided by two winners, what would the expectation value of the $1 ticket he bought have been, at the time he bought it?

9. The following notice is a real one, distributed to all the parents in the school attended by the son of one of the authors of this book:

> **Emerson School Raffle—Up, Up and Away!**
>
> We are all winners!
>
> 4 lucky people will walk away with lots of cash!
>
> | | |
> |---|---|
> | 1st Prize | $1,000 |
> | 2nd Prize | $400 |
> | 3rd Prize | $250 |
> | 4th Prize | $100 |
>
> Chances of winning are good—Only 4,000 tickets were printed!
>
> Everyone will benefit from the great new sports equipment we will be able to buy with the money raised!

In this raffle, supposing all the tickets were sold, what was the expectation value of each ticket costing $1?

***10.** The probability of the shooter winning in craps is .493, slightly less than even, as we proved in the preceding section. In casinos, a bet that the shooter will win is a bet on what is called the "Pass" line. We could all become rich, it would seem, if only we bet consistently *against* the shooter, on the "Don't Pass" line. But of course there is no such line; one cannot simply bet against the shooter, because the house will not take so unprofitable a bet. Yet usually one can place a bet called "Don't Pass–Bar 3," which wins if the shooter loses, unless the shooter loses by rolling a 3, in which case this bet loses also. What is the expectation value of a $100 bet on the "Don't Pass–Bar 3" line?

SUMMARY

In all inductive arguments the conclusion is supported by the premises with only some degree of probability, usually described simply as "more" or "less" probable in the case of scientific hypotheses. We explained in this chapter how a *quantitative* measure of probability, stated as a fraction between 0 and 1, can be assigned to many inductive conclusions.

Two alternative conceptions of probability, both permitting this quantitative assignment, were presented in Section 14.1.

- The *relative frequency* theory, according to which probability is defined as the relative frequency with which members of a class exhibit a specified attribute.

- The a *priori theory,* according to which the probability of an event's occurring is determined by dividing the number of ways in which the event can occur by the number of equipossible outcomes.

Both theories accommodate the development of a calculus of probability, introduced in Section 14.2, with which the probability of a complex event can be computed if the probability of its component events can be determined. Two basic theorems, the *product theorem* and the *addition theorem,* are used in this probability calculus.

If the complex event of interest is a joint occurrence, the probability of two or more components both occurring, the *product* theorem is applied. The product theorem asserts that if the component events are *independent,* the probability of their joint occurrence is equal to the product of their separate probabilities. But if the component events are *not independent,* the general product theorem applies, in which the probability of (*a* and *b*) is equal to the probability of (*a*) multiplied by the probability of (*b* if *a*).

If the complex event of interest is an alternative occurrence (the probability of at least one of two or more events), the *addition* theorem is applied. The addition theorem asserts that if the component events *are mutually exclusive,* their probabilities are summed to determine their alternative occurrence. But if the component events *are not mutually exclusive,* the probability of their alternative occurrence may be computed either:

- by analyzing the favorable cases into mutually exclusive events and summing the probabilities of those successes; or
- by determining the probability that the alternative occurrence will not occur and subtracting that fraction from 1.

In Section 14.3 we explained how the calculus of probability can be put to use in everyday life, allowing us to calculate the relative merits of alternative investments or wagers. We must consider both the *probability* of each of the various possible outcomes of an investment as well as the *return* received in the event of each. For each outcome, the anticipated return is multiplied by the fraction that represents the probability of that outcome occurring; those products are then summed to calculate the expectation value of that investment.

Solutions to Selected Exercises

Chapter 5

SECTION 5.3 *Exercises on p. 187*

1. S = historians;
P = extremely gifted writers whose works read like first-rate novels.
Form: Particular affirmative.

5. S = members of families that are rich and famous;
P = persons of either wealth or distinction.
Form: Particular negative.

10. S = people who have not themselves done creative work in the arts;
P = responsible critics on whose judgments we can rely.
Form: Universal negative.

SECTION 5.4 *Exercises on p. 193*

1. Quality: affirmative; quantity: particular; subject and predicate terms both undistributed.

5. Quality: negative; quantity: universal; subject and predicate terms both distributed.

10. Quality: affirmative; quantity: universal; subject term distributed, predicate term undistributed.

SECTION 5.5 *Exercises on p. 198*

1. If we assume that (a) is true, then:
(b), which is its contrary, is false, and
(c), which is its subaltern, is true, and
(d), which is its contradictory, is false.

If we assume that (a) is false, then:
(b), which is its contrary, is undetermined, and
(c), which is its subaltern, is undetermined, and
(d), which is its contradictory, is true.

SECTION 5.6 *Exercises on pp. 205–207*

A. p. 205

1. No reckless drivers who pay no attention to traffic regulations are people who are considerate of others. Equivalent.

5. Some elderly persons who would be incapable of doing an honest day's work are professional wrestlers. Equivalent.

B. p. 205

1. Some college athletes are not nonprofessionals. Equivalent.

5. No objects suitable for boat anchors are objects weighing less than fifteen pounds. Equivalent.

C. p. 205

1. All nonpessimists are nonjournalists. Equivalent.

5. Some residents are not citizens. Equivalent.

D. p. 205

1. False

5. Undetermined

10. False

E. p. 206

1. False

5. Undetermined
10. False

F. p. 207

1. Undetermined
5. False
10. Undetermined
15. True

G. p. 207

1. Undetermined
5. Undetermined
10. True
15. Undetermined

SECTION 5.7 *Exercises on pp. 214–215*

E. p. 215

Step (1) to step (2) is invalid: (1) asserts the falsehood of an **I** proposition; (2) asserts the truth of its corresponding **O** proposition. In the traditional interpretation, corresponding **I** and **O** propositions are subcontraries and cannot both be false. Therefore, if the **I** proposition in (1) is false, the **O** proposition in (2) would have to be true, in *that* interpretation. But because both **I** and **O** propositions do have existential import, both *can* be false (in the Boolean interpretation) if the subject class is empty. The subject class *is* empty in this case, because there are no mermaids. Hence the inference from the falsehood of (1) to the truth of (2) is invalid. Corresponding **I** and **O** propositions are not subcontraries in the Boolean interpretation, but the inference from (1) to (2) assumes that they are.

SECTION 5.8 *Exercises on pp. 221–222*

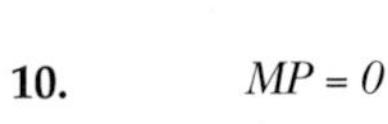

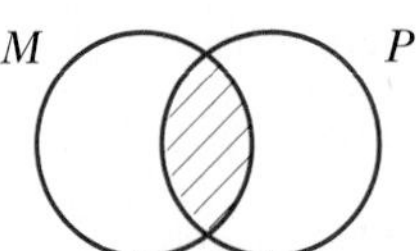

15. $PM \neq 0$

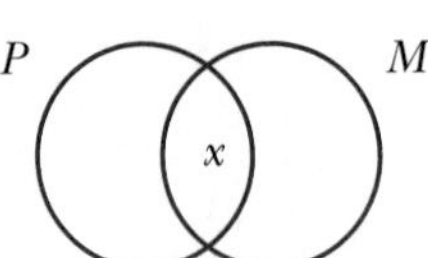

20. $P\bar{M} = 0$

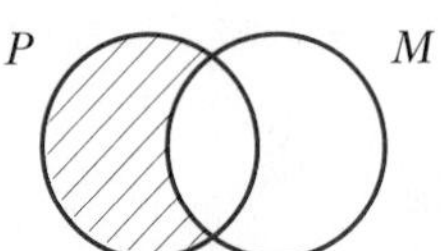

Chapter 6

SECTION 6.1 *Exercises on pp. 228–230*

5. STEP 1: The conclusion is: Some conservatives are not advocates of high tariff rates.

STEP 2: Major term: advocates of high tariff rates.

STEP 3: Major premise: All advocates of high tariff rates are Republicans.

STEP 4: Minor premise: Some Republicans are not conservatives.

STEP 5: This syllogism written in standard form:
All advocates of high tariff rates are Republicans.
Some Republicans are not conservatives.
Therefore some conservatives are not advocates of high tariff rates.

STEP 6: The three propositions of this syllogism are, in order: **A, O, O.** The middle term, Republicans, is the predicate term of the major premise and the subject term of the minor premise, so the syllogism is in the fourth figure. Thus its mood and figure are **AOO–4.**

10. STEP 1: The conclusion is: No sports cars are automobiles designed for family use.

STEP 2: Major term: Automobiles designed for family use.

STEP 3: Major premise: All automobiles designed for family use are vehicles intended to be driven at moderate speeds.

STEP 4: Minor premise: No sports cars are vehicles intended to be driven at moderate speeds.

STEP 5: This syllogism written in standard form:
All automobiles designed for family use are vehicles intended to be driven at moderate speeds.
No sports cars are vehicles intended to be driven at moderate speeds.
Therefore no sports cars are automobiles designed for family use.

STEP 6: The three propositions of this syllogism are, in order, **A**, **E**, **E**. The middle term, vehicles intended to be driven at moderate speeds, is the predicate term of both the major and the minor premise, so the syllogism is in the second figure. Thus its mood and figure are **AEE-2.**

SECTION 6.2 *Exercises on pp. 232–233*

5. One possible refuting analogy is this: All unicorns are mammals, so some mammals are not animals, because no animals are unicorns.

10. One possible refuting analogy is this: All square circles are circles, and all square circles are squares, therefore some circles are squares.

SECTION 6.3 *Exercises on pp. 242–244*

A. p. 242

5. No *P* is *M*.
Some *M* is *S*.
∴ Some *S* is not *P*.

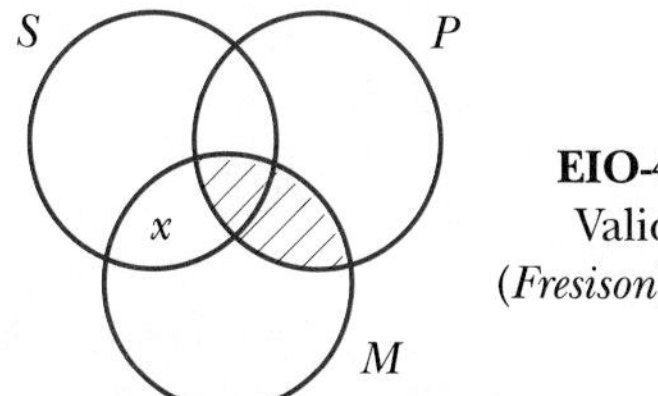

EIO-4
Valid
(*Fresison*)

10. Some *P* is *M*.
All *M* is *S*.
∴ Some *S* is *P*.

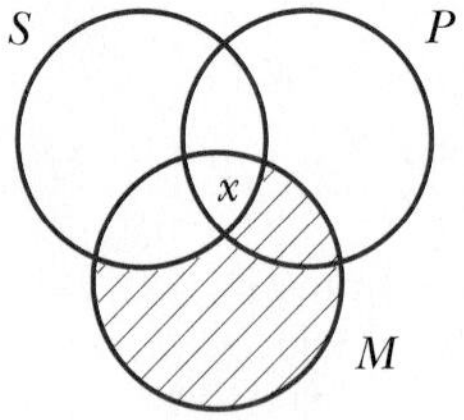

IAI-4
Valid
(*Dimaris*)

15. No *M* is *P*.
Some *S* is *M*.
∴ Some *S* is not *P*.

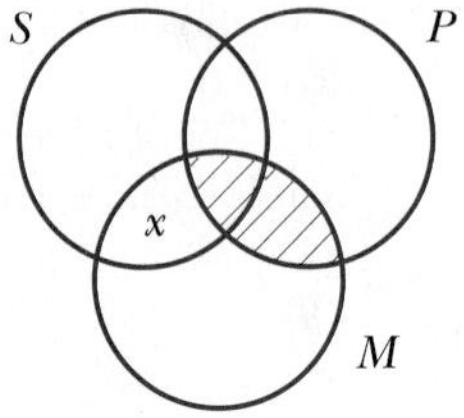

EIO-1
Valid
(*Ferio*)

B. p. 243

1. Some reformers are fanatics.
All reformers are idealists.
∴ Some idealists are fanatics.

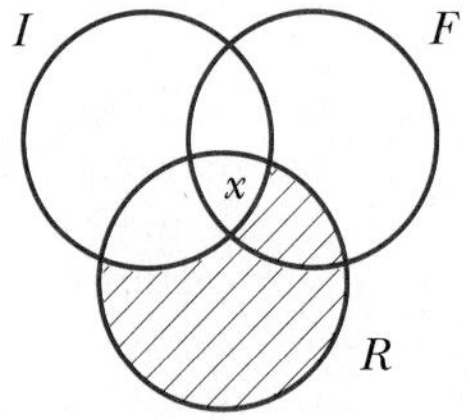

IAI-3
Valid
(*Disamis*)

5. No pleasure vessels are underwater craft.
All underwater craft are submarines.
∴ No submarines are pleasure vessels.

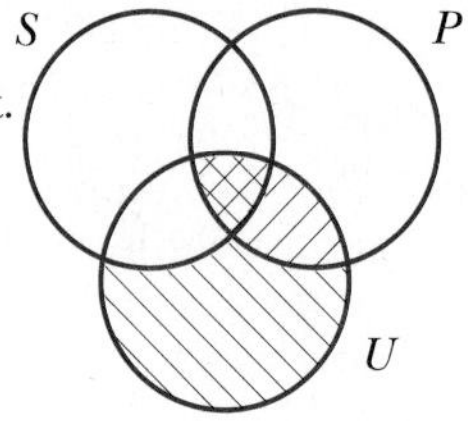

EAE-4
Invalid

10. All labor leaders are true liberals.
No weaklings are true liberals.
∴ No weaklings are labor leaders.

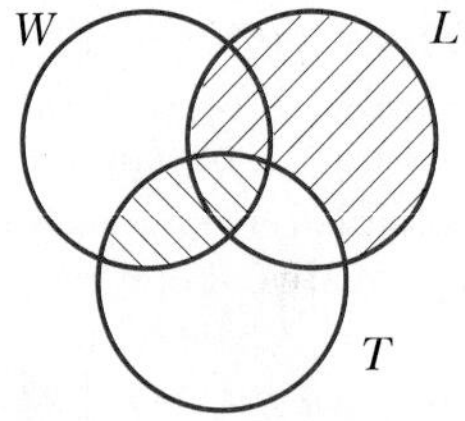

AEE-2
Valid
(*Camestres*)

SECTION 6.4 *Exercises on pp. 252–255*

A. p. 252

5. Commits the fallacy of the illicit minor. Breaks Rule 3.
10. Commits the fallacy of the illicit major. Breaks Rule 3.
15. Commits the fallacy of the illicit minor. Breaks Rule 3.

B. pp. 252–254

5. Commits the existential fallacy. Breaks Rule 6.
10. Commits the fallacy of the illicit minor. Breaks Rule 3.

C. pp. 254–255

5. Commits the fallacy of the illicit minor. Breaks Rule 3.

10. Commits the fallacy of four terms. (There is an equivocation on the term "people who like it," which has a very different meaning in the conclusion from the one it has in the premise.) Breaks Rule 1.

CHAPTER 6 APPENDIX *Exercises on p. 264*

5. Plainly this is possible in the first figure, where **AII-1,** which is valid, has only one term distributed, and that term only once. It also is possible in the third figure, where **AII–3** (as well as **IAI–3**) are valid and also have only one term distributed, and distributed only once. It also is possible in the fourth figure, where **IAI–4,** which is valid, has only one term distributed, and distributed only once. But where the middle term is the predicate term of both premises, in the second figure, it is not possible. Consider: To avoid breaking Rule 2, which requires that the middle term be distributed in at least one premise, one of the premises in this figure must be negative. But then, by Rule 5, the conclusion would have to be negative and would distribute its predicate. Thus, if only one term can be distributed only once, in the second figure that would have to be in the conclusion; but if the distributed term can be distributed only once, that would break Rule 3, because if it is distributed in the conclusion it must be distributed in the premises.

10. None. If the middle term were distributed in both premises, then, in the first figure, the minor premise would have to be negative, whence (by Rule 5) the conclusion would have to be negative, so by Rule 3 the major premise would have to be negative, in violation of Rule 4. In the second figure, both premises would have to be negative, in violation of Rule 4. In the third figure both premises would have to be universal, so the minor premise would have to be negative by Rule 3, and by Rule 5 the conclusion would be negative—so by Rule 3 the major premise would have to be negative, also in violation of Rule 4. In the fourth figure the major premise would have to be negative, and so by Rule 3 the major premise would be universal, whence (by Rule 3) the minor premise would have to be negative, also in violation of Rule 4.

Chapter 7

SECTION 7.2 *Exercises on pp. 271–272*

5. Where
E = explosives
F = flammable things (note that "flammable" and "inflammable" are *synonyms!*)
S = safe things

this syllogism translates into standard form thus:

All *E* is *F*.
No *F* is *S*.
Therefore no *S* is *E*.

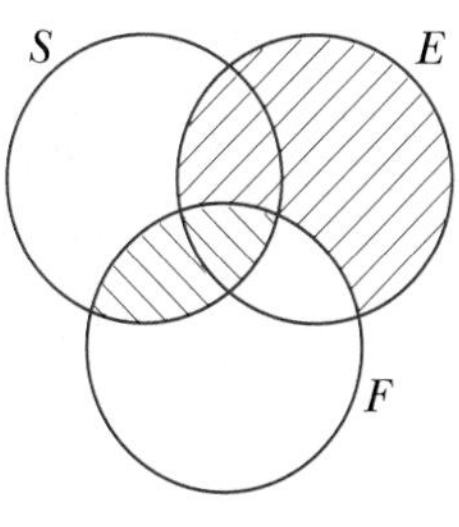

Exhibited in a Venn diagram, this syllogism (in *Camenes*) is shown to be valid.

10. Where
O = objects over six feet long
D = difficult things to store
U = useful things

this syllogism translates into standard form thus:

All *O* are *D*.
No *D* are *U*.
Therefore no *U* are *O*.

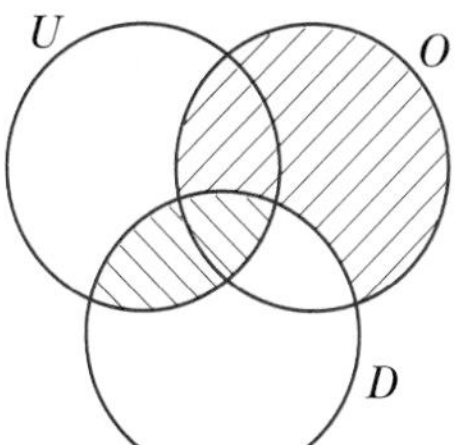

Exhibited in a Venn diagram, this syllogism (in *Camenes*) is shown to be valid.

SECTION 7.3 *Exercises on pp. 280–281*

5. All Junkos are the best things that money can buy.

10. No people who face the sun are people who see their own shadows.

15. No candidates of the Old Guard are persons supported by the Young Turks. (Or: No Young Turks are supporters of candidates of the Old Guard.)

20. All people who love well are people who pray well.

25. All soft answers are things that turn away wrath.

SECTION 7.4 *Exercises on pp. 283–287*

A. p. 283

5. All cases in which she gives her opinion are cases in which she is asked to give her opinion.

10. No times when people do not discuss questions freely are times when people are most likely to settle questions rightly.

B. pp. 284–287

5. No syllogisms that have two negative premises are valid syllogisms.
Some valid syllogisms are not unsound arguments.
∴ Some unsound arguments are syllogisms that have two negative premises.

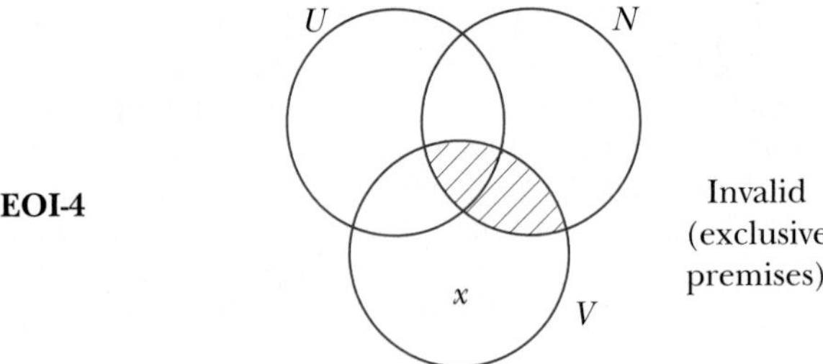

10. No persons who are truly objective are persons likely to be mistaken.
All persons likely to be mistaken are persons who ignore the facts.
∴ No persons who ignore the facts are persons who are truly objective.

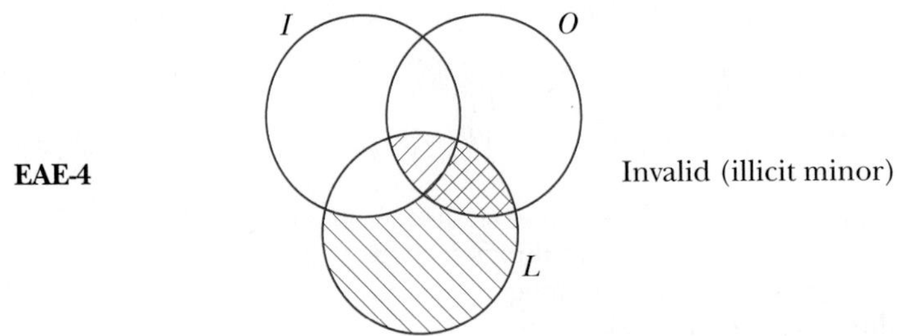

15. All things interesting to engineers are approximations.
No approximations are irrationals.
∴ No irrationals are things interesting to engineers.

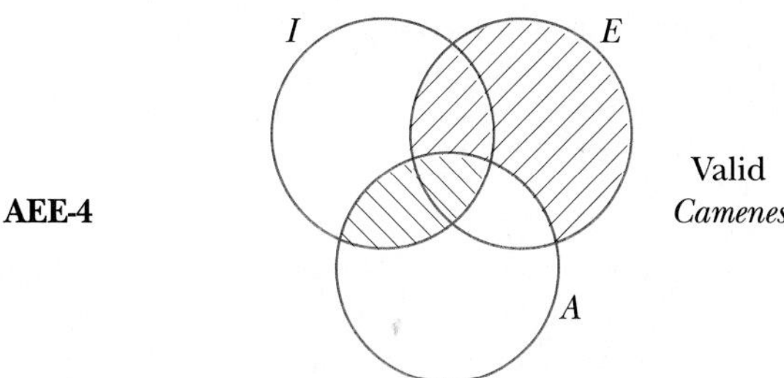

20. No times that Bill goes to work are times that Bill wears a sweater.
This morning is a time that Bill wears a sweater.
∴ This morning is not a time that Bill goes to work.

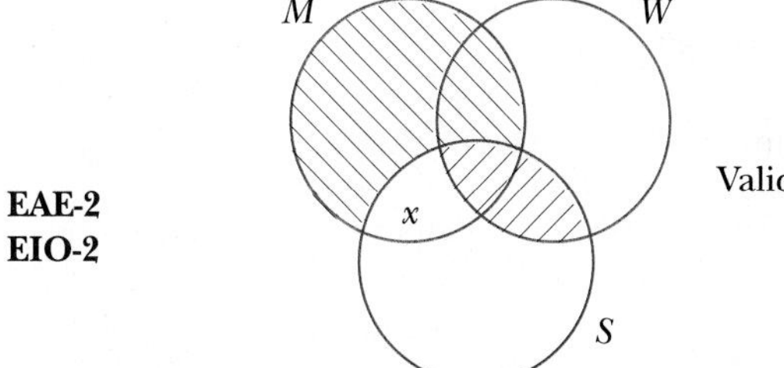

25. All valid syllogisms are syllogisms that distribute their middle terms in at least one premise.
This syllogism is a syllogism that distributes its middle term in at least one premise.
∴ This syllogism is a valid syllogism.

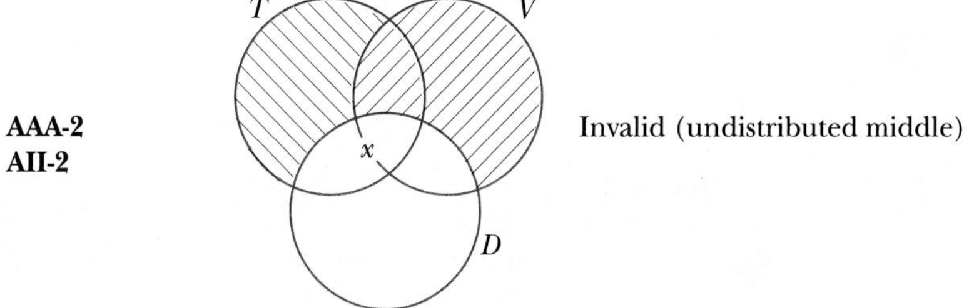

30. All situations in which much money is involved are situations in which competition is stiff.
This situation is a situation in which much money is involved.
∴ This situation is a situation in which competition is stiff.

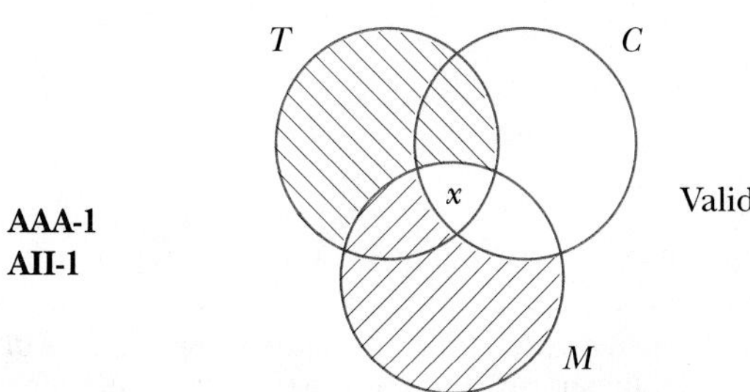

35. All invalid syllogisms are syllogisms that commit an illicit process.
This syllogism is not a syllogism that commits an illicit process.
∴ This syllogism is not an invalid syllogism.

AEE-2

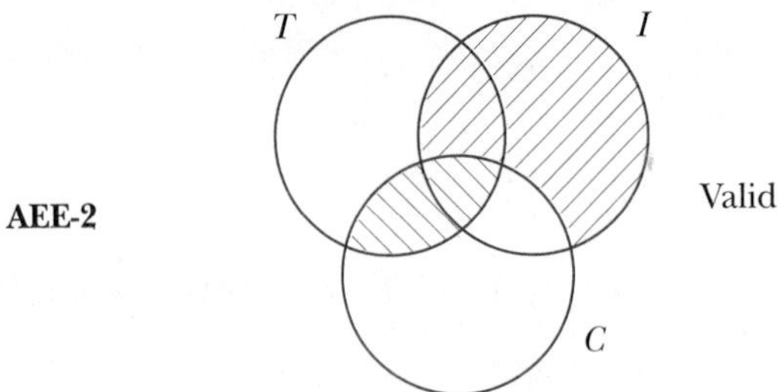

Valid

SECTION 7.5 *Exercises on pp. 290–293*

5. Third order.
Those persons whom you respect you do not hate.
Those persons who are vicious competitors you respect.
∴ Those persons who are vicious competitors you do not hate.

AAA-1

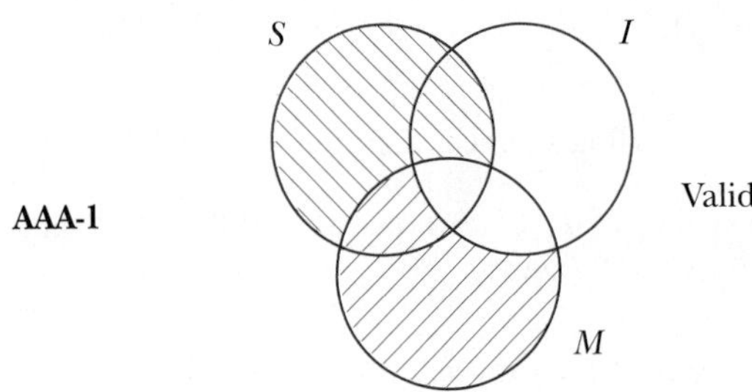

Valid

Valid third-order enthymeme in *Barbara*.

10. Second order.
No enthymemes are complete arguments.
This argument is an enthymeme.
∴ This argument is not a complete argument.

EAE-1
EIO-1

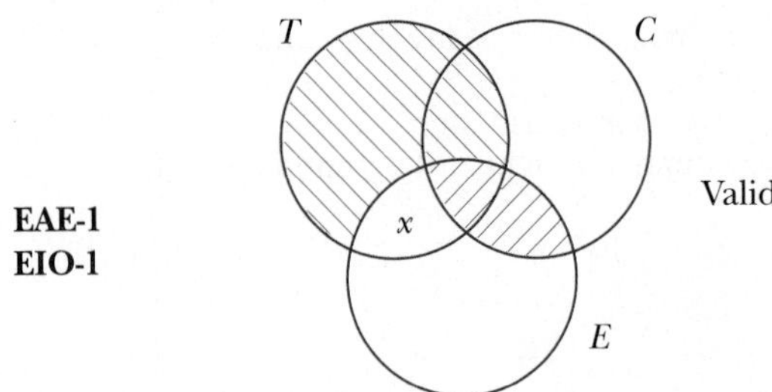

Valid

Sound enthymeme in *Ferio*, because the missing minor premise is obviously true.

15. First order. Valid, in *Darii*.
All species that tend to increase at a greater rate than their means of subsistence are species that are occasionally subject to a severe struggle for existence.

Man is a species that tends to increase at a greater rate than its means of subsistence.
∴ Man is a species that is occasionally subject to a severe struggle for existence.

AAA-1
AII-1

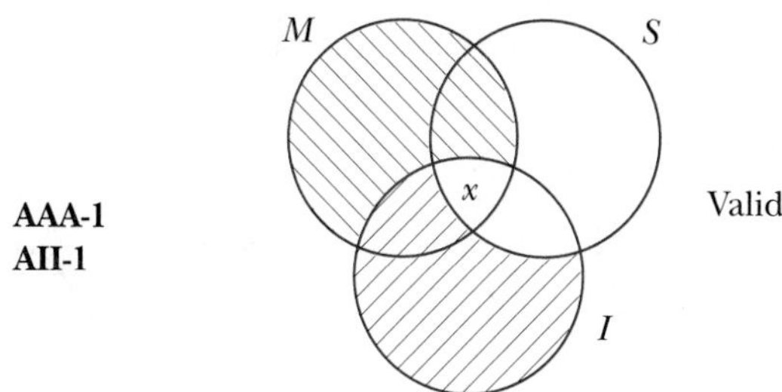

Valid

20. First order. Valid, in *Barbara*.
All that betters the condition of the vast majority of the people is desirable.
All productivity betters the condition of the vast majority of the people.
∴ All productivity is desirable.

AAA-1

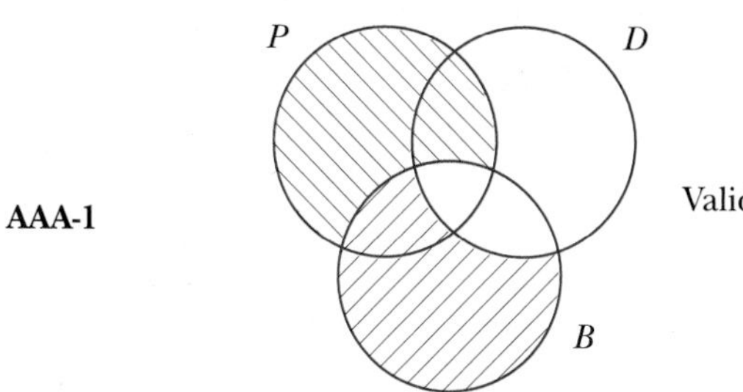

Valid

25. First order. Valid, in *Barbara*.
All people who are admitted to do what they do by necessity by the man who says that all things come to pass by necessity are people who cannot be criticized by the man who says that all things come to pass by necessity.
All who deny that all things come to pass by necessity are people who are admitted to do what they do by necessity by the man who says that all things come to pass by necessity.
∴ All who deny that all things come to pass by necessity are people who cannot be criticized by the man who says that all things come to pass by necessity.

AAA-1

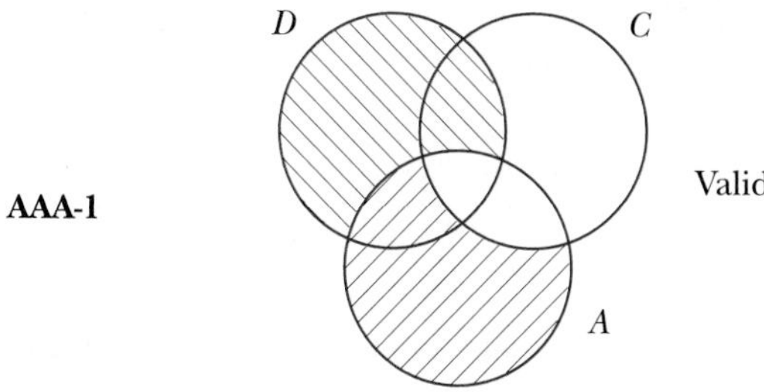

Valid

SECTION 7.6 *Exercises on pp. 295–297*

A. pp. 295–297

5. (1′) All interesting poems are poems that are popular among people of real taste.
(4′) No affected poems are poems that are popular among people of real taste.

(2′) All modern poems are affected poems.
(5′) All poems on the subject of soap bubbles are modern poems.
(3′) All poems of yours are poems on the subject of soap bubbles.
∴ No poems of yours are interesting poems.

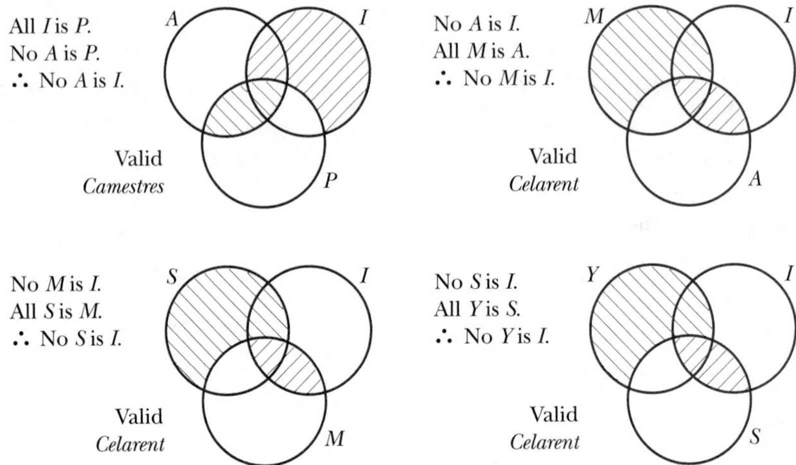
All *I* is *P*.
No *A* is *P*.
∴ No *A* is *I*.
A
I
P
Valid
Camestres
No *A* is *I*.
All *M* is *A*.
∴ No *M* is *I*.
M
I
A
Valid
Celarent
No *M* is *I*.
All *S* is *M*.
∴ No *S* is *I*.
S
I
M
Valid
Celarent
No *S* is *I*.
All *Y* is *S*.
∴ No *Y* is *I*.
Y
I
S
Valid
Celarent

Valid

B. p. 297

(1′) All those who read *The Times* are those who are well educated.
(3′) No creatures who cannot read are those who are well educated.
(2′) All hedgehogs are creatures who cannot read.
∴ No hedgehogs are those who read *The Times*.

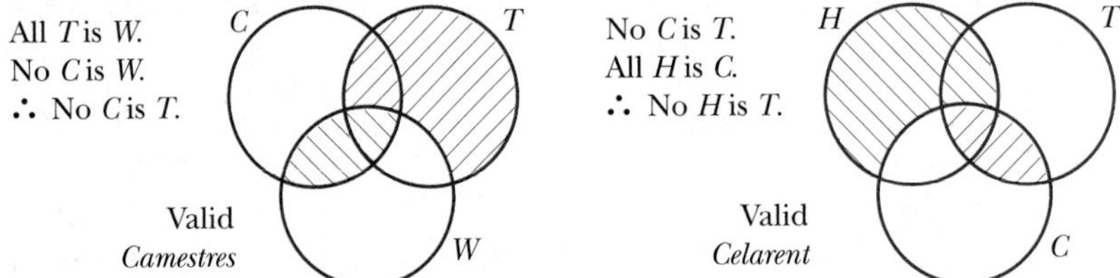
All *T* is *W*.
No *C* is *W*.
∴ No *C* is *T*.
C
T
W
Valid
Camestres
No *C* is *T*.
All *H* is *C*.
∴ No *H* is *T*.
H
T
C
Valid
Celarent

Valid

5. (2′) These sorites are examples not arranged in regular order, like the examples I am used to.
(4′) No examples not arranged in regular order, like the examples I am used to, are examples I can understand.
(1′) All examples I do not grumble at are examples I can understand.
(5′) All examples that do not give me a headache are examples I do not grumble at.
(3′) All easy examples are examples that do not give me a headache.
∴ These sorites are not easy examples.

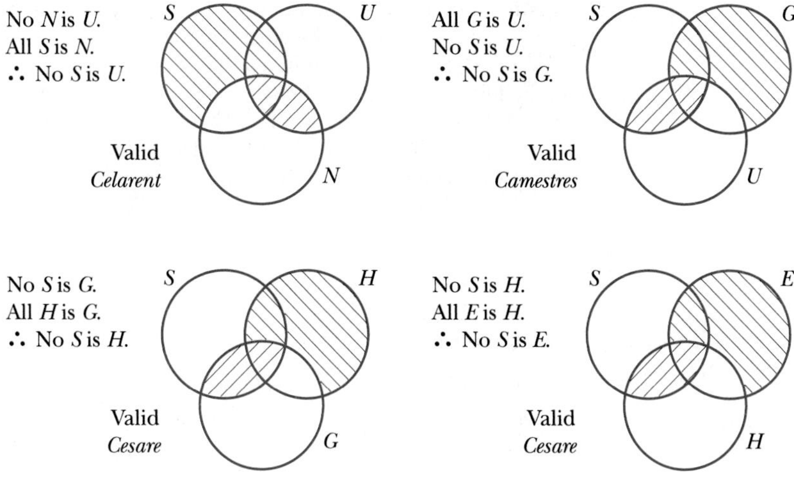
No N is U.
All S is N.
∴ No S is U.
S
U
N
Valid
Celarent
All G is U.
No S is U.
∴ No S is G.
S
G
U
Valid
Camestres
No S is G.
All H is G.
∴ No S is H.
S
H
G
Valid
Cesare
No S is H.
All E is H.
∴ No S is E.
S
E
H
Valid
Cesare

Valid

SECTION 7.7 *Exercises on pp. 302–305*

5. Mixed hypothetical syllogism, *modus ponens*. Valid.

10. Disjunctive syllogism. Valid.

15. Mixed hypothetical syllogism, *modus tollens*. Valid.

20. Two arguments are present here: The first is a pure hypothetical syllogism, the second is a mixed hypothetical syllogism of form *modus tollens*. Both are valid.

SECTION 7.8 *Exercises on pp. 309–312*

5. Very easy to go between the horns here. Plausible to grasp by either horn.

10. Impossible to go between the horns. It is plausible to grasp it by either horn, arguing either (a) that when desiring to preserve we may be motivated simply by inertia and seek to rest in the status quo, even while admitting that a change would not be worse and might even be better—but just "not worth the trouble of changing" or (b) that when desiring to change we may be motivated simply by boredom with the status quo, and seek a change even while admitting that a change might not be better and might even be worse—but "let's have a little variety." These are psychological rather than political or moral considerations, but the original dilemma appears to be itself psychological. The usual rebutting counterdilemma could be used here: When desiring to preserve, we do not wish to bring about something better; when desiring to change, we do not wish to prevent a change to the worse. It is a question, however, how plausible this is.

15. There were in theory a number of ways to go between the horns here: Between defiance and obedience to the Court decision there are many degrees of partial compliance short of full obedience but not outright full defiance. Either horn could be grasped, at least in theory: An emergency situation in the international sphere might prevent defiance from being followed by impeachment; and it is logically possible that the evidence produced by obedience to the order might not have been sufficient to persuade the Congress to impeach.

20. This is a rather informal version of Pascal's argument, which has been much discussed for more than three hundred years. If it is interpreted as having the disjunctive premise that either God exists or God does not exist, then it is obviously impossible to go between the horns. But each of the horns can be grasped to refute the given argument. It might be argued that if you live a life of conspicuous virtue even though you are not a believer, you will not be condemned to spend eternity in the flames of Hell. Or it might be argued that if you live as a believer you will suffer the loss of all those earthly pleasures that you might otherwise have enjoyed, and that that is a very grave penalty indeed.

Chapter 8

SECTION 8.2 *Exercises on pp. 327–331*

A. pp. 327–328

1. True. **5.** True. **10.** True. **15.** False. **20.** True. **25.** False.

B. pp. 328–329

1. True. **5.** False. **10.** True. **15.** True. **20.** False. **25.** False.

C. p. 329

1. True. **5.** True. **10.** False. **15.** False. **20.** True. **25.** False.

D. pp. 329–331

1. $I \bullet \sim L$ **5.** $\sim I \bullet \sim L$ **10.** $\sim (E \vee J)$
15. $\sim I \vee L$ **20.** $(I \bullet E) \vee \sim (J \bullet S)$ **25.** $(L \bullet E) \bullet (S \bullet J)$

SECTION 8.3 *Exercises on pp. 339–341*

A. p. 339

1. True. **5.** False. **10.** True. **15.** False. **20.** False. **25.** True.

B. p. 340

1. True. **5.** False. **10.** False. **15.** True. **20.** False. **25.** True.

C. pp. 340–341

1. $A \supset (B \supset C)$ **5.** $(A \bullet B) \supset C$ **10.** $\sim[A \supset (B \bullet C)]$
15. $B \supset (A \vee C)$ **20.** $B \vee C$ **25.** $(\sim C \bullet \sim D) \supset (\sim B \vee A)$

SECTION 8.4 *Exercises on pp. 344–346*

e. 10 is the specific form of *e*.
o. 3 has *o* as a substitution instance, and 24 is the specific form of *o*.

SECTION 8.7 *Exercises on pp. 355–357*

A. p. 355

1.

p	q	$p \supset q$	$\sim q$	$\sim p$	$\sim q \supset \sim p$
T	T	T	F	F	T
T	F	F	T	F	F
F	T	T	F	T	T
F	F	T	T	T	T

Valid

5.

p	q	$p \supset q$
T	T	T
T	F	F
F	T	T
F	F	T

Invalid (shown by second row)

10.

p	q	$p \bullet q$
T	T	T
T	F	F
F	T	F
F	F	F

Valid

15.

p	q	r	$q \supset r$	$p \supset (q \supset r)$	$p \supset r$	$q \supset (p \supset r)$	$p \vee q$	$(p \vee q) \supset r$
T	T	T	T	T	T	T	T	T
T	T	F	F	F	F	F	T	F
T	F	T	T	T	T	T	T	T
T	F	F	T	T	F	T	T	F
F	T	T	T	T	T	T	T	T
F	T	F	F	T	T	T	T	F
F	F	T	T	T	T	T	F	T
F	F	F	T	T	T	T	F	T

Invalid (shown by fourth and sixth rows)

20.

p	q	r	s	$p \bullet q$	$p \supset q$	$(p \bullet q) \supset r$	$r \supset s$	$p \supset (r \supset s)$	$(p \supset q) \bullet [(p \bullet q) \supset r]$	$p \supset s$
T	T	T	T	T	T	T	T	T	T	T
T	T	T	F	T	T	T	F	F	T	F
T	T	F	T	T	T	F	T	T	F	T
T	T	F	F	T	T	F	T	T	F	F
T	F	T	T	F	F	T	T	T	F	T
T	F	T	F	F	F	T	F	F	F	F
T	F	F	T	F	F	T	T	T	F	T
T	F	F	F	F	F	T	T	T	F	F
F	T	T	T	F	T	T	T	T	T	T
F	T	T	F	F	T	T	F	T	T	T
F	T	F	T	F	T	T	T	T	T	T
F	T	F	F	F	T	T	T	T	T	T
F	F	T	T	F	T	T	T	T	T	T
F	F	T	F	F	T	T	F	T	T	T
F	F	F	T	F	T	T	T	T	T	T
F	F	F	F	F	T	T	T	T	T	T

Valid

B. pp. 355–356

1. $(A \vee B) \supset (A \bullet B)$
$A \vee B$
$\therefore A \bullet B$

has the specific form

$(p \vee q) \supset (p \bullet q)$
$p \vee q$
$\therefore p \bullet q$

p	q	$p \vee q$	$p \bullet q$	$(p \vee q) \supset (p \bullet q)$
T	T	T	T	T
T	F	T	F	F
F	T	T	F	F
F	F	F	F	T

Valid

5. $(I \vee J) \supset (I \bullet J)$ has the specific form $(p \vee q) \supset (p \bullet q)$
$\sim(I \vee J)$ — $\sim(p \vee q)$
$\therefore \sim(I \bullet J)$ — $\therefore \sim(p \bullet q)$

p	q	$p \vee q$	$p \bullet q$	$(p \vee q) \supset (p \bullet q)$	$\sim(p \vee q)$	$\sim(p \bullet q)$
T	T	T	T	T	F	F
T	F	T	F	F	F	T
F	T	T	F	F	F	T
F	F	F	F	T	T	T

Valid (Note: Fallacy of denying the antecedent is *not* committed here!)

10. $U \supset (V \vee W)$ has the specific form $p \supset (q \vee r)$
$(V \bullet W) \supset \sim U$ — $(q \bullet r) \supset \sim p$
$\therefore \sim U$ — $\therefore \sim p$

p	q	r	$q \vee r$	$p \supset (q \vee r)$	$q \bullet r$	$\sim p$	$(q \bullet r) \supset \sim p$
T	T	T	T	T	T	F	F
T	T	F	T	T	F	F	T
T	F	T	T	T	F	F	T
T	F	F	F	F	F	F	T
F	T	T	T	T	T	T	T
F	T	F	T	T	F	T	T
F	F	T	T	T	F	T	T
F	F	F	F	T	F	T	T

Invalid (shown by second and third rows)

C. pp. 356–357

1.

$A \supset (B \bullet C)$ | | $p \supset (q \bullet r)$
$\sim B$ | has the specific | $\sim q$
$\therefore \sim A$ | form | $\therefore \sim p$

p	q	r	$q \bullet r$	$p \supset (q \bullet r)$	$\sim q$	$\sim p$
T	T	T	T	T	F	F
T	T	F	F	F	F	F
T	F	T	F	F	T	F
T	F	F	F	F	T	F
F	T	T	T	T	F	T
F	T	F	F	T	F	T
F	F	T	F	T	T	T
F	F	F	F	T	T	T

Valid

5.

$M \supset (N \supset O)$ | | $p \supset (q \supset r)$
N | has the specific | q
$\therefore O \supset M$ | form | $\therefore r \supset p$

p	q	r	$q \supset r$	$p \supset (q \supset r)$	$r \supset p$
T	T	T	T	T	T
T	T	F	F	F	T
T	F	T	T	T	T
T	F	F	T	T	T
F	T	T	T	T	F
F	T	F	F	T	T
F	F	T	T	T	F
F	F	F	T	T	T

Invalid (shown by fifth row)

10.

$G \supset (I \bullet D)$		$p \supset (q \bullet r)$
$(I \vee D) \supset B$	has the specific	$(q \vee r) \supset s$
$\therefore G \supset B$	form	$\therefore p \supset s$

p	q	r	s	q • r	p ⊃ (q • r)	q v r	(q v r) ⊃ s	p ⊃ s
T	T	T	T	T	T	T	T	T
T	T	T	F	T	T	T	F	F
T	T	F	T	F	F	T	T	T
T	T	F	F	F	F	T	F	F
T	F	T	T	F	F	T	T	T
T	F	T	F	F	F	T	F	F
T	F	F	T	F	F	F	T	T
T	F	F	F	F	F	F	T	F
F	T	T	T	T	T	T	T	T
F	T	T	F	T	T	T	F	T
F	T	F	T	F	T	T	T	T
F	T	F	F	F	T	T	F	T
F	F	T	T	F	T	T	T	T
F	F	T	F	F	T	T	F	T
F	F	F	T	F	T	F	T	T
F	F	F	F	F	T	F	T	T

Valid

SECTION 8.8 *Exercises on pp. 361–362*

A. pp. 361–362

1. *c* is the specific form of 1.

5. *c* has 5 as a substitution instance, and *i* is the specific form of 5.

10. *e* has 10 as a substitution instance.

B. p. 362

1.

p	q	$p \supset q$	$p \supset (p \supset q)$	$[p \supset (p \supset q)] \supset q$
T	T	T	T	T
T	F	F	F	T
F	T	T	T	T
F	F	T	T	F

Contingent

5.

p	q	$\sim q$	$q \bullet \sim q$	$p \supset (q \bullet \sim q)$	$p \supset [p \supset (q \bullet \sim q)]$
T	T	F	F	F	F
T	F	T	F	F	F
F	T	F	F	T	T
F	F	T	F	T	T

Contingent

10.

p	*q*	*r*	*s*	*p* ⊃ *q*	*r* ⊃ *s*	(*p* ⊃ *q*) • (*r* ⊃ *s*)	*q* v *s*	[(*p* ⊃ *q*) (*r* ⊃ *s*)] • (*q* v *s*)	*p* v *r*	{[(*p* ⊃ *q*) • (*r* ⊃ *s*)] • (*q* v *s*)} ⊃ (*p* v *r*)
T	T	T	T	T	T	T	T	T	T	T
T	T	T	F	T	F	F	T	F	T	T
T	T	F	T	T	T	T	T	T	T	T
T	T	F	F	T	T	T	T	T	T	T
T	F	T	T	F	T	F	T	F	T	T
T	F	T	F	F	F	F	F	F	T	T
T	F	F	T	F	T	F	T	F	T	T
T	F	F	F	F	T	F	F	F	T	T
F	T	T	T	T	T	T	T	T	T	T
F	T	T	F	T	F	F	T	F	T	T
F	T	F	T	T	T	T	T	T	F	F
F	T	F	F	T	T	T	T	T	F	F
F	F	T	T	T	T	T	T	T	T	T
F	F	T	F	T	F	F	F	F	T	T
F	F	F	T	T	T	T	T	T	F	F
F	F	F	F	T	T	T	F	F	F	T

Contingent

C. p. 362
1.

p	*q*	*p* ⊃ *q*	~*q*	~*p*	~*q* ⊃ ~*p*	(*p* ⊃ *q*) ≡ (~*q* ⊃ ~*p*)
T	T	T	F	F	T	T
T	F	F	T	F	F	T
F	T	T	F	T	T	T
F	F	T	T	T	T	T

Tautology

5.

p	q	$p \vee q$	$p \bullet (p \vee q)$	$[p \equiv [p \bullet (p \vee q)]$
T	T	T	T	T
T	F	T	T	T
F	T	T	F	T
F	F	F	F	T

Tautology

10.

p	q	$p \supset q$	$p \vee q$	$(p \vee q) \equiv q$	$(p \supset q) \equiv [(p \vee q) \equiv q]$
T	T	T	T	T	T
T	F	F	T	F	T
F	T	T	T	T	T
F	F	T	F	T	T

Tautology

15.

p	q	r	$q \vee r$	$p \bullet (q \vee r)$	$p \bullet q$	$p \bullet r$	$(p \bullet q) \vee (p \bullet r)$	$[p \bullet (q \vee r)] \equiv [(p \bullet q) \vee (p \bullet r)]$
T	T	T	T	T	T	T	T	T
T	T	F	T	T	T	F	T	T
T	F	T	T	T	F	T	T	T
T	F	F	F	F	F	F	F	T
F	T	T	T	F	F	F	F	T
F	T	F	T	F	F	F	F	T
F	F	T	T	F	F	F	F	T
F	F	F	F	F	F	F	F	T

Tautology

20.

p	q	$p \supset q$	$q \supset p$	$(p \supset q) \bullet (q \supset p)$	$p \bullet q$	$\sim p$	$\sim q$	$\sim p \bullet \sim q$	$(p \bullet q) \vee (\sim p \bullet \sim q)$	$[(p \supset q) \bullet (q \supset p)] \equiv [(p \bullet q) \vee (\sim p \bullet \sim q)]$
T	T	T	T	T	T	F	F	F	T	T
T	F	F	T	F	F	F	T	F	F	T
F	T	T	F	F	F	T	F	F	F	T
F	F	T	T	T	F	T	T	T	T	T

Tautology

Chapter 9

SECTION 9.2 *Exercises on pp. 379–380*

1. Absorption (Abs.)
5. Constructive Dilemma (C.D.)
10. Hypothetical Syllogism (H.S.)
15. Conjunction (Conj.)
20. Hypothetical Syllogism (H.S.)

SECTION 9.3 *Exercises on pp. 382–383*

1. **3.** 1, Simp.
4. 3, Add.
5. 2, 4, M.P.
6. 3, 5, Conj.

5. **5.** 2, 4, M.P.
6. 1, 5, Conj.
7. 3, 4, D.S.
8. 6, 7, C.D.

10. **6.** 4, 5, Conj.
7. 3, 6, M.P.
8. 7, 1, H.S.
9. 2, 8, Conj.
10. 9, 4, C.D.

SECTION 9.4 *Exercises on pp. 385–386*

5. **1.** $M \vee N$
2. $\sim M \bullet \sim O$
$\therefore N$
3. $\sim M$ — 2, Simp.
4. N — 1,3, D.S.

10. **1.** $A \supset B$
2. $(A \bullet B) \supset C$
$\therefore A \supset C$
3. $A \supset (A \bullet B)$ — 1, Abs.
4. $A \supset C$ — 3,2, H.S.

15. **1.** $(P \supset Q) \bullet (R \supset S)$
2. $(P \vee R) \bullet (Q \vee R)$
$\therefore Q \vee S$
3. $P \vee R$ — 2, Simp.
4. $Q \vee S$ — 1,3, C.D.

20. **1.** $(\sim H \vee I) \vee J$
2. $\sim(\sim H \vee I)$
$\therefore J \vee \sim H$
3. J — 1,2, D.S.
4. $J \vee \sim H$ — 3, Add.

25. **1.** $(W \bullet X) \supset (Y \bullet Z)$
2. $\sim[(W \bullet X) \bullet (Y \bullet Z)]$
$\therefore \sim(W \bullet X)$
3. $(W \bullet X) \supset [(W \bullet X) \bullet (Y \bullet Z)]$ — 1, Abs.
4. $\sim(W \bullet X)$ — 3,2, M.T.

30. **1.** $Q \supset (R \vee S)$
2. $(T \bullet U) \supset R$
3. $(R \vee S) \supset (T \bullet U)$
$\therefore Q \supset R$
4. $Q \supset (T \bullet U)$ — 1,3, H.S.
5. $Q \supset R$ — 4,2, H.S.

SECTION 9.5 *Exercises on pp. 387–393*

A. pp. 387–389

5. **1.** $N \supset [(N \bullet O) \supset P]$
2. $N \bullet O$
$\therefore P$
3. N — 2, Simp.
4. $(N \bullet O) \supset P$ — 1,3, M.P.
5. P — 4,2, M.P.

10. **1.** $E \vee \sim F$
2. $F \vee (E \vee G)$
3. $\sim E$
$\therefore G$
4. $\sim F$ — 1,3, D.S.
5. $E \vee G$ — 2,4, D.S.
6. G — 5,3, D.S.

15. **1.** $(Z \bullet A) \supset B$
2. $B \supset A$
3. $(B \bullet A) \supset (A \bullet B)$
$\therefore (Z \bullet A) \supset (A \bullet B)$
4. $B \supset (B \bullet A)$ — 2, Abs.
5. $B \supset (A \bullet B)$ — 4,3, H.S.
6. $(Z \bullet A) \supset (A \bullet B)$ — 1,5, H.S.

B. pp. 389–390

5. **1.** $(Q \supset R) \bullet (S \supset T)$
2. $(U \supset V) \bullet (W \supset X)$
3. $Q \vee U$
$\therefore R \vee V$
4. $Q \supset R$ — 1, Simp.
5. $U \supset V$ — 2, Simp.
6. $(Q \supset R) \bullet (U \supset V)$ — 4,5, Conj.
7. $R \vee V$ — 6,3, C.D.

10. **1.** $(N \vee O) \supset P$
2. $(P \vee Q) \supset R$
3. $Q \vee N$
4. $\sim Q$
$\therefore R$
5. N — 3,4, D.S.
6. $N \vee O$ — 5, Add.
7. P — 1,6, M.P.
8. $P \vee Q$ — 7, Add.
9. R — 2,8, M.P.

C. pp. 391–393

5. **1.** $C \supset R$
2. $(C \bullet R) \supset B$
3. $(C \supset B) \supset \sim S$
4. $S \vee M$
$\therefore M$
5. $C \supset (C \bullet R)$ — 1, Abs.
6. $C \supset B$ — 5,2, H.S.
7. $\sim S$ — 3,6, M.P.
8. M — 4,7, D.S.

10. **1.** $O \supset \sim M$
2. O
3. $B \supset \sim N$
4. B
5. $(\sim M \bullet \sim N) \supset F$
6. $(B \bullet F) \supset G$
$\therefore G$
7. $\sim M$ — 1,2, M.P.
8. $\sim N$ — 3,4, M.P.
9. $\sim M \bullet \sim N$ — 7,8, Conj.
10. F — 5,9, M.P.
11. $B \bullet F$ — 4,10, Conj.
12. G — 6,11, M.P.

SECTION 9.6 *Exercises on pp. 399–400*

5. Material Equivalence (Equiv.)
10. Association (Assoc.)
15. Distribution (Dist.)
20. De Morgan's Theorem (De M.)

SECTION 9.8 *Exercises on pp. 406–421*

A. pp. 406–407

5. **3.** 2, Dist.
4. 3, Com.
5. 4, Simp.
6. 5, Taut.
7. 1, Assoc.
8. 7,6, D.S.
9. 8, Impl

10. **3.** 2, Trans.
4. 3, Exp.
5. 1, D.N.
6. 5, Com.
7. 6, Dist.
8. 7, Com.
9. 4, 8, C.D.
10. 9, Com.
11. 10, D.N.
12. 11, De M.

B. pp. 409–410

5. **1.** $\sim K \vee (L \supset M)$
$\therefore (K \bullet L) \supset M$
2. $K \supset (L \supset M)$ 1, Impl.
3. $(K \bullet L) \supset M$ 2, Exp.

10. **1.** $Z \supset A$
2. $\sim A \vee B$
$\therefore Z \supset B$
3. $A \supset B$ 2, Impl.
4. $Z \supset B$ 1,3, H.S.

15. **1.** $(O \vee P) \supset (Q \vee R)$
2. $P \vee O$
$\therefore Q \vee R$
3. $O \vee P$ 2, Com.
4. $Q \vee R$ 1,3, M.P.

20. **1.** $I \supset [J \vee (K \vee L)]$
2. $\sim[(J \vee K) \vee L]$
$\therefore \sim I$
3. $\sim[J \vee (K \vee L)]$ 2, Assoc.
4. $\sim I$ 1,3, M.T.

25. **1.** $A \vee B$
2. $C \vee D$
$\therefore [(A \vee B) \bullet C] \vee [(A \vee B) \bullet D]$
3. $(A \vee B) \bullet (C \vee D)$ 1,2, Conj.
4. $[(A \vee B) \bullet C] \vee$
$[(A \vee B) \bullet D]$ 3, Dist.

30. **1.** $\sim[(B \supset \sim C) \bullet (\sim C \supset B)]$
2. $(D \bullet E) \supset (B \equiv \sim C)$
$\therefore \sim(D \bullet E)$
3. $\sim(B \equiv \sim C)$ 1, Equiv.
4. $\sim(D \bullet E)$ 2,3, M.T.

C. pp. 410–412

5. **1.** $[(K \vee L) \vee M] \vee N$
$\therefore (N \vee K) \vee (L \vee M)$
2. $[K \vee (L \vee M)] \vee N$ 1, Assoc.
3. $N \vee [K \vee (L \vee M)]$ 2, Com.
4. $(N \vee K) \vee (L \vee M)$ 3, Assoc.

10. **1.** $(Z \vee A) \vee B$
2. $\sim A$
$\therefore Z \vee B$
3. $(A \vee Z) \vee B$ 1, Com.
4. $A \vee (Z \vee B)$ 3, Assoc.
5. $Z \vee B$ 4,2, D.S.

15. **1.** $[R \supset (S \supset T)] \bullet [(R \bullet T) \supset U]$
2. $R \bullet (S \vee T)$
$\therefore T \vee U$
3. $(R \bullet S) \vee (R \bullet T)$ 2, Dist.
4. $[(R \bullet S) \supset T] \bullet$
$[(R \bullet T) \supset U]$ 1, Exp.
5. $T \vee U$ 4,3, C.D.

D. pp. 412–414

5.

1.	$K \supset L$	
	$\therefore K \supset (L \vee M)$	
2.	$\sim K \vee L$	1, Impl.
3.	$(\sim K \vee L) \vee M$	2, Add.
4.	$\sim K \vee (L \vee M)$	3, Assoc.
5.	$K \supset (L \vee M)$	4, Impl.

10.

1.	$Z \supset A$	
2.	$Z \vee A$	
	$\therefore A$	
3.	$A \vee Z$	2, Com.
4.	$\sim\sim A \vee Z$	3, D.N.
5.	$\sim A \supset Z$	4, Impl.
6.	$\sim A \supset A$	5, 1, H.S.
7.	$\sim\sim A \vee A$	6, Impl.
8.	$A \vee A$	7, D.N.
9.	A	8, Taut.

E. pp. 416–417

1.

1.	$A \supset \sim B$	
2.	$\sim(C \bullet \sim A)$	
	$\therefore C \supset \sim B$	
3.	$\sim C \vee \sim\sim A$	2, De M.
4.	$C \supset \sim\sim A$	3, Impl.
5.	$C \supset A$	4, D.N.
6.	$C \supset \sim B$	5, 1, H.S.

5.

1.	$[(M \bullet N) \bullet O] \supset P$	
2.	$Q \supset [(O \bullet M) \bullet N]$	
	$\therefore \sim Q \vee P$	
3.	$[O \bullet (M \bullet N)] \supset P$	1, Com.
4.	$[(O \bullet M) \bullet N] \supset P$	3, Assoc.
5.	$Q \supset P$	2, 4, H.S.
6.	$\sim Q \vee P$	5, Impl.

10.

1.	$[H \vee (I \vee J)] \supset (K \supset J)$	
2.	$L \supset [I \vee (J \vee H)]$	
	$\therefore (L \bullet K) \supset J$	
3.	$[(I \vee J) \vee H] \supset (K \supset J)$	1, Com.
4.	$[I \vee (J \vee H)] \supset (K \supset J)$	3, Assoc.
5.	$L \supset (K \supset J)$	2, 4 H.S.
6.	$(L \bullet K) \supset J$	5, Exp.

15.

1.	$(Z \supset Z) \supset (A \supset A)$	
2.	$(A \supset A) \supset (Z \supset Z)$	
	$\therefore A \supset A$	
3.	$[(Z \supset Z) \supset (A \supset A)] \vee \sim A$	1, Add.
4.	$\sim A \vee [(Z \supset Z) \supset (A \supset A)]$	3, Com.
5.	$A \supset [(Z \supset Z) \supset (A \supset A)]$	4, Impl.
6.	$A \supset \{A \bullet [(Z \supset Z) \supset (A \supset A)]\}$	5, Abs.
7.	$\sim A \vee \{A \bullet [(Z \supset Z) \supset (A \supset A)]\}$	6, Impl.
8.	$(\sim A \vee A) \bullet \{\sim A \vee [(Z \supset Z) \supset (A \supset A)]\}$	7, Dist.
9.	$\sim A \vee A$	8, Simp.
10.	$A \supset A$	9, Impl.

20.

1.	$(R \vee S) \supset (T \bullet U)$	
2.	$\sim R \supset (V \supset \sim V)$	
3.	$\sim T$	
	$\therefore \sim V$	
4.	$\sim T \vee \sim U$	3, Add.
5.	$\sim(T \bullet U)$	4, De M.
6.	$\sim(R \vee S)$	1, 5, M.T.
7.	$\sim R \bullet \sim S$	6, De M.
8.	$\sim R$	7, Simp.
9.	$V \supset \sim V$	2, 8, M.P.
10.	$\sim V \vee \sim V$	9, Impl.
11.	$\sim V$	10, Taut.

F. pp. 417–420

1. **1.** $\sim N \vee A$
2. N
$\therefore A$
3. $N \supset A$ — 1, Impl.
4. A — 3, 2, M.P.

5. **1.** $R \supset A$
$\therefore R \supset (A \vee W)$
2. $\sim R \vee A$ — 1, Impl.
3. $(\sim R \vee A) \vee W$ — 2, Add.
4. $\sim R \vee (A \vee W)$ — 3, Assoc.
5. $R \supset (A \vee W)$ — 4, Impl.

10. **1.** $(G \bullet S) \supset D$
2. $(S \supset D) \supset P$
3. G
$\therefore P$
4. $G \supset (S \supset D)$ — 1, Exp.
5. $S \supset D$ — 4, 3, M.P.
6. P — 2, 5, M.P.

15. **1.** $M \supset \sim C$
2. $\sim C \supset \sim A$
3. $D \vee A$
$\therefore \sim M \vee D$
4. $M \supset \sim A$ — 1,2, H.S.
5. $A \vee D$ — 3, Com.
6. $\sim\sim A \vee D$ — 5, D.N.
7. $\sim A \supset D$ — 6, Impl.
8. $M \supset D$ — 4,7, H.S.
9. $\sim M \vee D$ — 8, Impl.

20. **1.** $P \supset \sim M$
2. $C \supset M$
3. $\sim L \vee C$
4. $(\sim P \supset \sim E) \bullet (\sim E \supset \sim C)$
5. $P \vee \sim P$
$\therefore \sim L$
6. $(\sim E \supset \sim C) \bullet (\sim P \supset \sim E)$ — 4, Com.
7. $\sim P \supset \sim E$ — 4, Simp.
8. $\sim E \supset \sim C$ — 6, Simp.
9. $\sim P \supset \sim C$ — 7,8, H.S.
10. $\sim M \supset \sim C$ — 2, Trans.
11. $P \supset \sim C$ — 1, 10, H.S.
12. $(P \supset \sim C) \bullet (\sim P \supset \sim C)$ — 11,9, Conj.
13. $\sim C \vee \sim C$ — 12,5, C.D.
14. $\sim C$ — 13, Taut.
15. $C \vee \sim L$ — 3, Com.
16. $\sim L$ — 15,14, D.S.

G. pp. 420–421

5. **1.** $(H \vee \sim H) \supset G$
$\therefore G$
2. $[(H \vee \sim H) \supset G] \vee \sim H$ — 1, Add.
3. $\sim H \vee [(H \vee \sim H) \supset G]$ — 2, Com.
4. $H \supset [(H \vee \sim H) \supset G]$ — 3, Impl.
5. $H \supset \{H \bullet [(H \vee \sim H) \supset G]\}$ — 4, Abs.
6. $\sim H \vee \{H \bullet [(H \vee \sim H) \supset G]\}$ — 5, Impl.
7. $(\sim H \vee H) \bullet \{\sim H \vee [(H \vee \sim H) \supset G]\}$ — 6, Dist.
8. $\sim H \vee H$ — 7, Simp.
9. $H \vee \sim H$ — 8, Com.
10. G — 1,9, M.P.

SECTION 9.9 *Exercises on pp. 423–424*

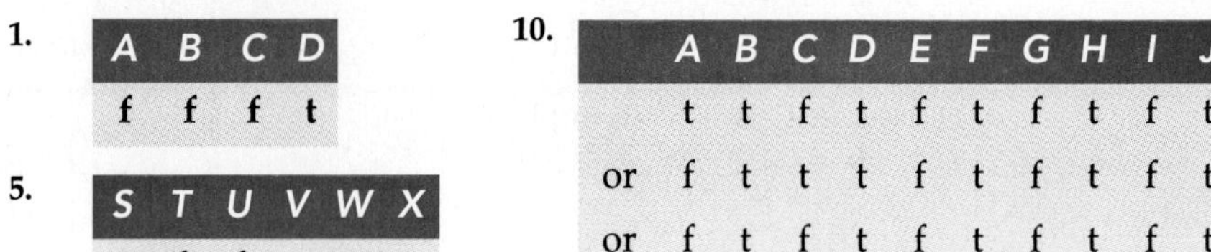

1.

A	B	C	D
f	f	f	t

5.

S	T	U	V	W	X
t	f	f	t	t	t

10.

	A	B	C	D	E	F	G	H	I	J
	t	t	f	t	f	t	f	t	f	t
or	f	t	t	t	f	t	f	t	f	t
or	f	t	f	t	f	t	f	t	f	t

or any of thirteen other truth-value assignments.

SECTION 9.10 *Exercises on pp. 427–431*

A. pp. 427–428

1.

1.	$(A \supset B) \cdot (C \supset D)$	
	$\therefore (A \cdot C) \supset (B \vee D)$	
2.	$A \supset B$	1, Simp.
3.	$\sim A \vee B$	2, Impl.
4.	$(\sim A \vee B) \vee D$	3, Add.
5.	$\sim A \vee (B \vee D)$	4, Assoc.
6.	$[\sim A \vee (B \vee D)] \vee \sim C$	5, Add.
7.	$\sim C \vee [\sim A \vee (B \vee D)]$	6, Com.
8.	$(\sim C \vee \sim A) \vee (B \vee D)$	7, Assoc.
9.	$(\sim A \vee \sim C) \vee (B \vee D)$	8, Com.
10.	$\sim(A \cdot C) \vee (B \vee D)$	9, De M.
11.	$(A \cdot C) \supset (B \vee D)$	10, Impl.

5.

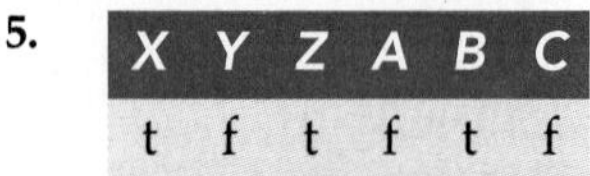

X	Y	Z	A	B	C
t	f	t	f	t	f

10.

	A	B	C	D	E	F	G
	f	f	t	t	f	t	t
or	f	f	t	f	f	t	t
or	f	f	f	t	f	t	t
or	f	f	f	f	f	t	t

B. pp. 428–430

1.

1.	$C \supset (M \supset D)$	
2.	$D \supset V$	
3.	$(D \supset A) \cdot \sim A$	
	$\therefore M \supset \sim C$	
4.	$D \supset A$	3, Simp.
5.	$\sim A \cdot (D \supset A)$	3, Com.
6.	$\sim A$	5, Simp.
7.	$\sim D$	4,6, M.T.
8.	$(C \cdot M) \supset D$	1, Exp.
9.	$\sim(C \cdot M)$	8,7, M.T.
10.	$\sim C \vee \sim M$	9, De M.
11.	$\sim M \vee \sim C$	10, Com.
12.	$M \supset \sim C$	11, Impl.

5. $(I \bullet S) \supset (G \bullet P)$
$[(S \bullet \sim I) \supset A] \bullet (A \supset P)$
$I \supset S$
$\therefore P$

proved invalid by

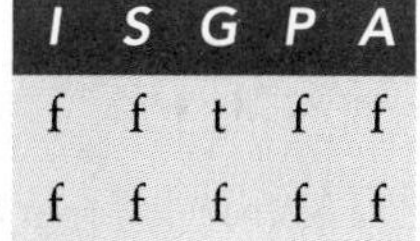

	I	S	G	P	A
	f	f	t	f	f
or	f	f	f	f	f

10. $(H \supset A) \bullet (F \supset C)$
$A \supset (F \bullet E)$
$(O \supset C) \bullet (O \supset M)$
$P \supset (M \supset D)$
$P \bullet (D \supset G)$
$\therefore H \supset G$

proved invalid by

H	A	C	F	E	O	M	P	D	G
t	t	t	t	t	f	f	t	f	f

15. **1.** $(J \vee A) \supset [(S \vee K) \supset (\sim I \bullet Y)]$
2. $(\sim I \vee \sim M) \supset E$
$\therefore J \supset (S \supset E)$
3. $\sim(J \vee A) \vee [(S \vee K) \supset (\sim I \bullet Y)]$ — 1, Impl.
4. $[(S \vee K) \supset (\sim I \bullet Y)] \vee \sim(J \vee A)$ — 3, Com.
5. $[(S \vee K) \supset (\sim I \bullet Y)] \vee (\sim J \bullet \sim A)$ — 4, De M.
6. $\{[(S \vee K) \supset (\sim I \bullet Y)] \vee \sim J\} \bullet$
$\{[(S \vee K) \supset (\sim I \bullet Y)] \vee \sim A\}$ — 5, Dist.
7. $[(S \vee K) \supset (\sim I \bullet Y)] \vee \sim J$ — 6, Simp.
8. $[\sim(S \vee K) \vee (\sim I \bullet Y)] \vee \sim J$ — 7, Impl.
9. $\sim(S \vee K) \vee [(\sim I \bullet Y) \vee \sim J]$ — 8, Assoc.
10. $[(\sim I \bullet Y) \vee \sim J] \vee \sim(S \vee K)$ — 9, Com.
11. $[(\sim I \bullet Y) \vee \sim J] \vee (\sim S \bullet \sim K)$ — 10, De M.
12. $\{[(\sim I \bullet Y) \vee \sim J] \vee \sim S\} \bullet$
$\{[(\sim I \bullet Y) \vee \sim J] \vee \sim K\}$ — 11, Dist.
13. $[(\sim I \bullet Y) \vee \sim J] \vee \sim S$ — 12, Simp.
14. $(\sim I \bullet Y) \vee (\sim J \vee \sim S)$ — 13, Assoc.
15. $(\sim J \vee \sim S) \vee (\sim I \bullet Y)$ — 14, Com.
16. $[(\sim J \vee \sim S) \vee \sim I] \bullet [(\sim J \vee \sim S) \vee Y]$ — 15, Dist.
17. $(\sim J \vee \sim S) \vee \sim I$ — 16, Simp.
18. $[(\sim J \vee \sim S) \vee \sim I] \vee \sim M$ — 17, Add.
19. $(\sim J \vee \sim S) \vee (\sim I \vee \sim M)$ — 18, Assoc.
20. $\sim(J \bullet S) \vee (\sim I \vee \sim M)$ — 19, De M.
21. $(J \bullet S) \supset (\sim I \vee \sim M)$ — 20, Impl.
22. $(J \bullet S) \supset E$ — 21, 2, H.S.
23. $J \supset (S \supset E)$ — 22, Exp.

C. p. 431

5. **1.** $(R \vee \sim R) \supset W$
$\therefore W$
2. $[(R \vee \sim R) \supset W] \vee \sim R$ — 1, Add.
3. $\sim R \vee [(R \vee \sim R) \supset W]$ — 2, Com.
4. $R \supset [(R \vee \sim R) \supset W]$ — 3, Impl.
5. $R \supset \{R \bullet [(R \vee \sim R) \supset W]\}$ — 4, Abs.
6. $\sim R \vee \{R \bullet [(R \vee \sim R) \supset W]\}$ — 5, Impl.

7. $(\sim R \vee R) \bullet \{\sim R \vee [(R \vee \sim R) \supset W]\}$ 6, Dist.
8. $\sim R \vee R$ 7, Simp.
9. $R \vee \sim R$ 8, Com.
10. W 1,9, M.P.

SECTION 9.11 *Exercises on pp. 433–434*

A. p. 433

5. **1.** $D \supset (Z \supset Y)$
2. $Z \supset (Y \supset \sim Z)$
$\therefore \sim D \vee \sim Z$
3. $\sim(\sim D \vee \sim Z)$ I. P. (Indirect proof)
4. $\sim\sim D \bullet \sim\sim Z$ 3, De M.
5. $D \bullet \sim\sim Z$ 4, D.N.
6. $D \bullet Z$ 5, D.N.
7. D 6, Simp.
8. $Z \supset Y$ 1, 7, M. P.
9. $Z \bullet D$ 6, Com.
10. Z 9, Simp.
11. $Y \supset \sim Z$ 2, 10, M. P.
12. Y 8, 10, M. P.
13. $\sim Z$ 11, 12, M. P.
14. $Z \bullet \sim Z$ 10, 13, Conj.

Chapter 10

SECTION 10.4 *Exercises on pp. 451–453*

A. pp. 451–452

5. $(\exists x)(Dx \bullet \sim Rx)$
10. $(x)(Cx \supset \sim Fx)$
15. $(x)(Vx \supset Cx)$
20. $(x)(Cx \equiv Hx)$

B. p. 453

5. $[(\exists x)(Gx \bullet \sim Sx)] \bullet [(\exists x)(Dx \bullet \sim Bx)]$
10. $(x)(\sim Bx \supset \sim Wx)$

C. p. 453

1. $(\exists x)(Ax \bullet \sim Bx)$
5. $(\exists x)(Ix \bullet \sim Jx)$
10. $(\exists x)(Sx \bullet \sim Tx)$

SECTION 10.5 *Exercises on pp. 461–463*

A. p. 461–462

5. **1.** $(x)(Mx \supset Nx)$
2. $(\exists x)(Mx \bullet Ox)$
$\therefore (\exists x)(Ox \bullet Nx)$
3. $Ma \bullet Oa$ 2, **E.I.**
4. $Ma \supset Na$ 1, **U.I.**
5. Ma 3, Simp.
6. Na 4,5, M.P.
7. $Oa \bullet Ma$ 3, Com.
8. Oa 7, Simp.
9. $Oa \bullet Na$ 8,6, Conj.
10. $(\exists x)(Ox \bullet Nx)$ 9, **E.G.**

10. **1.** $(x)(Bx \supset \sim Cx)$
2. $(\exists x)(Cx \bullet Dx)$
$\therefore (\exists x)(Dx \bullet \sim Bx)$
3. $Ca \bullet Da$ 2, **E.I.**
4. $Ba \supset \sim Ca$ 1, **U.I.**
5. Ca 3, Simp.
6. $\sim\sim Ca$ 5, D.N.
7. $\sim Ba$ 4,6, M.T.
8. $Da \bullet Ca$ 3, Com.

9.	Da	8, Simp.
10.	$Da \bullet {\sim}Ba$	9,7, Conj.
11.	$(\exists x)(Dx \bullet {\sim}Bx)$	10, **E.G.**

B. pp. 462–463

1.

1.	$(x)(Ax \supset {\sim}Bx)$	
2.	Bc	
	$\therefore {\sim}Ac$	
3.	$Ac \supset {\sim}Bc$	1, **U.I.**
4.	${\sim}{\sim}Bc$	2, D.N.
5.	${\sim}Ac$	3,4, M.T.

5.

1.	$(x)(Mx \supset Nx)$	
2.	$(\exists x)(Ox \bullet Mx)$	
	$\therefore (\exists x)(Ox \bullet Nx)$	
3.	$Oa \bullet Ma$	2, **E.I.**
4.	$Ma \supset Na$	1, **U.I.**
5.	Oa	3, Simp.
6.	$Ma \bullet Oa$	3, Com.
7.	Ma	6, Simp.
8.	Na	4,7, M.P.
9.	$Oa \bullet Na$	5,8, Conj.
10.	$(\exists x)(Ox \bullet Nx)$	9, E.G.

10.

1.	$(x)(Ax \supset Rx)$	
2.	${\sim}Rs$	
	$\therefore {\sim}As$	
3.	$As \supset Rs$	1, **U.I.**
4.	${\sim}As$	3,2, M.T.

SECTION 10.6 *Exercises on pp. 466–468*

A. pp. 466–467

5.

$(\exists x)(Mx \bullet {\sim}Nx)$	logically	$(Ma \bullet Na) \lor (Mb \bullet Nb)$
$(\exists x)(Mx \bullet Ox)$	equivalent	$(Ma \bullet Oa) \lor (Mb \bullet Ob)$
$\therefore (x)(Ox \supset Nx)$	in $\boxed{a, b}$ to	$\therefore (Oa \supset Na) \bullet (Ob \bullet Nb)$

proved invalid by

Ma	Mb	Na	Nb	Oa	Ob
t	t	t	f	t	t

or any of several other truth-value assignments.

10.

$(\exists x)(Bx \bullet {\sim}Cx)$	logically	$(Ba \bullet {\sim}Ca) \lor (Bb \bullet {\sim}Cb)$
$(x)(Dx \supset {\sim}Cx)$	equivalent	$(Da \supset {\sim}Ca) \bullet (Db \supset {\sim}Cb)$
$\therefore (x)(Dx \supset Bx)$	in $\boxed{a, b}$ to	$\therefore (Da \supset Ba) \bullet (Db \supset Bb)$

proved invalid by

Ba	Bb	Ca	Cb	Da	Db
f	t	f	f	t	t

B. pp. 467–468

1.

$(x)(Ax \supset Bx)$
$(x)(Cx \supset Bx)$
$\therefore (x)(Ax \supset Cx)$

logically equivalent in $\boxed{a}$ to

$Aa \supset Ba$
$Ca \supset Ba$
$\therefore Aa \supset Ca$

proved invalid by

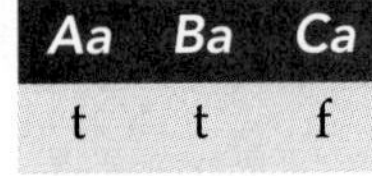

Aa	Ba	Ca
t	t	f

5.

$(\exists x)(Mx \bullet Nx)$
$(\exists x)(Ox \bullet {\sim}Nx)$
$\therefore (x)(Ox \supset {\sim}Mx)$

logically equivalent in $\boxed{a, b}$ to

$(Ma \bullet Na) \vee (Mb \bullet Nb)$
$(Oa \bullet {\sim}Na) \vee (Ob \bullet Nb)$
$\therefore (Oa \supset {\sim}Ma) \bullet (Ob \supset {\sim}Mb)$

proved invalid by

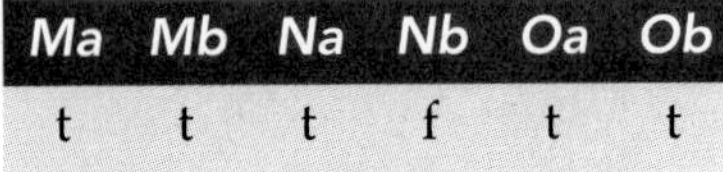

Ma	Mb	Na	Nb	Oa	Ob
t	t	t	f	t	t

or any of several other truth-value assignments.

10.

$(x)(Mx \supset Sx)$
$(x)(Wx \supset Mx)$
$\therefore (x)(Sx \supset Wx)$

logically equivalent in $\boxed{a}$ to

$Ma \supset Sa$
$Wa \supset Ma$
$\therefore Sa \supset Wa$

proved invalid by

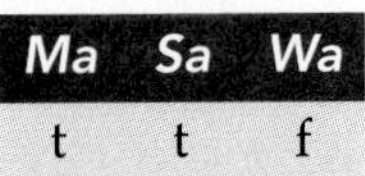

Ma	Sa	Wa
t	t	f

SECTION 10.7 *Exercises on pp. 472–477*

A. pp. 472–473

5. $(x)Gx \supset (Wx \equiv Lx)$
10. $(x)\{Ax \supset [(Bx \supset Wx) \bullet (Px \supset Sx)]\}$

B. pp. 473–474

1.

1.	$(x)[(Ax \vee Bx) \supset (Cx \bullet Dx)]$	
	$\therefore (x)(Bx \supset Cx)$	
2.	$(Ay \vee By) \supset (Cy \bullet Dy)$	1, **U.I.**
3.	${\sim}(Ay \vee By) \vee (Cy \bullet Dy)$	2, Impl.
4.	$[{\sim}(Ay \vee By) \vee Cy] \bullet [{\sim}(Ay \vee By) \vee Dy]$	3, Dist.
5.	${\sim}(Ay \vee By) \vee Cy$	4, Simp.
6.	$Cy \vee {\sim}(Ay \vee By)$	5, Com.
7.	$Cy \vee ({\sim}Ay \bullet {\sim}By)$	6, De M.
8.	$(Cy \vee {\sim}Ay) \bullet (Cy \vee {\sim}By)$	7, Dist.
9.	$(Cy \vee {\sim}By) \bullet (Cy \vee {\sim}Ay)$	8, Com.
10.	$Cy \vee {\sim}By$	9, Simp.
11.	${\sim}By \vee Cy$	10, Com.
12.	$By \supset Cy$	11, Impl.
13.	$(x)(Bx \supset Cx)$	12, **U.G.**

5.

$(\exists x)(Sx \bullet Tx)$
$(\exists x)(Ux \bullet {\sim}Sx)$
$(\exists x)(Vx \bullet {\sim}Tx)$
$\therefore (\exists x)(Ux \bullet Vx)$

logically equivalent in $\boxed{a, b, c}$ to

$(Sa \bullet Ta) \vee (Sb \bullet Tb) \vee (Sc \bullet Tc)$
$(Ua \bullet {\sim}Sa) \vee (Ub \bullet {\sim}Sb) \vee (Uc \bullet {\sim}Sc)$
$(Va \bullet {\sim}Ta) \vee (Vb \bullet {\sim}Tb) \vee (Vc \bullet {\sim}Tc)$
$\therefore (Ua \bullet Va) \vee (Ub \bullet {\sim}Vb) \vee (Uc \bullet Vc)$

proved invalid by

Sa	*Sb*	*Sc*	*Ta*	*Tb*	*Tc*	*Ua*	*Ub*	*Uc*	*Va*	*Vb*	*Vc*
t	f	t	t	t	f	f	t	f	t	f	t

or any of several other truth-value assignments.

10.

$(x)[(Sx \vee Tx) \supset \sim(Ux \vee Vx)]$
$(\exists x)(Sx \bullet \sim Wx)$
$(\exists x)(Tx \bullet \sim Xx)$
$(x)(\sim Wx \supset Xx)$
$\therefore (\exists x)(Ux \bullet \sim Vx)$

logically equivalent in $\boxed{a, b}$ to

$[(Sa \vee Ta) \supset \sim(Ua \vee Va) \bullet$
$[(Sb \vee Tb) \supset \sim(Ub \vee Vb)]$
$(Sa \bullet \sim Wa) \vee (Sb \bullet \sim Wb)$
$(Ta \bullet \sim Xa) \vee (Tb \bullet \sim Xb)$
$(\sim Wa \supset Xa) \bullet (\sim Wb \supset Xb)$
$\therefore (Ua \bullet \sim Va) \vee (Ub \bullet \sim Vb)$

and proved invalid by

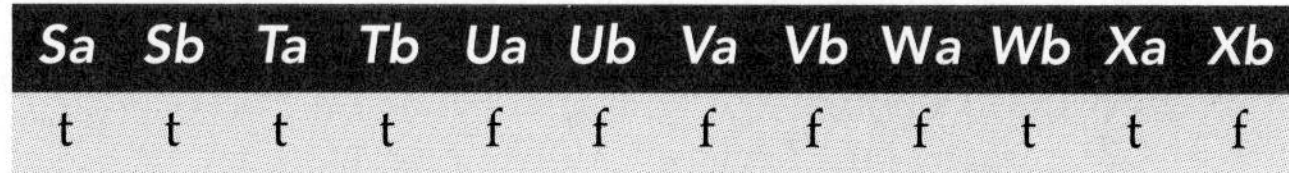

Sa	*Sb*	*Ta*	*Tb*	*Ua*	*Ub*	*Va*	*Vb*	*Wa*	*Wb*	*Xa*	*Xb*
t	t	t	t	f	f	f	f	f	t	t	f

or any of several other truth-value assignments.

C. pp. 474–475

1.

1.	$(x)[(Ax \vee Bx) \supset Cx]$	
2.	$(x)(Vx \supset Ax)$	
	$\therefore (x)(Vx \supset Cx)$	
3.	$(Ay \vee By) \supset Cy$	1, **U.I.**
4.	$Vy \supset Ay$	2, **U.I.**
5.	$\sim Vy \vee Ay$	4, Impl.
6.	$(\sim Vy \vee Ay) \vee By$	5, Add.
7.	$\sim Vy \vee (Ay \vee By)$	6, Assoc.
8.	$Vy \supset (Ay \vee By)$	7, Impl.
9.	$Vy \supset Cy$	8,3, H.S.
10.	$(x)(Vx \supset Cx)$	9, **U.G.**

5.

$(x)\{[Ex \bullet (Ix \vee Tx)] \supset \sim Sx\}$
$(\exists x)(Ex \bullet Ix)$
$(\exists x)(Ex \bullet Tx)$
$\therefore (x)(Ex \supset \sim Sx)$

This argument is logically equivalent in $\boxed{a, b}$ to

$\{[Ea \bullet (Ia \vee Ta)] \supset \sim Sa\} \bullet \{[Eb \bullet (Ib \vee Tb)] \supset \sim Sb\}$
$(Ea \bullet Ia) \vee (Eb \bullet Ib)$
$(Ea \bullet Ta) \vee (Eb \bullet Tb)$
$\therefore (Ea \supset \sim Sa) \bullet (Eb \supset \sim Sb)$

which is proved invalid by

	Ea	*Eb*	*Ia*	*Ib*	*Ta*	*Tb*	*Sa*	*Sb*
	t	t	t	f	t	f	f	t
or	t	t	f	t	f	t	t	f

10. **1.** $(x)[Bx \supset (Ix \supset Wx)]$
2. $(x)[Bx \supset (Wx \supset Ix)]$
$\therefore (x)\{Bx \supset [(Ix \vee Wx) \supset (Ix \bullet Wx)]\}$

3.	$By \supset (Iy \supset Wy)$	1, **U.I.**
4.	$By \supset (Wy \supset Iy)$	2, **U.I.**
5.	$[By \supset (Iy \supset Wy)] \bullet [By \supset (Wy \supset Iy)]$	3,4, Conj.
6.	$[\sim By \vee (Iy \supset Wy)] \bullet [\sim By \vee (Wy \supset Iy)]$	5, Impl.
7.	$\sim By \vee [(Iy \supset Wy) \bullet (Wy \supset Iy)]$	6, Dist.
8.	$\sim By \vee (Iy \equiv Wy)$	7, Equiv.
9.	$\sim By \vee [(Iy \bullet Wy) \vee (\sim Iy \bullet \sim Wy)]$	8, Equiv.
10.	$\sim By \vee [(\sim Iy \bullet \sim Wy) \vee (Iy \bullet Wy)]$	9, Com.
11.	$\sim By \vee [\sim(Iy \vee Wy) \vee (Iy \bullet Wy)]$	10, De M.
12.	$By \supset [(Iy \vee Wy) \supset (Iy \bullet Wy)]$	11, Impl.
13.	$(x)\{Bx \supset [(Ix \vee Wx) \supset (Ix \bullet Wx)]\}$	12, **U.G.**

D. pp. 475–477

1. **1.** $(x)[(Cx \bullet \sim Tx) \supset Px]$
2. $(x)(Ox \supset Cx)$
3. $(\exists x)(Ox \bullet \sim Px)$
$\therefore (\exists x)(Tx)$

4.	$Oa \bullet \sim Pa$	3, **E.I.**
5.	$Oa \supset Ca$	2, **U.I.**
6.	$(Ca \bullet \sim Ta) \supset Pa$	1, **U.I.**
7.	Oa	4, Simp.
8.	Ca	5,7, M.P.
9.	$\sim Pa \bullet Oa$	4, Com.
10.	$\sim Pa$	9, Simp.
11.	$Ca \supset (\sim Ta \supset Pa)$	6, Exp.
12.	$\sim Ta \supset Pa$	11,8, M.P.
13.	$\sim\sim Ta$	12,10, M.T.
14.	Ta	13, D.N.
15.	$(\exists x)(Tx)$	14, **E.G.**

5. $(\exists x)(Dx \bullet Ax)$
$(x)[Ax \supset (Jx \vee Cx)]$
$(x)(Dx \supset \sim Cx)$
$(x)[(Jx \bullet Ix) \supset \sim Px]$
$(\exists x)(Dx \bullet Ix)$
$\therefore (\exists x)(Dx \bullet \sim Px)$

This argument is logically equivalent in [a, b] to

$(Da \bullet Aa) \vee (Db \bullet Ab)$
$[Aa \supset (Ja \vee Ca)] \bullet [Ab \supset (Jb \vee Cb)]$
$(Da \supset \sim Ca) \bullet (Db \supset \sim Cb)$
$[(Ja \bullet Ia) \supset \sim Pa] \bullet [(Jb \bullet Ib) \supset \sim Pb]$
$(Da \bullet Ia) \vee (Db \bullet Ib)$
$\therefore (Da \bullet \sim Pa) \vee (Db \bullet \sim Pb)$

proved invalid by

	Da	Db	Aa	Ab	Ja	Jb	Ca	Cb	Ia	Ib	Pa	Pb
	t	t	t	f	t	f	f	f	f	t	t	t
or	t	t	f	t	f	t	f	f	t	f	t	t

10.

1.	(∃*x*)(*Cx* • *Rx*)	
2.	(*x*)[*Rx* ⊃ (*Sx* ∨ *Bx*)]	
3.	(*x*)[*Bx* ⊃ (*Dx* ∨ *Px*)]	
4.	(*x*)(*Px* ⊃ *Lx*)	
5.	(*x*)(*Dx* ⊃ *Hx*)	
6.	(*x*)(~*Hx*)	
7.	(*x*){[(*Cx* • *Rx*) • *Fx*] ⊃ *Ax*}	
8.	(*x*)(*Rx* ⊃ *Fx*)	
9.	(*x*)[*Cx* ⊃ ~(*Lx* • *Ax*)]	
	∴ (∃*x*)(*Cx* • *Sx*)	
10.	*Ca* • *Ra*	1, **E.I.**
11.	*Ra* • *Ca*	10, Com.
12.	*Ra*	11, Simp.
13.	*Ra* ⊃ *Fa*	8, **U.I.**
14.	*Fa*	13,12, M.P.
15.	(*Ca* • *Ra*) • *Fa*	10,14, Conj.
16.	[(*Ca* • *Ra*) • *Fa*] ⊃ *Aa*	7, **U.I.**
17.	*Aa*	16,15, M.P.
18.	*Ca* ⊃ ~(*La* • *Aa*)	9, **U.I.**
19.	*Ca*	10, Simp.
20.	~(*La* • *Aa*)	18,19, M.P.
21.	~*La* ∨ ~*Aa*	20, De M.
22.	~*Aa* ∨ ~*La*	21, Com.
23.	*Aa* ⊃ ~*La*	22, Impl.
24.	~*La*	23,17, M.P.
25.	*Pa* ⊃ *La*	4, **U.I.**
26.	~*Pa*	25,24, M.T.
27.	*Da* ⊃ *Ha*	5, **U.I.**
28.	~*Ha*	6, **U.I.**
29.	~*Da*	27,28, M.T.
30.	~*Da* • ~*Pa*	29,26, Conj.
31.	~(*Da* ∨ *Pa*)	30, De M.
32.	*Ba* ⊃ (*Da* ∨ *Pa*)	3, **U.I.**
33.	~*Ba*	32,31, M.T.
34.	*Ra* ⊃ (*Sa* ∨ *Ba*)	2, **U.I.**
35.	*Sa* ∨ *Ba*	34,12, M.P.
36.	*Ba* ∨ *Sa*	35, Com.
37.	*Sa*	36,33, D.S.
38.	*Ca* • *Sa*	19,37, Conj.
39.	(∃*x*)(*Cx* • *Sx*)	38, **E.G.**

15.

1.	(*x*)(*Ox* ⊃ *Sx*)	
2.	(*x*)(*Lx* ⊃ *Tx*)	
	∴ (*x*)[(*Ox* ∨ *Lx*) ⊃ (*Sx* ∨ *Tx*)]	
3.	*Oy* ⊃ *Sy*	1, **U.I.**
4.	*Ly* ⊃ *Ty*	2, **U.I.**
5.	~*Oy* ∨ *Sy*	3, Impl.
6.	(~*Oy* ∨ *Sy*) ∨ *Ty*	5, Add.
7.	~*Oy* ∨ (*Sy* ∨ *Ty*)	6, Assoc.
8.	(*Sy* ∨ *Ty*) ∨ ~*Oy*	7, Com.
9.	~*Ly* ∨ *Ty*	4, Impl.
10.	(~*Ly* ∨ *Ty*) ∨ *Sy*	9, Add.
11.	~*Ly* ∨ (*Ty* ∨ *Sy*)	10, Assoc.
12.	~*Ly* ∨ (*Sy* ∨ *Ty*)	11, Com.
13.	(*Sy* ∨ *Ty*) ∨ ~*Ly*	12, Com.

14.	$[(Sy \vee Ty) \vee \sim Oy] \bullet [(Sy \vee Ty) \vee \sim Ly]$	8,13, Conj.
15.	$(Sy \vee Ty) \vee (\sim Oy \bullet \sim Ly)$	14, Dist.
16.	$(\sim Oy \bullet \sim Ly) \vee (Sy \vee Ty)$	15, Com.
17.	$\sim(Oy \vee Ly) \vee (Sy \vee Ty)$	16, De M.
18.	$(Oy \vee Ly) \supset (Sy \vee Ty)$	17, Impl.
19.	$(x)[(Ox \vee Lx) \supset (Sx \vee Tx)]$	18, **U.G.**

Chapter 14

SECTION 14.2 *Exercises on pp. 595–603*

A. pp. 595–597

5. $\frac{1}{4} \times \frac{1}{3} \times \frac{1}{2} \times \frac{1}{1} = \frac{1}{24}$

The component events here are not independent, but in this case each success (in reaching the right house) *increases* rather than decreases the probability of the next success, because the number of available houses is fixed. After three men reach the correct house, the fourth (having to go to a different house) *must* succeed!

10. The probability that all four students will identify the same tire may be calculated in two different ways—just as the solution to Exercise 6 in this same set may be reached in two different ways.

Suppose that the first student, A, names the front left tire. The probability of his doing so, *after having done so*, is 1. Now the probability of the second student, B, naming that tire is $\frac{1}{4}$, there being four tires all (from B's point of view) equipossibly the one that A had named. The same is true of student C, and of student D. Therefore, regardless of which tire A does happen to name (front left, or any other), the probability that all four students will name the same tire is $1 \times \frac{1}{4} \times \frac{1}{4} \times \frac{1}{4} = \frac{1}{64}$ or .016.

The same result could be achieved by first specifying a particular tire (say, the front left tire) and asking: What is the probability of all four students naming that specified tire? This would be $\frac{1}{4} \times \frac{1}{4} \times \frac{1}{4} \times \frac{1}{4} = .004$. But the condition specified in the problem, that all four name the *same* tire, would be satisfied if all named the front left, or if all named the front right, or if all named the rear left, or if all named the rear right tire. So, if we were to approach the problem in this way, we also would need to inquire as to the probability of *either* the one or the other of these four outcomes—a calculation requiring the addition theorem, explained in Section 14.2B, for alternative outcomes. Because the four successful outcomes are mutually exclusive, we can simply sum the four probabilities: .004 + .004 + .004 + .004 = .016. The two ways of approaching the problem must yield exactly the same result, of course.

This dual analysis applies likewise to the three patients arriving at a building with five entrances, in Exercise 6. One may calculate $1 \times \frac{1}{5} \times \frac{1}{5} = \frac{1}{25}$; or (using the addition theorem discussed in Section 14.2B,) one may calculate $\frac{1}{5} \times \frac{1}{5} \times \frac{1}{5} = \frac{1}{125}$ and then add $\frac{1}{125} + \frac{1}{125} + \frac{1}{125} + \frac{1}{125} + \frac{1}{125} = \frac{1}{25}$.

B. pp. 602–603

1. Probability of losing with a 2, a 3, or a 12 is $\frac{4}{36}$ or $\frac{1}{9}$
Probability of throwing a 4, and then a 7 before another 4, is $\frac{3}{36} \times \frac{6}{9} = \frac{1}{18}$
Probability of throwing a 10, and then a 7 before another 10, is likewise $\frac{1}{18}$
Probability of throwing a 5, and then a 7 before another 5, is $\frac{4}{36} \times \frac{6}{10} = \frac{1}{15}$
Probability of throwing a 9, and then a 7 before another 9, is likewise $\frac{1}{15}$
Probability of throwing a 6, and then a 7 before another 6, is $\frac{5}{36} \times \frac{6}{11} = \frac{5}{66}$
Probability of throwing an 8, and then a 7 before another 8, is likewise $\frac{5}{66}$
Sum of the probabilities of the exclusive ways of the shooter's losing is $\frac{251}{495}$
So the shooter's chance of winning is $1 - \frac{251}{495} = \frac{244}{495}$ or .493.

5. Yes. You lose the bet only if you throw a 2, or a 3, or a 4, or a 5, on *both* rolls of the die. On each throw, the chance of getting one of those four numbers is $\frac{4}{6}$ or $\frac{2}{3}$. The chance of losing the bet is therefore $\frac{2}{3} \times \frac{2}{3}$, or $\frac{4}{9}$. Your chance of winning the bet, therefore, is $1 - \frac{4}{9} = \frac{5}{9} = .556$.

10. **Challenge to the Reader**
This problem, which has been the focus of some controversy, may be analyzed in two different ways.

First analysis:

a. There are 28 possible pairs in the abbreviated deck consisting of four kings and four aces. Of these 28 possible pairs, only seven (equipossible) pairs contain the ace of spades. Of these seven pairs, three contain two aces. If we know that the pair drawn contains the ace of spades, the probability that this pair contains two aces is $\frac{3}{7}$.

b. However, if we know only that one of the cards in the pair is an ace, we know only that the pair drawn is one of the 22 (equipossible) pairs that contain at least one ace. Of these 22 pairs, six contain two aces. Therefore, if we know only that the pair contains an ace, the probability that the pair drawn contains two aces is $\frac{6}{22}$ or $\frac{3}{11}$.

In this first analysis, the probabilities in the two cases are different.

Second analysis:

a. If one of the cards of the pair drawn is known to be the ace of spades, there are seven other possible cards with which the pair may be completed. Of these seven, three are aces. Therefore, if we know that one of the cards drawn is the ace of spades, the probability that this pair contains two aces is $\frac{3}{7}$.

b. If we know only that one of the cards drawn is an ace, we know that it is either the ace of spades, or the ace of hearts, or the ace of diamonds, or the ace of clubs. If it is the ace of spades, the analysis immediately preceding applies, and the probability that this pair contains two aces is again $\frac{3}{7}$.

If the ace is the ace of hearts, the same analysis applies; as it does if the card drawn is the ace of diamonds, or the ace of clubs. Therefore, even if we know only that an ace is one of the cards drawn, the probability that the pair contains two aces remains $\frac{3}{7}$.

In this second analysis, the probabilities in the two cases are the same. Which of these two analyses do you believe to be correct? Why?

SECTION 14.3 *Exercises on pp. 609–611*

1. a. $3.82

   b. $19,100,000.00

   But note: This was a *very* unusual set of circumstances!

5. This problem requires only a straightforward use of the product theorem. The probability of selecting, at random, just those two cows out of four is the probability of selecting one of that pair on the first choosing ($\frac{1}{2}$), times the probability of selecting the other one of that pair on the second choosing, where the first already had been selected ($\frac{1}{3}$). So the calculation is $\frac{1}{2} \times \frac{1}{3} = \frac{1}{6}$.

10. The calculation of the bettor's chances of winning on the "Don't Pass-Bar 3" line is the probability of the player's losing when the game is played according to the normal rules, *with the provision that he does not lose if he gets a 3 on the first roll*. The probability of a 3 on the first roll is $\frac{2}{36}$ or .056. The probability of the player losing on the normal rules is .507, as was shown in Section 14.2B. Therefore the probability of the player losing, barring the loss on a first-roll 3,

is .507 − .056 = .451. Because this is the probability of the player's losing if he cannot lose by getting a 3 on the first roll, it is the probability of the bettor winning on the "Don't Pass-Bar 3" line. So the expected value of a $100 bet on the "Don't Pass-Bar 3" line is .451 × $200 = $90.20.

Note that this bet, which the house will gladly accept, is substantially less favorable to the bettor than simply betting on the pass line—that is, simply betting on the player to win. The expected value of such a $100 wager (i.e., on the player to win according to normal rules) is .493 × $200 = $98.60.

A

Absorption: A rule of inference; one of nine elementary valid argument forms. If p implies q, absorption permits the inference that p implies *both* p and q. Symbolized as: $p \supset q$, therefore $p \supset (p \bullet q)$, 376

Abusive *ad hominem* argument, 128–29

Accent: An informal fallacy, committed when a term or phrase has a meaning in the conclusion of an argument different from its meaning in one of the premises, the difference arising chiefly from a change in emphasis given to the words used, 160–63

Accident: An informal fallacy, committed when a generalization is applied to individual cases that it does not properly govern, 150. *See also* Converse accident

Adams, Henry, 50

Ad baculum (appeal to force): An informal fallacy in which an inappropriate appeal to force is used to support the truth of some conclusion, 131–33

Addition (Add.): A rule of logical inference, one of nine elementary valid argument forms. Given any proposition p, addition permits the inference that p *or* q. Also called "logical addition," 377–79

Addition theorem: In the calculus of probability, a theorem used to determine the probability of a complex event consisting of one or more alternative occurrences of simple events whose probabilities are known, 597–602; for exclusive alternatives, 601

Addresses on War (Sumner), 82

Ad hoc: A term with several meanings, used to characterize hypotheses. It may mean only that the hypothesis was constructed after the facts it purports to explain; it may mean that the hypothesis is merely descriptive. Most commonly, "*ad hoc*" is used pejoratively, describing a hypothesis that serves to explain only the facts it was invented to explain and has no other testable consequences, 574

Ad hominem (argument against the person): An informal fallacy in which the object of attack is not the merits of some position, but the person who takes that position, 127–31; abusive, 128–29; circumstantial, 129–31

Ad ignorantiam (argument from ignorance): An informal fallacy in which a conclusion is supported by an illegitimate appeal to ignorance, as when it is supposed that something is likely to be true because we cannot prove that it is false, 142–44

Ad misericordiam (appeal to pity): An informal fallacy in which the support given for some conclusion is an inappropriate appeal to the mercy or altruism of the audience, 124–25

Ad populum (appeal to emotion): An informal fallacy in which the support given for some conclusion is an inappropriate appeal to popular belief, or to the emotions of the audience, 121–25

Advancement of Learning, The (Bacon), 518

Adventure of Silver Blaze, The (Doyle), 303

Adventures of Huckleberry Fin, The (Twain), 156

Ad verecundiam (appeal to inappropriate authority): An informal fallacy in which the appeal to authority is illegitimate, because the authority appealed to has no special claim to expertness on the matter in question, 145–46

Affirmative conclusion from a negative premise, Fallacy of, 248

Affirming the consequent: A formal fallacy, so named because the categorical premise in the argument affirms the consequent rather than the antecedent of the conditional premise. Symbolized as: $p \supset q$, q, therefore p, 300, 353

Affluent Society, The (Galbraith), 49

Against the Logicians (Sextus Empiricus), 303

Against the Physicists (Sextus Empiricus), 311

Age of Reason, The (Paine), 76

Agre, Peter, 584

Agreement, Method of: A pattern of inductive inference in which it is concluded that, if two or more instances of a phenomenon have only one circumstance in common, that one common circumstance is the cause (or effect) of the phenomenon under investigation, 520–25

Aim and Structure of Physical Theory, The (Duhem), 112

Alev, Imam Fatih, 137

Alford, Henry, 170

Alice's Adventures in Wonderland (Carroll), 427, 503

Alroy, Daniel, 51

Alternative occurrences: In probability theory, a complex event that consists of the occurrence of any one of two or more simple component events. (*E.g.*, the complex event of getting either a spade or a club in the random drawing of a playing card), 592, 597–603

Ambiguity: Uncertainty of meaning, often leading to disputes or to mistakes when the same word or phrase has two (or more) distinct meanings, and the context does not make clear which meaning is intended, 84–7, 91

Ambiguity, Fallacies of: Informal fallacies (of Equivocation, Amphiboly, Accent, Composition and Division) each of which may arise because of some ambiguity that leads to a shift or confusion of meanings within the course of an argument. Also called "sophisms," 157–67; accent, 160–63; amphiboly, 159–60; composition, 163–64; division, 164–67; equivocation, 157–59

Ambiguous middle: A formal fallacy, so-called because the mistake in some syllogism arises from a shift, within the argument, in the meaning of the middle term, 240

American Journal of Medical Science (Smith), 77

American Notebooks (Hawthorne), 83

Amiel, Henri-Frederic, 76

Amiel's Journal (Amiel), 76

Amphiboly: A kind of ambiguity arising from the loose, awkward, or mistaken way in which words are combined, leading to alternative possible meanings of a statement. Also, the name of a fallacy when an argument incorporates an amphibolous statement that is true as used in one occurrence, but false as used in another occurrence of the statement in that argument, 159–60

Analects, The (Confucius), 112

Analogical argument: A kind of inductive argument in which it is concluded that two entities are alike in some respect, on the ground that they are alike in some other respect or respects, 483–91; criteria for appraising, 492–96

Analogy: A likeness drawn between two or more entities in one or more respects. Analogies are used to enhance description and to aid in explanation—and also are widely used in inductive argument, 483, 485; argument by, 483–91; characteristics of argument by, 487; nonargumentative, 485

Analytical definition. *See* Definition by genus and difference

Analyzing arguments, 37–70

Anatomy of an Illness (Cousins), 311

Anecdotes of Samuel Johnson (Piozzi), 168

Animals without Backbones (Buchsbaum), 500

Annabel Lee (Poe), 74

Annals (Tacitus), 81

Antecedent: In a hypothetical proposition ("*If ... then ...*") the component that immediately follows the "if." Sometimes called the *implicans* or the *protasis*, 331, 335–37

Apodosis: The consequent in a hypothetical proposition, 331

Apology (Plato), 311

Apparently verbal but really genuine disputes, 84

***A priori* theory of probability:** A theory in which the probability ascribed to a simple event is a fraction between 0 and 1, of which the denominator is the number of equipossible outcomes, and the numerator is the number of outcomes in which the event in question occurs. Thus on the *a priori* theory, the probability of drawing a spade at random from a deck of playing cards is 13/52, 589–90, 591, 609

Aquinas, Thomas, 10, 46, 285, 303

Argument: Any group of propositions of which one is claimed to follow from the others, which are regarded as providing support or grounds for the truth of that one, 4, 6–9; by analogy, 483–503; analysis of, 37–69; complex, 7, 53–59; conclusion of, 7–8; deductive, 26–30, 180; diagramming, 41–53; explanations and, 19–26; inductive, 26–30, 482–83; interwoven, 37, 45; invalid, 31–35, 421–24; in ordinary language, 414; paraphrasing, 37–41, 44; premise of, 7–8; recognizing, 12–19; sound, 34; syllogistic, 230–33; valid, 31–35

Argument form: An array of symbols exhibiting logical structure; it contains statement variables but no statements, such that when statements are consistently substituted for the statement variables, the result is an argument, 342–56; common invalid, 353–54; common valid, 349–53; truth tables and, 347–49; "valid" and "invalid," precise meaning of, 346–47

Aringarosa, Bishop, 125

Aristotelian logic: The traditional account of syllogistic reasoning, in which certain interpretations of categorical propositions are presupposed. Often contrasted with the modern symbolic, or Boolean interpretation of categorical propositions, 180

Aristotle, 82, 114, 115, 143, 160, 168, 171, 181, 186, 209, 286, 303, 316, 440

Armour, Stacy, 550

Arnett, Cliff, 129

Arnold, Matthew, 113

Art of Scientific Discovery, The (Gore), 539

Association (Assoc.): An expression of logical equivalence; a rule of inference that permits the valid regrouping of simple propositions. According to it $[p \vee (q \vee r)]$ may be replaced by $[(p \vee q) \vee r]$ and vice versa, and $[p \bullet (q \bullet r)]$ may be replaced by $[(p \bullet q) \bullet r]$ and vice versa, 396

Astell, Mary, 487

Asyllogistic arguments: Arguments in which one or more of the component propositions is of a form more complicated than the **A, E, I** and **O** propositions of the categorical syllogism, and whose analysis therefore requires logical tools more powerful than those provided by Aristotelian logic, 278, 468–77

Attitude, agreement/disagreement in, 79–81

Austen, Jane, 8

Authority, appeal to. *See* Ad verecundiam

Autocrat of the Breakfast-Table, The (Holmes), 76

Ayer, Alfred J., 287, 502

B

Bacon, Francis, 11, 76, 518

Baird, Donna D., 524

Baker, Howard, 132

Baker Motley, Constance, 128

Baranovsky, Anatole M., 171

Barbara: The traditional name of one of the 15 valid standard-form categorical syllogisms. A syllogism in the form Barbara has the mood and figure **AAA-1;** that is to say, all three of its propositions are **A** propositions, and it is in the first figure because the middle term is

the subject of the major premise and the predicate of the minor premise, 261, 282, 291

Baroko: The traditional name of one of the 15 valid standard-form categorical syllogisms. A syllogism in the form Baroko has the mood and figure **AOO-2;** that is to say, the minor premise and conclusion are **O** propositions, the major premise is an **A** proposition, and it is in the second figure because the middle term is the predicate of both the major and the minor premise, 257, 262, 279

Barr, Stephen M., 507

Basic Laws of Arithmetic, The (Frege), 490

Bawer, Bruce, 137

Begging the question (*petitio principii*): An informal fallacy in which the conclusion of an argument is stated or assumed in any one of the premises, 152–54

Belief, agreement/disagreement in, 79–81

Bellow, Saul, 146

Belvedere (Escher), 178

Bentham, Jeremy, 8

Berkeley, George, 285

Bernstein, Anya, 49

Berra, Yogi, 427

Bettelheim, Bruno, 19

Biconditional statement or proposition: A compound statement or proposition that asserts that its two component statements have the same truth value, and therefore are materially equivalent. So named because, since the two component statements are either both true or both false, they must imply one another. A biconditional statement form is symbolized "$p \equiv q$," which may be read as "p if and only if q," 360, 444, 464

Bierce, Ambrose, 108, 111, 168

Bin Laden, Osama, 129, 130, 508

Blair, Tony, 49

Bodin, Jean, 23

Bokardo: The traditional name of one of the 15 valid standard-form categorical syllogisms. A syllogism in the form Bokardo has the mood and figure **OAO-3;** that is to say, its major premise and conclusion are **O** propositions, its minor premise is an **A** proposition, and it is in the third figure because the middle term is the subject of both the minor and the major premise, 263

Bonaparte, Napoleon, 453

Boole, George, 208, 209

Boolean interpretation: The modern interpretation of categorical propositions, adopted in this book, and named after the English logician George Boole (1815–1864). In the Boolean interpretation, often contrasted with the Aristotelian interpretation, universal propositions (**A** and **E** propositions) do not have existential import, 208, 212, 223

Boolean Square of Opposition, 216–17

Brahe, Tycho, 570

Breyer, Stephen, 96

Bright, John, 78

Brill, Steve, 506

Brinkley, Alan, 49

Broad, C.D., 304

Broder, David, 126

Brooks, David, 39, 453

Brooks, John, 284

Browne, Malcolm W., 490

Bruce, Thomas, 489

Bruggemann, Edward, 172

Bruno, Giordano, 581

Buchsbaum, Ralph, 500

Buckvar, Eric, 488

Burke, Edmund, 75

Bush, George W., 134, 298

Buss, David M., 488

Butler, Joseph, 173

Butler, Samuel, 110

C

Calculus of probability: A branch of mathematics that can be used to compute the probabilities of complex events from the probabilities of their component events, 591–603

Callahan, J.J., 304

Camenes: The traditional name of one of the 15 valid standard-form categorical syllogisms. A syllogism in the form Camenes has the mood and figure **AEE-4;** that is to say, its minor premise and conclusion are **E** propositions, its major premise is an **A** proposition, and it is in the fourth figure because the middle term is the predicate of the major premise and the subject of the minor premise, 261

Camestres: The traditional name of one of the 15 valid standard-form categorical syllogisms. A syllogism in the form Camestres has the mood and figure **AEE-2;** that is to say, its minor premise and conclusion are **E** propositions, its major premise is an **A** proposition, and it is in the second figure because the middle term is the predicate of both the major and the minor premise, 261, 283, 290

Campbell, C. Arthur, 304

Candlish, Stewart, 302

Cargill, Michelle, 551

Carroll, James, 527

Carroll, Lewis, 74, 158, 295, 427, 503

Case, Anne, 552

Categorical proposition: A proposition that can be analyzed as being about classes, or categories, affirming or

Dollar, Steve, 453

Dot: The symbol for conjunction, •, meaning "and," 318

Double negation: An expression of logical equivalence; a rule of inference that permits the valid mutual replacement of any symbol by the negation of the negation of that symbol. Symbolized as $p \stackrel{T}{\equiv} \sim\sim p$, 364, 394, 397

Douglas, Stephen, 31

Douglass, Frederick, 142

Doyle, A. Conan, 59, 288, 303

Doyle, T., 24

Dubois, W.E.B., 74

Dubos, René, 488

Duhem, Pierre, 112

Duns Scotus, 287

Du Pre, Jacqueline, 110

Dworkin, Roneld, 23, 509

Dyson, Freeman, 292

E

Eddington, Arthur, 501, 566

Education of Henry Adams, The (Adams), 50

Edwards, Jonathan, 173

Einstein, Albert, 566, 567, 568, 569, 570, 571

Elementary valid argument: Any one of a set of specified deductive arguments that serves as a rule of inference and that may therefore be used in constructing a formal proof of validity, 374

Emotion, appeal to (argument *ad populum*), 121–25

Emotive language, 71–72, 79–84

Engels, Friedrich, 44, 114

Enthymeme: An argument that is stated incompletely, the unstated part of it being taken for granted. An enthymeme may be of the first, second, or third order, depending upon whether the unstated proposition is the major premise, the minor premise, or the conclusion of the argument, 18–19, 287–93

Equivocation: An informal fallacy in which two or more meanings of the same word or phrase have been confused. If used with one of its meanings in one of the propositions of the argument but with a different meaning in another proposition of the argument, a word is said to have been used equivocally, 157–59

Erasmus, Desiderius, 81

Eratosthenes, 564–65

Escher, M.C., 2, 178, 480

Essay Concerning Civil Government (Locke), 114

Essay in Defence of the Female Sex, An (Astell), 487

Essay on Civil Disobedience, An (Thoreau), 84

Essay on the Extinction of the Soul (Chen), 501

Essays (Bacon), 76

Ethics (Spinoza), 59, 79, 94, 113

Euathlus, 308–09

Euphemisms, 79

Euripides, 78

Example, definitions by, 99–101

Exceptive proposition: A proposition that asserts that all members of some class, with the exception of the members of one of its subclasses, are members of some other class. Exceptive propositions are in reality compound, because they assert both a relation of class inclusion, and a relation of class exclusion. *E.g.* "All persons except employees are eligible" is an exceptive proposition in which it is asserted both that "All nonemployees are eligible," and that "No employees are eligible," 278–79, 469–70

Excluded middle, Principle of: The principle that asserts that any statement is either true or false; sometimes called one of the laws of thought, 368, 369

Exclusive disjunction, or strong disjunction: A logical relation meaning "or," that may connect two component statements. A compound statement asserting exclusive disjunction says that at least one of the disjuncts is true *and* that at least one of the disjuncts is false. It is contrasted with an "inclusive" (or "weak") disjunction, which says that at least one of the disjuncts is true and that they may both be true, 321, 337

Exclusive premises, Fallacy of: A formal fallacy, committed when a syllogism breaks the rule that forbids two negative premises, 247

Exclusive propositions: Propositions which assert that the predicate applies exclusively to the subject named. *E.g.* "None but generals wear stars" asserts that the predicate, wearing stars, applies only to generals, 277

Existential fallacy: Any mistake in reasoning that arises from assuming illegitimately that some class has members. It is a formal fallacy when, in a standard-form categorical syllogism, a particular conclusion is inferred from two universal premises, 213, 248

Existential Generalization (E.G.): A rule of inference in the theory of quantification that says that from any true substitution instance of a propositional function we may validly infer the existential quantification of the propositional function, 459, 460

Existential import: An attribute of those propositions which normally assert the existence of objects of some specified kind. Particular propositions (**I** and **O** propositions) always have existential import; thus the proposition "Some dogs are obedient" asserts that there are dogs. Whether universal propositions (**A** and **E** propositions) have existential import is an issue on which the Aristotelian and Boolean interpretations of propositions differ, 208

Existential Instantiation (E.I.): A rule of inference in the theory of quantification that says that we may (with some restrictions) validly infer from the existential quantification of a propositional function the truth of

F

J

K

L

M

N

Q

R

S

U

V

W

Z